THE WORKS
OF
VICTOR HUGO

THE WORKS
OF
VICTOR HUGO

The Hunchback
of Notre-Dame

Les Miserables

LONGMEADOW PRESS

This 1991 edition is published by Longmeadow Press,
201 High Ridge Road, Stamford, Connecticut 06904
by special arrangement with W.S. Konecky Associates.

ISBN 0-681-41056-6

10 9 8 7 6 5 4 3 2

Manufactured in the U.S.A.

THE HUNCHBACK OF NOTRE-DAME

CONTENTS

BOOK I

Contents

THE HUNCHBACK OF NOTRE-DAME

BOOK I

CHAPTER I

THE GREAT HALL OF THE PALACE OF JUSTICE

IT is this day three hundred and forty-eight years six months and nineteen days since the good people of Paris were awakened by a grand peal from all the bells in the three districts of the Cité, the Université, and the Ville. The 6th of January, 1482, was, nevertheless, a day of which history has not preserved any record. There was nothing worthy of note in the event which so early set in motion the bells and the citizens of Paris. It was neither an assault of the Picards or the Burgundians, nor a procession bearing the shrine of some saint, nor a mutiny of the students, nor an entry of "our most redoubted lord, Monsieur the King," nor even an execution of rogues of either sex before the Palace of Justice of Paris. Neither was it an arrival of some bedizened and befeathered embassy, a sight of frequent occurrence in the fifteenth century. It was but two days since the last cavalcade of this kind, that of the Flemish ambassadors commissioned to conclude a marriage between the Dauphin and Margaret of Flanders, had made its entry into Paris, to the great annoyance of the Cardinal de Bourbon, who, in order to please the King, had been obliged to receive this vulgar squad of Flemish burgomasters with a good grace, and to entertain them at his Hôtel de Bourbon with a "goodly morality, mummery, and farce," while a deluge of rain drenched the magnificent tapestry at his door.

What set in motion all the population of Paris on the 6th of January was the double solemnity, united from time immemorial, of the Epiphany and the Festival of Fools. On that day there was to be an exhibition of fireworks in the Place de Grève, a may-tree planted at the chapel of Braque, and a mystery performed at the

11

The Hunchback of Notre-Dame

Palace of Justice. Proclamation had been made to this effect on the preceding day, with sound of trumpet in the public places, by the Provost's officers in fair coats of purple camlet, with large white crosses on the breast.

That morning, therefore, all the houses and shops remained shut, and crowds of citizens of both sexes were to be seen wending their way toward one of the three places specified above. Be it, however, observed, to the honour of the taste of the cockneys of Paris, that the majority of this concourse were proceeding toward the fireworks, which were quite seasonable, or to the mystery which was to be represented in the great hall of the palace, well covered in and sheltered, and that the curious agreed to let the poor leafless may shiver all alone beneath a January sky in the cemetery of the chapel of Braque.

All the avenues to the Palace of Justice were particularly thronged, because it was known that the Flemish ambassadors, who had arrived two days before, purposed to attend the representation of the mystery, and the election of the Pope of Fools, which was also to take place in the great hall.

It was no easy matter on that day to get into this great hall, though it was then reputed to be the largest room in the world. To the spectators at the windows the palace yard crowded with people had the appearance of a sea, into which five or six streets, like the mouths of so many rivers, disgorged their living streams. The waves of this sea, incessantly swelled by fresh accessions, broke against the angles of the houses, projecting here and there like promontories into the irregular basin of the Place. In the centre of the lofty Gothic façade of the palace the grand staircase, with its double current ascending and descending, poured incessantly into the Place like a cascade into a lake. Great were the noise and the clamour produced by the cries of some, the laughter of others, and the trampling of the thousands of feet. From time to time this clamour and noise were redoubled; the current which propelled the crowd toward the grand staircase turned back, agitated and whirling about. It might be a dash made by an archer, or the horse of one of the Provost's sergeants kicking and plunging to restore order—an admirable manoeuvre, which the Provosty bequeathed to the constablery, the constablery to the *maréchaussée,* and the *maréchaussée* to the present *gendarmerie* of Paris.

Doors, windows, loopholes, the roofs of the houses, swarmed with

12

thousands of calm and honest faces gazing at the palace and at the crowd, and desiring nothing more; for most of the good people of Paris are quite content with the sight of the spectators; nay, a blank wall, behind which something or other is going forward, is to us an object of great curiosity.

If it could be given to us mortals living in this year of grace to mingle in imagination with those Parisians of the fifteenth century, and to enter with them, shoved, elbowed, hustled, that immense hall of the palace so straitened for room on the 6th of January, 1482, the sight would not be destitute either of interest or of charm; and all that we should see round us would be so ancient as to appear absolutely new. If the reader pleases, we will endeavour to retrace in imagination the impressions which he would have felt with us on crossing the threshold of the great hall, amid this motley crowd, coated, gowned, or clothed in the paraphernalia of office.

In the first place, how one's ears are stunned with the noise!— how one's eyes are dazzled! Overhead is a double roof of pointed arches, ceiled with carved wood, painted sky-blue, and studded with *fleurs de lis* in gold; underfoot, a pavement of alternate squares of black and white marble. A few paces from us stands an enormous pillar, then another, and another; in all, seven pillars, intersecting the hall longitudinally, and supporting the thrust of the double-vaulted roof. Round the first four pillars are shops, glistening with glass and jewellery; and round the other three, benches worn and polished by the hose of the pleaders and the gowns of the attorneys. Along the lofty walls, between the doors, between the windows, between the pillars, is ranged the interminable series of all the kings of France ever since Pharamond: the indolent kings with pendent arms and downcast eyes; the valiant and warlike kings with heads and hands boldly raised toward heaven. The tall, pointed windows are glazed with panes of a thousand hues; at the outlets are rich doors, finely carved; and the whole, ceiling, pillars, walls, wainscot, doors, statues, covered from top to bottom with a splendid colouring of blue and gold, which, already somewhat tarnished at the time we behold it, was almost entirely buried in dust and cobwebs in the year of grace 1549, when du Breul still admired it by tradition.

Now figure to yourself that immense oblong hall, illuminated by the dim light of a January day, stormed by a motley and noisy crowd, pouring in along the walls, and circling round the pillars, and you will have a faint idea of the general outline of the picture, the curious details of which we shall endeavour to delineate more precisely.

It is certain that if Ravaillac had not assassinated Henry IV there would have been no documents of his trial deposited in the Rolls Office of the Palace of Justice, and no accomplices interested in the destruction of those documents; consequently no incendiaries obliged, for want of better means, to burn the Rolls Office in order to burn the documents, and to burn the Palace of Justice in order to burn the Rolls Office; of course there would have been no fire in 1618. The old palace would still be standing with its old great hall; and I might then say to the reader, "Go, look at it," and thus we should both be spared trouble, myself the trouble of writing, and him that of perusing, an indifferent description. This demonstrates the novel truth—that great events have incalculable consequences.

It is, indeed, possible that the accomplices of Ravaillac had no hand in the fire of 1618. There are two other plausible ways of accounting for it; first, the great "star of fire, a foot broad, and a foot and a half high," which fell, as everybody knows, from the sky upon the Palace on the 7th of March, after midnight; secondly, this stanza of Théophile:

> Certes, ce fut un triste jeu,
> Quand à Paris dame Justice,
> Pour avoir mangé trop d'épice,
> Se mit tout le palais en feu.[1]

Whatever may be thought of this threefold explanation, political, physical, and poetical, of the burning of the Palace of Justice in 1618, the fact of the fire is unfortunately most certain. Owing to this catastrophe, and, above all, to the successive restorations which have swept away what it spared, very little is now left of this elder Palace of the Louvre, already so ancient in the time of Philip the Fair that the traces of the magnificent buildings erected by King Robert, and described by Hegaldus, had then to be sought for. What has become of the Chancery Chamber, where St Louis con-

[1] In Paris 'twas but sorry sport
When Justice, prey to greediness,
Gorged upon bribes unto excess
And set on fire her own High Court.

summated his marriage?—the garden where he administered justice, habited in a camlet coat, a surcoat of linsey-woolsey without sleeves, and a mantle over all, of black serge, reclining upon carpets with Joinville? Where is the chamber of the Emperor Sigismond?—that of Charles IV?—that of John Lackland? Where is the flight of steps from which Charles VI promulgated his edict of amnesty?—the slab whereon Marcel murdered, in the presence of the Dauphin, Robert de Clermont and the Maréchal de Champagne?—the wicket where the bulls of the Anti-Pope Benedict were torn in pieces, and whence those who had brought them were taken, coped and mitred in derision, and carried in procession through all Paris?—the great hall, with its gilding, its azure, its pointed arches, its statues, its pillars, its immense vaulted roof, cut and carved all over?—and the gilded chamber?—and the stone lion at the gate, kneeling, with head lowered and tail between his legs, like the lions of King Solomon's throne, in the reverential attitude which befits strength in the presence of justice?—and the beautiful doors?—and the painted windows?—and the chased iron-work which discouraged Biscornette?—and the delicate carvings of du Hancy? What has time, what have men, done with these wonders? What has been given to us for all these—for all this ancient French history, for all this Gothic art?—the heavy elliptic arches of Monsieur de Brosse, the clumsy architect of the porch of Saint Gervais—so much for art; and as for history, we have the traditions of the great pillar, which still reverberates with the gossip of the Patrus. This is no great matter. Let us return to the veritable great hall of the veritable old palace.

One of the extremities of this prodigious parallelogram was occupied by the famous marble table, hewn out of a single piece, so long, so broad, and so thick that, as the ancient land-gods say, in a style that might have given an appetite to Gargantua, "never was there seen in the world slice of marble to match it"; and the other by the chapel where Louis XI placed his own effigy kneeling before the Virgin, and to which, reckless of leaving two vacant niches in the file of royal statues, he removed those of Charlemagne and St. Louis, saints whom he conceived to possess great influence with heaven as Kings of France. This chapel, still new, having been built scarcely six years, was in that charming style of delicate architecture, wonderful sculpture, and sharp, deep carving, which marks with us the conclusion of the Gothic era, and prevails till about the middle of the sixteenth century in the fairy fantasies of the revival of the art. The small rose mullion over the porch was in particular a masterpiece of lightness and delicacy; you would have taken it for a star of lacework.

In the middle of the hall, opposite to the great door, an enclosed platform lined with gold brocade, backed against the wall, and to which a private entrance had been made by means of a window from the passage to the gilded chamber, was erected expressly for the Flemish envoys, and the other distinguished personages invited to the representation of the mystery.

On this marble table, according to established usage, the mystery was to be performed. Arrangements for this purpose had been made early in the morning. The rich marble floor, scratched all over by the heels of the clerks of the Basoche, supported a cage of wood-work of considerable height, the upper floor of which, exposed to view from every part of the hall, was to serve for the stage, while the lower, masked by hangings of tapestry, formed a sort of dressing-room for the actors. A ladder, undisguisedly placed outside, was to be the channel of communication between the two, and its rude steps were to furnish the only medium as well for entrances as for exits. There was no movement, however abrupt and unexpected, no piece of stage-effect so sudden, but had to be executed by the intervention of this ladder. Innocent and venerable infancy of the art of machinery!

Four sergeants of the Bailiff of Paris, whose duty it was to superintend all the amusements of the people, as well on festivals as on days of execution, were stationed one at each corner of the marble table.

It was not till the great clock of the palace had struck the hour of twelve that the performance was to begin—a late hour, to be sure, for a theatrical representation, but it had been found necessary to suit it to the convenience of the ambassadors.

Now, the whole assembled multitude had been waiting ever since the morning. Many of these good, sight-loving folks had, indeed, been shivering from daybreak before the steps of the palace; nay, some declared that they had passed the night under the great porch, to make sure of getting in. The crowd increased every moment, and, like water that rises above its level, began to mount along

The Palace of Justice

the walls, to swell about the pillars, to cover the entablatures, the cornices, all the salient points of the architecture, all the rilievos of the sculpture. Accordingly, the weariness, the impatience, the freedom of a day of licence, the quarrels occasioned every moment by a sharp elbow or a hobnailed shoe, and the tediousness of long waiting, gave, long before the hour at which the ambassadors were to arrive, a sharp, surly note to the clamour of the populace, kicked, cuffed, jostled, squeezed, and wedged together almost to suffocation. Nothing was to be heard but complaints and imprecations against the Flemings, the Provost of the Merchants, the Cardinal de Bourbon, the Bailiff of the Palace, Madame Margaret of Austria, the sergeant-vergers, the cold, the heat, the bad weather, the Bishop of Paris, the Pope of Fools, the pillars, the statues, this closed door, that open window—all to the great amusement of the groups of scholars and servingmen scattered through the crowd, who mingled with all this discontent their sarcasms and mischievous sallies, which, like pins thrust into a wound, produced no small aggravation of the general ill-humour.

There was among others a knot of these merry wights, who, after knocking the glass out of one of the windows, had boldly seated themselves on the entablature, and thence cast their eyes and their jokes alternately within and without, among the crowd in the hall and the crowd in the Place. From their mimicries, their peals of laughter, and the jeers which they exchanged from one end of the hall to the other with their comrades, it was evident that these young clerks felt none of the weariness and *ennui* which overpowered the rest of the assembly, and that they well knew how to extract from the scene before them sufficient amusement to enable them to wait patiently for the promised spectacle.

"Why, 'pon my soul, 'tis you, Joannes Frollo de Molendino!" cried one of them, a youth with a fair complexion, a handsome face, and an arch look, perched on the acanthi of a capital; "you are rightly named, Jehan du Moulin, for your arms and legs are exactly like the four sails of a windmill. How long have you been here?"

"By the devil's mercy," replied Joannes Frollo, "more than four hours, and I hope they will be counted into my time of purgatory. I heard the King of Sicily's eight chanters strike up the first verse of High Mass at seven o'clock in the Sainte-Chapelle."

17

The Hunchback of Notre-Dame

"Rare chanters, forsooth!" rejoined the other, "with voices sharper than their pointed caps! The King, before he founded a Mass to Monsieur St John ought to have ascertained whether Monsieur St John is fond of Latin chanted with a Provençal twang."

"And it was to employ those cursed singers of the King of Sicily that he did it!" cried an old woman among the crowds at the foot of the window. "Only think! A thousand livres Parisis for one Mass, and granted out of the tax on the sea-fish sold in the market of Paris, into the bargain!"

"Silence!" ejaculated a lusty, portly personage, who was holding his nose by the side of the fishwoman. "How could the King help founding a Mass? Would you have him fall ill again?"

"Admirably spoken, Sire Gilles Lecornu, master-furrier of the King's robes!" shouted the little scholar clinging to the capital.

A general peal of laughter from his comrades greeted the unlucky name of the poor master-furrier of the King's robes.

"Lecornu! Gilles Lecornu!"[1] cried some of them.

"*Cornutus et hirsutus*,"[2] said another.

"Ay, no doubt," replied the little demon of the capital. "What is there to laugh at? An honourable man, Gilles Lecornu, brother of Master Jehan Lecornu, provost of the King's household, son of Master Mahiet Lecornu, first porter of the wood of Vincennes, all citizens of Paris, all married from father to son!"

A fresh explosion of mirth succeeded; all eyes were fixed on the fat master-furrier, who, without uttering a word in reply, strove to withdraw himself from the public gaze. But in vain he puffed and struggled till he was covered with perspiration; the efforts which he made served only to wedge in his bloated apoplectic face, purple with rage and vexation, the more firmly between the shoulders of his neighbours.

At length one of these, short, pursy, and venerable as himself, had the courage to take his part.

"What an abomination! That scholars should dare to talk thus to a citizen! In my time they would have been scourged with rods and burned with them afterward."

The whole band burst out, "Soho! who sings that tune! What screech-owl of ill omen is that?"

[1] Lecornu, "horned."
[2] *Cornutus et hirsutus*, "horned and shaggy or hairy."

The Palace of Justice

"Stay; I know him," said one; " 'tis Master Andry Musnier."

"One of the four sworn booksellers to the Université," said another.

"Everything goes by fours at that shop," cried a third: "the four nations, the four faculties, the four festivals, the four proctors, the four electors, the four booksellers."

"Musnier, we will burn thy books!"

"Musnier, we will beat thy servingman!"

"Musnier, we will tear thy wife's rags off her back!"

"The good fat Mademoiselle Oudarde."

"Who is as fresh and as buxom as though she were a widow."

"The devil fetch you all!" muttered Master Andry Musnier.

"Master Andry," rejoined Jehan, still perched on his capital, "hold thy tongue, man, or I will drop upon thy head."

Master Andry lifted his eyes, appeared to be measuring for a moment the height of the pillar, estimating the weight of the wag, mentally multiplying this weight by the square of the velocity, and he held his tongue.

Jehan, master of the field of battle, triumphantly continued, "I would do it too, though I am the brother of an archdeacon."

"Pretty gentry those belonging to our universities! not even to enforce respect for our privileges on such a day as this!"

"Down with the Rector, the electors, and the proctors!" cried Joannes.

"Let us make a bonfire to-night with Master Andry's books in the Champ Gaillard!" exclaimed another.

"And the desks of the scribes!" said his neighbour.

"And the wands of the beadles!"

"And the chair of the Rector!"

"Down," responded little Jehan, "down with Master Andry, the beadles, and the scribes! down with the theologians, the physicians, and the decretists! down with the proctors, the electors, and the Rector!"

"This must surely be the end of the world!" murmured Master Andry, clapping his hands to his ears.

"The Rector! There goes the Rector!" cried one of those at the window.

All eyes were instantly turned toward the Place.

"Is it really our venerable Rector, Master Thibaut?" inquired

The Hunchback of Notre-Dame

Jehan Frollo du Moulin, who, from his position on the pillar within, could not see what was passing without.

"Yes, yes," replied the others, " 'tis he! 'Tis Master Thibaut, the Rector!"

It was, in fact, the Rector and all the dignitaries of the Université, going in procession to meet the embassy, and at that moment crossing the palace-yard. The scholars who had taken post at the window greeted them as they passed with sarcasms and ironical plaudits. The Rector, who was at the head of his company, received the first volley, which was a sharp one.

"Good morrow, Mr Rector! Soho! good morrow, then!"

"How has he managed to get hither—the old gambler? How could he leave his dice?"

"Ho, there! Mr Rector Thibaut, how often did you throw double-six last night?"

"How he trots along on his mule! I declare the beast's ears are not so long as his master's!"

"Oh, what a cadaverous face—all haggard and wrinkled and wizened with the love of gaming and dicing!"

Presently it came to the turn of the other dignitaries.

"Down with the beadles! down with the mace-bearers!"

"Robin Poussepain, who is that yonder?"

"It is Gilbert le Suilly, Chancellor of the College of Autun."

"Here, take my shoe; you are better placed than I am; throw it at his head."

"*Saturnalitias mittimus ecce nuces.*" [1]

"Down with the six theologians in their white surplices!"

"Are they the theologians? Why, I took them for the six white geese given by St. Geneviève to the Cité for the fief of Roogny."

"Down with the physicians!"

"May the devil strangle the proctor of the German nation!"

"And the chaplains of the Sainte-Chapelle, with their grey amices!"

"Ho, there, Masters of Arts! you in smart black copes, and you in smarter red ones!"

"What a rare tail they make to the Rector!"

"You would suppose it was a Doge of Venice going to marry the sea."

[1] "Lo, we send thee Saturnalian nuts."

The Palace of Justice

Meanwhile, Master Andry Musnier, sworn bookseller to the Université, inclining his lips toward the ear of Master Gilles Lecornu, master-furrier of the King's robes, "I tell you, sir," he whispered, "it is the end of the world. Never were known such excesses of the scholars; it is the cursed inventions of the age that ruin everything—artillery, serpentines, bombards, and, above all, printing, that other pestilence from Germany. No more manuscripts! no more books! Printing is cutting up the bookselling trade. The end of the world is certainly at hand."

"I perceive so," said the master-furrier, "because velvets have become so common."

At this moment the clock struck twelve.

"Aha!" said the whole assembled multitude with one voice. The scholars were mute; and there ensued a prodigious bustle, a general movement of feet and heads, a grand detonation of coughing and nose-blowing; each individual took his station, and set himself to rights. Profound silence succeeded; every neck was outstretched, every mouth open, every eye fixed on the marble table; but nothing was to be seen, save the four sergeants of the bailiff, who still stood there, stiff and motionless as four painted statues. Every face then turned toward the platform reserved for the Flemish ambassadors; the door remained shut, and the platform empty. The crowd had been waiting ever since morning for three things: noon, the Flanders embassy, and the mystery. Noon alone had been punctual to its time. This was rather too bad.

They waited one, two, three, five minutes, a quarter of an hour; nothing came. Not a creature appeared either on the platform or on the stage. Meanwhile impatience grew into irritation. Angry words went round, at first, it is true, in a low tone. "The mystery! the mystery!" was faintly muttered. A storm, which as yet only rumbled at a distance, began to gather over the crowd. It was Jehan du Moulin who drew down the first spark.

"The mystery, and let the Flemings go to the devil!" shouted he, with all his might, twisting like a snake about his capital. The crowd clapped their hands. "The mystery!" they repeated, "and send Flanders to all the devils!"

"Let us instantly have the mystery," resumed the scholar, "or I recommend that we should hang the Bailiff of the Palace by way of comedy and morality."

"Well said!" cried the people; "and let us begin with hanging the sergeants!"

Prodigious were the acclamations that followed. The four poor devils turned pale, and began to look at each other. The crowd moved toward them, and they saw the frail wooden balustrade which separated them from the people already bending and giving way to the pressure of the multitude.

The moment was critical. "Down, down with them!" was the cry, which resounded from all sides. At this instant the tapestry of the dressing-room, which we have described above, was thrown open, and forth issued a personage, the mere sight of whom suddenly appeased the crowd, and, as if by magic, changed its indignation into curiosity.

"Silence! silence!" was the universal cry.

The personage in question, shaking with fear in every limb, advanced to the edge of the marble table, with a profusion of bows, which, the nearer he approached, more and more resembled genuflexions. Meanwhile, tranquillity was pretty well restored; nothing was to be heard but that slight noise which always rises from even a silent crowd.

"Messieurs les bourgeois, and *mesdemoiselles les bourgeoises,"* said he, "we are to have the honour of declaiming and performing, before his Eminence Monsieur the Cardinal, a very goodly morality, called *The Good Judgment of Madame the Virgin Mary.* The part of Jupiter will be enacted by myself. His Eminence is at this moment attending the most honourable the embassy of Monsieur the Duke of Austria, which is detained till now to hear the speech of Monsieur the Rector of the Université, at the gate of Baudets. The moment his Eminence the Cardinal arrives we shall begin."

It is very certain that nothing but the interposition of Jupiter saved the necks of the four unlucky sergeants of the Bailiff of the Palace. Had we even the honour of inventing this most true history, and were we in consequence responsible for it before the tribunal of criticism, it is not against us that the classic precept of antiquity, *Nec Deus intersit,*[1] could at this moment be adduced. For the rest, the costume of his godship was very superb, and had contributed not a little to quiet the crowd by engrossing all their attention. He was attired in a brigandine of black velvet with

[1] "Ever let a God intervene."

gilt studs; on his head he wore a helmet, adorned with silver gilt buttons; and, but for the rouge and the thick beard, which divided his face between them; for the roll of gilt pasteboard, garnished all over with stripes of tinsel, which he held in his hand, and in which the practised eye easily recognized the thunderbolt of Jove; but for his flesh-coloured legs, and feet sandaled after the Greek fashion, he might have sustained a comparison for his stately port with a Breton archer of the corps of Monsieur de Berry.

CHAPTER II

PIERRE GRINGOIRE

WHILE he was speaking, however, the universal satisfaction, nay, admiration, excited by his costume, was dispelled by his words; and when he arrived at that unfortunate conclusion, "The moment his Eminence the Cardinal arrives we shall begin," his voice was drowned by the hootings of the multitude.

"The mystery! the mystery! Begin immediately!" shouted the people. And, amid the tempest of voices was heard that of Joannes de Molendino, which pierced through the uproar like a fife in a band of rough music: "Begin immediately!" screeched the young scholar.

"Down with Jupiter and the Cardinal de Bourbon!" vociferated Robin Poussepain and the other clerks perched in the window.

"The morality immediately!" repeated the populace; "this instant! or the sack and the cord for the comedians and the Cardinal!"

Poor Jupiter, affrighted, aghast, pale beneath his rouge, dropped his thunderbolt, took off his helmet, and bowed, trembling and stammering: "His Eminence—the ambassadors—Madame Margaret of Flanders——" He knew not what to say. In good sooth he was afraid of being hanged—hanged by the populace for waiting, hanged by the Cardinal for not waiting: on either side he had the same prospect; that is to say, the gallows. Luckily for him another person came forward to extricate him from this dilemma, and to assume the responsibility.

An individual who had stationed himself within the balustrade, in the vacant space left round the marble table, and whom no one had yet perceived, so completely was his tall slender figure screened from sight by the diameter of the pillar against which he had been leaning—this individual, tall and slender, as we have said, fair, pale, still young, though his forehead and cheeks were already wrinkled, with sparkling eyes and smiling lips, habited in black serge worn threadbare with age, approached the marble table, and made a sign to the horror-stricken actor, who was too much engrossed to notice him.

He advanced a step farther. "Jupiter!" said he; "my dear Jupiter!" Still the other heard him not. At length the tall pale man, losing his patience, called out almost under his very nose, "Michel Giborne!"

"Who calls me?" said Jupiter, starting like one suddenly awakened.

"I," replied the personage in black.

"Aha!" said Jupiter.

"Begin immediately," rejoined the other. "Comply with the wish of the audience. I undertake to pacify Monsieur the Bailiff, who will pacify Monsieur the Cardinal."

Jupiter breathed again.

"Gentlemen citizens," cried he with all the force of his lungs to the crowd who continued to hoot him, "we shall begin forthwith."

"*Evoe, Jupiter! Plaudite cives!*" [1] shouted the scholars.

"Hurrah! hurrah!" cried the populace.

A clapping of hands that was absolutely deafening ensued; and, after Jupiter had retired behind his tapestry, the hall still shook with acclamations.

Meanwhile the unknown personage, who had so magically laid the tempest, had modestly withdrawn into the penumbra of his pillar, where he would no doubt have remained invisible, motionless, and mute as before, but for two young females, who, being in the front rank of the spectators, had remarked his colloquy with Michel Giborne—Jupiter.

"Master!" said one of them, beckoning him to come to her.

"Hold your tongue, my dear Liénarde," said her neighbour, a buxom, fresh-coloured damsel, gaily attired in her Sunday bravery,

---

[1] "Hurrah for Jupiter! Applaud, ye citizens!"

Pierre Gringoire

"he is not a clerk, but a layman; you must not call him *master,* but *messire.*"

"Messire!" said Liénarde.

The unknown advanced to the balustrade. "What would you with me, my pretty damsels?" inquired he eagerly.

"Oh! nothing," said Liénarde, quite confused: "it is my neighbour, Gisquette la Gencienne, who wants to speak to you."

"Not so," replied Gisquette, blushing; "it was Liénarde who called you *master,* and I told her she must say *messire.*"

The two young females cast down their eyes. The other, who desired nothing better than to engage them in conversation, surveyed them with a smile.

"Then you have nothing to say to me?"

"Oh, dear, no!" answered Gisquette.

"Nothing," said Liénarde.

The tall fair young man was just retiring, but the two inquisitive girls had no mind to let him go so easily.

"Messire," said Gisquette, with the impetuosity of a sluice that is opened, or of a woman who has taken her resolution, "you must know that soldier who is to play the part of the Virgin Mary in the mystery?"

"You mean the part of Jupiter?" rejoined the unknown.

"Ah, yes!" said Liénarde; "she is mad, I think. You know Jupiter, then?"

"Michel Giborne?" answered the pale man. "Yes, madam."

"What a goodly beard he has!" said Liénarde.

"Will it be fine—what they are going to say up there?" timidly inquired Gisquette.

"Mighty fine, I assure you," replied the unknown, without the least hesitation.

"What will it be?" said Liénarde.

"*The Good Judgment of Madame the Virgin,* a morality, an't please you, madam."

"Ah! that's a different thing," rejoined Liénarde.

A short silence ensued; it was broken by the unknown informant. "This morality is quite a new piece; it has never been performed."

"Then," said Gisquette, "it is not the same that was given two years ago, at the entry of Monsieur the Legate, in which three handsome young girls enacted the parts of——"

25

"Of sirens," continued Liénarde.

"And quite naked," added the young man.

Liénarde modestly cast down her eyes; Gisquette looked at her and did the same. He then proceeded, with a smile, "That was a pleasant sight enough; this morality to-day was composed expressly for the Princess of Flanders."

"Will there be any love-songs in it?" asked Gisquette.

"Oh, fie! in a morality!" said the unknown; "they would be inconsistent with the character of the piece. If it were a mummery, well and good."

"What a pity!" exclaimed Gisquette. "On that day there were wild men and women at the conduit of Ponceau, and they fought together, and put themselves into a great many attitudes, singing little songs all the while."

"What is fit for a legate," drily replied the unknown, "may not be fit for a princess."

"And near them," resumed Liénarde, "was a band of musicians playing delightful tunes."

"And, for the refreshment of passengers," continued Gisquette, "the conduit threw out wine, milk, and hypocras, at three mouths, for everyone to drink that listed."

"And a little below the Ponceau," proceeded Liénarde, "at the Trinity, the Passion was represented in dumb-show."

"If I recollect right," cried Gisquette, "it was Christ on the cross, and the two thieves on the right and left."

Here the young gossips, warming at the recollection of the entry of Monsieur the Legate, began to speak both together.

"And farther on, at the Porte aux Peintres, there were other characters magnificently dressed."

"And at the conduit of Saint-Innocent a hunter pursuing a doe with a great noise of dogs and horns."

"And then, at the shambles, those scaffolds representing Dieppe!"

"And when the Legate passed, you know, Gisquette, how our people attacked it, and all the English had their throats cut."

"And then the superb personages at the Pont au Change, which was covered all over with an awning."

"And as the Legate passed more than two hundred dozen of all sorts of birds were let loose upon the bridge. What a fine sight that was, Liénarde!"

Pierre Gringoire

"This will be a finer to-day," remarked the interlocutor, who seemed to listen to them with impatience.

"You promise us, then, that this mystery will be a very fine one?" said Gisquette.

"Certainly," replied he, adding, with a degree of emphasis, "I made it myself."

"Indeed!" exclaimed the girls in amazement.

"Indeed!" responded the poet, bridling up a little; "that is to say, there are two of us; Jehan Marchand, who sawed the planks and put together the woodwork of the theatre, and I who wrote the piece. My name is Pierre Gringoire."

The author of *The Cid* could not have said with greater pride, Pierre Corneille.

Our readers may probably have perceived that some time must have elapsed between the moment when Jupiter disappeared behind the tapestry and that in which the author of the new morality revealed himself so abruptly to the simple admiration of Gisquette and Liénarde. It was an extraordinary circumstance that the crowd, a few minutes before so tumultuous, now waited most meekly on the faith of the comedian; which proves that everlasting truth, confirmed by daily experience in our theatres, that the best way to make the public wait with patience is to affirm that you are just going to begin.

At any rate, the young scholar Joannes did not fall asleep at his post.

"Soho, there!" he shouted all at once, amid the quiet expectation which had succeeded the disturbance. "Jupiter, Madame the Virgin, puppets of the devil, are ye making your game of us? The mystery! the mystery! Begin at once, or look to yourselves!"

This was quite enough to produce the desired effect. A band of instruments, high and low, in the interior of the theatre, began to play; the tapestry was raised, and forth came four persons, bepainted and bedecked with various colours, who climbed the rude stage-ladder, and, on reaching the upper platform, drew up in a row before the audience, to whom they paid the usual tribute of a low obeisance. The symphony ceased, and the mystery commenced.

The performers, having been liberally repaid for their obeisances with applause, began, amid solemn silence on the part of the audience, a prologue, which we gladly spare the reader. On this occasion,

27

as it often happens at the present day, the public bestowed much more attention on the dresses of the performers than on the speeches which they had to deliver; and, to confess the truth, the public were in the right. All four were habited in robes half white and half yellow, which differed in nothing but the nature of the stuff; the first being of gold and silver brocade, the second of silk, the third of woollen, and the fourth of linen. The first of these personages carried a sword in the right hand, the second two gold keys, the third a pair of scales, and the fourth a spade; and, to assist those dull perceptions which might not have seen clearly through the transparency of these attributes, there was embroidered in large black letters at the bottom of the robe of brocade, "MY NAME IS NOBILITY"; at the bottom of the silken robe, "MY NAME IS CLERGY"; at the bottom of the woollen robe, "MY NAME IS TRADE"; and at the bottom of the linen robe, "MY NAME IS LABOUR." The sex of the two male characters, Clergy and Labour, was sufficiently indicated to every intelligent spectator by the shortness of their robes and the fashion of their caps, whilst the two females had longer garments and hoods upon their heads.

Any person, too, must have been exceedingly perverse or impenetrably obtuse, not to gather from the prologue that Labour was wedded to Trade, and Clergy to Nobility; and that the two happy couples were the joint possessors of a magnificent golden dolphin, which they intended to adjudge to the most beautiful of women. Accordingly, they were travelling through the world in quest of this beauty; and, after successively rejecting the Queen of Golconda, the Princess of Trebisond, the daughter of the great Khan of Tartary, and many others, Labour and Clergy, Nobility and Trade, had come to rest themselves upon the marble table of the Palace of Justice; at the same time bestowing on the honest auditory as many maxims and apophthegms as could in those days have been picked up at the Faculty of Arts, at the examinations, disputations, and acts, at which masters take their caps and their degrees.

All this was really exceedingly fine; but yet, among the whole concourse upon whom the four allegorical personages were pouring, as if in emulation of each other, torrents of metaphors, there was not a more attentive ear, a more vehemently throbbing heart, a wilder-looking eye, a more outstretched neck, than the eye, the ear, the neck, and the heart of the author, of the poet, of the worthy

Pierre Gringoire

Pierre Gringoire, who a few moments before could not deny himself the pleasure of telling his name to two handsome girls. He had retired a few paces from them, behind his pillar; and there he listened, he watched, he exulted. The hearty applause which had greeted the opening of his prologue still rang in his ears; and he was completely absorbed in that kind of ecstatic contemplation with which an author sees his ideas drop one by one from the lips of the actor, amid the silence of a vast assembly.

With pain we record it, this first ecstasy was soon disturbed. Scarcely had Gringoire raised to his lips the intoxicating cup of joy and triumph, when it was dashed with bitterness.

A ragged mendicant, who could make nothing by his vocation, lost as he was among the crowd, and who had, probably, not found a sufficient indemnity in the pockets of his neighbours, conceived the idea of perching himself upon some conspicuous point, for the purpose of attracting notice and alms. During the delivery of the prologue he had accordingly scrambled, by the aid of the pillars of the reserved platform, up to the cornice which ran round it below the balustrade, and there he seated himself silently, soliciting the notice and pity of the multitude by his rags and a hideous sore which covered his right arm.

The prologue was proceeding without molestation, when, as ill luck would have it, Joannes Frollo, from the top of his pillar, espied the mendicant and his grimaces. An outrageous fit of laughter seized the young wag, who, caring little about interrupting the performance and disturbing the profound attention of the audience, merrily cried, "Only look at that rapscallion begging yonder!"

Reader, if you have ever thrown a stone into a pond swarming with frogs, or fired a gun at a covey of birds, you may form some conception of the effect produced by this incongruous exclamation, amid the general silence and attention. Gringoire started as at an electric shock; the prologue stopped short, and every head turned tumultuously toward the mendicant, who, so far from being disconcerted, regarded this incident as a favourable opportunity for making a harvest, and began to drawl out, in a doleful tone, and with half closed eyes, "Charity, if you please!"

"Why, upon my soul," resumed Joannes, " 'tis Clopin Trouillefou! Hoho! my fine fellow, you found the wound on your leg in the way, and so you've clapped it on your arm, have you?"

The Hunchback of Notre-Dame

As he spoke, he threw, with the dexterity of a monkey, a piece of small coin into the greasy hat which the beggar held with his ailing arm. The latter pocketed, without wincing, both the money and the sarcasm, and continued in a lamentable tone, "Charity, if you please!"

This episode considerably distracted the attention of the audience; and a number of the spectators, with Robin Poussepain and all the clerks at their head, loudly applauded this extempore duet, performed in the middle of the prologue by the scholar with his squeaking voice and the mendicant with his monotonous descant.

Gringoire was sorely displeased. On recovering from his first stupefaction, he bawled out lustily to the four actors on the stage, "Why the devil do ye stop? Go on! go on!" without even condescending to cast a look of disdain at the two interrupters.

At this moment he felt a twitch at the skirt of his surtout; he turned round in an ill humour, and had some difficulty in raising a smile, which, however, he could not suppress. It was the plump, handsome arm of Gisquette la Gencienne, thrust through the balustrade, which thus solicited his attention.

"Sir," said the damsel, "will they go on with the mystery?"

"Most certainly," replied Gringoire, not a little shocked at the question.

"In that case, Messire," she resumed, "will you have the courtesy to explain to me——"

"What they are going to say?" asked Gringoire, interrupting her. "Well, listen."

"No," rejoined Gisquette, "but what they have been saying so far."

Gringoire started, like a person with a wound which had been probed to the quick.

"A plague on the stupid wench!" he muttered between his teeth.

Gisquette had completely ruined herself in his good opinion.

The actors had, meanwhile, obeyed his injunction; and the public, seeing that they had resumed the performance, began again to listen, but not without losing a great many beauties, from the abrupt division of the piece into two parts, and the species of soldering which they had to undergo. Such, at least, was the painful reflec-

30

Pierre Gringoire

tion mentally made by Gringoire. Tranquillity, however, was gradually restored; the scholar held his tongue, the beggar counted the money in his hat, and the piece proceeded swimmingly.

It was, in truth, a masterly work; and we verily believe that managers might avail themselves of it at the present day, with some modifications. The plot was simple; and Gringoire, in the candid sanctuary of his own bosom, admired its clearness. As the reader may easily conceive, the four allegorical characters were somewhat fatigued with their tour through the three parts of the world, without finding an opportunity of disposing, agreeably to their intentions, of their golden dolphin. Thereupon followed a panegyric on the marvellous fish, with a thousand delicate allusions to the young bridegroom of Margaret of Flanders, at that moment sadly shut up at Amboise, and never dreaming that Labour and Clergy, Nobility and Trade, had been making a tour of the world on his account. The said dolphin, then, was young, handsome, bold, and, above all, —magnificent origin of every royal virtue!—the son of the Lion of France. I declare that this bold metaphor is truly admirable; and that the natural history of the theatre is not at all startled, on an occasion of this kind, that a dolphin should be the offspring of a lion. It is precisely these out-of-the-way and Pindaric medleys that are evidences of enthusiasm. Critical justice, nevertheless, requires the admission that the poet ought to have developed this original idea in the compass of somewhat less than two hundred verses. It is true that the mystery was to last from the hour of twelve till that of four, according to the ordinance of Monsieur the Provost, and that it was absolutely necessary to say something or other. Besides, the audience listened very patiently.

All at once, in the midst of a quarrel between Mademoiselle Trade and Madame Nobility, at the moment when Master Labour was delivering this emphatic line:

More stately beast was ne'er in forest seen,

the door of the reserved platform, which had hitherto remained so unseasonably closed, was still more unseasonably thrown open, and the sonorous voice of the usher abruptly announced, *"His Eminence Monseigneur the Cardinal de Bourbon!"*

31

CHAPTER III

MONSEIGNEUR THE CARDINAL

POOR Gringoire! the noise of all the big double petards at St John's, the discharge of a hundred matchlocks, the detonation of that famous serpentine of the Tour de Billy, which, at the siege of Paris, on the 29th of September, 1465, killed seven Burgundians by one shot, nay, the explosion of all the gunpowder in the magazine at the gate of the Temple, would not have so shocked his ear at the solemn and dramatic moment as these few words from the lips of an usher: *"His Eminence Monseigneur the Cardinal de Bourbon!"*

Not that Pierre Gringoire either feared or disdained Monsieur the Cardinal; he had neither that weakness nor that arrogance. A genuine eclectic, as we should say nowadays, Gringoire possessed one of those firm and elevated, calm and moderate minds, which always know how to steer a middle course, and are full of reason and liberal philosophy, at the same time that they make much of cardinals —an admirable race, widely separated from that of the philosophers; to whom Wisdom, like another Ariadne, seems to have given a ball of thread which they keep winding up from the commencement of the world, through the labyrinth of human affairs. We find them always and everywhere the same, that is to say, ever accommodating themselves to the times. And, without reckoning our Pierre Gringoire, who might be their representative in the fifteenth century, if we were to bestow on him that illustration which he deserves, it was certainly their spirit which animated Father du Breul, when he wrote, in the sixteenth, these simply sublime words, worthy of all ages: "I am a Parisian by nation, and a parrhisian by speech; for *parrhisia,* in Greek, signifies liberty of speech, the which I have used even unto Messeigneurs the Cardinals, uncle and brother of Monseigneur the Prince of Conty: at the same time with respect for their high dignity, and without giving offence to anyone of their retinue, which, methinks, is saying a great deal."

There was, then, neither hatred of the Cardinal nor disdain of his presence in the disagreeable impression which it made on Pierre Gringoire. On the contrary, our poet had too much good sense,

Monseigneur the Cardinal

and too threadbare a frock, not to feel particularly anxious that many an allusion in his prologue, and particularly the eulogy on the dolphin, the son of the Lion of France, should find its way to the ear of a most eminent personage. But it is not interest that predominates in the noble nature of poets. Supposing the entity of the poet to be represented by the number 10; it is certain that a chemist, on analysing it, would find it to be composed of one part interest and nine parts vanity. Now, at the moment when the door opened for the Cardinal the nine parts of Gringoire's vanity, swollen and inflated by the breath of popular admiration, were in a state of such prodigious enlargement as completely to smother that imperceptible particle of interest which we just now discovered in the constitution of poets; a most valuable ingredient, nevertheless, the ballast of reality and of humanity, without which they would never descend to this lower world. Gringoire was delighted to see, to feel, in some measure, a whole assembly, of varlets, it is true—but what does that signify?—stupefied, petrified, and stricken as it were insensible, by the immeasurable speeches which succeeded each other in every part of his epithalamium. I affirm that he participated in the general happiness, and that, unlike La Fontaine, who, on the first representation of his comedy of *The Florentine,* inquired, "What paltry scribbler wrote this rhapsody?" Gringoire would gladly have asked his neighbour, "Who is the author of this masterpiece?" Now, imagine what must have been the effect produced upon him by the abrupt and unseasonable arrival of the Cardinal.

What he had reason to apprehend was but too soon realized. The entry of his Eminence upset the auditory. All heads turned mechanically toward the platform. Not another word was to be heard. "The Cardinal! the Cardinal!" was upon every tongue. The unlucky prologue was cut short a second time.

The Cardinal paused for a moment on the threshold of the platform, with supercilious looks surveying the auditory. Meanwhile the tumult increased, each striving to raise his head above his neighbour's to obtain a better view of his Eminence.

He was, in fact, a very distinguished personage, the sight of whom was well worth any other comedy. Charles, Cardinal de Bourbon, Archbishop and Count of Lyons, Primate of the Gauls, was at once allied to Louis XI through his brother Pierre, Lord of Beaujeu, who was married to the King's eldest daughter, and to Charles the

33

Bold by his mother, Agnes of Burgundy. Now, the predominant, the distinctive, trait in the character of the Primate of the Gauls was a courtier-spirit and devotedness to power. The reader may form some conception of the numberless embarrassments in which he had been involved by this twofold relationship, and of the temporal rocks among which his spiritual bark had been obliged to luff that it might not be wrecked either against Louis or against Charles, that Charybdis and Scylla which had engulfed the Duke of Nemours and the Constable of Saint-Pol. Thanks to heaven, he had contrived pretty well to escape the dangers of the voyage, and had arrived at Rome without obstruction. But, though he was in port, and precisely because he was in port, he could never call to mind without agitation the various chances of his political life, so long harassed by labours and alarms. Accordingly, he was accustomed to say that the year 1467 had been to him both black and white; thereby meaning that he had lost in that year his mother the Duchess of Bourbonnais, and his cousin the Duke of Burgundy, and that one mourning had consoled him for the other.

In other respects he was a good sort of man; he led a jovial life as cardinal, loved to make merry with the growth of the royal vineyard of Chaillot, did not hate the jocund Richarde la Garmoise and Thomasse la Saillarde, bestowed alms on young damsels rather than on wrinkled hags, and for all these reasons was a great favourite with the populace of Paris. Wherever he went he was surrounded by a little court of bishops and abbots of high families, wenchers and boon companions, who had no objection to join in a carouse; and more than once the pious souls of Saint-Germain d'Auxerre, as they passed in the evening under the illumined windows of the Cardinal's residence, had been scandalized on hearing the same voices which had chanted vespers to them a few hours before lustily singing, to the clatter of glasses, the bacchanalian song of Benedict XII, that Pope who added a third crown to the tiara—*Bibamus papaliter.*[1]

It was no doubt this popularity, to which he was so justly entitled, that preserved him at his entrance from any unfavourable demonstrations on the part of the crowd, which a moment before had been so dissatisfied, and by no means disposed to pay respect to a cardinal on the very day that they were going to elect a Pope. But the Pari-

[1] "Let us drink like a Pope."

Monseigneur the Cardinal

sians are not apt to bear malice; and besides, by insisting on the commencement of the performance, the honest citizens had gained a victory over the Cardinal, and this triumph was enough for them. Moreover, Monsieur the Cardinal de Bourbon was a comely man; he had a superb scarlet robe, which he wore very gracefully. Of course he had in his favour all the women, that is to say, the better half of the audience. It would be decidedly unjust and in bad taste to hoot a cardinal for coming to the play a little after the time prescribed, when he is a handsome man and wears his scarlet robe in a graceful manner.

He entered, therefore, bowed to the audience with that hereditary smile which the great have for the people, and proceeded slowly toward his armchair covered with scarlet velvet, apparently thinking of something very different from the scene before him. His train, which we should nowadays call his staff, of abbots and bishops followed him as he advanced to the front of the platform, to the no small increase of the tumult and curiosity of the spectators. Each was eager to point them out, to tell their names, to recognize at least one of them—Monsieur the Bishop of Marseilles, Alaudet, if I recollect rightly; or the Dean of Saint-Denis; or the Abbot of Saint-Germain des Prés, that libertine brother of one of the mistresses of Louis XI; but, as may be supposed, with abundance of blunders and mistakes. As for the scholars, they swore lustily. It was their day, their Feast of Fools, their saturnalia, the annual orgies of the Basoche [1] and of the schools. There was no turpitude but was authorized on that day. Was it not then the least they could do to swear at their ease, and to curse a little in the name of God, on so fine a day, in the good company of churchmen and loose women? Accordingly they made good use of the licence, and amid the general uproar horrible was the clamour of the blasphemies and enormities proceeding from the tongues thus let loose—the tongues of clerks and scholars restrained during the rest of the year by the fear of the red-hot iron of St Louis. Poor St Louis! how they set him at nought in his own Palace of Justice! Each of them had fixed upon a black, grey, white, or purple cassock for his butt among the new occupants of the platform. As for Joannes Frollo de Molendino, he, as brother of an archdeacon, boldly attacked the scarlet;

[1] The company of clerks of the Parliament of Paris.

35

and, fixing his audacious eyes on the Cardinal, he sang at the top of his voice, *"Cappa repleta mero!"* [1]

All these circumstances, which we here reveal for the edification of the reader, were so smothered by the general tumult as to pass unnoticed by the reverend group on the platform. Had it, indeed, been otherwise the Cardinal would not have heeded them, so deeply were the liberties of that day engrafted on the manners of the age. He was, moreover, wholly preoccupied—and his countenance showed it—by another solicitude, which closely pursued him, and, indeed, entered the platform almost at the same time with him, namely, the Flanders embassy.

Not that he was a profound politician, and was calculating the possible consequences of the marriage of his cousin Margaret of Burgundy with his cousin Charles, Dauphin of Vienne; or how long the good understanding patched up between the Duke of Austria and the King of France was likely to last; or how the King of England would take the slight offered to his daughter. These matters gave him no uneasiness, and he enjoyed himself every evening over the royal growth of Chaillot, without ever dreaming that a few bottles of the same wine—first doctored a little, it is true, by Coictier the physician—cordially presented to Edward IV by Louis XI would one day rid Louis XI of Edward IV. The most honourable the embassy of Monsieur the Duke of Austria brought upon the Cardinal none of these cares; but it vexed him in another way. It was in truth rather hard, as we have already observed at the beginning of this book, that he, Charles de Bourbon, should be obliged to give hearty welcome and good entertainment to paltry citizens; he, a cardinal, to burgomasters; he, a Frenchman, a boon companion, to Flemings fond of beer—and that, too, in public. This was certainly one of the most disagreeable tasks he had ever undertaken to please the King.

He turned, therefore, toward the door, and with the best grace in the world—so well had he studied his part—when the usher with his sonorous voice announced Messieurs the Envoys of Monsieur the Duke of Austria. It is scarcely necessary to remark that all the spectators did the same.

The forty-eight ambassadors of Maximilian of Austria, headed by

[1] "A cloak stuffed with old wine!"

36

Monseigneur the Cardinal

the reverend father in God, Jehan, Abbot of Saint-Bertin, Chancellor of the Golden Fleece, and Jacques de Goy, Sieur Dauby, High Bailiff of Ghent, then entered two and two, with a gravity which formed a remarkable contrast amid the volatile ecclesiastical retinue of Charles de Bourbon. Deep silence pervaded the assembly, broken only by stifled laughter at the mention of the uncouth names and all the petty titles which each of these personages repeated with imperturbable solemnity to the usher, who then flung them, names and qualities pell-mell and cruelly mangled, among the crowd. There was Master Loys Roelof, *échevin* of the city of Louvain; Messire Clays d'Etuelde, *échevin* of Brussels; Messire Paul de Baeust, Sieur de Voirmizelle, President of Flanders; Master Jehan Coleghens, burgomaster of the city of Antwerp; Master George de la Moere, and Master Gheldolf van der Hage, *échevins* of the city of Ghent; and the Sieur de Bierbecque, Jehan Pinnock, Jehan Dymaerzelle, etc. etc. bailiffs, *échevins,* burgomasters; burgomasters, *échevins,* bailiffs; all stiff, starched, formal, tricked out in velvets and damasks, and ensconced in caps of black velvet with prodigious tassels of Cyprus gold thread; fine Flemish heads after all, with austere but goodly faces, of the same family as those which Rembrandt has brought out, so grave and so expressive, from the dark ground of his night-piece; personages who all had it written on their brows that Maximilian of Austria had good reason "to place full confidence," as his manifesto declared, "in their discretion, firmness, experience, loyalty, and rare qualities."

There was, however, one exception. This was a sharp, intelligent, crafty-looking face, a physiognomy compounded of that of the monkey and the diplomatist, toward the owner of which the Cardinal advanced three steps with a low bow, and whose name, nevertheless, was plain Guillaume Rym, councillor and syndic of the city of Ghent.

Few persons there knew who this Guillaume Rym was. He was a man of rare genius, who in times of revolution would have raised himself to distinction, but was forced in the fifteenth century to resort to the hollow ways of intrigue, and to live *in the saps,* as saith the Duke of Saint-Simon. For the rest, he was duly appreciated by the first *sapper* in Europe; he wrought in familiar concert with Louis XI, and frequently lent a helping hand to the King in his secret necessities—circumstances absolutely unknown to the crowd, who marvelled at the respect paid by the Cardinal to so insignificant a person as the Flemish syndic.

CHAPTER IV

MASTER JACQUES COPPENOLE

WHILE the syndic of Ghent and his Eminence were exchanging a low obeisance and a few words in a still lower tone a man of lofty stature, with jolly face and broad shoulders, stepped forward for the purpose of entering abreast with Guillaume Rym; they looked for all the world like a bulldog beside a fox. His felt cap and leathern vest were conspicuous amid the velvets and silks which surrounded him. Assuming that he was some groom who had mistaken the way, the usher stopped him.

"No admittance here, my friend," said he.

The man in the leathern vest pushed him back.

"What means the fellow?" cried he in a voice which drew the attention of the whole hall to this strange colloquy. "Dost not see that I belong to them?"

"Your name?" asked the usher.

"Jacques Coppenole."

"Your quality?"

"Hosier; at the sign of the Three Chains in Ghent."

The usher was staggered. To have to announce bailiffs and burgomasters and *échevins* was bad enough; but a hosier!—no—he could not make up his mind to that. The Cardinal was upon thorns. The whole assembly was all eye and ear. For two days his Eminence had been taking pains to lick these Flemish bears, in order to make them a little more producible in public, and his failure was galling. Meanwhile Guillaume Rym, with his sly smile, stepped up to the usher, and said in a very low whisper, "Announce Master Jacques Coppenole, clerk to the *échevins* of the city of Ghent."

"Usher," said the Cardinal in a loud tone, "announce Master Jacques Coppenole, clerk to the *échevins* of the most noble city of Ghent."

Master Jacques Coppenole

Now, it is very certain that Guillaume Rym, had he been left to himself, would have shuffled off the difficulty, but Coppenole had heard the Cardinal.

"No, by the Rood!" cried he, with his voice of thunder, "Jacques Coppenole, hosier. Hark ye, usher, neither more nor less. By the Rood! hosier—that's quite fine enough! Monsieur the Archduke has more than once sought his gloves among my hose."

A burst of laughter and applause ensued. A witticism or a pun is instantly comprehended in Paris, and consequently sure to be applauded. Coppenole, be it moreover observed, was one of the people, and the assembly by which he was surrounded belonged to the same class. The communication between them was in consequence prompt, electric, and hearty. The lofty bravado of the Flemish hosier, at the same time that it humbled the courtiers, awakened in all those plebeian minds a sense of dignity, still but vague and indistinct in the fifteenth century. This hosier, who had just held Monsieur the Cardinal at defiance, was their equal—a soothing reflection to poor devils accustomed to pay obedience and respect to the servants of the very sergeants of the bailiff of the Abbot of Sainte-Geneviève, the train-bearer of the Cardinal.

Coppenole bowed haughtily to the Cardinal, who returned the obeisance of the high and mighty burgher, dreaded by Louis XI. Then, while Guillaume Rym, a "cunning man and spiteful," as saith Philippe de Comines, looked after both with a smile of conscious superiority, they proceeded to their places—the Cardinal mortified and disconcerted; Coppenole, calm and proud, thinking, no doubt, that his title of hosier was as good as any other, and that Mary of Burgundy, the mother of that Margaret whose marriage Coppenole had come to negotiate, would have felt less dread of him as a cardinal than as a hosier; for it was not a cardinal who would have raised the people of Ghent against the favourites of the daughter of Charles the Bold; it was not a cardinal who would have steeled the multitude by a word against her tears and her entreaties, when the Princess of Flanders proceeded to the very foot of the scaffold to beg their lives of her subjects; while the hosier had but to lift his finger and off went your heads, ye most illustrious gentlemen, Guy d'Hymbercourt, and Chancellor Guillaume Hugonet!

The poor Cardinal's ordeal, however, was not yet over; he was doomed to drink to the very dregs the cup of penance for being in such company. The reader has, perhaps, not forgotten the impudent beggar, who at the commencement of the prologue perched himself beneath the fringe of the Cardinal's gallery. The arrival of the illustrious guests had not dislodged him from his roost, and while the prelates and the ambassadors were packing themselves, like real Flemish herrings, in the boxes of the gallery, he had placed himself at his ease, and carelessly crossed his legs over the architrave. Nobody, however, had at first noticed this extraordinary piece of insolence, the universal attention being directed to another quarter. Neither was he, on his part, aware of what was going forward in the hall; there he sat, rocking to and fro with the utmost unconcern, repeating, from force of habit, the refrain of "Charity, if you please!" Of a certainty he was the only one in the whole assembly who had not deigned to turn his head at the altercation between Coppenole and the usher. Now, as luck would have it, the hosier of Ghent, with whom the people already sympathized so strongly, and on whom all eyes were fixed, took his seat in the first row in the gallery, just above the mendicant. Great was, nevertheless, their astonishment, at seeing the Flemish ambassador, after taking a survey of the fellow nestled under his nose, slap him familiarly on his shoulder covered with tatters. The mendicant turned sharply round; surprise, recognition, pleasure, were expressed in both faces; and then, without caring a pinch of snuff for the spectators, the hosier and the scurvy rogue shook hands, and began to talk in a low tone, while the rags of Clopin Trouillefou, clapped against the cloth of gold with which the gallery was hung, produced the effect of a caterpillar upon an orange.

The novelty of this singular scene excited such a burst of merriment in the hall that the Cardinal could not help noticing it. He leaned forward, and as, from the place where he sat he had but a very imperfect view of the squalid figure of Trouillefou, he naturally supposed that he was soliciting alms. Incensed at his audacity, he cried, "Monsieur Bailliff of the Palace, throw me that varlet into the river."

"Cross of God! Monseigneur the Cardinal!" exclaimed Coppenole, "that varlet is a friend of mine."

"Hurrah! hurrah!" shouted the crowd. From that moment Master Coppenole had "great influence over the populace at Paris, as well as at Ghent; for," adds Philippe de Comines, "men of that kidney

Master Jacques Coppenole

are sure to have it, when they are so beyond measure disorderly."

The Cardinal bit his lips. Turning to his neighbour, the Abbot of Sainte-Geneviève, he said in an undertone, "Right pleasant ambassadors these, sent to us by Monsieur the Archduke to announce Madame Margaret!"

"Your Eminence," replied the Abbot, "is throwing away your civilities upon these Flemish hogs: *margaritas ante porcos.*" [1]

"Say rather," answered the Cardinal, with a smile, *"porcos ante Margaritam."* [2]

The whole petty cassocked Court was in raptures at this sally. The Cardinal felt somewhat relieved; he was now quits with Coppenole; he too had gained applause for his pun.

Now, let such of our readers as are capable of generalizing an image and an idea, to adopt the phraseology of the present day, permit us to ask if they have formed a clear conception of the spectacle presented at the moment to which we are calling their attention, by the vast parallelogram of the great hall of Paris. In the middle of the hall, backed against the western wall, a wide and magnificent gallery hung with gold brocade, into which, through a small doorway with pointed arch, advance in procession a number of grave personages, successively announced by a bawling usher. On the front seats are already many venerable figures, muffled in ermine, velvet, and scarlet. On the floor of the hall, in front and on either side of the gallery, which maintains a dignified silence, a great crowd and a great uproar. A thousand vulgar eyes fixed on every face in the gallery; a thousand whispers at every name. The scene, forsooth, is a curious one, and well deserving the attention of the spectators. But what is that kind of scaffold yonder at the farther end, on which are seen four party-coloured figures? And who is that pale-faced man in a black frock at the foot of it? Why, courteous reader, that is poor Pierre Gringoire and his prologue. We had all quite and clean forgotten him; and this was precisely what he was afraid of.

From the moment that the Cardinal entered Gringoire had not ceased to bestir himself for the salvation of his prologue. At first he enjoined the actors, who were in a state of suspense, to proceed

---

1 "Pearls before swine."
2 "Swine before a pearl." (A pun on the meaning of the word Margaret—"a pearl.")

and to raise their voices; then, perceiving that nobody listened to them, he ordered them to stop; and for the quarter of an hour that the interruption had lasted he had been incessantly bustling about, calling upon Gisquette and Liénarde to encourage their neighbours to call for the continuation of the prologue—but all in vain. Not a creature would turn away from the Cardinal, the embassy, and the gallery, the sole centre of that vast circle of visual rays. There is also reason to believe, and we record it with regret, that the audience was beginning to be somewhat tired of the prologue, at the moment when his Eminence arrived and made such a terrible diversion. After all, the gallery exhibited precisely the same spectacle as the marble table—the conflict between Labour and Clergy, Nobility and Trade. And many people liked much better to see them without disguise, living, breathing, acting, elbowing one another, in that Flemish embassy, in that episcopal court, under the Cardinal's robe, under the vest of Coppenole, than talking in verse, painted, tricked out, resembling effigies of straw stuffed into the yellow and white tunics in which Gringoire had enwrapped them.

When, however, our poet perceived that some degree of tranquillity was restored, he devised a stratagem for regaining the public attention.

"Sir," said he, turning to a jolly citizen, whose face was the image of patience, "don't you think they had better go on?"

"With what?" asked the other.

"Why, with the mystery," replied Gringoire.

"Just as you please," rejoined his neighbour.

This demi-approbation was quite enough for Gringoire. Mingling as much as possible with the crowd, he began to shout with all his might, "The mystery; the mystery! go on with the mystery!"

"The devil!" said Joannes de Molendino; "what is it they are singing down yonder?" (Gringoire was, in fact, making as much noise as half a dozen persons.) "I say, comrades, the mystery is over, is it not? They want to begin it again; we'll not suffer that."

"No, no," cried all the scholars. "Down with the mystery! down with it!"

This only served to redouble Gringoire's activity, and he bawled louder than ever, "Go on! go on!"

This clamour drew the attention of the Cardinal.

Master Jacques Coppenole

"Mr Bailiff of the Palace," said he to a stout man in black, stationed a few paces from him, "are those knaves in a holy-water font, that they make such an infernal racket?"

The Bailiff of the Palace was a sort of amphibious magistrate, a kind of bat of the judicial order, a something between the rat and the bird, the judge and the soldier.

He stepped up to his Eminence, and sorely dreading his anger, he explained to him with faltering tongue the popular inconsistency, how that noon had arrived before his Eminence, and that the comedians had been forced to begin without waiting for him.

The Cardinal laughed outright. "By my faith!" he exclaimed; "the Rector of the Université should have done the same! What say you, Master Guillaume Rym?"

"Monseigneur," answered Master Guillaume Rym, "we ought to be glad that we have escaped half of the play. The loss is so much gained."

"May those fellows continue their farce?" asked the bailiff.

"Go on, go on," said the Cardinal; " 'tis the same to me."

The bailiff advanced to the front of the gallery, and enjoined silence by a motion of his hand. "Burgesses and inhabitants," he cried, "to satisfy those who wish the piece to proceed, and those who are desirous that it should finish, his Eminence orders it to be continued."

The characters on the stage resumed their cue, and Gringoire hoped that at any rate the rest of his piece would be heard out. This hope, however, was destined, like his other illusions, to be very soon blasted. Silence was, indeed, in some degree restored among the audience, but Gringoire had not observed that, at the moment when the Cardinal ordered the mystery to be continued, the gallery was far from full, and that after the Flemish envoys had taken their seats other persons, forming part of the train, kept coming in, and the names and qualities of these, proclaimed every now and then by the bawling voice of the usher, broke in upon his dialogue and made great havoc with it. Gringoire was the more incensed at this strange accompaniment, which rendered it difficult to follow the piece, because he felt that the interest increased as it proceeded, and that his work needed nothing but to be heard. Indeed, a more ingenious and more dramatic plot could scarcely be invented. The four characters of the prologue were bewailing their mortal embarrassment when Venus appeared to them in person, attired in a robe embroidered with the arms of the Cité of Paris. She came to prefer her claim to the dolphin promised to the most beautiful female: it was supported by Jupiter, whose thunder was heard rumbling in the dressing-room, and the goddess had well-nigh carried her point, that is to say, without metaphor, established her right to the hand of Monsieur the Dauphin, when a child, in a dress of white damask, and holding a daisy—diaphanous personification of the Princess of Flanders—entered the lists against Venus. This unexpected incident produced an instant change in the state of affairs. After some controversy Venus, Margaret, and the whole party agreed to refer the matter to the decision of the Holy Virgin. There was another striking part, that of Don Pedro, King of Mesopotamia; but owing to so many interruptions it was difficult to discover its connexion with the plot of the piece.

All these beauties were unfortunately neither appreciated nor understood. The moment the Cardinal entered it was as if an invisible and magic thread had suddenly drawn all eyes from the marble table to the gallery, from the southern extremity to the west side of the hall. Nothing could break the spell thrown over the audience; every eye remained fixed on one point, and the newcomers and their confounded names, and their faces, and their dresses, created an endless diversion. This was most mortifying. Excepting Gisquette and Liénarde, who turned about from time to time when Gringoire pulled them by the sleeve, and the pursy, patient neighbour, not a creature listened, or even looked at the poor forsaken morality.

With what anguish of spirit did he see his whole edifice of glory and poesy tumbling down piecemeal! To think that the same auditory, which had been on the point of rebelling against Monsieur the Bailiff from impatience to hear his work, now that they might witness its performance, cared nothing at all about it! A performance, too, which had begun amid such unanimous applause! Oh! the incessant flowing and ebbing of popular favour! How near they had been to hanging the sergeants of the bailiff! What would he not have given for the return of that delicious moment!

The brutal monologue of the usher ceased at last; all the company

Master Jacques Coppenole

had arrived. Gringoire breathed once more, and the actors proceeded with spirit. All at once, what should Master Coppenole the hosier do, but rise from his seat? and Gringoire stood aghast to hear him, amid the breathless attention of the spectators, commence this abominable harangue:

"Gentlemen burgesses and yeomen of Paris, I know not, by the Rood, what we are about here. Down there, on yonder stage, I see some mountebanks, who appear disposed to fight. I cannot tell whether this is what you call a mystery; let it be what it will, it is not amusing. They bang one another with their tongues, and that is all. Here have I been waiting this quarter of an hour for the first blow; but nothing comes of it. They are cravens only who clapperclaw each other with abuse. You should have sent to London or Rotterdam for bruisers, and, by my faith! you would have had thumps which you would have heard all over the place; but these are contemptible. They might have given us at least a morris-dance or some other mummery. To be sure nothing was said about that; they promised me that I should see the Festival of Fools and the election of Pope. We have our Pope of Fools at Ghent too, and, by the Rood, in this respect we are not behind your famous city. But the way we do is this—we collect a crowd, such as there is here; then every one that likes puts his head in turn through a hole, and grins at the others, and he who makes the ugliest face is chosen Pope by acclamation—that's it. 'Tis a diverting sight, I assure you. Shall we choose your Pope after the fashion of my country? 'Twill be more amusing at any rate than listening to those praters. If they like to come and grin through the hole, why, let them. What say you, gentlemen burgesses? We have here a sufficiently grotesque specimen of both sexes to raise a hearty laugh in the Flemish fashion; and we have ugly faces enough among us to expect a capital grimace."

Gringoire would fain have replied, but horror, indignation, stupefaction, deprived him of utterance. Besides, the motion of the popular hosier was hailed with such enthusiasm by the citizens, flattered with the appellation of *yeomen*, that resistance would have been useless. All that he could now do was to swim with the current.

CHAPTER V

QUASIMODO

IN the twinkling of an eye everything was ready for carrying the idea of Coppenole into effect. Burgesses, scholars, and lawyers' clerks had fallen to work. The little chapel opposite to the marble table was chosen for the scene of the grimaces. Having broken the glass in the pretty little round window over the door, they agreed that the competitors should put their heads through the circle of stone that was left. To enable them to reach it two hogsheads were brought and set one upon the other. It was determined that all candidates, whether men or women,—for women were eligible—should hide their faces, and keep them covered in the chapel till the moment of exhibiting them, that the impression of the grimace might be the stronger. In a few minutes the chapel was full of competitors, and the door was shut upon them.

Coppenole from his place ordered, directed, superintended, all the arrangements. During the uproar the Cardinal, not less disconcerted than Gringoire, having excused himself on the plea of business and vespers, retired with his retinue; while the crowd which his coming had so strongly agitated, was scarcely aware of his departure. Guillaume Rym was the only person that noticed the discomposure of his Eminence. The popular attention, like the sun, pursued its revolution; setting out from one end of the hall, after pausing some time in the middle, it was now at the other extremity. The marble table, the brocaded gallery, had each had their moment; it was now the turn of Louis XI's chapel. The field was open to every species of fun; the Flemings and the populace alone were left.

The grimaces began. The first face that presented itself at the window with its red eyes and widely gaping mouth, and forehead puckered up in wrinkles, like hussar boots in the time of the Emperor,[1] caused such convulsions of inextinguishable laughter, that Homer would have taken these ruffians for immortal gods. A second and a third grimace succeeded—then another and another, followed by redoubled shouts of laughter and stampings and clatterings of glee. The crowd was seized with a sort of frantic intoxication, a

---

1 Napoleon.

Quasimodo

supernatural kind of fascination, of which it would be difficult to convey any idea to the reader of our own days. Imagine a series of visages successively presenting every geometric figure, from the triangle to the trapezium—from the cone to the polyhedron; every human expression, from rage to lechery; all ages, from the wrinkles of the new-born infant to those of the hag at the point of death; all the religious phantasmagorias from Faunus to Beelzebub; all the brute profiles, from the distended jaw to the beak, from the snout of the hog to the muzzle of the bull. Imagine all the grotesque heads of the Pont Neuf, those nightmares petrified under the hand of Germain Pilon, suddenly starting into life, and coming one after another to stare you in the face with flaming eyes; all the masks of the carnival of Venice passing in succession before your eyeglass—in a word, a human kaleidoscope.

The orgies became more and more uproarious. Teniers could have given but an imperfect idea of the scene. Fancy Salvator Rosa's battle turned into a bacchanalian piece. There were no longer any distinctions of ranks and persons,—no longer scholars, ambassadors, men, or women—all were lost in the general licence. The great hall was one vast furnace of effrontery and jollity; where every mouth was a cry, every eye a flash, every face a contortion, every individual a posture; all was howling and roaring. The extraordinary faces which in turn presented themselves at the window acted like so many brands thrown upon a blazing fire; and from all this effervescent crowd issued, like vapour from a furnace, a sharp, shrill, hissing noise, as from an immense serpent.

Meanwhile Gringoire, the first moment of dejection over, had recovered his spirits; he had braced himself against adversity. "Go on!" said he for the third time to his speaking machines, the comedians, and then paced to and fro, with long strides, before the marble table. He almost felt tempted to exhibit himself in his turn at the round window of the chapel, were it but to enjoy the pleasure of grinning at the ungrateful populace. But no, said he mentally, no revenge! that were unworthy of us. Let us struggle manfully to the last: the power of poesy is mighty over the populace: I will bring them back. We shall see which will conquer—the grimaces or the *belles-lettres*.

Alas poor Gringoire! he was left to be the only spectator of his play: every back was turned upon him.

The Hunchback of Notre-Dame

I am wrong: the fat patient man whom he had previously consulted in a critical moment was still turned toward the theatre. As for Gisquette and Liénarde, they had long deserted.

Gringoire was touched to the bottom of his heart by the constancy of his only spectator. He went up and spoke to him, at the same time gently shaking his arm; for the good man was leaning upon the balustrade and napping a little.

"Sir," said Gringoire, "I am exceedingly obliged to you."

"Sir," replied the fat man, with a yawn, "for what?"

"I see," rejoined the poet, "that you are quite annoyed by all this uproar, which prevents your hearing comfortably. But, never mind; your name will be handed down to posterity: may I ask what it is?"

"Renauld Château, Keeper of the Seal of the Châtelet of Paris, at your service."

"Sir, you are the only representative of the Muses in this assembly," said Gringoire.

"You are too polite, sir," replied the Keeper of the Seal of the Châtelet.

"You are the only one," resumed Gringoire, "who has paid any attention to the piece. What do you think of it?"

"Why, to tell the truth," answered the pursy magistrate, only half awake, "it is stupid enough."

Gringoire was forced to be content with this opinion; for thunders of applause, mingled with prodigious shouts, cut short their conversation. The Pope of Fools was elected. "Hurrah! hurrah! hurrah!" cried the people on all sides.

It was, in truth, a countenance of miraculous ugliness which at this moment shone forth from the circular aperture. After all the faces, pentagonal, hexagonal and heteroclite, that had followed each other at this window, without realizing the idea of the grotesque which the crowd had set up in their frantic imaginations, it required nothing short of the sublimely monstrous grimace which had just dazzled the multitude to obtain their suffrages. Master Coppenole himself applauded; and Clopin Trouillefou, who had been a candidate—and God knows what intensity of ugliness his features could attain—confessed himself conquered. We shall do the same: we shall not attempt to give the reader any idea of that tetrahedron nose, of that horseshoe mouth, of that little left eye, stubbled up with an eyebrow of carrotty bristles, while the right was

Quasimodo

completely overwhelmed and buried by an enormous wen; of those irregular teeth, jagged here and there like the battlements of a fortress; of that horny lip, over which one of those teeth protruded, like the tusk of an elephant; of that forked chin; and, above all, of the expression, that mixture of spite, wonder, and melancholy, spread over these exquisite features. Imagine such an object, if you can.

The acclamation was unanimous: the crowd rushed to the chapel. The lucky Pope of Fools was brought out in triumph, and it was not till then that surprise and admiration were at their height: what had been mistaken for a grimace was his natural visage; indeed, it might be said that his whole person was but one grimace. His prodigious head was covered with red bristles; between his shoulders rose an enormous hump, which was counterbalanced by a protuberance in front; his thighs and legs were so strangely put together that they touched at no one point but the knees, and seen in front, resembled two sickles joined at the handles; his feet were immense, his hands monstrous; but, with all this deformity, there was a formidable air of strength, agility, and courage, constituting a singular exception to the eternal rule, which ordains that force, as well as beauty, shall result from harmony. He looked like a giant who had been broken in pieces and ill soldered together.

When this sort of Cyclops appeared on the threshold of the chapel, motionless, squat, almost as broad as high, "the square of his base," as a great man expresses it, the populace instantly recognized him by his coat, half red and half purple, sprinkled with silver bells, and, more especially, by the perfection of his ugliness, and cried out with one voice: "It is Quasimodo the bell-ringer! It is Quasimodo the hunchback of Notre-Dame! Quasimodo the one-eyed! Quasimodo the bandy-legged! Hurrah! hurrah!" The poor devil, it seems, had plenty of surnames to choose among.

"Let pregnant women take care of themselves!" cried the scholars. The women actually covered their faces.

"Oh, the ugly ape!" cried one.

"And as mischievous as ugly," said another.

" 'Tis the devil himself!" exclaimed a third.

"I am so unlucky as to live near Notre-Dame, and I hear him at night prowling about in the gutters."

"What! with the cats?"

"He is always on our roofs."

49

The Hunchback of Notre-Dame

"The other night he came and grinned at me through my garret window. I thought it was a man: I was dreadfully frightened."

"I am sure he attends the witches' sabbaths. He once left a broom on my leads."

"Oh, the ugly hunchback!"

"Faugh!"

The men, on the contrary, were delighted. There was no end to their applause. Quasimodo, the object of all the tumult, was still standing at the door of the chapel, gloomy and grave, exhibiting himself to the popular admiration, when Robin Poussepain came up close to him and laughed him in the face. Quasimodo, without uttering a word, caught him up by the waist, and hurled him to the distance of ten paces among the crowd.

Master Coppenole, astonished at the feat, approached him. "Cross of God!" he exclaimed. "Holy Father!—why thou art the finest piece of ugliness I ever beheld. Thou deservest to be Pope at Rome as well as at Paris."

As he thus spoke he sportively clapped his hand on the monster's shoulder. Quasimodo did not stir. Coppenole continued: "My fine fellow, I should like to have a tussle with thee, were it to cost me a new *douzain* of twelve Tournois. What sayest thou?"

Quasimodo made no reply. "Cross of God!" cried the hosier, "art thou deaf?" Quasimodo really *was* deaf.

Presently, beginning to feel annoyed by Coppenole's manner, he turned toward him with so formidable a grin that the Flemish giant recoiled, like a bulldog from a cat. A circle of terror and respect, having a radius of at least fifteen geometric paces, was left vacant around this strange personage.

An old woman informed Coppenole that Quasimodo was deaf.

"Deaf!" cried the hosier, with a Flemish horse-laugh. "By the Rood! he is an accomplished Pope!"

"Ha!" said Jehan, who had at length descended from his pillar to obtain a closer view of the new Pope, " 'tis my brother's bell-ringer!—Good morrow, Quasimodo!"

"A devil of a fellow!" sighed Robin Poussepain, aching all over from the effects of his fall. "He appears—he is hunchbacked. He walks—he is bandy-legged. He looks at you—he is one-eyed. You talk to him—he is deaf! And what use does this Polyphemus make of his tongue, I wonder?"

"He can talk when he likes," said the old woman. "He became deaf with ringing the bells. He is not dumb."

"He lacks that qualification," observed Jehan.

"And he has an eye too much," added Robin Poussepain.

"Not so," rejoined Jehan tartly; "a one-eyed man is more incomplete than one who is quite blind."

Meanwhile all the mendicants, all the lackeys, all the cutpurses together with the scholars, went in procession to the storeroom of the Basoche to fetch the pasteboard tiara and the mock robe of the Pope of Fools. Quasimodo suffered them to be put upon him with a kind of proud docility. He was then required to sit down on a party-coloured litter. Twelve officers of the Fraternity of Fools hoisted it upon their shoulders; and a sort of disdainful exultation overspread the morose countenance of the Cyclops, when he saw beneath his feet all those heads of straight, handsome, well-shaped men. The roaring and ragged procession then moved off, to pass, according to custom, through the galleries in the interior of the palace, before it paraded the streets and public places of the Cité.

CHAPTER VI

LA ESMERALDA

WE have great satisfaction in apprising the reader that, during the whole of this scene, Gringoire and his play had maintained their ground. His actors, egged on by him, had continued the performance of his comedy, and he had continued to listen to them. In spite of the uproar he was determined to go through with it, not despairing of being able to recall the attention of the public. This glimmer of hope became brighter when he saw Quasimodo, Coppenole, and the obstreperous retinue of the Pope of Fools leaving the hall. The crowd rushed out after them. "Excellent!" said he; "we shall get rid of all those troublesome knaves." Unluckily these were the whole assembly. In the twinkling of an eye the great hall was empty.

To tell the truth, a few spectators still lingered behind, some dispersed, others in groups round the pillars, old men, women, or children, who had had enough of the uproar and tumult. Some of the scholars too remained astride of the entablature of the windows, where they had a good view of the Place.

"Well," thought Gringoire, "there are quite as many as I want to hear the conclusion of my mystery. Their number, indeed, is but small; but they are a select, a lettered, audience."

At that moment a symphony, destined to produce a striking effect at the arrival of the Holy Virgin, was not forthcoming. Gringoire perceived that his musicians had been pressed into the service of the Pope of Fools. "Skip that," said he, with the composure of a stoic.

He approached a knot of citizens who seemed to be talking about his play. The fragment of their conversation which he overheard was as follows:—

"Master Cheneteau, you know the Hôtel de Navarre, which belonged to Monsieur de Nemours?"

"Yes; opposite to the chapel of Braque."

"Well! the exchequer has just leased it to Guillaume Alexandre, the history-writer, for six livres eight sols Parisis per annum."

"How rents are rising!"

"Bah!" ejaculated Gringoire, with a sigh—"the others are listening, at any rate."

"Comrades," all at once shouted one of the young scapegraces in the windows, "La Esmeralda! La Esmeralda in the Place!"

This intimation produced a magic effect. All who were left in the hall ran to the windows, clambering up the walls to obtain a sight and repeating, "La Esmeralda! La Esmeralda!" Thunders of applause arose at the same moment from the Place.

"What can they mean by La Esmeralda?" said Gringoire, clasping his hands in despair. "Gracious heaven! it seems to have come to the turn of the windows now!"

Turning toward the marble table he perceived that the performance was at a stand. It was precisely the moment when Jupiter should have appeared with his thunderbolt; but Jupiter was standing stock-still at the foot of the stage.

"Michel Giborne!" cried the incensed poet, "mind thy business! what art thou doing? make haste up!"

"Alas!" replied Jupiter, "one of the scholars has run away with the ladder."

Gringoire looked: it was even so. The communication with the stage was completely cut off. "The varlet!" murmured he. "And why did he take the ladder?"

"To go and see La Esmeralda," answered Jupiter, in a doleful tone. " 'Stay,' said he, 'here's a ladder that's of no use,' and off he scampered with it."

This was the final blow. Gringoire received it with resignation. "The devil take you!" said he to the performers. "If I am paid you shall be."

With downcast looks he then made his retreat, but not till the very last, like a general who has been soundly beaten. "A pretty pack of asses and boobies, these Parisians!" he muttered between his teeth as he descended the winding staircase of the palace. "They come to hear a mystery, and will not listen to it. They will pay attention to everything and everybody—to Clopin Trouillefou, to the Cardinal, to Coppenole, to Quasimodo, to the devil! but on the Holy Virgin they have none to bestow. Had I known, ye gaping oafs, I should have given you Virgin Maries, I warrant me! Turn your backs on such a piece! Homer, it is true, begged his bread in the Greek towns; and Naso [1] died in exile among the Moscovites. But the devil flay me if I comprehend what they mean by their La Esmeralda. And what kind of word is it to begin with? It must surely be Egyptian!"

[1] Ovid.

BOOK II

CHAPTER I

FROM CHARYBDIS INTO SCYLLA

NIGHT comes on early in the month of January. It was already dusk when Gringoire left the palace. To him the nightfall was doubly welcome, as he purposed seeking some obscure and sequestered street, where he might muse unmolested, and where philosophy might apply the first dressing to the poet's wound. In fact, philosophy was his only refuge; for he knew not where he should find a lodging. After the signal failure of his dramatic attempt he durst not return to that which he had occupied in the Rue Grenier-sur-l'Eau, opposite to the Port au Foin, having made sure that Monsieur the Provost would give him such a remuneration for his labour as would enable him to pay Master Guillaume Doulx-Sire, farmer of the customs on beasts with cloven hoofs, for the six months' lodging which he owed him; that is to say, twelve sols Parisis— twelve times the value of all that he possessed in the world, including his hose, shirt, and doublet. Having considered for a moment, sheltering *ad interim* under the little gateway of the prison of the treasurer of the Sainte-Chapelle, what quarters he should select for the night, having all the pavements of Paris to choose among, he recollected having noticed, in the preceding week, a horsing-stone at the door of a counsellor of the Parliament, in the Rue de la Savaterie, and having said to himself that this stone would be, in case of emergency, an excellent pillow for a beggar or a poet. He thanked Providence for having sent this seasonable idea; but, as he was preparing to cross the palace-yard, for the purpose of entering the tortuous labyrinth of the Cité, with its ancient winding streets, such as those of la Barillerie, la Vielle-Draperie, la Savaterie, la Juiverie, and others, still standing, with their houses nine stories high, he saw the procession of the Pope of Fools coming out of the palace, and advancing across the court toward him, with loud shouts, the glare of numerous torches, and his own band of music. This sight tore open afresh the wounds of his self-love: he took to his heels. In the

54

From Charybdis into Scylla

keen mortification of his dramatic miscarriage everything that reminded him of the festival held that day touched him to the quick.

He resolved to make the Pont Saint-Michel. Boys were running to and fro letting off squibs and crackers. "Curse the fireworks!" ejaculated Gringoire, and he bent his steps toward the Pont au Change. To the houses at the end of the bridge were attached three large pieces of canvas, with likenesses of the King, the Dauphin, and Margaret of Flanders; and six smaller, on which were portrayed the Duke of Austria, and the Cardinal de Bourbon, and Monsieur de Beaujeu, and Madame Jeanne of France, and Monsieur the Bastard of Bourbon, and I know not whom besides—the whole lighted by torches. A crowd of spectators was admiring these performances.

"Happy painter, Jehan Fourbault!" said Gringoire with a deep sigh, as he turned his back on the productions of that artist. There was a street just before him: it appeared to be so dark and so deserted that he hoped there to be out of hearing as well as out of sight of all the festivities; he entered it. Presently his foot struck against some obstacle; he stumbled and fell. It was the bole of the may-tree, which the clerks of the Bosoche had placed, in the morning, at the door of a president of the Parliament, in honour of the day. Gringoire bore with fortitude this new misfortune; he picked himself up, and pursued his way across the river. Leaving behind him the Civil and Criminal Court of the Parliament, and pursuing his way along the high wall of the King's gardens, upon the unpaved strand, where he was ankle-deep in mud, he arrived at the western point of the Cité, and surveyed for some time the islet of the cattle-ferry, which has since given place to the Pont Neuf with its bronze horse. The islet appeared to him in the dark like a black mass, beyond the white narrow stripe of water which separated him from it. By the glimmer of a faint light might be indistinctly discerned the kind of cabin in the shape of a beehive which afforded shelter to the ferryman during the night.

"Happy ferryman!" thought Gringoire—"thou dreamest not of glory, thou writest no epithalamiums! what to thee are the marriages of kings and duchesses of Burgundy!—while I, a poet, am hooted, and shiver with cold, and owe twelve sous, and the sole of my shoe is so thin that it might serve for the horn of a lantern. Thanks to thee, ferryman! thy cabin refreshes the eye and causes me to forget Paris."

He was awakened from his almost lyric ecstasy by the explosion of a double petard, suddenly fired from the happy cabin. It was the ferryman taking his share in the rejoicings of the day. The report made Gringoire shudder.

"Accursed festival!" cried he, "wilt thou pursue me whithersoever I go, even to the cabin of the ferryman?" He then looked at the Seine flowing at his feet, and a horrible temptation came over him. "Ah!" said he, "how gladly would I drown myself, only the water is so cold!"

He then formed a desperate resolution. Since he found it impossible to escape the Pope of Fools, the paintings of Jehan Fourbault, the may-trees, the squibs, and the petards, he determined to proceed to the Place de Grève, and to penetrate boldly into the very heart of the rejoicings. "At any rate," thought he, "I shall be able to get a warm at the bonfire, and perhaps a supper on some of the fragments of the collation provided at the public larder of the city."

CHAPTER II

THE PLACE DE GRÈVE

NOTHING but a scarcely perceptible vestige of the Place de Grève, as it then existed, now remains. This is the charming turret which occupies the north angle of the Place, and which, already buried beneath the ignoble plaster that encases the fine outlines of its sculptures, will probably soon disappear, engulfed by the inundation of new buildings which is so rapidly swallowing up all the ancient structures of Paris.

Those who, like ourselves, cannot pass through the Place de Grève without bestowing a look of pity and sympathy on that poor turret, cooped up between two paltry erections of the time of Louis XV, may easily figure to themselves the general aspect of the edifice to which it belonged, and recompose in imagination the entire ancient Gothic Place of the fifteenth century.

It was then, as at present, an irregular trapezium, bordered on one side by the quay, and on the three others by a series of lofty, narrow, and gloomy houses. By day, the spectator might admire the variety of these edifices, covered with sculptures or carving, and ex-

The Place de Grève

hibiting complete specimens of the various styles of domestic architecture of the Middle Ages, of the period between the fifteenth and the eleventh centuries; from the square window, which had already begun to supersede the pointed arch, to the semicircular Roman arch, which had been supplanted by the pointed, and which was still extant in the ground-floor of that ancient house of the Tour-Roland, at the angle of the Place next to the Seine, by the Rue de la Tannerie. By night, all that could be distinguished of that mass of buildings was the dark jagged outline of the roofs stretching their chain of acute angles round the Place. For one of the radical differences of the cities of that time and the cities of the present day is that now the fronts face the streets and places, whereas then it was the gables. During the last two centuries the houses have turned round.

In the centre of the east side of the Place rose a heavy and hybrid structure in three compartments. It was called by three names, which explain its history, its destination, and its architecture: the Maison au Dauphin, because Charles V when Dauphin had resided there; La Marchandise, because it served for the Hôtel de Ville; and the Maison aux Pilliers, from the row of massive pillars which supported its three stories. The city there found all that is requisite for a good city like Paris; a chapel for saying prayers in; a hall for giving audience and occasionally snubbing the servants of the King; and in the lofts an arsenal well stored with artillery. For the citizens of Paris know that it is not sufficient in every conjuncture to plead and to pray for the franchises of the Cité, and therefore they always keep in reserve a good rusty arquebuse or two in a loft in the Hôtel de Ville.

The Grève wore at that time the same sinister aspect that it still retains, owing to the unpleasant ideas which it excites, and the gloomy Hôtel de Ville of Dominique Bocador, which occupies the site of the Maison aux Pilliers. A permanent gibbet and a pillory, or, as they were called in those days, "a justice and a ladder," placed side by side in the middle of the pavement conferred no particular attractions on this fatal spot, where so many human beings full of health and life have been suddenly cut off; where fifty years later was generated that fever of St Vallier, that disease produced by fear of the scaffold, the most monstrous of all diseases, because it did not proceed from God but from man.

The Hunchback of Notre-Dame

It is consolatory, be it observed by the way, to think that the punishment of death, which three hundred years ago still encumbered the Grève, the Halles, the Place Dauphin, the Croix du Trahoir, the Swine Market, the hideous Montfaucon, the barrier of the Sergens, the Place aux Chats, the gate of Saint-Denis, Champeaux, the gate of Baudets, and the gate of Saint-Jacques, with its iron wheels, its stone gibbets, and all its apparatus for executions, permanently imbedded in the pavement—to say nothing of the numberless "ladders" of the Provosts, the Bishop, the chapters, the abbots, the priors, possessing the power of life and death, or of the judicial drownings in the river Seine—it is consolatory, I say, to think that, at the present day, this ancient sovereign-paramount of feudal society, stripped successively of all the pieces of its armour, its luxury of pains and penalties, its penal spirit and tendency, its torture, for which is caused a new leathern bed to be made every five years at the Grand Châtelet, almost outlawed from our cities and our land, hunted from code to code, driven from place to place, should have in our immense Paris but an ignominious corner of the Grève, but one miserable, furtive, timid, shamefaced guillotine, which always seems as if fearful of being taken in the act, so speedily does it hurry away after striking the fatal blow.

CHAPTER III

THE POET PUZZLED

WHEN Pierre Gringoire reached the Place de Grève he was quite benumbed with cold. He had gone over the Pont aux Meuniers to avoid the crowd at the Pont au Change and the flags of Jehan Fourbault; but the wheels of all the Bishop's mills had splashed him so unmercifully as he passed that his frock was drenched: it seemed, moreover, as if the failure of his play had rendered him still more chilly than ever. Accordingly he hastened toward the bonfire which blazed magnificently in the middle of the Place. A large assemblage of people formed a circle round it.

"Cursed Parisians!" said he to himself; for Gringoire, like a genuine dramatic poet, was addicted to soliloquies; "there they are, shutting me out from the fire! And yet I am in great need of a comfortable chimney-corner. My shoes leak, and all those infernal mills showering upon me into the bargain! The devil take the Bishop of Paris and his mills! I would fain know what a bishop has to do with a mill! does he expect to be obliged to turn miller some day or other? If he needs nothing but my malison for that I give it to him, and to his cathedral, and to his mills, with all my heart. Stop a moment, let's see if these boobies will sheer off presently. But what are they doing there, I want to know? Warming themselves —fine amusement! Gaping at the bonfire—pretty sight, forsooth!"

On looking more closely he perceived that the circle was much larger than it needed to have been, had the persons composing it been desirous of warming themselves at the King's fire; and that the assemblage of spectators was not drawn together solely by the beauty of the hundred blazing faggots. In an extensive space left open between the crowd and the fire there was a young girl dancing.

Whether this young girl was a human being, or a fairy, or an angel Gringoire, sceptical philosopher and satirical poet as he was, could not at the first moment decide, so completely was he fascinated by the dazzling vision. She was not tall, though she appeared to be so from the slenderness and elegance of her figure. Her complexion was dark, but it was easy to divine that by daylight her skin must have the beautiful golden tint of the Roman and Andalusian women. Her small foot too was Andalusian. She danced, whirled, turned round, on an old Persian carpet, carelessly spread on the pavement; and every time her radiant face passed before you as she turned her large black eyes flashed lightning.

Every eye was fixed upon her, every mouth open; and in truth, while she was thus dancing, what with the sound of the tambourine, which her two plump exquisitely shaped arms held above her head, her bodice of gold without folds, her spotted robe which swelled with the rapidity of her motions, her bare shoulders, her finely turned legs which her petticoat now and then discovered, her black hair, her eyes of flame, she was a supernatural creature.

"Verily," thought Gringoire, "it is a salamander, a nymph, a goddess, a bacchanal of Mount Menalæus!" At that moment one of the tresses of the salamander's hair got loose, and a piece of brass which had been fastened to it dropped to the ground. "Ha! no," said he, "'tis a gipsy!" The illusion was at an end.

She began dancing again. She picked up from the ground two swords, which she balanced on their points upon her forehead, and made them turn round one way, while she turned the other. She was in fact a gipsy, neither more nor less. But though the spell was dissolved, still the whole scene was not without fascination and charm for Gringoire: the bonfire threw a crude red, trembling light on the wide circle of faces and on the tawny brow of the girl, and at the extremity of the Place cast a faint tinge, mingled with their wavering shadows, upon the ancient, black, and furrowed façade of the Maison aux Pilliers on the one hand, and upon the stone arms of the gibbet on the other.

Among the thousand faces to which this light communicated a scarlet hue there was one which seemed to be more deeply absorbed in the contemplation of the dancer than any of the others. It was the face of a man, austere, calm, and sombre. This man, whose dress was concealed by the surrounding crowd, appeared to be no more than thirty-five years of age; he was, nevertheless, bald, and had merely at his temples a few tufts of thin and already grey hair. His ample and lofty brow began to be furrowed with wrinkles; but in his deep-sunk eyes there was an expression of extraordinary youth, ardent life, and profound passion. He kept them intently fixed on the Bohemian; and while the lively girl of sixteen was delighting all the other spectators by her dancing and her capers his reverie seemed to become more and more gloomy. At times a smile and a sigh would meet upon his lips, but the smile was by far the sadder of the two. The girl at length paused, panting with her exertions, and the people applauded with enthusiasm.

"Djali!" said the Bohemian, and up started a pretty little white goat, a nimble, lively, glossy creature, with gilt horns, gilt hoofs, and a gilt collar, which Gringoire had not yet perceived, and which had, till then, been lying at the corner of the carpet watching her mistress dance. "Djali," said the girl, "it is your turn now"; and, seating herself, she gracefully held the tambourine before the animal. "Djali," continued she, "what month are we in?" The goat raised her foreleg and struck one stroke upon the tambourine. It was actually the first month. The crowd applauded. "Djali," said the girl, turning the tambourine a different way, "what day of the month is this?" Djali again raised her little gilt hoof, and struck six blows upon the instrument. "Djali," continued the Egyptian, again changing the position of the tambourine, "what o'clock is it?" Djali gave seven blows. At that moment the clock of the Maison aux Pilliers struck seven. The people were astounded.

"There is sorcery at the bottom of this!" said a sinister voice in the crowd. It was that of the bald man, who never took his eyes off the Bohemian. She shuddered and turned away; and thunders of applause burst forth and drowned the morose exclamation. They had the effect of effacing it so completely from her mind that she continued to question her goat.

"Djali, show me how Master Guichard Grand Remy, captain of the city pistoleers, does in the Candlemas procession." Djali raised herself on her hind-legs, and began bleating and walking with such comic gravity that the whole circle of spectators roared with laughter at this parody upon the interested devotion of the captain of the pistoleers.

"Djali," resumed the girl, emboldened by the increasing applause, "show me how Master Jacques Charmolue, the King's Attorney in the Ecclesiastical Court, preaches." The goat sat down on her rump, and began bleating and shaking her forepaws in such a grotesque way, that, in gesture, accent, attitude, everything excepting bad French and worse Latin, it was Jacques Charmolue to the life. The crowd applauded more loudly than ever.

"Sacrilege! profanation!" ejaculated the bald man. The gipsy turned round once more. "Ah!" said she, "it is that hateful man!" then lengthening her lower lip beyond the upper she gave a pout that seemed to be habitual to her, turned upon her heel, and began to collect the donations of the multitude in her tambourine. Silver and copper coins of all sorts and sizes were showered into it. She came to Gringoire, who so readily thrust his hand into his pocket that she stopped. "The devil!" muttered the poet fumbling in his pocket and finding the reality; that is, nothing. The graceful girl stood still before him, looking at him with her large eyes, and holding out her tambourine. Big drops of perspiration started from Gringoire's brow. If he had had Peru in his pocket he would certainly have given it to the dancer: but Gringoire had no Peru there, and, besides, America was not yet discovered. An unexpected incident luckily relieved him.

"Wilt thou begone, Egyptian grasshopper?" cried a sharp voice issuing from the darkest corner of the Place. The young girl turned about in alarm. It was not the voice of the bald man; it was the voice of a woman, a devout and spiteful voice. This exclamation, which frightened the gipsy, excited the merriment of a troop of boys who were strolling near the spot. " 'Tis the crazy woman in the Tour-Roland," cried they, with shouts of laughter; " 'tis Sacky who is scolding. Perhaps she has had no supper. Let us run to the city larder and see if we can get something for her!" And away they scampered to the Maison aux Pilliers.

Meanwhile Gringoire had taken advantage of the girl's agitation to sneak off. The shouts of the boys reminded him that he had not supped either. He thought that he too might as well try his luck at the larder. But the young rogues ran too fast for him: when he arrived everything was cleared away; there was not a scrap of any kind left.

It is not pleasant to be obliged to go to bed without supper, and still less agreeable to have no bed to go to as well as no supper to eat. Such was Gringoire's predicament. He found himself closely pressed on all sides by necessity, and he thought necessity unnecessarily harsh. He had long since discovered this truth, that Jupiter created man in a fit of misanthropy, and that, throughout the whole life of the philosopher, his destiny keeps his philosophy in a state of siege. For his own part, he had never seen the blockade so complete: he heard his stomach beat a parley; and he declared it a scurvy trick of malicious destiny to take his philosophy by famine.

In this melancholy reverie he became more and more absorbed, when a strange kind of song, but remarkably sweet, suddenly roused him from it. It was the Egyptian girl who was singing. Her voice, like her dancing and her beauty, was indefinable, something pure, sonorous, aerial, winged, as it were. There were continual gushes of melody, unexpected cadences, then simple phrases interspersed with harsh and hissing tones; now leaps which would have confused a nightingale, but in which harmony was nevertheless preserved; and presently soft undulations of octaves, which rose and fell like the bosom of the young singer. Her fine face followed with extraordinary versatility all the caprices of her song, from the wildest inspiration to the chastest dignity. You would have taken her at one time for a maniac, at another for a queen.

The song of the gipsy had disturbed Gringoire's reverie, but as the swan disturbs the water: he listened with a kind of rapture and a forgetfulness of everything. It was the first respite from suffering that he had enjoyed for several hours. That respite was a short one. The same female voice which had interrupted the dancing of the gipsy was now raised to interrupt her singing. "Cease thy chirping, cricket of hell!" it cried, still issuing from the darkest corner of the Place. The poor *cricket* stopped short. "Curse thy screeching, thou bird of foul omen!" exclaimed Gringoire, clapping his hands to his ears. The other spectators also began to murmur. "The devil take the hag!" cried more than one, and the invisible spoil-sport might have had to rue her aggressions against the Bohemian had not their attention been at that moment diverted by the procession of the Pope of Fools, which, after parading through the principal streets, was now entering the Place de Grève with all its torches and its clamour.

This procession, which set out, as the reader has seen, from the palace, was joined in its progress by all the idle ragamuffins, thieves, and vagabonds in Paris; accordingly it exhibited a most respectable appearance when it reached the Grève.

Egypt marched first, headed by the Duke on horseback, with his counts on foot, holding his bridle and stirrups. They were followed by the Egyptians of both sexes, pell-mell, with their young children crying at their backs: all of them, duke, counts, and commons, in rags and tatters. Next came the kingdom of Slang, that is to say, all the rogues and thieves in France, drawn up according to their respective dignities, the lowest walking first. Thus they moved on, four by four, with the different insignia of their degrees in this strange faculty, most of them cripples, some having lost legs, others arms. Amid the conclave of grand dignitaries it was difficult to distinguish the King of these ruffians, crouched in a little car drawn by two huge dogs. After the kingdom of Slang came the empire of Galilee. The Emperor, Guillaume Rousseau, marched majestically in his purple robe stained with wine, preceded by dancers performing military dances and scuffling together, and surrounded by his mace-bearers and subordinate officers. Lastly came the Basoche, the company of lawyers' clerks, with their may-trees garlanded with flowers, in their black gowns, with music worthy of the Sabbath, and large candles of yellow wax. In the centre of this multitude the officers of the fraternity of Fools bore upon their shoulders a hand-barrow, more profusely beset with tapers than the shrine of

The Hunchback of Notre-Dame

Sainte-Geneviève in time of pestilence; and on this throne glittered, with crosier, cope, and mitre, the new Pope of Fools, the bell-ringer of Notre-Dame, Quasimodo the hunchback.

Each of the divisions of this grotesque procession had its particular band of music. The Egyptians played upon their African balafos and tambourines. The men of Slang, a race by no means musical, had advanced no farther than the viol, the goat's horn, and the Gothic rebec of the twelfth century. The empire of Galilee was but little before them; the highest stretch of its music was some wretched air of the infancy of the art, still imprisoned in the *do, re, mi*. It was round the Pope of Fools that all the musical excellences of the age were commingled in one magnificent cacophony. It consisted only of viols, treble, alto, and tenor, besides flutes and instruments of brass. Our readers may not recollect that this was poor Gringoire's orchestra.

It is impossible to convey any idea of the look of pride and self-complacency which had overspread Quasimodo's dull and hideous countenance during this triumphal procession from the palace to the Grève. It was the first gratification of self-love that he had ever experienced. Hitherto he had met with nothing but humiliation, contempt for his condition, disgust of his person. Thus, deaf as he was, he enjoyed like a real Pope the acclamations of that crowd which he hated because he knew that he was hated by it. It mattered not to him that his subjects were a mob of cripples, mendicants, thieves, ruffians—still they were subjects, and he was a sovereign. He took in earnest all those ironical plaudits, all that mock reverence and respect, with which, we must however observe, there was mingled on the part of the crowd a certain degree of real fear; for the hunchback was strong, the bandy-legged dwarf was active, the deaf bell-ringer was spiteful, three qualities which tend to temper ridicule.

That the new Pope of Fools was conscious of the sentiments which he felt and of the sentiments which he inspired is more than we can undertake to assert. The mind which was lodged in that defective body had necessarily a touch of imperfection and of deafness. He had therefore but a vague, indistinct, confused, perception of what he felt at that moment: enough for him that joy prevailed, pride predominated. That gloomy and unhappy visage was encircled by a halo of delight.

The Poet Puzzled

It was, therefore, not without surprise and alarm that at the moment when Quasimodo, in this state of half intoxication, was borne triumphantly past the Maison aux Pilliers, his attendants beheld a man suddenly dart from among the crowd, and with an angry gesture snatch from his hands his crosier of gilt wood, the mark of his newly conferred dignity. This rash man was the bald-headed personage, who, mingled in the group of spectators, had thrilled the poor gipsy-girl by his exclamation of menace and abhorrence. He was attired in the ecclesiastical habit. At the moment when he issued from among the crowd, Gringoire, who had not before noticed him, recognized in him an old acquaintance. "Hold!" said he, with a cry of astonishment. "Sure enough it is my master in Hermes, Dom Claude Frollo the Archdeacon! What the devil would he be at with that one-eyed monster? He will eat him up."

Shrieks of terror burst from the crowd, as the formidable Quasimodo leaped from the litter to the ground; and the women turned away their faces that they might not see the Archdeacon torn in pieces. With one bound he was before the priest; he looked at him, and dropped upon his knees. The priest pulled off his tiara, broke his crosier, and tore his cope of tinsel. Quasimodo remained kneeling, bowed his head, and clasped his hands. Then ensued between them a strange dialogue of signs and gestures, for neither of them spoke: the priest erect, irritated, threatening, imperious—Quasimodo at his feet, humble, submissive, suppliant. And yet it is certain that Quasimodo could have crushed the priest with his thumb.

At length the Archdeacon, shaking the brawny shoulder of Quasimodo, motioned him to rise and follow him. Quasimodo rose. The Fraternity of Fools, their first stupor over, were for defending their Pope, who had been so unceremoniously dethroned. The Egyptians, the beggars, and the lawyers' clerks, crowded yelping round the priest. Quasimodo, stepping before the priest, clenched his athletic fists; and, as he eyed the assailants, he gnashed his teeth like an angry tiger. The priest resumed his sombre gravity, made a sign to Quasimodo, and withdrew in silence. Quasimodo went before, opening a passage for him through the crowd.

When they were clear of the populace a number of curious and idle persons began to follow them. Quasimodo then fell into the rear; and, facing the enemy, walked backward after the Archdeacon, square, massive, bristly, picking up his limbs, licking his

65

tusk, growling like a wild beast, and producing immense oscillations in the crowd with a gesture or a look. They pursued their way down a dark and narrow street, into which no one durst venture to follow them; the formidable figure of Quasimodo securing an unmolested retreat.

" 'Tis wonderful, by my faith!" exclaimed Gringoire; "but where the devil shall I find a supper?"

CHAPTER IV

SERIOUS RESULTS OF FOLLOWING A PRETTY GIRL IN THE STREET AT NIGHT

GRINGOIRE took it into his head to follow the gipsy-girl at all hazards. He saw her with her goat turn into the Rue de Coutellerie, and to the same street he directed his course. "Why not?" said he to himself by the way.

Gringoire, a practical philosopher of the streets of Paris, had remarked that nothing is so conducive to reverie as to follow a pretty woman without knowing whither she is going. In this voluntary resignation of free-will, in this submission of one whim to another, there is a mixture of fantastic independence and blind obedience, a something intermediate between slavery and liberty, which was pleasing to Gringoire, a man of a mind essentially mixed, indecisive, and complex, incessantly suspended between all human passions and propensities, and incessantly neutralizing them one by another. He was fond of comparing himself with the tomb of Mohammed, attracted in contrary directions by two loadstones, and eternally wavering between the ceiling and the pavement, between rising and sinking, between zenith and nadir.

Nothing tends so much to produce a disposition to follow passengers, and especially those of the fair sex, in the streets as the circumstance of having neither home nor harbour. Gringoire, therefore, walked pensively on after the girl, who quickened her pace and made her pretty little goat trot along by her side when she saw the shopkeepers retiring to their houses, and the tavern-keepers, who had alone kept open on that day, shutting up for the night. "After all" —this was what he thought, or something very much like it—"she must lodge somewhere. The gipsies are very good-natured. Who Knows——" The ellipsis was filled by I cannot tell what pleasing visions.

Meanwhile, from time to time, as he passed the last groups of tradesmen shutting their doors, he caught some fragments of their conversation, which broke the chain of his pleasing hypotheses. Two old men, for instance, would accost one another in this manner:

"Master Thibaut Fernicle, do you know that it is very cold?" Gringoire had known that ever since the beginning of winter.

"It is, indeed, Master Boniface Disome! Are we going to have such another winter as we had three years ago, in '80, when wood cost six sous the cord?"

"Pooh! that is nothing, Master Thibaut, to the winter of 1407, when the frost lasted from Martinmas to Candlemas; ay, and the cold was so bitter that the pen of the clerk of the Parliament froze in the great chamber every three words he wrote!"

Farther on a couple of female neighbours would be chatting at their windows, while the fog made their candles crackle again.

"Has your husband told you of the accident, Mademoiselle La Boudrague?"

"No; but what is it, Mademoiselle Turquant?"

"You know the horse of Monsieur Gilles Godin, notary to the Châtelet; well, he took fright at the Flemings and their procession, and knocked over Master Philippot Avrillot, the invalid of the Célestins."

"Indeed!"

"As true as you are there."

The windows would then close again: but Gringoire had, nevertheless, lost the thread of his ideas. Luckily, however, he soon recovered and quickly reunited it, thanks to the gipsy-girl and her Djali, who still pursued their way before him—two elegant, delicate, charming creatures, whose small feet, handsome shapes, and graceful manners he admired, almost confounding them in his imagination; regarding them both as young girls for intelligence and their fondness for each other, and thinking them both goats for agility, dexterity, and lightness of foot.

The Hunchback of Notre-Dame

The streets, in the meantime, became every moment darker and more deserted. The curfew had long since rung; and it was only at rare intervals that a passenger was met on the pavement, or a light seen at the windows. Gringoire, in following the Egyptian, had involved himself in that inextricable labyrinth of lanes and alleys and crossways surrounding the ancient sepulchre of the Holy Innocents, and which resembles a skein of thread entangled by a playful cat. "Here are streets which have very little logic!" said Gringoire, lost in their thousand meanders, through which, however, the girl proceeded as along a way that was well known to her, and at a more and more rapid pace. For his part, he should not have had the remotest conception of where he was had he not perceived, on turning a corner, the octagon mass of the pillory of the Halles, the black open-work top of which was distinctly defined against a window still lighted in the Rue Verdelet.

He had, by this time, begun to attract the notice of the young girl: she had more than once turned her head and looked at him with some uneasiness; nay, she had stopped short and taken advantage of a ray of light issuing from the half-open door of a bakehouse, to scrutinize him attentively from head to foot. Gringoire had seen her, after this survey, pout her lip as she had done before; then she passed on.

This pretty grimace set Gringoire about inquiring what it might denote. It certainly conveyed an expression of disdain and dislike. He began, in consequence, to hang his head, as if to count the stones of the pavement, and to drop farther behind, when, on reaching the corner of a street into which she had turned, he was startled by a piercing shriek. The street was extremely dark; a wick steeped in oil, burning in an iron cage at the foot of the Blessed Virgin at the angle of the street, nevertheless enabled Gringoire to distinguish the Bohemian struggling in the grasp of two men, who were striving to stifle her cries. The poor little goat, terrified at this attack, dropped her head, presented her horns, and bleated.

"Watch! watch!" shouted Gringoire, boldly advancing. One of the men who held the girl turned upon him. It was the formidable visage of Quasimodo. Gringoire did not run away, neither did he advance another step. Quasimodo went up to him and dealt him a backhanded blow that sent him reeling three or four yards and stretched him sprawling upon the pavement; then, darting back,

Following a Pretty Girl

he caught up the young girl, and bore her off across one of his arms like a silken scarf. His companion followed, and the poor goat ran after the three, bleating in a most plaintive manner.

"Murder! murder!" cried the unfortunate gipsy-girl.

"Halt, scoundrels, and let the wench go!" suddenly roared, in a voice of thunder, a horseman who came dashing along out of the next street. It was the captain of the archers of the King's Ordnance, armed *cap-à-pie,* and his drawn sword in his hand. He snatched the Bohemian out of the grasp of the stupefied Quasimodo, laid her across his saddle, and at the moment when the formidable hunchback, recovering from his surprise, would have rushed upon him to regain his prey fifteen or sixteen archers, who followed close at the heels of their captain, came up armed with quarterstaves. It was a part of a company of the King's Ordnance which did the duty of counter-watch, by the order of Messire Robert d'Estouteville, Keeper of the Provosty of Paris.

Quasimodo was surrounded, seized, and bound. He bellowed, he foamed, he kicked, he bit; and had it been daylight no doubt his face alone, rendered doubly hideous by rage, would have sufficed to scare away the whole detachment: but night disarmed him of his most formidable weapon, his ugliness. His companion had disappeared during the struggle.

The Bohemian gracefully raised herself upon the officer's saddle. Clapping her two hands upon his shoulders, she looked at him intently for a few moments, as if charmed with his handsome face, and grateful for the seasonable succour which he had afforded her. Then, giving a sweeter tone than usual to her sweet voice, she inquired, "What is your name, sir?"

"Captain Phœbus de Châteaupers, at your service, my dear," replied the officer, drawing himself up to his full height.

"Thank you," said she; and while the captain was turning up his whiskers *à la bourguignonne* she slid down the horse's side to the ground, and vanished with the swiftness of lightning.

69

CHAPTER V

A CHAPTER OF ACCIDENTS

GRINGOIRE, stunned by his fall, was extended on the pavement before the good Virgin at the corner of the street. By degrees he came to himself. At first he was floating for some minutes in a kind of dreamy reverie, which was rather soothing, though the aerial figures of the Bohemian and her goat were coupled with the weight of the ungentle fist of Quasimodo. This state was of short duration. A painful sensation of cold in that part of his body which was in contact with the pavement suddenly awoke him and recalled his mind to the surface. "Whence comes this cold?" said he sharply to himself. He then perceived that he was nearly in the middle of the kennel.

"Devil of a hunchbacked Cyclops!" muttered he, and attempted to rise, but he was so stunned and bruised that he was forced to remain where he was. His hand, however, was at liberty. He held his nose and resigned himself to his fate.

"The mud of Paris," thought he—for he had decidedly made up his mind to it that the kennel would be his bed—"the mud of Paris is particularly offensive: it must contain a great deal of volatile and nitrous salt. Besides, it is the opinion of Nicolas Flamel and of the alchemists . . ."

The word "alchemists" suggested to his mind the idea of the Archdeacon Claude Frollo. He bethought him of the violent scene which he had just witnessed; he recollected that the Bohemian was struggling between two men, that Quasimodo had a companion; and the stately and morose figure of the Archdeacon passed confusedly before his imagination. "That would be extraordinary!" thought he. And with this datum and upon this foundation he began to erect the fantastic edifice of hypothesis, that card-house of philosophers. Then, suddenly recalled once more to reality, "Egad!" cried he, "I am freezing!"

The place, in fact, was becoming less and less tenable. Each particle of the water in the kennel carried off a particle of radiating caloric from the loins of Gringoire; and the equilibrium between the

70

A Chapter of Accidents

temperature of his body and the temperature of the kennel began to be established in a way that was far from agreeable. All at once he was assailed by an annoyance of a totally different kind.

A party of boys, of those little bare-legged savages, who have in all ages padded the pavement of Paris by the name of *gamins,* and who when we were boys too threw stones at us in the evening as we left school, because our trousers were not in tatters like their own; a party of these ragged urchins ran toward the spot where Gringoire lay, laughing and whooping and hallooing, and caring very little whether they disturbed the neighbourhood or not. They were dragging after them something like an enormous bag; and the mere clattering of their wooden shoes would have been enough to wake the dead. Gringoire, who was not absolutely dead, propped himself up a little to see what was the matter.

"Halloo! Hennequin Dandèche!—halloo, Jehan Pincebourde," they bawled at the top of their voices, "old Eustache Moubon, the ironmonger at the corner, is just dead. We have got his *paillasse* and are going to make a bonfire of it!"

So saying, they threw down the *paillasse* precisely upon Gringoire, close to whom they had stopped without seeing him. At the same time one of them took a handful of straw, and went to light it at the Virgin's lamp.

"'Sdeath!" grumbled Gringoire, "I am likely to be hot enough presently!"

Between fire and water he was certainly in a critical situation. He made a supernatural effort, the effort of a coiner who is going to be boiled and strives to escape. He raised himself upon his feet, threw back the *paillasse* upon the urchins and hobbled away as fast as he was able.

"Holy Virgin!" cried the boys, " 'tis the ironmonger's ghost!" and off they scampered in their turn.

The *paillasse* was left in possession of the field of battle. Belleforêt, Father Le Juge, and Corrozet relate that on the following day it was picked up with great pomp by the clergy of the quarter, and carried to the treasure-house of the church of Sainte-Opportune, where the sacristan, down to the year 1789, made a very handsome income with the grand miracle performed by the statue of the Virgin at the corner of the Rue Mauconseil, which had, by its mere presence,

71

in the memorable night between the 6th and the 7th of January, 1482, exorcised the spirit of Jehan Moubon, which, to play the devil a trick, had when he died maliciously hid itself in his *paillasse*.

CHAPTER VI

THE BROKEN JUG

AFTER running for some time as fast as his legs would carry him, without knowing whither, knocking his head against many a corner of a street, plunging into many a kennel, dashing through many a lane, turning into many a blind alley, seeking a passage through all the meanders of the old pavement of the Halles, exploring, in his panic, what is termed in the exquisite Latin of the charters *tota via, cheminum, et viaria*,[1] our poet stopped short, in the first place for want of breath, and in the next collared, as it were, by a dilemma, which just occurred to his mind. "It seemeth to me, Master Pierre Gringoire," said he to himself, clapping his finger to the side of his nose, "that you are running about like a blockhead. The young rogues were not a whit less afraid of you than you of them. It seemeth to me, I tell you, that you heard their wooden shoes clattering off to the south, while you are scudding away to the north. Now, either they have run away, and then the *paillasse,* which they have no doubt left behind in their fright, is precisely the hospitable bed for which you have been running about ever since morning, and which the Virgin, blessed be her name! miraculously sends to reward you for having composed in honour of her a morality accompanied by triumphs and mummeries: or the boys have not run away; in that case they have set fire to the *paillasse;* and a good fire is the very next thing you want to warm, to dry, and to cheer you. In either case, a good fire, or a good bed, the *paillasse* is a gift of heaven. It was perhaps for this very reason that the Virgin at the corner caused the death of Jehan Moubon; and it is stupid of you to run your legs off in this manner, like a Picard from a Frenchman, leaving behind what you are seeking before you. You are a fool for your pains."

[1] "Every way, highway and byway."

The Broken Jug

He turned, and, with eyes and ears on the alert, strove to steer his way back to the lucky *paillasse,* but in vain. His course was incessantly checked by intersections of houses, blind alleys, spots where several streets terminated, and where he was forced to pause in doubt and hesitation, more perplexed and more entangled in the intricacies of those dark narrow lanes and courts than he would have been in the maze of the Hôtel des Tournelles itself. At length, losing all patience he solemnly ejaculated, "Curse these branching streets! the devil must have made them in the image of his fork."

This exclamation relieved him a little, and a kind of reddish light which he perceived at the extremity of a long narrow lane helped to cheer his spirits. "God be praised!" said he; "yonder it is. Yonder is my *paillasse* burning!" And comparing himself with the mariner who is wrecked in the night, *"Salve,"* he piously ejaculated, *"salve maris stella!"* [1]

Whether this fragment of the seaman's hymn was addressed to the Blessed Virgin or to the *paillasse* is more than we can take it upon us to decide.

Before he had proceeded many steps down the long lane, which was sloping and unpaved, and which became more and more muddy the farther he went, he perceived something that had a most extraordinary appearance. Here and there, all the way along it, crawled a number of indistinct and shapeless masses, proceeding toward the light at the bottom of the lane.

Nothing makes a man so adventurous as an empty pocket. Gringoire continued to advance, and soon came up with the hindmost of these strange figures, which was leisurely wriggling itself along after the others. On a near approach he perceived that it was only a wretched cripple in a bowl, who was hopping along upon both hands. At the moment when he was passing this species of spider with human face it accosted him in a lamentable tone: *"La buona mancia, signor! la buona mancia!"* [2]

"The devil fetch thee," said Gringoire, "and me along with thee, if I know what thou meanest!" And he walked on.

He overtook another of those moving masses. This was a cripple too—a man who had suffered such mutilation in legs and arms that the complicated system of crutches and wooden legs by which he was

---

1 "Hail, star of the sea!"
2 "Charity, sir, charity!"

supported gave him the appearance of a walking scaffold. Gringoire, who was fond of lofty and classic comparisons, likened him in imagination to the living tripod of Vulcan.

This living tripod took off its hat to him as he passed, but held it up under Gringoire's chin, like a barber's basin, at the same time bawling in his ear, *"Señor caballero, para comprar un pedaso de pan!"* [1]

"This fellow," said Gringoire, "seems to be talking too; but 'tis an odd language, and he must be cleverer than I am if he understands it."

He would have quickened his pace, but for the third time something obstructed the way. This something, or rather this somebody, was a little blind man, with Jewish face and long beard, who, rowing on in the space round him with a stick, and towed by a great dog, sang out with nasal twang and Hungarian accent, *"Facitote caritatem."* [2]

"Come," said Pierre Gringoire, "here is one at least who speaks a Christian language. I must have a most benevolent look for people to ask charity of me in this manner, in the present meagre state of my purse. My friend," continued he, turning toward the blind man, "it is not a week since I sold my last shirt, or as you understand no language but Cicero's, *Vendidi hebdomade nuper transita meam ultimam chemisam."*

This said, he turned his back on the blind man, and pursued his way. At the same time, however, the blind man quickened his pace, and in a trice up came the two cripples, in great haste, with a tremendous clatter of bowl and crutches upon the pavement. All three, jostling each other at the heels of poor Gringoire, opened upon him at once.

"Caritatem!" [3] sang the blind man.

"La buona mancia!" [4] sang the man of the bowl.

The other cripple joined in the concert with *"Un pedaso de pan!"* [5] Gringoire stopped his ears. "Oh, tower of Babel!" exclaimed he. He began to run for it. The blind man ran. The man of the

---

[1] "Sir Cavalier, something with which to buy a piece of bread!"
[2] "Give alms."
[3] "Charity!"
[4] "Spare a trifle!"
[5] "A morsel of bread!"

bowl ran. The man with wooden legs ran. Presently he was surrounded by halt and lame and blind, by one-armed and one-eyed, and lepers with their hideous sores, some issuing from houses, others from the adjoining courts, and others from cellars, howling, bellowing, yelping, hobbling, rushing toward the light, and bedraggled with mire like snails after a shower.

Gringoire, still followed by his three persecutors, and not knowing what to think of the matter, walked on in some alarm amid the others, turning aside, and, passing the cripples on crutches, stepping over the heads of those in bowls, and entangled in this crowd of limping, shuffling wretches, like the English captain who found himself suddenly surrounded by a prodigious host of land-crabs.

The idea occurred to him to try to return. But it was too late. The whole legion had closed behind him, and his three mendicants stuck to him like bird-lime. He proceeded, therefore, propelled at once by this irresistible tide, by fear, and by a dizziness, which made the whole scene appear to him like a horrible dream.

At length he reached the extremity of the lane. It opened into a spacious place, where a thousand scattered lights flickered in the confused haze of night. Gringoire pursued his way into it, hoping by the lightness of his heels to escape from the three infirm spectres who stuck so closely to him.

"Onde vas hombre?" [1] cried the cripple upon crutches, throwing them down, and running after him on two as goodly legs as ever stepped upon the pavement of Paris. At the same moment the other cripple, standing bolt upright upon his feet, clapped his heavy bowl cased with iron upon Gringoire's head, by way of cap, and the blind man stared him in the face with a pair of flaming eyes.

"Where am I?" cried the affrighted poet.

"In the Cour des Miracles," replied a fourth spectre, who had joined them.

"Miracles, upon my soul!" rejoined Gringoire, "for here are blind who see, and lame who run."

A sinister laugh was their only answer.

The poor poet cast his eyes round him. He was actually in that dreaded Cour des Miracles, into which no honest man had ever penetrated at such an hour, a magic circle, in which the officers of the

---

[1] "Where is the man off to?"

75

The Hunchback of Notre-Dame

Châtelet and the sergeants of the Provost who ventured within it were disposed of in a trice; the haunt of thieves; a hideous wen on the face of Paris; a sewer disgorging every morning and receiving every night that fetid torrent of vice, mendicity, and roguery which always overflows the streets of great capitals; a monstrous hive, to which all the drones of the social order retired at night with their booty; the hospital of imposture, where the gipsy, the unfrocked monk, the ruined scholar, the blackguards of all nations, Spaniards, Italians, Germans, of all religions, Jews, Christians, Mohammedans, idolaters, covered with painted wounds, beggars by day, transmogrified themselves into banditti at night; immense robing-room, in short, whither all the actors of that eternal comedy which theft, prostitution, and murder are performing in the streets of Paris, resorted at that period to dress and to undress.

It was a spacious area, irregular, and ill-paved, like all the open places of Paris in those days. Fires, round which swarmed strange-looking groups, were blazing here and there. All was bustle, confusion, uproar. Coarse laughter, the crying of children, the voices of women, were intermingled. The hands and heads of this multitude, black upon a luminous ground, were making a thousand antic gestures. A dog which looked like a man, or a man who looked like a dog, might be seen from time to time passing over the place on which trembled the reflection of the fires, interspersed with broad ill-defined shadows. The limits between races and species seemed to be done away with in this city, as in a pandemonium. Men, women, brutes, age, sex, health, disease all seemed to be in common among these people. They were jumbled, huddled together, laid upon one another; each there partook of everything.

The faint and flickering light of the fires enabled Gringoire to distinguish, in spite of his agitation, all round the immense place a hideous circumference of old houses, the decayed, worm-eaten, ruinous fronts of which, each perforated by one or two small lighted windows, appeared to him in the dark like enormous heads of old hags ranged in a circle, watching the witches' sabbath rites and winking their eyes. It was like a new world, unknown, unheard of, deformed, creeping, crawling, fantastic.

Gringoire—more and more terrified; held by the three mendicants as by three vices; deafened by a crowd of other faces bleating and barking round him—the unlucky Gringoire strove to rally his presence of mind, and to recollect whether it was Saturday or not. But his efforts were vain: the thread of his memory and of his thoughts was broken, and, doubting everything, floating between what he saw and what he felt, he asked himself this puzzling question:—"If I am, can this be? if this is, can I be?"

At this moment a distinct shout arose from amid the buzzing crowd by which he was surrounded: "Lead him to the King! lead him to the King!"

"Holy Virgin!" muttered Gringoire—"the King of this place!— why, he can be nothing but a goat."

"To the King! to the King!" repeated every voice.

He was hurried away. The rabble rushed to lay hands on him, but the three mendicants held him fast in their gripe, tearing him away from the others, and bawling, "He is ours!" The poor poet's doublet, previously in wretched plight, was utterly ruined in this struggle.

While crossing the horrible place the vertigo which had confused his senses was dispelled. He had taken but a few steps before a conviction of the reality flashed upon him. He began to become used to the atmosphere of the place. At that moment there had risen from his poetic brain, and perhaps, to speak quite simply and prosaically, from his empty stomach, a fume, a vapour, which, spreading itself between objects and him, had permitted him to catch a glimpse of them only in the distorting haze of the nightmare, in that darkness of dreams which shows all outlines as shaking, all forms as grinning, all objects as heaped together in preposterous groups, dilating things into chimeras and men into phantoms. By degrees this hallucination gave place to views less wild and less exaggerating. Reality burst upon him, paining his eyes, treading upon his toes, and demolishing piecemeal the whole frightful poesy by which he had at first fancied himself to be surrounded. He could not help perceiving that he was not walking in the Styx, but in the mud; that he was not elbowed by demons, but by robbers; that his soul was not in danger, but merely his life, because he lacked that excellent mediator between the ruffian and the honest man—the purse. In short, upon examining the scene more closely and more coolly he fell from the witches' sabbath down to the tavern. The Cour des Miracles was in fact nothing but a tavern, but a tavern for ruffians, quite as much stained with blood as with wine.

The Hunchback of Notre-Dame

The sight which presented itself when his ragged escort had at length brought him to the place of his destination was not calculated to carry him back to poetry, were it even the poetry of hell. It was more than ever the prosaic and brutal reality of the tavern. If our history did not pertain to the fifteenth century we should say that Gringoire had descended from Michelangelo to Callot.

Round a great fire which burned upon a large circular hearth, and the flames of which rose among the red-hot bars of a trivet unoccupied at the moment, sundry crazy tables were placed here and there at random; for the waiter had not deigned to study geometrical symmetry in their arrangement, or to take care at least that they should not intersect each other at too unusual angles. On these tables shone pots flowing with wine and beer, and round these pots were grouped a great many jolly faces, empurpled by the fire and by drink. Here a man with huge paunch and jovial phiz was whistling the while he took off the bandages from a false wound, and removed the wrappers from a sound and vigorous knee, which had been swathed ever since morning in a dozen ligatures. At the back of him was a shrivelled wretch, preparing with suet and bullock's blood his black pudding for the ensuing day. Two tables off, a sharper, in the complete dress of a pilgrim, was twanging a stave of a religious hymn. In another place a young rogue was taking a lesson in epilepsy from an old cadger, who was also teaching him the art of foaming at the mouth by chewing a bit of soap. By the side of these a dropsical man was ridding himself of his protuberance, while four or five canters of the other sex were quarrelling about a child they had stolen in the course of the evening. Circumstances these, which, two centuries later, "appeared so ridiculous to the Court," as Sauval tells us, "that they furnished pastime for the King, and were introduced into a royal *ballet,* called *Night,* divided into four parts, and performed upon the stage of the Petit-Bourbon."—"Never," adds a spectator of this performance, "were the sudden metamorphoses of the Cour des Miracles more successfully represented."

From every quarter burst forth the coarse laugh and the obscene song. Each did just as he pleased, swearing and descanting, without listening to his neighbour. The pots jingled, quarrels arose, and broken mugs occasioned a destruction of rags.

A large dog was seated on his rump looking at the fire. Young children were present at these orgies. The stolen boy was crying

The Broken Jug

bitterly. Another, a stout fellow about four years old, was sitting on a high bench, dangling his legs at the table, which reached up to his chin, and saying not a word. A third was gravely spreading with his finger the melted tallow which ran from a candle upon the table. The last, a little urchin, crouching in the dirt, was almost lost in a kettle, which he was scraping with a tile, and from which he was extracting sounds that would have thrown Stradivarius into a swoon.

Near the fire stood a hogshead, and upon this hogshead was seated a mendicant. This was the King upon his throne. The three vagabonds who held Gringoire led him before the hogshead, and for a moment the whole motley assemblage was silent, excepting the kettle inhabited by the boy. Gringoire durst not breathe or raise his eyes.

"Hombre, quita tu sombrero," [1] said one of the three fellows in whose clutches he was, and before he knew what was meant one of the others took off his hat—a shabby covering, it is true, but still useful either against sun or rain. Gringoire sighed.

"What varlet have we here?" asked the King. Gringoire shuddered. This voice, though it now had a tone of menace, reminded him of another which had that very morning given the first blow to his mystery, by drawling out amid the audience, "Charity, if you please!" He raised his eyes. It was Clopin Trouillefou himself.

Clopin Trouillefou, invested with the insignia of royalty, had not a rag more or a rag less than usual. The sore on his arm had disappeared. He held in his hand one of the whips composed of thongs of white leather which were used by the vergers in those days to keep back the crowd. On his head he wore a cap of such peculiar form that it was difficult to tell whether it was a child's biggin or a king's crown—so much are the two things alike. Gringoire, however, had regained some hope, though without knowing why, on recognizing in the King of the Cour des Miracles the provoking beggar of the great hall.

"Master," he stammered forth, "my lord—sire—what ought I to call you?" he at length asked, having arrived at the culminating point of his *crescendo,* and not knowing how to get higher or to descend again.

"Call me your Majesty, or comrade, or what thou wilt. But make haste. What hast thou to say in thy defence?"

[1] "Take off your hat, man!"

79

The Hunchback of Notre-Dame

"In thy defence!" thought Gringoire: "I don't half like that."

"It was I—I—I—" he resumed, with the same hesitation as before, "who, this morning——"

"By the devil's hoofs!" cried Clopin, interrupting him, "thy name, knave, and nothing more. Mark me. Thou art in the presence of three mighty sovereigns, myself, Clopin Trouillefou, King of Thunes, and supreme ruler of the realm of Slang; Mathias Hunyadi Spicali, Duke of Egypt and Bohemia, that sallow old crone whom thou seest yonder, with a clout round his head; and Guillaume Rousseau, Emperor of Galilee, the porpoise who is too busy with that trull to attend to us. We are thy judges. Thou hast entered our territories without being one of our subjects; thou hast violated the privileges of our city. Thou must be punished, unless thou art a prig, a cadger, or a stroller—or, to use the gibberish of those who call themselves honest people, a thief, a beggar, or a vagrant. Art thou any of these? justify thyself: state thy qualities."

"Alas!" sighed Gringoire, "I have not that honour. I am the author——"

"Enough!" exclaimed Trouillefou, without suffering him to proceed. "Thou shalt be hanged. And quite right too, messieurs honest citizens! As you deal by our people among you so we will deal by yours among us. The law which you make for the Vagabonds, the Vagabonds will enforce with you. 'Tis your fault if it is a harsh one. It is but proper that an honest man should now and then be seen grinning through a hempen collar—that makes the thing honourable. Come, my friend, divide thy rags with a good grace among these wenches. I will have thee hanged to amuse the vagabonds, and thou shalt give them thy purse to drink. If thou hast any mummery to make go down into the cellar; there is a capital crucifix in stone, which we picked up at Saint-Pierre-aux-Bœufs. Thou hast four minutes to settle the affairs of thy soul."

This was an alarming announcement.

"Well said upon my life! Clopin Trouillefou preaches like his Holiness the Pope," cried the Emperor of Galilee, breaking his pot to prop up his table.

"Most puissant Emperors and Kings," said Gringoire quite coolly —I never could make out how he recovered sufficient firmness to talk so resolutely—"you cannot mean what you say. My name is Pierre

The Broken Jug

Gringoire; I am the poet, whose morality was represented this morning in the great hall of the Palace."

"Oho! master!" said Clopin. "I was there too. But, comrade, because we were annoyed by thee in the morning, is that any reason why thou shouldst not be hung to-night?"

"I shall be puzzled to get myself out of the scrape," thought Gringoire. He made nevertheless another effort.

"I do not see," said he, "why poets should not be classed among the vagabonds. Æsop was a vagabond, Homer a beggar, Mercury a thief."

Clopin interrupted him. "I verily believe thou thinkest to bamboozle us with thy palaver. 'Sdeath! as thou must be hanged, make no more ado."

"Pardon me, most illustrious King of Thunes," replied Gringoire, disputing the ground inch by inch: "is it worth while—only one moment—you will not condemn me unheard——"

His voice was absolutely drowned by the uproar which prevailed around him. The little urchin continued to scrape his kettle with greater energy than ever; and, to mend the matter, an old woman had just placed on the red-hot trivet a frying-pan full of fat, which yelped and cackled over the fire like a dog that has been pipe-tailed by a troop of mischievous boys.

Clopin Trouillefou appeared to be conferring for a moment with the Duke of Egypt and the Emperor of Galilee, who was quite drunk. He then cried out sharply, "Silence, there!" and, as the kettle and the frying-pan paid no attention to him, but continued their duet, he leaped from his hogshead, gave one kick to the kettle, which rolled away with the boy to the distance of ten paces, and another to the frying-pan, which upset all the fat into the fire. He then gravely reascended his throne, caring no more for the smothered crying of the child than for the grumbling of the hag, whose supper had gone off in a blaze.

Trouillefou made a sign, and the Duke, the Emperor, and the high dignitaries of the kingdom of Cant ranged themselves round him in a semicircle, the centre of which was occupied by Gringoire, who was still held fast by his captors. It was a semicircle of rags and tatters and tinsel, of forks and hatchets, of bare brawny arms and legs, of squalid, bloated, stupid-looking faces. In the middle of this round table of ragamuffins Clopin Trouillefou, like the Doge of this Senate, like the chief of this clan, like the Pope of this conclave, overawed in the first place by the whole height of his hogshead, and in the next by a certain haughty, ferocious, and formidable look, which made his eye sparkle, and corrected the bestial type of the vagabond race in his savage profile. You would have taken him for a wild boar among domestic swine.

"Fellow," said he to Gringoire, stroking his deformed chin with his horny hand, "I see no reason why thou shouldst not be hanged. Thou seemest, indeed, to have a dislike to it, but that is natural enough; you citizens are not used to it. You have too frightful an idea of the thing. After all, we mean thee no harm. There is one way to get out of the scrape for the moment. Wilt thou be one of us?"

The reader may conceive what effect this proposition must have produced upon Gringoire, who saw that he had no chance of saving his life, and began to make up his mind to the worst. He caught eagerly at the proposed alternative.

"Certainly, most assuredly I will," said he.

"Thou consentest," rejoined Clopin, "to enrol thyself among the men of Slang?"

"The men of Slang, decidedly so," answered Gringoire.

"Thou acknowledgest thyself one of the crew?" proceeded the King of Thunes.

"One of the crew."

"A subject of the kingdom of Cant?"

"Of the kingdom of Cant."

"A Vagabond?"

"A Vagabond."

"With all thy soul?"

"With all my soul."

"Take notice," said the King, "thou shalt nevertheless be hanged."

"The devil!" ejaculated the poet.

"Only," continued Clopin, with imperturbable gravity, "thou shalt be hanged not quite so soon, and with more ceremony, at the cost of the good city of Paris, on a fair stone gibbet, and by the hands of honest men. That is some consolation."

"As you say," replied Gringoire.

"There are some other advantages which thou wilt enjoy. As

The Broken Jug

one of the crew thou wilt not have to pay rates, either for lamp, scavenger, or poor, to which the honest burgesses of Paris are liable."

"Be it so!" said the poet. "I am a Vagabond, a subject of the kingdom of Cant, one of the crew, a man of Slang, anything you please; nay, I was all of these before, august King of Thunes, for I am a philosopher; *et omnia in philosophia, omnes in philosopho continentur,*[1] you know."

The august King of Thunes knitted his brow. "What do you take me for, my friend? What Hungary Jew gibberish are you talking now? I know nothing of Hebrew. One may be a ruffian without being a Jew."

Gringoire strove to slip in an excuse between these brief sentences cut short by anger. "I beg your Majesty's pardon: it is not Hebrew, but Latin."

"I tell thee," rejoined Clopin furiously. "I am not a Jew, and I will have thee hanged, varlet; ay, and that little Jew pedlar beside thee, whom I hope some day to see nailed to a counter, like a piece of base coin as he is."

As he thus spoke he pointed to the little bearded Hungarian Jew, who, acquainted with no other language but that in which he had accosted Gringoire, was surprised at the ill-humour which the King of Thunes appeared to be venting upon him.

At length King Clopin became somewhat more calm. "Knave," said he to our poet, "thou hast a mind then to become a Vagabond?"

"Undoubtedly," replied Gringoire.

"'Tis not enough to have a mind," said his surly Majesty: "goodwill puts not one more onion into the soup. To be admitted into our brotherhood, thou must prove that thou art fit for something. Show us thy skill at picking a pocket."

"Anything you please," said the poet.

Clopin made a sign. Several of the Vagabonds left the circle, and presently returned. They brought two poles, each having a flat horizontal piece of wood fastened at the lower extremity, upon which it stood upright on the ground. Into the upper ends of these two poles the bearers fitted a crossbar, and the whole then formed a very handy portable gibbet, which Gringoire had the satisfaction to see set up before his face in a trice. Nothing was wanting, not even the cord, which dangled gracefully from the crossbar.

[1] "All things are included in philosophy, all men in the philosopher."

The Hunchback of Notre-Dame

"What are they about now?" said Gringoire to himself, while his heart sunk within him. A tinkling of small bells put an end to his anxiety. It was the figure of a man, a kind of scarecrow, in a red dress so profusely bestudded with little bells that they would have sufficed for the caparison of thirty Castilian mules, which the Vagabonds were suspending by the neck from the rope. The tinkling of these thousand bells, occasioned by the swinging of the rope, gradually subsided, and at length ceased entirely with the motion of the effigy.

Clopin pointed to a crazy stool placed under the figure.

"Get upon that!" said he to Gringoire.

"'Sdeath!" rejoined the poet, "I shall break my neck. Your stool halts like a distich of Martial's; it has one hexameter and one pentameter foot."

"Get up, knave!" repeated Clopin.

Gringoire mounted the stool, and after some oscillations of head and arms recovered his centre of gravity.

"Now," continued the King of Thunes, "cross thy right leg over the left and stand on tiptoe."

"*Morbleu!*" cried Gringoire, "then you absolutely insist on it that I shall break some of my limbs?"

Clopin shook his head. "Hark ye, my friend, thou talkest too much for me. In two words this is what thou hast to do. Thou must stand on tiptoe as I tell thee, so as to reach the pocket of the figure. Thou must take out a purse that is in it, and if thou canst do this without making any of the bells speak 'tis well: thou shalt be a Vagabond. We shall then have nothing to do but to baste thee soundly for a week or so."

"*Ventre-Dieu!*" exclaimed Gringoire. "And if the bells should give mouth in spite of me?"

"Why, then thou shalt be hanged; dost thou comprehend me?"

"Not at all," answered Gringoire.

"Well then I tell thee once more. Thou must pick the pocket of that figure of a purse, and if a single bell stirs while thou art about it thou shalt be hanged. Dost thou understand that?"

"I do," said Gringoire. "And then?"

"If thou art clever enough to prig the purse without setting the bells a-clattering thou art a Canter, and shalt be soundly thrashed every now and then for a week. Thou understandest that, no doubt?"

The Broken Jug

"But what better shall I be? Hanged in one case, beaten in the other?"

"And a Canter!" rejoined Clopin, "a Canter! Is that nothing? It is for thy own benefit that we shall beat thee, to enure thee to blows."

"Many thanks to you!" replied the poet.

"Come, bear a hand!" said the King, stamping upon his hogshead, which sounded like a big drum. "To thy task, knave! And recollect, if I hear but a single bell thou shalt change places with that figure."

The crew applauded Clopin's words, and ranged themselves in a circle round the gallows with so pitiless a laugh that Gringoire saw he amused them too much not to have to fear the worst from them. The only hope he had left was the most precarious chance of succeeding in the ticklish task imposed upon him. Before he set about it he addressed a fervent prayer to the effigy which he was going to rob, and which he would have softened as easily as the Vagabonds. The myriad of bells with their little copper tongues seemed to him so many gaping jaws of serpents, ready to bite and to hiss.

"Oh!" said he aside, "is it possible that my life depends on the slightest vibration of the smallest of these bells?" He tried the effect of a last effort upon Trouillefou. "And if there should come a gust of wind?"

"Thou shalt be hanged," replied the King of Thunes without hesitation.

Finding that there was neither respite, nor reprieve, nor any possible evasion for him, he went resolutely to work. Crossing his right leg over the left, and raising himself on tiptoe he stretched out his arm; but at the moment when he touched the effigy he found himself tottering upon the stool which had but three legs: he lost his balance, mechanically caught at the figure, and fell plump on the ground, stunned by the fatal jingle of the thousand bells of the figure, which, yielding to the impulsion of his hand, at first turned round upon itself, and then swung majestically between the two poles.

"*Malédiction!*" cried he as he fell, and he lay like one dead, with his face toward the ground. He heard, however, the horrid chime above his head, the diabolical laugh of the Canters, and the voice of

85

Trouillefou, who said, "Pick up the varlet, and hang him out of hand."

He rose. They had already taken down the effigy to make room for him. The Vagabonds made him once more mount the stool. Clopin stepped up to him, put the rope about his neck, and, patting him on the shoulder, "Farewell, my friend!" said he. "Thou canst not escape now, even with the devil's luck and thine own."

The word *"Mercy!"* died away on the lips of Gringoire. He glanced round him, but there was no hope: they were all laughing.

"Bellevigne de l'Etoile," said the King of Thunes to a porpoise of a fellow, who stepped forth from the ranks, "scramble up to that crossbar." The monster mounted with an agility for which no one would have given him credit, and Gringoire, raising his eyes, beheld him with terror crouching on the crossbeam over his head.

"Now," resumed Clopin, "the moment I clap my hands, thou, Andry the Red, kick away the stool; thou, François Chante-Prune, pull the varlet's legs, and thou, Bellevigne, spring upon his shoulders—all three at once, d'ye hear?"

Gringoire shuddered.

"Are ye there?" said Clopin Trouillefou to the three ruffians, ready to rush upon the unfortunate poet. The wretched man passed a moment of horrid suspense, while Clopin carelessly kicked into the fire a few twigs which the flame had not consumed. "Are ye there?" he repeated, opening his hands for the decisive clap.

He stopped short, as if a sudden thought had occurred to him. "Wait a moment!" said he, "I forgot. . . . It is customary with us not to hang a blade till the women have been asked whether any of them will have him. Comrade, this is thy last chance."

Gringoire breathed once more. It was the second time that he had come to life within the last half-hour. He durst not, therefore, place much reliance upon this reprieve.

Clopin again mounted his hogshead. "This way, gentlefolks!" cried he. "Is there any strumpet among you, who will have this knave? Come forward and see! A husband for nothing! Who wants one?"

Gringoire, in this wretched plight, looked far from tempting. The female mumpers showed no eagerness to accept the offer. The unhappy man heard them answer one after another, "No, no, hang him, and that will be a pleasure for us all."

The Broken Jug

Three of them, however, stepped forward from among the crowd to take a look at him. The first was a strapping broad-faced wench. She closely examined the deplorable doublet and the threadbare frock of the philosopher. She shrugged her shoulders. "Queer toggery!" grumbled she. Then, turning to Gringoire, "Where is thy cloak?"

"I have lost it," answered he.

"Thy hat?"

"They have taken it from me."

"Thy shoes?"

"They are nearly worn out."

"Thy purse?"

"Alas!" stammered Gringoire, "I have not a *denier* left."

"Hang then, and be thankful!" replied the wench, turning on her heel and striding away.

The second, an old wrinkled hag, dark, and hideously ugly, walked round Gringoire. He almost trembled lest she should take a fancy to him. At length she muttered to herself. "He is as lean as a carrion," and away she went.

The third was young, fresh-looking, and not ill-favoured. "Save me!" said the poor devil to her in a low tone. She surveyed him for a moment with a look of pity, cast down her eyes, twitched her petticoat, and stood for a moment undecided. He narrowly watched all her motions. It was the last glimmer of hope. "No," said she at last; "no; Guillaume Long-Joue would beat me," and she rejoined the crowd.

"Comrade," said Clopin, "thou art unlucky." Then, standing up on his hogshead, "Will nobody bid?" cried he, imitating the manner of an auctioneer, to the high diversion of the crew. "Will nobody bid? once, twice, three times!" and then, turning to the gallows, with a nod of the head, "Gone!"

Bellevigne de l'Etoile, Andry the Red, and François Chante-Prune again surrounded the gibbet. At that moment cries of "La Esmeralda! La Esmeralda!" arose among the Vagabonds. Gringoire shuddered and turned the way from which the clamour proceeded. The crowd opened and made way for a bright and dazzling figure. It was the gipsy-girl.

"La Esmeralda!" ejaculated Gringoire, struck amid his agitation at the sudden manner in which that magic name connected his scattered recollections of the events of the day. This extraordinary creature appeared by her fascination and beauty to exercise sovereign sway over the Cour des Miracles itself. Its inmates of both sexes respectfully drew back for her to pass, and at sight of her their brutal faces assumed a softer expression. With light step she approached the sufferer. Her pretty Djali followed at her heels. Gringoire was more dead than alive. She eyed him for a moment in silence.

"Are you going to hang this man?" said she gravely to Clopin.

"Yes, sister," replied the King of Thunes, "unless thou wilt take him for thy husband."

Her lower lip was protruded into the pretty pout already described. "I will take him," said she.

Gringoire was now thoroughly convinced that he had been in a dream ever since morning, and that this was but a continuation of it. The shock, though agreeable, was violent. The noose was removed, the poet was dismounted from the stool, on which he was obliged to sit down, so vehement was his agitation.

The Duke of Egypt, without uttering a word, brought an earthenware jug. The gipsy-girl handed it to Gringoire. "Drop it on the ground," said she to him. The jug broke into four pieces.

"Brother," said the Duke of Egypt, placing a hand upon the head of each, "she is thy wife. Sister, he is thy husband. For four years. Go."

CHAPTER VII

A WEDDING-NIGHT

IN a few moments our poet found himself in a small room with a vaulted ceiling, very snug and very warm, seated at a table, which appeared to desire nothing better than to draw a few loans from a cupboard, suspended close by, having a prospect of a good bed, and a *tête-à-tête* with a handsome girl. The adventure was like absolute enchantment. He began seriously to take himself for the hero of some fairy-tale; and looked round from time to time to see whether the chariot of fire drawn by griffins, which could alone have conveyed him with such rapidity from Tartarus to Paradise, was still there. Now and then, too, he would fix his eyes on the

A Wedding-night

holes in his doublet, as if to satisfy himself of his identity. His reason, tossed to and fro in imaginary space, had only this thread to hold by.

The girl appeared to take no notice of him; she moved backward and forward, setting things to rights, talking to her goat, and now and then pouting her lip. At length she sat down near the table, and Gringoire had a good opportunity to scrutinize her.

You have been a child, reader, and may perhaps have the good fortune to be so still. I dare say you have often (I know I have, for whole days together, ay, and some of the best-spent days of my life) followed from bush to bush on the bank of a stream, on a fine sunshiny day, some beautiful green-and-blue dragon-fly, darting off every moment at acute angles, and brushing the ends of all the branches. You remember with what ardent curiosity your attention and your eyes were fixed on those fluttering wings of purple and azure, amid which floated a form rendered indistinct by the very rapidity of its motion. The aerial creature, confusedly perceived through this flickering of wings, appeared to you chimerical, imaginary, a thing neither to be touched nor seen. But when at length it settled on the point of a rush, and, holding your breath the while, you could examine those delicate wings of gauze, that long robe of enamel, those two globes of crystal, what astonishment did you not feel, and what fear lest this beautiful figure should again vanish into an airy undefinable phantom! Recollect these impressions, and you will easily conceive what Gringoire felt on contemplating in a visible and palpable form that Esmeralda of whom he had till then had but a glimpse amid the whirling dance and a crowd of spectators.

He became more and more absorbed in his reverie. "This, then," thought he, while his eye vaguely followed her motions, "is La Esmeralda! a celestial creature!—a street-dancer! So much and so little. It was she who gave the finishing stroke to my mystery this afternoon, and it is she who saves my life to-night. My evil genius! my good angel! A sweet girl, upon my word!—and who must love me to distraction to have taken me in this manner. For," said he, rising all at once with that candour which formed the groundwork of his character and of his philosophy, "I know not exactly how it has come to pass, but I am her husband."

With this idea in his head and in his eyes he approached the girl with such ardent impetuosity that she drew back. "What do you want with me?" inquired she.

"Can you ask such a question, adorable Esmeralda?" rejoined Gringoire in so impassioned a tone that he was astonished at it himself.

The Egyptian opened her large eyes. "I know not what you mean," said she.

"What!" replied Gringoire, warming more and more, and thinking that after all it was but a virtue of the Cour des Miracles that he had to do with; "am I not thine, my sweet friend? art thou not mine." With these words he fondly threw his arm round her waist.

The drapery of the Bohemian glided through his hands like the skin of an eel. Bounding from one end of the cell to the other, she stooped, and raised herself again, with a little dagger in her hand, before Gringoire could see whence it came, with swollen lip, distended nostril, cheeks as red as an apricot, and eyes flashing lightning. At the same moment the little white goat placed itself before her in the attitude of attack, presenting to Gringoire two very pretty but very sharp gilt horns. All this was done in a twinkling.

Our philosopher stood petrified, alternately eyeing the goat and her mistress. "Holy Virgin!" he at length ejaculated, when surprise allowed him to speak, "what a couple of vixens!"

"And you," said the Bohemian, breaking silence on her part, "must be a very impudent fellow."

"Pardon me," replied Gringoire, smiling. "But why did you take me for your husband?"

"Ought I to have let you be hanged?"

"Then," rejoined the poet, somewhat disappointed in his amorous hopes, "you had no other intention in marrying me but to save me from the gallows?"

"And what other intention do you suppose I could have had?"

Gringoire bit his lips. "Go to," said he to himself, "I am not so triumphant in love affairs as I imagined. But then, of what use was it to break the poor jug?"

Meanwhile Esmeralda's dagger and the horns of her goat were still upon the defensive.

"Mademoiselle Esmeralda," said the poet, "let us capitulate. I am not a clerk to the Châtelet, and shall not provoke you thus to

A Wedding-night

carry a dagger in Paris, in the teeth of the Provost's ordinances and prohibitions. You must, nevertheless, be aware that Noël Lescrivain was sentenced a week ago to pay a fine of ten sous Parisis for having carried a short sword. But that is no business of mine, so to return to the point—I swear to you by my hopes of Paradise not to approach you without your permission and consent; but for heaven's sake give me some supper."

In reality Gringoire, like Despreaux, was not of a very amorous temperament. He belonged not to that chivalric and military class who take young damsels by assault. In love, as in all other affairs, he was for temporizing and pursuing middle courses; and to him a good supper with an agreeable companion appeared, especially when he was hungry, an excellent interlude between the prologue and the winding up of a love adventure.

The Egyptian made no reply. She gave her disdainful pout, raised her head like a bird, and burst into a loud laugh: the pretty little dagger vanished as it had come, so that Gringoire could not discover where the bee concealed its sting.

In a moment a loaf of rye-bread, a slice of bacon, some wrinkled apples, and a jug of beer were set out upon the table. Gringoire fell to with much avidity, as if all his love had been changed into appetite. His hostess, seated before him, looked on in silence, visibly engaged with some other thought, at which she smiled from time to time, while her soft hand stroked the head of the intelligent goat, closely pressed between her knees. A candle of yellow wax lighted this scene of voracity and reverie.

The first cravings of his stomach being appeased, Gringoire felt a degree of false shame on perceiving that there was only one apple left. "Do you not eat something, Mademoiselle Esmeralda?" said he. She replied in the negative by a shake of the head, and her pensive looks were fixed on the vaulted ceiling of the cell.

"What the devil can she be thinking of?" said Gringoire to himself, turning his eyes in the same direction as hers. "It is impossible that yon ugly head carved on the groining can thus engross her attention. Surely I may stand a comparison with that."

"Mademoiselle," said he, raising his voice. She appeared not to hear him. "Mademoiselle Esmeralda!" he again began in a still louder tone, to just as little purpose. The spirit of the damsel was elsewhere, and the voice of Gringoire had not the power to recall it.

Luckily for him the goat interfered, and began to pull her mistress gently by the sleeve. "What do you want, Djali?" said the Egyptian sharply, starting like one awakened out of a sound sleep.

"She is hungry," said Gringoire, delighted at the opportunity of opening the conversation.

La Esmeralda began crumbling some bread, which Djali gracefully ate out of the hollow of her hand. Gringoire, without giving her time to resume her reverie, ventured upon a delicate question. "Then you will not have me for your husband?" said he.

The damsel looked at him intently for a moment, and then replied, "No."

"For your lover?" asked Gringoire.

She pouted her lip, and again replied, "No."

"For your friend?" continued Gringoire.

She again fixed her eyes steadfastly upon him. "Perhaps," said she, after a moment's reflection.

This "perhaps," so dear to philosophers, emboldened Gringoire. "Do you know what friendship is?" he inquired.

"Yes," replied the Egyptian; "it is to be as brother and sister, two souls which touch each other without uniting, like two fingers of the same hand."

"And love?" proceeded Gringoire.

"Oh! love!" said she, and her voice trembled, and her eye sparkled. "It is to be two and yet but one—it is a man and a woman blending into an angel—it is heaven itself."

The street-dancer, as she uttered these words, appeared invested with a beauty which powerfully struck Gringoire, and seemed in perfect unison with the almost Oriental exaggeration of her language. A faint smile played upon her pure and rosy lips; her bright and serene brow was now and then clouded for a moment, according to the turn of her thoughts, as a mirror is by the breath; and from her long dark, downcast eyelashes emanated a sort of ineffable light, which imparted to her profile that ideal sweetness which Raphael subsequently found at the mystic point of intersection of virginity, maternity, and divinity.

Gringoire nevertheless proceeded. "And what should one be," said he, "to please you?"

"A man."

"What am I, then?"

A Wedding-night

"A man has a helmet on his head, a sword in his fist, and gold spurs at his heels."

"So then," rejoined Gringoire, "without a horse one cannot be a man. Do you love anyone?"

She remained pensive for a moment, and then said with a peculiar kind of expression, "I shall soon know that."

"Why not to-night?" replied the poet tenderly. "Why not me?"

She eyed him with a serious look. "Never can I love any man but one who is able to protect me."

Gringoire blushed and made sure that this stroke was aimed at him. It was evident that the girl was alluding to the little assistance he had afforded her in the critical situation in which she had found herself two hours before. At the recollection of this circumstance, which his own subsequent adventures had banished from his mind, he struck his forehead.

"Indeed," said he, "I ought to have begun with that subject. Forgive the confusion of my ideas. How did you contrive to escape from Quasimodo's clutches?"

This question made the gipsy-girl shudder. "Oh, the horrid hunchback!" she exclaimed, covering her face with her hands, and she shivered as from the effect of intense cold.

"Horrid, indeed!" said Gringoire, without relinquishing his idea; "but how did you get away from him?"

La Esmeralda smiled, sighed, and made no reply.

"Do you know why he followed you?" resumed Gringoire, seeking to return to his question by a roundabout way.

"I do not," said the girl. "But," added she sharply, "you followed me too; why did you follow me?"

"In good sooth," replied Gringoire, "I do not know either."

Both were then silent. Gringoire took up his knife and began to cut the table. The damsel smiled and seemed to be looking at something through the wall. All at once she commenced singing in a voice scarcely articulate:

> Quando las pintadas aves
> Mudas estan, y la tierra. [1]

She then abruptly broke off and began to caress her Djali.

"That is a pretty creature of yours," observed Gringoire.

[1] "When the speckled birds are moulting, and the cock also."

93

" 'Tis my sister," replied she.

"Why are you called La Esmeralda?" inquired the poet.

"I can't tell."

"No, sure!"

She drew from her bosom a small oblong bag, attached to a necklace of small red seeds, and emitting a very strong scent of camphor. The outside was green silk, and in the middle of it there was a large bead of green glass in imitation of emerald.

"Perhaps it is on account of this," said she.

Gringoire extended his hand to lay hold of the bag, but she started back. "Don't touch it," said she; " 'tis an amulet. You might do an injury to the charm, or the charm to you."

The curiosity of the poet was more and more excited. "Who gave you that?" he asked.

She laid her finger upon her lips and replaced the amulet in her bosom. He ventured upon further questions, but could scarcely obtain answers to them.

"What is the meaning of La Esmeralda?"

"I know not," said she.

"To what language does the word belong?"

"It is Egyptian, I believe."

"I thought so," said Gringoire. "You are not a native of France?"

"I don't know."

"Are your parents living?"

She began singing to the tune of an old song:

> My father's a bird,
>   And my mother's his mate;
> I pass the broad waters
>   Without boat or bait.

"How old were you when you came to France?"

"I was quite a child."

"And to Paris?"

"Last year. At the moment we were entering the Papal Gate I saw the yellowhammers flying in a line over our heads. It was then the end of August, and I said, 'We shall have a sharp winter.'"

"And so we have," said Gringoire, delighted with this commence-

94

ment of conversation; "I have done nothing but blow my fingers since it set in. Why, then, you possess the gift of prophecy?"

"No," replied she, relapsing into her laconic manner.

"The man whom you call the Duke of Egypt is the chief of your tribe, I presume?"

"Yes."

"And yet it was he who married us," timidly observed the poet.

Her lip exhibited the accustomed pout. "I don't even know your name," said she.

"My name, if you wish to know it, is Pierre Gringoire."

"I know a much finer," said she.

"How unkind!" replied the poet. "Never mind; you shall not make me angry. You will, perhaps, love me when you are better acquainted with me; and you have related your history to me with such candour that I cannot withhold mine from you.

"You must know then that my name is Pierre Gringoire, and that my father held the situation of notary at Gonesse. He was hanged by the Burgundians, and my mother was murdered by the Picards, at the siege of Paris twenty years ago: so, at six years old I was left an orphan with no other sole to my foot but the pavement of Paris. I know not how I passed the interval between six and sixteen. Here, a fruitwoman gave me an apple or a plum; there, a baker tossed me a crust of bread; at night I threw myself in the way of the watch, who picked me up and put me in prison, where I found at least a bundle of straw. In spite of this kind of life I grew tall and slim, as you see. In winter I warmed myself in the sunshine, under the porch of the Hôtel de Sens, and I thought it very absurd that the bonfires of St John should be deferred nearly to the dog-days. At sixteen I began to think of adopting a profession, and successively tried my hand at everything. I turned soldier, but was not brave enough; I became a monk, but was not devout enough, and, besides, I could not drink hard enough. In despair I apprenticed myself to a carpenter, but was not strong enough. I had a much greater fancy to be a schoolmaster; true, I had not learned to read, but what of that? After some time I discovered that, owing to some deficiency or other, I was fit for nothing, and therefore set up for a poet. This is a profession to which a man who is a vagabond may always betake himself, and it is better than to thieve, as some young rogues of my acquaintance advised me to do. One day, as good luck would have it, I met with Dom Claude Frollo, the reverend Archdeacon of Notre-Dame, who took a liking to me, and to him I owe it that I am this day a learned man, not unpractised either in scholastics, poetics, or rhythmics, nor even in hermetics, that sophia of all sophias. I am the author of the mystery that was performed to-day before a prodigious concourse of people, with immense applause, in the great hall of the Palace of Justice. I have also written a book of six hundred pages on the prodigious comet of 1465, which turned a man's brain, and have distinguished myself in other ways. Being somewhat of an artillery carpenter, I assisted in making the great bombard which, you know, burst at the bridge of Charenton, on the day that it was tried, and killed twenty-four of the spectators. So you see I am no bad match. I know a great many very curious tricks, which I will teach your goat, for instance, to mimic the Bishop of Paris, that cursed Pharisee whose mills splash the passengers all along the Pont aux Meuniers. And then my mystery will bring me in a good deal of hard cash, if I can get paid for it. In short, I am wholly at your service, damsel, my body and soul, my science and my learning, ready to live with you in any way you please, chastely or jovially, as husband and wife, if you think proper, as brother and sister, if you like it better."

Gringoire paused, waiting the effect of his address on his hearer. Her eyes were fixed on the ground.

"Phœbus," said she in an undertone, and then turning to the poet—"Phœbus, what does that mean?"

Gringoire, though unable to discover what connexion there could be between the subject of his speech and this question, was not displeased to have an opportunity of displaying his erudition. "It is a Latin word," said he, "and means the sun."

"The sun!" she exclaimed.

"It is the name of a certain handsome archer, who was a god," added Gringoire.

"A god!" repeated the Egyptian, and there was in her tone something pensive and impassioned.

At this moment one of her bracelets, having accidentally become loose, fell to the ground. Gringoire instantly stooped to pick it up; when he raised himself the damsel and the goat were gone. He heard the sound of a bolt, upon a door communicating no doubt with an adjoining cell, which fastened on the inside.

"No matter, so she has left me a bed!" said our philosopher. He explored the cell. It contained not any piece of furniture fit to lie down upon, excepting a long coffer, and the lid of this was carved in such a manner as to communicate to Gringoire, when he stretched himself upon it, a sensation similar to that experienced by Micromegas when he lay at his full length upon the Alps.

"Well," said he, accommodating himself to this uncomfortable couch as well as he could, " 'tis of no use to grumble. But at any rate this is a strange wedding-night!"

BOOK III

CHAPTER I

NOTRE-DAME

THE church of Notre-Dame at Paris is doubtless a sublime and majestic edifice. But notwithstanding the beauty which it has retained even in its old age one cannot help feeling grief and indignation at the numberless injuries and mutilations which time and man have inflicted on the venerable structure, regardless of Charlemagne who laid the first stone of it and of Philip Augustus who laid the last.

On the face of this aged queen of our cathedrals we always find a scar beside a wrinkle. *Tempus edax, homo edacior* [1]—which I should translate thus: "Time is blind, man stupid."

If we had leisure to examine with the reader, one by one, the different traces of destruction left upon the ancient church we should find that Time had had much less hand in them than men, and especially professional men.

In the first place, to adduce only some capital examples, there are assuredly few more beautiful specimens of architecture than that façade, where the three porches with their pointed arches; the plinth embroidered and fretted with twenty-eight royal niches; the immense central mullioned window, flanked by its two lateral windows, like the priest by the deacon and the sub-deacon; the lofty and light gallery of open-work arcades supporting a heavy platform upon its slender pillars; lastly, the two dark and massive towers with their slated penthouses—harmonious parts of a magnificent whole, placed one above another in five gigantic stages—present themselves to the eye in a crowd yet without confusion, with their innumerable details of statuary, sculpture, and carving powerfully contributing to the tranquil grandeur of the whole—a vast symphony of stone, if we may be allowed the expression; the colossal product of the combination of all the force of the age; in which the fancy of the workman, chastened by the genius of the artist, is seen starting forth in a hundred

---

[1] "Time is voracious, and man even more so."

Notre-Dame

forms upon every stone: in short, a sort of human Creation, mighty and fertile as the Divine Creation, from which it seems to have borrowed the twofold character of variety and eternity.

What we here say of the façade must be said of the whole church; and what we say of the cathedral of Paris must be said of all the churches of Christendom in the Middle Ages. But to return to the façade of Notre-Dame, such as it appears to us at present, when we piously repair thither to admire the solemn and gorgeous cathedral, which, to use the language of the chroniclers, "by its vastness struck terror into the spectator."

That façade, as we now see it, has lost three important accessories: in the first place, the flight of eleven steps which raised it above the level of the ground; in the next, the lower range of statues which filled the niches of the three porches, and the upper range of twenty-eight more ancient sovereigns of France which adorned the gallery of the first storey, beginning with Childebert and ending with Philip Augustus, holding in his hand "the imperial globe."

Time, by a slow and irresistible progress raising the level of the city, occasioned the removal of the steps; but if this rising tide of the pavement of Paris has swallowed up, one after another, those eleven steps which added to the majestic height of the edifice, Time has given to the church more perhaps than it has taken away; for it is Time that has imparted to the façade that sombre hue of antiquity which makes the old age of buildings the period of their greatest beauty.

But who has thrown down the two ranges of statues?—who has left the niches empty?—who has inserted that new and bastard pointed arch in the middle of the beautiful central porch?—who has dared to set up that tasteless and heavy door of wood, carved in the style of Louis XV, beside the arabesques of Biscornette? The men, the architects, the artists, of our own days.

And, if we step within the edifice, who has thrown down that colossal St Christopher, proverbial among statues for the same reason as the great hall of the palace among halls, and the steeple of Strasburg among steeples? who has brutally swept away those myriads of statues which peopled all the intercolumniations of the nave and the choir, kneeling, standing, on horseback, men, women, children, kings, bishops, soldiers, of stone, marble, gold, silver, copper, and even wax? Not Time, most assuredly.

And who has substituted for the old Gothic altar, splendidly encumbered with shrines and reliquaries, that heavy sarcophagus of marble with its cherubs and its clouds, looking for all the world like a stray specimen from the Val de Grâce or the Invalids? Who has stupidly inserted that clumsy anachronism of stone in the Carlovingian pavement of Hercandus? Is it not Louis XIV fulfilling the vow of Louis XIII?

And who has put cold white glass instead of those deeply coloured panes, which caused the astonished eyes of our ancestors to pause between the rose of the great porch and the pointed arches of the chancel? What would a sub-chorister of the sixteenth century say on beholding the yellow plaster with which our Vandal archbishops have bedaubed their cathedral? He would recollect that this was the colour with which the executioner washed over the houses of criminals; he would recollect the Hôtel du Petit-Bourbon, thus beplastered with yellow on account of the treason of the Constable, "and a yellow of so good quality," saith Sauval, "and so well laid on, that more than a century hath not yet faded its colour"; he would imagine that the sacred fane has become infamous, and flee from it as fast as he could.

And if we go up into the cathedral, without pausing over the thousand various barbarisms, what has been done with that charming little belfry, which stood over the point of intersection of the transept, and which, neither less light nor less bold than its neighbour, the steeple of the Sainte-Chapelle (likewise destroyed) rose, light, elegant, and sonorous, into the air, overtopping the towers? It was amputated (1787) by an architect of taste, who deemed it sufficient to cover the wound with that large plaster of lead, which looks for all the world like the lid of a saucepan.

It is thus that the wonderful art of the Middle Ages has been treated in almost every country, especially in France. In its ruins we may distinguish three kinds of injuries, which have affected it in different degrees: in the first place Time, which has here and there chapped and everywhere worn its surface; in the next, revolutions, political and religious, which, blind and furious by nature, have rushed tumultuously upon it, stripped it of its rich garb of sculptures and carvings, broken its open-work and its chains of arabesques and fanciful figures, torn down its statues, sometimes on account of their mitres, sometimes on account of their crowns; lastly, the fashions, more and more silly and grotesque, which since the splendid deviations of the Renaissance have succeeded each other in the necessary decline of architecture. The fashions have in fact done more mischief than revolutions. They have cut into the quick; they have attacked the very bones of the art; they have hacked, hewn, mangled, murdered, the building, in the form as well as in the symbol, in its logic not less than in its beauty. And then they have restored—a presumption from which at least time and revolutions have been exempt. In the name of *good taste,* forsooth, they have impudently clapped upon the wounds of Gothic architecture their paltry gewgaws of a day, their ribands of marble, their pompons of metal, a downright leprosy of egg-moulding, voltures, spirals, draperies, garlands, fringes, flames of stone, clouds of bronze, plethoric Cupids, chubby cherubs, which begin to eat into the face of art in the oratory of Catharine de' Medici, and put it to death two centuries later, writhing and grinning in the boudoir of the Dubarry.

Thus, to sum up the points to which we have directed attention, three kinds of ravages nowadays disfigure Gothic architecture: wrinkles and warts on the epidermis—these are the work of Time; wounds, contusions, fractures, from brutal violence—these are the work of revolutions from Luther to Mirabeau; mutilations, amputations, dislocations of members, *restorations*—this is the barbarous Greek and Roman work of professors, according to Vitruvius and Vignole. That magnificent art which the Vandals produced the academies have murdered. With Time and revolutions, whose ravages are, at any rate, marked by impartiality and grandeur, has been associated a host of architects, duly bred, duly certificated, and duly sworn, despoiling with the discernment of bad taste, substituting the chicories of Louis XV for the Gothic lacework, for the greater glory of the Parthenon. This is truly the ass's kick to the expiring lion; the old oak throwing out its leafy crown, to be bitten, gnawed, and torn by caterpillars.

How widely different this from the period when Robert Cenalis, comparing Notre-Dame at Paris with the famous temple of Diana at Ephesus, "so highly extolled by the ancient heathen," pronounced the Gallican cathedral "more excellent in length, breadth, height, and structure."

Notre-Dame, however, is not what may be called a complete building, nor does it belong to any definite class. It is not a Roman

The Hunchback of Notre-Dame

church neither is it a Gothic church. Notre-Dame has not, like
the abbey of Tournus, the heavy, massive squareness, the cold naked-
ness, the majestic simplicity, of edifices which have the circular
arch for their generative principle. It is not, like the cathedral of
Bourges, the magnificent, light, multiform, efflorescent, highly decorated production of the pointed arch. It cannot be classed
among that ancient family of churches, gloomy, mysterious,
low, and crushed as it were by the circular arch; quite hieroglyphic, sacerdotal, symbolical; exhibiting in their decorations
more lozenges and zigzags than flowers, more flowers than animals,
more animals than human figures; the work not so much of the architect as of the bishop; the first transformation of the art, impressed all over with theocratic and military discipline, commencing
in the Lower Empire and terminating with William the Conqueror.
Neither can our cathedral be placed in that other family of churches,
light, lofty, rich in painted glass and sculptures; sharp in form,
bold in attitude; free, capricious, unruly, as works of art; the second
transformation of architecture, no longer hieroglyphic, unchangeable,
and sacerdotal, but artistical, progressive, and popular, beginning
with the return from the Crusades and ending with Louis XI.
Notre-Dame is not of pure Roman extraction, like the former, neither
is it of pure Arab extraction, like the latter.

It is a transition edifice. The Saxon architect had set up the first
pillars of the nave, when the pointed style, brought back from the
Crusades, seated itself like a conqueror upon those broad Roman capitals designed to support circular arches only. The pointed style,
thenceforward mistress, constructed the rest of the church; but, unpractised and timid at its outset, it displays a certain breadth and
flatness, and dares not yet shoot up into steeples and pinnacles, as it
has since done in so many wonderful cathedrals. You would say
that it is affected by the vicinity of the heavy Roman pillars.

For the rest, those edifices of the transition from the Roman to
the Gothic style are not less valuable as studies than the pure types
of either. They express a shade of the art which would be lost but
for them—the engrafting of the pointed upon the circular style.

Notre-Dame at Paris is a particularly curious specimen of this
variety. Every face, every stone, of the venerable structure is a
page not only of the history of the country, but also of the history of
art and science. Thus, to glance merely at the principal details,

while the little Porte Rouge attains almost to the limits of the Gothic delicacy of the fifteenth century, the pillars of the nave by their bulk and heaviness carry you back to the date of the Carlovingian abbey of Sainte-Germain-des-Prés. You would imagine that there were six centuries between that doorway and those pillars. There are none, down to the alchemists themselves, but find in the symbols of the grand porch a satisfactory compendium of their science, of which the church of Saint-Jacques-de-la-Boucherie was so complete an hieroglyphic. Thus the Roman abbey and the philosophical church, Gothic art and Saxon art, the heavy round pillar, which reminds you of Gregory VII, Papal unity and schism, Sainte-Germain-des-Prés and Sainte-Jacques-de-la-Boucherie—are all blended, combined, amalgamated, in Notre-Dame. This central mother-church is a sort of chimera among the ancient churches of Paris; it has the head of one, the limbs of another, the trunk of a third, and something of them all.

These hybrid structures, as we have observed, are not the less interesting to the artist, the antiquary, and the historian. They show how far architecture is a primitive art, inasmuch as they demonstrate (what is also demonstrated by the Cyclopean remains, the Pyramids of Egypt, the gigantic Hindu pagodas) that the grandest productions of architecture are not so much individual as social works, rather the offspring of nations in labour than the inventions of genius; the deposit left by a people; the accumulations formed by ages; the residuum of the successive evaporations of human society—in short, a species of formation. Every wave of time superinduces its alluvium, every generation deposits its stratum upon the structure, every individual brings his stone. Such is the process of the beavers, such that of the bees, such that of men. The great emblem of architecture, Babel, is a beehive.

Great edifices, like great mountains, are the work of ages. It is frequently the case that art changes while they are still in progress. The new art takes the structure as it finds it, encrusts itself upon it, assimilates itself to it, proceeds with it according to its own fancy, and completes it if it can. The thing is accomplished without disturbance, without effort, without reaction, agreeably to a natural and quiet law. Certainly there is matter for very thick books, and often for the universal history of mankind, in those successive inoculations of various styles at various heights upon the same structure.

The Hunchback of Notre-Dame

The man, the artist, the individual, are lost in these vast masses without any author's name, while human skill is condensed and concentrated in them. Time is the architect, the nation is the mason.

To confine our view here to Christian European architecture, that younger sister of the grand style of the East, it appears to us like an immense formation divided into three totally distinct zones laid one upon another: the Roman [1] zone, the Gothic zone, and the zone of the Renaissance, which we would fain call the Græco-Roman. The Roman stratum, which is the most ancient and the lowest, is occupied by the circular arch, which again appears, supported by the Greek column, in the modern and uppermost stratum of the Renaissance. The pointed style is between both. The edifices belonging exclusively to one of these three strata are absolutely distinct, one, and complete. Such are the abbey of Jumièges, the cathedral of Rheims, the church of Sainte-Croix at Orleans. But the three zones blend and amalgamate at their borders, like the colours in the solar spectrum. Hence the complex structures, the transition edifices. The one is Roman at the foot, Gothic in the middle, Græco-Roman at the top. The reason is that it was six centuries in building. This variety is rare; the castle of Etampes is a specimen of it. But the edifices composed of two formations are frequent. Such is Notre-Dame at Paris, a building in the pointed style, the first pillars of which belong to the Roman zone, like the porch of Saint-Denis, and the nave of Saint-Germain-des-Prés. Such too is the charming semi-Gothic capitular hall of Bocherville, exhibiting the Roman stratum up to half its height. Such is the cathedral of Rouen, which would be entirely Gothic were it not for the extremity of its central steeple, which penetrates into the zone of the Renaissance. [2]

For the rest, all these shades, all these differences, affect only the surface of edifices; it is but art which has changed its skin. The constitution itself of the Christian church is not affected by them. There is always the same internal arrangement, the same logical disposition of parts. Be the sculptured and embroidered outside of a

[1] This is the same that is likewise called, according to countries, climates, and species, Lombard, Saxon, and Byzantine. These four are parallel and kindred varieties, each having its peculiar character, but all derived from the same principle—the circular arch.

[2] It was precisely this part of the steeple, which was of wood, that was destroyed by the fire of heaven in 1823.

cathedral what it may, we invariably find underneath at least the germ and rudiment of the Roman basilica. It uniformly expands itself upon the ground according to the same law. There are without deviation two naves, intersecting each other in the form of a cross, and the upper extremity of which, rounded into an apse, forms the chancel; and two aisles for processions and for chapels, a sort of lateral walking-places, into which the principal nave disgorges itself by the intercolumniations. These points being settled, the number of the chapels, porches, towers, pinnacles, is varied to infinity, according to the caprice of the age, the nation, and the art. Accommodation for the exercises of religion once provided and secured, architecture does just what it pleases. As for statues, painted windows, mullions, arabesques, open-work, capitals, bas-reliefs—it combines all these devices agreeably to the system which best suits itself. Hence the prodigious external variety in those edifices within which reside such order and unity. The trunk of the tree is unchangeable, the foliage capricious.

CHAPTER II

A BIRD'S-EYE VIEW OF PARIS

WE have just attempted to repair for the reader the admirable church of Notre-Dame at Paris. We have briefly touched upon most of the beauties which it had in the fifteenth century, and which it no longer possesses; but we have omitted the principal, namely, the view of Paris then enjoyed from the top of the towers.

It was in fact when, after groping your way up the dark spiral staircase with which the thick wall of the towers is perpendicularly perforated, and landing abruptly on one of the two lofty platforms deluged with light and air, that a delightful spectacle burst at once upon the view—a spectacle *sui generis,* of which some conception may easily be formed by such of our readers as have had the good fortune to see one of the few Gothic towns still left entire, complete, homogeneous, such as Nuremberg in Bavaria, Vittoria in Spain, or even smaller specimens, provided they are in good preservation, as Vitré in Bretagne, and Nordhausen in Prussia.

The Hunchback of Notre-Dame

The Paris of three hundred and fifty years ago, the Paris of the fifteenth century, was already a gigantic city. We modern Parisians in general are much mistaken in regard to the ground which we imagine it has gained. Since the time of Louis XI Paris has not increased above one-third; and certainly it has lost much more in beauty than it has acquired in magnitude.

The infant Paris was born, as everybody knows, in that ancient island in the shape of a cradle which is now called the Cité. The banks of that island were its first enclosure; the Seine was its first ditch. For several centuries Paris was confined to the island, having two bridges, the one on the north, and the other on the south, and two *têtes-de-ponts,* which were at once its gates and its fortresses —the Grand Châtelet on the right bank and the Petit Châtelet on the left. In process of time, under the kings of the first dynasty, finding herself straitened in her island and unable to turn herself about, she crossed the water. A first enclosure of walls and towers then began to encroach upon either bank of the Seine beyond the two Châtelets. Of this ancient enclosure some vestiges were still remaining in the past century; nothing is now left of it but the memory and here and there a tradition. By degrees the flood of houses, always propelled from the heart to the extremities, wore away and overflowed this enclosure. Philip Augustus surrounded Paris with new ramparts. He imprisoned the city within a circular chain of large, lofty, and massive towers. For more than a century the houses, crowding closer and closer, raised their level in this basin, like water in a reservoir. They began to grow higher; storey was piled upon storey; they shot up, like any compressed liquid, and each tried to lift its head above its neighbour's, in order to obtain a little fresh air. The streets became deeper and deeper, and narrower and narrower: every vacant place was covered and disappeared. The houses at length overleaped the wall of Philip Augustus, and merrily scattered themselves at random over the plain, like prisoners who had made their escape. There they sat themselves down at their ease and carved themselves gardens out of the fields. As early as 1367 the suburbs of the city had spread so far as to need a fresh enclosure, especially on the right bank: this was built for it by Charles V. But a place like Paris is perpetually increasing. It is such cities alone that become capitals of countries. They are reservoirs, into which all the geographical, political, moral, and intellectual channels of a country, all the natural inclined planes of its population, discharge themselves; wells of civilization, if we may be allowed the expression, and drains also, where all that constitutes the sap, the life, the soul, of a nation is incessantly collecting and filtering, drop by drop, age by age. The enclosure of Charles V consequently shared the same fate as that of Philip Augustus. By the conclusion of the fifteenth century it was overtaken, passed, and the suburbs kept travelling onward. In the sixteenth it seemed to be visibly receding more and more into the ancient city, so rapidly did the new town thicken on the other side of it. Thus, so far back as the fifteenth century, to come down no farther, Paris had already worn out the three concentric circles of walls which, from the time of Julian the Apostate, lay in embryo, so to speak, in the Grand Châtelet and the Petit Châtelet. The mighty city had successively burst its four mural belts, like a growing boy bursting the garments made for him a year ago. Under Louis XI there were still to be seen ruined towers of the ancient enclosures, rising at intervals above this sea of houses, like the tops of hills from amid an inundation, like the archipelagos of old Paris submerged beneath the new.

Since that time Paris has, unluckily for us, undergone further transformation, but it has overleaped only one more enclosure, that of Louis XV, a miserable wall of mud and dirt, worthy of the king who constructed it and the poet by whom it was celebrated:

Le mur murant Paris rend Paris murmurant.

In the fifteenth century Paris was still divided into three totally distinct and separate cities, each having its own physiognomy, individuality, manners, customs, privileges, and history: the Cité, the Université, and the Ville. The Cité, which occupied the island, was the mother of the two others, and cooped up between them, like— reader, forgive the comparison—like a little old woman between two handsome strapping daughters. The Université covered the left bank of the Seine from the Tournelle to the Tour de Nesle, points corresponding the one with the Halle aux Vins, and the other with the Mint, of modern Paris. Its enclosure encroached considerably upon the plain where Julian had built his baths. It included the hill of Sainte-Geneviève. The highest point of this curve of walls was the Papal Gate, which stood nearly upon the site of the present Panthéon. The Ville, the most extensive of the three divisions.

stretched along the right bank. Its quay ran, with several interruptions indeed, along the Seine, from the Tour de Billy to the Tour du Bois, that is to say, from the spot where the Grenier d'Abondance now stands to that occupied by the Tuileries. These four points at which the Seine intersected the enclosure of the capital, the Tournelle and the Tour de Nesle on the left, and the Tour de Billy and the Tour du Bois on the right, were called by way of eminence "the four towers of Paris." The Ville penetrated still farther into the fields than the Université. The culminating point of the enclosure of the Ville was at the gates of Saint-Denis and Saint-Martin, the sites of which remain unchanged to this day.

Each of these great divisions of Paris was, as we have observed, a city, but a city too special to be complete, a city which could not do without the two others. Thus they had three totally different aspects. The Cité, properly so called, abounded in churches; the Ville contained the palaces; and the Université, the colleges. Setting aside secondary jurisdictions, we may assume generally that the island was under the Bishop, the right bank under the Provost of the Merchants, the left under the Rector of the Université, and the whole under the Provost of Paris, a royal and not a municipal officer. The Cité had the cathedral of Notre-Dame, the Ville the Louvre and the Hôtel de Ville, and the Université the Sorbonne. The Ville contained the Halles, the Cité the Hôtel-Dieu, and the Université the Pré aux Clercs. For offences committed by the students on the left bank in their Pré aux Clercs they were tried at the Palace of Justice on the island, and punished on the right bank at Montfaucon: unless the Rector, finding the Université strong and the King weak, chose to interfere; for it was the privilege of the scholars to be hung in their own quarter.

Most of these privileges, be it remarked by the way, and some of them were more valuable than that just mentioned, had been extorted from different sovereigns by riots and insurrections. This is the invariable course—the King never grants any boon but what is wrung from him by the people.

In the fifteenth century that part of the Seine comprehended within the enclosure of Paris contained five islands: the Ile Louviers, then covered with trees, and now with timber, the Ile aux Vaches, and the Ile Notre-Dame, both uninhabited and belonging to the Bishop (in the seventeenth century these two islands were converted into one, which has been built upon and is now called the Ile Saint-Louis; lastly the Cité, and at its point the islet of the Passeur aux Vaches, since buried under the platform of the Pont Neuf. The city had at that time five bridges; three on the right, the Pont Notre-Dame and the Pont au Change of stone, and the Pont aux Meuniers of wood; two on the left, the Petit Pont of stone, and the Pont Saint-Michel of wood; all of them covered with houses. The Université had six gates, built by Philip Augustus; these were, setting out from the Tournelle, the gate of Saint-Victor, the gate of Bordelle, the Papal Gate, and the gates of Saint-Jacques, Saint-Michel, and Saint-Germain. The Ville had six gates, built by Charles V, that is to say, beginning from the Tour de Billy, the gates of Saint-Antoine, the Temple, Saint-Martin, Saint-Denis, Montmartre, and Saint-Honoré. All these gates were strong and handsome too, a characteristic which does not detract from strength. A wide, deep ditch, supplied by the Seine with water, which was swollen by the floods of winter to a running stream, encircled the foot of the wall all round Paris. At night the gates were closed, the river was barred at the two extremities of the city by stout iron chains, and Paris slept in quiet.

A bird's-eye view of these three towns, the Cité, the Université, and the Ville, exhibited to the eye an inextricable knot of streets strangely jumbled together. It was apparent, however, at first sight that these three fragments of a city formed but a single body. The spectator perceived immediately two long parallel streets without break or interruption crossing the three cities, nearly in a right line, from one end to the other, from south to north, perpendicularly to the Seine, incessantly pouring the people of the one into the other, connecting, blending, them together and converting the three into one. The first of these streets ran from the gate of Saint-Jacques to the gate of Saint-Martin; it was called in the Université Rue Saint-Jacques, in the Cité Rue de la Juiverie, and in the Ville Rue Saint-Martin: it crossed the river twice by the name of Petit Pont and Pont Notre-Dame. The second, named Rue de la Harpe on the left bank, Rue de la Barillerie on the island, Rue Saint-Denis on the right bank, Pont Saint-Michel over one arm of the Seine, and Pont au Change over the other, ran from the gate of Saint-Michel in the Université to the gate of Saint-Denis in the Ville. Still, though they bore so many different names, they formed in reality only two streets, but the two mother-streets, the two great arteries of Paris. All the other veins of the triple city were fed by or discharged themselves into these.

Besides these two principal diametrical streets crossing Paris breadthwise and common to the entire capital, the Ville and the Université had each its chief street running longitudinally parallel with the Seine, and in its course intersecting the two arterial streets at right angles. Thus in the Ville you might go in a direct line from the gate of Saint-Antoine to the gate of Saint-Honoré; and in the Université from the gate of Saint-Victor to the gate of Saint-Germain. These two great thoroughfares, crossed by the two former, constituted the frame upon which rested the mazy web of the streets of Paris, knotted and jumbled together in every possible way. In the unintelligible plan of this labyrinth might moreover be distinguished, on closer examination, two clusters of wide streets, which ran, expanding like sheaves of corn, from the bridges to the gates. Somewhat of this geometrical plan subsists to this day.

What then was the aspect of this whole, viewed from the summit of the towers of Notre-Dame in 1482? That is what we shall now attempt to describe. The spectator, on arriving breathless at that elevation, was dazzled by the chaos of roofs, chimneys, streets, bridges, belfries, towers, and steeples. All burst at once upon the eye—the carved gable, the sharp roof, the turret perched upon the angles of the walls, the stone pyramid of the eleventh century, the slated obelisk of the fifteenth, the round and naked keep of the castle, the square and fretted tower of the church, the great and the small, the massive and the light. The eye was long bewildered amid this labyrinth of heights and depths in which there was nothing but had its originality, its reason, its genius, its beauty, nothing but what had issued from the hand of art, from the humblest dwelling, with its painted and carved wooden front, elliptical doorway, and overhanging storeys, to the royal Louvre, which then had a colonnade of towers. But when the eye began to reduce this tumult of edifices to some kind of order the principal masses that stood out from among them were these.

To begin with the Cité. "The island of the Cité," says Sauval, who amid his frivolous gossip has occasionally some good ideas, "the island of the Cité is shaped like a great ship which hath taken the ground and is stuck fast in the mud, nearly in the middle of the channel of the Seine." We have already stated that in the fifteenth century this ship was moored to the two banks of the river by five bridges. This resemblance to a vessel had struck the heralds of those times; for it is to this circumstance, and not to the siege of the Normans, that, according to Favyn and Pasquier, the ship blazoned in the ancient arms of Paris owes its origin. To those who can decipher it heraldry is an algebra, a language. The entire history of the second half of the Middle Ages is written in heraldry; as the history of the first half in the imagery of the Roman churches: 'tis but the hieroglyphics of the feudal system succeeding those of theocracy.

The Cité, then, claimed the first notice, with its stern to the east and its head to the west. Turning toward the latter, you had before you a countless multitude of old roofs, above which rose the widely swelling lead-covered cupola of the Sainte-Chapelle, like the back of an elephant supporting its castle. In this case, indeed, the place of the tower was occupied by the lightest, the boldest, the most elegant steeple that ever allowed the sky to be seen through its cone of lacework. Just in front of Notre-Dame three streets disgorged themselves into the Parvis, a handsome square of old houses. On the south side of this square was the Hôtel-Dieu, with its grim, wrinkled, overhanging front, and its roof which seemed to be covered with warts and pimples. Then, to the right and to the left, to the east and to the west, within the narrow compass of the Cité, rose the steeples of its twenty-one churches of all dates, of all forms, of all dimensions, from the low and crazy Roman campanile of Saint-Denis-du-Pas to the slender spires of Saint-Pierre-aux-Bœufs and Saint-Landry. Behind Notre-Dame, to the north, the cloisters unfolded themselves with their Gothic galleries; to the south the semi-Roman palace of the Bishop; to the east the open area called the Terrain. Amid this mass of buildings the eye might still distinguish, by the lofty mitres of stone which crowned the topmost windows, then placed in the roofs even of palaces themselves, the mansion given by the city in the time of Charles VI to Juvénal des Ursins; a little farther on, the tarred sheds of the market of Palus; beyond that the new choir of Saint-Germain-le-Vieux, lengthened in 1458 at the expense of one end of the Rue aux Feboes; and then, at intervals, an open space thronged with people; a pillory erected at the corner of a street; a fine piece of the pavement of Philip Augustus, composed of magnificent slabs, channelled for the sake of the horses and laid in the middle of the way; a vacant back court with one of those transparent staircase turrets which were constructed in the fifteenth century, and a specimen of which may still be seen in the Rue des Bourdonnais. Lastly, on the right of the Sainte-Chapelle, toward the west, the Palace of Justice was seated with its group of towers on the bank of the river. The plantations of the King's gardens, which covered the western point of the Cité, intercepted the view of the islet of the Passeur. As for the water, it was scarcely to be seen at either end of the Cité from the towers of Notre-Dame; the Seine being concealed by the bridges, and the bridges by the houses.

When the eye passed these bridges, whose roofs were green with moss, the effect not so much of age as of damp from the water, if it turned to the left, toward the Université, the first building which struck it was a clump of towers, the Petit Châtelet, the yawning gateway of which swallowed up the end of the Petit Pont: then, if it followed the bank of the river from east to west, from the Tournelle to the Tour de Nesle, it perceived a long line of houses with carved beams projecting, storey beyond storey, over the pavement, an interminable zigzag of tradesmen's houses, frequently broken by the end of a street, and from time to time also by the front or perhaps the angle of some spacious stone mansion, seated at its ease, with its courts and gardens, amid this multitude of narrow, closely crowded dwellings, like a man of consequence among his dependents. There were five or six of these mansions on the quay, from the Logis de Lorraine, which divided with the Bernardines the extensive enclosure contiguous to the Tournelle, to the Hôtel de Nesle, whose principal tower was the boundary of Paris, and whose pointed roofs for three months of the year eclipsed with their black triangles corresponding portions of the scarlet disk of the setting sun.

On this side of the Seine there was much less traffic than on the other; the students made more noise and bustle there than the artisans, and there was no quay, properly speaking, except from the bridge of Saint-Michel to the Tour de Nesle. The rest of the bank of the Seine was in some places a naked strand, as beyond the Bernardines; in others a mass of houses standing on the brink of the water, as between the two bridges.

Great was the din here kept up by the washerwomen: they gabbled, shouted, sang, from morning till night, along the bank, and soundly beat their linen, much the same as they do at present. Among the sights of Paris this is by no means the dullest.

The Université brought the eye to a full stop. From one end to the other is a homogeneous, compact whole. Those thousand roofs, close, angular, adhering together, almost all composed of the same geometrical element, seen from above, presented the appearance of a crystallization of one and the same substance. The capricious ravines of the streets did not cut this pie of houses into too disproportionate slices. The forty-two colleges were distributed among them in a sufficiently equal manner. The curious and varied summits of these beautiful buildings were the production of the same art as the simple roofs which they overtopped; in fact, they were but a multiplication by the square of the cube of the same geometrical figure. They diversified the whole, therefore, without confusing it; they completed without overloading it. Geometry is a harmony. Some superb mansions, too, made here and there magnificent inroads among the picturesque garrets of the left bank; the Logis de Nevers, the Logis de Rome, the Logis de Reims, which have been swept away; the Hôtel de Cluny, which still subsists for the consolation of the artist, and the tower of which was so stupidly uncrowned some years ago. That Roman palace with beautiful circular arches, near Cluny, was the baths of Julian. There were likewise many abbeys, of a more severe beauty than the great houses, but neither less handsome nor less spacious. Those which first struck the eye were the Bernardines with their three steeples; Sainte-Geneviève, the square tower of which, still extant, excites such regret for the loss of the rest; the Sorbonne, half college, half monastery, an admirable nave of which still survives; the beautiful quadrangular cloister of the Mathurins; its neighbour, the cloister of Saint-Benoi; the Cordeliers, with their three enormous gables, side by side; and the Augustines, the graceful steeple of which made the second indentation (the Tour de Nesle being the first) on this side of Paris, setting out from the west. The colleges, which are in fact the intermediate link between the cloister and the world, formed the mean in the series of buildings between the mansions and the abbeys, with an austerity full of elegance, a sculpture less gaudy than that of the palaces, an architecture less serious than that of the convents. Unfortunately scarcely any vestiges are left of these edifices, in which Gothic art steered with such precision a middle course between luxury and economy. The churches—and they were both numerous and splendid in the Université, and of every age of architecture, from the circular arches of Saint-Julian to the pointed ones of Saint-Severin—the churches overtopped all; and, like an additional harmony in this mass of harmonies, they shot up every instant above the slashed gables, the open-work pinnacles and belfries, and the airy spires, the line of which also was but a magnificent exaggeration of the acute angle of the roofs.

The site of the Université was hilly. To the south-east the hill of Sainte-Geneviève formed an enormous wen; and it was a curious sight to see from the top of Notre-Dame that multitude of narrow, winding streets, now called *le pays latin,* those clusters of houses, which, scattered in all directions from the summit of that eminence, confusedly covered its sides down to the water's edge, seeming some of them to be falling, others to be climbing up again, and all to be holding fast by one another. An incessant stream of thousands of black specks crossing each other on the pavement, caused everything to appear in motion to the eye: these were the people diminished by distance and the lofty position of the spectator.

Lastly, in the intervals between those roofs, those spires, and those numberless peculiarities of buildings, which waved, notched, twisted, the outline of the Université in so whimsical a manner, were to be seen, here and there, the mossy fragment of a massive wall, a solid round tower, an embattled gateway, belonging to the enclosure of Philip Augustus. Beyond these were green fields and highroads, along which were a few straggling houses, which became thinner and thinner in the distance. Some of these suburban hamlets were already places of consequence. Setting out from the Tournelle, there was first the Bourg Saint-Victor, with its bridge of one arch over the Bièvre, its abbey, where was to be seen the epitaph of Louis the Fat, and its church with an octagon steeple flanked by four belfries of the eleventh century; then the Bourg Saint-Marceau which had already three churches and a convent; then, leaving the mill of the Gobelins and its four white walls on the left, there was the Faubourg Saint-Jacques, with its beautiful sculptured cross; the church of Saint-Jacques-du-Haut-Pas, a charming pointed Gothic structure; Saint-Magloire, a beautiful nave of the fourteenth century, converted by Napoleon into a magazine for hay; Notre-Dame des-Champs, containing Byzantine mosaics. Lastly, after leaving in the open country the Carthusian convent, a rich structure contemporary with the Palace of Justice, and the ruins of Vauvert, the haunt of dangerous persons, the eye fell, to the west, upon the three Roman pinnacles of Saint-Germain-des-Prés. The village of Saint-Germain, already a large parish, was composed of fifteen or twenty streets in the rear; the sharp spire of Saint-Sulpice marked one of the corners of the bourg. Close to it might be distinguished the quadrangular enclosure of the Fair of Saint-Germain, the site of the present market; next, the pillory of the abbey, a pretty little circular tower well covered with a cone of lead; the tile-kiln was farther off, so were the Rue du Four, which led to the manorial oven, the mill, and the hospital for lepers, a small detached building but indistinctly seen. But what particularly attracted attention and fixed it for some time on this point was the abbey itself. It is certain that this monastery, which had an air of importance both as a church and as a lordly residence, this abbatial palace, where the bishops of Paris deemed themselves fortunate to be entertained for a night, that refectory to which the architect had given the air, the beauty, and the splendid window of a cathedral, that elegant chapel of the Virgin, that noble dormitory, those spacious gardens, that port-cullis, that draw-bridge, that girdle of battlements cut out to the eye upon the greensward of the surrounding fields, those courts where men-at-arms glistened among copes of gold—the whole collected and grouped round three lofty spires with circular arches, firmly seated upon a Gothic choir, formed a magnificent object against the horizon.

When at length, after attentively surveying the Université, you turn to the right bank, to the Ville, the character of the scene suddenly changes. The Ville, in fact, much more extensive than the Université, was also less compact. At the first sight you perceived that it was composed of several masses remarkably distinct. In the first place, to the east, in that part of the town which is still named after the marsh into which Cæsar was enticed by Camulogenes, there was a series of palaces. Four nearly contiguous mansions, the Hôtels de Jouy, Sens, Barbeau, and the Logis de la Reine, mirrored their slated roofs, diversified with slender turrets, in the waters of the Seine. Those four buildings filled the space between the Rue des Nonaindières and the abbey of the Célestins, the spire of which gracefully relieved their line of gables and battlements. Some greenish walls upon the water's edge, in front of these buildings, did not prevent the eye from catching the beautiful angles of their fronts, their large quadrangular windows with stone frames and transoms, the pointed arches of their porches, surcharged with statues, and all those charming freaks of architecture which give to Gothic art the air of resorting to fresh combinations in every building. In the rear of these palaces ran in all directions, sometimes palisaded and embattled like a castle, sometimes embowered in great trees like a Carthusian convent, the immense and multiform enclosure of that marvellous Hôtel de Saint-Pol, where the King of France had superb accommodation for twenty-two princes equal in rank to the Dauphin and the Duke of Burgundy, with their attendants and retinues, without reckoning distinguished nobles, or the Emperor when he visited Paris, or the lions which had their residence apart from the royal habitation. Be it here remarked that the apartments of a prince in those days consisted of not fewer than eleven rooms, from the hall of parade to the oratory, exclusively of galleries and baths and stoves, and other "superfluous places" attached to each set of apartments; to say nothing of the private gardens of each of the King's guests; of the kitchens, the cellars, the servants' rooms, the general refectories of the household; of the offices where there were twenty-two general laboratories, from the bakehouse to the wine-cellar; of places appropriated to games of every sort, the mall, tennis, the ring; of aviaries, fish-ponds, menageries, stables, libraries, arsenals, foundries. Such was then the palace of a king, a Louvre, an Hôtel de Saint-Pol. It was a city within a city.

From the tower where we have taken our station the Hôtel de Saint-Pol, though almost half concealed by the four great buildings above-mentioned, was still a right goodly sight. The three mansions which Charles V had incorporated with his palace, though skilfully united to the principal building by long galleries with windows and small pillars, might be perfectly distinguished. These were the Hôtel du Petit-Muce, with the light balustrade which gracefully bordered its roof; the residence of the Abbot of Saint-Maur, having the appearance of a castle, a strong tower, portcullises, loopholes, bastions, and over the large Saxon doorway the escutcheon of the Abbot; the mansion of the Count d'Etampes, the keep of which, in ruin at the top, appeared jagged to the eye like the comb of a cock;

clumps of old oaks here and there forming tufts like enormous cauliflowers; swans disporting themselves in the clear water of the fishponds, all streaked with light and shade; the dwelling of the lions with its low pointed arches supported by short Saxon pillars, its iron grating, and its perpetual bellowing; beyond all these the scaly spire of the Ave Maria; on the left the residence of the Provost of Paris, flanked by four turrets of delicate workmanship; at the bottom, in the centre, the Hôtel de Saint-Pol, properly so called, with its numerous façades, its successive embellishments from the time of Charles V, the hybrid excrescences with which the whims of architects had loaded it in the course of two centuries, with all the apses of its chapels, all the gables of its galleries, a thousand weathercocks marking the four winds, and its two lofty contiguous towers, whose conical roofs, surrounded at their base with battlements, looked like sharp-pointed hats with the brims turned up.

Continuing to ascend that amphitheatre of palaces spread out far over the ground, after crossing a deep ravine parting the roofs of the Ville the eye arrived at the Logis d'Angoulême, a vast pile erected at various periods, parts of which were quite new and white, and harmonized no better with the whole than a red patch upon a blue doublet. At the same time the remarkably sharp and elevated roof of the modern palace, covered with lead, upon which glistening encrustations of gilt copper rolled themselves in a thousand fantastic arabesques, that roof so curiously damasked, gracefully lifted itself from amid the embrowned ruins of the ancient building, whose old clumsy towers, bellying like casks, and cracked from top to bottom, were ready to tumble to pieces with age. In the rear rose the forest of spires of the Palais des Tournelles. There was not a view in the world, not excepting Chambord or the Alhambra, more aerial, more impressive, more magical, than this wood of pinnacles, belfries, chimneys, weathercocks, spirals, screws, lanterns, perforated as if they had been struck by a nipping-tool, pavilions and turrets, all differing in form, height, and altitude. You would have taken it for an immense chessboard of stone.

To the right of the Tournelles that cluster of enormous towers, black as ink, running one into another, and bound together, as it were, by a circular ditch; that keep containing many more loopholes than windows; that drawbridge always up, that portcullis always down—that is the Bastille. Those black muzzles protruding between the battlements, and which you take at a distance for gutters, are cannon.

At the foot of the formidable edifice, just under its guns, is the gate of Saint-Antoine, hidden between its two towers.

Beyond the Tournelles, as far as the wall of Charles V, the royal parks were spread out, diversified with rich patches of verdure and flowers, amid which might be recognized by its labyrinth of trees and alleys the famous garden which Louis XI gave to Coictier. The doctor's observatory rose above the maze in the form of a detached massive column, having a small room for its capital. In this laboratory were concocted terrible astrological predictions. The site of it is now occupied by the Place Royale.

As we have already observed, the quarter of the palace of which we have endeavoured to give the reader some idea filled the angle which the wall of Charles V formed with the Seine to the east. The centre of the Ville was occupied by a heap of houses of the inferior class. Here in fact the three bridges of the Cité disgorged themselves on the right bank, and bridges make houses before palaces. This accumulation of dwellings of tradesmen and artisans, jammed together like cells in a hive, had its own beauty. There is something grand in the houses of a capital as in the waves of the sea. In the first place the streets, crossing and entwining, formed a hundred amusing figures; the environs of the Halles looked like a star with a thousand rays. The streets of Saint-Denis and Saint-Martin, with their numberless ramifications, ran up one beside the other like two thick trees intermingling their branches; and then the streets of la Plâtrerie, la Verrerie, and la Tixeranderie, wound over the whole. There were some handsome buildings that overtopped the petrified undulation of this sea of roofs. At the head of the Pont aux Changeurs, behind which the Seine was seen foaming under the wheels of the Pont aux Meuniers, there was the Châtelet, no longer a Roman castle as in the time of Julian the Apostate, but a feudal castle of the thirteenth century, and of stone so hard that in three hours the pickaxe could not chip off a piece larger than your fist. There too was the rich square tower of Saint-Jacques-de-la-Boucherie, with its angles all blunted by sculptures, and already an object of admiration, though it was not finished till the fifteenth century. It had not then those four monsters which, perched to this day at the corners of the roof, look like four sphinxes, giving to modern Paris the enigma of the ancient to unravel. They were not erected till the year 1526 by Rault, the sculptor, who had twenty francs for his labour.—There was the Maison aux Pilliers, of which we have conveyed some idea to the reader; there was Saint-Gervaise, since spoiled by a porch *in good taste;* there was Saint-Méry, whose old pointed arches were little less than circular; there was Saint-Jean, the magnificent spire of which was proverbial; there were twenty other buildings which did not disdain to bury their marvels in this chaos of deep, black, narrow streets. Add to these the sculptured stone crosses, more numerous even than the gibbets, the burying-ground of the Innocents, the architectural enclosure of which was to be seen at a distance above the roofs; the pillory of the Halles, the top of which was perceptible between two chimneys of the Rue de la Cossonerie; the 'ladder' of the Croix du Trahoir, in its crossing always black with people; the circular walls of the Halle au Blé; the remains of the ancient enclosure of Philip Augustus, to be distinguished here and there, drowned by the houses, towers overgrown with ivy, gates in ruins, crumbling and shapeless fragments of walls; the quay, with its thousand shops and its bloody slaughterhouses; the Seine covered with craft, from the Port au Foin to the For-L'Évêque, and you will have a faint image of the central trapezium of the Ville as it was in 1482.

Besides these two quarters, the one of palaces, the other of houses, the Ville presented a third feature—a long zone of abbeys, which bordered almost its whole circumference from west to east, and formed a second enclosure of convents and chapels within that of the fortifications which encompassed Paris. Thus, immediately adjoining to the park of Tournelles, between the Rue Saint-Antoine and the old Rue du Temple, there was the church of Sainte-Catherine with its immense extent of gardens and cultivated grounds, which were bordered only by the wall of Paris. Between the old and the new Rue du Temple there was the Temple, a grim tall cluster of gloomy towers, standing in the centre of a vast embattled enclosure. Between the Rue Neuve du Temple and the Rue Saint-Martin was the abbey of Saint-Martin, amid its gardens—a superb fortified church, whose girdle of towers and tiara of steeples were surpassed in strength and splendour by Saint-Germain-des-Prés alone. Between the streets of Saint-Martin and Saint-Denis was the enclosure of the Trinity; and lastly, between the streets of Saint-Denis and Montorgueil, the Filles Dieu. Beside the latter were to be seen the tumbledown roofs and the unpaved area of the Cour des Miracles. It was the only profane link that intruded itself into this chain of convents.

The fourth and last compartment, which was sufficiently obvious of itself in the agglomeration of buildings on the right bank which occupied the western angle of the enclosure and covered the margin of the river, was a new knot of palaces and mansions that had sprung up at the foot of the Louvre. The old Louvre of Philip Augustus, that immense building whose great tower rallied round it twenty-three other towers, without reckoning turrets, appeared at a distance to be enchased in the Gothic summits of the Hôtel d'Alençon and of the Petit Bourbon. That hydra of towers, the giant guardian of Paris, with its twenty-four heads ever erect, with its monstrous ridges, cased in lead or scaled with slate, and glistening all over with the reflection of metals, terminated in a striking manner the configuration of the Ville to the west.

Thus, an immense 'island' as the Romans termed it, of common houses, flanked on the right and left by clusters of palaces, crowned, the one by the Louvre, the other by the Tournelles, begirt on the north by a long belt of abbeys and cultivated enclosures, the whole blended and amalgamated to the eye; above these thousands of buildings, whose tiled and slated roofs formed so many strange chains, the tattooed, figured, carved steeples and spires of the forty-four churches of the right bank; myriads of streets running in all directions, bounded on the one hand by a high wall with square towers (the wall of the Université had circular towers); on the other by the Seine intersected by bridges and studded with craft—such was the Ville in the fifteenth century.

Beyond the walls there were suburbs crowding about the gates, but the houses composing them were less numerous and more scattered than in those belonging to the Université. In the rear of the Bastille there were a score of huts grouped about the Croix Faubin, with its curious sculptures, and the abbey of Saint-Antoine-des-Champs, with its flying buttresses; then Popincourt, lost in the cornfields; then La Courtille, a jovial hamlet of pothouses; the Bourg Saint-Laurent, with its church, whose steeple seemed at a distance to belong to the gate of Saint-Martin, with its pointed towers; the Faubourg, Saint-Denis, with the vast enclosure of

A Bird's-eye View of Paris

Saint-Ladre; beyond the gate of Montmartre, La Grange Batelière, belted with white walls; behind it, with its chalky declivities, Montmartre, which had then almost as many churches as windmills, but has retained the mills only; for the material bread is nowadays in more request than the spiritual. Lastly, beyond the Louvre were seen the Faubourg Saint-Honoré, already a very considerable place, stretching away into the fields, La Petite Bretagne embosomed in wood, and the Marché aux Pourceaux, in the centre of which stood the horrible cauldron for boiling the coiners of counterfeit money. Between La Courtille and Saint-Laurent your eye has already remarked, on the summit of a height squatted upon desert plains, a kind of building resembling at a distance a colonnade in ruins. This was neither a Parthenon, nor a temple of the Olympian Jupiter—it was Montfaucon.

Now, if the enumeration of so many edifices, concise as we have purposely made it, has not effaced in the mind of the reader the general image of old Paris as fast as we constructed it, we will compress our description into a few words. In the centre, the island of the Cité resembling in figure an enormous tortoise; its bridges scaly with slates protruding like feet from beneath the grey shell of roofs. On the left the dense, compact, bristling trapezium of the Université; on the right the vast semicircle of the Ville, in which gardens and buildings were much more intermingled. The three divisions, Cité, Université, and Ville, marbled by streets without number: the Seine, the "nourishing Seine," as Father du Breul calls it, studded with boats and islands and intersected by bridges, running across the whole. All round an immense plain chequered by handsome villages and cultivated lands bearing all sorts of crops; on the left Issy, Vanvres, Vaugirard, Montrouge, Gentilly, with its round tower and its square tower; on the right twenty others, from Conflans to Ville-l'Évêque. At the horizon a border of hills arranged in a circle, like the rim of the basin. Lastly, in the distance, to the east, Vincennes and its seven quadrangular towers; to the south Bicêtre and its pointed turrets; to the north Saint-Denis and its spire; to the west Saint Cloud and its keep. Such was the Paris seen from the top of the towers of Notre-Dame by the ravens living in the year 1482.

The Paris of that time was not merely a handsome city; it was a homogeneous city, an architectural and historical production of the

The Hunchback of Notre-Dame

Middle Ages, a chronicle of stone. It was a city formed of two strata only, the bastard Roman and the Gothic, for the pure Roman had long before disappeared, excepting at the Baths of Julian, where it still peered above the thick crust of the Middle Ages. As for the Celtic stratum, no specimens of that were now to be found even in digging wells.

Fifty years later, when the Renaissance came to blend with this unity so severe and yet so diversified the dazzling luxury of its fantasies and its systems, its extravagancies of Roman arches, Greek columns, and Gothic ellipses, its sculpture so delicate and so ideal, its particular style of arabesques and acanthi, its architectural paganism contemporaneous with Luther, Paris was perhaps still more beautiful, though less harmonious to the eye and the mind. But this splendid moment was of short duration; the Renaissance was not impartial; it was not content with building up, it wanted to throw down: it is true enough that it needed room. Thus Gothic Paris was complete but for a minute. Scarcely was Saint-Jacques-de-la-Boucherie finished when the demolition of the old Louvre was begun.

Since that time the great city has been daily increasing in deformity. The Gothic Paris, which swept away the bastard Roman, has been in its turn swept away; but can anyone tell what Paris has succeeded it?

There is the Paris of Catharine de' Medici at the Tuileries, the Paris of Henry II at the Hôtel de Ville; two edifices still in a grand style; the Paris of Henry IV at the Place Royale—fronts of brick with stone quoins, and slated roofs—tricoloured houses; the Paris of Louis XIII at Val de Grâce—a squat, clumsy style, something paunch-bellied in the column and hunchbacked in the dome; the Paris of Louis XIV at the Invalides, grand, rich, gilded, and cold; the Paris of Louis XV at Saint-Sulpice—volutes, knots of ribands, clouds, vermicellies, chicories, and the Lord knows what, all in stone; the Paris of Louis XVI at the Panthéon—a wretched copy of Saint-Peter's at Rome; the Paris of the Republic, at the School of Medicine—a poor Greek and Roman style, resembling the Coliseum or the Parthenon as the constitution of the year 3 does the laws of Minos—it is called in architecture, *the Messidor style;* the Paris of Napoleon, at the Place Vendôme—this is sublime—a column of bronze made of cannon; the Paris of the Restoration, at the Exchange—a very white colonnade supporting a very smooth frieze; the whole is square and cost twenty millions.

With each of these characteristic structures a certain number of houses scattered over the different quarters range themselves by a similarity of style, fashion, and attitude: these are easily distinguished by the eye of the connoisseur. Possessing this skill, you discover the spirit of an age and the physiognomy of a king even in the knocker of a door.

The Paris of the present day has no general physiognomy. It is a collection of specimens of various ages, the finest of which have disappeared. The capital increases only in houses, and what houses! At the rate that Paris is now going on it will be renewed every fifty years. Thus the historical signification of its architecture is daily becoming obliterated. The monuments of past times are becoming more and more rare, and you fancy you see them engulfed one after another in the deluge of houses. Our fathers had a Paris of stone; our children will have a Paris of plaster.

As for the modern structures of new Paris we would rather abstain from any mention of them. Not that we admire them quite as much as is fitting. Monsieur Soufflot's Sainte-Geneviève is certainly the most beautiful Savoy cake that ever was made in stone. The Palais de la Légion d'Honneur is also a most remarkable piece of pastry. The dome of the Halle au Blé is an English jockey-cap on a large scale. The towers of Saint-Sulpice are two big clarinets, and that is as good a shape as any other: the telegraph, writhing and grinning, forms a charming accession upon their roof. Saint-Roch has a porch comparable for magnificence to that of Saint-Thomas d'Aquin alone. It has also a Calvary in alto-relievo in a cellar, and a sun of gilt wood. These are absolutely wonderful things. The lantern in the labyrinth of the Jardin des Plantes is also a most ingenious work. As for the Exchange, which is Greek in its colonnade, Roman in the circular arches of its doors and windows, and belongs to the Renaissance style in its great elliptic vault—it is indubitably a most pure and classic structure; in proof of which it is crowned by an attic, such as was never seen at Athens—a beautiful straight line, gracefully broken here and there by stove-pipes. Add to this that if it is a rule that the architecture of an edifice should be adapted to its purpose in such a manner that this purpose may be obvious on a

mere inspection of the building, we cannot too highly admire a
structure which is equally suitable for a king's palace, a House of
Commons, a town-hall, a college, a riding-house, an academy, a ware-
house, a court of justice, a museum, a barrack, a sepulchre, a temple, a theatre. And after all it is an Exchange. A building ought
moreover to be adapted to the climate. This is evidently designed
expressly for our cold and rainy atmosphere. It has a roof nearly
flat as in the East, so that in winter, after snow, it is necessary to
sweep the roof, and it is most certain that a roof is intended to be
swept. As for that purpose to which we referred just now, it fulfils
it marvellously well: in France it is an Exchange, in Greece it would
have been a temple.

These are no doubt most splendid structures. Add to them a great
many handsome streets, amusing and diversified as the Rue de Rivoli, and I despair not that Paris, viewed from a balloon, may some
day present to the eye that richness of lines, that luxury of details,
that diversity of aspects, a certain combination of the grand with the
simple, of the beautiful with the unexpected, which characterizes a
draught-board.

Admirable, however, as the Paris of the present day appears to
you, build up and put together again in imagination the Paris of
the fifteenth century; look at the light through that surprising host
of steeples, towers, and belfries; pour forth amid the immense city,
break against the points of its islands, compress within the arches of
the bridges, the current of the Seine, with its large patches of green
and yellow, more changeable than a serpent's skin; define clearly the
Gothic profile of this old Paris upon an horizon of azure, make its
contour float in a wintry fog which clings to its innumerable chimneys; drown it in deep night, and observe the extraordinary play of
darkness and light in this sombre labyrinth of buildings; throw
into it a ray of moonlight, which shall show its faint outline and
cause the huge heads of the towers to stand forth from amid the
mist; or revert to that dark picture, touch up with shade the thousand acute angles of the spires and gables, and make them stand out,
more jagged than a shark's jaw, upon the copper-coloured sky of
evening. Now compare the two.

And if you would receive from the ancient city an impression
which the modern cannot produce ascend on the morning of some
high festival, at sunrise on Easter or Whitsunday, to some elevated

point from which you may overlook the whole capital, and listen to the awakening of the bells. Behold at a signal proceeding from heaven, for 'tis the Sun himself that gives it, those thousand churches trembling all at once. At first solitary tinkles pass from church to church, as when musicians give notice that they are going to begin. Then see, for at certain times the ear too seems to be endued with sight—see how, all of a sudden, at the same moment, there rises from each steeple as it were a column of sound, a cloud of harmony. At first the vibration of each bell rises straight, pure, and in a manner separate from that of the others, into the splendid morning sky; then, swelling by degrees, they blend, melt, amalgamate into a magnificent concert. It is now but one mass of sonorous vibrations, issuing incessantly from the innumerable steeples, which floats, undulates, bounds, whirls over the city, and expands far beyond the horizon the deafening circle of its oscillations. That sea of harmony, however, is not a chaos. Vast and deep as it is, it has not lost its transparency: you see in it each group of notes that has flown from the belfries, winding along apart; you may follow the dialogue, by turns low and shrill; you may see the octaves skipping from steeple to steeple; you watch them springing light, winged, sonorous, from the silver bell, dropping dull, faint, and feeble from the wooden; you admire the rich gamut incessantly running up and down the seven bells of Saint-Eustache; you see clear and rapid notes dart about in all directions, make three or four luminous zigzags, and vanish like lightning. Down yonder, the abbey of Saint-Martin sends forth its harsh, sharp tones; here the Bastille raises its sinister and husky voice; at the other extremity it is the great tower of the Louvre, with its counter-tenor. The royal chimes of the palace throw out incessantly on all sides resplendent trills, upon which falls, at measured intervals, the heavy toll from the belfry of Notre-Dame, which makes them sparkle like the anvil under the hammer. From time to time you see tones of all shapes, proceeding from the triple peal of Saint-Germain-des-Prés passing before you. Then again, at intervals, this mass of sublime sounds opens and makes way for the *strette* of the Ave Maria, which glistens like an aigrette of stars. Beneath, in the deepest part of the concert, you distinguish confusedly the singing within the churches, which rises through the vibrating pores of their vaults. Verily this is an opera which is well worth listening to. In an ordinary way, the noise issuing from Paris in the daytime is the talking of the city; at night it is the breathing of the city; in this case it is the singing of the city. Lend your ear then to this *tutti* of steeples; diffuse over the whole the buzz of half a million of human beings, the eternal murmur of the river, the infinite piping of the wind, the grave and distant quartette of the four forests placed like immense organs on the four hills of the horizon; soften down, as with a demi-tint, all that is too shrill and too harsh in the central mass of sound—and say if you know anything in the world more rich, more gladdening, more dazzling, than that tumult of bells; than that furnace of music; than those ten thousand brazen tones breathed all at once from flutes of stone three hundred feet high; than that city which is but one orchestra; than that symphony rushing and roaring like a tempest.

BOOK IV

CHAPTER I

THE FOUNDLING

SIXTEEN years before the period of the events recorded in this history, one fine morning—it happened to be Quasimodo Sunday—a living creature was laid after Mass in the church of Notre-Dame in the wooden bed walled into the porch on the left hand, opposite to the great image of St Christopher which faced the kneeling figure sculptured in stone of Antoine des Essarts, knight, till 1413, when both saint and sinner were thrown down. On this wooden bed it was customary to expose foundlings to the public charity. Anyone took them who felt so disposed. Before the wooden bed was a copper basin to receive the alms of the charitable.

The living creature which lay upon this hard couch on the morning of Quasimodo Sunday, in the year of our Lord 1467, appeared to excite a high degree of curiosity in the considerable concourse of persons who had collected round it. They consisted chiefly of the fair sex, being almost all of them old women.

In the front row, nearest to the bed, were four whom from their grey cassock you would judge to belong to some religious sisterhood. I see no reason why history should not transmit to posterity the names of these four discreet and venerable matrons. They were Agnès la Herme, Jehanne de la Tarme, Henriette la Gaultière, and Gauchère la Violette, all four widows, and sisters of the chapel of Étienne Haudry, who had left their house with the permission of their superior, and agreeably to the statutes of Pierre d'Ailly, for the purpose of attending divine service.

If, however, these good creatures were observing the statutes of Pierre d'Ailly, they were certainly violating at the moment those of Michel de Brache and the Cardinal of Pisa, which most inhumanly imposed upon them the law of silence.

"What is that, sister?" said Agnès to Gauchère, looking intently at the little creature, yelping and writhing on the wooden couch, and terrified at the number of strange faces.

127

"What will the world come to," said Jehanne, "if that is the way they make children nowadays?"

"I don't pretend to know much about children," rejoined Agnès, "but it must be a sin to look at that thing."

" 'Tis not a child, Agnès—'tis a misshapen ape," observed Gauchère.

" 'Tis a miracle!" ejaculated La Gaultière.

"Then," remarked Agnès, "this is the third since Lætare Sunday, for it is not a week since we had the miracle of the scoffer of the pilgrims punished by Our Lady of Aubervilliers, and that was the second miracle of the month."

"This foundling, as they call it, is a real monster of abomination," resumed Jehanne.

"He bellows loud enough to deafen a chanter," continued Gauchère.

"And to pretend that Monsieur de Reims could send this fright to Monsieur de Paris!" added La Gaultière, clasping her hands.

"I cannot help thinking," said Agnès la Herme, "that it is some brute, something between a Jew and a beast—something in short that is not Christian, and ought to be drowned or burned."

"I do hope," resumed La Gaultière, "that nobody will apply for it."

"Good God!" exclaimed Agnès, "how I pity the poor nurses at the foundling hospital in the lane yonder going down to the river, close by the archbishop's, if this little monster should be carried to them to be suckled! Why, I declare, I would rather suckle a vampire!"

"Poor la Herme! what a simpleton she is!" rejoined Jehanne. "Don't you see, sister, that this little monster is at least four years old, and that he would like a lump of meat a deal better than your breast?"

In fact, "this little monster"—we should be puzzled ourselves to call it anything else—was not a new-born infant. It was a little, shapeless, moving mass, tied up in a hempen bag, marked with the initials of Guillaume Chartier, the then Bishop of Paris, and leaving the head alone exposed. And that head was so deformed as to be absolutely hideous: nothing was to be seen upon it but a forest of red hair, one eye, a mouth, and teeth. The eye wept, the mouth

The Foundling

cried, and the teeth seemed sadly in want of something to bite. The whole was struggling in the sack, to the no small wonderment of the crowd incessantly coming and going and increasing round it.

Dame Aloïse de Gondelaurier, a noble and wealthy lady, who held by the hand a sweet little girl about six years old, and had a long veil hanging from the gold peak of her bonnet, stopped before the bed, and for a moment surveyed the unfortunate creature, while her charming little daughter Fleur-de-Lys, dressed entirely in silk and velvet, pointing with her delicate finger to each letter of the permanent inscription attached to the wooden bed, spelt the words "ENFANTS TROUVÉS [FOUNDLINGS]."

"I really thought," said the lady, turning away with disgust, "that children only were exposed here."

As she turned her back she threw into the basin a silver florin, which rang among the liards, and made the poor sisters of the chapel of Étienne Haudry lift their eyes in astonishment.

A moment afterward the grave and learned Robert Mistricolle, the King's prothonotary, passed with an enormous missal under one arm, and his wife, Damoiselle Guillemette la Mairesse, under the other, thus having at his side two regulators, the one spiritual, the other temporal.

"A foundling!" he exclaimed, after intently examining the object—"found apparently on the bank of the Phlegeton."

"He seems to have but one eye," observed Damoiselle Guillemette; "and there is a great wart over the other."

" 'Tis no wart," replied Master Robert Mistricolle, "but an egg, which contains another demon exactly like this, with another little egg, containing a third devil, and so on."

"La! how know you that?" asked Guillemette.

"I know it of a certainty," replied the prothonotary.

"Mr. Prothonotary," inquired Gauchère, "what prophesy you from this kind of foundling?"

"The greatest calamities," replied Mistricolle.

"Gracious heaven!" exclaimed an old woman who stood by, "no wonder we had such a pestilence last year, and that the English, it is said, are going to land in force at Harfleur!"

"Perhaps that may not prevent the Queen from coming to Paris in September," rejoined another; "trade is very flat already."

"I am of opinion," cried Jehanne de la Tarme, "that it would be better for the people of Paris if that little sorcerer were lying upon a faggot than upon a plank."

"Ay—a bonny blazing one!" added the old dame.

"That might be more prudent," observed Mistricolle.

For some moments a young priest had been listening to the comments of the women and the prothonotary. He was a man of an austere countenance, with an ample brow and piercing eye. Pushing aside the crowd without speaking, he examined "the little sorcerer," and extended his hand over him. It was high time, for all the pious bystanders were agog for the "bonny blazing faggot."

"I adopt this child," said the priest.

He wrapped him in his cassock and carried him away. The bystanders looked after him with horror, till he had passed the Porte Rouge which then led from the church to the cloisters, and was out of sight.

When they had recovered from their first astonishment Jehanne de la Tarme, stooping till her lips were near the ear of La Gaultière, "Sister," whispered she, "did I not tell you that yon young clerk, Monsieur Claude Frollo, is a sorcerer?"

CHAPTER II

CLAUDE FROLLO

CLAUDE FROLLO was, in fact, no ordinary personage. He belonged to one of those families who, in the impertinent language of the last century, were called indiscriminately *haute bourgeoisie* or *petite noblesse*. This family had inherited from the Paclets the fief of Tirechappe, which was held under the Bishop of Paris, and the twenty-one houses of which had been in the thirteenth century the subject of so many pleadings before the official. Claude Frollo, as possessor of this fief, was one of the one hundred and forty-one seigneurs who claimed manorial rights in Paris and its suburbs; and as such his name was long to be seen registered between the Hôtel de Tancarville, belonging to Master François le Rez, and the Collège de Tours, in the cartulary preserved in the church of Saint-Martin-des-Champs.

Claude Frollo

Claude Frollo had from his childhood been destined by his parents for the Church. He was taught to read Latin, to cast down his eyes, and to speak low. While quite a boy, his father had placed him in the Collège de Torchi in the Université; and there he had grown up on the missal and the lexicon.

For the rest, he was a dull, grave, serious boy, who studied assiduously, and learned quickly. He made but little noise in his recreations, had mingled but little in the bacchanals of the Rue du Fourre, and had not cut a figure in that mutiny of the year 1463, which the chroniclers have gravely recorded under the title of "Sixth Disturbance of the Université." He had scarcely ever been known to rally the poor scholars of Montaigu for the little hoods, after which they were nicknamed (Capettes), or the bursars of the Collège de Dormans for their shaven crowns and their tricoloured frock of grey, blue, and purple cloth—*azurini coloris et bruni,* as saith the charter of the Cardinal des Quatres-Couronnes.

On the other hand, he was assiduous in his attendance on the upper and lower schools of the Rue Saint-Jean-de-Beauvais. The first scholar whom the Abbé of Saint-Pierre-de-Val, at the moment of commencing his lecture on the canon law, perceived invariably stationed opposite to his chair by a pillar of the school of Saint-Vendregesile, was Claude Frollo, provided with his ink-horn, chewing his pen, scribbling upon his knee, and in winter blowing his fingers. The first auditor whom Messire Miles d'Isliers, doctor in divinity, saw entering every Monday morning, quite out of breath, on the opening of the door of the school of Chef-Saint-Denis, was Claude Frollo. Accordingly, at the age of sixteen the young clerk might have posed a father of the Church in mystic theology, a father of the council in canonical theology, and a doctor of the Sorbonne in scholastic theology.

Having passed through theology, he had fallen upon the capitularies of Charlemagne, and, with his keen appetite for knowledge, had devoured decretals after decretals, those of Théodore Bishop of Hispala, of Bouchard Bishop of Worms, of Yves Bishop of Chartres; then the decree of Gratian, which succeeded the capitularies of Charlemagne; then the collection of Gregory IX; then Honorius III's epistle *Super Specula*; [1] till he made himself perfectly familiar with that long and tumultuous period, in which the canon law

[1] *Upon the Mirror.*

and the civil law were struggling and labouring amid the chaos of the Middle Ages—a period opening with Théodore in 618, and closing with Pope Gregory in 1227.

Having dispatched the decretals, he proceeded to medicine and the liberal arts. He studied the science of herbs and the science of unguents; he became skilful in the cure of fevers and of contusions, of wounds and of imposthumes. He was qualified alike to practise in medicine and in chirurgery. He passed through all the degrees of Licentiate, Master, and Doctor, of Arts. He studied the learned languages, Latin, Greek, Hebrew, the triple sanctuary at that time but little frequented. He had a real fever for acquiring and hoarding up knowledge; and it seemed to the young man as if life had but one object, namely, to learn.

It was about this time that the intense heat of the summer of 1466 generated that destructive pestilence which swept away more than forty thousand human beings in the viscounty of Paris, and among others, saith Jean de Troyes, "Master Arnoul, the King's astrologer, a right honest, wise, and agreeable man." A rumour reached the Université that the Rue Tirechappe in particular was afflicted with this malady. There, in the midst of their fief, dwelt the parents of Claude. The young scholar hastened in great alarm to the paternal residence. On reaching it, he learned that his father and mother had died the preceding night. An infant brother was still alive, and crying, abandoned in his cradle. This babe was the only member of Claude's family that was left to him; he took the child in his arms, and quitted the house absorbed in thought. Hitherto he had lived only in learning and science; he now began to live in life.

This catastrophe was a crisis in the existence of Claude. An orphan and head of a family at nineteen, he felt himself rudely roused from the reveries of the schools to the realities of the world. Moved with pity, he conceived a passionate fondness for this helpless infant brother—a strange and delightful thing, this human affection, to him who heretofore had loved nothing but books.

This affection developed itself to an extraordinary degree: in a soul so new to the feeling it was like a first love. Separated from childhood from his parents, whom he had scarcely known, cloistered and as it were spellbound by his books, eager above all things to study and to learn, exclusively attentive till then to his understanding which expanded itself in science, to his imagination which grew up

Claude Frollo

in letters, the young scholar had not yet had time to find out where his heart lay. That little brother, without father or mother, that infant which dropped all at once from the sky into his arms, made a new man of him. He perceived that there was something in the world besides the speculations of the Sorbonne and the verses of Homer; that human beings have need of affections; that life without love is but a dry wheel, creaking and grating as it revolves. He fancied, it is true, for he was at an age when one illusion only gives place to another, that the family affections, the ties of blood, were alone needful for him, and that the love of his little brother was sufficient to fill his heart for his whole life.

He gave himself up therefore to the love of his little Jehan with the passion of a character already ardent, energetic, and concentrated. This poor, frail, fair, delicate creature, this orphan without any protector but an orphan, moved him to the bottom of his soul; and, grave thinker as he was, he began to muse upon Jehan with feelings of infinite compassion. He bestowed on him all possible care and attention, just as if he had been something exceedingly fragile and exceedingly valuable. He was more than a brother to the infant: he became a mother to him.

Little Jehan was still a nursling when he lost his mother: Claude put him out to nurse. Besides the fief of Tirechappe he had inherited from his father a mill situated on a hill near the Château de Winchestre, since corrupted to Bicêtre. The miller's wife was just suckling a fine boy; it was not far from the Université, and Claude carried little Jehan to her himself.

Thenceforward the thought of his little brother became not only a recreation, but even the object of his studies. He resolved to devote himself entirely to the care of him, and never to have any other wife, or any other child, but the happiness and prosperity of his brother. He attached himself therefore more strongly than ever to his clerical vocation. His merit, his learning, his condition of immediate vassal of the Bishop of Paris, threw the doors of the Church wide open to him. At the age of twenty, by a special dispensation of the Holy See, he was a priest, and as the youngest of the chaplains of Notre-Dame he performed the service of the altar called, on account of the lateness of the Mass said there, *altare pigrorum*.[1]

There, more than ever absorbed by his beloved books, which he

[1] "The sluggards' altar."

never quitted but to run for an hour to the mill, this mixture of learning and austerity, so uncommon at his age, quickly gained him the admiration and the respect of the convent. From the cloister his reputation for learning spread among the people, and among some of them it even procured him the character of a sorcerer—a frequent circumstance in that superstitious age.

It was at the moment when he was returning on Quasimodo Sunday from saying Mass at "the altar of the lazy," which stood by the door of the choir on the right, near the image of the Blessed Virgin, that his attention was attracted by the group of old women cackling round the bed of the foundlings. He approached the unfortunate little creature, so hated and so threatened. Its distress, its deformity, its destitution, the thought of his young brother, the idea which suddenly flashed across his mind, that if he were to die his poor little Jehan too might perhaps be mercilessly thrown upon the same spot, assailed his heart all at once: it melted with pity, and he carried away the boy.

When he had taken the child out of the sack he found him to be, in fact, a monster of deformity. The poor little wretch had a prodigious wart over his left eye, his head was close to his shoulders, his back arched, his breastbone protruded, and his legs were twisted; but he appeared lively, and though it was impossible to tell what language he attempted to speak, his cry indicated a tolerable degree of strength and health. This extreme ugliness only served to increase the compassion of Claude; and he vowed in his heart to bring up this boy for the love of his brother, that, whatever might be in the time to come the faults of little Jehan, he might have the benefit of this charity done in his behalf. It was a humane act, placed, as it were, to the account of his brother, one of the little stock of good works which he determined to lay up for him beforehand, in case the young rogue should some day run short of that kind of coin, the only one taken at the toll-gate of Paradise.

He baptized his adopted child and named him Quasimodo, either to commemorate the day on which he had found him, or to express the incomplete and scarcely finished state of the poor little creature. In truth, Quasimodo, with one eye, hunchback, and crooked legs, was but an apology for a human being.

CHAPTER III

THE BELL-RINGER OF NOTRE-DAME

NOW, by the year 1482 Quasimodo had grown up. He had been for several years bell-ringer to the cathedral of Notre-Dame, thanks to his foster-father, Claude Frollo, who had become Archdeacon of Josas, thanks to his diocesan, Messire Louis de Beaumont, who had been appointed Bishop of Paris in 1472, thanks to his patron Olivier le Daim, barber to Louis XI, by the Grace of God, King, etc. etc. etc.

In process of time a curious attachment grew up between the bell-ringer and the church. Cut off for ever from society by the double fatality of his unknown parentage and his distorted form, imprisoned from childhood within these impassable boundaries, the poor fellow was accustomed to see no object in the world beyond the religious walls which had taken him under their protection. Notre-Dame had been successively, to him, as he grew up and expanded, his egg, his nest, his home, his country, the universe.

A sort of mysterious and pre-existent harmony had grown up between this creature and the edifice. While still quite a child he crawled about, twisting and hopping in the shade of its arches, he appeared, with his human face and his limbs scarcely human, a native reptile of that dark damp pavement, among the grotesque shadows thrown down upon it by the capitals of the Roman pillars.

As he grew up the first time that he mechanically grasped the rope in the tower, and, hanging to it, set the bell in motion, the effect upon his foster-father was like that produced upon a parent by the first articulate sounds uttered by his child.

Thus, by little and little, his spirit expanded in harmony with the cathedral; there he lived, there he slept; scarcely ever leaving it, and, being perpetually subject to its mysterious influence, he came at last to resemble it, to be encrusted with it, to form, as it were, an integral part of it. His salient angles dovetailed, if we may be allowed the expression, into the receding angles of the building, so that he seemed to be not merely its inhabitant, but to have taken its form and pressure. Between the ancient church and him there were an instinctive sympathy so profound, and so many magnetic affinities, that he stuck to it in some measure as the tortoise to its shell.

It is scarcely necessary to say how familiar he had made himself with the whole cathedral in so long and so intimate a cohabitation. There was no depth that Quasimodo had not fathomed, no height that he had not scaled. Many a time had he climbed up the façade composed of several elevations, assisted only by the projections of the sculpture. Often might he have been seen crawling up the outside of the towers, like a lizard up a perpendicular wall: those twin giants, so tall, so threatening, so formidable, produced in him neither vertigo, fright, nor sudden giddiness. So gentle did they appear under his hand, and so easy to climb that you would have said he had tamed them. By dint of leaping, scrambling, gliding, struggling, among the precipices of the venerable cathedral, he had become something between a monkey and a mountain goat, just as the boy of Calabria swims before he can walk, and makes the sea his playfellow.

Not the person only but also the mind of Quasimodo appeared to be moulded by the cathedral. What manner of soul was his? What line had it acquired, what form had it received, within its gnarled envelope, in the course of his fantastic life? Quasimodo was born one-eyed, humpbacked, lame. It was not without great difficulty and great patience that Claude Frollo had taught him to speak; but there was a fatality attached to the unhappy foundling. Having become ringer of the bells of Notre-Dame at the age of fourteen, a fresh infirmity had come upon him: the volume of sound had broken the drum of his ear, and deafness was the consequence. Thus the only gate which nature had left wide open between him and the world was suddenly closed, and for ever. In closing, it shut out the only ray of light and joy that still reached his soul, which was now wrapped in profound darkness. The melancholy of the poor fellow became incurable and complete as his deformity. His deafness rendered him in some measure dumb also: for the moment he lost his hearing, he resolved to avoid the ridicule of others by a silence which he never broke but when he was alone. He voluntarily tied up that tongue, which Claude Frollo had taken such pains to loosen: hence, when necessity forced him to speak, his tongue was benumbed, awkward, and like a door the hinges of which have grown rusty.

If then we were to attempt to penetrate through this thick and obdurate bark to the soul of Quasimodo; if we could sound the

depths of this bungling piece of organization; if we were enabled
to hold a torch behind these untransparent organs, to explore the
gloomy interior of this opaque being, to illumine its obscure corners
and its unmeaning *cul-de-sacs,* and to throw all at once a brilliant
light upon the spirit enchained at the bottom of this den; we should
doubtless find the wretch in some miserable attitude, stunted and
rickety, like the prisoners under the leads of Venice, who grow old,
doubled up in a box of stone, too low to stand up and too short to
lie down in.

It is certain that the spirit pines in a misshapen form. Quasimodo scarcely felt within him the blind movements of a soul made
in his own image. The impressions of objects underwent a considerable refraction before they reached the seat of thought. His brain
was a peculiar medium: the ideas which entered it came out quite
twisted. The reflection resulting from this refraction was necessarily
divergent and devious. Hence a thousand optical illusions, a thousand aberrations of judgment, a thousand byways into which his
sometimes silly, sometimes crazy, imagination would wander.

The first effect of this vicious organization was to confuse the view
which he took of things. He received scarcely a single direct perception. The exterior world appeared to him at a greater distance
than it does to us. The second result of his misfortune was that it
rendered him mischievous. He was, in truth, mischievous because
he was savage; he was savage because he was ugly. There was logic
in his nature, as there is in ours. His strength, developed in a most
extraordinary manner, was another cause of his propensity to mischief. *Malus puer robustus,*[1] says Hobbes. We must nevertheless
do him justice: malice was probably not innate in him. From his
earliest intercourse with men he had felt, and afterward he had
seen, himself despised, rejected, cast off. Human speech had never
been to him aught but a jeer or a curse. As he grew up he had
found nothing but hatred about him. He had adopted it. He had
acquired the general malignity. He had picked up the weapon with
which he had been wounded.

After all, he turned toward mankind with reluctance: his
cathedral was enough for him. It was peopled with figures of
marble, with kings, saints, bishops, who at least did not laugh in
his face, and looked upon him only with an air of tranquillity and

[1] "A sturdy boy is a naughty boy."

benevolence. The other statues, those of monsters and demons, bore no malice against him. They were too like him for that. Their raillery was rather directed against other men. The saints were his friends, and blessed him; the monsters were his friends, and guarded him; he would therefore pass whole hours crouched before one of these statues, and holding solitary converse with it. If anyone came by he would run off like a lover surprised in a serenade.

The cathedral was not only his society but his world—in short, all nature to him. He dreamed of no other trees than the painted windows, which were always in blossom; of no other shades than the foliage of stone adorned with birds in the Saxon capitals; of no other mountains than the colossal towers of the church; of no other ocean than Paris which roared at their feet.

But that which he loved most of all in the maternal edifice, that which awakened his soul and caused it to spread its poor wings, otherwise so miserably folded up in its prison, that which even gave him at times a feeling of happiness, was the bells. He loved them, he caressed them, he talked to them, he understood them—from the chimes in the steeple of the transept to the great bell above the porch. The belfry of the transept and the two towers were like three immense cages, in which the birds that he had reared sang for him alone. It was these same birds, however, which had deafened him: but mothers are often fondest of the child which has caused them the greatest pain. It is true that theirs were the only voices he could still hear. On this account the great bell was his best beloved. He preferred her before all the other sisters of this noisy family, who fluttered about him on festival days. The name of this great bell was Mary. She was placed in the southern tower, along with her sister Jacqueline, a bell of inferior size, enclosed in a cage of less magnitude by the side of her own. This Jacqueline was called after the wife of Jehan Montague, who gave her to the church; a gift which, however, did not prevent his losing his head at Montfaucon. In the second tower were six other bells; and, lastly, the six smallest dwelt in the steeple of the transept, with the wooden bell, which was only rung between noon on Holy Thursday and the morning of Easter Eve. Thus Quasimodo had fifteen bells in his seraglio, but big Mary was his favourite.

It is impossible to form a conception of his joy on the days of the great peals. The instant the Archdeacon let him off, and said

The Bell-ringer

"Go," he ran up the winding staircase of the belfry quicker than another could have gone down. He hurried, out of breath, into the aerial chamber of the great bell, looked at her attentively and lovingly for a moment; then began to talk kindly to her, and patted her with his hand, as you would do a good horse which you are going to put on his mettle. He would pity her for the labour she was about to undergo. After these first caresses he shouted to his assistants in a lower story of the tower to begin. They seized the ropes, the windlass creaked, and slowly and heavily the enormous cone of metal was set in motion. Quasimodo, with heaving bosom, watched the movement. The first shock of the clapper against the wall of brass shook the woodwork upon which it was hung. Quasimodo vibrated with the bell. "Vah!" he would cry, with a burst of idiot laughter. Meanwhile the motion of the bell was accelerated, and as the angle which it described became more and more obtuse the eye of Quasimodo glistened and shone out with a more phosphoric light. At length the grand peal began: the whole tower trembled; rafters, leads, stones, all groaned together, from the piles of the foundation to the trefoils of the parapet. Quasimodo then boiled over with delight; he foamed at the mouth; he ran backward and forward; he trembled with the tower from head to foot. The great bell, let loose, and, as it were, furious with rage, turned its enormous throat first to one side and then to the other side of the tower, and thence issued a roar that might be heard four leagues round. Quasimodo placed himself before this open mouth; he crouched down and rose up, as the bell swung to and fro, inhaled its boisterous breath, and looked by turns at the abyss two hundred feet deep below him, and at the enormous tongue of brass which came ever and anon to bellow in his ear. This was the only speech that he could hear, the only sound that broke the universal silence to which he was doomed. He would spread himself out in it like a bird in the sun. All at once the frenzy of the bell would seize him; his look became wild; he would watch the rocking engine, as a spider watches a fly, and suddenly leap upon it. Then, suspended over the abyss, carried to and fro in the formidable oscillation of the bell, he seized the brazen monster by the earlets, strained it with his knees, spurred it with his heels, and with the whole weight and force of his body increased the fury of the peal. While the tower began to quake he would shout and grind his teeth, his red hair bristled up, his breast heaved and puffed like the bellows of a forge, his eye flashed fire, and the monstrous bell neighed breathless under him. It was then no longer the bell of Notre-Dame and Quasimodo: it was a dream, a whirlwind, a tempest, vertigo astride of uproar; a spirit clinging to a winged monster; a strange centaur, half man, half bell; a species of horrible Astolpho, carried off by a prodigious hippogriff of living brass.

The presence of this extraordinary being seemed to infuse the breath of life into the whole cathedral. A sort of mysterious emanation seemed—at least so the superstitious multitude imagined—to issue from him, to animate the stones of Notre-Dame, and to make the very entrails of the old church heave and palpitate. When it was known that he was there it was easy to fancy that the thousand statues in the galleries and over the porches moved and were instinct with life. In fact, the cathedral seemed to be a docile and obedient creature in his hands; waiting only his will to raise her mighty voice; being possessed and filled with Quasimodo as with a familiar genius. He might be said to make the immense building breathe. He was, in fact, everywhere; he multiplied himself at all the points of the edifice. At one time the spectator would be seized with affright, on beholding at the top of one of the towers an odd-looking dwarf, climbing, twining, crawling on all fours, descending externally into the abyss, leaping from one projecting point to another, and fumbling in the body of some sculptured Gorgon: it was Quasimodo unnesting the crows. At another, the visitor stumbled, in some dark corner of the church, upon a crouching, grim-faced creature, a sort of living chimera—it was Quasimodo musing. At another time might be seen under a belfry an enormous head and a bundle of ill-adjusted limbs furiously swinging at the end of a rope—it was Quasimodo ringing the vespers or the angelus. Frequently, at night, a hideous figure might be seen wandering on the delicate open-work balustrade which crowns the towers and runs round the apsis—it was still the hunchback of Notre-Dame. At such time, according to the reports of the gossips of the neighbourhood, the whole church assumed a fantastic, supernatural, frightful aspect; eyes and mouths opened here and there; the dogs, and the dragons, and the griffins of stone, which keep watch day and night with outstretched neck and open jaws round the monstrous cathedral, were heard to bark and howl. At Christmas, while the great bell, which seemed to rattle in the throat, summoned the pious to the midnight Mass, the gloomy façade of the cathedral wore such a strange and sinister air, that the grand porch seemed to swallow the multitude, while the rose-window above it looked on. All this proceeded from Quasimodo. Egypt would have taken him for the god of the temple; the Middle Ages believed him to be its demon: he was the soul of it. To such a point was he so that to those who knew that Quasimodo once existed Notre-Dame now appears deserted, inanimate, dead. You feel that there is something wanting. This immense body is void; it is a skeleton: the spirit has departed; you see its place, and that is all. It is like a skull: the sockets of the eyes are still there, but the eyes themselves are gone.

CHAPTER IV

THE DOG AND HIS MASTER

THERE was, however, one human being whom Quasimodo excepted from his antipathy, and to whom he was as much, nay, perhaps more strongly attached than to his cathedral—that being was Claude Frollo.

The thing was perfectly natural. Claude Frollo had taken pity on him, adopted him, supported him, brought him up. It was between Claude Frollo's legs that, when quite small, he had been accustomed to seek refuge when teased by boys or barked at by dogs. Claude Frollo had taught him to speak, to read, to write. To crown all Claude Frollo had made him bell-ringer.

The gratitude of Quasimodo was in consequence profound, impassioned, unbounded; and though the countenance of his foster-father was frequently gloomy and morose, though his way of speaking was habitually short, harsh, and imperious, never had this gratitude ceased for a moment to sway him. The Archdeacon had in Quasimodo the most submissive of slaves, the most docile of attendants, the most vigilant of warders. After the poor bell-ringer had lost his hearing Claude Frollo and he conversed in a language of signs, mysterious, and understood by themselves alone. Thus the Archdeacon was the only human creature with whom Quasimodo had kept up communication. There were but two things in the world with which he still had intercourse—Notre-Dame and Claude Frollo.

The Hunchback of Notre-Dame

Nothing on earth can be compared with the empire of the Arch-deacon over the bell-ringer, and the attachment of the bell-ringer to the Archdeacon. A sign from Claude, and the idea of giving him pleasure would have sufficed to make Quasimodo throw himself from the top of the towers of Notre-Dame. It was truly extraordinary to see all that physical strength, which had attained such a surprising development in Quasimodo, placed implicitly by him at the disposal of another. It bespoke undoubtedly filial submission, domestic attachment; but it proceeded also from the fascination which mind exercises upon mind. It was an imperfect, distorted, defective organization, with head abased and supplicating eyes, before a superior, a lofty, a commanding, intelligence; but, above all, it was gratitude—but gratitude so carried to its extreme limit that we know not what to compare it with. This virtue is not one of those of which the most striking examples are to be sought among men. We shall therefore say that Quasimodo loved the Archdeacon as never dog, never horse, never elephant, loved his master.

In 1482 Quasimodo was about twenty, Claude Frollo about thirty-six. The one had grown up, the other began to grow old.

Claude Frollo was no longer the simple student of the Collège de Torchi, the tender protector of an orphan child, the young and thoughtful philosopher, so learned and yet so ignorant. He was an austere, grave, morose churchman, second chaplain to the Bishop, Archdeacon of Josas, having under him the two deaneries of Mont-lhéry and Châteaufort, and one hundred and seventy-four parish priests. He was a sombre and awe-inspiring personage, before whom trembled the singing boys in albs and long coats, the precentors, the brothers of Saint-Augustin, the clerk, who officiated in the morning services at Notre-Dame, as he stalked slowly along beneath the lofty arches of the choir, majestic, pensive, with arms folded and head so bowed upon his bosom that no part of his face was to be seen but his bald and ample forehead.

Dom Claude Frollo, however, had not meanwhile abandoned either the sciences or the education of his young brother, those two occupations of his life: but time had dashed those fond pursuits with the bitterness of disappointment. Little Jehan Frollo, surnamed du Moulin, from the place where he had been nursed, had not as he grew up taken that bent which Claude was solicitous to give him. His brother had reckoned upon a pious, docile, and virtuous pupil; but the youth, like those young trees which in spite of all the gardener's efforts obstinately turn toward the quarter from which they receive air and sun, grew and flourished, and threw out luxuriant branches toward idleness, ignorance, and debauchery alone. Reckless of all restraint, he was a downright devil, who often made Dom Claude knit his brow, but full of shrewdness and drollery, which as often made him laugh. Claude had placed him in the same Collège de Torchi where he had passed his early years in study and retirement; and it was mortifying to him that this sanctuary, formerly edified by the name of Frollo, should now be scandalized by it. On this subject he frequently read Jehan very severe and very long lectures, to which the latter listened with exemplary composure. After all, the young scapegrace had a good heart: when the lecture was over he nevertheless returned quietly to his profligate courses. At one time it was a newcomer whom he worried into the payment of his footing—a precious tradition which has been carefully handed down to the present day; at another he had instigated a party of the students to make a classic attack upon some tavern, where, after beating the keeper with bludgeons, they merrily gutted the house, staving in even the wine-pipes of the cellar. Then again there would be a long report in Latin, which the sub-monitor of Torchi carried in woful wise to Dom Claude with this painful marginal annotation: *Rixa; prima causa vinum optimum potatum.*[1] Lastly it was asserted— Oh, horror of horrors in a lad of sixteen!—that his excesses ofttimes carried him into the Rue de Glatigny itself.

Grieved and thwarted by these circumstances in his human affections, Claude had thrown himself with so much the more ardour into the arms of science, who at least does not laugh you in the face, and always repays you, though sometimes in rather hollow coin, for the attentions which you have bestowed on her. Thus he became more and more learned, and at the same time, by a natural consequence, more and more rigid as a priest, more and more gloomy as a man.

As Claude Frollo had from his youth travelled through almost the entire circle of human knowledge, positive, external, and lawful, he was forced, unless he could make up his mind to stop where he was, to seek further food for the insatiable cravings of his understanding. The antique symbol of the serpent biting its tail is peculiarly appropriate to science; and it appears that Claude Frollo knew this

[1] "A brawl; first cause, wine-bibbing."

from experience. Several grave persons affirmed that after exhausting the *fas*[1] of human knowledge he had dared to penetrate into the *nefas*.[2] He had, it was said, tasted successively all the apples of the tree of knowledge, and had at last bitten at the forbidden fruit. He had taken his place by turns, as our readers have seen, at the conferences of the theologians in the Sorbonne, at the meetings of the philosophers at the image of Saint-Hilaire, at the disputes of the decretists at the image of Saint-Martin, at the congregations of the physicians at the holy-water font of Notre-Dame. All the allowable and approved dishes which those four great kitchens, called the four faculties, could elaborate and set before the understanding he had feasted upon, and satiety had supervened before his hunger was appeased. He had then dug farther and deeper, beneath all that finite, material, limited science; he had perhaps risked his soul, and had seated himself in the cavern at that mysterious table of the alchemists and astrologers, one end of which is occupied in the Middle Ages by Averroës, Guillaume de Paris, and Nicolas Flamel, while the other, lighted by the chandelier with seven branches, runs on to Solomon, Pythagoras, and Zoroaster. So, at least, it was conjectured, either rightly or wrongly.

It is certain that the Archdeacon frequently visited the churchyard of the Innocents, where, to be sure, his parents lay buried with the other victims of the pestilence of 1466; but then he appeared to take much less notice of the cross at the head of their grave than of the tomb erected close by it for Nicolas Flamel and Claude Pernelle.

It is certain that he had often been seen walking along the Rue des Lombards and stealthily entering a small house which formed the corner of the Rue des Écrivains and the Rue Marivaulx. It was the house built by Nicolas Flamel in which he died about the year 1417, and which, having been ever since uninhabited, was beginning to fall to ruin, so worn were the walls by the alchemists and the professors of the occult science from all countries, who resorted thither and scratched their names upon them. Some of the neighbours even affirmed that they had once seen through a hole the Archdeacon digging and turning over the mould in the two cellars, the jambs of which had been covered with verses and hieroglyphics by Flamel himself. It was supposed that Master Nicolas had buried the philos-

[1] Lawful.
[2] Unlawful.

ophers' stone in one of these cellars; and for two centuries the alchemists, from Magistri to Father Pacifique, never ceased delving
and rummaging, till the house, weakened and undermined by their
researches, at last tumbled about their ears.

It is certain, moreover, that the Archdeacon was smitten with a
strange passion for the emblematic porch of Notre-Dame, that page
of conjuration written in stone by Bishop Guillaume of Paris, who
has no doubt been damned for having prefixed so infernal a frontis-
piece to the sacred poem everlastingly chanted by the rest of the edifice.   It was also believed that the Archdeacon had discovered the
hidden meaning of the colossal St Christopher, and of the other tall
enigmatical statue which then stood at the entrance of the Parvis,
and which the people called in derision Monsieur Legris.   But a
circumstance which everybody might have remarked was his sitting
hours without number on the parapet of the Parvis, contemplating
the sculptures of the porch, sometimes examining the foolish virgins
with their lamps reversed, sometimes the wise virgins with their
lamps upright; at others calculating the angle of vision of the raven
on the left-hand side of the porch, looking at some mysterious spot
in the church, where the philosophers' stone is certainly concealed,
if it is not in Nicolas Flamel's cellar.   It was, be it observed by the
way, a singular destiny for the church of Notre-Dame at that period
to be thus loved in different degrees and with such ardour by two
beings so dissimilar as Claude and Quasimodo—loved by the one,
scarcely more than half man, for its beauty, its majesty, the harmonies resulting from its grand whole; loved by the other, with a
mind cultivated to the utmost and a glowing imagination, for its
mystic signification, for its hidden meaning, for the symbol concealed
beneath the sculptures of its façade, like the first text under the
second of a palimpsest, in short, for the riddle which it incessantly
propounds to the understanding.

Lastly, it is certain that the Archdeacon had fitted up for himself
in the tower nearest to the Grève, close to the belfry, a small and
secret cell, which none, it was said, but the Bishop durst enter without his permission.   This cell had been made of old almost at the
top of the tower, among the ravens' nests, by Bishop Hugo of Besan-
çon, who had there practised the black art in his time.   None knew
what that cell contained; but from the Terrain there had often been
seen at night, through a small window at the back of the tower, a

strange, red, intermitting light, appearing, disappearing, and reappearing at short and equal intervals, apparently governed by the blast of a bellows, and proceeding rather from the flame of a fire than that of a lamp or candle. In the dark this had a singular effect at that height, and the goodwives would say, "There's the Archdeacon puffing away again: hell is crackling up yonder!"

These, after all, were no very strong proofs of sorcery; still there was sufficient smoke to authorize the conclusion that there must be some fire: at any rate the Archdeacon had that formidable reputation. It is nevertheless but just to state that the science of Egypt, necromancy, magic, even the whitest and the most innocent, had not a more inveterate enemy, a more pitiless accuser, before the officials of Notre-Dame. Whether this horror was sincere or merely the game played by the rogue who is the first to cry, "Stop thief!" it did not prevent his being considered by the learned heads of the chapter as a soul lost in the mazes of the Cabala, groping in the darkness of the occult sciences, and already in the vestibule of hell. The people held much the same opinion; all who possessed any sagacity regarded Quasimodo as the demon and Claude Frollo as the conjuror. It was evident that the bell-ringer had engaged to serve the Archdeacon for a specific time, at the expiration of which he would be sure to carry off his soul by way of payment. Accordingly the Archdeacon, in spite of the extreme austerity of his life, was in bad odour with all good Christians, and there was not a devout nose among them but could smell the magician.

And if, as he grew older, chasms were formed in his science, neither had his heart remained free from them; at least there was good reason to believe so on surveying that face in which the workings of his spirit were discernible only through a dark cloud. Whence was that broad bald brow, that head always bent down, that bosom for ever heaved by sighs? What secret thought caused his lips to smile with such a bitter expression, at the very moment when his knitted brows approached one another like two bulls preparing for the fight? Why was the remnant of his hair already grey? What inward fire was it that at times burst from his eyes, so as to make them look like holes perforated in the wall of a furnace?

These symptoms of a violent moral preoccupation had acquired an unusual degree of intensity at the period of the occurrences related in this history. More than one of the singing-boys had fled affrighted

The Dog and his Master

on meeting him alone in the church, so strange and alarming were his looks. More than once, during the service in the choir, the priest in the next stall to his had heard him mingle unintelligible parentheses with the responses. More than once the laundress of the Terrain, employed to wash for the chapter, had observed, not without horror, marks as if scratched by claws or finger-nails upon the surplice of Monsieur the Archdeacon of Josas.

In other respects his austerity was redoubled, and never had he led a more exemplary life. From disposition as well as profession he had always kept aloof from women; he seemed now to dislike them more than ever. At the mere rustling of a silk petticoat his hood was over his eyes. On this point he was so strict that when the King's daughter, the Lady of Beaujeu, came in the month of December 1481 to see the cloisters of Notre-Dame he seriously opposed her admission, reminding the Bishop of the statute of the Black Book, dated on the vigil of St Bartholomew, 1334, which forbids access to the cloister to every woman "whatsoever, whether old or young, mistress or servant." Whereupon the Bishop was forced to appeal to the ordinance of Otho the Legate, which excepts "certain ladies of quality, who cannot be refused without scandal"— *aliquæ magnates mulieres quæ sine scandalo evitari non possunt.* Still the Archdeacon protested, alleging that the ordinance of the legate, which dated from 1207, was anterior by one hundred and twenty-seven years to the Black Book, and consequently annulled in point of fact by the latter; and he actually refused to appear before the princess.

It was moreover remarked that his horror of the Egyptians and Zingari seemed to have become more vehement for some time past. He had solicited from the Bishop an edict expressly prohibiting the Bohemians to come and dance and play in the area of the Parvis; and he had recently taken the pains to search through the musty archives of the official for cases of wizards and witches sentenced to the flames or the gallows for practising the black art in association with cats, swine, or goats.

147

BOOK V

CHAPTER I

ANCIENT ADMINISTRATION OF JUSTICE

A VERY lucky wight was, in the year of grace 1482, that doughty personage Robert d'Estouteville, knight, Sieur of Beyne, Baron of Ivry and Saint-Andry in La Marche, councillor and chamberlain of the King, and Keeper of the Provosty of Paris. It was then nearly seventeen years agone that the King had on the 7th of November, 1465, the year of the great comet, conferred on him the important appointment of Provost of Paris, which was considered rather as a dignity than an office. It was a marvellous thing that in '82 there should still be a gentleman holding a commission under the King whose appointment dated from the time of the marriage of the natural daughter of Louis XI with the Bastard of Bourbon. On the same day that Robert d'Estouteville had succeeded Jacques de Villiers in the provostship of Paris Master Jean Dauvet superseded Messire Hélye de Thorrettes as first president of the Court of Parliament, Jean Jouvénel des Ursins supplanted Pierre de Morvilliers in the office of Chancellor of France, and Regnault des Dormans turned Pierre Puy out of the post of Master of Requests in Ordinary to the King's household. And how many presidents, chancellors, and masters, had Robert d'Estouteville seen since he had held the provostship of Paris? It was "given to him to keep," said the letters patent, and well had he kept it forsooth. So closely had he clung to it, so completely had he identified himself with it, that he had escaped the results of that mania for changing his servants which possessed Louis XI, a jealous, niggardly, and laborious sovereign, who thought to keep up the elasticity of his power by frequent removals and appointments. Nay, more, the gallant knight had obtained the reversion of his place for his son, and for two years past the name of the noble Jacques d'Estouteville, Esquire, figured beside his own at the head of the register of the Ordinary of the Provosty of Paris. Rare, indeed, and signal favour! It is true that Robert d'Estouteville was a good soldier, that he had

Ancient Administration of Justice

loyally raised the banner against the *league of the public welfare,*
and that he had presented the Queen with a most wonderful stag
made of sweetmeats on the day of her entry into Paris. He was,
moreover, on terms of friendship with Messire Tristan l'Ermite,
Provost of the Marshals of the King's household. The situation of
Messire Robert was, of course, rather enviable. In the first place
he enjoyed a handsome salary to which hung, like supernumerary
bunches of grapes to his vine, the revenues of the civil and criminal
registries of the provostship, and also the civil and criminal revenues
of the Court of the Châtelet, to say nothing of the tolls collected at
the bridge of Mante and Corbeil, and other minor perquisites. Add
to this the pleasure of riding in the city cavalcades and processions,
and showing off among the half-scarlet, half-tawny robes of the city
officers his fine military armour, which you may still admire sculptured on his tomb in the abbey of Valmont in Normandy, and his
morion which had received many a dint, at Montlhéry. And then,
was it nothing to have the entire supremacy over the keeper, the warden, the gaoler, and the two auditors of the Châtelet, the sixteen com-
missaries of the sixteen quarters, the hundred and twenty horse-
patrols, the hundred and twenty vergers, and the whole of the watch
of the city? Was it nothing to administer justice, civil and criminal,
to have a right to burn, to hang, to draw, besides the inferior jurisdiction "in the first instance," as the charters express it, in that viscounty of Paris and the seven noble bailiwicks thereto appertaining?
Can you conceive anything more gratifying than to issue orders and
pass sentence, as Messire Robert d'Estouteville daily did in the
Grand Châtelet beneath the wide elliptic arches of Philip Augustus?
or to go, as he was accustomed, every evening to that charming house
situate in the Rue Galilee, in the purlieus of the Palais Royal,
which he held in right of his wife Madame Ambroise de Loré, to
rest from the fatigue of having sent some poor devil to pass the
night in "that little lodge in the Rue de l'Escorcherie, which the
provosts and *échevins* were wont to make their prison; the same being eleven feet long, seven feet four inches in width, and eleven feet
high."

Not only had Messire Robert d'Estouteville his particular court
as Provost and Viscount of Paris, but he had also a finger in the
infliction of the sentences decreed by the King himself. There was
not a head of any distinction but passed through his hands before it

was delivered up to the executioner. It was he who fetched the Duke de Nemours from the Bastille Saint-Antoine to convey him to the Halles, and Monsieur de Saint-Pol, who, on his way to the Grève, exclaimed loudly and bitterly against his fate, to the great delight of the Provost who was no friend to the Constable.

Here certainly were reasons more than sufficient to make a man satisfied with his life, and yet on the morning of January 7th, 1482, Messire Robert d'Estouteville awoke in an abominable bad temper. And the cause of this bad temper he would have been puzzled to tell himself. Was it because the sky was gloomy? Did his old belt of Montlhéry constrict with too military a pressure his provostship's goodly corporation? Had he seen a troop of ragamuffins in doublets without shirts, in hats without crowns, with wallet and flask at their side, passing along the street under his window, and setting him at defiance? Was it that vague presentiment of the three hundred and seventy livres, sixteen sols, eight deniers, of which the future King Charles VIII in the following year docked the revenues of the provostship? The reader has his choice; for our own part we are inclined to believe that he was in a bad temper merely because he was in a bad temper.

Besides, it was the morrow of a public festivity, a day of annoyance to everybody, and more especially to the magistrate whose duty it was to clear away all the filth, material and figurative, made by a *fête* at Paris. And then, too, he had to sit for the trial of offenders at the Grand Châtelet. Now we have remarked that judges in general arrange matters so that the days on which they have to perform their judicial functions are their days of ill-humour, that they may be sure to have somebody on whom they can conveniently vent it in the name of the King, of the law, and of justice.

Meanwhile the proceedings had commenced without him. His deputies did the business for him, according to custom: and ever since the hour of eight in the morning some scores of citizens of both sexes, crowded into a dark corner of the court of the Châtelet, between a strong oaken barrier and the wall, gazed with great edification at the spectacle of civil and criminal justice administered somewhat pell-mell and quite at random by Master Florian Barbedienne, auditor to the Châtelet, and lieutenant of Monsieur the Provost.

It was a small, low hall, with vaulted ceiling; at the farther end stood a table draped in fleurs-de-lis, a large empty armchair of carved oak, reserved for the Provost, and on the left a stool for the auditor, Master Florian. Below was the clerk busily writing. In front were the people, and before the door and the table a posse of the Provost's men in frocks of purple camlet with white crosses. Two sergeants of the Parloir aux Bourgeois, in their jackets half scarlet and half blue, stood sentry before a low closed door, which was seen behind the table. A single pointed window, of scanty dimensions, set in the thick wall, threw the faint light of a January morning on two grotesque figures—the fantastic demon of stone sculptured by way of ornament to the groining of the ceiling and the judge seated at the extremity of the hall.

Figure to yourself seated at the Provost's table, lolling upon his elbows between two piles of papers, his feet upon the skirt of his plain brown cloth robe, furred with white lamb-skin, which encircled his jolly rubicund visage and double chin, Master Florian Barbedienne, auditor to the Châtelet.

Now, the said auditor was deaf. A trifling defect in an auditor. Master Florian, nevertheless, gave judgment without appeal, and very consistently too. It is most certain that it is quite sufficient for a judge to appear to listen; and this condition, the only essential one for strict justice, the venerable auditor fulfilled the more exactly inasmuch as no noise could divert his attention.

For the rest, he had among the auditory a merciless comptroller of his sayings and doings in the person of our young friend, Jehan Frollo du Moulin, who was sure to be seen everywhere in Paris except before the professors' chairs.

"Look you," said he in a low tone to his companion Robin Poussepain, who was grinning beside him while he commented on the scenes that were passing before them—"there is the pretty Jehanneton du Buisson of the Marché Neuf! Upon my soul he condemns her too, the old brute! He must have no more eyes than ears. Fifteen sous four deniers Parisis for having worn two strings of beads! 'Tis paying rather dear, though.—Soho! two gentlemen among these varlets! Aiglet de Soins, and Hutin de Mailly—two esquires, *corpus Christi!* Ha! they have been dicing. When shall we see our rector here? To pay a fine of one hundred livres to the King! Bravo Barbedienne!—May I be my brother the Archdeacon, if this shall prevent me from gaming; gaming by day, gaming by night, gaming while I live, gaming till I die, and staking my soul after my shirt!

The Hunchback of Notre-Dame

—By'r Lady, what damsels! one after another, pretty lambs! Ambroise Lécuyère, Isabeau la Paynette, Bérarde Gironin, I know them all, by my fay! Fined, fined, fined! That will teach you to wear gilt belts! Ten sous Parisis, coquettes! Oh, the old deaf imbecile! Oh, Florian, the blockhead! Oh, Barbedienne, the booby! There he is at his feast! Fines, costs, charges, damages, stocks, pillory, imprisonment, are Christmas cakes and St John's marchpane to him! Look at him, the hog!—Get on! What, another light o' love! Thibaud la Thibaude, I declare! For being seen out of the Rue Glatigny!—Who is that young fellow? Gieffroy Mabonne, one of the bowmen of the guard—for swearing an oath, forsooth! A fine for you, La Thibaude! A fine for you, Gieffroy! But ten to one the old stupid will confound the two charges and make the woman pay for the oath, and the soldier for incontinence!—Look, look, Robin! what are they bringing in now? By Jupiter, there are all the hounds in the pack! That must be a fine head of game! A wild boar, surely! And so it is, Robin, so it is! And a rare one too, God wot!—Gramercy! 'tis our prince, our Pope of Fools, our bell-ringer, our one-eyed, hunchbacked, bandy-legged Quasimodo!"

Sure enough it was Quasimodo, bound, corded, pinioned. The party of the Provost's men who surrounded him were accompanied by the captain of the watch in person, having the arms of France embroidered on the breast of his coat and those of the city on the back. At the same time there was nothing about Quasimodo, save and except his deformity, which could justify this display of halberts and arquebusses; he was silent, sullen, and quiet. His only eye merely gave from time to time an angry glance at the bonds which confined him.

Meanwhile Master Florian was intently perusing the endorsement of a paper containing the charges alleged against Quasimodo, which had been handed to him by the clerk. By means of this precaution, which he was accustomed to take before he proceeded to an examination, he acquainted himself beforehand with the name, condition, and offence of the prisoner; was enabled to have in readiness replies to expected answers; and succeeded in extricating himself from all the sinuosities of the interrogatory without too grossly exposing his infirmity. To him therefore the endorsement was like the dog to the blind man. If, however, his infirmity chanced to betray itself now and then by some incoherent apostrophe or some unintelligible question, with the many it passed for profoundness, with some few for imbecility. In either case the honour of the magistracy remained unimpeached; for it is better that a judge should be reputed profound or imbecile than deaf. Accordingly he took great pains to conceal his deafness from observation, and in general he was so successful as at last to deceive himself on this point. This is more easily done than it may be imagined. Every hunchback holds his head erect, every stammerer is fond of spouting, every deaf person talks in a low tone. For his part he believed that he was somewhat hard of hearing; and this was the only concession that he made on this point to public opinion in moments of perfect frankness and self-examination.

After ruminating awhile on Quasimodo's affair he threw back his head and half closed his eyes, to give himself a look of the more majesty and impartiality, so that at that moment he was both deaf and blind—a twofold condition without which there is no perfect judge. In this magisterial attitude he commenced his examination.

"Your name?"

Now, here was a case which the law had not provided for—the deaf interrogating the deaf.

Quasimodo, unaware of the question addressed to him, continued to look steadfastly at the judge without answering. The deaf judge, equally unaware of the deafness of the accused, conceiving that he had answered, as persons in his situation generally did, went on, agreeably to his mechanical routine, "Very well; your age?"

Quasimodo maintained the same silence as before. The judge again supposing that he had answered his question, continued, "Now your business?"

Still Quasimodo was silent. The people who witnessed this curious scene began to whisper and to look at one another.

"That will do," rejoined the imperturbable auditor, when he presumed that the accused had finished his third answer. "You are accused before us, in the first place, of making a nocturnal disturbance; secondly, of an assault upon the person of a loose woman; thirdly, of disloyalty, sedition, and resistance to the archers of the guard of our lord the King. What have you to say for yourself on these points?—Clerk, have you taken down the prisoner's answers thus far?"

The Hunchback of Notre-Dame

At this unlucky question a roar of laughter burst from both clerk and audience, so vehement, so loud, so contagious, so universal, that neither of the deaf men could help noticing it. Quasimodo merely turned about and shrugged his hump with disdain; while Master Florian, equally astonished, and supposing that the mirth of the spectators had been provoked by some disrespectful reply of the prisoner's, rendered visible to him by the rising of his shoulders, indignantly exclaimed: "For that answer, fellow, you deserve a halter. Know you to whom you speak?"

This sally was not likely to check the explosion of the general mirth. So odd and so ridiculous did it appear to all, that the fit of laughter spread to the very sergeants of the Parloir aux Bourgeois, a sort of knaves of spades, proverbial for stupidity. Quasimodo alone preserved his gravity, for this very sufficient reason, that he had not the least notion of what was passing around him. The judge, more and more exasperated, thought fit to proceed in the same strain, hoping thereby to strike the prisoner with a terror that should react upon the audience.

"How dare you thus insult the auditor of the Châtelet, the deputy superintendent of the police of Paris, appointed to inquire into crimes, offences, and misdemeanours; to control all trades; to prevent forestalling and regrating; to cleanse the city of filth and the air of contagious diseases; to repair the pavements; in short, to pay continual attention to the public welfare, and that too without wages or hope of salary! Do you know that I am Florian Barbedienne, own lieutenant of Monsieur the Provost, and, moreover, Commissary, Comptroller, examiner . . ."

The Lord knows when Master Florian would have finished this flight of eloquence had not the low door behind him suddenly opened and afforded passage to the Provost himself. Master Florian did not stop short at his entrance, but, turning half round upon his heel, and abruptly directing to the Provost the harangue which a moment before he was launching forth against Quasimodo—"Monseigneur," said he, "I demand such punishment as it shall please you to pronounce upon the prisoner here present for audacious and heinous contempt of justice."

Out of breath with the exertion, he sat down and began to wipe off the perspiration which trickled from his forehead and fell in big drops upon the parchments spread out before him. Messire Robert d'Estouteville knitted his brows and commanded attention with a gesture so imperious and expressive that Quasimodo had some inkling of what was meant.

"What hast thou done to be brought hither, varlet?" said the Provost sternly.

The poor devil, supposing that the Provost was inquiring his name, broke his habitual silence, and in a harsh and guttural voice replied, "Quasimodo."

The answer was so incongruous with the question as once more to excite the risibility of the bystanders, when Messire Robert, flushed with rage, exclaimed, "Art thou making thy game of me too, thou arrant knave?"

"Bell-ringer at Notre-Dame," replied Quasimodo, conceiving that the judge had inquired his profession.

"Bell-ringer!"—roared the Provost, who had got up that morning, as we have observed, in such an ill-humour as not to need the further provocation of these cross-grained answers—"bell-ringer! I'll have such a peal rung on thy back as shall make thee rue thy impertinence. Dost thou hear, varlet?"

"If you want to know my age," said Quasimodo, "I believe I shall be twenty next Martinmas."

This was too provoking—the Provost lost all patience. "What, wretch! dost thou defy the Provost! Here, vergers, take this fellow to the pillory of the Grève; let him be flogged and then turn him for an hour. 'Sdeath, he shall pay for his insolence, and my pleasure is that this sentence be proclaimed by four trumpeters in the seven castellanies of the Viscounty of Paris."

The clerk instantly fell to work to record the sentence.

"*Ventre-Dieu!* but that's a just sentence!" cried Jehan Frollo du Moulin, from his corner.

The Provost turned about, and again fixed his flashing eyes on Quasimodo, "I verily believe," said he, "that the knave has dared to swear in our presence.—Clerk, add a fine of twelve deniers Parisis for the oath, and let half of it be given to the church of Saint-Eustache."

In a few minutes the sentence was drawn up. The language was simple and concise. The practice of the Provosty and Viscounty of Paris had not then been laid down by the president Thibaut Baillet, and Roger Barmne, King's advocate; it was not then obstructed by that forest of quirks, cavils, and quibbles which these two lawyers planted before it at the commencement of the sixteenth century. Everything about it was clear, explicit, expeditious. It was all straightforward work, and you perceived at once at the end of every path, uninterrupted by bushes or roundabout ways, the pillory, the gibbet, and the wheel. You knew at least what you had to expect.

The clerk handed the sentence to the Provost, who affixed his seal, and left the hall to continue his round of the courts in a mood which was likely to increase the population of the gaols of Paris. Jehan Frollo and Robin Poussepain laughed in their sleeves, while Quasimodo looked on with an air of calm indifference.

While Master Florian Barbedienne was in his turn reading the sentence, previously to his signing it, the clerk, feeling compassion for the wretched victim and hoping to obtain some mitigation of his punishment, approached as near as he could to the ear of the auditor and said, pointing at the same time to Quasimodo— "The poor fellow is deaf."

He conceived that this community of infirmity might awaken Master Florian's lenity in behalf of the culprit. But, in the first place, as we have already mentioned, Master Florian was by no means anxious to have it known that he was deaf; and, in the next, he was so hard of hearing as not to catch a single syllable of what the clerk said to him. Pretending, nevertheless, to hear, he replied: "Aha! that is a different thing, I did not know that. In this case let him have another hour in the pillory"; and he signed the sentence with this alteration.

"That's right!" cried Robin Poussepain, who owed Quasimodo a grudge; "this will teach him to handle people roughly."

CHAPTER II

THE TROU AUX RATS

WITH the reader's permission we shall conduct him back to the Place de Grève, which we yesterday quitted with Gringoire to follow La Esmeralda.

It is the hour of ten in the morning: the appearance of the Place indicates the morrow of a festival. The pavement is strewn with wrecks—rags, ribands, feathers, drops of wax from the torches, fragments of the public banquet. A good many citizens are lounging about, kicking the half-consumed cases of the fireworks, admiring the Maison aux Pilliers, extolling the beautiful hangings of the preceding day, and looking at the nails which had held them. The vendors of cider and beer are trundling their barrels among the groups. A few pedestrians, urged by business, bustle along at a quick rate. The shopkeepers are calling to one another from their doors and conversing together. The *fête*, the ambassadors, Coppenole, the Pope of Fools, were in every mouth; each striving to crack the best jokes and to laugh the loudest. And yet four sergeants on horseback, who have just posted themselves at the four sides of the pillory, have already gathered round them a considerable portion of the populace, who were kicking their heels about the Place in the hopes of enjoying the amusement of an execution.

Now, if the reader after surveying this lively and noisy scene which is performing all over the Place turns his eye toward the ancient half-Gothic, half-Roman building, called the Tour-Roland, which forms the corner of the quay to the west, he may perceive at the angle of the façade a large public breviary, richly illuminated, sheltered from the rain by a small penthouse, and secured from thieves by an iron grating, which, nevertheless, does not prevent your turning over the leaves. Beside this breviary is a narrow-pointed unglazed window, looking out upon the Place, and defended by two crossbars of iron—the only aperture for the admission of air and light to a small cell without a door, formed in the basement of the wall of the old building, and full of a quiet the more profound, a silence the more melancholy, from its very contiguity to a public place, and that the most populous and the most noisy in Paris.

This cell had been noted in Paris for three centuries, ever since Madame Rolande of the Tour-Roland, out of affection for her father, who had fallen in the Crusades, caused it to be cut out of the wall of her own house, for the purpose of shutting herself up in it for ever, keeping no part of her mansion but this hole, the door of which was walled up and the window open winter and summer, and giving all the rest to the poor and to God. In this anticipated tomb the disconsolate lady had awaited death for twenty years, praying night and day for the soul of her father, lying upon ashes, without so much as a stone for a pillow, habited in black sackcloth, and subsisting solely upon the bread and water which the pity of the passengers induced them to deposit on her window-sill, thus living upon charity, after giving away her all. At her death, at the moment of quitting this for her last sepulchre, she bequeathed it for ever to afflicted females, maids, wives, or widows, who should have occasion to pray much for themselves or others, and who should wish to bury themselves alive, on account of some heavy calamity or some extraordinary penance. The tears and blessings of the poor embalmed her memory, but to their great disappointment their pious benefactress could not be canonized for want of patronage sufficiently powerful. Such of them as were not most religiously disposed had hoped that the thing would be more easily accomplished in Paradise than at Rome, and had therefore at once prayed to God instead of the Pope in behalf of the deceased. Most of them had been content to hold her memory sacred and to make relics of her rags. The city had endowed in honour of this lady a public breviary, which was attached to the wall near the window of the cell, that passengers might stop from time to time, were it only that they might be induced to recite a prayer, that the prayer might make them think of alms, and that the poor recluses, the successive inmates of Madame Rolande's cell, might not absolutely perish of hunger and neglect.

In the cities of the Middle Ages tombs of this sort were not rare. In the most frequented street, in the most crowded and noisy market, in the midst of the highways, almost under the horses' feet and the cart-wheels, you frequently met with a cellar, a cave, a well, a walled and grated cabin, in which a human being, self-devoted to some everlasting sorrow, to some signal expiation, spent night and day in prayer. And none of those reflections which would be awakened in us at the present time by this strange sight, this horrid cell, a sort of intermediate link between a house and a grave, between the cemetery and the city; that being cut off from all community with mankind, and henceforth numbered among the dead; that lamp consuming its last drop of oil in obscurity; that spark of life glimmering in a grave; that voice of incessant prayer in a cage of stone; that face for ever turned toward the next world; that eye already lit by another sun; that ear pressed against the side of the tomb; that soul a prisoner in this body; this body a prisoner in this dungeon, and the moaning of that afflicted soul within this twofold envelope of flesh and granite—none of these ideas presented themselves to the multi-

The Trou aux Rats

tude in those days. The unreasoning and far from subtle Piety of
that period could not see so many facets in a religious act. She took
the thing in the lump; and honoured, venerated, upon occasion sanc-
tified, the sacrifice, but without analyzing the sufferings, or bestowing on them more than a moderate degree of pity. She carried from
time to time a pittance to the wretched penitent, peeping through
the hole to see if he were still alive; but she knew not his name;
she scarcely knew how many years it was since he had begun to die;
and to the inquiries of the stranger respecting the living skeleton who
was rotting in such a cabin, cave, or cellar the neighbours merely replied, "It is the recluse."

Thus at that day people saw everything with the naked eye, without magnifying-glass, without exaggeration, without metaphysics.
The microscope had not yet been invented either for material or for
spiritual things.

Instances of this kind of seclusion in the heart of cities, though
they raised but little wonder, were yet frequent, as we have just
observed. In Paris there was a considerable number of these cells
for praying to God and doing penance; and almost all of them were
occupied. The clergy, it is true, disliked to see them empty, as that
implied lukewarmness in their flocks; and lepers were placed in them
when no penitents offered themselves. Besides the cell of the Grève
there was one at Montfaucon, another at the charnel-house of the
Innocents; a third, I do not exactly remember where, at the Logis
Clichon, I believe; and others at various places, where you still find
traces of them in traditions, though the buildings have been swept
away. On the hill of Sainte-Geneviève a kind of medieval Job sang
for thirty years the seven penitential psalms, upon a dunghill at the
bottom of a cistern, beginning afresh as soon as he had finished, and
raising his voice highest at night; and to this day the antiquary imag-
ines that he hears his voice as he enters the Rue du Puits-qui-parle.[1]

But to return to the cell of the Tour-Roland. It is right to mention that ever since the death of Madame Rolande it had seldom been
for any length of time without a tenant. Many a woman had come
thither to mourn, some their indiscretions, and others the loss of
parents or lovers. Parisian scandal, which pervades everything,
even such things as least concern it, declared that very few widows
had been seen among the number.

[1] "The Street of the Talking Well."

The Hunchback of Notre-Dame

According to the fashion of the age, a Latin legend inscribed upon the wall indicated to the lettered passenger the pious destination of this cell. Down to the middle of the sixteenth century it was customary to explain the object of a building by a short motto placed over the door. Thus in France there may still be read over the postern of the seignorial house of Tourville, *Sileto et spera*:[1] in Ireland, beneath the coat of arms over the grand entrance to Fortescue castle, *Forte scutum salus ducum*;[2] in England, over the principal door of the hospitable mansion of Earl Cowper, *Tuum est.*[3] In those days every building was a thought.

As there was no door to the cell of the Tour-Roland, there had been engraved in Roman capitals, underneath the window, these two words, *Tu, ora.*[4] Hence the people, whose plain common sense never looks for profound meanings in things, and who scruple not to translate *Ludovico Magno* by *Porte Saint-Denis*, gave to this dark, damp, loathsome hole the name of *Trou aux Rats,*[5] an interpretation less sublime perhaps than the other, but certainly more picturesque.

CHAPTER III

SISTER GUDULE

AT the period of which we are treating the cell of the Tour-Roland was occupied. If the reader is desirous of knowing by whom he has only to listen to the conversation of three honest gossips, who, at the moment at which we have directed his attention to the Trou aux Rats, were going to the very spot, proceeding from the Châtelet along the riverside toward the Grève.

Two of them were dressed like wives of respectable citizens of Paris. Their fine white neckerchiefs; their linsey-woolsey petticoats, striped red and blue; their white worsted stockings, with coloured clocks, pulled up tight upon the leg; their square-toed shoes of

---

1 "Be silent and hope."
2 "A strong shield is the safety of the leaders."
3 "It is thine."
4 "Pray, thou."
5 "The rat-hole."

tawny leather with black soles; and above all their headdress, a sort of high cap of tinsel loaded with ribands and lace, still worn by the women of Champagne, and also by the grenadiers of the Russian Imperial Guard—indicated that they belonged to that class of wealthy trades-folk which comes between what lackeys call *a woman* and what they style *a lady*. They wore neither gold rings nor gold crosses, evidently not on account of poverty, but simply for fear of the sumptuary laws. Their companion was attired nearly in the same fashion, but in her dress and manner there was something which betrayed the countrywoman. The height of her belt above the hips told that she had not been long in Paris. Add to this a plaited neckerchief, bows of ribands at her shoes, the stripes of her petticoat running breadthwise instead of lengthwise, and various other enormities equally abhorrent to good taste.

The first two walked with the step peculiar to the women of Paris who are showing the lions to their provincial friends. The third held a big boy by one hand, while he carried a large cake in the other. The boy did not care to keep up with her, but suffered himself to be dragged along, and stumbled every moment, to the no small alarm of his mother. It is true that he paid much greater attention to the cake than to the pavement. Some weighty reason no doubt prevented his taking a bite, for he did no more than look wistfully at it. It was cruel to make a Tantalus of the podgy rascal.

Meanwhile the three damoiselles—for the term 'dames' was then reserved for noble females—were talking all at once.

"Let us make haste, Damoiselle Mahiette," said the youngest, who was also the lustiest of the three, to her country friend. "I am afraid we shall be too late. We were told at the Châtelet that he was to be put in the pillory forthwith."

"Pooh! pooh! What are you talking of, Damoiselle Oudarde Musnier?" replied the other Parisian. "He is to stay two hours in the pillory. We shall have plenty of time. Have you ever seen anyone in the pillory, my dear Mahiette?"

"Yes," answered Mahiette, "at Reims."

"Your pillory at Reims! why, 'tis not worth mentioning. A wretched cage, where they turn nothing but clodpoles!"

"Clodpoles, forsooth!" rejoined Mahiette, "in the Cloth Market at Reims! We have had some noted criminals there, however—people who had murdered both father and mother. Clodpoles, indeed! What do you take us for, Gervaise?"

It is certain that the provincial lady felt somewhat nettled at the attack on the honour of her pillory. Luckily the discreet Damoiselle Oudarde gave a seasonable turn to the conversation.

"What say you, Mahiette," she asked, "to our Flemish ambassadors? Have you ever had any like them at Reims?"

"I confess," replied Mahiette, "that Paris is the only place for seeing Flemings such as they."

"And their horses, what beautiful animals, dressed out as they are in the fashion of their country!"

"Ah, my dear!" exclaimed Mahiette, assuming in her turn an air of superiority, "what would you say had you been at Reims at the coronation in the year '61, and seen the horses of the princes and of the King's retinue! There were housings and trappings of all sorts; some of damask cloth and fine cloth of gold garnished with sable; others of velvet furred with ermine; others all covered with jewellery and large gold and silver bells. Think of the money that all this must have cost! And then the beautiful pages that were upon them!"

"Heyday!" cried Oudarde, "what is there to do yonder? See what a crowd is collected at the foot of the bridge! There seems to be something in the midst of them that they are looking at."

"Surely I hear the sound of a tambourine," said Gervaise. "I dare say it is young Esmeralda playing her antics with her goat. Quick, Mahiette, and pull your boy along. You are come to see the curiosities of Paris. Yesterday you saw the Flemings; to-day you must see the Egyptian."

"The Egyptian!" exclaimed Mahiette, starting back, and forcibly grasping the arm of her son. "God forbid! she might steal my boy. Come, Eustache!"

With these words she began to run along the quay toward the Grève, till she had left the bridge at a considerable distance behind her. Presently the boy, whom she dragged after her, tripped and fell upon his knees; she stopped to recover breath, and Oudarde and Gervaise overtook her.

"That Egyptian steal your boy!" said Gervaise; "beshrew me if this be not a strange fancy!"

Mahiette shook her head with a pensive look.

Sister Gudule

"And what is still more strange," observed Oudarde, "Sister Gudule has the same notion of the Egyptians."

"Who is Sister Gudule?" inquired Mahiette.

"You must be vastly ignorant at your Reims not to know that," replied Oudarde. "Why, the recluse of the Trou aux Rats."

"What! the poor woman to whom we are carrying the cake?"

Oudarde nodded affirmatively. "Just so. You will see her presently at her window on the Grève. She holds just the same opinion as you of those Egyptian vagabonds, who go about drumming on tambourines and telling fortunes. Nobody knows why she has such a horror of the Zingari and Egyptians. But you, Mahiette, wherefore should you take to your heels thus at the mere sight of them?"

"Oh!" said Mahiette, clasping her boy's head in both her hands, "I would not for the world that the same thing should happen to me as befell Paquette la Chantefleurie."

"Ah! you must tell us that story, good Mahiette," said Gervaise, taking her by the arm.

"I will," answered Mahiette; "but how ignorant you must be in your Paris not to know that! But we need not stop while I tell you the story.—You must know, then, that Paquette la Chantefleurie was a handsome girl of eighteen just when I was so myself, that is, eighteen years ago, and it is her own fault that she is not at this day, like me, a hearty, comely mother of six and thirty, with a husband and a boy. She was the daughter of Guybertaut, minstrel of Reims, the same that played before King Charles VII at his coronation, when he went down our river Vesle from Sillery to Muison, and the Maid of Orleans was in the barge with him. Paquette's father died while she was quite an infant; so she had only her mother, who was the sister of Monsieur Matthieu Pradon, master-brazier here at Paris, in the Rue Parin-Garlin, who died only last year. You see she came of a good family. The mother was unluckily a kind, easy woman, and taught Paquette nothing but to do a little needlework and make herself finery, which helped to keep them very poor. They lived at Reims, in the Rue de Folle Peine. In '61, the year of the coronation of our King Louis XI, whom God preserve! Paquette was so lively and so handsome that everybody called her La Chantefleurie. Poor girl! what beautiful teeth she had! and how she would laugh that she might show them! Now a girl that laughs a great deal is in the way to cry; fine teeth spoil fine eyes. Chantefleurie and her mother had great difficulty in earning a livelihood; since the death of the old minstrel their circumstances had been getting worse and worse; their needlework brought them no more than six deniers a week. How different from the time when old Guybertaut received twelve sols Parisis for a single song, as he did at the coronation! One winter—it was that of the same year '61—when the poor creatures had neither cord-wood nor faggots, the weather was very cold, which gave Chantefleurie such a beautiful colour that she was admired by all the men, and this led to her ruin.—Eustache, don't meddle with the cake!—We all knew what had happened as soon as we saw her come to church one Sunday with a gold cross at her breast. And, look you, she was not fifteen at the time. Her first lover was the young Vicomte de Cormontreuil, whose castle is about three-quarters of a league from Reims; and when she was deserted by him she took up first with one and then with another, till at last all men became alike to her. Poor Chantefleurie!" sighed Mahiette, brushing away a tear that started from her eye.

"There is nothing very extraordinary in this history," said Gervaise; "nor, as far as I can see, has it anything to do with Egyptians or children."

"Have patience," replied Mahiette; "you will soon see that it has. In '66, it will be sixteen years this very month on St Paul's Day, Paquette was brought to bed of a little girl. How delighted she was, poor thing! She had long been wishing for a child. Her mother, good soul, who had always winked at her faults, was now dead; so that Paquette had nothing in the world to love, and none to love her. For five years, ever since her fall, she had been a miserable creature, poor Chantefleurie! She was alone, alone in this life, pointed at and hooted in the streets, cuffed by the beadles, teased by little ragged urchins. By this time she was twenty—an age at which, it is said, loose women begin to be old. Her way of life scarcely brought her in more than her needlework had formerly done; the winter had set in sharp, and wood was again rare on her hearth, and bread in her cupboard. She was, of course, very sorrowful, very miserable, and her tears wore deep channels in her cheeks. But in her degraded and forlorn condition it seemed to her that she should be less degraded and less forlorn, if she had anything or anyone in the world that she could love, and that could love her. She felt that this must needs be a child, because nothing but a child could be innocent enough for that. Women of her class must have either a lover or a child to engage their affections, or they are very unhappy. Now, as Paquette could not find a lover she set her whole heart upon a child, and prayed to God night and day for one. And he took compassion on her, and gave her a little girl. Her joy is not to be described. How she did hug and fondle her infant! It was quite a tempest of tears and kisses. She suckled it herself, made it clothes out of her own, and henceforward felt neither cold nor hunger. Her beauty returned. An old maid makes a young mother. In a short time she again betook herself to her former loose courses, and laid out all the money she received on frocks and caps and lace and little satin bonnets, and all sorts of finery for her child.—Monsieur Eustache, haven't I told you not to meddle with that cake? It is certain that little Agnes—that was the name given to the child at her christening—was more bedizened with ribands and embroidery than a princess. Among other things she had a pair of little shoes, such as I'll be bound Louis XI never had. Her mother had made and embroidered them herself with the utmost art and skill of her needle. A prettier pair of little rose-coloured shoes was never seen. They were not longer than my thumb, and you must have seen the child's tiny feet come out or you would never believe they could go into them. But then those feet were so small, so pretty, so rosy— more so than the satin of the shoes. When you have children, Oudarde, you will know that nothing is so pretty as those delicate little feet and hands."

"I desire nothing better," said Oudarde, with a sigh; "but I must wait till it is the good pleasure of Monsieur Andry Musnier."

"Paquette's baby," resumed Mahiette, "had not merely handsome feet. I saw it when but four months old. Oh! it was a love! Her eyes were larger than her mouth, and she had the most beautiful dark hair, which already began to curl. What a superb brunette she would have made at sixteen! Her mother became every day more and more dotingly fond of her. She hugged her, she kissed her, she tickled her, she washed her, she pranked her up—she was ready to eat her. In the wildness of her joy she thanked God for the gift. But it was her tiny rosy feet above all that she was never tired of admiring. She would pass whole hours in putting on them the little shoes, taking them off again, gazing at them, and pressing them to her lips."

The Hunchback of Notre-Dame

"The story is well enough," said Gervaise in an undertone; "but where are the Egyptians?"

"Why, here," replied Mahiette. "One day a party of very strange-looking people on horseback arrived at Reims. They were beggars and vagabonds, who roved about the country, headed by their duke and their counts. Their visage was tawny; they had curly hair, and wore silver rings in their ears. The women were uglier than the men. Their complexion was darker. They went bareheaded; a shabby mantle covered the body, an old piece of sackcloth was tied about the shoulders, and their hair was like a horse's tail. The children, who were tumbling about upon their laps, were enough to frighten an ape. These hideous people had come—so it was said—straight from Egypt to Reims through Poland; the Pope had confessed them, and ordered them by way of penance to wander for seven years together through the world without lying in a bed; and they claim ten livres Tournois of all archbishops, bishops, and crosiered and mitred abbots, by virtue of a Bull of the Pope. They came to Reims to tell fortunes in the name of the King of Algiers and the Emperor of Germany. This was quite enough, as you may suppose, to cause them to be forbidden to enter the city. The whole band then encamped without more ado on the mill-hill, by the old chalk-pits, and all Reims went to see them. They looked at your palm and foretold wonderful things. At the same time there were various reports about their stealing children, cutting purses, and eating human flesh. Prudent persons said to the simple, 'Go not near them,' and yet went themselves in secret. It was quite the rage. The fact is, they told things which would have astonished a cardinal. Mothers were not a little proud of their children after the Egyptians had read all sorts of marvels written in their hands in Pagan gibberish. One had an emperor, another a Pope, a third a great captain. Poor Chantefleurie was seized with curiosity; she was anxious to know her luck, and whether little Agnes should one day be Empress of Armenia or something of that sort. She carried her to the encampment of the Egyptians; the women admired the infant, they fondled her, they kissed her with their dark lips, they were astonished at her tiny hand, to the no small delight of the poor mother. But above all they extolled her delicate feet and her pretty little shoes. The child was not quite a year old. She had begun to lisp a word or two, laughed at her mother like a little madcap, and

166

was plump and fat and played a thousand engaging antics. But she was frightened at the Egyptians and fell a-crying. Her mother kissed and cuddled her, and away she went overjoyed at the good luck which the fortune-tellers had promised her Agnes. She was to be a beauty, a paragon, a queen. She returned to her garret in the Rue Folle Peine quite proud of her burden. Next day she softly slipped out for a moment while the infant lay asleep on the bed, leaving the door ajar, and ran to tell an acquaintance in the Rue Séchesserie how that there would come a time when her dear little Agnes would have the King of England and the Archduke of Ethiopia to wait upon her at table, and a hundred other marvellous things. On her return, not hearing the child cry as she went upstairs, she said to herself. 'That's lucky! baby is asleep yet.' She found the door wider open than she had left it; she went in hastily and ran to the bed. Poor mother! the infant was gone, and nothing belonging to it was left except one of its pretty little shoes. She rushed out of the room, darted downstairs, screaming, 'My child! my child! who has taken my child?' The house stood by itself, and the street was a lonely one; nobody could give her any clue. She went through the town, searching every street; she ran to and fro the whole day, distracted, maddened, glaring in at the doors and windows, like a wild beast that has lost her young. Her dress was in disorder, her hair hung loose down her back, she was fearful to look at, and there was a fire in her eyes that dried up her tears. She stopped the passengers, crying, 'My child! my child! my dear little child! Tell me where to find my child, and I will be your slave, and you shall do with me what you please.' It was quite pitiful, Oudarde, and I assure you I saw a very hard-hearted man, Master Ponce Lacabre the attorney, shed tears at it. Poor, poor mother! In the evening she went home. While she was away a neighbour had seen two Egyptian women slip slily up her stairs with a large bundle and presently come down again, shut the door, and hurry off. After they were gone cries as if of a child had been heard proceeding from Paquette's lodging. The mother laughed with joy, flew upstairs, dashed open the door, and went in. Only think, Oudarde, instead of her lovely baby, so smiling, and so plump, and so ruddy, there she found a sort of little monster, a hideous, deformed, one-eyed, limping thing, squalling, and creeping about the floor. She covered her eyes in horror. 'Oh,' said she, 'can it be that the witches have changed my Agnes into this frightful animal?' Her neighbours took the little imp away forthwith; he would have driven her mad. He was the misshapen child of some Egyptian or other, who had given herself up to the devil. He appeared to be about four years old, and talked a language which was not a human language—such words were never before heard in this world. Chantefleurie snatched up the tiny shoe, all that was left her of all that she had loved. She lay so long, without moving, without speaking, apparently without breathing, that everybody thought she was dead. All at once she trembled in every limb; she covered the precious relic with passionate kisses, and burst into a fit of sobs, as if her heart was going to break. I assure you we all wept along with her. 'Oh, my baby!' said she, 'my dear little baby! where art thou?' It made one's heart bleed. I can't help crying still at the thought of it. Our children, you see, are as the very marrow of our bones. Oh, my Eustache, my poor Eustache, if I were to lose thee, what would become of me! At length Chantefleurie suddenly sprang up, and ran through the streets of Reims, shouting, 'To the camp of the Egyptians! Let the witches be burnt!' The Egyptians were gone. It was dark night; nobody could tell which way they had gone. Next day, which was Sunday, there were found on a heath between Gueux and Tilloy, about two leagues from Reims, the remains of a large fire, bits of ribands which had belonged to the dress of Paquette's child, and several drops of blood. There could be no further doubt that the Egyptians had the night before held their Sabbath on this heath, and feasted upon the child in company with their master, Beelzebub. When Chantefleurie heard these horrid particulars she did not weep; she moved her lips, as if to speak, but could not. The day after her hair was quite grey, and on the next she had disappeared."

"A frightful story, indeed," exclaimed Oudarde, "and enough to draw tears from a Burgundian!"

"I am no longer surprised," said Gervaise, "that you are so dreadfully afraid of the Egyptians."

"You did quite right," replied Oudarde, "to get out of their way with Eustache, especially as these are Egyptians from Poland."

"Not so," said Gervaise; "it is said that they come from Spain and Catalonia."

Sister Gudule

"At any rate," answered Oudarde, "it is certain that they are Egyptians."

"And not less certain," continued Gervaise, "that their teeth are long enough to eat little children. And I should not be surprised if La Esmeralda were to pick a bit now and then, though she has such a small, pretty mouth. Her white goat plays so many marvellous tricks that there must be something wrong at bottom."

Mahiette walked on in silence. She was absorbed in that reverie which is a sort of prolongation of a doleful story, and which continues till it has communicated its vibration to the inmost fibres of the heart. "And did you never know what became of Chantefleurie?" asked Gervaise. Mahiette made no reply. Gervaise repeated the question, gently shaking her arm and calling her by her name.

"What became of Chantefleurie?" said she, mechanically repeating the words whose impression was still fresh upon her ear. Then making an effort to recall her attention to the sense of those words: "Ah!" said she sharply, "it was never known what became of her."

After a pause she added: "Some said they saw her leave Reims in the dusk of the evening by the Porte Fléchembault; and others at daybreak by the old Porte Basée. Her gold cross was found hanging on the stone cross in the field where the fair is held. It was this trinket that occasioned her fall in '61. It was a present from the handsome Vicomte de Cermontreuil, her first admirer. Paquette never would part with it, distressed as she had often been. She clung to it as to life. Of course, when we heard how and where it was found we all concluded that she was dead. Yet there are persons who declared they had seen her on the road to Paris walking barefoot upon the flints. But, in this case, she must have gone out at the gate of Vesle, and all these accounts cannot be true. My own opinion is that she did actually go by the gate of Vesle, not only out of the town, but out of the world."

"I don't understand you," said Gervaise.

"The Vesle," replied Mahiette, with a melancholy smile, "is our river."

"Poor Chantefleurie!" said Oudarde, shuddering, "drowned!"

"Drowned!" replied Mahiette. "Ah! how it would have spoiled good Father Guybertaut's singing, while floating in his bark beneath the bridge of Tinqueux, had he been told that his dear little Paquette

169

would some day pass under that same bridge, but without song and without bark!"

"And the little shoe?" said Gervaise.

"Disappeared with the mother," replied Mahiette.

Oudarde, a comely, tender-hearted woman, would have been satisfied to sigh in company with Mahiette; but Gervaise, who was of a more inquisitive disposition, had not got to the end of her questions.

"And the monster?" said she all at once, resuming her inquiries.

"What monster?" asked Mahiette.

"The little Egyptian monster, left by the witches at Chantefleurie's in exchange for her child. What was done with it? I hope you drowned that too."

"Oh, no!" replied Mahiette.

"Burnt then, I suppose? The best thing too that could be done with a witch's child."

"Nor that either, Gervaise. The archbishop had compassion on the Egyptian boy; he carefully took the devil out of him, blessed him, and sent him to Paris to be exposed in the wooden cradle at Notre-Dame as a foundling."

"Those bishops," said Gervaise grumblingly, "because they are learned men, never do anything like other people. Only think, Oudarde, to pop the devil into the place of the foundlings! for it is quite certain that this little monster could be nothing else. Well, Mahiette, and what became of him at Paris? No charitable person would look at him, I reckon."

"I don't know," replied her country friend. "Just at that time my husband bought the place of notary at Beru, about two leagues from Reims, and, being fully engaged with our own business, we lost sight of the matter."

Amid such conversation the worthy trio reached the Place de Grève. Engrossed by the subject of their discourse, they had passed the Tour-Roland without being aware of it, and turned mechanically toward the pillory, round which the concourse of people was every moment increasing. It is probable that the scene which at this moment met their view would have made them completely forget the Trou aux Rats and their intention of calling there, had not Eustache whom Mahiette still led by the hand, as if apprised by some instinct that they had passed the place of their destination, cried, "Mother, now may I eat the cake?"

Sister Gudule

Had the boy been less hasty, that is to say, less greedy, he would have waited till the party had returned to the house of Master Andry Musnier, Rue Madame la Valence in the Université, when there would have been the two branches of the Seine and the five bridges of the Cité between the cake and the Trou aux Rats, before he had ventured the timid question, "Mother, now may I eat the cake?"

That very question, an imprudent one at the moment when it was put by Eustache, roused Mahiette's attention.

"Upon my word," said she, "we are forgetting the recluse. Show me your Trou aux Rats, that I may carry her the cake."

"Let's go at once," said Oudarde; "'tis a charity."

This was far from agreeable to Eustache. "She shan't have my cake," said he, dashing his head against his two shoulders by turns, which in a case of this kind is a signal token of displeasure.

The three women turned back, and, having arrived at the Tour-Roland, Oudarde said to the other two: "We must not all look in at the hole at once lest we should frighten Sister Gudule. Do you pretend to be reading the *Dominus* in the breviary, while I peep in at the window—she knows something of me. I will tell you when to come."

She went up by herself to the window. The moment she looked in profound pity took possession of every feature, and her open, good-humoured face changed colour and expression as suddenly as if it had passed out of the sunshine into the moonlight; a tear trembled in her eye and her mouth was contracted as when a person is going to weep. A moment afterward she put her finger upon her lips, and made a sign for Mahiette to come and look.

Mahiette went in silence and on tiptoe, as though approaching the bed of a dying person. It was in truth a melancholy sight that presented itself to the two women, while they looked in without stirring or breathing at the barred window of the Trou aux Rats.

The cell was small, wider than deep, with a vaulted ceiling, and seen from within resembled the hollow of a large episcopal mitre. Upon the stone floor, in one angle, a woman was seated or, rather, crouched. Her chin rested upon her knees, while her arms and clasped hands encircled her legs. Doubled up in this manner, wrapped in brown sackcloth, her long, lank grey hair falling over her face down to her feet, she presented at first sight a strange figure standing out from the dark ground of the cell, a sort of dun triangle

171

which the ray entering at the window showed like one of those spectres seen in dreams, half shadow and half light, pale, motionless, gloomy, cowering upon a grave or before the grating of a dungeon. It was neither woman, nor man, nor living creature; it had no definite form; it was a shapeless figure, a sort of vision in which the real and the fantastic were contrasted like light and shade. Scarcely could there be distinguished under her streaming hair the forbidding profile of an attenuated face; scarcely did the ample robe of sackcloth which enfolded her permit the extremity of a bare foot to be seen peeping from beneath it and curling up on the hard cold pavement. The faint likeness of the human form discernible under this garb of mourning made one shudder.

This figure, which you would have supposed to be embedded in the stone floor, appeared to have neither motion, nor breath, nor thought. Without other clothing save the sackcloth, in the month of January, barefoot upon a pavement of granite, without fire, in the gloom of a dungeon, the oblique aperture of which admitted only the chill blast but not the cheering sun, she seemed not to suffer, not even to feel. You would have thought that she had turned herself to stone with the dungeon, to ice with the season. Her hands were clasped, her eyes fixed. At the first glance you would have taken her for a spectre, at the second for a statue.

At intervals, however, her livid lips opened for the purpose of breathing, and quivered; but they looked as dead and as will-less as leaves driven by the blast. Meanwhile those haggard eyes cast a look, an ineffable look, a profound, melancholy, imperturbable look, steadfastly fixed on a corner of the cell which could not be seen from without; a look which seemed to connect all gloomy thoughts of that afflicted spirit with some mysterious object.

Such was the creature to whom was given from her garb the familiar name of Sacky, and from her dwelling that of the Recluse.

The three women—for by this time Gervaise had joined Oudarde and Mahiette—peeped in at the window. Their heads intercepted the faint light that entered the dungeon, but yet the wretched being whom they deprived of it appeared not to notice them. "Let us not disturb her," said Oudarde softly; "she is praying."

Mahiette scrutinized all this time that wan, withered deathlike face, under its veil of hair, with an anxiety that increased every moment, and her eyes filled with tears. "It would indeed be most extra-

Sister Gudule

ordinary!" muttered she. Putting her head between the bars of the aperture she was enabled to see the corner upon which the eye of the unhappy recluse was still riveted. When she drew back her head from the window her cheeks were bathed with tears.

"What do you call this woman?" said she to Oudarde, who replied, "We call her Sister Gudule."

"For my part," rejoined Mahiette, "I call her Paquette la Chantefleurie."

Then, laying her finger upon her lips, she made a sign to the astonished Oudarde to put her head through the aperture and look. Oudarde did so, and beheld in the corner upon which the eye of the recluse was fixed in gloomy ecstasy a tiny shoe of pink satin, embroidered all over with gold and silver. Gervaise looked in after Oudarde, and the three women fell a-weeping at the sight of the unfortunate mother. Neither their looks, however, nor their tears, were noticed by the recluse. Her hands remained clasped, her lips mute, her eyes fixed, and that look thus bent on the little shoe was enough to cut anyone who knew her story to the heart.

The three women gazed without uttering a word; they durst not speak even in a whisper. This profound silence, this intense sorrow, this utter forgetfulness of all but one object, produced upon them the effect of a high altar at Easter or Christmas. It awed them too into silence, into devotion: they were ready to fall on their knees.

At length Gervaise, the most inquisitive, and of course the least tender-hearted of the three, called to the recluse, in hopes of making her speak, "Sister! Sister Gudule!" Thrice did she repeat the call, raising her voice every time. The recluse stirred not; it drew from her neither word, nor look, nor sigh, nor sign of life.

"Sister! Sister St Gudule!" said Oudarde in her turn, in a kinder and more soothing tone. The recluse was silent and motionless as before.

"A strange woman!" exclaimed Gervaise. "I verily believe that a bombard would not awaken her."

"Perhaps she is deaf!" said Oudarde, sighing.

"Perhaps blind," added Gervaise.

"Perhaps dead," ejaculated Mahiette.

It is certain that if the spirit had not yet quitted that inert, lethargic, and apparently inanimate frame, it had at least retired to and shut itself up in recesses which the perceptions of the external organs could not reach.

"What shall we do to rouse her?" said Oudarde. "If we leave the cake in the window some boy will run away with it."

Eustache, whose attention had till this moment been taken up by a little cart drawn by a great dog, which had just passed along, all at once perceived that his mother and her friends were looking through the window at something; and, curious to learn what it was, he clambered upon a post, and, thrusting his red, chubby face in at the aperture, he cried, "Only look mother! who is that?"

At the sound of the child's clear, fresh, sonorous voice the recluse started. She instantly turned her head; her long, attenuated fingers drew back the hair from her brow, and she fixed her sad, astonished, distracted eyes upon the boy. That look was transient as lightning. "Oh, my God!" she instantly exclaimed, burying her face in her lap; and it seemed as if her harsh voice rent itself a passage from her chest, "at least keep those of others out of my sight!"

This shock, however, had, as it were, awakened the recluse. A long shudder thrilled her whole frame; her teeth chattered; she half raised her head, and, taking hold of her feet with her hands as if to warm them, she ejaculated, "Oh! how cold it is!"

"Poor creature," said Oudarde, with deep compassion, "would you like a little fire?"

She shook her head in token of refusal.

"Well, then," rejoined Oudarde, offering her a bottle, "here is some hippocras, which will warm you."

Again she shook her head, looked steadfastly at Oudarde, and said, "Water!"

Oudarde remonstrated. "No, sister," said she, "that is not fit drink for January. Take some of this hippocras and a bit of the cake we have brought you."

She pushed aside the cake, which Mahiette held out to her. "Some brown bread," was her reply.

"Here," said Gervaise, catching the charitable spirit of her companions, and taking off her cloak; "here is something to keep you warm. Put it over your shoulders."

She refused the cloak as she had done the bottle and the cake, with a single word, "Sackcloth."

Sister Gudule

"But surely," resumed the kind-hearted Oudarde, "you must have perceived that yesterday was a day of public rejoicing."

"Ah! yes, I did," replied the recluse; "for the last two days I have had no water in my pitcher." After a pause she added: "Why should the world think of me who do not think of it? When the fire is out the ashes get cold."

As if fatigued with the effort of speaking she dropped her head upon her knees. The simple Oudarde conceived that in the concluding words she was again complaining of cold. "Do have a fire, then," said she.

"Fire!" exclaimed the recluse, in a strange tone: "and would you make one for the poor baby who has been underground these fifteen years?"

Her limbs shook, her voice trembled, her eyes flashed: she raised herself upon her knees; all at once she extended her white, skinny hand towards the boy. "Take away that child," cried she. "The Egyptian will presently pass."

She then sank upon her face, and her forehead struck the floor with a sound like that of a stone falling upon it. The three women concluded that she was dead. Presently, however, she began to stir, and they saw her crawl upon hands and knees to the corner where the little shoe was. She was then out of their sight, and they durst not look after her; but they heard a thousand kisses and a thousand sighs, mingled with piercing shrieks, and dull, heavy thumps, as if from a head striking against a wall: at last, after one of these blows, so violent as to make all three start, they heard nothing more.

"She must have killed herself!" said Gervaise, venturing to put her head in at the aperture. "Sister! Sister Gudule!"

"Sister Gudule!" repeated Oudarde.

"Good God!" exclaimed Gervaise—"she does not stir. She must be dead!—Gudule! Gudule!"

Mahiette, shocked to such a degree that she could scarcely speak, made an effort. "Wait a moment," said she. Then going close to the window, "Paquette!" she cried, "Paquette la Chantefleurie!"

A boy who thoughtlessly blows a lighted cracker which hangs fire, and makes it explode in his eyes, is not more frightened than was Mahiette at the effect of this name thus abruptly pronounced.

The recluse shook all over, sprang upon her feet, and bounded to

175

the window, her eyes at the same time flashing fire, with such vehemence that the three women retreated to the parapet of the quay. The haggard face of the recluse appeared pressed against the bars of the window. "Aha!" she cried, with a horrid laugh, " 'tis the Egyptian that calls me!"

The scene which was just then passing at the pillory caught her eye. Her brow wrinkled with horror, she stretched both her skeleton arms out of her cell, and cried with a voice unlike that of a human being: "So it is thou, spawn of Egypt, it is thou, child-stealer, that callest me. Cursed be thou! cursed!—cursed!—cursed!"

CHAPTER IV

THE PILLORY

THESE words were, if we may so express it, the point of junction of two scenes which had thus far been acting contemporaneously, each on its particular stage; the one, that which has just been detailed, at the Trou aux Rats; the other, which we are about to describe, at the pillory. The first had been witnessed only by the three women with whom the reader has just made acquaintance; the spectators of the other consisted of the crowd which we some time since saw collecting in the Place de Grève round the pillory and the gallows.

This crowd, to whom the appearance of the four sergeants posted at the four corners of the pillory ever since nine in the morning intimated that some poor wretch was about to suffer, if not capital punishment, yet flogging, the loss of ears, or some other infliction—this crowd had increased so rapidly that the sergeants had been obliged more than once to keep it back by means of their horses' heels and the free use of their whips.

The mob, accustomed to wait whole hours for public executions, did not manifest any vehement impatience. They amused themselves with gazing at the pillory, a very simple contrivance, consisting of a cube of masonry some ten feet high, hollow within. A rude flight of steps of rough stone led to the upper platform, upon which was seen a horizontal wheel of oak. Upon this wheel the culprit was bound upon his knees and with his hands tied behind him. An axle of timber, moved by a capstan concealed from sight within the little building, caused the wheel to revolve in the horizontal plane, and thus exhibited the culprit's face to every point of the Place in succession. This was called *turning* a criminal.

Thus, you see, the pillory of the Grève was by no means so interesting an object as the pillory of the Halles. There was nothing architectural, nothing monumental about it: it had no roof with iron cross, no octagon lantern, no slender pillars spreading at the margin of the roof into capitals of acanthi and flowers, no fantastic and monstrous waterspouts, no carved woodwork, no delicate sculpture deeply cut in stone.

Here the eye was forced to be content with four flat walls and two buttresses of unhewn stone, and a plain, bare gibbet, likewise of stone, standing beside it. The treat would have been a sorry one for the lovers of Gothic architecture. It is true, however, that no people ever held works of art in less estimation than the Parisian populace in the Middle Ages, and that they cared not a pin about the beauty of a pillory.

The culprit, tied to the tail of a cart, was at length brought forward; and when he had been hoisted upon the platform, where he could be seen from all points of the Place, bound with cords and thongs upon the wheel of the pillory, a prodigious hooting, mingled with laughter and acclamations, burst from the mob. They had recognized Quasimodo.

It was a strange reverse for the poor fellow to be pilloried on the same spot, where the preceding day he had been hailed and proclaimed Pope and Prince of Fools, escorted by the Duke of Egypt, the King of Thunes, and the Emperor of Galilee. So much is certain, that there was not a creature in that concourse, not even himself, alternately the object of triumph and of punishment, who could clearly make out the connexion between the two situations. Gringoire and his philosophy were lacking to the spectacle.

Presently Michel Noiret, sworn trumpeter of our lord the King, commanded silence and proclaimed the sentence agreeably to the ordinance of the Provost. He then fell back behind the cart with his men in their official liveries.

Quasimodo never stirred; he did not so much as frown. All resistance, indeed, on his part was rendered impossible by what was then called in the language of criminal jurisprudence, "the vehemence and the firmness of the bonds," which means that the chains and the thongs probably cut into the very flesh. He had suffered himself to be led, and pushed, and carried, and lifted, and bound again and again. His face betrayed no other emotion than the astonishment of a savage or an idiot. He was known to be deaf; you would have supposed him to be blind also.

He was placed on his knees upon the circular floor. His doublet and shirt were taken off, and he allowed himself to be stripped to the waist without opposition. He was enmeshed in a fresh series of thongs: he suffered himself to be bound and buckled; only from time to time he breathed hard, like a calf whose head hangs dangling over the tail of a butcher's cart.

"The stupid oaf!" exclaimed Jehan Frollo du Moulin to his friend Robin Poussepain, for the two students had followed the culprit as a matter of course, "he has no more idea of what they are going to do than a ladybird shut up in a box."

A loud laugh burst from the mob when they beheld Quasimodo's naked hump, his camel breast, and his scaly and hairy shoulders. Amid all this mirth a man of short stature and robust frame, clad in the livery of the city, ascended the platform and placed himself by the side of the culprit. His name was quickly circulated among the crowd. It was Master Pierrat Torterue, sworn torturer of the Châtelet.

The first thing he did was to set down upon one corner of the pillory an hour-glass, the upper division of which was full of red sand, that dropped into the lower half. He then threw back his cloak, and over his left arm was seen hanging a whip composed of long white, glistening thongs, knotted, twisted, and armed with sharp bits of metal. With his left hand he carelessly turned up the right sleeve of his shirt as high as the elbow. At length he stamped with his foot. The wheel began to turn. Quasimodo shook in his bonds. The amazement suddenly expressed in his hideous face drew fresh shouts of laughter from the spectators.

All at once, at the moment when the wheel in its revolution presented the mountain shoulders of Quasimodo to Master Pierrat, he raised his arm; the thin lashes hissed sharply in the air like so many vipers, and descended with fury upon the back of the unlucky wight.

Quasimodo started like one awakened from a dream. He began

to comprehend the meaning of the scene, he writhed in his bonds; a violent contraction of surprise and pain distorted the muscles of his face, but he heaved not a single sigh. He merely turned his head, first one way, then the other, balancing it the while, like a bull stung in the flank by a gadfly.

A second stroke succeeded the first, then came a third, and another, and another. The wheel continued to turn and the blows to fall. The blood began to trickle in a hundred little streams down the swart shoulders of the hunchback; and the slender thongs, whistling in the air in their rotation, sprinkled it in drops over the gaping crowd.

Quasimodo had relapsed, in appearance at least, into his former apathy. He had endeavoured, at first quietly and without great external effort, to burst his bonds. His eye was seen to flash, his muscles to swell, his limbs to gather themselves up, and the thongs, cords, and chains to stretch. The effort was mighty, prodigious, desperate; but the old shackles of the Provost proved too tough. They cracked, and that was all. Quasimodo sank down exhausted. Stupor gave place in his countenance to an expression of deep despondency. He closed his only eye, dropped his head upon his breast, and counterfeited death.

Thenceforward he stirred not. Nothing could make him flinch —neither the blood which oozed from his lacerated back, nor the lashes which fell with redoubled force, nor the fury of the executioner, roused and heated by the exercise, nor the hissing and whizzing of the horrible thongs. At length an usher of the Châtelet, habited in black, and mounted upon a black horse, who had taken his station by the steps at the commencement of the flogging, extended his ebony wand toward the hour-glass. The executioner held his hand; the wheel stopped; Quasimodo's eye slowly opened.

Two attendants of the sworn torturer's washed the bleeding back of the sufferer, rubbed it with a sort of ointment, which in an incredibly short time closed all the wounds, and threw over him a kind of yellow frock shaped like a priest's cope; while Pierrat Torterue drew through his fingers the thongs saturated with blood which he shook off upon the pavement.

Quasimodo's punishment was not yet over. He had still to remain in the pillory that hour which Master Florian Barbedienne had so judiciously added to the sentence of Messire Robert d'Estouteville;

to the great glory of the old physiological and psychological pun: *Surdus absurdus*.[1] The hour-glass was therefore turned, and the hunchback left bound as before, that justice might be fully satisfied.

The populace, especially in a half-civilized era, are in society what the boy is in a family. So long as they continue in this state of primitive ignorance, of moral and intellectual minority, so long you may say of them as of the mischievous urchin— "That age is without pity." We have already shown that Quasimodo was generally hated, for more than one good reason, it is true. There was scarcely a spectator among the crowd, but either had or imagined that he had ground to complain of the malicious hunchback of Notre-Dame. His appearance in the pillory had excited universal joy; and the severe punishment which he had undergone, and the pitiful condition in which it had left him, so far from softening the populace, had but rendered their hatred more malignant by arming it with the sting of mirth.

Thus when the "public vengeance" was once satisfied—according to the jargon still used by gownsmen—it was the turn of private revenge to seek gratification. Here, as in the great hall, the women were most vehement. All bore him some grudge—some for his mischievous disposition, and others for his ugliness: the latter were the most furious. A shower of abuse was poured upon him, accompanied by hootings, and imprecations, and laughter, and here and there by stones.

Quasimodo was deaf, but he was sharp-sighted, and the fury of the populace was expressed not less energetically in their countenance than in their words. Besides, the pelting of the stones explained the meaning of the bursts of laughter. This annoyance passed for a while unheeded; but by degrees that patience, which had braced itself up under the lash of the executioner, gave way under all these stings of petty insects. The bull of the Asturias, which scarcely deigns to notice the attacks of the picador, is exasperated by the dogs and the banderillos.

At first he slowly rolled around a look of menace at the crowd; but, shackled as he was, this look could not drive away the flies which galled his wound. He then struggled in his bonds, and his furious contortions made the old wheel of the pillory creak upon its axis. This served only to increase the jeers and derisions of the populace.

[1] "A deaf man is absurd."

The Pillory

The wretched sufferer, finding, like a chained beast, that he could not break his collar, again became quiet; though at times a sigh of rage heaved all the cavities of his chest. Not a blush, not a trace of shame, was to be discerned in his face. He was too far from the social state and too near to the state of nature to know what shame is. Besides, is it possible that disgrace can be felt by one cast in a mould of such extreme deformity? But rage, hatred, despair, slowly spread over that hideous face a cloud which gradually became more and more black, more and more charged with an electricity that darted in a thousand flashes from the eye of the Cyclops.

This cloud, however, cleared off for a moment at the appearance of a mule bearing a priest. The instant he caught a glimpse of this mule and this priest in the distance, the face of the poor sufferer assumed a look of gentleness. The rage which had contracted it was succeeded by a strange smile, full of ineffable meekness, kindness, tenderness. As the priest approached this smile became more expressive, more distinct, more radiant. The prisoner seemed to be anticipating the arrival of a deliverer; but the moment the mule was near enough to the pillory for its rider to recognize the sufferer the priest cast down his eyes, wheeled about, clapped spurs to his beast, as if in a hurry to escape a humiliating appeal, and by no means desirous of being known or addressed by a poor devil in such a situation. This priest was the Archdeacon Claude Frollo.

Quasimodo's brow was overcast by a darker cloud than ever. For some time a smile mingled with the gloom, but it was a smile of bitterness, disappointment, and deep despondency. Time passed. For an hour and a half at least he had been exposed to incessant ill-usage—lacerated, jeered, and almost stoned. All at once he again struggled in his chains with a redoubled effort of despair that made the whole machine shake; and, breaking the silence which he had hitherto kept, he cried in a hoarse and furious voice, more like the roaring of a wild beast than the articulate tones of a human tongue, "Water!"

This cry of distress, heard above the shouts and laughter of the crowd, so far from exciting compassion, served only to heighten the mirth of the good people of Paris, who surrounded the pillory, and who, to confess the truth, were in those days not much less cruel or less brutalized than the disgusting crew of Vagabonds whom we have already introduced to the reader; these merely formed, in fact, the

181

lowest stratum of the populace. Not a voice was raised round the unhappy sufferer, but in scorn and derision of his distress. It is certain that at this moment he was still more grotesque and repulsive than pitiable; his face empurpled, and trickling with perspiration, his eye glaring wildly, his mouth foaming with rage and agony, and his tongue lolling out of it. It must also be confessed that had any charitable soul of either sex been tempted to carry a draught of water to the wretched sufferer, so strongly was the notion of infamy and disgrace attached to the ignominious steps of the pillory that it would have effectually deterred the good Samaritan.

In a few minutes Quasimodo surveyed the crowd with anxious eye, and repeated in a voice more rugged than before, "Water!" He was answered with peals of laughter.

"There is water for thee, deaf varlet," cried Robin Poussepain throwing in his face a sponge soaked in the kennel. "I am in thy debt."

A woman hurled a stone at his head. "That will teach thee to waken us at night," said she, "with thy cursed bells."

"Take that to drink thy liquor out of!" shouted a fellow, throwing at him a broken jug, which hit him upon the chest. "It was the sight of thy frightful figure that made my wife have a child with two heads."

"Water!" roared the panting Quasimodo for the third time.

At that moment he saw the populace make way. A young female, in a strange garb, approached the pillory. She was followed by a little white goat with gilt horns, and carried a tambourine in her hand. Quasimodo's eye sparkled. It was the Bohemian whom he had attempted to carry off the preceding night, and he had a confused notion that for this prank he was suffering his present punishment, though in fact it was because he had the misfortune to be deaf and to be tried by a deaf judge. He thought that she was coming to take revenge also, and to give him her blow as well as the rest.

He watched her with nimble foot ascend the steps. He was choked with rage and vexation. Had the lightning of his eye possessed the power, it would have blasted the Egyptian before she reached the platform. Without uttering a word she approached the sufferer, who vainly writhed to avoid her; and loosing a gourd from her girdle, she gently lifted it to the parched lips of the exhausted wretch.

The Pillory

A big tear was seen to start from his dry and bloodshot eye, and to trickle slowly down his deformed face so long contracted by despair. It was perhaps the first that he had shed since he arrived at manhood.

Meanwhile he forgot to drink. The Egyptian pouted her pretty lip with impatience, and then put the neck of the gourd between Quasimodo's jagged teeth; he drank greedily, for his thirst was extreme.

When he had finished the hunchback protruded his dark lips, no doubt to kiss the kind hand which had brought so welcome a relief; but the damsel, perhaps recollecting the violent assault of the foregoing night, quickly drew back her hand with the same start of terror that a child does from a dog which he fears will bite him. The poor fellow then fixed on her a look full of reproach and unutterable woe.

Under any circumstances it would have been a touching sight to see this girl, so fresh, so pure, so lovely, and at the same time so weak, humanely hastening to the relief of so much distress, deformity, and malice. On a pillory this sight was sublime. The populace themselves were moved by it, and began clapping their hands and shouting, "Huzza! huzza!"

It was precisely at this moment that the recluse perceived from the window of her den the Egyptian on the pillory, and pronounced upon her that bitter imprecation— "Cursed be thou, spawn of Egypt! cursed! cursed! cursed!"

La Esmeralda turned pale, and with faltering step descended from the pillory. The voice of the recluse still pursued her, "Get thee down! get thee down, Egyptian child-stealer! thou wilt have to go up again one of these days!"

"Sacky is in one of her moods to-day," said the people, grumbling; and that was all they did. Women of her class were then deemed holy and reverenced accordingly. Nobody liked to attack persons who were praying night and day.

The time of Quasimodo's punishment having expired, he was released, and the mob dispersed.

Mahiette and her two companions had reached the foot of the Grand Pont on their return, when she suddenly stopped short. "Bless me!" she exclaimed, "what has become of the cake, Eustache?"

"Mother," said the boy, "while you were talking with the woman

183

in that dark hole, a big dog came and bit a great piece out of it, so I ate some too."

"What, sir," she asked, "have you eaten it all?"

"It was the dog, Mother. I told him to let it alone, but he didn't mind me—so I just took a bite too."

" 'Tis a sad, greedy boy!" said his mother, smiling and scolding at once. "Look you, Oudarde, not a cherry or an apple in our garden is safe from him; so his grandfather says he will make a rare captain.—I'll trim you well, Master Eustache!—go along, you greedy glutton!"

BOOK VI

CHAPTER I

THE DANGER OF TRUSTING A GOAT WITH A SECRET

SEVERAL weeks had elapsed. It was now the beginning of March. The sun, which Dubartas, that classic ancestor of periphrasis, had not yet styled "the grandduke of candles," shone forth brightly and cheerily. It was one of those spring days which are so mild and so beautiful that all Paris, pouring into the public places and promenades, keeps them as holidays. On days so brilliant, so warm, and so serene there is a particular hour at which the curious spectator should go to admire the porch of Notre-Dame. It is the moment when the sun, already sinking in the west, looks the cathedral almost full in the face. His rays, becoming more and more horizontal, slowly withdraw from the pavement of the Place, and mount along the pinnacled façade, causing its thousands of figures in relief to stand out from their shadows, while the great central rose-window glares like the eye of a Cyclops, tinged by the reflections of the forge. It was now just that hour.

Opposite to the lofty cathedral, glowing in the sunset upon a stone balcony, over the porch of a rich Gothic building which formed the angle of the Place and the Rue du Parvis, some young and handsome women were chatting, laughing, and disporting themselves. By the length of their veils, which fell from the top of their pointed caps, encircled with pearls, to their heels; by the fineness of the embroidered neckerchief which covered their shoulders, but without wholly concealing the delicate contours of their virgin bosoms; by the richness of their petticoats, which surpassed that of their upper garments; by the gauze, the silk, the velvet, with which their dress was trimmed; and above all by the whiteness of their hands, which showed them to be unused to labour; it was easy to guess that they belonged to noble and wealthy families. It was, in fact, Damoiselle Fleur-de-Lys de Gondelaurier and her companions, Diane de Christeuil, Amelotte de Montmichel, Colombe de Gaillefontaine, and little de Champchevrier, who were staying at the house of the Dame de

185

Gondelaurier, a widow lady, on account of the expected visit of Monseigneur de Beaujeu and his consort who were to come to Paris in April for the purpose of selecting ladies of honour for the Dauphiness Marguerite. Now, all the gentry for a hundred miles round were anxious to obtain this favour for their daughters; and with this view numbers had already brought or sent them to Paris. Those mentioned above had been placed by their parents under the care of the discreet and venerable Dame Aloïse de Gondelaurier, widow of an officer of the King's crossbowmen, who resided with her only daughter in her own house in the Place du Parvis.

The balcony adjoined an apartment hung with rich fawn-coloured Flanders leather stamped with gold borders. The parallel beams which crossed the ceiling amused the eye by a thousand grotesque carvings, painted and gilt. On richly carved coffers were here and there blazoned splendid coats-of-arms; while a boar's head in Delft ware crowned a magnificent buffet, indicating that the mistress of the house was the wife or widow of a knight-bannaret. At the farther end, by a high fireplace, surrounded with escutcheons and armorial insignia, sat, in a rich armchair of crimson velvet, the Dame de Gondelaurier, whose age of fifty-five years was as legibly inscribed upon her dress as upon her face. By her side stood a young man, of a bold but somewhat vain and swaggering look—one of those handsome fellows to whom all the women take a liking, though the grave man and the physiognomist shrug their shoulders at them. This young cavalier wore the brilliant uniform of captain of the archers of the King's Ordnance, which so closely resembles the costume of Jupiter described at the outset of this history that we need not tire the reader with a second description of it.

The damsels were seated partly in the room, partly in the balcony, some on cushions of Utrecht velvet, others on oaken stools, carved with flowers and figures. Each of them held on her lap a portion of a large piece of tapestry, on which they were all working together, while the other part lay upon the matting that covered the floor.

They were chatting together, in that low tone and with those titters so common in a party of young girls when there is a young man among them. He whose presence was sufficient to set at work the self-love of all this youthful company, appeared himself to care very little about it; and while these beauties were each striving to engage his attention he seemed to be busily engaged himself in polishing the buckle of his belt with his leathern glove.

Now and then the old lady spoke to him in a very low tone, and he answered as well as he could, with a sort of awkward and forced politeness. From her smiles, from various other little significant tokens, and from the nods and winks which Dame Aloïse directed toward her daughter, Fleur-de-Lys, while softly speaking to the Captain, it was easy to see that he was an accepted lover, and that a match was on foot and would no doubt be speedily concluded between the young officer and Fleur-de-Lys. It was easy too to see from his coldness and embarrassment that, on his side at least, it was anything but a love-match. The good lady, who, fond mother as she was, doted upon her daughter, did not perceive the indifference of the Captain, and strove by her words and gestures to make him notice the grace with which Fleur-de-Lys plied her needle, or her distaff.

"Look, nephew," said she, plucking him by the sleeve, in order to whisper in his ear—"look at her now, as she stoops."

"Yes, indeed," replied the young man, relapsing into his former cold and irksome silence.

A moment afterward he was required to stoop again. "Did you ever," said Dame Aloïse, "see a more charming and engaging face than your betrothed? Is it possible to be fairer? Are not her hands and arms perfect models? And her neck, has it not all the elegance of a swan's?"

"No doubt," he replied, thinking of something else all the while.

"Why don't you go and talk to her, then?" retorted the lady, pushing him toward Fleur-de-Lys. "Go and say something to her. You are grown mighty shy all at once."

Now we can assure the reader that neither shyness nor modesty was to be numbered among the Captain's defects. He attempted, however, to do as he was desired.

"Fair cousin," said he, stepping up to Fleur-de-Lys, "what is the subject of this tapestry which you are working?"

"Fair cousin," answered Fleur-de-Lys, in a peevish tone, "I have told you three times already that it is the grotto of Neptune."

It was evident that the Captain's cold and absent manner had not escaped the keen observation of Fleur-de-Lys, though it was not perceived by her mother. He felt the necessity of making an attempt at conversation.

"And what is it intended for?" he inquired.

"For the abbey of Saint-Antoine-des-Champs," replied Fleur-de-Lys, without raising her eyes.

The Captain lifted up a corner of the tapestry. "And pray, my fair cousin," said he, "who is this big fellow, in the disguise of a fish, blowing the trumpet with puffed-out cheeks?"

"That is Triton," answered she.

In the tone of Fleur-de-Lys' brief replies there was still something that betokened displeasure. The Captain was more and more at a loss what to say. He stooped down over the tapestry. "A charming piece of work, by my fay!" cried he.

At this exclamation, Colombe de Gaillefontaine, another beautiful girl, of a delicately fair complexion, in a dress of blue damask, timidly ventured to address a question to Fleur-de-Lys, in the hope that the handsome Captain would answer it. "My dear Gondelaurier," said she, "have you seen the tapestries in the Hôtel de la Roche-Guyon?"

"Is not that the building next to the garden of the Louvre?" asked Diane de Christeuil, with a laugh. This young lady, be it observed, had remarkably handsome teeth, and consequently never spoke without laughing.

"And near that great old tower of the ancient wall of Paris?" inquired Amelotte de Montmichel, a charming brunette, with ruddy cheek and dark curling hair, who had a habit of sighing as the other of laughing, without knowing why.

At this moment Bérangère de Champchevrier, a little sylph of seven years, looking down upon the Place through the rails of the balcony, cried: "Oh! look, Godmother Fleur-de-Lys! look at that pretty dancer dancing on the pavement and playing on the tambourine among the people down yonder!"

"Some Egyptian, I dare say," replied Fleur-de-Lys, carelessly turning her head toward the Place.

"Let's see! let's see!" cried her lively companions, running to the front of the balcony, while Fleur-de-Lys, thinking of the coldness of her lover, slowly followed, and the Captain, released by this incident, which cut short a conversation that embarrassed him not a little, returned to the farther end of the apartment with the satisfaction of a soldier relieved from duty. The service of the gentle Fleur-de-Lys was nevertheless easy and delightful; and so it had formerly appeared to him: but now the prospect of a speedy marriage became every day more and more disagreeable. The fact is, he was of a rather inconstant disposition, and if the truth must be told, rather low in his tastes. Though of high birth, he had contracted more than one of the habits of the common soldier. He was fond of the tavern, and felt comfortable only among coarse language, military gallantries, easy beauties, and easy conquests. He had, nevertheless, received from his family some education and polish; but he had been thrown into the army too young, too young placed in garrison, and the varnish of the gentleman was daily wearing off by the hard friction of his guardsman's sword-belt. Though he still paid occasional visits to his relatives, from a slight feeling of human respect that was still left him, he found himself doubly embarrassed when he called upon Fleur-de-Lys; in the first place, because he distributed his love so promiscuously that he reserved a very small portion of it for her; and in the second, because in the company of so many handsome, well-bred, and modest women he was under constant apprehension lest his tongue, habituated to oaths and imprecations, should all at once get the better of the rein and launch out into the language of the tavern. Highly did he pique himself withal upon elegance in dress and appointments, and comeliness of person. The reader must reconcile these things as well as he can; I am but the historian.

The Captain, then, had stood for some moments, lost in thought, or not thinking at all, leaning in silence on the carved mantelpiece, when Fleur-de-Lys, suddenly turning round, addressed him. After all, it went sorely against the grain with the poor girl to pout at him.

"Did you not tell us, cousin, of a little Bohemian whom you rescued one night, about two months ago, from the hands of a dozen robbers?"

"I think I did, cousin," replied the Captain.

"I should not wonder," she resumed, "if it was the Bohemian dancing yonder in the Parvis. Come and see whether you know her, Cousin Phœbus."

In this gentle invitation to come to her and the tone in which it was uttered he detected a secret desire of reconciliation. Captain Phœbus de Châteaupers—for this is the personage whom the reader has had before him since the commencement of this chapter—advanced with slow steps toward the balcony. "Look," said Fleur-de-

189

Lys, softly grasping the Captain's arm—"look at yon girl dancing in that circle. Is she your Bohemian?"

Phœbus looked. "Yes," said he, "I know her by her goat."

"Oh! what a pretty little goat!" exclaimed Amelotte, clapping her hands in admiration.

"Are its horns of real gold?" asked Bérangère.

"Godmother," she began again, having all at once raised her bright eyes, which were in constant motion, to the top of the towers of Notre-Dame—"who is that man in black up yonder?"

All the young ladies looked up. A man was indeed lolling upon his elbows on the topmost balustrade of the northern tower, overlooking the Grève. It was a priest, as might be known by his dress, which was clearly distinguishable, and his head was supported by both his hands. He was motionless as a statue. His eye was fixed on the Place as intently as that of a hawk on a starling's nest which it has discovered.

" 'Tis the Archdeacon of Josas," said Fleur-de-Lys.

"You must have good eyes to know him at this distance," observed Gaillefontaine.

"How he looks at the dancing-girl!" exclaimed Diane de Christeuil.

"Let the Egyptian beware!" said Fleur-de-Lys. "The Archdeacon is not fond of Egypt."

" 'Tis a pity that man looks at her so," added Amelotte de Montmichel; "for she dances delightfully."

"Good Cousin Phœbus," abruptly cried Fleur-de-Lys, "since you know this Bohemian, just call her up. It will amuse us."

"Yes, do!" exclaimed all the young ladies, clapping their hands.

"Where is the use of it?" rejoined Phœbus. "She has no doubt forgotten me, and I know not even her name. However, as you wish it, ladies, I will try." Leaning over the balustrade of the balcony, he called out, "Child!"

The dancer had paused for a moment. She turned her head in the direction from which the voice proceeded; her sparkling eye fell upon Phœbus, and she stood motionless.

"Child!" repeated the Captain, beckoning her to come to him.

The girl still looked steadfastly at him; she then blushed deeply, as if every drop of blood had rushed to her cheeks, and, taking her tambourine under her arm, she made her way through the circle of astonished spectators toward the house to which she was summoned.

with slow, faltering step, and with the agitated look of a bird unable to withstand the fascination of a serpent.

A moment afterward the tapestry hung before the door was raised, and the Bohemian appeared at the threshold of the apartment, out of breath, flushed, flurried, with her large eyes fixed on the floor; she durst not advance a step farther. Bérangère clapped her hands.

Meanwhile the dancer stood motionless at the door of the room. Her appearance had produced a singular effect upon the party of young ladies. It is certain that all of them were more or less influenced by a certain vague and indistinct desire of pleasing the handsome officer; that the splendid uniform was the point at which all of their coquetries were aimed; and that ever since his entrance there had been a sort of secret rivalry among them, of which they were themselves scarcely conscious, but which nevertheless betrayed itself every moment in all they said and did. As, however, they all possessed nearly the same degree of beauty, they fought with equal weapons, and each might cherish a hope of victory. The coming of the Bohemian suddenly destroyed this equilibrium. Her beauty was so surpassing that at the moment when she appeared at the entrance of the room she seemed to shed over it a sort of light peculiar to herself. In this close apartment, overshadowed by hangings and carvings, she appeared incomparably more beautiful and radiant than in the public place—like a torch which is carried out of the broad daylight into the dark. In spite of themselves, the young ladies were dazzled. Each felt wounded, as it were, in her beauty. Their battle-front—reader, excuse the term—was changed accordingly, though not a single word passed between them. The instincts of women apprehend and answer one another much more readily than the understandings of men. An enemy had come upon them; of this they were all sensible, and therefore they all rallied. One drop of wine is sufficient to redden a whole glass of water; to tinge a whole company of pretty women with a certain degree of ill-humour merely introduce a woman prettier still, especially when there is but one man in the party.

The reception of the Bohemian was of course marvellously cold. They surveyed her from head to foot, then looked at each other with an expression which told their meaning as plainly as words could have done. Meanwhile the stranger, daunted to such a degree that she durst not raise her eyes, stood waiting to be spoken to.

The Captain was the first to break silence. "A charming creature, by my fay!" cried he. "What think you of her, my pretty cousin?"

This ejaculation, which a more delicate admirer would at least have uttered in a less audible tone, was not likely to disperse the feminine jealousies arrayed against the Bohemian.

"Not amiss," replied Fleur-de-Lys to the Captain's question, with affected disdain. The others whispered together.

At length Madame Aloïse, who felt not the less jealousy because she was jealous on behalf of her daughter, accosted the dancer. "Come hither, my girl," said she. The Egyptian advanced to the lady.

"My pretty girl," said Phœbus, taking a few steps toward her, "I know not whether you recollect me——"

"Oh, yes!" said she, interrupting him, with a smile and a look of inexpressible kindness.

"She has a good memory," observed Fleur-de-Lys.

"How was it," resumed Phœbus, "that you slipped away in such a hurry the other night? Did I frighten you?"

"Oh, no!" said the Bohemian.

In the accent with which this "Oh, no!" was uttered immediately after the "Oh, yes!" there was an indefinable something which wounded Fleur-de-Lys to the quick.

"In your stead," continued the Captain, whose tongue ran glibly enough in talking to one, whom from her occupation he took to be a girl of loose manners, "you left me a grim-faced, one-eyed, hunchbacked fellow—the Bishop's bell-ringer, I think they say. Some will have it that the Archdeacon, and others that the devil, is his father. He has a comical name—I have forgotten what—taken from some festival or other. What the devil did that owl of a fellow want with you, hey?"

"I don't know," answered she.

"Curse his impudence!—a rascally bell-ringer run away with a girl, like any viscount! A common fellow poach on the game of gentlemen! Who ever heard of such a thing! But he paid dearly for it. Master Pierrat Torterue is the roughest groom that ever trimmed a varlet; and I assure you, if that can do you any good, he curried the bell-ringer's hide most soundly."

The Danger of Trusting a Goat

"Poor fellow!" said the Bohemian, who at the Captain's words could not help calling to mind the scene at the pillory.

"Zounds!" cried the Captain, laughing outright, "that pity is as well bestowed as a feather on a pig's rump. May I be as portly as a Pope, if——" He stopped short. "I beg pardon, ladies, I was going to talk folly."

"Fie, sir!" said Gaillefontaine.

"He is only talking to that creature in her own language," said Fleur-de-Lys in an undertone, her vexation increasing every moment. Nor was it diminished when she saw the Captain, enchanted with the Bohemian and still more with himself, make a pirouette, repeating with blunt, soldierlike gallantry, "A fine girl, upon my soul!"

"But very uncouthly dressed," said Diane de Christeuil, smiling to show her beautiful teeth.

This remark was a new light to her companions. It showed them the assailable side of the Egyptian; as they could not carp at her beauty, they fell foul of her dress.

"How comes it, child," said Montmichel, "that you run about the streets in this manner, without veil or ruff?"

"That's an alarmingly short skirt," exclaimed Gaillefontaine.

"My dear," said Fleur-de-Lys, in a tone of anything but kindness, "the officers of the Châtelet will take you up for wearing that gilt belt."

"Child, child," resumed Christeuil, with an anything but amiable smile, "if you were to cover your arms decently with sleeves they would not be so sunburnt."

It was in truth a sight worthy of a more intelligent spectator than Phœbus, to see how these fair damsels, with their keen and envenomed tongues, twisted, glided, and writhed round the dancing-girl; they were at once cruel and graceful; they spitefully fell foul of her poor but whimsical toilet of tinsel and spangles. There was no end to their laughs and jeers and sarcasms. You would have taken them for some of those young Roman ladies who amused themselves with thrusting gold pins into the breasts of a beautiful slave; or they might be likened to elegant greyhounds, turning, with distended nostrils and glaring eyes, round a poor fawn, which the look of their master forbids them to devour.

193

The Hunchback of Notre-Dame

What after all was a poor street-dancer to these scions of distinguished families! They seemed to take no account of her presence, and talked of her before her face, and even to herself, as of an object at once very disgusting, very mean, and very pretty.

The Bohemian was not insensible to their stinging remarks. From time to time the glow of shame or the flash of anger flushed her cheek or lit up her eye; a disdainful word seemed to hover upon her lips; her contempt expressed itself in that pout with which the reader is already acquainted; but she stood motionless, fixing upon Phœbus a troubled and yet gentle look. In that look there was also an expression of tenderness and anxiety. You would have said that she restrained her feelings for fear of being turned out.

Meanwhile Phœbus laughed and began to take the part of the Bohemian, with a mixture of impertinence and pity. "Let them talk as they like, my dear," said he, clanking his gold spurs; "your dress is certainly somewhat whimsical and out of the way, but for such a charming creature as you are, what does that signify?"

"Dear me!" exclaimed the fair Gaillefontaine, bridling up, with a sarcastic smile, "how soon the gentlemen archers of the King's Ordnance take fire at bright Egyptian eyes!"

"Why not?" said Phœbus.

At this reply, carelessly uttered by the Captain, Colombe laughed, so did Diane, so did Amelotte, so did Fleur-de-Lys, though not without a tear in her eye. The Bohemian, who had hung down her head at the remark of Colombe de Gaillefontaine, raised her eyes glistening with joy and pride, and again fixed them on Phœbus. She was passing beautiful at that moment.

The old lady, who watched this scene, felt offended, though she knew not why. "Holy Virgin!" cried she, all at once, "what have I got about me? Ah! the nasty beast!"

It was the goat which, in springing toward her mistress had entangled her horns in the load of drapery which fell upon the feet of the noble lady when she was seated. This was a diversion. The Bohemian without saying a word disengaged the animal.

"Oh! here is the pretty little goat with golden feet!" cried Bérangère, leaping for joy.

The Bohemian crouched upon her knees, and pressed her cheek against the head of the nuzzling goat, while Diane, stooping to the

194

The Danger of Trusting a Goat

ear of Colombe, whispered: "How very stupid of me not to think of it sooner! Why, it is the Egyptian with the goat. It is reported that she is a witch, and that her goat performs the most amazing tricks."

"Well," said Colombe, "the goat must perform one of its miracles and amuse us in its turn."

Diane and Colombe eagerly addressed the Egyptian.

"Child," said they, "make your goat perform a miracle for us."

"I know not what you mean," replied the dancer.

"A miracle, a piece of magic, or witchcraft, in short."

"I don't understand you," she rejoined, and again began fondling the pretty creature, repeating, "Djali! Djali!"

At this moment Fleur-de-Lys remarked a small embroidered leathern bag hung round the neck of the goat. "What is that?" she asked the Egyptian.

The girl raised her large eyes toward her, and gravely answered, "That is my secret."

"I should like to know what your secret is," thought Fleur-de-Lys.

The good lady had meanwhile risen. "Girl," said she sharply, "if neither you nor your goat have any dance to show us why do you stay here?"

The Bohemian, without making any reply, drew leisurely toward the door. The nearer she approached it the more slowly she moved. An invincible loadstone seemed to detain her. All at once she turned her eyes glistening with tears toward Phœbus and stood still.

"By my fay!" cried the Captain, "you shan't get off thus. Come back and give us a dance. By the by, what is your name, my pretty dear?"

"La Esmeralda," said the dancing-girl, whose eyes were still fixed upon him.

At this strange name the young ladies burst into a loud laugh.

"A terrible name that for a girl!" said Diane.

"You see plainly enough," observed Amelotte, "that she is a witch."

"My girl," said Dame Aloïse in a solemn tone, "your parents never found that name for you in the font."

While this scene was passing Bérangère had enticed the goat into a corner of the room with a marchpane. They were at once the best friends in the world. The inquisitive girl loosed the little bag from the neck of the animal, opened it, and emptied its contents upon the mat: they consisted of an alphabet, each letter being separately inscribed upon a small piece of box-wood. No sooner were these playthings spread out upon the mat than, to the astonishment of the child, the goat—one of whose miracles this no doubt was—sorted out certain letters with her golden foot, arranged them and shuffled them gently together, in a particular order, so as to make a word, which the animal formed with such readiness that she seemed to have had a good deal of practice in putting it together. Bérangère, clapping her hands in admiration, suddenly exclaimed, "Godmother Fleur-de-Lys, come and see what the goat has done!"

Fleur-de-Lys ran to her and shuddered. The letters which the goat had arranged upon the floor formed the name PHŒBUS.

"Was it the goat that did this?" she asked in a tremulous voice.

"Yes, indeed it was, Godmother," replied Bérangère. It was impossible to doubt the fact.

"The secret is out," thought Fleur-de-Lys.

At the outcry of the child all who were present, the mother and the young ladies, and the Bohemian, and the officer, hastened to the spot. The dancing-girl saw at once what a blunder the goat had made. She changed colour, and began to tremble, like one who had committed some crime, before the Captain, who eyed her with a smile of astonishment and gratification.

For a moment the young ladies were struck dumb. "Phœbus!" they at length whispered one another, "why, that is the name of the Captain!"

"You have a wonderful memory," said Fleur-de-Lys to the petrified Bohemian. Then bursting into sobs, "Oh!" she faltered, in a tone of anguish, covering her face with both her fair hands, "she is a sorceress!" the while a voice, in still more thrilling accents, cried in the recesses of her heart— "She is a rival!" She sank fainting on the floor.

"My daughter! my daughter!" shrieked the affrighted mother. "Get thee gone, child of perdition!" said she to the Bohemian.

La Esmeralda picked up the unlucky letters in the twinkling of an eye, made a sign to her Djali, and retired at one door, while Fleur-de-Lys was borne away by another.

Captain Phœbus, being left by himself, wavered for a moment between the two doors, and then followed the gipsy-girl.

A Priest and a Philosopher

CHAPTER II

A PRIEST AND A PHILOSOPHER ARE TWO DIFFERENT PERSONS

THE priest, whom the young ladies had observed on the top of the north tower stooping over the Place, and intently watching the motions of the Bohemian, was in fact the Archdeacon Claude Frollo.

Our readers have not forgotten the mysterious cell which the Archdeacon had reserved for himself in that tower. I know not, be it remarked by the way, whether this is not the same cell, the interior of which may still be seen through a small square aperture on the east side, at about the height of a man, on the platform from which the towers rise. It is a small room, naked, empty, dilapidated, the ill-plastered walls of which are at the present day *adorned* with yellow engravings representing the fronts of cathedrals. This hole is, I presume, inhabited conjointly by bats and spiders, and consequently a double war of extermination is carried on there against the unfortunate flies.

Every day, an hour before sunset, the Archdeacon ascended the staircase of the tower, and shut himself up in this cell, where he frequently passed whole nights. On this day, just as he had reached the low door of his retreat, and put into the lock the little complicated key which he always carried with him in the pouch hanging at his side, the sounds of a tambourine and castanet struck his ear.

These sounds came from the Place du Parvis. The cell, as we have already stated, had but one window, looking upon the roof of the church. Claude Frollo hastily withdrew the key, and the next moment he was on the top of the tower, in the attitude of profound reverie in which the young ladies had perceived him.

There he was, grave, motionless, absorbed—all eye, all ear, all thought. All Paris was at his feet, with the thousand spires of its buildings, and its circular horizon of gentle hills, with its river winding beneath its bridges, and its population pouring through its streets, with its cloud of smoke, and its mountain-chain of roofs crowding close upon Notre-Dame with their double slopes of mail; but in this whole city the Archdeacon's eye sought but one point of the pave-

197

ment, the Place du Parvis, and among the whole multitude but one
figure, the Bohemian.

It would have been difficult to decide what was the nature of that
look, and of the fire that flashed from it. It was a fixed look, but
full of tumult and perturbation. And yet, from the profound quies-
cence of his whole body, scarcely shaken now and then by a mechanical shudder, as a tree by the wind; from the stiffness of his arms,
more marble-like than the balustrade upon which they leant; from
the petrified smile which contracted his face, you would have said
that Claude Frollo had nothing alive about him but his eyes.

The Bohemian was dancing; she made the tambourine spin round
on the tip of her finger, and threw it up in the air while she danced
Provençal sarabands—light, agile, joyous, and not aware of the
weight of that formidable look which fell straight upon her head.

The crowd thronged about her; from time to time a man habited
in a yellow and red loose coat went round the circle of spectators
to keep them back; he then seated himself in a chair, at the distance
of a few paces from the dancer, taking the head of the goat upon his
knees. This man seemed to be the companion of the Bohemian; but
Claude Frollo could not from his elevated station distinguish his
features.

From the moment that the Archdeacon perceived this stranger,
his attention seemed to be divided between the dancer and him, and
the gloom which overspread his countenance became deeper and
deeper. All at once, he started up, and a thrill shook his whole
frame. "Who can that man be?" he muttered—"till now I have
always seen her alone!"

He then darted beneath the winding vault of the spiral staircase
and descended. In passing the door of the belfry which was ajar,
he beheld an object which struck him: it was Quasimodo, leaning
out at one of the apertures of those slated penthouses which resemble enormous blinds, and intently looking down at the Place.
So entirely was he engrossed by the scene that he was not aware of the
passing of his foster-father. "Strange!" murmured Claude. "Can
it be the Egyptian that he is watching so earnestly?" He continued
to descend. In a few minutes the Archdeacon, full of care, sallied
forth into the Place by the door at the foot of the tower.

"What is become of the Bohemian?" he inquired, mingling with a
group of spectators whom the tambourine had collected.

A Priest and a Philosopher

"I know not," replied one of them; "I have but just missed her. I rather think she is gone to give them a dance in yon house opposite, from which some one called to her."

Instead of the Egyptian, upon the same carpet on which but a moment before she had been cutting her capricious capers, the Archdeacon now found only the man in the red and yellow surtout, who, to earn in his turn a few pieces of small coin, moved round the circle, with his elbows against his hips, his head thrown back, his face flushed, his neck stretched, and a chair between his teeth. On this chair was tied a cat, which a neighbour had lent for the purpose, and which, being frightened, was swearing lustily.

"By Our Lady!" exclaimed the Archdeacon, at the moment when the mountebank passed him with his pyramid of chair and cat; "what is Pierre Gringoire about here?"

The stern voice of the Archdeacon threw the poor fellow into such a commotion that he lost the balance of his edifice, and chair and cat tumbled pell-mell upon the heads of the persons nearest to him, amid the inextinguishable laughter of the rest.

In all probability Master Pierre Gringoire—for sure enough it was he—would have had an ugly account to settle with the mistress of the cat and the owners of all the bruised and scratched faces round him, had he not availed himself of the confusion to slip away to the church after the Archdeacon, who had motioned him to follow.

The cathedral was already dark and deserted, and the lamps in the chapels began to twinkle like stars amid the gloom. The great rose-window of the front alone, whose thousand colours were lit up by a ray of the setting sun, glistened in the dark like a cluster of diamonds, and threw its dazzling reflection on the farther extremity of the nave.

After they had advanced a few steps from the entrance Dom Claude, stopping short with his back against a pillar, looked steadfastly at Gringoire. In this look there was nothing to excite dread in Gringoire, deeply as he was ashamed of having been caught by a grave and learned personage in that Merry Andrew garb. The look of the priest had in it nothing sarcastic or ironical; it was serious, calm, and piercing. The Archdeacon first broke silence.

"Come hither, Master Pierre. There are many things which I want you to explain. In the first place, how happens it that I have

199

not seen you for these two months, and that I find you in the public
streets, in goodly garb forsooth, half red and half yellow, like a
Caudebec apple?"

"Messire," dolefully replied Gringoire, "it is indeed strange array; and one in which I feel about as comfortable as a cat in a coco-
nut-shell cap. 'Tis a sad thing, I admit, to let the gentlemen of the
watch run the risk of belabouring under this sorry disguise the shoulders of a Pythagorean philosopher. But how can I help it, my reverend master? The blame rests with my old coat, which basely forsook me in the depth of winter, upon pretext that it was dropping to
tatters. What could I do? Civilization is not yet so far advanced
that one may go stark naked, as Diogenes of old wished to do. Besides, a very keen wind was blowing at the time, and the month of
January is not a likely season to attempt to introduce this new
fashion with any hope of success. This wrapper offered itself; I
took it, and gave up my old black frock, which, for an hermetic
philosopher like me, was far from being hermetically close. So here
I am in mountebank's garb, like Saint Genest. 'Tis an eclipse, to
be sure. But Apollo, you know, tended swine for Admetus."

"A respectable profession truly, this that you have taken up!" replied the Archdeacon.

"I allow, master, that it is better to philosophize or poetize, to
blow up the flame in the furnace or to receive it from heaven, than
to carry cats about the streets. Accordingly, when I heard your exclamation, I was stupid as an ass before a spit. But what would you
have, Messire? A poor devil must live one day as well as another;
and the finest Alexandrines that ever were penned cannot stay the
hungry stomach so well as a crust of bread. You know, for example,
that famous epithalamium which I composed for Madame Margaret
of Flanders, and the Cité refuses to pay me for it on the ground
that it was not good enough, as if one could furnish tragedies like
those of Sophocles at four crowns apiece. Of course, I was ready
to perish with hunger. Luckily, I knew that I was pretty strong in
the jaw, so says I to this jaw— 'Try feats of strength and balancing; work and keep thyself.' A band of beggars, who are my very
good friends, have taught me twenty different herculean feats, and
now I give to my teeth every night the bread which they have helped
to earn in the day. After all, I grant that it is a sorry employment
of my intellectual faculties, and that man was not made to play the

A Priest and a Philosopher

tambourine and to carry chairs between his teeth. But, my reverend master, in order to live one must get a livelihood."

Dom Claude listened in silence. All at once his hollow eye assumed an expression so searching and so piercing that Gringoire felt that look penetrate to the inmost recesses of his soul.

"Well, Master Pierre; but how happens it that you are now in the company of that Egyptian dancing-girl?"

"Gramercy!" replied Gringoire, "it is because she is my wife and I am her husband."

The gloomy eyes of the priest glared like fire. "Wretch! Is this really so?" cried he, furiously grasping Gringoire's arm. "Hast thou so completely forsaken thy God as to become the husband of that creature?"

"By my hope of Paradise, Monseigneur," answered Gringoire, trembling in every joint, "I swear that she allows me no more familiarity than if I were an utter stranger."

"What are you talking, then, about husband and wife?" rejoined the priest.

Gringoire lost no time in relating to him as concisely as possible the circumstances with which the reader is already acquainted, his adventure in the Cour des Miracles, his marriage with the broken jug, and the course of life which he had since followed. From his account, it appeared that the Bohemian had never shown him more kindness than she had done on the first night. " 'Tis a provoking thing, though," said he, as he finished his story; "but it is owing to a strange notion, which those Egyptians have put into her head."

"What mean you?" asked the Archdeacon, whose agitation had gradually subsided during this narrative.

"It is rather difficult to explain my meaning," replied the poet. " 'Tis a superstition. My wife, as I am informed by an old fellow whom we call among ourselves the Duke of Egypt, is a child that has been either lost or found, which is the same thing. She has a charm hung round her neck which, they say, will some day cause her to find her parents, but which would lose its virtue if the girl were to lose hers."

"So, then," rejoined Claude, whose face brightened up more and more, "you really believe, Master Pierre, that this creature is yet virtuous?"

The Hunchback of Notre-Dame

"What chance, Dom Claude, can a man have against a superstition? This, I tell you, is what she has got into her head. I consider this nun-like chastity, which keeps itself intact among those Bohemian females, who are not remarkable for that quality, as a very rare circumstance indeed. But she has three things to protect her: the Duke of Egypt, who has taken her under his safeguard; her whole tribe, who hold her in extraordinary veneration, like another Notre-Dame; and a certain little dagger, which the hussy always carries about her somewhere or other, notwithstanding the ordinances of the Provost, and which is sure to be in her hands if you but clasp her waist. She is a saucy wasp, I can tell you."

The Archdeacon pursued his cross-examination of Gringoire. In the estimation of the latter La Esmeralda was a handsome, fascinating, inoffensive creature, with the exception of the pout peculiar to her; a simple warm-hearted girl, exceedingly ignorant, and exceedingly enthusiastic; fond above all things of dancing, of noise, of the open air; a sort of human bee, having invisible wings at her feet, and living in a perpetual whirl. She owed this disposition to the wandering life which she had always led. Gringoire had contrived to learn as much as this, that she had travelled over Spain and Catalonia, and as far as Sicily; nay, he believed that she had been carried by the caravan of Zingari to which she belonged into the Kingdom of Algiers. The Bohemians, so Gringoire said, were vassals of the King of Algiers, as chief of the nation of the white Moors. So much was certain that La Esmeralda had come to France while very young by way of Hungary. From all these countries the girl had brought scraps of odd jargons, snatches of old songs, and foreign ideas, which made her language as curious a piece of patchwork as her dress, half Parisian, and half African. For the rest, she was a favourite with the people of those quarters of the city which she frequented, for her sprightliness, her gracefulness, her personal attractions, her dancing, and her singing. She had a notion that in the whole city there were but two persons who hated her, and of whom she often spoke with terror—the wretched recluse of the Tour-Roland, who, for some reason or other, bore an implacable enmity to the Egyptians, and cursed the poor dancing-girl whenever she passed her cell, and a priest, whom she never met without being frightened by his looks and language. This last intimation disturbed

A Priest and a Philosopher

the Archdeacon not a little, though Gringoire scarcely noticed his agitation; so completely had the lapse of two months effaced from the memory of the thoughtless poet the singular circumstances of that night when he first met with the Egyptian, and the presence of the Archdeacon on that occasion. There was nothing else that the young dancer had reason to be afraid of; she never told fortunes, so that she was safe from prosecutions for witchcraft, so frequently instituted against the gipsy-women. And then Gringoire was as a brother to her, if not a husband. After all, the philosopher bore this kind of Platonic marriage with great resignation. At any rate, he was sure of lodging and bread. Every morning he sallied forth from the headquarters of the Vagabonds, mostly in company with the Egyptian; he assisted her in collecting her harvest of small coin in the streets; at night he returned with her to the same room, allowed her to lock herself up in her own cell, and slept the sleep of the righteous—"a very easy life," said he, "considering all things, and very favourable to reverie." And then, in his soul and conscience, the philosopher was not sure that he was not over head and ears in love with the Bohemian. He loved her goat almost as dearly. It was a charming, gentle, clever, intelligent creature—in short, a learned goat. There was nothing more common in the Middle Ages than those learned animals, which excited general wonder, and frequently brought their instructors to the stake. The sorceries of the golden-hoofed goat, however, were but very innocent tricks. These Gringoire explained to the Archdeacon, who appeared to be deeply interested by those particulars. It was sufficient, he said, in most cases, to hold the tambourine to the animal in such or such a way, to make it do what you wished. It had been trained to these performances by the girl, who was so extremely clever at the business that she had taken only two months to teach the goat to put together with movable letters the word "Phœbus."

"Phœbus!" exclaimed the priest; "why Phœbus?"

"God knows," replied Gringoire. "Possibly she may imagine that this word possesses some secret magic virtue. She frequently repeats it in an undertone when she thinks she is alone."

"Are you sure," inquired Claude, with his piercing look, "that it is only a word, and not a name?"

"Name! whose name?" said the poet.

"How should I know?" rejoined the priest.

"I'll just tell you, Messire, what I am thinking. These Bohemians are a sort of Guebres, and worship the sun—Dan Phœbus."

"That is not so clear to me as to you, Master Pierre."

"At any rate, 'tis a point which I care very little about. Let her mutter her Phœbus as much as she pleases. So much is certain, that Djali is almost as fond of me as of her mistress."

"What is Djali?"

"Why, that is the goat."

The Archdeacon rested his chin upon the points of his fingers, and for a moment appeared to be lost in thought. Then, suddenly turning toward Gringoire— "Thou wilt swear," said he, "that thou hast never touched her?"

"What! the goat?" asked Gringoire.

"No, the girl."

"Oh! my wife! I swear I never did."

"And thou art often alone with her?"

"Every evening for a full hour."

Dom Claude knitted his brow. "Oh! oh! *Solus cum sola non cogitabantur orare Paternoster.*" [1]

"Upon my life I might say the *Pater,* and the *Ave Maria,* and the *Credo in Deum Patrem omnipotentem,* and she would take no more notice of me than a pig of a church."

"Swear to me, by the soul of thy mother," cried the Archdeacon, with vehemence, "that thou hast not touched this creature with the tip of thy finger."

"I am ready to swear it by the body of my father also. But, my reverend master, allow me to ask a question in my turn."

"Speak."

"How can this concern you?"

The pale face of the Archdeacon crimsoned like the cheek of a bashful girl. He paused for a moment before he replied, with visible embarrassment— "Listen, Master Pierre Gringoire. You are not yet eternally lost, as far as I know. I take an interest in your welfare. Let me tell you, then, that the moment you but lay a hand on that Egyptian, that child of the devil, you become the vassal of Satan. 'Tis the body, you know, that always plunges the soul into perdition. Woe betide you if you approach this creature! That is all. Now get thee gone!" cried the priest, with a terrible look; and,

[1] "A man and a maid alone together don't think about paternosters."

pushing the astonished Gringoire from him by the shoulders, he retreated with hasty step beneath the gloomy arcades of the cathedral.

CHAPTER III

THE BELLS

EVER since the morning that Quasimodo underwent the punishment of the pillory the good people who dwelt in the neighbourhood of Notre-Dame fancied that they perceived a great abatement in his ardour for bell-ringing. Before that event the bells were going on all occasions; there were long tollings which lasted from prime to compline, chimes for High Mass, merry peals for a wedding or a christening, mingling in the air like an embroidery of all sorts of charming sounds. The old church, all quaking and all sonorous, seemed to keep up a perpetual rejoicing. You felt incessantly the presence of a spirit of noise and caprice, speaking by all these brazen mouths. This spirit seemed now to have forsaken its abode: the cathedral appeared sullen and silent; holidays, funerals, and the like were attended merely by the tolling which the ritual required, and no more; of the double sound which pervades a church, that of the organ within and of the bells without, the former alone was left. You would have said that there was no longer any musician in the belfries. Quasimodo, nevertheless, was still there. But what ailed him? Were rage and vexation on account of what he had suffered still rankling in his heart? Did he still feel in imagination the lash of the executioner, and had the despondency occasioned by such treatment extinguished even his fondness for the bells?—or was it possible that big Mary had a rival in the heart of the bell-ringer of Notre-Dame, and that she and her fourteen sisters were neglected for a more beautiful and a more lovely object?

It so happened that in this year of grace 1482 the Annunciation fell upon Tuesday the 25th of March. On that day the air was so light and serene that Quasimodo felt some reviving affection for his bells. He went up therefore into the north tower, while below the beadle threw wide open the doors of the church, which were at that time formed of enormous slabs of oak, covered with hide, bordered with nails of iron gilt, and adorned with carvings "most cunningly wrought."

The Hunchback of Notre-Dame

Having reached the high loft of the belfry, Quasimodo gazed for some time at the six bells with a sad shake of the head, as if lamenting that some other object had intruded itself into his heart between them and him. But when he had set them in motion, when he felt this bunch of bells swinging in his hand; when he saw, for he could not hear, the palpitating octave running up and down that sonorous scale, like a bird hopping from twig to twig; when the demon of Music, that demon which shakes a glittering quiver of *stretti,* trills, and *arpeggios,* had taken possession of the poor deaf bell-ringer, he was once more happy, he forgot all his troubles, his heart expanded, and his face brightened up.

He paced to and fro, he clapped his hands, he ran from rope to rope, he encouraged the six chimers with voice and gesture, as the leader of an orchestra spurs on intelligent performers.

"Go on, Gabrielle, go on," said he, "pour thy flood of sound into the Place, for 'tis a holiday.—Don't lag, Thibauld; no idling! Move, move; art thou rusty, lazybones?—Well done! quick, quick! peal it lustily: make them all deaf like me! That's right, bravely done, Thibauld!—Guillaume, Guillaume, thou art the biggest, and Pasquier the least, and yet Pasquier beats thee hollow. Those who can hear, I'll engage, hear more of him than of thee. Well done! well done, my Gabrielle; harder and harder still!—Soho! you two Sparrows up there! I do not hear you give out the least chirp. Of what use is it to have those brazen mouths, if ye but yawn when ye ought to sing? There, work away! 'Tis the Annunciation. The cheery sunshine requires a merry peal. Poor Guillaume! thou art quite out of breath, my big fellow!"

He was thus engaged in egging on his bells, which all six bounded and shook their shining haunches, like a noisy team of Spanish mules, urged first this way then that by the apostrophes of the driver. All at once, casting down his eye between the large slates which like scales cover the perpendicular wall of the belfry to a certain height, he descried in the Place a young girl quaintly clad, who stopped and spread upon the ground a carpet on which a little goat came and planted itself. A circle of spectators was soon formed round them. This sight suddenly changed the current of his ideas, and congealed his musical enthusiasm as a breath of air congeals melted rosin. He paused, turned his back to his bells, and, leaning forward from beneath the slated penthouse, eyed the dancing-girl with that pensive,

kind, nay tender, look, which had once before astonished the Archdeacon. Meanwhile the bells, left to themselves, abruptly ceased
all at once, to the great disappointment of the lovers of this kind of
music, who were listening with delight to the peal from the Pont au
Change, and went away as sulky as a dog to which you have held
a piece of meat and given a stone.

CHAPTER IV

CLAUDE FROLLO'S CELL

ONE fine morning in the same month of March, I believe it
was Saturday, the 29th, the festival of St Eustache, it so
happened that our young friend Jehan Frollo du Moulin
perceived, while dressing himself, that his breeches, containing his
purse, gave out no metallic sound. "Poor purse!" said he, drawing
it forth from his pocket; "not one little Parisis! How cruelly thou
hast been gutted by dice, Venus, and the tavern! There thou art,
empty, wrinkled, flaccid. Thou art like the bosom of a fury. I
would just ask you, Messire Cicero and Messire Seneca, whose dog's-
eared works lie scattered on the floor, of what use is it to me to
know, better than a master of the mint or a Jew of the Pont aux
Changeurs, that a gold crown is worth thirty-five unzains, at twenty-
five sous eight deniers Parisis each, if I have not a single miserable
black liard to risk on the double-six! O Consul Cicero! this is not
a calamity from which one may extricate one's self with periphrases,
with *quemadmodums* and *verumenimveros.*" [1]

He began to put on his clothes in silent sadness. While lacing his
buskins a thought occurred to him, but he gave it up immediately.
Again it presented itself, and he put on his vest the wrong side out,
an evident sign of some violent inward struggle. At length, dashing
his cap upon the ground, he exclaimed— "Yes, I will go to my
brother; I shall get a lecture, but then I shall get a crown."

Then hastily throwing on his surcoat trimmed with fur, and picking up his cap, he rushed out of the room. He went down the Rue
de la Harpe toward the Cité. As he passed the Rue de la Huchette

[1] "How's" and "verily's."

his olfactory nerves were gratified by the smell of the joints incessantly roasting there, and he cast a sheep's eye at the gigantic apparatus which one day drew from Calatagirone, the Franciscan, this
pathetic exclamation—*Veramente, queste rotisserie sono cosa stu-
penda!* [1] But Jehan had not wherewithal to get a breakfast, and
with a deep sigh he pursued his course under the gateway of the
Petit Châtelet, that enormous cluster of massive towers which guarded
the entrance to the city.

He did not even take the time to throw a stone in passing, as it was
then customary, at the mutilated statue of that Perinet Leclerc, who
had surrendered the Paris of Charles VI to the English—a crime for
which his effigy, defaced by stones and covered with mud, did penance
for three centuries, at the corner of the Rues de la Harpe and de
Bussy, as in a perpetual pillory.

Having crossed the Petit Pont, Jehan at length found himself before Notre-Dame. Again he wavered in his purpose, and he walked
for a few moments round the statue of Monsieur Legris, repeating
to himself— "I am sure of the lecture, but shall I get the crown?"

He stopped a verger who was coming from the cloisters. "Where
is the Archdeacon of Josas?" he inquired.

"I believe he is in his closet in the tower," replied the verger;
"and I would not advise you to disturb him there, unless you have
a message from some such person as the Pope or Monsieur the
King."

Jehan clapped his hands. "By Jupiter!" he exclaimed—"a fine
opportunity for seeing that famous den of sorcery!"

Determined by this reflection, he resolutely entered at the little
black door, and began to ascend the winding stairs leading to the
upper storeys of the tower. "We shall see," said he to himself by
the way. "By the whiskers of the Blessed Virgin, it must be a
curious place, that cell which my reverend brother keeps so carefully
to himself. They say that he has a roaring fire there sometimes to
cook the philosopher's stone at. By my fay, I care no more about
the philosopher's stone than any old pebble, and I would rather find
a savoury omelette on his furnace than the biggest philosopher's stone
in the world!"

Having reached the pillar gallery, he stood puffing for a moment,

[1] "In sooth, these cook-shops are prodigious!"

208

and then swore at the endless stairs by I know not how many million cartloads of devils. Having somewhat vented his spleen, he recommenced his ascent by the little door of the north tower, which is now shut against the public. Just after he had passed the bell-room he came to a lateral recess in which there was a low, pointed door. "Humph!" said the scholar; "this must be the place, I suppose."

The key was in the lock, and the door not fastened; he gently pushed it open far enough to look in.

The reader has no doubt turned over the admirable works of Rembrandt, that Shakespeare of painting. Among so many wonderful engravings there is one, in particular, representing Dr Faustus, as it is conjectured, which you cannot look at without being dazzled. The scene is a dark cell, in the middle of which is a table covered with hideous objects—skulls, globes, alembics, compasses, parchments with hieroglyphics. Before this table is the doctor dressed in a long gown, and with his fur cap pulled down to his very eyebrows. The lower part of his person is not to be seen. Half risen from his immense armchair, he leans with his clenched fists upon the table, and is looking with curiosity and terror at a large luminous circle, composed of magic letters, which glares upon the opposite wall, like the solar spectrum in a dark room. This cabalistic sun seems to tremble to the eye, and fills the gloomy cell with its mysterious radiance. It is terrible, and it is beautiful.

A scene not unlike the cell of Dr Faustus presented itself to the view of Jehan, when he ventured to look in at the half-open door. This, too, was a gloomy hole into which the light was very sparingly admitted. It contained, too, a great armchair and a large table, compasses, alembics, skeletons of animals hanging from the ceiling, a globe lying upon the floor pell-mell with glass jars, filled with liquids of various colours, skulls placed on parchments scrawled over with figures and letters, thick manuscripts wide open and heaped one upon another—in short all the rubbish of science—and the whole covered with dust and cobwebs; but there was no circle of luminous letters, no doctor in ecstasy contemplating the flaming vision as the eagle gazes at the sun.

The cell, however, was not unoccupied. A man seated in the armchair was stooping over the table. His back was turned to Jehan, who could see no more than his shoulders and the hinder part of his head; but he had no difficulty to recognize that bald crown, on which nature had made an everlasting tonsure, as if to mark by this outward symbol the irresistible clerical vocation of the Archdeacon.

The door had opened so softly that Dom Claude was not aware of the presence of his brother. The young scapegrace took advantage of this circumstance to examine the cell for a few moments. To the left of the armchair and beneath the small window was a large furnace, which he had not remarked at the first glance. The ray of light which entered at the aperture passed through a circular cobweb, in the centre of which the motionless insect architect looked like the hub of this wheel of lace. On the furnace lay in disorder all sorts of vessels, glass phials, and retorts. There was no fire in the furnace, nor did it appear to have been lighted for a considerable time. A glass mask, which Jehan observed among the implements of alchemy, and which no doubt served to protect the Archdeacon's face when he was at work upon any dangerous substance, lay in one corner, covered with dust, and as it were forgotten. By its side was a pair of bellows equally dusty, the upper surface of which bore this legend inlaid in letters of copper: *Spira, spera.*

Other mottoes in great number were inscribed, according to the custom of the hermetic philosophers, upon the walls, some written with ink and others cut as if with a graver. Gothic, Hebrew, Greek, and Roman letters were all mixed together; the inscriptions ran into one another, the more recent effacing the older, and all dovetailing like the boughs of a clump of trees, or pikes in a battle. They composed in fact a confused medley of all human philosophies, reveries, and knowledge. There was one here and there which was conspicuous above the rest like a pennon among the heads of lances. Most of them were short Latin or Greek mottoes, such as the Middle Ages were so clever at devising: *Unde? inde?—Homo homini monstrum.* *—Astra, castra; nomen, numen.—Μέγα βιβλίον, μέγα κακόν.—Sapere aude.—Flat ubi vult,*[1] etc. There were also by the way Hebrew scrawls, which Jehan, who knew very little of Greek, could not decipher, and the whole was crossed in all directions by stars, figures of men and beasts, and triangles, which intersected one another, and contributed not a little to make the wall of the cell resemble a sheet

---

[1] "Whence? Thence?" "Man is a monster to men." "The stars my camp, the name, my god." "The bigger the book, the greater the evil." "To learn, listen." "It bloweth where it listeth."

of paper upon which a monkey has been scribbling with a pen.

In other respects the cell exhibited a general appearance of neglect and dilapidation; and from the state of the utensils it might be inferred that the master had long been diverted from his usual pursuits by other occupations.

This master, meanwhile, bending over a vast manuscript adorned by grotesque paintings, appeared to be tormented by an idea which incessantly obtruded itself upon his meditations. So at least Jehan judged, on hearing him utter this soliloquy, with the pensive pauses of one in a brown study who thinks aloud:

"Yes, so Manou asserted and Zoroaster taught. The sun is the offspring of fire, the moon of the sun: fire is the soul of the universe. Its elementary atoms are incessantly overflowing and pouring upon the world in innumerable currents. At the points where these currents intersect one another in the atmosphere they produce light; at their points of intersection in the earth they produce gold. —Light, gold—one and the same thing!—From the state of fire to the concrete state.—The difference between the visible and palpable, between the fluid and solid in the same substance, between steam and ice, nothing more.—This is not a dream—'tis the general law of nature. But how is science to set about detecting the secret of this general law? Why, this light which floods my hand is gold! These same atoms, which expand according to a certain law, need but be condensed according to a certain other law.—How is this to be done?—Some have proposed to effect it by burying a ray of the sun.—Averroës—yes, it was Averroës—buried one under the first pillar on the left, in the sanctuary of the Koran, in the grand mosque at Cordova; but the vault must not be opened to see whether the operation has been successful for the space of eight thousand years."

"The devil!" said Jehan to himself—" 'tis a long while to wait for a crown!"

"Others have thought," continued the Archdeacon, "that it would be better to operate upon a ray of Sirius. But it is very difficult to obtain one of his rays pure, on account of the simultaneous presence of the other stars, whose light mingles with it. Flamel conceives that it is more simple to operate upon terrestial fire.—Flamel! what a name for an adept!—*Flamma*—yes, fire. That is all.—The diamond is in charcoal, gold is in fire.—But how is it to be extracted? —Magistri affirms that there are certain names of women possessing so sweet and so mysterious a charm, that it is sufficient to pronounce them during the operation.—Let us see what Manou says on the subject: 'Where women are honoured the gods are pleased; where they are despised it is useless to pray to the gods.—The mouth of a woman is constantly pure; it is a running water, a ray of sunshine.—The name of a woman ought to be agreeable, soft, imaginary; to terminate with long vowels and to be like words of blessing.'—Yes, the philosopher is right: thus, La Maria, La Sophia, La Esmeral—— Damnation! always—always—that thought!"

He closed the book with violence. He passed his hand over his brow, as if to chase away the idea which annoyed him; and then took up a nail and a small hammer, the handle of which was curiously painted with cabalistic letters.

"For some time past," said he, with a bitter smile, "I have failed in all my experiments. One fixed idea haunts me and pierces my brain like a red-hot iron. I have not even been able to discover the secret of Cassiodorus, who made a lamp to burn without wick and without oil. A simple matter, nevertheless!"

"*Peste!*" muttered Jehan.

"One single miserable thought, then," continued the priest, "is sufficient to make a man weak or mad! Oh! how Claude Pernelle would laugh at me!—She who could not for a moment divert Nicolas Flamel from the prosecution of the great work! But have I not in my hand the magic hammer of Zéchiélé! At every blow which the dread rabbi in the recesses of his cell struck upon this nail with this hammer some one of his enemies whom he had doomed to destruction sank into the earth which swallowed him up. The King of France himself, having one night knocked for a frolic at his door, sank up to his knees in the pavement of Paris.—This happened not three centuries ago.—Well, I have the hammer and the nail; but then these tools are not more formidable in my hands than a rule in the hands of a carpenter.—And yet I should possess the same power could I but discover the magic word pronounced by Zéchiélé while striking the nail."

"Nonsense!" thought Jehan.

"Let's see! let's try!" resumed the Archdeacon, with vehemence. "If I succeed, a blue spark will fly from the head of the nail—*Emen-Hétan! Emen-Hétan!*—That's not it—*Sigéani! Sigéani!*—May this nail open a grave for every man named Phœbus . . .!—Curses on it! for ever and ever the same idea!"

He angrily threw down the hammer, and then sunk forward in his armchair upon the table, so that the enormous back completely hid him from Jehan's sight. For a few minutes he saw no part of him but his hand convulsively clenched upon a book. All at once Dom Claude rose, took up a pair of compasses, and engraved in silence on the wall in capital letters the Greek word 'ANATKH.[1]

"My brother is mad," said Jehan to himself. "It would have been much more simple to write *Fatum*. Everybody is not obliged to understand Greek."

The Archdeacon returned, seated himself again in his armchair, and laid his head on both his hands, like one whose head aches to such a degree that he cannot hold it up.

The student watched his brother with astonishment. He, who carried his heart in his hand, who observed no other law in the world but the good law of nature, who let his passions run off by his inclinations, and in whom the lake of powerful emotions was always dry, so assiduous was he every morning in making new channels to drain it—he knew not how furiously this sea of human passions ferments and boils when it is refused any outlet; how it swells, how it rises, how it overflows; how it heaves in inward convulsions, till it has broken down its dikes and burst its bed. The austere and icy envelope of Claude Frollo, that cold surface of inaccessible virtue, had always deceived Jehan. The jovial scholar never dreamt of the lava, deep and furious, which boils beneath the snowy crest of Etna.

We know not whether these ideas occurred to him at the moment; but, volatile as he was, he apprehended that he had seen more than he ought to have seen, that he had surprised the soul of his elder brother in one of its most secret attitudes, and that he must take good care not to let Claude perceive it. Perceiving that the Archdeacon had relapsed into his former stupor, he softly drew back his head and took several steps outside the door, that his footfall might apprise the Archdeacon of his arrival.

"Come in," cried his brother, from within the cell; "I have been waiting for you. Come in, Master Jacques."

[1] Destiny, fatality.

The scholar boldly entered. The Archdeacon, to whom such a visitor in such a place was anything but welcome, started at the sight of him. "What! is it you, Jehan?"

"'Tis a J at any rate," said the student, with his ruddy, impudent, jovial face.

The countenance of Dom Claude resumed its stern expression. "What brings you hither?"

"Brother," replied the scholar, assuming as humble, modest, and decorous an air as he could, and twirling his cap on his fingers with a look of innocence, "I am come to ask of you . . ."

"What?"

"A little wholesome advice, which I much need." Jehan durst not add—"and a little money which I need still more." This last member of the sentence he forbore to utter.

"Sir," said the Archdeacon, in an austere tone, "I am highly displeased with you."

"Alas!" sighed the student.

Dom Claude made his chair describe one fourth of a circle, and looked steadfastly at Jehan. "I wanted to see you," said he.

This was an ominous exordium. Jehan prepared himself for a fierce attack.

"Every day, Jehan, complaints are brought to me of your misconduct. What have you to say for yourself about that beating which you gave to the young Vicomte Albert de Ramonchamp?"

"Oh!" replied Jehan, "a mere bagatelle! The scurvy page amused himself with making his horse run in the mud for the purpose of splashing the scholars."

"And what excuse have you to make," resumed the Archdeacon, "about that affair with Mahiet Targel, whose gown you tore? *Tunicam dechiraverunt*,[1] says the complaint."

"Pooh! only one of the sorry Montaigu hoods! that's all!"

"The complaint says *tunicam* and not *capettam*. Have you not learned Latin?"

Jehan made no reply.

"Yes," continued the priest, "the study of letters is at a low ebb now. The Latin language is scarcely understood, the Syriac unknown, the Greek so hateful that it is not accounted ignorance even

[1] "They have torn the robe."

214

in the greatest scholars to skip a Greek word without pronouncing it, and to say, *Græcum est, non legitur.*" [1]

Jehan boldly raised his eyes. "Brother," said he, "would you like me to explain in simple French the Greek word written there upon the wall?"

"Which word?"

"ANATKH!"

A slight flush tinged the pallid cheek of the Archdeacon, like the puff of smoke which betokens the secret commotions of a volcano. The student scarcely perceived it.

"Well, Jehan," stammered the elder brother with some effort, "what is the meaning of that word?"

"FATALITY."

Dom Claude turned pale, and the scholar carelessly continued: "And that word underneath, engraven by the same hand, 'Avαγνεία, signifies 'impurity.' You see, I do know something of Greek."

The Archdeacon was silent. The Greek lesson had made him thoughtful. Young Jehan, who had all the art of a spoiled child, deemed it a favourable moment for hazarding his request. Assuming, therefore, as soothing a tone as possible, he thus began: "My good brother, surely you will not look morose and take a dislike to me merely on account of a few petty bruises and thumps given in fair fight to a pack of little chits and monkeys—*quibusdam marmosetis.* You see, I do know something of Latin, brother Claude."

But this canting hypocrisy had not its accustomed effect upon the stern senior. It did not remove a single wrinkle from the brow of the Archdeacon. "Come to the point," said he drily.

"Well, then," replied Jehan, screwing up his courage; "it is this —I want money."

At this straightforward declaration the countenance of the Archdeacon all at once assumed a magisterial and paternal expression.

"You know, Monsieur Jehan," said he, "that our fief of Tire-chappe produces no more, deducting ground rent and other outgoings for the twenty-one houses, than thirty-nine livres, eleven sous, six deniers Parisis. This is half as much again as in the time of the Paclets, but 'tis no great deal."

"I want money," repeated Jehan stoically.

[1] "It is Greek, it is not read."

The Hunchback of Notre-Dame

"You know that the official has decided that our twenty-one houses are liable to the payment of fines to the bishopric, and that to relieve ourselves from this homage we must pay the most reverend Bishop two marks in silver gilt at the rate of six livres Parisis. Now I have not yet been able to save these two marks, as you well know."

"I know that I want money," repeated Jehan for the third time.

"And what would you do with it?"

At this question a glimmer of hope danced before the eyes of Jehan. He resumed his soft and fawning manner.

"Look you, my dear brother Claude, it is not for any bad purpose that I make this application. It is not to play the gallant in taverns with your unzains, or to parade the streets of Paris in a suit of gold brocade with a lackey at my heels. No, brother; it is for an act of charity."

"What act of charity?" inquired Claude, with some surprise.

"There are two of my friends who have proposed to purchase baby-linen for the child of a poor widow in Haudry's almshouses; it is a real charity. It would cost three florins, and I wish to contribute my share."

"A likely story!" observed the sagacious Claude. "What sort of baby-linen must it be to cost three florins—and that too for the infant of one of the Haudry widows! Since when have those widows had young infants to provide clothes for?"

"Well, then," cried Jehan, once more arming himself with his usual impudence, "I want money to go at night to see Isabeau la Thierrye."

"Dissolute wretch!" exclaimed the priest.

"Ἀναγνεία," said Jehan.

This word, which stared the scholar in the face on the wall of the cell produced an extraordinary effect on the priest. He bit his lips, and his anger was extinguished in a deep blush.

"Get you gone!" said he to Jehan; "I expect some one."

Jehan made another attempt. "Brother Claude, give me at least one petit Parisis to get something to eat."

"Where are you in Gratian's decretals?" asked Dom Claude.

"I have lost my exercises."

"Where are you in the Latin humanities?"

"Somebody has stolen my Horace."

"Where are you in Aristotle?"

Claude Frollo's Cell

"By my fay, brother!—which of the Fathers of the Church is it who says that heretics have in all ages sought refuge under the briars of Aristotle's metaphysics? Faugh upon Aristotle! I will not tear my religion to rags against his metaphysics."

"Young man," replied the Archdeacon, "at the last entry of the King there was a gentleman called Philippe de Comines, who had embroidered on the trappings of his horse this motto, which I counsel you to ponder well: *Qui non laborat non manducet.*" [1]

The scholar continued silent for a moment, with his finger on his ear, his eye fixed upon the floor, and a look of vexation. All at once turning toward Claude with the brisk motion of a water-wagtail, "Then, my good brother," said he, "you refuse me a sou to buy me a crust at the baker's?"

"Qui non laborat non manducet."

At this inflexible answer of the Archdeacon's Jehan covered his face with his hands, sobbed like a woman, and cried in a tone of despair, "Ο το το το το τοῖ!"

"What is the meaning of that?" asked Claude, surprised at this vagary.

"Why," said the scholar, after rubbing his eyes with his knuckles to give them the appearance of weeping—"it is Greek—'tis an anapæst of Æschylus, which expresses grief to the life."

He then burst into a laugh so droll and so ungovernable that the Archdeacon could not help smiling. It was in fact Claude's fault: why had he so utterly spoiled the boy?

"Nay, now, my good brother Claude," resumed Jehan, "only look at my worn-out buskins. Did you ever see a more lamentable sight?"

The Archdeacon had quickly resumed his former sternness. "I will send you new buskins, but no money."

"Only one poor petit Parisis, brother!" besought Jehan. "I will learn Gratian by heart, I will be a good Christian, a real Pythagoras of learning and virtue. One petit Parisis, pray! Would you let me fall a prey to hunger which is staring me in the face?"

Dom Claude shook his wrinkled brow. *"Qui non laborat——"*

"Well, then," cried Jehan, interrupting him, "jollity for ever! I will game, I will fight, I will be a Voss-pot, I will frequent lights o' love."

[1] "He that will not work, neither shall he eat."

217

So saying, he threw up his cap, and snapped his fingers like casta-nets. The Archdeacon eyed him with gloomy look.

"Jehan," said he, "you are on a very slippery descent. Know you whither you are going?"

"To the tavern," said Jehan.

"The tavern leads to the pillory."

" 'Tis a lantern like any other; and it was perhaps the one with which Diogenes found his man."

"The pillory leads to the gallows."

"The gallows is a balance, which has a man at one end and all the world at the other. 'Tis a fine thing to be the man."

"The gallows leads to hell."

"That is a rousing fire."

"Jehan, Jehan, the end will be bad."

"The beginning at least will have been good."

At this moment the sound of a footfall was heard on the stairs.

"Silence!" said the Archdeacon; "here is Master Jacques. Hark ye, Jehan," added he, in a lower tone, "be sure not to mention what you shall have seen and heard here. Quick! hide yourself under this furnace, and don't so much as breathe."

The scholar crept under the furnace. Here an excellent idea occurred to him. "By the by, brother Claude, I must have a florin for not breathing."

"Silence! you shall have it."

"But give it me now."

"There, take it!" said the Archdeacon angrily, throwing him his pouch. Jehan crawled as far as he could under the furnace, and the door opened.

CHAPTER V

THE TWO MEN IN BLACK

THE person who entered had a black gown and a gloomy look. Our friend Jehan, who had contrived to arrange him-self in his hiding-place in such a manner as to hear and see all that passed, was struck at the first glance by the perfect sadness of the garb and the countenance of the visitor. A certain gentleness at the same time overspread that face; but it was the gentleness of a cat or a judge. The man was very grey, wrinkled, and hard upon sixty, with white eyebrows, hanging lip, and large hands. When Jehan saw that it was nobody, that is to say, in all probability some physician or magistrate, and that his nose was at a great distance from his mouth, a sure sign of stupidity, he shrank back in his hole, vexed at the prospect of having to pass an indefinite time in so confined a posture and in such scurvy company.

The Archdeacon meanwhile had not even risen to this personage. He motioned to him to be seated on a stool near the door, and after a few moments' silence, in which he seemed to be pursuing a previous meditation, he said with the tone of a patron to his client, "Good morrow, Master Jacques."

"Good morrow, master," replied the man in black.

In the two ways of pronouncing on the one hand that "Master Jacques," and on the other that "master" by way of eminence, there was so much difference as between "monseigneur" and "monsieur"; it clearly bespoke the teacher and the disciple.

"Well," resumed the Archdeacon, after another silence, which Master Jacques took care not to interrupt, "have you succeeded?"

"Alas! master," said the other, with a sorrowful smile, "I keep puffing away. More ashes than I want, but not an atom of gold."

A gesture of displeasure escaped Dom Claude.

"I was not talking of that, Master Jacques Charmolue, but of the proceedings against your sorcerer, Marc Cenaine, I think you called him, the butler of the Cour des Comptes. Doth he confess his guilt. Has the torture produced the desired effect?"

"Alas! no," replied Master Jacques, still with his sad smile; "we have not that consolation. The man is as hard as flint. We might boil him in the Swine Market before he would confess. However, we are sparing no pains to get at the truth; his joints are all dislocated. We are trying everything we can think of, but all to no purpose. Oh, he is a terrible fellow! He fairly puzzles me."

"Have you found nothing further in his house?"

"Yes," said Master Jacques, groping in his pouch; "this parchment. There are words upon it which pass our comprehension: and yet Monsieur Philippe Lheulier, the criminal advocate, knows something of Hebrew, which he picked up in the affair of the Jews at Brussels."

As he thus spoke Master Jacques unrolled the parchment.

"Give it to me," said the Archdeacon. He threw his eye over it. "Pure magic, Master Jacques!" he exclaimed. *"Emen-Hétan*—that is the cry of the witches on their arrival at their sabbath meetings. *Per ipsum, et cum ipso, et in ipso* [1]—that is the command which chains down the devil in hell. *Hax, pax, max*—that belongs to medicine—a form against the bite of mad dogs. Master Jacques, you are the King's Proctor in the Ecclesiastical Court: this parchment is abominable."

"We will apply the torture again. But here is something else," added Master Jacques, fumbling a second time in his pouch, "that we have found at Marc Cenaine's."

It was a vessel of the same family as those which covered Dom Claude's furnace. "Aha!" said the Archdeacon; "a crucible of alchemy!"

"I must confess," resumed Master Jacques, with his timid and awkward smile, "that I tried it upon the furnace, but with no better luck than with my own."

The Archdeacon examined the vessel. "What has he engraved on his crucible? *Och, och*—the word that drives away fleas. This Marc Cenaine is an ignoramus. I can easily believe that you will not make gold with this. 'Tis fit to put in your alcove in summer, and that is all."

"Talking of blunders," said the King's Proctor, "I have been examining the porch below before I came up: is your reverence quite sure that the one of the seven naked figures at the feet of Our Lady, with wings at his heels, is Mercury?"

"Certainly," replied the priest: "so it is stated by Augustin Nypho, the Italian doctor, who had a bearded demon that revealed everything to him. But we will go down presently, and I will explain this to you by the text."

"Many thanks, master," said Charmolue, with a very low obeisance. "But I had well-nigh forgotten—when doth it please you that I should order the young sorceress to be apprehended?"

"What sorceress?"

"That Bohemian, you know, who comes every day to dance in the Parvis, in despite of the prohibition of the official. She has a goat which is possessed, and has the devil's own horns, and reads, and

[1] "By itself, and with itself, and in itself."

The Two Men in Black

writes, and understands mathematics, and would be enough to bring all Bohemia to the gallows. The indictment is quite ready. A handsome creature, upon my soul, that dancer! The brightest black eyes! A pair of Egyptian carbuncles! When shall we begin?"

The Archdeacon turned pale as death. "I will tell you," stammered he, with a voice scarcely articulate. Then with an effort he added, "For the present go on with Marc Cenaine."

"Never fear," said Charmolue, smiling. "As soon as I get back I will have him strapped down again to the leathern bed. But 'tis a devil of a fellow: he tires Pierrat Torterue himself, and his hands are bigger than mine. The windlass will be the best thing to set to work upon him."

Dom Claude appeared to be absorbed in gloomy reverie. Suddenly turning to Charmolue, "Master Pierrat . . . Master Jacques, I would say, go on with Marc Cenaine."

"Ay, ay, Dom Claude. Poor man, he will have suffered a martyrdom. But then what an idea, to go to the Sabbath! a butler of the Cour des Comptes, who ought to know the text of Charlemagne's ordinance. As for the girl—Smelarda, as they call her—I shall await your orders— Ah, true! and when we are at the porch you will also explain to me what the gardener in low relief at the entrance of the church is meant for! Is it not the Sower? Hey, master! What think you?"

Dom Claude, engrossed by his own reflections, attended not to the speaker. Charmolue, following the direction of his eye, perceived that it was mechanically fixed upon a large spider's web stretched across the window. At that moment a giddy fly, attracted by the March sun, flew into the net and became entangled in it. At the shock given to his web, an enormous spider rushed forth from his central cell, and then at one leap sprang upon the fly, which he doubled up with his forelegs, while with his hideous sucker he attacked the head. "Poor fly!" said the Proctor, and raised his hand to rescue it. The Archdeacon, suddenly starting up, held back his arm with convulsive violence.

"Master Jacques!" cried he, "meddle not with fatality!"

The Proctor turned about in alarm: it seemed as if his arm was held by iron pincers. The eye of the priest was fixed, wild, glaring, and gazed intently upon the horrible little group of the fly and the spider.

"Oh, yes, yes!" resumed the priest, with a voice that seemed to proceed from his very bowels—"this is an emblem of the whole affair. —It is young, it flies about, it is merry, it seeks the open air, the spring sunshine, liberty. Oh, yes! But it is stopped at the fatal window; it is caught in the toils of the spider, the hideous spider! Poor dancing-girl! poor predestined fly! Be quiet, Master Jacques! it is fatality!—Alas, Claude! thou art the spider. Claude, thou art the fly too! Thou didst seek science, the light, the sunshine; thou desiredst only to reach the free air, the broad day light of eternal truth; but while darting toward the dazzling window, which opens into the other world, a world of brightness, intelligence, and science, blind fly, silly doctor, thou didst not perceive that subtle spider's web, spread by Fate between the light and thee; thou rushedst into it, and now, with mangled head and broken wings, thou strugglest in the iron grip of fatality!—Master Jacques! Master Jacques! let the spider alone!"

"I assure you," said Charmolue, who stared at him without comprehending his meaning, "that I will not meddle with it. But, for mercy's sake, master, loose my arm! you have a hand like a vice."

The Archdeacon heard him not. "Oh, fool! fool," he again began, without taking his eyes for a moment off the window. "And if thou couldst have broken through those formidable meshes with thy delicate wings dost thou imagine that thou couldst then have attained the light? How wouldst thou have passed that glass which is beyond it, that transparent obstacle, that wall of crystal harder than brass, which separates all philosophies from truth? Oh, vanity of science! how many sages come fluttering from afar to dash their heads against it! how many systems come buzzing to rush pell-mell against this eternal window!"

He paused. The concluding reflections, which had insensibly diverted his mind from himself to science, appeared to have restored him to a degree of composure. Jacques Charmolue brought him back completely to a feeling of reality by asking him this question: "By the by, master, when will you come and help me to make gold? I am not lucky at it."

The Archdeacon shook his head with a bitter smile. "Master Jacques," he replied, "read the *Dialogus de Energia et Operatione*

Dæmonum,[1] by Michael Psellus. What we are about is not absolutely innocent."

"Speak lower, master," said Charmolue. "I thought as much myself. But a man may be allowed to dabble a little in hermetics when he is but King's Proctor in the Ecclesiastical Court at thirty crowns Tournois per annum. Only let us speak lower."

At that moment sounds resembling those made in mastication, proceeding from beneath the furnace, struck the alarmed ear of Charmolue.

"What is that?" he asked.

It was the scholar who, cramped in his hiding-place and heartily weary of it, had there found a hard crust and a cube of mouldy cheese, and fallen foul of them without ceremony, by way of consolation and breakfast. As he was very hungry he made a great noise, and smacked his chops so audibly at every munch as to excite alarm in the Proctor.

" 'Tis only my cat," said the Archdeacon sharply, "regaling herself under there with a mouse."

This explanation satisfied Charmolue. "In fact, master," he replied, with a respectful smile, "every great philosopher has had his familiar animal. As Servius says, you know: *Nullus enim locus sine genio est.*" [2]

Dom Claude, apprehensive of some new prank of Jehan's, reminded his worthy disciple that they had some figures on the porch to study together; and both left the cell, to the great relief of the scholar, who began seriously to fear that his knees and his chin would grow together.

CHAPTER VI

RESULTS OF SEVEN OATHS SWORN IN THE OPEN STREET

TE Deum laudamus!" exclaimed Master Jehan, sallying forth from his hole; "the two screech-owls are gone. Och! och! —Hax! pax! max!—the fleas!—the mad dogs!—the devil! —I've had quite enough of their talk! my head rings like a belfry.

1 *"Dialogue upon the Powers and Works of Demons."*
2 "There is no place without its genius."

The Hunchback of Notre-Dame

Let us be off too and turn my good brother's moneys into bottles!"

He cast a look of kindness and admiration into the interior of the precious pouch, adjusted his dress, wiped his buskins, brushed the ashes from his sleeves, whistled a tune, cut a caper, looked round to see if there was anything else in the cell that he could make free with, picked up here and there on the furnace some amulet of glass, fit to be given by way of trinket to Isabeau la Thierrye, opened the door which his brother as a last indulgence had left unlocked, and which he in his turn left open as the last trick he could play him, and descended the winding stairs, hopping like a bird.

He stamped with his foot when he found himself again on the ground. "Oh, good and honourable pavement of Paris!" he exclaimed—"cursed stairs that would give a breathing to the angels of Jacob's ladder themselves! What was I thinking of to squeeze myself into that stone gimlet which pierces the sky, and all to eat mouldy cheese and to see the steeples of Paris through a loophole!"

He had moved but a few steps when he perceived the two screech-owls, *alias* Dom Claude and Master Jacques Charmolue, contemplating one of the sculptures of the porch. He approached them on tiptoe, and heard the Archdeacon say in a very low tone to his companion, "it was Guillaume de Paris who had a Job engraved upon that stone of the colour of lapis lazuli, and gilt on the edges. Job represents the philosopher's stone."

"What is that to me?" said Jehan to himself—"I have got the purse."

At this moment he heard a loud and sonorous voice behind him pour forth a formidable volley of oaths: *"Sang Dieu! Ventre-Dieu! Bedieu! Corps de Dieu! Nombril de Belzébuth! Nom d'un pape! Corne et tonnerre!"*

"Upon my soul," cried Jehan, "that can be nobody but my friend Captain Phœbus!"

The name Phœbus struck the ear of the Archdeacon at the moment when he was explaining to the King's Proctor the dragon hiding his tail in a bath whence issue smoke and a royal head. Dom Claude shuddered, stopped short, to the great surprise of Charmolue, turned round, and saw his brother Jehan accosting a tall officer at the door of the Gondelaurier mansion.

It was in fact Captain Phœbus de Châteaupers. He was leaning against the angle of the house and swearing like a pagan.

224

Results of Seven Oaths

"By my fay, Captain Phœbus," said Jehan grasping his hand, "you swear with marvellous emphasis."

"Blood and thunder!" replied the Captain.

"Blood and thunder to you!" rejoined the scholar. "But, I say, gentle Captain, what has occasioned this overflow of fair words?"

"I beg your pardon, my good comrade Jehan," cried Phœbus, shaking him by the hand, "a horse at the top of his speed cannot stop short. Now, I was swearing at full gallop. I have just come from those affected prudes, and whenever I leave them I have my throat full of oaths; I am forced to turn them out or they would choke me outright—blood and thunder!"

"Will you come and drink with me?" asked the scholar.

This proposal pacified the Captain. "I fain would," said he, "but I have no money."

"Well, but I have."

"Aha! let us see!"

Jehan exhibited the pouch to the wondering gaze of the Captain. Meanwhile the Archdeacon, who had left Charmolue quite astounded, had approached and stopped within a few paces of them, watching both without their being aware of it, so entirely was their attention engrossed by the pouch.

"A purse in your pocket, Jehan," cried Phœbus, "is like the moon in a bucket of water. You see it, but it is not there: 'tis only the shadow. Nothing but pebbles in it, I wager."

"There are the pebbles that I pave my pocket with," replied Jehan drily; and so saying he emptied the pouch upon a post close by, with the air of a Roman saving his country.

"By heaven!" muttered Phœbus; "real moneys! 'tis absolutely dazzling."

Jehan retained his grave and dignified attitude. A few liards had rolled into the mud; the Captain in his enthusiasm stooped to pick them up. He counted the pieces, and, turning with a solemn look toward his companion, "Do you know, Jehan," said he, "that there are twenty-three sous Parisis? Whom have you had the luck to lighten last night in the Rue Coupe-Gueule?"

Jehan threw back the long light hair that curled about his face, and half closed his disdainful eyes. "'Tis a good thing," said he, "to have a brother who is an archdeacon and a simpleton."

"*Corne de Dieu!*" exclaimed Phœbus. "The worthy fellow!"

The Hunchback of Notre-Dame

"Let us go and drink," said Jehan.

The two friends then bent their steps toward the tavern known by the sign of La Pomme d'Eve. It is superfluous to say that they had first picked up the money, and that the Archdeacon followed them.

The Archdeacon followed them with wild and gloomy look. Was this the Phœbus whose accursed name had, ever since his interview with Gringoire, haunted all his thoughts? He knew not, but at any rate it was a Phœbus, and this magic name sufficed to lure the Archdeacon to follow the two reckless companions with stealthy step, listening to their conversation and watching their slightest gestures with intense anxiety. Indeed, nothing was more easy than to hear all they said, so loud was the tone in which they carried on their conversation about duels and harlots, flagons and drunken frolics.

At the turning of a street the sound of a tambourine was wafted to them from a crossing at a little distance. Dom Claude heard the officer say to his brother, "Blood and thunder! let us quicken our pace!"

"Why, Phœbus?"

"I am afraid lest the Bohemian should see me."

"What Bohemian?"

"The girl with the goat."

"La Smeralda?"

"The same, Jehan. I always forget her devil of a name. Let us make haste: she would know me again. I don't wish that girl to speak to me in the street."

"Are you then acquainted with her, Phœbus?"

Here the Archdeacon saw Phœbus grin, stoop to Jehan's ear, and whisper a few words in it. The Captain then burst into a loud laugh, and tossed his head with a triumphant air.

"Indeed!" said Jehan.

"Upon my soul!" replied Phœbus.

"To-night?"

"This very night."

"Are you sure she will come?"

"You must be silly, Jehan. Not the least doubt of it."

"Captain Phœbus, you are a lucky fellow!"

The Archdeacon heard every syllable of this conversation. His teeth chattered. A shudder, visible to the eye, thrilled his whole

226

frame. He paused for a moment; leaned against a post, like a drunken man, and again followed the two boon companions.

CHAPTER VII

THE GOBLIN-MONK

THE celebrated tavern, called La Pomme d'Eve, was situated in the Université, at the corner of Rue de la Rondelle and Rue du Bâtonnier. It was a very spacious but very low room, with a double roof, the central return of which was supported by a massive wooden pillar painted yellow; the floor covered with tables, bright tin jugs hanging up against the wall, plenty of topers, plenty of disreputable women, a window next to the street, a vine at the door, and over the door a creaking square of sheet-iron, upon which were painted a woman and an apple, rusted with rain and turning upon an iron spike. This kind of weathercock, which looked toward the pavement, was the sign of the house.

It was nightfall, and the tavern, full of candles, glared at a distance like a forge in the dark; the sounds of carousal, swearing, altercation, mixed with the jingle of glasses, issued from the broken panes. Through the haze which covered the window, in consequence of the heat of the room, might be discerned swarms of confused figures, from which burst from time to time roars of laughter. The pedestrians whose business called them that way passed this noisy window without casting their eyes on it; but at intervals some little ragged urchin would stand on tiptoe to look in, and shout the old doggrel couplet with which it was usual in those days to greet drunkards:

> Aux Houls,
> Saouls, saouls, saouls!

One man, however, kept incessantly walking to and fro before the noisy tavern, narrowly watching all goers and comers, and never moving farther from it than a sentry from his box. He was muffled up in a cloak to the very eyes. This cloak he had just bought at a shop contiguous to the tavern, no doubt as a protection from the cold of the March evenings, perhaps also to conceal his dress. From time to time he paused before the window, looked through the small lozenge-shaped panes bordered with lead, listened, and stamped.

The Hunchback of Notre-Dame

At length the tavern door opened. It was this that he appeared to be waiting for. Two persons who had been drinking there came out. The ray of light which escaped at the door fell for a moment upon their jovial faces. The man in the cloak stationed himself under a porch on the other side of the street to watch them.

"The clock has just struck seven," exclaimed one of the topers; "that is the time for my appointment."

"I tell you," replied his companion, with an articulation far from distinct, "that I don't live in the Rue des Mauvaises Paroles—*indignus qui inter verba mala habitat*.[1] I lodge in the Rue Jean-Pain-Mollet. You are more horned than a unicorn, if you say to the contrary."

"Jehan, my friend, you are drunk," said the other.

His companion rejoined, staggering, "That is what you are pleased to say, Phœbus; but it is proved that Plato had the profile of a hound."

The reader has no doubt already recognized in the two jolly topers the captain and the scholar. The man who was watching them in the dark appeared also to have recognized them; for with slow step he followed all the zigzags into which the Captain was drawn by his companion. The former, more inured to tipling, was none the worse for liquor. The man in the cloak, listening to them attentively, was enabled to catch the whole of the following interesting conversation.

"Body o' Bacchus! Mr. Bachelor, try to walk straight; you know I must leave you. It is seven o'clock, I tell you, and I have an appointment."

"Then go, leave me!—I see the stars and darts of fire. You are like the castle of Dampmartin, bursting with laughter."

"By my grandmother's warts, Jehan, the nonsense you talk is too absurd. By the by, Jehan, have you any money left?"

"Mr. Rector, there is no fault—the little shambles, *parva boucheria*."

"Jehan, my friend Jehan, you know I have an assignation with that damsel at the end of the Pont Saint-Michel. Surely, Jehan, we have not drunk all the parson's money. See if you have not one Parisis left."

[1] "He is unworthy who dwelleth among evil words."

The Goblin-Monk

"The consciousness of having spent the other hours to good purpose is an excellent sauce to the table."

"Fire and fury! A truce to cross purposes, Jehan. Tell me, have you any money left? I must have some, or, by heaven, I will rifle your pockets."

"Why, sir, the Rue Galiache is a street that has the Rue de la Verrerie at one end, and the Rue de la Tixeranderie at the other."

"Quite right, my dear friend Jehan, so it has. But, for heaven's sake! rally your senses. It is seven o'clock, and I want but one sou Parisis."

"Silence, now—silence to the song, and attention to the chorus:

> "When it shall befal the cats
> To be eaten up by rats,
> Then the King of Arras city
> Shall be master—more's the pity!
> When at St John's tide the sea,
> Wide and warm although it be,
> Shall be frozen firm and fast,
> As if done by winter's blast;
> Then the folks from Arras, they
> O'er the ice shall trudge away."

"Scholar of Antichrist!" cried Phœbus, "may thy brains be dashed out with thine own books!" At the same time he gave the intoxicated student a violent push which sent him reeling against the wall, where he presently sunk gently upon the pavement of Philip Augustus. From a relic of that brotherly compassion which is never wholly banished from the heart of a toper, Phœbus rolled Jehan with his foot upon one of those pillows of the poor which Providence keeps ready in the corners of all the streets of Paris, and which the wealthy disdainfully stigmatize with the name of dunghills. The Captain placed Jehan's head on an inclined plane of cabbage-stalks, and the scholar instantly began snoring in a magnificent bass. Yet was not the Captain's heart wholly free from animosity. "So much the worse for thee if the devil's cart picks thee up as it passes!" said he to the sleeping scholar, and away he went.

The man in the cloak, who had kept following him, paused for a moment before the helpless youth, as if undecided what to do:

then, heaving a deep sigh, he continued to follow the Captain.

Like them we will leave Jehan sleeping beneath the canopy of heaven, and speed after them, if it so please the reader.

On reaching the Rue Saint-André-des-Arcs Captain Phœbus perceived that some one was following him. Chancing to turn his eyes, he saw a kind of shadow creeping behind him along the walls. He stopped; the figure stopped: he walked on; the figure walked on too. He felt but little alarm at this discovery. "Pooh!" said he to himself, "I have not a single sou."

He halted in front of the college of Autun, where he had commenced what he called his studies, close to the statue of Cardinal Pierre Bertrand, on the right of the porch, and looked round him. The street was absolutely deserted. Nothing was to be seen but the figure, which approached him with slow steps, so slow that he had abundant time to observe that it had a cloak and a hat. When very near to him it stopped and remained motionless as the statue of Cardinal Bertrand; intently fixing upon him, however, a pair of eyes glaring with that vague light which issues at night from those of a cat.

The Captain was brave, and would not have cared a rush for a robber with a cudgel in his fist. But this walking statue, this petrified man, thrilled him with horror. There were at that time in circulation a number of stories of a goblin-monk who haunted at night the streets of Paris; these stories crowded confusedly upon his memory. He stood stupefied for some minutes, and at length broke silence by a forced laugh. "If you are a robber, as I hope," said he, "you are somewhat like a heron attacking a nutshell. I am the hopeful sprig of a ruined family, my dear fellow. Seek some better game. In the chapel of that college there is some wood of the true Cross, which is kept in the treasure-room."

The hand of the figure was stretched from beneath the cloak, and grasped the arm of Phœbus with the force of an eagle's talons. "Captain Phœbus de Châteaupers!" said the spectre at the same moment.

"What, the devil!" cried Phœbus, "you know my name!"

"Not only your name," replied the mysterious stranger in a sepulchral tone; "you have an assignation this evening."

"I have," answered the astounded Phœbus.

The Goblin-Monk

"At the hour of seven."

"In a quarter of an hour."

"At Falourdel's at the Pont Saint-Michel."

"Precisely so."

"To meet a woman."

"I plead guilty."

"Whose name is . . ."

"La Smeralda," said Phœbus gaily, having by degrees recovered his levity.

At that name the spectre shook the Captain's arm with violence. "Captain Phœbus de Châteaupers, thou liest!"

Whoever could have seen at that moment the flushed face of the Captain, the backward bound which he made with such force as to disengage his arm from the grip in which it was held, the fierce look with which he clapped his hand to the hilt of his sword, and the motionless attitude of the cloaked figure—whoever had witnessed this would have been frightened. It was something like the battle between Don Juan and the statue.

"Hell and fury!" cried the Captain. "That is a word to which the ear of a Châteaupers is not accustomed. Thou darest not repeat it."

"Thou liest!" said the spectre drily.

The Captain gnashed his teeth. Goblin-monk, phantom, superstitious tales—were all forgotten at the moment. In his eyes it was but a man and an insult. "Bravely said!" stammered he, half choked with rage. He drew his sword, and in a faltering voice— for rage makes one tremble, as well as fear—cried: "Here! on the spot! this very moment! draw—draw! The blood of one of us must dye this pavement!"

Meanwhile the other neither flinched nor stirred. When he saw his adversary on guard and ready for the combat: "Captain Phœbus," said he, in a tone tremulous with vexation; "you forget your engagement."

In men like Phœbus gusts of passion are like boiling milk, the ebullition of which a drop of cold water is sufficient to allay. At those few simple words the Captain dropped the weapon which glistened in his hand.

"Captain," continued the stranger, "to-morrow, the day after to-

231

morrow, a month, a year, ten years hence, you will find me ready to cut your throat; but first go to your assignation."

"In fact," said Phœbus, as if seeking to capitulate with himself; "a sword and a girl are two delightful things to encounter in a meeting; but I don't see why I should give up one for the other when I may have both."

He returned his sword to the scabbard.

"Go to your assignation," repeated the unknown.

"Many thanks, sir, for your courtesy," replied Phœbus, with some embarrassment. "It is very true that it will be time enough to-morrow to slash and cut buttonholes in Father Adam's doublet. I am beholden to you for allowing me one more agreeable quarter of an hour. I did hope, to be sure, to put you to bed in the kennel, and yet be in time for my appointment, especially as in such cases it is genteel to make the damsels wait a little. But you appear to be a hearty fellow, and it is safest to put off our meeting till to-morrow. So I shall go to my assignation, which is for the hour of seven, as you know."—Here Phœbus tapped his forehead. "Ah! I forgot! I must have money, and I have not a single sou left."

"Here is money," said the stranger.

Phœbus felt the cold hand of the unknown slip into his a large piece of money. He could not help taking the coin, and pressing that hand.

"By heaven!" he exclaimed, "you are a good fellow!"

"One condition!" said the stranger. "Prove to me that I was wrong, and that you spoke the truth. Conceal me in some corner, where I may see whether the girl is really the same whose name you mentioned."

"Oh!" replied Phœbus, "that will make no difference to me."

"Come along, then," rejoined the figure.

"At your service," said the Captain. "For aught I know, you may be the devil *in propria persona:* but let us be good friends to-night; to-morrow I will pay you my debts, both of the purse and the sword."

They walked away with hasty steps. In a few minutes the noise of the river apprised them that they were on the Pont Saint-Michel, at that time covered with houses. "I will first introduce you," said Phœbus to his companion, "and then go and fetch the wench, who is to wait for me near the Petit Châtelet." That companion made no reply; since they had been walking side by side he had not uttered a word. Phœbus stopped before a low door, against which he kicked violently. A light glimmered through the crevices of the door. "Who's there?" cried a mumbling voice.—"*Corps-Dieu! Tête-Dieu! Ventre-Dieu!*" replied the Captain. The door instantly opened, and discovered an old woman and a lamp, both of which trembled. The hag was bent almost double, and dressed in rags. Her head shook, and her hands, face, and neck were covered with wrinkles. She had very small eyes; her lips receded owing to the loss of her teeth, and all round her mouth she had long white hairs resembling the whiskers of a cat. The interior of her dwelling corresponded in appearance with herself. The walls were of plaster; the ceiling was formed of the black rafters and floor of the room above; the fireplace was dismantled, and every corner displayed a drapery of cobwebs. Two or three rickety tables and stools occupied the middle of the floor; a dirty boy was playing in the ashes, and at the farther end the stairs, or rather ladder, led up to a trap-door in the ceiling. On entering this den, the Captain's mysterious companion drew his cloak up to his eyes, while Phœbus kept swearing like a Turk. He put into the hand of the old woman the coin which had been given to him by the stranger. The crone, who called him, "Monseigneur" at every other word, deposited the crown in a drawer. While her back was turned the ragged urchin rose from the hearth, slily went to the drawer, took out the piece of money, and put a dry leaf which he had pulled from a faggot in its place.

The hag beckoned to the two gentlemen, as she called them, to follow, and ascended the ladder before them. On reaching the room above she set the lamp upon a coffer; and Phœbus opened a door that led to a dark closet. "This way, my good fellow," said he to his companion. The man in the cloak complied without uttering a word; the door closed upon him; he heard Phœbus bolt it, and a moment afterward go downstairs with the old woman. The light disappeared along with them.

The Hunchback of Notre-Dame

CHAPTER VIII

UTILITY OF WINDOWS LOOKING TOWARD THE RIVER

CLAUDE FROLLO—for we presume that the reader, more intelligent than Phœbus, has discovered that the spectre-monk was no other than the Archdeacon—Claude Frollo groped about for a few moments in the dark hole in which the Captain had bolted him. It was in fact a loft such as builders sometimes leave in the roof above the outer walls of a house. The vertical section of this kennel, as Phœbus had aptly called it, would have given a triangle. It had neither window nor loophole, and the inclined plane of the roof would not permit a person to stand upright in it. Claude therefore crouched in the dust and the mortar that crunched under him. His brain seemed to be on fire; but what passed at that moment in the dark soul of the Archdeacon none but God and himself could ever know.

In what fatal order did he arrange in imagination La Esmeralda, Phœbus, Jacques Charmolue, his young brother, whom he so loved yet whom he had left in the mud, his Archdeacon's gown, his reputation perhaps, staked as it was at Falourdel's—all these images, all these adventures? I cannot tell. But it is certain that these ideas formed in his mind a horrible group.

He waited a full quarter of an hour. To him this interval appeared an age. All at once he heard the stairs creak; some one was coming up. The trap-door opened; a light was discernible. In the crazy door of the loft there was a crevice to which he applied his eye. It was wide enough to allow him to see all that passed in the adjoining room. The hag first made her appearance, with the lamp in her hand, then Phœbus, turning up his whiskers, then a third face, that of the beautiful and graceful Esmeralda. The priest saw it rise above the floor like a dazzling apparition. Claude trembled; a cloud darkened his eyes; his arteries beat with violence; he was stunned with a rushing as of a mighty wind; everything about him seemed to whirl round; and presently sight and hearing forsook him.

When he came to himself Phœbus and La Esmeralda were alone,

Utility of Windows

sitting on the wooden coffer by the side of the lamp, which threw a strong light upon their two youthful faces, and enabled the Archdeacon to discover a truckle-bed at the farther extremity of the garret.

Beside this bed was a window, through the panes of which, broken like a spider's web by a shower of rain, he could see a patch of sky, and the moon couched on a bed of light fleecy clouds.

The damsel was flushed, confused, palpitating. Her long downcast eyelashes shaded her crimsoned cheeks. The face of the officer, to which she durst not raise her eyes, was radiant with delight. Unconsciously, and with a charming semblance of childishness, she traced unmeaning lines on the lid of the coffer with the tip of her finger, and then looked at the finger which had been thus employed. Her feet could not be seen; the little goat was cowering upon them.

An amorous chit-chat is a very commonplace sort of thing. It is a perpetual *I love you*—a phrase musical enough to the parties concerned, but exceedingly bald and insipid to indifferent persons, when not adorned with a few *fiorituri*. Claude, however, was not an indifferent listener.

"Oh! do not despise me, Monseigneur Phœbus!" said the girl, without raising her eyes. "I fear that what I am doing is wrong."

"Despise you, my pretty dear!" replied the officer, with a consequential air of gallantry; "despise you! and why?"

"For having followed you."

"I perceive, my beauty, that we don't understand one another. I ought, by rights, not to despise you, but to hate you."

The girl looked at him in alarm. "Hate me! what, then, have I done?"

"For wanting so much wooing."

"Alas!" said she . . . "I am breaking a vow . . . I shall never find my parents again . . . The charm will lose its virtue. But no matter! What need have I at present of father or mother?"

As she thus spoke, she fixed on the Captain her large dark eyes, moist with delight and tenderness.

"Devil take me if I understand!" exclaimed Phœbus.

La Esmeralda was silent for a moment; a tear then trickled from her eye, a sigh burst from her lips, and she said, "Oh, monseigneur, I love you!"

The Hunchback of Notre-Dame

There was round this young girl such an odour of chastity, such a charm of virtue, that Phœbus did not feel quite at ease by her side. This confession, however, emboldened him. "You do love me!" said he, with transport, throwing his arm round the waist of the Egyptian, having only waited for such an occasion.

"Phœbus," resumed the Bohemian, gently removing from her waist the tenacious hand of the Captain, "you are kind, you are generous, you are handsome; you saved me, who am but a poor foundling. I have long been dreaming about an officer saving my life. It was you that I dreamt of before I knew you; the officer of my dreams had a handsome uniform like you, the look of a gentleman, and a sword. Your name is Phœbus; 'tis a fine name; I love your name, I love your sword. Draw your sword, Phœbus—let me look at it."

"Strange girl!" said the Captain, unsheathing his sword with a smile. The Egyptian looked at the handle, and at the blade, examined with especial curiosity the cipher on the hilt, and kissed the weapon, saying, "You belong to a brave man."

As she bent over it Phœbus availed himself of this opportunity to imprint a kiss upon her beautiful neck. The girl suddenly raised her head, with a face crimsoned like a cherry. The priest gnashed his teeth in the dark.

"Captain Phœbus," the Egyptian again began, "let me talk to you. Just stand up and walk, and let me hear your spurs rattle. Gemini! how handsome you are!"

The Captain rose in compliance with her wish, and said in a tone of rebuke, yet with a smile of satisfaction, "Why, how childish you are! . . . But, my dear, did you ever see me in my State uniform?"

"Ah, no!" replied she.

"You would say that is handsome."

Phœbus went and again seated himself beside her, but much closer than before.

"Hark you, my dear . . ."

The Egyptian patted his lips with her pretty hand, with the grace and playfulness of a child. "No, no, I won't hearken to you. Do you love me? I want you to tell me if you love me."

"Do I love thee, angel of my life?" exclaimed the Captain, half sinking upon his knee. "I love thee, and never loved any but thee."

The Captain had so often repeated this declaration in many a similar conjuncture, that he brought it out without boggling or making a single blunder. At this impassioned apostrophe the Egyptian raised her eyes with a look of angelic happiness toward the dirty ceiling which here usurped the place of heaven. "Oh!" she softly murmured, "this is the moment at which one ought to die!"

Phœbus thought it a seasonable moment for stealing another kiss, which inflicted fresh torment on the miserable Archdeacon in his hiding-place.

"To die!" cried the amorous Captain. "What are you talking of, my angel! Why, 'tis the very time to live, or Jupiter is a cheat! Die at such a moment as this! A good joke, by the devil's horns . . . No, no, that won't do. Hark ye, my dear Similar . . . I beg pardon, Esmenarda . . . but you have such a prodigiously outlandish name, that I can't beat it into my head."

"Good God!" said the poor girl, "and I thought it a pretty name just because of its outlandishness. But, since you dislike it, I will change it to whatever you please."

"Nay, my darling, don't think about such trifles! 'tis a name one must get used to, that's all. When once I have learned it by heart, I shall say it offhand. But listen, my dear Similar, I passionately adore you. I cannot tell how much I love you; and I know a damsel who is bursting with rage about it."

"Who is that?" inquired the jealous girl.

"That is nothing to the purpose," said Phœbus. "Do you love me?"

"Do I?" said she.

"Well, that is enough. You shall see how I love you too. May the great devil Neptunus spit me upon his prong, if I don't make you the happiest girl in the world! We will have a pretty little cot somewhere or other. My archers shall parade under your windows. They are all on horseback, and Captain Mignon's are fools to them. I will take you to the Grange de Rully—'tis a magnificent sight. Eighty thousand stand of arms; thirty thousand suits of bright armour, cuirasses or brigandines; the sixty-seven banners of the trades; the standards of the Parliament, the Chambre des Comptes, the workers of the Mint—in short, a devil of a train. I will take you to see the lions in the Hôtel du Roi, which all the women are very fond of."

For some moments the damsel, absorbed in her own charming

thoughts, was drinking in the intoxicating tones of his voice, without attending to the meaning of his words.

"Oh! you shall be so happy!" continued the Captain, at the same time examining the buckle of her belt.

"What are you about?" said she sharply, roused from her reverie.

"Nothing," replied Phœbus; "I was only saying that you must lay aside this strange mountebank dress when you are with me."

"When I am with you, my Phœbus!" said the girl affectionately; and again she became silent and thoughtful. All at once she turned toward him. "Phœbus," said she, with an expression of infinite love, "instruct me in thy religion."

"My religion!" cried the Captain, bursting into a laugh. "I instruct you in my religion! Blood and thunder! What do you want with my religion?"

"That we may be married," replied the Egyptian.

The Captain's face assumed a mixed expression of surprise, disdain, and licentious passion. "Pooh!" said he; "what should we marry for?"

The Bohemian turned pale, and sorrowfully drooped her head.

"My sweet one," resumed Phœbus tenderly, "these are silly notions. Of what use is marriage? Do people love one another the less for not having mangled Latin in the shop of a priest?" As he thus spoke in his kindest tones, his eye glistened more and more.

Dom Claude, meanwhile, was watching all that passed. The planks of which the door was made were so decayed as to leave large chasms for his hawk's eye. The priest quivered and boiled at the scene. The sight of the beauteous girl thus *tête-à-tête* with the ardent officer seemed to infuse molten lead into his veins. An extraordinary commotion took place within him. Whoever could have seen, at that moment, the face of the unhappy man closely pressed against the crevices of the door, would have taken it for the face of a tiger looking through the bars of a cage at some jackal devouring a gazelle. His eye flamed like a candle through the chasms.

All at once Phœbus snatched away the neckerchief of the Egyptian. The poor girl, who had continued pale and thoughtful, started up, and hastily retreated from the enterprising officer. Casting a glance at her bare shoulders, blushing, confused, and dumb with shame, she crossed her two finely turned arms over her bosom to conceal it. But for the flush that crimsoned her cheeks, whoever had seen her thus silent, motionless, and with downcast eyes, would have taken her for a statue of Modesty.

This attack of the Captain's upon her toilet had uncovered the mysterious amulet which she wore about her neck.

"What is that?" said he, seizing this pretext for approaching the beautiful creature whom his vehemence had just alarmed.

"Touch it not," answered she sharply; "'tis my protector. It is this that will enable me to find my family, if I do nothing unworthy of it. Oh leave me, Captain, I beseech you! Ah, Mother! my poor Mother! where art thou? Help, help thy child!—Pray, Captain Phœbus, give me my neckerchief!"

"Oh, mademoiselle!" said Phœbus, stepping back, in a tone of indifference, "I see plainly that you love me not."

"Not love him!" exclaimed the unhappy girl, at the same time clinging to the Captain, and making him sit down by her. "Not love thee, my Phœbus! Cruel man to say so! Wouldst thou break my heart? . . . I am thine. Of what use to me is the amulet! what need have I of a mother! to me thou art father and mother, since I love thee! Phœbus, my beloved Phœbus, look at me; thou wilt not put away from thee one who comes to place herself in thy hands! My soul, my life, my all, are thine. So I am but loved, I shall be the proudest and the happiest of women. And when I am grown old and ugly, Phœbus, when I shall be no longer fit for thee to love, then permit me to be thy servant. Others shall then embroider scarfs for thee, but thou wilt let me clean thy boots and thy spurs, and brush thy uniform. Thou wilt grant me that indulgence, wilt thou not, my Phœbus? Meanwhile take me; let me belong to thee, and be the only object of thy love! We Egyptians want nothing else but air and love."

As she thus spoke she threw her arms round the neck of the officer, and with a sweet smile and tearful eye fixed upon him a beseeching look. The Captain pressed his burning lips to her bosom.

All at once above the head of the Captain she beheld another head —a livid, green, convulsive face, with the look of one of the damned; close to this face was a hand holding a dagger. It was the face and the hand of the priest. Unperceived by them, he had contrived to break open the crazy door, and there he was!

The girl was struck speechless and motionless with horror by this terrible apparition; like a dove raising her head at the moment when a falcon with glaring eyes is looking into her nest. She had not even the power to shriek. She saw the dagger descend upon the Captain, and rise again reeking. "Perdition!" he exclaimed, and fell. She swooned.

At the moment when her eyes closed, and her senses were forsaking her, she thought that she felt a kiss, burning as a hot iron, impressed upon her lips. On coming to herself, she was surrounded by soldiers belonging to the watch. The Captain was carried away bathed in his blood. The priest was gone. The window at the farther end of the chamber, which looked toward the river, was wide open. A cloak, supposed to belong to the officer, was picked up, and she heard the men saying to one another: " 'Tis a sorceress who has stabbed a captain."

BOOK VII

CHAPTER I

THE COIN TRANSFORMED INTO A DRY LEAF

FOR upward of a month Gringoire and the whole of the crew in the Cour des Miracles had been in a state of extreme anxiety. La Esmeralda was missing. They knew neither what had become of her, which sorely grieved the Duke of Egypt and his vagabond subjects, nor what had become of her goat, which redoubled Gringoire's sorrow. One night the girl had disappeared, and all researches had proved bootless; no traces of her could be discovered. Some of the mendicant tribe had told Gringoire that they had met her that evening, near the Pont Saint-Michel, walking along with an officer; but this husband after the fashion of Bohemia was an incredulous philosopher; and, besides, he knew better than anyone else how well his wife could defend herself. He had had abundant opportunities of judging what invincible chastity resulted from the two combined virtues of the amulet and the Egyptian, and had mathematically calculated the resistance of that chastity to the second power. He was therefore quite easy on that point.

But for this very reason he was the more puzzled to account for her disappearance. So deeply did he take it to heart that he would have fretted the flesh off his bones, had it been possible for him to become thinner than he was. He had forgotten everything else, even his literary pursuits, not excepting his great work *De Figuris Regularibus et Irregularibus,*[1] which he intended to get printed with the first money he should have. For he was over head and ears in love with printing, ever since he had seen the *Didaskalon* of Hugo Saint-Victor, printed with the celebrated types of Vindelin of Spire.

One day, while sorrowfully passing the Tournelle, a prison for criminals, he perceived a concourse of people about one of the doors of the Palace of Justice. "What is going forward here?" he asked a young man who was coming out.

"I know not, sir," answered the young man. "I am told that

[1] *Concerning Regular and Irregular Figures.*

they are trying a woman for murdering an officer of the King's Ordnance. As there seems to be something of sorcery in the business the Bishop and the official have interfered, and my brother, the Archdeacon of Josas, devotes all his time to it. I wanted to speak to him, but could not get at him for the crowd, which vexed me exceedingly, as I am in great need of money."

"Alas, sir!" said Gringoire, "I wish it was in my power to lend you some; but my breeches are all in holes, not with crowns or any other coin, I can assure you."

He durst not tell the young man that he knew his brother, the Archdeacon, whom he had never called upon since the scene in the church—a neglect of which he felt ashamed.

The scholar went his way, and Gringoire followed the crowd who were ascending the great staircase. In his estimation there was nothing like a criminal trial for dispelling melancholy, the judges being in general so amusingly stupid. The people with whom he had mingled moved on and elbowed one another in silence. After a slow and tiresome shuffling along an endless passage, which ran winding through the palace like the intestinal canal of the old structure, he arrived at a low door opening into a hall, which, from his tall stature, he was enabled to overlook above the undulating heads of the crowd.

The hall was spacious and dark, which made it appear still larger. The day was declining; the tall pointed windows admitted but a faint light, which expired before it reached the vaulted roof, an enormous trellis of carved woodwork, the thousand figures of which seemed to move confusedly in the dark. There were already several lighted candles here and there upon the tables, which threw their rays upon the heads of clerks poring over heaps of papers. The anterior part of the hall was occupied by the crowd; on the right and left were lawyers seated at tables; at the farther end, upon a raised platform, a great number of judges, men with immovable and sinister-looking faces, the last rows of whom were scarcely discernible for the darkness. The walls were sprinkled with abundance of fleur-de-lis. A large crucifix was indistinctly seen above the judges, and on every side an array of pikes and halberts, which the light of the candles seemed to tip with fire.

"Sir," said Gringoire to one of his neighbours, "who are all those persons ranged in rows yonder, like prelates in council?"

The Coin Transformed

"Sir," answered the neighbour, "those are the counsellors of the great chamber on the right, and the counsellors of inquiry on the left; the masters in black gowns, and the messires in red ones."

"And who is that great red porpoise above them?" inquired Gringoire.

"That is Monsieur the President."

"And those rams behind him?" continued Gringoire, who, as we have already observed, was not fond of magistrates; perhaps owing to the grudge which he bore the Palace of Justice ever since his dramatic miscarriage.

"They are the Masters of Requests of the King's household."

"And that boar in front of them?"

"The clerk to the Court of Parliament."

"And that crocodile, on the right?"

"Master Philippe Lheulier, Advocate Extraordinary to the King."

"And that great black cat on the left?"

"Master Jacques Charmolue, the King's Proctor in the Ecclesiastical Court, with the gentlemen of the officiality."

"But, I pray you, sir, what are all these worthy folks about here?"

"They are trying somebody."

"Who is it? I do not see the accused."

"It is a young woman, sir. She stands with her back toward us, and we can't see her for the crowd. Why, there she is, where you see that group of halberts."

"Do you know her name?" asked Gringoire.

"No, sir, I am but just come; but I presume that there is sorcery in the case, as the official attends the trial."

"Come on!" said our philosopher—"let us watch all these lawyers banqueting on human flesh! 'Tis a sight as well as any other."

Here the bystanders imposed silence on the interlocutors. An important witness was under examination.

"Gentlemen," said an old woman in the middle of the hall, who was so muffled up as to look like a walking bundle of rags—"gentlemen, it is as true that my name is Falourdel, and that I have kept house for forty years at the Pont Saint-Michel, and regularly paid rent, taxes, and rates. A poor old woman now, gentlemen, but once reckoned handsome, though I say it. One night I was spinning, when there comes a knock at my door. I asked 'Who's there?' and there was such a swearing! I opened the door: two men came in; a man in black, with a comely officer. Nothing was to be seen of the man in black but his eyes, for all the world like two burning coals: all the rest of him was cloak and hat. 'St Martha's room!' said they to me. That is my room upstairs, gentlemen, my best room. They gave me a crown. I put it into my drawer, saying to myself: 'It will serve to-morrow to buy tripe with at the shambles of the Gloriette.' Well, we went upstairs, and while my back was turned the man in black was gone. This staggered me a little. The officer, as handsome a gentleman as you would wish to set eyes on, went downstairs with me, and out he goes. By the time I had spun a quarter of a bobbin in he comes again with a pretty poppet of a damsel, who would have dazzled you like the sun if she had been properly attired. She had with her a goat, a large goat; it might be black, it might be white, I don't recollect now. The girl —that was no concern of mine—but the goat put me out, I must say . . . I don't like those animals; they have got a beard and horns . . . too like a man . . . and then the thing smells of witch-craft. However, I said nothing, and why should I? Had not I got the crown? And all right too, my lord, wasn't it? So I took the Captain and the girl to the room upstairs, and left them alone, that is to say, with the goat. I went down, and fell to spinning again . . . But I ought to tell you that my house has a ground floor and a floor above: the back of it looks to the river, like all the other houses on the bridge, and the windows both of the ground floor and the chamber open toward the water. Well, as I said just now, I began spinning again. I can't tell, not I, why I thought of the goblin-monk which the goat had put into my head—and then the girl was dressed in such a strange fashion! . . . Well, all at once I heard such a scream upstairs, and something fall upon the floor, and the window open. I ran to mine which is below, and saw a black figure drop before my eyes, and tumble into the water. It was a spectre in the habit of a priest. The moon was shining bright, so I saw it as plain as I see you now. It swam away toward the city. I was all over of a tremble, and called the watch. When those gentlemen came in they did not know what to make of it at first, and, being rather fuddled, they fell to beating me. I soon set them right. We went up, and what should we find but my best chamber drenched with blood, the Captain laid at full length with a dagger in his bosom, the girl shamming dead, and the goat frightened out

The Coin Transformed

of its wits! 'A pretty job!' said I; 'it will take me a fortnight to get the floor clean again—scour and scrub it as I will.' They carried away the officer—poor young man!—and the girl with her bosom all bare. . . . But, worse than all, next day, when I went to the drawer for the crown to buy tripe, lo and behold! I found nothing but a withered leaf where I had left it!"

The old woman ceased speaking. A murmur of horror arose from the auditory. "The spectre, the goat, and all that, look very like sorcery," said Gringoire to a neighbour. "Ay, and the withered leaf," added another. "No doubt," observed a third, "it was a witch colleagued with the goblin-monk to rob the officer."—Gringoire himself could scarcely help thinking that there was some probability in the conjecture.

"Witness," said the president in a dignified manner, "have you nothing further to communicate to the court?"

"No, my lord," replied the old woman, "only that in the report my house is called a crazy filthy hovel, which is a scandalous falsehood. To be sure, the houses on the bridge are not so goodly as some, but yet the butchers like to live in them, and they are people well to do in the world, and their wives are as proper comely women as you would wish to see."

The magistrate whom Gringoire had likened to a crocodile now rose. "Silence!" said he. "I beg you, my lord and gentlemen, to bear in mind that a dagger was found upon the accused. Witness, have you brought with you the leaf into which the crown given you by the demon was changed?"

"Yes, sir," she replied, "here it is."

An usher handed the dead leaf to the crocodile, who gave a sinister shake of the head, and passed it to the president; and the president sent it to the King's Proctor in the Ecclesiastical Court; so that it went the round of the hall. "Upon my word, a birch leaf!" ejaculated Master Jacques Charmolue; "a fresh proof of sorcery!"

A counsellor then rose and spoke. "Witness," said he, "two men went upstairs together at your house; a man in black, who immediately disappeared, and whom you afterwards saw swimming in the Seine, in the habit of a priest, and the officer. Which of the two gave you the crown?"

The old woman considered for a moment. "It was the officer," said she.

245

A murmur again ran through the court. "Aha!" thought Gringoire, "that alters the case materially."

Master Philippe Lheulier, Advocate Extraordinary to the King, again interposed. "Let me remind you, my lord and gentlemen, that the officer, in his deposition, taken in writing by his bedside, while admitting that he had a confused idea, at the moment when he was accosted by the man in black, that it might be the goblin-monk, added, that the phantom had strongly pressed him to keep his appointment with the accused; and, when the said Captain observed that he had no money, he gave him the crown with which the officer paid the witness Falourdel. The crown therefore is a coin of hell."

This conclusive observation appeared to dispel all the lingering doubts of Gringoire and the other sceptics among the audience.

"Gentlemen are in possession of the papers," added the King's Advocate, sitting down; "they can refer to the deposition of Captain Phœbus de Châteaupers."

At that name the accused rose. Her head was seen above the crowd. To his horror, Gringoire recognized La Esmeralda.

She was pale; her hair, once so gracefully plaited, and studded with sequins, was dishevelled; her lips were livid, her eyes hollow. Alas! what a change!

"Phœbus!" exclaimed she wildly, "where is he?—Oh, my lords, before you put me to death, for mercy's sake tell me if he still lives!"

"Silence, prisoner!" replied the president; "we have nothing to do with that."

"If you have any pity tell me if he is alive!" she resumed, clasping her attenuated hands; and her chains were heard to rustle along her dress.

"Well," said the King's Advocate drily, "he is dying.—Are you satisfied?"

The unhappy girl sank down again upon her seat, voiceless, tearless, white as a waxen image.

The president stooped toward a man placed at his feet, who had a gold-laced cap, a black gown, a chain about his neck, and a wand in his hand. "Usher, bring in the second prisoner."

All eyes turned toward a small door which opened, and, to the extreme agitation of Gringoire, in walked a pretty goat with gilt horns and hoofs. The elegant creature stopped for a moment on the threshold, stretching out her neck, as if, perched on the point of some rock, she was overlooking a vast plain beneath her. All at once she descried the Bohemian, and, springing over the table and the head of a clerk of the court, in two leaps she was at her knees; she then nestled gracefully on the feet of her mistress, soliciting a word or a caress: but the prisoner remained motionless, and poor Djali herself could not obtain even a look.

"Nay, by my fay! 'tis the same nasty beast," cried old Falourdel. "I could swear positively to them both."

"If it so pleaseth you, my lord and gentlemen," began Charmolue, "we will proceed to the examination of the second prisoner."

The second prisoner was the goat, sure enough. Nothing was more common in those days than to indict animals for sorcery. In the accounts of the provosty for 1466 we find, among others, the curious details of the costs of the trial of Gillet-Soulart and his sow, "executed for their crimes at Corbeil." Every item is there: the charge for the place of confinement made for the sow, the five hundred bundles of wood carried to the port of Morsant, the three quarts of wine and the bread, the last meal of the sufferer, fraternally shared by the executioner, even to the eleven days' keep and subsistence of the sow at eight deniers Parisis each. Sometimes, indeed, our pious ancestors went still farther than animals. The capitularies of Charlemagne and Louis le Débonnaire decree the infliction of severe punishments upon those luminous phantoms which have the audacity to appear in the air.

The Proctor of the Ecclesiastical Court then pronounced this solemn denunciation: "If the demon which possesses this goat, and which has withstood all the exorcisms that have been tried, persists in his wicked courses, and shocks the court with them, we forewarn him that we shall be forced to demand that he be sentenced to the gallows or the stake."

Cold perspiration covered the face of Gringoire. Charmolue took from a table the tambourine of the Egyptian, held it in a particular way to the goat, and asked, "What hour is it?"

The goat eyed him with intelligent look, raised her gilt foot and struck seven strokes. It was actually seven o'clock. A shudder of terror thrilled the crowd. Gringoire could no longer contain himself.

"The creature will be her own destruction!" he exclaimed aloud. "See you not that she knows not what she does?"

The Hunchback of Notre-Dame

"Silence among the lieges in the court!" cried the usher sternly.

Jacques Charmolue, by shifting the tambourine in various ways, made the goat exhibit several other tricks respecting the day of the month, month of the year, and so forth, which the reader has already witnessed; and, from an optical delusion peculiar to judicial proceedings, the very same spectators, who had perhaps many a time applauded the innocent pranks of Djali in the streets, were horror-stricken at them within the walls of the Palace of Justice. The goat was decidedly a devil.

But when the King's Proctor had emptied out upon the table a little leathern bag filled with detached letters which Djali had about her neck, and the goat was seen sorting out with her foot the separate letters of the fatal name "Phœbus," the spells to which the Captain had fallen a victim appeared to be irresistibly demonstrated, in the opinion of all; and the Bohemian, that exquisite dancer, who had so often enchanted the gazers with her graceful performances, was an odious witch.

The poor girl, meanwhile, exhibited not the least sign of life: neither the fond evolutions of her Djali, nor the threats of the judges, nor the muttered imprecations of the audience, were noticed by her. In order to rouse her a sergeant went to her, and shook her most unmercifully, while the president, raising his voice in a solemn tone, thus spoke: "Girl, you are of Bohemian race, addicted to unrighteous deeds. In company with the bewitched goat, your accomplice, implicated in this indictment, you did, on the night of the 29th of March last, in concert with the powers of darkness, and by the aid of charms and unlawful practices, stab and slay Phœbus de Châteaupers, Captain of the Archers of the King's Ordnance. Do you persist in denying this?"

"Oh, horror of horrors!" exclaimed the prisoner, covering her face with her hands. "Oh, my Phœbus! This is hell indeed!"

"Do you persist in denying it?" asked the president coldly.

"Do I deny it!" said she in a fearful tone, and with flashing eye, as she rose from her seat.

"Then," proceeded the president calmly, "how do you explain the facts laid to your charge?"

In broken accents, she replied: "I have already told you. I know not. It was a priest—a priest, a stranger to me—an infernal priest who haunts me!"

"There it is!" resumed the judge—"the goblin-monk."

"Oh, sirs, have pity upon me! I am but a poor girl . . ."

"Of Egypt," continued the judge.

Master Jacques Charmolue, in his gentlest, softest tone, then said, "In consequence of the painful obstinacy of the prisoner, I demand the application of the torture."

"Granted," said the president.

The unhappy girl shook all over. She rose, however, at the order of the halberdiers, and, preceded by Charmolue and the officers of the officiality, walked with tolerably firm step, between two files of partisans, toward a low door, which suddenly opened, and closed after her. To Gringoire it seemed as though she had been swallowed up by the gaping jaws of some monster. As soon as she had disappeared a plaintive bleating was heard. It was the poor goat bewailing the loss of her mistress.

The proceedings were suspended. A counsellor observed that the judges must be fatigued, and that they would be detained a long time if they waited for the conclusion of the torture; to which the president replied that a magistrate ought to have learned to sacrifice personal convenience to his duty.

"The provoking hussy!" said an old judge, "to bring the torture upon herself just now, when we ought to be at supper!"

CHAPTER II

SEQUEL TO THE COIN TRANSFORMED INTO A DRY LEAF

HAVING ascended and descended some steps in passages so dark that they were lighted in broad day by lamps, La Esmeralda, still surrounded by her dismal escort, was thrust by the sergeants of the palace into a room of sinister aspect. This room, of circular shape, occupied the ground floor of one of the towers that at the present day still perforate the stratum of modern edifices with which new Paris has covered the old city. There were no windows in this dungeon, neither was there any other aperture than the low entrance closed by a strong iron door. At the same time there was no want of light; in the massive substance of the wall there was a furnace, in which burned a large fire that threw a red glare over the den, and quite eclipsed the light of a miserable candle placed in the corner. The iron portcullis, which served as a door to the furnace, was drawn up at that moment, so that at its flaming mouth there were to be seen only the lower extremities of its bars, resembling a row of black, sharp, parted teeth; which made the furnace look like the mouth of one of those dragons of the legends vomiting fire and smoke. By the light which it suffused, the prisoner perceived round the room a variety of instruments, the uses of which were unknown to her. In the middle was a leathern mattress laid almost flat upon the floor, on which hung a thong with a buckle, fastened to a copper ring, which a grotesque monster sculptured in the keystone of the vaulted ceiling held between his teeth. Tongs, pincers, broad ploughshares, lay pell-mell, heating in the fire in the interior of the furnace. Its blood-red flare presented to the eye in the whole circumference of the chamber nought but an assemblage of fearful objects. This Tartarus was merely called *the chamber of the question.*

On the bed was carelessly seated Pierrat Torterue, the "sworn torturer." His assistants, two square-faced gnomes, with leathern aprons and linen breeches, were stirring the coals under the iron implements.

The poor girl had need to muster her courage; on entering this den she was struck with horror. The sergeants of the Bailiff of the Palace ranged themselves on one side, and the priests of the officiality on the other. In one corner was a table, at which sat a clerk with pen, ink, and paper.

Master Jacques Charmolue approached the Egyptian with one of his kindest smiles. "My dear child," said he, "do you persist in your denial?"

"Yes," she replied, in a voice scarcely audible.

"In that case," rejoined Charmolue, "it will be very painful to us to *question* you more urgently than we would. Take the trouble to sit down on this bed. Master Pierrat, give place to this young woman, and shut the door."

Pierrat rose growling. "If I shut the door," muttered he, "my fire will go out."

"Well, then, my good fellow," replied Charmolue, "leave it open."

The Sequel

Meanwhile La Esmeralda remained standing. That leathern bed, on which so many wretched creatures had writhed in agony, frightened her. Horror thrilled the very marrow of her bones; there she stood bewildered, stupefied. At a sign from Charmolue the two assistants laid hold of her, and placed her in a sitting posture on the bed. Those men did not hurt her, but when they grasped her, when the leather touched her, she felt all her blood flow back to her heart. She looked wildly round the room. She fancied that she saw those ugly implements of torture—which were, among the instruments of all kinds that she had hitherto seen, what bats, millepedes, and spiders are among birds and reptiles—quitting their places and advancing from every part of the room toward her, to crawl over her, and to bite, pinch, and sting her.

"Where is the doctor?" asked Charmolue.

"Here," answered a man in a black gown, whom she had not yet noticed.

She shuddered.

"Demoiselle," resumed the smooth tongue of the Proctor of the Ecclesiastical Court, "for the third time, do you persist in denying the charges preferred against you?"

This time her voice failed; she was able only to nod an affirmative.

"You persist!" cried Charmolue. "I am very sorry for it, but I am obliged to perform the duty of my office."

"Mr Proctor," said Pierrat abruptly, "what shall we begin with?"

Charmolue paused for a moment, with the ambiguous grimace of a poet at a loss for a rime. "With the buskin," he at length replied.

The unfortunate girl felt herself so totally abandoned by God and man, that her head sank upon her bosom, like something inert and destitute of animation. The torturer and the physician approached her together; at the same time the two assistants began to rummage in their hideous arsenal. At the clanking of the horrible irons the unhappy girl shivered like a dead frog subjected to the action of galvanism. "Oh, my Phœbus!" murmured she, in so low a tone as to be inaudible. She then relapsed into her former insensibility and deathlike silence. This sight would have rent any other heart than the hearts of judges. The wretched being to whom all this tremendous apparatus of saws, wheels, and pulleys was about

251

to be applied; the being about to be consigned to the iron grip of executioners and pincers, was that gentle, tender, frail creature— poor grain of millet, given up by human justice to be ground in the horrible mill of the torture!

Meanwhile the horny hands of Pierrat's men had brutally stripped that beautiful leg, and that small elegant foot, which had so often delighted the bystanders with their gracefulness and agility in the streets of Paris. "'Tis a pity!" muttered the torturer, surveying those graceful and delicate forms. Had the Archdeacon been present, he would assuredly have bethought him at that moment of his symbol of the spider and the fly. Presently the poor girl saw through the cloud that spread itself before her eyes the *buskin* approaching; presently her foot was hidden from sight in the iron-bound apparatus. Terror then restored her strength. "Take it off!" cried she wildly, at the same time starting up. "For mercy's sake!" She sprang from the bed with the intention of throwing herself at the feet of the King's Proctor; but, her leg being confined in the heavy block of oak sheathed with iron, she sank down powerless as a bee having its wings loaded with lead. On a sign from Charmolue she was replaced on the bed, and two coarse hands fastened round her slender waist the thong that hung from the ceiling.

"For the last time," said Charmolue, with his imperturbable benignity, "do you confess the crimes laid to your charge?"

"I am innocent."

"Then how do you explain the circumstances alleged against you?"

"Alas, sir, I know not."

"You deny them?"

"Everything!"

"Begin," said Charmolue to Pierrat.

Pierrat turned a screw; the buskin became more and more contracted, and the wretched sufferer gave one of those horrible shrieks which baffle the orthography of every human language.

"Hold!" said Charmolue to Pierrat.—"Do you confess?" he then asked the Egyptian.

"Everything!" cried the miserable girl. "I confess—mercy! mercy!"

In defying the torture she had not calculated her strength. Poor thing! her life had till then been so bright, so cheery, so joyous!— the first pang overcame her.

The Sequel

"Humanity obliges me to inform you," observed the King's Proctor, "that, though you confess, you have nothing but death to expect."

"I wish for it," said she. And she sank back upon the leathern bed, suspended, as if lifeless, by the thong buckled round her waist.

"So, my pretty!—hold up a little!" said Master Pierrat, raising her. "You look like the golden sheep about the neck of Monsieur of Burgundy."

Jacques Charmolue again raised his voice. "Clerk, write.—Bohemian girl, you confess your participation in the feasts, sabbaths, and practices of hell, with demons, sorcerers, and witches? Answer."

"Yes," said she in so low a tone as to be scarcely heard.

"You confess that you have seen the ram, which Beelzebub displays in the clouds to summon his children to their sabbath, and which is seen only by sorcerers?"

"Yes."

"You confess that you have had commerce with the devil in the shape of the goat implicated in these proceedings?"

"Yes."

"Lastly, you declare and confess that, instigated by, and with the assistance of the devil and the goblin-monk, you did, on the night of the 29th of March last, kill and slay a captain, named Phœbus de Châteaupers?"

She fixed her glazed eyes upon the magistrate, and replied, as if mechanically, without shock or convulsion, "Yes."—It was evident that her spirit was utterly broken.

"Write, clerk," said Charmolue. Then turning to Pierrat's men, "Loose the prisoner," he proceeded, "and let her be taken back into court." When the buskin was removed the Proctor examined her foot, still numbed with the pain. "Come, come," said he, " 'tis not much the worse. You cried out in time. You would soon be able to dance as well as ever, my beauty!" Then addressing the priests of the officiality, "Justice is enlightened at last," said he. " 'Tis a consolation, gentlemen! and the damsel will bear witness that we have shown her all possible lenity."

CHAPTER III

CONCLUSION OF THE COIN TRANSFORMED INTO A DRY LEAF

WHEN she again entered the court, pale and halting, she was greeted with a general buzz of pleasure. On the part of the auditory, it arose from that feeling of gratified impatience which is experienced at the theatre, at the conclusion of the last interlude of a play, when the curtain rises, and the fifth act begins; and on the part of the judges, from the prospect of being soon dismissed to their suppers. The poor little goat too bleated for joy. She would have run to her mistress, but she had been tied to a bench.

It was now dark night. The candles, having received no accession to their number, gave so faint a light that the walls of the court were not discernible. The darkness enveloped objects in a sort of haze. A few unfeeling faces of judges alone were with difficulty distinguishable. Opposite to them, at the other extremity of the long hall, they could perceive an undefined patch of white moving along the dark floor. It was the prisoner.

She advanced with faltering steps to her place. When Charmolue had magisterially resumed possession of his, he sat down; presently rising again, he said, without too strongly betraying the vanity of success: "The accused has confessed the crime."

"Bohemian girl," began the president, "you have confessed, then, all your misdeeds of magic, of prostitution, and of murder committed on the body of Phœbus de Châteaupers?"

Her heart was wrung, and she was heard to sob in the dark. "Whatever you please," answered she faintly, "only put me to death soon!"

"Mr Proctor," said the president, "the court is ready to hear your requisitions."

Master Charmolue produced a tremendous roll of paper, from which he began to read with abundant gesticulation, and the exaggerated emphasis of the bar, a Latin oration, in which all the evidence was built upon Ciceronian periphrases, flanked by quotations from Plautus, his favourite comic writer. We are sorry that

254

Conclusion

we cannot treat the reader to this delectable composition. The orator delivered it with wonderful action. Before he had finished the exordium big drops of perspiration trickled from his brow, and his eyes appeared to be starting from his head. All at once he stopped short in the middle of a sentence. His look, which was wont to be so bland, nay even so stupid, became terrific. "Gentlemen," cried he—now deigning to speak in French, for it was not in his manuscript—"to such a degree is Satan mixed up in this business, that yonder he is personally present at our proceedings, and making a mock of their majesty!" As he thus spoke, he pointed with his finger at the little goat, which, observing the gesticulations of Charmolue, had seated herself upon her rump, and was imitating as well as she could, with her forepaws and her bearded head, the pathetic pantomime of the King's Proctor in the Ecclesiastical Court. The reader will recollect that this was one of her most diverting tricks. This incident, the last proof, produced a powerful effect. To put an end to this scandal the goat's legs were bound, and the King's Proctor resumed the thread of his eloquent harangue. It was very long, but the winding up was admirable. He concluded with requiring that the prisoner should be condemned, in the first place to pay a certain pecuniary indemnity; in the second, to do penance before the grand porch of Notre-Dame; and thirdly, to be taken with her goat to the Place de Grève, and there executed.

He put on his cap and sat down.

A man in a black gown, near the prisoner, then rose; it was her advocate. The judges, feeling in want of their supper, began to murmur.

"Be brief," said the president.

"My lord," replied the advocate, "since the prisoner has confessed the crime I have but a few words to offer. In the Salic law there is this clause: 'If a witch have eaten a man, and she be convicted of it, she shall pay a fine of eight thousand deniers, which make two hundred sous in gold.' May it please the court then to sentence my client to pay this fine."

"That clause is become obsolete," said the Advocate Extraordinary to the King.

"*Nego!*" replied the advocate of the prisoner.

"To the vote!" said a counsellor; "the crime is proved, and it is late."

The question was put to the vote without leaving the court. The judges decided offhand; they were pressed for time. Their capped heads were seen uncovered one after another in the dusk, as the question was put to them successively in a low tone by the judge. The poor prisoner appeared to be looking at them; but her dim eye no longer saw the objects before it.

The clerk of the court began writing, and then handed a long parchment to the president. The unhappy girl heard a bustle among the people, pikes clashing together, and a chilling voice pronounce these words:

"Bohemian girl, on such day as it shall please our lord the King, at the hour of noon, you shall be drawn in a tumbrel, stripped to your shift, barefoot, with a rope about your neck, to the great porch of the church of Notre-Dame, and shall there do penance, holding in your hand a wax taper of two pounds' weight; and thence you shall be taken to the Place de Grève, and there hanged by the neck on the gallows of the Cité; and this your goat likewise; and you shall pay to the official three gold lions in reparation of the crimes by you committed and by you confessed, of sorcery, magic, incontinence, and murder done upon the body of Sieur Phœbus de Châteaupers. God receive your soul!"

"Oh! it must be a dream!" murmured the prisoner, and she felt rough hands bearing her away.

CHAPTER IV

LASCIATE OGNI SPERANZA [1]

IN the Middle Ages when a building was complete there was almost as much of it underground as above. A palace, a fortress, a church, had always a double basement, unless it stood upon piles like Notre-Dame. Under a cathedral there was a kind of subterranean church, low, dark, mysterious, blind, and mute, beneath the upper nave, which was resplendent with light and rang with the pealing of organs and bells, night and day; sometimes it was a catacomb. In palaces, in bastilles, it was a prison, sometimes a sepulchre, and sometimes both together. These mighty

[1] "Hope no more."

edifices, the mode of whose formation and *vegetation* we have elsewhere described, had not merely foundations, but, as it were, roots,
which shot out into the soil in chambers, in galleries, in staircases,
like the building above them. Thus churches, palaces, bastilles,
were buried up to the middle in the ground. The vaults of a building were another building, to which you descended instead of ascending, and which clapped its subterraneous storeys beneath the exterior storeys of the edifice, like those woods and mountains which
appear reversed in the mirror of a lake beneath the woods and mountains rising from its banks.

At the Bastille Saint-Antoine, at the Palace of Justice, at the
Louvre, these subterraneous edifices were prisons. The storeys of
these prisons became more and more contracted and gloomy the lower
you descended. They were so many zones pervaded by different
shades of horror. Dante could not find anything more suitable for
his hell. These funnels of dungeons usually terminated in a deep
hole gradually widening from the bottom upward, in which Dante
has placed his Satan, but where society confined culprits under sentence of death. When once a miserable wretch was thus buried,
farewell to light, to air, to life, to every hope; there was no leaving
the place but for the gallows or the stake. Sometimes the prisoner
was left to moulder there; human justice called this *forgetting*. The
condemned felt himself cut off from his kind by a superincumbent
mountain of stones and a host of gaolers; and the entire prison, the
massive fortress, was but one enormous complicated lock, which shut
him out from the living world.

Into a dungeon of this kind—the *oubliettes* dug by Saint Louis,
the *in pace* of the Tournelle—La Esmeralda was thrust after her
condemnation, no doubt for fear of escape, with the colossal Palace
of Justice over her head. Poor girl! she could not have stirred the
smallest of the stones of which it was built. There needed not such
a profusion of misery and torture to crush so frail a creature.

There she was, wrapt in darkness, buried, entombed, immured.
Whoever had beheld her in this state after having seen her sporting
and dancing in the sun would have shuddered. Cold as night, cold
as death, not a breath of air in her dark locks, not a human sound
in her ear, not a glimmer of light in her eyes, weighted down with
chains, bent double, crouched beside a pitcher and a loaf of bread,
on a little straw, in the pool formed beneath her by the water that

dripped from the walls of her dungeon, motionless and scarcely breathing—what more could she suffer? Phœbus, the sun, the daylight, the free air, the streets of Paris, the dances which had won her such applause; her love-prattle with the officer; then the priest, the dagger, the blood, the torture, the gallows; all this had again passed before her mind, sometimes like a gay and golden vision, at others like a hideous nightmare: but it was now no more than a horrible and indistinct struggle, which was veiled in darkness, or than distant music played above on the earth, and which was not heard at the depth into which the unfortunate creature was sunk. Since she had been there she had not waked, she had not slept. In this profound wretchedness, in the gloom of this dungeon, she could no more distinguish waking from sleeping, dream from reality, than night from day. She had ceased to feel, to know, to think; at the utmost she mused. Never had living creature been plunged so deeply into nothingness.

Thus torpid, frozen, petrified, she had scarcely noticed the noise of a trapdoor, which had opened twice or thrice somewhere near her, but without admitting a glimmer of light, and at which a hand had thrown down to her a crust of black bread. It was nevertheless the sole communication still left to her with mankind—the periodical visit of the gaoler. Her ear was mechanically directed to the only sound that now engaged it; above her head the wet filtered through the mossy stones of the vaulted roof, and a drop of water fell from it at equal intervals. She listened stupidly to the noise made by this drop falling into the pool of water by her side. This was the only motion still perceptible round her, the only clock that marked the lapse of time, the only noise that reached her of all the noises that are made on the face of the earth. Not but that she did indeed feel from time to time, in this dark and disgusting abode, something cold crawling about on her foot or her arm, and she could not help shuddering.

How long she had been in this place she knew not. She had a recollection of a sentence of death passed somewhere upon somebody; she remembered that she had then been borne away, and that she had awoke chilled with cold, in darkness and in silence. She had crawled about on her hands; iron rings had then galled her ankle and chains had rattled. She had ascertained that there was a solid wall all round her, that under her there was a pavement covered with

Lasciate Ogni Speranza

water, and a bundle of straw. She had then seated herself on this straw, and sometimes, for change of posture, on the lowest of the stone steps that led down to her dungeon. At one time she had tried to count the dark minutes measured by the drop of water; but presently her mind discontinued of itself this melancholy task imposed by a diseased brain, and it left her in a state of stupor.

At length, one day, or one night—for midnight and noonday were of the same colour in this sepulchre—she heard above her a louder noise than that usually made by the gaoler, when he brought her loaf and her pitcher of water. She raised her head, and saw a reddish ray entering through a cranny in a kind of trapdoor placed in the vaulted roof of the *in pace*. At the same time the heavy iron bars rattled; the door grated on its rusty hinges; it turned, and she saw a lantern, a hand, and the nether extremities of two figures, the door being too low for her to perceive their heads. The light so painfully affected her that she closed her eyes.

When she opened them again the door was shut, a lantern was placed on one of the steps, and something like a human form stood before her. A black wrapper descended to its feet; a hood of the same colour concealed the face. Nothing was to be seen of the person, not even the hands. The figure looked like a long black winding-sheet standing upright, under which something might be perceived moving. For some minutes she kept her eyes intently fixed on this spectral shape. Neither spoke. You would have taken them for two statues confronting each other. Two things only gave signs of life in the dungeon: the wick of the lantern which crackled owing to the dampness of the atmosphere, and the drip of the roof breaking this irregular crepitation by its monotonous plash, which caused the light of the lantern to dance in concentric rings on the oily surface of the pool.

At length the prisoner broke silence.

"Who are you?"

"A priest."

The word, the accent, the voice made her shudder.

"Are you prepared?" asked the priest, in a low tone.

"For what?"

"To die."

"Oh!" said she; "will it be soon?"

"To-morrow."

Her head, which she had raised with a look of joy, again sank upon her bosom. " 'Tis a long time till then," murmured she. "Why not to-day? What difference could it have made to them?"

"You must be very unhappy, then?" said the priest after a moment's silence.

"I am very cold," she replied. She clasped her feet with her hands, and her teeth chattered.

The priest seemed from beneath the hood to cast his eyes round the dungeon. "Without light! without fire! in the water! 'Tis horrible!"

"Yes," answered she, with that air of timidity which suffering had imparted; "everybody enjoys the light. Why should I be thrust into darkness?"

"Do you know," resumed the priest, after another pause, "why you are here?"

"I think I did know," said she, passing her attenuated fingers over her brow, as if to assist her memory, "but I don't now."

All at once, she burst out crying like a child. "I want to leave this place, sir. I am cold, I am afraid, and there are loathsome things which crawl up me."

"Well, come along with me."

With these words the priest took hold of her arm. The wretched girl was chilled to her inmost vitals, yet that hand produced a sensation of cold.

"Oh!" murmured she, "it is the icy hand of death! who are you then?"

The priest pushed back his hood. She looked at him. It was that sinister face which had so long haunted her, that demon-head which had appeared to her at Falourdel's above the head of her adored Phœbus, that eye which she had last seen glistening near a dagger.

This apparition, always so baneful to her, and which had thus hurried her on from misery to misery, roused her from her stupor. The thick veil which seemed to have spread itself over her memory was rent asunder. All the circumstances of her dismal adventure, from the night-scene at Falourdel's to her condemnation at the Tournelle, rushed at once upon her mind, not vague and confused as at the time of their occurrence, but distinct, fresh, palpitating, terrible. These recollections, almost obliterated by the excess of her sufferings, were revived by the sombre figure before her; as the invisible words written with sympathetic ink upon white paper are brought out quite fresh on its being held to the fire. All the wounds of her heart seemed to be torn open afresh, and to bleed at once.

"Ha!" cried she, with a convulsive tremor, and holding her hands over her eyes, "it is the priest!" Presently dropping her enfeebled arms, she remained sitting, her head bent forward, her eye fixed on the ground, mute and trembling. The priest looked at her with the eye of a hawk, which has long been descending in silence from the topmost height of the heavens, in circles gradually more and more contracted round a poor lark squatting in the corn, and, having suddenly pounced like winged lightning upon his prey, clutches the panting victim in his talons.

She began to murmur in a faint tone: "Finish! finish! Give the last blow!" and she bowed down her head with terror, like the lamb awaiting the fatal stroke from the hand of the butcher.

At length he asked, "Are you afraid of me, then?"

She made no reply.

"Are you afraid of me?" he repeated.

Her lips were compressed as though she smiled.

"Yes," said she, "the executioner jeers the condemned. For months he has been haunting, threatening, terrifying me! But for him, oh, God, how happy I should be! 'Tis he who has hurled me into this abyss—'tis he who killed *him*—who killed my Phœbus!" Sobbing vehemently, she raised her eyes to the priest. "Who are you, wretch?" she exclaimed. "What have I done to you? Why should you hate me thus? What grudge have you against me?"

"I *love* thee!" said the priest.

Her tears suddenly ceased. She eyed him with the vacant stare of an idiot. He had meanwhile sunk upon his knees, and gazed upon her with eye of fire.

"Dost thou hear? I *love* thee!" he repeated.

"Ah! what love!" ejaculated the unhappy creature, shuddering.

"The love of the damned," he replied.

Both remained silent for some minutes, overwhelmed by their emotions; he frantic, she stupid.

"Listen," at length said the priest, who had all at once recovered a wonderful degree of composure; "thou shalt know all. I will tell thee what hitherto I have scarcely dared tell myself, when I secretly examined my conscience, in those hours of night on which rests such thick darkness, that it seems as if God could no longer see us. Listen. Before I saw thee I was happy."

"And I!" she sighed forth faintly.

"Interrupt me not.—Yes, I was happy, or at least I fancied that I was so. I was innocent. No head was lifted so high and so proudly as mine. Priests and doctors consulted me. Science was all in all to me; it was a sister, and a sister sufficed me. In spite, however, of my determination to acknowledge no other influence, that power of nature, which, silly youth as I was, I had hoped to crush for life, had more than once convulsively shaken the chain of those iron vows which bind me, miserable man that I am, to the cold stones of the altar. But, fasting, prayer, study, the mortifications of the cloister, restored to the spirit the dominion over the passions. I shunned women. Besides, I needed but to open a book, and all the impure vapours of my brain were dispelled by the splendour of science. In a few minutes the dark things of earth fled far away, and I found myself calm and serene in the soothing light of everlasting truth. So long as the demon sent only vague shadows of women to attack me, so long as they passed casually before my eyes, at church, in the streets, in the fields, and scarcely recurred to my thoughts, I vanquished him with ease. Alas! if victory has not remained with me, it is the fault of God, who has not made man equal in strength to the demon.—List to me. One day . . ."

The priest paused, and deep sighs burst from his bosom. He resumed:

"One day I was sitting at the window of my cell. I was reading. The window looked upon an open place. I heard the sound of a tambourine. Vexed at being disturbed in my reverie, I cast my eyes upon the place. What I there saw, and what others saw besides me, was not a sight made for human eyes. There, in the middle of the pavement—it was noon—brilliant sunshine—a creature was dancing—a creature so beautiful that she might have served as a model for the mother of the Graces. Her eyes were black and splendid; amid her dark hair there were locks which, saturated as it were by the sun's beams, shone like threads of gold. Round her head, in her black tresses, there were pieces of metal, which sparkled in the sun, and formed a coronet of stars for her brow. Her azure robe, besprinkled with a thousand spangles, glistened like a summer night.

Lasciate Ogni Speranza

Her feet in their rapid movements appeared indistinct like the spokes of a wheel that is whirling quickly round. Her brown and supple arms were tied and untied round her body like two scarfs. Her figure was of surpassing beauty. Oh, the resplendent form, which had something luminous about it even in the broad sunlight! Surprised, charmed, intoxicated, I could not forbear watching thee; I looked till I shuddered: I felt that the hand of Fate was upon me."

The priest, oppressed by emotion, again paused for a moment. He then proceeded:

"Half fascinated already, I endeavoured to grasp at something to break my fall. I recollected the snares which Satan had previously spread for me. The creature before me possessed that superhuman beauty which can proceed only from heaven or from hell. She was not a mere girl, moulded of common clay, and faintly lighted within by the flickering ray of woman's soul. It was an angel, but an angel of darkness—of fire, not of light. At the moment when these thoughts were crossing my brain I saw near her a goat, a beast which associates with witches. It looked at me and laughed. The noontide sun tipped its horns with flame. I then perceived the snare of the demon, and had no further doubt that thou wert come from hell, and come for my perdition. I believed so."

The priest here looked steadfastly in the face of the prisoner, and coldly added, "I believe so still.

"Meanwhile the charm began to operate by degrees. Thy dancing turned my brain. I felt the mysterious spell upon me. All that should have waked in my soul was lulled to sleep; and, like men perishing in the snow, I took pleasure in yielding to this slumber. All at once I heard thee begin to sing. What could I do? Thy singing was more fascinating than thy dancing. I would have fled. Impossible. I was riveted, rooted, to the spot. I was forced to remain till thou hadst finished. My feet were ice, my head a furnace. At length, perhaps in pity to me, thy song ceased, and I saw thee depart. The reflection of the dazzling vision, the sounds of the enchanting music, vanished by degrees from my eyes, and died away in my ears. I then sank into the corner of the window, stiff and helpless as a fallen statue. The vesper bell awoke me; I fled: but alas! something had fallen within me which I could not raise up; something had come upon me, from which I could not flee!"

He made another pause and thus proceeded:

The Hunchback of Notre-Dame

"Yes, from that day I was possessed with a spirit that was strange to me. I had recourse to my remedies—the cloister, the altar, occupation, books. Follies! Oh, how hollow science sounds when you dash against it in despair a head filled with passions. Knowest thou, maiden, what thenceforth I always saw between the book and me? Thee, thy shadow, the image of the luminous apparition which had one day passed before me. But that image had no longer the same colour; it was sombre, dark, gloomy, like the black circle which long dances before the eye that has been imprudent enough to gaze at the sun.

"Haunted by it incessantly, incessantly hearing thy song ringing in my ears, incessantly seeing thy feet dancing upon my breviary, my dreams by night, as well as my thoughts by day, being full of thee. I was desirous to behold thee again, to touch thee, to know who thou wert, to ascertain whether thou resemblest the ideal image impressed upon my mind, to dispel perhaps the phantasm by the reality. At all events, I hoped that a new impression would efface the first; for the first had become intolerable to me. I sought thee. Again I beheld thee. When I had seen thee twice I wished to see thee a thousand times, to have thee always in my sight. Then—who can stop himself on the steep descent to perdition?—then was I no longer my own master. I became a vagrant, like thyself. I waited for thee beneath porches, I lurked at the corners of streets, I watched thee from my tower. Each night, on examining myself, I found that I was more helpless, more spellbound, more bewitched, more undone.

"I learned who thou wert; Egyptian, Bohemian, Gitana, Zingara. How could I longer doubt that there was witchcraft in the case! I hoped that the law would break the charm. A sorceress had bewitched Bruno d'Ast: he caused her to be burned, and was cured. I knew him. I resolved to try the same remedy. In the first place I obtained an ordinance forbidding thee to appear in the precincts of our church, hoping to forget thee if I should see thee no more. Reckless of this prohibition thou camest as usual. Then did I conceive the idea of carrying thee off. One night I attempted to put it into execution. There were two of us. We had thee already in our clutches when that odious officer came up and rescued thee. Thus did he commence thy sufferings, mine, and his own. At length, not knowing what to do, I denounced thee to the official.

Lasciate Ogni Speranza

I thought that I should be cured, as Bruno d'Ast was. I had also a confused notion that a judicial process would deliver thee into my power; that in a prison I should have thee, should hold thee; that there thou couldst not escape me. When one is doing evil 'tis madness to stop half-way. The extremity of guilt has its delirium of rapture.

"I should perhaps have renounced my design; my hideous idea would perhaps have evaporated from my brain without producing any result. I imagined that it would depend on me to follow up or to stop the proceedings whenever I pleased. But every wicked thought is inexorable, and hurries to become a fact; and where I fancied myself all-powerful Fate proved more mighty than I. Alas! alas! it was Fate that caught thee, and threw thee among the terrible works of the machine which I had secretly constructed. List to me. I have nearly done.

"One day—another day of lovely sunshine—I saw a man walking before me, who pronounced thy name, who laughed, and whose eyes glistened with unhallowed fire. I followed him—thou knowest the rest."

He ceased speaking. "Oh, my Phœbus!" was all that the poor girl could utter.

"Not that name!" said the priest, seizing her arm with violence. "Name not that name! Wretched as we are, 'tis that name which has undone us; or rather, we are undoing one another through the unaccountable freaks of fatality! . . . Thou art suffering, I know it. Thou art chilled; the darkness blinds thee; the dungeon clasps thee: but perhaps thou hast still some light in the recesses of thy soul, were it but thy childish love for that empty man who plays with thy heart—while I, I carry a dungeon within me; within me is the chill of winter, the chill of despair; darkness enwraps my soul. Knowest thou all that I have suffered? I was present at thy trial. Yes, one of those priest's cowls covered torments unequalled but by those of the damned. I was there when that savage beast—oh! I foreboded not the torture!—bore thee off to his den. I saw thee stripped, and thy delicate limbs grasped by the infamous hands of the executioner. I saw thy foot, which I would have given an empire to kiss, that foot by which to have been trampled upon had been to me happiness, I saw it encased in the horrible buskin, which converts the members of a living being into a bloody jelly.

The Hunchback of Notre-Dame

At the shriek which was forced from thee I plunged into my bosom a dagger that I carried beneath my wrapper. Look, it still bleeds."

He threw open his cassock. His breast was lacerated as by the claw of a tiger. The prisoner recoiled in horror.

"O maiden!" said the priest; "take pity on me! Thou deemest thyself miserable. Alas! thou knowest not what misery is. It is to love a woman—to be a priest—to be hated—to love with all the energies of your soul—to feel that you would give for the least of her smiles your blood, your life, your character, your salvation, immortality and eternity, this world and the next—to regret that you are not a king, an emperor, an archangel, that you might throw a greater slave at her feet; to clasp her night and day in your sleeping, and in your waking, dreams—to see her fond of a soldier's uniform, and to have nothing to offer her but the wretched cassock, which is to her an object of fear and disgust—to be present, with a heart bursting with jealousy and rage, while she lavishes on a silly braggart the treasures of love and beauty—to think of that delicious form till you writhe for whole nights on the floor of your cell, and to see all the endearments which you have reserved for her in imagination end in torture—these, these are pincers heated in the fire of hell! Happy in comparison is he who is sawn asunder between two planks, or quartered by horses! Knowest thou what agony it is when, during the long nights, your arteries boil, your heart is bursting, your head splitting, and your teeth tear your own flesh; when you are turned incessantly as upon a red-hot gridiron by those inexorable tormentors, love, jealousy, despair! Mercy, maiden! relax for a moment; or, if it must be so, torture me with one hand, but touch me gently with the other. Have pity on me, girl! have pity on me!"

The priest rolled in the water on the floor, and dashed his head against the stone steps of the dungeon. The Egyptian listened to him, looked at him. When he ceased speaking, breathless and exhausted, she repeated in a low tone, "Oh, my Phœbus!"

Th priest crawled toward her upon his knees. "I implore thee," he cried, "if thou hast any compassion, repulse me not. I love thee —I am miserable. When thou utterest that name it is as if thou wert rending all the fibres of my heart. Only have pity. If thou goest to perdition I must go with thee. All that I have done I have done for this. The place where thou art wilt be to me a Paradise; the sight of thee is more entrancing than that of heaven. Oh, say, wilt thou not have me? I should have thought that the day when a woman could reject such love the mountains would dissolve. Oh, if thou wouldst, how happy might we yet be! We would flee . . . I would enable thee to escape . . . we would seek that spot where there are the most trees, the most sunshine, the most azure sky."

She interrupted him with a loud thrilling laugh. "Look, Father, you have blood upon your fingers!"

The priest, motionless for some moments, as if petrified, looked steadfastly at his hand.

"Why, yes," he at length replied with unwonted mildness, "abuse me, jeer me, overwhelm me!—but come, come! Let us lose no time. It will be to-morrow, I tell thee. The gibbet of the Grève—thou knowest the gibbet—it is always ready. It is horrible—to see thee drawn in that cart! Oh, mercy, mercy! Never did I feel as at this moment how dearly I love thee! Oh, come along with me! Thou shalt take thine own time to love me after I have saved thee. Thou shalt hate me as long as thou wilt. Only come. To-morrow! to-morrow! the gallows! Oh, save thyself—spare me!"

In a state approaching to madness, he seized her arm, and would have hurried her along. She fixed her eyes intently upon him. "What is become of my Phœbus?" she inquired.

"Ah!" said the priest, loosing her arm from his grasp, "you have no pity!"

"What is become of Phœbus?" repeated she coldly.

"He is dead," replied the priest.

"Dead!" said she, still cold and passionless, "then why persuade me to live?"

He heard her not. "Oh, yes!" said he, as if talking to himself, "he must be dead. I struck home. The point must have reached his heart."

The girl rushed upon him like an enraged tigress, and thrust him toward the steps with supernatural force: "Begone, monster! begone, murderer! leave me to die! May the blood of us both mark thy brow with an everlasting stain! . . . Be thine, priest! Never! never! Nothing shall bring us together, not even hell itself. Avaunt, accursed!—never!"

The priest had stumbled upon the steps. Silently disengaging his feet from the skirts of his cassock, he picked up his lantern and began slowly to ascend to the door: he opened it and went forth. The prisoner gazed after him. All at once his head again appeared stooping over the stairs. His face was ghastly. With a rattle of rage and despair he cried, "I tell thee he is dead!"

She fell with her face to the ground; and no sound was then to be heard in the dungeon save the plash of the dropping water, which rippled the pool amid the profound darkness.

CHAPTER V

THE MOTHER

I CANNOT conceive anything in the world more delightful than the ideas awakened in the heart of a mother at the sight of her child's little shoe, especially if it be a holiday, a Sunday, a baptismal, shoe; a shoe embroidered down to the very sole; a shoe upon which the infant has never yet stepped. This shoe is so small and so pretty; it is so impossible for it to walk, that it seems to the mother as though she saw her child. She smiles at it, she kisses it, she talks to it; she asks herself if a foot can really be so small; and, if the infant should be absent, the pretty shoe is sufficient to set the sweet and fragile little creature before her eyes. She fancies she sees it—she does see it—all alive, all joyous, with its delicate hands, its round head, its pure lips, its serene eyes, the white of which is blue. If it be winter, there it is, crawling upon the carpet, climbing laboriously upon a stool, and the mother trembles lest it should approach too near to the fire. If it be summer, it is creeping about in the court-yard or in the garden, looking innocently and fearlessly at the big dogs and the big horses, pulling up the grass growing between the stones, playing with the shells and the flowers, and making the gardener scold on finding sand on his borders and mould on his paths. All about it is bright, joyous, and playful, like itself, even to the very breeze and the sunshine, which sport together in the locks of its soft hair. All this the little shoe sets before the mother, and it makes her heart melt like wax before the fire.

But when the child is lost these thousand images of joy, delight, and affection, which crowd round the little shoe, are transformed into as many frightful things. The pretty little embroidered shoe

268

The Mother

then becomes but an instrument of torture, which is incessantly racking the heart of the mother. It is still the same fibre that vibrates—the deepest and the most keenly sensitive fibre—not under the caresses of an angel, but in the grip of a demon.

One morning when the sun of May was rising in one of those deep blue skies, beneath which Garofalo loved to picture the taking down from the Cross, the recluse of the Tour-Roland heard the rumbling of wheels, the tramp of horses, and the clanking of iron in the Place de Grève. The noise scarcely roused her; she tied her hair over her ears that she might not hear it, and again fell to gaze upon her knees at the inanimate object which she had thus adored for fifteen years. To her this little shoe was, as we have already observed, the universe. Her thoughts were wrapped up in it, never to be parted from it but by death. How many bitter imprecations, how many touching complaints, how many earnest prayers she had addressed to heaven on the subject of this charming little shoe of rose-coloured satin, was known to the cell of the Tour-Roland alone. Never were keener sorrows poured forth over object so pretty and so delicate. On this particular morning her grief seemed to burst forth with greater violence than usual; and she was heard from without bewailing herself with a loud and monotonous voice which wrung the heart.

"Oh, my child!" said she, "my child! my poor dear little child!—never, no never shall I see thee more!—and still it seems as if it had happened but yesterday. Oh, my God! my God! better she had not been given to me at all than to have her taken from me so soon! And yet Thou must know that our children are a part of ourselves, and that a mother who has lost her child is tempted not to believe in God. . . . Ah! wretch that I was, to go out that day! . . . Oh, Lord! Lord! to snatch her from me thus, Thou couldst never have seen me with her, when I warmed her, all glee, before the fire, when she ceased sucking to laugh in my face, when I made her little feet step up my bosom to my very lips! Hadst Thou seen this, oh, my God! Thou wouldst have had pity on my joy; Thou wouldst not have ravished from me the only love that was left in my heart! Was I then so vile a wretch, O Lord! that Thou couldst not look at me before condemning me?—Alas! alas! there is the shoe, but where is the foot? where is the child? My child! my own child! what have they done with thee! O Lord, give me back my child! My knees have been flayed for these fifteen years in praying to Thee: is not this enough? Restore her to me for a day, an hour, a minute, only one minute, O Lord! and then cast me forth to the Evil One to all eternity. Oh, did I but know where to find Thee, I would grasp the skirts of Thy garment with both these hands, and not let Thee go till Thou hadst given me back my child! Behold her pretty little shoe! Hast Thou no compassion? Canst Thou doom a wretched mother to fifteen years of such torment as this? Blessed Virgin of heaven! they have stolen my child; they have devoured her on the moor; they have drunk her blood; they have gnawed her bones. Kind Virgin, have pity on me! My child! I want my child! What is it to me that she is in Paradise? I want none of your angels; I want my child. Oh, I will writhe upon the ground, I will dash my head against the stones, I will gladly seal my own perdition, so thou wilt but restore to me my child! Thou seest how these arms are torn! Has then the good God no compassion? Oh, let them give me but black bread and salt, provided I have my daughter; she will be to me both meat and drink, and warmth and sunshine. I confess that I am but a vile sinner, but my child was making me pious. Out of love to her I was amending my life, and I saw thee through her smile as through the opened heavens . . . oh that I could but once more, only once, put this pretty shoe on her rosy little foot, I would die blessing thee, Holy Virgin!—But no—fifteen years!—she must be grown up now!—Unfortunate girl! 'tis too certain that I shall never see thee more, not even in heaven, for there I shall never enter. Oh, what anguish!—to say, there is her shoe and that is all."

The wretched creature threw herself upon that shoe, a source of solace and of sorrow for so many years; and she sobbed as though her heart would break, just as she had done on the very first day. Grief like this never grows old. Though the garments of mourning become threadbare and lose their colour, the heart remains black as ever.

At this moment the brisk and merry voices of boys passed before her cell. At the sight or the sound of children the unhappy mother would always dart into the darkest nook of her sepulchre, with such precipitation that you would think she was striving to bury her head in the wall, in order that she might not hear them. On this occasion, contrary to her custom, she started up and listened attentively. One of the boys was just saying to another, "They are going to hang an Egyptian to-day."

With the sudden bound of the spider, that we lately saw rushing upon the fly entangled in his net, she sprang to the aperture which looked, as the reader knows, toward the Place de Grève. A ladder was actually reared against the permanent gallows, and the hangman was engaged in adjusting the chains, which had become rusty with the wet. A few people were standing round.

The laughing troop of boys was already far off. The recluse looked about for some passenger whom she might question. She perceived close to her cell a priest, who feigned to be reading in the public breviary, but whose thoughts were much less engaged by the book than by the gibbet, toward which he glanced from time to time with wild and gloomy look. She recognized in him the Archdeacon of Josas, an austere and holy man.

"Father," she inquired, "whom are they going to hang, yonder?"

The priest looked at her without answering. She repeated the question. "I know not," said he.

"Some boys," rejoined the recluse, "said just now that it was an Egyptian."

"I believe so," replied the priest.

Paquette la Chantefleurie burst into an hysterical laugh.

"Sister," said the Archdeacon, "you seem to hate the Egyptians with all your heart."

"Hate them!" cried the recluse; "why, they are witches, child-stealers! They devoured my little girl, my child, my only child! They ate my heart along with her—I have none now!"

The priest eyed her coldly.

"There is one in particular," she resumed, "that I hate and that I have cursed; a young girl about the same age that my child would have been now had they not eaten her. Whenever this young viper passes my cell she sets all my blood a-boiling."

"Well, then, sister, rejoice," said the priest, cold as the statue on a sepulchre; " 'tis for her that these preparations are being made."

His head sunk upon his bosom, and he slowly withdrew.

The recluse waved her arms in triumph. "Thanks, Sir Priest," cried she. "I told her what she would come to."

She then began with hurried step to pace to and fro before her window, her hair dishevelled, her eye glaring, dashing against the wall with her shoulder, with the wild air of a caged she-wolf, which has long been hungry and is aware that the hour for her repast is approaching.

CHAPTER VI

THREE HUMAN HEARTS DIFFERENTLY CONSTITUTED

PHŒBUS, meanwhile, was not dead. Men of that kind are hard to kill. When Master Philippe Lheulier, Advocate Extraordinary to the King, said to poor Esmeralda, "He is dying"—he was either misinformed or joking. When the Archdeacon repeated to her after condemnation, "He is dying"—the fact was that he knew nothing about the matter; but he believed it, he had no doubt of it, he made sure of it, he hoped it. It would have gone too much against the grain to give good tidings of his rival to the woman of whom he was enamoured. Every man in his place would have done the same.

Not that Phœbus's wound was not severe, but the injury was less serious than the Archdeacon flattered himself it was. The master-chirurgeon to whose house the soldiers of the watch had immediately carried him was for above a week under apprehensions for his life, and had even told him so in Latin. Youth, however, enabled him to get the better of it; and, as it frequently happens, notwithstanding prognostics and diagnostics, nature had amused herself in saving the patient in spite of the doctor's teeth. It was while lying on the master-chirurgeon's truckle-bed that he had undergone the first interrogatories of Philippe Lheulier and the inquisitors of the official, which had annoyed him exceedingly. One fine morning, therefore, finding himself better, he had left his gold spurs in payment at the chirurgeon's and decamped without beat of drum. This circumstance, however, had not in the least affected the judicial proceedings. Justice in those days cared but little about propriety and accuracy in a criminal process; provided that the accused were hung, it was perfectly satisfied. Now, the judges had evidence sufficient against Esmeralda. They believed Phœbus to be dead, and that was quite enough.

Phœbus, on his part, had not fled far. He had merely rejoined his company, in garrison at Queue-en-Brie, in the Ile de France, a few relays from Paris. He felt no inclination whatever to come forward personally in this process. He had a vague impression that he should cut a ridiculous figure in it. At bottom, he knew not what to think of the whole affair. Irreligious and superstitious, like every soldier who is nothing but a soldier, when he called to mind all the circumstances of this adventure he could not tell what to make of the goat, of the odd way in which he had first met with La Esmeralda, of the not less strange manner in which she had betrayed her love, of her being an Egyptian, and, lastly, of the goblin-monk. He imagined that in this history there was much more of magic than of love, probably a sorceress, perhaps the devil; in short, a comedy, or to use the language of those days, a mystery, of a very disagreeable nature, in which he played an extremely awkward part —that of the butt for blows and laughter. The Captain was quite dashed: he felt the sort of shame which La Fontaine so admirably compares with that of a fox caught by a hen. He hoped, besides, that the affair would not be bruited abroad, that in his absence his name would scarcely be mentioned in connexion with it, or at any rate not beyond the pleadings at the Tournelle. Neither was he far wrong in this expectation: there were then no newspapers; and as scarcely a week passed but there was some coiner boiled, some witch hanged, or some heretic burned, at one of the numberless *justices* of Paris, people were so accustomed to see the old feudal Themis, with bare arms and tucked-up sleeves, performing her office at the gallows and the pillory, that they scarcely took any notice of such events. In those days the higher classes scarcely knew the name of the sufferer who was carried past to the corner of the street, and the populace at most regaled itself with this coarse fare. An execution was a familiar incident in the public ways, like the oven of the baker, or the butcher's slaughter-house. The hangman was but a kind of butcher, a shade darker than the other.

Phœbus therefore soon set his mind at ease respecting the sorceress Esmeralda, or Similar, as he called her, the wound inflicted by the Bohemian or the goblin-monk—he cared not which—and the issue of the proceedings. But no sooner was his heart vacant on this score than the image of Fleur-de-Lys returned thither. The heart of Captain Phœbus, like the philosophy of those times, abhorred a vacuum.

The Hunchback of Notre-Dame

Besides, Queue-en-Brie was a very stupid place, a village of blacksmiths and dairy-women with chapped hands, a long line of crazy cottages bordering both sides of the highroad for a mile. Fleur-de-Lys was his last passion but one, a handsome girl with a good dower. One fine morning, therefore, being quite convalescent, and presuming that the affair with the Bohemian must after the lapse of two months be completely blown over and forgotten, the amorous cavalier came swaggering to the door of the Gondelaurier mansion. He took no notice of a numerous concourse assembled in the Place du Parvis, before the porch of Notre-Dame: he recollected that it was the month of May, and, supposing that the people might be drawn together by some religious holiday or procession, he fastened his horse to the ring at the gate and gaily went upstairs to his fair betrothed.

She was alone with her mother. Fleur-de-Lys had always felt sore about the scene with the sorceress, her goat, her cursed alphabet, and the long absences of Phœbus: nevertheless, at the entrance of her truant he looked so well, had such a new uniform, such a smart shoulder-belt, and so impassioned an air, that she reddened with pleasure. The noble demoiselle was herself more charming than ever. Her magnificent light hair was admirably plaited; she was attired completely in sky-blue, which so well suits women of a fair complexion—a piece of coquetry which she had been taught by Colombe—and her eye swam in that languor of love which suits them so much better.

Phœbus, who had so long set eyes on nothing superior in beauty to the wenches of Queue-en-Brie, was transported with Fleur-de-Lys; and this imparted such a warmth and such a tone of gallantry to his manner that his peace was instantly made. Madame de Gondelaurier herself, maternally seated as usual in her great armchair, had not the heart to scold him; and as for the reproaches of Fleur-de-Lys, they expired in accents of tenderness.

The young lady was seated near the window, still working away at her grotto of Neptune. The Captain leant over the back of her chair, and in an undertone she commenced her half-caressing, half-scolding inquiries.

"What have you been doing with yourself for these two months, you naughty man?"

"I swear," replied Phœbus, who did not relish the question, "you

274

are so beautiful that an archbishop could not help falling in love with you."

She could not forbear smiling. "Beautiful, forsooth! My beauty is nothing to the purpose, sir; I want an answer to my question."

"Well, then, my dear cousin, I was ordered away to keep garrison."

"Where, if you please? and why not come to bid me adieu?"

"At Queue-en-Brie."

Phœbus was delighted that the first question enabled him to shirk the second.

"But that is close by, sir. How is it that you have not been once to see me?"

Here Phœbus was seriously embarrassed. "Why . . . our duty . . . and, besides, charming cousin, I have been ill."

"Ill!" she exclaimed, in alarm.

"Yes, wounded."

"Wounded!"

The poor girl was thunderstruck.

"Oh, you need not frighten yourself about that," said Phœbus carelessly; "it was nothing. A quarrel, a scratch with a sword; how can that concern you?"

"Not concern me?" cried Fleur-de-Lys, raising her beautiful eyes swimming in tears. "Oh, in saying so you do not say what you think. How came you by the scratch you talk of? I insist on knowing all."

"Well then, my fair cousin, I had a squabble with Mahé Fédy —you know him—the lieutenant of Saint-Germain-en-Laye, and each of us ripped up a few inches of the other's skin. That is all."

The mendacious Captain well knew that an affair of honour always raises a man in the estimation of a woman. Accordingly, Fleur-de-Lys turned about and looked him in the face with emotions of fear, pleasure, and admiration. Still she was not completely satisfied.

"Ah, Phœbus," said she, "how I rejoice that you are quite well again! I do not know your Mahé Fédy—but he is a scurvy fellow. And what was the cause of this quarrel?"

Here Phœbus, whose imagination was not the most fertile, began to be puzzled how to get out of the dilemma.

"Oh, I hardly recollect—a mere nothing, a word about a horse—but, fair cousin," cried he, in order to change the conversation, "what is the occasion of this bustle in the Parvis? Only look," he continued, stepping to the window, "what a crowd there is in the Place!"

"I know not," replied Fleur-de-Lys. "I did hear that a witch is to do penance this morning before the church, and to be hung afterwards."

The Captain made so sure that the affair with La Esmeralda was long since over that he took but little interest in the information given to him by Fleur-de-Lys. He nevertheless asked her one or two questions.

"What is the name of this witch?"

"I know not," answered she.

"And what do they say she has done?"

"I know not," said she, with another shrug of her fair shoulders.

"Oh, my God!" said the mother, "there are nowadays so many sorcerers and witches that they burn them, I verily believe, without knowing their names. You might as well ask the name of every cloud in the sky. But what need we care? God Almighty will be sure to keep a correct list." Here the venerable lady rose and advanced to the window.—"Bless me! there is indeed a crowd, as you say, Phœbus. Why, the very roofs are covered with the populace! Do you know, Phœbus, this reminds me of my young days, of the entry of King Charles VII, when there was as great a crowd as this—only the people were much more comely than now. Every spot was thronged with them even to the battlements of the gate of Saint-Antoine. The King had the Queen on the crupper behind him, and after their Highnesses, came all the ladies riding in the same way behind their lords. A procession of all the gentlemen of France with their banners waving in the air. Ah! well-a-day! 'tis sad to think that all this pomp has been, and that nothing of it is now left!"

The lovers were not listening to the worthy dowager. Phœbus had again planted himself behind his betrothed, and was leaning over the back of her chair, wandering over so much of her neck as was not covered by her dress. Dazzled by that skin which shone like satin, the Captain said within himself, "How can one love any but a fair woman?" Both kept silence. The lady gave him from time to time a look of delight and fondness; and their hair mingled together in the spring sunshine.

"Phœbus," said Fleur-de-Lys abruptly, in a low tone, "we are to be married in three months; swear that you never loved any other but me."

"I do swear it, beautiful angel!" replied Phœbus, and his impassioned look concurred with the emphatic accent of his words to convince Fleur-de-Lys. It is possible that at the moment he himself believed what he asserted.

Meanwhile the good mother, pleased to see the young people on such excellent terms, had left the apartment to attend to some domestic matter or other. Phœbus perceived her absence, which emboldened the enterprising Captain. Fleur-de-Lys loved him; she was betrothed to him; she was alone with him: his former fondness for her was revived, if not in all its freshness, at any rate in all its ardour. I know not precisely what ideas crossed his mind; but so much is certain, that Fleur-de-Lys became suddenly alarmed at the expression of his countenance. She looked around her—her mother was gone!

"Bless me!" said she, flushed and agitated. "I am very hot!"

"Why," replied Phœbus, "I dare say it is almost noon. The sun is troublesome. I will draw the curtains."

"No, no!" cried the trembling damsel; "on the contrary, I have need of air"; and rising, she ran to the window, and stepped out on the balcony. Phœbus followed her thither.

The Place du Parvis, in front of Notre-Dame, into which, as the reader knows, this balcony looked, exhibited at this moment a sinister and singular spectacle, which quickly changed the nature of the timid Fleur-de-Lys' alarm. An immense crowd, which flowed back into all the adjacent streets, covered the Place, properly so called. The low wall which encompassed the Parvis would not have been sufficient to keep it clear, had it not been thickly lined by sergeants of the Onze-vingts and arquebusiers, with their pieces in their hands. The wide portals of the church were closed, contrasting with the numberless windows round the Place, which, thrown open up to the very roofs, displayed thousands of heads heaped one above another, nearly like piles of cannon-balls in a park of artillery. The surface of this crowd was grey, squalid, dirty. The sight which it was awaiting was evidently one of those which have the privilege of calling together all that is most disgusting in the population. Nothing could be more hideous than the noise that arose from this assemblage of sallow caps and unkempt heads. In this concourse there were more women than men, more laughing than crying.

Ever and anon some harsh or shrill voice was heard above the general din to this effect:

"I say, Mahiet Baliffre, is she to be hanged yonder?"

"No, simpleton—only to do penance there in chemise.—The priest is going to fling Latin in her face. 'Tis always done here, at noon precisely. If you want to see the hanging you must e'en go to the Grève."

"I will go afterwards."

.   .   .   .

"Is it true, La Boucombry, that she refused a confessor?"

"I am told so, La Bechaine."

"Only think, the pagan!"

.   .   .   .

"It is the custom, sir. The Bailiff of the Palace is bound to deliver over the culprit for execution, if of the laity, to the Provost of Paris; but if a clerk, to the official of the bishopric."

"I thank you, sir."

.   .   .   .

Such were the dialogues carried on at this moment among the spectators collected by the ceremony.

"Oh, my God! the poor creature!" exclaimed Fleur-de-Lys, surveying the populace with a sorrowful look. The Captain was too much engaged with her to notice the rabble.

At this moment the clock of Notre-Dame slowly struck twelve. A murmur of satisfaction pervaded the crowd. Scarcely had the last vibration of the twelfth stroke subsided when the vast assemblage of heads was broken into waves like the sea in a gale of wind, and one immense shout of "There she is!" burst simultaneously from pavement, windows, and roofs.

Fleur-de-Lys covered her eyes with her hands that she might not see.

Three Human Hearts

"Will you go in, charmer?" asked Phœbus.

"No," she replied; and those eyes which she had shut for fear she opened again out of curiosity.

A cart, drawn by a strong Norman bay, and completely sur-sounded by horsemen in purple livery, marked with white crosses, had just issued from the Rue Saint-Pierre-aux-Bœufs and entered the Place. The sergeants of the watch opened a passage for it through the populace with staves, with which they laid lustily about them. Beside the cart rode certain officers of justice and police, who might be known by their black dress, and the awkward manner in which they sat their horses. At their head paraded Master Jacques Charmolue. In the fatal vehicle was seated a young girl, with her hands tied behind her, and no priest at her side. She was stripped to her chemise: her long black hair—for it was not then customary to cut it off till the culprit was at the foot of the gallows —fell loosely over her bosom and her half-uncovered shoulders.

Through this flowing hair, more glossy than a raven's plumage, might be seen twisting a grey, knotty cord, which fretted her del-icate skin, and twined itself round the neck of the poor girl like an earthworm upon a flower. Beneath this cord glistened a little amu-let adorned with green beads, which had been left her no doubt because it is usual to refuse nothing to those who are going to die. The spectators in the windows could see at the bottom of the cart her naked legs, which she strove to conceal beneath her, as if by a last instinct of womanly modesty. At her feet there was a little goat, also bound. The prisoner held with her teeth her chemise, which was not properly fastened. Her misery seemed to be greatly aggravated by her being thus exposed nearly naked to the public gaze. Alas! it is not for such tremors that modesty is made!

"Only look, fair cousin," said Fleur-de-Lys sharply to the Cap-tain—"'tis that Bohemian hussy with the goat."

As she thus spoke she turned round toward Phœbus. His eyes were fixed on the cart. He was unusually pale.

"What Bohemian with the goat?" said he, faltering.

"What!" rejoined Fleur-de-Lys, "don't you recollect?"

"I know not what you mean," said Phœbus, interrupting her.

He was stepping back to return to the room; but Fleur-de-Lys, whose jealousy, some time since so strongly excited by this same Egyptian, was anew awakened, cast on him a look full of penetration and mistrust. She had a confused recollection at the moment of having heard that a Captain was implicated in the proceedings against this sorceress.

"What ails you?" said she to Phœbus; "one would suppose that the sight of this creature had given you a shock."

"Me! not the least in the world!" stammered Phœbus, with a forced grin.

"Then stay!" rejoined she imperiously, "and let us look on till all is over."

The unlucky Captain was obliged to stay. He recovered somewhat of his assurance on observing that the prisoner never raised her eyes from the bottom of the cart. It was but too surely La Esmeralda. On this last step of misfortune and ignomiiny she was still beautiful; her large black eyes appeared still larger, on account of the hollowness of her cheeks; her livid profile was pure and sublime. She resembled what she had been, as a Virgin of Masaccio's resembles a Virgin of Raphael's—feebler, thinner, more attenuated.

For the rest, there was nothing about her, excepting her modesty, but was left, as it were, to chance, so deeply was she overwhelmed by stupor and despair. At each jolt of the cart her form rebounded like an inanimate thing; her look was dull and inert. A tear glistened in her eye; but it was motionless, and looked as if it were frozen.

Meanwhile the sombre cavalcade had passed through the crowd, amid shouts of joy and attitudes of curiosity. In order to deserve the character of faithful historians, we must nevertheless record that many of the mob, ay, and of the hardest hearted too, on seeing her so beautiful and so forlorn, were moved with pity. The cart had now reached the Parvis.

It stopped before the central porch. The escort ranged itself on either side. The mob kept silence; and amid this silence, full of solemnity and anxiety, the folding doors of the great porch turned as if spontaneously upon their hinges, which creaked with a shrill sound like that of a fife, affording a view of the whole length of the church, vast, gloomy, hung with black, dimly lighted by a few tapers glimmering in the distance upon the high altar, and opening like the mouth of a cavern upon the Place resplendent with the glorious sunshine. At the farthest extremity, in the dusk of the chancel, was

Three Human Hearts

faintly seen a colossal silver cross relieved upon black cloth which fell behind it from the roof to the pavement. The whole nave was vacant. Heads of priests were however seen confusedly moving about in the distant stalls of the choir; and at the moment when the great door opened there burst from the church a grave, loud, and monotonous chant, hurling, as it were, in gusts, fragments of doleful psalms at the head of the condemned one.

Non timebo millia populi circumdantis me: exsurge, Domine; salvum me fac, Deus!
Salvum me fac, Deus, quoniam intraverunt aquæ usque ad animam meam.
Infixus sum in limo profundi; et non est substantia. [1]

At the same time another voice singly struck up on the steps of the high altar this melancholy offertory:—

Qui verbum meum audit, et credit ei qui misit me, habet vitam æternam et in judicium non venit; sed transit à morte in vitam.[2]

These chants sung by aged men, lost in the darkness, over that beautiful creature, full of youth and life, caressed by the warm air of spring, and inundated with the sunlight, belonged to the Mass for the dead. The populace listened devoutly.

The terrified girl, fixing her eyes on the dark interior of the church, seemed to lose both sight and thought. Her pale lips moved, as if in prayer; and when the executioner's man went to assist her to alight from the cart he heard her repeating in a faint voice the word, *"Phœbus!"*

Her hands were unbound, and she alighted, accompanied by her goat, which had also been untied, and bleated for joy on finding itself at liberty; and she was then made to walk barefoot on the hard pavement to the foot of the steps leading to the porch. The rope which was fastened about her neck trailed behind her; you would have taken it for a snake that was following her.

The chanting in the church ceased. A large gold crucifix and a

1 "I shall not fear though thousands compass me about; arise, Lord, and save me. Save me, O Lord, for the waters have overwhelmed my very soul. I am caught in the deep mire, and my goods are gone from me."
2 Whoso heareth my words, and believeth in Him that sent me, he shall have everlasting life, and does not come to judgment, but passes from death to life."

file of tapers began to move in the dusk. The sound of the halberts of the party-coloured Swiss was heard; and in a few moments a long procession of priests in copes, and deacons in dalmatics, slowly advanced chanting toward the prisoner, and expanded itself before her eyes and those of the mob. But hers were riveted on him who walked at its head immediately after the bearer of the crucifix. "Oh!" she muttered to herself, shuddering, "there he is again! The priest!"

It was actually the Archdeacon. On his left was the sub-chanter, and on his right the chanter bearing the staff of his office. He advanced, with head thrown back, and eyes fixed and open, chanting with a loud voice:

De ventre inferi clamavi, et exaudisti vocem meam.
Et projecisti me in profundum, in corde maris, et flumen circumdedit me.[1]

At the moment when he appeared in the broad daylight beneath the lofty pointed arch of the portal, covered with an ample cope of silver marked with a black cross, he was so pale that sundry of the crowd imagined it must be one of the marble bishops kneeling on the sepulchral monuments in the choir, who had risen and come to receive on the brink of the tomb her who was about to die.

She, not less pale, not less statue-like, was scarcely aware that a heavy lighted taper of yellow wax had been put into her hand; she had not heard the squeaking voice of the clerk reading the form of the penance; when told to say *Amen* she had said *Amen*. Neither did she recover any life or any strength till she saw the priest make a sign to those who had her in custody to retire, and advance alone toward her. She then felt the blood boil in her head, and a spark of indignation was rekindled in that soul, already cold, benumbed, stupefied.

The Archdeacon approached her slowly; even in this extremity she saw him survey her nearly naked form with an eye sparkling with pleasure, desire, and jealousy. In a loud voice he thus addressed her, "Bohemian girl, have you prayed God to pardon your crimes and misdemeanours?" Then stooping—as the spectators imagined, to receive her last confession—he whispered, "Wilt thou be mine? I can even yet save thee!"

[1] "I called from the deep and Thou heardest my voice; Thou didst plunge me into the deep, in the heart of the sea, and the floods compassed me about."

She eyed him steadfastly. "Go to the fiend, thy master, or I will inform of thee!"

He grinned horribly a ghastly smile. "They will not believe thee," he replied. "Thou wilt but add scandal to guilt. Answer quickly, wilt thou have me?"

"What hast thou done with my Phœbus?"

"He is dead," said the priest.

At that moment the wretched Archdeacon raised his head mechanically, and saw on the other side of the Place the Captain standing in the balcony with Fleur-de-Lys. He shuddered, passed his hand over his eyes, looked again, muttered a malediction, and all his features were violently contracted.

"Well then, die!" said he. "No one shall have thee." Then, lifting his hand over the Egyptian, he pronounced these words in a loud and solemn tone: *"I nunc anima anceps, et sit tibi Deus misericors!"* [1]

This was the dreadful form with which it was customary to conclude these gloomy ceremonies. It was the signal given by the priest to the executioner. The populace fell on their knees.

"Kyrie eleison!" said the priests, who stopped beneath the porch.

"Kyrie eleison!" repeated the crowd with a murmur that rose above their heads like the rumbling of an agitated sea.

"Amen!" said the Archdeacon.

He turned his back on the prisoner; his head sank upon his bosom; his hands crossed each other; he rejoined the train of priests, and presently receded from sight with the crucifix, the tapers, and the copes, beneath the dusky arches of the cathedral; and his sonorous voice expired by degrees in the choir, while chanting this verse of anguish: *"Omnes gurites tui et fluctus tui super me transierunt."* [2]

At the same time the intermitting stamp of the iron-shod shafts of the halberts of the Switzers, dying away between the intercolumniations of the nave, produced the effect of a clock-hammer striking the last hour of the doomed one.

Meanwhile the doors of Notre-Dame were left open, displaying to view the church empty, deserted, in mourning, taperless, and voiceless. The condemned girl stood motionless in her place, awaiting what was to be done with her. One of the vergers was obliged

[1] "Go, wavering soul! And may God be merciful unto thee!"
[2] "All thy whirlpools, O Lord, and all Thy waves, have gone over me!"

to intimate as much to Master Charmolue, who, during the whole of this scene, had been studying the bas-relief of the great porch, representing, according to some, the sacrifice of Abraham, according to others, the alchemical operation, the angel being typified by the sun, the fire by the bundle of sticks, and the operator by Abraham. It was with some difficulty that he was roused from this contemplation; but at length he turned about, and at a sign which he made two men in yellow dresses, the executioner's assistants, approached the Egyptian to tie her hands again.

The unfortunate creature, at the moment for reascending the fatal cart and setting out on her last stage, was probably seized by some keen repining after life. She raised her dry but inflamed eyes toward heaven, toward the sun, toward the silvery clouds, studded here and there with trapeziums and triangles of azure, and then cast them down around her upon the earth, upon the crowd, upon the houses.

All at once, while the men in yellow were pinioning her arms, she gave a startling scream, a scream of joy. In the balcony at the corner of the Place she had descried *him,* her friend, her lord, her Phœbus, just as he looked when alive. The judge had told her a falsehood! the priest had told her a falsehood! 'twas he himself —she could not possibly doubt it. There he stood, living, moving, habited in his brilliant uniform, with the plume on his head and the sword by his side.

"Phœbus!" she cried; "my Phœbus!"—and she would have stretched out toward him her arms trembling with love and transport, but they were bound.

She then saw the Captain knit his brow; a young and handsome girl who leant upon him looked at him with disdainful lip and angry eye; Phœbus then uttered a few words, which she was too far off to hear; both hastily retired from the balcony into the room, and the window was immediately closed.

"Phœbus!" cried she wildly, "dost thou too believe it?" A horrible idea had just flashed upon her. She recollected that she had been condemned for the murder of Captain Phœbus de Châteaupers. She had borne up thus far against everything. This last shock was too violent. She fell senseless upon the pavement.

"Come!" said Charmolue, "carry her to the cart, and let us make an end of the business!"

Three Human Hearts

No person had yet observed in the gallery of the royal statues, immediately above the pointed arches of the porch, a strange-looking spectator, who had till then been watching all that passed, with attitude so motionless, head so outstretched, visage so deformed, that, but for his apparel, half red and half purple, he might have been taken for one of those stone monsters, at whose mouths the long gutters of the cathedral have for these six hundred years disgorged themselves. This spectator had not lost a single incident of the tragedy that had been acting ever since noon before the porch of Notre-Dame; and in the very first moments he had, unobserved, securely tied to one of the small pillars of the gallery a knotted rope, the end of which reached the pavement. This done, he had set himself to watch as quietly as before, hissing from time to time at the jackdaws as they flew past him. All at once, at the moment when the executioner's assistants were preparing to obey the phlegmatic order of Charmolue, he strode across the balustrade of the gallery, seized the rope with feet, knees, and hands, glided down the façade like a drop of rain down a pane of glass; ran up to the two men with the swiftness of a cat that has fallen from a roof; felled both of them to the ground with his enormous fists; bore off the Egyptian on one arm, as a girl would her doll, and at one bound he was in the church, holding up the young girl above his head and shouting with terrific voice— "Sanctuary! sanctuary!" This was all done with the rapidity of lightning.

"Sanctuary! sanctuary!" repeated the mob, and the clapping of ten thousand hands caused Quasimodo's only eye to sparkle with joy and exultation.

This shock brought La Esmeralda to her senses. She opened her eyes, looked at Quasimodo, and instantly closed them again, as if horror-stricken at the sight of her deliverer.

Charmolue stood stupefied—so did the executioners and the whole escort. Within the walls of Notre-Dame the prisoner was secure from molestation. The cathedral was a place of refuge. Human justice dared not cross its threshold.

Quasimodo paused under the great porch. His large feet seemed as firmly rooted in the pavement of the church as the massive Roman pillars. His huge head, with its profuse covering of hair, appeared to be thrust down into his shoulders, like that of the lion, which too has a copious mane and no neck. He held the damsel, palpitating all over, hanging from his horny hands like a white drapery; but he carried her with as much care as if he was fearful of bruising or disturbing her. He felt, you would have thought, that a thing so delicate, so exquisite, so precious, was not made for such hands as his. At times he looked as though he dared not touch her even with his breath. Then, all at once, he would clasp her closely in his arms, against his angular bosom, as his treasure, as his all, as the mother of that girl would herself have done. His Cyclops eye bent down upon her, shed over her a flood of tenderness, of pity, of grief, and was suddenly raised flashing lightning. At this sight the women laughed and cried; the crowd stamped with enthusiasm, for at that moment Quasimodo was really beautiful. Yes, he was beautiful—he, that orphan, that foundling, that outcast; he felt himself august and strong; he looked in the face that society from which he was banished, and from which he had made so signal a conquest; the human justice from which he had snatched its victim; those judges, those executioners, all that force of the King's, which he, the meanest of the mean, had foiled with the force of God!

And then, how touching was that protection afforded by a being so deformed to a being so unfortunate as the girl condemned to die and saved by Quasimodo! It was the two extreme miseries of nature and society meeting and assisting each other.

After a triumph of a few minutes, however, Quasimodo hastened into the interior of the church with his burden. The people, fond of daring deeds, followed him with their eyes along the dusky nave, regretting that he had so soon withdrawn himself from their acclamations. All at once he was again descried at one of the extremities of the gallery of the Kings of France; he ran along it, like a maniac, holding up his prize in his arms, and shouting— "Sanctuary!" The populace greeted him with fresh applause. Having traversed the gallery he again penetrated into the interior of the church. Presently afterward he again appeared on the upper platform, still bearing the Egyptian in his arms, still running like one frantic, still shouting— "Sanctuary." Again the mob applauded. At length he made his third appearance on the top of the tower of the great bell: there he seemed to show proudly to the whole city her whom he had saved, and his thundering voice—that voice which was heard so seldom, and which he himself never heard—made the air ring with the thrice-repeated shout of— "Sanctuary! Sanctuary! Sanctuary!"

"Hurrah! Hurrah!" cried the populace on their part; and this prodigious acclamation was heard on the other side of the river by the crowd collected in the Place de Grève, and by the recluse, who was still waiting with her eyes riveted on the gallows.

BOOK VIII

CHAPTER I

A HIGH FEVER

CLAUDE FROLLO was no longer in Notre-Dame, when his foster-son cut thus abruptly the fatal noose in which the unhappy Archdeacon had caught the Egyptian, and was himself caught. On returning to the sacristy he had stripped off the alb, the cope, and the stole, thrown them all into the hands of the stupefied beadle, hurried out at the private door of the cloisters, ordered a boatman of the Terrain to carry him across the river, and wandered among the hilly streets of the Université, meeting at every step parties of men and women, hastening joyously toward the Pont Saint-Michel, "in hopes of being in time to see the sorceress hanged!" Pale and haggard, blinded and more bewildered than an owl let loose and pursued by a troop of boys in broad daylight, he knew not where he was, what he did, whether he was awake or dreaming. He walked, he ran, heedless whither, taking any street at random, still driven onward by the Grève, the horrible Grève, which he vaguely knew to be behind him.

In this manner he pursued his way along the hill of Sainte-Geneviève, and left the town by the gate of Saint-Victor. So long as he could see, on turning round, the line of towers enclosing the Université, and the scattered houses of the suburb, he continued to flee; but when at length the inequality of the ground had completely shut out that hateful Paris from his view, when he could fancy himself a hundred leagues off, in the country, in a desert, he paused, and felt as though he breathed once more.

A crowd of frightful ideas then rushed upon his mind. He saw plainly into the recesses of his soul, and shuddered. He thought of that unhappy girl who had undone him, and whom he had undone. With haggard eye he followed the double winding way along which fatality had urged their two destinies to the point of intersection, where it had pitilessly dashed them against one another. He thought of the folly of eternal vows, of the vanity of chastity, science, reli-

288

gion, and virtue. He wilfully plunged into evil thoughts, and as he immersed himself in them he felt a Satanic laugh arising within him.

And when, while thus diving into his soul, he saw how large a space nature had there prepared for the passions, he laughed still more bitterly. He stirred up from the bottom of his heart all its hatred and all its malignity; and he perceived, with the cold indifference of a physician examining a patient, that this hatred and this malignity were but vitiated love; that love, the source of every virtue in man, was transformed into horrid things in the heart of a priest, and that one so constituted as he in making himself a priest made himself a demon. He then laughed more hideously than ever, and all at once he again turned pale on considering the darkest side of his fatal passion, that corroding, venomous, rancorous, implacable love, which had consigned the one to the gallows, the other to perdition.

And then he laughed again on bethinking him that Phœbus was not dead; that he was still alive, gay, and joyous; that he had a smarter uniform than ever, and a new mistress whom he took to see the old one hanged. He laughed still more heartily on reflecting that, among all the living beings whose death he had wished for, the Egyptian, the only creature whom he did not hate, was also the only one who had not escaped him.

He bethought him of the plight in which the woman whom he loved had been exposed to the gaze of the crowd, of the entire population of Paris. He wrung his hands on reflecting how that woman, that beauteous girl, that virgin lily, that being all modesty and purity, whom he durst not approach without trembling, and a glimpse of whom to himself alone would have been a supreme happiness, had been exhibited in the broad face of day to the populace, to the vilest of the rabble of Paris, to lackeys, vagabonds, mendicants, thieves. He wept for rage at the mysteries of love exposed, profaned, sullied, withered for ever.

And when he strove to picture to himself the felicity which he might have found upon earth if she had not been a Bohemian, and if he had not been a priest, if Phœbus had not existed, and if she had not loved him; when he considered that a life of serenity and affection might have been possible for him also. even for him; that, at that very moment, there were here and there on the earth happy couples engaged in fond converse in orange groves, on the banks of murmuring streams, in the presence of a setting sun, or of a starry sky; and that, had it pleased God, he might have formed with her one of those blessed couples, his heart dissolved in tenderness and despair.

She formed the subject of his every thought. It was this fixed idea that haunted him incessantly, that tortured him, that racked his brain, and gnawed his vitals. He felt not regret; he felt not remorse; all that he had done he was ready to do again: he would rather see her in the hands of the hangman than in the arms of the Captain. But so acute was his anguish that at times he tore off his hair by handfuls.

There was one moment among others when it came into his mind that possibly at that very instant the hideous chain which he had seen in the morning might be drawing its iron noose round that neck so slender and so graceful. This idea made the perspiration start from every pore.

There was another moment when, laughing diabolically at himself the while, his imagination represented to him at once La Esmeralda as on the first day he had seen her, all life, all mirth, all joy, dressed and adorned, agile, dancing, harmonious, and La Esmeralda of the last hour, stripped, the rope about her neck, slowly ascending with bare feet the rough ladder to the gibbet: this twofold picture was drawn before him with such force as to extort from him a terrible shriek.

While this hurricane of despair was bending, breaking, shivering, overthrowing, uprooting everything in his soul, his eye ranged over the scene round him. At his feet some hens were ferreting among the bushes, and picking up the burnished insects that were running about in the sun; overhead groups of dapple-grey clouds were sprinkled upon an azure sky; on the horizon the steeple of the abbey of Saint-Victor pierced the curve of the hill with its slated obelisk, and the miller of Copeaux watched the labouring sails of his mills turning round, whistling the while. All this active, organized, tranquil life displayed around him in a thousand forms gave him pain. Again he began to flee.

This flight from nature, from life, from himself, from man, from God, from everything, lasted till evening. Sometimes he threw himself on his face upon the earth and tore up the young corn with his fingers; at others he paused along some lone village street, and his thoughts were so insupportable that he grasped his head with both hands, as though striving to wrench it from his shoulders in order to dash it upon the ground.

The sun was near setting when, on examining himself afresh, he found that he was almost mad. The storm which had been raging within him from the moment when he had lost the hope and the will to save the Egyptian had not left in his mind a single sound thought or idea. His reason was laid prostrate, nay almost utterly destroyed. His mind retained but two distinct images, La Esmeralda and the gibbet; all the rest was black. These two images formed a horrible group; and the more he fixed on them so much attention and thought as he was yet master of, the more they seemed to increase, according to a fantastic progression, the one in charm, in grace, in beauty, in light—the other in horror: so that at last La Esmeralda appeared like a star, the gibbet like an enormous fleshless arm.

It is remarkable that, during the whole of this torture, he never conceived any serious idea of putting an end to himself. The wretched man was tenacious of life. It is possible that he really saw hell gaping before him.

The day meanwhile continued to decline. The living principle which still existed within him began to think confusedly of returning. He conceived that he was far from Paris, but on examining the objects around he found that he had turned short after passing the bounds of the Université. The steeple of Saint-Sulpice and the three tall spires of Saint-Germain-des-Prés shot up above the horizon on his right. He proceeded in that direction. When he heard the challenge of the men-at-arms of the abbot around the embattled circumvallation of Saint-Germain, he turned off, took a path which presented itself between the abbey-mill and the lazar-house of the hamlet, and presently found himself on the margin of the Pré-aux-Clercs. This meadow was celebrated for the squabbles which took place there night and day; it was, so saith the chronicler, the *hydra* of the poor monks of Saint-Germain. The Archdeacon was apprehensive lest he should meet some one; he was afraid of every human face; he had avoided the Université and the hamlet of Saint-Germain; he wished to make it as late as possible before he entered the streets. He proceeded along the Pré-aux-Clercs, took the lonely path which separated it from the Dieu Neuf, and at length reached the bank of the river. There Dom Claude found a boatman who for a few deniers took him up the Seine to the point of the Cité, and set him ashore upon that vacant tongue of land, where the reader has already seen Gringoire pondering, and which extended beyond the King's gardens parallel with the isle of the cattle-ferryman.

The monotonous rocking of the boat and the murmur of the water had somewhat lulled the wretched Claude. When the boatman had left him he remained standing stupidly upon the strand, looking straight forward. All the objects he beheld seemed to dance before his eyes, forming a sort of phantasmagoria. It is no uncommon thing for the fatigue of excessive grief to produce this effect upon the mind.

The sun had set behind the tall Tour de Nesle. It was just twilight. The sky was white; the water of the river was white; and between these the left bank of the Seine, upon which his eyes were fixed, extended its sombre mass, which, gradually diminished by the perspective, pierced the haze of the horizon like a black arrow. It was covered with houses, of which nothing was distinguishable but the obscure profile, standing out in strong relief in the dark from the light ground of the sky and the water. Lights began to glimmer here and there in the windows. This immense black obelisk, thus bounded by the two white sheets of the sky and the river, of great breadth at this place, produced on Dom Claude a singular effect, which may be compared with that which would be experienced by a man lying down on his back at the foot of the steeple of Strasburg Cathedral, and looking at its enormous shaft piercing above his head the penumbra of the twilight; only in this Claude was standing and the obelisk lying. But as the river, in reflecting the sky, lengthened the abyss beneath him, the immense promontory shot forth into space like any church-steeple, and the impression was the same. That impression was rendered the more striking and extraordinary by the circumstance that this steeple was two leagues high—a colossal, immeasurable, unparalleled object; a tower of Babel; an edifice such as human eye never beheld. The chimneys of the houses, the battlements of the walls, the angles of the roofs, the steeple of the Augustines, the Tour de Nesle, all those salient points which indented the profile of the immense obelisk, heightened the illusion by presenting to the eye a grotesque semblance of the fretwork of a rich and fantastic sculpture. Claude, in the state of hallucination in which

A High Fever

he then was, fancied that he saw—saw with his bodily eyes—the tower of hell: the thousand lights gleaming from bottom to top of this frightful tower appeared to him so many entrances to the immense furnace within; and the voices and sounds which issued from it, the shrieks and moans of the damned. A deep fear came over him; he covered his ears with his hands that he might not hear, turned his back that he might not see, and hurried away from the terrible vision. But the vision was within him.

On entering the streets the passengers who jostled one another by the light of the shop-fronts appeared like spectres incessantly going and coming round him. Strange noises rang in his ears; extraordinary fancies disturbed his mind. He saw neither houses nor pavement, neither men, women, nor carriages, but a chaos of confused objects blending one with another. At the corner of the Rue de la Barillerie there was a grocer's shop, the penthouse of which was hung all along, according to immemorial custom, with tin hoops, to which were attached imitation candles of wood: these, being shaken by the wind, clattered like castanets. He imagined that he heard the skeletons of Montfaucon clashing together in the dark.

"Oh!" muttered he, "the night-wind is driving them one against another, and mingling the clank of their chains with the rattling of their bones. She is there too, perhaps, among them!"

Distracted, he knew not whither he went. Presently he was upon the Pont Saint-Michel. He perceived a light in the window of a ground-floor room; he approached it. Through a cracked pane he beheld a mean apartment, which awakened confused recollections in his mind. In this apartment, faintly lighted by a lamp, he saw a fair, fresh-coloured, jovial-looking youth, who, loudly laughing the while, was toying with a young woman whose dress was far from demure; and near the lamp was seated an old woman spinning and singing, or rather squalling, a song. In the intervals when the laughter ceased, snatches of the old woman's song reached the ear of the priest; the tenor of it was frightful and not very intelligible.

The old woman was Falourdel, the girl was a wanton, and the youth was his brother Jehan. He continued to watch them. He saw Jehan go to a window at the farther end of the room, open it, and look out on the quay, where a thousand illumined windows glanced in the distance; and he heard him say while shutting the window— " 'Pon my soul, 'tis dark night. The citizens are lighting up their candles, and God Almighty his stars."

Jehan then went back to his companion, and held up a bottle which stood on the table. "Zounds!" he cried, "empty already!—and I have no more money." So saying he came forth from the house. Dom Claude had but just time to throw himself on the ground that he might not be met, looked in the face, and recognized by his brother. Luckily the street was dark and the scholar not sober. "Oho!" said he; "here is one who has been enjoying himself to-day." With his foot he shook Dom Claude, who held in his breath.

"Dead drunk!" resumed Jehan. "Full enough, it seems. A proper leech loosed from a cask. Bald too!" added he, stooping— "an old man! *Fortunate senex!*" [1]

Dom Claude then heard him move away, saying, "Never mind! Reason is a fine thing, though; and very lucky is my brother the Archdeacon in being prudent and having money."

The Archdeacon then rose, and ran without stopping towards Notre-Dame, the enormous towers of which he saw lifting themselves in the dark above the houses. At the moment when, quite breathless, he reached the Place du Parvis, he paused, and durst not raise his eyes to the fatal edifice. "Oh!" said he, in a low tone, "is it true, then, that such a thing could have happened here to-day? —this very morning?"

He ventured, however, to look at the church. The façade was dark; the sky behind it glistened with stars. The crescent of the moon, which had not been long above the horizon, was seen at that moment on the top of the right-hand tower, and seemed to be perched like a luminous bird on the edge of the parapet, cut out into large trefoils.

The door of the cloisters was shut, but the Archdeacon always carried about him the key of the tower in which was his laboratory. Availing himself of it, he entered the church. He found the interior dark and silent as the grave. From the large shadows which fell from all sides in broad sheets he knew that the hangings put up for the morning's ceremony had not been removed. The great silver cross glistened amid the gloom, dotted with sparkling points, like the Milky Way of this sepulchral night. The tall windows of the choir

---

[1] "Fortunate old man!"

A High Fever

showed above the black drapery the upper extremity of their pointed arches, the panes of which, admitting a faint ray of moonlight, had but those doubtful colours of night, a sort of violet, white, and blue, the tint of which is elsewhere found only on the faces of the dead. The Archdeacon, perceiving all around the choir these livid points of arches, fancied that he beheld a circle of ghastly faces staring at him.

With hurried step he began to flee across the church. It then seemed to him that the church too moved, breathed, lived; that each massive column was transformed into an enormous leg, stamping the ground with its broad stone foot, and that the gigantic cathedral was but a sort of prodigious elephant, puffing and walking, with pillars for legs, the two towers for trunks, and the immense sheet of black cloth for a caparison.

Thus the fever or the frenzy of the wretched priest had attained such a degree of intensity that to him the external world was but a kind of Apocalypse, visible, palpable, terrific.

For a moment he felt somewhat relieved. On entering one of the aisles he perceived a reddish light behind a cluster of pillars. He ran toward it as toward a star. It was the poor lamp which night and day threw a dim light on the public breviary of Notre-Dame, beneath its iron grating. He hurried to the sacred book, in hopes of finding in it some consolation or encouragement. It was open at this passage of Job, which caught his fixed eye, "Then a spirit passed before my face; the hair of my flesh stood up."

On reading this fearful text he felt much the same as a blind man whose fingers are pricked by the staff which he has picked up. His knees failed him, and he sank upon the pavement, thinking of her who had that day suffered death. Such volumes of blasting vapours enveloped his brain that it seemed as if his head had been turned into one of the chimneys of hell.

He must have remained for a long time in this attitude, neither thinking nor feeling, helpless and passive in the hand of the demon. At length, recovering some degree of consciousness, he thought of seeking refuge in the tower, near his trusty Quasimodo. He rose, and, being afraid, he took the lamp of the breviary to light him. This was a sacrilege; but he no longer regarded such a trifle as that.

He slowly ascended the staircase of the tower, filled with a secret dread, which was communicated to the passengers who now and then crossed the Parvis, on seeing the mysterious light of this lamp mounting so late from loophole to loophole to the top of the tower.

All at once he felt a cool air upon his face, and found himself under the doorway of the uppermost gallery. The night was cold. The sky was mottled with clouds, the large white masses of which, overlapping each other at the edges, and being compressed at the corners, resembled the ice of a river that has broken up in winter. The crescent moon, imbedded in those clouds, looked like a celestial ship surrounded by these aërial sheets of ice.

He cast down his eye between the iron railing of the dwarf colonnade which unites the two towers, and for a moment contemplated through the veil of mist and smoke the vast extent of the roofs of Paris, sharp, countless, crowded together, and small as the ripples of a calm sea in a summer night. The moon gave but a faint light, which imparted an ashy tint to earth and sky.

At this moment the clock raised its loud and solemn voice. It was midnight. The priest thought of noon: it was again twelve o'clock. "Oh!" muttered he to himself, "she must be cold by this time!"

All at once a gust of wind extinguished his lamp, and at the same moment he saw something white, a shade, a human form, a female, appear at the opposite angle of the tower. He shuddered. By the side of this female there was a little goat, which mingled her bleating with the last tones of the bell. He had the courage to look at her— 'twas she herself!

She was pale; she was sad. Her hair fell over her shoulders, as in the morning; but there was no rope about her neck; her hands were not bound; she was free, she was dead.

She was habited in white, and had a white veil over her head. She came toward him slowly, looking up at the sky, and followed by the supernatural goat. He was petrified: he would have fled, but was unable. All he could do was to recede a step for every one that she advanced. He retreated in this manner till he was beneath the dark vault of the staircase. His blood curdled at the idea that she might perhaps come that way too; if she had, he might have died of fright.

She did in fact approach so near as the door of the staircase, where she paused for a few moments; she cast a fixed look into the darkness, but without appearing to discern the priest, and passed on. She seemed to him taller than when alive; he saw the moonshine through her white robe; he heard her breath.

When she was gone he began to descend the stairs as slowly as he had seen the spectre move. Horror-stricken, his hair erect, still holding the extinguished lamp in his hand, he fancied himself a spectre; and, while descending the winding stairs, he heard a voice, laughing and repeating distinctly in his ear, "A spirit passed before my face; the hair of my flesh stood up."

CHAPTER II

THE SANCTUARY

IN the Middle Ages every town, and till the time of Louis XII every town in France, had its sanctuaries. Amid the deluge of penal laws and barbarous jurisdictions which inundated that division of Paris which we have specially called the Cité, these sanctuaries were a kind of islands, which rose above the level of human justice. Every criminal who took refuge there was saved. There were in a district almost as many sanctuaries as places of execution. It was the abuse of impunity going hand in hand with the abuse of punishment—two bad things, which strove to correct one another. The palaces of the King, the mansions of the princes, but above all, the churches, had the right of sanctuary. Sometimes that right was conferred for a time on a whole city which needed repeopling. Louis XI made Paris a sanctuary in 1467.

When he had once set foot in the sanctuary the criminal was sacred, but he was obliged to beware of leaving it; one step out of the island-asylum plunged him again into the sea. The wheel, the gallows, the rack, kept strict guard round his retreat, and watched their prey incessantly as sharks prowl round a ship. Condemned persons thus rescued have been known to grow grey in a cloister, on the staircase of a palace, in the garden of an abbey, in the porch of a church: in this way the sanctuary was a prison as well as any place that bore the name. It sometimes happened that a solemn ordinance of the Parliament violated the sanctuary, and gave up the condemned to the executioner; but the case was rare. The Parliaments were jealous of the bishops, and when the gowns of the two professions chanced to come into collision that of the Church generally had the worst of it. At times, however, as in the affair of the assassins of Petit-Jean, the executioner of Paris, and in that of Emery Rousseau, the murderer of Jean Valleret, Justice overleaped the Church, and passed on to the execution of its sentences; but unless authorized by an ordinance of the Parliament woe to him who forcibly violated a sanctuary. Everybody knows what was the fate of Robert de Clermont, Marshal of France, and Jean de Châlons, Marshal of Champagne; and yet the party, in whose case they had interfered, one Perrin Marc, was but a moneychanger's man and a scurvy assassin: but then the two marshals had broken open the doors of Saint-Méry. There was the enormity!

Such was the respect with which sanctuaries were invested that, according to tradition, it occasionally extended to brute animals. Aymoin relates that a stag, hunted by Dagobert, having taken refuge near the tomb of Saint-Denis, the dogs stopped short, merely barking at him.

The churches had in general a cell appropriated to the reception of fugitives. In 1407 Nicolas Flamel had built for such persons, in the church of Saint-Jacques-de-la-Boucherie, a chamber which cost him four livres six sous sixteen deniers Parisis.

At Notre-Dame it was a small cell on the top of the aisle, under the flying-buttresses, facing the cloisters, on the very spot where the wife of the present keeper of the towers has made herself a garden, which is to the hanging gardens of Babylon what a lettuce is to a palm-tree, or a portress to Semiramis.

Here it was that, after his wild and triumphant course through towers and galleries, Quasimodo deposited La Esmeralda. So long as this race lasted the damsel had not recovered her senses; half stupefied, half awake, she was sensible of nothing but that she was mounting into the air, that she was floating, flying in it, that something was lifting her above the earth. From time to time she heard the loud laugh and the harsh voice of Quasimodo at her ear; she opened her eyes, and then beneath her she confusedly saw Paris speckled with its thousand roofs of slate and tile, like red and blue

The Sanctuary

mosaic-work, and above her head the hideous but joyful face of Quasimodo. Again her eyes closed, she imagined that all was over, that she had been executed during her swoon, and that the deformed spirit who had governed her destiny had seized and borne her away.

But when the panting bell-ringer had laid her down in the cell of sanctuary, when she felt his huge hands gently loosing the cord that galled her arms, she experienced that kind of shock which abruptly wakens those on board a ship that runs aground in the middle of a dark night. Her ideas awoke also and returned to her one by one. She saw that she was in the church; she recollected having been snatched out of the hand of the executioner; that Phœbus was alive, and that he no longer loved her; and these two ideas, one of which imparted such bitterness to the other, presenting themselves at once to the poor girl, she turned toward Quasimodo, who remained standing beside her, and whose aspect frightened her, saying, "Why did you save me?"

He looked anxiously at her, as if striving to guess what she said. She repeated the question. He then cast on her a look deeply sorrowful, and withdrew. She was lost in astonishment.

A few moments afterward he returned, bringing a bundle which he laid at her feet. It contained apparel which charitable women had left for her at the door of the church. She then cast down her eyes at herself, saw that she was almost naked, and blushed. Life had fully returned. Quasimodo seemed to participate in this feeling of modesty. Covering his face with his large hand, he again retired, but with slow step.

She hastened to dress herself. It was a white robe with a white veil—the habit of a novice of the Hôtel Dieu. She had scarcely finished before Quasimodo returned. He brought a basket under one arm and a mattress under the other. The basket contained a bottle, bread, and some other provisions. He set down the basket, and said, "Eat!"—He spread the mattress on the floor, and said, "Sleep!" It was his own dinner, his own bed, that the bell-ringer had brought her.

The Egyptian lifted her eyes to his face to thank him; but she could not utter a word. The poor fellow was absolutely hideous. She drooped her head with a thrill of horror. "Ah!" said he, "I frighten you, I see. I am ugly enough, God wot. Do not look at,

299

but only hearken to, me.—In the daytime you shall stay here; at night you can walk about all over the church. But stir not a step out of it either by night or by day, or they will catch you and kill you, and it will be the death of me."

Moved at this address, she raised her head to reply, but he was gone. Once more she was alone, pondering on the singular words of this almost monstrous being, and struck by the tone of his voice, at once so harsh and so gentle.

She then began to examine her cell. It was a chamber some six feet square, with a small aperture for a window, and a door opening upon the slightly inclined plane of the roof, composed of flat stones. Several gutters, terminating in heads of animals, seemed to bend down over it, and to stretch out their necks to look in at the hole. On a level with its roof she perceived a thousand chimney-tops, disgorging the smoke of all the fires of Paris. Melancholy prospect for the poor Egyptian, a foundling, rescued from the gallows; an unfortunate young creature, who had neither country, nor family, nor home!

At the moment when the idea of her forlorn situation wrung her heart more keenly than ever, she felt a hairy shaggy head rubbing against her hands and her knees. She shuddered—everything now alarmed her—and looked. It was the poor goat, the nimble Djali, which had escaped along with her at the moment when Quasimodo dispersed Charmolue's brigade, and had been at her feet nearly an hour, lavishing caresses on her mistress, without obtaining a single glance. The Egyptian covered the fond animal with kisses. "Oh, Djali!" said she, "how I have forgotten thee! And yet thou thinkest of me. Thou, for thy part, at least, art not ungrateful." At the same time, as if an invisible hand had removed the obstruction which had so long repressed her tears, she began to weep, and as the big drops trickled down her cheeks she felt the keenest and bitterest portion of her sorrows leaving her along with them.

Evening came on. The night was so beautiful, the moonlight so soft, that she ventured to take a turn in the high gallery which runs round the church. She felt somewhat refreshed by her walk, so calm did the earth appear to her, beheld from that elevation.

CHAPTER III

A HUMAN HEART IN A FORM SCARCELY HUMAN

NEXT morning she perceived on awakening that she had slept. This singular circumstance surprised her—it was so long that she had been unaccustomed to sleep! The sun, peeping in at her window, threw his cheering rays upon her face. But besides the sun she saw at this aperture an object that affrighted her—the unlucky face of Quasimodo. She involuntarily closed her eyes, but in vain; she still fancied that she saw through her rosy lids that visage so like an ugly mask. She kept her eyes shut. Presently she heard a hoarse voice saying very kindly: "Don't be afraid. I am your friend. I came to see you sleep. What harm can it do you, if I come to look at you when your eyes are shut? Well, well, I am going. There, now, I am behind the wall. Now you can open your eyes."

There was something still more plaintive than these words in the accent with which they were uttered. The Egyptian, affected by them, opened her eyes. He was actually no longer at the window. She went to it, looked out, and saw the poor hunchback cowering under the wall, in an attitude of grief and resignation. She made an effort to overcome the aversion which he excited. "Come!" said she kindly to him. Observing the motion of her lips, Quasimodo imagined that she was bidding him to go away. He then rose and retired, with slow and halting step and drooping head, without so much as daring to raise his eyes, filled with despair, to the damsel. "Come then!" she cried; but he continued to move off. She then darted out of the cell, ran to him, and took hold of his arm. On feeling her touch, Quasimodo trembled in every limb. He lifted his supplicating eye, and, finding that she drew him toward her, his whole face shone with joy and tenderness. She would have made him go into her cell, but he insisted on staying at her threshold. "No, no," said he, "the owl never enters the nest of the lark."

She then seated herself gracefully on her bed, with her goat at her feet. Both remained for some minutes motionless, contemplating in silence, he so much beauty, she so much ugliness. Every moment she discovered in Quasimodo some new deformity. Her look wandered from his knock-knees to his hunch back, from his hunch back to his only eye. She could not conceive how a creature so awkwardly put together could exist. At the same time an air of such sadness and gentleness pervaded his whole figure that she began to be reconciled with it.

He was the first to break silence. "Did you not call me back?" said he.

"Yes!" replied she, with a nod of affirmation.

He understood the sign. "Alas!" said he, as if hesitating to finish, "you must know, I am deaf."

"Poor fellow!" exclaimed the Bohemian, with an expression of pity.

He smiled sadly. "You think nothing else was wanting, don't you? Yes, I am deaf. That is the way in which I am served. It is terrible, is it not?—while you—you are so beautiful!"

The tone of the poor fellow conveyed such a profound feeling of his wretchedness that she had not the heart to utter a word. Besides, he would not have heard her. He then resumed: "Never till now was I aware how hideous I am. When I compare myself with you I cannot help pitying myself, poor unhappy monster that I am! I must appear to you like a beast.—You, you are a sunbeam, a drop of dew, a bird's song!—I, I am something frightful, neither man nor brute, something harder, more shapeless, and more trampled upon, than a flint."

He then laughed, and scarcely could there be aught in the world more cutting than this laugh. He continued: "Yes, I am deaf: but you will speak to me by gestures, by signs. I have a master who talks to me in that way. And then I shall know your meaning from the motion of your lips, from your look."

"Well, then," replied she smiling, "tell me why you have saved me?"

He looked steadfastly at her while she spoke.

"I understand," rejoined he; "you ask me why I saved you. You have forgotten a wretch who attempted one night to carry you off, a wretch to whom, the very next day, you brought relief on the vile pillory. A draught of water and a look of pity are more than I could repay with my life. You have forgotten that wretch—but he has not forgotten."

She listened to him with deep emotion. A tear started into the eye of the bell-ringer, but it did not fall. He appeared to make a point of repressing it. "Look you," he again began, when he no longer feared lest that tear should escape him—"we have very high towers here; a man falling from one of them would be dead almost before he reached the pavement. When you wish to be rid of me, tell me to throw myself from the top—you have but to say the word; nay, a look will be sufficient."

He then rose. Unhappy as was the Bohemian, this grotesque being awakened compassion even in her. She made him a sign to stay.

"No, no," said he, "I must not stay too long. I am ill at ease. It is out of pity that you do not turn your eyes from me. I will seek some place where I can look at you without your seeing me; that will be better."

He drew from his pocket a small metal whistle. "Take this," said he: "when you want me, when you wish me to come, when you have the courage to see me, whistle with this. I shall hear that sound."

He laid the whistle on the floor and retired.

CHAPTER IV

EARTHENWARE AND CRYSTAL

TIME passed on. Tranquillity returned by degrees to the soul of La Esmeralda. Excessive grief, like excessive joy, is too violent to last. The human heart cannot continue long in either extremity. The Bohemian had suffered so much that of the feelings she had lately experienced astonishment alone was left.

Along with security hope began to revive within her. She was out of society, out of life, but she had a vague feeling that it might not be impossible for her to return to them. She was like one dead, keeping in reserve a key to her tomb.

The terrible images which had so long haunted her were leaving her by degrees. All the hideous phantoms, Pierrat Torterue, Jacques Charmolue, had faded from her mind—all of them, even the priest himself. And then, Phœbus was yet living: she was sure of it; she had seen him. To her the life of Phœbus was everything. After the series of fatal shocks which had laid waste all her affections she had found but one sentiment in her soul which they had not overthrown —her love for the Captain. Love is like a tree: it shoots of itself; it strikes its roots deeply into our whole being, and frequently continues to put forth green leaves over a heart in ruins. And there is this unaccountable circumstance attending it, that the blinder that passion the more tenacious it is. Never is it stronger than when it is most unreasonable.

No doubt La Esmeralda did not think of the Captain without pain. No doubt it was terrible that he too should have made such a mistake, that he too should have thought the thing possible, that he too should have believed the wound to be inflicted by one who would have given a thousand lives for his sake. Still there was no reason to be angry with him: had she not confessed the crime? had she not, frail creature as she was, yielded to the torture? All the fault was hers. She ought to have suffered them to tear her in pieces rather than make such an admission. After all, could she see Phœbus but once more, for a single minute; a word, a look, would suffice to undeceive him and bring back the truant. This she had not the least doubt of. There were, at the same time, several singular circumstances about which she puzzled herself—the accident of Phœbus's presence at the penance; the young female in whose company he was. She was, no doubt, his sister. An improbable explanation, but she was satisfied with it, because she must needs believe that Phœbus still loved her, and loved but her. Had he not sworn it? What more could she require, simple and credulous as she was? And then, in this affair, were not appearances much more against her than against him? She waited therefore—she hoped.

We may add, too, that the church, that vast church which saved her, which enveloped her on all sides, which guarded her, was itself a sovereign anodyne. The solemn lines of that architecture, the religious attitude of all the objects around her, the serene and pious thoughts which transpired, as it were, through all the pores of that pile, acted upon her unknown to herself. The edifice, moreover, had sounds of such majesty and such blessing that they soothed her broken spirit. The monotonous chant of the officiating priests; the responses of the congregation, sometimes inarticulate, sometimes thundering; the harmonious shiver of the windows; the organ bursting forth like a hundred trumpets; the three belfries buzzing like hives of immense bees; all that orchestra, with its gigantic gamut incessantly ascending and descending from a crowd below to a bell-tower above, lulled her memory, her imagination, her sorrows. The bells more especially had this soothing effect. It was like a mighty magnetism which those vast engines poured over her in broad waves. Accordingly each successive sunrise found her most serene, more comfortable, and less pale. In proportion as her inward wounds healed her face recovered its grace and beauty, but chastened with more sedateness, more repose. Her former character returned also— even somewhat of her cheerfulness, her pretty pout, her fondness for her goat and for singing, and her modesty. In the morning she shrunk into a corner of her cell to dress herself, lest any inmate of neighbouring garrets should espy her through the window.

When the thoughts of Phœbus allowed her time the Egyptian would sometimes think of Quasimodo. He was the only bond, the only link, the only communication, that was left her with mankind, with the living. The unfortunate girl was more completely cut off from the world than Quasimodo. As for the strange friend whom chance had given her, she knew not what to make of him. She would frequently reproach herself for not feeling sufficient grati-tude to blind her to his imperfections; but decidedly she could not accustom herself to the poor bell-ringer. He was too hideous.

She had left on the floor the whistle that he had given her. Quasi-modo, nevertheless, looked in from time to time, on the succeeding days. She strove as much as she could to conceal her aversion when he brought her the basket of provisions or the pitcher of water; but he was sure to perceive the slightest movement of that kind, and then he went sorrowfully away.

One day he came just at the moment when she was fondling Djali. For a while he stood full of thought before the graceful group of the goat and the Egyptian. At length, shaking his huge misshapen head: "My misfortune," said he, "is that I am too much like a hu-man creature. Would to God that I had been a downright beast, like that goat!"

She cast on him a look of astonishment. "Oh!" he replied to that look—"well do I know why," and immediately retired.

Another time, when he came to the door of the cell, which he never entered, La Esmeralda was singing an old Spanish ballad; she knew not the meaning of the words, but it dwelt upon her ear because the Bohemian women had lulled her with it when quite a child. At the abrupt appearance of that ugly face the damsel stopped short, with an involuntary start in the middle of her song. The unhappy bell-ringer dropped upon his knees at the threshold of the door, and with a beseeching look clasped his clumsy, shapeless hands. "Oh!" said he sorrowfully, "go on, I pray you, and drive me not away." Not wishing to vex him, the trembling girl continued the ballad. By degrees her alarm subsided, and she gave herself up entirely to the impression of the melancholy tune which she was singing; while he remained upon his knees, with his hands joined as in prayer, scarcely breathing, his look intently fixed on the sparkling orbs of the Bohemian. You would have said that he was listening to her song with his eyes.

On another occasion, he came to her with an awkward and bashful air. "Hearken to me," said he, with effort; "I have something to say to you."—She made a sign to him that she was listening. He then began to sigh, half opened his lips, appeared for a moment ready to speak, looked at her, shook his head, and slowly retired, pressing his hand to his brow, and leaving the Egyptian in amazement.

Among the grotesque heads sculptured in the wall there was one for which he showed a particular predilection, and with which he seemed to exchange brotherly looks. The Egyptian once heard him address it in these words, "Oh! why am I not of stone, like thee?"

At length one morning La Esmeralda, having advanced to the parapet of the roof, was looking at the Place, over the sharp roof of Saint-Jean-le-Rond. Quasimodo was behind her. He stationed himself there on purpose to spare the damsel the disagreeable spectacle of his ungainly person. On a sudden the Bohemian shuddered; a tear and a flash of joy sparkled at once in her eyes; she fell on her knees, and extended her arms in anguish toward the Place, crying, "Phœbus! come! come! one word, a single word, for God's sake! Phœbus! Phœbus!"—Her voice, her face, her attitude, her whole figure, had the agonizing expression of a shipwrecked person who is making signals of distress to a distant vessel sailing gaily along in the sunshine.

Quasimodo, bending forward, perceived that the object of this wild and tender appeal was a young and handsome horseman, a captain, glistening with arms and accoutrements, who passed caracoling through the Place, and bowing to a fair lady smiling in her balcony. The officer was too far off to hear the call of the unhappy girl.

But the poor deaf bell-ringer understood it. A deep sigh heaved his breast; he turned round; his heart was swollen with the tears which he repressed; he dashed his convulsive fists against his head; and when he removed them there was in each of them a handful of red hair.

The Egyptian paid no attention to him. Gnashing his teeth, he said, in a low tone, "Perdition! That is how one ought to look, then! One need but have a handsome outside!"

She continued meanwhile upon her knees, and cried, with vehement agitation, "Oh! there he alights! He is going into that house!—Phœbus! Phœbus!—He does not hear me!—Phœbus!—Oh! the spiteful woman to talk to him at the same time that I do!—Phœbus! Phœbus!"

The deaf bell-ringer watched her. He comprehended this pantomime. The poor fellow's eye filled with tears, but he suffered none of them to escape. All at once he gently pulled her sleeve. She turned round. He had assumed a look of composure, and said to her, "Shall I go and fetch him?"

She gave a cry of joy. "Oh! go, go! run! quick! that captain! that captain! bring him to me! I will love thee!" She clasped his knees. He could not help shaking his head sorrowfully. "I will go and bring him to you," said he, in a faint voice. He then retired and hurried down the staircase, stifled with sobs.

When he reached the Place nothing was to be seen but the fine horse fastened to the gate of the Gondelaurier mansion. The Captain had just entered. He looked up to the roof of the church. La Esmeralda was still at the same place, in the same posture. He made her a sad sign with his head, and leaned with his back against one of the pillars of the porch, determined to await the Captain's departure.

In that house it was one of those festive days which precede a wedding. Quasimodo saw many persons enter, but nobody came out. Every now and then he looked up at the roof; the Egyptian did not stir any more than he. A groom came and untied the horse, and led him to the stable. The whole day passed in this manner, Quasimodo at the pillar, La Esmeralda on the roof, and Phœbus no doubt at the feet of Fleur-de-Lys.

The Hunchback of Notre-Dame

At length night arrived; a night without a moon, a dark night.
To no purpose did Quasimodo keep his eye fixed on La Esmeralda;
she soon appeared to be but a white spot in the twilight, which became more and more indistinct, till it was no longer discernible amid
the darkness.

Quasimodo saw the front windows of the Gondelaurier mansion
lighted up from top to bottom; he saw the other windows of the
Place lighted up one after another; he saw them darkened again
to the very last of them, for he remained the whole evening at
his post. Still the officer came not forth. When all the passengers had retired to their homes, and not a light was to be seen in
any of the windows, Quasimodo was left quite alone, in absolute
darkness.

The windows of the Gondelaurier mansion, however, continued
lighted, even after midnight. Quasimodo, motionless and attentive,
saw a multitude of living and dancing shadows passing over the
many-coloured panes. Had he not been deaf, in proportion as the
noises of Paris subsided, he would have heard more and more distinctly sounds of festivity, mirth, and music within the mansion.

About one in the morning the company began to break up. Quasimodo, enveloped in darkness, watched all the guests as they came
out under the porch lighted with torches. The Captain was not
among them.

He was filled with sad thoughts. Ever and anon he looked up at
the sky, as if tired of waiting. Large, heavy, ragged, black clouds
hung like crape hammocks beneath the starry cope of night. You
would have said that they were the cobwebs of the firmament. In
one of those moments he all at once saw the glazed door of the balcony
mysteriously open. Two persons came forth, and shut it after them
without noise. It was a man and a woman. It was with some difficulty that Quasimodo recognized in the one the handsome Captain, in
the other the young lady whom he had seen in the morning welcoming
the officer from the window. The Place was quite dark; and a double crimson curtain, which had collapsed again behind the door at the
moment of its shutting, scarcely suffered a gleam of light from the
apartment to reach the balcony.

The young Captain and the lady, as far as our deaf watchman
could judge—for he could not hear a word they said—appeared to
indulge in a very tender *tête-à-tête*. The young lady seemed to have

permitted the officer to throw his arm round her waist, and feebly withstood a kiss.

Quasimodo witnessed from below this scene, which it was the more delightful to see, inasmuch as it was not intended to be witnessed. He, however, contemplated that happiness, that beauty, with bitterness of soul. After all, nature was not silent in the poor fellow, and his vertebral column, confoundedly twisted as it was, nevertheless thrilled like any other. He thought of the miserable portion which Providence had allotted to him; that woman, love, and its pleasures, would be for ever passing before his eyes, but that he should never do more than witness the felicity of others. But what afflicted him most in this sight, and mingled anger with his vexation, was to think what the Egyptian must suffer if she beheld it. To be sure, the night was very dark; La Esmeralda, if she had staid in the same place—and he had no doubt of that—was at a considerable distance; and it was quite as much as he could do himself to distinguish the lovers in the balcony. This was some consolation.

Meanwhile their conversation became more and more animated. The young lady appeared to beseech the officer not to require more of her. Quasimodo could discern her fair hands clasped, her smiles mingled with tears, her looks uplifted to heaven, and the eager eyes of the Captain bent down upon her.

Luckily, for the resistance of the lady was becoming more and more feeble, the door of the balcony suddenly opened; an aged lady appeared; the fair one looked confused, the officer vexed, and all three went in.

A moment afterward a horse was prancing beneath the porch, and the brilliant officer, wrapped in his cloak, passed swiftly before Quasimodo. The bell-ringer suffered him to turn the corner of the street, and then ran after him with the agility of a monkey, crying, "Ho! Captain!"

The Captain pulled up. "What would the varlet with me?" said he, on spying in the dark the uncouth figure limping toward him.

Quasimodo, on coming up to him, boldly laid hold of the horse's bridle. "Follow me, Captain," said he; "there is one who would speak with you."

"By Mahound's horns!" muttered Phœbus; "methinks I have seen this rascally scarecrow somewhere or other. Halloo! fellow! let go the bridle."

"Captain," replied the deaf bell-ringer; "ask me not who it is."

"Loose my horse, I tell you," cried Phœbus angrily. "What means the rogue, hanging thus from my bridle-rein. Dost thou take my horse for a gallows, knave?"

Quasimodo, so far from relaxing his hold of the bridle, was preparing to turn the horse's head the contrary way. Unable to account for the opposition of the Captain, he hastened to give him this explanation. "Come, Captain; 'tis a woman who is waiting for you—a woman who loves you."

"A rare varlet!" said the Captain; "to suppose that I am obliged to go to all the women who love me, or say they do. After all, perhaps, she is like thyself with that owl's face.—Tell her who sent thee that I am going to be married, and that she may go to the devil."

"Hark ye, monseigneur," cried Quasimodo, thinking with a word to overcome his hesitation; "'tis the Egyptian whom you are acquainted with."

This intimation made a strong impression upon Phœbus, but not of the kind that the speaker anticipated. It will be recollected that our gallant officer had retired with Fleur-de-Lys a few moments before Quasimodo rescued the condemned girl from the clutches of Charmolue. In all his subsequent visits to the Logis Gondelaurier he had carefully abstained from mentioning that woman, the recollection of whom was, besides, painful to him; and Fleur-de-Lys, on her part, had not deemed it politic to tell him that the Egyptian was alive. Phœbus believed, therefore, that poor *Similar* was dead, and that she must have been so for a month or two. Add to this that for some moments the Captain had been pondering on the extreme darkness of the night, on the supernatural ugliness and sepulchral voice of the strange messenger: it was past midnight; the street was as lonely as on the evening that the spectre-monk had accosted him, and his horse snorted at the sight of Quasimodo.

"The Egyptian!" he exclaimed with almost a feeling of terror. "What, then, art thou from the other world?" At the same time he clapped his hand to the hilt of his dagger.

"Quick! quick!" said the dwarf, striving to lead the horse; "this way!"

Phœbus dealt him a smart stroke with his whip across the arm. Quasimodo's eye flashed. He made a movement, as if to rush upon the Captain; but, instantly restraining himself, he said, "Oh! how happy you are since there is somebody who loves you!" laying particular emphasis on the word *somebody*. "Get you gone!" added he, loosing the bridle.

Phœbus clapped spurs to his horse, at the same time swearing lustily. Quasimodo looked after him till he was lost in the darkness. "Oh!" said the poor fellow—"to refuse such a trifle as that!"

He returned to Notre-Dame, lighted his lamp, and ascended the tower. As he expected, the Bohemian was still in the same place. The moment she saw him she ran to meet him. "Alone!" she exclaimed, sorrowfully clasping her hands.

"I could not meet with him," said Quasimodo drily.

"You should have waited all night," she replied angrily.

He saw her look of displeasure, and comprehended the reproach. "I will watch him better another time," said he, drooping his head.

"Go thy way!" cried she.

He left her. She was dissatisfied with him. He had rather be ill-used by her than give her pain. He therefore kept all the mortification to himself.

From that day he avoided the presence of the Egyptian. He ceased to come to her cell. At most she sometimes caught a glimpse of the bell-ringer on the top of a tower, with his eye fixed in melancholy mood upon her; but the moment he was aware that she saw him he was gone.

Truth obliges us to state that she grieved very little about this voluntary absence of the poor hunchback. At the bottom of her heart she was glad of it. Quasimodo did not deceive himself on this point.

She saw him not, but she felt the presence of a good genius around her. Her fresh supplies of provisions were brought by an invisible hand while she was asleep. One morning she found over her window a cage with birds. Above her cell there was a sculptured figure which frightened her, as she had more than once signified to Quasimodo. One morning—for all these things were done at night—it was gone; it had been broken off. Whoever had clambered up to this piece of sculpture must have risked his life.

Sometimes, in the evening, she heard the voice of some unseen person beneath the penthouse of a belfry singing a wild, sad strain, as if to lull her to sleep. They were verses without rime, such as a deaf man might make.

One morning, on opening her eyes, she saw two nosegays standing in her window. One was in a bright, handsome crystal vase, but cracked. The water with which it was filled had run out, and the flowers were faded. The other was a pot of coarse common stoneware, but which retained all the water, and the flowers in it were fresh and fragrant. I know not whether it was done intentionally, but La Esmeralda took the faded nosegay, and carried it all day at her bosom. On that day she heard not the voice singing from the tower—a circumstance that gave her very little concern. She passed whole days in fondling Djali, in watching the door of the Logis Gondelaurier, in talking to herself of Phœbus, and in feeding the swallows with crumbs of bread.

For some time she had neither seen nor heard Quasimodo. The poor bell-ringer seemed to have entirely forsaken the church. One night, however, unable to sleep for thinking of her handsome captain, she heard a sigh near her cell. Somewhat alarmed, she rose, and by the light of the moon she saw a shapeless mass lying outside across the doorway. It was Quasimodo asleep upon the stones.

CHAPTER V

THE KEY OF THE PORTE ROUGE

MEANWHILE public rumour had communicated to the Archdeacon the miraculous manner in which the Egyptian had been saved. When apprised of this, he knew not how he felt. He had made up his mind to the death of La Esmeralda, and was therefore easy on that point: he had drained the cup of misery to the dregs. The human heart—Dom Claude had deeply meditated on these matters—cannot contain more than a certain quantity of despair. When a sponge is thoroughly soaked the sea may pass over it without introducing into it one additional drop.

Now, the sponge being filled by the death of La Esmeralda, Dom Claude could not experience keener suffering in this world. But to know that she was living, and Phœbus too, was to be exposed anew to the vicissitudes, the shocks, the torments of life; and Claude was weary of them all.

On hearing these tidings he shut himself up in his cell in the cloisters. He attended neither the conferences of the chapter nor the usual offices. He closed his door against all, not excepting the Bishop; and continued to seclude himself in this manner for several weeks. It was reported that he was ill. So he really was.

What was he doing while thus shut up? Under what thoughts was the wretched Archdeacon struggling? Was he engaged in a last conflict with his indomitable passion? Was he combining a final plan of death for her and perdition for himself?

His Jehan, his beloved brother, his spoiled child, came to his door, knocked, swore, entreated, mentioned his name ten times over —Claude would not open to him.

He passed whole days with his face close to the panes of his window. From that window, situated as we have said in the cloisters, he could see the cell of La Esmeralda; he perceived the girl herself with her goat, sometimes with Quasimodo. He remarked the little attentions of the uncouth hunchback, his respectful manners and his submissive demeanour toward the Egyptian. He recollected—for he had a good memory, and memory is the tormentor of the jealous —he recollected the extraordinary look of the bell-ringer at the dancing-girl on a particular evening. He asked himself what motive could have instigated Quasimodo to rescue her. He witnessed a thousand little scenes between the Bohemian and the hunchback, the pantomime of which, beheld at a distance, and commented on by his passion, appeared to him exceedingly tender. He then vaguely felt awakening within him a jealousy such as he had no conception of, a jealousy which made him blush for shame and indignation. For the Captain—it was not surprising; but for such an object as that! The idea distracted him.

His nights were terrible. Since he knew that the Egyptian was alive the cold ideas of spectre and tomb which haunted him for a whole day were dispelled, and the flesh regained its dominion over him. He writhed upon his bed when he reflected that the lovely brunette was so near a neighbour to him.

Every night his frenzied imagination pictured to him La Esmeralda in all those attitudes which had made the blood boil most vehemently in his veins. He saw her stretched upon the wounded Captain, her eyes closed, her beautiful bosom covered with his blood, at the moment of transport, when the Archdeacon had imprinted on her pale lips that kiss which had felt to the unfortunate girl, though

313

half dead, like the touch of a burning coal. Again he saw her stripped by the rough hands of the torturers; he saw them expose her finely shaped leg, and her white supple knee, while they encased her delicate little foot in the screw-buskin. He further saw that ivory knee alone left uncovered by the horrible apparatus. Lastly, he figured to himself the forlorn damsel, the rope about her neck, with bare feet, bare shoulders, bare bosom, as he had seen her on the day of penance. These images made his blood boil, and a thrill run through his whole frame.

One night, among others, they inflamed him to such a degree that, leaping out of his bed, he threw a surplice over him, and quitted his cell, with his lamp in his hand, half naked, wild, and his eyes glaring like fire.

He knew where to find the key of the Porte Rouge, the communication between the cloisters and the church; and, as the reader knows, he always carried about him a key of the staircase to the towers.

CHAPTER VI

SEQUEL TO THE KEY OF THE PORTE ROUGE

ON that night La Esmeralda had fallen asleep in her lodge, forgetful of the past, and full of hope and pleasing thoughts. She had slept for some time, dreaming, as she was wont, of Phœbus, when she seemed to hear a kind of noise about her. Her sleep was always light and unquiet—a bird's sleep; the least thing awoke her. She opened her eyes. The night was very dark. She nevertheless saw at the window a face looking at her; there was a lamp which threw a light upon this apparition. At the moment when the figure saw that it was perceived by La Esmeralda it blew out the lamp. The girl, however, had had time to get a glimpse of it; her eyelids closed with affright. "Oh!" she cried in a faint voice—"the priest!"

All her past miseries flashed upon her again like lightning. She fell back on her bed frozen with horror. A moment afterward, she felt something touch her, which made her shudder. She raised herself furiously into a sitting posture. The priest clasped her in both his arms. She would have shrieked, but could not.

The Sequel

"Begone, murderer! begone, monster!" said she, in a voice faint and tremulous with rage and terror.

"Mercy! mercy!" muttered the priest, pressing his lips to her shoulders.

Seizing with both hands the hair remaining on his bald head, she strove to prevent his kisses, as though they had been the bites of a mad dog.

"Mercy! mercy!" repeated the wretched priest. "If thou didst but know what my love for thee is!—it is fire; it is molten lead; it is a thousand daggers in my heart!" And he held her two arms with superhuman force.

"Loose me!" cried she distractedly, "or I will spit in thy face!"

He loosed his hold. "Strike me; heap indignities upon me; do what thou wilt! but, for mercy's sake, love me!"

She then struck him with childish rage. "Begone! demon!" said she, while her taper fingers bent in order to scratch his face.

"Love me! for pity love me!" cried the wretched priest, grappling her, and returning her blows with kisses.

She soon found that he was too strong for her. " 'Tis time to put an end to this!" said he, gnashing his teeth.

Palpitating, exhausted, vanquished, she made a last effort, and began to cry, "Help! help!—a vampire! a vampire!"

No one came. Djali alone was awakened, and bleated with affright.

"Be silent," said the panting priest.

All at once, having fallen on the floor in the struggle, the hand of the Egyptian touched something cold, that felt like metal. It was Quasimodo's whistle. She seized it with a convulsion of hope, lifted it to her lips, and whistled with all the force she had left. The whistle gave out a clear, shrill, piercing sound.

"What is that?" inquired the priest.

Almost at the same moment he felt himself grasped by a vigorous arm. The cell was dark: he could not discern who held him thus; but he heard teeth gnashing with rage, and there was just sufficient light scattered amid the darkness to enable him to see the broad blade of a cutlass glistening above his head.

The priest imagined that he perceived the figure of Quasimodo. He supposed that it could be no other. He recollected having stumbled on entering against a bundle of something lying across the door-

315

way outside. Still, as the newcomer uttered not a word, he knew not what to believe. He caught the arm which held the cutlass, crying, "Quasimodo!"—forgetful, in this moment of distress, that Quasimodo was deaf.

In the twinkling of an eye the priest was stretched on the floor, and felt a leaden knee pressing upon his breast. From the angular pressure of that knee he recognized Quasimodo; but what could he do? How was he to make himself known to the assailant? Night rendered the deaf monster blind.

He gave himself up for lost. The girl, with as little pity as an enraged tigress, interposed not to save him. The cutlass was descending upon his head. The moment was critical. All at once his adversary appeared to hesitate. "No," said a muttering voice— "no blood upon her!" It was actually the voice of Quasimodo.

The priest then felt a huge hand dragging him by the leg out of the cell; it was there that he was to die. Luckily, for him, the moon had just burst forth. When they were past the door her pale beams fell upon the head of the priest. Quasimodo looked at his face, was seized with a trembling, relaxed his grasp, and started back.

The Egyptian, who had advanced to the threshold of the cell, saw with surprise the actors suddenly exchanging characters. It was now the priest's turn to threaten, Quasimodo's to supplicate. The priest, having furiously assailed the hunchback with gestures of anger and reproach, at length motioned him to retire. Quasimodo stood for a moment with bowed head, and then, falling on his knees before the door of the Egyptian, "Monseigneur," said he, in a tone of gravity and resignation, "kill me first, and do what you please afterward."

As he thus spoke he offered his cutlass to the priest. Beside himself with rage, the priest clutched at the weapon; but La Esmeralda was too quick for him. Snatching the cutlass from the hand of Quasimodo, and bursting into an hysterical laugh, "Come on!" said she to the priest.

She held the blade uplifted. The priest wavered. She would certainly have struck. "Thou darest not approach now, coward," she cried. Then, with unpitying look, and well aware that she should pierce the heart of the priest as with a thousand red-hot irons, she added, "Ah! I know that Phœbus is not dead!"

The priest, with a violent kick, overthrew Quasimodo, and rushed

The Sequel

quivering with rage to the vaulted staircase. When he was gone Quasimodo picked up the whistle which had been the means of saving the Egyptian. "It was getting rusty," said he, handing it to her. He then left her to herself.

The damsel, vehemently agitated by this violent scene, sank exhausted upon her bed, and sobbed aloud. Her horizon had again become overcast.

The priest, on his part, groped his way back to his cell. The thing was conclusive. Dom Claude was jealous of Quasimodo! With pensive look he repeated the fatal phrase, "Nobody shall have her!"

BOOK IX

CHAPTER I

GRINGOIRE HAS SEVERAL CAPITAL IDEAS ONE AFTER ANOTHER IN THE RUE DES BERNARDINS

A S soon as Gringoire perceived the turn which this whole affair was taking, and that decidedly halter, gibbet, and other unpleasant things would be the lot of the principal characters of this comedy, he felt no sort of inclination to interfere in it. The Vagabonds, with whom he had remained, considering that after all they were the best company in Paris, had continued to interest themselves for the Egyptian. This he thought perfectly natural in people who, like her, had no other prospect than Charmolue and Torterue, and who never soared like him into the regions of imagination between the two wings of Pegasus. From them he learned that she whom he had espoused over the broken jug had taken sanctuary in Notre-Dame, and he was very glad of it. He thought sometimes of the little goat and that was all. In the daytime he performed mountebank tricks for a livelihood, and at night he elucubrated a memorial against the Bishop of Paris, for he remembered the drenching he had got from his mills, and bore him a grudge for it. He was also engaged in a commentary upon the admired work of Baudry-le-Rouge, Bishop of Noyon and Tournay, *De Cupa Petarum,*[1] which had awakened in him a violent passion for architecture—a passion which had superseded in his heart the passion for hermetics; the one indeed was but a natural corollary to the other, since there is an intimate connexion between hermetics and masonry. Gringoire had passed from the love of an idea to the love of the form of an idea.

One day he had stopped near Saint-Germain-l'Auxerrois, at the corner of a building called the For-l'Évêque, which faced another named the For-le-Roi. At this For-l'Évêque there was a beautiful chapel of the fourteenth century, the choir of which looked toward the street. Gringoire was intently examining the sculptures on the

1 *"The Stone Cup."*

outside. It was one of those moments of absorbing, exclusive, supreme enjoyment, when the artist sees nothing in the world but his art, and sees the world in his art. All at once he felt a hand fall heavily upon his shoulder. He turned about. It was his old friend, his old master, the Archdeacon.

He was stupefied. It was a long time since he had seen the Archdeacon, and Dom Claude was one of those solemn and impassioned personages, the meeting with whom always deranges the equilibrium of the sceptical philosopher.

The Archdeacon kept silence for a few minutes, during which Gringoire had leisure to observe him. He found Dom Claude greatly altered—pale as a winter morning, his eyes sunk, his hair almost white. The priest at length broke this silence, saying, but in a grave, freezing tone, "How goes it with you, Master Pierre?"

"As to my health?" said Gringoire. "Why, I may say, so so. Upon the whole good. I take everything in moderation. You know, master, the secret of health recommended by Hippocrates—*cibi, potus, somni, venus, omnia moderata sint.*" [1]

"Then you have no troubles, Master Pierre?" rejoined the Archdeacon, looking steadfastly at Gringoire.

"No, i' faith, not I."

"And what are you doing now?"

"You see, master, I am examining the cut of these stones, and the way in which that bas-relief is chiselled."

The priest smiled. It was one of those bitter smiles, which lift up but one of the corners of the mouth. "And that amuses you?"

"'Tis Paradise!" exclaimed Gringoire. And, turning to the sculptures, with the dazzled look of a demonstrator of living phenomena, "Don't you think," said he, "that this metamorphosis in low relief, for example, is executed with great skill, patience, and delicacy? Look at this little pillar. About what capital did you ever see foliage more elegant and more highly finished? Look at those three medallions by Jean Maillevin. They are not first-rate works of that great genius; nevertheless, the truth to nature, and the sweetness of the faces, the gaiety of the attitudes and draperies, and that inexplicable charm which is blended with all the defects, render the miniature figures exceedingly lively and exceedingly delicate—per-

[1] "In food, drink, sleep, love, let there be moderation."

haps too much so. Do you not think that this is amusing?"

"Yes, I do," said the priest.

"And if you were to see the interior of the chapel!" resumed the poet, with his garrulous enthusiasm, "sculptures all over; tufted like a cauliflower. The choir is in a right godly style, and so peculiar that I never saw anything like it."

Dom Claude interrupted him. "You are happy, then?"

"Yes, upon my honour," replied Gringoire, with warmth. "At first I was fond of women, then of beasts, now of stones. They are quite as amusing as women and beasts, and much less treacherous."

The priest raised his hand to his brow. It was his habitual gesture. "Indeed!"

"Stay," said Gringoire, "you shall see that a man need not want pleasure." He took the arm of the priest, who made no resistance, and drew him into the staircase turret of the For-l'Évêque. "There is a staircase for you! Whenever I look at it I am happy. It is the simplest of its kind, and yet the most exquisite in Paris. Every step is rounded off underneath. Its beauty and simplicity consist in the overlapping parts, which for a foot or thereabout are let in, mortised, embedded, enchained, enchased, dovetailed one into another, and bite in such a way as to be not less solid than goodly."

"And you wish for nothing?"

"No."

"And regret nothing?"

"Neither wishes nor regrets. I have arranged my life."

"Man arranges," said Claude; "circumstances derange."

"I am a Pyrrhonian philosopher," replied Gringoire, "and I keep everything in equilibrium."

"And how do you earn a livelihood?"

"I still make epics and tragedies now and then; but what brings in most money is the trade you have seen me follow—carrying pyramids of chairs and so forth between my teeth."

"A scurvy trade for a philosopher."

"It has to do with the equilibrium," said Gringoire. "When you take an idea into your head you find it in everything."

"I know it," replied the Archdeacon.

After a pause the priest resumed, "You are nevertheless as poor as ever?"

"Poor enough, I grant you, but not unhappy."

Several Capital Ideas

At this moment the dialogue was interrupted by the trampling of horses, and a company of archers of the King's Ordnance, with raised lances, and an officer at their head, passed the end of the street. The cavalcade was brilliant, and the pavement rang beneath their tread.

"How you eye that officer!" said Gringoire to the Archdeacon. "I rather think I know him."

"What is his name?"

"I believe," said Claude, "his name is Phœbus de Châteaupers."

"Phœbus, a curious name! There is also a Phœbus Comte de Foix. I once knew a girl who never swore but by Phœbus."

"Come this way!" said the priest, "I have something to say to you."

Ever since the appearance of the archers some agitation was perceptible under the frozen exterior of the Archdeacon. He walked on, followed by Gringoire, who was wont to obey him, like all who had ever approached him, such was the ascendancy which he exercised. They proceeded in silence to the Rue des Bernardins, where a casual passenger only was at times to be seen. Here Dom Claude stopped short.

"What have you to say to me, master?" inquired Gringoire.

"Don't you think," said the Archdeacon, with a look of deep reflection, "that the dress of those archers who have just passed is finer than yours or mine?"

Gringoire shook his head. "By my fay! I like my red and yellow jacket better than those shells of iron and steel. A sorry pleasure, to make at every step the same noise that the Ironmongers' Quay would do in an earthquake!"

"Then, Gringoire, you have never envied those comely fellows in their habiliments of war?"

"Envied them!—for what, Mr Archdeacon?—for their strength, their armour, their discipline? Far preferable are philosophy and independence in rags. I had rather be the head of a fly than the tail of a lion."

"That is singular!" said the priest thoughtfully. "A goodly uniform is nevertheless goodly."

Gringoire, seeing him absorbed in thought, left him, and went up to the porch of a neighbouring house. Presently he returned, clapping his hands. "If you were not so deeply engaged with the goodly uniforms of the men-at-arms, Mr Archdeacon, I would beg of you to go and look at that door. I always said that the entrance to the Sieur Aubrey's house is not to be matched all the world over."

"Pierre Gringoire," said the Archdeacon, "what have you done with the young Egyptian dancing-girl?"

"La Esmeralda?—Why, how abruptly you change the conversation!"

"Was she not your wife?"

"Yes, after a fashion; by means of a broken jug we were joined together for four years. By the way," added Gringoire, with a half-bantering tone and look, "you seem to be always thinking of her."

"And do you never think of her now?"

"Very little. I am so busy! . . . But what a charming little goat that was!"

"Did not that Bohemian save your life?"

"True enough, by'r Lady!"

"Well, what is become of her? What have you done with her?"

"I can't tell. I believe they hanged her!"

"You believe?"

"I am not sure. When I saw that they were determined to hang somebody I got out of the way."

"Is that all you know about the matter?"

"Stop a moment! I was told that she had taken sanctuary in Notre-Dame, and that she was safe there, which I was very glad to hear; but I have not been able to ascertain whether her goat was saved along with her—and that is all I know about the matter."

"I can tell you more, then," cried Dom Claude, his voice, hitherto low almost to a whisper, rising to the loudness of thunder. "She has actually taken sanctuary in Notre-Dame. But in three days Justice will again seize her, and she will be hanged in the Grève. The Parliament has issued a decree."

"That is a pity!" said Gringoire.

In the twinkling of an eye the priest had relapsed into his former coldness and tranquillity.

"And," resumed the poet, "who the devil has amused himself with soliciting an order of restitution? Why could they not let the Parliament alone? What harm is there in it if a poor girl does seek shelter among the swallows' nests under the flying buttresses of Notre-Dame?"

"There are Satans in the world," rejoined the Archdeacon.

"'Tis infernally cross-grained!" observed Gringoire.

"Then she did save your life?" resumed the Archdeacon, after a pause.

"That was among my very good friends, the Vagabonds. She came in the nick of time, or I should have been hanged. They would have been sorry for it now."

"Will you then not try to do something for her?"

"I desire no better, Dom Claude, but perhaps I may get my own neck into an ugly noose!"

"What signifies that?"

"What signifies it! You are exceedingly kind, master! I have just begun two great works."

The priest struck his forehead. Notwithstanding the composure which he affected, a violent gesture from time to time betrayed his inward convulsions. "What can be done to save her?"

"Master," said Gringoire, "I answer, *Il padelt,* which is Turkish for *God is our hope.*"

"What can be done to save her?" repeated Claude thoughtfully.

Gringoire, in his turn, struck his brow. "Hark ye, master, I have no lack of imagination; I will devise expedients. Suppose we solicit the King's pardon."

"Pardon! of Louis XI!"

"Why not?"

"Take the bone from the hungry tiger."

Gringoire cast about for other expedients.

"Well, stop! Shall we make declaration that the girl is pregnant, and demand an examination of matrons?"

The pupil of the priest's hollow eye sparkled. "Pregnant, dolt! Knowest thou aught to that purpose?"

His look alarmed Gringoire. "Oh, no, not I!" he hastily replied. "Our marriage was literally *forismaritagium*—for I was shut out. At any rate we should obtain a respite."

"Stupid oaf! hold thy tongue!"

"Nay, don't be angry," muttered Gringoire. "One might obtain a respite; that would harm nobody, and would put forty deniers Parisis into the pockets of the matrons, who are poor women."

The priest heard him not. "At any rate," he muttered, "she must away! The order must be executed in three days! Besides, if there were no order, that Quasimodo! Who can account for the depraved tastes of women!" Then raising his voice: "Master Pierre," said he, "I have well weighed the matter; there is but one way to save her."

"And which?—I can see none for my part."

"Hark ye, Master Pierre; recollect that to her you owe your life. I will tell you frankly my idea. The church is watched night and day; only such persons as have been seen to enter are suffered to go out again. Of course you would be allowed to go in. You must come, I will take you to her. You must change clothes with her."

"So far, so good," observed the philosopher. "And then?"

"Why, then she will go away in your clothes, and you will remain in hers. You will be hanged perhaps; but she will escape."

Gringoire rubbed his brow with a profoundly serious look.

"I declare," said he, "that is an idea which would never have come into my head of itself."

At this unlooked-for proposition of Dom Claude's, the open and good-humoured countenance of the poet was overcast, like a smiling landscape of Italy when some unlucky blast dashes a cloud upon the sun.

"Well, Gringoire, what say you to this expedient?"

"I say, master, they will not hang me perhaps, but they will hang me to a certainty."

"That does not concern us."

"The devil!" exclaimed Gringoire.

"She saved your life. You are only paying a debt."

"How many of my debts besides that are unpaid!"

"Master Pierre, you absolutely must comply."

The Archdeacon spoke imperatively.

"Hark ye, Dom Claude," replied the dismayed poet, "you cling to this idea; but you are quite wrong. I see no reason why I should thrust my head into the halter instead of another."

"What is there, then, that so strongly attaches you to life?"

"Why, a thousand things."

"What are they?—I would ask."

"What are they? The fresh air, the blue sky, morning and evening, the warm sunshine, and the moonlight, my good friends the

Several Capital Ideas

Vagabonds, our romps with the good-natured damsels, the beautiful architectural works of Paris to study, three thick books to write— one of them against the Bishop and his mills—and I know not what besides. Anaxagoras said that he was in the world to admire the sun. And then I have the felicity to pass all my days from morn to eventide with a man of genius, to wit myself, which is exceedingly agreeable."

"A head fit for a bell!" muttered the Archdeacon.—"Well, but tell me, who saved this life which is so charming to thee? To whom is it owing that thou yet breathest this air, beholdest that sky, and canst amuse thy lark's spirit with extravagances and follies? What wouldst thou be but for her? And yet thou canst suffer her to die —her, to whom thou owest thy life—her, that beautiful, lovely, adorable creature, almost as necessary to the light of the world as the sun himself; whilst thou, half sage, half madman, rough sketch of something or other, a species of vegetable, who imaginest thou canst walk and think, thou wilt continue to live with the life of which thou hast robbed her, as useless as a candle at noonday! Nay, nay, have some feeling, Gringoire; be generous in thy turn. It was she who set the example."

The priest was warm. Gringoire listened to him at first with a look of indecision; presently he began to soften, and at last he put on a tragic grimace, which made his wan face look like that of a newborn infant which has the colic.

"You are pathetic," said he, brushing away a tear. "Well, I will think about it. 'Tis a droll idea, this of yours!" Pausing awhile, he continued— "After all, who knows! perhaps they will not hang me. Betrothal is not always followed by marriage. When they find me up yonder in the little cell, so grotesquely attired in cap and petticoat, perhaps they will only laugh.—And then, if they do hang me, why, death by the halter is like any other death, or, more correctly speaking, it is not like any other death. It is a death worthy of the sage who has oscillated all his life; a death, which is neither fish nor flesh, like the soul of the downright sceptic; a death impressed all over with Pyrrhonism and hesitation, which holds the middle place between heaven and earth, which leaves one in suspense. It is a philosophic death, and perhaps I was predestined to it. 'Tis magnificent to die as one has lived."

The priest interrupted him. "Are we agreed?"

"After all, what is death?" continued Gringoire, in the warmth of his excitement. "An unpleasant moment, a toll, a passage from little to nothing. When some one asked Cercidas of Megalopolis if he should like to die—'Why not?' he replied, 'for, after death, I shall see those great men, Pythagoras among the philosophers, Hecatæus among the historians, Homer among the poets, and Olympus among the musicians.'"

The Archdeacon held out his hand. "It is settled, then; you will come to-morrow?"

This gesture, and the question which accompanied it, brought Gringoire back from his digression. "Beshrew me, no!" said he, in the tone of a man awakening from sleep. "Be hanged!—too absurd! —I beg to be excused."

"Farewell, then!" and the Archdeacon added, muttering between his teeth, "I will find thee out again!"

"I don't wish that fellow to find me again," thought Gringoire, running after Dom Claude.—"Hold, Mr Archdeacon, no malice between old friends! You take an interest in that girl, my wife, I would say—quite right! You have devised a stratagem to withdraw her in safety from Notre-Dame, but to me your expedient is extremely disagreeable. A capital idea has just occurred to me. If I could propose a method of extricating her from the dilemma without entangling my own neck in the smallest running noose whatever—what would you say to it? Would that satisfy you? or must I absolutely be hanged before you are content?"

The priest tore off the buttons of his cassock with irritation. "Eternal babbler! what is thy proposal?"

"Yes," resumed Gringoire, talking to himself, and clapping his forefinger to his nose in the attitude of meditation—"that's it!— She is a favourite with the dark race.—They will rise at the first word.—Nothing easier.—A sudden attack.—In the confusion, carry her away!—To-morrow night . . . they will desire nothing better."

"Your proposal! Let us hear!" said the priest, shaking him.

Gringoire turned majestically toward him. "Leave me alone! you see I am composing." Having considered for a few moments longer, he clapped his hands in exultation, exclaiming, "Admirable! sure to succeed!"

"But the means?" inquired Claude angrily. Gringoire's face beamed with triumph.

"Come hither, then, and lend me your ear. 'Tis a right bold counter-mine, which will get all of us out of our trouble. By heaven! it must be confessed that I am no fool."

He stopped short.—"By the by, is the little goat with the girl?"

"Yes!—devil fetch thee!"

"They meant to have hanged her too—did they not?"

"What is that to me?"

"Yes, they meant to hang her. Why, it was only last month that they hanged a sow. The hangman likes that—he eats the meat afterwards. Hang my pretty Djali! Poor, dear, little lamb!"

"Malisons upon thee!" cried Dom Claude. "Thou thyself art the hangman. What means, dolt, hast thou devised for saving her? Must one tear thine idea from thee with pincers?"

"Gently, master, I will tell you."

Gringoire bent his lips to the Archdeacon's ear, and whispered very softly, at the same time casting an uneasy look from one end of the street to the other, though not a creature was passing. When he had finished, Dom Claude grasped his hand, and said coldly, "Good! to-morrow?"

"To-morrow," repeated Gringoire. The Archdeacon retired one way, while he went the other, saying to himself, in an undertone, "A rare business this, Monsieur Pierre Gringoire! No matter! It shall not be said that because one is little one shrinks from great undertakings. Bito carried a full-grown bull upon his shoulders; the wagtail, the nightingale, the swallow, cross the ocean."

CHAPTER II

BECOME A VAGABOND

THE Archdeacon on his return to the cloisters found his brother Jehan waiting for him at the door of his cell. The youth had amused himself, while waiting, by drawing with a piece of charcoal upon the wall a profile of his elder brother, enriched with an enormous nose.

Dom Claude scarcely looked at Jehan; his thoughts were otherwise engaged. The reckless, jovial countenance of Jehan, the radiance of which had so often restored serenity to the gloomy physiognomy of the priest, was now incapable of dispelling the mist which thickened daily over his corrupt, mephitic, and stagnant soul.

"Brother," said Jehan diffidently, "I am come to see you."

"What then?" replied the Archdeacon, without so much as lifting his eyes to him.

"Brother," resumed the young hypocrite, "you are so kind to me, and give me such good advice, that I cannot stay away from you."

"What then?" repeated Dom Claude.

"Alas, brother! you had great reason to say to me, 'Jehan, conduct yourself discreetly; Jehan, attend to your studies; Jehan, pass not the night out of college, without legitimate occasion and the leave of the master. Beat not the Picards. Rot not, like an unlettered ass, upon the straw of the school. Jehan, submit to punishment at the discretion of the master. Jehan, go to chapel every evening, and sing an anthem, with collect and prayer, to the blessed Virgin Mary.' Ah! what excellent counsels were these!"

"Well?"

"Brother, you see before you a sinner, a grievous sinner, a wretch, a libertine, a criminal, a reprobate. My dear brother, Jehan has trodden your gracious counsels like straw and litter underfoot. Severely am I punished for it; God Almighty is rigidly just. So long as I had money, I made merry, revelled in folly, and led a joyous life. How fascinating is debauchery in front, but oh! how ugly and deformed behind! Now I have not a coin left; I have sold my linen. My joyous life is over. The bright taper is put out; and I have but a scurvy tallow candle which stinks in my nostrils. The girls jeer at me. I have only water to drink. I am dunned by remorse and creditors."

"What more?" said the Archdeacon.

"Alas! my dear brother, I would fain turn me to a better life. I come to you full of contrition. I am penitent. I confess my faults. I have great reason to wish that I may one day become licentiate and sub-monitor of the Collège de Torchi. At this moment I feel an irresistible vocation to that office. But I have no ink, I have no pens, I have no paper, I have no books—I must buy more. To this end I am in great need of a little money, and I am come to you, brother, with a heart full of contrition."

"Is that all?"

"Yes," said the scholar. "A little money."

"I have none."

"Well then, brother," replied Jehan, with a grave and at the same time a determined look, "I am sorry to have to inform you that very fair offers have been made to me from another quarter. You will not give me some money?"

"No."

"Then I will become a Vagabond." In uttering this monstrous resolution he assumed the look of Ajax expecting the thunderbolt to descend upon his head.

"Become a Vagabond then," coldly replied the Archdeacon.

Jehan made a low obeisance, and skipped whistling down the cloister stairs.

At the moment when he was passing through the court of the cloisters, beneath the window of his brother's cell, he heard it open, and, looking up, saw the stern face of the Archdeacon protruded through the aperture. "Go to the devil!" said Dom Claude; "that is the last money thou shalt have from me."

At the same time the priest threw at Jehan a purse which made a great bump on the scholar's forehead, and with which Jehan went his way, at once growling and pleased, like a dog pelted with marrowbones.

CHAPTER III

L'ALLEGRO

THE reader has not perhaps forgotten that part of the Cour des Miracles was enclosed by the ancient wall surrounding the Ville, many of the towers of which had begun so early as this period to fall to ruin. One of these towers had been converted into a place of entertainment by the Vagabonds. At the bottom was a tavern, and the upper floors were appropriated to other purposes. This tower was the busiest and consequently the most disgusting part of this resort of the crew. It was a kind of monstrous hive, where an incessant buzz was kept up night and day. At night, when all the rest of the colony was buried in sleep, when not a single light was to be seen in the windows of the crazy buildings encompassing the place, when no sound was to be heard issuing from the innumerable dens swarming with thieves, harlots, and stolen or bastard children, the jovial tower might always be known by the noise that was made there, by the crimson light, which, gleaming at once from the chimneys, the windows, and the crevices in the cracked walls, issued, as it were, from every pore.

The cellar, therefore, was the tavern. The descent to it was by a low door and stairs as rugged as a classic Alexandrine. Over the door there was by way of sign a wondrous daubing representing a number of new sous and dead hens (*des sous neufs et des poulets tués*) with this pun underneath: *Aux sonneurs pour les trépassés.*[1]

One evening, at the moment when the curfew-bell was ringing in every belfry in Paris, the sergeants of the watch, had they chanced to enter the redoubtable Cour des Miracles, might have remarked that there was a greater tumult than usual in the tavern of the Vagabonds, and that the inmates were both drinking and swearing more lustily. In the open space without were numerous groups conversing in a subdued tone, as when some important enterprise is planning; and here and there a varlet was crouching, and whetting some rusty weapon or other upon a paving-stone.

In the tavern itself, however, wine and gaming were so powerful a diversion to the ideas which on that evening engrossed the vagabond crew, that it would have been difficult to discover from the conversation of the topers the nature of their project. They merely appeared to be in higher spirits than ordinary, and between the legs of each was seen glistening some weapon or other—a billhook, a hatchet, a thick bludgeon, or the supporter of an old arquebus.

The room, of circular form, was very spacious; but the tables were so close, and the customers so numerous, that all the contents of the tavern, men and women, benches and beer-jugs, those who were drinking, those who were sleeping, those who were gaming, the able-bodied and the cripple, seemed to be tumbled together pell-mell, with just as much order and harmony as a heap of oyster-shells. A few tallow candles were burning on the tables, but the real luminary of the tavern, that which performed the part of the chandelier at the Opera House, was the fire. This cellar was so damp that the fire was never suffered to go out even in summer. It was an immense fire-place, with carved mantel, bristling with clumsy andirons and other culinary apparatus, containing one of those large fires of wood and

---

[1] "To the bell-ringers for the dead."

turf mixed, which at night in the village streets produce, by their glare on the opposite walls, the appearances of the windows of a smithy. A large dog, sitting gravely in the ashes, was turning a spit laden with viands before the fire.

Notwithstanding the confusion, after the first glance there might be distinguished in this multitude three principal groups crowding round three personages with whom the reader is already acquainted. One of these personages, grotesquely bedizened with many a piece of Eastern frippery, was Matthias Hunyadi Spicali, Duke of Egypt and Bohemia. The varlet was seated on a table, his legs crossed, his finger uplifted, imparting in a loud voice sundry lessons in black and white magic to many a gaping face around him. Another party had drawn closely about our old friend, the valiant King of Thunes, who was armed to the very teeth. Clopin Trouillefou, with grave look and in a low voice, was superintending the pillage of a large hogshead full of arms, which stood with head knocked out before him, and from which stores of hatchets, swords, coats of mail, hunting-knives, spear-heads, saws, augers, were disgorged like apples and grapes from a cornucopia. Each took from the heap what he pleased—one a helmet, another a long rapier, a third a cross or basket-hilted dagger. The very children armed themselves, and there were even little urchins cuirassed and accoutred, running between the legs of the topers like large beetles.

Lastly, a third party, the most noisy, the most jovial, and the most numerous, occupied the benches and tables, amidst which a treble voice was swearing and holding forth from beneath a heavy suit of armour complete from head to heel. The individual who had thus encased himself was so empanoplied by his martial accoutrements, that no part of his person could be seen, save a saucy red snub nose, a lock of light hair, rosy lips, and daring eyes. He had his belt stuck full of daggers, a long sword at his thigh, a rusty arbalest on his left, a large jug of wine before him, to say nothing of a trollop with open bosom on his right. Every mouth round him was laughing, cursing, drinking.

Add to these twenty secondary groups, the attendants, male and female, running about with plates and jugs, the gamesters, lolling over the billiards, the merils, and the dice, the impassioned game of the tringlet; the quarrels in one corner, the kisses in another; and you will have some idea of the whole, over which flickered the glare of a huge blazing fire, which made a thousand broad, grotesque shadows dance on the walls of the tavern.

As for the noise, it was like that within a bell in a grand peal.

Amid all this din, upon the bench in the chimney-corner was seated a philosopher absorbed in meditation, his feet in the ashes, and his eye fixed on the burning brands. It was Pierre Gringoire.

"Come, make haste, arm yourselves! we shall start in an hour!" said Clopin Trouillefou to his crew.

Two card-players were quarrelling. "Knave," cried the more rubicund of the two, holding up his fist at the other, "I will mark thee with the club. Thou shalt be qualified to succeed Mistigri in the card-parties of Monseigneur the King."

"Oaf," roared a Norman, who might easily be known by his nasal twang, "we are crammed together here like the saints of Callouville!"

"My sons," said the Duke of Egypt to his auditors, in his falsetto, "the witches of France go to the Sabbath without broom or aught else to ride on, merely with a few magical words; those of Italy always have a goat at the door waiting for them. They are all obliged to go out of the house through the chimney."

The voice of the young warrior in armour was heard above the uproar. "Hurrah! Hurrah!" cried he, "my first feat of arms to-day! A Vagabond! Zounds! what am I but a Vagabond! Pour me out some drink! My friends, my name is Jehan Frollo du Moulin, and I am a gentleman. I could lay any wager that if Jupiter were a *gendarme* he would be fond of plunder. We are going, brothers, on a rare expedition. We are valiant fellows. Lay siege to the church, break open the doors, carry off the damsel, rescue her from the judges, save her from the priests, dismantle the cloisters, burn the bishop in his palace—why, we shall do it all in less time than a burgomaster takes to eat a basin of soup. Our cause is a righteous one; we'll plunder Notre-Dame; that's flat. We'll hang Quasimodo. Do you know Quasimodo, fair gentlewomen. Have ye seen him puffing upon the great bell on a Whit-Sunday? By Beelzebub's horns, that is grand! You would take him for a devil astride of a ghoul.—I say, my friends, I am a Vagabond to my heart's core, a canter in my soul, a cadger born. I have been well off, and have run through my fortune. My father wanted to make me an officer, my mother a sub-dean, my aunt a counsellor of Inquisition, my

L'Allegro

grandmother prothonotary to the King, my grand-aunt Keeper of the Short Robe: while I—I have chosen to be a Vagabond. I told my father so; he flung his malison in my face; and my mother, who —poor old lady—began to cry and sputter like that stake on the fire. A merry life though a short one, say I! Tavernière, my darling, let us change our wine; I have some money left yet. I don't like the Surène; it cuts my throat. *Corbœuf!* I'd almost as lieve swallow knives."

Meanwhile the rabble applauded with bursts of laughter; and as the tumult swelled round him the scholar shouted, "How delightful! —*populi debacchantis populosa debacchatio!*" [1] His eye swimming in ecstasy, he then fell achanting in the tone of a canon at vespers; but, suddenly stopping short, he cried, "Here, you devil's taverner, give me some supper!"

Then followed a moment of comparative quiet, during which the Duke of Egypt raised his shrill voice, while instructing his Bohemians. "The weasel is called Aduine; the fox, Bluefoot; the wolf, Greyfoot or Goldfoot; the bear, the old man, or the grandfather.— The cap of a gnome renders you invisible, and enables you to see invisible things.—Every toad that is baptized ought to be dressed in red or black velvet, with a bell about its neck and a bell at each foot. The godfather must take hold of the head; the godmother of the rump."

Meanwhile the crew continued to arm themselves at the other end of the tavern, amid such whispers as these:

"Poor Esmeralda!" said a Bohemian—"she is our sister—we must release her."

"Is she still in Notre-Dame?" asked a Jewish-looking pedlar.

"Ay, by the Mass!"

"Well then, comrades!" cried the pedlar, "to Notre-Dame! the sooner the better! In the chapel of Saint-Féréol and Saint-Ferrution there are two statues, one of St John Baptist, the other of St Antony, both of gold, weighing together seventeen marks fifteen esterlins, and the pedestals of silver gilt seventeen marks five ounces. I know this to a certainty—I am by trade a goldsmith."

By this time Jehan's supper was set before him. Falling to with an excellent appetite, he exclaimed, "By Saint-Voult-de-Lucques!

---

[1] "The ravings of the people, popular fury."

—the people call him Saint-Goguelu,—I am the happiest fellow in Paris, though I have renounced the half of a house situate, lying, and being in Paradise, promised me by my brother the Archdeacon. Look at that simpleton, gazing at me with the smooth look of an archduke. There is another on my left with tusks so long that they hide his chin. Body o' Mahound! comrade! thou hast the very air and odour of a bone-dealer; and yet hast the assurance to clap thyself down so near me! I am noble, my friend. Trade is incompatible with nobility. Go thy ways!—Soho! you there! what are ye fighting for? What, Baptiste Croque-Oison, art not afraid to risk thy goodly nose against the clumsy fists of that booby? Knowest thou not, simpleton, *non cuiquam datum est habere nasum?* [1]—Thou art truly divine, Jacqueline Rouge-Oreille! what a pity that thou art bald! Girls, keep those mischievous brats quiet, and snuff the candles. By Mahound! what have I got here! A hair in the omelette! Goodly hostelry of Beelzebub, where the girls use forks as combs!"

So saying, he dashed his plate on the pavement, and began singing with all his might one of the peculiar songs of the lawless crew of whom he had become a worthy associate.

"I reck not,
God wot,
Of laws or vows,
Of hearth or house,
Of God or king,
Or any such thing."

Clopin Trouillefou had meanwhile finished his distribution of arms. He went up to Gringoire, who, with his feet on the andiron, appeared to be in a brown study. "Friend Pierre," said the King of Thunes, "what the devil art thinking of?"

Gringoire turned toward him with a melancholy smile. "I am fond of the fire, my dear sir," said he, "not for the trivial reason that it warms our feet or cooks our soup, but because there are sparks in it. Sometimes I pass whole hours watching those sparks. I discover a thousand things in those stars which sprinkle the black chimney-back. Those stars are worlds too."

"Thunder and death, if I understand thee!" cried the King of Thunes. "Dost know what hour it is?"

[1] "It is not given to every one to have a nose."

L'Allegro

"Not I," answered Gringoire.

Clopin then went to the Duke of Egypt. "Comrade Matthias," said he, "it lacks not quite one quarter of an hour. I am told the King is in Paris."

"One reason more why we should get our sister out of their clutches," replied the old Bohemian.

"Thou speakest like a man, Matthias," rejoined Trouillefou. "Besides, we shall get on swimmingly. No resistance to fear in the church. The canons are mere hares, and we are strong. The officers of the Parliament will be finely taken in to-morrow when they go to look for her. By the Pope's nose! they shall not hang the comely damsel."

With these words Clopin sallied forth from the tavern.

Gringoire, roused from his meditations, had begun to contemplate the wild and noisy scene around him, muttering between his teeth, "*Luxuriosa res vinum et tumultuosa ebrietas.*[1] What good reason have I to abstain from liquor! and how admirably St Benedict observes, *Vinum apostatare facit etiam sapientes!*"[2]

At that moment Clopin returned, and shouted with a voice of thunder, "Midnight!"

At this signal, which had the effect of the sound to horse upon a regiment in halt, all the Vagabond crew, men, women, and children, poured in a torrent out of the tavern, with a loud noise of arms and the clanking of iron implements.

The moon was overcast. The Cour des Miracles was quite dark. Not a light was to be seen. It was nevertheless filled with a multitude of both sexes, who talked in low tones together. A vast buzz was to be heard, and all sorts of weapons were seen glistening in the dark. Clopin mounted a huge stone. "To your ranks, ye men of Cant," he cried. "To your ranks, Egypt! To your ranks, Galilee!" A bustle ensued amid the darkness. The immense multitude appeared to be forming in column. In a few minutes the King of Thunes again raised his voice. "Now, silence in passing through the streets! No torch is to be lit till we are at Notre-Dame. March!"

In less than ten minutes the horsemen of the watch fled panic-stricken before a long black procession descending in profound si-

[1] "Wine is a thing of luxury, drunkenness of tumult."
[2] "To abjure wine also makes wise men."

lence toward the Pont au Change, along the winding streets which run in all directions through the massive quarter of the Halles.

CHAPTER IV

A BLUNDERING FRIEND

THAT same night Quasimodo could not sleep. He had just gone his last round in the church. He had not remarked that at the moment when he was fastening the doors the Archdeacon had passed, or the ill-humour he had shown on seeing him employed in carefully bolting and padlocking the immense iron bars, which gave to the large folding-doors the solidity of a wall. Dom Claude appeared that night to be more deeply absorbed in thought than usual. Ever since the nocturnal adventure in the cell he had treated Quasimodo with great harshness; but, in spite of this usage, nay, even though he sometimes went so far as to strike him, nothing could shake the submission, the patience, the devoted resignation, of the faithful bell-ringer. From the Archdeacon he would take anything, abuse, threats, blows, without murmuring a reproach, without uttering a complaint. The utmost that he did was to watch the Archdeacon with anxiety when he ascended the staircase of the tower; but Claude had of himself cautiously abstained from appearing again in the presence of the Egyptian.

That night, then, Quasimodo, after taking a glance at his bells, at Mary, at Jacqueline, at Thibault, whom he had lately so miserably neglected, went up to the top of the northern tower and there, placing his well-closed dark lantern on the leads, he began to take a survey of Paris.

The night, as we have already said, was very dark. Paris, which at this period was scarcely lighted at all, presented to the eye a confused aggregate of black masses, intersected here and there by the pallid curve of the Seine. Quasimodo could discern no light but in the window of a distant building, the vague and sombre outline of which was visible above the roofs in the direction of the gate of Saint-Antoine. There too was some one who kept vigil.

While his eye ranged over this expanse of haze and darkness an unaccountable feeling of apprehension and uneasiness gained upon him. For several days past he had been upon his guard. He had observed suspicious-looking men prowling incessantly about the church, and keeping their eyes fixed on the young girl's place of refuge. He imagined that some plot against the unfortunate refugee might be on foot, and that the hatred of the people might be directed against her as it was against himself. So he stood on the watch, upon his tower, *revant dans son revoir*,[1] as Rabelais expresses it, gazing by turns at the cell and at the city, keeping sure guard, like a good dog, with a heart full of distrust.

All at once, while he was scrutinizing the great city with the eye which Nature, by way of compensation, had made so piercing that it almost supplied the deficiency of the other organs, it seemed to him that the outline of the quay of La Vielle Pelleterie had an extraordinary appearance; that there was a motion at that point; that the black line of the parapet, defined upon the white surface of the water, was not straight and steady like that of the other quays; but that it undulated to the eye, like the waves of a river, or like the heads of a moving multitude. This struck him as strange. He redoubled his attention. The movement appeared to be toward the Cité. It lasted some time on the quay, then subsided by degrees, as if that which caused it were entering the interior of the Ile: it afterward ceased entirely, and the outline of the quay again became straight and motionless.

While Quasimodo was making all sorts of conjectures, the movement seemed to reappear in the Rue du Parvis, which runs into the Cité, perpendicularly to the façade of Notre-Dame. At last, notwithstanding the intense darkness, he perceived the head of a column approaching through this street, and the next moment a crowd spread itself over the Place du Parvis, where nothing could be distinguished but that it was a crowd.

This sight was alarming. It is probable that this singular procession, which seemed to make a point of avoiding observation, was equally careful to maintain profound silence; yet it could not help making some noise, were it only by the tramping of feet. But even this sound reached not the ear of Quasimodo; and this vast multitude, of which he could scarcely see anything, and of which he heard absolutely nothing, though all was bustle and motion so near to him,

---

[1] "Dreaming in his dream-place."

must have had the effect of an army of the dead, mute, impalpable, and shrouded in vapour. It appeared to him as if a mist full of human beings was approaching, and that what he saw moving were shadows of the shades.

Then were his apprehensions revived, and the idea of an attempt against the gipsy-girl again occurred to his mind. He had a confused foreboding of mischief. At this critical moment he began to consider what course he had best pursue, and with more judgment and decision than might have been expected from a brain so imperfectly organized. Ought he to wake the Egyptian? to assist her to escape? How? which way? the streets were invested; the church was backed by the river. There was no boat, no outlet. He had, therefore, but one course—to die on the threshold of Notre-Dame; at any rate to make all the resistance in his power until succour should arrive, and not to disturb the slumbers of La Esmeralda; the unfortunate creature would be awakened time enough to die. This resolution once taken, he set about examining the enemy with greater composure.

The crowd seemed to increase every moment in the Parvis. He presumed, however, that the noise they made must be very slight, because the windows in the streets and the Place remained closed. All at once a light appeared, and in an instant seven or eight lighted torches rose above the heads of the multitude, shaking their tufts of flame amid the darkness. Then did Quasimodo distinctly perceive a frightful rabble of men and women in rags, armed with scythes, pikes, pickaxes, and halberts, with their thousand glistening heads. Here and there black forks projected like horns over hideous faces. He had some vague recollection of this mob, and fancied that he had seen those faces some months before, when he was elected Pope of Fools. A man, who held a torch in one hand and a cudgel in the other, got upon a post, and appeared to be haranguing them. At the same time this strange army made some evolutions, as if certain divisions were taking their respective stations about the church. Quasimodo picked up his lantern, and went down to the platform between the towers, to obtain a nearer view and to arrange his means of defence.

Clopin Trouillefou, on his arrival before the lofty portal of Notre-Dame, had, in fact, ranged his troops in order of battle. Though he expected no resistance, yet he resolved, like a prudent general, to preserve such order as would enable him to face about in case of need against any sudden attack of the watch or of the Onze-vingts. Accordingly, he drew up his brigade in such a way that, had you seen it from above, or at a distance, you would have taken it for the Roman triangle at the battle of Ecnomus, the boar's head of Alexander, or the famous wedge of Gustavus Adolphus. The base of this triangle rested upon the farthest side of the Place, so as to block up the Rue du Paris; one of its sides faced the Hôtel Dieu, and the other the Rue Saint-Pierre-aux-Bœufs. Trouillefou had placed himself at the apex, with the Duke of Egypt, our friend Jehan, and the boldest of the Vagabonds.

An enterprise of this kind was by no means uncommon in the towns of the Middle Ages. Police, as we understand the term, there was none. Neither was there in populous cities, and in capitals more particularly, any sole, central, regulating power. The feudal system had constituted these large communities after a strange fashion. A city was an assemblage of a thousand seigneuries, which cut it up into compartments of all forms and all dimensions. Hence a thousand contradictory polices, that is to say, no police at all. In Paris, for instance, independently of the one hundred and forty-one seigneurs claiming manorial rights, there were twenty-five who claimed the right of administering justice, from the Bishop of Paris, who had five hundred streets, down to the Prior of Notre-Dame-des-Champs, who had four. The paramount authority of the King was but nominally recognized by all these feudal justiciaries. Louis XI, that indefatigable workman, who so largely commenced the demolition of the feudal edifice, continued by Richelieu and Louis XIV for the interest of royalty, and completed by Mirabeau for the benefit of the people—Louis XI had certainly endeavoured to break this web of seigneuries spread out over Paris, by violently hurling against it at random two or three ordinances of general police. Thus, in 1465, the inhabitants were ordered as soon as it was dark to place lighted candles in their windows, and to shut up their dogs, upon pain of the gallows. The same year they were enjoined to block the streets at night with iron chains, and forbidden to carry daggers or offensive weapons out of doors after dusk; but, in a short time, all these attempts at municipal legislation fell into neglect. The old structure of feudal jurisdiction was left standing. Bailiwicks and seigneuries without number carved out the city among them, crossing, jostling, entangling themselves with, and dovetailing into, one another. There was an endless confusion of watches, under-watches, and counter-watches, in defiance of which robbery, plunder, and sedition, were carried on by main force. Amid this disorder, then, it was no un-common thing for a part of the rabble to make an attack upon a palace, a mansion, a house, in the most populous parts of the city. The neighbours in general abstained from interfering in the affair, unless the pillage extended to their own property. They shut their ears to the firing, closed their shutters, barricaded their doors, left the quarrel to be settled by or without the watch; and the next morn-ing the talk in Paris would be, "Stephen Barbette's was broken open last night," or "the Maréchal de Clermont was seized," etc. Thus not only the royal habitations, the Louvre, the Palace, the Bastille, the Tournelles, but the mere seigneurial residences, the Petit-Bour-bon, the Hôtel de Sens, and the Hôtel d'Angoulême, had their walls and their battlements, their portcullises and their gates. The churches were protected by their sanctity. Some of them, however, were fortified; but Notre-Dame was not of the number. The abbey of Saint-Germain-des-Près was embattled like a baronial castle, and it expended more bronze on cannon than on bells. But to return to Notre-Dame:

As soon as the first arrangements were terminated—and we must say, for the honour of the Vagabond discipline, that Clopin's orders were executed in silence, and with admirable precision—the worthy chief of the band mounted upon the parapet of the Parvis, and raised his harsh and husky voice, turning his face toward Notre-Dame, and at the same time waving his torch, the flame of which, blown about by the wind, and ever and anon almost drowned in its own smoke, now reddened the façade of the church, and presently left it buried in darkness.

"To thee, Louis de Beaumont, Bishop of Paris, counsellor to the court of Parliament, I, Clopin Trouillefou, King of Thunes, Grand Coësre, Prince of Slang, Bishop of Fools, give this notice: Our sis-ter, falsely condemned for magic, has taken sanctuary in thy church. Thou owest her safeguard and protection. Now, the court of Parlia-ment wishes to lay hold of her again, and thou consentest thereto; therefore, O Bishop, are we come to thee. If thy church is sacred, our sister is sacred also; if our sister is not sacred, neither is thy church. We summon thee, then, to surrender the girl to us if thou

wouldst save thy church; or, we will take the girl ourselves and
plunder thy church. This will be still better. In testimony
whereof I here plant my banner. So God keep thee, Bishop of
Paris!"

Unluckily Quasimodo could not hear these words, which were pronounced with a sort of wild and sombre majesty. One of the Vagabonds delivered his banner to Clopin, who solemnly planted it between two paving-stones. It was a pitchfork, on the prongs of which
hung a lump of bleeding carrion.

This done, the King of Thunes turned round and surveyed his
army, a savage throng, whose eyes glistened almost as much as
their pikes. After a moment's pause he gave the word of onset.
"Forward! my lads! To your business, blackguards!" was the cry
of Clopin Trouillefou.

Thirty stout men, fellows with brawny limbs and the faces of
blacksmiths, sprang from the ranks, bearing sledgehammers, pincers,
and crowbars in their hands and on their shoulders. They made for
the great door of the church, ascended the steps, and were presently
crouching down beneath the arch, at work with their pincers and
their levers. A crowd of the Vagabonds followed to assist or to look
on. The eleven steps of the porch were thronged by them. The
door, however, held firm. "Devil!" said one, "it is tough and obstinate!"—" 'Tis old, and its joints are stiff," said another.—"Courage,
comrades!" replied Clopin. "I'll wager my head against an old
shoe that you will have opened the door, taken the girl, and stripped
the high altar before there is a beadle awake. Hold, I think the
lock is giving way."

Clopin was interrupted at this moment by a tremendous crash
behind him. He turned round. An enormous beam had fallen
from the sky; it had crushed a dozen of the Vagabonds on the steps
of the church, and rebounded on the pavement with the noise of a
cannon, breaking a score or two of legs among the crowd of beggars,
who, with cries of horror, scampered off in every direction. The
area of the Parvis was cleared in a twinkling. The blacksmiths,
though protected by the depth of the porch, abandoned the door,
and Clopin himself fell back to a respectful distance from the
church. "I have had a narrow escape," cried Jehan; "I was in
the wind of it, by Jove! but Peter the Butcher is butchered."

It is impossible to describe the fright and consternation which fell with that beam upon the *banditti*. For some minutes they stood staring up at the sky, more astounded at the piece of timber than they would have been by the arrival of twenty thousand of the King's archers. "The devil!" exclaimed the Duke of Egypt, "this does look like magic!"—"It must surely be the moon that has thrown us this log," said Andry the Red.—"Why, then, methinks, the moon is a good friend to our Lady, the Virgin," observed François Chante-Prune.—"Thousand Popes!" cried Clopin, "ye are a parcel of fools!" but still he knew not how to account for the fall of the beam.

Meanwhile nothing was to be seen on the façade, the top of which was too high for the light of the torches to reach it. The ponderous beam lay in the middle of the Parvis, and nothing was heard save the groans of the wretches who had been mangled by its shock upon the steps. The first panic over, the King of Thunes at length fancied that he had made a discovery, which appeared plausible to his companions. *"Ventre-Dieu!"* cried he, "are the canons defending themselves? If so, sack! sack!"—"Sack! sack!" responded the whole crew, with a tremendous hurrah; and a furious discharge of cross bows and arquebuses was levelled at the façade of the church.

The report of the firearms awoke the peaceful inhabitants of the neighbouring houses; sundry windows might be seen opening, nightcaps popping out, and hands holding candles. "Fire at the windows!" roared out Clopin. The windows were shut in an instant, and the poor citizens, who had scarcely had time to cast a hasty and timid glance upon this scene of flash and tumult, returned to perspire with fright by the sides of their spouses, asking themselves whether the witches' sabbath was now held in the Parvis, or whether there was another attack of the Burgundians, as in '64. The men were apprehensive of robbery, the women of rape, and all trembled.

"Sack! sack!" repeated the men of Slang, but they durst not advance. They looked first at the church and then at the beam. The beam did not stir, and the church retained its calm and lonely air, but something had frozen the courage of the Vagabonds.

"To work, then, scoundrels!" cried Trouillefou. "Force the door!" Not a soul moved a finger. "Pretty fellows, these," said Clopin, "who are frightened out of their wits by a bit of wood!"— "Captain," rejoined an old smith, "it is not the bit of wood that frightens us, but the door is all clamped with iron bars. The pincers are of no use."—"What want you then to break it open?" in-

A Blundering Friend

quired Clopin.—"We want a battering-ram."—"Here it is then,"
cried the King of Thunes, stepping boldly up to the formidable beam,
and setting his foot upon it; "the canons themselves have sent you
one. Thank you, canons," he added, making a mock obeisance toward the church.

This bravado produced the desired effect. The charm of the beam
was broken; picked up like a feather by two hundred vigorous arms,
it was dashed with fury against the great door, which the Vagabonds
had in vain attempted to force. In the dim light thrown by the few
torches upon the Place this long beam and its supporters might have
been taken for an immense beast with hundreds of legs butting at a
giant of stone.

At the shock of the beam the half-metallic door resounded like an
immense drum; it yielded not, but the whole cathedral shook,
and the innermost cavities of the edifice were heard to groan. At
the same instant a shower of stones began to rain upon the assailants.
"Hell and the devil!" cried Jehan; "are the towers shaking their
balustrade upon us?" But the impulse was given; the King of
Thunes was right; it was decidedly the Bishop defending his citadel,
and the Vagabonds only battered the door with the more fury, in
spite of the stones which were cracking skulls in all directions. It
is remarkable that these stones fell one by one, but so closely did they
follow each other, that the assailants always felt two at a time, one at
their legs, the other on their heads. There were few of them that
did not tell; already a large heap of killed and wounded lay bleeding and palpitating under the feet of their comrades, who, nothing
daunted, filled up their ranks as fast as they were thinned. The
long beam continued to batter at regular intervals, the door to groan,
and the stones to shower down. The reader need not be told that
this unexpected resistance, which so exasperated the Vagabonds, proceeded from Quasimodo. Chance had unluckily favoured the courageous hunchback.

When he had descended to the platform between the towers his
brain was all in confusion. For some minutes he ran along the gallery to and fro like a maniac, looking down at the compact mass of
banditti ready to burst into the church, and calling upon God and
the devil to save the Egyptian. He had a thought of mounting to the
southern belfry and ringing the alarm-bell; but before he could have
made big Mary utter a single sound the church might have been

broken open ten times over. It was just at this moment that the smiths were coming up to the door with their tools. What was to be done?

All at once he recollected that workmen had been engaged the whole day in repairing the wall, timbers, and roof of the southern tower. To that tower Quasimodo hastened. The lower rooms were full of materials. There were piles of stones, rolls of lead, bundles of laths, massive beams, and heaps of gravel; it was, in short, a complete arsenal.

There was no time to be lost. The crowbars and hammers were at work below. With a strength increased tenfold by the sense of danger he hoisted up the heaviest and longest beam that he could find, shoved it out of a small window, and over the angle of the balustrade surrounding the platform, and fairly launched it into the abyss. The enormous mass, in this fall of one hundred and sixty feet, grazed the wall, breaking the sculptures, and turned over and over several times in its descent. At length it reached the ground; terrible shrieks succeeded; and the black beam, rebounding on the pavement, looked like a serpent writhing and darting upon its prey.

Quasimodo saw the Vagabonds scattered by the fall of the beam, like ashes before the wind. He took advantage of their consternation; and while they fixed a superstitious stare upon the log fallen as they thought from the sky, and put out the eyes of the stone saints of the porch by the discharge of their arrows and firearms, Quasimodo fell to work in silence to carry stones, rubbish, gravel, and even the bags of tools belonging to the masons, to the edge of the balustrade over which he had already hoisted the beam. As soon as they commenced battering the door, the shower of stones began to fall, and the Vagabonds imagined that the church was tumbling about their ears. Anyone who could have seen Quasimodo at that moment would have been seized with dread. Besides the projectiles, which he had piled upon the balustrade, he had carried a heap of stones to the platform itself; so that as soon as the former were exhausted he might have recourse to the latter. There he was, then, stooping and rising, stooping and rising again, with an activity absolutely inconceivable. His huge head, more like that of a gnome than of a human being, was at times bent over the balustrade; then an enormous stone would fall, then another, and another. From time to time, too, he would follow a thumping stone with his eye; and when it did good execution, he would grunt out, "Hun!"

The Vagabonds, however, were nothing daunted. More than twenty times the massive door against which their attack was directed had trembled under the weight of the oaken ram, multiplied by the force of a hundred men. The panels were cracked, the carving flew off in shivers, the hinges at every blow sprang up from their pivots, the planks began to start, and the wood was pounded to powder between the braces of iron; luckily for Quasimodo there was more iron than wood. He was aware, nevertheless, that the door could not hold out long. Though he could not hear it, yet every stroke of the ram reverberated in the caverns, and in the inmost recesses of the church. From his lofty station he saw the assailants, flushed with triumph and with rage, shaking their fists at the gloomy façade, and for his own sake as well as for the Egyptian's he coveted the wings of the daws, which flew off in flocks above his head. His ammunition was not effective enough to repel the assailants.

At this moment of anguish he remarked, a little lower down than the balustrade from which he crushed the men of Slang, two long gutters of stone which disgorged themselves immediately over the great door. The inner orifice of these gutters opened on the level of the platform. An idea struck him. He ran to his bell-ringer's lodge for a faggot, placed it over the hole of the two spouts, laid upon it several bundles of laths and rolls of lead, a kind of ammunition to which he had not yet resorted; and, as soon as all was arranged, he set fire to the faggot with his lantern.

During this interval, as the stones had ceased falling, the Vagabonds no longer looked up; and the ruffians, panting like dogs baying the wild boar in his den, crowded tumultuously round the great door, shattered by the battering engine, but still standing. They awaited with a thrill of impatience the last grand blow, the blow that was to shiver it in pieces. Each was striving to get nearest to the door, that he might be first to dart into the rich magazine of treasures, which had been accumulating in the cathedral for three centuries. They roared with joy as they reminded one another of all the beautiful silver crucifixes, the rich copes of brocade, the monuments of silver gilt, the magnificence of the choir, the gorgeous festivals, at Christmas, gay with torches, at Easter, shining in the sun—all those splendid solemnities when shrines, chandeliers, pyxes, tabernacles, reliquaries, embossed the altars with a crest of gold and diamonds. Assuredly at this moment the canters and whiners, the limpers, and tremblers, and tumblers, thought much less of the rescue of the Egyptian than of the plunder of Notre-Dame. For our own parts, we verily believe that with a great proportion of them La Esmeralda was merely a pretext, if, however, robbers need any pretext.

All on a sudden, while they were grouping themselves for a last effort about the engine, each holding his breath and stiffening his muscles to throw all his strength into the decisive blow, a howling, more hideous than that which followed the fall of the fatal beam, burst from among them. Those who were not yelling and yet alive looked round. Two streams of molten lead were pouring from the top of the building upon the thickest part of the crowd. This sea of men had subsided beneath the boiling metal, which had made, at the points where it fell, two black and smoking holes in the rabble, such as hot water would make in a snowdrift. Here the dying were writhing, half calcined and roaring with agony. All round these two principal streams a shower of horrible rain was scattered over the assailants, and the drops pierced their skulls like gimlets of fire. The clamour was horrible. The Vagabonds, throwing the beam upon the dead and dying, fled pell-mell, the bold and the timid together, and the Parvis was cleared a second time.

All eyes were raised to the top of the building. They beheld an amazing sight. In the uppermost gallery, above the central rose window, a vast body of flame, accompanied by showers of sparks, ascended between the two towers—a fierce and irregular flame, patches of which were every now and then carried off by the wind along with the smoke. Below this fire, below the sombre balustrade, with its glowing red open-work ornaments, two spouts, in the shape of the jaws of monsters, incessantly vomited those silver streams, which stood out distinctly against the dark mass of the lower façade. As they approached the ground, those two streams spread like water poured through the holes of the rose of a watering-pot. Above the flames the enormous towers, each showing two sides deeply contrasted, the one quite black, the other quite red, appeared still larger from the immense shadows which they threw toward the sky. Their numberless sculptures of devils and dragons assumed a grisly aspect. The flickering of the flame gave an appearance of motion to them.

A Blundering Friend

Gorgons seemed to be laughing, waterspouts yelping, salamanders puffing fire, and griffins sneezing in the smoke. And among the monsters thus awakened from their sleep of stone by the flames and by the din there was one that moved from place to place, and passed from time to time in front of the fire, like a bat before a candle.

A silence of terror fell upon the army of the Vagabonds, during which might be heard the cries of the canons shut up in their cloisters, and more alarmed than horses in a burning stable, together with the sound of windows stealthily opened and more quickly shut, a bustle in the interior of the houses and in the Hôtel Dieu, the wind in the flame, the last rattle of the dying, and the continuous pattering of the leaden rain upon the pavement.

Meanwhile, the principal of the Vagabonds had retired to the porch of the Gondelaurier mansion, and were holding consultation. The Duke of Egypt, seated on a post, contemplated with religious awe the resplendent blaze burning at the height of two hundred feet in the air. Clopin Trouillefou struck his clumsy fists together with rage. "Impossible to break in!" muttered he to himself.—"An enchanted church!" grumbled the old Bohemian, Mathias Hunyadi Spicali.—"By the Pope's whiskers," exclaimed a grey-headed ragamuffin who had been a soldier, "those two church gutters beat the portcullis of Lectoure at spewing lead out and out!"—"Do you see that demon passing to and fro before the fire?" cried the Duke of Egypt.—"Egad," said Clopin, " 'tis that cursed bell-ringer, that Quasimodo."—"And I tell you," replied the Bohemian, shaking his head, "it is the spirit Sabnac, the demon of fortification. He appears in the form of an armed soldier with a lion's head. He changes men into stones, and builds towers with them. He has the command of fifty legions. I know him well—'tis he, sure enough."

"Is there then no way of forcing that infernal door?" cried the King of Thunes, stamping violently on the pavement. The Duke of Egypt pointed mournfully to the two streams of boiling lead, which still continued to streak the dark façade. "Churches have been known," observed he with a sigh, "to defend themselves in this manner without the aid of man. It is now about forty years since Sainte-Sophia at Constantinople threw down the crescent of Mohammed three times running by shaking her domes, which are her heads. Guillaume de Paris, who built this, was a magician."

"Shall we then give it up for a bad job, like a scurvy set of poltroons?" said Clopin. "Shall we leave our sister behind, to be hanged to-morrow by these cowled wolves?"

"And the sacristy too, where are cartloads of gold?" added a rapscallion, whose name we regret our inability to record.

"Beard of Mahound!" ejaculated Trouillefou.

"Let us make one more trial," said the preceding speaker.

Again Mathias Hunyadi shook his head. "We shall not get in at the door, that's certain."

"I shall go back," said Clopin. "Who will come with me? By the by, where is little Jehan, the student, who had cased himself up to the eyes in steel?"

"Dead, no doubt," replied some one. "I have not heard his laugh for some time."

The King of Thunes knitted his brow. "More's the pity! He carried a bold heart under that iron shell.—And Master Pierre Gringoire, what is become of him?"

"Captain Clopin," said Andry the Red, "he sneaked off as soon as we had reached the Pont aux Changeurs."

Clopin stamped. "'Sdeath! the coward! To urge us into this affair and then leave us in the lurch!"

"Captain," cried Andry the Red, who was looking down the Rue de Parvis, "yonder comes the little scholar."

"Thanks be to Pluto!" rejoined Clopin. "But what the devil is he dragging after him?"

It was actually Jehan, who was advancing as expeditiously as he could for his heavy warlike accoutrements and a long ladder which, with the aid of half a dozen of the gang, he was trailing along the pavement, more out of breath than an ant dragging a blade of grass twenty times as long as itself.

"Victory! *Te Deum!*" shouted the scholar.

Clopin went up to him. "What, in the devil's name, are you going at with that ladder?"

"I have got it," replied Jehan, panting and blowing. "I knew where it was kept—under the shed belonging to the lieutenant's house. I am acquainted with one of the maids there, who thinks me a perfect Cupid. The poor girl came down half naked to let me in—and here is the ladder."

"I see," said Clopin; "but what are you going to do with it?"

Jehan eyed him with a look of spite and importance, and snapped

A Blundering Friend

his fingers like castanets. At that moment he was really sublime. His head was cased in one of those surcharged helmets of the fifteenth century, which daunted the enemy by their fantastic appendages. His was bestudded with ten iron beaks, so that he might have disputed the formidable epithet δεκεμβολος with Nestor's Homeric ship.

"What am I going to do with it, august King of Thunes? Do you see that row of statues, which look so like idiots, there above the three porches?"

"Yes, what then?"

"That is the gallery of the Kings of France."

"And what of that?" said Clopin.

"Just listen. At the end of that gallery there is a door, which is always on the latch. With this ladder I will mount to it, and then I am in the church."

"Let me go up first, boy."

"No, no, comrade. I brought the ladder. You shall be second, if you will."

"May Beelzebub strangle thee!" cried Clopin peevishly. "I will not be second to any man."

"Then, my dear fellow, seek a ladder for yourself."

Jehan started again, dragging his ladder along and shouting, "This way, my lads!"

In an instant the ladder was raised and placed against the balustrade of the lower gallery, above one of the side doors, amid loud acclamations from the crowd of the Vagabonds, who thronged to the foot of it to ascend. Jehan maintained his right to go up first. The gallery of the Kings of France is at this present time about sixty feet above the pavement. The eleven steps up to the porch then increased the height. Jehan mounted slowly, being impeded by his heavy armour, laying hold of the ladder with one hand, and having his arbalest in the other. When he was about half-way up he cast a melancholy look at the dead bodies that covered the steps and the pavement. "By my fay," said he, "a heap of carcasses that would not disgrace the fifth book of the *Iliad*." He then continued to ascend, followed by the Vagabonds. Had you seen this line of cuirassed backs undulating in the dark, you would have taken it for an immense serpent with iron scales rearing itself against the church.

The scholar at length touched the balcony and nimbly leaped upon it. He was greeted by a general shout from the whole gang. Thus master of the citadel, he joined in the hurrahs, but all at once he was struck dumb with horror. He perceived Quasimodo crouching in the dark behind one of the royal statues, and his eye flashing fire.

Before a second of the besiegers could set foot on the gallery, the formidable hunchback sprang to the top of the ladder, and, without uttering a word, caught hold of the two sides with his nervous hands, and pushed them from the wall with superhuman force. The long ladder, bending under the load of the escalading party, whose piercing shrieks rent the air, stood upright for a moment, and seemed to hesitate; then, all at once taking a tremendous lurch, it fell with its load of *banditti* more swiftly than a drawbridge when the chains that held it have broken. An immense imprecation ensued; presently all was silent, and here and there a mangled wretch crawled forth from beneath the heap of the dead. Quasimodo, leaning with his two elbows upon the balustrade, looked quietly on.

Jehan Frollo found himself in a critical situation. Separated from his comrades by a perpendicular wall of eighty feet, he was alone in the gallery with the formidable bell-ringer. While Quasimodo was playing with the ladder the scholar had run to the postern, which he expected to find upon the latch. He was disappointed. The dwarf had locked it after him when he went down to the gallery. Jehan then hid himself behind one of the stone kings, holding his breath, and eyeing the monstrous hunchback with a look of horror, like the man who, having scraped acquaintance with the wife of a keeper of wild beasts, went one night in pursuance of an assignation, and, climbing over the wrong wall, found himself all at once face to face with a prodigious white bear. For some moments he was not observed by Quasimodo, who at length chancing to turn his head, and perceiving the scholar, suddenly started up.

Jehan prepared himself for a rude encounter, but the hunchback stood stockstill, merely fixing his eye intently upon the scholar. "Hoho!" said Jehan, "why dost thou look at me so spitefully?" With these words the harebrained youth slyly adjusted his arbalest. "Quasimodo," cried he, "I will change thy surname; instead of the deaf thou shalt henceforth be called the blind." The feathered shaft whizzed and pierced the left arm of the bell-ringer. Quasimodo heeded it no more than he would have done the scratch of a pin. He laid hold of the quarrel, drew it from his arm, and calmly broke it

A Blundering Friend

upon his massive knee: he then dropped rather than threw the pieces over the balustrade. Jehan had not time to discharge a second. Quasimodo, having broken the arrow, suddenly drew in his breath, leaped like a grasshopper, and fell upon the scholar, whose armour was flattened against the wall by the shock. A tremendous sight was then seen in the chiaroscuro produced by the faint light of the torches.

Quasimodo grasped with his left hand the two arms of the scholar, who forbore even to struggle, so completely did he feel himself overpowered. With his right the hunchback took off in silence, and with ominous deliberation, the different parts of his armour one after another—helmet, cuirass, arm-pieces, sword, daggers. He looked for all the world like an ape picking a walnut. He threw the iron shell of the scholar, piece by piece, at his feet.

When Jehan found himself stripped, disarmed, powerless, in the hands of his irresistible antagonist he began to laugh him impudently in the face, with all the thoughtless gaiety of a boy of sixteen. But he did not laugh long. Quasimodo was seen standing upon the parapet of the gallery, holding the scholar by the leg with one hand, and swinging him round over the abyss like a sling. Presently was heard a sound like that of a coconut broken by being dashed against a wall; something was seen falling, but it was stopped one third of the way down by a projecting part of the building. It was a dead body that stuck there, bent double, the back broken, and the skull empty.

A cry of horror burst from the Vagabonds— "Revenge!" shouted Clopin.—"Sack! sack!" responded the multitude. "Storm! storm!" Then followed prodigious yells, intermingled with all languages, all dialects, all accents. The death of poor Jehan kindled a fury in the crowd. They were filled with shame and indignation at having been so long held in check before a church by a hunchback. Rage found ladders and multiplied the torches; and in a few moments Quasimodo beheld with consternation a fearful rabble mounting on all sides to the assault of Notre-Dame. Some had ladders, others knotted ropes, while such as could not procure either scrambled up by the aid of the sculptures, holding by each other's rags. There were no means of withstanding this rising tide of grim faces, to which rage gave a look of twofold ferocity. The perspiration trickled down their begrimed brows; their eyes flashed; all these hideous figures were now closing in upon Quasimodo. You would have imagined that some other church had sent its gorgons, its demons, its dragons, its most fantastic monsters, to the assault of Notre-Dame.

Meanwhile the Place was illumined with a thousand torches. A flood of light suddenly burst upon the scene of confusion, which had till then been buried in darkness. The fire kindled on the platform was still burning, and illumined the city to a considerable distance. The enormous outline of the two towers, projected afar upon the roofs of the houses, formed a large patch of shadow amid all this light. The city seemed to be in a bustle. Distant alarm-bells were proclaiming that there was something amiss. The Vagabonds were shouting, yelling, swearing, climbing; and Quasimodo, powerless against such a host of enemies, shuddering for the Egyptian, seeing so many ferocious faces approaching nearer and nearer to the gallery, prayed to heaven for a miracle, at the same time wringing his hands in despair.

CHAPTER V

THE RETREAT WHERE MONSIEUR LOUIS OF FRANCE SAYS HIS PRAYERS

THE reader has, perhaps, not forgotten that Quasimodo, the moment before he perceived the nocturnal band of the Vagabonds, while surveying Paris from the top of his tower, had discovered but a single light, which illumined a window in the uppermost floor of a lofty and gloomy building by the gate of Saint-Antoine. This building was the Bastille. That light was the candle of Louis XI.

The King had actually been for two days past in Paris. He was to leave it again on the day after the morrow for his fortress of Montilz-lez-Tours. His visits to his good city of Paris were rare and short; for there he felt that he had not trap-doors, gibbets, and Scottish archers enough about him.

He had come that day to sleep in the Bastille. He disliked the great chamber which he had at the Louvre, five fathoms square, with its great chimney-piece, adorned with twelve great beasts and thirteen great prophets, and its great bed, twelve feet by eleven. He was lost amid all this grandeur. This burgher King gave the preference to the Bastille, with its humble chamber and bed. Besides, the Bastille was stronger than the Louvre.

This chamber which the King had reserved for himself in the famous State prison was spacious, and occupied the topmost floor of a turret in the keep. It was an apartment of circular form, the floor covered with shining straw matting; the rafters of the ceiling adorned with *fleurs-de-lis* of pewter gilt, the spaces between them coloured; wainscoted with rich woods, sprinkled with rosettes of tin, painted a fine, lively green composed of orpine and woad.

There was but one long and pointed window, latticed with brass wire and iron bars, and somewhat darkened besides by beautiful stained glass, exhibiting the arms of the King and those of the Queen, each pane of which cost twenty-two sous.

There was but one entrance, a modern door, with elliptic arch, covered on the inside with cloth, and having without one of those porches of Irish wood, frail structures of curious workmanship, which were still very common in old buildings one hundred and fifty years ago. "Though they disfigure and encumber the places," says Sauval peevishly, "yet will not our ancient folk put them away, but they preserve them in spite of every one."

In this chamber was to be seen none of the furniture of ordinary apartments, neither tables upon trestles, nor benches, nor forms, nor common stools, in the shape of a box, nor those of a better sort, standing upon columns and counter-columns, at four sous apiece. Nothing was to be seen there save a very magnificent folding armchair; the woodwork was adorned with roses painted on a red ground; and the seat was of scarlet Spanish leather, garnished with silk fringe, and studded with a thousand golden nails. This solitary chair indicated that one person only had a right to sit down in that apartment. Near the chair and close to the window was a table covered with a cloth on which were the figures of birds. On this table were a portfolio spotted with ink, sundry parchments, pens, and a chased silver cup. At a little distance stood a chafing-dish, and a *prie-Dieu,* covered with crimson velvet embossed with studs of gold. Lastly, at the farthest part of the room there was a simple bed, of yellow and scarlet damask, without lace or any trimming but plain fringe. This bed, famed for having witnessed the sleep or the sleeplessness of Louis XI, was to be seen two hundred years ago in the house of a councillor of State.

Such was the chamber commonly called, "The retreat where Monsieur Louis of France said his prayers."

At the moment of our ushering the reader into this retreat it was very dark. An hour had elapsed since the tolling of the curfew; it was night, and there was only one flickering wax candle upon the table, to light five persons, who formed several groups in the chamber.

The first on whom the light fell was a personage superbly dressed in hose, scarlet close-bodied coat striped with silver, and a surtout of cloth of gold with black designs, and trimmed with fur. This splendid costume, upon which the light played, seemed to be braided with flame at all its folds. The wearer had his arms embroidered at the breast in gaudy colours; a chevron, with a deer passant in the base of the shield. The escutcheon was supported on the dexter side by an olive-branch, and on the sinister by a buck's horn. This personage carried in his belt a rich dagger, the hilt of which, of silver gilt, was chased in the form of a crest, and terminated in a count's coronet. He carried his head high, had a haughty bearing and an ill-natured look. At the first glance you discovered in his countenance an expression of arrogance, at the second of cunning.

He stood bareheaded, with a long paper in his hand, before the armchair, on which was seated a person, shabbily dressed, his body ungracefully bent, one knee crossed over the other, and his elbow upon the table. Figure to yourself, on the seat of rich Cordova leather, a pair of slender thighs and spindle-shanks, apparelled in black knitted woollen stuff; a body wrapped in a surtout of fustian, trimmed with fur, which showed much more leather than hair; lastly, to crown all, an old greasy hat of the coarsest black cloth, in the band of which were stuck a number of small leaden figures. This, with a dirty skull-cap, which suffered scarcely a hair to straggle from beneath it, was all that could be seen of the seated personage. His head was so bent forward upon his breast as to throw into the shade the whole of his face, excepting the tip of his nose, on which a ray of light fell; it was evidently a long one. The wrinkled, attenuated hand indicated that he was old. It was Louis XI.

At some distance behind the two persons we have described two men, dressed in the Flemish fashion, were conversing in a low voice. It was not so dark where they stood, but that one who attended the representation of Gringoire's mystery would have recognized in them two of the principal Flemish envoys, Guillaume Rym, the sagacious syndic of Ghent, and Jacques Coppenole, the popular hosier. It will be recollected that these two persons were mixed up with the secret politics of Louis XI.

Lastly, at the opposite end of the room, near the door, in the dark, stood, motionless as a statue, a short, thick-set man, in military attire, with coat-of-arms embroidered on the breast, whose square face without brow, eyes on a level with the top of the head, and ears hidden by two large penthouses of straight hair, partook at once of the dog's and the tiger's.

All were uncovered excepting the King.

The nobleman standing near the King was reading to him a long memorial, to which his Majesty seemed to listen attentively. The two Flemings were whispering together.

"By the Rood!" muttered Coppenole, "I am tired of standing. Are no chairs allowed here?"

Rym answered by a shake of the head, accompanied by a discreet smile.

"God's Cross!" resumed Coppenole, who was quite miserable to be obliged to speak in so low a tone, "I have a good mind to clap myself down on the floor, as I might do at home."

"Nay, Master Jacques, prithee do no such thing."

"Hey-day, Master Guillaume! must one keep on one's legs all the while one is here, then?"

"Even so, or on your knees," replied Rym.

At that moment the King raised his voice. They were silent.

"Fifty sous the gowns of our servingmen, and twelve livres the cloaks of the clerks of our crown! Why, 'tis throwing gold away by tons! Are you distraught, Olivier?"

As he thus spoke the old King raised his head. About his neck might then be seen glistening the golden shells of the collar of St Michael. The rays of the candle fell full upon his skinny and morose face. He snatched the paper from the hands of the reader.

"You will ruin us!" he cried, running his hollow eye over it. "What means all this? What need have we for such a prodigious establishment? Two chaplains, at the rate of ten livres each per month, and a clerk of the chapel at one hundred sous! A *valet-de-chambre*, at ninety livres by the year! Four esquires of the kitchen, at six score livres by the year, each! An overseer of the roast, another of the vegetables, another of the sauces, a head cook, a butler,

355

and two assistants, at ten livres each per month! Two scullions at eight livres! A groom and his two helpers at twenty-four livres the month! A porter, a pastrycook, a baker, two carters, at sixty livres by the year each! And the Marshal of the Forges, six score livres! And the Master of the Chamber of our Exchequer, twelve hundred livres! And the Comptroller, five hundred! And I know not how many more! 'Tis enough to drive one mad! To pay the wages of our servants France is plundered. All the ingots in the Louvre will melt away before such a fire of expense! We will sell our plate! And next year, if God and Our Lady [here he lifted his hat] grant us life, we will take our diet-drink out of a pewter pot."

As he thus spoke he cast a look at the silver cup which glistened upon the table. He coughed, and then proceeded: "Master Olivier, the princes who rule over great countries, such as kings and emperors, ought never to suffer habits of expense to creep into their households; for that fire runs farther and catches the provinces. Give me not occasion to repeat this, Master Olivier. Our expenditure increases every year. The thing likes us not. Why, *Pasque-Dieu!* till '79 it never exceeded thirty-six thousand livres; in '80 it amounted to forty-three thousand six hundred and nineteen livres—I have the exact sum in my head—in '81 to sixty-six thousand six hundred and eighty; and this year, by the faith of my body, it will not be under eighty thousand! Doubled in four years! Monstrous!"

He paused to take breath, and then began again with warmth: "I see about me none but people who fatten upon my leanness. Ye suck crowns out of me at every pore!"

All present maintained profound silence. It was one of those paroxysms which must be left to spend themselves. He continued:

"It is like that petition in Latin from the nobles of France, that we would re-establish what they call the great charges of the Crown! Charges, in good sooth! crushing charges! Ah, gentlemen! ye say that we are not a king to reign *dapifero nullo, buticulario nullo!* [1] We will show you, *Pasque-Dieu!* whether we are not a king!"

Here he smiled at the sense of his own power; his wrath was softened, and he turned toward the Flemings.

"Look you, Compère Guillaume, the Grand Master of the pantry, the Grand Chamberlain, the Grand Seneschal, are of less use than the meanest servingman. Remember that, Compère Coppenole!

[1] "No footman, no butler."

The Retreat

They are good for nothing. Such useless attendants on a king are very like the four evangelists about the dial of the great clock of the Palace, which Philip Brille has lately beautified. They are gilt, but they mark not the hour, and the hand can go without them."

For a moment he appeared thoughtful, and then, shaking his old head, he added, "No, no, by Our Lady, I am not Philip Brille, and I will not new-gild the grand vassals.—Go on, Olivier." The person to whom he spoke took up the paper, and began reading again with a loud voice:

"To Adam Tenon, clerk to the Keeper of the Seals of the Provosty of Paris, for silver, making and engraving said seals, which have been new made, because the former could no longer be used, by reason of their being old and worn out—twelve livres Parisis.

"To Guillaume Frère, the sum of four livres four sous Parisis, as his salary and wages for feeding the pigeons in the two dovecotes of the Hôtel des Tournelles, in the months of January, February, and March of this present year; and for this there have been given seven quarters of barley.

"To a Grey Friar, for confessing a criminal, four sous Parisis."

The King listened in silence. He coughed from time to time; he would then lift the cup to his lips and swallow a mouthful, at the same time making a wry face.

"In this year there have been made by order of justice, by sound of trumpet, in the public places of Paris, fifty-six proclamations— the account to be settled.

"For having made quest and search in certain places, both in Paris and elsewhere, after moneys which were said to be concealed there, but none found—forty-five livres Parisis."

"Bury a crown to dig up a sou!" said the King.

"For putting six panes of white glass in the place where the iron cage is at the Hôtel des Tournelles—thirteen sous.

"For two new sleeves to the King's old doublet—twenty sous.

"For a pot of grease to grease the King's boots—fifteen deniers.

"For new-making a sty for the King's black hogs—thirty livres Parisis.

"For sundry partitions, planks, and doors, made to shut up the lions at Saint-Pol—twenty-two livres."

"Costly beasts those!" said Louis XI. "No matter! 'tis a seemly magnificence in a king. There is a great red lion, which I am very

357

fond of for his engaging ways. Have you seen him, Master Guillaume?—It is right that princes should keep extraordinary animals. We kings ought to have lions for our dogs and tigers for our cats. What is great befits crowns. In the time of Jupiter's pagans, when the people offered to the churches a hundred oxen and a hundred sheep, the emperors gave a hundred lions and a hundred eagles. That was proud and magnificent. The kings of France have always had these bellowings round their throne; nevertheless, people must do me the justice to say that I spend less money in that way than my predecessors, and that I am exceedingly moderate on the score of lions, bears, elephants, and leopards.—Go on, Master Olivier. We wished to say thus much to our Flanders friends."

Guillaume Rym made a profound obeisance, while Coppenole, with his sulky mien, looked like one of those bears which his Majesty had been talking of. The King did not notice this. He sipped at the cup, and, spitting out the drink, exclaimed, "Faugh! the horrid tisane!" The reader proceeded:

"For the feed of a footpad shut up for these six months in the lodge of the slaughter-house, till it is settled what to do with him —six livres four sous."

"What is that?" said the King—"feed what ought to hang! *Pasque-Dieu!* not another sou will I give for *that* food.—Olivier, settle that business with Monsieur d'Estouteville, and this very night make me the needful preparation for wedding this gallant with the gallows.—Go on."

Olivier made a mark with his thumb-nail against the last item, and proceeded:

"To Henriet Cousin, Master Executioner of Paris, the sum of sixty sous Parisis, to him adjudged and ordered by Monseigneur the Provost of Paris, for that he did buy, at the command of the said Sieur the Provost, a great sword for executing and beheading persons condemned by justice for their misdeeds, and did provide a sheath and all thereunto appertaining, and likewise did get the old sword ground and repaired, by reason that it was broken and notched in doing justice upon Messire Louis of Luxembourg, as may more fully appear . . ."

The King interrupted the reader. "That is enough; I order that sum with all my heart. Those are expenses which I think not of. I never grudge moneys so laid out.—Go on."

The Retreat

"For new-making a great cage——"

"Ah!" said the King, grasping the arms of his chair with both hands, "I knew that I had come to this Bastille for something; stop, Master Olivier, I will look at that cage myself. You shall read the items, while I examine it.—Gentlemen of Flanders, come and look at it—'tis a curious thing."

He then rose, leant upon the arm of the reader, motioned to the kind of mute standing before the door to precede him, to the two Flemings to follow, and left the chamber.

The royal party was reinforced at the door of the retreat by men-at-arms encumbered with iron, and slender pages bearing torches. It pursued its way for some time through the interior of the sombre keep, perforated with staircases and corridors even into the substance of the walls. The Captain of the Bastille went first, to get the wickets opened for the old King, who, bent with age and infirmity, coughed as he walked along.

At each wicket every head was obliged to stoop excepting that of the old monarch. "Hum!" muttered he between his gums—for he had lost all his teeth—"we are already not far from the door of the tomb. At a low door the passenger must stoop."

At length, having passed the last wicket, so encumbered with locks and fastenings that it took nearly a quarter of an hour to open it, they entered a lofty and spacious hall, in the middle of which was discovered, by the light of the torches, a massive cube of masonry, iron, and timber. The interior was hollow. It was one of those famous cages for prisoners of State which were called "the King's daughters." In the sides of it were two or three small windows, so closely latticed with thick iron bars that the glass could not be seen. The door was a large stone slab, like a gravestone; one of those doors which are never used but to enter: only in this case the buried person was yet living.

The King began to walk slowly round the little edifice, examining it with care, while Master Olivier, who followed him, read aloud to this effect:

"For having new-made a great wooden cage of thick joists, girders, and planks, being nine feet long by eight wide, and seven feet from floor to ceiling, planed and clamped by strong iron clamps, the which hath been set in a chamber situate in one of the towers of the Bastide Saint-Antoine, in the which cage is put and kept, by com-

359

mand of our lord the King, a prisoner who aforetime dwelt in a cage that was old, crazy, and decayed.—There were used for the said new cage ninety-six joists, fifty-two uprights, ten girders, three fathoms in length; and there were employed nineteen carpenters, in squaring, cutting, and working all said timber in the court of the Bastide for twenty days———"

"Capital heart of oak!" said the King, rapping the wood with his knuckle.

"There were used for this cage," continued the reader, "two hundred and twenty thick iron clamps, of nine and eight feet, the rest of middling length, with the screws, nuts, and bands to the said clamps; the whole of the said iron weighing three thousand seven hundred and thirty-five pounds; besides eight stout holdfasts to fasten the said cage, with the nails, weighing together two hundred and eighteen pounds; without reckoning the iron grating to the windows of the chamber in which the cage is placed, the iron doors of that chamber, and other things . . ."

"A great deal of iron," said the King, "to repress the levity of one mind!"

"The whole amounts to three hundred seventeen livres five sous seven deniers."

"*Pasque-Dieu!*" exclaimed the King. At this imprecation, which was the favourite oath of Louis XI, some person appeared to rouse up within the cage. Chains were heard trailing upon the floor, and a faint voice, which seemed to issue from a tomb, cried, "Mercy, sire! mercy!" The person who thus spoke could not be seen.

"Three hundred seventeen livres five sous seven deniers!" repeated Louis XI.

The lamentable voice which issued from the cage had thrilled all present, including Master Olivier himself. The King alone appeared not to have heard it. At his command Master Olivier began reading again, and his Majesty coolly continued his examination of the cage.

"Besides the above, there has been paid to a mason who made the holes to receive the bars of the windows, and the floor of the chamber where the cage is, because the floor could not have borne this cage by reason of its weight—twenty-seven livres fourteen sous Parisis."

The voice again began moaning. "Mercy, for heaven's sake, sire!

The Retreat

—I assure your Majesty that it was the Cardinal d'Angers who did the treason, and not I."

"The mason is exorbitant," said the King. "Proceed Olivier."

Olivier continued:

"To a joiner for windows, bedstead, and other things—twenty livres two sous Parisis."

The voice likewise continued: "Alas! sire! will you not hear me? I protest that it was not I who wrote that thing to Monseigneur de Guyenne, but Cardinal Balue!"

"The joiner is dear," observed the King. "Is that all?"

"No, sire. To a glazier, for the windows of the said chamber, forty-six sous eight deniers Parisis."

"Pardon, sire! Is it not enough that all my goods have been given to my judges, my plate to Monsieur de Torcy, my library to Master Pierre Doriolle, my tapestry to the Governor of Roussillon? I am innocent. For fourteen years I have pined in an iron cage.— Mercy, sire! mercy! You will be rewarded for it in heaven."

"Master Olivier," said the King, "the total?"

"Three hundred sixty-seven livres eight sous three deniers Parisis."

"By Our Lady!" exclaimed the King, "an extravagant cage!"

Snatching the paper from the hand of Master Olivier, he looked by turns at the account and at the cage, and began to count upon his fingers. Meanwhile the prisoner continued wailing and sobbing. It was truly doleful in the dark. The bystanders looked at each other and turned pale.

"Fourteen years, sire! fourteen long years! ever since the month of April 1469. In the name of the Blessed Mother of God, sire, hearken to me. Your Majesty has all this time been enjoying the warmth of the sun. Am I never more to see the daylight? Be merciful, sire! Clemency is a right royal virtue, which turneth aside the current of wrath. Doth your Majesty believe that at the hour of death it is a great consolation to a king not to have left any offence unpunished? Besides, sire, it was not I, but Monsieur d'Angers, who was guilty of the treachery against your Majesty. Would that you saw the thick chain fastened to my leg, and the great iron ball at the end of it, much heavier than it need be!—Ah, sire! take pity on me!"

"Olivier," said the King, shaking his head, "I perceive that I am

361

charged twenty sous by the load for lime, though it may be bought for twelve. Send back this account."

Turning from the cage, he began to move toward the door of the chamber. The wretched prisoner judged from the receding torches and noise that the King was going. "Sire! sire!" cried he in tones of despair. The door shut. He saw nothing, he heard nothing save the husky voice of the gaoler chanting a stanza of a song of that day on the subject of his own misfortunes:

> Maître Jean Balue
> A perdu la vue
> De ses évêchés.
> Monsieur de Verdun
> N'en a plus pas un,
> Tous sont dépêchés.[1]

The King returned in silence to his retreat, followed by his train, who were thrilled by the last heart-rending wailings of the prisoner. His Majesty turned abruptly toward the Governor of the Bastille. "By the by," said he, "was there not some one in that cage?"

"In good sooth, sire, there was," replied the Governor, astonished at the question.

"Who, then?"

"The Bishop of Verdun."

The King knew that better than anybody else. But this was his way.

"Ah!" said he, as naturally as if he had but just thought of it; "Guillaume de Harancourt, a friend of Monsieur the Cardinal Balue's. Not a bad fellow for a bishop!"

The door of the retreat presently opened, and again closed upon the five personages to whom the reader was introduced at the beginning of this chapter, and who resumed their places, their whispering conversation, and their attitudes.

During the King's absence several dispatches had been laid upon his table. He broke the seals of them himself, and hastily ran over one after another. He then made a sign to Master Olivier, who appeared to perform the office of minister, to take a pen, and, with-

[1] "Master Jean Balue has no more
The bishoprics he had before,
My lord of Verdun
He hath not one."

The Retreat

out communicating to him the contents of the dispatches, began in a low tone to dictate his answers, which Olivier wrote kneeling very incommodiously at the table.

Guillaume Rym watched him closely. The King spoke so low that the Flemings could catch no more than a few detached and scarcely intelligible fragments of his dictation, such as: "To maintain the fertile places by commerce, the barren by manufactures." —"To show the English lords our four pieces of Ordnance, the London, the Brabant, the Bourg-en-Bresse, and the Saint-Omer."—"The artillery causes war to be now carried on more judiciously."—"To our friend, Monsieur Bressuire."—"Armies cannot be kept without taxes——"

By and by he raised his voice. *"Pasque-Dieu!* Monsieur the King of Sicily seals his letters with yellow wax, like a King of France. Perhaps we are wrong to permit this. The greatness of houses is assured by the integrity of their prerogatives.—Note this, Compère Olivier."

Presently, "Oho!" said he, "the big message! What would our brother the Emperor?" Running his eye over the missive, he ever and anon interrupted his reading by interjections—"Certes, the Allmains are so great and so mighty that 'tis scarcely credible."— "But we forget the old saying: the finest county is Flanders; the finest duchy, Milan; the finest kingdom, France.—Is it not so, my Flemish friends?"

This time Coppenole bowed as well as Rym. The patriotism of the hosier was tickled.

The last dispatch made Monsieur Louis knit his brow. "What is this?" he exclaimed. "Grievances and complaints against our garrisons in Picardy! Olivier, write forthwith to Monsieur the Maréchal de Roualt—that discipline is relaxed—that the *gendarmes* of the guard, the nobles of the ban, the yeomen-archers, the Switzers, do infinite mischief to our lieges—that the soldier, not content with the provisions which he finds in the houses of the farmers, drives them out with grievous blows of sticks and staves to the city in quest of wine, fish, groceries, and other luxurious things—that Monsieur the King is acquainted with these proceedings—that it is our intention to protect our people from molestation, robbery, and plunder —that it is our will, by Our Lady!—that, moreover, it pleaseth us not that any musician, chirurgeon, or man-at-arms shall be attired like a prince in velvet, silks, and rings of gold—that these vanities are hateful to God—that we ourselves, who are a gentleman, are content with a doublet of cloth at sixteen sous the Paris ell—that messieurs the soldiers' boys may even come down to that price too.—Order and command.—To Monsieur de Roualt, our friend.—Right!"

This letter he dictated aloud, in a firm tone, and by fits and starts. At the moment when he had finished the door opened and a personage whose look bespoke vehement terror rushed into the chamber, crying, "Sire! sire! the people of Paris have risen in revolt!"

The stern features of Monsieur Louis were contracted; but all the visible signs of his emotion passed away like lightning. He restrained himself, and observed with calm austerity, "Compère Jacques, you come in rather abruptly!"

"Sire! sire! the mob is in rebellion!" replied Compère Jacques, breathless with haste and alarm.

The King, who had risen, seized him roughly by the arm, and whispered so as to be heard by him alone, with concentrated anger and a sidelong glance at the Flemings, "Be silent, or speak low!"

The newcomer comprehended his meaning, and began in a low tone as coherent a narrative as his fears would permit. The King listened with composure, while Guillaume Rym directed the attention of Coppenole to the face and the dress of the speaker, to his furred hood, his short cloak, and his black velvet gown, which bespoke a president of the Cour des Comptes.

No sooner had this personage communicated a few particulars to the King than Monsieur Louis burst into a loud laugh, exclaiming: "Is that all? Speak up, Compère Coictier! Be not afraid to open your mouth! Our Lady knows that I have no secrets from our good friends of Flanders."

"But, sire . . ."

"Speak up, I tell you, man!"

Compère Coictier was dumbfounded.

"Come!" resumed the King—"speak, sir!—there is a riot of the rabble in our good city of Paris?"

"Yes, sire."

"Directed, you say, against Monsieur the Bailiff of the Palace of Justice?"

"It is, apparently," said the *compère,* still stammering, quite disconcerted at the abrupt and unaccountable change which had taken place in the sentiments of the King.

"Where did the watch fall in with the mob?" inquired Louis.

"Going along the great Truanderie toward the Pont aux Changeurs. I met it myself, as I was coming hither in obedience to the commands of your Majesty. I heard some of them shouting, 'Down with the Bailiff of the Palace!'"

"And what complaint have they to make against the bailiff?"

"Why," said Compère Jacques, "he is their liege lord."

"Indeed!"

"Yes, sire. They are the ragamuffins of the Cour des Miracles; they have long been complaining of the bailiff whose vassals they are. They will not acknowledge his authority either in criminal or in civil matters."

"Ay, marry!" ejaculated the King, with a smile of satisfaction, which he strove in vain to disguise.

"In all their petitions to the Parliament," replied the Compère Jacques, "they pretend that they have but two masters: your Majesty and their God—who, I verily believe, is the devil."

"Eigh! eigh!" said the King.

He rubbed his hands, with an inward exultation, which beamed forth from his face; he could not dissemble his joy, though he endeavoured at times to compose himself. He completely puzzled all present, not excepting "Master Olivier." He kept silence for a moment, with a look of deep thought, but also of satisfaction.

"Are they numerous?" he all at once inquired.

"Indeed they are, sire," answered Compère Jacques.

"How many?"

"Six thousand, at least."

The King could not help ejaculating, "Good!" He then asked, "Are they armed?"

"With scythes, pikes, spades, arquebuses—all sorts of very dangerous weapons."

The King appeared not at all uneasy at this recapitulation. Compère Jacques deemed it his duty to add, "If your Majesty send not prompt succour to the bailiff he is lost."

"We will send," said the King, with a look of affected gravity. "'Tis well. Certes, we will send. Monsieur the bailiff is our friend. Six thousand! They are saucy rascals. Their boldness is marvellous, and hath sorely offended us. But we have few people about us to-night. It will be time enough in the morning."

"Instantly, sire!" exclaimed Compère Jacques, "or they will have leisure to plunder the bailiff's house, to pull down the seigneurie, and to hang the bailiff twenty times over. For the love of God, sire, send before morning!"

The King looked him full in the face: "I tell you, in the morning." It was one of those looks to which there is no replying.

For some moments Louis was silent. "Tell me, Compère Jacques," he again began—"for you must know what was . . ."—he corrected himself—"what is the feudal jurisdiction of the bailiff?"

"Sire, the Bailiff of the Palace has the Rue de la Calandre, as far as the Rue de l'Herberie, the Place Saint-Michel, and the Places vulgarly called the Mureaux, situate near the church of Notre-Dame-des-Champs"—here the King lifted the brim of his hat— "which mansions are thirteen in number; also the Cour des Miracles, the lazar-house called La Banlieue, and the whole line of causeway commencing at this lazar-house and ending at the gate of Saint-Jacques. Of all these parts he is the liege-lord, with the right of administering high, middle, and low justice."

"Hey-dey!" said the King, rubbing the side of his nose with his forefinger, "'tis a good slice of my fair city. So Monsieur the Bailiff was king of all that!"

He asked no more questions, but remained absorbed in thought, and talking to himself. "Very fine, Monsieur the Bailiff! you had there between your teeth a nice piece of our Paris!"

All at once he burst forth: *"Pasque-Dieu!* what mean those men who pretend to be liege-lords, judges, and masters here? who have their toll-bar at the end of every field? their gibbet and their hangman at every cross-street among our people? So that, like the Greek, who believed in as many gods as there were fountains, and the Persian, as he saw stars, the French have as many kings as they see gibbets. Egad! this is a frightful state of things. I like not the confusion. I would fain know if it be by the grace of God that there is at Paris any other liege-lord besides the king, any other justice besides our Parliament, any other emperor besides ourselves in this empire. By the faith of my soul, there must come a day when there shall be in France but one king, one liege-lord, one judge, one headsman as in Paradise there is but one God!"

The Retreat

Again he lifted his hat, and, still musing, continued with the look and accent of a huntsman letting slip and urging on his dogs: "Good! my people! well done! Down with these false lords! On them! on them! Sack, plunder, hang! You would fain be kings, messeigneurs, would you?"

Here he stopped short, bit his lips, as if to catch the thought which had half escaped him, fixing his piercing eye on each of the five personages around him in succession, and, suddenly seizing his hat with both hands, and looking steadfastly at it, he exclaimed, "Oh! I would burn thee, if thou knewest what there is in my head!"

Then, casting his eyes again around him, with the keen and restless look of a fox slily returning to his den: "It matters not: we will send succour to Monsieur the Bailiff. Unluckily we have but few troops here at this moment against such a mob. We must wait till morning. Order shall be restored in the city, and they shall hang out of the way all who are taken."

"By the by, sire," said Compère Coictier, "I forgot in my first alarm—the watch has taken two stragglers of the band. If your Majesty pleases to see them, they are below."

"Will I see them?" cried the King. *"Pasque-Dieu!* how couldst thou forget that! Run quick, Olivier, and fetch them!"

Master Olivier left the room, and presently returned with the two prisoners surrounded by archers of the Ordnance. The first had a bloated face and stupid idiot-like, drunken look. He was dressed in rags, and, in walking, he bent his knees and shuffled his feet. With the pale and smiling countenance of the other the reader is already familiar.

The King scrutinized them for a moment without saying a word, and then abruptly asked the first, "What is thy name?"

"Gieffroy Pincebourde."

"Thy profession?"

"A Vagabond."

"What wert thou going to do in that damnable sedition?"

The varlet stared at the King, swinging his arms with a besotted look. His was one of those misshapen heads, in which the understanding is almost as much cramped as a light beneath an extinguisher.

"I know not," said he. "The others went; so I went along."

The Hunchback of Notre-Dame

"Were ye not bound to attack with violence and to plunder your liege-lord the Bailiff of the Palace?"

"I know that we were going to take something from somebody—that is all!"

A soldier brought to the King a hedging-bill which had been found upon the prisoner.

"Ownest thou that weapon?" inquired the King.

"Yes; 'tis my bill: I am a vine-dresser."

"Knowest thou this man?" pointing to the other prisoner; "was he one of thy companions?"

"No: I know him not."

" 'Tis enough," said the King; and, beckoning to the silent personage stationed near the door, "Compère Tristan," said he, "there is a man for you."

Tristan the Hermit bowed. He gave some directions in a low tone to two archers, who took the wretched prisoner away.

The King meanwhile turned to the second prisoner, whose brow was covered with a cold perspiration. "Thy name?"

"Sire, Pierre Gringoire."

"Thy trade."

"A philosopher, sire."

"How darest thou, knave, to go and assault our friend Monsieur the Bailiff of the Palace, and what hast thou to say to this riot?"

"Sire, I had no hand in it."

"How now, varlet! hast thou not been apprehended by the watch in this goodly company?"

"No, sire; 'tis a mistake: it was quite an accident. I make tragedies. Sire, I conjure your Majesty to hear me. I am a poet. Men of my profession are addicted to walking the streets at night. It was the greatest chance in the world. I have been wrongfully apprehended; I am innocent of this commotion. Your Majesty found that I am not known to yon Vagabond. I beseech your Majesty . . ."

"Silence!" said the King, between two gulps of his diet-drink. "Thou stunnest one."

Tristan the Hermit stepped forward, and pointing to Gringoire: "Sire," he asked, "may we take him too?"—It was the first audible word that he had uttered.

368

The Retreat

"Why," replied the King, "I see no reason to the contrary."

"Alas, sire! I see a great many!" ejaculated Gringoire.

Our philosopher was at that moment greener than an olive. From the cold and indifferent look of the King he perceived that he had no resource but in something unusually pathetic, and, throwing himself at his feet, he cried with vehement gesticulation: "Sire, your Majesty will deign to hear me. Ah, sire! let not your wrath fall upon so humble an object as I am! The thunderbolts of God are not hurled against a lettuce. You, sire, are an august and most puissant monarch; have pity on a poor but honest man, who would be more puzzled to kindle a sedition than an icicle to give out a spark. Most gracious sovereign, clemency is a kingly virtue; whilst severity only exasperates the minds of men. The fierce blasts of the north cannot make the traveller throw off his cloak; the sun, gradually pouring forth his rays, warms him to such a degree that he is glad to strip himself to his shirt. I avouch to you, my sovereign lord and master, that I am not of the Vagabond crew, a thief, or a disorderly person. Sedition and robbery belong not to the train of Apollo. I am not a man to rush into those clouds which burst in thunders of insurrection. I am a faithful liege of your Majesty. The same jealousy which a husband has for the honour of his wife, the love which a son feels in return for the affection of a father, a good subject ought to have for the glory of his king; he ought to burn with zeal for his person, his house, his prosperity, to the exclusion of every other passion. Such, sire, is my political creed. Judge me not, then, from this coat out at elbows to be an accomplice in sedition and plunder. Pardon me sire, and on my knees will I pray to God, night and morning, for you. I am not very rich, it is true; indeed I am rather poor, but not vicious for all that. It is not my fault. Every one knows that great wealth is not to be gained by letters, and that the most learned have not always the largest fire in winter. The lawyers run away with all the grain, and leave nothing but the straw for the other scientific professions. I could repeat to you forty excellent proverbs on the ragged cloak of the philosopher. Oh, sire! clemency is the only light that can illumine the interior of a great soul. Clemency bears the torch before all the other virtues. Without it they are blind, and grope about in the dark for God. Mercy, which is the same thing as clemency, produces love in subjects, which is the most

369

effective guard for the person of the prince. What harm can it do to your Majesty, who dazzles all eyes, that there is one poor man more upon the earth—one poor innocent philosopher, floundering in the darkness of calamity, with empty pocket and empty stomach! Besides, sire, I am one of the learned. Great kings add a pearl to their crown by protecting letters. Hercules disdained not the title of Musagetes; Matthias Corvinus patronized Jean de Monroyal, the ornament of the mathematics. Now it is a bad way of patronizing letters to hang those who cultivate them. What a stain upon Alexander, if he had hanged Aristotle! That *trait* would not be a spot on the face of his reputation heightening its beauty, but a foul ulcer disfiguring it. Sire, I have composed a most pertinent epithalamium for Mademoiselle of Flanders and Monseigneur the most august Dauphin. That is not a brand of rebellion. Your Majesty perceives that I am not an ignorant varlet, that I have studied deeply, and that I have great natural eloquence. Have mercy then, sire! In so doing you will perform an act of gallantry to Our Lady; and I protest to you that I have a strong dislike to the idea of being hanged!"

As he thus spoke the disconsolate Gringoire kissed the King's slippers, and Guillaume Rym whispered Coppenole: "He does right to crawl the floor. Kings are like the Cretan Jupiter; they have no ears but in their feet." The hosier, without bestowing a thought on the Cretan Jupiter, replied with a grim smile, and his eye fixed on Gringoire, "Capital, by the Rood! Methinks I hear the Chancellor Hugonet begging his life of me!"

When Gringoire at length ceased, out of breath with his harangue, he lifted his eyes, trembling, toward the King, who was scratching with his nail a spot on the knee of his breeches; his Majesty then sipped at his drink. He uttered not a word, however; and this silence kept Gringoire on the rack. At length the King fixed his eye upon him. "What an eternal prater!" said he. Then turning to Tristan the Hermit: "Bah! let the varlet go!"

Gringoire fell backward, overpowered with joy.

"Let him go!" grumbled Tristan. "Will it not please your Majesty to have him shut up awhile in a cage?"

"*Compère,*" rejoined Louis XI, "dost think it is for such birds that we make cages costing three hundred sixty-seven livres eight sous three deniers? Dismiss me this *paillard* forthwith."—Mon-

The Retreat

sieur Louis was fond of this term, which, with *Pasque-Dieu,* constituted the whole stock of his jocularity—"and turn him out with a sound drubbing."

"Ah!" ejaculated Gringoire, "what a magnanimous king!" and, for fear of a counter-order, he hastened toward the door, which Tristan opened for him with a very ill grace. The soldiers went out with him, driving him before them with kicks and thumps, which Pierre bore like a genuine stoic.

The good-humour of the King, ever since he had been informed of the insurrection against the bailiff, manifested itself in all he did. This unusual clemency was no slight sign of it. Tristan the Hermit looked as surly in his corner as a dog when you have shown him a bone and taken it away again.

The King, meanwhile, was playfully drumming the march of Pont-Audemer with his fingers on the arm of his chair. This prince was a dissembler, but he could conceal his troubles much better than his joy. These external manifestations of delight at any agreeable tidings were sometimes carried to a great length; as at the death of Charles the Bold, when he vowed to present a silver balustrade to Saint-Martin-de-Tours; and at his accession to the throne, when he forgot to give directions for the funeral of his father.

"Eh, sire!" suddenly exclaimed Jacques Coictier, "what is become of the acute fit of illness for which your Majesty commanded my services?"

"Oh!" said the King, "I am really in great pain, *compère.* I have a ringing in my ears, and rakes of fire are harrowing my breast."

Coictier took the hand of the King, and felt his pulse with a most self-sufficient look.

"See, Coppenole," said Rym, in a low tone, "there he is between Coictier and Tristan. These are his whole court. A physician for himself, a hangman for all besides."

While feeling the King's pulse Coictier assumed a look of more and more alarm. Louis eyed him with some anxiety. Coictier's countenance assumed a darker and darker shade. The worthy man had nothing to live upon but the ill health of the King; this resource he cultivated with his utmost skill.

"Indeed!" he at length muttered; "but this is serious!"

"Is it not?" said the King in alarm.

371

"Pulse quick, irregular, intermittent," continued the physician. *"Pasque-Dieu!"*

"In less than three days this might prove fatal."

"Our Lady!" ejaculated the King. "And what remedy, *compère?*"

"I will consider of it, sire."

He desired the King to put out his tongue, shook his head, and made a rueful face. In the midst of these grimaces, "Egad, sire!" he abruptly began, "I have to tell you that a receivership of vacant benefices has fallen in, and to remind you that I have a nephew."

"Thy nephew shall have my receivership, Compère Jacques," replied the King; "but relieve me from this fire in my chest."

"Since your Majesty is so gracious," rejoined the physician, "you will not refuse me a little aid toward the building of my house in the Rue Saint-André-des-Arcs."

"Eh!" said the King.

"My money is all run out," continued the doctor, "and it were indeed a pity that the house should lack a roof: not for the sake of the house, which is quite simple and burgher-like; but for the paintings of Jehan Fourbault, wherewith the ceilings are enlivened. There is a Diana flying in the air, but so excellent, so delicate, with action so natural, head-gear so neat and crowned with a crescent, and flesh so white, that she is enough to tempt them that examine her too closely. There is a Ceres too—another goddess of rare beauty. She is seated upon sheaves of wheat, having upon her head a gay garland of ears entwined with salsify and other flowers. Nothing was ever seen more lovely than her eyes, more neatly turned than her limbs, more noble than her air, or more graceful than her drapery. She is one of the most innocent and perfect beauties that the pencil hath ever produced."

"Bloodsucker!" muttered the King, "what is it thou wouldst have?"

"I lack a roof for these paintings, sire; the cost will be trifling, but I have no money."

"How much will it cost?"

"Why—a roof of copper, embellished with figures and gilt—two thousand livres at the utmost."

"Ah! the murderer!" exclaimed the King. "He never draws me a tooth but he makes a diamond of it for himself."

The Retreat

"Shall I have my roof?" said Coictier.

"Yes; and go to the devil!—but cure me first."

Jacques Coictier made a profound obeisance. "Sire," said he, "nothing but a repellent can save you. We will rub your loins with that fine specific composed of cerate, an Armenian bolus, white of egg, oil, and vinegar. You must continue your drink, and we will answer for your Majesty."

A lighted candle attracts more than one moth. Master Olivier, seeing the liberality of the King, and deeming it a favourable opportunity, approached in his turn. "Sire . . ."

"How now?" said Louis XI.

"Sire, your Majesty knows that Simon Radin is dead."

"What then?"

"He was counsellor of Justice to the Exchequer."

"Well?"

"His place is vacant, sire."

As he thus spoke the haughty face of Master Olivier had relinquished its arrogant expression, and assumed a cringing air—the only change of which a courtier's features are susceptible. The King looked him full in the face. "I understand," said he drily.

"Master Olivier," he again began, after a brief pause, "Maréchal de Boucicaut used to say, 'There are no gifts to be got but from the King, no fish to be caught but in the sea.' I perceive that you are of the same way of thinking as Monsieur de Boucicaut. Now listen to this. We have a good memory. In '68 we made you groom of our chamber; in '69 keeper of the castle of the bridge of Saint-Cloud, at a salary of one hundred livres Tournois; you wanted them to be Parisis. In November '73, by letters issued at Gergeaule, we appointed you keeper of the wood of Vincennes, in the room of Gilbert Acle, esquire; in '75 ranger of the forest of Rouvray-lez-Saint-Cloud, in the room of Jacques le Maire; in '78 we were graciously pleased, by letters patent with double seal of green wax, to grant a yearly sum of ten livres Parisis to you and your wife, upon the Place aux Marchands, situate at the school of Saint-Germain; in '79 we made you ranger of the forest of Senart, in the room of poor Jehan Daiz; then captain of the castle of Loches, then governor of Saint-Quentin, then captain of the bridge of Meulan, from which you have taken the style of count. Out of the fine of five sous paid by every barber who shaves on a holiday, three sous go to you, and we have your leavings. We have been pleased to change your name from *le Mauvais,* which accorded but too well with your mien. In '74 we granted you, to the great displeasure of our nobility, coat-armour of a thousand colours, which makes you a breast like a peacock's. *Pasque-Dieu!* are you not content yet? Is not the draught of fishes miraculous enough? Are you not afraid lest another salmon should sink your boat? Pride will be your downfall, *compère.* Pride always has ruin and shame close at its heels. Think of this, and be quiet."

These words, uttered with a stern look, caused the angry visage of Master Olivier to resume its former insolence. "'Tis plain," murmured he, almost aloud, "that the King is ill to-day. He gives everything to the physician."

Louis, so far from being exasperated at this impertinence, again began with a degree of mildness: "Hold, I forgot that I made you my ambassador to Ghent to Madame Marie.—Yes, gentlemen," added the King, turning toward the Flemings, "this man was my ambassador.—There now, *compère,*" continued he, addressing Master Olivier, "we will not fall out: we are old friends. It is very late; we have finished our business. Shave me."

Our readers were probably not prepared till this moment to recognize in "Master Olivier" that terrible Figaro, whom Providence, the great dramatist, so curiously mixed up with the long and bloody comedy of Louis XI. We shall not here attempt to portray that singular face. This royal barber had three names. At court he was politely called Olivier le Daim; by the people, Olivier the Devil. His real name was Olivier le Mauvais.

Olivier le Mauvais, then, stood motionless, looking doggedly at the King, and stealing sidelong glances at Jacques Coictier.—"Yes, yes! the physician!" he muttered between his teeth.

"Ah, yes, the physician!" repeated Louis XI, with singular mildness—"the physician has more influence than thou. And very naturally. He has our whole body in his grip, while thou layest hold of us by the chin only. Come, my poor barber, think no more of it. What wouldst thou say, and what would become of thy office, if I were a king like Chilperic, who had a beard which he was in the habit of grasping in his hand?—Now, *compère,* fetch your things, and shave me."

The Retreat

Olivier, seeing that the King was determined not to be put out of temper, left the room grumbling to comply with his orders.

The King rose, went to the window, and hastily opening it, cried, clapping his hands, and with extraordinary agitation— "Ah, yes! the sky over the city is all in a glow. The bailiff's house must be on fire. It cannot be anything else. Well done, my good people!—at length ye lend me a hand to crush their lordships." Then turning toward the Flemings— "Only come and look, gentlemen. Is not that a fire yonder?"

The two citizens of Ghent approached. "'Tis a great fire too," said Guillaume Rym.

"By the Rood!" cried Coppenole, whose eyes all at once sparkled, "that reminds me of the burning of the Seigneur d'Hymbercourt's house. There must be a fine insurrection yonder."

"Think you so, Master Coppenole?" said the King, with a look of scarcely less delight than that of the hosier. "'Twill be difficult to quell, no doubt."

"By the Mass, sire, your Majesty will get a great many companies of men-at-arms thinned in doing it."

"Ah!—I!—that alters the case!" rejoined the King. "If I pleased . . ."

"If this riot be what I suppose," boldly replied the hosier, "your pleasing will be to no purpose."

"*Compère,*" said Louis XI, "with two companies of my guard and one piece of ordnance one might soon put down the rabble."

The hosier, regardless of the signs made to him by his colleague, appeared determined to contradict the King. "The Switzers too were rabble," said he. "The Duke of Burgundy, being a proud gentleman, held this rabble dog-cheap. At the battle of Grandson, he cried, 'Gunners, fire on yon base-born varlets!' and he swore by St. George. But Scharnachthal, the avenger, rushed upon the goodly Duke with his mace and his men; and at the onslaught of peasants clad in buffalo-hides the shining Burgundian army was shivered like a pane of glass by a stone. I know not how many knights were slain by the rabble; and Monsieur de Château-Guyon, the most illustrious of the Burgundian nobles, was found dead with his tall grey charger in a small meadow."

"My friend," rejoined the King, "you are talking of a battle: we have to do with a riot. Why, I would put an end to it in the twinkling of an eye."

"It may be, sire," replied the other, with indifference; "but in that case the people's time is not come."

Guillaume Rym thought it right to interfere. "Master Coppenole, you are speaking to a mighty monarch."

"I know it," gravely replied the hosier.

"Let him talk away, my friend Rym," said the King; "I like this frankness. My father, Charles VII, was accustomed to say that Truth was sick. Now, I fancied that she was dead, and had not found a confessor. Master Coppenole is making me sensible of my mistake."

Then, laying his hand familiarly upon Coppenole's shoulder, he proceeded: "You were saying, Master Jacques . . ."

"I was saying, sire, that perhaps you are right—that the hour of the people here is not yet come."

Louis fixed upon him his piercing eye. "And when will that hour arrive?"

"You will hear it strike."

"By what clock, pray?"

Coppenole, with grave but tranquil look, drew the King close to the window. "Listen, sire. Here is a castle-keep, there a bell-tower, cannon, burghers, soldiers. When the bell-tower shall buzz, when the cannon shall roar, when the keep shall fall with a mighty crash, when the burghers and the soldiers shall shout and slay one another, then shall the hour have struck."

The face of Louis XI became gloomy and thoughtful. For a moment he was silent; he then patted with his hand the thick wall of the tower, as though it had been the flank of a favourite charger. "Oh, no!" said he, "thou wilt not fall so easily, my good Bastille!" Then turning sharply toward the bold Fleming: "Master Jacques," said he, "have you ever seen an insurrection?"

"I have made one," answered the hosier.

"How do you set about making an insurrection?" inquired the King.

"Why," replied Coppenole, "the thing is not at all difficult. There are a hundred ways. In the first place the city must be discontented. That is not a rare circumstance. And then the character of the inhabitants. Those of Ghent are disposed to sedition. They are always attached to the son of the reigning prince, but never to the prince himself. Well, I will suppose that some morning some one comes into my shop and says to me: 'Father Coppenole, here is this, that, and the other; the demoiselle of Flanders is determined to save her ministers; the high bailiff has doubled the toll for grinding corn' —or anything else—no matter what. Incontinently I leave my work, and out I go into the street, and shout— 'To arms!' There is always some cask or hogshead lying about. I leap upon it, and I tell, in the first words that come, what I have upon my heart; and when one belongs to the people, sire, one always has something upon the heart. Then the lieges assemble, they shout, they ring the alarm-bell, they arm themselves with weapons taken from the soldiers, the market-people join them, and they fall to work. And this will always be the way, while there are lords in the seigneuries, burghers in the burghs, and peasants in the country."

"And against whom do ye thus rebel?" inquired the King. "Against your bailiffs? against your liege-lords?"

"Sometimes one, sometimes the other, just as it happens; sometimes too against the Duke."

Monsieur Louis returned to his chair. "Aha!" said he, with a smile; "here they have got no farther than the bailiffs!"

At that moment Olivier le Daim returned. He was followed by two pages bearing the requisites for the King's toilet; but what struck Louis XI was the circumstance of his being accompanied also by the Provost of Paris and the officer of the watch, whose countenances bespoke alarm. The face of the spiteful barber also wore a look of dismay, but an expression of pleasure lurked beneath it. He it was who spoke. "Begging your Majesty's pardon," said he, "I bring calamitous tidings."

The King, turning sharply round, tore the mat on the floor with the legs of his chair. "What have you to say?"

"Sire," replied Olivier le Daim, with the malignant look of a man who rejoices in the opportunity of striking a severe blow, "it is not against the Bailiff of the Palace that the insurrection of the populace is directed."

"And against whom, then?"

"Against yourself, sire?"

The aged monarch started upon his feet, upright as a young man. "Explain, Olivier, explain! And beware of thy head, *com-*

père; for I swear by the cross of Saint-Lo that if thou liest the sword which cut off the head of Monsieur de Luxembourg is not so notched but it shall hack off thine!"

This was a formidable oath. In all his life Louis XI had sworn but twice by the cross of Saint-Lo. Olivier opened his lips to reply. "Sire . . ."

"Down on thy knees!" cried the King vehemently, interrupting him. "Tristan, look to this man!"

Olivier fell on his knees. "Sire," said he coldly, "a witch has been sentenced to death by your court of Parliament. She has taken sanctuary in Notre-Dame. The people have risen to remove her by force. The Provost and the officer of the watch, who have just come from the spot, are here to contradict me if I speak not truth. It is to Notre-Dame that the rabble are laying siege."

"Soho!" ejaculated the King, in a low tone, pale and trembling with rage. "Notre-Dame, is it? They are besieging Our Lady, my good mistress, in her own cathedral!—Rise, Olivier. Thou art right. I give thee Simon Radin's place. Thou art right. It is myself whom they are assailing. The witch is under the safeguard of the church, the church is under my safeguard. I verily believed that the bailiff was the object of their attack. It is myself, after all!"

Then, as if his passion had suddenly restored to him the vigour of youth, he began to pace the floor with hasty strides. He no longer laughed; he was terrible to behold as he stalked to and fro. The fox was turned into an hyena. He seemed to be choked, and incapable of utterance; his lips moved, and his scraggy fists were clenched. All at once he raised his head; his hollow eye glared, and his voice burst forth like the blast of a trumpet: "Cut them in pieces, Tristan! cut all those knaves in pieces! Go, my friend Tristan! slay, and spare not!"

This explosion over, he returned to his seat, and said with cold, concentrated rage: "Here, Tristan!—We have with us in this Bastille the Vicomte de Gif's fifty lances, making together three hundred horse: take them. There is also Captain de Châteaupers' company of the archers of our Ordnance: take them. You are provost of the farriers; you have your own people: take them. At the Hôtel Saint-Pol you will find forty archers of the new guard of Monsieur the Dauphin: take them. And with all this force hasten forthwith

The Retreat

to Notre-Dame.—So, so, messieurs of the mob of Paris, it is at the crown of France, at the sanctity of Our Lady, and at the peace of this commonwealth, that your blows are aimed!—Exterminate, Tristan! exterminate! Spare not one of them but for Montfaucon!"

Tristan bowed: "It shall be done, sire." After a pause he asked, "What shall I do with the sorceress?"

"Ah!" said he, musing at this question—"the sorceress!—Monsieur d'Estouteville, what would the people with her?"

"Sire," replied the Provost of Paris, "I should imagine that, as the people are gone to take her from her sanctuary in Notre-Dame, they are offended because she is unpunished, and mean to hang her."

For a while the King appeared to be lost in thought; then turning to Tristan: *"Compère,"* said he, "exterminate the people, and hang the sorceress."

"Excellent!" whispered Rym to Coppenole; "punish the people for the intention, and carry that intention into effect!"

" 'Tis enough, sire," answered Tristan. "But if the sorceress be still in Notre-Dame, is she to be removed in despite of sanctuary?"

"Pasque-Dieu! sanctuary!" ejaculated the King, rubbing his forehead. "And yet the witch must be hanged."

Here, as if actuated by a sudden idea, he fell upon his knees before his chair, took off his hat, laid it upon the seat, and devoutly fixed his eyes on one of the leaden figures with which it was garnished. "Oh!" he began with clasped hands, "my gracious patroness, Our Lady of Paris, forgive me. I will do it but this once. That criminal must be punished. I assure you, Holy Virgin, my good mistress, that she is a sorceress who is not worthy of your kind protection. You know, madam, that many very pious princes have transgressed the privilege of churches for the glory of God and the necessity of the state. St Hugh, a bishop of England, allowed King Edward to take a magician in his church. St Louis of France, my master, violated for the same purpose the church of Monsieur St Paul; and Monsieur Alphonse, son of the King of Jerusalem, the church of the Holy Sepulchre itself. Forgive me then for this time, Our Lady of Paris! I will never do so again, and I will give you a goodly statue of silver, like that which I gave last year to Our Lady of Ecouys. Amen!"

He made the sign of the Cross, rose, put on his hat, and said to Tristan: "Lose not a moment, *compère*. Take Monsieur de Châteaupers along with you. Let the alarm-bell be rung. Quell the rabble. Hang the sorceress. That is settled. I expect you to bear the costs of the execution. Report to me upon it.—Come, Olivier, I shall not get to bed to-night. Shave me."

Tristan the Hermit bowed and retired. The King then motioned Rym and Coppenole to withdraw. "God keep you, my good friends of Flanders. Go, take a little rest: the night is far spent; indeed we are nearer to morning than evening."

Both accordingly retired, and on reaching their apartments, to which they were escorted by the captain of the Bastille, Coppenole said to Guillaume Rym: "By the Rood! I have had enough of this coughing king. I have seen Charles of Burgundy drunk; he was not so ill-conditioned as Louis XI sick."

"Master Jacques," replied Rym, " 'tis because the wine of kings is not so cruel as their diet-drink."

CHAPTER VI

A NARROW ESCAPE

ON leaving the Bastille Gringoire scudded down the Rue Saint-Antoine with the swiftness of a runaway horse. When he had reached the Baudoyer gate he walked straight up to the stone cross which stood in the middle of the open space, as though he had been able to discern in the dark the figure of a man in a dark dress and cowl, seated on the steps of the cross. "Is it you, master?" said Gringoire.

The black figure started up. "Death and perdition! You make my blood boil, Gringoire. The warder on the tower of Saint-Gervais has just cried half-past one."

"Why," replied Gringoire, " 'tis not my fault, but that of the watch and the King. I have had a narrow escape. I was on the point of being hanged. I am predestined to it, I fancy."

"Thou art never in time for anything," said the other; "but let us be gone. Hast thou the watchword?"

"Only think, master—I have seen the King! I have just come from him. He wears fustian breeches. 'Tis quite an adventure!"

"Eternal babbler! What care I for thy adventure! Hast thou the watchword of the Vagabonds?"

"Be easy; I have."

" 'Tis well. We should not else be able to reach the church. The rabble block up all the streets. Luckily they seem to have met with resistance. We shall perhaps yet arrive in time."

"Yes, master, but how are we to get into the church?"

"I have a key to the towers."

"And how shall we get out?"

"Behind the cloisters there is a postern opening upon the Terrain, and so to the river. I have taken the key of it, and I moored a boat there this morning."

"I have had a most lucky escape from the gallows indeed!" said Gringoire exultingly.

"Never mind that now! come along, quick!" rejoined the other. Both then proceeded at a rapid pace toward the Cité.

CHAPTER VII

CHÂTEAUPERS TO THE RESCUE!

THE reader probably recollects the critical situation in which we left Quasimodo. The brave hunchback, assailed on all sides, had lost, if not all courage, at least all hope of saving, not himself—he never once thought of himself—but the Egyptian. He ran in consternation to the gallery. The church was on the point of being carried by the mob. All at once the tramp of horses in full gallop was heard in the neighbouring streets; and presently a wide column of horsemen riding at speed and a long file of torches poured with a tremendous noise into the Place like a hurricane. "France! France for ever! Châteaupers to the rescue! Down with the rascals!" The affrighted Vagabonds faced about.

Quasimodo, who could not hear the din, saw the naked swords, the torches, the pikeheads, the whole column of cavalry, at the head of which he recognized Captain Phœbus. He observed the confusion of the rabble, the consternation of some, and the alarm of the stoutest; and, at the sight of this unexpected succour, he mustered strength enough to throw down the foremost of the assailants, who were already striding over into the gallery.

The mob defended themselves with the valour of despair. Taken in flank by the Rue Saint-Pierre-aux-Bœufs and in rear by the Rue du Parvis, with their backs toward Notre-Dame, which they were still assailing and which Quasimodo defended, at once besiegers and besieged, they were in the singular situation in which Count Henri d'Harcourt subsequently found himself at the famous siege of Turin, in 1640, between Prince Thomas of Savoy whom he was besieging, and the Marquis de Leganez, who was blockading him; *Taurinum obsessor idem et obsessus,*[1] as his epitaph has it.

The conflict was terrible. As Father Mathieu observes, "Wolf's flesh requires dogs' teeth." The King's troops, amid whom Phœbus de Châteaupers conducted himself valiantly, gave no quarter: what escaped the point of the sword was cut down by the edge. The rabble, badly armed, foamed and bit. Men, women, children, darting at the flanks and chests of the horses, clung to them like cats with tooth and nail. Some thrust torches into the faces of the archers; while others, catching them by the neck with iron hooks, pulled them from their horses and cut them in pieces. One in particular was remarked with a huge scythe, mowing away at the legs of the horses. It was a fearful sight. Snuffling a stave with nasal twang, he kept his scythe incessantly going. At each stroke he formed about him a large semicircle of dismembered limbs. In this manner he wrought his way into the thickest of the cavalry with the deliberate movement, the swaying of the head, and the regular expiration of a mower cutting a field of clover. It was Clopin Trouillefou. The fire of an arquebus laid him prostrate.

Meanwhile windows were thrown open. The neighbours, hearing the shouts of the men-at-arms, took part in the affair, and showers of balls were discharged from every storey upon the rabble. The Parvis was filled with a dense smoke, which the musketry streaked ever and anon with fire. Through this smoke were faintly seen the façade of Notre-Dame, and the decrepit Hôtel Dieu, with a number of pale-faced patients gazing from the top of its roof studded with dormer windows.

The Vagabonds at length gave way, discomfited by weariness, the want of proper weapons, the consternation of that surprise, the fir-

---

[1] "He oppressed the people of Turin and was oppressed by them."

Châteaupers to the Rescue!

ing from the windows, and the furious onslaught of the King's troops. Forcing the line of their assailants, they fled in all directions, leaving the Parvis strewed with dead.

When Quasimodo, who had been busily engaged the whole time, perceived their defeat, he fell on his knees and lifted his hands to heaven; then, frantic with joy he flew with the swiftness of a bird to the little cell, the access to which he had so gallantly defended. He had now but one thought—to throw himself at the feet of her whom he had saved for the second time. When he reached the cell he found it empty.

BOOK X

CHAPTER I

THE LITTLE SHOE

AT the moment when the Vagabonds attacked the church La Esmeralda was asleep. It was not long before she was roused by the constantly increasing noise round the cathedral and the uneasy bleating of her goat, which had awoke before her. She sat up, listening and looking about; then, alarmed by the light and the uproar, she hurried out of the cell to see what was the matter. The aspect of the Place, the scene exhibited there, the confusion of this nocturnal assault, the hideous appearance of the rabble, hopping about like a host of frogs, faintly discerned in the dark, the harsh croaking of this uncouth mob, the few torches dancing to and fro in the obscurity, like will-o'-the-wisps gambolling over the misty surface of bogs, produced all together the effect of a mysterious battle between the phantoms of the witches' sabbath and the stone monsters of the church. Imbued from infancy with the superstitions of the gipsy tribe, her first idea was that she had caught the strange beings peculiar to night in their unhallowed pranks. She then hurried back in affright to her cell, to bury her face in the bed-clothes, and to shut out if possible the terrific vision.

The first fumes of fear having gradually dispersed, she found, from the incessantly increasing din and divers other tokens of reality, that she was invested not by spectres but by creatures of flesh and blood. Her terror then, without being augmented, changed its form. She had conceived a notion of the possibility of a popular sedition to tear her from her asylum. The prospect of still losing her life, her hopes, her Phœbus, which her imagination held forth to her, the absolute nothingness of her own strength, her forlorn situation, cut off from all support, all chance of flight—these and a thousand other thoughts overwhelmed her. She fell upon her knees, laying her head covered with her clasped hands upon the bed, filled with thrilling apprehensions; and, Egyptian, idolater, and pagan as she was, she began with heavy sobs to implore mercy of the God of

The Little Shoe

Christians and to pray to Our Lady, her protectress. For, be one's creed what it will, there are moments in life when one is always of the religion of the temple near which one happens to be.

In this attitude she remained for a considerable time, trembling indeed more than she prayed, her blood curdling at the indications of the nearer and nearer approach of that infuriated multitude, utterly at a loss to account for their proceedings, ignorant of what they were doing and what they meant to do, but anticipating some terrible catastrophe.

Amid this anguish she heard a footstep close to her. She looked up. Two men, one of whom carried a lantern, had just entered her cell. She gave a faint shriek.

"Fear nothing," said a voice, which was not unknown to her; "it is I."

"And who are you?" she inquired.

"Pierre Gringoire."

That name gave her fresh courage. She lifted her eyes and saw that it actually was the poet. But at his side stood a black figure, muffled up from head to foot, which struck her mute.

"Ah!" resumed Gringoire, in a tone of reproach, "Djali knew me before you did!"

The little goat had, in fact, not waited for Gringoire to mention his name. No sooner did he enter than she fondly rubbed against his knees, covering the poet with endearments and white hair; for she was shedding her coat. Gringoire returned her caresses.

"Who is that with you?" said the Egyptian, in a low tone.

"Be easy," answered Gringoire. " 'Tis one of my friends."

The philosopher, setting down the lantern, crouched upon the floor, clasped Djali in his arms, and cried with enthusiasm, "Oh! 'tis a darling creature, with its engaging ways, and withal shrewd, ingenious, and learned as a grammarian! Come, my Djali, let us see if thou hast not forgotten thy diverting tricks. How does Master Jacques Charmolue do——?"

The man in black would not suffer him to finish. He stepped up to Gringoire, and roughly pushed him on the shoulder. Gringoire rose. "Ah! true!" said he; "I had well-nigh forgotten that we are in haste. But yet, master, that is no reason for hurting people so.—— My poor dear child, your life is in danger, and Djali's too. They

385

mean to hang you again. We are your friends, and are come to save you. Follow us."

"Is it true?" cried she in extreme agitation.

"Quite true, I assure you. Come quick!"

"I will," stammered she. "But how is it that your friend does not speak?"

"Why," said Gringoire, "the fact is, that his father and mother were fantastic people, and made him of a reserved disposition."

She was obliged to be satisfied with this explanation. Gringoire took her by the hand; his companion picked up the lantern and walked on before. The young creature was stupefied with fear. She suffered Gringoire to lead her away. The goat went with them, frisking about, and so overjoyed to see the poet again, that she thrust her head every moment against his legs with such force as to make him stagger. "Such is life," said the philosopher, whenever he had well-nigh fallen; "it is often our best friends that throw us down!"

They rapidly descended the tower stairs, passed through the church, dark, solitary, but ringing with the uproar, which produced a fearful contrast, and went out by the Porte Rouge into the cloister court. The cloisters were deserted; the canons had fled to the Bishop's palace, where they were praying together: the court was empty, with the exception of a few affrighted servingmen, squatting in the dark corners. Gringoire and his companions proceeded toward the postern leading out of that court to the Terrain. The man in black unlocked it with a key which he brought with him. The reader is aware that the Terrain was a slip of land inclosed with walls, belonging to the chapter of Notre-Dame, forming the eastern extremity of the island, in the rear of the cathedral. They found this spot entirely deserted. At that distance already there was less tumult in the air. The various noises of the assault reached them more blended, more softened down. The breeze which followed the current of the river shook the leaves of the only tree standing on the point of the Terrain, the rustling of which was already audible; but they were yet at a very little distance from the danger. The buildings nearest to them were the Bishop's palace and the cathedral. There was evidently a great bustle within the former. Its gloomy front was streaked with lights darting from window to window; as when you have burned a sheet of paper there remains a dun edifice of ashes upon which bright sparks play a thousand capricious gambols. Be-

The Little Shoe

side it, the enormous towers of Notre-Dame, thus seen from behind, with the long nave from which they rise, standing out in black relief from the red glare which filled the Parvis, looked like the two gigantic andirons of a fire of the Cyclops.

So much of Paris as could be seen on all sides oscillated to the eye in one of those shadows mingled with light which we find in pictures of Rembrandt's.

The man with the lantern proceeded directly to the point of the Terrain. At that spot there was, at the water's edge, a decayed fence, composed of stakes crossed with laths, upon which a few sickly branches of a low vine were spread like the fingers of an open hand. Behind, and in the shade cast by this trellis, lay a small skiff. The man made a sign to Gringoire and his companion to get in. The goat followed him. The man then stepped in himself, cut the rope which moored the skiff, pushed off from the shore with a long pole, seated himself in the fore-part, and, taking up two oars, began to row out toward the middle of the river. In this place the Seine is very rapid, so that he had some difficulty to work off from the point of the island.

The first thing Gringoire did, after getting into the boat, was to take his seat at the stern and to lift the goat upon his knees. Her mistress, in whom the stranger excited undefinable apprehensions, sat down by the poet, pressing close to his side.

When our philosopher felt the boat moving, he clapped his hands, and kissed Djali's forehead. "Oh!" he exclaimed, "we are all four saved!" With the look of a profound thinker, he added, "One is indebted sometimes to fortune, sometimes to stratagem, for the successful issue of great undertakings."

The skiff slowly pursued its way toward the right bank. The girl watched the mysterious unknown with secret terror. He had carefully masked the light of his dark lantern; and he was faintly seen in the fore-part of the skiff, like a spectre. His cowl, still down, formed a sort of visor, and every time that, in rowing, he opened his arms, from which hung wide black sleeves, they looked like two prodigious bat's wings. He had not yet uttered a word, or suffered a breath to escape him. He made no other noise in the boat than what proceeded from the working of the oars, which blended with the rush of the thousand ripples against the side of the vessel.

"Odds my life!" suddenly exclaimed Gringoire, "we are as merry

as so many owls! Mute as Pythagoreans or fish! *Pasque-Dieu,*
my friends, I wish somebody would talk to me.—The human voice
is music to the human ear. By the by, that saying belongs not to
me but to Didymus of Alexandria, and a most pertinent one it is.
Certes, Didymus of Alexandria was no ordinary philosopher.—One
word, my dear child! speak to me, I beseech you.—Do you know, my
love, that the Parliament has supreme jurisdiction over sanctuaries,
and that you ran as great risk in your cell in Notre-Dame as the little bird trochylus, which builds its nest in the jaws of the crocodile?
—The moon is breaking out again, master! 'Tis to be hoped we
shall not be perceived.—We are doing a praiseworthy action to be
sure in saving the demoiselle, and yet we should be hanged in the
King's name if they were to catch us.—Alas! human actions have
two handles, to lay hold by. What is condemned in one is applauded
in another. Many a man censures Catiline and admires Cæsar.
Is it not so, master? What say you to that philosophy? For my
part, I possess the philosophy of instinct, of nature, *ut apes geome-
triam.*[1]—What, will nobody answer me? How dull ye both are! I
am obliged to talk to myself. That is what we call in tragedy a soliloquy.—*Pasque-Dieu!* let me tell you I have just seen Louis XI,
and have learned that oath from him. *Pasque-Dieu!* then, what an
uproar they are still making in the Cité!—He is a mean old king,
that Monsieur Louis. He has not yet paid me for my epithalamium,
and it was a mere chance that he did not order me to be hanged to-
night, which would have annoyed me exceedingly. He is stingy
toward men of merit. He ought to read the four books by Salvianus
of Cologne, *Adversus avaritiam.*[2] In good sooth, 'tis a close-fisted
king in his dealings with men of letters, and commits very barbarous
cruelties. He is a very sponge in sucking up the money drained
from the people. His revenues are like the belly fattening by the
leanness of all the other members. Complaints of the hardness of
the times are therefore treated as murmurs against the prince. Under this mild godly old gentleman the gibbets crack with the weight
of the condemned, the blocks are clotted with putrefying gore, the
prisons are bursting like cows in a clover-field. This king has a hand
that takes and a hand that hangs. He is attorney-general to Monseigneur Gibbet and my lady Gabelle. The great are despoiled of

[1] "As the bees do geometry."
[2] *Against avarice.*

their dignities, and the humble incessantly loaded with fresh burdens. 'Tis an exorbitant prince. I cannot love this monarch. What say you, master?"

The man in black did not interrupt the censures of the garrulous poet. He continued to struggle against the violence of the current which separates the prow of the Cité from the poop of the Ile de Notre-Dame, which we now call the Ile de Saint-Louis.

"By the by, master," Gringoire began again abruptly, "at the moment when we had passed through the enraged rabble and reached the Parvis, did you remark that unlucky little wight, whose brains your hunchback was in a fair way to dash out against the balustrade of the gallery of the kings? I am too near-sighted to recognize him. Perchance you know who it was."

The unknown answered not a word. But he suddenly ceased rowing, his arms sank, as if broken, his head drooped upon his breast, and La Esmeralda heard him sigh convulsively. She had heard sighs of that kind before.

The skiff, left to itself, drifted for some moments at the will of the current. At length the man in black roused himself, and again began pulling against the stream. He doubled the point of the Ile de Notre-Dame, and rowed toward the landing-place of the Port au Foin.

"Ah!" said Gringoire, "yonder is the Logis Barbeau.—Only look, master, at that group of black roofs which form such singular angles —there, beneath that mass of low, streaky, dirty-looking clouds, in which the moon appears smashed and spread about like the yolk of a broken egg. 'Tis a goodly mansion that! It has a chapel with vaulted roof, beautified with excellent sculptures. You may see above it the belfry, with its rare and delicate tracery. There is also a pleasant garden, containing a fish-pond, an aviary, an echo, a mall, a maze, a house for wild beasts, and many shady alleys particularly agreeable to Venus. There is likewise a rogue of a tree called 'The Lovers' Tree,' because it served for the trysting-place of a famous princess and a gay and witty Constable of France.—Alas! we poor philosophers are to a constable what a bed of cabbages or turnips is to a grove of laurels. What signifies it after all! For the great, as for us, life is a medley of good and ill. Pain is ever by the side of pleasure as the spondee by the dactyl.—I must tell you the history of the Logis Barbeau, master; it finished in a tragical way.

The Hunchback of Notre-Dame

It was in 1319, under Philip V, who reigned longer than any other King of France. The moral of the history is that the temptations of the flesh are hurtful and pernicious. Beware of looking too hard at the wife of your neighbour, much as your senses may be tickled by her beauty.—Zounds! what an uproar they are making yonder!"

The tumult around Notre-Dame was in fact raging with increased vehemence. They listened. Shouts of victory were distinctly heard. All at once a hundred torches, which made the helmets of the men-at-arms glisten, appeared on all parts of the church, on the towers, the galleries, the flying buttresses. These torches seemed to be employed in searching after something; and presently distant shouts of "The Egyptian!—the sorceress!—death to the Egyptian!"—were plainly heard by the fugitives.

The unhappy girl drooped her head upon her hands, and the unknown began to row furiously toward the shore. Our philosopher was meanwhile musing. He hugged the goat in his arms, and sidled gently away from the Bohemian, who pressed closer and closer to him, as to the only asylum that was now left her.

It is certain that Gringoire was in a cruel dilemma. He considered that, as the law then stood, the goat would be hanged too if she were retaken; that it would be a great pity—poor dear Djali!—that two condemned ones thus clinging to him were more than he could manage; that, besides, his companion desired nothing better than to take charge of the Egyptian. A violent conflict ensued among his thoughts, in which, like Homer's Jupiter, he weighed by turns the Egyptian and the goat; and he looked first at one and then at the other with eyes brimful of tears, muttering at the same time between his teeth: "And yet I cannot save you both!"

A shock apprised them that the skiff had reached the shore. The Cité still rang with the appalling uproar. The unknown rose, stepped up to the Egyptian, and offered her his arm to assist her to land. She refused it and clung to the sleeve of Gringoire, who, on his part, engaged with the goat, almost pushed her away. She then sprang without help out of the boat. She was so alarmed that she knew not what she was doing or whither she was going. She stood stupefied for a moment, with her eyes fixed on the water. When she came to herself a little she was alone on the quay with the unknown. It appeared that Gringoire had taken advantage of the instant of landing to steal away with the goat among the cluster of houses composing the Rue Grenier-sur-l'Eau.

The poor Egyptian shuddered on finding herself alone with that man. She strove to speak, to cry out, to call Gringoire; but her tongue refused its office, and not a sound issued from her lips. All at once, she felt the hand of the unknown upon hers. Her teeth chattered and she turned paler than the moon's ray which fell upon her. The man spoke not a word. With hasty step he began to move toward the Place de Grève, drawing her along by the hand. At that moment she had a vague feeling that Fate is an irresistible power. She had lost all elasticity, and followed mechanically, running while he walked. The quay at this spot is rising ground; to her it seemed as if she were going downhill.

She looked round on all sides. Not a passenger was to be seen. The quay was absolutely deserted. She heard no sound, she perceived no movement of men but in the tumultuous and roaring Cité, from which she was parted only by an arm of the Seine, and whence her name, mingled with cries of death, was wafted to her ear. The rest of Paris lay scattered round her in vast masses of shade.

Meanwhile the unknown continued to drag her along with the same silence and the same rapidity. She had no recollection of the places through which he took her. In passing a lighted window she suddenly made an effort to resist, and cried, "Help! help!"

The window opened; the inmate of the room appeared at it in his shirt and nightcap, with a lamp in his hand, looked out with drowsy eyes upon the quay, muttered a few words, which she could not catch, and reclosed the window. She felt as though the last glimmer of hope was extinguished.

The man in black uttered not a syllable; he held her tightly, and began to quicken his pace. She ceased to resist, and followed him spiritless and helpless.

From time to time she mustered a little strength, and in a voice broken from the jolting of the rugged pavement and from her being out of breath, owing to the rapid rate at which she was drawn along, she asked, "Who are you?—Who are you?" He made no reply.

Proceeding thus along the quay, they arrived at a large open space. The moon shone faintly. It was the Grève. In the middle of it stood a sort of black cross—it was the gibbet. She now knew where she was.

The Hunchback of Notre-Dame

The man stopped, turned toward her, and raised his cowl. "Oh!" stammered she, petrified with horror, "I knew that it must be he!"

It was in truth the priest. He looked like a ghost. Moonlight produces this effect. It seems as if by that light one beholds only the spectres of objects.

"List to me!" said he; and she shuddered at the sound of that fatal voice, which she had not heard for so long a time. He continued, with frequent pauses and in broken sentences which betoken violent inward agitation,— "List to me! Here we are. I would speak to thee. This is the Grève. We go no farther. Fate delivers us up into the hands of each other. Thy life is at my disposal; my soul at thine. Here is a place and a night beyond which one sees nothing. List to me, then. I would tell thee . . . but not a word about thy Phœbus"—as he spoke he paced to and fro, like a man who cannot remain quietly on one spot, and drew her after him—"talk not to me of him. If thou but utterest that name, I know not what I shall do; it will be terrible."

Having proceeded thus far, like a body recovering its centre of gravity, he stood still, but his words betrayed not the less perturbation. His voice became more and more faint.

"Turn not thy head from me thus. List to me. 'Tis a serious business. First, I would tell thee what has passed. 'Tis no matter for laughter, I protest to thee. But what was I saying? Ah, yes! An order has been issued by the Parliament which consigns thee again to the gallows. I have rescued thee from their hands. But yonder they are searching for thee. Look."

He pointed toward the Cité. It was evident, in fact, that the search was continued. The noise drew nearer. The tower of the lieutenant's house, facing the Grève, was full of bustle and lights; and the soldiers might be seen running on the opposite quay with torches, shouting, "The Egyptian! where is the Egyptian? Death! death!"

"Thou seest that they are in pursuit of thee, and that I am not deceiving thee. Maiden, I love thee! Open not thy lips; answer me not, if it is to tell me that thou hatest me. I am determined not to hear that. I have aided thine escape. Let me complete the work. I can save thee. Everything is prepared. All depends on thy will. Whatever thou wilt shall be done."

The Little Shoe

He interrupted himself with vehemence— "No! that is not what I meant to say." Then running, and drawing her along after him, for he still kept hold of her, he went straight to the foot of the gibbet, and, pointing to it, said coldly, "Choose between us."

She tore herself from his clasp, and, throwing herself on the pavement, clasped the foot of the fatal machine; then, half turning her head, she looked over her shoulder at the priest. The priest stood motionless, his finger still raised toward the gibbet, like a statue.

"I feel less horror of that than of you," at length said the Egyptian.

He slowly dropped his arm, and cast his eyes upon the pavement in deep dejection. "Yes," said he; "if these stones could speak, they would say— 'There is the most miserable of men!'"

"I love you," he again began. The girl, kneeling before the gibbet, covered by her long flowing hair, allowed him to proceed without interruption. His accent was now soft and plaintive, woefully contrasting with the lofty sternness of his features.

"I love you. Nothing can be more true. No fire can be fiercer than that which consumes my heart. Ah! maiden, night and day— yes, night and day—doth this claim no pity? 'Tis a love, a torture, night and day, I tell thee. Oh! my poor child, this is an agony worthy of compassion, I assure thee. I would speak kindly to thee, thou seest. I would have thee not feel such horror of me. And then, if a man loves a woman it is not his fault. What! thou wilt never take compassion on me, then? Thou wilt hate me for ever? 'Tis this that makes me cruel—ay, hateful to myself! Thou wilt not even deign to look at me. Thou art thinking perhaps of something else, while I am talking to thee and trembling on the brink of the eternity of both. At any rate, talk not to me of thine officer! Were I to throw myself at thy knees; were I to kiss, not thy feet— thou wouldst not suffer me—but the ground beneath them; were I to sob like a child, and to tear from my bosom not words, but my heart and my entrails, to tell thee how I love thee, all would be in vain—all!—And yet thou hast in thy soul nought but what is kind and tender. Thou art all goodness, all gentleness, all compassion, all charms. Alas! to me alone art thou unfeeling. Oh! what a fatality."

He buried his face in his hands. La Esmeralda heard him weep;

it was for the first time. His figure, thus upright and shaken by sobs, was more pitiable and more humble than if he had knelt. He continued to weep thus for some time.

"Alas!" he proceeded, this first paroxysm over, "I am at a loss for words. And yet I had well pondered what I should say to thee. Now I tremble and shudder; I shrink back at the decisive moment; I feel some superior power that overwhelms me and makes me stammer. Oh! I shall sink on the pavement unless thou take pity on me, on thyself. Condemn not both of us. Would that thou knewest how I love thee, and what a heart is mine. Oh! what an abandonment of all virtue, what a desperate desertion of myself! A doctor, I make a mock at science; a gentleman, I disgrace my name; a priest, I violate the most solemn vows, and renounce my God!—and all for thy sake, enchantress; and thou rejectest the wretched one! Oh! I must tell thee all—still more, something even yet more horrible—most horrible!"

As he uttered the concluding words his look became quite wild. He kept silence for a moment, and then began again, as if speaking to himself, in a loud tone, "Cain, what hast thou done with thy brother?"

Again he paused, and then continued: "What have I done with him, Lord? I have taken him unto me, I have fed him, I have brought him up, I have loved him, I have idolized him, and—I have slain him!—Yes, Lord, he it was whose head was but now dashed before mine eyes against the stones of thy temple, and it was on my account, and on account of this woman, on her account . . ."

His eye flashed wildly. His voice became more and more faint: he repeated several times, and with pauses of some length, like a bell prolonging its last vibration: "On her account . . . on her account . . ." His lips continued to move, but his tongue ceased to articulate any audible sound. All at once he sank down and remained motionless upon the ground, with his head bowed to his knees.

A slight movement made by the girl to draw her foot from under him brought him to himself. He passed his hand slowly over his hollow cheeks, and looked vacantly for some moments at his fingers which were wet.—"What!" he muttered; "have I wept?"

Turning abruptly toward the Egyptian, with irrepressible anguish, he said: "And hast thou coldly beheld me weep? Knowest

The Little Shoe

thou, girl, that those tears are lava? Is it then true that thy sex are not moved by anything that can befall the man they hate? Wert thou to see me die, thou wouldst laugh. But I—I wish not thy death! One word! a single word of kindness! Tell me not that thou lovest me; say only that thou wishest me well: it shall suffice— I will save thee. Otherwise . . . oh! the time passes. I implore thee by all that is sacred, wait not till I am again transformed into stone, like that gibbet which also claims thee! Consider that I hold both our fates in my hand, that I am mad—oh! it is terrible—that I may let all drop, and that there is beneath us a bottomless abyss, down which I shall follow thee in thy fall to all eternity! One kind word! one word! but a single word!"

She opened her lips to answer. He fell on his knees before her, to catch with adoration the words, perhaps of sympathy, which should drop from her mouth. "You are a murderer!" said she.

The priest clasped her furiously in his arms, and burst forth into a terrific laugh. "Murderer though I be," cried he, "I will have thee. Thou wilt not have me for a slave; thou shalt have me for a master. Thou shalt be mine. I have a den to which I will drag thee. Thou shalt come, thou must come, with me, or I will deliver thee up! Thou must die, girl, or be mine—be the priest's, the apostate's, the murderer's!—The choice rests with thyself—decide instantly; for I will not submit to farther humiliations."

His eye sparkled with passion and rage. The girl's neck was flushed beneath the touch of his burning lips.

"Loose me, monster!" cried she. "Oh! the hateful poisonous monk! Loose me, or I will tear out thy scurvy grey hair and dash it in thy face!"

He reddened, turned pale, released her from his grip, and eyed her with a gloomy look. She deemed herself victorious, and continued: "I tell thee I belong to my Phœbus, that 'tis Phœbus I love, that 'tis Phœbus who is handsome! As for thee, priest, thou art old, thou art ugly! Go thy way!"

He gave a violent shriek, like a wretch to whose flesh a red-hot iron is applied. "Die then!" said he, gnashing his teeth. She noticed the infernal malignity of his look, and would have fled. He caught her again, shook her, threw her down, and with rapid strides proceeded toward the angle of the Tour-Roland, dragging her after him along the pavement by her beautiful arms.

The Hunchback of Notre-Dame

On reaching that point he turned toward her. "Once more," said he, "wilt thou be mine?"

She replied firmly, "No."

He then cried aloud: "Gudule! Sister Gudule! Here is the Egyptian! Revenge thyself on her!"

The damsel felt herself suddenly seized by the wrist. She looked; it was a skeleton arm thrust through a hole in the wall, which held her like a vice.

"Hold fast!" said the priest, " 'tis the Egyptian, who has run away. Let her not escape. I will fetch the sergeants; thou shalt see her hanged."

These inhuman words were answered by a guttural laugh from within the wall, "Ha! ha! ha!" The Egyptian saw the priest run off toward the bridge of Notre-Dame. The tramp of horses was heard in that direction.

The girl presently recognized the malicious recluse. Panting with terror, she strove to release herself. She writhed, she made many a bound of agony and despair, but the recluse held her with supernatural force. The bony fingers meeting round her wrist clasped her as firmly as if that hand had been riveted to her arm. More efficient than a chain or a ring of iron, it was a pair of living and intelligent pincers issuing from a wall.

Against that wall La Esmeralda sank exhausted, and then the fear of death came over her. She thought of the pleasure of life, of youth, of the look of the sky, of the scenery of nature, of love, of Phœbus, of all that was past and all that was to come, of the priest who was gone to denounce her, of the gibbet which stood there, and the hangman who would presently arrive. Then did she feel the horror mounting to the very roots of her hair, and she heard the sinister laugh of the recluse, who said in a low tone, "Thou art going to be hanged! Ha! ha! ha!"

She turned half dead toward the aperture and saw the sallow face of the recluse between the bars. "What harm have I done to you?" said she, in a faint voice.

The recluse made no reply, but began to mutter, with a singing, irritating, and jeering intonation, "Gipsy-girl! gipsy-girl! gipsy-girl!"

The wretched Esmeralda drooped her head, conceiving that it was not a human being with which she had to deal.

The Little Shoe

Suddenly the recluse exclaimed, as if the girl's question had taken all the intermediate time to reach her understanding: "What harm hast thou done me, dost thou ask? What harm hast thou done me, Egyptian! Why, listen. I had a child, seest thou? a little child, an infant, I tell thee—a pretty little girl.—My Agnes," she resumed, kissing something in the dark.—"Well; they stole my child; they took my child away; they ate my child. That is the harm thou hast done me."

The damsel replied, like the lamb in the fable, "Most probably I was not even born then."

"Oh, yes!" rejoined the recluse, "thou must have been born. Thou wert one of them. She would be about thy age.—Just! 'Tis fifteen years that I have been here: fifteen years have I suffered; fifteen years have I prayed; fifteen years have I dashed my head against these four walls.—I tell thee it was Egyptians who stole my babe, and ate her afterward.—Hast thou a heart?—then fancy to thyself what it is to have a child that sucks, that sleeps, that plays! It is so innocent!—Well, it was such an infant that they stole from me and killed, God wot. Now it is my turn; I will feast on the Egyptian.—Oh, how I would bite thee if I could get my head between the bars! Only think—while the poor little thing was asleep! And if they had even wakened her when they took her up, her crying would have been to no purpose; I was not there. Ah, ye Egyptian mothers! ye ate my child! Come and see how I will serve yours."

She then began to laugh or to gnash her teeth—for both had nearly the same expression on that furious face. The day began to dawn. A grey light faintly illumined this scene, and the gibbet in the middle of the Place became more and more distinct. On the other side, toward the bridge of Notre-Dame, the poor condemned one imagined that she heard the tramp of horses approaching.

"Madame!" cried she, clasping her hands and sinking on her knees, dishevelled, overwhelmed, distracted with terror, "take pity on me. They are coming. I never harmed you. Would you have me die that horrid death before your face? You are compassionate, I am sure. 'Tis too frightful! Loose me—let me try to escape. Have mercy! I should not like to die thus!"

"Give me back my child," said the recluse.

"Mercy! Mercy!"

"Give me my child."

The Hunchback of Notre-Dame

"Let me go, for heaven's sake!"

"Give me my child."

The poor girl sank down, overcome, exhausted, with the glazed eye of one who is already in the grave. "Alas!" stammered she, "you seek your child, and I seek my parents!"

"Give me my little Agnes," continued Gudule. "Thou knowest not where she is?—then die!—I tell thee, I was a light o' love; I had a child; they took it away—those accursed Egyptians! 'Tis plain then thou must die. When thy Egyptian mother comes to ask for thee I will say to her, 'Mother, look at that gibbet!'—Or, give me back my child—knowest thou where she is, where my little daughter is? Stay, I will show thee. There is her shoe, all that is left me of her. Knowest thou where is its fellow? If thou dost, tell me, and if it is at the end of the world, I will fetch it, if I crawl thither on hands and knees."

As she thus spoke, putting her other hand out at the aperture, she showed the little embroidered shoe to the Egyptian. It was already light enough for her to distinguish its form and colours.

"Let me look at that shoe," said the girl, shuddering. "Gracious God!" At the same time, with the hand that was at liberty, she tore open the little bag adorned with green beads which she wore about her neck.

"Go to! go to!" muttered Gudule; "fumble away in thy infernal amulet!" Then stopping short, and trembling in every joint, she cried with a voice issuing from her very bowels— "My child! My child!"

The Egyptian had taken out of the bag a little shoe that was the precise fellow to the other. To this little shoe was attached a piece of parchment, upon which was written this legend:

> When the fellow thou shalt find,
> Thy mother is not far behind.

In the twinkling of an eye the recluse had compared the two shoes, read the inscription upon the parchment, and, thrusting her face, beaming with celestial joy, against the bars of the window, shouted, "My daughter! my daughter!"

"My mother! my mother!" responded the Egyptian.

Who could describe the scene?

The wall and the iron bars were between them.

The Little Shoe

"Oh! this wall!" cried the recluse. "To see her, yet not be able to clasp her to my heart! Thy hand! give me thy hand!"

The girl put her hand through the window; the recluse seized it, fastened her lips to it and stood absorbed in that kiss, giving no other sign of life but a sigh which from time to time heaved her bosom. Meanwhile tears gushed from her eyes, in silence, and in the dusk, like a shower at night. The poor mother poured forth upon that adored hand the dark deep well-spring of tears which was within her, and from which her sorrows had been oozing drop by drop for fifteen years.

All at once she raised her head, threw back the long grey hair from her face, and, without saying a word, began to pull and thrust at the bars of her window more furiously than a lioness. The bars defied her utmost strength. She then went to a corner of her cell, fetched a large paving-stone which served her for a pillow, and dashed it against them with such violence as to shiver one of them into several pieces. A second blow drove out the old iron cross which barricaded the window. With both hands she then pulled out the rusty fragments of the bars. There are moments when the hands of a woman possess superhuman force.

The passage being cleared—and this was accomplished in less than a minute—she clasped her daughter in her arms and drew her into the cell. "Come!" murmured she; "let me drag thee from the abyss!"

She set her down gently upon the floor, then caught her up again, and, carrying her in her arms, as if she had still been her infant Agnes, she paced her narrow cell, intoxicated, frantic with joy, shouting, singing, kissing the girl, talking to her, laughing, weeping, all at once and with vehemence.

"My child! my dear child!" cried she. "I have got my child! here she is! The gracious God has restored her to me. Come, all of you, and see that I have got my daughter again! Lord Jesus, how beautiful she is. The Almighty made me wait fifteen years, but it was to give her back to me in beauty.—After all then the Egyptians did not eat thee! Who could have said so? My child, my dear little child, kiss me! Oh, those good Egyptians! How I love the Egyptians!—And it is thou thyself! And this was the reason why my heart always leaped within me whenever thou wert passing. Fool that I was to take this for hatred! Forgive me, my

399

Agnes, forgive me! Thou must have thought me very spiteful, didst thou not? Ah! how I love thee!—And the pretty mark on thy neck!—hast thou it still? Let us see. Yes, there it is! Oh! how handsome thou art grown. It was from thy mother thou hadst those large bright eyes! Kiss me, darling! I do love thee!—What care I whether other mothers have children!—I can laugh at them now. Let them come. Here is mine. Here is—her neck, her eyes, her hair, her hand. Show me anything more charming than this! Yes, yes, she will have plenty of lovers, I will answer for it. I have sorrowed for fifteen years. All my beauty has left me and gone to her. Kiss me, love!"

In this strain she ran on, uttering a thousand extravagant things, disheveling the poor girl's dress so as to make her blush, stroking her silken hair with her hand, kissing her foot, her knee, her brow, her eyes, and extolling every feature. The damsel suffered her to do as she pleased, repeating at intervals, in a low and infinitely sweet tone: "Oh, Mother!"

"Ah, my darling," the recluse again began, interrupting herself at every word with kisses, "how I shall love thee! We will leave this place. How happy we shall be! I have some property at Reims, in our own country. Dost thou remember Reims? Ah, no! how shouldst thou! thou wert then quite an infant. If thou didst but know how pretty thou wert at four months old! Tiny feet which people came out of curiosity to see all the way from Epernay, which is fifteen miles off! We shall have a house and a field. Thou shalt sleep in my bed. My God! my God! who would have believed it! I have got my daughter again!"

"Oh, Mother!" said the girl, at length recovering power to speak amid her emotion, "the Egyptian woman told me this. There was a good woman of our tribe who died last year, and who always took care of me like a nurse. It was she who fastened this little bag about my neck. She always said: 'My dear, never part with this trinket. It is a treasure. It will enable thee to find thy mother again. Thou carriest thy mother about thy neck.'—The Egyptian foretold it, you see."

The recluse again clasped her daughter in her arms. "Come, let me kiss thee! how sweetly thou saidst that! When we go into the country we will give those little shoes to an infant Jesus in the church. We certainly owe so much as that to the kind Holy Vir-

The Little Shoe

gin. But what a charming voice thou hast! When thou wert speaking to me just now it was like music. Ah! Lord God! I have found my child again! And yet who would believe the story! Surely nothing can kill one, since I have not died of joy."

She then began to clap her hands, laughing, and exclaiming, "How happy we shall be!"

At that moment the cell rang with the clank of arms and the tramp of horses, which seemed to be advancing from the bridge of Notre-Dame along the quay. The Egyptian threw herself in unutterable anguish into the arms of the recluse.

"Save me!" she shrieked; "save me, Mother! they are coming!"

The recluse turned pale. "Oh, heavens! what sayst thou! I had forgotten! they are searching for thee! What hast thou done, then?"

"I know not," answered the unfortunate girl; "but I am condemned to die."

"Die!" cried Gudule reeling, as if stricken by a thunderbolt. "Die!" she slowly repeated, fixing her glazed eye upon her daughter.

"Yes, Mother," replied the affrighted girl, "they mean to put me to death. They are coming to take me. That gibbet is for me. Save me! save me! They are coming! Save me!"

For some moments the recluse remained motionless as a statue; she then shook her head doubtingly, and suddenly burst into a loud laugh, her old terrific laugh: "No, no, thou must be dreaming. It cannot be. To lose her for fifteen years, and then to find her for a single minute! And they would take her from me again, now that she is grown up and handsome, and talks to me and loves me! They would now come to devour her before my face—mine, who am her mother! Oh, no! such things are not possible. God Almighty would not permit such doings."

By this time the cavalcade had apparently halted. A distant voice was heard calling out, "This way, Messire Tristan! The priest says that we shall find her at the Trou aux Rats." The tramp of the horses began again.

The recluse started up with a shriek of despair. "Away! begone, my child! I now recollect it all. Thou art right. 'Tis for thy death. Curses on them! Away!"

She put her head out at the window and quickly drew it back again. "Stay!" said she, in a low, doleful voice, convulsively grasp-

401

ing the hand of the Egyptian, who was more dead than alive. "Stay! hold thy breath! The Place is full of soldiers. Thou canst not get away. It is too light."

Her eyes were dry and inflamed. For a moment she remained silent; but with hurried step she paced up and down her cell, stopping now and then, and tearing out handfuls of her grey hair, which she dashed upon the floor.

"They are coming!" she exclaimed all at once. "I will talk to them. Hide thyself in this corner. They will not see thee. I will tell them that I let thee go; that thou hast run away—that I will!"

Catching up the girl in her arms, she carried her to a corner of the cell which could not be seen from without. Here she made her crouch down, taking care that neither foot nor hand should protrude beyond the dark shadow, loosed her black hair, which she spread over her white robe to conceal it, and placed before her the water-jug and paving-stone, the only movables that she possessed, fondly imagining that they would help to hide her. This done, she was more calm, knelt down, and prayed. Day had not yet so far broken but that dim obscurity still pervaded the Trou aux Rats.

At that moment the voice of the priest, that infernal voice, passed very close to the cell, crying, "This way, Captain Phœbus de Châteaupers!"

At that name, at that voice, La Esmeralda made a slight movement. "Stir not!" said Gudule.

She had scarcely uttered the words when a tumult of horses and men was heard outside the cell. The mother hastily rose and posted herself before the window to intercept the view of the interior. She beheld a numerous body of armed men, foot and horse, drawn up in the Grève. Their commander alighted, and advanced toward her. He was a man of truculent aspect. "Old woman," said he, "we are seeking a sorceress to hang her; we were told that thou hadst her."

The poor mother, assuming a look of as much indifference as she could, answered, "I know not what you mean."

"*Tête-Dieu!*" cried the other, "what kind of story did that crazed archdeacon tell us? Where is he?"

"Monseigneur," said one of the soldiers, "he has slipped away."

"Come, come, old crone," resumed the commandant, "let us have the truth! A sorceress was given to thee to hold. What hast thou done with her?"

The recluse, apprehensive lest by denying everything she might awaken suspicion, replied in a tone of affected sincerity and surliness, "If you mean a young girl that I was desired to hold just now, all I can tell you is that she bit me, and I let her go. Leave me alone, I pray you."

The countenance of the commandant betrayed a feeling of disappointment.

"Tell me no lies, old scarecrow," rejoined he. "I am Tristan the Hermit, the *compère* of the King. Tristan, the Hermit, dost hear? 'Tis a name," he added, looking round at the Place de Grève, "which has an echo here."

"If you were Satan the Hermit," replied Gudule, regaining some hope, "I should have nothing else to tell you, neither should I be afraid of you."

"*Tête-Dieu!*" cried Tristan, "there's a hag for you! So, the young sorceress has escaped! And which way is she gone?"

"Down the Rue du Mouton, I believe," answered Gudule in a careless tone.

Tristan turned his head, and motioned to his troop to prepare to start. The recluse began to breathe again.

"Monseigneur," said one of the archers, all at once, "ask the old witch why the bars of her window are broken in this fashion."

That question once more overwhelmed the heart of the wretched mother with anguish. She nevertheless retained some presence of mind. "They were always so," stammered she.

"Pooh!" replied the archer, "they formed but yesterday a fair black cross, fit to remind a man of his prayers."

Tristan cast a sidelong glance at the recluse. "By my fay," said he, "the hag does begin to look confused."

The wretched woman felt that all depended on keeping up a bold face, and, while her soul was racked with mortal anguish, she fell a-laughing. Mothers have this kind of force. "Pshaw!" said she, "that fellow is drunk. It is more than a year since the tail of a cart laden with stones was backed against my window, and broke the grating. How I did abuse the driver!"

"'Tis true enough," said another archer, "I was present."

Wherever you may be you are sure to meet with people who have seen everything. This unexpected testimony somewhat revived the recluse, who felt, during this interrogatory like one forced to cross an abyss on the edge of a knife; but she was doomed to a continual alternation of hope and alarm.

"If it was a cart that did this," replied the first soldier, "the stumps of the bars would be driven inward, whereas, these are bent outwards."

"Aha!" said Tristan to the archer, "thou hast a nose like an inquisitor to the Châtelet. What hast thou to say to that, woman?"

"Good God!" she exclaimed, driven to extremity, and in a voice in spite of herself akin to that of weeping, "I assure you, monseigneur, that it was a cart which broke those bars. That man saw it, you hear. Besides, what has this to do with your Egyptian?"

"Hum!" grumbled Tristan.

"The devil!" resumed the first soldier, flattered by the commendation of the Provost; "the fractures of the iron are quite fresh."

Tristan shook his head. She turned pale. "How long is it, say you, since this affair of the cart?"

"A month—a fortnight, perhaps—monseigneur. I cannot recollect exactly."

"She said at first above a year," observed the soldier.

"That looks suspicious," said the Provost.

"Monseigneur," she exclaimed, still standing close to the window and trembling lest they should think of putting in their heads and looking about the cell; "monseigneur, I swear to you that it was a cart which broke this ironwork. I swear it by the angels in Paradise. If it was not a cart, may I deny God, and may eternal perdition be my lot!"

"Thou art in good earnest in that oath," said Tristan, with a scrutinizing look.

The poor creature felt her assurance forsaking her by degrees. She was so confounded as to make awkward blunders, and she perceived with terror that she was not saying what she ought to have said.

A soldier now came up, crying: "Monseigneur, the old witch lies. The girl has not been in the Rue du Mouton. The chain has been up all night, and the keeper has not seen a creature pass."

Tristan, whose look became every moment more threatening, turned to the recluse, "What hast thou to say to this?"

"I know not, monseigneur," replied she, still striving to make head against this new incident; "I may be mistaken. In fact, I almost think she must have crossed the water."

"Why, that is the very contrary way," said the Provost. "Besides, 'tis not likely that she would have gone back to the Cité, where search was making for her. Thou liest, hag!"

"And then," added the first soldier, "there is no boat either on this side of the water or on the other."

"She must have swum over," replied the recluse, defending the ground inch by inch.

"Who ever heard of women swimming!" cried the soldier.

"*Tête-Dieu!* old woman, thou liest! thou liest!" exclaimed Tristan, with vehemence. "I have a good mind to let the young sorceress go, and to take thee instead. A quarter of an hour's torture will bring the truth out of thy throat. Come, thou shalt go along with us."

"As you please, monseigneur," said she, eagerly catching at these words. "Go to, go to! The torture! I am ready. Take me. Let us be gone forthwith!"—Meanwhile, thought she, my daughter will have opportunity to escape.

" 'Sblood!" cried the Provost, "what eagerness for torture! The mad creature completely puzzles me."

An old grey-headed sergeant of the watch advanced from the ranks. "Mad indeed! monseigneur," said he, addressing the Provost. "If she has let loose the Egyptian, 'tis not her fault, for she is not fond of the Egyptians. For these fifteen years that I have belonged to the watch I have heard her every night cursing the Bohemian women with bitter and endless execrations. If the one we are seeking be, as I suppose, the dancing-girl with the goat, I know that she hates her above all."

Gudule made an effort, and repeated, "Above all."

The unanimous testimony of the men belonging to the watch confirmed the representation of the old sergeant. Tristan the Hermit, despairing of being able to extract any information from the recluse, turned his back upon her, and with inexpressible anxiety she beheld him slowly proceeding toward his horse. "Come," muttered he between his teeth, "let us be off and pursue our search. I will not sleep till the Egyptian is hanged."

He nevertheless paused for some time before he mounted his horse. Gudule wavered between life and death, on seeing him cast round the Place the restless look of a hound, which is aware that the lair of the game is near at hand and is unwilling to leave the spot. At length he shook his head and vaulted into the saddle. The heart of Gudule, so cruelly oppressed, once more expanded, and, casting an eye upon her daughter, at whom she had not dared to look while the soldiers were there, she ejaculated in a low tone, "Saved!"

The poor girl had remained all this time in her corner, without stirring, without breathing, and having the image of death before her eyes. She had not lost any incident of the scene between Gudule and Tristan, and she had shared all the agonies endured by her mother. She had heard the successive snappings of the threads by which she was suspended over the abyss; twenty times she expected to see them all break; and she at length began again to breathe and to feel herself upon solid ground. At this moment she heard a voice saying to the Provost, "Corbœuf! Mr Provost, 'tis no business of mine, who am a soldier, to hang witches. The beggarly crew are beneath one. I leave you to attend to it alone. You must permit me to go and rejoin my company, because it is without a captain." That voice was the voice of Phœbus de Châteaupers.—What she then felt is not to be described. He was there, then, her friend, her protector, her refuge, her Phœbus! She sprang up, and, before her mother could prevent her, darted to the window, crying, "Phœbus! my Phœbus! come hither!"

Phœbus was gone; he had just turned at a gallop the corner of the Rue de la Coutellerie. But Tristan was there still.

The recluse rushed upon her daughter with the roar of a wild beast. Striking her nails into her neck she drew her back with violence. A mother tigress is not very particular. But it was too late. Tristan had seen her.

"Eigh! eigh!" cried he, with a grin which discovered all his teeth, and made his face resemble the muzzle of a wolf, "two mice in the trap!"

"I suspected as much," said the soldier.

"Thou art an excellent cat!" replied Tristan, patting him on the shoulder. "Come," added he, "where is Henriet Cousin?"

A man who had neither the garb nor the look of a soldier stepped forth from the ranks. He wore a dress half grey and half brown, and leathern sleeves; had lank hair, and carried a coil of rope in his huge fist. This man always accompanied Tristan, who always accompanied Louis XI.

"My friend," said Tristan the Hermit, "I presume that yonder is the sorceress whom we are seeking. Thou wilt hang her forthwith. Hast thou thy ladder?"

"There is one under the shed of the Maison aux Pilliers," replied the man. "Is it at this *justice* that we are to do the business?" continued he, pointing to the stone gibbet.

"Yes."

"Ho! ho! ho!" rejoined the man, with a more vulgar, more bestial grin than even that of the Provost, "we shan't have far to go."

"Make haste," said Tristan, "and laugh afterward."

Ever since Tristan had espied the girl, and all hope was at an end, the recluse had not uttered a word. She had thrown the poor Egyptian, half dead, in the corner of the cell, and posted herself again at the window, with her two hands like claws resting upon the corner of the entablature. In this attitude, her eyes, which had again become wild and fierce, were seen to wander fearlessly over the surrounding soldiers. At the moment when Henriet Cousin reached the cell, her look was so ferocious, that he started back.

"Monseigneur," said he, returning to the Provost, "which are we to take?"

"The young one."

"So much the better; for yon old hag looks like a Tartar."

"Poor dancing-girl with the goat!" sighed the veteran sergeant of the watch.

Once more Henriet Cousin approached the window. His eye quailed before that of the mother. "Madam . . ." he began very timidly.

"What wouldst thou?" cried she, interrupting him, in a low but resolute tone.

" 'Tis not you I want," said he; " 'tis the other."

"What other?"

"The young one."

She shook her head, crying, "There is nobody, I tell thee—nobody! —nobody!"

"There is," replied the executioner, "and well you know it. Let me take the girl. I will not harm you."

"Oh! thou wilt not harm me!" said she, with a terrible laugh.

"Let me take the other, madam; 'tis by the order of Monsieur the Provost."

With a frantic air she repeated, "There is nobody!—nobody!"

"I tell you there is," replied the executioner. "We all saw that there were two of you."

"Look then!" said the recluse, grinning. "Put thy head in at the hole."

The hangman eyed her nails, and durst not venture.

"Make haste!" cried Tristan, who had drawn up his men in a semicircle round the Trou aux Rats, and posted himself on horseback near the gibbet.

Henriet returned once more to the Provost, quite at a loss how to proceed. He had laid his rope upon the ground, and, with a clownish air, twirling his hat upon his hand— "Monseigneur," he asked, "how are we to get in?"

"By the door."

"There is none."

"By the window."

"It is too small."

"Enlarge it, then," said Tristan angrily. "Hast thou not pickaxes?"

The mother watched them from her den, still leaning against the window-sill. She had ceased to hope; she knew not what she would have, but she would not have them take her daughter from her.

Henriet Cousin went to the shed of the Maison aux Pilliers to fetch his tools. He also brought from the same place a ladder, which he immediately set up against the gibbet. Five or six of the Provost's men armed themselves with mattocks and crowbars, and Tristan proceeded with them to the cell.

"Old woman," said the Provost, in a stern voice, "yield up the girl to us quietly."

She gave him such a look as though she understood not what he said.

"*Tête-Dieu!*" resumed Tristan, "what reason canst thou have for preventing this sorceress from being hanged according to the King's pleasure?"

The wretched woman burst into one of her wild laughs. "What reason have I? 'Tis my *daughter*!" The accent with which she uttered that word made even Henriet Cousin himself shudder.

"I am sorry for it," replied the Provost, "but it is the good pleasure of the King."

"What is thy King to me?" cried she, redoubling her terrible laugh. "I tell thee it is my daughter!"

"Break down the wall," said Tristan.

Nothing more was required to make the opening sufficiently wide than to displace one massive stone under the window. When the mother heard the mattocks and the crowbars sapping her fortress she gave a terrific scream; and then began to run round her cell with frightful swiftness—one of the habits of a wild beast, which she had contracted from confinement. She said nothing, but her eyes flashed fire. The soldiers were thrilled to their hearts' core. All at once she caught up her paving-stone in both hands, laughed, and hurled it at the workmen. The stone, feebly thrown—for her hands trembled—missed them all and rolled to the feet of Tristan's horse. She gnashed her teeth.

Meanwhile, though the sun had not yet risen, it was broad daylight; the old decayed chimneys of the Maison aux Pilliers were tinged of a beautiful roseate hue. It was the hour at which the earliest windows of the great city open cheerily upon the roofs. Certain of the inhabitants—sundry costermongers riding on their asses to the markets—began to cross the Grève. They paused for a moment before the party of soldiers collected around the Trou aux Rats, surveyed them with looks of astonishment, and pursued their way.

The recluse had sat down in front of her daughter, covering her with her body, listening with fixed eye to the poor girl, who stirred not, who spake not, save that she murmured in a low tone, "Phœbus! Phœbus!"

In proportion as the work of the besiegers seemed to advance, the mother mechanically drew back, and pressed the girl closer and closer against the wall. All at once she saw the stone shake—for she kept strict watch, and never took her eyes from it—and she heard the voice of Tristan encouraging the labourers. This roused her from the stupor into which she had sunk for some minutes, and she cried—the while her voice sometimes rent the ear like a saw, sometimes stammered as if all the maledictions thronging forth at once were jostling one another upon her lips— "Ho! ho! ho! But this is horrible. Robbers, do ye really mean to take my daughter from me? I tell you it is my daughter! Oh, the cowards! Oh, the hangman's lackeys! Oh, the journeymen murderers! Help! help! fire! But will they rob me of my child in this manner? Can such a thing be suffered by the Almighty?"

Then turning to Tristan, with foaming lips, glaring eyes, on all fours like a panther, and bristling with rage: "Come a little nearer to rob me of my daughter! Dost thou not comprehend that this woman tells thee it is her daughter! Knowest thou what it is to be the mother of a child? And if thou hast young ones, when they howl hast thou not within thee something that yearns at their cry?"

"Down with the stone!" said Tristan; "it is loosened."

The crowbars displaced the ponderous stone. It was, as we have said, the mother's last rampart. She threw herself upon it; she would have held it fast; she scratched it with her nails; but the massive block, set in motion by six men, slipped from her grasp, and glided gently to the ground along the iron levers.

The mother, seeing an entry made, threw herself athwart the aperture, barricading the breach with her body, waving her arms, striking her head against the top of the window, and shouting with a voice so husky with fatigue that it could scarcely be heard, "Help! fire! fire!"

"Now take the girl," said Tristan, as cool as ever.

The mother glared at the soldiers so fiercely that they were much more disposed to fall back than to advance.

"On, there!" shouted the Provost. "Henriet Cousin, on!"

Not a creature stirred a step.

The Provost exclaimed, "What! men-at-arms afraid of a woman!"

"Monseigneur," said Henriet, "call you that a woman?"

"She has the mane of a lion," said another.

"Advance!" replied the Provost, "the gap is large enough. Enter three abreast, as at the breach of Pontoise. Let us finish the business. By the death of Mahound! the first that recoils I will cut in two."

Placed between the Provost and the mother, and threatened by both, the soldiers hesitated for a moment; then, making their choice, they advanced toward the Trou aux Rats.

When the recluse saw this she suddenly raised herself upon her knees, threw back her long hair from her face, and dropped her lank and lacerated hands upon her thighs. Big tears started from her eyes, trickling one by one down the wrinkles in her cheeks, like a torrent along the bed which it has wrought for itself. At the same time she began to speak, but in a voice so suppliant, so meek, so subdued, so cutting, that more than one old trooper who could have eaten human flesh had to wipe his eyes.

"Gentlemen, and Messieurs Sergeants, one word! There is one thing that I must tell you. It is my daughter, look you—my dear little girl, whom I had lost. Listen—it is a strange story. I am no stranger to messieurs the sergeants. They were always very kind to me at the time when the boys in the streets pelted me with stones, because I was a light o' love. You will leave me my child when you know all. I was a poor unfortunate girl. The Bohemians stole my infant. Stay, here is her shoe, which I have kept for fifteen years. Her foot was no bigger than that. La Chantefleurie, Rue Folle-Peine, at Reims—perhaps you know that name. Well, I was she. You will take pity on me, will you not, gentlemen? The Egyptians stole her from me, and hid her away for these fifteen years. I thought she was dead. Only think, my good friends, I thought she was dead. I have lived here these fifteen years, in this den, without fire in winter. It is hard, is it not? The poor dear little shoe! I have prayed so earnestly that God Almighty has heard me. This very morning He has restored my daughter to me. 'Tis a miracle of His doing. She was not dead, you see. You will not take her from me, I am sure. If it were myself I should not say a word— but as for her, a girl of sixteen, give her time to see the sun! What harm has she done to you? None whatever. Nor I either. Did you but know that I have none but her, that I am getting old, that she was a blessing bestowed on me by the Holy Virgin herself! And then you are all so kind-hearted! You knew not that it was my daughter, till I told you. Oh! how I love her! Monseigneur High Provost, I would rather be stabbed to the heart than have a scratch upon her nail! You look like a good, kind gentleman. What I tell you explains everything—is it not so? Oh, monseigneur! if you ever had a mother! You are the captain; leave me my child! Consider that I am praying to you on my knees, as one prays to Jesus Christ. I ask nothing of anyone. I am from Reims, gentlemen. I have a little spot left me by my uncle, Mahiet Pradon. I am not a beggar. I want nothing but my child! God Almighty, who is the Master of us all, gave her not to me for nothing. The King, you say! the King! How could it pleasure him were you to kill my daughter! And then the King is merciful! 'Tis my daughter! mine, I tell you! she is not the King's! she is not yours. I will be gone; we will both go. Who would stop two weak women, one of them the mother, the other the daughter. Let us pass, then! we are from Reims. Oh! you are very kind, Messieurs Sergeants; I love you all. You will not take my darling from me—'tis impossible. Is it not? quite impossible! My child! My own dear child!"

We shall not attempt to convey any idea of her gestures, of her tone, of the tears which she swallowed as she spoke, of her hands which she clasped and then wrung, of the cutting smiles, the moans, the sighs, the heartrending shrieks which she blended with this wild, rambling, and incoherent harangue. When she had done Tristan the Hermit knitted his brow, but it was to conceal a tear which started into his tiger-like eye. Conquering this weakness, however, he said in a dry tone, "The King wills it."

Then, bending to the ear of Henriet Cousin, he whispered, "Finish out of hand!" The redoubtable Provost himself perhaps felt even his heart fail him.

The hangman and the sergeants entered the cell. The mother made no resistance; she merely crawled toward her daughter, and threw herself headlong upon her. The Egyptian saw the soldiers approaching. The horror of death roused her. "Mother," cried she, in a tone of inexpressible anguish, "Mother, they are coming; defend me!" "Yes, my love, I will defend thee," replied the mother in a faint voice; and, clasping her closely in her arms, she covered her with kisses. Mother and daughter, as they thus lay on the ground, presented a sight that was truly pitiable.

Henriet Cousin laid hold of the girl round the body. When she felt the touch of his hand she shuddered, "Ugh!" and fainted. The hangman, from whose eyes big tears fell drop by drop upon her, attempted to lift her, but was prevented by the mother, who had entwined her arms round her daughter's waist, and clung so firmly to her child, that it was impossible to part them. Henriet Cousin, therefore, dragged the girl out of the cell, and the mother after her —the latter, too, with her eyes shut, and apparently insensible.

The Little Shoe

The sun was just then rising, and a considerable number of people collected thus early in the Place were striving to make out what it was that the hangman was thus dragging along the pavement toward the gibbet; for it was Tristan's way to prevent the near approach of spectators at executions.

There was not a creature at the windows. There were only to be seen on the top of that tower of Notre-Dame which overlooks the Grève, two men standing out in dark relief from the clear morning sky, who appeared to be looking on.

Henriet Cousin stopped with what he was dragging at the foot of the fatal ladder, and scarcely breathing, so deeply was he affected, he slipped the cord about the lovely neck of the girl. The unfortunate creature felt the horrid touch of the rope. She opened her eyes, and beheld the hideous arm of the stone gibbet extended over her head. Rousing herself, she cried in a loud and heartrending voice, "No! no! I will not." The mother, whose face was buried in her daughter's garments, uttered not a word; her whole body was seen to tremble, and she was heard to kiss her child with redoubled fervency. The hangman took advantage of this moment to wrench asunder her arms with which she had clung to the condemned girl. Either from exhaustion, or despair, she made no resistance. He then lifted the damsel on his shoulder, from which the charming creature hung gracefully on either side, and began to ascend the ladder.

At that moment the mother, crouched on the pavement, opened her eyes. Without uttering any cry, she sprang up with a terrific look; then, like a beast of prey, she seized the hand of the hangman and bit him. It was like lightning. The executioner roared with pain. Some of the sergeants ran to him. With difficulty they extricated his bleeding hand from the teeth of the mother. She maintained profound silence. They thrust her back in a brutal manner, and it was remarked that her head fell heavily upon the pavement. They lifted her up, but again she sank to the ground.—She was dead.

The hangman, who had not set down the girl, continued to mount the ladder.

CHAPTER II

LA CREATURA BELLA BIANCO VESTITA [1]

WHEN Quasimodo ascertained that the cell was vacant, that the Egyptian was not there, and that while he was defending her she had been taken away, he grasped his head with both hands, and stamped with rage and astonishment; he then began to run all over the church in quest of the Bohemian, setting up strange shouts at every corner, and strewing his red hair upon the pavement. It was the very moment when the King's archers entered the cathedral victorious, also seeking the Egyptian. Quasimodo assisted them, having no suspicion—poor deaf creature!—of their fatal intentions; it was the Vagabond crew whom he regarded as the enemies of the Egyptian. He himself conducted Tristan the Hermit to every possible place of concealment, opened for him all the secret doors, the double-bottomed altars, and the back sacristies. Had the unfortunate girl been still there he must inevitably have betrayed her. When Tristan was tired of the unsuccessful search—and on such occasions he was not soon tired—Quasimodo continued it alone. He traversed the church twenty times, a hundred times, lengthwise and breadthwise, from top to bottom, mounting, descending, running, calling, crying, shouting, ferreting, rummaging, poking his head into every hole, thrusting a torch into every dark corner, distracted, mad. At length, when he was sure, quite sure, that she was no longer there, that she had been stolen away from him, he slowly ascended the tower-stairs, those stairs which he had mounted with such transport and exultation on the day that he saved her. He again passed that way, with drooping head, voiceless, tearless, almost unbreathing. The church was once more clear, and silence again reigned within it. The archers had quitted the sacred edifice to track the sorceress in the Cité. Quasimodo, left alone in the vast cathedral, ringing but a few moments before with the clamours of the besiegers, returned toward the cell, where the Egyptian had slept so many weeks under his guardianship. As he approached it he could not help fancying that he might perhaps find her there again. When, at the turn of the gallery which opens upon the roof of the

[1] "The beautiful creature clad in white" (Dante).

aisles, he perceived the narrow cabin with its small window and its little door, clapped under a great flying buttress, like a bird's nest under a bough, his heart failed him, poor fellow! and he leant against a pillar, lest he should fall. He imagined that she might perhaps have returned thither; that a good genius had no doubt brought her back; that this little cell was too quiet, too safe, too charming for her not to be there; and he durst not take another step for fear of destroying the illusion. "Yes," said he to himself, "perhaps she is asleep, or praying. Let us not disturb her." At length he mustered courage, advanced on tiptoe, looked in, entered. Empty! the cell was still empty! The unhappy hunchback slowly paced round it, lifted up the bed and looked under it, as though she could have been hidden between the mattress and the floor. He then shook his head and remained for a while in a state of stupor. All at once he furiously trampled upon his torch, and without word or sigh he franticly dashed his head against the wall, and fell swooning on the pavement.

When his senses returned he threw himself upon the bed, he rolled upon it, he wildly kissed the spot where La Esmeralda had lain; he remained thus for some minutes as motionless as if life had fled: he then rose, bathed in perspiration, panting, beside himself, and began to beat his head against the wall with the frightful regularity of a pendulum, and the resolution of one who is determined to dash out his brains. At length he fell a second time exhausted. Presently he crawled on his knees out of the cell, and crouched opposite to the door in an attitude of despair. In this state he continued for above an hour, without stirring, his eye fixed on the vacant cell, more gloomy and more thoughtful than a mother seated between an empty cradle and a full coffin. He uttered not a word; only at long intervals a sob violently shook his whole body, but it was a sob without tears, like those of summer lightnings which make no noise.

It appears that then, seeking in his doleful reverie to discover who could thus unexpectedly have carried off the Egyptian, he bethought himself of the Archdeacon. He recollected that none but Dom Claude had a key to the staircase leading to the cell; he called to mind his nocturnal attempts upon the damsel, in the first of which he, Quasimodo, himself had assisted, and the second of which he had frustrated; he called to mind a thousand other circumstances, and soon felt not the least doubt that it was the Archdeacon who had taken the girl from him. Such, however, was his respect for the priest, so deeply had gratitude, affection, love, for that man struck root in his heart, that even at this moment they withstood the pull of jealousy and despair.

He considered that the Archdeacon had done this, and instead of the mortal rancour with which the thought would have filled his heart for any other, the moment it fixed upon Claude Frollo, it only aggravated his grief. At this moment, when the dawn began to whiten the flying buttresses, he descried on a higher storey of the cathedral, at the angle formed by the outer balustrade which runs round the apsis, a figure in motion. The face of this figure was turned toward him. He recognized the person. It was the Archdeacon. Claude's step was grave and deliberate. He looked not before him as he walked toward the north tower; but his face was turned askance toward the right bank of the Seine, as if he were striving to see something over the intervening roofs. The owl frequently has this oblique attitude, flying in one direction and looking in another. The priest thus passed on above Quasimodo without perceiving him.

The hunchback, petrified by this sudden apparition, watched till he lost sight of him at the door of the staircase of the north tower. The reader already knows that this is the tower which commands a view of the Hôtel de Ville. Quasimodo rose and followed the Archdeacon.

He went up the stairs to ascend the tower, for the purpose of ascertaining why the priest ascended it; if indeed the poor bell-ringer, who knew not what he did, or what he wished, could be said to have any purpose. He was full of rage and full of apprehension. The Archdeacon and the Egyptian clashed together in his heart.

When he had reached the top of the tower, before he issued from the darkness of the staircase and stepped out upon the platform, he looked cautiously about to discover where the priest was. Claude had his back toward him. A balustrade of open-work surrounds the platform of the steeple. The priest, whose eyes were bent upon the town, was leaning with his breast against that corner of the balustrade which looks down upon the bridge of Notre-Dame.

Quasimodo stole with wolf's step behind him, to see what he was thus looking at. The attention of the priest was so completely engrossed that he perceived not the approach of the hunchback.

Paris, viewed from the towers of Notre-Dame in the cool dawn of a summer morning, is a delectable and a magnificent sight; and the Paris of that period must have been eminently so. It was then the month of July. The sky was perfectly serene. A few lingering stars were going out at different points, and there was still a very bright one in the east in the lightest part of the firmament. The sun was just rising. Paris began to be astir. A very white and a very pure light touched the eastward faces of its myriad houses and made them conspicuous to the eye. The giant shadows of the steeples extended from roof to roof, from one end of the great city to the other. There were quarters which already began to send forth various sounds. Here was heard the hammer of the smith, there that of the carpenter, and yonder the complicated creaking of a cart as it passed along the street. A few columns of smoke issued from different points of this vast surface of roofs, as from the fissures of an immense solfatara. The river which dashes its waters against the piers of so many bridges, and the points of so many islands, was streaked with lines of silver. Around the Cité, beyond the ramparts, the horizon melted into a wide circle of fleecy vapours, through which might be faintly discerned the indefinite line of the plains and the graceful swelling of the hills. All sorts of sounds floated confusedly over this half-awakened city. Toward the east the morning breeze drove across the sky a few white tufts rent from the mantle of mist that enwrapped the hills.

In the Parvis certain stirring housewives, with milk-jugs in their hands, pointed out to each other with astonishment the shattered state of the great portal of Notre-Dame; and the two streams of lead congealed in the interstices between the stones of the pavement. These were the only vestiges of the tumult of the past night. The fire kindled by Quasimodo between the towers was extinguished. Tristan had already caused the Place to be cleared, and the dead to be thrown into the Seine. Such kings as Louis XI take care to have the pavement speedily washed after a massacre.

Outside the balustrade of the tower, below the very point where the priest had stopped, there was one of those stone gutters fantastically carved, with which Gothic edifices are bristled, and in a crevice of this gutter were two fine wallflowers in blossom, which waved, and, as if they were animated by the breeze, seemed to be sportively bowing to each other. Above the towers, aloft in the air, small birds were heard twittering and screaming.

The Hunchback of Notre-Dame

But the priest neither heard nor saw any of these things. He was one of those who take no notice either of mornings, or of birds, or of flowers. His contemplation was engrossed by one point only of that immense horizon, which presented so many aspects around him.

Quasimodo burned with impatience to inquire what he had done with the Egyptian; but the Archdeacon seemed at that moment to be out of the world. With him it was evidently one of those critical moments of life, when a man would not feel the earth crumbling beneath his feet. He remained motionless and silent, with his eyes invariably fixed on a particular spot; and this silence and this motionless attitude had something so formidable that the savage bell-ringer himself shuddered before and durst not disturb it. All he could do therefore, and this was one way of questioning the Archdeacon, was to follow the direction of his eye; and thus guided, that of the unhappy hunchback fell upon the Place de Grève.

He now perceived what the priest was looking at. The ladder was set up against the permanent gibbet. There were a few people in the Place and a great number of soldiers. A man was dragging along the pavement something white to which something black was clinging. This man stopped at the foot of the gibbet. What then took place he could not clearly discern; not that the sight of his only eye was at all impaired, but a party of soldiers prevented his distinguishing what was going forward. Besides, at that moment the sun burst forth and poured such a flood of light above the horizon that every point of Paris, steeples, chimneys, gables, seemed to be set on fire at one and the same moment.

Meanwhile the man began to mount the ladder. Quasimodo now saw distinctly again. He carried across his shoulder a woman, a young woman dressed in white; this young woman had a rope about her neck. Quasimodo knew her. It was the Egyptian!

The man reached the top of the ladder. There he arranged the rope. The priest, in order to see the better, now knelt down upon the balustrade.

The man suddenly kicked away the ladder, and Quasimodo, who had not breathed for some moments, saw the unfortunate girl, with the man mounted upon her shoulders, dangling at the end of the rope within two or three yards of the pavement. The rope spun round several times, and Quasimodo saw the body of the Egyptian shaken by terrible convulsions. The priest, on his part, with outstretched neck and eyes starting from his head, contemplated the terrific group of the man and the young girl, the spider and the fly.

At this most awful moment, a demon laugh, a laugh such as one only who has ceased to be human is capable of, burst forth upon the livid face of the priest. Quasimodo heard not this laugh, but he saw it. The bell-ringer recoiled a few steps from the Archdeacon, then suddenly rushing furiously upon him, thrust him with his two huge hands into the abyss, over which Dom Claude was leaning. "Damnation!" cried the priest as he fell.

The gutter beneath caught him and broke the fall. He clung to it with eager hands, and was just opening his mouth to give a second cry when he beheld the formidable and avenging face of Quasimodo protruded over the balustrade above his head. He was then silent.

The abyss was beneath him—a fall of more than two hundred feet —and the pavement! In this terrible situation, the Archdeacon uttered neither word nor groan. Only he writhed upon the edge of the gutter, and made astonishing efforts to hoist himself on to it. But his hands had no hold of the granite, and his toes merely streaked the blackened wall without finding the least support. All who have ever been up the towers of Notre-Dame know that the stone bulges immediately under the balustrade. It was against the retreating slope that the wretched Archdeacon exhausted himself in fruitless efforts. He had not to do with a perpendicular wall, but a wall that receded from him.

Quasimodo might have withdrawn him from the gulf by merely reaching him his hand; but he did not so much as look at him. He looked at the Grève. He looked at the Egyptian. He looked at the gibbet. The hunchback was leaning upon the balustrade, at the very spot which the Archdeacon had just before occupied; and there, never turning his eye from the only object which existed for him at that moment, he was motionless and mute as one thunderstruck; while a stream flowed in silence from that eye, which till then had not shed a single tear.

The Archdeacon meanwhile began to pant. The perspiration trickled from his bald brow, the blood oozed from his fingers' ends; the skin was rubbed from his knees against the wall. He heard his cassock, which hung by the gutter, crack and rip at every movement that he made. To crown his misery, that gutter terminated in a leaden pipe which bent with his weight. The Archdeacon felt it slowly giving way. The wretched man said to himself, that when his cassock should be rent, when the leaden pipe should yield, he must fall, and horror thrilled his entrails. At times he wildly eyed a sort of narrow ledge, formed about ten feet below him by the excrescences of the sculpture of the church, and in his distress he prayed to heaven in the recesses of his soul to permit him to end his life on this space of two square feet, were it even to last a hundred years. Once he glanced at the abyss beneath him; when he raised his head his eyes were closed and his hair standing erect.

There was something frightful in the silence of these two persons. While the Archdeacon, at the distance of a few feet, was experiencing the most horrible agonies, Quasimodo kept his eye fixed on the Grève and wept.

The Archdeacon, perceiving that all his exertions served but to shake the only frail support that was left him, determined to stir no more. There he was, clasping the gutter, scarcely breathing, absolutely motionless save that mechanical convulsion of the abdomen which supervenes in sleep, when you dream that you are falling. His fixed eyes glared in a wild and ghastly manner. Meanwhile he began to lose his hold; his fingers slipped down the gutter: he felt his arms becoming weaker and weaker, and his body heavier and heavier. The leaden pipe which supported him bent more and more every moment toward the abyss. Beneath him he beheld— fearful sight!—the roof of Saint-Jean-le-Rond, diminutive as a card bent in two. He eyed one after another the passionless sculptures of the tower, suspended like himself over the abyss, but without fear for themselves or pity for him. All about him was stone: before his eyes gaping monsters; under him, at the bottom of the gulf, the pavement; over his head, Quasimodo weeping.

In the Parvis several groups of curious spectators were calmly puzzling their brains to divine who could be the maniac that was amusing himself in this strange manner. The priest heard them say, for their voices reached him, clear and sharp, "By'r Lady, he must break his neck!"

Quasimodo wept.

At length the Archdeacon, foaming with rage and terror, became sensible that all was useless. He nevertheless mustered all his remaining strength for a last effort. Setting both his knees against the wall, he hooked his hands into a cleft in the stones, and succeeded in raising himself about a foot; but this struggle caused the leaden beak which supported him to give way suddenly. His cassock was ripped up from the same cause. Feeling himself sinking, having only his stiffened and crippled hands to hold by, the wretched man closed his eyes, and presently his fingers relaxed their grasp. Down he fell!

Quasimodo watched him falling.

A fall from such a height is rarely perpendicular. The Archdeacon, launched into the abyss, fell at first head downward and with outstretched arms, and then whirled several times over and over; dropping upon the roof of a house, and breaking some of his bones. He was not dead when he reached it, for the bell-ringer saw him strive to grapple the ridge with his fingers; but the slope was too steep, and his strength utterly failed him. Sliding rapidly down the roof, like a tile that has got loose, down he went, and rebounded on the pavement. He stirred no more.

Quasimodo then raised his eye to the Egyptian, dangling from the gallows. At that distance he could see her quiver beneath her white robe in the last convulsive agonies of death; he then looked down at the Archdeacon, stretched at the foot of the tower, with scarcely a vestige of the human form about him, and, heaving a deep sigh, he cried, "There is all I ever loved!"

CHAPTER III

THE MARRIAGE OF CAPTAIN PHŒBUS

TOWARD the evening of the same day, when the judicial officers of the Bishop came to remove the mangled corpse of the Archdeacon from the pavement of the Parvis, Quasimodo was not to be found in Notre-Dame.

Many rumours were circulated respecting this affair. The general opinion was that the day had arrived when, according to agreement, Quasimodo, or the devil, was to carry away Claude Frollo, the sorcerer. It was presumed that he had smashed the body to get at the soul, just as monkeys crack the shell of a nut to get at the kernel.

For this reason the Archdeacon was not interred in consecrated ground.

Louis XI died in the month of August in the following year, 1483.

As for Pierre Gringoire, he contrived to save the goat, and to gain applause as a tragic writer. It appears that, after dabbling in astrology, philosophy, architecture, alchemy, and all sorts of vain pursuits, he reverted to tragedy, which is the most vain of all. This he called *"having come to a tragic end."* In the accounts of the Ordinary for 1483 may be found the following entry relative to his dramatic triumphs:

> To Jehan Marchand and Pierre Gringoire, carpenter and composer, who made and composed the mystery enacted at the Châtelet of Paris at the entry of Monsieur the Legate, and arranged the characters, habited and equipped as by the said mystery was required; and also for having made the scaffolds which were necessary thereto, one hundred livres.

Phœbus de Châteaupers likewise "came to a tragic end": he married.

CHAPTER IV

THE MARRIAGE OF QUASIMODO

WE have just said that on the day when the Egyptian and the Archdeacon died Quasimodo was not to be found in Notre-Dame. He was never seen afterward, nor was it ever known what became of him.

In the night following the execution of La Esmeralda the hangman and his assistants took down her body from the gibbet, and conveyed it, according to custom, to the vault of Montfaucon.

Montfaucon, as we are told by Sauval, was "the most ancient and the most superb gallows in the kingdom." Between the faubourgs of the Temple and Saint-Martin, about one hundred and sixty fathoms from the walls of Paris, and a few crossbow-shots from La Courtille, was seen at the top of a gentle, imperceptible rise, yet sufficiently elevated to be seen for several leagues round, a building of strange form, nearly resembling a Celtic cromlech, and where also human victims were sacrificed.

Conceive on the top of a mound of chalk, a clumsy parallelopipedon

The Marriage of Quasimodo

of masonry, fifteen feet high, forty long, and thirty wide, with a door, an outer railing, and a platform; upon this platform sixteen massive pillars of unhewn stone, thirty feet high, ranged in form of a colonnade round three of the four sides of the masonry which supports them, connected at top by strong beams, from which at certain distances hang chains, each having a skeleton dangling at the end of it; round about it in the plain a stone cross and two gibbets of secondary rank, which seem to spring up like shoots from the central stock; above all these in the air crows perpetually flying—and you will have a picture of Montfaucon.

At the conclusion of the fifteenth century this formidable gibbet, which dated from 1328, was already very decrepit: the beams were rotten; the chains eaten up with rust; the pillars green with moss; there were wide interstices between the courses of the stone; and grass grew upon the untrodden platform. The profile of this edifice upon the sky was a horrible one, especially at night, when the faint moonlight fell upon those bleached skulls, or when the night-breeze, shaking the chains and the skeletons, made them rattle in the dark. The presence of this gibbet was sufficient to induce a belief that all the environs were haunted.

The stonework which served as a base to the odious edifice was hollow. Here had been formed a vast vault, closed by an old crazy iron gate, into which were thrown not only the human remains taken from the chains of Montfaucon, but the bodies of all the wretches executed at the other permanent gibbets of Paris. In this vast charnel-house, in which so many human carcases and so many crimes have mouldered together, many of the great of the world, and many innocent persons, have successively laid their bones, from Enguerraud de Marigni, who made a present of Montfaucon, and who was a good man, to Admiral de Coligni with whom it was closed, and who also was a good man.

Respecting the mysterious disappearance of Quasimodo, all that we have been able to discover is this:

About a year and a half or two years after the events with which this history concludes, when search was made in the vault of Montfaucon for the body of Olivier le Daim, who had been hung two days previously, and to whom Charles VIII had granted the favour to be interred in better company at Saint-Laurent, among these hideous carcases were found two skeletons in a singular posture. One of these skeletons, which was that of a woman, had still upon it some fragments of a dress that had once been white; and about the neck was a necklace of the seeds of adrezarach, and a little silk bag braided with green beads, which was open and empty. These things were of so little value that the hangman no doubt had not thought it worth his while to take them. The other, by which this first was closely embraced, was the skeleton of a man. It was remarked that the spine was crooked, the head depressed between the shoulders, and one leg shorter than the other. There was however no rupture of the vertebræ of the neck, and it was evident that the person to whom it belonged had not been hanged. He must have come hither and died in the place. When those who found this skeleton attempted to disengage it from that which it held in its grasp it crumbled to dust.

LES
MISERABLES

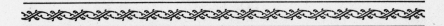

CONTENTS

CONTENTS

I. THE GOOD BISHOP

In 1815, M. Charles François-Bienvenu Myriel was Bishop of D——. He was a man of seventy-five, and had occupied the bishopric of D—— since 1806.

M. Myriel was the son of a counsellor of the Parlement of Aix. His father, intending him to inherit his place, had contracted a marriage for him at the early age of eighteen or twenty. Charles Myriel, notwithstanding this marriage, had, it was said, been an object of much attention. His person was admirably moulded; although of slight figure, he was elegant and graceful; all the earlier part of his life had been devoted to the world and to its pleasures. The revolution came, events crowded upon each other; the parliamentary families, decimated, hunted, and pursued, were soon dispersed. M. Charles Myriel, on the first outbreak of the revolution, emigrated to Italy. His wife died there of a lung complaint with which she had been long threatened. They had no children. What followed in the fate of M. Myriel? The decay of the old French society, the fall of his own family, the tragic sights of '93, still more fearful, perhaps, to the exiles who beheld them from afar, magnified by fright—did these arouse in him ideas of renunciation and of solitude? No one could have answered; all that was known was that when he returned from Italy he was a priest.

In 1804, M. Myriel was curé of B—— (Brignolles). He was then an old man, and lived in the deepest seclusion.

Near the time of the coronation, a trifling matter of business belonging to his curacy—what it was, is not now known precisely—took him to Paris. Among other personages of authority he went to Cardinal Fesch on behalf of his parishioners.

One day, when the emperor had come to visit his uncle, the worthy curé, who was waiting in the ante-room, happened to be in the way of his Majesty. Napoleon noticing that the old man looked at him with a certain curiousness, turned around and said brusquely:

"Who is this good man who looks at me?"

"Sire," said M. Myriel, "you behold a good man, and I a great man. Each of us may profit by it."

That evening the emperor asked the cardinal the name of the curé, and some time afterwards M. Myriel was overwhelmed with surprise on learning that he had been appointed Bishop of D——.

When M. Myriel came to D—— he was accompanied by an old lady, Mademoiselle Baptistine, who was his sister, ten years younger than himself.

Their only domestic was a woman of about the same age as Mademoiselle Baptistine, who was called Madame Magloire.

Mademoiselle Baptistine was a tall, pale, thin, sweet person. She fully realised the idea which is expressed by the word "respectable." She had never been pretty; her whole life, which had been but a succession of pious works, had produced upon her a kind of transparent whiteness, and in growing old she had acquired what may be called the beauty of goodness. She was more a spirit than a virgin mortal.

Madame Magloire was a little, white, fat, jolly, bustling old woman, always out of breath, caused first by her activity, and then by the asthma.

M. Myriel, upon his arrival, was installed in his episcopal palace with the honours ordained by the imperial decrees, which class the bishop next in rank to the field-marshal.

The bishop's palace at D—— was contiguous to the hospital: the palace was a spacious and beautiful edifice, in truth a lordly dwelling: there was an air of grandeur about everything, the apartments of the bishop, the court of honour, which was very large, with arched walks after the antique Florentine style; and a garden planted with magnificent trees.

The hospital was a low, narrow, one story building with a small garden. Three days after the bishop's advent he visited the hospital; when the visit was ended, he invited the director to oblige him by coming to the palace.

"Monsieur," he said to the director of the hospital, "how many patients have you?"

"Twenty-six, monseigneur."

"That is as I counted them," said the bishop.

"The beds," continued the director, "are very much crowded."

"I noticed it."

"The wards are but small chambers, and are not easily ventilated."

"It seems so to me."

"And then, when the sun does shine, the garden is very small for the convalescents."

"That was what I was thinking."

"Of epidemics we have had typhus fever this year; two years ago we had military fever, sometimes one hundred patients, and we did not know what to do."

"That occurred to me."

"What can we do, monseigneur?" said the director; "we must be resigned."

This conversation took place in the dining gallery on the ground floor.

The bishop was silent a few moments: then he turned suddenly towards the director.

"Monsieur," he said, "how many beds do you think this hall alone would contain?"

"The dining hall of monseigneur!" exclaimed the director, stupefied.

The bishop ran his eyes over the hall, seemingly taking measure and making calculations.

"It will hold twenty beds," said he to himself; then raising his voice, he said:

"Listen, Monsieur Director, to what I have to say. There is evidently a mistake here. There are twenty-six of you in five or six small rooms: there are only three of us, and space for sixty. There is a mistake, I tell you. You have my house and I have yours. Restore mine to me; you are at home."

Next day the twenty-six poor invalids were installed in the bishop's palace, and the bishop was in the hospital.

M. Myriel had no property, his family having been impoverished by the revolution. His sister had a life estate of five hundred francs, which in the vicarage sufficed for her personal needs. M. Myriel received from the government as bishop a salary of fifteen thousand francs. The day on which he took up his residence in the hospital building, he resolved to appropriate this sum once for all to the following uses:

"For the little seminary, fifteen hundred livres.
Mission congregation, one hundred livres.
For the Lazaristes of Montdidier, one hundred livres.
Congregation of the Saint-Esprit, one hundred and fifty livres.
Seminary of foreign missions in Paris, two hundred livres.
Religious establishments in the Holy Land, one hundred livres.
Maternal charitable societies, three hundred livres.
For that of Arles, fifty livres.
For the amelioration of prisons, four hundred livres.
For the relief and deliverance of prisoners, five hundred livres.
For the liberation of fathers of families imprisoned for debt, one thousand livres.
Additions to the salaries of poor schoolmasters of the diocese, two thousand livres.
Public storehouse of Hautes-Alpes, one hundred livres.
Association of the ladies of D—— of Manosque and Sisteron for the gratuitous instruction of poor girls, fifteen hundred livres.
For the poor, six thousand livres.
My personal expenses, one thousand livres.
Total, fifteen thousand livres."

M. Myriel made no alteration in this plan during the time he held the see of D——. About three months after the installation, the bishop said one day, "With all this I am very much cramped." "I think so too," said Madame Magloire: "Monseigneur has not even asked for the sum due him by the department for his carriage expenses in town, and in his circuits in the diocese. It was formerly the custom with all bishops."

"Yes!" said the bishop; "you are right, Madame Magloire."

He made his application.

Some time afterwards the conseil-général took his claim into consideration and voted him an annual stipend of three thousand francs under this head: "Allowance to the bishop for carriage expenses, and travelling expenses for pastoral visits."

The bourgeoisie of the town were much excited on the subject, and in regard to it a senator of the empire, formerly a member of the Council of Five Hundred, an advocate of the Eighteenth Brumaire, now provided with a rich senatorial seat near D——, wrote to M. Bigot de Préameneu, Minister of Public Worship, a fault-finding, confidential epistle, from which we make the following extract:—

"Carriage expenses! What can he want of it in a town of less than 4000 inhabitants? Expenses of pastoral visits! And what good do they do, in the first place; and then, how is it possible to travel by post in this mountain region? There are no roads; he can go only on horseback. Bah! this whole priesthood! Monsieur le Comte, things will never be better till the emperor delivers us from these macaroni priests. Down with the pope! As for me, I am for Cæsar alone," etc.

This application, on the other hand, pleased Madame Magloire exceedingly. "Good," said she to Mademoiselle Baptistine; "Monseigneur began with others, but he has found at last that he must end by taking care of himself. He has arranged all his charities, and so now here are three thousand francs for us."

The same evening the bishop wrote and gave to his sister a note couched in these terms:

Carriage and Travelling Expenses

"For beef broth for the hospital, fifteen hundred livres.
For the Aix Maternal Charity Association, two hundred and fifty livres.
For the Draguignan Maternal Charity Association, two hundred and fifty livres.
For Foundlings, five hundred livres.
For Orphans, five hundred livres.
Total, three thousand livres."

Such was the budget of M. Myriel.

It being the custom that all bishops should put their baptismal names at the head of their orders and pastoral letters, the poor people of the district had chosen by a sort of affectionate instinct, from among the names of the bishop, that which was expressive to them, and they always called him Monseigneur Bienvenu. We shall follow their example and shall call him thus; besides, this pleased him. "I like this name," said he; "Bienvenu counterbalances Monseigneur."

The bishop, after converting his carriage into alms, none the less regularly made his round of visits, and in the diocese of D—— this was a wearisome task. There was very little plain, a good deal of mountain; and hardly any roads, as a matter of course; thirty-two curacies, forty-one vicarages, and two hundred and eighty-five subcuracies. To visit all these is a great labour, but the bishop went through with it. He travelled on foot in his own neighbourhood, in a cart when he was in the plains, and in a *cacolet*, a basket strapped on the back of a mule, when in the mountains.

One day he arrived at Senez, formerly the seat of a bishopric, mounted on an ass. His purse was very empty at the time, and would not permit any better conveyance. The mayor of the city came to receive him at the gate of the episcopal residence, and saw him dismount from his ass with astonishment and mortification. Several of the citizens stood near by, laughing. "Monsieur Mayor," said the bishop, "and Messieurs citizens, I see what astonishes you; you think that it shows a good deal of pride for a poor priest to use the same conveyance which was used by Jesus Christ. I have done it from necessity, I assure you, and not from vanity."

In his visits he was indulgent and gentle, and preached less than he talked. In the cantons where the necessitous were treated with severity he would say, "Look at the people of Briançon. They have given to the poor, and to widows and orphans, the right to mow their meadows three days before any one else. When their houses are in ruins they rebuild them without cost. And so it is a country blessed of God. For a whole century they have not had a single murderer."

In villages where the people were greedy for gain at harvest time, he would say, "Look at Embrun. If a father of a family, at harvest time, has his sons in the army, and his daughters at service in the city, and he is sick, the priest recommends him in his sermons, and on Sunday, after mass, the whole population of the village, men, women, and children, go into the poor man's field and harvest his crop, and put the straw and the grain into his granary."

One day he preached this sermon in the cathedral:—

"My very dear brethren, my good friends, there are in France thirteen hundred and twenty thousand peasants' cottages that have but three openings; eighteen hundred and seventeen thousand that have two, the door and one window; and finally, three hundred and forty-six thousand cabins, with only one opening—the door. And this is in consequence of what is called the excise upon doors and windows. In these poor families, among the aged women and the little children, dwelling in these huts, how abundant is fever and disease? Alas! God gives light to men; the law sells it. I do not blame the law, but I bless God. In Isère, in Var, and in the Upper and the Lower Alps, the peasants have not even wheelbarrows, they carry the manure on their backs; they have no candles, but burn pine knots, and bits of rope soaked in pitch. And the same is the case all through the upper part of Dauphiné. They make bread once in six months, and bake it with the refuse of the fields. In the winter it becomes so hard that they cut it up with an axe, and soak it for twenty-four hours, before they can eat it. My brethren, be compassionate; behold how much suffering there is around you."

In company one day he heard an account of a criminal case that was about to be tried. A miserable man, through love for a woman and for the child she had borne him, had been making false coin, his means being exhausted. At that time counterfeiting was still punished with death. The woman was arrested for passing the first piece that he had made. She was held a prisoner, but there was no proof against her lover. She alone could testify against him, and convict him by her confession. She denied his guilt. They insisted, but she was obstinate in her denial. In this state of the case, the *procureur du roi* devised a shrewd plan. He represented to her that her lover was unfaithful, and by means of fragments of letters skillfully put together, succeeded in persuading the unfortunate woman that she had a rival, and that this man had deceived her. At once exasperated by jealousy, she denounced her lover, confessed all, and proved his guilt. He was to be tried in a few days, at Aix, with his accomplice, and his conviction was certain. The story was told, and everybody was in ecstasy at the adroitness of the officer. The bishop listened to all this in silence. When it was finished he asked:

"Where are this man and woman to be tried?"

"At the Assizes."

"And where is the *procureur du roi* to be tried?"

A tragic event occurred at D——. A man had been condemned to death for murder. The unfortunate prisoner was a poorly educated, but not entirely ignorant man, who had been a juggler at fairs, and a public letter-writer. The people were greatly interested in the trial. The evening before the day fixed for the execution of the condemned, the almoner of the prison fell ill. A priest was needed to attend the prisoner in his last moments. The curé was sent for, but he refused to go, saying, "That does not concern me. I have nothing to do with such drudgery, or with that mountebank; besides, I am sick myself; and moreover it is not my place." When this reply was reported to the bishop, he said, "The curé is right. It is not his place, it is mine."

He went, on the instant, to the prison, went down into the dungeon of the "mountebank," called him by his name, took him by the hand, and talked with him. He passed the whole day with him, forgetful of food and sleep, praying to God for the soul of the condemned, and exhorting the condemned to join with him.

On the morrow when they came for the poor man, the bishop was with him. He followed him, and showed himself to the eyes of the crowd in his violet camail, with his bishop's cross about his neck, side by side with the miserable being, who was bound with cords.

He mounted the cart with him, he ascended the scaffold with him. The sufferer, so gloomy and so horror-stricken in the evening, was now radiant with hope. He felt that his soul was reconciled, and he trusted in God. The bishop embraced him, and at the moment when the axe was about to fall, he said to him, "Whom man kills, him God restoreth to life; whom his brethren put away, he findeth the Father. Pray, believe, enter into life! The Father is there."

There were those in the city who said the bishop's conduct was affectation, but such ideas were confined to the upper classes. The people, who do not look for unworthy motives in holy works, admired.

As to the bishop, the sight of the guillotine was a shock to him, from which it was long before he recovered. By times he would talk to himself, and in an undertone mutter dismal monologues. One evening his sister overheard and preserved the following: "I did not believe that it could be so monstrous. It is wrong to be so absorbed in the divine law as not to perceive the human law. Death belongs to God alone. By what right do men touch that unknown thing?"

With the lapse of time these impressions faded away, and were probably effaced. Nevertheless it was remarked that the bishop ever after avoided passing by the place of execution.

The house which he occupied consisted of a ground floor and a second story; three rooms on the ground floor, three on the second story, and an attic above. Behind the house was a garden of about a quarter of an acre. The two women occupied the upper floor; the bishop lived below. The first room, which opened upon the street, was his dining-room, the second was his bedroom, and the third his oratory. You could not leave the oratory without passing through the bedroom, and to leave the bedroom you must pass through the dining-room. At one end of the oratory there was an alcove closed in, with a bed for the country curés when business or the wants of their parish brought them to D——.

At half-past eight in the evening he took supper with his sister, Madame Magloire standing behind them and waiting on the table. Nothing could be more frugal than this meal. If, however, the bishop had one of his curés to supper, Madame Magloire improved the occasion to serve her master with some excellent fish from the lakes, or some fine game from the mountain.

There was a stable in the garden, which was formerly the hospital kitchen, where the bishop now kept a couple of cows, and invariably, every morning, he sent half the milk they gave to the sick at the hospital. "I pay my tithes," said he.

It had been the ambition of Mademoiselle Baptistine to be able to buy a parlour lounge, with cushions of Utrecht velvet, roses on a yellow ground, while the mahogany should be in the form of swans' necks. But this would have cost at least five hundred francs, and as she had been able to save only forty-two francs and ten sous for the purpose in five years, she had finally given it up. But who ever does attain to his ideal?

Nothing could be plainer in its arrangements than the bishop's bed-chamber. A window, which was also a door, opening upon the garden; facing this, the bed, an iron hospital-bed, with green serge curtains; in the shadow of the bed, behind a screen, the toilet utensils, still betraying the elegant habits of the man of the world; two doors, one near the chimney, leading into the oratory, the other near the book-case, opening into the dining-room. The book-case, a large closet with glass doors, filled with books; the fire-place, cased with wood painted to imitate marble, usually without fire; in the fire-place, a pair of andirons ornamented with two vases of flowers, once plated with silver, which was a kind of episcopal luxury; above the fire-place, a copper crucifix, from which the silver was worn off, fixed upon a piece of thread-bare black velvet in a wooden frame from which the gilt was almost gone; near the window, a large table with an inkstand, covered with confused papers and heavy volumes. In front of the table was the straw armchair, and before the bed, a prie-dieu from the oratory.

He had at his window an antique curtain of coarse woolen stuff, which finally became so old that, to save the expense of a new one, Madame Magloire was obliged to put a large patch in the very middle of it. This patch was in the form of a cross. The bishop often called attention to it. "How fortunate that is," he would say.

We must confess that he still retained six silver dishes and a silver soup ladle, which Madame Magloire contemplated every day with new joy as they shone on the coarse, white, linen table-cloth. And as we are drawing the portrait of the Bishop of D— just as he was, we must add that he had said, more than once, "It would be difficult for me to give up eating from silver."

With this silver ware should be counted two large, massive silver candlesticks which he inherited from a great-aunt. These candlesticks held two wax-candles, and their place was upon the bishop's mantel. When he had any one to dinner, Madame Magloire lighted the two candles and placed the two candlesticks upon the table.

There was in the bishop's chamber, at the head of his bed, a small cupboard in which Madame Magloire placed the six silver dishes and the great ladle every evening. But the key was never taken out of it.

The garden was laid out with four walks, crossing at the drain-well in the centre. There was another walk round the garden, along the white wall which enclosed it. These walks left four square plats which were bordered with box. In three of them Madame Magloire cultivated vegetables; in the fourth the bishop had planted flowers, and here and there were a few fruit trees. Madame Magloire once said to him with a kind of gentle reproach: "Monseigneur, you are always anxious to make everything useful, but yet here is a plat that is of no use. It would be much better to have salads there than bouquets." "Madame Magloire," replied the bishop, "you are mistaken. The beautiful is as useful as the useful." He added after a moment's silence, "perhaps more so."

This plat, consisting of three or four beds, occupied the bishop nearly as much as his books. He usually passed an hour or two there, trimming, weeding, and making holes here and there in the ground, and planting seeds. He was as much averse to insects as a gardener would have wished. He made no pretensions to botany, and knew nothing of groups or classification; he did not study plants, he loved flowers. He had much respect for the learned, but still more for the ignorant; and he watered his beds every summer evening with a tin watering-pot painted green.

Not a door in the house had a lock. The door of the dining-room was formerly loaded with bars and bolts like the door of a prison. The bishop had had all this iron-work taken off, and the door, by night as well as by day, was closed only with a latch. The passer-by, whatever might be the hour, could open it with a simple push. At first the two women had been very much troubled at the door being never locked; but Monseigneur de D—— said to them: "Have bolts on your own doors, if you like." They shared his confidence at last, or at least acted as if they shared it. Madame Magloire alone had occasional attacks of fear.

It occurred to a worthy curé to ask one day, probably at the instigation of Madame Magloire, if monseigneur did not fear that some evil would befall a house so poorly defended. The bishop touched him gently on the shoulder, and said:[1] "*Nisi Dominus custodierit domum, in vanum vigilant qui custodiunt eam.*"

And then he changed the subject.

He very often said: "There is a bravery for the priest as well as a bravery for the colonel of dragoons. Only," added he, "ours should be quiet."

After the destruction of the band of Gaspard Bès, which had infested the gorges of Ollivolles, one of his lieutenants, Cravatte, took refuge in the mountains. He concealed himself for some time with his bandits in the county of Nice, then made his way to Piedmont, and suddenly reappeared in France in the neighbourhood of Barcelonnette. He concealed himself in the caverns of the Joug de l'Aigle, from which he made descents upon the hamlets and villages by the ravines of Ubaye and Ubayette.

He even pushed as far as Embrun, and one night broke into the cathedral and stripped the sacristy. His robberies desolated the country. The gendarmes were put upon his trail, but in vain. He was a bold wretch. In the midst of all this terror, the bishop arrived. He was making his visit to Chastelar. The mayor came to see him and urged him to turn back. Cravatte held the mountains as far as Arche and beyond; it would be dangerous even with an escort. It would expose three or four poor gendarmes to useless danger.

"And so," said the bishop, "I intend to go without an escort."

"Do not think of such a thing," exclaimed the mayor.

"I think so much of it, that I absolutely refuse the gendarmes, and I am going to start in an hour."

"Alone?"

"Alone."

"Monseigneur, you will not do it."

"There is on the mountain," replied the bishop, "a humble little commune, that I have not seen for three years; and they are good friends of mine, kind and honest peasants. They own one goat out of thirty that they pasture. They make pretty woolen thread of various colours, and they play their mountain airs upon small six-holed flutes. They need some one occasionally to tell them of the goodness of God. What would they say of a bishop who was afraid?"

"But, monseigneur, the brigands?"

"True," said the bishop, "I am thinking of that. You are right. I may meet them. They too must need some one to tell them of the goodness of God."

"Monseigneur, but it is a band! a pack of wolves!"

[1] Unless God protects a house, they who guard it watch in vain.

"Monsieur Mayor, perhaps Jesus has made me the keeper of that very flock. Who knows the ways of providence?"

"Monseigneur, they will rob you."

"I have nothing."

"They will kill you."

"A simple old priest who passes along muttering his prayer? No, no; what good would it do them?"

"Oh, my good sir, suppose you should meet them!"

"I should ask them for alms for my poor."

"Monseigneur, do not go. In the name of heaven! you are exposing your life."

"Monsieur Mayor," said the bishop, "I am not in the world to care for my life, but for souls."

He would not be dissuaded. He crossed the mountain on a mule, met no one, and arrived safe and sound among his "good friends" the shepherds. He remained there a fortnight, preaching, administering the holy rites, teaching and exhorting. When he was about to leave, he resolved to chant a Te Deum with pontifical ceremonies. But what could be done? there was no episcopal furniture. They could only place at his disposal a paltry village sacristy with a few old robes of worn-out damask, trimmed with imitation-galloon.

"No matter," said the bishop. "Monsieur le curé, at the sermon announce our Te Deum. That will take care of itself."

While they were in this embarrassment, a large chest was brought to the parsonage, and left for the bishop by two unknown horsemen, who immediately rode away. The chest was opened; it contained a cope of cloth of gold, a mitre ornamented with diamonds, an archbishop's cross, a magnificent crosier, all the pontifical raiment stolen a month before from the treasures of Our Lady of Embrun. In the chest was a paper on which were written these words: "*Cravatte to Monseigneur Bienvenu.*"

"I said that it would take care of itself," said the bishop. Then he added with a smile: "To him who is contented with a curé's surplice, God sends an archbishop's cope."

"Monseigneur," murmured the curé, with a shake of the head and a smile, "God—or the devil."

The bishop looked steadily upon the curé, and replied with authority: "God!"

As to what became of the "treasures" of the Cathedral of Embrun, it would embarrass us to be questioned on that point. There were among them very fine things, and very tempting, and very good to steal for the benefit of the unfortunate. Stolen they had already been by others. Half the work was done; it only remained to change the course of the theft, and to make it turn to the side of the poor. We can say nothing more on the subject. Except that there was found among the bishop's papers a rather obscure note, that reads as follows: "*The question is, whether this ought to be returned to the cathedral or to the hospital.*"

The senator heretofore referred to was an intelligent man, who had made his way in life with a directness of purpose which paid no attention to all those stumbling-blocks which constitute obstacles in men's path, known as conscience, sworn faith, justice, and duty; he had advanced straight to his object without once swerving in the line of his advancement and his interest. He was not a bad man at all, doing all the little kindnesses that he could to his sons, sons-in-law, and relatives generally, and even to his friends.

At some semi-official ceremony, Count * * * (this senator) and M. Myriel remained to dinner with the prefect. At dessert, the senator, a little elevated, though always dignified, exclaimed:

"Parbleu, Monsieur Bishop; let us talk. It is difficult for a senator and a bishop to look each other in the eye without winking. We are two augurs. I have a confession to make to you; I have my philosophy."

"And you are right," answered the bishop.

The senator, encouraged by this, proceeded:—

"Monsieur Bishop, the Jehovah hypothesis tires me. It is good for nothing except to produce people with scraggy bodies and empty heads. Down with this great All, who torments me! Hail, Zero! who leaves me quiet. My head is not turned with your Jesus, who preaches in every corn-field renunciation and self-sacrifice. It is the advice of a miser to beggars. Renunciation, for what? Self-sacrifice, to what? I do not see that one wolf immolates himself for the benefit of another wolf. Let us dwell, then, with nature. That man has another life, elsewhere, above, below, anywhere—I don't believe a single word of it. Ah! I am recommended to self-sacrifice and renunciation, that I should take care what I do; that I must break my head over questions of good and evil, justice and injustice. Why? Because I shall have to render an account for my acts. When? After death. What a fine dream! Did I exist before my birth? No. Shall I, after my death? No. What am I? A little dust, aggregated by an organism. I must eat or be eaten, and I choose to eat. Such is my philosophy. I tell you, Monsieur Bishop, I do not allow myself to be entangled with nonsense. But it is necessary there should be something for those who are below us, the bare-foots, knife-grinders, and other wretches. Legends are given them to swallow, about the soul, immortality, paradise, and the stars. They munch that; they spread it on their dry bread. He who has nothing besides, has the good God—that is good for the people."

The bishop clapped his hands.

"That is the idea," he exclaimed. "This materialism is an excellent thing, and truly marvellous; reject it who will. Ah! when one has it, he is a dupe no more; he does not stupidly allow himself to be exiled like Cato, or stoned like Stephen, or burnt alive like Joan of Arc. Those who have succeeded in procuring this admirable materialism have the happiness of feeling that they are irresponsible, and of thinking that they can devour everything in quietness—places, sinecures, honours, power rightly or wrongly acquired, lucrative recantations, useful treasons, savoury capitulations of conscience, and that they will enter their graves with their digestion completed. How agreeable it is! I do not say that for you, Monsieur Senator. Nevertheless, I cannot but felicitate you. You great lords have, you say, a philosophy of your own, for your special benefit—exquisite, refined, accessible to the rich alone; good with all sauces, admirably seasoning the pleasures of life. This philosophy is found at great depths, and brought up by special search. But you are good princes, and you are quite willing that the belief in the good God should be the philosophy of the people, much as goose with onions is the turkey with truffles of the poor."

A little while before, the bishop performed an act which the whole town thought far more perilous than his excursion across the mountains infested by the bandits.

In the country near D——, there was a man who lived alone. This man, to state the startling fact without preface, had been a member of the National Convention. His name was G——.

The little circle of D—— spoke of the conventionist with a certain sort of horror. A conventionist, think of it; that was in the time when folks thee-and-thoued one another, and said "citizen." This man came very near being a monster; he had not exactly voted for the execution of the king, but almost; he was half a regicide. But as he had not voted for the king's execution, he was not included in the sentence of exile, and could remain in France.

He lived about an hour's walk from the town, far from any hamlet or road, in a secluded ravine of a very wild valley. He had no neighbours or even passers-by. Since he had lived there the path which led to the place had become overgrown, and people spoke of it as of the house of a hangman.

At last, one day the news was circulated in the town that the young herdsboy who served the conventionist G—— in his retreat, had come for a doctor; that the old wretch was dying, that he was motionless, and could not live through the night. "Thank God!" added many.

The bishop took his cane, put on his overcoat, because his cassock was badly worn, as we have said, and besides the night wind was evidently rising, and set out.

The sun was setting; it had nearly touched the horizon when the bishop reached the accursed spot. He jumped over a ditch, cleared a hedge, made his way through a brush fence, found himself in a dilapidated garden, and after a bold advance across the open ground, suddenly, behind some high brushwood, he discovered the retreat.

It was a low, poverty-stricken hut, small and clean, with a little vine nailed up in front.

Before the door in an old chair on rollers, there sat a man with white hair, looking with smiling gaze upon the setting sun.

The young herdsboy stood near him, handing him a bowl of milk.

While the bishop was looking, the old man raised his voice.

"Thank you," he said, "I shall need nothing more"; and his smile changed from the sun to rest upon the boy.

The bishop stepped forward. At the sound of his footsteps the old man turned his head, and his face expressed as much surprise as one can feel after a long life.

"This is the first time since I have lived here," said he, "that I have had a visitor. Who are you, monsieur?"

"My name is Bienvenu-Myriel," the bishop replied.

The old man continued half-smiling. "Then you are my bishop?"

"Possibly."

"Come in, monsieur."

The conventionist extended his hand to the bishop, but he did not take it. He only said:

"I am glad to find that I have been misinformed. You do not appear to me very ill."

"Monsieur," replied the old man, "I shall soon be better."

He paused and said:

"I shall be dead in three hours."

Then he continued:

"I am something of a physician; I know the steps by which death approaches; yesterday my feet only were cold; to-day the cold has crept to my knees, now it has reached the waist; when it touches the heart, all will be over. The sunset is lovely, is it not? I should like to live until the dawn, but I know I have scarcely life for three hours. Be it so: I shall die in the starlight."

The old man turned towards the herdsboy:

"Little one, go to bed: thou didst watch the other night: thou art weary."

The child went into the hut.

The old man followed him with his eyes, and added, as if speaking to himself: "While he is sleeping, I shall die: the two slumbers keep fit company."

The bishop was not as much affected as he might have been: it was not his idea of godly death. This conventionist after all, this representative of the people, had been a power on the earth; and perhaps for the first time in his life the bishop felt himself in a humour to be severe.

"I congratulate you," he said, in a tone of reprimand. "At least you did not vote for the execution of the king."

The conventionist did not seem to notice the bitter emphasis placed upon the words "at least." The smile vanished from his face, and he replied:

"Do not congratulate me too much, monsieur; I did vote for the destruction of the tyrant."

And the tone of austerity confronted the tone of severity.

"What do you mean?" asked the bishop.

"I mean that man has a tyrant, Ignorance. I voted for the abolition of that tyrant. That tyrant has begotten royalty, which is authority springing from the False, while science is authority springing from the True. Man should be governed by science."

"And conscience," added the bishop.

"The same thing: conscience is innate knowledge."

The conventionist went on:

"As to Louis XVI.: I said no. I do not believe that I have the right to kill a man, but I feel it a duty to exterminate evil. I voted for the downfall of the tyrant; that is to say, for the abolition of prostitution for woman, of slavery for man, of night for the child. In voting for the republic I voted for that: I voted for fraternity, for harmony, for light. I assisted in casting down prejudices and errors: their downfall brings light! We caused the old world to fall; the old world, a vase of misery, reversed, becomes an urn of joy to the human race."

"Joy alloyed," said the bishop.

"You might say joy troubled, and, at present, after this fatal return of the blast which we call 1814, joy disappeared. Alas! the work was imperfect I admit; we demolished the ancient order of things physically, but not entirely in the idea. To destroy abuses is not enough; habits must be changed."

"You have demolished, but I distrust a demolition effected in anger!"

"Justice has its anger, Monsieur Bishop, and the wrath of justice is an element of progress. Whatever may be said, the French revolution is the greatest step in advance taken by mankind since the advent of Christ; incomplete it may be, but it is sublime. It made the waves of civilisation to flow over the earth; it was good. The French revolution is the consecration of humanity."

The bishop could not help murmuring: "Yes, '93!"

The conventionist raised himself in his chair.

"Ah! you are there! '93! I was expecting that. A cloud had been forming for fifteen hundred years; at the end of fifteen centuries it burst. You condemn the thunderbolt."

Without perhaps acknowledging it to himself, the bishop felt that he had been touched; however, he made the best of it, and replied:

"The judge speaks in the name of justice, the priest in the name of pity, which is only a more exalted justice. A thunderbolt should not be mistaken."

And he added, looking fixedly at the conventionist: "Louis XVII?"

"Louis XVII. Let us see! For whom do you weep?—for the innocent child? It is well; I weep with you. For the royal child? I ask time to reflect. To my view the brother of Cartouche, an innocent child, hung by a rope under his arms in the Place de Grève till he died, for the sole crime of being the brother of Cartouche, is a no less sad sight than the grandson of Louis XV., an innocent child, murdered in the tower of the Temple for the sole crime of being the grandson of Louis XV."

"Monsieur," said the bishop, "I dislike this coupling of names."

"Cartouche or Louis XV.; for which are you concerned?"

There was a moment of silence; the bishop regretted almost that he had come, and yet he felt strangely and inexplicably moved.

The conventionist resumed: "Oh, Monsieur Priest! you do not love the harshness of the truth, but Christ loved it. He took a scourge and purged the temple; his flashing whip was a rude speaker of truths. He was not pained at coupling the dauphin of Barabbas with the dauphin of Herod. Monsieur, innocence is its own crown! Innocence has only to act to be noble! She is as august in rags as in the fleur de lys."

"That is true," said the bishop, in a low tone.

"I repeat," continued the old man; "you have mentioned Louis XVII. Let us weep together for all the innocent, for all the martyrs, for all the children, for the low as well as for the high. I am one of them, but then, as I have told you, we must go further back than '93, and our tears must begin before Louis XVII. I will weep for the children of kings with you, if you will weep with me for the little ones of the people."

"I weep for all," said the bishop.

"Equally," exclaimed G——, "and if the balance inclines, let it be on the side of the people; they have suffered longer."

There was silence again, broken at last by the old man.

"Yes, Monsieur, it is for a long time that the people have been suffering, and then, sir, that is not all; why do you come to question me and to speak to me of Louis XVII.? I do not know you. You are a bishop, a prince of the church, one of those men who are covered with gold, with insignia, and with wealth, who have palaces, and who roll in your carriages in the name of Jesus Christ who went bare-footed. You are a prelate; rents, palaces, horses, valets, a good table, all the sensualities of life, you have these like all the rest, and you enjoy them like all the rest; very well, but that says too much or not enough; that does not enlighten me as to your intrinsic worth, you who come probably with the claim of bringing me wisdom. To whom am I speaking? Who are you?"

The bishop replied with mildness:

"Monsieur, be it so. But explain to me how my palace and my lackeys prove that pity is not a virtue, that kindness is not a duty, and that '93 was not inexorable?"

The old man passed his hand across his forehead as if to dispel a cloud.

"Before answering you," said he, "I beg your pardon. I have done wrong, monsieur; you are in my house, you are my guest. I owe you courtesy. You are discussing my ideas; it is fitting that I confine myself to combating your reasoning. Your riches and your enjoyments are advantages that I have over you in the debate, but it is not in good taste to avail myself of them. I promise you to use them no more."

"I thank you," said the bishop.

The conventionist began to gasp; the agonising asthma, which mingles with the latest breath, made his voice broken; nevertheless, his soul yet appeared perfectly lucid in his eyes. He continued:

"Let us have a few more words here and there—I would like it. Outside of the revolution which, taken as a whole, is an immense human affirmation, '93, alas! is a reply. You think it inexorable, but the whole monarchy, monsieur? Monsieur, monsieur, forget not this; the French revolution had its reasons. Its wrath will be pardoned by the future; its result is a better world. From its most terrible blows comes a caress for the human race. I must be brief. I must stop. I have too good a cause; and I am dying."

And, ceasing to look at the bishop, the old man completed his idea in these few tranquil words:

"Yes, the brutalities of progress are called revolutions. When they are over, this is recognised: that the human race has been harshly treated, but that it has advanced."

The conventionist thought that he had borne down successively one after the other all the interior intrenchments of the bishop. There was one left, however, and from this, the last resource of Monseigneur Bienvenu's resistance, came forth these words:

"Progress ought to believe in God. The good cannot have an impious servitor. An atheist is an evil leader of the human race."

The old representative of the people looked up into the sky, raised his finger towards heaven, and said:

"The infinite exists. It is there. If the infinite had no *me*, the *me* would be its limit; it would not be the infinite; in other words, it would not be. But it is. Then it has a *me*. This *me* of the infinite is God."

The dying man pronounced these last words as if he saw some one. When he ceased, his eyes closed. The effort had exhausted him. It was evident that he had lived through in one minute the few hours that remained to him. The last moment was at hand.

The bishop perceived it, time was pressing. He drew closer to the dying man.

"This hour is the hour of God. Do you not think it would be a source of regret, if we should have met in vain?"

The conventionist re-opened his eyes.

"Monsieur Bishop," said he, with a deliberation which perhaps came still more from the dignity of his soul than from the ebb of his strength, "I have passed my life in meditation, study, and contemplation. I was sixty years old when my country called me, and ordered me to take part in her affairs. I obeyed. There were abuses, I fought them; there were tyrannies, I destroyed them; there were rights and principles, I proclaimed and confessed them. I was not rich; I am poor. I was one of the masters of the state, the vaults of the bank were piled with specie, so that we had to strengthen the walls or they would have fallen under the weight of gold and of silver; I dined in the Rue de l'Arbre-Sec at twenty-two sous for the meal. I succoured the oppressed, I solaced the suffering. True, I tore the drapery from the altar; but it was to staunch the wounds of the country. I have, on occasion, protected my own adversaries, your friends. There is at Peteghem in Flanders, at the very place where the Merovingian kings had their summer palace, a monastery of Urbanists, the Abbey of Sainte Claire in Beaulieu, which I saved in 1793; I have done my duty according to my strength, and the good that I could. After which I was hunted, hounded, pursued, persecuted, slandered, railed at, spit upon, cursed, proscribed. For many years now, with my white hairs, I have perceived that many people believed they had a right to despise me. Now I am eighty-six years old; I am about to die. What have you come to ask of me?"

"Your benediction," said the bishop. And he fell upon his knees.

This "pastoral visit" was of course an occasion for criticism. One day a dowager addressed this sally to him. "Monseigneur, people ask when your Grandeur will have the red bonnet." "Oh! ho! that is a high colour," replied the bishop. "Luckily those who despise it in a bonnet, venerate it in a hat."

We should be very much deceived if we supposed from this that Monseigneur Bienvenu was "a philosopher bishop," or "a patriot curé." His meeting, which we might almost call his communion with the conventionist G——, left him in a state of astonishment which rendered him still more charitable; that was all.

Some time after the elevation of M. Myriel to the episcopacy, the emperor made him a baron of the empire. Called by Napoleon to the synod of the bishops of France and Italy, convoked at Paris, M. Myriel was one of the ninety-five bishops who were present. But he attended only one sitting. Bishop of a mountain diocese, living in rusticity and privation, he seemed to bring among these eminent personages ideas that changed the temperature of the synod. He returned very soon to D——. When asked about this sudden return, he answered: "*I annoyed them. Those prelates are princes. I am only a poor peasant bishop.*"

The fact is, that he was disliked. Among other strange things, he had dropped the remark one evening when he happened to be at the house of one of his colleagues of the highest rank: "What fine clocks! fine carpets! fine liveries! This must be very uncomfortable. Oh! how unwilling I should be to have all these superfluities crying for ever in my ears: 'There are people who hunger! there are people who are cold! there are poor! there are poor!' "

II. JEAN VALJEAN RETURNS

AN HOUR BEFORE SUNSET, on the evening of a day in the beginning of October, 1815, a man travelling afoot entered the little town of D——. It would have been hard to find a passer-by more wretched in appearance. He was a man of middle height, stout and hardy, in the strength of maturity; he might have been forty-six or seven. A slouched leather cap half hid his face, bronzed by the sun and wind, and dripping with sweat. His shaggy breast was seen through the coarse yellow shirt which at the neck was fastened by a small silver anchor; he wore a cravat twisted like a rope; coarse blue trousers, worn and shabby, white on one knee, and with holes in the other; an old ragged grey blouse, patched on one side with a piece of green cloth sewed with twine: upon his back was a well-filled knapsack, strongly buckled and quite new. In his hand he carried an enormous knotted stick: his stockingless feet were in hobnailed shoes; his hair was cropped and his beard long.

The sweat, the heat, his long walk, and the dust, added an indescribable meanness to his tattered appearance.

This man must have walked all day long; for he appeared very weary. Some women of the old city which is at the lower part of the town, had seen him stop under the trees of the boulevard Gassendi, and drink at the fountain which is at the end of the promenade. He must have been very thirsty, for some children who followed him, saw him stop not two hundred steps further on and drink again at the fountain in the market-place.

When he reached the corner of the Rue Poichevert he turned to the left and went towards the mayor's office. He went in, and a quarter of an hour afterwards he came out.

There was then in D——, a good inn called *La Croix de Colbas*. The traveller turned his steps towards this inn, and went at once into the kitchen, which opened out of the street. All the ranges were fuming, and a great fire was burning briskly in the chimney-place. Mine host, who was at the same time head cook, was going from the fire-place to the sauce-pans, very busy superintending an excellent dinner for some wagoners who were laughing and talking noisily in the next room. Whoever has travelled knows that nobody lives better than wagoners. A fat marmot, flanked by white partridges and goose, was turning on a long spit before the fire; upon the ranges were cooking two large carps from Lake Lauzet, and a trout from Lake Alloz.

The host, hearing the door open, and a new-comer enter, said, without raising his eyes from his ranges—

"What will monsieur have?"

"Something to eat and lodging."

"Nothing more easy," said mine host, but on turning his head and taking an observation of the traveller, he added, "for pay."

The man drew from his pocket a large leather purse, and answered,

"I have money."

"Then," said mine host, "I am at your service."

The man put his purse back into his pocket, took off his knapsack and put it down hard by the door, and holding his stick in his hand, sat down on a low stool by the fire. D—— being in the mountains, the evenings of October are cold there.

However, as the host passed backwards and forwards, he kept a careful eye on the traveller.

"Is dinner almost ready?" said the man.

"Directly," said mine host.

While the new-comer was warming himself with his back turned, the worthy innkeeper took a pencil from his pocket, and then tore off the corner of an old paper which he pulled from a little table near the window. On the margin he wrote a line or two, folded it, and handed the scrap of paper to a child, who appeared to serve him as lackey and scullion at the same time. The innkeeper whispered a word to the boy and he ran off in the direction of the mayor's office.

The traveller saw nothing of this.

He asked a second time: "Is dinner ready?"

"Yes; in a few moments," said the host.

The boy came back with the paper. The host read with attention, then thought for a moment. Then he took a step towards the traveller, who seemed drowned in troublous thought.

"Monsieur," said he, "I cannot receive you."

The traveller half rose from his seat.

"Why? Are you afraid I shall not pay you, or do you want me to pay in advance? I have money, I tell you."

"It is not that."

"What then?"

"I have no room."

"Well, put me in the stable," quietly replied the man.

"I cannot."

"Why?"

"Because the horses take all the room."

"Well," responded the man, "a corner in the garret; a truss of straw: we will see about that after dinner."

"I cannot give you any dinner."

This declaration, made in a measured but firm tone, appeared serious to the traveller. He got up.

"Ah, bah! but I am dying with hunger. I have walked since sunrise; I have travelled twelve leagues. I will pay, and I want something to eat."

"I have nothing," said the host.

The man burst into a laugh, and turned towards the fire-place and the ranges.

"Nothing! and all that?"

"All that is engaged."

"By whom?"

"By those persons, the wagoners."

"How many are there of them?"

"Twelve."

"There is enough there for twenty."

"They have engaged and paid for it all in advance."

The man sat down again and said, without raising his voice: "I am at an inn. I am hungry, and I shall stay."

The host bent down his ear, and said in a voice which made him tremble: "Go away!"

At these words the traveller, who was bent over, poking some embers in the fire with the iron-shod end of his stick, turned suddenly around, and opened his mouth, as if to reply, when the host, looking steadily at him, added in the same low tone: "Stop, no more of that. Shall I tell you your name? your name is Jean Valjean, now shall I tell you *who* you are? When I saw you enter, I suspected something. I sent to the mayor's office, and here is the reply. Can you read?" So saying, he held towards him the open paper, which had just come from the mayor. The man cast a look upon it; the innkeeper, after a short silence, said: "It is my custom to be polite to all: Go!"

The man bowed his head, picked up his knapsack, and went out.

He took the principal street; he walked at random, slinking near the houses like a sad and humiliated man: he did not once turn around. If he had turned, he would have seen the innkeeper of the *Croix de Colbas*, standing in his doorway with all his guests, and the passers-by gathered about him, speaking excitedly, and pointing him out; and from the looks of fear and distrust which were exchanged, he would have guessed that before long his arrival would be the talk of the whole town.

The good inn was closed against him: he sought a tavern in the Rue Chaffaut.

The traveller did not dare to enter by the street door; he slipped into the court, stopped again, then timidly raised the latch, and pushed open the door.

"Who is it?" said the host.

"One who wants supper and a bed."

"All right: here you can sup and sleep."

He seated himself near the fireplace and stretched his feet out towards the fire, half dead with fatigue: an inviting odour came from the pot. All that could be seen of his face under his slouched cap assumed a vague appearance of comfort, which tempered the sorrowful aspect given him by long-continued suffering.

His profile was strong, energetic, and sad; a physiognomy strangely marked: at first it appeared humble, but it soon became severe. His eye shone beneath his eyebrows like a fire beneath a thicket.

However, one of the men at the table had put up his horse at the inn before entering the tavern of the Rue de Chaffaut. He beckoned to the tavern-keeper to come to him; they exchanged a few words in a low voice.

The tavern-keeper returned to the fire, and said harshly:

"You are going to clear out from here!"

The stranger turned round and said mildly,

"Ah! Do you know?"

"Yes."

"They sent me away from the other inn."

"And we turn you out of this."

"Where would you have me go?"

"Somewhere else."

The man took up his stick and knapsack, and went off. As he went out, some children who had followed him from the *Croix de Colbas*, and seemed to be waiting for him, threw stones at him. He turned angrily and threatened them with his stick, and they scattered like a flock of birds.

He passed the prison: an iron chain hung from the door attached to a bell. He rang.

The grating opened.

"Monsieur Turnkey," said he, taking off his cap respectfully, "will you open and let me stay here to-night?"

A voice answered:

"A prison is not a tavern: get yourself arrested and we will open."

The grating closed.

He went into a small street where there are many gardens, some enclosed only by hedges. Among them he saw a pretty little one-story house, where there was a light in the window. He looked in. It was a large whitewashed room, with a bed draped with calico, and a cradle in the corner. A table was set in the centre of the room; a brass lamp lighted the coarse white table-cloth; a tin mug full of wine shone like silver, and the brown soup-dish was smoking. At this table sat a man about forty years old, with a joyous, open countenance, who was trotting a little child upon his knee. Near by him a young woman was suckling another child; the father was laughing, the child was laughing, and the mother was smiling.

The traveller rapped faintly on the window.

No one heard him. He rapped a second time.

He heard the woman say, "Husband, I think I hear some one rap."

"No," replied the husband.

He rapped a third time. The husband got up, took the lamp, and opened the door.

He was a tall man, half peasant, half mechanic. He wore a large leather apron that reached to his left shoulder, and formed a pocket containing a hammer, a red handkerchief, a powder-horn, and all sorts of things which the girdle held up.

"Monsieur," said the traveller, "I beg your pardon; for pay can you give me a plate of soup and a corner of the shed in your garden to sleep in? Tell me; can you, for pay?"

"Who are you?" demanded the master of the house.

The man replied: "I have come from Puy-Moisson; I have walked all day; I have come twelve leagues. Can you, if I pay?"

"I wouldn't refuse to lodge any proper person who would pay," said the peasant; "but why do you not go to the inn?"

"There is no room."

"Bah! That is not possible. It is neither a fair nor a market-day."

The traveller replied hesitatingly: "I don't know; he didn't take me."

"Have you been to that place in the Rue Chaffaut?"

The embarrassment of the stranger increased; he stammered: "They didn't take me either."

The peasant's face assumed an expression of distrust: he looked over the new-comer from head to foot, and suddenly exclaimed, with a sort of shudder: "Are you the man!"

He looked again at the stranger, stepped back, put the lamp on the table, and took down his gun.

His wife started up, and, clasping her two children, precipitately took refuge behind her husband. The man advanced to the door and said:

"Get out!"

"For pity's sake, a glass of water."

"A gun shot," said the peasant, and then he closed the door violently, and the man heard two heavy bolts drawn. A moment afterwards the window-shutters were shut, and noisily barred.

Night came on apace; the cold Alpine winds were blowing; by the light of the expiring day the stranger perceived in one of the gardens which fronted the street a kind of hut which seemed to be made of turf. He was suffering both from cold and hunger. He had resigned himself to the latter; but there at least was a shelter from the cold. He got down and crawled into the hut. It was warm there and he found a good bed of straw. He rested a moment motionless from fatigue; then, as his knapsack on his back troubled him, and it would make a good pillow, he began to unbuckle the straps. Just then he heard a ferocious growling and looking up saw the head of an enormous bull-dog at the opening of the hut.

It was a dog-kennel!

He was himself vigorous and formidable; seizing his stick, he made a shield of his knapsack, and got out of the hut as best he could, but not without enlarging the rents of his already tattered garments. He threw himself rather than seated himself on a stone, and it appears that some one who was passing heard him exclaim, "I am not even a dog!"

Then he arose, and began to tramp again, taking his way out of the town, hoping to find some tree or haystack beneath which he could shelter. When he thought he was far away from all human habitation he raised his eyes, and looked about him inquiringly. He was in a field: before him was a low hillock covered with stubble, which after the harvest looks like a shaved head. The sky was very dark; it was not simply the darkness of night, but there were very low clouds, which seemed to rest upon the hills, and covered the whole heavens. There are moments when nature appears hostile.

He retraced his steps; on passing by the Cathedral square, he shook his fist at the church. At the corner of this square stands a printing-office; exhausted with fatigue, and hoping for nothing better, he lay down on a stone bench in front of this printing-office.

Just then an old woman came out of the church. She saw the man lying there in the dark and said:

"What are you doing there, my friend?"

He replied harshly, and with anger in his tone:

"You see, my good woman, I am going to sleep."

The good woman, who really merited the name, was Madame la Marquise de R——.

"Upon the bench?" said she.

"For nineteen years I have had a wooden mattress," said the man; "tonight I have a stone one."

"You have been a soldier?"

"Yes, my good woman, a soldier."

"Why don't you go to the inn?"

"Because I have no money."

"Alas!" said Madame de R——, "I have only four sous in my purse."

"Give them then." The man took the four sous, and Madame de R—— continued:

"You cannot find lodging for so little in an inn. But have you tried? You cannot pass the night so. You must be cold and hungry. They should give you lodging for charity."

"I have knocked at every door."

"Well, what then?"

"Everybody has driven me away."

The good woman touched the man's arm and pointed out to him, on the other side of the square, a little low house beside the bishop's palace.

"You have knocked at every door?" she asked.

"Yes."

"Have you knocked at that one there?"

"No."

"Knock there."

That evening, after his walk in the town, the Bishop of D—— remained quite late in his room. He was busy with his great work on Duty, which unfortunately is left incomplete. At eight o'clock he was still at work, writing with some inconvenience on little slips of paper, with a large book open on his knees, when Madame Magloire, as usual, came in to take the silver from the panel near the bed. A moment after, the bishop, knowing that the table was laid, and that his sister was perhaps waiting, closed his book and went into the dining-room.

This dining-room was an oblong apartment, with a fireplace, a door upon the street, and a window opening into the garden.

Madame Magloire had just finished placing the plates.

While she was arranging the table, she was talking with Mademoiselle Baptistine.

One can readily fancy these two women, both past their sixtieth year: Madame Magloire, small, fat, and quick in her movements; Mademoiselle Baptistine, sweet, thin, fragile, a little taller than her brother, wore a silk puce colour dress, in the style of 1806, which she had bought at that time in Paris, and which still lasted her. To borrow a common mode of expression, which has the merit of saying in a single word what a page would hardly express, Madame Magloire had the air of a peasant, and Mademoiselle Baptistine that of a lady.

Just as the bishop entered, Madame Magloire was speaking with some warmth. She was talking upon a familiar subject, the means of fastening the front door.

It seems that while Madame Magloire was out making provision for supper, she had heard in sundry places talk that an ill-favoured runaway, a suspicious vagabond, had arrived and was lurking somewhere in the town. It was the part of every one to shut up, bolt, and bar his house properly, and *secure his door thoroughly.*

Madame Magloire dwelt upon these last words; but the bishop was thinking of something else. He did not hear a word of what was let fall by Madame Magloire, and she repeated it. Then Mademoiselle Baptistine, endeavouring to satisfy Madame Magloire without displeasing her brother, ventured to say timidly:

"Brother, do you hear what Madame Magloire says?"

"I heard something of it indistinctly," said the bishop. Then turning his chair half round, putting his hands on his knees, and raising towards the old servant his cordial and good-humoured face, which the firelight shone upon, he said: "Well, well! what is the matter? Are we in any great danger?"

Then Madame Magloire began her story again, unconsciously exaggerating it a little. It appeared that a bare-footed gipsy man, a sort of dangerous beggar, was in the town. A man with a knapsack and a rope, and a terrible-looking face.

"Indeed!" said the bishop.

This readiness to question her encouraged Madame Magloire; it seemed to indicate that the bishop was really well-nigh alarmed. She continued triumphantly: "Yes, monseigneur; it is true. There will something happen to-night in the town: everybody says so. If one goes out, it is dark as a pocket. And I say, monseigneur, and mademoiselle says also—"

"Me?" interrupted the sister; "I say nothing. Whatever my brother does is well done."

Madame Magloire went on as if she had not heard this protestation:

"We say that this house is not safe at all; and if monseigneur will permit me, I will go and tell Paulin Musebois, the locksmith, to come and put the old bolts in the door again; they are there, and it will take but a minute. I say we must have bolts, were it only for to-night."

At this moment there was a violent knock on the door.

"Come in!" said the bishop.

The door opened quickly, quite wide, as if pushed by some one boldly and with energy.

A man entered.

He came in, took one step, and paused, leaving the door open behind him. He had his knapsack on his back, his stick in his hand, and a rough, hard, tired, and fierce look in his eyes.

Madame Magloire had not even the strength to scream. She stood trembling with her mouth open.

The bishop looked upon the man with a tranquil eye.

As he was opening his mouth to speak, the man, leaning with both hands on his club, glanced from one to another in turn, and said in a loud voice:

"See here! My name is Jean Valjean. I am a convict; I have been nineteen years in the galleys. Four days ago I was set free, and started for Pontarlier, which is my destination; during those four days I have walked from Toulon. To-day I have walked twelve leagues. When I reached this place this evening I went to an inn, and they sent me away on account of my yellow passport, which I had shown at the mayor's office, as was necessary. I went to another inn; they said: 'Get out!' It was the same with one as with another; nobody would have me. I went to the prison, and the turnkey would not let me in. I crept into a dog-kennel, the dog bit me, and drove me away as if he had been a man; you would have said that he knew who I was. I went into the fields to sleep beneath the stars: there were no stars;

I thought it would rain, and there was no good God to stop the drops, so I came back to the town to get the shelter of some doorway. There in the square I lay down upon a stone; a good woman showed me your house, and said: 'Knock there!' I have knocked. What is this place? Are you an inn? I have money; my savings, one hundred and nine francs and fifteen sous which I have earned in the galleys by my work for nineteen years. I will pay. What do I care? I have money. I am very tired—twelve leagues on foot, and I am so hungry. Can I stay?"

"Madame Magloire," said the bishop, "put on another plate."

The man took three steps, and came near the lamp which stood on the table. "Stop," he exclaimed; as if he had not been understood, "not that, did you understand me? I am a galley-slave—a convict—I am just from the galleys." He drew from his pocket a large sheet of yellow paper, which he unfolded. "There is my passport, yellow as you see. That is enough to have me kicked out wherever I go. Will you read it? I know how to read, I do. I learned in the galleys. There is a school there for those who care for it. See, here is what they have put in the passport: 'Jean Valjean, a liberated convict, native of ——,' you don't care for that, 'has been nineteen years in the galleys; five years for burglary; fourteen years for having attempted four times to escape. This man is very dangerous.' There you have it! Everybody has thrust me out; will you receive me? Is this an inn? Can you give me something to eat, and a place to sleep? Have you a stable?"

"Madame Magloire," said the bishop, "put some sheets on the bed in the alcove."

Madame Magloire went out to fulfil her orders.

The bishop turned to the man:

"Monsieur, sit down and warm yourself: we are going to take supper presently, and your bed will be made ready while you sup."

At last the man quite understood; his face, the expression of which till then had been gloomy and hard, now expressed stupefaction, doubt, and joy.

"True? What! You will keep me? you won't drive me away? a convict! You call me *Monsieur* and don't say 'Get out, dog!' as everybody else does. I thought that you would send me away, so I told first off who I am. Oh! the fine woman who sent me here! I shall have a supper! a bed like other people with mattress and sheets—a bed! It is nineteen years that I have not slept on a bed. You are really willing that I should stay? You are good people! Besides I have money: I will pay well. I beg your pardon, Monsieur Innkeeper, what is your name? I will pay all you say. You are a fine man. You are an innkeeper, an't you?"

"I am a priest who lives here," said the bishop.

"A priest," said the man. "Oh, noble priest! Then you do not ask any money? You are the curé, an't you? the curé of this big church? Yes, that's it. How stupid I am; I didn't notice your cap."

While speaking, he had deposited his knapsack and stick in the corner, replaced his passport in his pocket, and sat down. Mademoiselle Baptistine looked at him pleasantly. He continued:

"You are humane, Monsieur Curé; you don't despise me. A good priest is a good thing. Then you don't want me to pay you?"

"No," said the bishop, "keep your money. How much have you? You said a hundred and nine francs, I think."

"And fifteen sous," added the man.

"One hundred and nine francs and fifteen sous. And how long did it take you to earn that?"

"Nineteen years."

"Nineteen years!"

The bishop sighed deeply.

The man continued: "I have all my money yet. In four days I have spent only twenty-five sous which I earned by unloading wagons at Grasse. As you are an abbé, I must tell you, we have an almoner in the galleys. And then one day I saw a bishop; monseigneur, they called him. He said mass in the centre of the place on an altar; he had a pointed gold thing on his head, that shone in the sun; it was noon. We could not see him well. He spoke to us, but he was not near enough, we did not understand him. That is what a bishop is."

While he was talking, the bishop shut the door, which he had left wide open.

Madame Magloire brought in a plate and set it on the table.

"Madame Magloire," said the bishop, "put this plate as near the fire as you can." Then turning towards his guest, he added: "The night wind is raw in the Alps; you must be cold, monsieur."

Every time he said this word monsieur, with his gently solemn, and heartily hospitable voice, the man's countenance lighted up. *Monsieur* to a convict, is a glass of water to a man dying of thirst at sea. Ignominy thirsts for respect.

"The lamp," said the bishop, "gives a very poor light."

Madame Magloire understood him, and going to his bedchamber, took from the mantel the two silver candlesticks, lighted the candles, and placed them on the table.

"Monsieur Curé," said the man, "you are good; you don't despise me. You take me into your house; you light your candles for me, and I hav'n't hid from you where I come from, and how miserable I am."

The bishop, who was sitting near him, touched his hand gently and said: "You need not tell me who you are. This is not my house; it is the house of Christ. I tell you, who are a traveller, that you are more at home here than I; whatever is here is yours. What need have I to know your name? Besides, before you told me, I knew it."

The man opened his eyes in astonishment:

"Really? You knew my name?"

"Yes," answered the bishop, "your name is my brother."

"Stop, stop, Monsieur Curé," exclaimed the man. "I was famished when I came in, but you are so kind that now I don't know what I am; that is all gone."

Meantime Madame Magloire had served up supper; it consisted of soup made of water, oil, bread, and salt, a little pork, a scrap of mutton, a few figs, a green cheese, and a large loaf of rye bread. She had, without asking, added to the usual dinner of the bishop a bottle of fine old Mauves wine.

The bishop's countenance was lighted up with this expression of pleasure, peculiar to hospitable natures. "To supper!" he said briskly, as was his habit when he had a guest. He seated the man at his right. Mademoiselle Baptistine, perfectly quiet and natural, took her place at his left.

The bishop said the blessing, and then served the soup himself, according to his usual custom. The man fell to, eating greedily.

Suddenly the bishop said: "It seems to me something is lacking on the table."

The fact was, that Madame Magloire had set out only the three plates which were necessary. Now it was the custom of the house, when the bishop had any one to supper, to set all six of the silver plates on the table, an innocent display. This graceful appearance of luxury was a sort of childlikeness which was full of charm in this gentle but austere household, which elevated poverty to dignity.

Madame Magloire understood the remark; without a word she went out, and a moment afterwards the three plates for which the bishop had asked were shining on the cloth, symmetrically arranged before each of the three guests.

In order to give an idea of what passed at this table, we cannot do better than to transcribe here a passage in a letter from Mademoiselle Baptistine in which the conversation between the convict and the bishop is related with charming minuteness.

. . . .

"This man paid no attention to any one. He ate with the voracity of a starving man. After supper, however, he said:

" 'Monsieur Curé, all this is too good for me, but I must say that the wagoners, who wouldn't have me eat with them, live better than you.'

"Between us, the remark shocked me a little. My brother answered:

" 'They are more fatigued than I am.'

" 'No,' responded this man; 'they have more money. You are poor, I can see. Perhaps you are not a curé even. Are you only a curé? Ah! if God is just, you well deserve to be a curé.'

" 'God is more than just,' said my brother.

"A moment after he added:

" 'Monsieur Jean Valjean, you are going to Pontarlier?'

" 'A compulsory journey.'

"I am pretty sure that is the expression the man used. Then he continued:

" 'I must be on the road to-morrow morning at daybreak. It is a hard journey. If the nights are cold, the days are warm.'

" 'You are going,' said my brother, 'to a fine country. During the revolution, when my family was ruined, I took refuge first in Franche-Comté, and supported myself there for some time by the labour of my hands. There I found plenty of work, and had only to make my choice. There are paper-mills, tanneries, distilleries, oil-factories, large clock-making establishments, steel manufactories, copper foundries, at least twenty iron foundries.' Then he broke off and addressed me:

" 'Dear sister, have we not relatives in that part of the country?'

"I answered:

" 'We had; among others Monsieur Lucenet, who was captain of the gates at Pontarlier under the old régime.'

" 'Yes,' replied my brother, 'but in '93, no one had relatives; every one depended upon his hands. I laboured. They have, in the region of Pontarlier, where you are going, Monsieur Valjean, a business which is quite patriarchal and very charming, sister. It is their dairies, which they call *fruitières*.'

"Then my brother, while helping this man at table, explained to him in detail what these *fruitières* were;—that they were divided into two kinds: the *great barns*, belonging to the rich, and where there are forty or fifty cows, which produce from seven to eight thousand cheeses during the summer; and the associated *fruitières*, which belong to the poor; these comprise the peasants inhabiting the mountains, who put their cows into a common herd, and divide the proceeds.

"My brother gave him all these details as if he wished that this man should understand, without advising him directly, and abruptly, that it would be an asylum for him. One thing struck me. This man was what I have told you. Well! my brother, during the supper, and during the entire evening, with the exception of a few words about Jesus, when he entered, did not say a word which could recall to this man who he himself was, nor indicate to him who my brother was. He thought, doubtless, that this man, who called himself Jean Valjean, had his wretchedness too constantly before his mind; that it was best not to distress him by referring to it, and to make him think, if it were only for a moment, that he was a common person like any one else, by treating him thus in the ordinary way. Is not this really understanding charity? and is it not the wisest sympathy, when a man has a suffering point, not to touch upon it at all? It seems to me that this was my brother's inmost thought. At any rate, he took supper with this Jean Valjean with the same air and manner that he would have supped with Monsieur Gédéon, the provost, or with the curé of the parish."

After having said good-night to his sister, Monseigneur Bienvenu took one of the silver candlesticks from the table, handed the other to his guest, and said to him:

"Monsieur, I will show you to your room."

As may have been understood from what has been said before, the house was so arranged that one could reach the alcove in the oratory only by passing through the bishop's sleeping chamber. Just as they were passing through this room Madame Magloire was putting up the silver in the cupboard at the head of the bed. It was the last thing she did every night before going to bed.

The bishop left his guest in the alcove, before a clean white bed.

"Come," said the bishop, "a good night's rest to you: to-morrow morning, before you go, you shall have a cup of warm milk from our cows."

"Thank you, Monsieur l'Abbé," said the man.

Scarcely had he pronounced these words of peace, when suddenly he made a singular motion which would have chilled the two good women of the house with horror, had they witnessed it. Even now it is hard for us to understand what impulse he obeyed at that moment. Did he intend to give a warning or to throw out a menace? Or was he simply obeying a sort of instinctive impulse, obscure even to himself? He turned abruptly towards the old man, crossed his arms, and casting a wild look upon his host, exclaimed in a harsh voice:

"Ah, now, indeed! You lodge me in your house, as near you as that!"

He checked himself, and added, with a laugh, in which there was something horrible:

"Have you reflected upon it? Who tells you that I am not a murderer?"

The bishop responded:

"God will take care of that."

Then with gravity, moving his lips like one praying or talking to himself, he raised two fingers of his right hand and blessed the man, who, however, did not bow; and without turning his head or looking behind him, went into his chamber.

When the alcove was occupied, a heavy serge curtain was drawn in the oratory, concealing the altar. Before this curtain the bishop knelt as he passed out, and offered a short prayer.

As to the man, he was so completely exhausted that he did not even avail himself of the clean white sheets; he blew out the candle with his nostril, after the manner of convicts, and fell on the bed, dressed as he was, into a sound sleep.

Jean Valjean was born of a poor peasant family of Brie. In his childhood he had not been taught to read: when he was grown up, he chose the occupation of a pruner at Faverolles. His mother's name was Jeanne Mathieu, his father's Jean Valjean or Vlajean, probably a nickname, a contraction of *Voilà Jean.*

He had lost his parents when very young. His mother died of malpractice in a milkfever: his father, a pruner before him, was killed by a fall from a tree. Jean Valjean now had but one relative left, his sister, a widow with seven children, girls and boys. This sister had brought up Jean Valjean, and, as long as her husband lived, she had taken care of her younger brother. Her husband died, leaving the eldest of these children eight, the youngest one year old. Jean Valjean had just reached his twenty-fifth year: he took the father's place, and, in his turn, supported the sister who reared him. His youth was spent in rough and ill-recompensed labour: he never was known to have a sweetheart; he had not time to be in love.

At night he came in weary and ate his soup without saying a word. While he was eating, his sister, *Mère Jeanne*, frequently took from his porringer the best of his meal; a bit of meat, a slice of pork, the heart of the cabbage, to give to one of her children. He went on eating, his head bent down nearly into the soup, his long hair falling over his dish, hiding his eyes, he did not seem to notice anything that was done. At Faverolles, not far from the house of the Valjeans, there was on the other side of the road a farmer's wife named Marie Claude; the Valjean children, who were always famished, sometimes went in their mother's name to borrow a pint of milk, which they would drink behind a hedge, or in some corner of the lane, snatching away the pitcher so greedily one from another, that the little girls would spill it upon their aprons and their necks; if their mother had known of this exploit she would have punished the delinquents severely. Jean Valjean, rough and grumbler as he was, paid Marie Claude; their mother never knew it, and so the children escaped.

He earned in the pruning season eighteen sous a day: after that he hired out as a reaper, workman, teamster, or labourer. He did whatever he could find to do. His sister worked also, but what could she do with seven little children? It was a sad group, which misery was grasping and closing upon, little by little. There was a very severe winter; Jean had no work, the family had no bread; literally, no bread, and seven children.

One Sunday night, Maubert Isabeau, the baker on the Place de l'Eglise, in Faverolles, was just going to bed when he heard a violent blow against the barred window of his shop. He got down in time to see an arm thrust through the aperture made by the blow of a fist on the glass. The arm seized a loaf of bread and took it out. Isabeau rushed out; the thief used his legs valiantly; Isabeau pursued him and caught him. The thief had thrown away the bread, but his arm was still bleeding. It was Jean Valjean.

All that happened in 1795. Jean Valjean was brought before the tribunals of the time for "burglary at night, in an inhabited house." He had a gun which he used as well as any marksman in the world, and was something of a poacher, which hurt him, there being a natural prejudice against poachers. Jean Valjean was found guilty: the terms of the code were explicit. Jean Valjean was sentenced to five years in the galleys.

On the 22nd of April, 1796, a great chain was riveted at the Bicêtre. Jean Valjean was a part of this chain. While they were with heavy hammer-strokes behind his head riveting the bolt of his iron collar, he was weeping. The tears choked his words, and he only succeeded in saying from time to time: "*I was a pruner at Faverolles.*" Then sobbing as he was, he raised his right hand and lowered it seven times, as if he was touching seven heads of unequal height, and at this gesture one could guess that whatever he had done, had been to feed and clothe seven little children.

He was taken to Toulon, at which place he arrived after a journey of twenty-seven days, on a cart, the chain still about his neck. At Toulon he was dressed in a red blouse, all his past life was effaced, even to his name. He was no longer Jean Valjean: he was Number 24,601. What became of the sister? What became of the seven children? Who troubled himself about that?

Near the end of his fourth year, his chance of liberty came to Jean Valjean. His comrades helped him as they always do in that dreary place, and he escaped. He wandered two days in freedom through the fields; if it is freedom to be hunted, to turn your head each moment, to tremble at the least noise, to be afraid of everything, of the smoke of a chimney, the passing of a man, the baying of a dog, the gallop of a horse, the striking of a clock, of the day because you see, and of the night because you do not; of the road, of the path, the bush, of sleep. During the evening of the second day he was retaken; he had neither eaten nor slept for thirty-six hours. The maritime tribunal extended his sentence three years for this attempt, which made eight.

In the sixth year his turn of escape came again; he tried it, but failed again. He did not answer at roll-call, and the alarm cannon was fired. At night the people of the vicinity discovered him hidden beneath the keel of a vessel on the stocks; he resisted the galley guard which seized him. Escape and resistance. This the provisions of the special code punished by an addition of five years, two with the double chain, thirteen years. The tenth year his turn came round again; he made another attempt with no better success. Three years for this new attempt. Sixteen years. And finally, I think it was in the thirteenth year, he made yet another, and was retaken after an absence of only four hours. Three years for these four hours. Nineteen years. In October 1815, he was set at large: he had entered in 1796 for having broken a pane of glass, and taken a loaf of bread.

Jean Valjean entered the galleys sobbing and shuddering: he went out hardened; he entered in despair: he went out sullen.

He recognised, that he was not an innocent man, unjustly punished. He acknowledged that he had committed an extreme and a blamable action; that the loaf perhaps would not have been refused him, had he asked for it; that at all events it would have been better to wait, either for pity, or for work; that it is not altogether an unanswerable reply to say: "could I wait when I was hungry?" that, in the first place, it is very rare that any one dies of actual hunger; and that, fortunately or unfortunately, man is so made that he can suffer long and much, morally and physically, without dying; that he should, therefore, have had patience; that that would have been better even for those poor little ones; that it was an act of folly in him, poor, worthless man, to seize society in all its strength, forcibly by the collar, and imagine that he could escape from misery by theft; in short, that he had done wrong.

Then he asked himself:

If he were the only one who had done wrong in the course of his fatal history? If, in the first place, it were not a grievous thing that he, a workman, should have been in want of work; that he, an industrious man, should have lacked bread. If, moreover, the fault having been committed and avowed, the punishment had not been savage and excessive. If there were not a greater abuse, on the part of the law, in the penalty, than there had been, on the part of the guilty, in the crime. If the discharge of the penalty were not the effacement of the crime; and if the result were not to reverse the situation, to replace the wrong of the delinquent by the wrong of the repression, to make a victim of the guilty, and a creditor of the debtor, and actually to put the right on the side of him who had violated it. If that penalty, taken in connection with its successive extensions for his attempts to escape, had not at last come to be a sort of outrage of the stronger on the weaker, a crime of society towards the individual, a crime which was committed afresh every day, a crime which had endured for nineteen years.

He questioned himself if human society could have the right alike to crush its members, in the one case by its unreasonable carelessness, and in the other by its pitiless care; and to keep a poor man for ever between a lack of work, an excess of punishment.

If it were not outrageous that society should treat with such rigid precision those of its members who were most poorly endowed in the distribution of wealth that chance had made, and who were, therefore, most worthy of indulgence.

These questions asked and decided, he condemned society and sentenced it to his hatred.

Anger may be foolish and absurd, and one may be irritated when in the wrong; but a man never feels outraged unless in some respect he is at bottom right. Jean Valjean felt outraged.

There was at Toulon a school for the prisoners conducted by some not very skilful friars, where the most essential branches were taught to such of these poor men as were willing. He was one of the willing ones. He went to school at forty and learned to read, write, and cipher. He felt that to increase his knowledge was to strengthen his hatred.

We must not omit one circumstance, which is, that in physical strength he far surpassed all the other inmates of the prison. At hard work, at twisting a cable, or turning a windlass, Jean Valjean was equal to four men. At one time, while the balcony of the City Hall of Toulon was undergoing repairs, one of Puget's admirable caryatides, which support the balcony, slipped from its place, and was about to fall, when Jean Valjean, who happened to be there, held it up on his shoulder till the workmen came.

His suppleness surpassed his strength. Certain convicts, always planning escape, have developed a veritable science of strength and skill combined,—the science of the muscles. To scale a wall, and to find a foothold where you could hardly see a projection, was play for Jean Valjean. Given an angle in a wall, with the tension of his back and his knees, with elbows and hands braced against the rough face of the stone, he would ascend, as if by magic, to a third story. Sometimes he climbed up in this manner to the roof of the galleys.

He talked little, and never laughed. Through the diseased perceptions of an incomplete nature and a smothered intelligence, he vaguely felt that a monstrous weight was over him. In that pallid and sullen shadow in which he crawled, whenever he turned his head and endeavoured to raise his eyes, he saw, with mingled rage and terror, forming, massing, and mounting up out of view above him with horrid escarpments, a kind of frightful accumulation of things, of laws, of prejudices, of men, and of acts, which was no other than that prodigious pyramid we call civilisation. Here and there in that shapeless and crawling mass he distinguished some detail vividly clear, here the jailer with his staff, here the gendarme with his sword, yonder the mitred archbishop; and on high, in a sort of blaze of glory, the emperor crowned and resplendent. All this, laws, prejudices, acts, men, things, went and came above him, marching over him and crushing him with an indescribably tranquil cruelty and inexorable indifference. Souls sunk to the bottom of possible misfortune, and unfortunate men lost in the lowest depths, feel upon their heads the whole weight of that human society, so formidable to him who is without it, so terrible to him who is beneath it.

If a millet seed under a millstone had thoughts, doubtless it would think what Jean Valjean thought.

Sometimes in the midst of his work in the galleys he would stop, and begin to think. All that had happened to him would appear absurd; all that surrounded him would appear impossible. He would say to himself: "it is a dream." He would look at the jailer standing a few steps from him; the jailer would seem to be a phantom; all at once this phantom would give him a blow with a stick.

For him the external world had scarcely an existence. It would be almost true to say that for Jean Valjean there was no sun, no beautiful summer days, no radiant sky, no fresh April dawn. Some dim window light was all that shone in his soul.

To sum up, in conclusion, what can be summed up and reduced to positive results, of all that we have been showing, we will make sure only of this, that in the course of nineteen years, Jean Valjean, the inoffensive pruner of Faverolles, the terrible galley-slave of Toulon, had become capable, thanks to the training he had received in the galleys, of two species of crime; first, a sudden, unpremeditated action, full of rashness, all instinct, a sort of reprisal for the wrong he had suffered; secondly, a serious, premeditated act, discussed by his conscience, and pondered over with the false ideas which such a fate will give. He had as motives, habitual indignation, bitterness of soul, a deep sense of injuries suffered, a reaction even against the good, the innocent, and the upright, if any such there are. The beginning as well as the end of all his thoughts was hatred of human law; that hatred which, if it be not checked in its growth by some providential event, becomes, in a certain time, hatred of society, then hatred of the human race, and then hatred of creation, and reveals itself by a vague and incessant desire to injure some living being, it matters not who. So, the passport was right which described Jean Valjean as *a very dangerous man.*

When the time for leaving the galleys came, and when there were sounded in the ear of Jean Valjean the strange words: *You are free!* the moment seemed improbable and unreal; a ray of living light, a ray of the true light of living men, suddenly penetrated his soul. But this ray quickly faded away. Jean Valjean soon saw what sort of liberty that is which has a yellow passport.

He had calculated that his savings, during his stay at the galleys, would amount to a hundred and seventy-one francs. It is proper to say that he had forgotten to take into account the compulsory rest on Sundays and holydays, which, in nineteen years, required a deduction of about twenty-four francs. However that might be, his savings had been reduced, by various local charges, to the sum of a hundred and nine francs and fifteen sous, which was counted out to him on his departure.

He understood nothing of this, and thought himself wronged, or to speak plainly, robbed.

The day after his liberation, he saw before the door of an orange flower distillery at Grasse, some men who were unloading bags. He offered his services. They were in need of help and accepted them. He set at work. He was intelligent, robust, and handy; he did his best; the foreman appeared to be satisfied. While he was at work, a gendarme passed, noticed him, and asked for his papers. He was compelled to show the yellow passport. That done, Jean Valjean resumed his work. A little while before, he had asked one of the labourers how much they were paid per day for this work, and the reply was: *thirty sous.* At night, as he was obliged to leave the town next morning, he went to the foreman of the distillery, and asked for his pay. The foreman did not say a word, but handed him fifteen sous. He remonstrated. The man replied: *"That is good enough for you."* He insisted. The foreman looked him in the eyes and said: *"Look out for the lock-up!"*

There again he thought himself robbed.

Society, the state, in reducing his savings, had robbed him by wholesale. Now it was the turn of the individual, who was robbing him by retail.

As the cathedral clock struck two, Jean Valjean awoke.

What awakened him was too good a bed. For nearly twenty years he had not slept in a bed, and, although he had not undressed, the sensation was too novel not to disturb his sleep.

He could not get to sleep again, and so he began to think. Many thoughts came to him, but there was one which continually presented itself, and which drove away all others. He had noticed the six silver plates and the large ladle that Madame Magloire had put on the table.

Those six silver plates took possession of him. There they were, within a few steps. At the very moment that he passed through the middle room to reach the one he was now in, the old servant was placing them in a little cupboard at the head of the bed. He had marked that cupboard well: on the right, coming from the dining-room. They were solid; and old silver. With the big ladle, they would bring at least two hundred francs, double what he had got for nineteen years' labour.

His mind wavered a whole hour, and a long one, in fluctuation and in struggle. The clock struck three. He opened his eyes, rose up hastily in bed, reached out his arm and felt his haversack, which he had put into the corner of the alcove, then he thrust out his legs and placed his feet on the ground, and found himself, he knew not how, seated on his bed.

In that hideous meditation, he thought, too, he knew not why, and with that mechanical obstinacy that belongs to reverie, of a convict named Brevet, whom he had known in the galleys, and whose trousers were only held up by a single knit cotton suspender. The checked pattern of that suspender came continually before his mind.

He would perhaps have remained there until daybreak, if the clock had not struck the quarter or the half-hour. The clock seemed to say to him: "Come along!"

He rose to his feet, hesitated for a moment longer, and listened; all was still in the house; he walked straight and cautiously towards the window, which he could discern. The night was not very dark; there was a full moon, across which large clouds were driving before the wind. This produced alternations of light and shade, out-of-doors eclipses and illuminations, and in-doors a kind of glimmer.

On reaching the window, Jean Valjean examined it. It had no bars, opened into the garden, and was fastened, according to the fashion of the country, with a little wedge only. He opened it; but as the cold, keen air rushed into the room, he closed it again immediately. He looked into the garden with that absorbed look which studies rather than sees. The garden was enclosed with a white wall, quite low, and readily scaled. Beyond, against the sky, he distinguished the tops of trees at equal distances apart, which showed that this wall separated the garden from an avenue or a lane planted with trees.

When he had taken this observation, he turned like a man whose mind is made up, went to his alcove, took his haversack, opened it, fumbled in it, took out something which he laid upon the bed, put his shoes into one of his pockets, tied up his bundle, swung it upon his shoulders, put on his cap, and pulled the vizor down over his eyes, felt for his stick, and went and put it in the corner of the window, then returned to the bed, and resolutely took up the object which he had laid on it. It looked like a short iron bar, pointed at one end like a spear. Could it be a lever? Could it be a club?

In the day-time, it would have been seen to be nothing but a miner's drill. At that time, the convicts were sometimes employed in quarrying stone on the high hills that surround Toulon, and they often had miners' tools in their possession.

He took the drill in his right hand, and holding his breath, with stealthy steps, he moved towards the door of the next room, which was the bishop's, as we know. On reaching the door, he found it unlatched. The bishop had not closed it.

Jean Valjean listened. Not a sound.

He pushed the door with the end of his finger, with the stealthy and timorous carefulness of a cat.

It yielded gradually and silently. The opening was wide enough for him to pass through; but a small table near the door barred the entrance.

He pushed the door harder than before. This time a rusty hinge suddenly sent out into the darkness a harsh and prolonged creak.

Jean Valjean shivered. The noise of this hinge sounded in his ears as clear and terrible as the trumpet of the Judgment Day.

He stopped, and dropped from his tiptoes to his feet. It seemed impossible that the horrible sound of this incensed hinge had not shaken the whole house with the shock of an earthquake: the old man would arise; the two old women would scream; help would come; in a quarter of an hour the town would be alive with it, and the gendarmes in pursuit.

He stood still, petrified like the pillar of salt, not daring to stir. Some minutes passed. The door was wide open; he ventured a look into the room. Nothing had moved. He listened. Nothing was stirring in the house. He took one step and was in the room.

A deep calm filled the chamber. Here and there indistinct, confused forms could be distinguished; Jean Valjean advanced, carefully avoiding the furniture. At the further end of the room he could hear the equal and quiet breathing of the sleeping bishop.

Suddenly he stopped: he was near the bed, he had reached it sooner than he thought.

For nearly a half hour a great cloud had darkened the sky. At the moment when Jean Valjean paused before the bed the cloud broke as if purposely, and a ray of moonlight crossing the high window, suddenly lighted up the bishop's pale face. He slept tranquilly. He was almost entirely dressed, on account of the cold nights of the lower Alps, with a dark woollen garment which covered his arms to the wrists. His head had fallen on the pillow in the unstudied attitude of slumber; over the side of the bed hung his hand, ornamented with the pastoral ring. His entire countenance was lit up with a vague expression of content, hope, and happiness.

Jean Valjean was in the shadow with the iron drill in his hand. He did not remove his eyes from the old man. The only thing which was plain from his attitude and his countenance was a strange indecision. He appeared ready either to cleave this skull, or to kiss this hand.

In a few moments he raised his left hand slowly to his forehead and took off his hat.

The crucifix above the mantelpiece was dimly visible in the moonlight, apparently extending its arms towards both, with a benediction for one and a pardon for the other.

Suddenly Jean Valjean put on his cap, then passed quickly, without looking at the bishop, along the bed, straight to the cupboard which he perceived near its head; he raised the drill to force the lock; the key was in it; he opened it. The first thing he saw was the basket of silver. He took it, crossed the room with hasty stride, careless of noise, reached the door, entered the oratory, took his stick, stepped out, put the silver in his knapsack, threw away the basket, ran across the garden, leaped over the wall like a tiger, and fled.

The next day at sunrise, Monseigneur Bienvenu was walking in the garden. Madame Magloire ran towards him quite beside herself.

"Monseigneur, monseigneur," cried she, "does your greatness know where the silver basket is?"

"Yes," said the bishop.

"God be praised!" said she, "I did not know what had become of it."

The bishop had just found the basket on a flower-bed. He gave it to Madame Magloire and said: "There it is."

"Yes," said she, "but there is nothing in it. The silver?"

"Ah!" said the bishop, "it is the silver then that troubles you. I do not know where that is."

"Good heavens! it is stolen. That man who came last night stole it."

And in the twinkling of an eye, with all the agility of which her age was capable, Madame Magloire ran to the oratory, went into the alcove, and came back to the bishop. The bishop was bending with some sadness over a cochlearia des Guillons, which the basket had broken in falling. He looked up at Madame Magloire's cry:

"Monseigneur, the man has gone! the silver is stolen!"

The bishop was silent for a moment, then raising his serious eyes, he said mildly to Madame Magloire:

"Now first, did this silver belong to us?"

Madame Magloire did not answer; after a moment the bishop continued:

"Madame Magloire, I have for a long time wrongfully withheld this silver; it belonged to the poor. Who was this man? A poor man evidently."

"Alas! alas!" returned Madame Magloire. "It is not on my account or mademoiselle's; it is all the same to us. But it is on yours, monseigneur. What is monsieur going to eat from now?"

The bishop looked at her with amazement:

"How so! have we no tin plates?"

Madame Magloire shrugged her shoulders.

"Tin smells."

"Well, then, iron plates."

"Iron tastes."

"Well," said the bishop, "then, wooden plates."

In a few minutes he was breakfasting at the same table at which Jean Valjean sat the night before. While breakfasting, Monseigneur Bienvenu pleasantly remarked to his sister who said nothing, and Madame Magloire who was grumbling to herself, that there was really no need even of a wooden spoon or fork to dip a piece of bread into a cup of milk.

"Was there ever such an idea?" said Madame Magloire to herself, as she went backwards and forwards: "to take in a man like that, and to give him a bed beside him; and yet what a blessing it was that he did nothing but steal! Oh, my stars! it makes the chills run over me when I think of it!"

Just as the brother and sister were rising from the table, there was a knock at the door.

"Come in," said the bishop.

The door opened. A strange, fierce group appeared on the threshold. Three men were holding a fourth by the collar. The three men were gendarmes; the fourth Jean Valjean.

A brigadier of gendarmes, who appeared to head the group, was near the door. He advanced towards the bishop, giving a military salute.

"Monseigneur," said he—

At this word Jean Valjean, who was sullen and seemed entirely cast down, raised his head with a stupefied air—

"Monseigneur!" he murmured, "then it is not the curé!"

"Silence!" said a gendarme, "it is monseigneur, the bishop."

In the meantime Monsieur Bienvenu had approached as quickly as his great age permitted:

"Ah, there you are!" said he, looking towards Jean Valjean, "I am glad to see you. But! I gave you the candlesticks also, which are silver like the rest, and would bring two hundred francs. Why did you not take them along with your plates?"

Jean Valjean opened his eyes and looked at the bishop with an expression which no human tongue could describe.

"Monseigneur," said the brigadier, "then what this man said was true? We met him. He was going like a man who was running away, and we arrested him in order to see. He had this silver."

"And he told you," interrupted the bishop, with a smile, "that it had been given him by a good old priest with whom he had passed the night. I see it all. And you brought him back here? It is all a mistake."

"If that is so," said the brigadier, "we can let him go."

"Certainly," replied the bishop.

The gendarmes released Jean Valjean, who shrank back—

"Is it true that they let me go?" he said in a voice almost inarticulate, as if he were speaking in his sleep.

"Yes! you can go. Do you not understand?" said a gendarme.

"My friend," said the bishop, "before you go away, here are your candlesticks; take them."

He went to the mantelpiece, took the two candlesticks, and brought them to Jean Valjean.

"Now," said the bishop, "go in peace. By the way, my friend, when you come again, you need not come through the garden. You can always come in and go out by the front door. It is closed only with a latch, day or night."

Then turning to the gendarmes, he said:

"Messieurs, you can retire." The gendarmes withdrew.

Jean Valjean felt like a man who is just about to faint.

The bishop approached him, and said, in a low voice:

"Forget not, never forget that you have promised me to use this silver to become an honest man."

Jean Valjean, who had no recollection of this promise, stood confounded. The bishop had laid much stress upon these words as he uttered them. He continued, solemnly:

"Jean Valjean, my brother: you belong no longer to evil, but to good. It is your soul that I am buying for you. I withdraw it from dark thoughts and from the spirit of perdition, and I give it to God!"

Jean Valjean went out of the city as if he were escaping. He made all haste to get into the open country, taking the first lanes and bypaths that offered, without noticing that he was every moment retracing his steps. He wandered thus all the morning. He felt somewhat angry, he knew not against whom. He could not have told whether he were touched or humiliated. There came over him, at times, a strange relenting which he struggled with, and to which he opposed the hardening of his past twenty years. At times he would really have liked better to be in prison with the gendarmes, and that things had not happened thus; that would have given him less agitation. Although the season was well advanced, there were yet here and there a few late flowers in the hedges, the odour of which, as it met him in his walk, recalled the memories of his childhood. These memories were almost insupportable, it was so long since they had occurred to him.

As the sun was sinking towards the horizon, lengthening the shadow on the ground of the smallest pebble, Jean Valjean was seated behind a thicket in a large reddish plain, an absolute desert. There was no horizon but the Alps, not even the steeple of a village church. A by-path which crossed the plain passed a few steps from the thicket.

In the midst of this meditation, he heard a joyous sound. He saw coming along the path a little Savoyard, a dozen years old, singing, with his hurdy-gurdy at his side, and his marmot box on his back.

Always singing, the boy stopped from time to time, and played at tossing up some pieces of money that he had in his hand, probably his whole fortune. Among them there was one forty-sous piece.

The boy stopped by the side of the thicket without seeing Jean Valjean, and tossed up his handful of sous; until this time he had skilfully caught the whole of them upon the back of his hand. This time the forty-sous piece escaped him, and rolled towards the thicket, near Jean Valjean.

Jean Valjean put his foot upon it.

The boy, however, had followed the piece with his eye, and had seen where it went.

He was not frightened, and walked straight to the man.

"Monsieur," said the little Savoyard, with that childish confidence which is made up of ignorance and innocence, "my piece?"

"What is your name?" said Jean Valjean.

"Petit Gervais, monsieur."

"Get out," said Jean Valjean.

"Monsieur," continued the boy, "give me my piece."

Jean Valjean dropped his head and did not answer.

"My piece!" exclaimed the boy, "my white piece! my silver!"

Jean Valjean did not appear to understand. The boy took him by the collar of his blouse and shook him. And at the same time he made an effort to move the big, iron-soled shoe which was placed upon his treasure.

"I want my piece! my forty-sous piece!"

The child began to cry. Jean Valjean raised his head. He still kept his seat. His look was troubled. He looked upon the boy with an air of wonder, then reached out his hand towards his stick, and exclaimed in a terrible voice: "Who is there?"

"Me, monsieur," answered the boy. "Petit Gervais! me! me! give me my forty sous, if you please! Take away your foot, monsieur, if you please!" Then becoming angry, small as he was, and almost threatening:

"Come, now, will you take away your foot? Why don't you take away your foot?"

"Ah! you here yet!" said Jean Valjean, and rising hastily to his feet, without releasing the piece of money, he added: "You'd better take care of yourself!"

The boy looked at him in terror, then began to tremble from head to foot, and after a few seconds of stupor, took to flight and ran with all his might without daring to turn his head or to utter a cry.

At a little distance, however, he stopped for want of breath, and Jean Valjean in his reverie heard him sobbing.

In a few minutes the boy was gone.

The sun had gone down.

The shadows were deepening around Jean Valjean. He had not eaten during the day; probably he had some fever.

He had remained standing, and had not changed his attitude since the child fled. His breathing was at long and unequal intervals. His eyes were fixed on a spot ten or twelve steps before him, and seemed to be studying with profound attention the form of an old piece of blue crockery that was lying in the grass. All at once he shivered; he began to feel the cold night air.

He pulled his cap down over his forehead, sought mechanically to fold and button his blouse around him, stepped forward and stooped to pick up his stick.

At that instant he perceived the forty-sous piece which his foot had half buried in the ground, and which glistened among the pebbles. It was like an electric shock. "What is that?" said he, between his teeth. He drew back a step or two, then stopped without the power to withdraw his gaze from this point which his foot had covered the instant before, as if the thing that glistened there in the obscurity had been an open eye fixed upon him.

He said: "Oh!" and began to walk rapidly in the direction in which the child had gone. After some thirty steps, he stopped, looked about, and saw nothing.

Then he called with all his might "Petit Gervais! Petit Gervais!"
And then he listened.

There was no answer.

A biting norther was blowing, which gave a kind of dismal life to everything about him. The bushes shook their little thin arms with an incredible
fury. One would have said that they were threatening and pursuing
somebody.

He began to walk again, then quickened his pace to a run, and from time
to time stopped and called out in that solitude, in a most desolate and
terrible voice:

"Petit Gervais! Petit Gervais!"

He met a priest on horseback. He went up to him and said:

"Monsieur curé, have you seen a child go by?"

"No," said the priest.

"Petit Gervais was his name?"

"I have seen nobody."

He took two five-franc pieces from his bag, and gave them to the priest.

"Monsieur curé, this is for your poor. Monsieur curé, he is a little fellow,
about ten years old, with a marmot, I think and a hurdygurdy. He went
this way. One of these Savoyards, you know?"

"I have not seen him."

"Petit Gervais? is his village near here? can you tell me?"

"If it be as you say, my friend, the little fellow is a foreigner. They
roam about this country. Nobody knows them."

Jean Valjean hastily took out two more five-franc pieces, and gave them
to the priest.

"For your poor," said he.

Then he added wildly:

"Monsieur abbé, have me arrested. I am a robber."

The priest put spurs to his horse, and fled in great fear.

Jean Valjean began to run again in the direction which he had first taken.

Finally, at a place where three paths met, he stopped. The moon had
risen. He strained his eyes in the distance, and called out once more "Petit
Gervais! Petit Gervais! Petit Gervais!" His cries died away into the mist,
without even awakening an echo. That was his last effort; his knees suddenly bent under him, as if an invisible power overwhelmed him at a blow,
with the weight of his bad conscience; he fell exhausted upon a great
stone, and exclaimed: "What a wretch I am!"

Then he burst into tears. It was the first time he had wept for nineteen
years.

When Jean Valjean left the bishop's house, as we have seen, his mood
was one that he had never known before. He set himself stubbornly in
opposition to the angelic deeds and the gentle words of the old man, "you
have promised me to become an honest man. I am purchasing your soul, I
withdraw it from the spirit of perversity, and I give it to God Almighty."
He felt dimly that the pardon of this priest was the hardest assault, and

the most formidable attack which he had yet sustained; that his hardness of heart would be complete, if it resisted this kindness; that if he yielded, he must renounce that hatred with which the acts of other men had for so many years filled his soul. Did a voice whisper in his ear that he had just passed through the decisive hour of his destiny, that there was no longer a middle course for him, that he must now, so to speak, mount higher than the bishop, or fall lower than the galley slave; that, if he would become good, he must become an angel; that, if he would remain wicked, he must become a monster?

In this frame of mind, he had met Petit Gervais, and stolen his forty sous. Why? He could not have explained it, surely; was it the final effect of the evil thoughts he had brought from the galleys, a result of what is called in physics *acquired force?* It was that, and it was also perhaps even less than that. We will say plainly, it was not he who had stolen, it was not the man, it was the beast which, from habit and instinct, had stupidly set its foot upon that money, while the intellect was struggling in the midst of so many new and unknown influences. When the intellect awoke and saw this act of the brute, Jean Valjean recoiled in anguish and uttered a cry of horror. The fact is, that in stealing this money from that child, he had done a thing of which he was no longer capable.

However that may be, this last misdeed had a decisive effect upon him; it rushed across the chaos of his intellect and dissipated it, set the light on one side and the dark clouds on the other, and acted upon his soul, in the condition it was in, as certain chemical reagents act upon a turbid mixture, by precipitating one element and producing a clear solution of the other.

Jean Valjean wept long. While he wept, the light grew brighter and brighter in his mind—an extraordinary light, a light at once transporting and terrible.

What did he do after weeping? Where did he go? Nobody ever knew. It is known simply that, on that very night, the stage-driver who drove at that time on the Grenoble route, and arrived at D—— about three o'clock in the morning, saw, as he passed through the bishop's street, a man in the attitude of prayer, kneel upon the pavement in the shadow, before the door of Monseigneur Bienvenu.

III. QUARTIER LATIN

IN 1817, FOUR YOUNG PARISIANS played "a good farce." These Parisians were, one from Toulouse, another from Limoges, the third from Cahors, and the fourth from Montauban; but they were students, and to say student is to say Parisian; to study in Paris is to be born in Paris.

These young men were remarkable for nothing; neither good nor bad, neither learned nor ignorant, neither talented nor stupid; handsome in that charming April of life which we call twenty. The first was called Félix

Tholomyès, of Toulouse; the second, Listolier, of Cahors; the third, Fameuil, of Limoges; and the last, Blacheville, of Montauban. Of course each had his mistress. Blacheville loved Favourite, so called, because she had been in England; Listolier adored Dahlia, who had taken the name of a flower as her *nom de guerre;* Fameuil idolised Zéphine, the diminutive of Josephine, and Tholomyès had Fantine, called *the Blonde,* on account of her beautiful hair, the colour of the sun.

Favourite, Dahlia, Zéphine, and Fantine were four enchanting girls, perfumed and sparkling, something of workwomen still, since they had not wholly given up the needle, agitated by love-affairs, yet preserving on their countenances a remnant of the serenity of labour, and in their souls that flower of purity, which in woman survives the first fall. One of the four was called the child, because she was the youngest; and another was called the old one—the Old One was twenty-three. To conceal nothing, the three first were more experienced, more careless, and better versed in the ways of the world than Fantine, the Blonde, who was still in her first illusion.

Favourite, having been in England, was the admiration of Zéphine and Dahlia.

What had attracted Listolier to Dahlia was her beautiful, rosy fingernails. How could such nails work! She who will remain virtuous must have no compassion for her hands. As to Zéphine, she had conquered Fameuil by her rebellious yet caressing little way of saying "yes, sir."

Fantine was one of those beings which are brought forth from the heart of the people. Sprung from the most unfathomable depths of social darkness, she bore on her brow the mark of the anonymous and unknown. She was born at M—— on M——. Who were her parents? None could tell, she had never known either father or mother. She was called Fantine —why so? because she had never been known by any other name. She was named after the pleasure of the first passer-by who found her, a mere infant, straying barefoot in the streets. Fantine was beautiful and remained pure as long as she could. She was a pretty blonde with fine teeth. She had gold and pearls for her dowry; but the gold was on her head and the pearls in her mouth.

She worked to live; then, also to live, for the heart too has its hunger, she loved.

She loved Tholomyès. To him, it was an amour; to her a passion.

Blacheville, Listolier, and Fameuil formed a sort of group of which Tholomyès was the head. He was the wit of the company.

Tholomyès was an old student of the old style; he was rich, having an income of four thousand francs—a splendid scandal on the Montagne Sainte-Geneviève. He was a good liver, thirty years old, and ill preserved. But in proportion as his youth died out, his gaiety increased; he replaced his teeth by jests, his hair by joy, his health by irony.

One day, Tholomyès took the other three aside, and said to them with an oracular gesture:

"For nearly a year, Fantine, Dahlia, Zéphine, and Favourite have been asking us to give them a surprise; we have solemnly promised them one. They are constantly reminding us of it, me especially. Just as the old women at Naples cry to Saint January, *'Faccia gialluta, fa o miracolo,* yellow face, do your miracle,' our pretty ones are always saying: 'Tholomyès, when are you going to be delivered of your surprise?' At the same time our parents are writing for us. Two birds with one stone. It seems to me the time has come. Let us talk it over."

Upon this, Tholomyès lowered his voice, and mysteriously articulated something so ludicrous that a prolonged and enthusiastic giggling arose from the four throats at once, and Blacheville exclaimed: "What an idea!"

The result of this mystery was a brilliant pleasure party, which took place on the following Sunday, the four young men inviting the four young girls.

It is difficult to picture to one's self, at this day, a country party of students and grisettes as it was forty-five years ago. Paris has no longer the same environs; the aspect of what we might call circum-Parisian life has completely changed in half a century. In place of the rude, one-horse chaise, we have now the railroad car; in place of the pinnace, we have now the steamboat; we say Fécamp to-day, as we then said Saint Cloud. The Paris of 1862 is a city which has France for its suburbs.

The four couples scrupulously accomplished all the country follies then possible. It was in the beginning of the holidays, and a warm, clear summer's day. The night before, Favourite, the only one who knew how to write, had written to Tholomyès in the name of the four: "It is lucky to go out early." For this reason, they rose at five in the morning. Then they went to Saint Cloud by the coach, looked at the dry cascade and exclaimed: "How beautiful it must be when there is any water!" breakfasted at the *Tête Noire,* amused themselves with a game of rings at the quincunx of the great basin, ascended to Diogenes' lantern, played roulette with macaroons on the Sèvres bridge, gathered bouquets at Puteaux, bought reed pipes at Neuilly, ate apple puffs everywhere, and were perfectly happy.

Tholomyès was excessively gay, but one felt the governing power in him. There was dictatorship in his joviality; his principal adornment was a pair of nankeen pantaloons, cut in the elephant-leg fashion, with under-stockings of copper-coloured braid; he had a huge ratten, worth two hundred francs, in his hand, and as he denied himself nothing, a strange thing called cigar in his mouth. Nothing being sacred to him, he was smoking.

"This Tholomyès is astonishing," said the others, with veneration. "What pantaloons! what energy!"

As to Fantine, she was joy itself. Her splendid teeth had evidently been endowed by God with one function—that of laughing. She carried in her hand rather than on her head, her little hat of sewed straw, with long, white strings. Her thick blond tresses, inclined to wave, seemed designed for the flight of Galatea under the willows. Her rosy lips babbled with enchantment. The corners of her mouth, turned up voluptuously like the antique masks of Erigone, seemed to encourage audacity; but her long, shadowy eyelashes were cast discreetly down.

Fantine was beautiful, without being too conscious of it. Fantine was joy; Fantine also was modesty.

That day was sunshine from one end to the other. The parterres of Saint Cloud were balmy with perfumes; the breeze from the Seine gently waved the leaves; the boughs were gesticulating in the wind; the bees were pillaging the jessamine; a whole crew of butterflies had settled in the milfoil, clover, and wild oats.

After breakfast, the four couples went to see, in what was then called the king's square, a plant newly arrived from the Indies, which at this time was attracting all Paris to Saint Cloud: it was a strange and beautiful shrub with a long stalk, the innumerable branches of which, fine as threads, tangled, and leafless, were covered with millions of little white blossoms. There was always a crowd admiring it.

When they had viewed the shrub, Tholomyès exclaimed, "I propose donkeys," and making a bargain with a donkey-driver, they returned through Vanvres and Issy. At Issy, they had an adventure. The park, Bien-National, was by sheer good luck open. They passed through the grating, visited the mannikin anchorite in his grotto, and tried the little, mysterious effects of the famous cabinet of mirrors. They swung stoutly in the great swing, attached to the two chestnut trees. Fantine alone refused to swing.

"I do not like this sort of airs," murmured Favourite, rather sharply.

They left the donkeys for a new pleasure, crossed the Seine in a boat, and walked from Passy to the Barrière de l'Etoile. They had been on their feet, it will be remembered, since five in the morning, but *bah! there is no weariness on Sunday*, said Favourite; *on Sunday fatigue has a holiday*.

From time to time Favourite exclaimed:

"But the surprise? I want the surprise."

"Be patient," answered Tholomyès.

They thought of dinner, and the happy eight, a little weary at last, stranded on Bombarda's, with two windows from which they could see, through the elms, the quai and the river; two tables, one loaded with a triumphant mountain of bouquets, interspersed with hats and bonnets, while at the other, the four couples were gathered round a joyous pile of plates, napkins, glasses, and bottles, jugs of beer and flasks of wine.

Crowds in their Sunday clothes were scattered over the great square and the square Marigny, playing games and going around on wooden horses; others were drinking; a few, printer apprentices, had on paper caps; their laughter resounded through the air. It was a time of undoubted peace and profound royal security; it was the time when a private and special report of Prefect of Police Anglès to the king on the faubourgs of Paris, ended with these lines: "Everything considered, sire, there is nothing to fear from these people. They are as careless and indolent as cats. The lower people of the provinces are restless, those of Paris are not so. They are all small men, sire, and it would take two of them, one upon the other, to make one of your grenadiers. There is nothing at all to fear on the side of the populace of the capital. It is remarkable that this part of the population has also decreased in stature during the last fifty years; and the people of the faubourgs of Paris are smaller than before the Revolution. They are not dangerous. In short, they are good canaille."

The simple police of the Restoration looked too hopefully on the people of Paris. They are by no means such good canaille as is believed. The Parisian is among Frenchmen what the Athenian was among Greeks. Nobody sleeps better than he, nobody is more frankly frivolous and idle than he, nobody seems to forget things more easily than he; but do not trust him, notwithstanding; he is apt at all sorts of nonchalance, but when there is glory to be gained, he is wonderful in every species of fury. Give him a pike, and he will play the tenth of August; give him a musket, and you shall have an Austerlitz. He is the support of Napoleon, and the resource of Danton. Is France in question? he enlists; is liberty in question? he tears up the pavement.

When the tocsin sounds, this dweller in the faubourgs will grow; this little man will arise, his look will be terrible, his breath will become a tempest, and a blast will go forth from his poor, frail breast that might shake the wrinkles out of the Alps. Thanks to the men of the Paris faubourgs, the Revolution infused into armies conquers Europe. He sings, it is his joy. Proportion his song to his nature, and you shall see! So long as he had the Carmagnole merely for his chorus, he overthrew only Louis XVI.; let him sing the Marseillaise, and he will deliver the world.

Fameuil and Dahlia hummed airs; Tholomyès drank, Zéphine laughed, Fantine smiled. Listolier blew a wooden trumpet that he had bought at Saint Cloud. Favourite looked tenderly at Blacheville, and said:

"Blacheville, I adore you."

This brought forth a question from Blacheville:

"What would you do, Favourite, if I should leave you?"

"Me!" cried Favourite. "Oh! do not say that, even in sport! If you should leave me, I would run after you, I would scratch you, I would pull your hair, I would throw water on you, I would have you arrested."

Blacheville, in ecstasy, leaned back in his chair, and closed both eyes with a satisfied air.

Dahlia, still eating, whispered to Favourite in the hubbub:

"Are you really so fond of your Blacheville, then?"

"I detest him," answered Favourite, in the same tone, taking up her fork. "He is stingy; I am in love with the little fellow over the way from where I live. He is a nice young man; do you know him? Anybody can see that he was born to be an actor! I love actors. It is all the same, I tell Blacheville that I adore him. How I lie! Oh, how I lie!"

Meantime, while some were singing, the rest were all noisily talking. Tholomyès interfered.

"Do not talk at random, nor too fast!" exclaimed he; "we must take time for reflection, if we would be brilliant. Gentlemen, no haste. Mingle dignity with festivity, eat with deliberation, feast slowly."

"Tholomyès, let us alone," said Blacheville.

"Down with the tyrant!" cried Fameuil.

"My friends!" exclaimed Tholomyès, in the tone of a man resuming his sway. "Collect yourselves. There must be a limit even to dinners. You like apple puffs, ladies; do not abuse them. There must be, even in puffs, good sense and art. Gluttony punishes the glutton. Indigestion is charged by God with enforcing morality on the stomach. And remember this: each of our passions, even love, has a stomach that must not be overloaded. We must in everything write the word *finis* in time; we must restrain ourselves, when it becomes urgent; we must draw the bolt on the appetite, play a fantasia on the violin, then break the strings with our own hand. The wise man is he who knows when and how to stop."

"Tholomyès," cried Blacheville, "you are drunk."

"The deuce I am!" said Tholomyès.

"Then be gay," resumed Blacheville.

"I agree," replied Tholomyès. "Everything is beautiful; the flies hum in the sunbeams. The humming-birds whizz in the sunshine. Kiss me, Fantine!"

And, by mistake, he kissed Favourite.

Tholomyès, now that he was started, would have been stopped with difficulty, had not a horse fallen down at this moment on the quai. The shock stopped short both the cart and the orator. It was an old, meagre mare, worthy of the knacker, harnessed to a very heavy cart. On reaching Bombarda's, the beast, worn and exhausted, had refused to go further. This incident attracted a crowd.

"Poor horse!" sighed Fantine.

Dahlia exclaimed:

"Here is Fantine pitying horses! was there ever anything so absurd?"

At this moment, Favourite, crossing her arms and turning round her head, looked fixedly at Tholomyès and said:

"Come! the surprise?"

"Precisely. The moment has come," replied Tholomyès. "Gentlemen, the hour has come for surprising these ladies. Ladies, wait for us a moment."

"It begins with a kiss," said Blacheville.

"On the forehead," added Tholomyès.

Each one gravely placed a kiss on the forehead of his mistress; after which they directed their steps towards the door, all four in file, laying their fingers on their lips.

Favourite clapped her hands as they went out.

"It is amusing already," said she.

"Do not be too long," murmured Fantine. "We are waiting for you."

The girls, left alone, leaned their elbows on the window sills and chattered together, bending their heads and speaking from one window to the other.

They saw the young men go out of Bombarda's, arm in arm; they turned round, made signals to them laughingly, then disappeared in the dusty Sunday crowd which takes possession of the Champs-Élysées once a week.

"What are they going to bring us?" said Zéphine.

"Surely something pretty," said Dahlia.

"I hope it will be gold," resumed Favourite.

They were soon distracted by the stir on the water's edge. It was the hour for the departure of the mails and diligences. Almost all the stagecoaches to the south and west, passed at that time by the Champs-Elysées. Every minute some huge vehicle, painted yellow and black, heavily loaded, noisily harnessed, distorted with mails, awnings, and valises, rushed through the crowd.

It so happened that one of these vehicles which could be distinguished with difficulty through the obscurity of the elms, stopped for a moment, then set out again on a gallop. This surprised Fantine.

"It is strange," said she. "I thought the diligences never stopped."

Favourite shrugged her shoulders:

"This Fantine is surprising; I look at her with curiosity. She wonders at the most simple things. Suppose that I am a traveller, and say to the diligence: 'I am going on; you can take me up on the quai in passing.' The diligence passes, sees me, stops and takes me up. This happens every day. You know nothing of life, my dear."

Some time passed in this manner. Suddenly Favourite started as if from sleep.

"Well!" said she, "and the surprise?"

"Yes," returned Dahlia, "the famous surprise."

"They are very long!" said Fantine.

As Fantine finished the sigh, the boy who had waited at dinner entered. He had in his hand something that looked like a letter.

"What is that?" asked Favourite.

"It is a paper that the gentlemen left for these ladies," he replied.

"Why did you not bring it at once?"

"Because the gentlemen ordered me not to give it to the ladies before an hour," returned the boy.

Favourite snatched the paper from his hands. It was really a letter.

"Stop!" said she. "There is no address; but see what is written on it:

"THIS IS THE SURPRISE."

She hastily unsealed the letter, opened it, and read (she knew how to read):

"Oh, our lovers!

"Know that we have parents. Parents—you scarcely know the meaning of the word, they are what are called fathers and mothers in the civil code, simple but honest. Now these parents bemoan us, these old men claim us, these good men and women call us prodigal sons, desire our return and offer

*to kill for us the fatted calf. We obey them, being virtuous. At the moment
when you read this, five mettlesome horses will be bearing us back to our
papas and mammas. The Toulouse diligence snatches us from the abyss, and
you are this abyss, our beautiful darlings! We are returning to society, to
duty and order, on a full trot, at the rate of three leagues an hour. It is
necessary to the country that we become, like everybody else, prefects,
fathers of families, rural guards, and councillors of state. Venerate us. We
sacrifice ourselves. Mourn for us rapidly, and replace us speedily. If this
letter rends you, rend it in turn. Adieu.*

"For nearly two years we have made you happy. Bear us no ill will for it."

"Signed: BLACHEVILLE,
FAMEUIL,
LISTOLIER,
FÉLIX THOLOMYÈS.

"P. S. The dinner is paid for."

The four girls gazed at each other.

Favourite was the first to break silence.

"Well!" said she, "it is a good farce all the same."

"It is very droll," said Zéphine.

"It must have been Blacheville that had the idea," resumed Favourite.
"This makes me in love with him. Soon loved, soon gone. That is the story."

"No," said Dahlia, "it is an idea of Tholomyès. This is clear."

"In that case," returned Favourite, "down with Blacheville, and long live
Tholomyès!"

"Long live Tholomyès!" cried Dahlia and Zéphine.

And they burst into laughter.

Fantine laughed like the rest.

An hour afterwards, when she had re-entered her chamber, she wept. It
was her first love, as we have said; she had given herself to this Tholomyès
as to a husband, and the poor girl had a child.

IV. FANTINE

THERE WAS, during the first quarter of the present century, at Montfermeil,
near Paris, a sort of chop-house; it is not there now. It was kept by a man
and his wife, named Thénardier. Above the door, nailed flat against the
wall, was a board, upon which something was painted that looked like
a man carrying on his back another man wearing the heavy epaulettes of a
general, gilt and with large silver stars; red blotches typified blood; the
remainder of the picture was smoke, and probably represented a battle.
Beneath was this inscription: To THE SERGEANT OF WATERLOO.

Nothing is commoner than a cart or wagon before the door of an inn;
nevertheless the vehicle, or more properly speaking, the fragment of a

vehicle which obstructed the street in front of the Sergeant of Waterloo one evening certainly would have attracted by its bulk the attention of any painter who might have been passing.

It was the fore-carriage of one of those drays for carrying heavy articles, used in wooded countries for transporting joists and trunks of trees: it consisted of a massive iron axle-tree with a pivot to which a heavy pole was attached, and which was supported by two enormous wheels. As a whole, it was squat, crushing, and misshapen: it might have been fancied a gigantic gun-carriage.

Under the axle-tree hung festooned a huge chain fit for a Goliath of the galleys.

Why was this vehicle in this place in the street, one may ask? First to obstruct the lane, and then to complete its work of rust. There is in the old social order a host of institutions which we find like this across our path in the full light of day, and which present no other reasons for being there.

The middle of the chain was hanging quite near the ground, under the axle; and upon the bend, as on a swinging rope, two little girls were seated.

The mother, a woman whose appearance was rather forbidding, was seated on the sill of the inn, swinging the two children by a long string, while she brooded them with her eyes for fear of accident with that animal but heavenly expression peculiar to maternity. At each vibration the hideous links uttered a creaking noise like an angry cry; the little ones were in ecstasies, the setting sun mingled in the joy, and nothing could be more charming than this caprice of chance which made of a Titan's chain a swing for cherubim.

Suddenly the mother heard a voice say quite near her ear:

"You have two pretty children there, madame."

A woman was before her at a little distance; she also had a child, which she bore in her arms. She was carrying in addition a large carpet-bag, which seemed heavy.

This woman's child was a little girl of two or three years. She might have entered the lists with the other little ones for coquetry of attire; she wore a head-dress of fine linen; ribbons at her shoulders and Valenciennes lace on her cap. She was charmingly rosy and healthful.

As to the mother, she seemed poor and sad; she had the appearance of a working woman who is seeking to return to the life of a peasant. She was young,—and pretty? It was possible, but in that garb beauty could not be displayed. Her hair, one blonde mesh of which had fallen, seemed very thick, but it was severely fastened up beneath an ugly, close, narrow nun's head-dress, tied under the chin. Laughing shows fine teeth when one has them, but she did not laugh. Her eyes seemed not to have been tearless for a long time. She was pale, and looked very weary, and somewhat sick. It was Fantine.

Ten months had slipped away since "the good farce."

What had passed during these ten months? We can guess.

After recklessness, trouble. Fantine had lost sight of Favourite, Zéphine, and Dahlia; the tie, broken on the part of the men, was unloosed on the part of the women; they would have been astonished if any one had said a fortnight afterwards they were friends. Fantine was left alone. The father of her child gone—Alas! such partings are irrevocable—she found herself absolutely isolated, with the habit of labour lost, and the taste for pleasure acquired.

Fantine could scarcely read, and did not know how to write. She had only been taught in childhood how to sign her name. She had a letter written by a public letter-writer to Tholomyès, then a second, then a third. Tholomyès had replied to none of them. What should she do? She had no one to ask.

The idea occurred to her of returning to her native village M— sur M—, there perhaps some one would know her, and give her work. She had already valiantly renounced her finery, was draped in calico, and had put all her silks, her gew-gaws, her ribbons, and laces on her daughter— the only vanity that remained. She sold all she had, which gave her two hundred francs; when her little debts were paid, she had but about eighty left. At twenty-two years of age, on a fine spring morning, she left Paris, carrying her child on her back.

We shall have no further need to speak of M. Félix Tholomyès. We will only say here, that twenty years later, under King Louis Philippe, he was a fat provincial attorney, rich and influential, a wise elector and rigid jury- man; always, however, a man of pleasure.

Towards noon, after having, for the sake of rest, travelled from time to time at a cost of three or four cents a league, in what they called then the Petites Voitures of the environs of Paris, Fantine reached Montfermeil.

As she was passing by the Thénardier chop-house, the two little children sitting in delight on their monstrous swing, had a sort of dazzling effect upon her, and she paused before this joyous vision. She thought she saw above this inn the mysterious "HERE" of Providence. These children were evidently happy: she gazed upon them, she admired them, so much affected that at the moment when the mother was taking breath between the verses of her song, she could not help saying what we have been reading.

"You have two pretty children there, madame."

The most ferocious animals are disarmed by caresses to their young. The mother raised her head and thanked her, and made the stranger sit down on the stone step, she herself being on the doorsill: the two women began to talk together.

"My name is Madame Thénardier," said the mother of the two girls: "we keep this inn."

This Madame Thénardier was a red-haired, browny, angular woman, of the soldier's wife type in all its horror, and, singularly enough, she had a lolling air which she had gained from novel-reading.

The traveller told her story, a little modified.

She said she was a working woman, and her husband was dead. Not being able to procure work in Paris she was going in search of it elsewhere;

in her own province; that she had left Paris that morning on foot; that carrying her child she had become tired, and meeting the Villemomble stage had got in; that from Villemomble she had come on foot to Mont-fermeil; that the child had walked a little, but not much, she was so young; that she was compelled to carry her, and the jewel had fallen asleep.

Mother Thénardier untied the children and took them from the swing saying:

"Play together, all three of you."

At that age acquaintance is easy, and in a moment the little Thénardiers were playing with the new-comer, making holes in the ground to their intense delight.

The two women continued to chat.

"What do you call your brat?"

"Cosette."

For Cosette read Euphrasie. But the mother had made Cosette out of it, by that sweet and charming instinct of mothers and of the people, who change Jósefa into Pepita, and Françoise into Sillette.

"How old is she?"

"She is going on three years."

"The age of my oldest."

The three girls were grouped in an attitude of deep anxiety and bliss; a great event had occurred; a large worm had come out of the ground; they were afraid of it, and yet in ecstasies over it.

"Children," exclaimed the Thénardier mother; "how soon they know one another. See them! one would swear they were three sisters."

These words were the spark which the other mother was probably awaiting. She seized the hand of Madame Thénardier and said:

"Will you keep my child for me?"

Madame Thénardier made a motion of surprise, which was neither con-sent nor refusal.

Cosette's mother continued:

"You see I cannot take my child into the country. Work forbids it. With a child I could not find a place there; they are so absurd in that district. It is God who has led me before your inn. The sight of your little ones, so pretty, and clean, and happy, has overwhelmed me. I said: there is a good mother; they will be like three sisters, and then it will not be long before I come back. Will you keep my child for me?"

"I must think over it," said Thénardier.

"I will give six francs a month."

Here a man's voice was heard from within:

"Not less than seven francs, and six months paid in advance."

"Six times seven are forty-two," said Thénardier.

"I will give it," said the mother.

"And fifteen francs extra for the first expenses," added the man.

"That's fifty-seven francs," said Madame Thénardier.

"I will give it," said the mother; "I have eighty francs. That will leave me enough to go into the country if I walk. I will earn some money there, and as soon as I have I will come for my little love."

The man's voice returned:

"Has the child a wardrobe?"

"That is my husband," said Thénardier.

"Certainly she has, the poor darling. I knew it was your husband. And a fine wardrobe it is too, an extravagant wardrobe, everything in dozens, and silk dresses like a lady. They are there in my carpet-bag."

"You must leave that here," put in the man's voice.

"Of course I shall give it to you," said the mother; "it would be strange if I should leave my child naked."

The face of the master appeared.

"It is all right," said he.

The bargain was concluded. The mother passed the night at the inn, gave her money and left her child, fastened again her carpet-bag, diminished by her child's wardrobe, and very light now, and set off next morning, expecting soon to return. These partings are arranged tranquilly, but they are full of despair.

When Cosette's mother had gone, the man said to his wife:

"That will do me for my note of 110 francs which falls due to-morrow; I was fifty francs short. Do you know I should have had a sheriff and a protest? You have proved a good mousetrap with your little ones."

The captured mouse was a very puny one, but the cat exulted even over a lean mouse.

What were the Thénardiers?

They belonged to that bastard class formed of low people who have risen, and intelligent people who have fallen, which lies between the classes called middle and lower, and which unites some of the faults of the latter with nearly all the vices of the former.

This Thénardier, if we may believe him, had been a soldier, a sergeant he said; he probably had made the campaign of 1815, and had even borne himself bravely according to all that appeared. The sign of his inn was an allusion to one of his feats of arms. He had painted it himself, for he knew how to do a little of everything—badly.

However, to be wicked does not insure prosperity—for the inn did not succeed well.

Thanks to Fantine's fifty-seven francs, Thénardier had been able to avoid a protest and to honour his signature. The next month they were still in need of money, and the woman carried Cosette's wardrobe to Paris and pawned it for sixty francs. When this sum was spent, the Thénardiers began to look upon the little girl as a child which they sheltered for charity, and treated her as such. Her clothes being gone, they dressed her in the cast-off garments of the little Thénardiers, that is in rags. They fed her a little better than the dog, and a little worse than the cat. Cosette ate under the table in a wooden dish like theirs.

Her mother, as we shall see hereafter, who had found a place at M——

sur M—— wrote, or rather had some one write for her, every month, inquiring news of her child. The Thénardiers replied invariably: "Cosette is doing wonderfully well."

The six months passed away: the mother sent seven francs for the seventh month, and continued to send this sum regularly month after month. The year was not ended before Thénardier said: "A pretty price that is. What does she expect us to do for her seven francs?" And he wrote demanding twelve francs. The mother assented, and forwarded the twelve francs.

There are certain natures which cannot have love on one side without hatred on the other. This Thénardier mother passionately loved her own little ones: this made her detest the young stranger. The woman was unkind to Cosette, Eponine and Azelma were unkind also. Children at that age are only copies of the mother; the size is reduced, that is all.

A year passed and then another.

People used to say in the village:

"What good people these Thénardiers are! They are not rich, and yet they bring up a poor child, that has been left with them."

Meantime Thénardier, having learned in some obscure way that the child was probably illegitimate, and that its mother could not acknowledge it, demanded fifteen francs a month, saying "that the 'creature' was growing and eating," and threatening to send her away. The mother paid the fifteen francs.

From year to year the child grew, and her misery also.

So long as Cosette was very small, she was the scapegoat of the two other children; as soon as she began to grow a little, that is to say, before she was five years old, she became the servant of the house.

Five years old, it will be said, that is improbable. Alas! it is true, social suffering begins at all ages. Cosette was made to run errands, sweep the rooms, the yard, the street, wash the dishes, and even carry burdens. The Thénardiers felt doubly authorised to treat her thus, as the mother, who still remained at M—— sur M——, began to be remiss in her payments. Some months remained due.

Had this mother returned to Montfermeil, at the end of these three years, she would not have known her child. Cosette, so fresh and pretty when she came to that house, was now thin and wan. She had a peculiar restless air. Sly! said the Thénardiers.

Injustice had made her sullen, and misery had made her ugly. It was a harrowing sight to see in the winter time the poor child, not yet six years old, shivering under the tatters of what was once a calico dress, sweeping the street before daylight with an enormous broom in her little red hands and tears in her large eyes.

In the place she was called the Lark. People like figurative names and were pleased thus to name this little being, not larger than a bird, trembling, frightened, and shivering, awake every morning first of all in the house and the village, always in the street or in the fields before dawn.

Only the poor lark never sang.

V. MONSIEUR MADELEINE

WHAT had become of this mother, in the meanwhile, who, according to the people of Montfermeil, seemed to have abandoned her child? where was she? what was she doing?

After leaving her little Cosette with the Thénardiers, she went on her way and arrived at M—— sur M——.

While Fantine had been slowly sinking deeper and deeper into misery, her native village had been prosperous.

From time immemorial the special occupation of the inhabitants of M—— sur M—— had been the imitation of English jets and German black glass trinkets. The business had always been dull in consequence of the high price of the raw material, which reacted upon the manufacture. At the time of Fantine's return to M—— sur M—— an entire transformation had been effected in the production of these "black goods." Towards the end of the year 1815, an unknown man had established himself in the city, and had conceived the idea of substituting gum-lac for resin in the manufacture; and for bracelets, in particular, he made the clasps by simply bending the ends of the metal together instead of soldering them.

This very slight change had reduced the price of the raw material enormously, and this had rendered it possible, first, to raise the wages of the labourer—a benefit to the country—secondly, to improve the quality of the goods—an advantage for the consumer—and thirdly, to sell them at a lower price even while making three times the profit—a gain for the manufacturer.

In less than three years the inventor of this process had become rich, which was well, and had made all around him rich, which was better. He was a stranger in the Department. Nothing was known of his birth, and but little of his early history.

On his arrival at M—— sur M—— he had the dress, the manners, and the language of a labourer only.

It seems that the very day on which he thus obscurely entered the little city of M—— sur M——, just at dusk on a December evening, with his bundle on his back, and a thorn stick in his hand, a great fire had broken out in the town-house. This man rushed into the fire, and saved, at the peril of his life, two children, who proved to be those of the captain of the gendarmerie, and in the hurry and gratitude of the moment no one thought to ask him for his passport. He was known from that time by the name of Father Madeleine. He was a man of about fifty, who always appeared to be preoccupied in mind, and who was good-natured; this was all that could be said about him.

Thanks to the rapid progress of this manufacture, to which he had given such wonderful life, M—— sur M—— had become a considerable centre of business. The profits of Father Madeleine were so great that by the end of the second year he was able to build a large factory, in which there were two immense workshops, one for men and the other for women: whoever was needy could go there and be sure of finding work and wages.

Father Madeleine had made his fortune, but, very strangely for a mere man of business, that did not appear to be his principal care. It seemed that he thought much for others, and little for himself. In 1820, it was known that he had six hundred and thirty thousand francs standing to his credit in the banking-house of Laffitte; but before setting aside this six hundred and thirty thousand francs for himself, he had expended more than a million for the city and for the poor.

At length, in 1819, it was reported in the city one morning, that upon the recommendation of the prefect, and in consideration of the services he had rendered to the country, Father Madeleine had been appointed by the king, Mayor of M—— sur M——. The next day Father Madeleine declined.

In the same year, 1819, the results of the new process invented by Madeleine had a place in the Industrial Exhibition, and upon the report of the jury, the king named the inventor a Chevalier of the Legion of Honour. Father Madeleine declined the Cross.

Decidedly this man was an enigma, and the good people gave up the field, saying, "After all, he is a sort of an adventurer."

As we have seen, the country owed a great deal to this man, and the poor owed him everything; his workmen in particular adored him. After he became rich, those who constituted "society" bowed to him as they met, and, in the city, he began to be called Monsieur Madeleine;—but his workmen and the children continued to call him *Father Madeleine,* and at that name his face always wore a smile. As his wealth increased, invitations rained in on him. "Society" claimed him. A thousand advances were made to him, but he refused them all.

And again the gossips were at no loss. "He is an ignorant man, and of poor education. No one knows where he came from. He does not know how to conduct himself in good society, and it is by no means certain that he knows how to read."

In 1820, the services that he had rendered to the region were so brilliant, and the wish of the whole population was so unanimous, that the king again appointed him mayor of the city. He refused again; but the principal citizens came and urged him to accept, and the people in the streets begged him to do so; all insisted so strongly that at last he yielded. It was remarked that what appeared most of all to bring him to this determination, was the almost angry exclamation of an old woman belonging to the poorer class, who cried out to him with some temper:

"A good mayor is a good thing. Are you afraid of the good you can do?"

Nevertheless he remained as simple as at first. He had grey hair, a serious eye, the brown complexion of a labourer, and the thoughtful countenance of a philosopher. He usually wore a hat with a wide brim, and a long coat of coarse cloth, buttoned to the chin. He fulfilled his duties as mayor, but beyond that his life was isolated. He talked with very few persons. His pleasure was to walk in the fields.

He always took his meals alone with a book open before him in which he read. As his growing fortune gave him more leisure, it seemed that he profited by it to cultivate his mind. It was remarked from year to year that his language became more polished, choicer, and more gentle.

Although he was no longer young, it was reported that he was of prodigious strength. He would help up a fallen horse, push at a stalled wheel, or seize by the horns a bull that had broken loose. He always had his pockets full of money when he went out, and empty when he returned. When he passed through a village the ragged little youngsters would run after him with joy, and surround him like a swarm of flies.

It was surmised that he must have lived formerly in the country, for he had all sorts of useful secrets which he taught the peasants. He showed them how to destroy the grain-moth by sprinkling the granary and washing the cracks of the floor with a solution of common salt, and how to drive away the weevil by hanging up all about the ceiling and walls, in the pastures, and in the houses, the flowers of the orviot. He had recipes for clearing a field of rust, of vetches, of moles, of doggrass, and all the parasitic herbs which live upon the grain. He defended a rabbit warren against rats, with nothing but the odour of a little Barbary pig that he placed there.

The children loved him because he knew how to make charming little playthings out of straw and cocoanuts.

Some pretended that he was a mysterious personage, and declared that no one ever went into his room, which was a true anchorite's cell furnished with hour-glasses, and enlivened with death's heads and cross-bones. So much was said of this kind that some of the more mischievous of the elegant young ladies of M—— sur M—— called on him one day and said: "Monsieur Mayor, will you show us your room? We have heard that it is a grotto." He smiled, and introduced them on the spot to this "grotto." They were well punished for their curiosity. It was a room very well fitted up with mahogany furniture, ugly as all furniture of that kind is, and the walls covered with shilling paper. They could see nothing but two candlesticks of antique form that stood on the mantel, and appeared to be silver, "for they were marked," a remark full of the spirit of these little towns.

It was also whispered that he had "immense" sums deposited with Laffitte, with the special condition that they were always at his immediate command, in such a way, it was added, that Monsieur Madeleine might arrive in the morning at Laffitte's, sign a receipt and carry away his two or three millions in ten minutes. In reality these "two or three millions" dwindled down, as we have said, to six hundred and thirty or forty thousand francs.

Near the beginning of the year 1821, the journals announced the decease of Monsieur Myriel, Bishop of D——, "surnamed *Monseigneur Bienvenu,*" who died in the odour of sanctity at the age of eighty-two years.

The announcement was reproduced in the local paper of M—— sur M——. Monsieur Madeleine appeared next morning dressed in black with crape on his hat.

This mourning was noticed and talked about all over the town. *"He wears black for the Bishop of D——,"* was the talk of the drawing-rooms; it elevated Monsieur Madeleine very much, and gave him suddenly, and in a trice, marked consideration. One evening, one of the dowagers of that little great world, curious by right of age, ventured to ask him: "The mayor is doubtless a relative of the late Bishop of D——?"

He said: "No, madame."

"But," the dowager persisted, "you wear mourning for him?"

He answered: "In my youth I was a servant in his family."

It was also remarked that whenever there passed through the city a young Savoyard who was tramping about the country in search of chimneys to sweep, the mayor would send for him, ask his name and give him money. The little Savoyards told each other, and many of them passed that way.

Little by little in the lapse of time all opposition had ceased. At first there had been, as always happens with those who rise by their own efforts, slanders and calumnies against Monsieur Madeleine, soon this was reduced to satire, then it was only wit, then it vanished entirely; respect became complete, unanimous, cordial, and there came a moment, about 1821, when the words Monsieur the Mayor were pronounced at M—— sur M—— with almost the same accent as the words Monseigneur the Bishop at D—— in 1815. People came from thirty miles around to consult Monsieur Madeleine. He settled differences, he prevented lawsuits, he reconciled enemies. Everybody, of his own will, chose him for judge.

One man alone, in the city and its neighbourhood, held himself entirely clear from this contagion, and, whatever Father Madeleine did, he remained indifferent, as if a sort of instinct, unchangeable and imperturbable, kept him awake and on the watch.

Often, when Monsieur Madeleine passed along the street, calm, affectionate, followed by the benedictions of all, it happened that a tall man, wearing a flat hat and an iron-grey coat, and armed with a stout cane, would turn around abruptly behind him, and follow him with his eyes until he disappeared, crossing his arms, slowly shaking his head, and pushing his upper with his under lip up to his nose, a sort of significant grimace which might be rendered by: "But what is that man? I am sure I have seen him somewhere. At all events, I at least am not his dupe."

This personage, grave with an almost threatening gravity, was one of those who, even in a hurried interview, command the attention of the observer.

His name was Javert, and he was one of the police.

Animals are nothing but the forms of our virtues and vices, wandering before our eyes, the visible phantoms of our souls. God shows them to us to make us reflect. Now, if we admit for a moment that there is in every man some one of the species of the animal creation, it will be easy for us to describe the guardian of the peace, Javert.

The peasants of the Asturias believe that in every litter of wolves there is one dog, which is killed by the mother, lest on growing up it should devour the other little ones. Give a human face to this dog son of a wolf, and you will have Javert.

Javert was born in a prison. His mother was a fortune-teller whose husband was in the galleys. He grew up to think himself without the pale of society, and despaired of ever entering it. He noticed that society closes its doors, without pity, on two classes of men, those who attack it and those who guard it; he could choose between these two classes only; at the same time he felt that he had an indescribable basis of rectitude, order, and honesty, associated with an irrepressible hatred for that gypsy race to which he belonged. He entered the police. He succeeded. At forty he was an inspector.

In his youth he had been stationed in the galleys at the South.

Before going further, let us understand what we mean by the words human face, which we have just now applied to Javert.

The human face of Javert consisted of a snub nose, with two deep nostrils, which were bordered by large bushy whiskers that covered both his cheeks. When Javert laughed, which was rarely and terribly, his thin lips parted, and showed, not only his teeth, but his gums; and around his nose there was a wrinkle as broad and wild as the muzzle of a fallow deer. Javert, when serious, was a bull-dog; when he laughed, he was a tiger. For the rest, a small head, large jaws, hair hiding the forehead and falling over the eyebrows, between the eyes a permanent central frown, a gloomy look, a mouth pinched and frightful, and an air of fierce command.

This man was a compound of two sentiments, very simple and very good in themselves, but he almost made them evil by his exaggeration of them; respect for authority and hatred of rebellion; and in his eyes, theft, murder, all crimes, were only forms of rebellion. In his strong and implicit faith he included all who held any function in the state, from the prime minister to the constable. He had nothing but disdain, aversion, and disgust for all who had once overstepped the bounds of the law. He was absolute, and admitted no exceptions.

Javert was like an eye always fixed on Monsieur Madeleine; an eye full of suspicion and conjecture. Monsieur Madeleine finally noticed it, but seemed to consider it of no consequence. He treated Javert as he did everybody else, at ease and with kindness.

From some words that Javert had dropped, it was guessed that he had secretly hunted up all the traces of his previous life which Father Madeleine had left elsewhere. Once he happened to say, speaking to himself: "I think I have got him!" Then for three days he remained moody without speaking a word. It appeared that the clue which he thought he had was broken.

One day, however, his strange manner appeared to make an impression upon Monsieur Madeleine.

Monsieur Madeleine was walking one morning along one of the unpaved alleys of M—— sur M——; he heard a shouting and saw a crowd at a little distance. He went to the spot. An old man, named Father Fauchelevent, had fallen under his cart, his horse being thrown down.

This Fauchelevent was one of the few who were still enemies of Monsieur Madeleine at this time. When Madeleine arrived in the place, the business of Fachelevent, who was a notary of long-standing, and very well-read for a rustic, was beginning to decline. Fauchelevent had seen this mere artisan grow rich, while he himself, a professional man, had been going to ruin. This had filled him with jealousy, and he had done what he could on all occasions to injure Madeleine. Then came bankruptcy, and the old man, having nothing but a horse and cart, as he was without family, and without children, was compelled to earn his living as a carman.

The horse had his thighs broken, and could not stir. The old man was caught between the wheels. Unluckily he had fallen so that the whole weight rested upon his breast. The cart was heavily loaded. Father Fauchelevent was uttering doleful groans. They had tried to pull him out, but in vain. An unlucky effort, inexpert help, a false push, might crush him. It was impossible to extricate him otherwise than by raising the waggon from beneath. Javert, who came up at the moment of the accident, had sent for a jack.

Monsieur Madeleine came. The crowd fell back with respect.

"Help," cried old Fauchelevent. "Who is a good fellow to save an old man?"

Monsieur Madeleine turned towards the bystanders:

"Has anybody a jack?"

"They have gone for one," replied a peasant.

"How soon will it be here?"

"We sent to Flachot Place, where there is a blacksmith; but it will take a good quarter of an hour at least."

"A quarter of an hour!" exclaimed Madeleine.

It had rained the night before, the road was soft, the cart was sinking deeper every moment, and pressing more and more on the breast of the old carman. It was evident that in less than five minutes his ribs would be crushed.

"We cannot wait a quarter of an hour," said Madeleine to the peasants who were looking on.

"We must!"

"But it will be too late! Don't you see that the waggon is sinking all the while?"

"It can't be helped."

"Listen," resumed Madeleine, "there is room enough still under the waggon for a man to crawl in, and lift it with his back. Is there nobody here who has strength and courage? Five louis d'ors for him!"

Nobody stirred in the crowd.

"Ten louis," said Madeleine.

The bystanders dropped their eyes. One of them muttered: "He'd have to be devilish stout. And then he would risk getting crushed."

"Come," said Madeleine, "twenty louis."

The same silence.

"It is not willingness which they lack," said a voice.

Monsieur Madeleine turned and saw Javert. He had not noticed him when he came.

Javert continued:

"It is strength. He must be a terrible man who can raise a waggon like that on his back."

Then, looking fixedly at Monsieur Madeleine, he went on emphasising every word that he uttered:

"Monsieur Madeleine, I have known but one man capable of doing what you call for."

Javert added, with an air of indifference, but without taking his eyes from Madeleine:

"He was a convict."

"Ah!" said Madeleine.

"In the galleys at Toulon."

Madeleine became pale.

Meanwhile the cart was slowly settling down. Father Fauchelevent roared and screamed:

"I am dying! my ribs are breaking! a jack! anything! oh!"

Madeleine looked around him:

"Is there nobody, then, who wants to earn twenty louis and save this poor old man's life?"

None of the bystanders moved. Javert resumed:

"I have known but one man who could take the place of a jack; that was that convict."

"Oh! how it crushes me!" cried the old man.

Madeleine raised his head, met the falcon eye of Javert still fixed upon him, looked at the immovable peasants, and smiled sadly. Then, without saying a word, he fell on his knees, and even before the crowd had time to utter a cry, he was under the cart.

They cried out to him: "Father Madeleine! come out from there!" Old Fauchelevent himself said: "Monsieur Madeleine! go away! I must die, you see that; leave me! you will be crushed too." Madeleine made no answer.

The bystanders held their breath. The wheels were still sinking and it had now become almost impossible for Madeleine to extricate himself.

All at once the enormous mass started, the cart rose slowly, the wheels came half out of the ruts. A smothered voice was heard, crying: "Quick! help!" It was Madeleine, who had just made a final effort.

They all rushed to the work. The cart was lifted by twenty arms. Old Fauchelevent was safe.

Madeleine arose. He was very pale, though dripping with sweat. His clothes were torn and covered with mud. All wept. The old man kissed his knees and called him the good God. He himself looked with tranquil eye upon Javert, who was still watching him.

Fauchelevent had broken his knee-pan in his fall. Father Madeleine had him carried to an infirmary that he had established for his workmen in the same building with his factory, which was attended by two sisters of charity. The next morning the old man found a thousand franc bill upon the stand by the side of the bed, with this note in the handwriting of Father Madeleine: *I have purchased your horse and cart.* The cart was broken and the horse was dead. Fauchelevent got well, but he had a stiff knee. Monsieur Madeleine, through the recommendations of the sisters and the curé, got the old man a place as gardener at a convent in the Quartier Saint Antoine at Paris.

Some time afterwards Monsieur Madeleine was appointed mayor. The first time that Javert saw Monsieur Madeleine clothed with the scarf which gave him full authority over the city, he felt the same sort of shudder which a bull-dog would feel who should scent a wolf in his master's clothes. . . .

Such was the situation of the country when Fantine returned. No one remembered her. Luckily the door of M. Madeleine's factory was like the face of a friend. She presented herself there, and was admitted into the workshop for women. The business was entirely new to Fantine; she could not be very expert in it, and consequently did not receive much for her day's work; but that little was enough, the problem was solved; she was earning her living.

She bought a mirror, delighted herself with the sight of her youth, her fine hair and her fine teeth, thought of nothing save Cosette and the possibilities of the future, and was almost happy. She hired a small room and furnished it on credit, a remnant of her habits of disorder.

Not being able to say that she was married, she took good care, as we have already intimated, not to speak of her little girl.

At first, as we have seen, she paid the Thénardiers punctually. As she only knew how to sign her name she was obliged to write through a public letter-writer.

She wrote often; that was noticed. They began to whisper in the women's workshop that Fantine "wrote letters," and that "she had airs." Beyond this, more than one was jealous of her fair hair and of her white teeth.

It was ascertained that she wrote, at least twice a month, and always to the same address, and that she prepaid the postage. They succeeded in learning the address: *Monsieur Thénardier, inn-keeper Montfermeil.* In short, it became known that Fantine had a child. "She must be that sort of a woman." And there was one old gossip who went to Montfermeil, talked with the Thénardiers, and said on her return: "For my thirty-five francs, I have found out all about it. I have seen the child!"

Fantine had been more than a year at the factory, when one morning the overseer of the workshop handed her, on behalf of the mayor, fifty francs, saying that she was no longer wanted in the shop, and enjoining her, on behalf of the mayor, to leave the city.

This was the very same month in which the Thénardiers, after having asked twelve francs instead of six, had demanded fifteen francs instead of twelve.

Fantine was thunderstruck. She faltered out some suppliant words. The overseer gave her to understand that she must leave the shop instantly. Fantine was moreover only a moderate worker. Overwhelmed with shame even more than with despair, she left the shop, and returned to her room. Her fault then was now known to all!

She felt no strength to say a word. She was advised to see the mayor; she dared not.

Monsieur Madeleine had known nothing of all this. It was Monsieur Madeleine's habit scarcely ever to enter the women's workshop.

He had placed at the head of this shop an old spinster whom the curé had recommended to him, and he had entire confidence in this overseer, a very respectable person, firm, just, upright, full of that charity which consists in giving, but not having to the same extent that charity which consists in understanding and pardoning. Monsieur Madeleine left everything to her. It was in the exercise of this full power, and with the conviction that she was doing right, that the overseer had framed the indictment, tried, condemned, and executed Fantine.

As to the fifty francs, she had given them from a fund that Monsieur Madeleine had entrusted her with for alms-giving and aid to work-women, and of which she rendered no account.

Fantine offered herself as a servant in the neighbourhood; she went from one house to another. Nobody wanted her. She could not leave the city. The second-hand dealer to whom she was in debt for her furniture, and such furniture! had said to her: "If you go away, I will have you arrested as a thief." The landlord, whom she owed for rent, had said to her: "You are young and pretty, you can pay." She divided the fifty francs between the landlord and the dealer, returned to the latter three-quarters of his goods, kept only what was necessary, and found herself without work, without position, having nothing but her bed, and owing still about a hundred francs.

She began to make coarse shirts for the soldiers of the garrison, and earned twelve sous a day. Her daughter cost her ten. It was at this time that she began to get behindhand with the Thénardiers.

However, an old woman, who lit her candle for her when she came home at night, taught her the art of living in misery. Behind living on a little, lies the art of living on nothing.

Fantine learned how to do entirely without fire in winter, how to give up a bird that eats a farthing's worth of millet every other day, how to make a coverlid of her petticoat, and a petticoat of her coverlid, how to save her candle in taking her meals by the light of an opposite window.

At first, Fantine was so much ashamed that she did not dare to go out. When she was in the street, she imagined that people turned behind her and pointed at her; the sharp and cold disdain of the passers-by penetrated her, body and soul, like a north wind.

In small cities an unfortunate woman seems to be laid bare to the sarcasm and the curiosity of all. In Paris, at least, nobody knows you, and that obscurity is a covering. Oh! how she longed to go to Paris! impossible.

She must indeed become accustomed to disrespect as she had to poverty. Little by little she learned her part. After two or three months she shook off her shame and went out as if there were nothing in the way. "It is all one to me," said she.

Excessive work fatigued Fantine, and the slight dry cough that she had increased. She had been discharged towards the end of winter; summer passed away, but winter returned.

Fantine earned too little. Her debts had increased. The Thénardiers, being poorly paid, were constantly writing letters to her. One day they wrote to her that her little Cosette was entirely destitute of clothing for the cold weather, that she needed a woollen skirt, and that her mother must send at least ten francs for that. In the evening she went into a barber's shop at the corner of the street, and pulled out her comb. Her beautiful fair hair fell below her waist.

"What beautiful hair!" exclaimed the barber.

"How much will you give me for it?" said she.

"Ten francs."

"Cut it off."

She bought a knit skirt and sent it to the Thénardiers.

This skirt made the Thénardiers furious. It was the money that they wanted. They gave the skirt to Eponine. The poor lark still shivered.

Fantine thought: "My child is no longer cold, I have clothed her with my hair." She put on a little round cap which concealed her shorn head, and with that she was still pretty.

One day she received from the Thénardiers a letter in these words: "Cosette is sick of an epidemic disease. A miliary fever they call it. The drugs necessary are dear. It is ruining us, and we can no longer pay for them. Unless you send us forty francs within a week the little one will die."

She burst out laughing, and said to her old neighbour:

"Oh! they are nice! forty francs! think of that! that is two Napoleons! Where do they think I can get them? Are they fools, these boors?

As she passed through the square, she saw many people gathered about an odd-looking carriage on the top of which stood a man in red clothes, declaiming. He was a juggler and a traveling dentist, and was offering to the public complete sets of teeth, opiates, powders, and elixirs.

Fantine joined the crowd and began to laugh with the rest at this harangue, in which were mingled slang for the rabble and jargon for the better sort. The puller of teeth saw this beautiful girl laughing, and suddenly called out: "You have pretty teeth, you girl who are laughing there. If you will sell me your two incisors, I will give you a gold Napoleon for each of them."

"What is that? What are my incisors?" asked Fantine.

"The incisors," resumed the professor of dentistry, "are the front teeth, the two upper ones."

"How horrible!" cried Fantine.

Fantine fled away and stopped her ears not to hear the shrill voice of the man who called after her: "Consider, my beauty! two Napoleons! how much good they will do you! If you have the courage for it, come this evening to the inn of the *Tillac d' Argent;* you will find me there."

Fantine returned home; she read again the Thénardiers' letter. In the evening she went out, and took the direction of the Rue de Paris where the inns are.

The next morning the two teeth were gone.

She sent the forty francs to Montfermeil.

And this was a ruse of the Thénardiers to get money. Cosette was not sick.

Fantine threw her looking-glass out of the window. Long before she had left her little room on the second story for an attic room with no other fastening than a latch; one of those garret rooms the ceiling of which makes an angle with the floor and hits your head at every moment. She no longer had a bed, she retained a rag that she called her coverlid, a mattress on the floor, and a worn-out straw chair. Her little rose-bush was dried up in the corner, forgotten. As fast as the heels of her stockings wore out she drew them down into her shoes. She mended her old, wornout corsets with bits of calico. Her creditors quarrelled with her and gave her no rest. She met them in the street; she met them again on her stairs. She passed whole nights in weeping and thinking. She had a strange brilliancy in her eyes, and a constant pain in her shoulder near the top of her left shoulder-blade. She coughed a great deal. She sewed seventeen hours a day; but a prison contractor, who was working prisoners at a loss, suddenly cut down the price, and this reduced the day's wages of free labourers to nine sous. Seventeen hours of work, and nine sous a day! Her creditors were more pitiless than ever. The second-hand dealer, who had taken back nearly all his furniture, was constantly saying to her: "When will you pay me, wench?"

Good God! what did they want her to do? She felt herself hunted down, and something of the wild beast began to develop within her. About the same time, Thénardier wrote to her that really he had waited with too much generosity, and that he must have a hundred francs immediately, or else little Cosette, just convalescing after her severe sickness, would be turned out of doors into the cold and upon the highway. "A hundred francs," thought Fantine. "But where is there a place where one can earn a hundred sous a day?"

"Come!" said she, "I will sell what is left."

The unfortunate creature became a woman of the town.

The holy law of Jesus Christ governs our civilisation, but it does not yet permeate it; it is said that slavery has disappeared from European civilisation. This is a mistake. It still exists: but it weighs now only upon woman, and it is called prostitution.

At the stage of this mournful drama at which we have now arrived, Fantine has nothing left of what she had formerly been. Life and social order have spoken their last word to her. All that can happen to her has happened. She has endured all, borne all, experienced all, suffered all, lost all, wept for all. She is resigned.

She believed so at least, but it is a mistake to imagine that man can exhaust his destiny, or can reach the bottom of anything whatever.

THERE is in all small cities, and there was at M—— sur M—— in particular, a set of young men who nibble their fifteen hundred livres of income in the country with the same air with which their fellows devour two hundred thousand francs a year at Paris. They are nobodies, who have a little land, a little folly, and a little wit, who would be clowns in a drawing-room, and think themselves gentlemen in a bar-room, who talk about "my fields, my woods, my peasants," hiss the actresses at the theatre to prove that they are persons of taste, have a dog who eats the bones under the table, and a mistress who sets the dishes upon it, hold fast to a sou, overdo the fashions, admire tragedy, despise women, grow stupid as they grow old, do no work, do no good, and not much harm.

Monsieur Félix Tholomyès, had he remained in his province and never seen Paris, would have been such a man.

In the early part of January, 1823, one evening when it had been snowing, one of these dandies, one of these idlers, very warmly wrapped in one of those large cloaks which completed the fashionable costume in cold weather, was amusing himself with tormenting a creature who was walking back and forth before the window of the officers' café, in a ball-dress, with her neck and shoulders bare, and flowers upon her head. The dandy was smoking, for that was decidedly the fashion.

Every time that the woman passed before him, he threw out at her, with a puff of smoke from his cigar, some remark which he thought was witty and pleasant as: "How ugly you are!" "Are you trying to hide?" "You have lost your teeth!" etc., etc. This gentleman's name was Monsieur Bamatabois. The woman, a rueful, bedizened spectre, who was walking backwards and forwards upon the snow, did not answer him, did not even look at him, but continued her walk in silence and with a dismal regularity that brought her under his sarcasm every five minutes. This failure to secure attention doubtless piqued the loafer, who, taking advantage of the moment when she turned, came up behind her with a stealthy step and stifling his laughter stooped down, seized a handful of snow from the side walk, and threw it hastily into her back between her naked shoulders. The girl roared with rage, turned, bounded like a panther, and rushed upon the man, burying her nails in his face, and using the most frightful words that ever fell from the off-scouring of a guard-house. These insults were thrown out in a voice roughened by brandy, from a hideous mouth which lacked the two front teeth. It was Fantine.

At the noise which this made, the officers came out of the café, a crowd gathered, and a large circle was formed, laughing, jeering and applauding, around this centre of attraction composed of two beings who could hardly be recognized as a man and a woman, the man defending himself, his hat knocked off, the woman kicking and striking, her head bare, shrieking, toothless, and without hair, livid with wrath, and horrible.

Suddenly a tall man advanced quickly from the crowd, seized the woman by her muddy satin waist, and said: "Follow me!"

The woman raised her head; her furious voice died out at once. Her eyes were glassy, from livid she had become pale, and she shuddered with a shudder of terror. She recognised Javert.

The dandy profited by this to steal away.

Javert dismissed the bystanders, broke up the circle, and walked off rapidly towards the Bureau of Police, dragging the poor creature after him. The flock of spectators, in a paroxysm of joy, followed with their jokes.

When they reached the Bureau of Police, which was a low hall warmed by a stove, and guarded by a sentinel, with a grated window looking on the street, Javert opened the door, entered with Fantine, and closed the door behind him, to the great disappointment of the curious crowd who stood upon tiptoe and stretched their necks before the dirty window of the guard-house.

On entering Fantine crouched down in a corner motionless and silent, like a frightened dog.

The sergeant of the guard placed a lighted candle on the table. Javert sat down, drew from his pocket a sheet of stamped paper, and began to write.

These women are placed by our laws completely under the discretion of the police. Javert was impassible; his grave face betrayed no emotion. He was, however, engaged in serious and earnest consideration. At this moment he felt that his policeman's stool was a bench of justice. He was conducting a trial. He was trying and condemning. The more he examined the conduct of this girl, the more he revolted at it. It was clear that he had seen a crime committed. He had seen, there in the street, society represented by a property holder and an elector, insulted and attacked by a creature who was an outlaw and an outcast. A prostitute had assaulted a citizen. He, Javert, had seen that himself. He wrote in silence.

When he had finished, he signed his name, folded the paper, and handed it to the sergeant of the guard, saying: "Take three men, and carry this girl to jail." Then turning to Fantine: "You are in for six months."

The hapless woman shuddered.

"Six months! six months in prison!" cried she. "Six months to earn seven sous a day! but what will become of Cosette! my daughter! my daughter!

Why, I still owe more than a hundred francs to the Thénardiers, Monsieur Inspector, do you know that?"

"Come," said Javert, "I have heard you. Haven't you got through? March off at once! you have your six months! thé Eternal Father in person could do nothing for you."

Javert turned his back.

The soldiers seized her by the arms.

A few minutes before a man had entered without being noticed. He had closed the door, and stood with his back against it, and heard the despairing supplication of Fantine.

When the soldiers put their hands upon the wretched being, he stepped forward out of the shadow and said:

"One moment, if you please!"

Javert raised his eyes and recognised Monsieur Madeleine. He took off his hat, and bowing with a sort of angry awkwardness:

"Pardon, Monsieur Mayor—"

This word, Monsieur Mayor, had a strange effect upon Fantine. She sprang to her feet at once like a spectre rising from the ground, pushed back the soldiers with her arms, walked straight to Monsieur Madeleine before they could stop her, and gazing at him fixedly, with a wild look, she exclaimed:

"Ah! it is you then who are Monsieur Mayor!"

Then she burst out laughing and spit in his face.

Monsieur Madeleine wiped his face and said:

"Inspector Javert, set this woman at liberty."

Javert felt as though he were on the point of losing his senses. He experienced, at that moment, blow on blow, and almost simultaneously, the most violent emotions that he had known in his life. To see a woman of the town spit in the face of a mayor was a thing so monstrous that in his most daring suppositions he would have thought it sacrilege to believe it possible. On the other hand, deep down in his thought, he dimly brought into hideous association what this woman was and what this mayor might be. But when he saw this mayor, this magistrate, wipe his face quietly and say: *set this woman at liberty*, he was stupefied with amazement; thought and speech alike failed him; the sum of possible astonishment had been overpassed.

The mayor's words were not less strange a blow to Fantine. She raised her bare arm and clung to the damper of the stove as if she were staggered. Meanwhile she looked all around and began to talk in a low voice, as if speaking to herself:

"At liberty! they let me go! I am not to go to prison for six months! Who was it said that? It is not possible that anybody said that. I misunderstood. That cannot be this monster of a mayor! Was it you, my good Monsieur Javert, who told them to set me at liberty? Oh! look now! I will tell you and you will let me go. This monster of a mayor, this old whelp of a mayor, he is the cause of all this. Think of it, Monsieur Javert, he turned me away! on account of a parcel of beggars who told stories in the workshop. Was not that horrible! To turn away a poor girl who does her work honestly. Since that I could not earn enough, and all the wretchedness has come. To begin with, there is a change that you gentlemen of the police ought to make— that is, to stop prison contractors from wronging poor people. I will tell you how it is; listen. You earn twelve sous at shirt making, that falls to nine sous, not enough to live. Then we must do what we can. For me, I had my little Cosette, and I had to be a bad woman. You see now that it is this beggar of a mayor who has done all this, and then, I did stamp on the hat of this gentleman in front of the officers' café. But he, he had spoiled my whole dress with the snow. We women, we have only one silk dress, for evening. See you, I have never meant to do wrong, in truth, Monsieur Javert, and I see everywhere much worse women than I am who are much more fortunate. Oh, Monsieur Javert, it is you who said that they must let me go, is it not? Go and inquire, speak to my landlord; I pay my rent, and he will surely tell you that I am honest. Oh dear, I beg your pardon, I have touched—I did not know it—the damper of the stove, and it smokes."

Monsieur Madeleine listened with profound attention. While she was talking, he had fumbled in his waistcoat, had taken out his purse and opened it. It was empty. He had put it back into his pocket. He said to Fantine:

"How much did you say that you owed?"

Fantine, who had only looked at Javert, turned towards him:

"Who said anything to you?"

Then addressing herself to the soldiers:

"Say now, did you see how I spit in his face? Oh! you old scoundrel of a mayor, you come here to frighten me, but I am not afraid of you. I am afraid of Monsieur Javert. I am afraid of my good Monsieur Javert!"

As she said this she turned again towards the inspector:

"Now, you see, Monsieur Inspector, you must be just. I know that you are just, Monsieur Inspector; in fact, it is very simple, a man who jocosely throws a little snow into a woman's back, that makes them laugh, the officers, they must divert themselves with something, and we poor things are only for their amusement. And then, you, you come, you are obliged to keep order, you arrest the woman who has done wrong, but on reflection, as you are good, you tell them to set me at liberty, that is for my little one, because six months in prison, that would prevent my supporting my child. Only never come back again, wretch! Oh! I will never come back again, Monsieur Javert!"

She put her hand upon the latch. One more step and she would be in the street.

Javert until that moment had remained standing, motionless, his eyes fixed on the ground.

The sound of the latch roused him. He raised his head with an expression of sovereign authority.

"Sergeant," exclaimed he, "don't you see that this vagabond is going off? Who told you to let her go?"

"I," said Madeleine.

Fantine had trembled and dropped the latch, as a thief who is caught, drops what he has stolen.

Javert turned towards the mayor, said to him, "Monsieur Mayor, that cannot be done."

"Why?" said Monsieur Madeleine.

"This wretched woman has insulted a citizen."

"Inspector Javert," replied Monsieur Madeleine, "listen. You are an honest man, and I have no objection to explain myself to you. The truth is this. I was passing through the square when you arrested this woman; there was a crowd still there; I learned the circumstances; I know all about it; it is the citizen who was in the wrong, and who, by a faithful police, would have been arrested."

Javert went on:

"This wretch has just insulted Monsieur the Mayor."

"That concerns me," said Monsieur Madeleine. "The insult to me rests with myself, perhaps. I can do what I please about it."

"I beg Monsieur the Mayor's pardon. The insult rests not with him, it rests with justice."

"Inspector Javert," replied Monsieur Madeleine, "the highest justice is conscience. I have heard this woman. I know what I am doing."

At these decisive words, Javert had the boldness to look the mayor in the eye, and said, but still in a tone of profound respect:

"I am very sorry to resist Monsieur the Mayor; it is the first time in my life, but he will deign to permit me to observe that I am within the limits of my own authority. I was there. This girl fell upon Monsieur Bamatabois, who is an elector and the owner of that fine house with a balcony, that stands at the corner of the esplanade, three stories high, and all of hewn stone. Indeed, there are some things in this world which must be considered. However that may be, Monsieur Mayor, this matter belongs to the police of the street; that concerns me, and I detain the woman Fantine."

At this Monsieur Madeleine folded his arms and said in a severe tone which nobody in the city had ever yet heard:

"The matter of which you speak belongs to the municipal police. By the terms of articles nine, eleven, fifteen, and sixty-six of the code of criminal law, I am the judge of it. I order that this woman be set at liberty."

Javert endeavoured to make a last attempt.

"But, Monsieur Mayor—"

"I refer you to article eighty-one of the law of December 13th, 1799, upon illegal imprisonment."

"Monsieur Mayor, permit—"

"Not another word."

"However—"

"Retire," said Monsieur Madeleine.

Javert received the blow, standing in front, and with open breast like a Russian soldier. He bowed to the ground before the mayor, and went out.

Fantine stood by the door and looked at him with stupor as he passed before her.

When Javert was gone, Monsieur Madeleine turned towards her, and said to her, speaking slowly and with difficulty, like a man who is struggling that he may not weep:

"I have heard you. I knew nothing of what you have said. I believe that it is true. I did not even know that you had left my workshop. Why did you not apply to me? But now: I will pay your debts, I will have your child come to you, or you shall go to her. You shall live here, at Paris, or where you will. I take charge of your child and you. You shall do no more work, if you do not wish to. I will give you all the money that you need. You shall again become honest and again become happy. More than that, listen. I declare to you from this moment, if all is as you say, and I do not doubt it, that you have never ceased to be virtuous and holy before God. Oh, poor woman!"

This was more than poor Fantine could bear. To have Cosette! to leave this infamous life! to live free, rich, happy, honest, with Cosette! She looked as if she were stupefied at the man who was speaking to her. Her limbs gave way, she threw herself on her knees before Monsieur Madeleine, and, before he could prevent it, she had seized his hand and carried it to her lips.

Then she fainted.

VI. JAVERT

MONSIEUR MADELEINE had Fantine taken to the infirmary, which was in his own house. He confided her to the sisters, who put her to bed. A violent fever came on, and she passed a part of the night in delirious ravings. Finally, she fell asleep.

Towards noon the following day, Fantine awoke. She heard a breathing near her bed, drew aside the curtain, and saw Monsieur Madeleine standing gazing at something above his head. His look was full of compassionate and supplicating agony. She followed its direction, and saw that it was fixed upon a crucifix nailed against the wall.

She gazed at him for a long while without daring to interrupt him; at last she said timidly:

"What are you doing?"

Monsieur Madeleine had been in that place for an hour waiting for Fantine to awake. He took her hand, felt her pulse, and said:

"How do you feel?"

"Very well. I have slept," she said. "I think I am getting better—this will be nothing."

Monsieur Madeleine had passed the night and morning in informing himself about Fantine. He knew all now, he had learned, he sighed deeply; but she smiled with this sublime smile from which two teeth were gone.

That same night, Javert wrote a letter. Next morning he carried this letter himself to the post-office of M—— sur M——. It was directed to Paris and bore this address: "To Monsieur Chabouillet, Secretary of Monsieur the Prefect of Police."

Monsieur Madeleine wrote immediately to the Thénardiers. Fantine owed them a hundred and twenty francs. He sent them three hundred francs, telling them to pay themselves out of it, and bring the child at once to M—— sur M——, where her mother, who was sick, wanted her.

This astonished Thénardier.

"The Devil!" he said to his wife, "we won't let go of the child. It may be that this lark will become a milch cow. I guess some silly fellow has been smitten by the mother."

He replied by a bill of five hundred and some odd francs. In this bill figured two incontestable items for upwards of three hundred francs, one of a physician and the other of an apothecary who had attended and supplied Eponine and Azelma during two long illnesses. Cosette, as we have said, had not been ill. This was only a slight substitution of names. Thénardier wrote at the bottom of the bill: "*Received on account three hundred francs.*"

Monsieur Madeleine immediately sent three hundred francs more, and wrote: "Make haste to bring Cosette."

"Christ!" said Thénardier, "we won't let go of the girl."

Meanwhile Fantine remained in the infirmary.

It was not without some repugnance, at first, that the sisters received and cared for "this girl." He who has seen the bas-reliefs at Rheims will recall the distension of the lower lip of the wise virgins beholding the foolish virgins. But in a few days Fantine had disarmed them. One day the sisters heard her say in her delirium: "I have been a sinner, but when I shall have my child with me, that will mean that God has pardoned me. While I was bad I would not have had my Cosette with me; I could not have borne her sad and surprised looks. It was for her I sinned, and that is why God forgives me."

Monsieur Madeleine came to see her twice a day, and at each visit she asked him:

"Shall I see my Cosette soon?"

He answered:

"Perhaps to-morrow. I expect her every moment."

And the mother's pale face would brighten.

"Has she not a child she is anxious to see?" said the doctor.

"Yes."

"Well then, make haste to bring her."

The Thénardiers, however, did not "let go of the child"; they gave a hundred bad reasons. Cosette was too delicate to travel in the winter time, and then there were a number of little petty debts, of which they were collecting the bills, etc., etc.

"I will send somebody for Cosette," said Monsieur Madeleine, "if necessary, I will go myself."

He wrote at Fantine's dictation this letter, which she signed. "Monsieur Thénardier:

"You will deliver Cosette to the bearer.

"He will settle all small debts.

"I have the honour to salute you with consideration.

"FANTINE."

In the meanwhile a serious matter intervened.

One morning Monsieur Madeleine was in his office arranging for some pressing business of the mayoralty, in case he should decide to go to Montfermeil himself, when he was informed that Javert, the inspector of police, wished to speak with him.

"Let him come in," said he.

Javert respectfully saluted the mayor, who had his back towards him. The mayor did not look up, but continued to make notes on the papers.

Javert advanced a few steps, and paused without breaking silence.

At last the mayor laid down his pen and turned partly round:

"Well, what is it? What is the matter, Javert?"

Javert remained silent a moment as if collecting himself; then raised his voice with a sad solemnity. "There has been a criminal act committed, Monsieur Mayor."

"What act?"

"An inferior agent of the government has been wanting in respect to a magistrate, in the gravest manner. I come, as is my duty, to bring the fact to your knowledge."

"Who is this agent?" asked Monsieur Madeleine.

"I," said Javert.

"And who is the magistrate who has to complain of this agent?"

"You, Monsieur Mayor."

Monsieur Madeleine straightened himself in his chair. Javert continued, with serious looks and eyes still cast down.

"Monsieur Mayor, six weeks ago, after that scene about that girl, I was enraged and I denounced you."

"Denounced me?"

"To the Prefecture of Police at Paris."

Monsieur Madeleine, who did not laugh much oftener than Javert, began to laugh:

"As a mayor having encroached upon the police?"

"As a former convict."

Javert, who had not raised his eyes, continued:

"I believed it. For a long while I had had suspicions. A resemblance, information you obtained at Faverolles, your immense strength; the affair of old Fauchelevent; your skill as a marksman; your leg which drags a little— and in fact I don't know what other stupidities; but at last I took you for a man named Jean Valjean."

"Named what? How did you call that name?"

"Jean Valjean. He was a convict I saw twenty years ago, when I was adjutant of the galley guard at Toulon. After leaving the galleys this Valjean, it appears, robbed a bishop's palace, then he committed another robbery with weapons in his hands, in a highway, on a little Savoyard. For eight years his whereabouts have been unknown, and search has been made for him. I fancied—in short, I have done this thing. Anger determined me, and I denounced you to the prefect."

M. Madeleine, who had taken up the file of papers again, a few moments before, said with a tone of perfect indifference: "And what answer did you get?"

"That I was crazy."

"Well!"

"Well; they were right."

"It is fortunate that you think so!"

"It must be so, for the real Jean Valjean has been found."

The paper that M. Madeleine held fell from his hand; he raised his head, looked steadily at Javert, and said in an inexpressible tone:

"Ah!"

Javert continued:

"I will tell you how it is, Monsieur Mayor. There was, it appears, in the country, near Ailly-le-Haut Clocher, a simple sort of fellow who was called Father Champmathieu. He was very poor. Nobody paid any attention to him. Such folks live, one hardly knows how. Finally, this last fall, Father Champmathieu was arrested for stealing cider apples from—, but that is of no consequence. There was a theft, a wall scaled, branches of trees broken. Our Champmathieu was arrested; he had even then a branch of an apple-tree in his hand. The rogue was caged. So far, it was nothing more than a penitentiary matter. But here comes in the hand of Providence. The jail being in a bad condition, the police justice thought it best to take him to Arras, where the prison of the department is. In this prison at Arras there was a former convict named Brevet, who is there for some trifle, and who, for his good conduct, has been made turnkey. No sooner was Champmathieu set down, than Brevet cried out: 'Ha, ha! I know that man. He is a *fagot*.'[1]

"'Look up here, my good man. You are Jean Valjean.' 'Jean Valjean, who is Jean Valjean?' Champmathieu plays off the astonished. 'Don't play ignorance,' said Brevet. 'You are Jean Valjean; you were in the galleys at Toulon. It is twenty years ago. We were there together.' Champmathieu denied it all. Faith! you understand; they fathomed it. The case was worked up and this was what they found. This Champmathieu thirty years ago was a pruner in divers places, particularly in Faverolles. There we lose trace of him. A long time afterwards we find him at Auvergne; then at Paris, where he is said to have been a wheelwright and to have had a daughter—a washerwoman, but that is not proven, and finally in this part of the country. Now before going to the galleys for burglary, what was Jean Valjean? A pruner. Where? At Faverolles.

[1]Former convict.

"Another fact. This Valjean's baptismal name was Jean; his mother's family name, Mathieu. Nothing could be more natural, on leaving the galleys, than to take his mother's name to disguise himself; then he would be called Jean Mathieu. He goes to Auvergne, the pronunciation of that region would make *Chan* of *Jean*—they would call him Chan Mathieu. Our man adopts it, and now you have him transformed into Champmathieu. You follow me, do you not? Search has been made at Faverolles; the family of Jean Valjean are no longer there. Nobody knows where they are. You know in such classes these disappearances of families often occur. You search, but can find nothing. Such people, when they are not mud, are dust. And then as the commencement of this story dates back thirty years, there is nobody now at Faverolles who knew Jean Valjean. But search has been made at Toulon. Besides Brevet there are only two convicts who have seen Jean Valjean. They are convicts for life; their names are Cochepaille and Chenildieu. These men were brought from the galleys and confronted with the pretended Champmathieu. They did not hesitate. To them as well as to Brevet it was Jean Valjean. Same age; fifty-four years old; same height; same appearance, in fact the same man; it is he. At this time it was that I sent my denunciation to the Prefecture at Paris. They replied that I was out of my mind, and that Jean Valjean was at Arras in the hands of justice. You may imagine how that astonished me; I who believed that I had here the same Jean Valjean. I wrote to the justice; he sent for me and brought Champmathieu before me."

"Well," interrupted Monsieur Madeleine.

Javert replied, with an incorruptible and sad face:

"Monsieur Mayor, truth is truth. I am sorry for it, but that man is Jean Valjean. I recognised him also."

Monsieur Madeleine said in a very low voice:

"Are you sure?"

Javert began to laugh with the suppressed laugh which indicates profound conviction.

"H'm, sure!"

He remained a moment in thought, mechanically taking up pinches of the powdered wood used to dry ink, from the box on the table, and then added:

"And now that I see the real Jean Valjean, I do not understand how I ever could have believed anything else. I beg your pardon, Monsieur Mayor."

In uttering these serious and supplicating words to him, who six weeks before had humiliated him before the entire guard, and had said "Retire!" Javert, this haughty man, was unconsciously full of simplicity and dignity. Monsieur Madeleine answered his request, by this abrupt question:

"And what did the man say?"

"Oh, bless me! Monsieur Mayor, the affair is a bad one. If it is Jean Valjean, it is a second offence. To climb a wall, break a branch, and take apples, for a child is only a trespass; for a man it is a misdemeanor; for a convict it is a crime. Scaling a wall and theft includes everything. It is not a case for a police court, but for the assizes. It is not a few days' imprisonment, but the galleys for life. But this man pretends not to understand, he says: 'I am Champmathieu: I have no more to say.' He puts on an appearance of astonishment; he plays the brute. Oh, the rascal is cunning! But it is all the same, there is the evidence. Four persons have recognised him, and the old villain will be condemned. It has been taken to the assizes at Arras. I am going to testify. I have been summoned."

Monsieur Madeleine had turned again to his desk, and was quietly looking over his papers, reading and writing alternately, like a man pressed with business. He turned again towards Javert:

"That will do, Javert. Indeed all these details interest me very little. We are wasting time, and we have urgent business, Javert; go at once to the house of the good woman Buseaupied, who sells herbs at the corner of Rue Saint Saulve; tell her to make her complaint against the carman Pierre Chesnelong. He is a brutal fellow, he almost crushed this woman and her child. He must be punished. Then you will go to Monsieur Charcellay, Rue Montre-de-Champigny. He complains that the gutter of the next house when it rains throws water upon his house, and is undermining the foundation. Then you will inquire into the offences that have been reported to me, at the widow Doris's, Rue Guibourg, and Madame Renée le Bossé's, Rue du Garraud Blanc, and make out reports. But I am giving you too much to do. Did you not tell me you were going to Arras in eight or ten days on this matter?"

"Sooner than that, Monsieur Mayor."

"What day then?"

"I think I told monsieur that the case would be tried to-morrow, and that I should leave by the diligence to-night."

Monsieur Madeleine made an imperceptible motion.

"And how long will the matter last?"

"One day at longest. Sentence will be pronounced at latest to-morrow evening. But I shall not wait for the sentence, which is certain; as soon as my testimony is given I shall return here."

"Very well," said Monsieur Madeleine.

And he dismissed him with a wave of his hand.

Javert did not go.

"Your pardon, monsieur," said he.

"What more is there?" asked Monsieur Madeleine.

"Monsieur Mayor, there is one thing more to which I desire to call your attention."

"What is it?"

"It is that I ought to be dismissed."

Monsieur Madeleine arose.

"Javert, you are a man of honour and I esteem you. You exaggerate your fault. Besides, this is an offence which concerns me. You are worthy of promotion rather than disgrace. I desire you to keep your place."

Javert looked at Monsieur Madeleine with his calm eyes, in whose depths it seemed that one beheld his conscience, unenlightened, but stern and pure, and said in a tranquil voice:

"Monsieur Mayor, I cannot agree to that."

"I repeat," said Monsieur Madeleine, "that this matter concerns me."

But Javert, with his one idea, continued:

"As to exaggerating, I do not exaggerate. This is the way I reason. I have unjustly suspected you. That is nothing. It is our province to suspect, although it may be an abuse of our right to suspect our superiors. But without proofs and in a fit of anger, with revenge as my aim, I denounced you as a convict—you, a respectable man, a mayor, and a magistrate. This is a serious matter, very serious. I have committed an offence against authority in your person, I, who am the agent of authority. If one of my subordinates had done what I have, I would have pronounced him unworthy of the service, and sent him away. Well, listen a moment, Monsieur Mayor; I have often been severe in my life towards others. It was just. I did right. Now if I were not severe towards myself, all I have justly done would become injustice. Should I spare myself more than others? No. Monsieur Mayor, I do not wish you to treat me with kindness. Your kindness, when it was for others, enraged me; I do not wish it for myself. That kindness which consists in defending a woman of the town against a citizen, a police agent against the mayor, the inferior against the superior, that is what I call ill-judged kindness. Such kindness disorganizes society. Good God, it is easy to be kind, the difficulty is to be just. Had you been what I thought, I should not have been kind to you; not I."

"We will see," said Monsieur Madeleine.

And he held out his hand to him.

Javert started back, and said fiercely:

"Pardon, Monsieur Mayor, that should not be. A mayor does not give his hand to a spy."

Then he bowed profoundly, and went towards the door. There he turned around: his eyes yet downcast.

"Monsieur Mayor, I will continue in the service until I am relieved."

VII. THE TRIAL

IN THE AFTERNOON following the visit of Javert, M. Madeleine went to see Fantine as usual.

Before going to Fantine's room, he sent for Sister Simplice.

The two nuns who attended the infirmary were called Sister Perpétue and Sister Simplice.

Sister Perpétue was an ordinary village-girl, who entered the service of God as she would have entered service anywhere. She was a nun as others are cooks. Sister Simplice in comparison was a sacramental taper by the side of a tallow candle. No one could have told Sister Simplice's age; she had never been young, and seemed as if she never should be old. She was a person—we dare not say a woman—gentle, austere, companionable, cold, and who had never told a lie. Never to have lied, never to have spoken, for any purpose whatever, even carelessly, a single word which was not the truth, the sacred truth, was the distinctive trait of Sister Simplice; it was the mark of her virtue. Sincere and pure as we may be, we all have the mark of some little lie upon our truthfulness. She had none. A little lie, an innocent lie, can such a thing exist? To lie is the absolute of evil. Satan has two names; he is called Satan, and he is called the Liar. Such were her thoughts. And as she thought, she practised.

Monsieur Madeleine took Sister Simplice aside and recommended Fantine to her with a singular emphasis, which the sister remembered at a later day.

On leaving the Sister, he approached Fantine.

That day she had more fever. As soon as she saw Monsieur Madeleine, she asked him:

"Cosette?"

He answered with a smile:

"Very soon."

Monsieur Madeleine, while with Fantine, seemed the same as usual. Only he stayed an hour instead of half an hour, to the great satisfaction of Fantine. He made a thousand charges to everybody that the sick woman might want for nothing. It was noticed that at one moment his countenance became very sombre. But this was explained when it was known that the doctor had, bending close to his ear, said to him: "She is sinking fast."

Then he returned to the mayor's office, and the office boy saw him examine attentively a road-map of France which hung in his room. He made a few figures in pencil upon a piece of paper.

From the mayor's office he went to the outskirts of the city, to a Fleming's, Master Scaufflaer, Frenchified into Scaufflaire, who kept horses to let and "chaises if desired."

Monsieur Madeleine found Master Scaufflaire at home busy repairing a harness.

"Master Scaufflaire," he asked, "have you a good horse?"

"Monsieur Mayor," said the Fleming, "all my horses are good. What do you understand by a good horse?"

"I understand a horse that can go twenty leagues in a day."

"The devil!" said the Fleming, "twenty leagues!"

"Yes."

"Before a chaise?"

"Yes."

"And how long will he rest after the journey?"

"He must be able to start again the next day in case of need."

"To do the same thing again?"

"Yes."

"The devil! and it is twenty leagues?"

Monsieur Madeleine drew from his pocket the paper on which he had pencilled the figures. He showed them to the Fleming. They were the figures, 5, 6, 8½.

"You see," said he. "Total, nineteen and a half, that is to say, twenty leagues."

"Monsieur Mayor," resumed the Fleming, "I have just what you want. My little white horse, you must have seen him sometimes passing; he is a little beast from Bas-Boulonnais. He is full of fire. They tried at first to make a saddle horse of him. Bah! he kicked, he threw everybody off. They thought he was vicious, they didn't know what to do. I bought him. I put him before a chaise; Monsieur, that is what he wanted; he is as gentle as a girl, he goes like the wind. But, for example, it won't do to get on his back. It's not his idea to be a saddle horse. Everybody has his peculiar ambition. To draw, but not to carry: we must believe that he has said that to himself."

"And he will make the trip?"

"Your twenty leagues, all the way at a full trot, and in less than eight hours. But there are some conditions."

"Name them."

"First, you must let him breathe an hour when you are half way; he will eat, and somebody must be by while he eats to prevent the tavern boy from stealing his oats; for I have noticed that at taverns, oats are oftener drunk by the stable boys than eaten by the horses."

"Somebody shall be there."

"Secondly—is the chaise for Monsieur the Mayor?"

"Yes."

"Monsieur the Mayor knows how to drive?"

"Yes."

"Well, Monsieur the Mayor will travel alone and without baggage, so as not to overload the horse."

"Agreed."

"But Monsieur the Mayor, having no one with him, will be obliged to take the trouble of seeing to the oats himself."

"So said."

"I must have thirty francs a day, the days he rests included. Not a penny less, and the fodder of the beast at the expense of Monsieur the Mayor."

Monsieur Madeleine took three Napoleons from his purse and laid them on the table.

"There is two days, in advance."

"Fourthly, for such a trip, a chaise would be too heavy; that would tire the horse. Monsieur the Mayor must consent to travel in a little tilbury that I have."

"I consent to that."

"It is light, but it is open."

"It is all the same to me."

"Has Monsieur the Mayor reflected that it is winter?"

Monsieur Madeleine did not answer; the Fleming went on:

"That it is very cold?"

Monsieur Madeleine kept silence.

Master Scaufflaire continued:

"That it may rain?"

Monsieur Madeleine raised his head and said:

"The horse and the tilbury will be before my door to-morrow at half-past four in the morning."

"That is understood, Monsieur Mayor," answered Scaufflaire, then scratching a stain on the top of the table with his thumb nail, he resumed with that careless air that Flemings so well know how to associate with their shrewdness:

"Why, I have just thought of it! Monsieur the Mayor has not told me where he is going. Where is Monsieur the Mayor going?"

The mayor had the same impassive and absent-minded air as ever.

"Monsieur Scaufflaire," said he, "at what sum do you value the horse and the tilbury that you furnish me?"

"Does Monsieur the Mayor wish to buy them?"

"No, but I wish to guarantee them to you. On my return you can give me back the amount. At how much do you value horse and chaise?"

"Five hundred francs, Monsieur Mayor!"

"Here it is."

Master Scaufflaire regretted terribly that he had not said a thousand francs. In fact, the horse and tilbury, in the lump, were worth a hundred crowns.

The Fleming called his wife, and related the affair to her. Where the deuce could the mayor be going? They talked it over. "He is going to Paris," said the wife. "I don't believe it," said the husband. Monsieur Madeleine had forgotten the paper on which he had marked the figures, and left it on the mantel. The Fleming seized it and studied it. Five, six, eight and a half? this must mean the relays of the post. He turned to his wife: "I have found it out." "How?" "It is five leagues from here to Hesdin, six from Hesdin to Saint Pol, eight and a half from Saint Pol to Arras. He is going to Arras."

Meanwhile Monsieur Madeleine had reached home. He went up to his room, and shut himself in, which was nothing remarkable, for he usually went to bed early. However, the janitress of the factory, who was at the same time Monsieur Madeleine's only servant, observed that his light was out at half-past eight, and she mentioned it to the cashier who came in, adding:

"Is Monsieur the Mayor sick? I thought that his manner was a little singular."

The cashier occupied a room situated exactly beneath Monsieur Madeleine's. He paid no attention to the portress's words, went to bed, and went to sleep. Towards midnight he suddenly awoke; he had heard, in his sleep, a noise overhead. It was a step that went and came, as if some one were

walking in the room above. A moment afterwards, the cashier heard something that sounded like the opening and shutting of a wardrobe, then a
piece of furniture was moved, there was another silence, and the step began again. The cashier rose up in bed, threw off his drowsiness, looked
out, and through his window-panes, saw upon an opposite wall the ruddy
reflection of a lighted window. From the direction of the rays, it could
only be the window of Monsieur Madeleine's chamber. The reflection
trembled as if it came rather from a bright fire than from a light. The
shadow of the sash could not be seen which indicated that the window was
wide open. Cold as it was, this open window was surprising. The cashier
fell asleep again. An hour or two afterwards he awoke again. The same
step, slow and regular, was coming and going constantly over his head.

The reflection continued visible upon the wall, but it was now pale and
steady like the light of a lamp or candle. The window was still open.

Let us see what was passing in Monsieur Madeleine's room.

The reader has doubtless divined that Monsieur Madeleine is none other
than Jean Valjean.

We have little to add to what the reader already knows, concerning
what had happened to Jean Valjean, since his adventure with Petit Gervais.
From that moment, we have seen, he was another man. What the bishop
had desired to do with him, that he had executed.

He succeeded in escaping from sight, sold the bishop's silver, keeping
only the candlesticks as souvenirs, glided quietly from city to city across
France, came to M—— sur M——, conceived the idea that we have described,
accomplished what we have related, gained the point of making himself un-
assailable and inaccessible, and thence forward, established at M—— sur
M——, having but two thoughts: to conceal his name, and to sanctify his
life; to escape from men and to return to God.

These two thoughts were associated so closely in his mind, that they
formed but a single one. Sometimes, however, there was a conflict between them. In such cases, it will be remembered, the man, whom all the
country around M—— sur M—— called Monsieur Madeleine, did not waver
in sacrificing the first to the second, his security to his virtue. Thus, in
despite of all reserve and of all prudence, he had kept the bishop's candlesticks, worn mourning for him, called and questioned all the little Savoyards who passed by, gathered information concerning the families at
Faverolles, and saved the life of old Fauchelevent, in spite of the disquiet-
ing insinuations of Javert.

Even while listening to Javert, his first thought was to go, to run, to
denounce himself, to drag this Champmathieu out of prison, and to put
himself in his place; it was painful and sharp as an incision into the living
flesh, but passed away, and he said to himself: "Let us see! Let us see!"

For the rest of the day he was in this state, a tempest within, a perfect
calm without; he took only what might be called precautionary measures.
He went according to his habit to the sick bed of Fantine, and prolonged

his visit, by an instinct of kindness, saying to himself that he ought to do so, and recommend her earnestly to the sisters, in case it should happen that he would have to be absent. He felt vaguely that it would perhaps be necessary for him to go to Arras; and without having in the least decided upon this journey, he said to himself that, entirely free from suspicion as he was, there would be no difficulty in being a witness of what might pass, and he engaged Scaufflaire's tilbury, in order to be prepared for any emergency.

Returning to his room he collected his thoughts.

"After all, if there is any harm done to anybody, it is in nowise my fault. Providence has done it all. This is what He wishes apparently. Have I the right to disarrange what He arranges? What is it that I ask for now? Why do I interfere? It does not concern me. How! I am not satisfied! But what would I have then? The aim to which I have aspired for so many years, my nightly dream, the object of my prayers to heaven, security, I have gained it. It is God's will. I must do nothing contrary to the will of God."

Thus he spoke in the depths of his conscience, hanging over what might be called his own abyss. He rose from his chair, and began to walk the room. "Come," said he, "let us think of it no more. The resolution is formed!" But he felt no joy.

For the first time within eight years, the unhappy man had just tasted the bitter flavour of a wicked thought and a wicked action.

He spit it out with disgust.

He continued to question himself. He sternly asked himself what he had understood by this: "My object is attained." He declared that his life, in truth, did have an object. But what object? to conceal his name? to deceive the police? was it for so petty a thing that he had done all that he had done? had he no other object, which was the great one, which was the true one? To save, not his body, but his soul. To become honest and good again. To be an upright man! was it not that above all, that alone, which he had always wished, and which the bishop had enjoined upon him! To close the door on his past? But he was not closing it, great God! he was re-opening it by committing an infamous act! for he became a robber again, and the most odious of robbers! he robbed another of his existence, his life, his peace, his place in the world, he became an assassin! he murdered, in a moral sense, a wretched man, he inflicted upon him that frightful life in death, that living burial, which is called the galleys!

He felt that the bishop was there, that the bishop was present all the more that he was dead, that the bishop was looking fixedly at him, that henceforth Mayor Madeleine with all his virtues would be abominable to him, and the galley slave, Jean Valjean, would be admirable and pure in his sight. That men saw his mask, but the bishop saw his face. That men saw his life, but the bishop saw his conscience. He must then go to Arras, deliver the wrong Jean Valjean, denounce the right one.

"Well," said he, "let us take this course! let us do our duty! Let us save this man!"

He took his books, verified them, and put them in order. He threw into the fire a package of notes which he held against needy small traders. He wrote a letter, which he sealed, and upon the envelope of which might have been read, if there had been any one in the room at the time: *Monsieur Laffitte, banker, Rue d'Artois, Paris.*

He drew from a secretary a pocket-book containing some banknotes and the passport that he had used that same year in going to the elections.

The letter to Monsieur Laffitte finished, he put it in his pocket as well as the pocket-book, and began to walk again.

He felt that he had reached the second decisive movement of his conscience, and his destiny; that the bishop had marked the first phase of his new life, and that this Champmathieu marked the second. After a great crisis, a great trial.

And then all at once he thought of Fantine.

Here was a new crisis.

"Ah! yes, indeed! so far I have only thought of myself! I have only looked to my own convenience! It is whether I shall keep silent or denounce myself, conceal my body or save my soul, be a despicable and respected magistrate, or an infamous and venerable galley slave: it is myself, always myself, only myself. But, good God! all this is egotism. Different forms of egotism, but still egotism! Suppose I should think a little of others? Let us see, let us examine! I denounce myself? I am arrested, this Champmathieu is released, I am sent back to the galleys; very well, and what then? what takes place here? Ah! here, there is a country, a city, factories, a business, labourers, men, women, old grandfathers, children, poor people! I have created all this, I keep it all alive; wherever a chimney is smoking, I have put the brands in the fire and the meat in the pot; I have produced ease, circulation, credit; before me there was nothing; I have aroused, vivified, animated, quickened, stimulated, enriched, all the country; without me, the soul is gone. I take myself away; it all dies. And this woman who has suffered so much, who is so worthy in her fall, all whose misfortunes I have unconsciously caused! And that child which I was going for, which I have promised to the mother! Do I not also owe something to this woman, in reparation for the wrong that I have done her? If I should disappear, what happens? The mother dies. The child becomes what she may. This is what comes to pass, if I denounce myself.

"How foolish, how absurd I was! What was I speaking of in denouncing myself? What! because it would have pleased me to do the grand and the generous! That is melodramatic after all! Must an entire country be let go to ruin! must a poor hapless woman perish in the hospital! must a poor little girl perish on the street! And all for this old whelp of an apple-thief, who, beyond all doubt, deserves the galleys for something else, if not for this. Fine scruples these, which save an old vagabond who has, after all, only a few years to live, and who will hardly be more unhappy in the galleys than in his hovel, and which sacrifice a whole population, mothers, wives, children! This poor little Cosette who has no one but me in the world, and who is doubtless at this moment all blue with cold in the hut of these Thénardiers! I should fail in my duty towards all these poor beings!"

He arose and resumed his walk. This time it seemed to him that he was satisfied.

He looked at himself in the little mirror that hung over his mantelpiece and said:

"Yes! To come to a resolution has solaced me! I am quite another man now!"

He took a few steps more, then he stopped short.

"Come!" said he, "I must not hesitate before any of the consequences of the resolution I have formed. There are yet some threads which knit me to this Jean Valjean. They must be broken!"

He felt in his pocket, drew out his purse, opened it, and took out a little key.

He put this key into a lock the hole of which was hardly visible, lost as it was in the darkest shading of the figures on the paper which covered the wall. A secret door opened; a kind of false press built between the corner of the wall and the casing of the chimney. There was nothing in this closet but a few refuse trifles; a blue smock-frock, an old pair of trousers, an old haversack, and a great thorn stick, iron-bound at both ends.

He had kept them, as he had kept the silver candlesticks, to remind him at all times of what he had been. But he concealed what came from the galleys, and left the candlesticks that came from the bishop in sight.

He cast a furtive look towards the door, then with a quick and hasty movement, without even a glance at these things which he had kept so religiously and with so much danger during so many years, he took the whole, rags, stick, haversack, and threw them all into the fire.

In a few seconds, the room and the wall opposite were lit up with a great, red, flickering glare. It was all burning; the thorn stick cracked and threw out sparks into the middle of the room.

The haversack, as it was consumed with the horrid rags which it contained, left something uncovered which glistened in the ashes. By bending towards it, one could have easily recognised a piece of silver. It was doubtless the forty sous piece stolen from the little Savoyard.

Suddenly his eyes fell upon the two silver candlesticks on the mantel, which were glistening dimly in the reflection.

"Stop!" thought he, "all Jean Valjean is contained in them too. They also must be destroyed."

He took the two candlesticks.

There was fire enough to melt them quickly into an unrecognisable ingot. A minute more, and they would have been in the fire.

At that moment, it seemed to him that he heard a voice crying within him: "Jean Valjean!" "Jean Valjean!"

His hair stood on end; he was like a man who hears some terrible thing.

"Yes! that is it, finish!" said the voice, "complete what you are doing! destroy these candlesticks! annihilate this memorial! forget the bishop!

forget all! ruin this Champmathieu, yes! very well. Applaud yourself! So it is arranged, it is determined, it is done. Behold a man, a greybeard who knows not what he is accused of, who has done nothing, it may be, an innocent man, whose misfortune is caused by your name, upon whom your name weighs like a crime, who will be taken instead of you; will be condemned, will end his days in abjection and in horror! very well. Be an honoured man yourself. Remain, Monsieur Mayor, remain honourable and honoured, enrich the city, feed the poor, bring up the orphans, live happy, virtuous, and admired, and all this time while you are here in joy and in the light, there shall be a man wearing your red blouse, bearing your name in ignominy, and dragging your chain in the galleys! Yes! this is a fine arrangement! Oh, wretch!"

The sweat rolled off his forehead. He looked upon the candlesticks with haggard eyes.

"Is there anybody here?" asked he, aloud and in a startled voice.

Then he continued with a laugh, which was like the laugh of an idiot:

"What a fool I am! there cannot be anybody here."

He put the candlesticks on the mantel.

Then he resumed this monotonous and dismal walk, which disturbed the man asleep beneath him in his dreams, and wakened him out of his sleep.

The clock struck three. For five hours he had been walking thus, almost without interruption, when he dropped into his chair. He fell asleep.

When he awoke, he was chilly. A wind as cold as the morning wind made the sashes of the still open window swing on their hinges. The fire had gone out. The candle was low in the socket. The night was yet dark.

He arose and went to the window. There were still no stars in the sky. From his window he could look into the court-yard and into the street. A harsh, rattling noise that suddenly resounded from the ground made him look down.

The noise he had heard was the sound of horse's hoofs upon the pavement. At that moment there was a low rap at the door of his room.

"Monsieur Mayor, it is just five o'clock."

"What is that to me?"

"Monsieur Mayor, it is the chaise."

"What chaise?"

"The driver says that he has come for Monsieur the Mayor."

"What driver?"

"Monsieur Scaufflaire's driver."

"Monsieur Scaufflaire?"

That name startled him as if a flash had passed before his face.

"Oh, yes!" he said, "Monsieur Scaufflaire!"

There was a long silence. He examined the flame of the candle with a stupid air, and took some of the melted wax from around the wick and rolled it in his fingers. The old woman was waiting. She ventured, however, to speak again:

"Monsieur Mayor, what shall I say?"

"Say that it is right, and I am coming down."

The postal service from Arras to M—— sur M—— was still performed at this time by the little mail waggons of the date of the empire. These mail waggons were two-wheeled cabriolets, lined with buckskin, hung upon jointed springs, and having but two seats, one for the driver, the other for the traveller. The wheels were armed with those long threatening hubs which keep other vehicles at a distance, and which are still seen upon the roads of Germany. The letters were carried in a huge oblong box placed behind the cabriolet and making a part of it. This box was painted black and the cabriolet yellow.

That night the mail that came down to M—— sur M—— by the road from Hesdin, at the turn of a street just as it was entering the city, ran against a little tilbury drawn by a white horse, which was going in the opposite direction, and in which there was only one person, a man wrapped in a cloak. The wheel of the tilbury received a very severe blow. The courier cried out to the man to stop, but the traveller did not listen and kept on his way at a rapid trot.

"There is a man in a devilish hurry!" said the courier.

At daybreak he was in the open country; the city of M—— sur M—— was a long way behind. He saw the horizon growing lighter; he beheld, without seeing them, all the frozen figures of a winter dawn pass before his eyes. It was broad day when he arrived at Hesdin. He stopped before an inn to let his horse breathe and to have some oats given him. The excellent animal had made five leagues in two hours, and had not turned a hair.

The stable boy who brought the oats stooped down suddenly and examined the left wheel.

"Have you come far?" said the boy.

"Five leagues from here."

"Ah!"

"Why do you say: ah?"

The boy stooped down again, was silent a moment, with his eye fixed on the wheel, then he rose up saying:

"To think that this wheel has just come five leagues, that is possible, but it is very sure that it won't go a quarter of a league now. Look for yourself."

The wheel in fact was badly damaged. The collision with the mail waggon had broken two spokes and loosened the hub so that the nut no longer held.

"My friend," said he to the stable-boy, "is there a wheelwright here?"

"Certainly, monsieur. There he is, close by. Hallo, Master Bourgaillard!"

The wheelwright came and examined the wheel, and made such a grimace as a surgeon makes at the sight of a broken leg.

"When can I start again?"

"To-morrow."

"To-morrow!"

"It is a good day's work. Is monsieur in a great hurry?"

"A very great hurry. I must leave in an hour at the latest."

"Impossible, monsieur."

"Well! in two hours."

"Impossible to-day. There are two spokes and a hub to be repaired. Monsieur cannot start again before to-morrow."

"My business cannot wait till to-morrow. Instead of mending this wheel, cannot it be replaced?"

"A wheel to exchange?"

"Yes."

"I have not a wheel made for your cabriolet. Two wheels make a pair. Two wheels don't go together haphazard."

"In that case, sell me a pair of wheels."

"Monsieur, every wheel doesn't go on to every axle."

"But try."

"It's of no use, monsieur. I have nothing but cart wheels to sell. We are a small place here."

"Have you a cabriolet to let?"

The wheelwright, at the first glance, had seen that the tilbury was a hired vehicle. He shrugged his shoulders.

"You take good care of the cabriolets that you hire! I should have one a good while before I would let it to you."

"Well, sell it to me."

"I have not one."

"What! not even a carriole? I am not hard to suit, as you see."

"We are a little place. True, I have under the old shed there," added the wheelwright, "an old chaise that belongs to a citizen of the place, who has given it to me to keep, and who uses it every 29th of February. I would let it to you, of course it is nothing to me. The citizen must not see it go by, and then, it is clumsy; it would take two horses."

"I will take two post-horses."

"Where is monsieur going?"

"To Arras."

"And monsieur would like to get there to-day?"

"I would."

"By taking post-horses?"

"Why not?"

"Well, by taking post-horses, monsieur will not reach Arras before to-morrow. We are a cross-road. The relays are poorly served, the horses are in the fields. The ploughing season has just commenced; heavy teams are needed, and the horses are taken from everywhere, from the post as well as elsewhere. Monsieur will have to wait at least three or four hours at each relay, and then they go at a walk. There are a good many hills to climb."

"Well, I will go on horseback. Unhitch the cabriolet. Somebody in the place can surely sell me a saddle."

"Certainly, but will this horse go under the saddle?"

"It is true, I had forgotten it, he will not."

"Then——"

"But I can surely find in the village a horse to let?"

"A horse to go to Arras at one trip?"

"Yes."

"It would take a better horse than there is in our parts. You would have to buy him too, for nobody knows you. But neither to sell nor to let, neither for five hundred francs nor for a thousand, will you find such a one."

"What shall I do?"

"The best thing to do, like a sensible man, is that I mend the wheel and you continue your journey to-morrow."

"Is there no mail that goes to Arras? When does it pass?"

"To-night. Both mails make the trip in the night, the up mail as well as the down."

"How! must you take a whole day to mend this wheel?"

"A whole day, and a long one!"

"If you set two workmen at it?"

"If I should set ten."

"If you should tie the spokes with cords?"

"The spokes I could, but not the hub. And then the tire is also in bad condition, too."

"Is there no livery stable in the city?"

"No."

"Is there another wheelwright?"

The stable boy and the wheelwright answered at the same time, with a shake of the head—

"No."

It was evident that Providence was in the matter. It was Providence that had broken the wheel of the tilbury and stopped him on his way. He had not yielded to this sort of first summons; he had made all possible efforts to continue his journey; he had faithfully and scrupulously exhausted every means; he had shrunk neither before the season, nor from fatigue, nor from expense; he had nothing for which to reproach himself. If he went no further, it no longer concerned him. It was now not his fault; it was, not the act of his conscience, but the act of Providence.

He breathed freely and with a full chest for the first time since Javert's visit. It seemed to him that the iron hand which had gripped his heart for twenty hours was relaxed.

It appeared to him that now God was for him, was manifestly for him. He said to himself that he had done all that he could, and that now he had only to retrace his steps, tranquilly.

If his conversation with the wheelwright had taken place in a room of the inn, it would have had no witnesses, nobody would have heard it, the matter would have rested there; but that conversation occurred in the street. Every colloquy in the street inevitably gathers a circle. After listening for a few minutes, a young boy whom no one had noticed, had separated from the group and ran away.

At the instant the traveller was making up his mind to go back, this boy returned. He was accompanied by an old woman.

"Monsieur," said the woman, "my boy tells me that you are anxious to hire a cabriolet."

The fatal hand had closed upon him again.

The old woman had, in fact, under a shed, a sort of willow carriole. He paid what was asked, left the tilbury to be mended at the blacksmith's against his return, had the white horse harnessed to the carriole, and resumed the route he had followed since morning.

He had lost a good deal of time at Hesdin, he wished to make it up. The little horse was plucky, and pulled enough for two; but it was February, it had rained, the roads were bad. And then, it was no longer the tilbury. The carriole ran hard, and was very heavy. And besides there were many steep hills.

At Saint Pol he drove to the nearest inn, and had the horse taken to the stable. As he had promised Scaufflaire, he stood near the manger while the horse was eating.

The innkeeper's wife came into the stable.

"Does not monsieur wish breakfast?"

"Be quick," said he, "I must start again. I am in a hurry."

A big Flemish servant girl waited on him in all haste. He looked at the girl with a feeling of comfort.

"This is what ailed me," thought he. "I had not breakfasted."

His breakfast was served. He seized the bread, bit a piece, then slowly put it back on the table, and did not touch anything more.

He returned to the stable to his horse.

An hour later he had left Saint Pol, and was driving towards Tinques, which is but five leagues from Arras.

He did not stop at Tinques. As he was driving out of the village, a countryman who was repairing the road, raised his head and said:

"Your horse is very tired."

The poor beast, in fact, was not going faster than a walk.

"How far is it from here to Arras?"

"Near seven long leagues."

"How is that? the post route only counts five and a quarter."

"Ah!" replied the workman, "then you don't know that the road is being repaired. You will find it cut off a quarter of an hour from here. You are not of these parts?"

"No."

"Stop, monsieur," the countryman continued, "do you want I should give you some advice? Your horse is tired; go back to Tinques. There is a good house there. Sleep there. You can go on to Arras to-morrow."

"I must be there to-night—this evening!"

"Then go back all the same to that inn, and take an extra horse. The boy that will go with the horse will guide you through the cross-roads."

He followed the countryman's advice, retraced his steps, and a half hour afterwards he again passed the same place, but at a full trot, with a good extra horse. A stable-boy, who called himself a postillion, was sitting upon the shaft of the carriole.

He felt, however, that he was losing time. It was now quite dark.

They were driving through a cross-path. The road became frightful. The carriole tumbled from one rut to the other. In one of the jolts the whiffle-tree broke.

"Monsieur," said the postillion, "the whiffle-tree is broken; I do not know how to harness my horse now, this road is very bad at night, if you will come back and stop at Tinques, we can be at Arras early to-morrow morning."

He answered: "Have you a piece of string and a knife?"

"Yes, monsieur."

He cut off the limb of a tree and made a whiffle-tree of it.

This was another loss of twenty minutes; but they started off at a gallop.

The plain was dark. A low fog, thick and black, was creeping over the hill-tops and floating away like smoke. There were glimmering flashes from the clouds. A strong wind came from the sea. The cold penetrated.

Some distant bell struck the hour. He asked the boy:

"What o'clock is that?"

"Seven o'clock, monsieur; we shall be in Arras at eight. We have only three leagues."

At this moment he thought for the first time, and it seemed strange that it had not occurred to him sooner; that perhaps all the trouble he was taking might be useless; that he did not even know the hour of the trial; that he should at least have informed himself of that; that it was foolish to be going on at this rate, without knowing whether it would be of any use. Then he figured out some calculations in his mind; that ordinarily the sessions of the courts of assize began at nine o'clock in the morning; that this case would not occupy much time; that he would get there after it was all over!

Meanwhile Fantine was in ecstasies.

She had passed a very bad night. In the morning, when the doctor came, she was delirious. He appeared to be alarmed, and asked to be informed as soon as Monsieur Madeleine came.

At noon the doctor came again, left a few prescriptions, inquired if the mayor had been at the infirmary, and shook his head.

Monsieur Madeleine usually came at three o'clock to see the sick woman. About half-past two, Fantine began to be agitated. In the space of twenty minutes, she asked the nun more than ten times: "My sister, what time is it?"

The clock struck three. At the third stroke, Fantine rose up in bed—ordinarily she could hardly turn herself—she joined her two shrunken and yellow hands in a sort of convulsive clasp, and the nun heard from her one of those deep sighs which seem to uplift a great weight. Then Fantine turned and looked towards the door.

Nobody came in; the door did not open.

She sat so for a quarter of an hour, her eyes fixed upon the door, motionless, and as if holding her breath. The sister dared not speak. The church clock struck the quarter. Fantine fell back upon her pillow.

She said nothing, and began to make folds in the sheet.

A half-hour passed, then an hour, but no one came; every time the clock struck, Fantine rose and looked towards the door, then she fell back.

Her thought could be clearly seen, but she pronounced no name, she did not complain, she found no fault.

The clock struck five. Then the sister heard her speak very low and gently: "But since I am going away to-morrow, he does wrong not to come to-day!"

Sister Simplice herself was surprised at Monsieur Madeleine's delay.

The clock struck six. Fantine did not appear to hear. She seemed no longer to pay attention to anything around her.

Sister Simplice sent a girl to inquire of the portress of the factory if the mayor had come in, and if he would not very soon come to the infirmary. The girl returned in a few minutes.

Fantine was still motionless, and appeared to be absorbed in her own thoughts.

The servant related in a whisper to Sister Simplice that the mayor had gone away that morning before six o'clock in a little tilbury drawn by a white horse, cold as the weather was; that he went alone, without even a driver, that no one knew the road he had taken, that some said he had been seen to turn off by the road to Arras, that others were sure they had met him on the road to Paris. That when he went away he seemed, as usual, very kind, and that he simply said to the portress that he need not be expected that night.

While the two women were whispering, with their backs turned towards Fantine's bed, the sister questioning, the servant conjecturing, Fantine, with that feverish vivacity of certain organic diseases, which unites the free movement of health with the frightful exhaustion of death, had risen to her knees on the bed. All at once she exclaimed:

"You are talking there of Monsieur Madeleine! why do you talk so low? what has he done? why does he not come?"

"My child," said the sister, "be calm, lie down again."

Fantine, without changing her attitude, resumed with a loud voice, and in a tone at once piercing and imperious:

"He cannot come. Why not? You know the reason. You were whispering it there between you. I want to know."

The servant whispered quickly in the nun's ear: "Answer that he is busy with the City Council."

Sister Simplice reddened slightly; it was a lie that the servant had proposed to her. On the other hand, it did seem to her that to tell the truth to the sick woman would doubtless be a terrible blow, and that it was dangerous in the state in which Fantine was. This blush did not last long. The sister turned her calm, sad eye upon Fantine, and said:

"The mayor has gone away."

Fantine sprang up and sat upon her feet. Her eyes sparkled. A marvellous joy spread over that mournful face.

"Gone away!" she exclaimed. "He has gone for Cosette!"

Then she stretched her hands towards heaven, and her whole countenance became ineffable. Her lips moved; she was praying in a whisper.

When her prayer was ended: "My sister," said she, "I am quite willing to lie down again, I will do whatever you wish; I was naughty just now, pardon me for having talked so loud; it is very bad to talk loud; I know it, my good sister, but see how happy I am. God is kind, Monsieur Madeleine is good; just think of it, that he has gone to Montfermeil for my little Cosette."

She lay down again, helped the nun to arrange the pillow, and kissed a little silver cross which she wore at her neck, and which Sister Simplice had given her.

"My child," said the sister, "try to rest now, and do not talk any more."

"He started this morning for Paris. Indeed he need not even go through Paris. Montfermeil is a little to the left in coming. You remember what he said yesterday, when I spoke to him about Cosette: *Very soon, very soon!* This is a surprise he has for me. You know he had me sign a letter to take her away from the Thénardiers. They will have nothing to say, will they? They will give up Cosette. Because they have their pay. The authorities would not let them keep a child when they are paid. My sister, do not make signs to me that I must not talk. I am very happy, I am doing very well. I have no pain at all. He will be here to-morrow with Cosette! How far is it from here to Montfermeil?"

The sister, who had no idea of the distance, answered: "Oh! I feel sure that he will be here to-morrow."

"To-morrow! to-morrow!" said Fantine, "I shall see Cosette to-morrow! See, good Sister of God, I am well now."

One who had seen her a quarter of an hour before could not have understood this. Now she was all rosy; she talked in a lively, natural tone; her whole face was only a smile.

"Well," resumed the nun, "now you are happy, obey me—do not talk any more."

Fantine laid her head upon the pillow, and said in a low voice:

"Yes, lie down again; be prudent now that you are going to have your child. Sister Simplice is right. All here are right."

The sister closed the curtains, hoping that she would sleep.

Between seven and eight o'clock the doctor came. Hearing no sound, he supposed that Fantine was asleep, went in softly, and approached the bed on tiptoe. He drew the curtains aside, and by the glimmer of the twilight he saw Fantine's large calm eyes looking at him.

She said to him: "Monsieur, you will let her lie by my side in a little bed, won't you?"

The doctor thought she was delirious. She added:

"Look, there is just room."

The doctor recommended silence, and that she should avoid all painful emotion. He prescribed an infusion of pure quinine, and, in case the fever should return in the night, a soothing potion. As he was going away he said to the sister: "She is better. If by good fortune the mayor should really come back to-morrow with the child, who knows? there are such astonishing crises; we have seen great joy instantly cure diseases; I am well aware that this is an organic disease, and far advanced, but this is all such a mystery! We shall save her perhaps!"

It was nearly eight o'clock in the evening when the carriole which we left on the road drove into the yard of the Hotel de la Poste at Arras. The man we have followed thus far, got out, answered the hospitalities of the inn's people with an absent-minded air, sent back the extra horse, and took the little white one to the stable himself.

This done, he left the hotel.

He was not acquainted in Arras, the streets were dark, and he went haphazard. A citizen came along with a lantern.

"Monsieur," said he, "the court house, if you please?"

"You are not a resident of the city, monsieur?" answered the citizen, who was an old man, "well, follow me, I am going right by the court house, that is to say, the city hall. For they are repairing the court house just now, and the courts are holding their sessions at the city hall, temporarily."

As they walked along, the citizen said to him:

"If monsieur wishes to see a trial, he is rather late. Ordinarily the sessions close at six o'clock."

However, when they reached the great square, the citizen showed him four long lighted windows on the front of a vast dark building.

"Faith, monsieur, you are in time, you are fortunate. Do you see those four windows? that is the court of assizes. There is a light there. Then they have not finished. The case must have been prolonged and they are having an evening session. Are you interested in this case? Is it a criminal trial? Are you a witness?"

He answered:

"I have no business; I only wish to speak to a lawyer."

"That's another thing," said the citizen. "Stop, monsieur, here is the door. The doorkeeper is up there. You have only to go up the grand stairway."

He followed the citizen's instructions, and in a few minutes found himself in a hall where there were many people, and scattered groups of lawyers in their robes whispering here and there. He felt no fear in addressing the first lawyer whom he met.

"Monsieur," said he, "how are they getting along?"

"It is finished," said the lawyer.

"Finished!"

The word was repeated in such a tone that the lawyer turned around.

"Pardon me, monsieur, you are a relative, perhaps?"

"No. I know no one here. And was there a sentence?"

"Of course. It was hardly possible for it to be otherwise."

"To hard labour?"

"For life."

He continued in a voice so weak that it could hardly be heard: "The identity was established, then?"

"What identity?" responded the lawyer. "There was no identity to be established. It was a simple affair. This woman had killed her child, the infanticide was proven, the jury were not satisfied that there was any premeditation; she was sentenced for life."

"It is a woman, then?" said he.

"Certainly. The Limosin girl. What else are you speaking of?"

"Nothing, but if it is finished; why is the hall still lighted up?"

"That is for the other case, which commenced nearly two hours ago."

"What other case?"

"Oh! that is a clear one also. It is a sort of a thief, a second offender, a galley slave, a case of robbery. I forget his name. He looks like a bandit. Were it for nothing but having such a face, I would send him to the galleys."

He approached several groups and listened to their talk. This man had stolen some apples, but that did not appear to be very well proven; what was proven was that he had been in the galleys at Toulon. This was what ruined his case.

An officer stood near the door which opened into the courtroom. He asked this officer:

"Monsieur, will the door be opened soon?"

"It will not be opened," said the officer.

"Why not?"

"Because the hall is full."

"What! there are no more seats?"

"Not a single one. The door is closed. No one can enter."

The officer added, after a silence: "There are indeed two or three places still behind Monsieur the Judge, but Monsieur the Judge admits none but public functionaries to them."

So saying, the officer turned his back.

He retired with his head bowed down, crossed the ante-chamber, and walked slowly down the staircase, seeming to hesitate at every step. Suddenly he opened his coat, drew out his pocket-book, took out a pencil, tore out a sheet, and wrote rapidly upon that sheet, by the glimmering light, this line: *Monsieur Madeleine, Mayor of M—— sur M——;* then he went up the stairs again rapidly, passed through the crowd, walked straight to the officer, handed him the paper, and said to him with authority: "Carry that to Monsieur the Judge."

Without himself suspecting it, the Mayor of M—— sur M—— had a certain celebrity. For seven years the reputation of his virtue had been extending throughout Bas-Boulonnais; it had finally crossed the boundaries of the little county, and had spread into the two or three neighbouring departments.

The Judge of the Royal Court of Douai, who was holding this term of the assizes at Arras, was familiar, as well as everybody else, with this name. When the officer, quietly opening the door which led from the counsel chamber to the court room, bent behind the judge's chair and handed him the paper, on which was written the line we have just read, adding: "*This gentleman desires to witness the trial*," the judge made a hasty movement of deference, seized a pen, wrote a few words at the bottom of the paper and handed it back to the officer, saying to him: "Let him enter."

The unhappy man heard, through his thoughts, some one saying to him: "Will monsieur do me the honour to follow me?"

In a few minutes he found himself alone in a kind of panelled cabinet, of a severe appearance, lighted by two wax candles placed upon a table covered with green cloth. The last words of the officer who had left him still rang in his ear: "Monsieur, you are now in the counsel chamber; you have but to turn the brass knob of that door and you will find yourself in the court room, behind the judge's chair."

The decisive moment had arrived.

Suddenly, he seized the knob; the door opened.

He was in the court room.

He took a step, closed the door behind him, mechanically, and remained standing, noting what he saw.

At one end of the hall, that at which he found himself, heedless judges, in threadbare robes, were biting their finger-nails, or closing their eyelids; at the other end was a ragged rabble; there were lawyers in all sorts of attitudes; soldiers with honest and hard faces; old, stained wainscoting, a dirty ceiling, tables covered with serge, which was more nearly yellow than green; doors blackened by finger-marks; tavern lamps, giving more smoke than light, on nails in the panelling; candles, in brass candlesticks, on the tables; everywhere obscurity, unsightliness, and gloom.

All eyes converged on a single point, a wooden bench placed against a little door, along the wall at the left hand of the judge. Upon this bench, which was lighted by several candles, was a man between two gendarmes.

This was the man.

He thought he saw himself, older, doubtless, not precisely the same in features, but alike in attitude and appearance, with that bristling hair, with those wild and restless eyeballs, with that blouse—just as he was on the day he entered D——, full of hatred, and concealing in his soul that hideous hoard of frightful thoughts which he had spent nineteen years in gathering upon the floor of the galleys.

He said to himself, with a shudder: "Great God! shall I again come to this?"

This being appeared at least sixty years old. There was something indescribably rough, stupid, and terrified in his appearance.

At the sound of the door, people had stood aside to make room. The judge had turned his head, and supposing the person who entered to be the mayor of M—— sur M——, greeted him with a bow. The prosecuting attorney, who had seen Madeleine at M—— sur M——, recognised him and bowed likewise. He scarcely perceived them.

Judges, clerk, gendarmes, a throng of heads, cruelly curious—he had seen all these once before, twenty-seven years ago. And by a tragic sport of destiny, which was agitating all his ideas and rendering him almost insane, it was another self before him. This man on trial was called by all around him, Jean Valjean!

A chair was behind him; he sank into it, terrified at the idea that he might be observed. When seated, he took advantage of a pile of papers on the judges' desk to hide his face from the whole room. He could now see without being seen.

He looked for Javert, but did not see him. The witnesses' seat was hidden from him by the clerk's table.

At the moment of his entrance, the counsel for the prisoner was finishing his plea. The attention of all was excited to the highest degree; the trial had been in progress for three hours. During these three hours, the spectators had seen a man, an unknown, wretched being, thoroughly stupid or thoroughly artful, gradually bending beneath the weight of a terrible probability. The counsel for the defence had established that the theft of the apples was not in fact proved. His client, whom in his character of counsel he persisted in calling Champmathieu, had not been seen to scale the wall or break off the branch. He had been arrested in possession of this branch (which the counsel preferred to call *bough*); but he said that he had found it on the ground. Where was the proof to the contrary? Undoubtedly this branch had been broken and carried off after the scaling of the wall, then thrown away by the alarmed marauder; undoubtedly, there had been a thief.—But what evidence was there that this thief was Champmathieu? One single thing. That he was formerly a convict.

The counsel would not deny that this fact unfortunately appeared to be fully proved; the defendant had resided at Faverolles; the defendant had been a pruner, the name of Champmathieu might well have had its origin in that of Jean Mathieu; all this was true, and finally, four witnesses had positively and without hesitation identified Champmathieu as the galley slave, Jean Valjean; to these circumstances and this testimony the counsel could oppose nothing but the denial of his client, an interested denial; but even supposing him to be the convict Jean Valjean, did this prove that he had stolen the apples? that was a presumption at most, not a proof. The accused, it was true, and the counsel "in good faith" must admit it, had adopted "a mistaken system of defence." He had persisted in denying everything, both the theft and the fact that he had been a convict. The man was evidently imbecile. Long suffering in the galleys, long suffering out of the galleys, had brutalised him, etc., etc.; if he made a bad defence, was this a reason for convicting him?

The time had come for closing the case. The judge commanded the accused to rise, and put the usual question: "Have you anything to add to your defence?"

The man, standing, and twirling in his hands a hideous cap, seemed not to hear.

The judge repeated the question.

This time the man heard, and appeared to comprehend. He started like one awakening from sleep, cast his eyes around him, looked at the spectators, the gendarmes, his counsel, the jurors, and the court, placed his huge fists on the bar before him, looked around again, and suddenly fixing his eyes upon the prosecuting attorney, began to speak.

"I have this to say: That I have been a wheelwright at Paris; that it was at M. Baloup's too. It is a hard life to be a wheelwright, you always work out-doors, in yards, under sheds when you have good bosses, never in shops, because you must have room, you see. In the winter, it is so cold that you thresh your arms to warm them; but the bosses won't allow that; they say it is a waste of time. It is tough work to handle iron when there is ice on the pavements. It wears a man out quick. You get old when you are young at this trade. A man is used up by forty. I was fifty-three; I was sick a good deal. I earned only thirty sous a day, they paid me as little as they could—the bosses took advantage of my age. Then I had my daughter, who was a washerwoman at the river. She earned a little for herself; between us two, we got on; she had hard work too. All day long up to the waist in a tub, in rain, in snow, with wind that cuts your face when it freezes, it is all the same, the washing must be done. But there is a hot lye that is terrible and ruins your eyes. She would come home at seven o'clock at night, and go to bed right away, she was so tired. Her husband used to beat her. She is dead. We wasn't very happy. She was a good girl; she never went to balls, and was very quiet. Look here, I am telling the truth. You have only to ask if 'tisn't so. I don't know what more you want of me."

The man ceased speaking, but did not sit down. He had uttered these sentences in a loud, rapid, hoarse, harsh, and guttural tone, with a sort of angry and savage simplicity. When he had finished, the auditory burst into laughter. He looked at them, and seeing them laughing and not knowing why, began to laugh himself.

That was an ill omen.

The judge, considerate and kindly man, raised his voice:

He reminded "gentlemen of the jury" that M. Baloup, the former master wheelwright by whom the prisoner said he had been employed, had been summoned, but had not appeared. He had become bankrupt, and could not be found. Then, turning to the accused, he adjured him to listen to what he was about to say, and added: "You are in a position which demands reflection. The gravest presumptions are weighing against you, and may lead to fatal results. Prisoner, on your own behalf, I question you a second time, explain yourself clearly on these two points. First, did you or did you not climb the wall of the Pierron close, break off the branch and steal the apples, that is to say, commit the crime of theft, with the addition of breaking into an inclosure? Secondly, are you or are you not the discharged convict, Jean Valjean?"

The prisoner shook his head with a knowing look, like a man who understands perfectly, and knows what he is going to say. He opened his mouth, turned towards the presiding judge, and said:

"In the first place—"

Then he looked at his cap, looked up at the ceiling, and was silent.

"Prisoner," resumed the prosecuting attorney, in an austere tone, "give attention. You have replied to nothing that has been asked you. Your agitation condemns you. It is evident that your name is not Champmathieu, but that you are the convict, Jean Valjean, disguised under the name at first, of Jean Mathieu, which was that of his mother; that you have lived in Auvergne; that you were born at Faverolles, where you were a pruner. It is evident that you have stolen ripe apples from the Pierron close, with the addition of breaking into the inclosure. The gentlemen of the jury will consider this."

The accused had at last resumed his seat; he rose abruptly when the prosecuting attorney had ended, and exclaimed:

"You are a very bad man, you, I mean. This is what I wanted to say. I couldn't think of it first off. I never stole anything. I am a man who don't get something to eat every day. I was coming from Ailly, walking alone after a shower, which had made the ground all yellow with mud, and I found a broken branch on the ground with apples on it; and I picked it up not knowing what trouble it would give me. It is three months that I have been in prison, being knocked about. More'n that, I can't tell. I never studied; I am a poor man. You are all wrong not to see that I didn't steal. I picked up off the ground things that was there. You talk about Jean Valjean, Jean Mathieu—I don't know any such people. They must be villagers. I have worked for Monsieur Baloup, Boulevard de l'Hopital. My name is Champmathieu. You must be very sharp to tell me where I was born. I don't know myself. I am tired of your everlasting nonsense. What is everybody after me for like a mad dog?"

The prosecuting attorney was still standing; he addressed the judge:

"Sir, in the presence of the confused but very adroit denegations of the accused, who endeavours to pass for an idiot, but who will not succeed in it—we will prevent him—we request that it may please you and the court to call again within the bar the convicts, Brevet, Cochepaille, and Chenildieu, and the police-inspector Javert, and to submit them to a final interrogation, concerning the identity of the accused with the convict Jean Valjean."

"I must remind the prosecuting attorney," said the presiding judge, "that police-inspector Javert, recalled by his duties to the chief town of a neighbouring district, left the hall, and the city also as soon as his testimony was taken."

"True," replied the prosecuting attorney; "in the absence of Monsieur Javert, I think it a duty to recall to the gentlemen of the jury what he said here a few hours ago. Javert is an estimable man, who does honour to inferior but important functions, by his rigorous and strict probity. These are the terms in which he testified: 'I do not need even moral presumptions and material proofs to contradict the denials of the accused. I recognise him perfectly. This man's name is not Champmathieu; he is a convict, Jean Valjean, very hard, and much feared. He was liberated at the expiration of his term, but with extreme regret. He served out nineteen years at hard labour for burglary; five or six times he attempted to escape. Besides the Petit Gervais and Pierron robberies, I suspect him also of a robbery committed on his highness, the late Bishop of D——. I often saw him when I was adjutant of the galley guard at Toulon. I repeat it; I recognise him perfectly.' "

This declaration, in terms so precise, appeared to produce a strong impression upon the public and jury. The prosecuting attorney concluded by insisting that, in the absence of Javert, the three witnesses, Brevet, Chenildieu, and Cochepaille, should be heard anew and solemnly interrogated.

The old convict Brevet was clad in the black and grey jacket of the central prisons. Brevet was about sixty years old; he had the face of a man of business, and the air of a rogue. They sometimes go together. He had become something like a turnkey in the prison—to which he had been brought by new misdeeds. He was one of those men of whom their superiors are wont to say, "He tries to make himself useful." The chaplain bore good testimony to his religious habits. It must not be forgotten that this happened under the Restoration.

"Brevet," said the judge, "you have suffered infamous punishment, and cannot take an oath."

Brevet cast down his eyes.

"Nevertheless," continued the judge, "even in the man whom the law has degraded there may remain, if divine justice permit, a sentiment of honour and equity. Prisoner, rise. Brevet, look well upon the prisoner; collect your remembrances, and say, on your soul and conscience, whether you still recognise this man as your former comrade in the galleys, Jean Valjean."

Brevet looked at the prisoner, then turned again to the court.

"Yes, your honour, I was the first to recognise him, and still do so. This man is Jean Valjean, who came to Toulon in 1796, and left in 1815. I left a year after. He looks like a brute now, but he must have grown stupid with age; at the galleys he was sullen. I recognise him now, positively."

"Sit down," said the judge. "Prisoner, remain standing."

Chenildieu was brought in, a convict for life, as was shown by his red cloak and green cap. He was undergoing his punishment in the galleys of Toulon, whence he had been brought for this occasion. He was a little man, about fifty years old, active, wrinkled, lean, yellow, brazen, restless, with a sort of sickly feebleness in his limbs and whole person, and immense force in his eye.

The judge addressed nearly the same words to him as to Brevet. The judge requested him to collect his thoughts, and asked him as he had Brevet, whether he still recognised the prisoner.

Chenildieu burst out laughing.

"Gad! do I recognise him! we were five years on the same chain. You're sulky with me, are you, old boy?"

"Sit down," said the judge.

The officer brought in Cochepaille; this other convict for life, brought from the galleys and dressed in red like Chenildieu, was a peasant from Lourdes, and a semi-bear of the Pyrenees. He had tended flocks in the mountains, and from shepherd had glided into brigandage. He was one of those unfortunate men whom nature turns out as wild beasts, and society finishes up into galley slaves.

"It is Jean Valjean," said Cochepaille. "The same they called Jean-the-Jack, he was so strong."

A buzz ran through the crowd and almost invaded the jury.

"Officers," said the judge, "enforce order. I am about to sum up the case."

At this moment there was a movement near the judge. A voice was heard exclaiming:

"Brevet, Chenildieu, Cochepaille, look this way!"

So terrible was this voice that those who heard it felt their blood run cold. All eyes turned towards the spot whence it came. A man, who had been sitting among the privileged spectators behind the court, had risen, pushed open the low door which separated the tribunal from the bar, and was standing in the centre of the hall. The judge, the prosecuting attorney, Monsieur Bamatabois, twenty persons recognised him, and exclaimed at once:

"Monsieur Madeleine!"

The clerk's lamp lighted up his face. He held his hat in hand; there was no disorder in his dress; his overcoat was carefully buttoned. He was very pale, and trembled slightly.

Before even the judge and prosecuting attorney could say a word, before the gendarmes and officers could make a sign, the man, whom all up to this moment had called Monsieur Madeleine, had advanced towards the witnesses, Cochepaille, Brevet, and Chenildieu.

"Do you not recognise me?" said he.

Monsieur Madeleine turned towards the jurors and court, and said in a mild voice:

"Gentlemen of the jury, release the accused. Your honour, order my arrest. He is not the man whom you seek; it is I. I am Jean Valjean."

The face of the judge was marked with sympathy and sadness; he exchanged glances with the prosecuting attorney, and a few whispered words with the assistant judges. He turned to the spectators and asked in a tone which was understood by all:

"Is there a physician here?"

The prosecuting attorney continued:

"Gentlemen of the jury, the strange and unexpected incident which disturbs the audience, inspires us, as well as yourselves, with a feeling we have no need to express. You all know, at least by reputation, the honourable Monsieur Madeleine, Mayor of M—— sur M——. If there be a physician in the audience, we unite with his honour the judge in entreating him to be kind enough to lend his assistance to Monsieur Madeleine and conduct him to his residence."

Monsieur Madeleine did not permit the prosecuting attorney to finish, but interrupted him with a tone full of gentleness and authority.

"I thank you, Monsieur Prosecuting Attorney, but I am not mad. You shall see. You were on the point of committing a great mistake; release that man. You can take me, since I am here. I have done my best. I have disguised myself under another name, I have become rich, I have become a mayor, I have desired to enter again among honest men. It seems that this cannot be. I have nothing more to add. Take me. Great God! the prosecuting attorney shakes his head. You say 'Monsieur Madeleine has gone mad;' you do not believe me. This is hard to be borne. Would that Javert were here. He would recognise me!"

He turned to the three convicts:

"Well! I recognise you, Brevet, do you remember—"

He paused, hesitated a moment, and said:

"Do you remember those checkered, knit suspenders that you had in the galleys?"

Brevet started as if struck with surprise, and gazed wildly at him from head to foot. He continued:

"Chenildieu, the whole of your left shoulder has been burned deeply, from laying it one day on a chafing dish full of embers, to efface the three letters T. F. P., which yet are still to be seen there. Answer me, is this true?"

"It is true!" said Chenildieu.

He turned to Cochepaille:

"Cochepaille, you have on your left arm, near where you have been bled, a date put in blue letters with burnt powder. It is the date of the landing of the emperor at Cannes, *March 1st*, 1815. Lift up your sleeve."

Cochepaille lifted up his sleeve; the date was there.

The unhappy man turned towards the audience and the court with a smile of triumph; it was also the smile of despair.

"You see clearly," said he, "that I am Jean Valjean."

"I will not disturb the proceeding further," continued Jean Valjean. "I am going, since I am not arrested. I have many things to do."

He walked towards the outer door. Not a voice was raised, not an arm stretched out to prevent him. It was never known who opened the door, but it is certain that the door was open when he came to it. On reaching it he turned and said:

"Monsieur the Prosecuting Attorney, I remain at your disposal."

He went out, and the door closed as it had opened.

Less than an hour afterwards, the verdict of the jury discharged from all accusation the said Champmathieu; and Champmathieu, set at liberty forthwith, went his way stupefied, thinking all men mad.

VIII. SISTER SIMPLICE

Day began to dawn. Fantine had had a feverish and sleepless night, yet full of happy visions; she fell asleep at daybreak. Sister Simplice, who had watched with her, took advantage of this slumber to go and prepare a new potion of quinine. The good sister had been for a few moments in the laboratory of the infirmary when suddenly she turned her head, and uttered a faint cry. M. Madeleine stood before her.

"How is the poor woman?"

"Better just now. But we have been very anxious indeed."

She explained what had happened, that Fantine had been very ill the night before, but was now better, because she believed that the mayor had gone to Montfermeil for her child.

"That is well," said he.

"Yes," returned the sister, "but now, Monsieur the Mayor, when she sees you without her child, what shall we tell her?"

He reflected for a moment, then said:

"God will inspire us."

"But, we cannot tell her a lie," murmured the sister, in a smothered tone.

The broad daylight streamed into the room, and lighted up the face of M. Madeleine.

The sister happened to raise her eyes.

"O God, monsieur," she exclaimed. "What has befallen you? Your hair is all white!"

Sister Simplice had no mirror; she rummaged in a case of instruments, and found a little glass which the physician of the infirmary used to discover whether the breath had left the body of a patient. M. Madeleine took the glass, looked at his hair in it, and said, "Indeed!"

He spoke the word with indifference, as if thinking of something else.

"Will not Monsieur the Mayor bring back her child?" asked the sister, scarcely daring to venture a question.

"Certainly, but two or three days are necessary."

"If she does not see Monsieur the Mayor here," continued the sister timidly, "she will not know that he has returned; it will be easy for her to have patience, and when the child comes, she will think naturally that Monsieur the Mayor has just arrived with her. Then we will not have to tell her a falsehood."

Monsieur Madeleine seemed to reflect for a few moments, then said with his calm gravity:

"No, my sister, I must see her. Perhaps I have not much time."

The nun did not seem to notice his "perhaps," which gave an obscure and singular significance to the words of Monsieur the Mayor. She answered, lowering her eyes and voice respectfully:

"In that case, she is asleep, but monsieur can go in."

He entered the chamber of Fantine, approached her bed, and opened the curtains. She was sleeping. Her long, fair eyelashes, the only beauty of her youth, quivered as they lay upon her cheek.

She opened her eyes, saw him, and said tranquilly, with a smile:

"And Cosette?"

He answered something mechanically, which he could never afterwards recall.

Happily, the physician came to the aid of M. Madeleine.

"My child," said he, "be calm, your daughter is here."

The eyes of Fantine beamed with joy, and lighted up her whole countenance.

"Oh!" she exclaimed, "bring her to me!"

"Not yet," continued the physician, "not at this moment. You have some fever still. The sight of your child will agitate you, and make you worse. We must cure you first."

She interrupted him impetuously.

"But I am cured! I tell you I am cured! I will see my child!"

"You see how you are carried away!" said the physician. "So long as you are in this state, I cannot let you have your child. It is not enough to see her, you must live for her. When you are reasonable, I will bring her to you myself."

The poor mother bowed her head.

"Sir, I ask your pardon. Once I would not have spoken as I have now, but so many misfortunes have befallen me that sometimes I do not know what I am saying. I will wait as long as you wish, but I am sure that it will not harm me to see my daughter."

Nevertheless, although restraining herself, she could not help addressing a thousand questions to M. Madeleine.

"Did you have a pleasant journey, Monsieur the Mayor? Oh! how good you have been to go for her! Tell me only how she is. Did she bear the journey well? Ah! she will not know me. In all this time, she has forgotten me, poor kitten! Tell me only, were her clothes clean? Did those Thénardiers keep her neat? How did they feed her?"

He took her hand. "Cosette is beautiful," said he. "Cosette is well; you shall see her soon, but be quiet. You talk too fast; and then you throw your arms out of bed, which makes you cough."

In fact, coughing fits interrupted Fantine at almost every word.

The physician had retired; Sister Simplice alone remained with them. But Fantine cried out:—

"I hear her! Oh, darling! I hear her!"

There was a child playing in the court—a little girl, running up and down to keep herself warm, singing and laughing in a loud voice. Fantine heard this little girl singing.

"Oh!" said she, "it is my Cosette! I know her voice!"

She began to count on her fingers.

"One, two, three, four. She is seven years old. In five years. She will have a white veil and open-worked stockings, and will look like a little lady. Oh, my good sister, you do not know how foolish I am; here I am thinking of my child's first communion!"

Suddenly she ceased speaking, and her eyes, dilated with terror, seemed to fasten on something before her at the other end of the room. She did not take her eyes from the object which she seemed to see, but touched his arm with one hand, and with the other made a sign to him to look behind him.

He turned, and saw Javert.

Let us see what had happened.

The half hour after midnight was striking when M. Madeleine left the hall of the Arras Assizes. He had returned to his inn just in time to take the mail-coach. A little before six in the morning he had reached M—— sur M——, where his first care had been to post his letter to M. Laffitte, then go to the infirmary and visit Fantine.

Immediately upon the discharge of Champmathieu the prosecuting attorney closeted himself with the judge. The first sensation being over, the judge made few objections. Justice must take its course. Then to confess the truth, although the judge was a kind man, and really intelligent, he was at the same time a strong, almost zealous royalist, and had been shocked when the mayor of M—— sur M——, in speaking of the debarkation at Cannes, said the *Emperor* instead of *Buonaparte*.

The order of arrest was therefore granted. The prosecuting attorney sent it to M—— sur M—— by a courier, at full speed, to police inspector Javert.

Javert was just rising when the courier brought him the warrant and order of arrest.

One who did not know Javert, on seeing him as he entered the hall of the infirmary, could have divined nothing of what was going on, and would have thought his manner the most natural imaginable. He was cool, calm, grave; his grey hair lay perfectly smooth over his temples, and he had ascended the stairway with his customary deliberation. But one who knew him thoroughly and examined him with attention, would have shuddered. The buckle of his leather cravat, instead of being on the back of his neck, was under his left ear. This denoted an unheard-of agitation.

He came unostentatiously, had taken a corporal and four soldiers from a station-house near-by, had left the soldiers in the court, had been shown to Fantine's chamber by the portress, without suspicion, accustomed as she was to see armed men asking for the mayor.

On reaching the room of Fantine, Javert turned the key, pushed open the door with the gentleness of a sick-nurse, or a police spy, and entered. Suddenly, Fantine raised her eyes, saw him, and caused Monsieur Madeleine to turn round.

Fantine had not seen Javert since the day the mayor had wrested her from him. Her sick brain accounted for nothing, only she was sure that he had come for her. She shrieked in anguish:

"Monsieur Madeleine, save me!"

Jean Valjean had risen. He said to Fantine in his gentlest and calmest tone:

"Be composed; it is not for you that he comes."

He then turned to Javert and said:

"I know what you want."

Javert answered:

"Hurry along."

At the exclamation of Javert, Fantine had opened her eyes again. But the mayor was there, what could she fear?

Javert advanced to the middle of the chamber, exclaiming:

"Hey, there; are you coming?"

The unhappy woman looked around her. There was no one but the nun and the mayor. To whom could this contemptuous familiarity be addressed?

Then she saw a mysterious thing, so mysterious that its like had never appeared to her in the darkest delirium of fever. She saw the spy Javert seize Monsieur the Mayor by the collar.

Jean Valjean did not attempt to disturb the hand which grasped the collar of his coat. He said:

"Javert—"

Javert interrupted him: "Call me Monsieur the Inspector!"

"Monsieur," continued Jean Valjean, "I would like to speak a word with you in private."

"Aloud, speak aloud," said Javert, "people speak aloud to me."

Jean Valjean went on, lowering his voice.

"It is a request that I have to make of you—"

"I tell you to speak aloud."

"But this should not be heard by any one but yourself."

"What is that to me? I will not listen."

Jean Valjean turned to him and said rapidly and in a very low tone:

"Give me three days! Three days to go for the child of this unhappy woman! You shall accompany me if you like."

"Are you laughing at me!" cried Javert. "Hey! I did not think you so stupid! You ask for three days to get away, and tell me that you are going for this girl's child! That is good!"

Fantine shivered.

"My child!" she exclaimed, "going for my child! Then she is not here! Sister, tell me, where is Cosette? I want my child! Monsieur Madeleine, Monsieur the Mayor!"

Javert stamped his foot.

"There is the other now! Hold your tongue, hussy! Miserable country, where galley slaves are magistrates and women of the town are nursed like countesses! Ha, but all this will be changed; it was time!"

He gazed steadily at Fantine, and added, grasping anew the cravat, shirt, and coat collar of Jean Valjean:

"I tell you that there is no Monsieur Madeleine, and that there is no Monsieur the Mayor. There is a robber, there is a brigand, there is a convict called Jean Valjean, and I have got him! That is what there is!"

Fantine started upright, supporting herself by her rigid arms and hands; she looked at Jean Valjean, then at Javert, and then at the nun; she opened her mouth as if to speak. She stretched out her arms in anguish, groping about her like one who is drowning; then sank suddenly back upon the pillow.

She was dead.

Jean Valjean put his hand on that of Javert which held him, and opened it as he would have opened the hand of a child; then he said:

"You have killed this woman."

"Have done with this!" cried Javert, furious, "I am not here to listen to sermons; save all that; the guard is below; come right along, or the hand-cuffs!"

There stood in a corner of the room an old iron bedstead in a dilapidated condition, which the sisters used as a camp-bed when they watched. Jean Valjean went to the bed, wrenched out the rickety head bar—a thing easy for muscles like his—in the twinkling of an eye, and with the bar in his clenched fist, looked at Javert. Javert recoiled towards the door.

Jean Valjean, his iron bar in hand, walked slowly towards the bed of Fantine. On reaching it, he turned and said to Javert in a voice that could scarcely be heard:

"I advise you not to disturb me now."

Javert trembled. He had an idea of calling the guard, but Jean Valjean might profit by his absence to escape. He remained, therefore, grasped the bottom of his cane, and leaned against the framework of the door without taking his eyes from Jean Valjean.

Jean Valjean rested his elbows upon the post, and his head upon his hand, and gazed at Fantine, stretched motionless before him. He remained thus, mute and absorbed, evidently lost to everything of this life. His countenance and attitude bespoke nothing but inexpressible pity.

Fantine's hand hung over the side of the bed. Jean Valjean knelt before this hand, raised it gently, and kissed it.

Then he rose, and, turning to Javert, said:

"Now, I am at your disposal."

Javert put Jean Valjean in the city prison.

The arrest of Monsieur Madeleine produced a sensation, or rather an extraordinary commotion, at M—— sur M——. We are sorry not to be able to disguise the fact that, on this single sentence, *he was a galley slave*, almost everybody abandoned him. In less than two hours, all the good he had done was forgotten, and he was "nothing but a galley slave." All day long, conversations like this were heard in every part of the town: "Don't you know, he was a discharged convict!" "He! Who?" "The mayor." "Well! I always did suspect him. The man was too good, too perfect, too sweet. He refused fees, and gave sous to every little blackguard he met. I always thought that there must be something bad at the bottom of all this."

"The drawing-rooms," above all, were entirely of this opinion.

An old lady, a subscriber to the *Drapeau Blanc*, made this remark, the depth of which it is almost impossible to fathom:

"I am not sorry for it. That will teach the Bonapartists!"

Three or four persons alone in the whole city remained faithful to his memory. The old portress who had been his servant was among the number.

On the evening of this same day, the worthy old woman was sitting in her lodge, still quite bewildered and sunk in sad reflections. There was no one in the house but the two nuns, Sister Perpétue and Sister Simplice, who were watching the corpse of Fantine.

Towards the time when Monsieur Madeleine had been accustomed to return, the honest portress rose mechanically, took the key of his room from a drawer, with the taper-stand that he used at night to light himself up the stairs, then hung the key on a nail from which he had been in the habit of taking it, and placed the taper-stand by its side, as if she were expecting him. She then seated herself again in her chair, and resumed her reflections. The poor old woman had done all this without being conscious of it.

More than two hours had elapsed when she started from her reverie and exclaimed, "Why, bless me! I have hung his key on the nail!"

Just then, the window of her box opened, a hand passed through the opening, took the key and stand, and lighted the taper at the candle which was burning.

The portress raised her eyes; she knew the hand, the arm, the coat-sleeve. "My God! Monsieur Mayor!" she exclaimed, "I thought you were—"

She stopped; the end of her sentence would not have been respectful to the beginning. To her, Jean Valjean was still Monsieur the Mayor.

He completed her thought.

"In prison," said he. "I was there; I broke a bar from a window, let myself fall from the top of a roof, and here I am. I am going to my room; go for Sister Simplice. She is doubtless beside this poor woman."

The old servant hastily obeyed.

He ascended the staircase which led to his room. On reaching the top, he left his taper standing on the upper stair, opened his door with little noise, felt his way to the window and closed the shutter, then came back, took his taper, and went into the chamber.

The precaution was not useless; it will be remembered that his window could be seen from the street.

He took from a wardrobe an old shirt which he tore into several pieces and in which he packed the two silver candlesticks. In all this there was neither haste nor agitation. And even while packing the bishop's candlesticks, he was eating a piece of black prisonbread.

Two gentle taps were heard at the door.

"Come in," said he.

It was Sister Simplice.

She was pale, her eyes were red, and the candle which she held trembled in her hand.

Jean Valjean had written a few lines on a piece of paper, which he handed to the nun, saying: "Sister, you will give this to the curé."

The paper was not folded. She cast her eyes on it.

"You may read it," said he.

She read: "I beg Monsieur the Curé to take charge of all that I leave here. He will please defray therefrom the expenses of my trial, and of the burial of the woman who died this morning. The remainder is for the poor."

She had scarcely finished when there was a loud noise on the staircase. They heard a tumult of steps ascending, and the old portress exclaiming in her loudest and most piercing tones:

"My good sir, I swear to you in the name of God, that nobody has come in here the whole day, and the whole evening; that I have not even once left my door!"

A man replied: "But yet, there is a light in this room."

They recognised the voice of Javert.

The chamber was so arranged that the door in opening covered the corner of the wall to the right. Jean Valjean blew out the taper, and placed himself in this corner.

Sister Simplice fell on her knees near the table.

The door opened.

Javert entered.

The whispering of several men, and the protestations of the portress were heard in the hall.

The nun did not raise her eyes. She was praying.

The candle was on the mantel, and gave but a dim light.

Javert perceived the sister, and stopped abashed.

It will be remembered that the very foundation of Javert, his element, the medium in which he breathed, was veneration for all authority. To him, ecclesiastical authority was the highest of all; he was devout, superficial, and correct, upon this point as upon all others. In his eyes, a priest was a spirit who was never mistaken, a nun was a being who never sinned.

This was the Sister Simplice, who had never lied in her life. Javert knew this.

"Sister," said he, "are you alone in this room?"

There was a fearful instant during which the poor portress felt her limbs falter beneath her. The sister raised her eyes, and replied:

"Yes."

Then continued Javert—"Excuse me if I persist, it is my duty—you have not seen this evening a person, a man—he has escaped, and we are in search of him—Jean Valjean—you have not seen him?"

The sister answered—"No."

She lied. Two lies in succession, one upon another, without hesitation, quickly, as if she were an adept in it.

"Your pardon!" said Javert, and he withdrew, bowing reverently.

The affirmation of the sister was to Javert something so decisive that he did not even notice the singularity of this taper, just blown out, and smoking on the table.

An hour afterwards, a man was walking rapidly in the darkness beneath the trees from M—— sur M—— in the direction of Paris. This man was Jean

Valjean. It has been established, by the testimony of two or three waggoners who met him, that he carried a bundle, and was dressed in a blouse.

A last word in regard to Fantine.

The curé thought best, and did well perhaps, to reserve out of what Jean Valjean had left, the largest amount possible for the poor. After all, who were in question?—a convict and a woman of the town. This was why he simplified the burial of Fantine, and reduced it to that bare necessity called the Potter's field.

And so Fantine was buried in the common grave of the cemetery, which is for everybody and for all, and in which the poor are lost. Happily, God knows where to find the soul. Fantine was laid away in the darkness with bodies which had no name; she suffered the promiscuity of dust. She was thrown into the public pit. Her tomb was like her bed.

IX. WATERLOO

ON A BEAUTIFUL MORNING in May, last year (1861), a traveller, he who tells this story, was journeying from Nivelles towards La Hulpe. He travelled a-foot. He was following, between two rows of trees, a broad road, undulating over hills, which, one after another, upheave it and let it fall again, like enormous waves. He had just passed a wood upon a hill, and at the corner of a crossroad, beside a sort of worm-eaten sign-post, bearing the inscription—*Old Toll-Gate, No.* 4—a tavern with this sign:—*The Four Winds. Echaleau, Private Café.*

Half a mile from this tavern, he reached the bottom of a little valley, where a stream flowed beneath an arch in the embankment of the road. At this point there was at the right, and immediately on the road, an inn, with a four-wheeled cart before the door, a great bundle of hop-poles, a plough, a pile of dry brush near a quickset hedge, some lime which was smoking in a square hole in the ground, and a ladder lying along an old shed with mangers for straw. A young girl was pulling weeds in a field, where a large green poster, probably of a travelling show at some annual fair, fluttered in the wind. At the corner of the inn, beside a pond, in which a flotilla of ducks was navigating, a difficult foot-path lost itself in the shrubbery. The traveller took this path.

At the end of a hundred paces, passing a wall of the fifteenth century, surmounted by a sharp gable of crossed bricks, he found himself opposite a great arched stone doorway, with rectilinear impost, in the solemn style of Louis XIV., and plain medallions on the sides. Over the entrance was a severe façade, and a wall perpendicular to the façade almost touched the doorway, flanking it at an abrupt right angle. On the meadow before the door lay three harrows, through which were blooming, as best they could, all the flowers of May. The doorway was closed. It was shut by two decrepit folding-doors, decorated with an old rusty knocker.

The sunshine was enchanting; the branches of the trees had that gentle tremulousness of the month of May which seems to come from the birds' nests rather than the wind. A spruce little bird, probably in love, was singing desperately in a tall tree.

The traveller paused and examined in the stone at the left of the door, near the ground, a large circular excavation like the hollow of a sphere. Just then the folding-doors opened, and a peasant woman came out.

She saw the traveller, and perceived what he was examining.

"It was a French ball which did that," said she.

And she added—

"What you see there, higher up, in the door, near a nail, is the hole made by a Biscay musket. The musket has not gone through the wood."

"What is the name of this place?" asked the traveller.

"Hougomont," the woman answered.

The traveller raised his head. He took a few steps and looked over the hedges. He saw in the horizon, through the trees, a sort of hillock, and on this hillock something which, in the distance, resembled a lion.

He was on the battle-field of Waterloo.

Hougomont—this was the fatal spot, the beginning of the resistance, the first check encountered at Waterloo by this great butcher of Europe, called Napoleon.

The traveller pushed open the door, elbowed an old carriage under the porch, and entered the court.

Near the arch opens another door in the wall, with keystones of the time of Henry IV., which discloses the trees of an orchard. Beside this door were a dung-hill, mattocks and shovels, some carts, an old well with its flagstone and iron pulley, a skipping colt, a strutting turkey, a chapel surmounted by a little steeple, a pear-tree in bloom, trained in espalier on the wall of the chapel; this was the court, the conquest of which was the aspiration of Napoleon. This bit of earth, could he have taken it, would perhaps have given him the world. The hens are scattering the dust with their beaks. You hear a growling: it is a great dog, who shows his teeth, and takes the place of the English.

The English fought admirably there. The storm of the combat is still in this court: the horror is visible there; the overturn of the conflict is there petrified; it lives, it dies; it was but yesterday. The walls are still in death agonies; the stones fall, the breaches cry out; the holes are wounds; the trees bend and shudder, as if making an effort to escape.

The English were barricaded; the French effected an entrance, but could not maintain their position. At the side of the chapel, one wing of the château, the only remnant which exists of the manor of Hougomont, stands crumbling, one might almost say disembowelled. The château served as donjon; the chapel served as block-house.

There was a massacre in the chapel. No mass has been said there since the carnage. The altar remains, however—a clumsy wooden altar, backed by a wall of rough stone. Four whitewashed walls, two little arched windows, a large wooden crucifix, above the crucifix a square opening in which is stuffed a bundle of straw; in a corner on the ground, an old glazed sash all broken, such is this chapel. Near the altar hangs a wooden statue of St. Anne of the fifteenth century; the head of the infant Jesus has been carried away by a musket-shot. The French, masters for a moment of the chapel, then dislodged, fired it. The flames filled this ruin; it was a furnace; the door was burned, the floor was burned, but the wooden Christ was not burned. The fire ate its way to his feet, the blackened stumps of which only are visible; then it stopped. A miracle, say the country people. The infant Jesus, decapitated, was not so fortunate as the Christ.

On coming out of the chapel, a well is seen at the left. There are two in this yard. You ask: why is there no bucket and no pulley to this one? Because no water is drawn from it now. Why is no more water drawn from it? Because it is full of skeletons. Three hundred dead were thrown into it. Perhaps with too much haste. Were they all dead? Tradition says no. It appears that on the night after the burial, feeble voices were heard calling out from the well.

Bauduin killed, Foy wounded, fire, slaughter, carnage, a brook made of English blood, of German blood, and of French blood, mingled in fury; a well filled with corpses, the regiment of Nassau and the regiment of Brunswick destroyed, Duplat killed, Blackmann killed, the English Guards crippled, twenty French battalions, out of the forty of Reille's corps, decimated, three thousand men, in this one ruin of Hougomont, sabred, slashed, slaughtered, shot, burned; and all this in order that to-day a peasant may say to a traveller: *Monsieur, give me three francs; if you like, I will explain to you the affair of Waterloo.*

Let us go back, for such is the story-teller's privilege, and place ourselves in the year 1815, a little before the date of the commencement of the action narrated in the first part of this book.

Had it not rained on the night of the 17th of June, 1815, the future of Europe would have been changed. A few drops of water more or less prostrated Napoleon. That Waterloo should be the end of Austerlitz, Providence needed only a little rain, and an unseasonable cloud crossing the sky sufficed for the overthrow of a world.

The battle of Waterloo—and this gave Blücher time to come up—could not be commenced before half-past eleven. Why? Because the ground was soft. It was necessary to wait for it to acquire some little firmness that the artillery could manœuvre.

Napoleon was an artillery officer, and he never forgot it. The foundation of this prodigious captain was the man who, in his report to the Directory upon Aboukir, said: *Such of our balls killed six men.* All his plans of battle were made for projectiles. On the 18th of June, 1815, he counted on his artillery the more because he had the advantage in numbers. Wellington had only a hundred and fifty-nine guns; Napoleon had two hundred and forty.

Both generals had carefully studied the plain of Mont Saint Jean, now called the plain of Waterloo. Already in the preceding year, Wellington, with the sagacity of prescience, had examined it as a possible site for a great battle. On this ground and for this contest Wellington had the favourable side, Napoleon the unfavourable. The English army was above, the French army below.

To sketch here the appearance of Napoleon, on horseback, glass in hand, upon the heights of Rossomme, at dawn on the 18th of June, 1815, would be almost superfluous. Before we point him out, everybody has seen him. This calm profile under the little chapeau of the school of Brienne, this green uniform, the white facings concealing the stars on his breast, the overcoat concealing the epaulets, the bit of red sash under the waistcoat, the leather breeches, the white horse with his housings of purple velvet with crowned N.'s and eagles on the corners, the Hessian boots over silk stockings, the silver spurs, the Marengo sword, this whole form of the last Cæsar lives in all imaginations, applauded by half the world, reprobated by the rest.

Everybody knows the first phase of this battle; the difficult opening, uncertain, hesitating, threatening for both armies, but for the English still more than for the French.

It had rained all night; the ground was softened by the shower; water lay here and there in the hollows of the plains as in basins; at some points the wheels sank in to the axles; the horses' girths dripped with liquid mud. Had not the wheat and rye spread down by that multitude of advancing carts filled the ruts and made a bed under the wheels, movement would have been impossible.

The affair opened late; when the first gun was fired, the English General Colville looked at his watch and noted that it was thirty-five minutes past eleven.

The battle was commenced with fury, by the left wing of the French at Hougomont. At the same time Napoleon attacked La Haie Sainte, and Ney pushed the right wing of the French against the left wing of the English which rested upon Papelotte. Papelotte was taken; La Haie Sainte was carried.

Note a circumstance. There were in the English infantry, particularly in Kempt's brigade, many new recruits. These young soldiers, before our formidable infantry, were heroic; these recruits exhibited something of French invention and French fury. This raw infantry showed enthusiasm. That displeased Wellington.

After the capture of La Haie Sainte, the battle wavered.

There is in this day from noon to four o'clock, an obscure interval; the middle of this battle is almost indistinct. Twilight was gathering. You could perceive in this mist the crossed shoulder-belts, the grenade cartridge boxes, the dolmans of the hussars, the red boots with a thousand creases, the heavy shakos festooned with fringe, the almost black infantry of Brunswick united with the scarlet infantry of England, the Scotch with bare knees and plaids, the large white gaiters of our grenadiers.

Towards four o'clock the situation of the English army was serious.

Hougomont yielding, La Haie Sainte taken, there was but one knot left, the centre. That still held; Wellington reinforced it.

The centre of the English army occupied the plateau of Mont Saint Jean, with the village behind it and in front the declivity, which at that time was steep. All about the plateau, the English had cut away the hedges here and there, made embrasures in the hawthorns, thrust the mouth of a cannon between two branches, made loopholes in the thickets. Their artillery was in ambush under the shrubbery. This labour was so well done that Haxo, sent by the emperor at nine o'clock in the morning to reconnoitre the enemy's batteries, saw nothing of it.

Wellington, anxious, but impassible, was on horseback, and remained the whole day in the same attitude, a little in front of the old mill of Mont Saint Jean. Wellington was frigidly heroic. The balls rained down. His aide-de-camp, Gordon, had just fallen at his side. The day was clearly going badly. Wellington cried to his old companions of Talavera, Vittoria, and Salamanca: *Boys! We must not be beat: what would they say of us in England!*

About four o'clock, the English line staggered backwards. All at once the regiments, driven by the shells and bullets of the French, fell back into the valley now crossed by the cow-path of the farm of Mont Saint Jean; the battle front of the English was slipping away, Wellington gave ground. Beginning retreat! cried Napoleon.

The emperor, although sick and hurt in his saddle by a local affliction, had never been in so good humour as on that day. The dark-browed man of Austerlitz was gay at Waterloo. The greatest, when foredoomed, present these contradictions; the perfect smile belongs to God alone.

Wellington had fallen back. It remained only to complete this repulse by a crushing charge. Napoleon, turning abruptly, sent off a courier at full speed to Paris to announce that the battle was won.

He ordered Milhaud's cuirassiers to carry the plateau of Mont Saint Jean. They were three thousand five hundred. They formed a line of half a mile. They were gigantic men on colossal horses. There were twenty-six squadrons, and they had behind them, as a support, the division of Lefebvre Desnouettes, the hundred and six gendarmes d'élite, the Chasseurs of the Guard, eleven hundred and ninety-seven men, and the Lancers of the Guard, eight hundred and eighty lances. They wore casques without plumes, and cuirasses of wrought iron, with horse pistols in their holsters, and long sabre-swords. In the morning, they had been the admiration of the whole army, when at nine o'clock, with trumpets sounding, and all the bands playing, *Veillons au salut de l'empire*, they came, in heavy column, one of their batteries on their flank, the other at their centre, and deployed in two ranks between the Genappe road and Frischemont, and took their position of battle.

Aide-de-camp Bernard brought them the emperor's order. Ney drew his sword and placed himself at their head. The enormous squadrons began to move.

All this cavalry, with sabres drawn, banners waving and trumpets sounding, formed in column by division, descended with an even movement and as one man—with the precision of a bronze battering-ram opening a breach—the hill of La Belle Alliance, sank into that formidable depth where so many men had already fallen, disappeared in the smoke, then, rising from this valley of shadow reappeared on the other side, still compact and serried, mounting at full trot, through a cloud of grape emptying itself upon them, the frightful acclivity of mud of the plateau of Mont Saint Jean.

Behind the crest of the plateau, under cover of the masked battery, the English infantry could not see the cuirassiers, and the cuirassiers could not see them. They listened to the rising of this tide of men. They heard the increasing sound of three thousand horses, the alternate and measured striking of their hoofs at full trot, the rattling of the cuirasses, the clicking of the sabres, and a sort of fierce roar of the coming host. There was a moment of fearful silence, then, suddenly, a long line of raised arms brandishing sabres appeared above the crest, with casques, trumpets, and standards, and three thousand faces with grey moustaches, crying, *Vive l'Empereur!*

All at once, at the left of the English, right, the head of the column of cuirassiers saw between themselves and the English a ditch, a grave. It was the sunken road of Ohain.

The second rank pushed in the first, the third pushed in the second; the horses reared, threw themselves over, fell upon their backs, and struggled with their feet in the air, piling up and overturning their riders. The force acquired to crush the English crushed the French. Here the loss of the battle began.

Was it possible that Napoleon should win this battle? We answer no. Why? Because of Wellington? Because of Blücher? No. Because of God.

It was time that this vast man should fall.

The excessive weight of this man in human destiny disturbed the equilibrium. The moment had come for incorruptible supreme equity to look to it. Reeking blood, overcrowded cemeteries, weeping mothers—these are formidable pleaders. When the earth is suffering from a surcharge, there are mysterious moanings from the deeps which the heavens hear.

Napoleon had been impeached before the Infinite, and his fall was decreed. He vexed God.

Waterloo is not a battle; it is the change of front of the universe.

At the same time with the ravine, the artillery was unmasked.

The cuirassiers had not even time to breathe. The disaster of the sunken road had decimated, but not discouraged them. They hurled themselves upon the English squares.

The English army was terribly shaken. There is no doubt, if they had not been crippled in their first shock by the disaster of the sunken road, the cuirassiers would have overwhelmed the centre, and decided the victory. Wellington, though three-fourths conquered, was struck with heroic admiration. He said in a low voice: "Splendid!"

The cuirassiers had not succeeded, in this sense, that the centre was not broken. All holding the plateau, nobody held it, and in fact it remained for the most part with the English. Wellington held the village and the crowning plain; Ney held only the crest and the slope. On both sides they seemed rooted in this funebral soil.

But the enfeeblement of the English appeared irremediable. The hæmorrhage of this army was horrible. Kempt, on the left wing, called for reinforcements. "*Impossible,*" answered Wellington; "*we must die on the spot we now occupy.*" Almost at the same moment Ney sent to Napoleon for infantry, and Napoleon exclaimed: "*Infantry! where does he expect me to take them! Does he expect me to make them?*"

The Iron Duke remained calm, but his lips were pale. At five o'clock Wellington drew out his watch, and was heard to murmur these sombre words: *Blücher, or night!*

It was about this time that a distant line of bayonets glistened on the heights beyond Frischemont.

The rest is known; the irruption of a third army, the battle thrown out of joint, eighty-six pieces of artillery suddenly thundering forth, a new battle falling at night-fall upon our dismantled regiments, the whole English line assuming the offensive and pushed forward, the gigantic gap made in the French army, the English grape and the Prussian grape lending mutual aid, extermination, disaster in front, disaster in flank, the guard entering into line amid this terrible crumbling.

Feeling that they were going to their death, they cried out: *Vive l'Empereur!* There is nothing more touching in history than this death-agony bursting forth in acclamations.

The sky had been overcast all day. All at once, at this very moment—it was eight o'clock at night—the clouds in the horizon broke, and through the elms on the Nivelles road streamed the sinister red light of the setting sun. The rising sun shone upon Austerlitz.

Each battalion of the guard, for this final effort, was commanded by a general. When the tall caps of the grenadiers of the guard with their large eagle plates appeared, symmetrical, drawn up in line, calm, in the smoke of that conflict, the enemy felt respect for France; they thought they saw twenty victories entering upon the field of battle, with wings extended, and those who were conquerors, thinking themselves conquered, recoiled; but Wellington cried: "*Up, guards, and at them!*" The red regiment of English guards, lying behind the hedges, rose up, a shower of grape riddled the tricoloured flag fluttering about our eagles, all hurled themselves forward, and the final carnage began.

Ney, desperate, great in all the grandeur of accepted death, bared himself to every blow in this tempest. He had his horse killed under him. Reeking with sweat, fire in his eyes, froth upon his lips, his uniform unbuttoned, one of his epaulets half cut away by the sabre stroke of a horse-guard, his badge of the grand eagle pierced by a ball, bloody, covered with mud, magnificent, a broken sword in his hand, he said: *"Come and see how a marshal of Frances dies upon the field of battle!"* But in vain, he did not die. Unhappy man! thou wast reserved for French bullets!

The route behind the guard was dismal.

The army fell back rapidly from all sides at once, from Hougomont, from La Haie Sainte, from Papelotte, from Planchenoit. The cry: *Treachery!* was followed by the cry: *Sauve qui peut!* A disbanding army is a thaw. The whole bends, cracks, snaps, floats, rolls, falls, crashes, hurries, plunges.

Napoleon gallops along the fugitives, harangues them, urges, threatens, entreats. The mouths, which in the morning were crying *vive l'Empereur,* are now agape; he is hardly recognised. The Prussian cavalry, just come up, spring forward, fling themselves upon the enemy, sabre, cut, hack, kill, exterminate. Teams rush off, the guns are left to the care of themselves; the soldiers of the train unhitch the caissons and take the horses to escape. They trample upon the living and the dead. A multitude fills roads, paths, bridges, plains, hills, valleys, woods, choked up by this flight of forty thousand men. Cries, despair, knapsacks and muskets cast into the rye, passage forced at the point of the sword; no more comrades, no more officers, no more generals; who now was flying in such wise? The Grand Army.

In the gathering night, on a field near Genappe, Bernard and Bertrand seized by a flap of his coat and stopped a haggard, thoughtful, gloomy man, who, dragged thus far by the current of the rout, had dismounted, passed the bridle of his horse under his arm, and, with bewildered eye, was returning alone towards Waterloo. It was Napoleon endeavouring to advance again, mighty somnambulist of a vanished dream.

Waterloo is a battle of the first rank won by a captain of the second.

What is truly admirable in the battle of Waterloo is England, English firmness, English resolution, English blood; the superb thing which England had there—may it not displease her—is herself. It is not her captain, it is her army.

Wellington, strangely ungrateful, declared in a letter to Lord Bathurst that his army, the army that fought on the 18th of June, 1815, was a "detestable army." What does this dark assemblage of bones, buried beneath the furrows of Waterloo, think of that?

England has been too modest in regard to Wellington. To make Wellington so great is to belittle England. Wellington was tenacious, that was his merit, but the least of his foot-soldiers or his horsemen was quite as firm as he. The iron soldier is as good as the Iron Duke. For our part, all our glorification goes to the English soldier, the English army, the English people. If trophy there be, to England the trophy is due. The Waterloo column would be more just if, instead of the figure of a man, it lifted to the clouds the statue of a nation.

But this great England will be offended at what we say here. She has still, after her 1688 and our 1789, the feudal illusion. She believes in hereditary right, and in the hierarchy. This people, surpassed by none in might and glory, esteems itself as a nation, not as a people. So much so that as a people they subordinate themselves willingly, and take a Lord for a head. Workmen, they submit to be despised; soldiers, they submit to be whipped. We remember that at the battle of Inkerman a sergeant who, as it appeared, had saved the army, could not be mentioned by Lord Raglan, the English military hierarchy not permitting any hero below the rank of officer to be spoken of in a report.

Waterloo, if we place ourselves at the culminating point of view of the question, is intentionally a counter-revolutionary victory. It is Europe against France; it is Petersburg, Berlin, and Vienna against Paris; it is the *status quo* against the initiative; it is the monarchies clearing the decks for action against indomitable French uprising. The final extinction of this vast people, for twenty-six years in eruption, such was the dream. It was the solidarity of the Brunswicks, the Nassaus, the Romanoffs, the Hohenzollerns, and the Hapsburgs, with the Bourbons. Divine right rides behind with Waterloo.

It is true that the empire having been despotic, royalty, by the natural reaction of things, was forced to become liberal, and also that a constitutional order has indirectly sprung from Waterloo, to the great regret of the conquerors. The fact is, that revolution cannot be conquered, and that being providential and absolutely decreed, it reappears continually, before Waterloo in Bonaparte, throwing down the old thrones, after Waterloo in Louis XVIII., granting and submitting to the charter. Would you realise what Revolution is, call it Progress; and would you realise what Progress is, call it To-morrow. To-morrow performs its work irresistibly, and it performs it from to-day. It always reaches its aim through unexpected means. Thus progress goes on. No tool comes amiss to this workman. It adjusts to its divine work, without being disconcerted, the man who strode over the Alps, and the good old tottering invalid of the Père Elysée. It makes use of the conqueror without, the cripple within. Waterloo, by cutting short the demolition of European thrones by the sword, has had no other effect than to continue the revolutionary work in another way. The saberers have gone out, the time of the thinkers has come.

Let us see in Waterloo only what there is in Waterloo. Of intentional liberty, nothing. The Counter-revolution was involuntarily liberal, as, by a corresponding phenomenon, Napoleon was involuntarily revolutionary. On the 18th June, 1815, Robespierre on horseback was thrown from the saddle. End of the dictatorship: the whole European system fell.

The empire sank into a darkness which resembled that of the expiring Roman world. Only, the barbarism of 1815, which should be called by its special name, the counter-revolution, was short-winded, soon out of breath, and soon stopped.

One of the most unquestionably safe forms of society in the nineteenth century was established in France and on the Continent. Europe put on the white cockade.

Man had been at once made greater and made less by Napoleon. The ideal, under this splendid material reign, had received the strange name of ideology. The people, however, that food for cannon so fond of the cannoneer, looked for a great man. "Napoleon is dead," said a visitor to an invalid of Marengo and Waterloo. "*He dead!*" cried the soldier; "*are you sure of that?*"

We return, for it is a requirement of this book, to the fatal field of battle.

When the last gun had been fired the plain of Mont Saint Jean remained deserted. The English occupied the camp of the French; it is the usual verification of victory to sleep in the bed of the vanquished. The Prussians, let loose upon the fugitives, pushed forward. Wellington went to the village of Waterloo to make up his report to Lord Bathurst.

Towards midnight a man was prowling or rather crawling along the sunken road of Ohain. He was, to all appearance, neither English nor French, peasant nor soldier, less a man than a ghoul, attracted by the scent of the corpses, coming to rifle Waterloo. Who was this man? Night, probably, knew more of his doings than day! He had no knapsack, but large pockets. From time to time he stooped down suddenly, stirred on the ground something silent and motionless, then rose up and skulked away.

The prowler passed an indescribably hideous review of the dead. He walked with his feet in blood.

Suddenly he stopped. A few steps before him, in the sunken road, at a point where the mound of corpses ended, from under this mass of men and horses appeared an open hand, lighted by the moon.

This hand had something upon a finger which sparkled; it was a gold ring.

The man stooped down, remained a moment, and when he rose again there was no ring upon that hand.

At this moment he experienced a shock. He felt that he was held from behind.

He turned; it was the open hand, which had closed, seizing the lapel of his capote.

An honest man would have been frightened. This man began to laugh.

"Oh," said he, "it's only the dead man. I like a ghost better than a gendarme. Is this dead man alive? Let us see."

He bent over again, rummaged among the heap, removed whatever impeded him, seized the hand, laid hold of the arm, disengaged the head, drew out the body. It was a cuirassier, an officer; a great gold epaulet protruded from beneath his cuirass, but he had no casque. A furious sabre cut had disfigured his face, where nothing but blood was to be seen. It did not seem, however, that he had any limbs broken; and by some happy chance, if the word is possible here, the bodies were arched above him in such a way as to prevent his being crushed. His eyes were closed.

He had on his cuirass the silver cross of the Legion of Honour.

The prowler tore off this cross, after which he felt the officer's fob, found a watch there, and took it. Then he rummaged in his vest and found a purse, which he pocketed.

When he had reached this phase of the succour he was lending the dying man, the officer opened his eyes.

"Thanks," said he feebly.

The rough movements of the man handling him, the coolness of the night, and breathing the fresh air freely, had roused him from his lethargy.

The prowler raised his head. The sound of a footstep could be heard on the plain; probably it was some patrol who was approaching.

The officer murmured, signs of suffering in his voice: "Who has gained the battle?"

"The English," answered the prowler.

The officer replied: "Search my pockets. You will there find a purse and a watch. Take them."

This had already been done. The prowler made a pretence of executing the command, and said: "There is nothing there."

"I have been robbed," replied the officer; "I am sorry. They would have been yours."

The step of the patrol became more and more distinct.

"Somebody is coming," said the prowler, making a movement as if he would go.

The officer, raising himself up painfully upon one arm, held him back.

"You have saved my life. Who are you?"

The prowler answered quick and low:

"I belong, like yourself, to the French army. I must go. If I am taken I shall be shot. I have saved your life. Help yourself now."

"What is your grade?"

"Sergeant."

"What is your name?"

"Thénardier."

"I shall not forget that name," said the officer. "And you, remember mine. My name is Pontmercy."

X. THE SHIP *ORION*

JEAN VALJEAN has been retaken.

We shall be pardoned for passing rapidly over the painful details. We shall merely reproduce a couple of items published in the newspapers of that day, the first from the *Drapeau Blanc*. It is dated the 25th of July, 1823:

"A district of the Pas-de-Calais has just been the scene of an extraordinary occurrence. A stranger in that department, known as Monsieur Madeleine, had, within a few years past, restored, by means of certain new processes, the manufacture of jet and black glass ware—a former local branch of industry. He had made his own fortune by it, and, in fact, that of the entire district. In acknowledgment of his services he had been appointed mayor. The police has discovered that Monsieur Madeleine was none other than an escaped convict, condemned in 1796 for robbery, and named Jean Val-jean. This Jean Valjean has been sent back to the galleys. It appears that previous to his arrest, he succeeded in withdrawing from Laffitte's a sum amounting to more than half a million which he had deposited there, and which it is said, by the way, he had very legitimately realised in his business. Since his return to the galleys at Toulon, it has been impossible to discover where Jean Valjean concealed this money."

The second article is from the *Journal de Paris* of the same date:

"An old convict, named Jean Valjean, has recently been brought before the Var Assizes, under circumstances calculated to attract attention. This villain had succeeded in eluding the vigilance of the police; he had changed his name, and had even been adroit enough to procure the appointment of mayor in one of our small towns in the North. He had established in this town a very considerable business, but was, at length, unmasked and arrested, thanks to the indefatigable zeal of the public authorities. He kept, as his mistress, a prostitute, who died of the shock at the moment of his arrest. This wretch, who is endowed with herculean strength, managed to escape, but, three or four days afterwards, the police retook him, in Paris, just as he was getting into one of the small vehicles that ply be-tween the capital and the village of Montfermeil (Seine-et-Oise). It is said that he had availed himself of the interval of these three or four days of freedom, to withdraw a considerable sum deposited by him with one of our principal bankers. The amount is estimated at six or seven hundred thousand francs. According to the minutes of the case, he has concealed it in some place known to himself alone, and it has been impossible to seize it; how-ever that may be, the said Jean Valjean has been brought before the assizes of the Department of the Var under indictment for an assault and robbery on the high road committed vi et armis some eight years ago. This bandit attempted no defence. It was proven by the able and eloquent representative of the crown that the robbery was shared in by others, and that Jean Valjean formed one of a band of robbers in the South. Con-sequently, Jean Valjean, being found guilty, was condemned to death. The criminal refused to appeal to the higher courts, and the king, in his inexhaustible clemency, deigned to commute his sentence to that of hard labour in prison for life. Jean Valjean was immediately forwarded to the galleys at Toulon."

Jean Valjean changed his number at the galleys. He became 9430.

Before proceeding further, it will not be amiss to relate, in some detail, a singular incident which took place, about the same time, at Montfermeil.

There exists, in the neighbourhood of Montfermeil, a very ancient super-stition. They believe, there, that the Evil One has, from time immemorial, chosen the forest as the hiding-place for his treasure. The good wives of the vicinity affirm that it is no unusual thing to meet, at sundown, in the secluded portions of the woods, a black-looking man, resembling a wag-goner or wood-cutter, shod in wooden shoes, clad in breeches and sack of coarse linen, and recognisable from the circumstance that, instead of a cap or hat, he has two immense horns upon his head. That certainly ought to render him recognisable. This man is constantly occupied in digging holes. There are three ways of dealing when you meet him.

The first mode is to approach the man and speak to him. Then you perceive that the man is nothing but a peasant, that he looks black because it is twilight, that he is digging no hole whatever, but is merely cutting grass for his cows; and that what had been taken for horns are nothing but his pitchfork which he carries on his back, and the prongs of which, thanks to the night perspective, seemed to rise from his head. You go home and die within a week. The second method is to watch him, to wait until he has dug the hole, closed it up, and gone away; then, to run quickly to the spot, to open it and get the "treasure" which the black-looking man has, of course, buried there. In this case, you die within a month. The third manner is not to speak to the dark man nor even to look at him, and to run away as fast as you can. You die within the year.

As all three of these methods have their drawbacks, the second, which, at least, offers some advantages, among others that of possessing a treasure, though it be but for a month, is the one generally adopted. Daring fellows, who never neglect a good chance, have, therefore, many times, it is asseverated, reopened the holes thus dug by the black-looking man, and tried to rob the Devil. What is this treasure of the Evil One? A penny—sometimes a crown; a stone, a skeleton, a bleeding corpse, sometimes a spectre twice folded like a sheet of paper in a portfolio, sometimes nothing.

It appears that, in our time, they find in addition sometimes a powder-horn with bullets, sometimes an old pack of brown and greasy cards which have evidently been used by the Devil. Whoever plays with these cards is sure to lose all he has, and as to the powder in the flask, it has the peculiarity of bursting your gun in your face.

Now, very shortly after the time when the authorities took it into their heads that the liberated convict Jean Valjean had, during his escape of a few days' duration, been prowling about Montfermeil, it was remarked, in that village, that a certain old road-labourer named Boulatruelle had "a fancy" for the woods. He would be met towards evening in the remotest glades and the wildest thickets, having the appearance of a person looking for something and, sometimes, digging holes. The good wives who passed that way took him at first for Beelzebub, then they recognised Boulatruelle, and were by no means reassured.

The village gossips said:—"It's plain that the Devil has been about, Boulatruelle has seen him and is looking for his treasure." The old women crossed themselves very often.

Thénardier made up a party and plied the old roadsman with drink. Boulatruelle drank enormously, but said little.

One morning about daybreak as he was going to his work, Boulatruelle had been surprised at seeing under a bush in a corner of the wood, a pickaxe and spade, *as one would say, hidden there*. However, he supposed that they were the pick and spade of old Six-Fours, the water-carrier, and thought no more about it. But, on the evening of the same day, he had seen, without being seen himself, for he was hidden behind a large tree, "a person who did not belong at all to that region, and whom he, Boulatruelle, knew very well"—or, as Thénardier translated it, "*an old comrade at the galleys*"—turn off from the high road towards the thickest part of the wood. Boulatruelle obstinately refused to tell the stranger's name. This person carried a package, something square, like a large box or a small trunk. Boulatruelle was surprised. Seven or eight minutes elapsed before it occurred to him to follow; he was too late. The person was already in the thick woods, night had come on, and Boulatruelle did not succeed in overtaking him.

Thereupon he made up his mind to watch the outskirts of the wood. "There was a moon." Two or three hours later, Boulatruelle saw this person come forth again from the wood, this time carrying now not the little trunk but a pick and a spade. Boulatruelle let the person pass unmolested, because, as he thought to himself, the other was three times as strong as he, was armed with a pickaxe, and would probably murder him, on recognising his countenance and seeing that he, in turn, was recognised. Touching display of feeling in two old companions unexpectedly meeting! But the pick and the spade were a ray of light to Boulatruelle; he hastened to the bushes, in the morning, and found neither one nor the other. He thence concluded that this person, on entering the wood, had dug a hole with his pick, had buried the chest, and had, then, filled up the hole with his spade. Now, as the chest was too small to contain a corpse, it must contain money; hence his continued searches. Boulatruelle had explored, sounded, and ransacked the whole forest, and had rummaged every spot where the earth seemed to have been freshly disturbed. But all in vain.

Nobody thought any more about it, at Montfermeil, excepting a few good gossips, who said: "Be sure the road-labourer of Gagny didn't make all that fuss for nothing: the devil was certainly there."

Towards the end of October, in that same year, 1823, the inhabitants of Toulon saw coming back into their port, in consequence of heavy weather, and in order to repair some damages, the ship *Orion*, which then formed a part of the Mediterranean squadron.

The year 1823 was what the Restoration has called the "time of the Spanish War."

That war was a great family affair of the Bourbons; sans-culottes revived, to the great alarm of all the old dowagers, under the name of *descamisados;* monarchists striving to impede progress, which they styled anarchy; the theories of '89 rudely interrupted in their undermining advances; a halt from all Europe, intimated to the French idea of revolution, making its tour of the globe; the spirit of liberty and of innovation reduced by bayonets; principles struck dumb by cannon-shot; France undoing by her arms what she had done with her mind; to cap the climax, the leaders on the other side sold, their troops irresolute; cities besieged by millions of money. It seemed clear that certain Spanish officers intrusted with the duty of resistance, yielded too easily; it appeared as if the generals rather than the battles had been won. It was war grown petty indeed, where you could read *Bank of France* on the folds of the flag.

In a still graver point of view, this war, which broke the military spirit of France, fired the democratic spirit with indignation. Since 1792, all the revolutions of Europe have been but the French Revolution: liberty radiates on every side from France. The war of 1823, an outrage on the generous Spanish nation, was, at the same time, an outrage on the French Revolution. This monstrous deed of violence France committed, but by compulsion; for, aside from wars of liberation, all that armies do they do by compulsion. The words *passive obedience* tell the tale. An army is a wondrous masterpiece of combination, in which might is the result of an enormous sum-total of utter weakness.

As to the Bourbons, the war of 1823 was fatal to them. They took it for a success. They did not see what danger there is in attempting to kill an idea by a military watchword. The Spanish campaign became in their councils an argument on behalf of violent measures and intrigues in favour of divine right. France having restored *el rey neto* in Spain, could certainly restore the absolute monarchy at home.

But let us return to the ship *Orion.*

A ship-of-the-line is one of the most magnificent struggles of human genius with the forces of nature. She has eleven claws of iron to grasp the rock at the bottom of the sea, and more wings and feelers than the butterfly to catch the breezes in the clouds. Ocean strives to lead her astray in the frightful sameness of his billows, but the ship has her compass, which is her soul, always counselling her and always pointing towards the north. In dark nights, her lanterns take the place of the stars. Thus, then, to oppose the wind, she has her ropes and canvas; against the water her timber; against the rock her iron, her copper, and her lead; against the darkness, light; against immensity, needle.

Every day, from morning till night, the quays of the port of Toulon were covered with a throng of saunterers and idlers, whose occupation consisted in gazing at the *Orion.* One morning, the throng witnessed an accident.

The crew was engaged in furling sail. The topman, whose duty it was to take in the starboard upper corner of the main top-sail, lost his balance. He was seen tottering; the dense throng assembled on the wharf of the arsenal uttered a cry, the man's head overbalanced his body, and he whirled over the yard, his arms outstretched towards the deep; as he went over, he grasped the man-ropes, first with one hand, and then with the other, and hung suspended in that manner. The sea lay far below him at a giddy depth. The shock of his fall had given to the man-ropes a violent swinging motion, and the poor fellow hung dangling to and fro at the end of this line, like a stone in a sling.

To go to his aid was to run a frightful risk. None of the crew, who were all fishermen of the coast recently taken into service, dared attempt it. In the meantime, the poor topman was becoming exhausted; his increasing weakness could be detected. All were now looking forward to the moment when he should let go of the rope, and, at instants, all turned their heads away that they might not see him fall.

Suddenly, a man was discovered clambering up the rigging with the agility of a wildcat. This man was clad in red—it was a convict; he wore a green cap—it was a convict for life. As he reached the round top, a gust of wind blew off his cap and revealed a head entirely white: it was not a young man.

In fact, one of the convicts employed on board in some prison task, had, at the first alarm, run to the officer of the watch, and asked permission to save the topman's life at the risk of his own. A sign of assent being given, with one blow of a hammer he broke the chain riveted to the iron ring at his ankle, then took a rope in his hand, and flung himself into the shrouds. Nobody, at the moment, noticed with what ease the chain was broken.

In a twinkling he was upon the yard. On reaching its extreme tip, he fastened one end of the rope he had with him, and let the other hang at full length. Thereupon, he began to let himself down by his hands along this rope, and then there was an inexpressible sensation of terror; instead of one man, two were seen dangling at that giddy height.

It was time; one minute more, and the seaman, exhausted and despairing, would have fallen into the deep. The convict firmly secured him to the rope to which he clung with one hand while he worked with the other. Finally, he was seen reascending to the yard, and hauling the sailor after him; he supported him there, for an instant, to let him recover his strength, and then, lifting him in his arms, carried him, as he walked along the yard, to the crosstrees, and from there to the round-top, where he left him in the hands of his mess-mates.

Then the throng applauded; old galley sergeants wept, women hugged each other on the wharves, and, on all sides, voices were heard exclaiming, "This man must be pardoned!"

He, however, slid down the rigging, and started to run along a lower yard. All eyes were following him. Suddenly, the throng uttered a thrilling outcry: the convict had fallen into the sea.

The fall was perilous. The frigate *Algesiras* was moored close to the *Orion*, and the poor convict had plunged between the two ships. It was feared that he would be drawn under one or the other. Four men sprang, at once, into a boat. The people cheered them on, and anxiety again took possession of all minds. The man had not again risen to the surface. He had disappeared in the sea, without making even a ripple, as though he had fallen into a cask of oil. They sounded and dragged the place until night, but not even the body was found.

The next morning, the *Toulon Journal* published the following lines:—"November 17, 1823. Yesterday, a convict at work on board of the *Orion*, on his return from rescuing a sailor, fell into the sea, and was drowned. His body was not recovered. This man was registered by the number 9430, and his name was Jean Valjean."

XI. PROMISE FULFILLED

IN 1823, MONTFERMEIL was nothing but a village in the woods. It was a peaceful and charming spot, and not upon the road to any place; the inhabitants cheaply enjoyed that rural life which is so easy of enjoyment. But water was scarce there on account of the height of the plateau. The end of the village towards Chelles found drinking-water only at a little spring on the side of the hill, about fifteen minutes' walk from Montfermeil.

This was the terror of the poor being whom the reader has not perhaps forgotten—little Cosette. It will be remembered that Cosette was useful to the Thénardiers in two ways, they got pay from the mother and work from the child. Thus when the mother ceased entirely to pay, we have seen why, in the preceding chapters, the Thénardiers kept Cosette. She saved them a servant. In that capacity she ran for water when it was wanted.

Christmas in the year 1823 was particularly brilliant at Montfermeil. Some jugglers from Paris had obtained permission from the mayor to set up their stalls in the main street of the village, and a company of pedlars had, under the same licence, put up their booths in the square before the church and even in the lane upon which the Thénardier chophouse was situated. This filled up the taverns and pot-houses, and gave to this little quiet place a noisy and joyous appearance.

On that Christmas evening, several men, waggoners and pedlars, were seated at table and drinking around four or five candles in the low hall of the Thénardier tavern. This room resembled all barrooms; tables, pewter-mugs, bottles, drinkers, smokers; little light, and much noise. Thénardier, the wife, was looking to the supper, which was cooking before a bright blazing fire; the husband, Thénardier, was drinking with his guests and talking politics.

Aside from the political discussions, the principal subjects of which were the Spanish war and the Duc d'Angoulême, local interludes were heard amid the hubbub:—

"Down around Nanterre and Suresnes wine is turning out well. Where they expected ten casks they are getting twelve. That is getting a good yield of juice out of the press."

Cosette was at her usual place, seated on the cross-piece of the kitchen table, near the fire-place; she was clad in rags; her bare feet were in wooden shoes, and by the light of the fire she was knitting woollen stockings for the little Thénardiers.

At intervals, the cry of a very young child, which was somewhere in the house, was heard above the noise of the bar-room. The mother had nursed him, but did not love him. When the hungry clamour of the brat became too much to bear:—"Your boy is squalling," said Thénardier, "why don't you go and see what he wants?" "Bah!" answered the mother; "I am sick of him." And the poor little fellow continued to cry in the darkness.

The reader has perhaps, since her first appearance, preserved some remembrance of this huge Thénardiess;—for such we shall call the female of this species,—large, blond, red, fat, brawny, square, enormous, and agile; she belonged, as we have said, to the race of those colossal wild women who posturise at fairs with paving-stones hung in their hair. She did everything about the house, the chamber-work, the washing, the cooking, anything she pleased, and played the deuce generally. Cosette was her only servant; a mouse in the service of an elephant. Everything trembled at the sound of her voice; windows and furniture as well as people. Her broad face, covered with freckles, had the appearance of a skimmer. She had a beard. She swore splendidly; she prided herself on being able to crack a nut with her fist. A tooth protruded from her mouth.

The other Thénardier was a little man, meagre, pale, angular, bony, and lean, who appeared to be sick, and whose health was excellent; here his knavery began. He smiled habitually as a matter of business, and tried to be polite to everybody, even to the beggar to whom he refused a penny. He had the look of a weazel, and the mien of a man of letters. He affected drinking with waggoners. Nobody ever saw him drunk. He smoked a large pipe. He wore a blouse, and under it an old black coat. He made pretensions to literature and materialism. There were names which he often pronounced in support of anything whatever that he might say: Voltaire, and, oddly enough, St. Augustine. He professed to have "a system."

It will be remembered that he pretended to have been in the service; he related with some pomp that at Waterloo, being sergeant in a Sixth or Ninth Light something, he alone, against a squadron of Hussars of Death, had covered with his body, and saved amid a shower of grape, "a general dangerously wounded." Hence the flaming picture on his sign, and the name of his inn, which was spoken of in the region as the "tavern of the sergeant of Waterloo." It was said in the village that he had studied for the priesthood.

Thénardier was fond of being thought learned. Nevertheless, the schoolmaster remarked that he made mistakes in pronunciation. He made out travellers' bills in a superior style, but practised eyes sometimes found them faulty in orthography. Thénardier was sly, greedy, lounging, and clever. He did not disdain servant girls, consequently his wife had no more of them. This giantess was jealous. It seemed to her that this little, lean, and yellow man must be the object of universal desire.

Every new-comer who entered the chop-house said, on seeing the Thénardiess: There is the master of the house. It was an error. She was not even *the mistress*. The husband was both master and mistress. He directed everything by a sort of invisible and continuous magnetic action. A word sufficed, sometimes a sign; the mastodon obeyed. Thénardier was to her, without her being really aware of it, a sort of being apart and sovereign. She had the virtues of her order of creation; never would she have differed in any detail with "Monsieur Thénardier"—nor—impossible supposition—would she have publicly quarrelled with her husband, on any matter whatever.

This woman loved nothing but her children, and feared nothing but her husband. She was a mother because she was a mammal. Her maternal feelings stopped with her girls, and, as we shall see, did not extend to boys. The man had but one thought—to get rich.

He did not succeed. His great talents had no adequate opportunity. Thénardier at Montfermeil was ruining himself, if ruin is possible at zero. In Switzerland, or in the Pyrenees, this penniless rogue would have become a millionaire. But where fate places the innkeeper he must browse. Thénardier owed about fifteen hundred francs, of pressing debts, which rendered him moody.

He had certain professional aphorisms which he inculcated in the mind of his wife. "The duty of the innkeeper," said he to her one day, emphatically, and in a low voice, "is to sell to the first comer, food, rest, light, fire, dirty linen, servants, fleas, and smiles; to charge for the open window, the closed window, the chimney corner, the sofa, the chair, the stool, the bench, the feather bed, the mattress, and the straw bed; to know how much the mirror is worn, and to tax that; and, by the five hundred thousand devils, to make the traveller pay for everything, even to the flies that his dog eats!"

Such were these two beings. Cosette, between them, was beaten unmercifully; that came from the woman. She went barefoot in winter; that came from the man.

Cosette ran up stairs and down stairs; washed, brushed, scrubbed, swept, ran, tired herself, got out of breath, lifted heavy things, and, puny as she was, did the rough work. The Thénardier chop-house was like a snare, in which Cosette had been caught. It was something like a fly serving spiders.

Four new guests had just come in.

Cosette was then thinking that it was late in the evening, that the bowls and pitchers in the rooms of the travellers who had arrived must be filled immediately, and that there was no more water in the cistern.

One thing comforted her a little; they did not drink much water in the Thénardier tavern. There were plenty of people there who were thirsty; but it was that kind of thirst which reaches rather towards the jug than the pitcher. Had anybody asked for a glass of water among these glasses of wine, he would have seemed a savage to all those men.

From time to time, one of the drinkers would look out into the street and exclaim:—"It is as black as an oven!" or, "It would take a cat to go along the street without a lantern to-night!" And Cosette shuddered.

All at once, one of the pedlars who lodged in the tavern came in, and said in a harsh voice:

"You have not watered my horse."

"Yes, we have, sure," said the Thénardiess.

"I tell you no, ma'am," replied the pedlar.

Cosette came out from under the table.

"Oh, yes, monsieur!" said she, "the horse did drink; he drank in the bucket, the bucket full, and 'twas me that carried it to him, and I talked to him."

This was not true. Cosette lied.

"Here is a girl as big as my fist, who can tell a lie as big as a house," exclaimed the pedlar. "I tell you that he has not had any water, little wench! He has a way of blowing when he has not had any water, that I know well enough."

Cosette persisted, and added in a voice stifled with anguish, and which could hardly be heard:

"But he did drink a good deal."

"Come," continued the pedlar, in a passion, "that is enough; give my horse some water, and say no more about it."

Cosette went back under the table.

"Well, of course that is right," said the Thénardiess; "if the beast has not had any water, he must have some."

Then looking about her:

"Well, what has become of that girl?"

Cosette came out of the kind of hole where she had hidden. The Thénardiess continued:

"Mademoiselle Dog-without-a-name, go and carry some drink to this horse."

"But, ma'am," said Cosette feebly, "there is no water."

The Thénardiess threw the street door wide open.

"Well, go after some!"

Cosette hung her head, and went for an empty bucket that was by the chimney corner.

The bucket was larger than she, and the child could have sat down in it comfortably.

The Thénardiess went back to her range, and tasted what was in the kettle with a wooden spoon, grumbling the while.

"There is some at the spring. She is the worst girl that ever was. I think 'twould have been better if I'd left out the onions."

Then she fumbled in a drawer where there were some pennies, pepper, and garlic.

"Here, Mamselle Toad," added she, "get a big loaf at the baker's, as you come back. Here is fifteen sous."

Cosette had a little pocket in the side of her apron; she took the piece without saying a word, and put it in that pocket.

Then she remained motionless, bucket in hand, the open door before her. She seemed to be waiting for somebody to come to her aid.

"Get along!" cried the Thénardiess.

Cosette went out. The door closed.

The row of booths extended along the street from the church as far as the Thénardier tavern. These booths were all illuminated with candles, burning in paper lanterns, which, as the schoolmaster of Montfermeil said, produced a magical effect. In retaliation, not a star was to be seen in the sky.

The last of these stalls, set up exactly opposite Thénardier's door, was a toy-shop, all glittering with trinkets, glass beads, and things magnificent in tin. In the first rank, and in front, the merchant had placed a great doll nearly two feet high, dressed in a robe of pink crape with golden wheat-ears on its head, which had real hair and enamel eyes. Eponine and Azelma had passed hours in contemplating it, and Cosette herself, furtively, it is true, had dared to look at it.

At the moment when Cosette went out, bucket in hand, all gloomy and overwhelmed as she was, she could not help raising her eyes towards this wonderful doll, *the lady,* as she called it

This whole booth seemed a palace to her; this doll was not a doll, it was a vision. It was joy, splendour, riches, happiness. Cosette was measuring with the sad and simple sagacity of childhood the abyss which separated her from that doll. She was saying to herself that one must be a queen, or at least a princess, to have a thing like that.

In this adoration, she forgot everything, even the errand on which she had been sent. Suddenly, the harsh voice of the Thénardiess called her back to the reality: "How, jade, haven't you gone yet? Hold on; I am coming for you! I'd. like to know what she's doing there? Little monster, be off!"

Cosette fled with her bucket, running as fast as she could.

She looked no more at booths, so long as she was in the lane. In the vicinity of the church, the illuminated stalls lighted the way, but soon the last gleam from the last stall disappeared. The poor child found herself in darkness. She shook the handle of the bucket as much as she could on her way. That made a noise, which kept her company.

Cosette thus passed through the labyrinth of crooked and deserted streets, which terminates the village of Montfermeil towards Chelles. As long as she had houses, or even walls, on the sides of the road, she went on boldly enough. From time to time, she saw the light of a candle through the cracks of a shutter; it was light and life to her; there were people there; that kept up her courage. However, as she advanced, her speed slackened as if mechanically. When she had passed the corner of the last house, Cosette stopped. It was Montfermeil no longer, it was the open country; dark and deserted space was before her. She looked with despair into this darkness where nobody was, where there were beasts, where there were perhaps ghosts. Then she seized her bucket again; fear gave her boldness:

"Pshaw," said she, "I will tell her there isn't any more water!" And she resolutely went back into Montfermeil.

She had scarcely gone a hundred steps when she stopped again. Now, it was the Thénardiess that appeared to her; the hideous Thénardiess, with her hyena mouth, and wrath flashing from her eyes. The child cast a pitiful glance before her and behind her. What could she do? What would become of her? Where should she go? Before her, the spectre of the Thénardiess; behind her, all the phantoms of night and of the forest. It was at the Thénardiess that she recoiled. She took the road to the spring again, and began to run. She ran out of the village; she ran into the woods, seeing nothing, hearing nothing. She did not stop running until out of breath, and even then she staggered on, desperate.

It was only seven or eight minutes' walk from the edge of the woods to the spring. Cosette knew the road,.from travelling it several times a day. A remnant of instinct guided her blindly. But she neither turned her eyes to the right nor to the left, for fear of seeing things in the trees and in the bushes. Thus she arrived at the spring.

It was a small natural basin, about two feet deep, surrounded with moss and that long figured grass called Henry Fourth's collars, and paved with a few large stones. A brook escaped from it with a gentle, tranquil murmur.

Cosette felt with her left hand in the darkness for a young oak which bent over the spring, swung herself from it, bent down and plunged the bucket in the water. When she was thus bent over, she did not notice that the pocket of her apron emptied itself into the spring. The fifteen-sous piece fell into the water. Cosette neither saw it nor heard it fall. She drew out the bucket almost full and set it on the grass.

This done, her strength was exhausted. She was anxious to start at once; but the effort of filling the bucket had been so great that it was impossible for her to take a step. She was compelled to sit down upon the grass.

A cold wind blew from the plain. The woods were dark. Great branches drew themselves up fearfully. The brambles twisted about like long arms seeking to seize their prey in their claws. The prospect was dismal.

Cosette felt that she was seized by this black enormity of nature. She had only one thought, to fly; to fly with all her might, across woods, across fields, to houses, to windows, to lighted candles. Her eyes fell upon the bucket that was before her. Such was the dread with which the Thénardiess inspired her, that she did not dare to go without the bucket of water. She grasped the handle with both hands. She could hardly lift the bucket.

She went a dozen steps in this manner, but the bucket was full, it was heavy, she was compelled to rest it on the ground. She breathed an instant, then grasped the handle again, and walked on, this time a little longer. But she had to stop again. After resting a few seconds, she started on. She walked bending forward, her head down, like an old woman: the weight of the bucket strained and stiffened her thin arms. The iron handle was numbing and freezing her little wet hands; from time to time she had to stop, and every time she stopped, the cold water that splashed from the bucket fell upon her naked knees. She was worn out with fatigue, and was not yet out of the forest. Arriving near an old chestnut tree which she knew, she made a last halt, longer than the others, to get well rested; meanwhile the poor little despairing thing could not help crying: "Oh! my God! my God!"

At that moment she felt all at once that the weight of the bucket was gone. A hand, which seemed enormous to her, had just caught the handle, and was carrying it easily. She raised her head. A large dark form, straight and erect, was walking beside her in the gloom. It was a man who had come up behind her, and whom she had not heard. This man, without saying a word, had grasped the handle of the bucket she was carrying.

The child was not afraid.

In the afternoon of that same Christmas-day, 1823, a man walked a long time in the most deserted portion of the Boulevard de l'Hôpital at Paris. This man had the appearance of some one who was looking for lodgings, and seemed to stop by preference before the most modest houses of this dilapidated part of the Faubourg Saint Marceau.

He wore a round hat, very old and carefully brushed, a long coat, completely threadbare, of coarse yellow cloth, a large waistcoat with pockets of antique style, black trousers worn grey at the knees, black woollen stockings, and thick shoes with copper buckles. One would have called him an old preceptor of a good family, returned from the emigration.

At a quarter past four, that is to say, after dark, he passed in front of the theatre of the Porte Saint Martin where the play that day was *The Two Convicts*. The poster, lit up by the reflection from the theatre, seemed to strike him, for, although he was walking rapidly, he stopped to read it. A moment after, he was in the *cul-de-sac* de la Planchette, and entered the *Pewter platter*, which was then the office of the Lagny stage.

The man asked:

"Have you a seat?"

"Only one, beside me, on the box," said the driver.

"I will take it."

"Get up then."

Before starting, however, the driver cast a glance at the poor apparel of the traveller, and at the smallness of his bundle, and took his pay.

About six o'clock in the evening they were at Chelles. The driver stopped to let his horses breathe.

"I will get down here," said the man.

He took his bundle and stick, and jumped down from the stage.

A moment afterwards he had disappeared.

The driver turned to the inside passengers:

"There," said he, "is a man who does not belong here, for I don't know him. He has an appearance of not having a sou; however, he don't stick about money; he pays to Lagny, and he only goes to Chelles."

The man had hurried rapidly in the darkness along the main street of Chelles; then he had turned to the left, before reaching the church, into the cross road leading to Montfermeil, like one who knew the country and had been that way before.

When he reached the wood, he slackened his pace, and began to look carefully at all the trees, pausing at every step, as if he were seeking and following a mysterious route known only to himself. There was a moment when he appeared to lose himself, and when he stopped, undecided. Finally he arrived, by continual groping, at a glade where there was a heap of large whitish stones. He made his way quickly towards these stones, and examined them with attention in the dusk of the night, as if he were passing them in review. A large tree, covered with these excrescences which are the warts of vegetation, was a few steps from the heap of stones. He went to this tree, and passed his hand over the bark of the trunk, as if he were seeking to recognise and to count all the warts.

Opposite this tree, which was an ash, there was a chestnut tree wounded in the bark, which had been staunched with a bandage of zinc nailed on. He rose on tip-toe and touched that band of zinc.

Then he stamped for some time upon the ground in the space between the tree and the stones, like one who would be sure that the earth had not been freshly stirred.

This done, he resumed his walk through the woods.

This was the man who had fallen in with Cosette.

Cosette, we have said, was not afraid.

The man spoke to her. His voice was serious, and was almost a whisper.

"My child, that is very heavy for you which you are carrying there."

"Yes, monsieur."

"Give it to me," the man continued, "I will carry it for you."

Cosette let go of the bucket. The man walked along with her.

"It is very heavy, indeed," said he to himself. Then he added:

"Little girl, how old are you?"

"Eight years, monsieur."

"And have you come far in this way?"

"From the spring in the woods."

"And are you going far?"

"A good quarter of an hour from here."

The man remained a moment without speaking, then he said abruptly:

"You have no mother then?"

"I don't know," answered the child.

Before the man had had time to say a word, she added:

"I don't believe I have. All the rest have one."

And after a silence, she added: "I believe I never had any."

"What is your name?" said the man.

"Cosette."

It seemed as if the man had an electric shock. He made another pause, then he began:

"Who is it that has sent you out into the woods after water at this time of night?"

"Madame Thénardier."

The man resumed with a tone of voice which he tried to render indifferent, but in which there was nevertheless a singular tremor:

"What does she do, your Madame Thénardier?"

"She is my mistress," said the child. "She keeps the tavern."

"The tavern," said the man. "Well, I am going there to lodge to-night. Show me the way."

"We are going there," said the child.

The man walked very fast. Cosette followed him without difficulty. She felt fatigue no more. From time to time, she raised her eyes towards this man with a sort of tranquillity and inexpressible confidence.

A few minutes passed. The man spoke:

"Is there no servant at Madame Thénardier's?"

"No, monsieur."

"Are you alone?"

"Yes, monsieur."

There was another interval of silence. Cosette raised her voice:

"That is, there are two little girls."

"What little girls?"

"Ponine and Zelma."

The child simplified in this way the romantic names dear to the mother.

"What are Ponine and Zelma?"

"They are Madame Thénardier's young ladies, her daughters."

"And what do they do?"

"Oh!" said the child, "they have beautiful dolls, things which there's gold in; they are full of business. They play, they amuse themselves."

"And you?"

"Me! I work."

She continued after an interval of silence:

"Sometimes, when I have finished my work and they are willing, I amuse myself also."

"How do you amuse yourself?"

"The best I can. They let me alone. But I have not many playthings. Ponine and Zelma are not willing for me to play with their dolls. I have only a little lead sword, not longer than that."

The child showed her little finger.

"And which does not cut?"

"Yes, monsieur," said the child, "it cuts lettuce and flies' heads."

As they drew near the tavern, Cosette timidly touched his arm:

"Monsieur?"

"What, my child?"

"Here we are close by the house."

"Well?"

"Will you let me take the bucket now?"

"What for?"

"Because, if madame sees that anybody brought it for me, she will beat me."

The man gave her the bucket. A moment after they were at the door of the chop-house.

Cosette could not help casting one look towards the grand doll still displayed in the toy-shop, then she rapped. The door opened. The Thénardiess appeared with a candle in her hand.

"Oh! it is you, you little beggar! you have taken your time! she has been playing, the wench!"

"Madame," said Cosette, trembling, "there is a gentleman who is coming to lodge."

The Thénardiess very quickly replaced her fierce air by her amiable grimace, a change at sight peculiar to innkeepers.

"Is it monsieur?" said she.

"Yes, madame," answered the man, touching his hat.

Rich travellers are not so polite. This gesture and the sight of the stranger's costume and baggage which the Thénardiess passed in review at a glance made the amiable grimace disappear and the fierce air reappear.

"Ah! my brave man, I am very sorry, but I have no room."

"Put me where you will," said the man, "in the garret, in the stable. I will pay as if I had a room."

"Forty sous."

"Forty sous. Well."

"In advance."

"Forty sous," whispered a waggoner to the Thénardiess, "but it is only twenty sous."

"It is forty sous for him," replied the Thénardiess in the same tone. "I don't lodge poor people for less."

"That is true," added her husband softly, "it ruins a house to have this sort of people."

Meanwhile the man, after leaving his stick and bundle on a bench, had seated himself at a table on which Cosette had been quick to place a bottle of wine and a glass. The man, who hardly touched his lips to the wine, was contemplating the child with a strange attention.

Cosette was ugly. Happy, she might, perhaps, have been pretty. Cosette was thin and pale; she was nearly eight years old, but one would hardly have thought her six. The light of the fire which was shining upon her, made her bones stand out and rendered her thinness fearfully visible. Her whole dress was nothing but a rag, which would have excited pity in the summer, and which excited horror in the winter. Her naked legs were red and rough. The hollows under her collar bones would make one weep. The whole person of this child, her gait, her attitude, the sound of her voice, expressed and uttered a single idea: fear.

Fear was spread all over her; she was, so to say, covered with it; fear drew back her elbows against her sides, drew her heels under her skirt, made her take the least possible room, prevented her from breathing more than was absolutely necessary, and had become what might be called her bodily habit, without possible variation, except of increase.

This fear was such that on coming in, all wet as she was, Cosette had not dared go and dry herself by the fire, but had gone silently to her work.

Suddenly, the Thénardiess exclaimed out:

"Oh! I forgot! that bread!"

Cosette had entirely forgotten the bread. She had recourse to the expedient of children who are always terrified. She lied.

"Madame, the baker was shut."

"You ought to have knocked."

"I did knock, madame. He didn't open."

"I'll find out to-morrow if that is true," said the Thénardiess. "Meantime give me back the fifteen-sous piece."

Cosette plunged her hand into her apron pocket, and turned white.

"Come," said the Thénardiess, "didn't you hear me?"

Cosette turned her pocket inside out; there was nothing there.

"Have you lost it, the fifteen-sous piece?" screamed the Thénardiess, "or do you want to steal it from me?"

At the same time she reached her arm towards the cowhide hanging in the chimney corner.

This menacing movement gave Cosette the strength to cry out:

"Forgive me! Madame! Madame! I won't do so any more!"

The Thénardiess took down the whip.

Meanwhile the man in the yellow coat had been fumbling in his waist-coat pocket.

"I beg your pardon, madame," said the man, "but I just now saw something fall out of the pocket of that little girl's apron and roll away. That may be it."

At the same time he stooped down and appeared to search on the floor.

"Just so, here it is," said he, rising.

And he handed a silver piece to the Thénardiess.

"Yes, that is it," said she.

That was not it, for it was a twenty-sous piece, but the Thénardiess put the piece in her pocket, and contented herself with casting a ferocious look at the child and saying:

"Don't let that happen again, ever."

A door now opened, and Eponine and Azelma came in.

They were really two pretty little girls, one with her well-polished auburn tresses, the other with her long black braids falling down her back, and both so lively, neat, plump, fresh, and healthy, that it was a pleasure to see them.

They went and sat down by the fire. They had a doll which they turned backwards and forwards. Eponine and Azelma did not notice Cosette. To them she was like the dog. These three little girls could not count twenty-four years among them all, and they already represented all human society; on one side envy, on the other disdain.

The doll of the Thénardier sisters was very much faded, and very old and broken; it appeared none the less wonderful to Cosette, who had never in her life had a doll, *a real doll*, to use an expression that all children will understand.

All at once, the Thénardiess, who was continually going and coming about the room, noticed that Cosette's attention was distracted, and that instead of working she was busied with the little girls who were playing.

"Ah! I've caught you!" cried she. "That is the way you work! I'll make you work with a cowhide, I will."

The stranger, without leaving his chair, turned towards the Thénardiess.

"Madame," said he, smiling diffidently. "Pshaw! let her play!"

On the part of any traveller who had eaten a slice of mutton, and drunk two bottles of wine at his supper, and who had not had the appearance of *a horrid pauper*, such a wish would have been a command. But that a man who wore that hat should allow himself to have a desire, and that a man who wore that coat should permit himself to have a wish, was what the Thénardiess thought ought not to be tolerated. She replied sharply:

"She must work, for she eats. I don't support her to do nothing."

"What is it she is making?" said the stranger, in that gentle voice which contrasted so strangely with his beggar's clothes and his porter's shoulders.

"Stockings, if you please. Stockings for my little girls who have none, worth speaking of, and will soon be going barefooted."

The man looked at Cosette's poor red feet, and continued:

"When will she finish that pair of stockings?"

"It will take her at least three or four good days, the lazy thing."

"And how much might this pair of stockings be worth, when it is finished?"

The Thénardiess cast a disdained glance at him.

"At least thirty sous."

"Would you take five francs for them?" said the man.

"Goodness!" exclaimed a waggoner who was listening, with a horse-laugh, "five francs? It's a humbug! five bullets!"

Thénardier now thought it time to speak.

"Yes, monsieur, if it is your fancy, you can have that pair of stockings for five francs. We can't refuse anything to travellers."

"You must pay for them now," said the Thénardiess, in her short and peremptory way.

"I will buy that pair of stockings," answered the man, "and," added he, drawing a five franc piece from his pocket and laying it on the table, "I will pay for them."

Then he turned towards Cosette.

"Now your work belongs to me. Play, my child."

The waggoner was so affected by the five franc piece, that he left his glass and went to look at it.

"It's so, that's a fact!" cried he, as he looked at it. "A regular hindwheel! and no counterfeit!"

Thénardier approached, and silently put the piece in his pocket.

The Thénardiess had nothing to reply. She bit her lips, and her face assumed an expression of hatred.

Meanwhile Cosette trembled. She ventured to ask:

"Madame, is it true? can I play?"

"Play!" said the Thénardiess in a terrible voice.

"Thank you, madame," said Cosette. And, while her mouth thanked the Thénardiess, all her little soul was thanking the traveller.

Thénardier returned to his drink. His wife whispered in his ear:

"What can that yellow man be?"

"I have seen," answered Thénardier, in a commanding tone, "millionaires with coats like that."

Cosette had taken from a little box behind her a few old rags, and her little lead sword.

Eponine and Azelma paid no attention to what was going on. They had just caught the kitten. They had thrown the doll on the floor, and Eponine, the elder, was dressing the kitten, in spite of her miaulings and contortions, with clothes and red and blue rags.

"Look! look, sister, this doll is more amusing than the other. She shall be my little girl; I will be a lady. I'll come to see you, and you must look at her. By and by you must see her whiskers, and you must be surprised. And then you must see her ears, and then you must see her tail, and you must say to me: 'Oh! my stars!' and I will say to you, 'Yes, madame, it is a little girl that I have like that.' Little girls are like that now."

Meanwhile, the drinkers were singing an obscene song, at which they laughed enough to shake the room. Thénardier encouraged and accompanied them.

While Eponine and Azelma were dressing up the cat, Cosette had dressed up the sword. That done, she had laid it upon her arm, and was singing it softly to sleep.

The Thénardiess approached the *yellow man.* "My husband is right," thought she; "it may be Monsieur Laffitte. Some rich men are so odd."

She came and rested her elbow on the table at which he was sitting.

"You see, monsieur," she pursued, putting on her sweetest look, "I am very willing the child should play, I am not opposed to it. But, you see, she is poor; she must work."

"The child is not yours, then?" asked the man.

"Oh dear! no, monsieur! It is a little pauper that we have taken in through charity. A sort of imbecile child. We do all we can for her, but we are not rich. We write in vain to her country; for six months we have had no answer. We think that her mother must be dead."

"Ah!" said the man.

"This mother was no great things," added the Thénardiess. "She abandoned her child."

The revellers continued to sing their songs, and the child, under the table, also sang hers.

All at once, Cosette stopped. She had just turned and seen the little Thénardiers' doll, which they had forsaken for the cat and left on the floor, a few steps from the kitchen table.

Then she let the bundled-up sword fall, and ran her eyes slowly around the room. The Thénardiess was whispering to her husband and counting some money, Eponine and Azelma were playing with the cat, the travellers were eating or drinking or singing, nobody was looking at her. She crept out from under the table on her hands and knees, darted quickly to the doll, and seized it. An instant afterwards she was at her place, seated, motionless, only turned in such a way as to keep the doll that she held in her arms in the shadow.

Nobody had seen her, except the traveller, who was slowly eating his meagre supper.

But in spite of Cosette's precautions, she did not perceive that one of the doll's feet *stuck out,* and that the fire of the fireplace lighted it up very vividly. This rosy and luminous foot which protruded from the shadow suddenly caught Azelma's eye, and she said to Eponine: "Oh! sister!"

Eponine got up, and without letting go of the cat, went to her mother and began to pull at her skirt.

"Mother," said the child, "look there."

The face of the Thénardiess assumed the peculiar expression which is composed of the terrible mingled with the commonplace and which has given this class of women the name of furies.

She cried with a voice harsh with indignation:

"Cosette!"

Cosette took the doll and placed it gently on the floor with a kind of veneration mingled with despair. Then she burst into tears.

Meanwhile the traveller arose. "What is the matter?" said he.

"Don't you see?" said the Thénardiess, pointing with her finger to the *corpus delicti* lying at Cosette's feet.

"Well, what is that?" said the man.

"That beggar," answered the Thénardiess, "has dared to touch the children's doll."

Here Cosette redoubled her sobs.

"Be still!" cried the Thénardiess.

The man walked to the street door, opened it, and went out.

As soon as he had gone, the Thénardiess profited by his absence to give Cosette under the table a severe kick.

The door opened again, and the man reappeared, holding in his hands the fabulous doll of which we have spoken. He stood it up before Cosette, saying:

"Here, this is for you."

There was a solemn silence in the whole bar-room.

"Well, Cosette," said the Thénardiess in a voice which was meant to be sweet, "a'n't you going to take your doll?"

Cosette looked upon the wonderful doll with a sort of terror.

"Is it true, is it true, monsieur?" said Cosette; "is the lady for me?"

The stranger nodded assent and put the hand of "the lady" in her little hand.

"I will call her Catharine," said she.

It was Eponine and Azelma now who looked upon Cosette with envy.

Cosette placed Catharine on a chair, then sat down on the floor before her, and remained motionless, without saying a word.

"Why don't you play, Cosette?" said the stranger.

"Oh! I am playing," answered the child.

This stranger, this unknown man, who seemed like a visit from Providence to Cosette, was at that moment the being which the Thénardiess hated more than aught else in the world. However, she was compelled to restrain herself. She sent her daughters to bed immediately, then asked the yellow man's *permission* to send Cosette to bed—*who is very tired today*, added she, with a motherly air. Cosette went to bed, holding Catharine in her arms.

Several hours passed away. The midnight mass was said, the revel was finished, the drinkers had gone, the room was deserted, the fire had gone out, the stranger still remained in the same place and in the same posture. The Thénardiers alone out of propriety and curiosity, had remained in the room.

"Is he going to spend the night like this?" grumbled the Thénardiess. When the clock struck two in the morning, she said to her husband: "I am going to bed, you may do as you like."

A good hour passed. The worthy innkeeper had read the *Courrier Français* at least three times, from the date of the number to the name of the printer. The stranger did not stir.

Thénardier moved, coughed, spit, blew his nose, and creaked his chair. The man did not stir. "Is he asleep?" thought Thénardier.

Finally, Thénardier took off his cap, approached softly, and ventured to say:—

"Is monsieur not going to repose?"

"Yes," said the stranger, "you are right. Where is your stable?"

"Monsieur," said Thénardier, with a smile, "I will conduct monsieur."

He took the candle, the man took his bundle and his staff, and Thénardier led him into a room on the first floor, which was very showy, furnished all in mahogany, with a high-post bedstead and red calico curtains.

"What is this?" said the traveller.

"It is properly our bridal chamber," said the innkeeper.

"I should have liked the stable as well," said the man, bluntly.

Thénardier did not appear to hear this not very civil answer.

He lighted two entirely new wax candles, which were displayed upon the mantel; a good fire was blazing in the fireplace. There was on the mantel, under a glass case, a woman's head-dress of silver thread and orange-flowers.

"What is this?" said the stranger.

"Monsieur," said Thénardier, "it is my wife's bridal cap."

Thénardier lied. When he hired this shanty to turn it into a chop-house, he found the room thus furnished, and bought this furniture, and purchased at second-hand these orange-flowers, thinking that the house would derive from them what the English call respectability.

The innkeeper retired to his room; his wife was in bed, but not asleep. When she heard her husband's step, she turned towards him and said:

"You know that I am going to kick Cosette out doors to-morrow!"

Thénardier coolly answered:

"You are, indeed!"

For his part, the traveller had put his staff and bundle in a corner. Then he drew off his shoes, took one of the two candles, blew out the other, pushed open the door, and went out of the room, looking about him as if he were searching for something. He passed through a hall, and came to the stairway. There he heard a very soft little sound, which resembled the breathing of a child. Guided by this sound he came to a sort of triangular nook beneath the stairs. There, among all sorts of old baskets and old rubbish, was a bed; if a mattress so full of holes as to show the straw, and a covering so full of holes as to show the mattress, can be called a bed. There were no sheets. This was placed on the floor immediately on the tiles. In this bed Cosette was sleeping.

The man approached and looked at her.

Cosette was sleeping soundly; she was dressed. In the winter she did not undress on account of the cold. She held the doll clasped in her arms; its large open eyes shone in the obscurity. From time to time she heaved a deep sigh, as if she were about to wake, and she hugged the doll almost convulsively.

An open door near Cosette's nook disclosed a large dark room. The stranger entered. At the further end, through a glass window, he perceived two little beds with very white spreads. They were those of Azelma and Eponine. Half hid behind these beds was a willow cradle without curtains, in which the little boy who had cried all the evening was sleeping.

The stranger was about to withdraw when his eye fell upon the fireplace. There was no fire, there were not even any ashes. What there was, however, attracted the traveller's attention. It was two little children's shoes, of coquettish shape and of different sizes. The traveller remembered the graceful and immemorial custom of children putting their shoes in the fireplace on Christmas night. Eponine and Azelma had taken good care not to forget this, and each had put one of her shoes in the fireplace.

The traveller bent over them.

The fairy—that is to say, the mother—had already made her visit, and shining in each shoe was a beautiful new ten-sous piece.

The man was on the point of going away, when he perceived further along, by itself, in the darkest corner of the fireplace, another object. He looked, and recognised a shoe, a horrid wooden shoe of the clumsiest sort, half broken and covered with ashes and dried mud. Cosette, with that touching confidence of childhood which can always be deceived without ever being discouraged, had also placed her shoe in the fireplace.

There was nothing in this wooden shoe.

The stranger fumbled in his waistcoat, bent over, and dropped into Cosette's shoe a gold Louis.

Then he went back to his room with stealthy tread.

On the following morning, at least two hours before day, Thénardier, seated at a table in the bar-room was making out the bill of the traveller in the yellow coat.

After some erasures, Thénardier produced this masterpiece.

Bill of Monsieur in No. 1.

Supper	3 frs.
Room	10 "
Candle	5 "
Fire	4 "
Service	1 "
Total	23 frs.

Service was written *servisse*.

"Twenty-three francs!" exclaimed his wife, with an enthusiasm mingled with some hesitation.

Thénardier lighted his pipe, and answered between two puffs:

"You'll give the bill to the man."

Then he went out.

He was scarcely out of the room when the traveller came in, his staff and bundle in his hand.

"Up so soon!" said the Thénardiess; "is monsieur going to leave us already?"

The traveller answered:

"Yes, madame, I am going away. Madame," added he, "what do I owe?"

The Thénardiess, without answering, handed him the folded bill.

The man unfolded the paper and looked at it; but his thoughts were evidently elsewhere.

"Madame," replied he, "do you do a good business in Montfermeil?"

"So-so, monsieur," answered the Thénardiess, stupefied at seeing no other explosion.

She continued in a mournful and lamenting strain:

"Oh! monsieur, the times are very hard. If we only had rich travellers now and then, like monsieur! We have so many expenses! Why, that little girl eats us out of house and home."

"What little girl?"

"Why, the little girl you know! Cosette! the lark, as they call her about here!"

"Ah!" said the man.

She continued:

"You see, monsieur, we don't ask charity, but we are not able to give it. Monsieur knows that the government demands a deal of money. And then I have my own girls. I have nothing to spend on other people's children."

"Suppose you were relieved of her?"

"Who? Cosette?"

"Yes."

"Ah, monsieur! my good monsieur! take her, keep her, take her away, carry her off, sugar her, stuff her, drink her, eat her, and be blessed by the holy Virgin and all the saints in Paradise!"

"Agreed."

"Really! you will take her away?"

"I will."

"Immediately?"

"Immediately. Call the child."

"Cosette!" cried the Thénardiess.

"In the meantime," continued the man, "I will pay my bill. How much is it?"

He cast a glance at the bill, and could not repress a movement of surprise.

"Twenty-three francs?"

The Thénardiess had had time to prepare herself for the shock. She replied with assurance:

"Yes, of course, monsieur! it is twenty-three francs."

The stranger placed five five-franc pieces upon the table.

"Go for the little girl," said he.

At this moment Thénardier advanced into the middle of the room and said:

"Monsieur owes twenty-six sous."

"Twenty-six sous!" exclaimed the woman.

"Twenty sous for the room," continued Thénardier coldly, "and six for supper. As to the little girl, I must have some talk with monsieur about that. Leave us, wife."

The Thénardiess was dazzled by one of those unexpected flashes which emanate from talent. She felt that the great actor had entered upon the scene, answered not a word, and went out.

As soon as they were alone, Thénardier offered the traveller a chair. The traveller sat down, but Thénardier remained standing, and his face assumed a singular expression of good-nature and simplicity.

"Monsieur," said he, "listen, I must say that I adore this child."

The stranger looked at him steadily.

"What child?"

Thénardier continued:

"How strangely we become attached! What is all this silver? Take back your money. This child I adore."

"Who is that?" asked the stranger.

"Oh, our little Cosette! And you wish to take her away from us? Indeed, I speak frankly, as true as you are an honourable man, I cannot consent to it. I should miss her. I have had her since she was very small. It is true, she costs us money; it is true she has her faults, it is true we are not rich, it is true I paid four hundred francs for medicines at one time when she was sick. But we must do something for God. She has neither father nor mother; I have brought her up. I have bread enough for her and for myself. In fact, I must keep this child. I feel the need of her prattle in the house."

The stranger was looking steadily at him all the while. He continued:

"Pardon me, excuse me, monsieur, but one does not give his child like that to a traveller. Isn't it true that I am right? After that, I don't say—you are rich and have the appearance of a very fine man—if it is for her advantage,—but I must know about it. You understand? I would not want to lose sight of her, I should want to know who she was with, that I might come and see her now and then, and that she might know that her good foster-father was still watching over her. I do not know even your name. If you should take her away, I should say, alas for the little Lark, where has she gone? I must, at least, see some poor rag of paper, a bit of a passport, something."

The stranger answered in a severe and firm tone.

"Monsieur Thénardier, people do not take a passport to come five leagues from Paris. If I take Cosette, I take her, that is all. You will not know my name, you will not know my abode, you will not know where she goes, and my intention is that she shall never see you again in her life. Do you agree to that? Yes or no?"

As demons and genii recognise by certain signs the presence of a superior God, Thénardier comprehended that he was to deal with one who was very powerful. Although during the evening he had been drinking with the waggoners, smoking, and singing bawdy songs, still he was observing the stranger all the while, watching him like a cat, and studying him like a mathematician. Not a gesture, not a movement of the man in the yellow coat had escaped him. Before even the stranger had so clearly shown his interest in Cosette, Thénardier had divined it. Why this interest? What was this man? Why, with so much money in his purse, this miserable dress?

He had been thinking it over all night. This could not be Cosette's father. Was it a grandfather? Then why did he not make himself known at once? This man evidently had no right to Cosette. Then who was he?

Thénardier did what great captains do at that decisive instant which they alone can recognise; he unmasked his battery at once.

"Monsieur," said he, "I must have fifteen hundred francs."

The stranger took from his side-pocket an old black leather pocket-book, opened it, and drew forth three bank bills which he placed upon the table. He then rested his large thumb on these bills, and said to the tavern-keeper,

"Bring Cosette."

Cosette, as soon as she awoke, had run to her wooden shoe. She had found the gold piece in it. She did not know that it was a piece of gold; she had never seen one before. Nevertheless this louis, which she had placed in the same pocket of her apron from which the fifteen-sous piece had fallen the night before, distracted her attention from her work. While sweeping the stairs, she stopped and stood there, forgetting her broom, occupied in looking at this shining star at the bottom of her pocket.

It was in one of these reveries that the Thénardiess found her.

Wonderful to tell, she did not give her a slap nor even call her a hard name.

"Cosette," said she, almost gently, "come quick."

An instant after, Cosette entered the bar-room.

The stranger took the bundle he had brought and untied it. This bundle contained a little woollen frock, an apron, a coarse cotton under-garment, a petticoat, a scarf, woollen stockings, and shoes—a complete dress for a girl of seven years. It was all in black.

"My child," said the man, "take this and go and dress yourself quick."

The day was breaking when those of the inhabitants of Montfermeil who were beginning to open their doors, saw pass on the road to Paris a poorly clad goodman leading a little girl dressed in mourning who had a pink doll in her arms.

No one recognised the man; as Cosette was not now in tatters, few recognised her.

Cosette walked seriously along, opening her large eyes, and looking at the sky. She had put her louis in the pocket of her new apron. From time to time she bent over and cast a glance at it, and then looked at the goodman. She felt somewhat as if she were near God.

The Thénardiess, according to her custom, had left her husband alone. She was expecting great events. When the man and Cosette were gone, Thénardier, after a good quarter of an hour, took her aside, and showed her the fifteen hundred francs.

"What's that?" said she.

It was the first time, since the beginning of their housekeeping, that she had dared to criticise the act of her master.

He felt the blow.

"True, you are right," said he; "I am a fool. Give me my hat."

He folded the three bank bills, thrust them into his pocket, and started in all haste, but he missed the direction and took the road to the right. Some neighbours of whom he inquired put him on the track; the Lark and the man had been seen to go in the direction of Livry. He followed this indication, walking rapidly and talking to himself.

"This man is evidently a millionaire dressed in yellow, and as for me, I am a brute. He first gave twenty sous, then five francs, then fifty francs, then fifteen hundred francs, all so readily. He would have given fifteen thousand francs. But I shall catch him."

They had the start of him, but a child walks slowly, and he went rapidly. And then the country was well known to him.

When he had passed the ponds, and reached the arch of the old aqueduct of the abbey of Chelles, he perceived above a bush, the man's hat. The bushes were low. Thénardier perceived that the man and Cosette were seated there. The man had sat down to give Cosette a little rest. The chop-house keeper turned aside the bushes, and suddenly appeared before the eyes of those whom he sought.

"Pardon me, excuse me, monsieur," said he, all out of breath; "but here are your fifteen hundred francs."

So saying, he held out the three bank bills to the stranger.

"What does that mean?"

Thénardier answered respectfully:

"Monsieur, that means that I take back Cosette."

Cosette shuddered, and hugged close to the goodman.

"Yes, monsieur, I take her back. I tell you I have reflected. Indeed, I haven't the right to give her to you. I am an honest man, you see. This little girl is not mine. She belongs to her mother. Her mother has confided her to me; I can only give her up to her mother. You will tell me: But her mother is dead. Well. In that case, I can only give up the child to a person who shall bring me a written order, signed by the mother, stating I should deliver the child to him. That is clear."

The man, without answering, felt in his pocket, and Thénardier saw the pocket-book containing the bank bills reappear.

The tavern-keeper felt a thrill of joy.

"Good!" thought he; "hold on. He is going to corrupt me!"

The man opened the pocket-book, and drew from it a little piece of paper, which he unfolded and presented open to the innkeeper, saying:

"You are right. Read that!"

Thénardier took the paper and read.

"M—— sur M——, March 25, 1823

"*Monsieur Thénardier:*
"*You will deliver Cosette to the bearer. He will settle all small debts.*
"*I have the honour to salute you with consideration.*

"FANTINE."

"You know that signature?" replied the man.

It was indeed the signature of Fantine. Thénardier recognised it.

Thénardier retreated in good order.

"This signature is very well imitated," he grumbled between his teeth. "Well, so be it!"

Then he made a desperate effort.

"Monsieur," said he, "it is all right. Then you are the person. But you must settle 'all small debts.' There is a large amount due to me."

The man rose to his feet, and said at the same time, snapping with his thumb and finger some dust from his threadbare sleeve:

"Monsieur Thénardier, in January the mother reckoned that she owed you a hundred and twenty francs; you sent her in February a memorandum of five hundred francs; you received three hundred francs at the end of February, and three hundred at the beginning of March. There has since elapsed nine months which, at fifteen francs per month, the price agreed upon, amounts to a hundred and thirty-five francs. You had received a hundred francs in advance. There remain thirty-five francs due you. I have just given you fifteen hundred francs."

Thénardier felt what the wolf feels the moment when he finds himself seized and crushed by the steel jaws of the trap. He did what the wolf does, he gave a spring.

"Monsieur-I-don't-know-your-name," said he resolutely, and putting aside this time all show of respect. "I shall take back Cosette or you must give me a thousand crowns."

The stranger said quietly:

"Come, Cosette."

He took Cosette with his left hand, and with the right picked up his staff, which was on the ground. Thénardier noted the enormous size of the cudgel, and the solitude of the place.

The man disappeared in the wood with the child, leaving the chop-house keeper motionless and non-plussed. As they walked away, Thénardier observed his broad shoulders, a little rounded, and his big fists.

Then his eyes fell back upon his own puny arms and thin hands. "I must have been a fool indeed," thought he, "not to have brought my gun."

Jean Valjean was not dead.

When he fell into the sea, or rather when he threw himself into it, he was, as we have seen, free from his irons. He swam under water to a ship at anchor to which a boat was fastened.

He found means to conceal himself in this boat until evening. At night he betook himself again to the water, and reached the land a short distance from Cape Brun.

There, as he did not lack for money, he could procure clothes. A little public-house supplied clothing for escaped convicts, a lucrative business. Then Jean Valjean, like all those joyless fugitives who are endeavouring to throw off the track the spy of the law and social fatality, followed an obscure and wandering path.

His first care, on reaching Paris, had been to purchase a mourning dress for a little girl of seven years, then to procure lodgings. That done, he had gone to Montfermeil.

On the evening of the same day that Jean Valjean had rescued Cosette from the clutches of the Thénardiess, he entered Paris again. He entered the city at night-fall, with the child, by the barrière de Monceaux. There he took a cabriolet, which carried him as far as the esplanade of the Observatory. There he got out, paid the driver, took Cosette by the hand, and both in the darkness of the night, through the deserted streets, walked towards the Boulevard de l'Hôpital.

The day had been strange and full of emotion for Cosette; they had eaten behind hedges bread and cheese bought at isolated chop-houses; they had often changed carriages, and had travelled short distances on foot. She did not complain; but she was tired, and Jean Valjean perceived it. He took her in his arms; Cosette, without letting go of Catharine, laid her head on Jean Valjean's shoulder, and went to sleep.

XII. THE OLD GORBEAU HOUSE

FORTY YEARS AGO, the solitary pedestrian who ventured into the unknown regions of La Salpêtrière and went up along the Boulevard as far as the Barrière d'Italie, reached certain points where it might be said that Paris disappeared. It was not the country, for there were houses and streets; it was not a city, the streets had ruts in them, like the highways, and grass grew along their borders; it was not a village, the houses were too lofty. It was the old quarter of the Horse Market.

Our pedestrian, if he trusted himself beyond the four tumbling walls of this Horse Market, would reach the corner of the Rue des Vignes-Saint-Marcel, a latitude not much explored. There, near a manufactory and between two garden walls, could be seen at the time of which we speak an old ruined dwelling.

On the inside of the door a brush dipped in ink had, in a couple of strokes of the hand, traced the number 52, and above the screen, the same brush had daubed the number 50, so that a new-comer would hesitate, asking: Where am I?

The letter-carriers called the house No. 50–52; but it was known, in the quarter, as Gorbeau House.

Before this Gorbeau tenement Jean Valjean stopped.

He fumbled in his waistcoat and took from it a sort of night-key, opened the door, entered, then carefully closed it again and ascended the stairway, still carrying Cosette.

At the top of the stairway he drew from his pocket another key, with which he opened another door. The chamber which he entered and closed again immediately was a sort of garret, rather spacious, furnished only with a mattress spread on the floor, a table, and a few chairs. A stove containing a fire, the coals of which were visible, stood in one corner. The street lamp of the boulevards shed a dim light through this poor interior. At the further extremity there was a little room containing a cot bed. On this Jean Valjean laid the child without waking her.

Jean Valjean bent down and kissed the child's hand.

Nine months before, he had kissed the hand of the mother, who also had just fallen asleep.

He knelt down by the bedside of Cosette.

Jean Valjean had never loved anything. For twenty-five years he had been alone in the world. He had never been a father, lover, husband, or friend. At the galleys, he was cross, sullen, abstinent, ignorant, and intractable. The heart of the old convict was full of freshness. His sister and her children had left in his memory only a vague and distant impression, which had finally almost entirely vanished. He had made every exertion to find them again, and, not succeeding, had forgotten them.

When he saw Cosette, when he had taken her, carried her away, and rescued her, he felt his heart moved. All that he had of feeling and affection was aroused and vehemently attracted towards this child.

Poor old heart, so young!

But, as he was fifty-five and Cosette was but eight years old, all that he might have felt of love in his entire life melted into a sort of ineffable radiance.

This was the second white vision he had seen. The bishop had caused the dawn of virtue on his horizon; Cosette evoked the dawn of love.

On her part, Cosette, too, unconsciously underwent a change, poor little creature! She was so small when her mother left her, that she could not recollect her now. As all children do, like the young shoots of the vine that cling to everything, she had tried to love. She had not been able to succeed. Everybody had repelled her—the Thénardiers, their children, other children. She had loved the dog; it died, and after that no person and no thing would have aught to do with her. She now felt sensations utterly unknown to her before—a sensation of budding and of growth.

Her kind friend no longer impressed as old and poor. In her eyes Jean Valjean was handsome, as the garret seemed pretty.

And, in truth, the mysterious impression produced upon Cosette, in the depths of the woods at Chelles, by the hand of Jean Valjean grasping her own in the darkness, was not an illusion but a reality. The coming of this man and his participation in the destiny of this child had been the advent of God.

In the meanwhile, Jean Valjean had well chosen his hiding-place. He was there in a state of security that seemed to be complete.

The lower floor of No. 50-52 was a sort of dilapidated shed; it served as a sort of stable for market gardeners, and had no communication with the upper floor. The upper floor contained several rooms and a few lofts, only one of which was occupied—by an old woman, who was maid of all work to Jean Valjean. All the rest was uninhabited.

From the earliest dawn, Cosette laughed, prattled, and sang. Jean Valjean had begun to teach her to read. Sometimes he would remember that it was with the intention of accomplishing evil that he had learned to read, in the galleys. This intention had now been changed into teaching a child.

From that time on, life seemed full of interest to him, men seemed good and just; he no longer, in his thoughts, reproached any one with any wrong; he saw no reason, now, why he should not live to grow very old, since his child loved him. He looked forward to a long future illuminated by Cosette with charming light.

Jean Valjean was prudent enough never to go out in the daytime. Every evening, however, about twilight, he would walk for an hour or two, sometimes alone, often with Cosette, selecting the most unfrequented side alleys of the boulevards and going into the churches at nightfall.

The old woman was housekeeper and cook, and did the marketing.

They lived frugally, always with a little fire in the stove, but like people in embarrassed circumstances. Jean Valjean still wore his yellow coat, his black pantaloons, and his old hat. On the street he was taken for a beggar; kind-hearted dames, in passing, would turn and hand him a penny. Jean Valjean accepted the penny and bowed humbly. It chanced, sometimes, also, that he would meet some wretched creature begging alms, and then, glancing about him to be sure no one was looking, he would stealthily approach the beggar, slip a piece of money, often silver, into his hand, and walk rapidly away. He began to be known in the quarter as *the beggar who gives alms*.

The old *landlady*, a crabbed creature, fully possessed with keen observation as to all that concerned her neighbours, watched Jean Valjean closely. She had questioned Cosette, who, knowing nothing, could tell nothing, further than that she came from Montfermeil. One morning this old female spy saw Jean Valjean go, with an appearance which seemed peculiar to the old busybody, into one of the uninhabited apartments of the building. She followed him with the steps of an old cat, and could see him without herself being seen, through the chink of the door directly opposite. Jean Valjean had, doubtless for greater caution, turned his back towards the door in question. The old woman saw him fumble in his pocket, and take from it a needle case, scissors, and thread, and then proceed to rip open the lining of one lapel of his coat and take from under it a piece of yellowish paper, which he unfolded. The beldame remarked with dismay, that it was a bank bill for a thousand francs.

A moment afterwards, Jean Valjean asked her to get this thousand-franc bill changed for him, adding that it was the half-yearly interest on his property which he had received on the previous day. "Where?" thought the old woman. He did not go out until six o'clock, and the government treasury is certainly not open at that hour. This bill of a thousand francs, commented upon and multiplied, gave rise to a host of breathless conferences among the gossips of the Rue des Vignes Saint Marcel.

Some days afterwards, it chanced that Jean Valjean, in his shirt-sleeves, was sawing wood in the entry. The old woman saw the coat hanging on a nail, and examined it. The lining had been sewed over. She felt it carefully and thought she could detect in the lapels and in the padding, thicknesses of paper. Other thousand-franc bills beyond a doubt!

There was, in the neighbourhood of Saint Médard, a mendicant to whom Jean Valjean often gave alms. Sometimes he spoke to him. Those who were envious of this poor creature said he was in the pay of the police. He was an old church beadle of seventy-five, who was always mumbling prayers.

One evening, as Jean Valjean was passing that way, unaccompanied by Cosette, he noticed the beggar sitting in his usual place, under the street lamp which had just been lighted. Jean Valjean walked up to him, and put a piece of money in his hand, as usual. The beggar suddenly raised his eyes, gazed intently at Jean Valjean, and then quickly dropped his head. This movement was like a flash; Jean Valjean shuddered; it seemed to him that he had just seen, by the light of the street-lamp, not the calm, sanctimonious face of the aged beadle, but a terrible and well-known countenance.

He scarcely dared to admit, even to himself, that he thought he had seen the face of Javert.

On the morrow, at nightfall, he went thither, again. The beggar was in his place. "Good day! Good day!" said Jean Valjean, with firmness, as he gave him the accustomed alms. The beggar raised his head and answered in a whining voice: "Thanks, kind sir, thanks!" It was, indeed, only the old beadle.

Jean Valjean now felt fully reassured. He even began to laugh. "What the deuce was I about to fancy that I saw Javert," thought he; "is my sight growing poor already?" And he thought no more about it.

Some days after, it might be eight o'clock in the evening, he was in his room, giving Cosette her spelling lesson, when he heard the door of the building open and close again. That seemed odd to him. The old woman, the only occupant of the house besides himself and Cosette, always went to bed at dark to save candles. Jean Valjean made a sign to Cosette to be silent. He heard some one coming up the stairs. Jean Valjean blew out his candle.

He sent Cosette to bed, telling her in a suppressed voice to lie down very quietly—and, as he kissed her forehead, the footsteps stopped. Jean Valjean remained silent and motionless, holding his breath in the darkness. He saw a light through the keyhole. There was, evidently, somebody outside with a candle who was listening.

A few minutes elapsed, and the light disappeared. But he heard no sound of footsteps, which seemed to indicate that whoever was listening at the door had taken off his shoes.

Jean Valjean threw himself on his bed without undressing, but could not shut his eyes that night.

At daybreak, as he was sinking into slumber from fatigue, he was aroused, again, by the creaking of the door of some room at the end of the hall, and then he heard the same footstep which had ascended the stairs, on the preceding night. The step approached. He started from his bed and placed his eye to the keyhole. It was a man, indeed, who passed by Jean Valjean's room, this time without stopping. The hall was still too dark for him to make out his features; but the man was tall, wore a long frock-coat, and had a cudgel under his arm. It was the redoubtable form of Javert.

At seven in the morning, when the old lady came to clear up the rooms, Jean Valjean eyed her sharply, but asked her no questions.

While she was doing her sweeping, she said:—

"Perhaps monsieur heard some one come in, last night?"

"Ah! yes, by the way, I did," he answered in the most natural tone. "Who was it?"

"It's a new lodger," said the old woman, "who has come into the house."

"And his name——?"

"Well, I hardly recollect now. Dumont or Daumont.— Some such name as that."

"And what is he—this M. Daumont?"

The old woman studied him, a moment, through her little foxy eyes, and answered:

"He's a gentleman living on his income like you."

At dusk, he went to the street-door and looked carefully up and down the boulevard. No one was to be seen. It is true that there might have been some one hidden behind a tree.

He went upstairs again.

"Come," said he to Cosette.

He took her by the hand and they both went out.

Jean Valjean had immediately left the boulevard and began to thread the streets, making as many turns as he could, returning sometimes upon his track to make sure that he was not followed.

The moon was full. Jean Valjean was not sorry for that. The moon, still near the horizon, cut large prisms of light and shade in the streets. Jean Valjean could glide along the houses and the walls on the dark side and observe the light side. He did not, perhaps, sufficiently realise that the obscure side escaped him. However, in all the deserted little streets in the neighbourhood of the Rue de Poliveau, he felt sure that no one was behind him.

Cosette walked without asking any questions. Jean Valjean knew, no more than Cosette, where he was going. He trusted in God, as she trusted in him. It seemed to him that he also held some one greater than himself by the hand; he believed he felt a being leading him, invisible.

He was not even absolutely sure that this was Javert, and then it might be Javert, and Javert not know that he was Jean Valjean. Was he not supposed to be dead? Nevertheless, he was determined not to enter Gorbeau House again.

As eleven o'clock struck in the tower of Saint Etienne du Mont, he crossed the Rue de Pontoise in front of the bureau of the Commissary of Police, which is at No. 14. Some moments afterwards, instinct made him turn his head. At this moment he saw distinctly—thanks to the commissary's lamp which revealed them—three men following him quite near, pass one after another under this lamp on the dark side of the street. One of these men entered the passage leading to the commissary's house.

"Come, child!" said he to Cosette, and he made haste to get out of the Rue de Pontoise. He made a circuit, went round the arcade des Patriarches, and plunged into the Rue des Postes.

The moon lighted up this square brightly. Jean Valjean concealed himself in a doorway, calculating that if these men were still following him, he could not fail to get a good view of them when they crossed this lighted space.

In fact, three minutes had not elapsed when the men appeared. There were now four of them; all were tall, dressed in long brown coats, with round hats, and great clubs in their hands.

They stopped in the centre of the square and formed a group like people consulting. The man who seemed to be the leader turned and energetically pointed in the direction in which Jean Valjean was; one of the others seemed to insist with some obstinacy on the contrary direction. At the instant when the leader turned, the moon shone full in his face. Jean Valjean recognised Javert perfectly.

Uncertainty was at an end for Jean Valjean; happily, it still continued with these men. He took advantage of their hesitation; it was time lost for them, gained for him. He came out from the doorway in which he was concealed, and made his way towards the region of the Jardin des Plantes. Cosette began to be tired; he took her in his arms, and carried her.

He doubled his pace.

He passed through the Rue de la Clef, then by the Fontaine de Saint Victor along the Jardin des Plantes by the lower streets, and reached the quay. The quay was deserted. The streets were deserted. Nobody behind him. He took breath.

He arrived at the bridge of Austerlitz, still a toll-bridge at this period.

"It is two sous," said the toll-keeper. "You are carrying a child who can walk. Pay for two."

He paid, annoyed that his passage should have attracted observation. All flight should be gliding.

A large cart was passing the Seine at the same time, and like him was going towards the right bank. This could be made of use. He could go the whole length of the bridge in the shade of this cart.

Towards the middle of the bridge, Cosette, her feet becoming numb, desired to walk. He put her down and took her by the hand.

The bridge passed, he perceived some wood-yards a little to the right and walked in that direction. To get there, he must venture into a large clear open space. He did not hesitate. Those who followed him were evidently thrown off his track, and Jean Valjean believed himself out of danger. Sought for, he might be, but followed he was not.

A little street, the Rue de Chemin Vert Saint Antoine, opened between two wood-yards inclosed by walls. This street was narrow, obscure, and seemed made expressly for him. Before entering it, he looked back.

From the point where he was, he could see the whole length of the bridge of Austerlitz.

Four shadows, at that moment, entered upon the bridge.

These shadows were coming from the Jardin des Plantes towards the right bank.

These four shadows were the four men.

Jean Valjean felt a shudder like that of the deer when he sees the hounds again upon his track.

But now, they no longer walked very fast. Cosette's step slackened Jean Valjean's pace. He took her up and carried her again. He took care to keep always on the dark side of the street. The two or three first times he turned, he saw nothing; on turning again, he thought he saw in the portion of the street through which he had just passed something which stirred.

He plunged forward rather than walked, hoping to find some side street by which to escape, and came to a wall.

This wall, however, did not prevent him from going further; it was a wall forming the side of a cross alley, in which the street Jean Valjean was then in came to an end.

He looked to the right. The alley ran out to a space between some buildings that were mere sheds or barns, then terminated abruptly. The end of this blind alley was plain to be seen—a great white wall.

The instant Jean Valjean decided to turn to the left, to try to reach the street which he saw at the end of the alley, he perceived, at the corner of the alley and the street towards which he was just going, a sort of black, motionless statue.

It was a man, who had just been posted there, evidently, and who was waiting for him, guarding the passage.

What he had seen moving in the obscurity some distance behind him, the moment before, was undoubtedly Javert and his squad. Javert probably had already reached the commencement of the street of which Jean Valjean was at the end. Javert, to all appearance, was acquainted with this little trap, and had taken his precautions by sending one of his men to guard the exit. To advance, was to fall upon that man. To go back, was to throw himself into Javert's hands. Jean Valjean looked up into the sky in despair.

A lime-tree lifted its branches above this corner, and the wall was covered with ivy towards the Rue Polonceau.

At this moment a muffled and regular sound began to make itself heard at some distance. Jean Valjean ventured to thrust his head a little way around the corner of the street. Seven or eight soldiers, formed in platoon, had just turned into the Rue Polonceau. He saw the gleam of their bayonets. They were coming towards him.

The soldiers, at whose head he distinguished the tall form of Javert, advanced slowly and with precaution. They stopped frequently. It was plain they were exploring all the recesses of the walls and all the entrances of doors and alleys.

Javert's two assistants marched in the ranks.

There was now only one thing possible.

Jean Valjean had this peculiarity, that he might be said to carry two knapsacks; in one he had the thoughts of a saint, in the other the formidable talents of a convict. He helped himself from one or the other as occasion required.

Among other resources, thanks to his numerous escapes from the galleys at Toulon, he had, it will be remembered, become master of that incredible art of raising himself, in the right angle of a wall, if need to be to the height of a sixth story; an art without ladders or props, by mere muscular strength, supporting himself by the back of his neck, his shoulders, his hips, and his knees, hardly making use of the few projections of the stone.

Jean Valjean measured with his eyes the wall above which he saw the lime tree.

The difficulty was Cosette. Cosette did not know how to scale a wall. To carry her was impossible.

He needed a cord. Jean Valjean had none. Where could he find a cord, at midnight, in the Rue Polonceau?

The despairing gaze of Jean Valjean encountered the lamp-post.

At this epoch there were no gas-lights in the streets of Paris. At nightfall the street lamps were raised and lowered by means of a rope traversing the street from end to end, running through the grooves of posts. The reel on which this rope was wound was inclosed below the lantern in a little iron box.

Jean Valjean, with the energy of a final struggle, crossed the street at a bound, entered the cul-de-sac, sprang the bolt of the little box with the point of his knife, and an instant after was back at the side of Cosette. He had a rope.

"Father," said she, in a whisper, "I am afraid. Who is it that is coming?"

"Hush!" answered the unhappy man, "it is the Thénardiess."

Cosette shuddered. He added:

"Don't say a word; I'll take care of her. If you cry, if you make any noise, the Thénardiess will hear you. She is coming to catch you."

Then, without any haste, but with a firm and rapid decision, he passed it around Cosette's body under the arms, attached his cravat to an end of the rope by means of the knot which seamen call a swallow-knot, took the other end of the rope in his teeth, took off his shoes and stockings and threw them over the wall, climbed upon the pile of masonry and began to raise himself in the angle of the wall and the gable with as much solidity and certainty as if he had the rounds of a ladder under his heels. Half a minute had not passed before he was on his knees on the wall.

Cosette watched him, stupefied.

All at once, she heard Jean Valjean's voice calling to her in a low whisper: "Put your back against the wall."

She obeyed.

"Don't speak, and don't be afraid," added Jean Valjean.

And she felt herself lifted from the ground.

Before she had time to think where she was she was at the top of the wall.

Jean Valjean seized her, put her on his back, took her little hands in his left hand, lay down flat and crawled along the top of the wall as far as the cut-off corner. As he had supposed, there was a building there, the roof of which sloped with a gentle inclination, and just reaching to the lime-tree.

He had just reached the inclined plane of the roof, and had not yet left the crest of the wall, when a violent uproar proclaimed the arrival of the patrol. He heard the thundering voice of Javert:

"Search the cul-de-sac! The Rue Droit Mur is guarded, the Petite Rue Picpus also. I'll answer for it if he is in the cul-de-sac."

The soldiers rushed into the Cul-de-sac Genrot.

Jean Valjean slid down the roof, keeping hold of Cosette, reached the lime-tree, and jumped to the ground. Whether from terror, or from courage, Cosette had not uttered a whisper. Her hands were a little scraped.

Jean Valjean found himself in a sort of garden, one of those gloomy gardens which seem made to be seen in the winter and at night. This garden was oblong, with a row of large poplars at the further end, some tall forest trees in the corners, and a clear space in the centre, where stood a very large isolated tree, then a few fruit trees, contorted and shaggy, like big bushes, some vegetable beds, a melon patch the glass covers of which shone in the moonlight, and an old well. There were here and there stone benches which seemed black with moss.

The large building of the Rue Droit Mur which ran back on the Petite Rue Picpus, presented upon this garden two square façades. All the windows were grated. No light was to be seen. On the upper stories there were shutters as in prisons. The shadow of one of these façades fell on the garden like an immense black pall.

Jean Valjean's first care had been to find his shoes, and put them on. Cosette trembled, and pressed closely to his side. They heard the tumultuous clamour of the patrol ransacking the cul-de-sac and the street, the clatter of their muskets against the stones, the calls of Javert to the watchmen he had stationed.

At the end of a quarter of an hour it seemed as though this stormy rumbling began to recede. Jean Valjean did not breathe.

He had placed his hand gently upon Cosette's mouth.

But the solitude about him was so strangely calm that that frightful din, so furious and so near, did not even cast over it a shadow of disturbance. It seemed as if these walls were built of the deaf stones spoken of in Scripture.

Suddenly, in the midst of this deep calm, a new sound arose; a celestial, divine, ineffable sound, as ravishing as the other was horrible. It was a hymn which came forth from the darkness, a bewildering mingling of prayer and harmony in the obscure and fearful silence of the night; voices of women, but voices with the pure accents of virgins, and artless accents of children; those voices which are not of earth, and which resemble those that the new-born still hear, and the dying hear already. This song came from the gloomy building which overlooked the garden.

Cosette and Jean Valjean fell on their knees.

The night wind had risen, which indicated that it must be between one and two o'clock in the morning. Poor Cosette did not speak.

"Are you sleepy?" said Jean Valjean.

"I am very cold," she answered.

A moment after she added:

"Is she there yet?"

"Who?" said Jean Valjean.

"Madame Thénardier."

Jean Valjean had already forgotten the means he had employed to secure Cosette's silence.

"Oh!" said he. "She has gone. Don't be afraid any longer."

The child sighed as if a weight were lifted from her breast.

The ground was damp, the wind freshened every moment. The goodman took off his coat and wrapped Cosette in it.

"Are you warmer, so?"

"Oh! yes, father!"

"Well, wait here a moment for me. I shall soon be back."

He went along by the large building, in search of some better shelter. He found doors, but they were all closed. All the windows of the ground-floor were barred.

As he passed the interior angle of the building, he noticed several arched windows before him, where he perceived some light. He rose on tiptoe and looked in at one of these windows. He thought he saw something, stretched out on the pavement, which appeared to be covered with a shroud, and which resembled a human form. It was lying with the face downwards, the arms crossed, in the immobility of death. One would have said, from a sort of serpent which trailed along the pavement, that this ill-omened figure had a rope about its neck.

He had the courage to press his forehead against the glass, and watch to see if the thing would move. He remained what seemed to him a long time in vain; the prostrate form made no movement. Suddenly he was seized with an inexpressible dismay, and he fled. It seemed to him that if he should turn his head he would see the figure walking behind him with rapid strides and shaking its arms.

Where was he? what was this strange house? A building full of nocturnal mystery, calling to souls in the shade with the voice of angels, and, when they came, abruptly presenting to them this frightful vision—promising to open the radiant gate of Heaven and opening the horrible door of the tomb. It was not a dream? He had to touch the walls to believe it.

He went to Cosette. She was sleeping.

He plainly perceived this truth, the basis of his life henceforth, that so long as she should be alive, so long as he should have her with him, he should need nothing except for her, and fear nothing save on her account. He did not even realise that he was very cold, having taken off his coat to cover her.

Meanwhile, he had heard for some time a singular noise. It sounded like a little bell that some one was shaking. This noise was in the garden. It resembled the dimly heard tinkling of cow-bells in the pastures at night.

He looked, and saw that there was some one in the garden.

Something which resembled a man was walking among the glass cases of the melon patch, rising up, stooping down, stopping, with a regular motion, as if he were drawing or stretching something upon the ground. This being appeared to limp.

Jean Valjean shuddered with the continual tremor of the outcast. He said to himself that perhaps Javert and his spies had not gone away, that they had doubtless left somebody on the watch in the street; that, if this man should discover him in the garden, he would cry thief, and would deliver him up.

While he was revolving these questions, he touched Cosette's hands. They were icy.

He called to her in a low voice:

"Cosette!"

She did not open her eyes.

He shook her smartly.

She did not wake.

"Could she be dead?" said he, and he sprang up, shuddering from head to foot.

He walked straight to the man whom he saw in the garden. He had taken in his hand the roll of money which was in his vest-pocket.

This man had his head down, and did not see him coming.

Jean Valjean approached, exclaiming:

"A hundred francs!"

The man started and raised his eyes.

"A hundred francs for you," continued Jean Valjean, "if you will give me refuge to-night."

The moon shone full in Jean Valjean's bewildered face.

"What, it is you, Father Madeleine!" said the man.

This name made Jean Valjean start back.

He was ready for anything but that. The speaker was an old man, bent and lame, dressed much like a peasant, who had on his left knee a leather knee-cap from which hung a bell. His face was in the shade, and could not be distinguished.

Meanwhile the goodman had taken off his cap, and was exclaiming, tremulously:

"Ah! my God! how did you come here, Father Madeleine? How did you get in, O Lord? Did you fall from the sky? There is no doubt, if you ever do fall, you will fall from there. And what has happened to you? You have no cravat, you have no hat, you have no coat? Do you know that you would have frightened anybody who did not know you? No coat? Merciful heavens! are the saints all crazy now? But how did you get in?"

"Who are you? and what is this house!" asked Jean Valjean.

"Oh! indeed, that is good now," exclaimed the old man. "I am the one you got the place for here, and this house is the one you got me the place in. What! you don't remember me?"

"No," said Jean Valjean. "And how does it happen that you know me?"
"You saved my life," said the man.

He turned, a ray of the moon lighted up his side face, and Jean Valjean recognised old Fauchelevent.

"Ah!" said Jean Valjean, "it is you? yes, I remember you."

"That is very fortunate!" said the old man, in a reproachful tone.

"And what are you doing here?" added Jean Valjean.

"Oh! I am covering my melons."

Old Fauchelevent had in his hand, indeed, at the moment when Jean Valjean accosted him, the end of a piece of awning which he was stretching out over the melon patch. It was this work which made him go through the peculiar motions observed by Jean Valjean.

He continued:

"I said to myself: the moon is bright, there is going to be a frost. Suppose I put their jackets on my melons? And," added he, looking at Jean Valjean, with a loud laugh, "you would have done well to do as much for yourself! But how did you come here?"

Jean Valjean, finding that he was known by this man, at least under his name of Madeleine, went no further with his precautions. He multiplied questions. Oddly enough their parts seemed reversed. It was he, the intruder, who put questions.

"And what is this bell you have on your knee?"

"That!" answered Fauchelevent, "that is so that they may keep away from me."

"How! keep away from you?"

Old Fauchelevent winked in an indescribable manner.

"Ah! Bless me! there's nothing but women in this house; plenty of young girls. It seems that I am dangerous to meet. The bell warns them. When I come they go away."

"What is this house?"

"Why, you know very well."

"No, I don't."

"Why, you got me this place here as gardener."

"Answer me as if I didn't know."

"Well, it is the Convent of the Petit Picpus, then."

Jean Valjean remembered. He repeated as if he were talking to himself: "The Convent of the Petit Picpus!"

"But now, really," resumed Fauchelevent, "how the deuce did you manage to get in, you, Father Madeleine? It is no use for you to be a saint, you are a man; and no men come in here."

"But you are here."

"There is none but me."

"But," resumed Jean Valjean, "I must stay here."

"Oh! my God," exclaimed Fauchelevent.

Jean Valjean approached the old man, and said to him in a grave voice: "Father Fauchelevent, I saved your life."

"I was first to remember it," answered Fauchelevent.

"Well, you can now do for me what I once did for you."

Fauchelevent grasped in his old wrinkled and trembling hands the robust hands of Jean Valjean, and it was some seconds before he could speak; at last he exclaimed:

"Oh! that would be a blessing of God if I could do something for you, in return for that! I save your life! Monsieur Mayor, the old man is at your disposal."

A wonderful joy had, as it were, transfigured the old gardener. A radiance seemed to shine forth from his face.

"What do you want me to do?" he added.

"I will explain. You have a room?"

"I have a solitary shanty, over there, behind the ruins of the old convent, in a corner that nobody ever sees. There are three rooms."

The shanty was in fact so well concealed that Jean Valjean had not seen it.

"Good," said Jean Valjean. "Now I ask of you two things."

"What are they, Monsieur Madeleine?"

"First, that you will not tell anybody what you know about me. Second, that you will not attempt to learn anything more."

"As you please. I know that you can do nothing dishonourable, and that you have always been a man of God. And then, besides, it was you that put me here. It is your place, I am yours."

"Very well. But now come with me. We will go for the child."

"Ah!" said Fauchelevent, "there is a child!"

He said not a word more, but followed Jean Valjean as a dog follows his master.

In half an hour Cosette, again become rosy before a good fire, was asleep in the old gardener's bed. Jean Valjean had put on his cravat and coat; his hat, which he had thrown over the wall, had been found and brought in. While Jean Valjean was putting on his coat, Fauchelevent had taken off his knee-cap with the bell attached, which now, hanging on a nail near a shutter, decorated the wall. The two men were warming themselves, with their elbows on a table, on which Fauchelevent had set a piece of cheese, some brown bread, a bottle of wine, and two glasses, and the old man said to Jean Valjean, putting his hand on his knee:

"Ah! Father Madeleine! you didn't know me at first? You save people's lives and then you forget them? Oh! that's bad; they remember you. You are ungrateful!"

The events, the reverse of which, so to speak, we have just seen, had been brought about under the simplest conditions.

When Jean Valjean, on the night of the very day that Javert arrested him at the death-bed of Fantine, escaped from the municipal prison of M—— sur M——, the police supposed that the escaped convict would start for Paris. Javert was summoned to Paris to aid in the investigation. Javert, in fact, was of great aid in the recapture of Jean Valjean.

He thought no more of Jean Valjean—with these hounds always upon the scent, the wolf of to-day banishes the memory of the wolf of yesterday—when, in December, 1823, he read a newspaper. Just as he finished the article which interested him, a name—the name of Jean Valjean—at the bottom of the page attracted his attention. The newspaper announced that the convict Jean Valjean was dead, and published the fact in terms so explicit, that Javert had no doubt of it. He merely said: *"That settles it."*

Some time afterwards it happened that a police notice was transmitted by the Prefecture of Seine-et-Oise to the Prefecture of Police of Paris in relation to the kidnapping of a child, which had taken place in the commune of Montfermeil. A little girl, seven or eight years old, the notice said, who had been confided by her mother to an innkeeper of the country, had been stolen by an unknown man; this little girl answered to the name of Cosette, and was the child of a young woman named Fantine, who had died at the Hospital, nobody knew when or where. This notice came under the eyes of Javert, and set him to thinking.

The name of Fantine was well known to him. He remembered that Jean Valjean had actually made him—Javert—laugh aloud by asking of him a respite of three days, in order to go for the child of this creature. He recalled the fact that Jean Valjean had been arrested at Paris, at the moment he was getting into the Montfermeil diligence. What was he doing in this region of Montfermeil? Nobody could divine. Javert understood it. The daughter of Fantine was there. Jean Valjean was going after her. Now this child had been stolen by an unknown man! Who could this man be? Could it be Jean Valjean? But Jean Valjean was dead. Javert, without saying a word to any one, took a trip to Montfermeil.

He expected to find great developments there; he found great obscurity. For the first few days, the Thénardiers, in their spite, had blabbed the story about. The disappearance of the Lark had made some noise in the village. However, Thénardier very soon arrived at the conclusion that it is never useful to set in motion the Procureur du Roi; that the first result of his complaints in regard to the *kidnapping* of Cosette would be to fix upon himself the keen eye of justice. And first of all, how should he explain the fifteen hundred francs he had received? He stopped short, and enjoined secrecy upon his wife, and professed to be astonished when anybody spoke to him of the *stolen child*. He knew nothing about it; undoubtedly he had made some complaint at the time that the dear little girl should be "taken away" so suddenly; he would have liked, for affection's sake, to keep her two or three days; but it was her "grandfather" who had come for her, the most natural thing in the world. It was upon this story that Javert fell on reaching Montfermeil. The grandfather put Jean Valjean out of the question.

Javert returned to Paris.

"Jean Valjean is really dead," said he, "and I am a fool."

He had begun to forget all this story, when, in the month of March, 1824, he heard an odd person spoken of who lived in the parish of Saint Médard, and who was called "the beggar who gives alms." This person, it was said, lived alone with a little girl eight years old, who knew nothing of herself except that she came from Montfermeil. Montfermeil! This name constantly recurring, excited Javert's attention anew. An old begging police spy, formerly a beadle, to whom this person had extended his charity, added some other details. "This man was very unsociable, never going out except at night, speaking to nobody, except to the poor sometimes, and allowing nobody to get acquainted with him. He wore a horrible old yellow coat which was worth millions, being lined all over with bank bills." This decidedly piqued Javert's curiosity. That he might get a near view of this fantastic rich man without frightening him away, he borrowed one day of the beadle his old frock.

"The suspicious individual" did indeed come to Javert thus disguised, and gave him alms; at that moment Javert raised his head, and the shock which Jean Valjean received, thinking that he recognised Javert, Javert received, thinking that he recognised Jean Valjean.

He followed the old man to Gorbeau House, and set "the old woman" talking, which was not at all difficult. The old woman confirmed the story of the coat lined with millions, and related to him the episode of the thousand-franc note. She had seen it! she had touched it! Javert hired a room. That very night he installed himself in it. He listened at the door of the mysterious lodger, hoping to hear the sound of his voice, but Jean Valjean perceived his candle through the key-hole and baulked the spy by keeping silence.

The next day Jean Valjean decamped. But Javert was waiting for him behind the trees of the boulevard with two men.

Javert had called for assistance from the Prefecture, but he had not given the name of the person he hoped to seize. That was his secret; and he kept it for three reasons; first, because the least indiscretion might give the alarm to Jean Valjean; next, because the arrest of an old escaped convict who was reputed dead, a criminal whom the records of justice had already classed for ever *among malefactors of the most dangerous kind,* would be a magnificent success which the old members of the Parisian police certainly would never leave to a new-comer like Javert, and he feared they would take his galley-slave away from him; finally, because Javert, being an artist, had a liking for surprises.

Let us say, in addition, that Javert had his own personal scruples; he was really in doubt.

Sadness, trouble, anxiety, weight of cares, this new sorrow of being obliged to fly by night, and to seek a chance asylum in Paris for Cosette and himself, the necessity of adapting his pace to the pace of a child, all this, without his knowing it even, had changed Jean Valjean's gait, and impressed upon his carriage such an appearance of old age that the police itself, incarnated in Javert, could be deceived. The impossibility of approaching too near, his dress of an old preceptor of the emigration, the declaration of Thénardier, who made him a grandfather; finally, the belief in his death at the galleys, added yet more to the uncertainty which was increasing in Javert's mind.

It was not until quite late that, thanks to the bright light which streamed from a bar-room, he decidedly recognised Jean Valjean.

A patrol passing, on its return to the station at the arsenal, he put it in requisition and took it along with him. The links of his chain were solidly welded. He was sure of success; he had now only to close his hand.

When he reached the centre of the web, the fly was no longer there.

Javert did not lose his presence of mind. Sure that the convict who had broken his ban could not be far away, he set watches, arranged traps and ambushes, and beat the quarter the night through. The first thing that he saw was the displacement of the lamp, the rope of which was cut. Precious indication, which led him astray, however, by directing all his researches towards the Cul-de-sac Genrot. There are in that cul-de-sac some rather low walls which face upon gardens the limits of which extend to some very large uncultivated grounds. Javert explored these gardens and these grounds, as if he were searching for a needle.

At daybreak, he left two intelligent men on the watch, and returned to the Prefecture of Police, crestfallen as a spy who has been caught by a thief.

XIII. THE REFUGE

NOTHING resembled more closely the commonest *porte-cochère* of the time than the *porte-cochère* of No. 62 Petite Rue Picpus. This door was usually half open in the most attractive manner, disclosing a court surrounded with walls bedecked with vines. Above the rear wall large trees could be seen. When a beam of sunshine enlivened the court, it was difficult to pass by No. 62 Petite Rue Picpus, without carrying away a pleasant idea. It was, however, a gloomy place of which you had had a glimpse.

The door smiled; the house prayed and wept.

If you succeeded in passing the porter, you entered on the right a little vestibule which led to a stairway shut in between two walls, and so narrow that but one person could pass at a time. If you did not allow yourself to be frightened by the yellow wall paper with the chocolate surbase that extended along the stairs, you reached the second story in a hall where the yellow hue and the chocolate plinth followed you with a peaceful persistency. You came to a door, all the more mysterious that it was not quite closed. You pushed it open, and found yourself in a little room about six feet square, the floor tiled, scoured, neat and cold, and the walls hung with fifteen-cent paper, nankeen-coloured paper with green flowers. A dull white light came from a large window with small panes which was at the left, and which took up the whole width of the room. You looked, you saw no one; you listened, you heard no step and no human sound. The wall was bare; the room had no furniture, not even a chair.

You looked again, and you saw in the wall opposite the door a quadrangular opening about a foot square, covered with a grate of iron bars crossing one another, black, knotted, solid, which formed squares, I had almost said meshes, less than an inch across. In case any living being had been so marvellously slender as to attempt to get in or out by the square hole, this grate would have prevented it. It did not let the body pass, but it did let the eyes pass, that is to say, the mind. This seemed to have been cared for, for it had been doubled by a sheet of tin inserted in the wall a little behind it, and pierced with a thousand holes more microscopic than those of a skimmer. At the bottom of this plate there was an opening cut exactly like the mouth of a letter-box. A piece of broad tape attached to a bell hung at the right of the grated opening.

If you pulled this tape, a bell tinkled and a voice was heard, very near you, which startled you.

"Who is there?" asked the voice.

It was a woman's voice, a gentle voice, so gentle that it was mournful.

Here again there was a magic word which you must know. If you did not know it, the voice was heard no more, and the wall again became silent as if the wild obscurity of the sepulchre had been on the other side.

If you knew the word, the voice added:

"Enter at the right."

You then noticed at your right, opposite the window, a glazed door surmounted by a glazed sash and painted grey. You lifted the latch, you passed through the door, and you were in a sort of theatre box, hardly made visible by the dim light of the glass door, narrow, furnished with two old chairs and a piece of tattered straw matting—a genuine box with its front to lean upon, upon which was a tablet of black wood. This box was grated, but it was not a grate of gilded wood as at the Opera; it was a monstrous trellis of iron bars frightfully tangled together, and bolted to the wall by enormous bolts which resembled clenched fists.

After a few minutes, when your eyes began to get accustomed to this cavernous light, you tried to look through the grate, but could not see more than six inches beyond. There you saw a barrier of black shutters, secured and strengthened by wooden cross-bars painted gingerbread colour. These shutters were jointed, divided into long slender strips, and covered the whole length of the grate. They were always closed.

In a few moments, you heard a voice calling to you from behind these shutters and saying:

"I am here. What do you want of me?"

It was a loved voice, perhaps sometimes an adored one. You saw nobody. You hardly heard a breath. It seemed as if it were a ghostly voice speaking to you across the portal of the tomb.

If you appeared under certain necessary conditions, very rare, the narrow strip of one of these shutters opened in front of you, and the ghostly voice became an apparition. Behind the grate, behind the shutter, you perceived, as well as the grate permitted, a head, of which you saw only the mouth and chin; the rest was covered with a black veil. You caught a glimpse of a black guimpe and an ill-defined form covered with a black shroud. This head spoke to you, but did not look at you and never smiled at you.

What you saw was the interior of a cloister.

It was the interior of that stern and gloomy house that was called the convent of the Bernardines of the Perpetual Adoration. This box where you were was the parlour. This voice, the first that spoke to you, was the voice of the portress, who was always seated, motionless and silent, on the other side of the wall, near the square aperture, defended by the iron grate and the plate with the thousand holes, as by a double visor.

Next to the rules of the Carmelites, who go bare-footed and never sit down, the most severe rules are those of the Bernardine-Benedictines of Martin Verga. They are clothed with a black guimpe, which, according to the express command of Saint Benedict, comes up to the chin. A serge dress with wide sleeves, a large woollen veil, and the fillet which comes down to the eyes, constitute their dress. It is all black, except the fillet, which is white. The novices wear the same dress, all in white. The professed nuns have in addition a rosary by their side.

The Bernardine-Benedictines of this Obedience abstain from meat all the year round, fast during Lent and many other days peculiar to them, rise out of their first sleep at one o'clock in the morning to read their breviary and chant matins until three, sleep in coarse woollen sheets at all seasons and upon straw, use no baths, never light any fire, scourge themselves every Friday, observe the rule of silence, speak to one another only at recreations, which are very short, and wear haircloth chemises for six months, from the fourteenth of September, the Exaltation of the Holy Cross, until Easter. These six months are a moderation—the rules say all the year; but this haircloth chemise, insupportable in the heat of summer, produced fevers and nervous spasms. It became necessary to limit its use. Even with this mitigation, after the fourteenth of September, when the nuns put on this chemise, they have three or four days of fever. Obedience, poverty, chastity, continuance in cloister; such are their vows, rendered much more difficult of fulfilment by the rules.

Each one of them in turn performed what they call *the reparation*. The reparation is prayer for all sins, for all faults, for all disorders, for all violations, for all iniquities, for all the crimes which are committed upon the earth. During twelve consecutive hours, from four o'clock in the afternoon till four o'clock in the morning, or from four o'clock in the morning till four o'clock in the afternoon, the sister who performs *the reparation* remains on her knees upon the stone before the holy sacrament, her hands clasped and a rope around her neck. When fatigue becomes insupportable, she prostrates herself, her face against the marble and her arms crossed; this is all her relief.

Moreover, there is always a nun on her knees before the holy sacrament. They remain for an hour. They are relieved like soldiers standing sentry. That is the Perpetual Adoration.

They never say *my* or *mine*. They have nothing of their own, and must cherish nothing. They say *our* of everything; thus: our veil, our chaplet; if they speak of their chemise, they say *our chemise*.

None are allowed to shut themselves up, and to have a *home*, a *room*. They live in open cells. When they meet one another, one says: *Praise and adoration to the most holy sacrament of the altar!* The other responds: *Forever.* The same ceremony when one knocks at another's door. Forever. Like all rituals, this becomes mechanical from habit; and one sometimes says *forever* before the other has had time to say, what is indeed rather lengthy, *Praise and adoration to the most holy sacrament of the altar!*

At the period to which this history relates, a boarding-school was attached to the convent. The pupils, austerities excepted, conformed to all the ritual. There are young women who, returned to the world, and after several years of marriage, have not yet succeeded in breaking off the habit of saying hastily, whenever there is a knock at the door: *Forever!* Like the nuns, the boarders saw their relatives only in the locutory. Even their mothers were not permitted to embrace them.

On Thursday these nuns heard high mass, vespers, and all the offices the same as on Sunday. As to the number and duration of their prayers, we cannot give a better idea than by quoting the frank words of one of themselves: *The prayers of the postulants are frightful, the prayers of the novices worse, and the prayers of the professed nuns still worse.*

The day on which a novice makes her profession she is dressed in her finest attire, with her head decked with white roses, and her hair glossy and curled; then she prostrates herself; a great black veil is spread over her, and the office for the dead is chanted. The nuns then divide into two files, one file passes near her, saying in plaintive accents: *Our sister is dead,* and the other file responds in ringing tones: *living in Jesus Christ!*

Those of the Petit Picpus had had a vault made under their high altar for the burial of their community. The *government,* as they call it, does not permit corpses to be deposited in this vault. They therefore were taken from the convent when they died. This was an affliction to them, and horrified them as if it were a violation.

Into this house it was that Jean Valjean had, as Fauchelevent said, "fallen from heaven."

He had crossed the garden wall at the corner of the Rue Polonceau. That angels' hymn which he had heard in the middle of the night, was the nuns chanting matins; that hall of which he had caught a glimpse in the obscurity, was the chapel; that phantom which he had seen extended on the floor was the sister performing the reparation; that bell the sound of which had so strangely surprised him was the gardener's bell fastened to old Fauchelevent's knee.

When Cosette had been put to bed, Jean Valjean and Fauchelevent had, as we have seen, taken a glass of wine and a piece of cheese before a blazing fire; then, the only bed in the shanty being occupied by Cosette, they had thrown themselves each upon a bundle of straw. Neither of them had slept.

Jean Valjean, feeling that he was discovered and Javert was upon his track, knew full well that he and Cosette were lost should they return into the city. Since the new blast which had burst upon him, had thrown him into this cloister, Jean Valjean had but one thought, to remain there. To live in an impossible place; that would be safety.

For his part, Fauchelevent was racking his brains. How did Monsieur Madeleine come there, with such walls! The walls of a cloister are not so easily crossed. How did he happen to be with a child? A man does not scale a steep wall with a child in his arms. Who was this child? Where did they both come from? Father Madeleine wore that air which discourages questions; and moreover Fauchelevent said to himself: "One does not question a saint." To him Monsieur Madeleine had preserved all his prestige. From some words that escaped from Jean Valjean, however, the gardener thought he might conclude that Monsieur Madeleine had probably failed on account of the hard times, and that he was pursued by his creditors; or it might be that he was compromised in some political affair and was concealing himself; which did not at all displease Fauchelevent, who had an old Bonapartist heart. But the mystery to which Fauchelevent constantly returned and over which he was racking his brains was, that Monsieur Madeleine should be there, and that this little girl should be with him. Fauchelevent saw nothing clearly except this: Monsieur Madeleine has saved my life. He said aside to himself: It is my turn now.

At daybreak, old Fauchelevent opened his eyes, and saw Monsieur Madeleine, who, seated upon his bunch of straw, was looking at Cosette as she slept. Fauchelevent half arose, and said:—

"Now that you are here, how are you going to manage to come in?"

This question summed up the situation.

"To begin with," said Fauchelevent, "you will not set foot outside of this room, neither the little girl nor you. One step in the garden, we are ruined."

"That is true."

"Monsieur Madeleine," resumed Fauchelevent, "you have arrived at a very good time; I mean to say very bad; there is one of these ladies dangerously sick. On that account they do not look this way much. She must be dying. They are saying the forty-hour prayers. For to-day we shall be quiet here; I do not answer for to-morrow."

"However," observed Jean Valjean, "this shanty is under the corner of the wall; it is hidden by a sort of ruin; there are trees; they cannot see it from the convent."

"And I add, that the nuns never come near it."

"Well?" said Jean Valjean.

The interrogation point which followed that well, meant: it seems to me that we can remain here concealed. This interrogation point Fauchelevent answered:—

"There are the little girls."

"What little girls?" asked Jean Valjean.

As Fauchelevent opened his mouth to explain the words he had just uttered, a single stroke of a bell was heard.

"The nun is dead," said he. "There is the knell."

And he motioned to Jean Valjean to listen.

The bell sounded a second time.

"It is the knell, Monsieur Madeleine. The bell will strike every minute, for twenty-four hours, until the body goes out of the church. You see they play. In their recreations, if a ball roll here, that is enough for them to come after it, in spite of the rules, and rummage all about here. Those cherubs are little devils."

"Who?" asked Jean Valjean.

"The little girls. You would be found out very soon. They would cry, 'What! a man!' But there is no danger to-day. There will be no recreation. The day will be all prayers. You hear the bell. As I told you, a stroke every minute. It is the knell."

"I understand, Father Fauchelevent. There are boarding scholars."

And Jean Valjean thought within himself:—

"Here, then, Cosette can be educated, too."

Fauchelevent exclaimed:—

"Zounds! they are the little girls for you! And how they would scream at sight of you! and how they would run! Here, to be a man, is to have the plague. You see how they fasten a bell to my leg, as they would to a wild beast."

Jean Valjean was studying more and more deeply. "The convent would save us," murmured he. Then he raised his voice:

"Yes, the difficulty is in remaining."

"No," said Fauchelevent, "it is to get out."

Jean Valjean felt his blood run cold.

"To get out?"

"Yes, Monsieur Madeleine, in order to come in, it is necessary that you should get out."

And, after waiting for a sound from the tolling bell to die away, Fauchelevent pursued:—

"It would not do to have you found here like this. Whence do you come? for me you have fallen from heaven, because I know you; but for the nuns, you must come in at the door."

Suddenly they heard a complicated ringing upon another bell.

"Oh!" said Fauchelevent. "They are going to the chapter. They always hold a chapter when anybody dies. She died at daybreak. It is usually at daybreak that people die. But cannot you go out the way you came in? Let us see; this is not to question you, but where did you come in?"

Make your way out of a forest full of tigers, and when out, fancy yourself advised by a friend to return. Jean Valjean imagined all the police still swarming in the quarter, officers on the watch, sentries everywhere, frightful fists stretched out towards his collar,—Javert, perhaps, at the corner of the square.

"Impossible," said he. "Father Fauchelevent, let it go that I fell from on high."

"Ah! I believe it, I believe it," replied Fauchelevent. "You have no need to tell me so. God must have taken you into his hand, to have a close look at you, and then put you down. Only he meant to put you into a monastery; he made a mistake. Hark! another ring; that is to warn the porter to go and notify the municipality. Your little one is asleep yet. What is her name?"

"Cosette."

"She is your girl? that is to say: you should be her grandfather?"

"Yes."

"For her, to get out will be easy. I have my door, which opens into the court. I knock; the porter opens. I have my basket on my back; the little girl is inside; I go out. Father Fauchelevent goes out with his basket—that is all simple. You will tell the little girl to keep very still. She will be under cover. I will leave her as soon as I can, with a good old friend of mine, a fruiteress, in the Rue du Chemin Vert, who is deaf, and who has a little bed. I will scream into the fruiteress's ear that she is my niece, and she must keep her for me till to-morrow. Then the little girl will come back with you; for I shall bring you back. It must be done. But how are you going to manage to get out?"

Jean Valjean shook his head.

"Let nobody see me, that is all, Father Fauchelevent. Find some means to get me out, like Cosette, in a basket, and under cover."

Fauchelevent scratched the tip of his ear with the middle finger of his left hand—a sign of serious embarrassment.

A third ring made a diversion.

"That is the death-physician going away," said Fauchelevent. "He has looked, and said she is dead; it is right. When the inspector has viséd the passport for paradise, the undertaker sends a coffin. I nail it up. That's a part of my gardening. A gardener is something of a gravedigger. They put her in a low room in the church which communicates with the street, and where no man can enter except the death-physician. I do not count the bearers and myself for men. In that room I nail the coffin. The bearers come and take her, and whip-up, driver: that is the way they go to heaven. They bring in a box with nothing in it, they carry it away with something inside. But what events since yesterday? Mother Crucifixion is dead, and Father Madeleine—"

"Is buried," said Jean Valjean, sadly smiling.

A fourth time the bell rang out. Fauchelevent quickly took down the knee-piece and bell from the nail, and buckled it on his knee.

"This time, it is for me. Monsieur Madeleine, do not stir, but wait for me. There is something new. If you are hungry, there is the wine, and bread and cheese."

And he went out of the hut, saying: "I am coming, I am coming."

Jean Valjean saw him hasten across the garden, as fast as his crooked leg would let him, with side glances at his melons the while.

In less than ten minutes, Father Fauchelevent, whose bell put the nuns to

flight as he went along, rapped softly at a door, and a gentle voice answered
—*Forever, Forever!* that is to say, *Come in.*

This door was that of the parlour allotted to the gardener, for use when
it was necessary to communicate with him. The prioress, seated in the only
chair in the parlour, was waiting for Fauchelevent.

A serious and troubled bearing is peculiar, on critical occasions, to priests
and monastics. At the moment when Fauchelevent entered, this double sign
of preoccupation marked the countenance of the prioress, the charming and
learned Mademoiselle de Blemeur, Mother Innocent, who was ordinarily
cheerful.

The gardener made a timid bow, and stopped at the threshold of the cell.
The prioress, who was saying her rosary, raised her eyes and said:

"Ah! it is you, Father Fauvent."

This abbreviation had been adopted in the convent.

"I am here, reverend mother."

"I wish to speak to you."

"And I, for my part," said Fauchelevent, with a boldness at which he was
alarmed himself, "I have something to say to the most reverend mother."

The prioress looked at him.

"Ah, you have a communication to make to me."

"A petition!"

"Well, what is it?"

Goodman Fauchelevent, ex-notary, belonged to that class of peasants who
are never disconcerted. A certain combination of ignorance and skill is very
effective; you do not suspect it, and you accede to it. The whole convent
thought him stupid—a great merit in religion. Moreover, he was regular in
his habits, and never went out except when it was clearly necessary on
account of the orchard and the garden. This discretion in his conduct was
counted to his credit. He had, nevertheless, learned the secrets of two men;
the porter of the convent, who knew the peculiarities of the parlour, and the
grave-digger of the cemetery, who knew the singularities of burial: in this
manner, he had a double-light in regard to these nuns—one upon their life,
the other upon their death.

The goodman, with the assurance of one who feels that he is appreciated,
began before the reverend prioress a rustic harangue, quite diffuse and very
profound. He spoke at length of his age, his infirmities, of the weight of
years henceforth doubly heavy upon him, of the growing demands of his
work, of the size of the garden, of the nights to be spent, like last night for
example, when he had to put awnings over the melons on account of the
moon; and finally ended with this: that he had a brother—(the prioress
gave a start)—a brother not young—(second start of the prioress, but a
reassured start)—that if it was desired, this brother could come and live with
him and help him; that he was an excellent gardener; that the community
would get good services from him, better than his own; that, otherwise, if
his brother were not admitted, as he, the oldest, felt that he was broken

down, and unequal to the labour, he would be obliged to leave, though with much regret; and that his brother had a little girl that he would bring with him, who would be reared under God in the house, and who, perhaps,— who knows?—would some day become a nun.

When he had finished, the prioress stopped the sliding of her rosary through her fingers, and said:

"Can you, between now and night, procure a strong iron bar?"

"For what work?"

"A stone is to be raised."

"Heavy?"

"The slab of the pavement at the side of the altar."

"The stone that covers the vault?"

"Yes."

"That is a piece of work where it would be well to have two men."

"Mother Ascension, who is as strong as a man, will help you."

"A woman is not a man. My brother is very strong."

"And the four mother choristers will assist you."

"And when the vault is opened?"

"It must be shut again."

"Is that all?"

"No."

"Give me your orders, most reverend mother."

"Fauvent, we have confidence in you."

"I am here to do everything."

"And to keep silent about everything."

"Yes, reverend mother."

The prioress, after a quivering of the underlip which resembled hesitation, spoke:

"You know that a mother died this morning."

The prioress was silent, moved her lips a moment as in a mental orison, and resumed:

"The mothers have carried her into the room of the dead, which opens into the church."

"I know."

"No other man than you can or must enter that room. Be watchful."

The prioress again made a little low murmur, probably sacred, then raised her voice.

"During her life, Mother Crucifixion worked conversions; after her death, she will work miracles."

"She will!" answered Fauchelevent.

"Father Fauvent, the community has been blessed in Mother Crucifixion. She had her consciousness to the last. She spoke to us, then she spoke to the angels. She gave us her last commands. If you had a little more faith, and if you could have been in her cell, she would have cured your leg by touching it. She smiled. We felt that she was returning to life in God. There was something of Paradise in that death."

Fauchelevent thought that he had been listening to a prayer.

"Amen!" said he.

"Father Fauvent, we must do what the dead wish."

The prioress counted a few beads on her chaplet. Fauchelevent was silent.

"Furthermore, she is more than a departed one; she is a saint."

"Like you, reverend mother."

"She slept in her coffin for twenty years, by the express permission of our Holy Father, Pius VII."

"He who crowned the Emp——Buonaparte."

For a shrewd man like Fauchelevent, the reminiscence was untoward. Luckily the prioress, absorbed in her thoughts, did not hear.

The prioress went on:

"Father Fauvent, Mother Crucifixion will be buried in the coffin in which she has slept for twenty years."

"I shall have to nail her up then in that coffin."

"Yes."

"And we will put aside the undertaker's coffin?"

"Precisely."

"I am at the disposal of the most reverend community."

"The four mother choristers will help you."

"To nail up the coffin I don't need them."

"No. To let it down."

"Where?"

"Into the vault."

"What vault?"

"Under the altar."

Fauchelevent gave a start.

"The vault under the altar!"

"Under the altar."

"But—"

"You will have an iron bar."

"Yes, but—"

"You will lift the stone with the bar by means of the ring."

"But—"

"We must obey the dead. To be buried in the vault under the altar of the chapel, not to go into profane ground, to remain in death where she prayed in life; this was the last request of Mother Crucifixion. She has asked it, that is to say, commanded it."

"But it is forbidden."

"Forbidden by men, enjoined by God."

"If it should come to be known?"

"We have confidence in you."

"Oh! as for me, I am like a stone in your wall. But, reverend mother, if the agent of the Health Commission—"

"St. Benedict II., in the matter of burial, resisted Constantine Pogonatus."

"However, the Commissary of Police—"

"Chonodemaire, one of the seven German kings who entered Gaul in the reign of Constantius, expressly recognised the right of conventuals to be inhumed in religion, that is to say, under the altar."

"But the Inspector of the Prefecture—"

"The world is nothing before the cross. Martin, eleventh general of the Carthusians, gave to his order this device: *Stat crux dum volvitur orbis.*"

"Amen," said Fauchelevent, imperturbable in this method of extricating himself whenever he heard any Latin.

The prioress drew breath, then turning towards Fauchelevent:

"Father Fauvent, is it settled?"

"It is settled, reverend mother."

"Can we count upon you?"

"I shall obey."

"It is well."

"I am entirely devoted to the convent."

"It is understood, you will close the coffin. The sisters will carry it into the chapel. The office for the dead will be said. Then they will return to the cloister. Between eleven o'clock and midnight, you will come with your iron bar. All will be done with the greatest secrecy."

"Reverend mother, I shall need a lever at least six feet long."

"Where will you get it?"

"Where there are gratings there are always iron bars. I have my heap of old iron at the back of the garden."

"About three-quarters of an hour before midnight; do not forget."

"Reverend mother?"

"What?"

"If you should ever have any other work like this, my brother is very strong. A Turk."

"You will do it as quickly as possible."

"I will do everything to prove my zeal for the community. This is the arrangement. I shall nail up the coffin. At eleven o'clock precisely I will be in the chapel. The mother choristers will be there. Mother Ascension will be there. Two men would be better. But no matter! I shall have my lever. We shall open the vault, let down the coffin, and close the vault again. After which, there will be no trace of anything. The government will suspect nothing. Reverend mother, is this all so?"

"No."

"What more is there, then?"

"There is still the empty coffin."

This brought them to a stand. Fauchelevent pondered. The prioress pondered.

"Father Fauvent, what shall be done with the coffin?"

"It will be put in the ground."

"Empty?"

Another silence. Fauchelevent made with his left hand that peculiar gesture, which dismisses an unpleasant question.

"Reverend mother, I nail up the coffin in the lower room in the church, and nobody can come in there except me, and I will cover the coffin with the pall."

"Yes, but the bearers, in putting it into the hearse and in letting it down into the grave, will surely perceive that there is nothing inside."

"Ah! the de——!" exclaimed Fauchelevent.

The prioress began to cross herself, and looked fixedly at the gardener. *Vil* stuck in his throat.

"Reverend mother, I will put some earth into the coffin. That will have the effect of a body."

"You are right. Earth is the same thing as man. So you will prepare the empty coffin?"

"I will attend to that."

The face of the prioress, till then dark and anxious, became again serene. She made him the sign of a superior dismissing an inferior.

"Father Fauvent, I am satisfied with you; to-morrow after the burial, bring your brother to me, and tell him to bring his daughter."

At the sound of Fauchelevent opening the door, Jean Valjean turned.

"Well?"

"All is arranged, and nothing is," said Fauchelevent. "I have permission to bring you in; but before bringing you in, it is necessary to get you out. That is where the cart is blocked! For the little girl, it is easy enough."

"You will carry her out?"

"And she will keep quiet?"

"I will answer for it."

"But you, Father Madeleine?"

And, after an anxious silence, Fauchelevent exclaimed:

"But why not go out the way you came in?"

Jean Valjean, as before, merely answered: "Impossible."

Fauchelevent, talking more to himself than to Jean Valjean, grumbled:

"There is another thing that torments me. I said I would put in some earth. But I think that earth inside, instead of a body, will not be like it; that will not do, it will shake about; it will move. The men will feel it. You understand, Father Madeleine, the government will find it out."

Jean Valjean stared at him, and thought that he was raving.

Fauchelevent resumed:

"How the d——ickens are you going to get out? For all this must be done to-morrow. To-morrow I am to bring you in. The prioress expects you."

Then he explained to Jean Valjean that this was a reward for a service that he, Fauchelevent, was rendering to the community. That the nun who died that morning had requested to be buried in the coffin which she had used as a bed, and interred in the vault under the altar of the chapel. That he, Fauchelevent, would nail up the coffin in the cell, raise the stone in the chapel, and let down the body into the vault. And that, in return for this, the prioress would admit his brother into the house as gardener and his niece as boarder. That his brother was M. Madeleine, and that his niece was Cosette. That the prioress had told him to bring his brother the next evening, after the fictitious burial at the cemetery. But that he could not bring M. Madeleine from the outside, if M. Madeleine were not outside. That that was the first difficulty. And then that he had another difficulty; the empty coffin.

"What is the empty coffin?" asked Jean Valjean.

Fauchelevent responded:

"The coffin from the administration."

"What coffin? and what administration?"

"A nun dies. The municipality physician comes and says: there is a nun dead. The government sends a coffin. The next day it sends a hearse and some bearers to take the coffin and carry it to the cemetery. The bearers will come and take up the coffin; there will be nothing in it."

"Put somebody in it."

"A dead body? I have none."

"No."

"What then?"

"A living body."

"What living body?"

"Me," said Jean Valjean.

"You!"

"Why not?"

Jean Valjean had one of those rare smiles which came over him like the aurora in a winter sky.

"You know, Fauchelevent, that you said: Mother Crucifixion is dead, and that I added: and Father Madeleine is buried. It will be so."

"Ah! good, you are laughing, you are not talking seriously."

"Very seriously. I must get out!"

"Undoubtedly."

"And I told you to find a basket and a cover for me also."

"Well!"

"The basket will be of pine, and the cover will be of black cloth."

"In the first place, a white cloth. The nuns are buried in white."

"Well, a white cloth."

Jean Valjean continued:

"The question is, how to get out without being seen. This is the means. But in the first place tell me, how is it done? where is this coffin?"

"The empty one?"

"Yes."

"Down in what is called the dead-room. It is on two trestles and under the pall."

"What is the length of the coffin?"

"Six feet."

"What is the dead-room?"

"It is a room on the ground floor, with a grated window towards the garden, closed on the outside with a shutter, and two doors; one leading to the convent, the other to the church."

"What church?"

"The church on the street, the church for everybody?"

"Have you the keys of those two doors?"

"No. I have the key of the door that opens into the convent; the porter has the key of the door that opens into the church."

"When does the porter open that door?"

"Only to let in the bearers, who come after the coffin; as soon as the coffin goes out, the door is closed again."

"Who nails up the coffin?"

"I do."

"Who puts the cloth on it?"

"I do."

"Are you alone?"

"No other man, except the police physician, can enter the dead-room. That is even written upon the wall."

"Could you, to-night, when all are asleep in the convent, hide me in that room?"

"No. But I can hide you in a little dark closet which opens into the dead-room, where I keep my burial tools, and of which I have the care and the key."

"At what hour will the hearse come after the coffin to-morrow?"

"About three o'clock in the afternoon. The burial takes place at the Vaugirard cemetery, a little before night. It is not very near."

"I shall remain hidden in your tool-closet all night and all the morning. And about eating? I shall be hungry."

"I will bring you something."

"You can come and nail me up in the coffin at two o'clock."

Fauchelevent started back, and began to snap his fingers.

"But it is impossible!"

"Pshaw! to take a hammer and drive some nails into a board?"

What seemed unheard-of to Fauchelevent was simple to Jean Valjean. Jean Valjean had been in worse straits. He who has been a prisoner knows the art of making himself small according to the dimensions of the place for escape. To live a long time in a box, to find air where there is none, to know how to be stifled without dying—that was one of the gloomy talents of Jean Valjean.

Fauchelevent, recovering a little, exclaimed:

"But how will you manage to breathe?"

"I shall breathe."

"In that box? Only to think of it suffocates me."

"You surely have a gimlet, you can make a few little holes about the mouth here and there, and you can nail it without drawing the upper board tight."

"Good! But if you happen to cough or sneeze?"

"He who is escaping never coughs and never sneezes."

And Jean Valjean added:

"Father Fanchelevent, I must either be taken here, or be willing to go out in the hearse. The only thing that I am anxious about, is what will be done at the cemetery."

"That is just what does not embarrass me," exclaimed Fauchelevent. "If you are sure of getting yourself out of the coffin, I am sure of getting you out of the grave. The gravedigger is a drunkard and a friend of mine. I will tell you what will take place. We shall arrive a little before dusk, three-quarters of an hour before the cemetery gates are closed. The hearse will go to the grave. I shall follow. I will have a hammer, a chisel, and some pincers in my pocket. The hearse stops, the bearers tie a rope around your coffin and let you down. The priest says the prayers, makes the sign of the cross, sprinkles the holy water, and is off. I remain alone with Father Mestienne. He is my friend, I tell you. One of two things; either he will be drunk, or he will not be drunk. If he is not drunk, I say to him: come and take a drink before the Good Quince is shut. I get him away. I lay him under the table, I take his card from him to return to the cemetery with, and I come back without him. You will have only me to deal with. If he is drunk, I say to him: be off. I'll do your work. He goes away, and I pull you out of the hole."

Jean Valjean extended his hand.

"It is settled, Father Fauchelevent. All will go well."

"Provided nothing goes amiss," thought Fauchelevent. "How terrible that would be!"

Next day, as the sun was declining, the scattered passers on the Boulevard du Maine took off their hats at the passage of an old-fashioned hearse, adorned with death's-heads, cross-bones, and teardrops. In this hearse there was a coffin covered with a white cloth, upon which was displayed a large black cross.

Fauchelevent limped behind the hearse, very well satisfied. His twin plots, one with the nuns, the other with M. Madeleine, had succeeded equally well. Jean Valjean's calmness had that powerful tranquillity which is contagious. Fauchelevent had now no doubt of success. What remained to be done was nothing.

Suddenly the hearse stopped; they were at the gate. It was necessary to exhibit the burial permit. The undertaker whispered with the porter of the cemetery. During this colloquy, an unknown man came and placed himself behind the hearse at Fauchelevent's side. He was a working-man, who wore a vest with large pockets, and had a pick under his arm.

Fauchelevent looked at this unknown man.

"Who are you?" he asked.

The man answered:

"The gravedigger."

"The gravedigger?"

"Yes."

"You!"

"Me."

"The gravedigger is Father Mestienne."

"He was."

"How! he was?"

"He is dead."

Fauchelevent was ready for anything but this, that a gravedigger could die. It is, however, true; gravediggers themselves die. By dint of digging graves for others, they open their own.

Fauchelevent remained speechless. He had hardly the strength to stammer out:

"But it's not possible!"

"It is so."

The gravedigger walked before him. He was one of those men who, though young, have an old appearance, and who, though thin, are very strong.

"Comrade!" cried Fauchelevent.

The man turned.

"I am the gravedigger of the convent."

"My colleague," said the man.

Fauchelevent, illiterate, but very keen, understood that he had to do with a very formidable species, a good talker.

He mumbled out:

"Is it so, Father Mestienne is dead?"

The man answered:

"Perfectly. The good God consulted his list of bills payable. It was Father Mestienne's turn. Father Mestienne is dead."

Fauchelevent repeated mechanically: "So he is dead, old Mestienne! I am sorry for it; he was a jolly fellow. But you too, you are a jolly fellow. Isn't that so, comrade? we will go and take a drink together, right away."

The man answered: "I have studied, I have graduated. I never drink."

The hearse had started, and was rolling along the main avenue of the cemetery.

"Are we not going to make each other's acquaintance?" stammered Fauchelevent.

"It is made. You are a peasant, I am a Parisian."

"We are not acquainted as long as we have not drunk together. He who empties his glass empties his heart. Come and drink with me. You can't refuse."

"Business first."

Fauchelevent said to himself: I am lost.

They were now only a few rods from the path that led to the nuns' corner.

The gravedigger continued:

"Peasant, I have seven youngsters that I must feed. As they must eat, I must not drink."

The hearse turned a huge cypress, left the main path, took a little one, entered upon the grounds, and was lost in a thicket. This indicated the immediate proximity of the grave. Fauchelevent slackened his pace, but could not slacken that of the hearse. Luckily the mellow soil, wet by the winter rains, stuck to the wheels, and made the track heavy.

He approached the gravedigger.

"They have such a good little Argenteuil wine," suggested Fauchelevent.

Here an observation is necessary. Fauchelevent, whatever was his anguish, proposed to drink, but did not explain himself on one point; who should pay? Ordinarily Fauchelevent proposed, and Father Mestienne paid. As for him, Fauchelevent, however excited he was, he did not care about paying.

The hearse advanced; Fauchelevent, full of anxiety, looked about him on all sides. Great drops of sweat were falling from his forehead.

The hearse stopped.

The choir-boy got out of the mourning carriage, then the priest.

One of the forward wheels of the hearse mounted on a little heap of earth, beyond which was seen an open grave.

Who was in the coffin? Jean Valjean.

Jean Valjean had arranged it so that he could live in it, and could breathe a very little.

Soon after Fauchelevent had finished nailing down the upper board, Jean Valjean had felt himself carried out, then wheeled along. By the diminished jolting, he had felt that he was passing from the pavement to the hard ground; that is to say, that he was leaving the streets and entering upon the boulevards. By a dull sound, he had divined that they were crossing the bridge of Austerlitz. At the first stop he had comprehended that they were entering the cemetery; at the second stop he had said: here is the grave.

He felt that hands hastily seized the coffin, then a harsh scraping upon the boards; he concluded that that was a rope which they were tying around the coffin to let it down into the excavation.

Then he felt a kind of dizziness.

Probably the bearer and the gravedigger had tipped the coffin and let the head down before the feet. He returned fully to himself on feeling that he was horizontal and motionless. He had touched the bottom.

He felt a certain chill.

A voice arose above him, icy and solemn. He heard some Latin words which he did not understand:

"*Qui dormiunt in terræ pulvere, evigilabunt; alii in vitam æternam, et alii in opprobrium, ut videant semper.*"

A child's voice said:

"*De profundis.*"

He heard upon the board which covered him something like the gentle patter of a few drops of rain. It was probably the holy water.

He thought: "This will soon be finished. The priest is going away.

Fauchelevent will take Mestienne away to drink. They will leave me. Then Fauchelevent will come back alone, and I shall get out. That will take a good hour."

The deep voice resumed.

"*Requiescat in pace.*"

And the child's voice said:

"*Amen.*"

Jean Valjean, intently listening, perceived something like receding steps. "Now there they go," thought he. "I am alone."

All at once he heard a sound above his head which seemed to him like a clap of thunder.

It was a spadeful of earth falling upon the coffin.

A second spadeful of earth fell.

One of the holes by which he breathed was stopped up.

A third spadeful of earth fell.

Then a fourth.

There are things stronger than the strongest man. Jean Valjean lost consciousness.

When the hearse had departed and the priest and the choir-boy had got into the carriage, and were gone, Fauchelevent, who had never taken his eyes off the gravedigger, saw him stoop, and grasp his spade, upright in the heap of earth.

Hereupon, Fauchelevent formed a supreme resolve.

Placing himself between the grave and the gravedigger, and folding his arms, he said:

"I'll pay for it!"

The gravedigger eyed him with amazement, and replied:

"What, peasant?"

Fauchelevent repeated:

"I'll pay for it!"

"For what?"

"For the wine."

"What wine?"

"At the Good Quince."

"Go to the devil!" said the gravedigger.

And he threw a spadeful of earth upon the coffin.

The coffin gave back a hollow sound. Fauchelevent felt himself stagger, and nearly fell into the grave. In a voice in which the strangling sound of the death-rattle began to be heard he cried:

"Come, comrade, before the Good Quince closes!"

The gravedigger took up another spadeful of earth. Fauchelevent continued:

"I'll pay," and he seized the gravedigger by the arm.

"Hark ye, comrade," he said, "I am the gravedigger of the convent, and have come to help you. It's a job we can do at night. Let us take a drink first."

And as he spoke, even while clinging desperately to this urgent effort, he asked himself, with some misgiving: "And even should he drink—will he get tipsy?"

"Good rustic," said the gravedigger, "if you insist, I consent. We'll have a drink, but after my work, never before it."

And he tossed his spade again. Fauchelevent held him.

"It is Argenteuil at six sous the pint!"

"Ah, bah!" said the gravedigger, "you're a bore. Ding-dong, ding-dong, the same thing over and over again; that's all you can say. Be off, about your business."

And he threw in the second spadeful.

Fauchelevent had reached that point where a man knows no longer what he is saying.

"Oh! come on, and take a glass, since I'm the one to pay," he again repeated.

"When we've put the child to bed," said the gravedigger.

He tossed in the third spadeful: then, plunging his spade into the earth, he added:

"You see, now, it's going to be cold to-night, and the dead one would cry out after us, if we were to plant her there without good covering."

At this moment, in the act of filling his spade, the gravedigger stooped low, and the pocket of his vest gaped open.

Fauchelevent slipped his hand from behind into the pocket, and took the white object it contained.

The gravedigger flung into the grave the fourth spadeful.

Just as he was turning to take the fifth, Fauchelevent, looking at him with imperturbable calmness, asked:

"By the way, my new friend, have you your card?"

The gravedigger stopped.

"What card?"

"The cemetery-gate will be closed."

"Well, what then?"

"Have you your card?"

"Oh! my card!" said the gravedigger, and he felt in his pocket.

"No!" said he, "no! I haven't got my card. I must have forgotten it."

"Fifteen francs fine!" said Fauchelevent.

The gravedigger turned green.

"Oh, good-gracious God, what a fool I am!" he exclaimed. "Fifteen francs fine!"

"Three hundred-sou pieces," said Fauchelevent.

The gravedigger dropped his spade.

"Come! come, recruit," said Fauchelevent, "never despair; there's nothing to kill oneself about, and feed the worms. Where do you live?"

"Just by the barrière. Fifteen minutes' walk. Number 87 Rue de Vaugirard."

"You have time to scamper home, get your card, come back, and the gatekeeper will let you in again. Having your card, there's nothing to pay. Then you can bury your dead man. I'll stay here, and watch him while you're gone, to see that he doesn't run away."

"I owe you my life, peasant!"

"Be off, then, quick!" said Fauchelevent.

When the gravedigger had disappeared through the bushes, Fauchelevent listened until his footsteps died away, and then, bending over the grave, called out in a low voice:

"Father Madeleine!"

No answer.

Fauchelevent clambered down into the grave, threw himself upon the head of the coffin, and cried out:

"Are you there?"

Silence in the coffin.

Fauchelevent, no longer able to breathe for the shiver that was on him, took his cold chisel and hammer, and wrenched off the top board. The face of Jean Valjean could be seen in the twilight, his eyes closed and his cheeks colourless.

Fauchelevent murmured in a voice low as a whisper:

"He is dead!"

Then the poor old man began to sob, talking aloud to himself the while, for it is a mistake to think that talking to one's self is not natural.

"It's Father Mestienne's fault. What did he die for, the fool? It was he who killed poor M. Madeleine. Father Madeleine! He is in the coffin. He's settled. There's an end of it. Now, what's the sense of such things? Good God! he's dead! Yes, and his little girl—what am I to do with her?"

At a distance, through the trees, a harsh grating sound was heard. It was the gate of the cemetery closing.

Fauchelevent again bent over Jean Valjean, but suddenly started back with all the recoil that was possible in a grave. Jean Valjean's eyes were open, and gazing at him.

"I was falling asleep," said Jean Valjean.

Fauchelevent dropped on his knees.

"Oh, blessed Virgin! How you frightened me!"

"I am cold," said Jean Valjean.

Fauchelevent thrust his hand into his pocket, and drew from it a flask which completed what the open air had begun. Jean Valjean took a swallow of brandy, and felt thoroughly restored.

He got out of the coffin, and assisted Fauchelevent to nail down the lid again. Three minutes afterwards, they were calm out of the grave.

After this, Fauchelevent was calm enough. He took his time. The cemetery was closed. There was no fear of the return of the gravedigger, at home, hunting up his "card," and rather unlikely to find it, as it was in Fauchelevent's pocket. Without his card, he could not get back into the cemetery.

Fauchelevent took the spade and Jean Valjean the pick, and together they buried the empty coffin.

When the grave was filled, Fauchelevent said to Jean Valjean:

"Come, let us go; I'll keep the spade, and you take the pick."

Jean Valjean found it hard to move and walk. In the coffin he had stiffened considerably, somewhat in reality like a corpse. He had, in some sort, to thaw himself out of the sepulchre.

They went out by the avenues the hearse had followed. When they reached the closed gate and the porter's lodge, Fauchelevent, who had the gravedigger's card in his hand, dropped it into the box, the porter drew the cord, the gate opened, and they went through.

"Father Madeleine," said Fauchelevent, as he went along, looking up at the houses, "you have better eyes than mine—which is number 87?"

"Here it is, now," said Jean Valjean.

"There's no one in the street," resumed Fauchelevent. "Give me the pick, and wait for me a couple of minutes."

Fauchelevent went in at number 87, ascended to the topmost flight, guided by the instinct which always leads the poor to the garret, and knocked, in the dark, at the door of a little attic room. A voice called: "Come in!"

The lodging of the gravedigger was, like all these shelters of the needy, an unfurnished but much littered loft. A packing-case of some kind—a coffin, perhaps—supplied the place of a bureau, a straw pallet the place of a bed, a butter-pot the place of water-cooler, and the floor served alike for chairs and table. In one corner, on a ragged old scrap of carpet, was a haggard woman, and a number of children were huddled together. The whole of this wretched interior bore the traces of recent overturn. The coverlets were displaced, the ragged garments scattered about, the pitcher broken, the mother had been weeping, and the children probably beaten; all traces of a headlong and violent search. It was plain that the gravedigger had been looking, wildly, for his card, and had made everything in the attic, from his pitcher to his wife, responsible for the loss.

But Fauchelevent was in too great a hurry for the end of his adventure, to notice this gloomy side of his triumph.

As he came in, he said:

"I've brought your spade and pick."

"What, it is you, peasant?"

"And, to-morrow morning, you will find your card with the gatekeeper of the cemetery. I found it on the ground when you had gone; I buried the corpse; I filled in the grave; I finished your job."

"Thanks, villager!" exclaimed the gravedigger in amazement. "The next time I will treat."

An hour later, in the depth of night, two men and a child stood in front of No. 62, Petite Rue Picpus. The elder of the men lifted the knocker and rapped.

It was Fauchelevent, Jean Valjean, and Cosette.

The porter, who had his instructions, opened the little side door and admitted all three.

The prioress, rosary in hand, was awaiting them. A mother, with her veil down, stood near her. A modest taper lighted the parlour.

The prioress scrutinised Jean Valjean. Then she proceeded to question:
"You are the brother?"

"Yes, reverend mother," replied Fauchelevent.

"What is your name?"

Fauchelevent replied:

"Ultimus Fauchelevent!"

He had, in reality, had a brother named Ultimus, who was dead.

"From what part of the country are you?"

Fauchelevent answered:

"From Picquigny, near Amiens."

"What is your age?"

Fauchelevent answered:

"Fifty."

"What is your business?"

Fauchelevent answered:

"Gardener."

"Are you a true Christian?"

Fauchelevent answered:

"All of our family are such."

"Is this your little girl?"

Fauchelevent answered:

"Yes, reverend mother."

"You are her father?"

Fauchelevent answered:

"Her grandfather."

The mother said to the prioress in an undertone:

"He answers well."

Jean Valjean had not spoken a word.

The prioress looked at Cosette attentively, and then said, aside to the mother—

"She will be homely."

The two mothers talked together very low for a few minutes in a corner of the parlour, and then the prioress turned and said—

"Father Fauvent, you will have another knee-cap and bell. We need two, now."

In fact, Jean Valjean was regularly installed; he had the leather knee-cap and the bell; henceforth his name was Ultimus Fauchelevent.

The strongest recommendation for Cosette's admission had been the remark of the prioress: *She will be homely*. The prioress having uttered this prediction, immediately took Cosette into her friendship and gave her a place in the school building as a charity pupil.

Cosette, at the convent, still very naturally thought herself Jean Valjean's daughter.

Jean Valjean succeeded in having the garments which she laid aside given to him. It was the same mourning suit he had carried for her to put on when she left the Thénardiers. It was not much worn. Jean Valjean rolled up these garments, as well as the woollen stockings and shoes, with much camphor and other aromatic substances of which there is such an abundance in convents, and packed them in a small valise which he managed to procure. He put this valise in a chair near his bed, and always kept the key of it in his pocket.

Father Fauchelevent was recompensed for his good deed; in the first place it made him happy, and then he had less work to do, as it was divided. Finally, as he was very fond of tobacco, he found the presence of M. Madeleine advantageous in another point of view; he took three times as much tobacco as before, and that too in a manner infinitely more voluptuous, since M. Madeleine paid for it. The nuns did not adopt the name of *Ultimus;* they called Jean Valjean *the other Fauvent.*

If those holy women had possessed the discrimination of Javert, they might have remarked, in course of time, that when there was any little errand to run outside for on account of the garden, it was always the elder Fauchelevent, old, infirm, and lame as he was, who went, and never the other. Jean Valjean was well satisfied to keep quiet and still. Javert watched the quarter for a good long month.

The convent was to Jean Valjean like an island surrounded by wide waters. It may be remembered that he knew all kinds of receipts and secrets of field-work. These he turned to account. Nearly all the orchard trees were wild stock; he grafted them and made them bear excellent fruit.

Cosette was allowed to come every day, and pass an hour with him. At the hours of recreation, Jean Valjean from a distance watched her playing and romping, and he could distinguish her laughter from the laughter of the rest.

For, now, Cosette laughed.

XIV. THE HOMELESS

PARIS begins with the cockney and ends with the *gamin,* two beings of which no other city is capable. All monarchy is comprised in the cockney; all anarchy in the *gamin.*

This pale child of the Paris suburbs lives, develops, and gets into and out of "scrapes," amid suffering, a thoughtful witness of our social realities and our human problems. He thinks himself careless, but he is not. He looks on, ready to laugh; ready, also, for something else. This little fellow will grow.

The *gamin,* in his perfect state, possesses all the policemen of Paris, and, always, upon meeting one, can put a name to the countenance. He reads their souls as an open book. He will tell you off-hand and without hesitating —Such a one is a *traitor;* such a one is *very cross;* such a one is *great;* such a one is *ridiculous;* "That chap thinks the Pont Neuf belongs to him, and hinders *people* from walking on the cornice outside of the parapets; that other one has a mania for pulling *persons'* ears."

The Paris *gamin* is respectful, ironical, and insolent. In the very presence of Jehovah, he would go hopping and jumping up the steps of Paradise. He is very good at boxing with both hands and feet. Every description of growth is possible to him. He plays in the gutter and rises from it by revolt; his effrontery is not cured by grape; he was a blackguard, lo! he is a hero!

The *gamin* is the expression of Paris, and Paris is the expression of the world.

About eight or nine years after the events narrated in the second part of this story, there was seen, on the Boulevard du Temple, and in the neighbourhood of the Château d'Eau, a little boy of eleven or twelve years of age, who would have realised with considerable accuracy the ideal of the *gamin* previously sketched, if, with the laughter of his youth upon his lips, his heart had not been absolutely dark and empty. This child was well muffled up in a man's pair of pantaloons, but he had not got them from his father, and in a woman's chemise, which was not an inheritance from his mother. Strangers had clothed him in these rags out of charity. Still, he had a father and a mother. But his father never thought of him, and his mother did not love him.

He was a boisterous, pallid, nimble, wide-awake, roguish urchin, with an air at once vivacious and sickly. He went, came, sang, played pitch and toss, scraped the gutters, stole a little, but he did it gaily, like the cats and the sparrows, laughed when people called him an errand-boy, and got angry when they called him a ragamuffin. He had no shelter, no food, no fire, no love, but he was light-hearted because he was free.

However, deserted as this lad was, it happened sometimes, every two or three months, that he would say to himself: "Come, I'll go and see my mother!" Then he would leave the Boulevard, the Cirque, the Porte Saint Martin, go down along the quays, cross the bridges, reach the suburbs, walk as far as the Saltpêtrière, and arrive—where? Precisely at that double number, 50-52, which is known to the reader, the Gorbeau building.

At the period referred to, the tenement No. 50-52, usually empty, and permanently decorated with the placard "Rooms to let," was, for a wonder, tenanted by several persons who, in all other respects, as is always the case at Paris, had no relation to or connection with each other. They all belonged to that indigent class which begins with the small bourgeois in embarrassed circumstances, and descends, from grade to grade of wretchedness, through the lower strata of society, until it reaches those two beings in whom all the material things of civilisation terminate, the scavenger and the ragpicker. The "landlady" of the time of Jean Valjean was dead, and had been replaced by another exactly like her.

Among those who lived in the building, the wretchedest of all were a family of four persons, father, mother, and two daughters nearly grown, all four lodging in the same garret room, one of those cells of which we have already spoken. The father, in renting the room, had given his name as Jondrette.

Now, this family was the family of our sprightly little bare-footed urchin. But on the Boulevard du Temple this boy went by the name of little Gavroche. Why was his name Gavroche? Probably because his father's name was Jondrette.

The room occupied by the Jondrettes in the Gorbeau tenement was the last at the end of the hall. The adjoining cell was tenanted by a very poor young man who was called Monsieur Marius.

Let us see who and what Monsieur Marius was.

In the Rue Boucherat, Rue de Normandie, and Rue de Saintonge, there still remain a few old inhabitants who preserve a memory of a fine old man named M. Gillenormand. This man was old when they were young.

He was a peculiar old man, and very truly a man of another age—the genuine bourgeois of the eighteenth century, a very perfect specimen, a little haughty, wearing his good old bourgeoisie as marquises wear their marquisates. He had passed his ninetieth year, walked erect, spoke in a loud voice, saw clearly, drank hard, ate, slept, and snored. He had every one of his thirty-two teeth. He wore glasses only when reading. He was of an amorous humour, but said that for ten years past he had decidedly and entirely renounced women. He was no longer pleasing, he said; he did not add: "I am too old," but, "I am too poor." He would say: "If I were not ruined, he! he!" His remaining income in fact was only about fifteen thousand livres.

He was superficial, hasty, easily angered. He got into a rage on all occasions, most frequently when most unseasonable. When anybody contradicted him he raised his cane; he beat his servants as in the time of Louis XIV. He had an unmarried daughter over fifty years old, whom he belaboured severely when he was angry, and whom he would gladly have horsewhipped. She seemed to him about eight years old.

He wore the costume of the *incroyables* of the Directory. He had thought himself quite young until then, and had kept up with the fashions. His coat was of light cloth, with broad facings, a long swallow tail, and large steel buttons. Add to this short breeches and shoe buckles. He always carried his hands in his pockets. He said authoritatively: *The French Revolution is a mess of scamps.*

Monsieur Gillenormand worshipped the Bourbons and held 1789 in horror; he was constantly relating how he saved himself during the Reign of Terror, and how, if he had not had a good deal of gaiety and a good deal of wit, his head would have been cut off. If any young man ventured to eulogise the republic in his presence, he turned black in the face, and was angry enough to faint. Sometimes he would allude to his ninety years of age, and say, *I really hope that I shall not see ninety-three twice.* At other times he intimated to his people that he intended to live a hundred years.

He had had two wives; by the first a daughter, who had remained unmarried, and by the second another daughter, who died when about thirty years old, and who had married for love, or luck, or otherwise, a soldier of fortune, who had served in the armies of the republic and the empire, had won the cross at Austerlitz, and been made colonel at Waterloo. "*This is the disgrace of my family,*" said the old bourgeois. He took a great deal of snuff, and had a peculiar skill in ruffling his lace frill with the back of his hand. He had very little belief in God.

Such was M. Luke Esprit Gillenormand, who had not lost his hair, which was rather grey than white, and always combed in dog's-ears. To sum up, and with all this, a venerable man.

He was of the eighteenth century, frivolous and great.

As to the two daughters of Monsieur Gillenormand, we have just spoken of them. They were born ten years apart. In their youth they resembled each other very little; and in character as well as in countenance, were as far from being sisters as possible.

The younger had married the man of her dreams, but she was dead. The elder was not married. Mademoiselle Gillenormand the elder could have given odds to an English miss. She was immodestly modest. She had one frightful reminiscence in her life: one day a man had seen her garter.

However, explain who can these ancient mysteries of innocence, she allowed herself to be kissed without displeasure, by an officer of lancers who was her grand-nephew and whose name was Théodule.

To prudery she added bigotry, a suitable lining. She was of the fraternity of the Virgin, wore a white veil on certain feast-days, muttered special prayers, revered "the holy blood," venerated "the sacred heart," remained for hours in contemplation before an old fashioned Jesuit altar in a chapel closed to the vulgar faithful, and let her soul fly away among the little marble clouds and along the grand rays of gilded wood.

There was besides in the house, between this old maid and this old man, a child, a little boy, always trembling and mute before M. Gillenormand. M. Gillenormand never spoke to this child but with stern voice, and sometimes with uplifted cane: "*Here! Monsieur—rascal, black-guard, come here! Answer me, rogue! Let me see you, scape-grace!*" etc. etc. He idolised him.

It was his grandson. We shall see this child again.

When M. Gillenormand lived in the Rue Servandoni, he frequented several very fine and very noble salons. Although a bourgeois, M. Gillenormand was welcome. As he was twice witty, first with his own wit, then with the wit which was attributed to him, he was even sought after and lionised. He went nowhere save on condition of ruling there.

M. Gillenormand was usually accompanied by his daughter, this long mademoiselle, then past forty, and seeming fifty, and by a beautiful little boy of seven, white, rosy, fresh-looking, with happy and trustful eyes, who never appeared in a salon without hearing a buzz about him: "How pretty he is! What a pity! poor child!" This child was the boy to whom we have but just alluded. They called him "poor child," because his father was "a brigand of the Loire."

This brigand of the Loire was M. Gillenormand's son-in-law, already mentioned, and whom M. Gillenormand called *the disgrace of his family.*

Whoever, at that day, had passed through the little city of Vernon, would have noticed a man of about fifty, a large scar upon his forehead extending down his cheek, bent, bowed down, older than his years, walking nearly every day with a spade and a pruning knife in one of those walled compartments which border the left bank of the Seine,—charming inclosures full of flowers of which one would say, if they were much larger, they are gardens, and if they were a little smaller, they are bouquets. He lived solitary and alone, in silence and in poverty, with a woman who was neither young nor old, neither beautiful nor ugly, neither peasant nor bourgeois, who waited upon him. Flowers were his occupation.

By dint of labour, perseverance, attention, and pails of water, he had succeeded in creating after the Creator, and had invented certain tulips and dahlias which seemed to have been forgotten by Nature. By break of day, in summer, he was in his walks, digging, pruning, weeding, watering, walking in the midst of his flowers. He was timid, so much so as to seem unsociable, he rarely went out, and saw nobody but the poor who rapped at his window, and his curé, Abbé Mabeuf, a good old man. Still, if any of the inhabitants of the city or strangers, whoever they might be, curious to see his tulips and roses, knocked at his little house, he opened his door with a smile. This was the brigand of the Loire.

Whoever had read the military memoirs, the biographies, the *Moniteur,* and the bulletins of the Grand Army, would have been struck by a name which appears rather often, the name of George Pontmercy. Pontmercy fought at Spires, at Worms, at Neustadt, at Turkheim, at Alzey, at Mayence where he was one of the two hundred who formed Houchard's rearguard. He with eleven others held their ground against the Prince of Hesse's corps behind the old rampart of Andernach. He was under Kleber at Marchiennes, and at the battle of Mont Palissel, where he had his arm broken by a musket-ball. Then he passed to the Italian frontier, and he was one of the thirty grenadiers who defended the Col di Tende with Joubert. Joubert was made Adjutant-General, and Pontmercy Second-Lieutenant. Pontmercy was by the side of Berthier in the midst of the storm of balls on that day of Lodi of which Bonaparte said: *Berthier was cannoneer, cavalier, and grenadier.* He saw his old general, Joubert, fall at Novi. In 1805, he was in that division which captured Günzburg from the Archduke Ferdinand. At Weltingen he received in his arms under a shower of balls Colonel Maupetit, who was mortally wounded at the head of the 9th Dragoons. He distinguished himself at Austerlitz in that wonderful march in echelon under the enemy's fire. When the cavalry of the Russian Imperial Guard crushed a battalion of the 4th of the Line, Pontmercy was one of those who revenged the repulse, and overthrew the Guard. The emperor gave him the cross. He was in the eighth corps, of the Grand Army, which Mortier commanded, and which took Hamburg. Then he saw Moscow, then the Beresina, then Lutzen, Bautzen, Dresden, Wachau, Leipsic, and the defiles of Glenhausen, then Montmirail, Chateau-Thierry, Caron, the banks of the Marne, the banks of the Aisne, and the formidable position at Laon. At Arney le Duc, a captain, he sabred ten cossacks, and saved, not his general, but his corporal. He was wounded on that occasion, and twenty-seven splinters were extracted from his left arm alone.

He accompanied Napoleon to the island of Elba. At Waterloo he led a squadron of cuirassiers in Dubois' brigade. He it was who took the colours from the Lunenburg battalion. He carried the colours to the emperor's feet. He was covered with blood. He had received, in seizing the colours, a sabre stroke across his face. The emperor, well pleased, cried to him: *You are a Colonel, you are a Baron, you are an Officer of the Legion of Honour!* Pontmercy answered: *Sire, I thank you for my widow.* An hour afterwards, he fell in the ravine of Ohain. Now who was this George Pontmercy? He was that very brigand of the Loire.

We have already seen something of his history. After Waterloo, Pontmercy, drawn out, as will be remembered, from the sunken road of Ohain, succeeded in regaining the army, and was passed along from ambulance to ambulance to the cantonments of the Loire.

The Restoration put him on half-pay, then sent him to a residence, that is to say under surveillance at Vernon. The king, Louis XVIII., ignoring all that had been done in the Hundred Days, recognised neither his position of officer of the Legion of Honour, nor his rank of colonel, nor his title of baron. He, on his part, neglected no opportunity to sign himself *Colonel Baron Pontmercy*. He had only one old blue coat, and he never went out without putting on the rosette of an officer of the Legion of Honour. The *procureur du roi* notified him that he would be prosecuted for "illegally" wearing this decoration. When this notice was given to him by a friendly intermediary, Pontmercy answered with a bitter smile: "I do not know whether it is that I no longer understand French, or you no longer speak it; but the fact is I do not understand you." Then he went out every day for a week with his rosette. Nobody dared to disturb him.

One morning, he met the *procureur du roi* in one of the streets of Vernon, went up to him and said: "Monsieur *procureur du roi*, am I allowed to wear my scar?"

He had nothing but his very scanty half-pay as chief of squadron. He hired the smallest house he could find in Vernon. He lived there alone; how we have just seen. Under the empire, between two wars, he had found time to marry Mademoiselle Gillenormand. The old bourgeois, who really felt outraged, consented with a sigh, saying: "*The greatest families are forced to it.*" In 1815, Madame Pontmercy, an admirable woman worthy of her husband, died, leaving a child. This child would have been the colonel's joy in his solitude; but the grandfather had imperiously demanded his grandson, declaring that, unless he were given up to him, he would disinherit him. The father yielded for the sake of the little boy, and not being able to have his child he set about loving flowers.

It was expressly understood that Pontmercy should never endeavour to see his son or speak to him, under pain of the boy being turned away, and disinherited. To the Gillenormands, Pontmercy was pestiferous. They intended to bring up the child to their liking. The colonel did wrong perhaps to accept these conditions, but he submitted to them, thinking that he was doing right, and sacrificing himself alone.

The inheritance from the grandfather Gillenormand was a small affair, but the inheritance from Mlle. Gillenormand the elder was considerable. This aunt, who had remained single, was very rich from the maternal side, and the son of her sister was her natural heir.

The salon of Madame de T. was all that Marius Pontmercy knew of the world. There were in Madame de T.'s salon some very venerable noble old ladies, and when they were all present, seated in a circle about a dying fire, dimly lighted by a green-shaded lamp, with their stern profiles, their grey or white hair, their long dresses of another age, the little Marius looked upon them with startled eyes, thinking that he saw, not women, but patriarchs and magi, not real beings, but phantoms. There were young people there, but they were slightly dead. Conserve, Conservatism, Conservative, was nearly all the dictionary.

These salons did not long maintain their purity. As early as 1818, doctrinaires began to bud out in them, a troublesome species. They opposed, and sometimes with a rare intelligence, destructive liberalism by conservative liberalism. We heard them say: "Be considerate towards royalism; it has done much real service. It has brought us back tradition, worship, religion, respect. The revolution, whose heirs we are, ought to comprehend all. To attack royalism is a misconception of liberalism. What a blunder, and what blindness!"

Marius Pontmercy went, like all children, through various studies. When he left the hands of Aunt Gillenormand, his grandfather entrusted him to a worthy professor, of the purest classic innocence. Marius had his years at college, then he entered the law-school. He was royalist, fanatical, and austere. He had little love for his grandfather, whose gaiety and cynicism wounded him, and the place of his father was a dark void.

For the rest, he was an ardent but cool lad, noble, generous, proud, religious, lofty; honourable even to harshness, pure even to unsociableness.

In 1827, Marius had just attained his eighteenth year. On coming in one evening, he saw his grandfather with a letter in his hand.

"Marius," said M. Gillenormand, "you will set out tomorrow for Vernon."

"What for?" said Marius.

"To see your father."

Marius shuddered. He had thought of everything but this, that a day might come, when he would have to see his father. Nothing could have been more unlooked for, more surprising, and, we must say, more disagreeable.

Marius, besides his feelings of political antipathy, was convinced that his father, the sabrer, as M. Gillenormand called him in the gentler moments, did not love him; that was clear, since he had abandoned him and left him to others.

The grandfather continued: "It appears that he is sick. He asks for you." And after a moment of silence he added:

"Start to-morrow morning. I think there is at the Cour des Fontaines a conveyance which starts at six o'clock and arrives at night. Take it. He says the case is urgent."

Then he crumpled up the letter and put it in his pocket. Marius could have started that evening and been with his father the next morning. A diligence then made the trip to Rouen from the Rue du Bouloi by night passing through Vernon. Neither M. Gillenormand nor Marius thought of inquiring.

The next day at dusk, Marius arrived at Vernon. Candles were just beginning to be lighted. He asked the first person he met for *the house of Monsieur Pontmercy.* For in his feelings he agreed with the Restoration, and he, too, recognised his father neither as baron nor as colonel.

The house was pointed out to him. He rang; a woman came and opened the door with a small lamp in her hand.

"Monsieur Pontmercy?" said Marius.

The woman remained motionless.

"Is he here?" asked Marius.

The woman gave an affirmative nod of the head.

"Can I speak with him?"

The woman gave a negative sign.

"But I am his son!" resumed Marius. "He expects me."

"He expects you no longer," said the woman.

Then he perceived that she was in tears.

She pointed to the door of a low room; he entered.

In this room, which was lighted by a tallow candle on the mantel, there were three men, one of them standing, one on his knees, and one stripped to his shirt and lying at full length upon the floor. The one upon the floor was the colonel.

The two others were a physician and a priest who was praying.

The colonel had been three days before attacked with a brain fever. At the beginning of the sickness, having a presentiment of ill, he had written to Monsieur Gillenormand to ask for his son. He had grown worse. On the very evening of Marius' arrival at Vernon, the colonel had had a fit of delirium; he sprang out of his bed in spite of the servant, crying: "My son has not come! I am going to meet him!" Then he had gone out of his room and fallen upon the floor of the hall. He had but just died.

The doctor had come too late, the curé had come too late. The son also had come too late.

Marius looked upon this man, whom he saw for the first time, and for the last—this venerable and manly face, these open eyes which saw not, this white hair, these robust limbs upon which he distinguished here and there brown lines which were sabre-cuts, and a species of red stars which were bullet-holes. He looked upon that gigantic scar which imprinted heroism upon this face on which God had impressed goodness. He thought that this man was his father and that this man was dead, and he remained unmoved.

The sorrow which he experienced was the sorrow which he would have felt before any other man whom he might have seen stretched out in death.

Mourning, bitter mourning was in that room. The servant was lamenting by herself in a corner, the curé was praying, and his sobs were heard; the doctor was wiping his eyes. This doctor, this priest, and this woman, looked at Marius through their affliction without saying a word; it was he who was the stranger. Marius, too little moved, felt ashamed and embarrassed at his attitude; he had his hat in his hand, he let it fall to the floor, to make them believe that grief deprived him of strength to hold it.

At the same time he felt something like remorse, and he despised himself for acting thus. But was it his fault? He did not love his father, indeed!

The colonel left nothing. The sale of his furniture hardly paid for his burial. The servant found a scrap of paper which she handed to Marius. It contained this, in the handwriting of the colonel:

"For my Son.—The emperor made me a baron upon the battlefield of Waterloo. Since the Restoration contests this title which I have bought with my blood, my son will take it and bear it. I need not say that he will be worthy of it." On the back, the colonel had added: "At this same battle of Waterloo, a sergeant saved my life. This man's name is Thénardier. Not long ago, I believe he was keeping a little tavern in a village in the suburbs of Paris, at Chelles or at Montfermeil. If my son meets him, he will do Thénardier all the service he can."

Not from duty towards his father, but on account of that vague respect for death in the heart of man, Marius took his paper.

No trace remained of the colonel. Monsieur Gillenormand had his sword and uniform sold to a second-hand dealer. The neighbours stripped the garden and carried off the rare flowers. The other plants became briery and scraggy, and died.

Marius remained only forty-eight hours at Vernon. After the burial, he returned to Paris and went back to his law, thinking no more of his father than if he had never lived. In two days the colonel had been buried, and in three days forgotten.

Marius wore crape on his hat. That was all.

Marius had preserved the religious habits of his childhood. One Sunday he had gone to hear mass at Saint Sulpice; he took his place behind a pillar and knelt down, without noticing it, before a Utrecht velvet chair, on the back of which this name was written: Monsieur Mabeuf, church-warden. The mass had hardly commenced when an old man presented himself and said to Marius:

"Monsieur, this is my place."

Marius moved away readily, and the old man took his chair.

After mass, Marius remained absorbed in thought a few steps distant; the old man approached him again and said: "I beg your pardon, monsieur, for having disturbed you a little while ago, but you must have thought me impertinent, and I must explain myself."

"Monsieur," said Marius, "it is unnecessary."

"Yes!" resumed the old man; "I do not wish you to have a bad opinion of me. You see I think a great deal of that place. It seems to me that the mass is better there. Why? I will tell you. To that place I have seen for ten years, regularly, every two or three months, a poor, brave father come, who had no other opportunity and no other way of seeing his child, being prevented through some family arrangements. He came at the hour when he knew his son was brought to mass. The little one never suspected that his father was here. He did not even know, perhaps, that he had a father, the innocent boy! The father, for his part, kept behind a pillar, so that nobody should see him. This poor man worshipped this little boy. I saw that. He had a father-in-law, a rich aunt, relatives, I do not remember exactly, who threatened to disinherit the child if he, the father, should see him. They were separated by political opinions. Certainly I approve of political opinions, but there are people who do not know where to stop. Bless me! because a man was at Waterloo he is not a monster. He lived at Vernon, where my brother is curé, and his name is something like Pontmarie, Montpercy. He had a handsome sabre cut."

"Pontmercy," said Marius, turning pale.

"Exactly; Pontmercy. Did you know him?"

"Monsieur," said Marius, "he was my father."

The old churchwarden clasped his hands, and exclaimed—

"Ah! you are the child! Yes, that is it; he ought to be a man now. Well! poor child, you can say that you had a father who loved you well."

Marius offered his arm to the old man, and walked with him to his house. Next day he said to Monsieur Gillenormand:—

"We have arranged a hunting party with a few friends. Will you permit me to be absent for three days?"

"Four," answered the grandfather; "go; amuse yourself."

And, with a wink, he whispered to his daughter—

"Some love affair!"

Marius was absent three days, then he returned to Paris, went straight to the library of the law-school, and asked for the file of the *Moniteur*.

He read the *Moniteur;* he read all the histories of the republic and the empire; the *Memorial de Sainte-Hélène;* all the memoirs, journals, bulletins, proclamations; he devoured everything. The first time he met his father's name in the bulletins of the grand army he had a fever for a whole week. He went to see the generals under whom George Pontmercy had served. The churchwarden, Mabeuf, gave him an account of the life at Vernon, the colonel's retreat, his flowers and his solitude. Marius came to understand fully this rare, sublime, and gentle man, this sort of lion-lamb who was his father.

In the meantime, engrossed in this study, which took up all his time, as well as all his thoughts, he hardly saw the Gillenormands more. At the hours of meals he appeared; then when they looked for him, he was gone. The aunt grumbled. The grandfather smiled. "Poh, poh! it is the age for the lasses!" Sometimes the old man added: "The devil! I thought that it was some gallantry. It seems to be a passion."

It was a passion, indeed. Marius was on the way to adoration for his father.

At the same time an extraordinary change took place in his ideas.

The republic, the empire, had been to him, till then, nothing but monstrous words. The republic, a guillotine in a twilight; the empire, a sabre in the night. He had looked into them, and there, where he expected to find only a chaos of darkness, he had seen, with a sort of astounding surprise, mingled with fear and joy, stars shining, Mirabeau, Vergniaud, Saint-Just, Robespierre, Camille Desmoulins, Danton, and a sun rising, Napoleon. He perceived then that up to that time he had comprehended his country no more than he had his father. He now saw, and on the one hand he admired, on the other he worshipped. When he thought of his former opinions, which seemed so ancient to him already, he became indignant at himself, and he smiled. From the rehabilitation of his father he had naturally passed to the rehabilitation of Napoleon.

This, however, we must say, was not accomplished without labour.

From childhood he had been imbued with the judgment of the party of 1814 in regard to Bonaparte. Now, like all new converts to a religion, his conversion intoxicated him, he plunged headlong into adhesion, and he went too far. Fanaticism for the sword took possession of him, and became complicated in his mind with enthusiasm for the idea. He did not perceive that along with genius he was admiring force, that is to say installing in the two compartments of his idolatry, on one side what is divine, and on the other what is brutal.

However this might be, a great step had been taken. Where he had formerly seen the fall of the monarchy, he now saw the advent of France.

All these revolutions were accomplished in him without a suspicion of it in his family.

When, in this mysterious labour, he had entirely cast off his old Bourbon and ultra skin, when he had shed the aristocrat, the jacobite, and the royalist, when he was fully revolutionary, thoroughly democratic, and almost republican, he went to an engraver on the Quai des Orfévres, and ordered a hundred cards bearing this name: *Baron Marius Pontmercy*.

However, as he knew nobody, and could not leave his cards at anybody's door, he put them in his pocket.

By another natural consequence, in proportion as he drew nearer to his father, his memory, and the things for which the colonel had fought for twenty-five years, he drew off from his grandfather. As we have mentioned, for a long time M. Gillenormand's capriciousness had been disagreeable to him. There was already between them all the distaste of a serious young man for a frivolous old man. Through affection and veneration for his father, Marius had almost reached aversion for his grandfather.

Nothing of this, however, as we have said, was betrayed externally. Only he was more and more frigid; laconic at meals, and scarcely ever in the house. When his aunt scolded him for it, he was very mild, and gave as an excuse his studies, courts, examinations, dissertations, etc. The grandfather did not change his infallible diagnosis: "In love? I understand it."

Marius was absent for a while from time to time.

"Where can he go to?" asked the aunt.

On one of these journeys, which were always very short, he went to Montfermeil in obedience to the injunction which his father had left him, and sought for the former sergeant of Waterloo, the innkeeper Thénardier. Thénardier had failed, the inn was closed, and nobody knew what had become of him. While making these researches, Marius was away from the house four days.

"Decidedly," said the grandfather, "he is going astray."

They thought they noticed that he wore something, upon his breast and under his shirt, hung from his neck by a black ribbon.

We have spoken of a lancer. He was a grand-nephew of M. Gillenormand's on the paternal side, who passed his life away from his family. Lieutenant Théodule Gillenormand fulfilled all the conditions required for what is called a handsome officer. He had "the waist of a girl," a way of trailing the victorious sabre, and a curling mustache. He came to Paris so rarely that Marius had never seen him. The two cousins knew each other only by name. Théodule was, we think we have mentioned, the favourite of Aunt Gillenormand, who preferred him because she did not see him.

One morning, Mlle. Gillenormand the elder had retired to her room as much excited as her placidity allowed. Marius had asked his grandfather again for permission to make a short journey, adding that he intended to set out that evening. "Go!" the grandfather had answered, and M. Gillenormand had added aside, lifting his eyebrows to the top of his forehead: "He is getting to be an old offender." Mlle. Gillenormand had returned to her room very much perplexed, dropping this exclamation point on the stairs: "That is pretty!" and this interrogation point: "But where can he be going?"

As a diversion from this curiosity which was giving her a little more agitation than she allowed herself, she took refuge in her talents, and began to festoon cotton upon cotton, in one of those embroideries of the time of the empire and the restoration in which a great many cab wheels appear. She had been sitting in her chair for some hours when the door opened. Mlle. Gillenormand raised her eyes; Lieutenant Théodule was before her making the regulation bow. She uttered a cry of pleasure. You may be old, you may be a prude, you may be a bigot, you may be his aunt, but it is always pleasant to see a lancer enter your room.

"You here, Théodule!" exclaimed she.

"On my way, aunt."

"Embrace me, then."

Aunt Gillenormand went to her secretary, and opened it.

"You stay with us at least all the week?"

"Aunt, I leave this evening."

"Impossible!"

"Mathematically."

"Stay, my dear Théodule, I beg you."

"The heart says yes, but my orders say no."

"Take this for your pains."

She put ten louis into his hand.

"You mean for my pleasure, dear aunt."

Théodule embraced her a second time, and she had the happiness of having her neck a little chafed by the braid of his uniform.

"Do you make the journey on horseback with your regiment?" she asked.

"No, aunt. I wanted to see you. I have a special permit. My servant takes my horse; I go by the diligence. And, speaking of that, I have a question to ask you."

"What?"

"My cousin, Marius Pontmercy, is travelling also, is he?"

"How do you know that?" exclaimed the aunt, her curiosity suddenly excited to the quick.

"On my arrival, I went to the diligence to secure my place in the coupé."

"Well?"

"A traveller had already secured a place on the impériale. I saw his name on the book."

"What name?"

"Marius Pontmercy."

"The wicked fellow!" exclaimed the aunt. "Ah! your cousin is not a steady boy like you. To think that he is going to spend the night in a diligence."

"Like me."

"But for you, it is from duty; for him, it is from dissipation."

Here, an event occurred in the life of Mademoiselle Gillenormand the elder; she had an idea. If she had been a man, she would have slapped her forehead. She apostrophised Théodule:

"Are you sure that your cousin does not know you?"

"Yes. I have seen him; but he has never deigned to notice me."

"Where does this diligence go?"

"To Les Andelys."

"Is there where Marius is going?"

"Unless, like me, he stops on the road. I get off at Vernon to take the branch for Gaillon. I know nothing of Marius' route."

"Listen, Théodule."

"I am listening, aunt."

"Well, Marius is often away."

"Eh! eh!"

"He sleeps away."

"Oh! oh!"

"We want to know what is at the bottom of it."

Théodule answered with the calmness of a man of bronze:

"Some petticoat."

"That is clear," exclaimed the aunt, who thought she heard Monsieur Gillenormand speak. She resumed:

"Do us a kindness. Follow Marius a little way. He does not know you, it will be easy for you. You can write us the account. It will amuse grandfather."

Théodule had no excessive taste for this sort of watching; but he was much affected by the ten louis, and he thought he saw a possible succession of them. He accepted the commission and said: "As you please, aunt." And he added aside: "There I am, a duenna."

Mademoiselle Gillenormand embraced him.

"You would not play such pranks, Théodule. You are obedient to discipline, you are the slave of your orders, you are a scrupulous and dutiful man, and you would not leave your family to go to see such a creature."

Marius, on the evening which followed this dialogue, mounted the diligence without suspecting that he was watched. As to the watchman, the first thing that he did, was to fall asleep.

At daybreak, the driver of the diligence shouted: "Vernon! Vernon relay! passengers for Vernon?" And Lieutenant Théodule awoke.

"Good," growled he, half asleep, "here I get off."

Then, his memory clearing up by degrees, an effect of awakening, he remembered his aunt, the ten louis, and the account he was to render of Marius' acts and deeds. It made him laugh.

At this moment a pair of black pantaloons getting down from the impériale, appeared before the window of the coupé.

"Can that be Marius?" said the lieutenant.

It was Marius.

A little peasant girl, beside the coach, among the horses and postillions, was offering flowers to the passengers. "Flowers for your ladies," cried she.

Marius approached her and bought the most beautiful flowers in her basket.

"Now," said Théodule leaping down from the coach, "there is something that interests me. Who the deuce is he going to carry those flowers to? It ought to be a mighty pretty woman for so fine a bouquet."

And, no longer now by command, but from personal curiosity, like those dogs who hunt on their own account, he began to follow Marius.

Marius walked towards the church.

"All right," said Théodule to himself. "The church! Nothing is so exquisite as an ogle which passes across the good God."

Marius did not go in, but went behind the building.

"The rendezvous is outside," said Théodule. "Let us see the lass."

And he advanced on tiptoe towards the corner which Marius had turned

Marius, his face hid in his hands, was kneeling in the grass, upon a grave. He had scattered his bouquet. At the end of the grave, at an elevation which marked the head, there was a black wooden cross, with this name in white letters: COLONEL BARON PONTMERCY.

The lass was a tomb.

It was here that Marius had come the first time that he absented himself from Paris. It was here that he returned every time that M. Gillenormand said: he sleeps out.

Lieutenant Théodule was absolutely disconcerted by this unexpected encounter with a sepulchre; he experienced a disagreeable and singular sensation which he was incapable of analysing, and which was made up of respect for a tomb mingled with respect for a colonel. He retreated, leaving Marius alone in the churchyard, and there was something of discipline in this retreat. Death appeared to him with huge epaulets, and he gave him almost a military salute. Not knowing what to write to his aunt, he decided to write nothing at all; and probably nothing would have resulted from the discovery made by Théodule in regard to Marius' amours, had not, by one of those mysterious arrangements so frequently accidental, the scene at Vernon been almost immediately followed by a sort of counter-blow at Paris.

Marius returned from Vernon early in the morning of the third day, was set down at his grandfather's, and, fatigued by the two nights passed in the diligence, feeling the need of making up for his lack of sleep by an hour at the swimming school, ran quickly up to his room, took only time enough to lay off his travelling coat and the black ribbon which he wore about his neck, and went away to the bath.

M. Gillenormand, who had risen early like all old persons who are in good health, had heard him come in, and hastened as fast as he could with his old legs, to climb to Marius' room. But the youth had taken less time to go down than the octogenarian to go up, and when Grandfather Gillenormand entered the garret room, Marius was no longer there.

The bed was not disturbed, and upon the bed were displayed without distrust the coat and the black ribbon.

"I like that better," said M. Gillenormand.

And a moment afterwards he entered the parlour where Mademoiselle Gillenormand the elder was already seated, embroidering her cab wheels.

The entrance was triumphal.

M. Gillenormand held in one hand the coat and in the other the neck ribbon, and cried:

"Victory! We are going to penetrate the mystery! here we are with the romance even. I have the portrait!"

In fact, a black shagreen box, much like to a medallion, was fastened to the ribbon.

"Let us see, father," said the old maid.

The box opened by pressing a spring. They found nothing in it but a piece of paper carefully folded.

"*From the same to the same,*" said M. Gillenormand, bursting with laughter. "I know what that is. A love-letter!"

"Ah! then let us read it!" said the aunt.

And she put on her spectacles. They unfolded the paper and read this:

"*For my son.*—The emperor made me a baron upon the battlefield of Waterloo. Since the restoration contests this title which I have bought with my blood, my son will take it and bear it. I need not say that he will be worthy of it."

The father and daughter felt chilled as by the breath of a death's head. They did not exchange a word. M. Gillenormand, however, said in a low voice, and as if talking to himself:

"It is the handwriting of that sabrer."

Just at that moment, a little oblong package, wrapped in blue paper, fell from a pocket of the coat. Mademoiselle Gillenormand picked it up and unfolded the blue paper. It was Marius' hundred cards. She passed one of them to M. Gillenormand, who read: *Baron Marius Pontmercy.*

The old man rang. Nicolette came. M. Gillenormand took the ribbon, the box, and the coat, threw them all on the floor in the middle of the parlour, and said:

"Take away those things."

A full hour passed in complete silence. The old man and the old maid sat with their backs turned to one another, and were probably, each on their side, thinking over the same things. At the end of that hour, Aunt Gillenormand said:

"Pretty!"

A few minutes afterwards, Marius made his appearance. His grandfather, holding one of his cards in his hand, exclaimed with his crushing air of sneering, bourgeois superiority:

"Stop! stop! stop! stop! stop! you are a baron now. I present you my compliments. What does this mean?"

Marius coloured slightly, and answered:

"It means that I am my father's son."

M. Gillenormand checked his laugh, and said harshly:

"Your father; I am your father."

"My father," resumed Marius with downcast eyes and stern manner, "was a humble and heroic man, who served the republic and France gloriously, who was great in the greatest history that men have ever made, who received twenty wounds, who died forgotten and abandoned, and who had but one fault; that was in loving too dearly two ingrates, his country and me."

This was more than M. Gillenormand could listen to. At the word, *Republic,* he rose, or rather, sprang to his feet. Every one of the words which Marius had pronounced, had produced the effect upon the old royalist's face, of a blast from a bellows upon a burning coal. From dark he had become red, from red purple, and from purple glowing.

"Marius!" exclaimed he, "abominable child! I don't know what your father was! I don't want to know! but what I do know is, that there was never anything but miserable wretches among all that rabble! they were all beggars, assassins, red caps, thieves! I say all! I say all!"

Marius knew not what to do. He was the priest who sees all his wafers thrown to the winds, the fakir who sees a passer-by spit upon his idol. His father had been trodden under foot and stamped upon in his presence, but by whom? by his grandfather. How should he avenge the one without outraging the other? On one hand a sacred tomb, on the other white hairs. He raised his eyes, looked straight at his grandfather, and cried in a thundering voice:

"Down with the Bourbons, and the great hog Louis XVIII.!"

Louis XVIII. had been dead for four years; but it was all the same to him.

The old man, scarlet as he was, suddenly became whiter than his hair. He turned towards a bust of the Duke de Berry which stood upon the mantel, and bowed to it profoundly with a sort of peculiar majesty. Then he walked twice, slowly and in silence, from the fireplace to the window and from the window to the fireplace, traversing the whole length of the room and making the floor crack as if an image of stone were walking over it. The second time, he bent towards his daughter, who was enduring the shock with the stupor of an aged sheep, and said to her with a smile that was almost calm:

"A baron like Monsieur and a bourgeois like me cannot remain under the same roof."

And all at once straightening up, pallid, trembling, terrible, his forehead swelling with the fearful radiance of anger, he stretched his arm towards Marius and cried to him:

"Be off."

Marius left the house.

The next day, M. Gillenormand said to his daughter:

"You will send sixty pistoles every six months to this blood-drinker, and never speak of him to me again."

Marius, for his part, departed in indignation. A circumstance had aggravated his exasperation still more. In hurriedly carrying away, at the old man's command, Marius' "things" to his room, Nicolette had, without perceiving it, dropped, probably on the garret stairs, which were dark, the black shagreen medallion which contained the paper written by the colonel. Neither the paper nor the medallion could be found. Marius was convinced that "Monsieur Gillenormand"—from that day forth he never named him otherwise—had thrown "his father's will" into the fire. He knew by heart the few lines written by the colonel, and consequently nothing was lost. But the paper, the writing, that sacred relic, all that was his heart itself. What had been done with it?

Marius went away without saying where he was going, and without knowing where he was going, with thirty francs, his watch, and a few clothes in a carpet bag. He hired a cabriolet by the hour, jumped in, and drove at random towards the Latin quarter.

XV. THE A B C

AT THAT PERIOD, apparently indifferent, something of a revolutionary thrill was vaguely felt. People were transformed almost without suspecting it, by the very movement of the time. Royalists became liberals, liberals became democrats.

There were not yet in France any of those underlying organisations like the German Tugenbund and the Italian Carbonari; but here and there obscure excavations were branching out. There was in Paris, among other affiliations of this kind, the Society of the Friends of the A B C—a society having as its aim, in appearance, the education of children; in reality, the elevation of men.

They declared themselves the Friends of the A B C. The *abaissé* [the abased] were the people. They wished to raise them up, a pun at which you should not laugh. Puns are sometimes weighty in politics, witness *Tu es Petrus et super hanc Petram.*

The Friends of the A B C were not numerous, it was a secret society in the embryonic state. They met in Paris, at two places, in a wine shop called *Corinthe,* and in a little coffeehouse called *Le Café Musain.* They smoked, drank, played, and talked very loud about everything, in whispers about something else.

Most of the Friends of the A B C were students, in thorough understanding with a few working-men. The names belong to history; Enjolras, Combeferre, Jean Prouvaire, Feuilly, Courfeyrac, Bahorel, Lesgle or Laigle, Joly, Grantaire.

These young men constituted a sort of family among themselves, by force of friendship. All except Laigle were from the South.

Enjolras, whom we have named first, the reason why will be seen by-and-by, was an only son and was rich.

Enjolras was a charming young man, who was capable of being terrible. He was angelically beautiful. He was officiating and militant; from the immediate point of view, a soldier of democracy; above the movement of the time, a priest of the ideal. His twenty-two years of age appeared seventeen; he was serious, he did not seem to know that there was on the earth a being called woman. He had but one passion, the right; but one thought, to remove all obstacles.

Beside Enjolras who represented the logic of the revolution, Combeferre represented its philosophy. Between the logic of the revolution and its philosophy, there is this difference—that its logic could conclude with war, while its philosophy could only end in peace. Combeferre completed and corrected Enjolras. He was lower and broader. His desire was to instil into all minds the broad principles of general ideas; he said "Revolution, but civilisation;" and about the steep mountain he spread the vast blue horizon. Hence, in all Combeferre's views, there was something attainable and practicable. Revolution with Combeferre was more respirable than with Enjolras. Enjolras expressed its divine right, and Combeferre its natural right. He desired that society should work without ceasing at the elevation of the intellectual and moral level; at the coming of knowledge, at bringing ideas into circulation, at the growth of the mind in youth; and he feared that the poverty of the methods then in vogue, the meanness of a literary world which was circumscribed by two or three centuries, called classical, the tyrannical dogmatism of official pedants, scholastic prejudices and routine, would result in making artificial oyster-beds of our colleges. He was learned, purist, precise, universal, a hard student, and at the same time given to musing, "even chimerical," said his friends. He believed in all the dreams: railroads, the suppression of suffering in surgical operations, the fixing of the image in the camera obscura, the electric telegraph, the steering of balloons. Little dismayed, moreover, by the citadels built upon all sides against the human race by superstitions, despotisms, and prejudices, he was one of those who think that science will at last turn the position. Enjolras was a chief; Combeferre was a guide.

Jean Prouvaire was yet a shade more subdued than Combeferre. Jean Prouvaire was addicted to love; he cultivated a pot of flowers, played on the flute, made verses, loved the people, mourned over woman, wept over childhood, confounded the future and God in the same faith. All day he pondered over social questions: wages, capital, credit, marriage, religion, liberty of thought, liberty of love, education, punishment, misery, association, property, production and distribution, the lower enigma which covers the human ant-hill with a shadow; and at night he gazed upon the stars. Like Enjolras, he was rich, and an only son.

Feuilly was a fan-maker, an orphan, who with difficulty earned three francs a day, and who had but one thought, to deliver the world. He had still another desire—to instruct himself; which he also called deliverance. He had taught himself to read and write; all that he knew, he had learned alone. Feuilly was a generous heart. He had an immense embrace. This orphan had adopted the people. Being without a mother, he had meditated upon his mother country. He was not willing that there should be any man upon the earth without a country. He nurtured within himself, with the deep divination of the man of the people, what we now call *the idea of nationality*. He had learned history expressly that he might base his indignation upon a knowledge of its cause. In this new upper room of utopists particularly interested in France, he represented the foreign nations. His specialty was Greece, Poland, Hungary, the Danubian Provinces, and Italy. He uttered these names incessantly, in season and out of season, with the tenacity of the right. The protest of the right against the fact, persists forever.

Courfeyrac had a father whose name was M. de Courfeyrac. We might almost, in what concerns Courfeyrac, stop here, and content ourselves with saying as to the remainder: Courfeyrac, see Tholomyès. Enjolras was the chief, Combeferre was the guide, Courfeyrac was the centre. The others gave more light, he gave more heat; the truth is, that he had all the qualities of a centre, roundness and radiance.

Bahorel was a creature of good humour and bad company, brave, a spendthrift, prodigal almost to generosity, talkative almost to eloquence, bold almost to effrontery; with fool-hardy waistcoats and scarlet opinions; a wholesale blusterer, that is to say, liking nothing so well as a quarrel unless it were a revolution; always ready to break a paving-stone, then to tear up a street, then to demolish a government, to see the effect of it; a student of the eleventh year. He had adopted for his motto: *never a lawyer.* He ate up in doing nothing a considerable allowance, something like three thousand francs. His parents were peasants, in whom he had succeeded in inculcating a respect for their son.

Bahorel, a capricious man, was scattered over several cafés; the others had habits, he had none. He loafed. To err is human. To loaf is Parisian.

In this conclave of young heads there was one bald member, Lesgle, or Laigle de Meaux. His comrades called him Bossuet.

His specialty was to succeed in nothing. On the other hand, he laughed at everything. At twenty-five he was bald. Bossuet was slowly making his way towards the legal profession, doing his law, in the manner of Bahorel. He lodged sometimes with one, sometimes with another, oftenest with Joly. Joly was studying medicine. He was two years younger than Bossuet.

Joly was a young Malade Imaginaire. What he had learned in medicine was rather to be a patient than a physician. At twenty-three, he thought himself a valetudinarian, and passed his time in looking at his tongue in a mirror. He declared that man is a magnet, like the needle, and in his room he placed his bed with the head to the south and the foot to the north, so that at night the circulation of the blood should not be interfered with by the grand magnetic current of the globe. All these young men, diverse as they were, and of whom, as a whole, we ought only to speak seriously, had the same religion: Progress.

Among all these passionate hearts and all these undoubting minds there was one sceptic. How did he happen to be there? from juxtaposition. The name of this sceptic was Grantaire, and he was a man who took good care not to believe anything. All these words: rights of the people, rights of man, social contract, French Revolution, republic, democracy, humanity, civilisation, religion, progress, were, to Grantaire, very nearly meaningless. A rover, a gambler, a libertine, and often drunk, he displeased these young thinkers by singing incessantly: *"I loves the girls and I loves good wine."*

Still, this sceptic had a fanaticism. This fanaticism was neither an idea, nor a dogma, nor an art, nor a science; it was a man: Enjolras. Grantaire admired, loved, and venerated Enjolras. In what way did Enjolras subjugate him? By ideas? No. By a character. He admired, by instinct, his opposite.

His soft, wavering, disjointed, diseased, deformed ideas attached themselves to Enjolras as to a backbone. His moral spine leaned upon that firmness.

On a certain afternoon, Laigle de Meaux was leaning lazily back against the doorway of the Café Musain. He had the appearance of a caryatid in vacation; leaning back is a way of lying down standing which is not disliked by dreamers.

Laigle de Meaux perceived, through all his somnambulism, a two-wheeled vehicle turning into the square. What did this cabriolet want? There was inside, beside the driver, a young man, and before the young man, a large carpet-bag. The bag exhibited to the passers this name, written in big black letters upon a card sewed to the cloth: MARIUS PONTMERCY.

This name changed Laigle's attitude. He straightened up and addressed this apostrophe to the young man in the cabriolet:

"Monsieur Marius Pontmercy?"

The cabriolet, thus called upon, stopped. The young man raised his eyes.

"Well?" said he.

"You are Monsieur Marius Pontmercy?"

"Certainly."

"I was looking for you," said Laigle de Meaux.

"How is that?" inquired Marius; for he had before him a face which he saw for the first time. "I do not know you."

"Nor I either. I do not know you," answered Laigle.

Marius was not in a pleasant humour just at that moment. He knit his brows; Laigle de Meaux, imperturbable, continued:

"You were not at school yesterday."

"You are a student?" inquired Marius.

"Yes, Monsieur. Like you. The day before yesterday I happened to go into the school. You know, one sometimes has such notions. The professor was about to call the roll. You know that they are very ridiculous just at that time. If you miss the third call, they erase your name. Sixty francs gone."

Marius began to listen. Laigle continued:

"It was Blondeau who was calling the roll. You know Blondeau; he slily commenced with the letter P. Suddenly, Blondeau calls *Marius Pontmercy;* nobody answers. Blondeau, full of hope, repeats louder: *Marius Pontmercy?* And he seizes his pen. I said to myself rapidly: Here is a brave fellow who is going to be erased. This is a real live fellow who is not punctual. He is not a good boy. He is an honourable idler who loafs, who pays his court to beauty, who is perhaps, at this very moment, with my mistress. Let us save him. Death to Blondeau! At that moment Blondeau dipped his pen, and repeated for the third time: *Marius Pontmercy!* I answered: *Present!* In that way you were not erased."

"Monsieur!—" said Marius.

"And I was," added Laigle de Meaux.

"I do not understand you," said Marius.

"Nothing more simple. I was near the chair to answer, and near the door to escape. The professor was looking at me with a certain fixedness. Suddenly, Blondeau, who must be the malignant nose of which Boileau speaks, leaps to the letter L. L is my letter; I am of Meaux, and my name is Lesgle. I answer: *Present!* Then Blondeau looks at me with the gentleness of a tiger, smiles, and says: If you are Pontmercy, you are not Laigle. So saying, he erases me."

"Monsieur, I am mortified—"

"Young man," said Laigle of Meaux, "let this be a lesson to you. In future, be punctual."

"I really am very sorry."

Laigle burst out laughing.

"And I, in raptures; I was on the brink of being a lawyer. This rupture saves me. I renounce the triumphs of the bar. I shall not defend the widow, and I shall not attack the orphan. I intend to pay you a solemn visit of thanks. Where do you live?"

"In this cabriolet," said Marius.

"A sign of opulence," replied Laigle calmly. "I congratulate you. You have here rent of nine thousand francs a year."

Just then Courfeyrac came out of the café.

Marius smiled sadly.

"I have been paying this rent for two hours, and I hope to get out of it; but I do not know where to go."

"Monsieur," said Courfeyrac, "come home with me."

"I should have priority," observed Laigle, "but I have no home."

In a few days, Marius was the friend of Courfeyrac. Marius, in Courfeyrac's presence, breathed freely, a new thing for him.

One morning, however, Courfeyrac abruptly put this question to him.

"By the way, have you any political opinions?"

"What do you mean?" said Marius, almost offended at the question.

"What are you?"

"Bonapartist democrat."

"Grey shade of quiet mouse colour," said Courfeyrac.

The next day, Courfeyrac introduced Marius to the Café Musain. Then he whispered in his ear with a smile: "I must give you your admission into the revolution." And he took him into the room of the Friends of the A B C.

Marius, up to this time solitary by habit and by taste, was a little bewildered at this flock of young men about him. All these different progressives attacked him at once, and perplexed him. He heard talk of philosophy, of literature, of art, of history, of religion, in a style he had not looked for. On abandoning his grandfather's opinions for his father's, he had thought himself settled; he now suspected, with anxiety, and without daring to confess it to himself, that he was not. The angle under which he saw all things was beginning to change anew. A certain oscillation shook the whole horizon of his brain, a strange internal moving-day.

It seemed that there were to these young men no "sacred things." Marius heard, upon every subject, a singular language annoying to his still timid mind. Of the conversations which Marius frequented and in which he sometimes took part, one shocked him severely.

This was held in the back room of the Café Musain. Nearly all the Friends of the A B C were together that evening. The large lamp was ceremoniously lighted. They talked of one thing and another, without passion and with noise. In the midst of the uproar Bossuet suddenly ended some apostrophe with this date:

"The 18th of June, 1815: Waterloo."

At this name, Waterloo, Marius, who was leaning on a table with a glass of water by him, took his hand away from under his chin, and began to look earnestly about the room.

"Pardieu," exclaimed Courfeyrac, "that number 18 is strange, and striking to me. It is the fatal number of Bonaparte. Put Louis before and Brumaire behind, you have the whole destiny of the man, with this expressive peculiarity, that the beginning is hard pressed by the end."

Enjolras, till now dumb, broke the silence, and thus addressed Courfeyrac: "You mean the crime by the expiation."

This word, *crime*, exceeded the limits of the endurance of Marius, already much excited by the abrupt evocation of Waterloo.

He rose, he walked slowly towards the map upon the wall, at the bottom of which could be seen an island, and said:

"Corsica. A little island which has made France truly great."

Enjolras, whose blue eye was not fixed upon anybody, and seemed staring into space, answered without looking at Marius:

"France needs no Corsica to be great. France is great because she is France."

Marius felt no desire to retreat; he turned towards Enjolras, and his voice rang with a vibration which came from the quivering of his nerves:

"God forbid that I should lessen France! but it is not lessening her to join her with Napoleon. Come, let us talk then. I am a newcomer among you, but I confess that you astound me. Where are we? who are we? who are you? who am I? Let us explain ourselves about the emperor. I hear you say Buonaparte, accenting the *u* like the royalists. I can tell you that my grandfather does better yet; he says Buonaparté. I thought you were young men. Where is your enthusiasm then? and what do you do with it? whom do you admire, if you do not admire the emperor? and what more must you have? He was everything. He had in his brain the cube of human faculties. He made codes like Justinian, he dictated like Cæsar, his conversation joined the lightning of Pascal to the thunderbolt of Tacitus, he made history and he wrote it, his bulletins are Iliads, he combined the figures of Newton with the metaphors of Mahomet. And all at once, startled Europe listened, armies set themselves in march, parks of artillery rolled along, bridges of boats stretched over the rivers, clouds of cavalry galloped in the hurricane, cries, trumpets, a trembling of thrones everywhere, the frontiers of the kingdoms oscillated upon the map, men saw him, him, standing erect in the horizon with a flame in his hands, unfolding in the thunder his two wings, the Grand Army and the Old Guard, and he was the archangel of war!"

All were silent, and Marius, almost without taking breath, continued with a burst of enthusiasm:

"Be just, my friends! to be the empire of such an emperor, what a splendid destiny for a people, when that people is France, and when it adds its genius to the genius of such a man! To appear and to reign, to march and to triumph, to have every capital for a magazine, to decree the downfall of dynasties, to transfigure Europe at a double quickstep, so that men feel, when you threaten, that you lay your hand on the hilt of the sword of God; to follow, in a single man, Hannibal, Cæsar, and Charlemagne, to be the people of one who mingles with your every dawn the glorious announcement of a battle gained! To conquer the world twice, by conquest and by resplendence, this is sublime, and what can be more grand?"

"To be free," said Combeferre.

Marius in his turn bowed his head: these cold and simple words had pierced his epic effusion like a blade of steel, and he felt it vanish.

That evening left Marius in a profound agitation, with a sorrowful darkness in his soul. He had but just attained a faith; could he so soon reject it? He decided within himself that he could not. He went no more to the Café Musain.

In this trouble in which his mind was plunged he scarcely gave a thought to certain serious phases of existence. The realities of life jogged his memory sharply; one morning, the keeper of the house entered Marius' room, and said to him:

"Monsieur Courfeyrac is responsible for you."

"Yes."

"But I am in need of money."

"Ask Courfeyrac to come and speak with me," said Marius.

Courfeyrac came; the host left them. Marius related to him what he had not thought of telling him before, that he was, so to speak, alone in the world.

"What are you going to do?"

"I have no idea."

"Have you any money?"

"Fifteen francs."

"Do you wish me to lend you some?"

"Never."

"Have you any clothes?"

"What you see."

"Have you any jewellery?"

"A watch."

"A silver one?"

"Gold, here it is."

"I know a dealer in clothing who will take your overcoat and one pair of trousers."

"That is good."

"You will then have but one pair of trousers, one waistcoat, one hat, and one coat."

"And my boots."

"What? you will not go barefoot? what opulence!"

"That will be enough."

"I know a watchmaker who will buy your watch."

"That is good."

"No, it is not good. What will you do afterwards?"

"What I must. Anything honourable at least."

"Do you know English?"

"No."

"Do you know German?"

"No."

"That is bad."

"Why?"

"Because a friend of mine, a bookseller, is making a sort of encyclopædia, for which you could have translated German or English articles. It is poor pay, but it gives a living."

"I will learn English and German."

"And in the meantime?"

"In the meantime I will eat my coats and my watch."

The clothes dealer gave twenty francs for the clothes. They went to the watchmaker. He gave forty-five francs for the watch.

"That is not bad," said Marius to Courfeyrac, on returning to the house; "with my fifteen francs, this makes eighty francs."

"The hotel bill?" observed Courfeyrac.

"Ah! I forgot," said Marius.

The host presented his bill, which amounted to seventy francs.

"I have ten francs left," said Marius.

"The devil," said Courfeyrac, "you will have five francs to eat while you are learning English, and five francs while you are learning German. That will be swallowing a language very rapidly or a hundred-sous piece very slowly."

Meanwhile Aunt Gillenormand, who was really a kind person on sad occasions, had finally unearthed Marius' lodgings.

One morning when Marius came home from the school, he found a letter from his aunt, and the *sixty pistoles*, that is to say, six hundred francs in gold, in a sealed box.

Marius sent the thirty louis back to his aunt, with a respectful letter, in which he told her that he had the means of living, and that he could provide henceforth for all his necessities. At that time he had three francs left.

The aunt did not inform the grandfather of this refusal, lest she should exasperate him. Indeed, had he not said: "Let nobody ever speak to me of this blood-drinker"?

Marius left the Porte Saint Jacques Hotel, unwilling to contract debt.

Life became stern to Marius. To eat his coats and his watch was nothing. He chewed that inexpressible thing which is called *the cud of bitterness*. A horrible thing, which includes days without bread, nights without sleep, evenings without a candle, a hearth without a fire, weeks without labour, a future without hope, a coat out at the elbows, an old hat which makes young girls laugh, the door found shut against you at night because you have not paid your rent, the insolence of the porter and the landlord, the jibes of neighbours, humiliations, self-respect outraged, any drudgery acceptable, disgust, bitterness, prostration—Marius learned how one swallows down all these things, and how they are often the only things that one has to swallow.

There was a period in Marius' life when he swept his own hall, when he bought a pennyworth of Brie cheese at the market-woman's, when he waited for nightfall to make his way to the baker's and buy a loaf of bread, which he carried furtively to his garret, as if he had stolen it. On several occasions, Aunt Gillenormand sent him the sixty pistoles. Marius always sent them back, saying that he had no need of anything.

He was still in mourning for his father, when the revolution which we have described was accomplished in his ideas. Since then, he had never left off black clothes. His clothes left him, however. A day came, at last, when he had no coat. His trousers were going also. What was to be done? Courfeyrac, for whom he also had done some good turns, gave him an old coat. But this coat was green. Then Marius did not go out till after night fall. Desiring always to be in mourning, he clothed himself with night.

Through all this, he procured admission to the bar. He was reputed to occupy Courfeyrac's room, which was decent, and where a certain number of law books, supported and filled out by some odd volumes of novels, made up the library required by the rules.

When Marius had become a lawyer, he informed his grandfather of it, in a letter which was frigid, but full of submission and respect. M. Gillenormand took the letter with trembling hands, read it, and threw it, torn in pieces, into the basket. Two or three days afterwards, Mademoiselle Gillenormand overheard her father, who was alone in his room, talking aloud. She listened: the old man said: "If you were not a fool, you would know that a man cannot be a baron and a lawyer at the same time."

It is with misery as with everything else. It gradually becomes endurable. This is the way in which Marius Pontmercy's life was arranged.

By dint of hard work, courage, perseverance, and will, he succeeded in earning by his labour about seven hundred francs a year. He had learned German and English; thanks to Courfeyrac, who introduced him to his friend the publisher, Marius translated from the journals, annotated republications, compiled biographies, etc. He lived on this. How? Not badly.

Marius occupied, at an annual rent of thirty francs, a wretched little room in the Gorbeau tenement, with no fireplace. He gave three francs a month to the old woman who had charge of the building, for sweeping his room and bringing him every morning a little warm water, a fresh egg, and a penny loaf of bread. His breakfast varied from two or four sous, as eggs were cheap or dear. At six o'clock in the evening he went down into the Rue Saint Jacques, to dine. He ate no soup. He took a sixpenny plate of meat, a threepenny half-plate of vegetables, and a threepenny dessert. For three sous, as much bread as he liked. As for wine, he drank water.

Thus, his food cost him twenty sous a day, which was three hundred and sixty-five francs a year. Add the thirty francs for his lodging, and the thirty-six francs to the old woman, and a few other trifling expenses, and for four hundred and fifty francs, Marius was fed, lodged, and waited upon. His clothes cost him a hundred francs, his linen fifty francs, his washing fifty francs; the whole did not exceed six hundred and fifty francs. This left him fifty francs. He was rich. He occasionally lent ten francs to a friend. Courfeyrac borrowed sixty francs of him once.

Marius always had two complete suits, one old "for every day," the other quite new, for special occasions. Both were black. He had but three shirts, one he had on, another in the drawer, the third at the washerwoman's. He renewed them as they wore out. They were usually ragged, so he buttoned his coat to his chin.

For Marius to arrive at this flourishing condition had required years. He had undergone everything, in the shape of privation; he had done everything, except get into debt. Rather than borrow, he did not eat.

By the side of his father's name, another name was engraven upon Marius' heart, the name of Thénardier. Marius, in his enthusiastic yet serious nature, surrounded with a sort of halo the man to whom, as he thought, he owed his father's life, that brave sergeant who had saved the colonel in the midst of the balls and bullets of Waterloo. Marius had learned at Montfermeil of the ruin and bankruptcy of the unlucky innkeeper. Since then, nobody could give him any news of Thénardier; it was thought he had gone abroad. His creditors had sought for him, also, with less love than Marius, but with as much zeal, and had not been able to put their hands on him.

This was the only debt which the colonel had left him, and Marius made it a point of honour to pay it. "What," thought he, "when my father lay dying on the field of battle, Thénardier could find him through the smoke and the grape, and bring him off on his shoulders, and yet he owed him nothing; while I, who owe so much to Thénardier, I cannot reach him. Oh! I will find him!"

Marius was now twenty years old. It was three years since he had left his grandfather. They remained on the same terms on both sides, without attempting a reconciliation, and without seeking to meet. And, indeed, what was the use of meeting? to come in conflict?

To tell the truth, Marius was mistaken as to his grandfather's heart. He imagined that M. Gillenormand had never loved him, and that this crusty and harsh yet smiling old man, who swore, screamed, stormed, and lifted his cane, felt for him at most only the affection, at once slight and severe, of the old men of comedy. Marius was deceived. There are fathers who do not love their children; there is no grandfather who does not adore his grandson. In reality, we have said, M. Gillenormand worshipped Marius. "But I could not do anything else than turn him away," said the grandfather.

Marius' life was solitary. From his taste for remaining outside of everything, and also from having been startled by its excesses, he had decided not to enter the group presided over by Enjolras. They had remained good friends; they were ready to help one another, if need were, in all possible ways; but nothing more. Marius had two friends, one young, Courfeyrac, and one old, M. Mabeuf. He inclined towards the old one. First he was indebted to him for the revolution through which he had gone; he was indebted to him for having known and loved his father.

M. Mabeuf was not, however, on that occasion anything more than the calm and passive agent of providence. He had enlightened Marius accidentally and without knowing it.

The day that M. Mabeuf said to Marius: "*Certainly, I approve of political opinions*," he expressed the real condition of his mind. All political opinions were indifferent to him, and he approved them all without distinction, provided they left him quiet. He did not understand how men could busy themselves with hating one another about such bubbles as the charter, democracy, legitimacy, the monarchy, the republic, etc., when there were in this world all sorts of mosses, herbs and shrubs, which they could look at, and piles of folios which they could pore over.

When he knew Pontmercy, there was this sympathy between the colonel and himself, that what the colonel did for flowers, he did for fruits. M. Mabeuf had succeeded in producing seedling pears as highly flavoured as the pears of Saint Germain. He had written and published a *Flora of the Environs of Cauteretz* with coloured illustrations, a highly esteemed work, the plates of which he owned and which he sold himself. He received fully two thousand francs a year for it; this was nearly all his income. Though poor, he had succeeded in gathering together, by means of patience, self-denial, and time, a valuable collection of rare copies. He never went out without a book under his arm, and he often came back with two.

Monsieur Mabeuf took Marius into favour, because Marius, being young and gentle, warmed his old age without arousing his timidity. When Marius was full of military glory, gunpowder, marches, and countermarches, and all those wonderful battles in which his father had given and received such huge sabre strokes he went to see Monsieur Mabeuf, and Monsieur Mabeuf talked with him about the hero from the floricultural point of view.

Towards 1830, his brother the curé died, and almost immediately after, as at the coming on of night, the whole horizon of Monsieur Mabeuf was darkened. By a failure—of a notary—he lost ten thousand francs, which was all the money that he possessed in his brother's name and his own.

He carried off his plates, his herbariums, his portfolios and his books, and established himself in a sort of cottage near La Saltpêtrière.

Marius had a liking for this open-hearted old man, who was being slowly seized by indigence. Marius went to see Monsieur Mabeuf once or twice a month.

It was Marius' delight to take long walks alone on the outer boulevards, or in the less frequented walks of the Luxembourg. It was in one of these walks that he had discovered the Gorbeau tenement, and its isolation and cheapness being an attraction to him, he had taken a room in it. He was only known in it by the name of Monsieur Marius.

Towards the middle of this year, 1831, the old woman who waited upon Marius told him that his neighbours, the wretched Jondrette family, were to be turned into the street. Marius, who passed almost all his days out of doors, hardly knew that he had any neighbours.

"Why are they turned out?" said he.

"Because they do not pay their rent; they owe for two terms."

"How much is that?"

"Twenty francs," said the old woman.

Marius had thirty francs in reserve in a drawer.

"Here," said he to the old woman, "there are twenty-five francs. Pay for these poor people, give them five francs, and do not tell them that it is from me."

It happened that the regiment to which Lieutenant Théodule belonged came to be stationed at Paris. This was the occasion of a second idea occurring to Aunt Gillenormand; she plotted to have Théodule supplant Marius.

One morning, as Monsieur Gillenormand was reading something like *La Quotidienne*, his daughter entered, and said in her softest voice, for the matter concerned her favourite:

"Father, Théodule is coming this morning to present his respects to you."

"Who is that,—Théodule?"

"Your grandnephew."

"Ah!" said the grandfather.

Then he resumed his reading, thought no more of the grandnephew who was nothing more than any Théodule, and very soon was greatly excited, as was almost always the case when he read. The "sheet" which he had, royalist indeed—that was a matter of course,—announced for the next day, without any mollification, one of the little daily occurrences of the Paris of that time; that the students of the schools of Law and Medicine would meet in the Square of the Pantheon at noon—to deliberate. It did not require much more to enrage Monsieur Gillenormand.

He thought of Marius, who was a student, and who, probably, would go, like the others, "to deliberate, at noon, in the Square of the Pantheon."

While he was dwelling upon this painful thought, Lieutenant Théodule entered, in citizen's dress, which was adroit, and was discreetly introduced by Mademoiselle Gillenormand.

Mademoiselle Gillenormand said aloud to her father:

"Théodule, your grandnephew."

And, in a whisper, to the lieutenant:

"Say yes to everything."

"Ah! it is you; very well, take a seat," said the old man.

And then, he entirely forgot the lancer.

Théodule sat down, and Monsieur Gillenormand got up.

Monsieur Gillenormand began to walk up and down with his hands in his pockets, talking aloud, and rubbing with his nervous old fingers the two watches which he carried in his two waistcoat pockets.

"This mess of snivellers! they meet together in the Square of the Pantheon. To go out and jaw in the open air about the National Guard! I will bet anything you please, a million against a fig, that they will all be fugitives from justice and discharged convicts."

"It is true," said Théodule.

Monsieur Gillenormand turned his head half around, saw Théodule, and continued.

"Why did you leave my house? To go out and be a republican. Pish! in the first place the people do not want your republic, they do not want it, they have good sense, they know very well that there always have been kings, and that there always will be, they know very well that the people, after all, is nothing but the people, they laugh at your republic, do you understand, idiot? And then they have cannon in the court of the Louvre. Such is the brigandage of these things."

"You are right, uncle," said Théodule.

M. Gillenormand resumed:

"Cannon in the court of the Museum! what for? Do you want to shoot down the Apollo Belvedere? And all these foolish brats have political opinions. They ought to be strictly forbidden to have any political opinions. They fabricate systems, they reform society, they demolish monarchy, they upset all laws, they put the garret into the cellar, and my porter in place of the king, they turn Europe topsy-turvy, they rebuild the world. It needed some final hiccough, France is giving it. Deliberate, you rogues. Such things will happen as long as they go and read the papers under the arches of the Odeon. All these journals are a pest. Oh! just heavens! you can be proud of having thrown your grandfather into despair, you can!"

"That is evident," said Théodule.

And taking advantage of M. Gillenormand's drawing breath, the lancer added magisterially: "There ought to be no journal but the *Moniteur* and no book but the *Annuaire Militaire*."

M. Gillenormand went on.

"Citizens, I tell you that your progress is a lunacy, that your humanity is a dream, that your revolution is a crime, that your republic is a monster. I tell you that, my goodmen!"

"Zounds," cried the lieutenant, "that is wonderfully true."

M. Gillenormand broke off a gesture which he had begun, turned, looked the lancer Théodule steadily in the eyes, and said:

"You are a fool."

XVI. COSETTE

MARIUS was now a fine-looking young man, of medium height, with heavy jet black hair, a high intelligent brow, large and passionate nostrils, a frank and calm expression, and an indescribable something beaming from every feature, which was at once lofty, thoughtful and innocent. In a difficult situation he possessed all the essentials of stupidity; another turn of the screw, and he could become sublime. His manners were reserved, cold, polished, far from free. But as his mouth was very pleasant, his lips the reddest and his teeth the whitest in the world, his smile corrected the severity of his physiognomy. At certain moments there was a strange contrast between this chaste brow and this voluptuous smile. His eye was small, his look great.

At the time of his most wretched poverty, he noticed that girls turned when he passed, and with a deathly feeling in his heart he fled or hid himself. He thought they looked at him on account of his old clothes, and that they were laughing at him; the truth is, that they looked at him because of his graceful appearance, and that they dreamed over it.

This wordless misunderstanding between him and the pretty girls he met, had rendered him hostile to society. There were, however, two women from whom Marius never fled, and whom he did not at all avoid. One was the old woman with the beard, who swept his room, and who gave Courfeyrac an opportunity to say: "As his servant wears her beard, Marius does not wear his." The other was a little girl that he saw very often, and that he never looked at.

For more than a year Marius had noticed in a retired walk of the Luxembourg, the walk which borders the parapet of the Pépinière, a man and a girl quite young, nearly always sitting side by side, on the same seat, at the most retired end of the walk. The man might be sixty years old; he seemed sad and serious; his whole person presented the robust but wearied appearance of a soldier retired from active service. Had he worn a decoration, Marius would have said: it is an old officer. His expression was kind, but it did not invite approach, and he never returned a look. He wore a blue coat and pantaloons, and a broad-brimmed hat, which always appeared to be new; a black cravat, and Quaker linen, that is to say, brilliantly white, but of coarse texture.

The first time the young girl that accompanied him sat down on the seat which they seemed to have adopted, she looked like a girl of about thirteen or fourteen, puny to the extent of being almost ugly, awkward, insignificant, yet promising, perhaps, to have rather fine eyes. She wore the dress, at once aged and childish, peculiar to the convent school-girl, an ill-fitting garment of coarse black merino. They appeared to be father and daughter.

For two or three days Marius scrutinised this old man, who was not yet an aged man, and this little girl, not yet a woman; then he paid no more attention to them. For their part they did not even seem to see him.

Courfeyrac had noticed them at some time or other, but finding the girl homely, had avoided them. Struck by the dress of the little girl and the hair of the old man, he had named the daughter *Mademoiselle Lanoire* [*Black*] and the father *Monsieur Leblanc* [*White*]. The students said: "Ah! Monsieur Leblanc is at his seat!" and Marius, like the rest, had found it convenient to call this unknown gentleman M. Leblanc.

Marius saw them thus nearly every day at the same hour during the first year. He found the man very much to his liking, but the girl rather disagreeable.

The second year, Marius broke off this habit of going to the Luxembourg, without really knowing why himself, and there were nearly six months during which he did not set foot in his walk. At last he went back again and saw, still on the same seat, this well known pair. When he came near them, he saw that it was indeed the same man, but it seemed to him that it was no longer the same girl. The woman whom he now saw was a noble, beautiful creature, with all the most bewitching outlines of woman, at that pure and fleeting moment which can only be translated by these two words: sweet fifteen. Beautiful chestnut hair, shaded with veins of gold, a brow which seemed chiselled marble, cheeks which seemed made of roses, a pale incarnadine, a flushed whiteness, an exquisite mouth. And that nothing might be wanting to this ravishing form, the nose was not beautiful, it was pretty; neither straight nor curved, neither Italian nor Greek; it was the Parisian nose.

At the first instant Marius thought it was another daughter of the same man, a sister doubtless of her whom he had seen before. But when the invariable habit of his promenade led him for the second time near the seat, and he had looked at her attentively, he recognised that she was the same. In six months the little girl had become a young woman; that was all.

And then she was no longer the school-girl with her plush hat, her merino dress, her shapeless shoes, and her red hands. She wore a dress of black damask, a mantle of the same, and a white crape hat. Her white gloves showed the delicacy of her hand which played with the Chinese ivory handle of her parasol, and her silk boot betrayed the smallness of her foot.

As to the man, he was still the same.

The second time that Marius came near her, the young girl raised her eyes; they were of a deep celestial blue, but in this veiled azure was nothing yet beyond the look of a child. She looked at Marius as she would have looked at any little monkey playing under the sycamores, or the marble vase which cast its shadow over the bench; and Marius also continued his promenade thinking of something else.

He passed four or five times more by the seat where the young girl was, without even turning his eyes towards her.

One day the air was mild, the Luxembourg was flooded with sunshine and shadow, the sky was as clear as if the angels had washed it in the morning, the sparrows were twittering in the depths of the chestnut trees.

Marius was thinking of nothing, he was living and breathing, he passed near this seat, the young girl raised her eyes, their glances met.

But what was there now in the glance of the young girl? Marius could not have told. There was nothing, and there was everything. It was a strange flash.

She cast down her eyes, and he continued on his way.

There is a time when every young girl looks thus. Woe to him upon whom she looks!

At night, on returning to his garret, Marius cast a look upon his dress, and for the first time perceived that he had the slovenliness, the indecency, and the unheard-of stupidity, to promenade in the Luxembourg with his "every day" suit, a hat broken near the band, coarse teamsters' boots, black pantaloons shiny at the knees, and a black coat threadbare at the elbows.

The next day, at the usual hour, Marius took from his closet his new coat, his new pantaloons, his new hat, and his new boots; he dressed himself in this panoply complete, put on his gloves, prodigious prodigality, and went to the Luxembourg.

When he entered the walk he saw M. Leblanc and the young girl at the other end. He buttoned his coat, stretched it down that there might be no wrinkles, noticed with some complaisance the lustre of his pantaloons, and marched upon the seat.

As he drew nearer, his step became slower and slower. Before he had reached the end of the walk, he stopped, and he did not know himself how it happened, but he turned back. He did not even say to himself that he would not go to the end. It was doubtful if the young girl could see him so far off, and notice his fine appearance in his new suit. However, he held himself very straight, so that he might look well, in case anybody who was behind should happen to notice him.

He reached the opposite end and then returned, and this time he approached a little nearer to the seat. He even came to within about three trees of it, but there he felt an indescribable lack of power to go further, and he hesitated. He thought he had seen the young girl's face bent towards him. Still he made a great and manly effort, conquered his hesitation, and continued his advance. In a few seconds, he was passing before the seat, erect and firm, blushing to his ears, without daring to cast a look to the right or the left, and with his hand in his coat like a statesman. At the moment he passed under the guns of the fortress, he felt a frightful palpitation of the heart. She wore, as on the previous day, her damask dress and her crape hat. He heard the sound of an ineffable voice, which might be "her voice." She was talking quietly. She was very pretty. He felt it, though he made no effort to see her. "She could not, however," thought he, "but have some esteem and consideration for me, if she knew that I was the real author of the dissertation on Marcos Obregon de la Ronda, which Monsieur François de Neufchâteau has put, as his own, at the beginning of his edition of *Gil Blas!*"

He passed the seat, went to the end of the walk, which was quite near, then turned and passed again before the beautiful girl. This time he was very pale. Indeed, he was experiencing nothing that was not very disagreeable. He walked away from the seat and from the young girl, and although his back was turned, he imagined that she was looking at him, and that made him stumble.

He made no effort to approach the seat again, he stopped midway of the walk, and sat down there—a thing which he never did—casting many side glances, and thinking, in the most indistinct depths of his mind, that after all it must be difficult for persons whose white hat and black dress he admired, to be absolutely insensible to his glossy pantaloons and his new coat.

At the end of a quarter of an hour, he rose, as if to recommence his walk towards this seat, which was encircled by a halo. He, however, stood silent and motionless. For the first time in fifteen months, he said to himself, that this gentleman, who sat there every day with his daughter, had undoubtedly noticed him, and probably thought his assiduity very strange.

Next day, Ma'am Bougon,—thus Courfeyrac designated the old portress-landlady of the Gorbeau tenement,—was stupefied with astonishment to see Monsieur Marius go out again with his new coat.

He went again to the Luxembourg, but did not get beyond his seat midway of the walk. He sat down there as on the day previous, gazing from a distance and seeing distinctly the white hat, the black dress. He did not stir from the seat, and did not go home until the gates of the Luxembourg were shut. Later, some weeks afterwards, when he thought of it, he could not remember where he had dined that night.

The next day, for the third time, Ma'am Bougon was thunderstruck. Marius went out with his new suit. "Three days running!" she exclaimed.

She made an attempt to follow him, but Marius walked briskly and with immense strides; it was a hippopotamus undertaking to catch a chamois. In two minutes she lost sight of him, and came back out of breath, three quarters choked by her asthma, and furious. "The silly fellow," she muttered, "to put on his handsome clothes every day and make people run like that!"

Marius had gone to the Luxembourg.

The young girl was there with Monsieur Leblanc. Marius approached as near as he could, seeming to be reading a book, but he was still very far off, then he returned and sat down on his seat, where he spent four hours watching the artless little sparrows as they hopped along the walk; they seemed to him to be mocking him.

Thus a fortnight rolled away. Marius went to the Luxembourg, no longer to promenade, but to sit down, always in the same place, and without knowing why.

She was indeed of a marvelous beauty.

On one of the last days of the second week, Marius was as usual sitting on his seat, holding in his hand an open book of which he had not turned a leaf for two hours. Suddenly he trembled. A great event was commencing at the end of the walk. Monsieur Leblanc and his daughter had left their seat, the daughter had taken the arm of the father, and they were coming slowly towards the middle of the walk where Marius was.

Marius closed his book, then he opened it, then he made an attempt to read. "O dear!" thought he, "I shall not have time to take an attitude."

"What are they coming by here for?" he asked himself. He would gladly have been very handsome, he would gladly have worn the cross of the Legion of Honour. He imagined that Monsieur Leblanc was hurling angry looks upon him. "Is he going to speak to me?" thought he. He bowed his head; when he raised it they were quite near him. The young girl looked at him steadily; it seemed to him that she reproached him for having been so long without coming to her, and that she said: "It is I who come."

She seemed more beautiful than she had ever seemed before. He felt as though he was swimming in the deep blue sky. At the same time he was horribly disconcerted, because he had a little dust on his boots.

He met Courfeyrac under the arches of the Odeon, and said: "Come and dine with me." They went to Rousseau's and spent six francs. Marius ate like an ogre. He gave six sous to the waiter. At dessert he said to Courfeyrac: "Have you read the paper? What a fine speech Audry de Puyraveau has made!"

He was desperately in love.

Isolation, pride, independence, a taste for nature, lack of everyday material activity, life in one's self, the secret struggles of chastity, and an ecstasy of goodwill towards the whole creation, had prepared Marius for this possession. His worship for his father had become almost a religion, and, like all religion, had retired into the depths of his heart. He needed something above that. Love came.

A whole month passed during which Marius went every day to the Luxembourg. When the hour came, nothing could keep him away. Marius lived in transports. It is certain that the young girl looked at him.

He finally grew bolder, and approached nearer to the seat. However he passed before it no more, obeying at once the instinct of timidity and the instinct of prudence, peculiar to lovers. He thought it better not to attract the "attention of the father." He formed his combinations of stations behind trees and the pedestals of statues, with consummate art, so as to be seen as much as possible by the young girl and as little as possible by the old gentleman. Sometimes he would stand for half an hour motionless behind some Leonidas or Spartacus with a book in his hand, over which his eyes, timidly raised, were looking for the young girl, while she, for her part, was turning her charming profile towards him, suffused with a smile. While yet talking in the most natural and quiet way in the world with the white-haired man, she rested upon Marius all the dreams of a maidenly and passionate eye.

We must, however, suppose that M. Leblanc perceived something of this at last, for often when Marius came, he would rise and begin to promenade. He had left their accustomed place, and had taken the seat at the other end of the walk, near the Gladiator, as if to see whether Marius would follow them. Marius did not understand it, and committed that blunder. "The father" began to be less punctual and did not bring "his daughter" every day. Sometimes he came alone. Then Marius did not stay. Another blunder.

Marius took no note of these symptoms. From the phase of timidity he had passed, a natural and inevitable progress, to the phase of blindness. His love grew. He dreamed of her every night. And then there came to him a good fortune for which he had not even hoped, oil upon the fire, double darkness upon his eyes. One night, at dusk, he found on the seat, which "M. Leblanc and his daughter" had just left, a handkerchief, a plain handkerchief without embroidery, but white, fine, and which appeared to him to exhale ineffable odours. He seized it in transport. This handkerchief was marked with the letters U. F. It was evidently her first name. Ursula, thought he, what a sweet name! He kissed the handkerchief, inhaled its perfume, put it over his heart, and at night went to sleep with it on his lips.

"I feel her whole soul in it!" he exclaimed.

This handkerchief belonged to the old gentleman, who had simply let it fall from his pocket.

For days and days after this piece of good fortune, he always appeared at the Luxembourg kissing this handkerchief and placing it on his heart. The beautiful child did not understand this at all, and indicated it to him by signs, which he did not perceive.

"Oh, modesty!" said Marius.

Since we have pronounced the word *modesty*, and since we conceal nothing, we must say that once, however, through all his ecstasy, "Ursula" gave him a very serious pang. It was upon one of the days when she prevailed upon M. Leblanc to leave the seat and to promenade on the walk. A brisk north wind was blowing, which swayed the tops of the plane trees. Father and daughter, arm in arm, had just passed before Marius' seat.

Suddenly a gust of wind, rather more lively than the rest, rushed upon the walk, and raised her skirt, almost to the height of the garter. A limb of exquisite mould was seen. Marius saw it. He was exasperated and furious.

The young girl had put down her dress with a divinely startled movement, but he was outraged none the less. True, he was alone in the walk. But there might have been somebody there. And if anybody had been there! could one conceive of such a thing? what she had done was horrible! Alas, the poor child had done nothing; there was but one culprit, the wind; and yet Marius was determined to be dissatisfied, and was jealous of his shadow.

When "Ursula," reaching the end of the walk, returned with M. Leblanc, and passed before the seat on which Marius had again sat down, Marius threw at her a cross and cruel look. The young girl slightly straightened back, with that elevation of the eyelids, which says: "Well, what is the matter with him?"

That was their first quarrel.

Marius had hardly finished this scene with her when somebody came down the walk. It was an Invalide, very much bent, wrinkled and pale with age, in the uniform of Louis XV., with the little oval patch of red cloth with crossed swords on his back, the soldier's Cross of Saint Louis, and decorated also by a coat sleeve in which there was no arm, a silver chain, and a wooden leg. Marius thought he could discern that this man appeared to be very much pleased. It seemed to him even that the old cynic, as he hobbled along by him, had addressed to him a very fraternal and very merry wink, as if by some chance they had been put into communication and had enjoyed some dainty bit of good fortune together. What had he seen to be so pleased, this relic of Mars? What had happened between this leg of wood and the other? Marius had a paroxysm of jealousy. "Perhaps he was by!" said he; "perhaps he saw!" And he would have been glad to exterminate the Invalide.

Time lending his aid, this anger of Marius passed away. He forgave her at last; but it was a great effort; he pouted at her three days.

Meanwhile, in spite of all that, and because of all that, his passion was growing, and was growing mad.

We have seen how Marius discovered, or thought he discovered, that Her name was Ursula. In three or four weeks Marius had devoured this piece of good fortune. He desired another. He wished to know where she lived.

He had committed one blunder in falling into the snare of the seat by the Gladiator. He had committed a second by not remaining at the Luxembourg when Monsieur Leblanc came there alone. He committed a third, a monstrous one. He followed "Ursula."

One night after he had seen them disappear at the porte-cochère, he entered after them, and said boldly to the porter:—

"Is it the gentleman on the first floor who has just come in?"

"No," answered the porter. "It is the gentleman on the third."

Another fact. This success made Marius still bolder.

"In front?" he asked.

"Faith!" said the porter, "the house is only built on the street."

"And what is this gentleman?"

"He lives on his income, monsieur. A very kind man, who does a great deal of good among the poor, though not rich."

"What is his name?" continued Marius.

The porter raised his head, and said:—

"Is monsieur a detective?"

Marius retired, much abashed, but still in great transports. He was getting on.

"Good," thought he. "I know that her name is Ursula, that she is the daughter of a retired gentleman, and that she lives there, in the third story, in the Rue de l'Ouest."

Next day Monsieur Leblanc and his daughter made but a short visit to the Luxembourg; they went away while it was yet broad daylight. Marius followed them, as was his custom. On reaching the porte-cochère, Monsieur Leblanc passed his daughter in, and then stopped, and before entering himself, turned and looked steadily at Marius. The day after that they did not come to the Luxembourg. Marius waited in vain all day.

At nightfall he went to the Rue de l'Ouest, and saw a light in the windows of the third story. He walked beneath these windows until the light was put out.

The next day nobody was at the Luxembourg. Marius waited all day, and then went to perform his night duty under the windows. That took him till ten o'clock in the evening. His dinner took care of itself. Fever supports the sick man, and love the lover.

He passed a week in this way. Monsieur Leblanc and his daughter appeared at the Luxembourg no more. Marius made melancholy conjectures; he dared not watch the porte-cochère during the day.

On the eighth day when he reached the house, there was no light in the windows. "What!" said he, "the lamp is not yet lighted. But yet it is dark. Or they have gone out?" He waited till ten o'clock. Till midnight. Till one o'clock in the morning. No light appeared in the third story windows, and nobody entered the house. He went away very gloomy.

On the morrow he found nobody at the Luxembourg, he waited; at dusk he went to the house. No light in the windows; the blinds were closed; the third story was entirely dark.

Marius knocked at the porte-cochère; went in and said to the porter:—
"The gentleman of the third floor?"
"Moved," answered the porter.
"Since when?"
"Yesterday."
"Where does he live now?"
"I don't know anything about it."
"He has not left his new address, then?"
"No."
And the porter, looking up, recognised Marius.
"What! it is you!" said he, but decidedly now, "you do keep bright lookout."

XVII. THE CAVE

EVERY HUMAN SOCIETY has what is called in the theatres *a third sub-stage*. The social soil is mined everywhere, sometimes for good, sometimes for evil. The dark caverns, these gloomy protectors of primitive Christianity, were awaiting only an opportunity to explode beneath the Cæsars, and to flood the human race with light. The catacombs, where the first mass was said, were not merely the cave of Rome; they were the cavern of the world.

There is under the social structure, this complex wonder of a mighty burrow,—of excavations of every kind. There is the religious mine, the philosophic mine, the political mine, the economic mine, the revolutionary mine. This pick with an idea, that pick with a figure, the other pick with a vengeance. They call and they answer from one catacomb to another. Utopias travel under ground in the passages. They branch out in every direction. They sometimes meet there and fraternize. Jean Jacques lends his pick to Diogenes, who lends him his lantern. Sometimes they fight. But nothing checks or interrupts the simultaneous activity, which goes to and fro, and up and down, and up again, in these dusky regions, and which slowly transforms the upper through the lower, and the outer through the inner. Society has hardly a suspicion of this vast unknown swarming of workers which, without touching its surface, changes its substance. What comes from all this deep delving? The future.

The deeper we sink, the more mysterious are the workers. To a degree which social philosophy can recognise, the work is good; beyond this degree it is doubtful and mixed; below, it becomes terrible. At a certain depth, the excavations become inpenetrable to the soul of civilisation, the respirable limit of man is passed; the existence of monsters becomes possible. The demon is dimly rough-hewn; every one for himself. The eyeless I howls, searches, gropes, and gnaws.

The savage outlines which prowl over this grave, half brute, half phantom, have no thought for universal progress, they ignore ideas and words, they have no care but for individual glut. They are almost unconscious, and there is in them a horrible defacement. From suffering these goblins pass to crime. What crawls in the third sub-stage is no longer the stifled demand for the absolute, it is the protest of matter.

We have just seen one of the compartments of the upper mine, the great political, revolutionary, and philosophic sap. There, it is true, men may be deceived and are deceived, but there error is venerable, so much heroism does it imply. For the sum of all work which is done there, there is one name: Progress.

The time has come to open other depths, the depths of horror.

There is beneath society, we must insist upon it, and until the day when ignorance shall be no more, there will be, the great cavern of evil.

This cave is beneath all, and is the enemy of all. It is hate universal. It does not undermine, in its hideous crawl, merely the social order of the time; it undermines philosophy, it undermines science, it undermines law, it undermines human thought, it undermines civilisation, it undermines revolution, it undermines progress. It goes by the naked names of theft, prostitution, murder, and assassination. It is darkness, and it desires chaos. It is vaulted in with ignorance. Destroy the cave Ignorance, and you destroy the mole Crime.

A quartette of bandits, Claquesous, Gueulemer, Babet, and Montparnasse, ruled from 1830 to 1835 over the third sub-stage of Paris.

Gueulemer was a Hercules without a pedestal. His cave was the Arche-Marion sewer. He was six feet high, and had a marble chest, brazen biceps, cavernous lungs, a colossus' body, and a bird's skull.

The diaphaneity of Babet contrasted with the meatiness of Gueulemer. Babet was thin and shrewd. He was transparent, but impenetrable. You could see the light through his bones, but nothing through his eye. He professed to be a chemist. He had been bar-keeper. He had played vaudeville at Saint Mihiel. He had been married, and had had children. What had become of his wife and children, he did not know. He had lost them as one loses his pocket-handkerchief.

What was Claquesous? He was night. Before showing himself, he waited till the sky was daubed with black. At night he came out of a hole, which he went into again before day. Where was this hole? Nobody knew. Was his name Claquesous? No. He said: "My name is Nothing-at-all." He was a ventriloquist.

Montparnasse was a child; less than twenty, with a pretty face, lips like cherries, charming black locks, the glow of spring in his eyes; he had all the vices and aspired to all the crimes. Montparnasse was a fashion-plate living in distress and committing murders. The cause of all the crimes of this young man was his desire to be well dressed. Frizzled, pomaded, with slender waist, hips like a woman, the bust of a Prussian officer, a buzz of admiration about him from the girls of the boulevard, an elaborately-tied cravat, a sling-shot in his pocket, a flower in his button-hole; such was this charmer of the sepulchre.

These four men were not four men; it was a sort of mysterious robber with four heads preying upon Paris by wholesale; it was the monstrous polyp of evil which inhabits the crypt of society.

By means of their ramifications and the underlying network of their relations, Babet, Gueulemer, Claquesous, and Montparnasse, controlled the general lying-in-wait business of the Department of the Seine. Originators of ideas in this line, men of midnight imagination came to them for the execution. The four villains being furnished with the single draft, they took charge of putting it on the stage. They worked upon scenario. They had a company of actors of darkness at the disposition of every cavernous tragedy.

What has become of these men? They still exist, and so long as society shall be what it is, they will be what they are. Under the dark vault of their cave, they are for ever reproduced from the ooze.

What is required to exorcise these goblins? Light. Light in floods. No bat resists the dawn. Illuminate the bottom of society.

SUMMER passed, then autumn; winter came. Neither M. Leblanc nor the young girl had set foot in the Luxembourg. Marius searched continually; he searched everywhere: he found nothing. He was no longer Marius the enthusiastic dreamer; he was a lost dog. It seemed to him that everything had disappeared.

He reproached himself a hundred times. Why did I follow her? I was so happy in seeing her only! She looked upon me; was not that infinite? She had the appearance of loving me. Was not that everything? I desired to have what? There is nothing more after that. I was a fool.

Once, confiding in a beautiful September sun, Marius allowed himself to be taken to the Bal de Sceaux, by Courfeyrac, Bossuet, and Grantaire, hoping, what a dream! that he might possibly find her there. We need not say that he did not see her whom he sought. "But yet it is here that all the lost women are to be found," muttered Grantaire.

At another time, an accidental meeting produced a singular effect upon him. In one of the little streets in the neighbourhood of the Boulevard des Invalides, he saw a man dressed like a labourer, wearing a cap with a long visor, from beneath which escaped a few locks of very white hair. Marius was struck by the beauty of this white hair, and noticed the man who was walking with slow steps and seemed absorbed in painful meditation. Strangely enough, it appeared to him that he recognised M. Leblanc. But why these working-man's clothes? what did that mean? what did this disguise signify? The man had taken some little side-street, and Marius could not find him again. "After all," said he to himself, "it is probably only a resemblance."

Marius still lived in the Gorbeau tenement. He paid no attention to anybody there.

At this time, there were no occupants remaining in the house but himself and those Jondrettes whose rent he had once paid. The other tenants had moved away or died, or had been turned out for not paying their rent.

One day, in the course of this winter, Marius went slowly up the boulevard towards the barrière. He was walking thoughtfully, with his head down.

Suddenly he felt that he was elbowed in the dusk; he turned, and saw two young girls in rags, one tall and slender, the other a little shorter, passing rapidly by, breathless, frightened, and apparently in flight; they had met him, had not seen him, and had jostled him in passing. Marius could see in the twilight their hair tangled and flying, their frightful bonnets, their tattered skirts, and their naked feet. As they ran they were talking to each other. The taller one said in a very low voice:

"The *cognes* came. They just missed *pincer* me at the *demi-cercle*."

The other answered: "I saw them. I *cavalé, cavalé, cavalé*."

Marius understood, through this dismal argot, that the gendarmes, or the city police, had not succeeded in seizing these two girls, and that the girls had escaped. They plunged in under the trees of the boulevard behind him. Marius was about to resume his course when he perceived a little greyish packet on the ground at his feet. He stooped down and picked it up. It was a sort of envelope which appeared to contain papers.

"Good," said he, "those poor creatures must have dropped this!"

He retraced his steps, he called, he did not find them; he concluded they were already beyond hearing, put the packet in his pocket and went to dinner.

In the evening, as he was undressing to go to bed, he happened to feel in his coat-pocket the packet which he had picked up on the boulevard. He had forgotten it. He thought it might be well to open it, and that the packet might perhaps contain the information necessary to restore it.

It was unsealed and contained four letters, also unsealed.

All four exhaled an odour of wretched tobacco.

The first letter was addressed: *To Madame, Madame the Marchioness de Grucheray, Square opposite the Chamber of Deputies, No.* ——

Marius said to himself that he should probably find in this letter the information of which he was in search, and that, moreover, as the letter was not sealed, probably it might be read without impropriety.

It was in these words:

"Madame the Marchioness:

"The virtue of kindness and piety is that which binds sosiety most closely. Call up your christian sentiment, and cast a look of compassion upon this unfortunate Spanish victim of loyalty and attachment to the sacred cause of legitimacy, which he has paid for with his blood, consecrated his fortune, wholy, to defend this cause, and to-day finds himself in the greatest missery. He has no doubt that your honourable self will furnish him assistance to preserve an existence extremely painful for a soldier of education and of honour full of wounds, reckons in advance upon the humanity which animmates you and upon the interest which Madame the Marchioness feels in a nation so unfortunate. Their prayer will not be in vain, and their memory will retain herr charming souvenir.

"From my respectful sentiments with which I have the honour to be
  "Madame,

    *"*DON ALVARÈS, *Spanish captain of cabalry, royalist refuge in France, who finds himself traveling for his country and ressources fail him to continue his travells."*

No address was added to the signature. Marius hoped to find the address in the second letter the superscription of which ran: *to Madame, Madame the Comtess de Montvernet, Rue Cassette, No. 9.* Marius read as follows:

"Madame the Comtess,

"It is an unfortunate mothur of a family of six children the last of whom is only eight months old. Me sick since my last lying-in, abandoned by my husband for five months haveing no ressources in the world the most frightful indigance.

"In the hope of Madame the Comtesse, she has the honour to be, Madame, with a profound respect,

*"*MOTHER BALIZARD.*"*

Marius passed to the third letter, which was, like the preceding, a begging one. Marius finally opened the fourth letter. There was on the address: *To the beneficent gentleman of the church of Saint Jacques du Haut Pas.* It contained these few lines:

"Beneficent man.

"If you will deign to accompany my daughter, you will see a misserable calamity, and I will show you my certificates.

"At the sight of these writings your generous soul will be moved with a sentiment of lively benevolence, for true philosophers always experience vivid emotions.

"Agree, compassionate man, that one must experience the most cruel

necessity, and that it is very painful, to obtain relief, to have it attested by authority, as if we were not free to suffer and to die of inanition while waiting for some one to relieve our missery. The fates are very cruel to some and too lavish or too careful to others.

"I await your presence or your offering, if you deign to make it, and I pray you to have the kindness to accept the respectful sentiments with which I am proud to be,

"Truly magnanimous man,
 "Your very humble
   And very obedient servant,
     "P. FABANTOU, dramatic artist."

After reading these letters, Marius did not find himself much wiser than before.

In the first place none of the signers gave his address.

Then they seemed to come from four different individuals, Don Alvarès, Mother Balizard, the poet Genflot, and the dramatic artist Fabantou; but, strangely enough, these letters were all four written in the same hand.

What was the conclusion from that, unless that they came from the same person?

Moreover, and this rendered the conjecture still more probable, the paper, coarse and yellow, was the same in all four, the odour of tobacco was the same, and although there was an evident endeavour to vary the style, the same faults of orthography were reproduced with a very quiet certainty, and Genflot, the man of letters, was no more free from them than the Spanish captain.

Marius put them back into the envelope, threw it into a corner, and went to bed.

About seven o'clock in the morning, he had got up and breakfasted, and was trying to set about his work when there was a gentle rap at his door.

"What do you want, Ma'am Bougon?" asked Marius, without raising his eyes from the books and papers on his table.

A voice, not Ma'am Bougon's, answered:

"I beg your pardon, Monsieur—"

It was a hollow, cracked, smothered, rasping voice, the voice of an old man, roughened by brandy and by liquors.

Marius turned quickly and saw a young girl.

In her early childhood, she must have been pretty. The grace of her youth was still struggling against the hideous old age brought on by debauchery and poverty.

"What do you wish, mademoiselle?"

The young girl answered with her voice like a drunken galley-slave's:

"Here is a letter for you, Monsieur Marius."

Without waiting for an invitation, she entered. Great holes in her skirt revealed her long limbs and her sharp knees. She was shivering.

She had really in her hand a letter which she presented to Marius.

Marius, in opening this letter, noticed that the enormously large wafer was still wet. The message could not have come far. He read:

"*My amiable neighbour, young man!*

"*I have lerned your kindness towards me, that you have paid my rent six months ago. I bless you, young man. My eldest daughter will tell you that we have been without a morsel of bread for two days, four persons, and my spouse sick. If I am not desseived by my thoughts, I think I may hope that your generous heart will soften at this exposure and that the desire will subjugate you of being propitious to me by deigning to lavish upon me some light gift.*

"*I am with the distinguished consideration which is due to the benefactors of humanity,*

"JONDRETTE

"*P. S. My daughter will await your orders, dear Monsieur Marius.*"

This letter, in the midst of the obscure accident which had occupied Marius' thoughts since the previous evening, was a candle in a cave. Everything was suddenly cleared up.

This letter came from the same source as the other four. It was the same writing, the same style, the same orthography, the same paper, the same odour of tobacco. The Spanish Captain Don Alvarès, the unfortunate mother Balizard, the dramatic poet Genflot, the old comedy writer Fabantou, were all four named Jondrette, if indeed the name of Jondrette himself was Jondrette.

During the now rather long time that Marius had lived in the tenement, he must have met the Jondrettes in the passage and on the stairs, more than once, but to him they were only shadows; he had taken so little notice that on the previous evening he had brushed against the Jondrette girls upon the boulevard without recognising them; and it was with great difficulty that this girl, who had just come into his room, awakened beneath his disgust and pity a vague remembrance of having met with her elsewhere.

Now he understood that the occupation of his neighbour Jondrette in his distress was to work upon the sympathies of benevolent persons; that he procured their addresses, and that he wrote under assumed names letters to people whom he deemed rich and compassionate.

Meantime, while Marius fixed upon her an astonished and sorrowful look, the young girl was walking to and fro in the room.

"Ah," said she, "you have a mirror!"

She went to the table.

"Ah!" said she, "books! I can read, I can."

She hastily caught up the book which lay open on the table, and read fluently:

"—General Bauduin received the order to take five battalions of his brigade and carry the château of Hougomont, which is in the middle of the plain of Waterloo—"

She stopped:

"Ah, Waterloo! I know that. It is a battle in old times. My father was there; my father served in the armies. We are jolly good Bonapartists at home, that we are. Against English, Waterloo is."

She put down the book, took up a pen, and exclaimed:

"And I can write, too!"

She dipped the pen in the ink, and turning towards Marius:

"Would you like to see? Here, I am going to write a word to show."

And before he had had time to answer, she wrote upon a sheet of blank paper which was on the middle of the table: "*The Cognes are here.*"

Then, throwing down the pen:

"There are no mistakes in spelling. You can look. We have received an education, my sister and I. We have not always been what we are. We were not made—"

Then she looked at Marius, and said to him:

"Do you know, Monsieur Marius, that you are a very pretty boy?"

She went to him, and laid her hand on his shoulder: "You pay no attention to me, but I know you, Monsieur Marius. I meet you here on the stairs, and then I see you visiting a man named Father Mabeuf, who lives out by Austerlitz, sometimes, when I am walking that way. That becomes you very well, your tangled hair."

Marius had drawn back quietly.

"Mademoiselle," said he, with cold gravity, "I have here a packet, which is yours, I think. Permit me to return it to you."

And he handed her the envelope, which contained the four letters.

She clapped her hands and exclaimed:

"We have looked everywhere!"

Then she snatched the packet, and opened the envelope, saying:

"Lordy, Lordy, haven't we looked, my sister and I? And you have found it! on the boulevard, didn't you? It must have been on the boulevard? You see, this dropped when we ran."

Meanwhile she had unfolded the petition addressed "to the beneficent gentleman of the church of Saint Jacques du Haut Pas."

"Here!" said she, "this is for the old fellow who goes to mass. And this too is the hour. I am going to carry it to him. He will give us something perhaps for breakfast."

Then she began to laugh, and added:

"Do you know what it will be if we have breakfast to-day? It will be that we shall have had our breakfast for day before yesterday, our dinner for day before yesterday, our breakfast for yesterday, our dinner for yesterday, all that at one time this morning. Yes! if you're not satisfied, stuff till you burst, dogs!"

This reminded Marius of what the poor girl had come to his room for.

He felt in his waistcoat, he found nothing there.

The young girl continued, seeming to talk as if she were no longer conscious that Marius was there present.

"Sometimes I go away at night. Sometimes I do not come back. Before coming to this place, the other winter, we lived under the arches of the bridges. We hugged close to each other so as not to freeze. My little sister cried. How chilly the water is! When I thought of drowning myself, I said: No; it is too cold. When one has not eaten, it is very queer."

After a thorough exploration of his pockets, Marius had at last got together five francs and sixteen sous. This was at the time all that he had in the world. "That is enough for my dinner to-day," thought he, "to-morrow we will see." He took the sixteen sous, and gave the five francs to the young girl.

For five years Marius had lived in poverty, in privation, in distress even, but he perceived that he had never known real misery. In fact, he who has seen the misery of man only has seen nothing, he must see the misery of woman; he who has seen the misery of woman only has seen nothing, he must see the misery of childhood.

When man has reached the last extremity, he comes, at the same time, to the last expedients. Woe to the defenceless beings who surround him! Fathers, mothers, children, brothers, sisters, men, women, girls, cling together, and almost grow together like a mineral formation, in that dark promiscuity of sexes, of relationships, of ages, of infancy, of innocence.

This young girl was to Marius a sort of messenger from the night. She revealed to him an entire and hideous aspect of the darkness.

Marius almost reproached himself with the fact that he had been so absorbed in his reveries and passion that he had not until now cast a glance upon his neighbours. Paying their rent was a mechanical impulse; everybody would have had that impulse; but he, Marius, should have done better. What! a mere wall separated him from these abandoned beings, who lived by groping in the night without the pale of the living. Undoubtedly they seemed very depraved, very corrupt, very vile, very hateful, even, but those are rare who fall without becoming degraded; there is a point, moreover, at which the unfortunate and the infamous are associated and confounded in a single word, a fatal word, Les Misérables; whose fault is it? And then, is it not when the fall is lowest that charity ought to be greatest?

While he thus preached to himself, Marius looked at the wall which separated him from the Jondrettes, as if he could send his pitying glance through that partition to warn those unfortunate beings. The wall was a thin layer of plaster, upheld by laths and joists, through which, as we have just seen, voices and words could be distinguished perfectly. None but the dreamer, Marius, would not have perceived this before. There was no paper hung on this wall, either on the side of the Jondrettes, or on Marius' side; its coarse construction was bare to the eye. Almost unconsciously, Marius examined this partition. Suddenly he noticed towards the top, near the ceiling, a triangular hole, where three laths left a space between them. The plaster which should have stopped this hole was gone, and by getting upon the bureau he could see through that hole into the Jondrettes' garret.

Pity has and should have its curiosity. This hole was a kind of Judas. It is lawful to look upon misfortune like a betrayer for the sake of relieving it. "Let us see what these people are," thought Marius, "and to what they are reduced."

He climbed upon the bureau, put his eye to the crevice, and looked.

DEN for den, those of beasts are preferable to those of men. Caverns are better than the wretched holes which shelter humanity.

Marius was poor and his room was poorly furnished, but even as his poverty was noble, his garret was clean. The den into which his eyes were at that moment directed, was abject, filthy, fetid, infectious, gloomy, unclean. All the furniture was a straw chair, a rickety table, a few old broken dishes, and in two of the corners two indescribable pallets; all the light came from a dormer window of four panes, curtained with spiders' webs. The walls had a leprous look, and were covered with seams and scars like a face disfigured by some horrible malady; a putrid moisture oozed from them. Obscene pictures could be discovered upon them coarsely sketched in charcoal.

The room which Marius occupied had a broken brick pavement; this one was neither paved nor floored; the inmates walked immediately upon the old plastering of the ruinous tenement, which had grown black under their feet. However, this room had a fireplace; so it rented for forty francs a year. In the fireplace there was a little of everything, a chafing-dish, a kettle, some broken boards, rags hanging on nails, a bird cage, some ashes, and even a little fire. Two embers were smoking sullenly.

The size of this garret added still more to its horror. It had projections, angles, black holes, recesses under the roof, bays, and promontories. Beyond were hideous, unfathomable corners, which seemed as if they must be full of spiders as big as one's fist, centipedes as large as one's foot, and perhaps even some unknown monsters of humanity.

By the table, upon which Marius saw a pen, ink, and paper, was seated a man of about sixty, small, thin, livid, haggard, with a keen, cruel, and restless air; a hideous harpy.

This man had a long grey beard. He was dressed in a woman's chemise, which showed his shaggy breast and his naked arms bristling with grey hairs. Below this chemise were a pair of muddy pantaloons and boots from which the toes stuck out.

He had a pipe in his mouth, and was smoking. There was no more bread in the den, but there was tobacco.

He was writing, probably some such letter as those which Marius had read.

As he wrote, the man talked aloud, and Marius heard his words:

"To think that there is no equality even when we are dead! Look at Père Lachaise! The great, those who are rich, are in the upper part, in the avenue of the acacias, which is paved. They can go there in a carriage. The low, the poor, the unfortunate, they are put in the lower part, where there is mud up to the knees, in holes, in the wet. They are put there so that they may rot sooner! You cannot go to see them without sinking into the ground."

Here he stopped, struck his fist on the table, and added, gnashing his teeth: "Oh! I could eat the world!"

A big woman, who might have been forty years old or a hundred, was squatting near the fireplace, upon her bare feet.

She also was dressed only in a chemise and a knit skirt patched with pieces of old cloth. A coarse tow apron covered half the skirt. Although this woman was bent and drawn up into herself, it could be seen that she was very tall. She had hideous hair, light red sprinkled with grey, that she pushed back from time to time with her huge shining hands.

Upon one of the pallets Marius could discern a slender little wan girl, the younger sister, doubtless, of the one who had come to his room.

Marius was about to get down from the sort of observatory which he had extemporised, when a sound induced him to remain.

The door of the garret was hastily opened. The eldest daughter appeared upon the threshold. On her feet she had coarse men's shoes, covered with mud, which had been spattered as high as her red ankles, and she was wrapped in a ragged old gown which Marius had not seen upon her an hour before, but which she had probably left at his door that she might inspire the more pity. She came in, pushed the door to behind her, stopped to take breath, for she was quite breathless, then cried with an expression of joy and triumph:

"He is coming!"

The father turned his eyes, the woman turned her head, the younger sister did not stir.

"Who?" asked the father.

"The gentleman!"

"The philanthropist?"

"Yes."

"Of the church of Saint Jacques?"

"Yes."

"He is going to come?"

"He is coming in a fiacre."

"In a fiacre. It is Rothschild?"

The father arose.

"How are you sure? if he is coming in a fiacre, how is it that you get here before him? you gave him the address, at least? you told him the last door at the end of the hall on the right?"

"Tut, tut, tut!" said the girl, "how you run on! I went into the church, he was at his usual place, I made a curtsey to him, and I gave him the letter, he read it and said to me: Where do you live, my child? I said: Monsieur, I will show you. He said to me: No, give me your address; my daughter has some purchases to make, I am going to take a carriage and I will get to your house as soon as you do. I gave him the address. When I told him the house, he appeared surprised and hesitated an instant, then he said: It is all the same, I will go. When mass was over, I saw him leave the church with his daughter. I saw them get into a fiacre. And I told him plainly the last door at the end of the hall on the right."

"And how do you know that he will come?"

"I just saw the fiacre coming into the Rue du Petit Banquier. That is what made me run."

The girl looked resolutely at her father, and showing the shoes which she had on, said:

"I tell you that I shall never put on these shoes again. I would rather go barefoot."

"You are right," answered the father, in a mild tone which contrasted with the rudeness of the young girl, "but they would not let you go into the churches; the poor must have shoes. People do not go to God's house barefooted," added he bitterly. Then returning to the subject which occupied his thoughts—

"And you are sure then, sure that he is coming?"

"He is at my heels," said she.

The man sprang up.

"Wife!" cried he, "you hear. Here is the philanthropist. Put out the fire."

The astounded woman did not stir.

The father, with the agility of a mountebank, caught a broken pot which stood on the mantel, and threw some water upon the embers.

Then turning to his elder daughter:

"You! unbottom the chair!"

He seized the chair, and with a kick he ruined the seat. His leg went through it.

As he drew out his leg, he asked his daughter:

"Is it cold?"

"Very cold. It snows."

The father turned towards the younger girl, who was on the pallet near the window, and cried in a thundering voice:

"Quick! off the bed, good-for-nothing! will you never do anything? break a pane of glass!"

The little girl sprang off the bed trembling.

"Break a pane of glass!" said he again.

The child was speechless.

"Do you hear me?" repeated the father, "I tell you to break a pane!"

The child, with a sort of terrified obedience, rose upon tiptoe and struck her fist into a pane. The glass broke and fell with a crash.

"Good," said the father.

He was serious, yet rapid. His eye ran hastily over all the nooks and corners of the garret.

You would have said he was a general, making his final preparations at the moment when the battle was about to begin.

The mother, who had not yet said a word, got up and asked in a slow, muffled tone, her words seeming to come out as if curdled:

"Dear, what is it you want to do?"

"Get into bed," answered the man.

His tone admitted of no deliberation. The mother obeyed, and threw herself heavily upon one of the pallets.

Meanwhile a sob was heard in a corner.

"What is that?" cried the father.

The younger daughter showed her bleeding fist. It was the mother's turn to cry out.

"You see now! what stupid things you are doing! breaking your glass, she has cut herself!"

"So much the better!" said the man. "I knew she would."

"How! so much the better?" resumed the woman.

"Silence!" replied the father. "I suppress the liberty of the press."

Then tearing the chemise which he had on, he made a bandage with which he hastily wrapped up the little girl's bleeding wrist.

That done, his eye fell upon the torn chemise with satisfaction.

"And the chemise too," said he, "all this has a good appearance."

An icy wind whistled at the window and came into the room. The mist from without entered and spread about like a whitish wadding picked apart by invisible fingers. Through the broken pane the falling snow was seen. The cold promised the day before by the Candlemas sun had come indeed.

The father cast a glance about him as if to assure himself that he had forgotten nothing. He took an old shovel and spread ashes over the moistened embers in such a way as to hide them completely.

Then rising and standing with his back to the chimney:

"Do you know," resumed the father, "that it is cold as a dog in this devilish garret? If this man should not come! Oh! that is it! he makes us wait for him! he says: Well! they will wait for me! that is what they are for!—Oh! how I hate them, these professed charitable men, who go to mass, and who think themselves above us, and who come to humiliate us, and to bring us clothes! as they call them! rags which are not worth four sous, and bread! that is not what I want of the rabble! I want money! But what now is he doing, your mug of a benevolent gentleman? is he coming? The brute may have forgotten the address! I will bet that the old fool—"

Just then there was a light rap at the door, the man rushed forward and opened it, exclaiming with many low bows and smiles of adoration:

"Come in, monsieur! deign to come in, my noble benefactor, as well as your charming young lady."

Marius had not left his place. What he felt at that moment escapes human language.

It was She.

Marius could hardly discern her through the luminous vapour which suddenly spread over his eyes. It was that sweet absent being, that star which had been his light. She appeared again in this gloom, in this garret, in this shapeless den, in this horror!

She was still the same, a little paler only; her delicate face was set in a violet velvet hat, her form was hidden under a black satin pelisse, below her long dress he caught a glimpse of her little foot squeezed into a silk buskin.

She was still accompanied by Monsieur Leblanc.

She stepped into the room and laid a large package on the table.

The elder Jondrette girl had retreated behind the door and was looking upon that velvet hat, that silk dress, and that charming happy face, with an evil eye.

The den was so dark that people who came from outdoors felt as if they were entering a cellar on coming in. The two newcomers stepped forward, therefore, with some hesitation. Monsieur Leblanc said to the father:

"Monsieur, you will find in this package some new clothes, some stockings, and some new coverlids."

"Our angelic benefactor overwhelms us," said Jondrette, bowing down to the floor. Then, stooping to his eldest daughter's ear, he added rapidly in a whisper:

"Well! what did I tell you? rags? no money. They are all alike! Tell me, how was the letter to this old blubber-lip signed?"

"Fabantou," answered the daughter.

"The dramatic artist, good!"

This was lucky for Jondrette, for at that very moment Monsieur Leblanc turned towards him and said to him, with the appearance of one who is trying to recollect a name:

"I see that you are indeed to be pitied, Monsieur—"

"Fabantou," said Jondrette quickly.

"Monsieur Fabantou, yes, that is it. I remember."

"Dramatic artist, monsieur, and who has had his successes."

Here Jondrette evidently thought the moment come to make an impression upon the "philanthropist." He exclaimed in a tone of voice which belongs to the braggadocio of the juggler at a fair, and, at the same time, to the humility of a beggar on the highway: "Pupil of Talma! Monsieur! I am a pupil of Talma! Fortune once smiled on me. Alas! now it is the turn of misfortune. Look, my benefactor, no bread, no fire. My poor darlings have no fire! My only chair unseated! A broken window! in such weather as is this! My spouse in bed! sick!"

"Poor woman!" said Monsieur Leblanc.

"My child injured!" added Jondrette.

The child, whose attention had been diverted by the arrival of the strangers, was staring at "the young lady," and had ceased her sobbing. Jondrette pinched her injured hand. The little one uttered loud cries.

The adorable young girl whom Marius in his heart called "his Ursula" went quickly to her:

"Poor, dear child!" said she.

"Look, my beautiful young lady," pursued Jondrette, "her bleeding wrist! It is an accident which happened in working at a machine by which she earned six sous a day. It may be necessary to cut off her arm."

"Indeed!" said the old gentleman alarmed.

The little girl, taking this seriously, began to sob again beautifully.

"Alas, yes, my benefactor!" answered the father.

For some moments, Jondrette had been looking at "the philanthropist" in a strange manner. Suddenly, taking advantage of a moment when the newcomers were anxiously questioning the smaller girl about her mutilated hand, he passed over to his wife who was lying in her bed, appearing to be overwhelmed and stupid, and said to her quickly and in a very low tone:

"Notice that man!"

Then turning towards M. Leblanc, and continuing his lamentation:

"You see, monsieur! my whole dress is nothing but a chemise of my wife's! and that all torn! in the heart of winter. I cannot go out, for lack of a coat. If I had a sign of a coat, I should go to see Mademoiselle Mars, who knows me, and of whom I am a great favourite. She is still living in the Rue de la Tour des Dames, is not she? You know, monsieur, we have played together in the provinces. I shared her laurels. Celimène would come to my relief, monsieur! But no, not a sou in the house! My wife sick, not a sou! My daughter dangerously injured, not a sou! My spouse has choking fits. She needs aid, and my daughter also! But the doctor! but the druggist! how can I pay them! not a penny! I would fall on my knees before a penny, monsieur! You see how the arts are fallen! And do you know, monsieur, my worthy monsieur, do you know what is going to happen to-morrow? To-morrow is the fatal day, the last delay that my landlord will give me; if I do not pay him this evening, to-morrow my eldest daughter, myself, my spouse with her fever, my child with her wound, we shall all four be turned out of doors, and driven off into the street, into the rain, upon the snow. You see, monsieur, I owe four quarters, a year! that is sixty francs."

Jondrette lied. Four quarters would have made but forty francs, and he could not have owed for four, since it was not six months since Marius had paid for two.

M. Leblanc took five francs from his pocket and threw them on the table.

Jondrette had time to mutter into the ear of his elder daughter: "That will not pay for my chair and my window! I must make my expenses!"

Meantime, M. Leblanc had taken off a large brown overcoat, which he wore over his blue surtout, and hung it over the back of the chair.

"Monsieur Fabantou," said he, "I have only these five francs with me; but I am going to take my daughter home, and I will return this evening; is it not this evening that you have to pay?"

Jondrette's face lighted up with a strange expression.

"Yes, my noble monsieur. At eight o'clock, I must be at my landlord's."

"I will be here at six o'clock, and I will bring you the sixty francs."

"My benefactor!" cried Jondrette.

M. Leblanc took the arm of the beautiful young girl, and turned towards the door:

"Till this evening, my friends," said he.

"Six o'clock," said Jondrette.

"Six o'clock precisely."

Just then the overcoat on the chair caught the eye of the elder daughter.

"Monsieur," said she, "you forget your coat."

Jondrette threw a crushing glance at his daughter, accompanied by a terrible shrug of the shoulders.

M. Leblanc turned and answered with a smile:

"I do not forget it, I leave it."

"O my patron," said Jondrette, "my noble benefactor, I am melting into tears! Allow me to conduct you to your carriage."

"If you go out," replied M. Leblanc, "put on this overcoat. It is really very cold."

Marius had lost nothing of all this scene, and yet in reality he had seen nothing of it. His eyes had remained fixed upon the young girl, his heart had, so to speak, seized upon her and enveloped her entirely, from her first step into the garret.

When she went out, he had but one thought, not to lose her again, at least, after having so miraculously found her! He leaped down from the bureau and took his hat. He ran to the stairs. There was nobody on the stairs. He hurried down, and reached the boulevard in time to see a fiacre turn the corner.

Marius rushed in that direction. When he reached the corner of the boulevard, he saw the fiacre again at a long distance; there was no means of reaching it; what should he do? run after it? impossible; and then from the carriage they would certainly notice a man running at full speed in pursuit of them, and the father would recognise him. Just at this moment, marvellous and unheard-of good fortune, Marius saw a public cab passing along the boulevard, empty.

Marius made a sign to the driver to stop, and cried to him:

"Right away!"

Marius had no cravat, he had on his old working coat, some of the buttons of which were missing, and his shirt was torn.

The driver stopped, winked, and reached his left hand towards Marius, rubbing his forefinger gently with his thumb.

"What?" said Marius.

"Pay in advance," said the driver.

Marius remembered that he had only sixteen sous with him.

"How much?" he asked.

"Forty sous."

"I will pay when I get back."

The driver made no reply, but to whistle and whip up his horse.

Marius saw the cab move away with a bewildered air. For the want of twenty-four sous he was losing his joy, his happiness, his love! he was falling back into night! he had seen, and he was again becoming blind. He thought bitterly, and it must indeed be said, with deep regret, of the five francs he had given that very morning to that miserable girl. Had he had those five francs he would have been saved. He returned to the old tenement in despair.

He might have thought that M. Leblanc had promised to return in the evening, and that he had only to take better care to follow him then; but in his rapt contemplation he had hardly understood it.

Just as he went up the stairs, he noticed on the other side of the boulevard, beside the deserted wall of the Rue de la Barrière des Gobelins, Jondrette in the "philanthropist's" overcoat, talking to one of those men of dangerous appearance, who, by common consent, are called *prowlers of the barrières;* men of equivocal faces, suspicious speech, who have an appearance of evil intentions, and who usually sleep by day, which leads us to suppose that they work by night.

These two men quietly talking while the snow was whirling about them in its fall made a picture which a policeman certainly would have observed, but which Marius hardly noticed.

Nevertheless, however mournful was the subject of his reflections, he could not help saying to himself that this prowler of the barrières with whom Jondrette was talking, resembled a certain Panchaud, alias Printanier, alias Bigrenaille, whom Courfeyrac had once pointed out to him, and who passed in the quartier for a very dangerous night-wanderer. This Panchaud, alias Printanier, alias Bigrenaille, figured afterwards in several criminal trials, and has since become a celebrated scoundrel. He was still at that time only a notorious scoundrel. He is now a matter of tradition among bandits and assassins. He was the head of a school near the close of the last reign. And in the evening, at nightfall, at the hour when crowds gather and speak low, he was talked about at the La Force in La Fosse aux Lions. You might even in that prison, just at the spot where that privy sewer, which served for the astonishing escape of thirty prisoners in broad day in 1843, passes under the encircling passage-way; you might, above the flagging of that sewer, read his name, PANCHAUD, audaciously cut by himself upon the outer wall in one of his attempts to escape. In 1832, the police already had him under their eye, but he had not yet really made his début.

Marius mounted the stairs of the old tenement with slow steps; just as he was going into his cell, he perceived in the hall the elder Jondrette girl. This girl was odious to his sight; it was she who had his five francs, it was too late to ask her for them, the cab was there no longer, the fiacre was far away. As to questioning her about the address of the people who had just come, that was useless; it was plain that she did not know, since the letter signed Fabantou was addressed *to the beneficent gentleman of the Church of Saint Jacques du Haut Pas.*

Marius went into his room and pushed to his door behind him.

It did not close; he turned and saw a hand holding the door partly open.

"Is it you?" said Marius almost harshly, "you again? What do you want of me?"

She seemed thoughtful and did not look at him. She had lost the assurance which she had had in the morning.

"Come now," said Marius. "What is it you want of me?"

She raised her mournful eyes, in which a sort of confused light seemed to shine dimly, and said to him:

"Monsieur Marius, you look sad. What is the matter with you?"

"There is nothing the matter with me."

"Yes!"

"No."

"I tell you there is!"

"Let me be quiet!"

Marius pushed the door anew, she still held it back.

"Stop," said she, "you are wrong. Though you may not be rich, you were good this morning. Be so again now. You gave me something to eat, tell me now what ails you. You are troubled at something, that is plain. I do not want you to be troubled. I may be useful. I help my father. When it is necessary to carry letters, go into houses, inquire from door to door, find out an address, follow somebody, I do it."

An idea came into Marius' mind. He approached the girl.

"Listen," said he to her, kindly.

"Oh! yes, talk softly to me! I like that better."

"Well," resumed he, "you brought this old gentleman here with his daughter."

"Yes."

"Do you know their address?"

"No."

"Find it for me."

The girl's eyes had become joyful; they now became dark.

"Is that what you want?" she asked.

"Yes."

"Do you know them?"

"No."

"That is to say," said she hastily, "you do not know her, but you want to know her."

This *them* which had become *her* had an indescribable significance and bitterness.

"Well, can you do it?" said Marius.

"You shall have the beautiful young lady's address."

There was again, in these words "the beautiful young lady," an expression which made Marius uneasy. He continued:

"Well, no matter! the address of the father and daughter. Their address, yes!"

She looked steadily at him.

"What will you give me?"

"Anything you wish!"

"Anything I wish?"

"Yes."

"You shall have the address."

She looked down, and then with a hasty movement closed the door. Marius was alone.

Suddenly he heard the loud, harsh voice of Jondrette pronounce these words, full of the strangest interest:

"I tell you that I am sure of it, and that I recognised him!"

Of whom was Jondrette talking? he had recognised whom? M. Leblanc? did Jondrette know him? Marius sprang upon the bureau, and resumed his place near the little aperture in the partition.

He again saw the interior of the Jondrette den.

Nothing had changed in the appearance of the family, except that the wife and daughters had opened the package, and put on the woollen stockings and underclothes. Two new coverlids were thrown over the two beds.

Jondrette had evidently just come in.

The woman, who seemed timid and stricken with stupor before her husband, ventured to say to him:

"What, really? you are sure?"

"Sure! It was eight years ago! but I recognise him! I recognised him immediately. What! it did not strike you?"

"No."

"I told you to pay attention. But it is the same height, the same face, hardly any older; there are some men who do not grow old; I don't know how they do it; it is the same tone of voice. He is better dressed, that is all! Ah! mysterious old devil, I have got you, all right!"

Suddenly he turned towards the woman, folded his arms, and exclaimed:

"And do you want I should tell you one thing? the young lady—"

"Well, what?" said the woman, "the young lady?"

Marius listened with an intense anxiety. His whole life was concentrated in his ears.

But Jondrette stooped down, and whispered to his wife. Then he straightened up and finished aloud:

"It is she!"

"That girl?" said the wife.

"I tell you it is she. You will see."

At this absolute affirmation, the woman appeared to Marius still more terrible than her husband. She was a swine with the look of a tigress.

"And do you want I should tell you one thing? My fortune is made."

The woman stared at him with that look which means: Has the man who is talking to me gone crazy?

He continued:

"Thunder! I want food for my hunger, I want drink for my thirst! to stuff! to sleep! to do nothing! I want to have my turn, I do! before I burst! I want to be a bit of a millionaire!"

He took a turn about the garret and added:

"Like other people."

"What do you mean?" asked the woman. .

He shook his head, winked and lifted his voice like a street doctor about to make a demonstration:

"What do I mean? listen!"

"Hist!" muttered the woman, "not so loud! if it means business nobody must hear."

"Pshaw! who is there to hear? our neighbour? I saw him go out just now. Besides, does he hear, the great stupid? and then I tell you that I saw him go out."

Nevertheless, by a sort of instinct, Jondrette lowered his voice, not enough, however, for his words to escape Marius.

"Listen attentively. He is caught, the Crœsus! it is all right. It is already done. Everything is arranged. I have seen the men. He will come this evening at six o'clock. There is nobody in the house. Our neighbour never comes back before eleven o'clock. The girls will stand watch. You shall help us. He will be his own executor."

"And if he should not be his own executor," asked the wife.

Jondrette made a sinister gesture and said:

"We will execute him."

And he burst into a laugh.

It was the first time that Marius had seen him laugh. This laugh was cold and feeble, and made him shudder.

Jondrette opened a closet near the chimney, took out an old cap and put it on his head after brushing it with his sleeve.

"Now," said he, "I am going out. I have still some men to see. Some good ones. You will see how it is going to work. I shall be back as soon as possible, it is a great hand to play, look out for the house."

And with his two fists in the two pockets of his trousers, he stood a moment in thought, then exclaimed:

"Do you know that it is very lucky indeed that he did not recognise me? If he had been the one to recognise me he would not have come back. He would escape us! It is my beard that saved me! my romantic beard! my pretty little romantic beard!"

And he began to laugh again.

He went to the window. The snow was still falling, and blotted out the grey sky.

"What villainous weather!" said he.

And pulling his cap over his eyes, he went out.

Hardly had he had time to take a few steps in the hall, when the door opened and his tawny and cunning face again appeared.

"I forgot," said he. "You will have a charcoal fire."

And he threw into his wife's apron the five-franc piece which the "philanthropist" had left him.

"A charcoal fire?" asked the woman.

"Yes."

"How many bushels?"

"Two good ones."

"That will be thirty sous. With the rest, I will buy something for dinner."

"The devil, no."

"Why?"

"The piece of a hundred sous is not to be spent."

"Why?"

"Because I shall have something to buy."

"What?"

"Something."

"How much will you need?"

"Where is there a tool store near here?"

"Rue Mouffetard."

"Oh! yes, at the corner of some street; I see the shop."

"But tell me now how much you will need for what you have to buy?"

"Fifty sous or three francs."

"There won't be much left for dinner."

"Don't bother about eating to-day. There is better business."

Jondrette closed the door, and Marius heard his steps recede along the hall and go rapidly down the stairs.

Just then the clock of Saint Médard struck one.

Marius, all dreamer as he was, was, as we have said, of a firm and energetic nature.

"I must put my foot on these wretches," said he.

Across the dark words which had been uttered, he saw distinctly but one thing, that an ambuscade was preparing, an ambuscade obscure, but terrible.

He got down from the bureau as quietly as he could, taking care to make no noise.

There was but one thing to be done.

He put on his presentable coat, tied a cravat about his neck, took his hat, and went out, without making any more noise than if he had been walking barefooted upon moss.

Once out of the house, he went to the Rue du Petit Banquier.

He was about midway of that street near a wall which bordered a broad field, he was walking slowly, and the snow deafened his steps; all at once he heard voices talking near him. He turned his head, the street was empty, there was nobody in it, it was broad daylight, and yet he heard voices distinctly.

It occurred to him to look over this wall.

There were in fact two men there with their backs to the wall, seated in the snow, and talking in a low tone.

These two were unknown to him; one was a bearded man in a blouse, and the other a long-haired man in tatters. The bearded man had on a Greek cap, the other was bare-headed, and there was snow in his hair.

The long-haired one jogged the other with his elbow, and said:

"With Patron-Minette, it can't fail."

"Do you think so?" said the bearded one; and the long-haired one replied:

"It will be a *fafiot* of five hundred *balles* for each of us, and the worst that can happen: five years, six years, ten years at most!"

The other answered hesitatingly, shivering under his Greek cap:

"Yes, it is a real thing. We can't go against such things."

"I tell you that the affair can't fail," replied the long-haired one. "Father What's-his-name's *maringotte* will be harnessed."

Then they began to talk about a melodrama which they had seen the evening before at La Gaîté.

Marius went on his way.

It seemed to him that the obscure words of these men, so strangely hidden behind that wall, and crouching down in the snow, were not perhaps without some connection with Jondrette's terrible projects. That must be *the affair*.

He went towards the Faubourg Saint Marceau, and asked at the first shop in his way where he could find a commissary of police.

Number 14, Rue de Pontoise, was pointed out to him.

Marius went thither.

Passing a baker's shop, he bought a two-sou loaf and ate it, foreseeing that he would have no dinner.

On his way he rendered to Providence its due. He thought that if he had not given his five francs to the Jondrette girl in the morning, he would have followed M. Leblanc's fiacre, and consequently known nothing of this, so that there would have been no obstacle to the ambuscade of the Jondrettes, and M. Leblanc would have been lost, and doubtless his daughter with him.

On reaching Number 14, Rue de Pontoise, he went upstairs and asked for the commissary of police.

"The commissary of police is not in," said one of the office boys; "but there is an inspector who answers for him. Would you like to speak to him? is it urgent?"

"Yes," said Marius.

The office boy introduced him into the commissary's private room. A man of tall stature was standing there, behind a railing, in front of a stove, and holding up with both hands the flaps of a huge overcoat with three capes. He had a square face, a thin and firm mouth, very fierce, bushy, greyish whiskers, and an eye that would turn your pockets inside out. You might have said of his eye, not that it penetrated, but that it ransacked.

This man's appearance was not much less ferocious or formidable than Jondrette's; it is sometimes no less startling to meet the dog than the wolf.

"What do you wish?" said he to Marius, without adding monsieur.

"The commissary of police?"

"He is absent. I answer for him."

"It is a very secret affair."

"Speak, then."

"And very urgent."

"Then speak quickly."

This man, calm and abrupt, was at the same time alarming and reassuring. He inspired fear and confidence. Marius related his adventure.—That a person whom he only knew by sight was to be drawn into an ambuscade that very evening; that occupying the room next the place, he, Marius Pontmercy, attorney, had heard the whole plot through the partition; that the scoundrel who had contrived the plot was named Jondrette; that he had accomplices, probably prowlers of the barrières, among others a certain Panchaud, alias Printanier, alias Bigrenaille; that Jondrette's daughters would stand watch; that there was no means of warning the threatened man, as not even his name was known; and finally, that all this was to be done at six o'clock that evening, at the most desolate spot on the Boulevard de l'Hôpital, in the house numbered 50-52.

At that number the inspector raised his head, and said coolly:

"It is then in the room at the end of the hall?"

"Exactly," said Marius, and he added, "Do you know that house?"

The inspector remained silent a moment, then answered, warming the heel of his boot at the door of the stove:

"It seems so."

He continued between his teeth, speaking less to Marius than to his cravat.

"There ought to be a dash of Patron-Minette in this."

That word struck Marius.

"Patron-Minette," said he. "Indeed, I heard that word pronounced."

And he related to the inspector the dialogue between the long-haired man and the bearded man in the snow behind the wall on the Rue du Petit Banquier.

The inspector muttered:

"The long-haired one must be Brujon, and the bearded one must be Demi-Liard, alias Deux-Milliards."

He had dropped his eyes again, and was considering.

"As to the Father What's-his-name, I have a suspicion of who he is. There, I have burnt my coat. They always make too much fire in these cursed stoves. Number 50-52. Old Gorbeau property."

Then he looked at Marius:

"You have seen only this bearded man and this long-haired man?"

"And Panchaud."

"You did not see a sort of little devilish rat prowling about there?"

"No."

"Nor a great, big, clumsy heap, like the elephant in the Jardin des Plantes?"

"No."

"Nor a villain who has the appearance of an old red cue?"

"No."

"As to the fourth nobody sees him, not even his helpers, clerks, and agents. It is not very surprising that you did not see him."

"No. What are all these beings?" inquired Marius.

The inspector relapsed into silence, then resumed:

"No. 50-52. I know the shanty. Impossible to hide ourselves in the interior without the artists perceiving us, then they would leave and break up the play. They are so modest! the public annoys them. None of that, none of that. I want to hear them sing, and make them dance."

This monologue finished, he turned towards Marius and asked him looking steadily at him:

"Will you be afraid?"

"Of what?" said Marius.

"Of these men?"

"No more than you!" replied Marius rudely, who began to notice that this police spy had not yet called him monsieur.

The inspector looked at Marius still more steadily and continued with a sententious solemnity:

"You speak now like a brave man and an honest man. Courage does not fear crime, and honesty does not fear authority."

Marius interrupted him:

"That is well enough; but what are you going to do?"

The inspector merely answered:

"The lodgers in that house have latch-keys to get in with at night. You must have one?"

"Yes," said Marius.

"Have you it with you?"

"Yes."

"Give it to me," said the inspector.

Marius took his key from his waistcoat, handed it to the inspector, and added:

"If you trust me you will come in force."

The inspector threw a glance upon Marius such as Voltaire would have thrown upon a provincial academician who had proposed a rhyme to him; with a single movement he plunged both his hands, which were enormous, into the two immense pockets of his overcoat, and took out two small steel pistols, of the kind called fisticuffs. He presented them to Marius, saying hastily and abruptly:

"Take these. Go back home. Hide yourself in your room; let them think you have gone out. They are loaded. Each with two balls. You will watch; there is a hole in the wall, as you have told me. The men will come. Let them go on a little. When you deem the affair at a point, and when it is time to stop it, you will fire off a pistol. Not too soon. The rest is my affair. A pistol shot in the air, into the ceiling, no matter where. Above all, not too soon. Wait till the consummation is commenced; you are a lawyer, you know what that is."

Marius took the pistols and put them in the side pocket of his coat.

"They make a bunch that way, they show," said the inspector. "Put them in your fobs rather."

Marius hid the pistols in his fobs.

"Now," pursued the inspector, "there is not a minute to be lost by anybody. What time is it? Half past two. Is it at seven?"

"Six o'clock," said Marius.

"I have time enough," continued the inspector, "but I have only enough. Forget nothing of what I have told you. Bang. A pistol shot."

"Be assured," answered Marius.

And as Marius placed his hand on the latch of the door to go out, the inspector called to him:

"By the way, if you need me between now and then, come or send here. You will ask for Inspector Javert."

XVIII. PATRON-MINETTE

EVENING had come; night had almost closed in; there was now but one spot in the horizon or in the whole sky which was lighted by the sun; that was the moon.

She was rising red behind the low dome of La Salpêtrière.

It was not now snowing; the moon, growing brighter and brighter, was getting clear of the haze, and its light, mingled with the white reflection from the fallen snow, gave the room a twilight appearance.

There was a light in the Jondrette den. Marius saw the hole in the partition shine with a red gleam which appeared to him bloody.

He was sure that this gleam could hardly be produced by a candle. However, there was no movement in their room, nobody was stirring there, nobody spoke.

Marius took his boots off and pushed them under his bed.

Some minutes passed. Marius heard the lower door turn on its hinges; a heavy and rapid step ascended the stairs and passed along the corridor, the latch of the garret was noisily lifted; Jondrette came in.

Several voices were heard immediately. The whole family was in the garret. Only they kept silence in the absence of the master, like the cubs in the absence of the wolf.

"It is me," said he.

Marius heard him put something heavy on the table, probably the chisel which he had bought.

"Ah, ha!" said Jondrette, "have you been eating here?"

"Yes," said the mother, "I had three big potatoes and some salt. I took advantage of the fire to cook them."

"Well," replied Jondrette, "to-morrow I will take you to dine with me. There will be a duck and the accompaniments. You shall dine like Charles X.; everything is going well?"

Then he added, lowering his voice:

"The mouse-trap is open. The cats are ready."

He lowered his voice still more, and said:

"Put that into the fire."

Marius heard a sound of charcoal, as if somebody was striking it with pincers or some iron tool, and Jondrette continued:

"Have you greased the hinges of the door, so that they shall not make any noise?"

"Yes," answered the mother.

"What time is it?"

"Six o'clock, almost. The half has just struck on Saint Médard."

"The devil!" said Jondrette, "the girls must go and stand watch. Come here, you children, and listen to me."

There was a whispering.

Jondrette's voice rose again:

"Has Burgon gone out?"

"Yes," said the mother.

"Are you sure there is nobody at home in our neighbour's room?"

"He has not been back to-day, and you know that it is his dinner time."

"You are sure?"

"Sure."

"It is all the same," replied Jondrette; "there is no harm in going to see whether he is at home. Daughter, take the candle and go."

Marius dropped on his hands and knees, and crept noiselessly under the bed.

Hardly had he concealed himself, when he perceived a light through the cracks of his door.

"P'pa," cried a voice, "he has gone out."

He recognised the voice of the elder girl.

"Have you gone in?" asked the father.

"No," answered the girl, "but as his key is in the door, he has gone out."

The father cried:

"Go in just the same."

The door opened, and Marius saw the tall girl come in with a candle. She had the same appearance as in the morning, except that she was still more horrible in this light.

She walked straight towards the bed. Marius had a moment of inexpressible anxiety, but there was a mirror nailed on the wall near the bed; it was to that she was going. She stretched up on tiptoe and looked at herself in it. A sound of old iron rattling was heard in the next room.

She smoothed her hair with the palm of her hand, and smiled at the mirror, taking alternately front and three-quarter views of herself.

"Well," cried her father, "what are you doing now?"

"I am looking under the bed and the furniture," answered she, continuing to arrange her hair; "there is nobody here."

"Booby!" howled the father. "Here immediately, and let us lose no time."

"I am coming! I am coming!" said she.

She cast a last glance at the mirror, and went out, shutting the door after her.

A moment afterwards, Marius heard the sound of the bare feet of the two young girls in the passage, and the voice of Jondrette crying to them. "Pay attention, now! one towards the barrière, the other at the corner of the Rue du Petit Banquier. Don't lose sight of the house door a minute, and if you see the least thing, here immediately! tumble along! You have a key to come in with."

The elder daughter muttered:

"To stand sentry barefoot in the snow!"

"To-morrow you shall have boots of beetle colour silk!" said the father.

They went down the stairs, and, a few seconds afterwards, the sound of the lower door shutting announced that they had gone out.

There were now in the house only Marius and the Jondrettes, and probably also the mysterious beings of whom Marius had caught a glimpse in the twilight behind the door of the untenanted garret.

Marius judged that the time had come to resume his place at the partition.

A candle was burning in a verdigrised candlestick, but it was not that which really lighted the room. The entire den was illuminated by the reflection of a large sheet iron furnace in the fireplace, which was filled with lighted charcoal. The furnace was red hot; a blue flame danced over it and helped to show the form of the chisel bought by Jondrette in the Rue Pierre Lombard, which was growing ruddy among the coals. In a corner near the door, and arranged as if for anticipated use, were two heaps which appeared to be, one a heap of old iron, the other a heap of ropes. All this would have made one, who had known nothing of what was going forward, waver between a very sinister and a very simple idea. The room seemed rather a smithy than a mouth of hell; but Jondrette, in that glare, had rather the appearance of a demon than of a blacksmith.

The Jondrette lair was, if the reader remembers what we have said of the Gorbeau house, admirably chosen for the theatre of a deed of darkness and violence, and for the concealment of a crime. It was the most retired room of the most isolated house of the most solitary boulevard in Paris.

Suddenly Jondrette raised his voice:

"By the way, now, I think of it. In such weather as this he will come in a fiacre. Light the lantern, take it, and go down. You will stay there behind the lower door. The moment you hear the carriage stop, you will open immediately, he will come up, you will light him up the stairs and above the hall, and when he comes in here, you will go down again immediately, pay the driver, and send the fiacre away."

"And the money?" asked the woman.

Jondrette fumbled in his trousers, and handed her five francs.

"What is that?" she exclaimed.

Jondrette answered with dignity:—

"It is the monarch which our neighbour gave this morning."

And he added:—

"Do you know? we must have two chairs here."

"What for?"

"To sit in."

Marius felt a shiver run down his back on hearing the woman make this quiet reply:—

"Pardieu! I will get our neighbour's."

And with rapid movement she opened the door of the den, and went out into the hall.

Marius physically had not the time to get down from the bureau, and go and hide himself under the bed.

"Take the candle," cried Jondrette.

"No," said she, "I have two chairs to bring. It is moonlight."

Marius heard the heavy hand of mother Jondrette groping after his key in the dark. The door opened.

The woman came in, took the only chairs which Marius had, and went out, slamming the door noisily behind her.

She went back into the den.

"Here are the two chairs."

"And here is the lantern," said the husband. "Go down quick."

Jondrette was left alone.

He arranged the two chairs on the two sides of the table, turned the chisel over in the fire, put an old screen in front of the fireplace, which concealed the furnace, then went to the corner where the heap of ropes was, and stooped down, as if to examine something. Marius then perceived that what he had taken for a shapeless heap, was a rope ladder, very well made, with wooden rounds, and two large hooks to hang it by.

This ladder and a few big tools, actual masses of iron, which were thrown upon the pile of old iron heaped up behind the door, were not in the Jondrette den in the morning, and had evidently been brought there in the afternoon, during Marius' absence.

"Those are smith's tools," thought Marius.

Had Marius been a little better informed in this line, he would have recognised, in what he took for smith's tools, certain instruments capable of picking a lock or forcing a door, and others capable of cutting or hacking,—the two families of sinister tools, which thieves call *cadets* and *fauchants*.

Jondrette had let his pipe go out—a sure sign that he was intensely absorbed—and had come back and sat down. The candle made the savage ends and corners of his face stand out prominently. There were contractions of his brows, and abrupt openings of his right hand, as if he were replying to the last counsels of a dark interior monologue. In one of these obscure replies which he was making to himself, he drew the table drawer out quickly towards him, took out a long carving knife which was hidden there, and tried its edge on his nail. This done, he put the knife back into the drawer, and shut it.

Marius, for his part, grasped the pistol which was in his right fob pocket, took it out, and cocked it.

The pistol in cocking gave a little clear, sharp sound.

Jondrette started, and half rose from his chair.

"Who is there?" cried he.

Marius held his breath; Jondrette listened a moment, then began to laugh, saying:—

"What a fool I am! It is the partition cracking."

Marius kept the pistol in his hand.

Just then the distant and melancholy vibration of a bell shook the windows. Six o'clock struck on Saint Médard.

Jondrette marked each stroke; at the sixth he snuffed the candle with his fingers.

The door opened.

Monsieur Leblanc appeared.

He laid four louis upon the table.

"Monsieur Fabantou," said he, "that is for your rent and your pressing wants. We will see about the rest."

"God reward you, my generous benefactor!" said Jondrette.

The snow which had been falling ever since morning, was so deep that they had not heard the fiacre arrive, and did not hear it go away.

Meanwhile Monsieur Leblanc had taken a seat.

Jondrette had taken possession of the other chair opposite Monsieur Leblanc.

Now, to form an idea of the scene which follows, let the reader call to mind the chilly night, the solitudes of La Salpêtrière covered with snow, and white in the moonlight, like immense shrouds, the flickering light of the street lamps here and there reddening these tragic boulevards and the long rows of black elms, not a passer perhaps within a mile around; the Gorbeau tenement at its deepest degree of silence, horror, and night; in that tenement, in the midst of these solitudes, in the midst of this darkness, the vast Jondrette garret lighted by a candle; and in this den two men seated at a table, Monsieur Leblanc tranquil, Jondrette smiling and terrible, his wife, the wolf dam, in a corner; and, behind the partition, Marius, invisible, alert, losing no word, losing no movement, his eye on the watch, the pistol in his grasp.

Marius was experiencing nothing but an emotion of horror, no fear. He clasped the butt of the pistol, and felt reassured. "I shall stop this wretch when I please," thought he.

He felt that the police was somewhere near by in ambush, awaiting the signal agreed upon, and all ready to stretch out its arm.

He hoped, moreover, that from this terrible meeting between Jondrette and Monsieur Leblanc some light would be thrown upon all that he was interested to know.

No sooner was Monsieur Leblanc seated than he turned his eyes towards the empty pallets.

"How does the poor little injured girl do?" he inquired.

"Badly," answered Jondrette with a doleful yet grateful smile, "very badly, my worthy monsieur. Her eldest sister has taken her to the Bourbe to have her arm dressed. You will see them, they will be back directly."

"Madame Fabantou appears to me much better," resumed Monsieur Leblanc.

"She is dying," said Jondrette. "But you see, monsieur! she has so much courage, that woman! She is not a woman, she is an ox."

The woman, touched by the compliment, retorted with the smirk of a flattered monster:

"You are always too kind to me, Monsieur Jondrette."

"Jondrette!" said M. Leblanc, "I thought that your name was Fabantou?"

"Fabantou or Jondrette!" replied the husband hastily. "Sobriquet as an artist!"

And, directing a shrug of the shoulders towards his wife, he continued with an emphatic and caressing tone of voice:

"Ah! how long we have always got along together, this poor dear and I! We are so unfortunate, my respected monsieur! What a degradation, when one has been what we were! Alas! we have nothing left from our days of prosperity! Nothing but one single thing, a painting, to which I cling, but yet which I shall have to part with, for we must live! item, we must live!"

While Jondrette was talking, with an apparent disorder which detracted nothing from the crafty and cunning expression of his physiognomy, Marius raised his eyes, and perceived at the back of the room somebody whom he had not before seen. A man had come in so noiselessly that nobody had heard the door turn on its hinges. This man had a knit woollen waistcoat of violet colour, old, worn-out, stained, cut, and showing gaps at all its folds, full trousers of cotton velvet, socks on his feet, no shirt, his neck bare, his arms bare and tattooed, and his face stained black. He sat down in silence and with folded arms on the nearest bed, and as he kept behind the woman, he was distinguished only with difficulty.

That kind of magnetic instinct which warns the eye made M. Leblanc turn almost at the same time with Marius. He could not help a movement of surprise, which did not escape Jondrette:

"Ah! I see!" exclaimed Jondrette, buttoning up his coat with a complacent air, "you are looking at your overcoat. It's a fit! my faith, it's a fit!"

"Who is that man?" said M. Leblanc.

"That man?" said Jondrette, "that is a neighbour. Pay no attention to him."

The neighbour had a singular appearance. However, factories of chemical products abound in Faubourg Saint Marceau. Many machinists might have their faces blacked. The whole person of M. Leblanc, moreover, breathed a candid and intrepid confidence. He resumed:

"Pardon me; what were you saying to me, Monsieur Fabantou?"

"I was telling you, monsieur and dear patron," replied Jondrette, leaning his elbows on the table, and gazing at M. Leblanc with fixed and tender eyes, similar to the eyes of a boa constrictor, "I was telling you that I had a picture to sell."

A slight noise was made at the door. A second man entered, and sat down on the bed behind the female Jondrette. He had his arms bare, like the first, and a mask of ink or of soot.

Although this man had, literally, slipped into the room, he could not prevent M. Leblanc from perceiving him.

"Do not mind them," said Jondrette. "They are people of the house. I was telling you, then, that I have a valuable painting left. Here, monsieur, look."

He got up, went to the wall, at the foot of which stood the panel of which we have spoken, and turned it round, still leaving it resting against the wall. It was something, in fact, that resembled a picture, and which the candle scarcely revealed. Marius could make nothing out of it, Jondrette being between him and the picture; he merely caught a glimpse of a coarse daub, with a sort of principal personage, coloured in the crude and glaring style of strolling panoramas and paintings upon screens.

"What is that?" asked M. Leblanc.

Jondrette exclaimed:

"A painting by a master; a picture of great price, my benefactor! I cling to it as to my two daughters, it calls up memories to me! but I have told you, and I cannot unsay it, I am so unfortunate that I would part with it."

Whether by chance, or whether there was some beginning of distrust, while examining the picture, M. Leblanc glanced towards the back of the room. There were now four men there, three seated on the bed, one standing near the door-casing; all four bare-armed, motionless, and with blackened faces.

Jondrette noticed that M. Leblanc's eye was fixed upon these men.

"They are friends. They live near by," said he. "They are dark because they work in charcoal. They are chimney doctors. Do not occupy your mind with them, my benefactor, but buy my picture. Take pity on my misery. I shall not sell it to you at a high price. How much do you estimate it worth?"

"But," said M. Leblanc, looking Jondrette full in the face and like a man who puts himself on his guard, "this is some tavern sign, it is worth about three francs."

Jondrette answered calmly:

"Have you your pocket-book here? I will be satisfied with a thousand crowns."

M. Leblanc rose to his feet, placed his back to the wall, and ran his eye rapidly over the room. He had Jondrette at his left on the side towards the window, and his wife and the four men at his right on the side towards the door. The four men did not stir, and had not even the appearance of seeing him.

"If you do not buy my picture, dear benefactor," said Jondrette, "I have only to throw myself into the river."

Suddenly this little man straightened up and became horrifying, he took a step towards M. Leblanc and cried to him in a voice of thunder:

"But all this is not the question! do you know me?"

The door of the garret had been suddenly flung open, disclosing three men in blue blouses with black paper masks. The first was spare and had a long iron-bound cudgel; the second, who was a sort of colossus, held by the middle of the handle, with the axe down, a butcher's pole-axe. The third, a broad-shouldered man, not so thin as the first, nor so heavy as the second, held in his clenched fist an enormous key stolen from some prison door.

It appeared that it was the arrival of these men for which Jondrette was waiting. A rapid dialogue commenced between him and the man with the cudgel, the spare man.

"Is everything ready?" said Jondrette.

"Yes," answered the spare man.

"Where is Montparnasse then?"

"The young primate stopped to chat with your daughter."

"Is there a fiacre below?"

"Yes."

"The *maringotte* is ready?"

"Ready."

"With two good horses?"

"Excellent."

"It is waiting where I said it should wait?"

"Yes."

"Good," said Jondrette.

M. Leblanc was very pale. He looked over everything in the room about him like a man who understands into what he has fallen, and his head, directed in turn towards all the heads which surrounded him, moved on his neck with an attentive and astonished slowness, but there was nothing in his manner which resembled fear. He had made an extemporised intrenchment of the table; and this man who, the moment before, had the appearance only of a good old man, had suddenly become a sort of athlete, and placed his powerful fist upon the back of his chair with a surprising and formidable gesture.

Three of the men had taken from the heap of old iron a large pair of shears, a steelyard bar, a hammer, and placed themselves before the door without saying a word.

Marius thought that in a few seconds more the time would come to interfere, and he raised his right hand towards the ceiling, in the direction of the hall, ready to let off his pistol-shot.

Jondrette, after his colloquy with the man who had the cudgel, turned again towards M. Leblanc and repeated his question, accompanying it with that low, smothered, and terrible laugh of his:

"You do not recognise me, then?"

M. Leblanc looked him in the face, and answered:

"No."

Then Jondrette came up to the table. He leaned forward over the candle, folding his arms, and pushing his angular and ferocious jaws up towards the calm face of M. Leblanc, like a wild beast about to bite, he cried:

"My name is not Fabantou, my name is not Jondrette, my name is Thénardier! I am the innkeeper of Montfermeil! do you understand me? Thénardier! now do you know me?"

"No more than before."

Marius did not hear this answer. When Jondrette had said: *My name is Thénardier*, Marius supported himself against the wall as if he had felt the chill of a sword-blade through his heart. Then his right arm, which was just ready to fire the signal shot, dropped slowly down, and at the moment that Jondrette had repeated: *Do you understand me? Thénardier!* Marius had almost dropped the pistol. Jondrette had not moved M. Leblanc, but he had completely unnerved Marius. That name of Thénardier, which M. Leblanc did not seem to know, Marius knew. Remember what that name was to him! that name he had worn on his heart, written in his father's will! he carried it in the innermost place of his thoughts, in the holiest spot of his memory, in that sacred command: "A man named Thénardier saved my life. If my son should meet him, he will do him all the good he can."

What! here was that Thénardier, here was that innkeeper of Montfermeil, for whom he had so long and so vainly sought! He had found him at last, and how? this saviour of his father was a bandit! this man, to whom he, Marius, burned to devote himself, was a monster! this deliverer of Colonel Pontmercy was in the actual commission of a crime, the shape of which Marius did not yet see very distinctly, but which looked like an assassination!

His father from the depths of his coffin commanded him to do all the good he could to Thénardier; for his father's life, saved in a storm of grape upon the heroic field of Waterloo, he was at last about to reward this man with the scaffold!

He held in his hand those beings who were moving there before his eyes. If he fired the pistol, M. Leblanc was saved and Thénardier was lost; if he did not, M. Leblanc was sacrificed, and, perhaps, Thénardier escaped.

Here Thénardier took a step towards the men who were before the door, and added with a shudder:

"When I think that he dares to come and talk to me, as if I were a cobbler!"

Then addressing M. Leblanc with a fresh burst of frenzy:

"And know this, too, monsieur philanthropist! I am an old French soldier; I ought to be decorated. I was at Waterloo, I was, and in that battle I saved a general, named the Comte de Pontmercy. This picture which you see, and which was painted by David at Bruqueselles, do you know who it represents? It represents me. David desired to immortalise that feat of arms. I have General Pontmercy on my back, and I am carrying him through the storm of grape. That is history. He has never done anything at all for me, this general; he is no better than other people. But, nevertheless, I saved his life at the risk of my own, and I have my pockets full of certificates. I am a soldier at Waterloo—name of a thousand names! And now that I have had the goodness to tell you all this, let us make an end of it; I must have some money; I must have a good deal of money, I must have an immense deal of money, or I will exterminate you, by the thunder of God!"

Marius had regained some control over his distress, and was listening. The last possibility of doubt had now vanished. It was indeed the Thénardier of the will. Marius shuddered at that reproach of ingratitude flung at his father, and which he was on the point of justifying so fatally. His perplexities were redoubled.

The picture by a master, the painting by David, was, the reader has guessed, nothing more than the sign of his chop-house, painted, as will be remembered, by himself, the only relic which he had saved from his shipwreck at Montfermeil.

Marius could now look at the thing, and in this daub he really made out a battle, a background of smoke, and one man carrying off another. It was the group of Thénardier and Pontmercy; the saviour sergeant, the colonel saved. Marius was as it were intoxicated; this picture in some sort restored his father to life; it was not now the sign of the Montfermeil inn, it was a resurrection.

Thénardier fixed his bloodshot eyes upon Monsieur Leblanc, and said in a low and abrupt tone:

"What have you to say before we begin to dance with you?"

Monsieur Leblanc said nothing. In the midst of this silence a hoarse voice threw in this ghastly sarcasm from the hall:

"If there is any wood to split, I am on hand!"

It was the man with the pole-axe who was making merry.

"What have you taken off your mask for?" cried Thénardier, furiously.

For some moments, Monsieur Leblanc had seemed to follow and to watch all the movements of Thénardier, who was walking to and fro with confidence inspired by feeling that the door was guarded. In his apostrophe to the man with the pole-axe, he turned his back to Monsieur Leblanc.

Monsieur Leblanc seized this opportunity, pushed the chair away with his foot, the table with his hand, and at one bound, with a marvellous agility, before Thénardier had had time to turn around he was at the window. To open it, get up and step through it, was the work of a second. He was half outside when six strong hands seized him, and drew him forcibly back into the room. The three "chimney doctors" had thrown themselves upon him. At the same time the Thénardiess had clutched him by the hair.

At the disturbance which this made, the other bandits ran in from the hall. One of the "chimney doctors," in whom Marius recognised Panchaud, alias Printanier, alias Bigrenaille, raised a sort of loaded club made of a bar of iron with a knob of lead at each end, over Monsieur Leblanc's head.

Marius could not endure this sight. "Father," thought he, "pardon me!" And his finger sought the trigger of the pistol. The shot was about to be fired, when Thénardier's voice cried:

"Do him no harm!"

M. Leblanc had knocked down two assailants, but four others seized the formidable old man by the arms and held him down.

They succeeded in throwing him over upon the bed nearest to the window.

"Now, the rest of you," continued Thénardier, "search him."

M. Leblanc seemed to have given up all resistance. They searched him. There was nothing upon him but a leather purse which contained six francs, and his handkerchief.

Thénardier put the handkerchief in his pocket.

"What! no pocket-book?" he asked.

"Nor any watch," answered one of the "chimney doctors."

"It is all the same," muttered, with the voice of a ventriloquist, the masked man who had the big key, "he is an old rough."

Thénardier went to the corner by the door and took a bundle of ropes which he threw to them.

"Tie him to the foot of the bed," said he, and perceiving the fellow who lay motionless, stretched across the room by the blow of M. Leblanc's fist:

"Is Boulatruelle dead?" asked he.

"No," answered Bigrenaille, "he is drunk."

"Sweep him into a corner," said Thénardier.

Two of the "chimney doctors" pushed the drunkard up to the heap of old iron with their feet.

"Babet, what did you bring so many for?" said Thénardier in a low tone to the man with the cudgel, "it was needless."

"What would you have?" replied the man with the cudgel, "they all wanted to be in. The season is bad. There is nothing doing."

The pallet upon which M. Leblanc had been thrown was a sort of hospital bed supported by four big roughly squared wooden posts. M. Leblanc made no resistance. The brigands bound him firmly, standing, with his feet to the floor, by the bed-post furthest from the window and nearest to the chimney.

When the last knot was tied, Thénardier took a chair and came and sat down nearly in front of M. Leblanc.

"Monsieur," said Thénardier.

And with a gesture dismissing the brigands who still had their hands upon M. Leblanc:

"Move off a little, and let me talk with monsieur."

They all retired towards the door. He resumed:

"Monsieur, you were wrong in trying to jump out the window. You might have broken your leg. Now, if you please, we will talk quietly. In the first place I must inform you of a circumstance I have noticed, which is that you have not yet made the least outcry."

Thénardier was right; this was true, although it had escaped Marius in his anxiety. M. Leblanc had only uttered a few words without raising his voice, and, even in his struggle by the window with the six bandits, he had preserved the most profound and the most remarkable silence. Thénardier continued:

"Indeed! you might have cried thief a little, for I should not have found it inconvenient. Murder! that is said upon occasion, and, as far as I am concerned, I should not have taken it in bad part. It is very natural that one should make a little noise when he finds himself with persons who do not inspire him with as much confidence as they might; you might have done it, and we should not have disturbed you. We would not even have gagged you. And I will tell you why. It is because this room is very deaf. That is all I can say for it, but I can say that. It is a cave. We could fire a bomb here, and at the nearest guardhouse it would sound like a drunkard's snore. It is a convenient apartment. But, you did not cry out, that was better, I make you my compliments for it, and I will tell you what I conclude from it: my dear monsieur, when a man cries out, who is it that comes? The police. And after the police? Justice. Well! you did not cry out; because you were no more anxious than we to see justice and the police come. It is because,—I suspected as much long ago,—you have some interest in concealing something. For our part we have the same interest. Now we can come to an understanding."

While speaking thus, it seemed as though Thénardier, with his gaze fixed upon Monsieur Leblanc, was endeavouring to thrust daggers into the very conscience of his prisoner. His language, marked by a sort of subdued and sullen insolence, was reserved and almost select; and in this wretch who was just before nothing but a brigand, one could now perceive the man who studied to be a priest.

The silence which the prisoner had preserved, this precaution which he had carried even to the extent of endangering his life, this resistance to the first impulse of nature, which is to utter a cry, all this, it must be said, since it had been remarked, was annoying to Marius, and painfully astonished him.

The observation of Thénardier, well founded as it was, added in Marius' eyes still more to the obscurity of the mysterious cloud that enveloped this strange and serious face to which Courfeyrac had given the nickname of Monsieur Leblanc. But whatever he might be, bound with ropes, surrounded by assassins, half buried, so to speak, in a grave which was deepening beneath him every moment, this man remained impassible; and Marius could not repress his admiration for that superbly melancholy face.

Here was evidently a soul inaccessible to fear, and ignorant of dismay. Here was one of those men who are superior to astonishment in desperate situations.

Thénardier quietly got up, went to the fireplace, took away the screen and thus revealed the furnace full of glowing coals in which the prisoner could plainly see the chisel at a white heat, spotted here and there with little scarlet stars.

Then Thénardier came back and sat down by Monsieur Leblanc.

"I continue," said he. "Now we can come to an understanding. Let us arrange this amicably. I do not want to ruin you, I am willing to go half way and make some sacrifice. I need only two hundred thousand francs."

Monsieur Leblanc did not breathe a word. Thénardier went on:

"You see I do not know the state of your fortune, but I know that you do not care much for money, and a benevolent man like you can certainly give two hundred thousand francs to a father of a family who is unfortunate. You will say: but I have not two hundred thousand francs with me. Oh! I am not exacting. I do not require that. I only ask one thing. Have the goodness to write what I shall dictate."

Here Thénardier paused, then he added, emphasising each word and casting a smile towards the furnace:

"I give you notice that I shall not admit that you cannot write."

A grand inquisitor might have envied that smile.

Thénardier pushed the table close up to Monsieur Leblanc, and took the inkstand, a pen, and a sheet of paper from the drawer, which he left partly open, and from which gleamed the long blade of the knife.

He laid the sheet of paper before Monsieur Leblanc.

The prisoner spoke at last:

"How do you expect me to write? I am tied."

"That is true, pardon me!" said Thénardier, "you are quite right."

And turning towards Bigrenaille:

"Untie monsieur's right arm."

Panchaud, alias Printanier, alias Bigrenaille, executed Thénardier's order. When the prisoner's right hand was free, Thénardier dipped the pen into the ink, and presented it to him.

"Remember, monsieur, that you are in our power, at our discretion, that no human power can take you away from here, and that we should be really grieved to be obliged to proceed to unpleasant extremities. I give you notice that you will remain tied until the person whose duty it will be to carry the letter which you are about to write, has returned. Have the kindness now to write."

"What?" asked the prisoner.

"I will dictate."

M. Leblanc took the pen.

Thénardier began to dictate:

"My daughter—"

The prisoner lifted his eyes to Thénardier.

"Put 'my dear daughter,' " said Thénardier. M. Leblanc obeyed. Thénardier continued:

"Come immediately—"

He stopped.

"You call her daughter, do you not?"

"Who?" asked M. Leblanc.

"Zounds!" said Thénardier, "the little girl, the Lark."

M. Leblanc answered without the least apparent emotion:

"I do not know what you mean."

"Well, go on," said Thénardier, and he began to dictate again.

"Come immediately, I have imperative need of you. The person who will give you this note is directed to bring you to me. I am waiting for you. Come with confidence."

M. Leblanc had written the whole. Thénardier added:

"Ah! strike out *come with confidence*, that might lead her to suppose that the thing is not quite clear and that distrust is possible."

M. Leblanc erased the three words.

"Now," continued Thénardier, "sign it. What is your name?"

The prisoner laid down the pen and asked:

"For whom is this letter?"

"You know very well," answered Thénardier, "for the little girl, I have just told you."

It was evident that Thénardier avoided naming the young girl in question. He said "the Lark," he said "the little girl," but he did not pronounce the name. The precaution of a shrewd man preserving his own secret before his accomplices. To speak the name would have been to give up the whole "affair" to them, and to tell them more than they needed to know.

He resumed:

"Sign it. What is your name?"

"Urbain Fabre," said the prisoner.

Thénardier, with the movement of a cat, thrust his hand into his pocket and pulled out the handkerchief taken from M. Leblanc. He looked for the mark upon it and held it up to the candle.

"U. F. That is it. Urbain Fabre. Well, sign U. F."

The prisoner signed.

"As it takes two hands to fold the letter, give it to me, I will fold it."

This done, Thénardier resumed:

"Put on the address, *Mademoiselle Fabre*, at your house. I know that you live not very far from here, in the neighbourhood of Saint Jacques du Haut Pas, since you go there to mass every day, but I do not know in what street. I see that you understand your situation."

The prisoner remained thoughtful for a moment, then he took the pen and wrote:

"Mademoiselle Fabre, at Monsieur Urbain Fabre's, Rue Saint Dominique d'Enfer, No. 17."

Thénardier seized the letter. "Wife!" cried he.

The Thénardiess sprang forward.

"Here is the letter. You know what you have to do. There is a fiacre below."

And addressing the man with the pole-axe:

"Here, since you have taken off your hide-your-nose, go with the woman. You will get up behind the fiacre. You know where you left the *maringotte*."

A minute had not passed when the snapping of a whip was heard, which grew fainter and rapidly died away.

There were now but five bandits left in the den with Thénardier and the prisoner. They were heaped together in a corner like brutes, and were silent. Thénardier was warming his feet. The prisoner had relapsed into his taciturnity.

Marius was waiting in an anxiety which everything increased. Who was this "little girl," whom Thénardier had also called the Lark? was it his "Ursula"? The prisoner had not seemed to be moved by this word, the Lark, and answered in the most natural way in the world: I do not know what you mean. On the other hand, the two letters U. F. were explained; it was Urbain Fabre, and Ursula's name was no longer Ursula. This Marius saw most clearly.

"At all events," said he, "if the Lark is she, I shall certainly see her, for the Thénardiess is going to bring her here. Then all will be plain. I will give my blood and my life if need be, but I will deliver her. Nothing shall stop me."

Nearly half an hour passed thus. Thénardier appeared absorbed in a dark meditation, the prisoner did not stir. Nevertheless Marius thought he had heard at intervals and for some moments a little dull noise from the direction of the prisoner.

Suddenly Thénardier addressed the prisoner:

"Monsieur Fabre, I think the Lark is really your daughter, and I find it quite natural that you should keep her. But my wife is going to find her. They will both get into the fiacre with my comrade behind. There is somewhere outside one of the barriers a *maringotte* with two very good horses harnessed. They will take your young lady there. She will get out of the carriage. My comrade will get into the *maringotte* with her, and my wife will come back here to tell us: 'It is done.' As to your young lady, no harm will be done her; the *maringotte* will take her to a place where she will be quiet, and as soon as you have given me the little two hundred thousand francs, she will be sent back to you. If you have me arrested, my comrade will give the Lark a pinch, that is all."

The prisoner did not utter a word. After a pause, Thénardier continued:

"It is very simple, as you see. There will be no harm done unless you wish there should be."

He stopped; the prisoner did not break the silence.

Appalling images passed before Marius' mind. What! this young girl whom they were kidnapping, they were not going to bring her here? One

of those monsters was going to carry her off into the gloom? where?—
And if it were she! And it was clear that it was she. Marius felt his heart
cease to beat. What was he to do? Fire off the pistol? put all these wretches
into the hands of justice? But the hideous man of the pole-axe would none
the less be out of all reach with the young girl.

In the midst of this silence they heard the sound of the door of the stairway which opened, then closed.

The prisoner made a movement in his bonds.

The Thénardiess burst into the room, red, breathless, panting, and cried,
striking her hands upon her hips both at the same time:

"False address!"

The bandit whom she had taken with her, came in behind her and
picked up his pole-axe again:

"False address?" repeated Thénardier.

She continued:

"Nobody! Rue Saint Dominique, number seventeen, no Monsieur Urbain
Fabre! They do not know who he is!"

She stopped for lack of breath, then continued:

"Monsieur Thénardier! this old fellow has cheated you! you are too good,
do you see! I would have cut up the *Margoulette* for you in quarters, to
begin with! and if he had been ugly, I would have cooked him alive! That
is how I would have fixed it! No wonder that they say men are stupider
than women! Nobody! number seventeen! It is a large porte-cochère! No
Monsieur Fabre! Rue Saint Dominique, full gallop, and drink-money to
the driver, and all!"

Marius breathed. She, Ursula or the Lark, was safe.

While his exasperated wife was vociferating, Thénardier had seated himself on the table; he sat a few seconds without saying a word, swinging his
right leg, which was hanging down, and gazing upon the furnace.

At last he said to the prisoner with a slow and singularly ferocious in-
flexion:

"A false address! what did you hope for by that?"

"To gain time!" cried the prisoner with a ringing voice.

And at the same moment he shook off his bonds; they were cut. The
prisoner was no longer fastened to the bed save by one leg.

Before the seven men had had time to recover themselves and spring
upon him, he had bent over to the fireplace, reached his hand towards the
furnace, then rose up, and now Thénardier, the Thénardiess, and the
bandits, thrown by the shock into the back part of the room, beheld him
with stupefaction, holding above his head the glowing chisel.

At the judicial inquest, to which the ambuscade in the Gorbeau tenement
gave rise in the sequel, it appeared that a big sou, cut and worked in a
peculiar fashion, was found in the garret, when the police made a descent
upon it; this big sou was one of those marvels of labour which the patience of the galleys produces. The unhappy man who aspires to deliverance finds the means to split a sou into two thin plates, to hollow out these

two plates without touching the stamp of the mint, and to cut a screw-thread upon the edge of the sou, so as to make the plates adhere anew. This screws and unscrews at will; it is a box. In this box, they conceal a watch-spring, and this watch-spring, well handled, cuts off rings of some size and bars of iron. The unfortunate convict is supposed to possess only a sou; no, he possesses liberty.

A big sou of this kind was found in two pieces in the room. There was also discovered a little saw of blue steel which could be concealed in the big sou. It is probable that when the bandits were searching the prisoner's pockets, he had this big sou upon him and succeeded in hiding it in his hand; and that afterwards, having his right hand free, he unscrewed it and used the saw to cut the ropes by which he was fastened, which would explain the slight noise and the imperceptible movements which Marius had noticed. Being unable to stoop down for fear of betraying himself, he had not cut the cords on his left leg.

The bandits had recovered from their first surprise.

"Be easy," said Bigrenaille to Thénardier. "He holds yet by one leg. I tied that shank for him."

The prisoner now raised his voice:

"You are pitiable, but my life is not worth the trouble of so long a defence. As to your imagining that you could make me write what I do not wish to write, that you could make me say what I do not wish to say—"

He pulled up the sleeve of his left arm, and added: "Here." At the same time he extended his arm, and laid upon the naked flesh the glowing chisel. They heard the hissing of burning flesh; the odour peculiar to chambers of torture spread through the den. Marius staggered, lost in horror; the brigands themselves felt a shudder; the face of the wonderful old man hardly contracted.

"Wretches," said he, "have no more fear for me than I have of you."

And drawing the chisel out of the wound, he threw it through the window, which was still open; the horrible glowing tool disappeared, whirling into the night, and fell in the distance, and was quenched in the snow.

The prisoner resumed:

"Do with me what you will."

He was disarmed.

"Lay hold of him," said Thénardier.

Two of the brigands laid their hands upon his shoulders, and the masked man with the ventriloquist's voice placed himself in front of him, ready to knock out his brains at the least motion.

At the same time Marius heard beneath him, at the foot of the partition, but so near that he could not see those who were talking, this colloquy, exchanged in a low voice:

"There is only one thing more to do."

"To kill him!"

"That is it."

It was the husband and wife who were holding counsel.

Thénardier walked towards the table, opened the drawer, and took out the knife.

Marius cast his eyes wildly about him; the last mechanical resource of despair. Suddenly he started.

At his feet, on the table, a clear ray of the full moon illuminated, and seemed to point out to him a sheet of paper. Upon that sheet he read this line, written in large letters that very morning, by the elder of the Thénardier girls:

"THE COGNES ARE HERE."

An idea, a flash crossed Marius' mind. He knelt down upon his bureau, reached out his arm, caught up the sheet of paper, quietly detached a bit of plaster from the partition, wrapped it in the paper, and threw the whole through the crevice into the middle of the den.

It was time. Thénardier had conquered his last fears, or his last scruples, and was moving towards the prisoner.

"Something fell!" cried the Thénardiess.

"What is it?" said the husband.

The woman had sprung forward, and picked up the piece of plaster wrapped in the paper. She handed it to her husband.

"How did this come in?" asked Thénardier.

"Egad!" said the woman, "how do you suppose it got in? It came through the window."

"I saw it pass," said Bigrenaille.

Thénardier hurriedly unfolded the paper, and held it up to the candle.

"It is Eponine's writing. The devil!"

He made a sign to his wife, who approached quickly, and he showed her the line written on the sheet of paper; then he added in a hollow voice:

"Quick! the ladder! leave the meat in the trap, and clear the camp!"

"Without cutting the man's throat?" asked the Thénardiess.

"We have not the time."

"Which way?" inquired Bigrenaille.

"Through the window," answered Thénardier. "As Ponine threw the stone through the window, that shows that the house is not watched on that side."

The brigands who were holding the prisoner let go of him; in the twinkling of an eye, the rope ladder was unrolled out of the window, and firmly fixed to the casing by the two iron hooks.

Thénardier rushed towards the window, but as he was stepping out, Bigrenaille seized him roughly by the collar.

"No; after us."

"After us!" howled the bandits.

"You are children," said Thénardier. "We are losing time."

"Well," said one of the bandits, "let us draw lots who shall go out first."

Thénardier exclaimed:

"Are you fools? are you cracked? Losing time, write our names! put them in a cap!—"

"Would you like my hat?" cried a voice from the door.

They all turned round. It was Javert.

He had his hat in his hand, and was holding it out smiling.

Javert, at nightfall, had posted his men and hid himself behind the trees on the Rue de la Barrière des Gobelins, which fronts the Gorbeau tenement on the other side of the boulevard. He commenced by opening his pocket to put into it the two young girls, who were charged with watching the approaches to the den. But he only bagged Azelma; Eponine had disappeared.

Then Javert put himself in rest, and listened for the signal agreed upon. The going and coming of the fiacre fretted him greatly. At last, he became impatient, and, having recognised several of the bandits who had gone in, he finally decided to go up without waiting for the pistol shot. It will be remembered that he had Marius' pass-key.

He had come at the right time.

The frightened bandits rushed for the arms which they had thrown down anywhere when they had attempted to escape. The Thénardiess seized a huge paving-stone which served for a cricket.

Javert put on his hat again, and stepped into the room, his arms folded, his cane under his arm, his sword in its sheath.

"Halt there," said he. "You will not pass out through the window, you will pass out through the door. It is less unwholesome. There are seven of you, fifteen of us. Be genteel."

Bigrenaille took a pistol which he had concealed under his blouse, and put it into Thénardier's hand, whispering in his ear:

"It is Javert. I dare not fire at that man. Dare you?"

"*Parbleu!*" answered Thénardier.

"Well, fire."

Thénardier took the pistol, and aimed at Javert.

Javert, who was within three paces, looked at him steadily, and contented himself with saying:

"Don't fire, now! it will flash in the pan."

Thénardier pulled the trigger. The pistol flashed in the pan.

"I told you so!" said Javert.

Bigrenaille threw his tomahawk at Javert's feet.

"You are the emperor of the devils! I surrender."

"And you?" asked Javert of the other bandits.

They answered:

"We, too."

Javert replied calmly:

"That is it, that is well, I said so, you are genteel."

"I only ask one thing," said Bigrenaille, "that I shan't be refused tobacco while I am in solitary."

"Granted," said Javert.

And turning round and calling behind him:

"Come in now!"

A squad of sergents de ville with drawn swords, and officers armed with axes and clubs, rushed in at Javert's call. They bound the bandits. This crowd of men, dimly lighted by a candle, filled the den with shadow.

"Handcuffs on all!" cried Javert.

"Come on, then!" cried a voice which was not a man's voice. The Thénardiess had intrenched herself in one of the corners of the window.

The sergents de ville and officers fell back.

She was holding the paving stone with both hands above her head.

"Take care!" she cried.

They all crowded back towards the hall. A wide space was left in the middle of the garret.

The Thénardiess cast a glance at the bandits who had allowed themselves to be tied, and muttered in a harsh and guttural tone:

"The cowards!"

Javert smiled, and advanced into the open space.

"Don't come near! get out," cried she, "or I will crush you!"

"What a grenadier!" said Javert; "mother, you have a beard like a man, but I have claws like a woman."

And he continued to advance.

The Thénardiess, her hair flying, braced her legs, bent backwards, and threw the paving stone wildly at Javert's head. Javert stooped, the stone passed over him, hit the wall behind, from which it knocked down a large piece of the plastering.

At that moment Javert reached the Thénardier couple. One of his huge hands fell upon the shoulder of the woman, and the other upon her husband's head.

"The handcuffs!" cried he.

The police officers returned in a body, and in a few seconds Javert's order was executed.

The Thénardiess, completely crushed, looked at her manacled hands and those of her husband, dropped to the floor and exclaimed, with tears in her eyes:

"My daughters!"

"They are provided for," said Javert.

Meanwhile the officers had found the drunken fellow who was asleep behind the door, and shook him. He awoke stammering.

"Is it over, Jondrette?"

"Yes," answered Javert.

The six manacled bandits were standing, three blackened, three masked.

"Keep on your masks," said Javert.

And, passing them in review with the eye of a Frederic II. at parade at Potsdam, he said to the three "chimney doctors":

"Good day, Bigrenaille. Good day, Brujon. Good day, Deux Milliards."

Then, turning towards the three masks, he said to the man of the pole-axe:

"Good day, Gueulemer."

And to the man of the cudgel:

"Good day, Babet."

And to the ventriloquist:

"Your health, Claquesous."

Just then he perceived the prisoner of the bandits, who, since the entrance of the police, had not uttered a word, and had held his head down.

"Untie monsieur!" said Javert, "and let nobody go out."

This said, he sat down with authority before the table, on which the candle and the writing materials still were, drew a stamped sheet from his pocket, and commenced his procès verbal.

When he had written the first lines, a part of the formula, which is always the same, he raised his eyes:

"Bring forward the gentleman whom these gentlemen had bound."

The officers looked about them.

"Well," asked Javert, "where is he now?"

The prisoner of the bandits, M. Leblanc, M. Urbain Fabre, the father of Ursula, or the Lark, had disappeared.

The door was guarded, but the window was not. As soon as he saw that he was unbound, and while Javert was writing, he had taken advantage of the disturbance, the tumult, the confusion, the obscurity, to leap out of the window.

An officer ran to the window; nobody could be seen outside.

The rope ladder was still trembling.

"The devil!" said Javert, between his teeth, "that must have been the best one."

The day following that in which these events took place in the house on the Boulevard de l'Hôpital, a child, who seemed to come from somewhere near the bridge of Austerlitz, went up by the cross alley on the right in the direction of the Barrière de Fontainebleau. Night had closed in. This child was pale, thin, dressed in rags, with tow trousers in the month of February, and was singing with all his might.

At the corner of the Rue du Petit Banquier, an old crone was fumbling in a manure-heap by the light of a street lamp; the child knocked against her as he passed, then drew back, exclaiming:

"Why! I took that for an enormous, enormous dog!"

The old woman rose up furious.

"Jail-bird!" muttered she. "If I had not been stooping over, I know where I would have planted my foot!"

The child was now at a little distance.

"K'sss! k'sss!" said he. "After all, Madame has not the style of beauty that suits me."

He went on his way and reached No. 50-52. Finding the door locked, he began to batter it with kicks, heroic and re-echoing kicks, that revealed rather the men's shoes which he wore, than the child's feet which he had.

Meantime, this same old woman was running after him with much clamour and many crazy gestures. What's the matter? what's the matter? Good God! They are staving the door down! They are breaking into the house!

Suddenly she stopped. She had recognised the *gamin*.

"What! it is that Satan!"

"Hullo, it is the old woman," said the child. "Good day, Burgonmuche. I have come to see my ancestors."

"There is nobody there, nosey."

"Pshaw!" said the child, "where is my father, then?"

"At La Force."

"Heigho! and my mother?"

"At Saint Lazare."

"Well! and my sisters?"

"At Les Madelonnettes."

The child scratched the back of his ear, looked at Ma'am Burgon and said:

"Ah!"

Then he turned on his heel, and a moment afterwards, the old woman heard him sing, as he disappeared under the black elms shivering in the wintry winds.

XIX. EPONINE

The Revolution of 1830 soon grounded. The years 1831 and 1832 are one of the most peculiar and most striking periods in history.

Who stops revolutions half-way? The bourgeoisie.

Why? Because the bourgeoisie is the interest which has attained to satisfaction.

There has been an attempt, an erroneous one, to make a special class of the bourgeoisie. The bourgeoisie is simply the contented portion of the people. The bourgeois is the man who has now time to sit down. A chair is not a caste.

But, by wishing to sit down, we may stop the progress even of the human race. That has often been the fault of the bourgeois.

As soon as the revolution strikes the shore, the able carve up the wreck. The able, in our age, have decreed to themselves the title of statesmen, so that this word, statesman, has come to be, in some sort, a word of argot. Indeed, let no one forget, wherever there is ability only, there is necessarily pettiness. To say "the able," amounts to saying, "mediocrity," just as saying, "statesmen," is sometimes equivalent to saying "traitors."

According to the able, therefore, revolutions such as the Revolution of July, are arteries cut; a prompt ligature is needed. The theory of the able is to give a success something of the sound of a catastrophe, in order that those who profit by it may tremble also, to moderate a step in advance with fear, to enlarge the curve of transition to the extent of retarding progress, to tame down this work, to denounce and restrain the ardencies of enthusiasm, to cut off the corners and the claws, to clog triumph, to swaddle the right, to wrap up the people-giant in flannel and hurry him to bed.

The year 1830 made Louis Philippe king. Lafayette undertook the coronation. He called it *the best of republics.*

Louis Philippe had been handsome, and, when old, was still fine looking; not always agreeable to the nation, he always was to the multitude; he pleased. He had this gift, a charm. Majesty he lacked; he neither wore the crown, though king, nor white hair, though an old man. His manners were of the old régime, and his habits of the new, a mixture of the noble and the bourgeois which was befitting to 1830.

He went rarely to chapel, not at all to the chase, never to the opera. Incorruptible by priests, dog-keepers, and danseuses; this entered into his popularity with the bourgeoisie. He had no court. He went out with his umbrella under his arm, and this umbrella for a long time was a portion of his glory.

To be Prince Equality, to bear within himself the contradiction of the Restoration and the Revolution, such was the fortune of Louis Philippe in 1830; never was there a more complete adaptation of a man to an event. Louis Philippe is 1830 made man. Moreover, he had in his favour that grand designation for the throne, exile. He had been proscribed, a wanderer, poor. He had lived by his labour. In Switzerland, this heir to the richest princely domains in France had sold an old horse, to procure food. At Reichenau he had given lessons in mathematics, while his sister Adelaide did sewing and embroidery. These memories associated with a king, rendered the bourgeoisie enthusiastic.

He was the friend of Lafayette; he had belonged to the Jacobin Club; Mirabeau had slapped him on the shoulder; Danton had said to him, "Young man!" At twenty-four years of age, in '93, being M. de Chartres, from the back of an obscure bench in the convention, he had been present at the trial of Louis XVI., so well named *that poor tyrant.*

The effect which the Revolution produced upon him was tremendous. His memory was like a living impression of those grand years, minute by minute. One day, before a witness whom it is impossible for us to doubt, he corrected from memory the whole letter A of the alphabetic list of the constituent assembly.

Louis Philippe was a king in broad day. While he reigned the press was free, the tribune was free, conscience and speech were free. The laws of September are clear and open. Knowing well the corroding power of light on privileges, he left his throne exposed to the light.

The government of 1830 had from the first a hard life. Born yesterday, it was obliged to fight to-day.

It was hardly installed when it began to feel on all sides vague movements directed against the machinery of July, still so newly set up, and so far from secure. Meanwhile, within the country, pauperism, proletariat, wages, education, punishment, prostitution, the lot of woman, riches, misery, production, consumption, distribution, exchange, money, credit, rights of capital, rights of labour, all these questions multiplied over society; a terrible steep.

Towards the end of April, 1832, fermentation became boiling. Glimpses were caught of a possible revolution. France looked to Paris; Paris looked to the Faubourg Saint Antoine.

The wine-shops of the Rue de Charonne, although the junction of the two epithets seems singular, applied to wine-shops, were serious and stormy.

In them the simple existence of the government was brought in question. The men there publicly discussed whether it were *the thing to fight or to remain quiet*. There were back shops where an oath was administered to working-men, that they would be in the streets at the first cry of alarm, and "that they would fight without counting the number of the enemy." Sometimes they went upstairs into a closed room, and there scenes occurred which were almost masonic.

In the lower rooms they read "subversive" pamphlets.

A carpenter, engaged on the Rue de Reuilly in nailing the boards of a fence about a lot on which a house was building, found in the lot a fragment of a torn letter, on which the following lines were still legible.

". . . The Committee must take measures to prevent recruiting in the sections for the different societies . . ."

And in a postscript:

"We have learned that there are muskets at No. 5 (bis) Rue du Faubourg Poissonière, to the number of five or six thousand, at an armourer's in that court. The section has no arms."

A mason going home, after his day's work, forgot a little package on a bench near the Bridge of Austerlitz. This package was carried to the guard-house. It was opened and disclosed two printed dialogues, a song entitled: *Working-men, associate*, and a tin box full of cartridges.

In a ditch on the boulevard, between Père Lachaise and the Barrière du Trône, at the most solitary spot, some children, playing, discovered under a heap of chips and rubbish a bag which contained a bullet-mould, a wooden mandrel for making cartridges, a wooden mortar in which there were some grains of hunting powder, and a little melting pot in the interior of which showed unmistakable traces of melted lead.

The government received word one day that arms had just been distributed in the Faubourg and two hundred thousand cartridges. The week afterwards thirty thousand cartridges were distributed. A remarkable thing, the police could not seize one. An intercepted letter contained: "The day is not distant when in four hours by the clock, eighty thousand patriots will be under arms."

All this fermentation was public, we might almost say tranquil. The imminent insurrection gathered its storm calmly in the face of the government. No singularity was wanting in this crisis, still subterranean, but already perceptible. Bourgeois talked quietly with working-men about the preparations.

A man entered a shop, drank, and went out, saying: "*Wine-merchant, what is due, the revolution will pay.*"

At a wine-shop opposite the Rue de Charonne, revolutionary officers were elected. The ballots were gathered in caps.

One day at a liquor-dealer's door in the Lenoir market, a man with a heavy beard and an Italian accent mounted on a block and read aloud a singular writing which seemed to emanate from a secret power. Groups formed about him and applauded. The passages which stirred the crowd most were caught and noted down. ". . . Our doctrines are trammelled, our proclamations are torn down, our posters are watched and thrown into prison . . ." ". . . The recent fall in cottons has converted many moderates . . ." "The future of the peoples is being worked out in our obscure ranks." ". . . Behold the statement of the matter: action or reaction, revolution or counter-revolution. For, in our times, there is no belief longer in inertia or in immobility. For the people or against the people, that is the question. There is no other." ". . . The day that we no longer suit you, crush us, but until then help us to go forward." All this in broad day.

Other acts, bolder still, were suspected by the people on account of their very boldness. On the 4th of April, 1832, a passer-by mounted the block at the corner of the Rue Sainte Marguerite, and cried:

"Down with property! The opposition of the left are cowards and traitors. When they want to be right, they preach revolution. They are democrats that they may not be beaten, and royalists that they may not fight. Distrust the republicans, citizen labourers."

"Silence, citizen spy!" cried a working-man.

This situation was, as we said in the beginning, rendered tangible and emphatic by the Faubourg Saint Antoine more than by any other portion of the population. There was the stitch in the side.

This old Faubourg, populous as an ant-hill, industrious, courageous, and choleric as a hive, was thrilling with the expectation and the desire for a commotion. Everything was in agitation, and yet labour was not interrupted on that account.

There are in that Faubourg bitter distresses hidden under garret roofs; there are there also ardent and rare intelligencies. And it is especially in reference to distress and intelligence that it is dangerous for extremes to meet.

The Faubourg Saint Antoine had still other causes of excitement, for it felt the rebound of the commercial crises, of the failures, the strikes, and stoppages, inherent in great political disturbances. In time of revolution misery is at once cause and effect. This population, full of proud virtue, filled with latent caloric to the highest point, always ready for an armed contest, prompt to explode, irritated, deep, mined, seemed only waiting for the fall of a spark. Whenever certain sparks are floating over the horizon, driven by the wind of events, we cannot but think of the Faubourg Saint Antoine and the terrible chance which has placed the powder-mill of sufferings and ideas at the gates of Paris.

The Faubourg Saint Antoine is a reservoir of people. Revolutionary agitation makes fissures in it through which flows popular sovereignty. This sovereignty may do harm; it makes mistakes like everything else; but, even when led astray, it is still grand.

In '93, according as the idea which was afloat was good or bad, according as it was the day of fanaticism or of enthusiasm, there came from the Faubourg Saint Antoine sometimes savage legions, sometimes heroic bands.

Savage. We must explain this word. What was the aim of those bristling men who in the demiurgic days of revolutionary chaos, raged, howling, wild, with tomahawk raised, and pike aloft, rushed over old overturned Paris? They desired the end of oppressions, the end of tyrannies, the end of the sword, labour for man, instruction for children, social gentleness for woman, liberty, equality, fraternity, bread for all, ideas for all. The Edenisation of the world, Progress; this holy, good, and gentle thing, progress, pushed to the wall and beside themselves, they demanded, terrible, half naked, a club in their grasp, and a roar in their mouth. They were savages, yes; but the savages of civilisation.

They proclaimed the right furiously; they desired, were it through fear and trembling, to force the human race into paradise. They seemed barbarians, and they were saviours. With the mask of night they demanded the light.

In contrast with these men, wild, we admit, and terrible, but wild and terrible for the good, there are other men, smiling, embroidered, gilded, beribboned, bestarred, in silk stockings, in white feathers, in yellow gloves, in varnished shoes, who, leaning upon a velvet table by the corner of a marble mantel, softly insist upon the maintenance and the preservation of the past, the middle ages, divine right, fanaticism, ignorance, slavery, the death penalty, and war, glorifying politely and in mild tones the sabre, the stake, and the scaffold. As for us, if we were compelled to choose between the barbarians of civilisation, and the civilisees of barbarism, we would choose the barbarians.

ALL were in conventicle at the Café Musain.

Enjorlas said, "It is well to know where we are and on whom we can rely. Let us then take a little account of the herd. How many are there of us? We cannot put this work off till to-morrow. Courfeyrac, you will see the Polytechnicians. It is their day out. To-day, Wednesday. Feuilly, will you not see the men of the Glacière? Combeferre has promised me to go to Picpus. Bahorel will visit the Estrapade. Prouvaire, the masons are growing lukewarm; you will bring us news from the lodge in the Rue de Grenelle Saint Honoré. Joly will go to Dupuytren's clinique, and feel the pulse of the Medical School. Bossuet will make a little tour in the Palace of Justice and chat with the young lawyers. I will take charge of the Cougourde."

"Then it is all arranged," said Courfeyrac.

"No."

"What more is there then?"

"The Barrière du Maine," answered Enjolras. "At the Barrière du Maine there are marble cutters, painters, assistants in sculptors' studios. It is an enthusiastic family, but subject to chills. I do not know what has ailed them for some time. They are thinking of other things. They are fading out. They spend their time in playing dominoes. Somebody must go and talk to them a little, and firmly too. They meet at Richefeu's. They can be found there between noon and one o'clock. We must blow upon these embers. I had counted on that absent-minded Marius for this, for on the whole he is good, but he does not come any more. I must have somebody for the Barrière du Maine. I have nobody left."

"I," said Grantaire, "I am here."

"You?"

"I."

"You to indoctrinate republicans! you, to warm up, in the name of principles, hearts that have grown cold!"

"Why not?"

"Is it possible that you can be good for anything?"

"Yes, I have a vague ambition for it," said Grantaire.

"Do you know anything about these comrades at Richefeu's?"

"Not much. We are on good terms, though."

"What will you say to them?"

"I will talk to them about Robespierre, faith. About Danton, about principles."

"You!"

"I. But you don't do me justice. When I am about it, I am terrible. I have read Prudhomme, I know the Contrat Social, I know my Constitution of the year Two by heart. 'The Liberty of the citizen ends where the Liberty of another citizen begins.' Do you take me for a brute? I have an old assignat in my drawer. The Rights of Man, the sovereignty of the people, zounds! I can repeat, for six hours at a time, watch in hand, superb things."

"Be serious," said Enjolras.

"I am savage," answered Grantaire.

Enjolras thought for a few seconds, and made the gesture of a man who forms his resolution.

"Grantaire," said he gravely, "I consent to try you. You shall go to the Barrière du Maine."

Grantaire lived in a furnished room quite near the Café Musain. He went out, and came back in five minutes. He had been home to put on a Robespierre waistcoat.

"Red," said he as he came in.

And, approaching Enjolras, he whispered in his ear:

"Set your mind at ease."

He jammed down his hat, resolutely, and went out.

A quarter of an hour later, the back room of the Café Musain was deserted. All the Friends of the A B C had gone, each his own way, to their business. Enjolras, who had reserved the Cougourde for himself, went out last.

One o'clock sounded from the belfry of Vaugirard when Enjolras reached the Richefeu smoking-room. A voice was ringing out in the mist, sharply answered by another voice. It was· Grantaire talking with an adversary whom he had found.

Grantaire was seated, opposite another figure, at a table of Saint Anne marble strewed with bran, and dotted with dominoes: he was striking the marble with his fist, and what Enjolras heard was this:

"Double six."

"Four."

"The beast! I can't play."

"You are done for. Two."

"Six."

"Three."

"Ace."

"Blank."

"Has he any chance! Ah! you have one chance! (Long reverie.) Two."

"Ace."

"Neither a five, nor an ace. That is bothering for you."

"Domino!"

HARDLY had Javert left the old ruin, carrying away his prisoners in three coaches, when Marius also slipped out of the house. It was only nine o'clock in the evening. Marius went to Courfeyrac's. Courfeyrac was no longer the imperturbable inhabitant of the Latin Quarter; he had gone to live in the Rue de la Verrerie "for political reasons." Marius said to Courfeyrac: "I have come to sleep with you." Courfeyrac drew a mattress from his bed, where there were two, laid it on the floor, and said: "There you are."

The next day, by seven o'clock in the morning, Marius went back to the tenement, paid his rent, and what was due to Ma'am Bougon, had his books, bed, table, bureau, and his two chairs loaded upon a hand-cart, and went off without leaving his address. Marius had two reasons for his prompt removal. The first was, that he now had a horror of that house; the second was, that he did not wish to figure in the trial and be brought forward to testify against Thénardier.

Javert thought that the young man, whose name he had not retained, had been frightened and had escaped, or, perhaps, had not even returned home at the time of the ambuscade; he made some effort to find him, but he did not succeed.

A month rolled away, then another. Marius was still with Courfeyrac. He knew from a young attorney, an habitual attendant in the ante-rooms of the court, that Thénardier was in solitary confinement. Every Monday Marius sent to the clerk of La Force five francs for Thénardier.

Marius, having now no money, borrowed the five francs of Courfeyrac. It was the first time in his life that he had borrowed money. This periodical five francs was a double enigma, to Courfeyrac who furnished them, and to Thénardier who received them. "To whom can it go?" thought Courfeyrac. "Where can it come from?" Thénardier asked himself.

Marius was in sore affliction. Everything had relapsed into darkness. He knew not even the name which he had thought he knew. Certainly it was no longer Ursula. And the Lark was a nickname. And what should he think of the old man? Was he really hiding from the police? The white-haired working-man whom Marius had met in the neighbourhood of the Invalides recurred to his mind. It now became probable that that working-man and M. Leblanc were the same man. He disguised himself then? This man had heroic sides and equivocal sides. Why had he not called for help? why had he escaped? was he, yes or no, the father of the young girl?

If you go up the Rue Saint Jacques, leave the barrière at your side, and follow the old interior boulevard to the left for some distance, you find a sort of field. Nobody goes there, hardly a cart or a waggon once in a quarter of an hour.

It happened one day that Marius' solitary walks conducted him to this spot. That day there was a rarity on the boulevard, a passer. Marius asked this traveller: "What is the name of this place?"

The traveller answered: "It is the Field of the Lark." After that word, "the Lark," Marius heard nothing more. The Lark was the appellation which, in the depths of Marius' melancholy, had replaced Ursula. "Yes," said he, "this is her field. I shall learn here where she lives."

This was absurd, but irresistible.

And he came every day to this Field of the Lark.

Javert's triumph in the Gorbeau tenement had seemed complete, but it was not so.

In the first place, and this was his principal regret, Javert had not made the prisoner prisoner. And then, Montparnasse had escaped.

Montparnasse, having met Eponine, who was standing sentry under the trees of the boulevard, had led her away. He was free. Javert "nabbed" her, trifling consolation; Eponine had rejoined Azelma at Les Madelonnettes.

Finally, on the trip from the Gorbeau tenement to La Force, one of the principal prisoners, Claquesous, had been lost. Nobody knew how it was done, the officers and sergeants "didn't understand it," he had changed into vapour, he had glided out of the handcuffs, he had slipped through the cracks of the carriage, the fiacre was leaky, and had fled; nothing could be said, save that on reaching the prison there was no Claquesous. Was there some secret connivance of the officers? However it might be, Claquesous was not found again. Javert appeared more irritated than astonished at it.

As to Marius, "that dolt of a lawyer," who was "probably frightened," and whose name Javert had forgotten, Javert cared little for him. Besides he was a lawyer, they are always found again. But was he a lawyer merely?

The trial commenced.

The police judge thought it desirable not to put one of the men of the Patron-Minette band into solitary confinement, hoping for some blabbing. This was Brujon, the long-haired man of the Rue du Petit Banquier. He was left in the Charlemagne court, and the watchmen kept their eyes upon him.

One night, a watchman saw through the peep-hole of the dormitory, Brujon sitting up in his bed and writing something by the light of the reflector. Brujon was put into the dungeon for a month, but they could not find what he had written. The police knew nothing more.

It is certain, however, that the next day "a postillion" was thrown from the Charlemagne court into the Fosse aux Lions, over the five-story building which separates the two courts.

Prisoners call a ball of bread artistically kneaded, which is sent *into Ireland*, that is to say, over the roof of a prison, from one court to the other, a postillion. Etymology: over England; from one county to the other; *into Ireland*. This ball falls in the court. He who picks it up opens it, and finds a letter in it addressed to some prisoner in the court. If it be a convict who finds it, he hands the letter to its destination; if it be a warden, or one of those secretly bribed prisoners who are called sheep in the prisons and foxes in the galleys, the letter is carried to the office and delivered to the police.

This time the postillion reached its address, although he for whom the message was destined was then *in solitary*. Its recipient was none other than Babet, one of the four heads of Patron-Minette.

The postillion contained a paper rolled up, on which there were only these two lines:

"Babet, there is an affair on hand in the Rue Plumet. A grating in a garden."

This was the thing that Brujon had written in the night.

In spite of spies, both male and female, Babet found means to send the letter from La Force to La Salpêtrière to "a friend" of his who was shut up there. This girl in her turn transmitted the letter to another who, she knew, had some relations with the Thénardiers and could, by going to see Eponine, serve as a bridge between La Salpêtrière and Les Madelonnettes.

It happened just at that very moment that Eponine and Azelma were released. Eponine went to the Rue Plumet, reconnoitred the grating and the garden, looked at the house, spied, watched, and, a few days after transmitted a biscuit to Babet's mistress at La Salpêtrière. A biscuit, in the dark symbolism of the prisons, signifies: *nothing to do*.

So that in less than a week after that, Babet and Brujon, meeting on the way from La Force, as one was going "to examination," and the other was returning from it: "Well," asked Brujon, "the Rue P.?" "Biscuit," answered Babet.

This was the end of that fœtus of crime, engendered by Brujon in La Force.

This abortion, however, led to results entirely foreign to Brujon's programme.

MARIUS now visited nobody, but he sometimes happened to meet Father Mabeuf.

The *Flora of Cauteretz* had absolutely no more sale. The experiments upon indigo had not succeeded in the little garden of Austerlitz, which was very much exposed. M. Mabeuf was not discouraged, however. He had obtained a bit of ground in the Jardin des Plantes, with a good exposure, to carry on, "at his own cost," his experiments upon indigo. For this he had put the plates of his *Flora* into pawn. He had reduced his breakfast to two eggs, and he left one of them for his old servant, whose wages he had not paid for fifteen months. And often his breakfast was his only meal. He laughed no more with his childlike laugh, he had become morose, and he now received no visits. Marius was right in not thinking to come. Sometimes, at the hour when M. Mabeuf went to the Jardin des Plantes, the old man and the young man met on the Boulevard de l'Hôpital. They did not speak, but sadly nodded their heads.

M. Mabeuf was at this time very nearly eighty years old. One night he saw a singular apparition.

He had come home while it was still broad day. Mother Plutarch, whose health was poor, was sick and gone to bed. He had dined on a bone on which a little meat was left, and a bit of bread which he had found on the kitchen table, and had sat down on a block of stone, which took the place of a seat in his garden.

Near this seat there rose, in the fashion of the old orchard-gardens, a sort of hut, in a ruinous condition, of joists and boards, a warren on the ground floor, a fruit-house above. There were no rabbits in the warren, but there were a few apples in the fruit-house. A remnant of the winter's store.

Father Mabeuf was looking over the book which he held in his hand, at his plants, and among others at a magnificent rhododendron which was one of his consolations; there had been four days of drought, wind, and sun, without a drop of rain; the stalks bent over, the buds hung down, the leaves were falling, they all needed to be watered; the rhododendron especially was a sad sight. Father Mabeuf was one of those to whom plants have souls. The old man had worked all day on his indigo bed, he was exhausted with fatigue, he got up nevertheless, put his books upon the bench, and walked, bent over and with tottering steps, to the well, but when he had grasped the chain, he could not even draw it far enough to unhook it. Then he turned and looked with a look of anguish towards the sky which was filling with stars.

The evening had that serenity which buries the sorrows of man under a strangely dreary yet eternal joy. The night promised to be as dry as the day had been.

"Stars everywhere!" thought the old man; "not the smallest cloud! not a drop of water."

At this moment he heard a voice which said:

"Father Mabeuf, would you like to have me water your garden?"

At the same time he heard a sound like that of a passing deer in the hedge, and he saw springing out of the shrubbery a sort of tall, slender girl, who came and stood before him, looking boldly at him.

Before Father Mabeuf, who was easily startled, could answer a word, this being had unhooked the chain, plunged in and drawn out the bucket, and filled the watering-pot, and the goodman saw this apparition with bare feet and a ragged skirt running along the beds, distributing life about her. The sound of the water upon the leaves filled Father Mabeuf's soul with transport. It seemed to him that now the rhododendron was happy.

When the first bucket was emptied, the girl drew a second, then a third. She watered the whole garden.

"God will bless you," said Father Mabeuf, "you are an angel, since you care for flowers."

"No," she answered, "I am the devil, but that is all the same to me."

The old man exclaimed:

"What a pity that I am so unfortunate and so poor, and that I cannot do anything for you!"

"You can do something," said she.

"What?"

"Tell me where M. Marius lives."

The old man did not understand.

"What Monsieur Marius?"

"A young man who used to come here."

M. Mabeuf had fumbled in his memory.

"Ah! yes,—" he exclaimed, "I know what you mean. Listen, now! Monsieur Marius—the Baron Marius Pontmercy, yes! he lives—or rather he does not live there now—ah! well, I don't know."

While he spoke, he had bent over to tie up a branch of the rhododendron, and he continued:

"Ah! I remember now. He passes up the boulevard very often, and goes toward the Field of the Lark. Go that way. He isn't hard to find."

When M. Mabeuf rose up, there was nobody there; the girl had disappeared.

He was decidedly a little frightened.

"Really," thought he, "if my garden was not watered, I should think it was a spirit."

A few days after this visit of a "spirit" to Father Mabeuf, one morning—it was Monday, the day on which Marius borrowed the hundred-sous piece of Courfeyrac for Thénardier—Marius had put this hundred-sous piece into his pocket, and before carrying it to the prison office, he had gone to the Field of the Lark.

He lived in the Field of the Lark rather than in Courfeyrac's room. That morning, he sat down on the bank of the brook of the Gobelins. The bright sun was gleaming through the new and glossy leaves.

He was thinking of "Her!" All at once he heard a voice which was known to him, say:

"Ah! there he is!"

He raised his eyes and recognised the unfortunate child who had come to his room one morning, the elder of the Thénardier girls, Eponine; he now knew her name. Singular fact, she had become more wretched and more beautiful, two steps which seemed impossible. She had accomplished a double progress towards the light, and towards distress. She was barefooted and in rags, as on the day when she had so resolutely entered his room, only her rags were two months older; the holes were larger, the tatters dirtier. It was the same rough voice, the same forehead tanned and wrinkled by exposure; the same free, wild, and wandering gaze. She had, in addition to her former expression, that mixture of fear and sorrow which the experience of a prison adds to misery.

She had spears of straw and grass in her hair, not like Ophelia from having gone mad through the contagion of Hamlet's madness, but because she had slept in some stable loft.

And with all this, she was beautiful.

Meantime, she had stopped before Marius with something which resembled a smile.

She stood for a few seconds, as if she could not speak.

"I have found you, then?" said she at last. "Father Mabeuf was right; it was on this boulevard. How I have looked for you! if you only knew? Do you know? I have been in the jug. A fortnight! They have let me out! seeing that there was nothing against me, and then I was not of the age of discernment. It lacked two months. Oh! how I have looked for you! it is six weeks now. You don't live down there any longer?"

"No," said Marius.

"Oh! I understand. On account of the affair. Such scares are disagreeable. You have moved. What! why do you wear such an old hat as that? a young man like you ought to have fine clothes. Do you know, Monsieur Marius? Father Mabeuf calls you Baron Marius, I forget what more. It's not true that you are a baron? barons are old fellows, they go to the Luxembourg in front of the château where there is the most sun, they read the *Quotidienne* for a sou. I went once for a letter to a baron's like that. He was more than a hundred years old. But tell me, where do you live now?"

Marius did not answer.

"Ah!" she continued, "you have a hole in your shirt. I must mend it for you."

She resumed with an expression which gradually grew darker:

"You don't seem to be glad to see me?"

Marius said nothing; she herself was silent for a moment, then exclaimed:

"But if I would, I could easily make you glad!"

"How?" inquired Marius. "What does that mean?"

"Ah! you used to speak more kindly to me!" replied she.

"Well, what is it that you mean?"

She bit her lip; she seemed to hesitate, as if passing through a kind of interior struggle. At last, she appeared to decide upon her course.

"So much the worse, it makes no difference. You look sad, I want you to be glad. But promise me that you will laugh, I want to see you laugh and hear you say: Ah, well! that is good. Poor Monsieur Marius! you know, you promised me that you would give me whatever I should ask—"

"Yes! but tell me!"

She looked into Marius' eyes and said:

"I have the address."

Marius turned pale. All his blood flowed back to his heart.

"What address?"

"The address you asked me for."

She added as if she were making an effort:

"The address—you know well enough!"

"Yes!" stammered Marius.

"Of the young lady!"

Having pronounced this word, she sighed deeply.

Marius sprang up from the bank on which he was sitting, and took her wildly by the hand.

"Oh! come! show me the way, tell me! ask me for whatever you will! Where is it?"

"Come with me," she answered. "I am not sure of the street and the number; it is away on the other side from here, but I know the house very well. I will show you."

She withdrew her hand and added in a tone which would have pierced the heart of an observer, but which did not even touch the intoxicated and transported Marius:

"Oh! how glad you are!"

A cloud passed over Marius' brow. He seized Eponine by the arm:

"Swear to me one thing!"

"Swear?" said she, "what does that mean? Ah! you want me to swear?"

And she laughed.

"Your father! promise me, Eponine! swear to me that you will not give this address to your father!"

She turned towards him with an astounded appearance.

"Eponine! How do you know that my name is Eponine?"

"Promise what I ask you!"

But she did not seem to understand.

"That is nice! you called me Eponine!"

Marius caught her by both arms at once.

"But answer me now, in heaven's name! pay attention to what I am saying, swear to me that you will not give the address you know to your father!"

"My father?" said she. "Oh! yes, my father! Do not be concerned on his account. He is in solitary. Besides, do I busy myself about my father!"

"But you don't promise me!" exclaimed Marius.

"Let me go then!" said she, bursting into a laugh, "how you shake me! Yes! yes! I promise you that! I swear to you that! What is it to me? I won't give the address to my father. There! will that do? is that it?"

"Nor to anybody?" said Marius.

"Nor to anybody."

"Now," added Marius, "show me the way."

"Right away?"

"Right away."

"Come. Oh! how glad he is!" said she.

After a few steps, she stopped.

"You follow too near me, Monsieur Marius. Let me go forward, and follow me like that, without seeming to. It won't do for a fine young man, like you, to be seen with a woman like me."

˙ She went on a few steps, and stopped again; Marius rejoined her. She spoke to him aside and without turning:

"By the way, you know you have promised me something?"

Marius fumbled in his pocket. He had nothing in the world but the five francs intended for Thénardier. He took it, and put it into Eponine's hand.

She opened her fingers and let the piece fall on the ground, and, looking at him with a gloomy look:

"I don't want your money," said she.

XX. THE SECRET HOUSE

TOWARDS the middle of the last century, a velvet-capped president of the Parlement of Paris having a mistress and concealing it, had *"une petite maison"* built in the Faubourg Saint Germain, in the deserted Rue de Blomet, now called the Rue Plumet.

This was a summer-house of but two stories; two rooms on the ground floor, two chambers in the second story, a kitchen below, a boudoir above, a garret next the roof, the whole fronted by a garden with a large iron grated gate opening on the street. This garden contained about an acre. This was all that the passers-by could see; but in the rear of the house there was a small yard, at the further end of which there was a low building, two rooms only and a cellar, a convenience intended to conceal a child and nurse in case of need. This building communicated, from the rear, by a masked door opening secretly, with a long narrow passage, paved, winding, open to the sky, bordered by two high walls, and which, concealed with wonderful art, and as it were lost between the inclosures of the gardens and fields, all the corners and turnings of which it followed, came to an end at another door, also concealed, which opened a third of a mile away, almost in another quartier, upon the unbuilt end of the Rue de Babylone.

The house, built of stone in the Mansard style, wainscoted, and furnished in the Watteau style, walled about with a triple hedge of flowers, had a discreet, coquettish, and solemn appearance about it, suitable to a caprice of love and of magistracy.

In the month of October, 1829, a man of a certain age hired the house as it stood, including, of course, the building in the rear, and the passage which ran out to the Rue de Babylone. He had the secret openings of the two doors of this passage repaired. The house was still nearly furnished with the president's old furniture. The new tenant had ordered a few repairs, and finally came and installed himself with a young girl and an aged servant, without any noise, rather like somebody stealing in than like a man who enters his own house. The neighbours did not gossip about it, for the reason that there were no neighbours.

This tenant, to partial extent, was Jean Valjean; the young girl was Cosette. The servant was a spinster named Toussaint, whom Jean Valjean had saved from the hospital and misery, and who was old, stuttering, and a native of a province, three qualities which had determined Jean Valjean to take her with him. He hired the house under the name of Monsieur Fauchelevent, gentleman. In what has been related hitherto, the reader doubtless recognised Jean Valjean even before Thénardier did.

Why had Jean Valjean left the convent of the Petit Picpus? What had happened?

Nothing had happened.

Jean Valjean was happy in the convent, so happy that his conscience at last began to be troubled. He saw Cosette every day, he said to himself that she was his, that nothing could take her from him, that this would be so indefinitely, that certainly she would become a nun, being every day gently led on towards it. Thus the convent was henceforth the universe to her as well as to him, he would grow old there and she would grow up there, she would grow old there and he would die there; no separation was possible.

In reflecting upon this, he at last began to find difficulties. He questioned himself. He said to himself that this child had a right to know what life was before renouncing it; that to cut her off, in advance, and, in some sort, without consulting her, from all pleasure, under pretence of saving her from all trial, to take advantage of her ignorance and isolation to give her an artificial vocation, was to outrage a human creature and to lie to God. And who knows but, thinking over all this some day, and being a nun with regret, Cosette might come to hate him? a final thought, which was insupportable to him. He resolved to leave the convent.

As to objections, there were none. Five years of sojourn between those four walls, and of absence from among men, had necessarily destroyed or dispersed the elements of alarm. He might return tranquilly among men. He had grown old, and all had changed. Who would recognize him now? And then, to look at the worst, there was no danger save for himself, and he had no right to condemn Cosette to the cloister for the reason that he had been condemned to the galleys. What, moreover, is danger in presence of duty? Finally, nothing prevented him from being prudent, and taking proper precautions.

As to Cosette's education, it was almost complete.

His determination once formed, he awaited an opportunity. It was not slow to present itself. Old Fauchelevent died.

Jean Valjean asked an audience of the reverend prioress, and told her that having received a small inheritance on the death of his brother, which enabled him to live henceforth without labour, he would leave the service of the convent, and take away his daughter; but that, as it was not just that Cosette, not taking her vows, should have been educated gratuitously, he humbly begged the reverend prioress to allow him to offer the community, as indemnity for the five years which Cosette had passed there, the sum of five thousand francs.

Thus Jean Valjean left the convent of the Perpetual Adoration.

On leaving the convent, he took in his own hands, and would not entrust to any assistant, the little box, the key of which he always had about him. Cosette laughed about it, and called this box *the inseparable,* saying: "I am jealous of it."

Jean Valjean nevertheless did not appear again in the open city without deep anxiety. He discovered the house in the Rue Plumet, and buried himself in it. He was henceforth in possession of the name of Ultimus Fauchelevent.

At the same time he hired two other lodgings in Paris, in order to change his abode on occasion, and not again find himself in such a strait as on the night when he had so miraculously escaped from Javert. These two lodgings were two very humble dwellings, and of a poor appearance, in two quartiers widely distant from each other, one in the Rue de l'Ouest, the other in the Rue de l'Homme Armé.

He went from time to time, now to the Rue de l'Homme Armé, and now to the Rue de l'Ouest, to spend a month or six weeks, with Cosette, without taking Toussaint. He was waited upon by the porters, and gave himself out for a man of some means of the suburbs, having a foothold in the city. This lofty virtue had three domiciles in Paris in order to escape from the police.

Still, properly speaking, he lived in the Rue Plumet, and he had ordered his life there in the following manner:

Cosette with the servant occupied the house; she had the large bedroom with painted piers, the boudoir with gilded mouldings, the president's parlour furnished with tapestry and huge arm-chairs; she had the garden. Jean Valjean had a bed put into Cosette's chamber with a canopy of antique damask in three colours, and an old and beautiful Persian carpet; to soften the severity of these magnificent relics, he had added to this curiosity shop all the little lively and graceful pieces of furniture used by young girls, an étagère, a bookcase and gilt books, a writing-case, a blotting-case, a work-table inlaid with pearl, a silver-gilt dressing-case, a dressing table in Japan porcelain. Long damask curtains of three colours, on a red ground, matching those of the bed, hung at the second story windows. On the first floor, tapestry curtains. All winter Cosette's Petite Maison was warmed from top to bottom. For his part, he lived in the sort of porter's lodge in the back-yard, with a mattress on a cot bedstead, a white wood table, two straw chairs, an earthen water-pitcher, a few books upon a board, his dear box in a corner, never any fire. He dined with Cosette, and there was a black loaf on the table for him. He said to Toussaint, when she entered their service: "Mademoiselle is the mistress of the house." "And you, m-monsieur?" replied Toussaint, astounded. "Me, I am much better than the master, I am the father."

Cosette had been trained to housekeeping in the convent, and she regulated the expenses, which were very moderate. Every day Jean Valjean took Cosette's arm, and went to walk with her. They went to the least frequented walk of the Luxembourg, and every Sunday to mass, always at Saint Jacques du Haut Pas, because it was quite distant. As that is a very poor quartier, he gave much alms there, and the unfortunate surrounded him in the church, which had given him the title of the superscription of the epistle of the Thénardiers: *To the benevolent gentleman of the church of Saint Jacques du Haut Pas.* He was fond of taking Cosette to visit the needy and the sick. No stranger came into the house in the Rue Plumet. Toussaint brought the provisions, and Jean Valjean himself went after the water to a watering trough which was near by on the boulevard.

There was on the Rue de Babylone door a box for letters and papers; but the three occupants of the summer-house on the Rue Plumet receiving neither papers nor letters, the entire use of the box, formerly the agent of amours and the confidant of a legal spark, was now limited to the notices of the receiver of taxes and the Guard warnings. For M. Fauchelevent belonged to the National Guard: he had not been able to escape the close meshes of the enrollment of 1831. The municipal investigation made at that time had extended even to the convent of the Petit Picpus, a sort of impenetrable and holy cloud from which Jean Valjean had come forth venerable in the eyes of his magistracy, and, in consequence, worthy of mounting guard.

Three or four times a year, Jean Valjean donned his uniform, and performed his duties, very willingly; it was a good disguise for him, which associated him with everybody else while leaving him solitary. Jean Valjean had completed his sixtieth year, the age of legal exemption; but he did not appear more than fifty; moreover, he had no desire to cavil; he had no civil standing; he was concealing his name, he was concealing his identity, he was concealing his age, he was concealing everything;

and, we have just said, he was very willingly a National Guard. To resemble the crowd who pay their taxes, this was his whole ambition.

We must note one incident, however. When Jean Valjean went out with Cosette, he dressed as we have seen, and had much the air of an old officer. When he went out alone, and this was most usually in the evening, he was always clad in the waistcoat and trousers of a working-man, and wore a cap which hid his face. Was this precaution, or humility? Both at once.

Neither Jean Valjean, nor Cosette, nor Toussaint, ever came in or went out except by the gate on the Rue de Babylone. Unless one had seen them through the grated gate of the garden, it would have been difficult to guess that they lived in the Rue Plumet. This gate always remained closed. Jean Valjean had left the garden uncultivated, that it might not attract attention.

In this he deceived himself, perhaps.

This garden, thus abandoned to itself for more than half a century, had become very strange and very pleasant. The passers-by of forty years ago stopped in the street to look at it, without suspecting the secrets which it concealed behind its fresh green thickets. More than one dreamer of that day has many a time allowed his eyes and his thoughts indiscreetly to penetrate through the bars of the ancient gate which was padlocked, twisted, tottering, secured by two green and mossy pillars, and grotesquely crowned with a pediment of indecipherable arabesque.

There was a stone seat in a corner, one or two mouldy statues, some trellises loosened by time and rotting upon the wall; dog-grass everywhere. Horticulture had departed, and nature had returned. Weeds were abundant. The heyday of the gilliflowers was splendid. The trees bent over towards the briers, the briers mounted towards the trees, the shrub had climbed, the branch had bowed, that which runs upon the ground had attempted to find that which blooms in the air, that which floats in the wind had stooped towards that which trails in the moss; trunks, branches, leaves, twigs, tufts, tendrils, shoots, thorns, were mingled, crossed, married, confounded; vegetation, in a close and strong embrace, had celebrated and accomplished there under the satisfied eye of the Creator, in this inclosure of three hundred feet square, the sacred mystery of its fraternity, symbol of human fraternity.

At night, a dreamy vapour arose from the garden and wrapped it around; a shroud of mist, a calm and celestial sadness, covered it; the intoxicating odour of honeysuckles and bindweed rose on all sides like an exquisite and subtle poison; you heard the last appeals of the woodpecker, and the wagtails drowsing under the branches; you felt the sacred intimacy of bird and tree; by day the wings rejoiced the leaves; by night the leaves protected the wings.

In winter, the bush was black, wet, bristling, shivering, and let the house be seen in part. You perceived, instead of the flowers in the branches and the dew in the flowers, the long silver ribbons of the snails upon the thick and cold carpet of yellow leaves; but in every way, under every aspect, in every season, spring, winter, summer, autumn, this little inclosure exhaled melancholy, contemplation, solitude, liberty, the absence of man, the presence of God, and the old rusty grating appeared to say: "This garden is mine!"

There was also in this solitude a heart which was all ready.

Cosette had left the convent, still almost a child; she was a little more than fourteen years old, and she was "at the ungraceful age"; as we have said, apart from her eyes, she seemed rather homely than pretty; she had, however, no ungraceful features, but she was awkward, thin, timid, and bold at the same time, a big child in short.

Her education was finished; that is to say, she had been taught religion, and also, and above all, devotion; then "history," that is, the thing which they call thus in the convent, geography, grammar, the participles, the kings of France, a little music, to draw profiles, etc., but further than this she was ignorant of everything, which is a charm and a peril. The soul of a young girl ought not to be left in obscurity; in after life there spring up too sudden and too vivid mirages.

Nothing prepares a young girl for passions like the convent. The convent turns the thoughts in the direction of the unknown. From thence visions, suppositions, conjectures, romances sketched out, longings for adventures, fantastic constructions, whole castles are built in the interior obscurity of the mind.

One day Cosette happened to look in her mirror, and she said to herself: "What!" It seemed to her almost that she was pretty. This threw her into strange anxiety. Up to this moment she had never thought of her face. She had seen herself in her glass, but she had not looked at herself. And then, she had often been told that she was homely; Jean Valjean alone would quietly say: "Why no! why! no!" And now suddenly her mirror said like Jean Valjean: "Why no!" She had no sleep that night. "If I were pretty!" thought she, "how funny it would be if I should be pretty!"

The next day she looked at herself, but not by chance, and she doubted. "Where were my wits gone?" said she, "no, I am homely." She had merely slept badly, her eyes were dark and she was pale. She had not felt very happy the evening before, in the thought that she was beautiful, but she was sad at thinking so no longer. She did not look at herself again, and for more than a fortnight she tried to dress her hair with her back to the mirror.

In the evening after dinner, she regularly made tapestry or did some convent work in the parlour, while Jean Valjean read by her side. Once, on raising her eyes from her work, she was very much surprised at the anxious way in which her father was looking at her.

At another time, she was passing along the street, and it seemed to her that somebody behind her, whom she did not see, said: "Pretty woman! but badly dressed." "Pshaw!" thought she, "that is not me. I am well dressed and homely." She had on at the time her plush hat and merino dress.

At last, she was in the garden one day, and heard poor old Toussaint saying: "Monsieur, do you notice how pretty mademoiselle is growing?" Cosette did not hear what her father answered. Toussaint's words threw her into a sort of commotion. She ran out of the garden, went up to her room, hurried to the glass, it was three months since she had looked at herself, and uttered a cry. She was dazzled by herself.

She was beautiful and handsome; she could not help being of Toussaint's and her mirror's opinion.

For his part, Jean Valjean felt a deep and undefinable anguish in his heart.

He had in fact, for some time past, been contemplating with terror that beauty which appeared every day more radiant upon Cosette's sweet face. This man who had passed through every distress, who had been almost evil, and who had become almost holy, who, after having dragged the chain of the galleys, now dragged the invisible but heavy chain of indefinite infamy, this man whom the law had not released, and who might be at any instant retaken, and led back from the obscurity of his virtue to the broad light of public shame, this man accepted all, excused all, pardoned all, blessed all, wished well to all, and only asked of Providence, of men, of the laws, of society, of nature, of the world, this one thing, that Cosette should love him!

That Cosette should continue to love him!

He said to himself: "How beautiful she is! What will become of me?"

From the morrow of the day on which she had said: "Really, I am handsome!" Cosette gave attention to her dress. She recalled the words of the passer: "Pretty, but badly dressed," she was horrified at the merino and ashamed of the plush.

Her father had never refused her anything. In less than a month little Cosette was not only one of the prettiest women, which is something, but one of "the best dressed" in Paris, which is much more.

Still, merely by simple inspection of Cosette's toilette, a woman would have recognised that she had no mother. Certain little proprieties, certain special conventionalities, were not observed by Cosette. A mother, for instance, would have told her that a young girl does not wear damask.

The first day that Cosette went out with her dress and mantle of black damask and her white crape hat she came to take Jean Valjean's arm, gay, radiant, rosy, proud, and brilliant. "Father," said she, "how do you like this?" Jean Valjean answered in a voice which resembled the bitter voice of envy: "Charming!" He seemed as usual during the walk. When they came back he asked Cosette:

"Are you not going to wear your dress and hat any more?"

This occurred in Cosette's room. Cosette turned towards the wardrobe where her boarding-school dress was hanging.

"That disguise!" said she. "Father, what would you have me do with it? Oh! to be sure, no, I shall never wear those horrid things again."

Jean Valjean sighed deeply.

From that day, he noticed that Cosette, who previously was always asking to stay in, saying: "Father, I enjoy myself better here with you," was now always asking to go out. Indeed, what is the use of having a pretty face and a delightful dress, if you do not show them?

He also noticed that Cosette no longer had the same taste for the back-yard. She now preferred to stay in the garden, walking even without displeasure before the grating. Jean Valjean, ferocious, did not set his foot in the garden. He stayed in his back-yard, like a dog.

Cosette, by learning that she was beautiful, lost the grace of not knowing it. But what she lost in ingenuous grace, she gained in pensive and serious charm.

It was at this period that Marius, after the lapse of six months, saw her again at the Luxembourg.

The power of a glance has been so much abused in love stories, that it has come to be disbelieved in. Few people dare now to say that two beings have fallen in love because they have looked at each other. Yet it is in this way that love begins, and in this way only. The rest is only the rest, and comes afterwards.

At that particular moment when Cosette unconsciously looked with this glance which so affected Marius, Marius had no suspicion that he also had a glance which affected Cosette.

For a long time now she had seen and scrutinised him as young girls scrutinise and see, while looking another way. Marius still thought Cosette ugly, while Cosette already began to think Marius beautiful. As he paid no attention to her, this young man was quite indifferent to her. Still she could not help saying to herself that he had beautiful hair, beautiful eyes, beautiful teeth, a charming voice, when she heard him talking with his comrades; that he walked with an awkward gait, if you will, but with a grace of his own; that he did not appear altogether stupid; that his whole person was noble, gentle, natural, and proud, and finally that he had a poor appearance, but that he had a good appearance.

On the day their eyes met and at last said abruptly to both those first obscure and ineffable things which the glance stammers out, Cosette at first did not comprehend. She went back pensively to the house in the Rue de l'Ouest, to which Jean Valjean, according to his custom, had gone to spend six weeks. The next day, on waking, she thought of this unknown young man, so long indifferent and icy; she was rather a little angry at this disdainful beau.

We remember Marius' hesitations, his palpitations, his terrors. He remained at his seat and did not approach, which vexed Cosette. One day she said to Jean Valjean: "Father, let us walk a little this way." Seeing that Marius was not coming to her, she went to him. Oddly enough, the first symptom of true love in a young man is timidity, in a young woman, boldness.

That day Marius went away confident, and Cosette anxious. From that day onward, they adored each other.

The first thing that Cosette felt was a vague yet deep sadness. It seemed to her that since yesterday her soul had become black. She no longer recognised herself. The whiteness of soul of young girls, which is composed of coldness and gaiety, is like snow. It melts before love, which is its sun.

Cosette did not know what love was. She had never heard the word uttered in its earthly sense. In the books of profane music which came into the convent, *amour* was replaced by *tambour*, or *Pandour*. This made puzzles which exercised the imagination of the girls, such as: *Oh! how delightful is the tambour!* or: *Pity is not a Pandour!* But Cosette had left while yet too young to be much concerned about the "tambour." She did not know, therefore, what name to give to what she now experienced. Is one less sick for not knowing the name of the disease?

She loved with so much the more passion as she loved with ignorance. She did not know that the love which presented itself was that which best suited the condition of her soul. It was a sort of far-off worship, a mute contemplation, a deification by an unknown votary. It was the apprehension of adolescence by adolescence, the dream of her nights become a romance and remaining a dream, the wished-for phantom realised at last, and made flesh, but still having neither name, nor wrong, nor stain, nor need, nor defect; in a word, a lover distant and dwelling in the ideal, a chimera having a form. Any closer and more palpable encounter would at this first period have terrified Cosette, still half buried in the magnifying mirage of the cloister. She had all the terrors of children and all the terrors of nuns commingled. In this condition, it was not a lover that she needed, it was not even an admirer, it was a vision. She began to adore Marius as something charming, luminous, and impossible.

As extreme artlessness meets extreme coquetry, she smiled upon him, very frankly.

She waited impatiently every day the hour for her walk, she found Marius there, she felt herself inexpressibly happy, and sincerely believed that she uttered her whole thought when she said to Jean Valjean: "What a delightful garden the Luxembourg is!"

The old and eternal mother, Nature, silently warned Jean Valjean of the presence of Marius. Jean Valjean shuddered in the darkest of his mind. Jean Valjean saw nothing, knew nothing, but Marius' ways were no longer at all natural. He had a book and pretended to be reading; why did he pretend? Formerly he came with his old coat, now he had his new coat on every day; it was not very certain that he did not curl his hair, he had strange eyes, he wore gloves; in short, Jean Valjean cordially detested this young man.

Cosette gave no ground for suspicion. Without knowing exactly what affected her, she had a very definite feeling that it was something, and that it must be concealed.

There was between the taste for dress which had arisen in Cosette and the habit of wearing new coats which had grown upon this unknown man, a parallelism which made Jean Valjean anxious. It was an accident perhaps, doubtless, certainly, but a threatening accident.

He had never opened his mouth to Cosette about the unknown man. One day, however, he could not contain himself, and with that uncertain despair which hastily drops the plummet into its unhappiness, he said to her: "What a pedantic air that young man has!"

Cosette answered with supreme calmness: "That young man!"

As if she saw him for the first time in her life.

"How stupid I am!" thought Jean Valjean. "She had not even noticed him. I have shown him to her myself."

O simplicity of the old! depth of the young!

Jean Valjean commenced a sullen war against Marius, which Marius, with the sublime folly of his passion and his age, did not guess. Jean Valjean spread around him a multitude of snares; he changed his hours, he changed his seat, he forgot his handkerchief, he went to the Luxembourg alone; Marius fell headlong into every trap; and to all these interrogation points planted upon his path by Jean Valjean he answered ingenuously, yes. Meanwhile Cosette was still walled in in her apparent unconcern and her imperturbable tranquillity, so that Jean Valjean came to this conclusion: "This booby is madly in love with Cosette, but Cosette does not even know of his existence!"

There was nevertheless a painful tremor in the heart. The moment when Cosette would fall in love might come at any instant. Does not everything begin by indifference?

Once only Cosette made a mistake, and startled him. He rose from the seat to go, after sitting there three hours, and she said: "So soon!"

Jean Valjean had not discontinued the promenades in the Luxembourg, not wishing to do anything singular, and above all dreading to excite any suspicion in Cosette; but during those hours so sweet to the two lovers, while Cosette was sending her smile to the intoxicated Marius, who perceived nothing but that, and now saw nothing in the world save one radiant, adored face, Jean Valjean fixed upon Marius glaring and terrible eyes. He who had come to believe that he was no longer capable of a malevolent feeling, had moments in which, when Marius was there, he thought that he was again becoming savage and ferocious, and felt opening and upheaving against this young man those old depths of his soul where there had once been so much wrath.

What? he was there, that creature. What did he come for? He came to pry, to scent, to examine, to attempt: he came to say, "Eh, why not?" he came to prowl about his, Jean Valjean's life!—to prowl about his happiness, to clutch it and carry it away!

Jean Valjean added: "Yes, that is it! what is he looking for? an adventure? What does he want? an amour! An amour!—and as for me! What! I, after having been the most miserable of men, shall be the most unfortunate; I shall have spent sixty years of life upon my knees; I shall have suffered all that a man can suffer; I shall have grown old without having been young; I shall have lived with no family, no relatives, no friends, no wife, no children! I shall have left my blood on every stone, on every thorn, on every post, along every wall; I shall have been mild, although the world was harsh to me, and good, although it was evil; I shall have become an honest man in spite of all; I shall have repented of the wrong which I have done, and pardoned the wrongs which have been done to me, and the moment that I am rewarded, the moment that it is over, the moment that I reach the end, the moment that I have what I desire, rightfully and justly; I have paid for it, I have earned it; it will all disappear, it will all vanish, and I shall lose Cosette, and I shall lose my life, my joy, my soul, because a great booby has been pleased to come and lounge about the Luxembourg."

Then his eyes filled with a strange and dismal light. It was no longer a man looking upon a man; it was not an enemy looking upon an enemy. It was a dog looking upon a robber.

The insanity of Marius continued. One day he followed Cosette to the Rue de l'Ouest. Another day he spoke to the porter: the porter in his turn spoke, and said to Jean Valjean: "Monsieur, who is that curious young man who has been asking for you?" The next day, Jean Valjean cast that glance at Marius which Marius finally perceived. A week after, Jean Valjean had moved. He resolved that he would never set his foot again either in the Luxembourg, or in the Rue de l'Ouest. He returned to the Rue Plumet.

Cosette did not complain, she said nothing, she asked no questions, she did not seek to know any reason; she was already at that point at which one fears discovery and self-betrayal. Jean Valjean did not understand the deep significance of Cosette's silence. He noticed only that she had become sad, and he became gloomy. There was on either side an armed inexperience.

Once he made a trial. He asked Cosette:

"Would you like to go to the Luxembourg?"

A light illumined Cosette's pale face.

"Yes," said she.

They went. Three months had passed. Marius went there no longer. Marius was not there.

The next day, Jean Valjean asked Cosette again:

"Would you like to go to the Luxembourg?"

She answered sadly and quietly:

"No!"

Jean Valjean was hurt by this sadness, and harrowed by this gentleness.

These two who had loved each other so exclusively, and with so touching a love, and who had lived so long for each other, were now suffering by each other, and through each other; without speaking of it, without harsh feeling, and smiling the while.

The more unhappy of the two was Jean Valjean. Youth, even in its sorrows, always has a brilliancy of its own.

Jean Valjean felt irresistibly that Cosette was escaping him. He would have been glad to hold her fast, to rouse her enthusiasm by something external and striking. He chanced once to see a general pass in the street on horseback in full uniform, Count Coutard, Commandant of Paris. He envied this gilded man, he thought that if Cosette saw him thus it would dazzle her, that when he should give his arm to Cosette and pass before the gate of the Tuileries they would present arms to him, and that that would so satisfy Cosette that it would destroy her inclination to look at the young men.

An unexpected shock came to him in the midst of these sad thoughts.

They sometimes made a pleasure excursion to go and see the sun rise, a gentle joy suited to those who are entering upon life and those who are leaving it. A walk at early dawn, to him who loves solitude, is equivalent to a walk at night, with the gaiety of nature added. The streets are empty and the birds are singing.

Jean Valjean's inclination was to go to unfrequented spots, to solitary nooks, to neglected places. There were at that time in the neighbourhood of the barrières of Paris some poor fields, almost in the city, where there grew in summer a scanty crop of wheat, and which in autumn, after this was gathered, appeared not to have been harvested, but stripped. Jean Valjean had a predilection for these fields. Cosette did not dislike them. To him it was solitude, to her it was liberty. There she became a little girl again, she could run and almost play, she took off her hat, laid it on Jean Valjean's knees, and gathered flowers. She looked at the butterflies upon the blossoms, but did not catch them; gentleness and tenderness are born with love, and the young girl who has in her heart a trembling and fragile idea, feels pity for a butterfly's wing. She wove garlands of wild poppies which she put upon her head, and which, lit up and illuminated in the sunshine, and blazing like a flame, made a crown of fire for her fresh and rosy face.

So one October morning, tempted by the deep serenity of the autumn of 1831, they had gone out, and found themselves at daybreak near the Barrière du Maine. It was not day, it was dawn; a few constellations here and there in the deep pale heavens, the earth all black, the sky all white. a shivering in the spears of grass, everywhere the mysterious thrill of the twilight. A lark, which seemed among the stars, was singing at this enormous height, and one would have said that this hymn from littleness to the infinite was calming the immensity. All was peace and silence; nobody upon the highway; on the footpaths a few scattered working-men, hardly visible, going to their work.

Suddenly, Cosette exclaimed: "Father, I should think somebody was coming down there."

Cosette was right. Some shapeless thing which came from the boulevard was entering upon the highway.

There were horses, wheels, cries; whips were cracking. It was in fact a waggon which had just turned out of the boulevard into the road, and which was making its way towards the barrière; a second, of the same appearance, followed it, then a third, then a fourth; seven vehicles turned in in succession, the horses' heads touching the rear of the waggons. Dark forms were moving upon these waggons, flashes were seen in the twilight as if of drawn swords, a clanking was heard which resembled the rattling of chains; it advanced, the voices grew louder, and it was as terrible a thing as comes forth from the cavern of dreams.

Seven waggons were moving in file upon the road. Six of them were of a peculiar structure. They resembled coopers' drays; they were a sort of long ladder placed upon two wheels, forming thills at the forward end. Each dray, or better, each ladder, was drawn by four horses tandem. Upon these ladders strange clusters of men were carried. Twenty-four on each waggon, twelve on each side, back to back, their faces towards the passers-by, their legs hanging down, these men had behind them something which clanked and which was a chain, and at their necks something which shone and which was an iron collar. Each had his collar, but the chain was for all; so that these twenty-four men, if they should chance to get down from the dray and walk, would be made subject to a sort of inexorable unity, and have to wiggle over the ground with the chain for a backbone, very much like centipedes. In front and rear of each waggon, two men, armed with muskets, stood, each having an end of the chain under his foot. The collars were square. The seventh waggon, a huge cart with racks, but without a cover, had four wheels and six horses, and carried a resounding pile of iron kettles, melting pots, furnaces, and chains, over which were scattered a number of men, who were bound and lying at full length, and who appeared to be sick. This cart, entirely exposed to view, was furnished with broken hurdles which seemed to have served in the ancient punishments.

These waggons kept the middle of the street. At either side marched a row of guards of infamous appearance, wearing three-pronged hats like the soldiers of the Directory, stained, torn, filthy, muffled up in Invalides' uniforms and hearse-boys' trousers, half grey and half blue, almost in tatters, with red epaulets, yellow cross-belts, sheath-knives, muskets, and clubs: a species of servant-soldiers. The one who appeared to be their chief had a horsewhip in his hand. All these details, blurred by the twilight, were becoming clearer and clearer in the growing light. At the head and the rear of the convoy, gendarmes marched on horseback, solemn, and with drawn swords.

This cortège was so long that when the first waggon reached the barrière, the last had hardly turned out of the boulevard.

A crowd, come from nobody knows where, and gathered in a twinkling, as is frequently the case in Paris, were pushing along the two sides of the highway and looking on. In the neighbouring lanes there were heard people shouting and calling each other, and the wooden shoes of the market gardeners who were running to see.

The men heaped upon the drays were silent as they were jolted along. They were livid with the chill of the morning. They all had tow trousers, and their bare feet were in wooden shoes. The rest of their costume was

according to the fancy of misery. Their dress was hideously variegated:
nothing is more dismal than the harlequin of rags. Felt hats jammed out
of shape, glazed caps, horrible cloth caps, and beside the linen monkey-
jacket, the black coat out at the elbows; several had women's hats; others
had baskets on their heads; hairy breasts could be seen, and through the
holes in their clothing tattooings could be discerned; behind the convoy
a troop of children were bursting with laughter.

This file of waggons, whatever it was, was dismal. It was evident that
to-morrow, that in an hour, a shower might spring up, that it would be
followed by another, and another, and that the worn-out clothing would be
soaked through; that once wet, these men would never get dry, once
chilled, they would never get warm again; that their tow trousers would be
fastened to their skin by the rain, that water would fill their wooden shoes,
that blows of the whip could not prevent the chattering of their jaws,
that the chain would continue to hold them by the neck, that their feet
would continue to swing.

The clubs did not spare even the sick, who lay tied with ropes and
motionless in the seventh waggon, and who seemed to have been thrown
there like sacks filled with misery.

Suddenly, the sun appeared; the immense radiance of the Orient burst
forth, and one would have said that it set all these savage heads on fire.
Their tongues were loosed, a conflagration of sneers, of oaths, and songs
burst forth.

As the songs and the blasphemy increased, he who seemed the captain of
the escort cracked his whip, and upon that signal, a fearful, sullen, and
promiscuous cudgelling, which sounded like hail, fell upon the seven waggons; many roared and foamed; which redoubled the joy of the gamins
who had collected, a swarm of flies upon these wounds.

Jean Valjean's eye had become frightful. All at once he remembered that
this was really the route, that this detour was usual to avoid meeting
the king, which was always possible on the Fontainebleau road, and that,
thirty-five years before, he had passed through this barrière.

Cosette was equally terrified. She did not comprehend; what she saw
did not seem possible to her; at last she exclaimed:

"Father! what can there be in those waggons?"

Jean Valjean answered:

"Convicts."

"And where are they going?"

"To the galleys."

At this moment the cudgelling, multiplied by a hundred hands, reached
its climax; blows with the flat of the sword joined in; it was a fury of
whips and clubs; the galley slaves crouched down, a hideous obedience
was produced by the punishment, and all were silent with the look of
chained wolves.

"Father, are they still men?"

"Sometimes," said the wretched man.

It was in fact the chain which, setting out before day from Bicêtre, took the Mans road to avoid Fontainebleau, where the king then was. This detour made the terrible journey last three or four days longer; but to spare the royal person the sight of the punishment, it may well be prolonged.

Jean Valjean, on the way back to the Rue de Babylone with Cosette, did not notice that she asked him other questions regarding what they had just seen; perhaps he was himself too much absorbed in his own dejection to heed her words or to answer them. But at night, as Cosette was leaving him to go to bed, he heard her say in an undertone, and as if talking to herself: "It seems to me that if I should meet one of those men in my path, O my God, I should die just from seeing him near me!"

Fortunately it happened that on the morrow of this tragic day there were, in consequence of some official celebration, fêtes in Paris, a review in the Champ de Mars, rowing matches upon the Seine, theatricals in the Champs Elysées, fireworks at l'Etoile, illuminations everywhere. Jean Valjean, doing violence to his habits, took Cosette to these festivities, for the purpose of diverting her mind from the memories of the day before, and of effacing under the laughing tumult of all Paris, the abominable thing which had passed before her. The review made the display of uniforms quite natural; Jean Valjean put on his National Guard uniform with the vague interior feeling of a man who is taking refuge.

Some days later, one morning, when the sun was bright, and they were both upon the garden steps, Cosette was picking a daisy in pieces. Jean Valjean was fascinated by the contemplation of her slender fingers upon that flower. A redbreast was twittering in the shrubbery beside them. White clouds were crossing the sky so gaily that one would have said they had just been set at liberty. Cosette continued picking her flower attentively; she seemed to be thinking of something; but that must have been pleasant. Suddenly she turned her head over her shoulder with the delicate motion of the swan, and said to Jean Valjean: "Father, what are they then, the galley slaves?"

Thus their life gradually darkened.

There was left to them but one distraction, and this had formerly been a pleasure: that was to carry bread to those who were hungry, and clothing to those who were cold. In these visits to the poor, in which Cosette often accompanied Jean Valjean, they found some remnant of their former lightheartedness; and, sometimes, when they had had a good day, when many sorrows had been relieved and many little children revived and made warm, Cosette, in the evening, was a little gay. It was at this period that they visited the Jondrette den.

The day after that visit, Jean Valjean appeared in the cottage in the morning, with his ordinary calmness, but with a large wound on his left arm, very much inflamed and very venomous, which resembled a burn, and which he explained in some fashion. This wound confined him within doors more than a month with fever. He would see no physician. When Cosette urged it: "Call the dog-doctor," said he.

Cosette dressed it night and morning with so divine a grace and so angelic a pleasure in being useful to him, that Jean Valjean felt all his old happiness return, his fears and his anxieties dissipate. He now said to himself: "I imagined all that. I am an old fool."

As soon as his wound was cured, he resumed his solitary and twilight walks.

It would be a mistake to believe that one can walk in this way alone in the uninhabited regions of Paris, and not meet with some adventure.

XXI. THE GARDEN

ONE EVENING little Gavroche had had no dinner; he remembered that he had had no dinner also the day before; this was becoming tiresome. He resolved that he would try for some supper.

In one of his preceding strolls, he had noticed an old garden haunted by an old man and an old woman, and in this garden a passable apple tree. Beside this apple tree, there was a sort of fruit-loft poorly inclosed where the conquest of an apple might be made. An apple is a supper; an apple is life. What ruined Adam might save Gavroche.

Gavroche directed his steps towards the garden; he found the lane, he recognised the apple tree, he verified the fruit-loft, he examined the hedge; a hedge is a stride. Day was declining, not a cat in the lane, the time was good. Gavroche sketched out the escalade, then suddenly stopped. Somebody was talking in the garden. Gavroche looked through one of the openings of the hedge.

Within two steps of him, at the foot of the hedge on the other side, precisely at the point where the hole he was meditating would have taken him, lay a stone which made a kind of seat, and on this seat the old man of the garden was sitting with the old woman standing before him. The old woman was muttering. Gavroche, who was anything but discreet, listened.

"Monsieur Mabeuf!" said the old woman.

"Mabeuf!" thought Gavroche, "that is a funny name."

The old man who was addressed made no motion. The old woman repeated:

"Monsieur Mabeuf."

The old man, without raising his eyes from the ground, determined to answer:

"What, Mother Plutarch?"

"Mother Plutarch!" thought Gavroche, "another funny name."

Mother Plutarch resumed, and the old man was forced to enter into the conversation:

"The landlord is dissatisfied."

"Why so?"

"There are three quarters due."

"In three months there will be four."

"He says he will turn you out of doors to sleep."

"I shall go."

"The grocery woman wants to be paid. She holds on to her wood. What will you keep warm with this winter? We shall have no wood."

"There is the sun."

"The butcher refuses credit, he will not give us any more meat."

"That is all right. I do not digest meat well. It is too heavy."

"What shall we have for dinner?"

"Bread."

"The baker demands something on account, and says no money, no bread."

"Very well."

"What will you eat?"

"We have the apples from the apple tree."

"But, monsieur, we can't live like that without money."

"I have not any."

The old woman went away, the old man remained alone. He began to reflect. Gavroche was reflecting on his side. It was almost night.

The first result of Gavroche's reflection was that instead of climbing over the hedge he crept under. The branches separated a little at the bottom of the bushes.

"Heigho," exclaimed Gavroche internally, "an alcove!" and he hid in it. He almost touched Father Mabeuf's seat. He heard the octogenarian breathe.

Then, for dinner, he tried to sleep.

Sleep of a cat, sleep with one eye. Even while crouching there Gavroche kept watch.

The whiteness of the twilight sky blanched the earth, and the lane made a livid line between two rows of dusky bushes.

Suddenly, upon that whitened band two dim forms appeared. One came before—the other, at some distance, behind.

"There are two fellows," growled Gavroche.

The first form seemed some old bourgeois bent and thoughtful, dressed more than simply, walking with the slow pace of an aged man, and taking his ease in the starry evening.

The second was straight, firm, and slight. It regulated its step by the step of the first; but in the unwonted slowness of the gait, dexterity and agility were manifest. This form had, in addition to something wild and startling, the whole appearance of what was then called a dandy; the hat was of the latest style, the coat was black, well cut, probably of fine cloth, and closely fitted to the form. The head was held up with a robust grace, and, under the hat, could be seen in the twilight the pale profile of a young man. This profile had a rose in its mouth. The second form was well known to Gavroche: it was Montparnasse.

As to the other, he could have said nothing about it, except that it was an old goodman.

Gavroche immediately applied himself to observation.

One of these two passers evidently had designs upon the other. Montparnasse hiding, at such an hour, in such a place—it was threatening. Gavroche felt his *gamin's* heart moved with pity for the old man.

What could he do? intervene? one weakness in aid of another? That would be ludicrous to Montparnasse. Gavroche could not conceal it from himself that, to this formidable bandit of eighteen, the old man first, the child afterwards, would be but two mouthfuls.

While Gavroche was deliberating, the attack was made, sharp and hideous. The attack of a tiger on a wild ass, a spider on a fly. Montparnasse, on a sudden, threw away the rose, sprang upon the old man, collared him, grasped him and fastened to him, and Gavroche could hardly restrain a cry. A moment afterwards, one of these men was under the other, exhausted, panting, struggling, with a knee of marble upon his breast. Only it was not altogether as Gavroche had expected. The one on the ground was Montparnasse; the one above was the goodman. All this happened a few steps from Gavroche.

The old man had received the shock and had returned it, and returned it so terribly that in the twinkling of an eye the assailant and assailed had changed parts.

"There is a brave Invalide!" thought Gavroche.

And he could not help clapping his hands. But it was a clapping of hands thrown away. It did not reach the two combatants, absorbed and deafened by each other, and mingling their breath in the contest.

There was silence. Montparnasse ceased to struggle. Gavroche said this aside: "Can he be dead?"

The goodman had not spoken a word, nor uttered a cry. He arose, and Gavroche heard him say to Montparnasse:

"Get up."

Montparnasse got up, but the goodman held him. Montparnasse had the humiliated and furious attitude of a wolf caught by a sheep.

Gavroche looked and listened, endeavouring to double his eyes by his ears. He was enormously amused.

The goodman questioned. Montparnasse responded.

"How old are you?"

"Nineteen."

"You are strong and well. Why don't you work?"

"It is fatiguing."

"What is your business?"

"Loafer."

"Speak seriously. Can I do anything for you? What would you like to be?"

"A robber."

There was a silence. The old man seemed to be thinking deeply, yet did not release Montparnasse.

From time to time the young bandit, vigorous and nimble, made the efforts of a beast caught in a snare. He gave a spring, attempted a trip, twisted his limbs desperately, endeavoured to escape. The old man did not appear to perceive it, and with a single hand held his two arms with the sovereign indifference of absolute strength.

Then, looking steadily upon Montparnasse, he gently raised his voice.

"My child, you are entering by laziness into the most laborious of existences. Ah! you declare yourself a loafer! prepare to labour. The hardest of all labour is robbery. Trust me, do not undertake this dreadful drudgery of being an idler. To become a rascal is not comfortable. It is not so hard to be an honest man. Go, now, and think of what I have said to you. And now, what did you want of me? my purse? here it is."

And the old man, releasing Montparnasse, put his purse in his hand, which Montparnasse weighed for a moment; after which, with the same mechanical precaution as if he had stolen it, Montparnasse let it glide gently into the back pocket of his coat.

All this said and done, the goodman turned his back and quietly resumed his walk.

"Blockhead!" murmured Montparnasse.

Who was this goodman? the reader has doubtless guessed.

Montparnasse, in stupefaction, watched him till he disappeared in the twilight. This contemplation was fatal to him.

Gavroche, with a side glance, made sure that Father Mabeuf, perhaps asleep, was still sitting on the seat. Then the urchin came out of his bushes, and began to creep along in the shade, behind the motionless Montparnasse. He reached Montparnasse thus without being seen or heard, gently insinuated his hand into the back pocket of the fine black cloth coat, took the purse, withdrew his hand, and, creeping off again, glided away like an adder into the darkness. Montparnasse, who had no reason to be upon his guard, and who was reflecting for the first time in his life, perceived nothing of it. Gavroche, when he had reached the point where Father Mabeuf was, threw the purse over the hedge, and fled at full speed.

The purse fell on the foot of Father Mabeuf. This shock awoke him. He stooped down, and picked up the purse. He did not understand it at all, and he opened it. It was a purse with two compartments; in one there were some small coins; in the other, there were six napoleons.

M. Mabeuf, very much startled, carried the thing to his housekeeper.

"This falls from the sky," said Mother Plutarch.

Cosette's grief, so poignant still, and so acute four or five months before, had, without her knowledge even, entered upon convalescence. Nature, Spring, her youth, her love for her father, the gaiety of the birds and the flowers, were filtering little by little, day by day, into this soul so pure and so young, something which almost resembled oblivion. Was the fire dying out entirely? or was it merely becoming a bed of embers? The truth is, that she had scarcely anything left of that sorrowful and consuming feeling.

One day she suddenly thought of Marius: "What!" said she, "I do not think of him now."

In the course of that very week she noticed, passing before the grated gate of the garden, a very handsome officer of lancers, waist like a wasp, ravishing uniform, cheeks like a young girl's, sabre under his arm, waxed moustaches, polished schapska. Moreover, fair hair, full blue eyes, plump, vain, insolent and pretty face; the very opposite of Marius. A cigar in his mouth. Cosette thought that this officer doubtless belonged to the regiment in barracks on the Rue de Babylone.

The next day, she saw him pass again. She noticed the hour.

Dating from this time, was it chance? she saw him pass almost every day.

The officer's comrades perceived that there was, in this garden so "badly kept," behind that wretched old-fashioned grating, a pretty creature that always happened to be visible on the passage of the handsome lieutenant, who is not unknown to the reader, and whose name was Théodule Gillenormand.

"Stop!" said they to him. "Here is a little girl who has her eye upon you; why don't you look at her?"

"Do you suppose I have the time," answered the lancer, "to look at all the girls who look at me?"

This was the very time when Marius was descending gloomily towards agony, and saying: "If I could only see her again before I die!" Had his wish been realised, had he seen Cosette at that moment looking at a lancer, he would not have been able to utter a word, and would have expired of grief.

Whose fault was it? Nobody's.

Marius was of that temperament which sinks into grief, and remains there; Cosette was of that which plunges in, and comes out again.

Cosette indeed was passing that dangerous moment, the fatal phase of feminine reverie abandoned to itself, when the heart of an isolated young girl resembles the tendrils of a vine which seize hold, as chance determines, of the capital of a column or the signpost of a tavern. A hurried and decisive moment, critical for every orphan, whether she be poor or whether she be rich, for riches do not defend against a bad choice; the real misalliance is that of souls.

In the first fortnight in April, Jean Valjean went on a journey. This, we know, happened with him from time to time, at very long intervals. He remained absent one or two days at the most. Where did he go? nobody knew, not even Cosette. It was generally when money was needed for the household expenses that Jean Valjean made these little journeys.

Jean Valjean then was absent. He had said: "I shall be back in three days."

In the evening, Cosette was alone in the parlour. To amuse herself, she had opened her piano and began to sing.

All at once it seemed to her that she heard a step in the garden.

It could not be her father, he was absent; it could not be Toussaint, she was in bed. It was ten o'clock at night.

She went to the window shutter which was closed and put her ear to it.

It appeared to her that it was a man's step, and that he was treading very softly.

She ran immediately up to the first story, into her room, opened a slide in her blind, and looked into the garden. The moon was full. She could see as plainly as in broad day.

There was nobody there.

She opened the window. The garden was absolutely silent and all that she could see of the street was as deserted as it always was.

She thought no more about it.

Cosette by nature was not easily startled. There was in her veins the blood of the gipsy and of the adventuress who goes bare foot. It must be remembered she was rather a lark than a dove. She was wild and brave at heart.

The next day, not so late, at nightfall, she was walking in the garden. She thought she heard for a moment a sound like the sound of the evening before, as if somebody were walking in the darkness under the trees, not very far from her; but she said to herself that nothing is more like a step in the grass than the rustling of two limbs against each other, and she paid no attention to it. Moreover, she saw nothing.

She had to cross a little green grass-plot to reach the steps. The moon, which had just risen behind her, projected, as Cosette came out from the shrubbery, her shadow before her upon this grass-plot.

Cosette stood still, terrified.

By the side of her shadow, the moon marked out distinctly upon the sward another shadow singularly frightful and terrible, a shadow with a round hat.

It was like the shadow of a man who might have been standing in the edge of the shrubbery, a few steps behind Cosette.

For a moment she was unable to speak, or cry, or call, or stir, or turn her head.

At last she summoned up all her courage and resolutely turned round.

There was nobody there.

She looked upon the ground. The shadow had disappeared.

She returned into the shrubbery, boldly hunted through the corners, went as far as the gate, and found nothing.

She felt her blood run cold. Was this also a hallucination? What! two days in succession? One hallucination may pass, but two hallucinations? What made her most anxious was that the shadow was certainly not a phantom. Phantoms never wear round hats.

The next day Jean Valjean returned. Cosette narrated to him what she thought she had heard and seen. She expected to be reassured, and that her father would shrug his shoulders and say: "You are a foolish little girl."

Jean Valjean became anxious.

"It may be nothing," said he to her.

He left her under some pretext and went into the garden, and she saw him examining the gate very closely.

In the night she awoke; now she was certain, and she distinctly heard somebody walking very near the steps under her window. She ran to her slide and opened it. There was in fact a man in the garden with a big club in his hand. Just as she was about to cry out, the moon lighted up the man's face. It was her father!

She went back to bed, saying: "So he is really anxious!"

Jean Valjean passed that night in the garden and the two nights following. Cosette saw him through the hole in her shutter.

The third night the moon was smaller and rose later, it might have been one o'clock in the morning, she heard a loud burst of laughter and her father's voice calling her:

"Cosette!"

She sprang out of bed, threw on her dressing-gown, and opened her window.

Her father was below on the grass-plot.

"I woke you up to show you," said he. "Look, here is your shadow in a round hat."

And he pointed to a shadow on the sward made by the moon, and which really bore a close resemblance to the appearance of a man in a round hat. It was a figure produced by a sheet-iron stove-pipe with a cap, which rose above a neighbouring roof.

Cosette also began to laugh, all her gloomy suppositions fell to the ground, and the next day, while breakfasting with her father, she made merry over the mysterious garden haunted by shadows of stove-pipes.

Jean Valjean became entirely calm again; as to Cosette, she did not notice very carefully whether the stove-pipe was really in the direction of the shadow which she had seen, or thought she saw, and whether the moon was in the same part of the sky. She made no question about the oddity of a stove-pipe which is afraid of being caught in the act, and which retires when you look at its shadow. Cosette was fully reassured.

A few days afterwards however, a new incident occurred.

In the garden, near the grated gate, on the street, there was a stone seat protected from the gaze of the curious by a hedge, but which, nevertheless, by an effort, the arm of a passer could reach through the grating and the hedge.

One evening in this same month of April, Jean Valjean had gone out; Cosette, after sunset, had sat down on this seat. The wind was freshening in the trees; Cosette rose, slowly made the round of the garden, walking in the grass which was wet with dew, and saying to herself: "One really needs wooden shoes for the garden at this hour. I shall catch cold."

She returned to the seat. Just as she was sitting down, she noticed in the place she had left a stone of considerable size which evidently was not there the moment before.

Somebody had put it there, an arm had passed through that grating; there was the stone. She did not touch it, fled without daring to look behind her, took refuge in the house, and immediately shut the glass-door of the stairs with shutter, bar, and bolt. She asked Toussaint:

"Has my father come in?"

"Not yet, mademoiselle."

Jean Valjean, a man given to thought and a night-walker, frequently did not return till quite late.

"Toussaint," resumed Cosette, "you are careful in the evening to bar the shutters well, upon the garden at least, and to really put the little iron things into the little rings which fasten?"

"Oh! never fear, mademoiselle."

Toussaint did not fail, and Cosette well knew it, but she could not help adding:

"Because it is so solitary about here!"

She had all the doors and windows carefully closed, made Toussaint go over the whole house from cellar to garret, shut herself up in her room, drew her bolts, looked under her bed, lay down, and slept badly. All night she saw the stone big as a mountain and full of caves.

At sunrise—the peculiarity of sunrise is to make us laugh at all our terrors of the night, and our laugh is always proportioned to the fear we have had—at sunrise Cosette, on waking, looked upon her fright as upon a nightmare, and said to herself: "What have I been dreaming about? This is like those steps which I thought I heard at night last week in the garden! It is like the shadow of the stove-pipe!"

The sun, which shone through the cracks of her shutters, and made the damask curtains purple, reassured her.

"There was no stone on the bench, any more than there was a man with a round hat in the garden; I dreamed the stone as I did the rest."

She dressed herself, went down to the garden, ran to the bench, and felt a cold sweat. The stone was there.

But what is fright by night is curiosity by day.

She raised the stone, which was pretty large. There was something underneath which resembled a letter.

It was a white paper envelope. There was no address on the one side, no wafer on the other. Still the envelope, although open, was not empty.

Cosette took out of the envelope paper which contained a few lines written in a rather pretty hand-writing, thought Cosette, and very fine. Cosette looked for a name, there was none; a signature, there was none. To whom was it addressed? to her probably, since a hand had placed the packet upon her seat. From whom did it come? She looked at the sky, the street, the acacias all steeped in light, some pigeons which were flying about a neighbouring roof, then all at once her eye eagerly sought the manuscript. This is what she read:

"The reduction of the universe to a single being, the expansion of a single being even to God, this is love.

———

"Love is the salutation of the angel to the stars.

———

"How sad is the soul when it is sad from love!

———

"What a void is the absence of the being who alone fills the world! Oh! how true it is that the beloved being becomes God! One would conceive that God would be jealous if the Father of all had not evidently made creation for the soul, and the soul for love!

———

"A glimpse of a smile under a white crape hat with a lilac coronet is enough, for the soul to enter into the palace of dreams.

———

"God is behind all things, but all things hide God. Things are black, creatures are opaque. To love a being, is to render her transparent.

———

"Certain thoughts are prayers. There are moments when, whatever be the attitude of the body, the soul is on its knees.

———

"Separated lovers deceive absence by a thousand chimerical things which still have their reality. They are prevented from seeing each other, they cannot write to each other; they find a multitude of mysterious means of correspondence. They commission the song of the birds, the perfume of flowers, the laughter of children, the light of the sun, the sighs of the wind, the beams of the stars, the whole creation. And why not? All the works of God were made to serve love. Love is powerful enough to charge all nature with its messages.

"O Spring! thou art a letter which I write to her.

———

"I met in the street a very poor young man who was in love. His hat was old, his coat was threadbare—there were holes at his elbows; the water passed through his shoes and the stars through his soul."

———

Now these pages, from whom could they come? Who could have written them?

Cosette did not hesitate for a moment. One single man.

He! She had always loved him, always adored him. "Oh, yes!" said she, "how I recognise all this! This is what I had already read in his eyes."

As she finished it for the third time, Lieutenant Théodule returned before the grating, and rattled his spurs on the pavement. Cosette mechanically raised her eyes. She thought him flat, stupid, silly, useless, conceited, odious, impertinent, and very ugly. The officer thought it his duty to smile. She turned away insulted and indignant. She would have been glad to have thrown something at his head.

She fled, went back to the house and shut herself up in her room to read over the manuscript again.

When evening came, Jean Valjean went out; Cosette dressed herself. She arranged her hair in the manner which best became her, and she put on a dress the neck of which, as it had received one cut of the scissors too much, was, as young girls say "a little immodest." It was not the least in the world immodest, but it was prettier than otherwise. She did all this without knowing why.

Did she intend to go out? no.

Did she expect a visit? no.

At dusk, she went down to the garden. Toussaint was busy in her kitchen, which looked out upon the back-yard.

She began to walk under the branches, putting them aside with her hand from time to time, because there were some that were very low.

She thus reached the seat.

The stone was still there.

She sat down, and laid her soft white hand upon that stone as if she would caress it and thank it.

All at once, she had that indefinable impression which we feel, though we see nothing, when there is somebody standing behind us.

She turned her head and arose.

It was he.

He was bareheaded. He appeared pale and thin. She hardly discerned his black dress. The twilight dimmed his fine forehead, and covered his eyes with darkness.

His hat was lying a few steps distant in the shrubbery.

Cosette drew back slowly, for she felt herself attracted forward. He did not stir. In retreating, she encountered a tree, and leaned against it. But for this tree, she would have fallen.

Then she heard his voice, that voice which she had never really heard, hardly rising above the rustling of the leaves, and murmuring:

"Pardon me, I am here. I could not live as I was, I have come. Have you read what I placed there, on this seat? do you recognise me at all? do not be afraid of me. It is a long time now, do you remember the day when you looked upon me? it was at the Luxembourg, near the Gladiator. And the day when you passed before me? it was the 16th of June and the 2nd of July. It will soon be a year. For a very long time now, I have not seen you at all. You lived in the Rue de l'Ouest, on the third floor front, in a new house, you see that I know! I followed you. What was I to do? And then you disappeared. I thought I saw you pass once when I was reading the papers under the arches of the Odéon. I ran. But no. It was a person who had a hat like yours. At night, I come here. Do not be afraid, nobody sees me. I come for a near look at your windows. I walk very softly that you may not hear, for perhaps you would be afraid. The other evening I was behind you, you turned round, I fled. Once I heard you sing. I was happy. Does it disturb you that I should hear you sing through the shutter? it can do you no harm. It cannot, can it? See, you are my angel, let me come sometimes; I believe I am going to die. If you but knew! I adore you! Pardon me, I am talking to you, I do not know what I am saying to you, perhaps I annoy you, do I annoy you?"

She took his hand and laid it on her heart. He felt the paper there, and stammered:

"You love me, then?"

She answered in a voice so low that it was no more than a breath which could scarcely be heard:

"Hush! you know it!"

And she hid her blushing head in the bosom of the proud and intoxicated young man.

He fell upon the seat, she by his side. There were no more words. The stars were beginning to shine. How was it that their lips met? How is it that the birds sing, that the snow melts, that the rose opens, that May blooms, that the dawn whitens behind the black trees on the shivering summit of the hills?

One kiss, and that was all.

Both trembled, and they looked at each other in the darkness with brilliant eyes.

They felt neither the fresh night, nor the cold stone, nor the damp ground, nor the wet grass, they looked at each other. They had clasped hands, without knowing it.

She did not ask him, she did not even think of it, in what way and by what means he had succeeded in penetrating into the garden. It seemed so natural to her that he should be there.

From time to time Marius' knee touched Cosette's knee, which gave them both a thrill.

Gradually they began to talk. The night was serene and splendid above their heads. These two beings told each other all their dreams, their frenzies, their ecstasies, their chimeras, their despondencies, how they had adored each other from afar, how they had longed for each other, their despair when they had ceased to see each other.

When they had finished, when they had told each other everything, she laid her head upon his shoulder, and asked him:

"What is your name?"

"My name is Marius," said he. "And yours?"

"My name is Cosette."

XXII. INSIDE THE ELEPHANT

SPRING IN PARIS is often accompanied with keen and sharp north winds, by which one is not exactly frozen, but frost-bitten; these winds, which mar the most beautiful days, have precisely the effect of those currents of cold air which enter a warm room through the cracks of an ill-closed window or door. It seems as if the dreary door of winter were partly open and the wind were coming in at it.

One evening when these winds were blowing harshly, to that degree that January seemed returned, and the bourgeois had resumed their cloaks, little Gavroche, always shivering cheerfully under his rags, was standing, as if in ecstasy, before a wig-maker's shop in the neighbourhood of the Orme Saint Gervais. He was adorned with a woman's woollen shawl, picked up nobody knows where, of which he had made a muffler. Little Gavroche appeared to be intensely admiring a wax bride, with bare neck and a head-dress of orange flowers, which was revolving behind the sash, exhibiting between two lamps, its smile to the passers; but in reality he was watching the shop to see if he could not "chiper" a cake of soap from the front, which he would afterwards sell for a sou to a hairdresser. It often happened that he breakfasted upon one of these cakes. He called this kind of work, for which he had some talent, "shaving the barbers."

As he was contemplating the bride and squinting at the cake of soap, he muttered between his teeth: "Tuesday. It isn't Tuesday. Is it Tuesday? Perhaps it is Tuesday. Yes, it is Tuesday."

Nobody ever discovered to what this monologue related.

If, perchance, this soliloquy referred to the last time he had dined it was three days before, for it was then Friday.

The barber in his shop, warmed by a good stove, was shaving a customer and casting from time to time a look towards this enemy, this frozen and brazen *gamin*, who had both hands in his pockets, but his wits evidently out of their sheath.

While Gavroche was examining the bride, the windows, and the Windsor soap, two children of unequal height, rather neatly dressed, and still smaller than he, one appearing to be seven years old, the other five, timidly turned the knob of the door and entered the shop, asking for something, charity, perhaps, in a plaintive manner which rather resembled a groan than a prayer. They both spoke at once and their words were unintelligible because sobs choked the voice of the younger, and the cold made the elder's teeth chatter. The barber turned with a furious face, and without leaving his razor, crowding back the elder with his left hand and the little one with his knee, pushed them into the street and shut the door saying:

"Coming and freezing people for nothing!"

The two children went on, crying. Meanwhile a cloud had come up; it began to rain.

Little Gavroche ran after them and accosted them:

"What is the matter with you, little brats?"

"We don't know where to sleep," answered the elder.

"Is that all?" said Gavroche. "That is nothing. Does anybody cry for that?"

And assuming, through his slightly bantering superiority, a tone of softened authority and gentle protection:

"*Momacques*, come with me."

"Yes, monsieur," said the elder.

And the two children followed him as they would have followed an archbishop. They had stopped crying.

Gavroche led them up the Rue Saint Antoine in the direction of the Bastille.

Gavroche, as he travelled on, cast an indignant and retrospective glance at the barber's shop.

"He has no heart, that *merlan*," he muttered. "He is an *Angliche*."

A girl, seeing them all three marching in a row, Gavroche at the head, broke into a loud laugh. This laugh was lacking in respect for the group.

"Good day, Mamselle Omnibus," said Gavroche to her.

A moment afterwards, the barber recurring to him, he added:

"I am mistaken in the animal; he isn't a *merlan*, he is a snake. Wig-maker, I am going after a locksmith, and I will have a rattle made for your tail."

This barber had made him aggressive. He splashed the polished boots of a passer with mud.

"Whelp!" cried the man, furious.

Gavroche lifted his nose above his shawl.

"Monsieur complains?"

"Of you!" said the passer.

"The bureau is closed," said Gavroche. "I receive no more complaints."

Meanwhile, continuing up the street, he saw, quite frozen under a porte-cochère, a beggar girl of thirteen or fourteen, whose clothes were so short that her knees could be seen. The little girl was beginning to be too big a girl for that. Growth plays you such tricks. The skirt becomes short at the moment that nudity becomes indecent.

"Poor girl!" said Gavroche. "She hasn't even any breeches. But here, take this."

And, taking off all that good woollen which he had about his neck, he threw it upon the bony and purple shoulders of the beggar girl, where the muffler became a shawl.

The little girl looked at him with an astonished appearance, and received the shawl in silence. At a certain depth of distress, the poor, in their stupor, groan no longer over evil, and are no longer thankful for good.

This done: "Brrr!" said Gavroche, shivering worse than St. Martin, who at least, kept half his cloak.

At this brrr! the storm, redoubling its fury, became violent. These malignant skies punish good actions.

"Ah," exclaimed Gavroche, "what does this mean? It rains again! Good God, if this continues, I withdraw my subscription."

And he continued his walk.

The two children limped along behind him.

As they were passing by one of those thick grated lattices which indicate a baker's shop, for bread like gold is kept behind iron gratings, Gavroche turned:

"Ah, ha, *mômes*, have we dined?"

"Monsieur," answered the elder, "we have not eaten since early this morning."

"You are then without father or mother?" resumed Gavroche, majestically.

"Excuse us, monsieur, we have a papa and mamma, but we don't know where they are."

"Sometimes that's better than knowing," said Gavroche, who was a thinker.

"It is two hours now," continued the elder, "that we have been walking; we have been looking for things in every corner, but we can find nothing."

"I know," said Gavroche. "The dogs eat up everything."

Still he asked them no questions. To be without a home, what could be more natural?

Gavroche stopped, and for a few minutes he had been groping and fumbling in all sorts of recesses which he had in his rags.

Finally he raised his head with an air which was only intended for one of satisfaction, but which was in reality triumphant.

"Let us compose ourselves. Here is enough for supper for three."

And he took a sou from one of his pockets.

Without giving the two little boys time for amazement, he pushed them both before him into the baker's shop, and laid his sou on the counter, crying:

"Boy! five centimes' worth of bread."

The man, who was the master baker himself, took a loaf and a knife.

"In three pieces, boy!" resumed Gavroche.

And seeing that the baker, after having examined the three costumes, had taken a black loaf, he thrust his finger deep into his nose with a respiration as imperious as if he had had the great Frederick's pinch of snuff at the end of his thumb, and threw full in the baker's face this indignant apostrophe:

"Whossachuav?"

Those of our readers who may be tempted to see in this summons of Gavroche to the baker a Russian or Polish word, or one of those savage cries which the Iowas and the Botocudos hurl at each other from one bank of a stream to the other in their solitudes, are informed that it is a phrase which they use every day (they, our readers), and which takes the place of this phrase: what is that you have? The baker understood perfectly well, and answered:

"Why! it is bread, very good bread of the second quality."

"White bread, boy! I am treating."

When the bread was cut, the baker put the sou in his drawer, and Gavroche said to the two children:

"Eat."

At the same time he handed each of them a piece of bread.

And, thinking that the elder, who appeared to him more worthy of his conversation, deserved some special encouragement, he added, giving him the largest piece:

"Stick that in your gun."

There was one piece smaller than the other two; he took it for himself.

The poor children were starving, Gavroche included. While they were tearing the bread with their fine teeth, they encumbered the shop of the baker who, now that he had received his pay, was regarding them ill-humouredly.

"Come into the street," said Gavroche.

They went on in the direction of the Bastille.

From time to time when they were passing before a lighted shop, the smaller one stopped to look at the time by a leaden watch suspended from his neck by a string.

"Here is decidedly a real canary," said Gavroche.

As they finished their pieces of bread and reached the corner of that gloomy Rue des Ballets, at the end of which the low and forbidding wicket of La Force is seen:

"Hullo, is that you, Gavroche?" said somebody.

"Hullo, is that you, Montparnasse?" said Gavroche.

A man had just accosted the *gamin,* and this man was none other than Montparnasse, disguised with blue eye-glasses, but recognisable by Gavroche.

"Hush!" said Montparnasse, "not so loud."

And he hastily drew Gavroche out of the light of the shops.

The two little boys followed mechanically, holding each other by the hand.

When they were under the black arch of a porte-cochère, sheltered from sight and from the rain, Montparnasse continued:

"I am going to find Babet."

"Ah!" said Gavroche, "her name is Babet."

"Not her, his."

"Ah, Babet!"

"Yes, Babet."

"I thought he was buckled."

"He has slipped the buckle," answered Montparnasse.

And he rapidly related to the *gamin* that, on the morning of that very day, Babet, having been transferred to the Conciergerie, had escaped. Gavroche admired the skill.

Montparnasse added a few particulars in regard to Babet's escape and finished with:

"Oh! that is not all."

Gavroche, while listening, had caught hold of a cane which Montparnasse had in his hand, he had pulled mechanically on the upper part, and the blade of a dagger appeared.

Montparnasse gave him a wink.

"The deuce!" resumed Gavroche, "then you are going to have a tussle with the *cognes?*"

"We don't know," answered Montparnasse with an indifferent air. "It is always well to have a pin about you."

Gavroche insisted:

"What is it you are going to do to-night?"

Montparnasse took up the serious line anew and said, biting his syllables: "Several things."

And abruptly changing the conversation: "Where are you going now?"

Gavroche showed his two protégés and said:

"I am going to put these children to bed."

"Where do they sleep?"

"At my house."

"Your house. Where is that?"

"At my house."

"You have a room then?"

"Yes, I have a room."

"And where is your room?"

"In the elephant," said Gavroche.

Montparnasse, although by nature not easily astonished, could not restrain an exclamation:

"In the elephant?"

"Well, yes, in the elephant!" replied Gavroche, "whossematruthat?"

This is also a word in the language which nobody writes and which everybody uses. Whossematruthat, signifies what is the matter with that?

The profound observation of the *gamin* recalled Montparnasse to calmness and to good sense. He appeared to return to more respectful sentiments for Gavroche's lodging.

"Indeed!" said he, "yes, the elephant. Are you well off there?"

"Very well," said Gavroche. "There, really *chenument*. There are no draughts of wind as there are under the bridges."

"How do you get in?"

"I get in."

"There is a hole then?" inquired Montparnasse.

"Zounds! But it mustn't be told. It is between the forelegs."

"And you climb up? Yes, I understand."

Meanwhile Montparnasse had become thoughtful.

"You recognised me very easily," he murmured.

He took from his pocket two little objects which were nothing but two quills wrapped in cotton and introduced one into each nostril. This made him a new nose.

"That changes you," said Gavroche, "you are not so ugly, you ought to keep so all the time."

"Joking aside," asked Montparnasse, "how do you like that?"

It was also another sound of voice. In the twinkling of an eye, Montparnasse had become unrecognisable.

"Oh! play us Punchinello!" exclaimed Gavroche.

The two little ones, who had not been listening till now, they had themselves been so busy in stuffing their fingers into their noses, were attracted by this name and looked upon Montparnasse with dawning joy and admiration.

Unfortunately Montparnasse was anxious.

He laid his hand on Gavroche's shoulder and said to him, dwelling upon his words:

"Listen to a digression, boy, if I were on the Square, with my *dogue*, my *dague*, and my *digue*, and if you were so prodigal as to offer me twenty great sous, I shouldn't refuse to *goupiner*[1] for them, but we are not on Mardi Gras."

This grotesque phrase produced a singular effect upon the *gamin*. He turned hastily, cast his small sparkling eyes about him with intense attention, and perceived, within a few steps, a sergent de ville, whose back was turned to them. Gavroche let an "ah, yes!" escape him, which he suppressed upon the spot, and shaking Montparnasse's hand:

"Well, good night," said he, "I am going to my elephant. On the supposition that you should need me some night, you will come and find me there. I live in the second story. There is no porter. You would ask for Monsieur Gavroche."

"All right," said Montparnasse.

And they separated, Montparnasse making his way towards the Grève and Gavroche towards the Bastille. The little five-year-old drawn along by his brother, whom Gavroche was drawing along, turned his head back several times to see "Punchinello" going away.

The unintelligible phrase by which Montparnasse had warned Gavroche of the presence of the sergent de ville, contained no other talisman than the syllable *dig* repeated five or six times under various forms. This syllable *dig*, not pronounced singly, but artistically mingled with the words of a phrase, means: *Take care, we cannot talk freely*. There was furthermore in Montparnasse's phrase a literary beauty which escaped Gavroche, that is *my dogue, my dague, and my digue*, an expression of the argot of the Temple, which signifies *my dog, my knife, and my wife*, very much used among the Pitres and the Queues Rouges of the age of Louis XIV., when Molière wrote and Callot drew.

Twenty years ago, there was still to be seen in the southeast corner of the Place de la Bastille, near the canal basin dug in the ancient ditch of the prison citadel, a grotesque monument which has now faded away from the memory of Parisians, and which is worthy to leave some trace, for it was an idea of the "member of the Institute, General-in-Chief of the Army of Egypt."

It was an elephant, forty feet high, constructed of framework and masonry, bearing on its back its tower, which resembled a house, formerly painted green by some house-painter, now painted black by the sun, the rain, and the weather. In that open and deserted corner of the Square, the broad front of the colossus, his trunk, his tusks, his size, his enormous

[1] To labour.

rump, his four feet like columns, produced at night, under the starry sky, a startling and terrible outline. It was a mysterious and mighty phantom, visibly standing by the side of the invisible spectre of the Bastille.

As they came near the colossus, Gavroche comprehended the effect which the infinitely great may produce upon the infinitely small, and said:

"Brats! don't be frightened."

Then he entered through a gap in the fence into the inclosure of the elephant. The two children, a little frightened, followed without saying a word.

Lying by the side of the fence was a ladder, which, by day, was used by the working-men of the neighbouring wood-yard. Gavroche set it up against one of the elephant's forelegs. About the point where the ladder ended, a sort of black hole could be distinguished in the belly of the colossus.

Gavroche showed the ladder and the hole to his guests, and said to them: "Mount and enter."

The two little fellows looked at each other in terror.

"You are afraid!" exclaimed Gavroche.

And he added:

"You shall see."

He clasped the elephant's wrinkled foot, and in a twinkling, without deigning to make use of the ladder, he reached the crevice. He entered it as an adder glides into a hole, and disappeared, and a moment afterwards the two children saw his pallid face dimly appearing like a faded and wan form, at the edge of the hole full of darkness.

"Well," cried he, "why don't you come up? you'll see how nice it is!"

The little ones urged each other forward. The *gamin* made them afraid and reassured them at the same time, and then it rained very hard.

The elder clambered up the rounds of the ladder. Gavroche encouraged him with the exclamations of a fencing master to his scholars, or of a muleteer to his mules:

"Don't be afraid! That's it! Come on!"

And when he came within his reach he caught him quickly by the arm and drew him up.

"Now," said Gavroche, "wait for me. Monsieur, have the kindness to sit down."

And, going out by the crevice as he had entered, he let himself glide with the agility of a monkey along the elephant's leg, he dropped upon his feet in the grass, caught the little five-year-old by the waist and set him half way up the ladder, then he began to mount up behind him, crying to the elder:

"I will push him; you pull him."

In an instant the little fellow was lifted, pushed, dragged, pulled, stuffed, crammed into the hole without having had time to know what was going on. And Gavroche, entering after him, pushing back the ladder with a kick so that it fell upon the grass, began to clap his hands, and cried:

"Here we are! Hurrah for General Lafayette!"

This explosion over, he added:

"Brats, you are in my house."

Gavroche was in fact at home.

The bourgeois in their Sunday clothes, who passed by the elephant of the Bastille, frequently said, eyeing it scornfully with their goggle eyes: "What's the use of that?" The use of it was to save from the cold, the frost, the hail, the rain, to protect from the wintry wind, a little being with no father or mother, with no bread, no clothing, no asylum. This idea of Napoleon, disdained by men, had been taken up by God.

The hole by which Gavroche had entered was a break hardly visible from the outside, concealed as it was, and as we have said, under the belly of the elephant.

"Let us begin," said Gavroche, "by telling the porter that we are not in."

And plunging into the obscurity with certainty, like one familiar with his room, he took a board and stopped the hole.

A sudden light made the children wink; Gavroche had just lighted one of those bits of string soaked in resin which are called cellar-rats. The cellar-rat, which made more smoke than flame, rendered the inside of the elephant dimly visible.

Gavroche's two guests looked about them, and felt something like what Jonah must have felt in the Biblical belly of the whale. An entire and gigantic skeleton enveloped them. Above, a long dusky beam, from which projected at regular distances massive encircling timbers, represented the vertebral column with its ribs, stalactites of plaster hung down like the viscera, and from one side to the other huge spider-webs made dusty diaphragms.

The debris fallen from the elephant's back upon his belly had filled up the concavity, so that they could walk upon it as upon a floor.

The smaller one hugged close to his brother and said in a low tone:

"It is dark."

This word made Gavroche cry out.

"What is that you are driving at?" he exclaimed. "Are we humbugging? Must you have the Tuileries? would you be fools? Are you the brats of the pope's headwaiter?"

A little roughness is good for alarm. It is reassuring. The two children came close to Gavroche.

Gavroche, paternally softened by this confidence, passed "from the grave to the gentle," and addressing himself to the smaller:

"Goosy," said he to him, accenting the insult with a caressing tone, "it is outside that it is dark. Outside it rains, here it doesn't rain; outside it is cold, here there isn't a speck of wind; outside there are heaps of folks, here there isn't anybody; outside there isn't even a moon, here there is my candle, by jinks!"

The two children began to regard the apartment with less fear; but Gavroche did not allow them much longer leisure for contemplation.

"Quick," said he.

And he pushed them towards what we are very happy to be able to call the bottom of the chamber.

His bed was there.

Gavroche's bed was complete. That is to say, there was a mattress, a covering, and an alcove with curtains.

The mattress was a straw mat, the covering a large blanket of coarse grey wool, very warm and almost new. The alcove was like this:

Three rather long laths, sunk and firmly settled into the rubbish of the floor, that is to say of the belly of the elephant, two in front and one behind, and tied together by a string at the top, so as to form a pyrimidal frame. This frame supported a fine trellis of brass wire which was simply hung over it, but artistically applied and kept in place by fastenings of iron wire, in such a way that it entirely enveloped the three laths. A row of large stones fixed upon the ground all about this trellis so as to let nothing pass. This trellis was nothing more nor less than a fragment of those copper nettings which are used to cover the bird-houses in menageries. Gavroche's bed under this netting was as if in a cage.

It was this netting which took the place of curtains.

Gavroche removed the stones a little which kept down the netting in front, and the two folds of the trellis which lay one over the other opened.

"On your hands and knees!" said Gavroche.

He made his guests enter the cage carefully, then he went in after them, creeping, pulled back the stones, and hermetically closed the opening.

They were all three stretched upon the straw.

Small as they were, none of them could have stood up in the alcove. Gavroche still held the cellar rat in his hand.

"Now," said he, "*pioncez!* I am going to suppress the candelabra."

"Monsieur," inquired the elder of the two brothers, of Gavroche, pointing to the netting, "what is that?"

"That," said Gavroche, "is for the rats, *pioncez!*"

However, he felt it incumbent upon him to add a few words for the instruction of these beings of a tender age, and he continued:

"They are things from the Jardin des Plantes. They are used for ferocious animals. Tsaol (it is a whole) magazine full of them. Tsony (it is only) to mount over a wall, climb by a window and pass under a door. You get as much as you want."

While he was talking, he wrapped a fold of the coverlid about the smaller one, who murmured:

"Oh! that is good! it is warm!"

Gavroche looked with satisfaction upon the coverlid.

"That is also from the Jardin des Plantes," said he. "I took that from the monkeys."

And, showing the elder the mat upon which he was lying, a very thick mat and admirably made, he added:

"That was the giraffe's."

After a pause, he continued:

"The beasts had all this. I took it from them. They didn't care. I told them: It is for the elephant."

He was silent again and resumed:

"We get over the walls and we make fun of the government. That's all."

The two children looked with a timid and stupefied respect upon this intrepid and inventive being, a vagabond like them, isolated like them, wretched like them, who was something wonderful and all-powerful, who seemed to them supernatural, and whose countenance was made up of all the grimaces of an old mountebank mingled with the most natural and most pleasant smile.

"Monsieur," said the elder timidly, "you are not afraid then of the sergents de ville?"

Gavroche merely answered:

"*Môme!* we don't say sergents de ville, we say *cognes.*"

The smaller boy had his eyes open, but he said nothing. As he was on the edge of the mat, the elder being in the middle, Gavroche tucked the coverlid under him as a mother would have done, and raised the mat under his head with some old rags in such a way as to make a pillow. Then he turned towards the elder:

"Eh! we are pretty well off, here!"

"Oh, yes," answered the elder, looking at Gavroche with the expression of a rescued angel.

The two poor little soaked children were beginning to get warm.

"Ah, now," continued Gavroche, "what in the world were you crying for?"

And pointing out the little one to his brother:

"A youngster like that, I don't say, but a big boy like you, to cry is silly; it makes you look like a calf."

"Well," said the child, "we had no room, no place to go."

"Listen to me," continued Gavroche, "you must never whine any more for anything. I will take care of you. You will see what fun we have. In the summer we will go swimming in the Basin, we will run on the track before the Bridge of Austerlitz all naked, that makes the washerwomen mad. They scream, they scold, if you only knew how funny they are! We will go to see the skeleton man. He is alive. And then I will take you to the theatre. I have tickets, I know the actors, I even played once in a piece. We ran about under a cloth, that made the sea. I will have you engaged at my theatre. We will go and see the savages. They're not real, those savages. They have red tights which wrinkle, and you can see their elbows darned with white thread. After that, we will go to the Opera. We will go in with the claqueurs. The claque at the Opera is very select. I wouldn't go with the claque on the boulevards. At the Opera, just think, there are some who pay twenty sous, but they are fools. And then we will go to see the guillotining. I will show you the executioner. He lives in the Rue des Marias. Monsieur Sanson. There is a letter-box on his door. Oh! we have famous fun!"

At this moment, a drop of wax fell upon Gavroche's finger, and recalled him to the realities of life.

"The deuce!" said he, "there's the match used up. Attention! I can't spend more than a sou a month for my illumination. When we go to bed, we must go to sleep. We haven't time to read the romances of Monsieur Paul de Kock. Besides the light might show through the cracks of the porte-cochère, and the *cognes* couldn't help seeing."

"And then," timidly observed the elder who alone dared to talk with Gavroche and reply to him, "a spark might fall into the straw, we must take care not to burn the house up."

The storm redoubled. They heard, in the intervals of the thunder, the tempest beating against the back of the colossus; but Gavroche burst into a laugh.

"Be calm, children. Don't upset the edifice. That was fine thunder; give us some more. That wasn't any fool of a flash. Bravo God! by jinks! that is most as good as it is at the theatre."

This said, he restored order in the trellis, gently pushed the two children to the head of the bed, pressed their knees to stretch them out at full length, and exclaimed:

"As God is lighting his candle, I can blow out mine. Children, we must sleep, my young humans. It is very bad not to sleep. I'm going to extinguish. Are you all right?"

"Yes," murmured the elder, "I feel as if I had feathers under my head."

The two children hugged close to each other. Gavroche finished arranging them upon the mat, and pulled the coverlid up to their ears, then repeated for the third time the injunction in hieratic language:

"*Pioncez!*"

And he blew out the taper.

Hardly was the light extinguished when a singular tremor began to agitate the trellis under which the three children were lying. It was a multitude of dull rubbings, which gave a metallic sound, as if claws and teeth were grinding the copper wire. This was accompanied by all sorts of little sharp cries.

The little boy of five, hearing this tumult over his head, and shivering with fear, pushed the elder brother with his elbow, but the elder brother had already "*pioncé*," according to Gavroche's order. Then the little boy ventured to accost Gavroche, but very low, and holding his breath:

"Monsieur?"

"Hey?" said Gavroche, who had just closed his eyes.

"What is that?"

"It is the rats," answered Gavroche.

And he laid his head again upon the mat.

The rats, in fact, which swarmed by thousands in the carcase of the elephant, had been held in awe by the flame of the candle so long as it burned, but as soon as this cavern, which was, as it were, their city, had been restored to night, smelling there what the good story-teller Perrault calls "some fresh meat," they had rushed in en masse upon Gavroche's tent, climbed to the top, and were biting its meshes as if they were seeking to get through this new-fashioned mosquito bar.

Still the little boy did not go to sleep.

"Monsieur!" he said again.

"Hey?" said Gavroche.

"What are the rats?"

"They are mice."

This explanation reassured the child a little. He had seen some white mice in the course of his life, and he was not afraid of them. However, he raised his voice again:

"Monsieur?"

"Hey?" replied Gavroche.

"Why don't you have a cat?"

"I had one," answered Gavroche, "I brought one here, but they ate her up for me."

This second explanation undid the work of the first, and the little fellow again began to tremble. The dialogue between him and Gavroche was resumed for the fourth time.

"Monsieur!"

"Hey?"

"Who was it that was eaten up?"

"The cat."

"Who was it that ate the cat?"

"The rats."

"The mice?"

"Yes, the rats."

The child, dismayed by these mice who ate cats, continued:

"Monsieur, would those mice eat us?"

"Golly!" said Gavroche.

The child's terror was complete. But Gavroche added:

"Don't be afraid! they can't get in. And when I am here. Here, take hold of my hand. Be still and *pioncez!*"

Gavroche at the same time took the little fellow's hand across his brother. The child clasped his hand against his body, and felt safe. Courage and strength have such mysterious communications.

The hours of the night passed away. Darkness covered the immense Place de la Bastille; a wintry wind, which mingled with the rain, blew in gusts, the patrolmen ransacked the doors, alleys, yards, and dark corners, and, looking for nocturnal vagabonds, passed silently by the elephant; the monster, standing, motionless, with open eyes in the darkness, appeared to be in reverie and well satisfied with his good deeds, and he sheltered from the heavens and from men the three poor sleeping children.

Towards the end of the hour which immediately precedes daybreak, a man turned out of the Rue Saint Antoine, running, crossed the Square, turned the great inclosure of the Column of July, and glided between the palisades under the belly of the elephant. Had any light whatever shone upon this man, from his thoroughly wet clothing, one would have guessed that he had passed the night in the rain. When under the elephant he raised a grotesque call, which belongs to no human language and which a parrot alone could reproduce. He twice repeated this call, of which the following orthography gives but a very imperfect idea:

"Kirikikiou!"

At the second call, a clear, cheerful young voice answered from the belly of the elephant:

"Yes!"

Almost immediately the board which closed the hole moved away, and gave passage to a child, who descended along the elephant's leg and dropped lightly near the man. It was Gavroche. The man was Montparnasse.

As to this call, *kirikikiou*, it was undoubtedly what the child meant by, *You will ask for Monsieur Gavroche*.

On hearing it he had waked with a spring, crawled out of his "alcove," separating the netting a little, which he afterwards carefully closed again, then he had opened the trap and descended.

The man and the child recognised each other silently in the dark; Montparnasse merely said:

"We need you. Come and give us a lift."

The *gamin* did not ask any other explanation.

"I'm on hand," said he.

And they both took the direction of the Rue Saint Antoine, whence Montparnasse came, winding their way rapidly through the long file of market waggons which go down at that hour towards the market.

The market gardeners, crouching among the salads and vegetables, half asleep, buried up to the eyes in the boots of their waggons on account of the driving rain, did not even notice these strange passers-by.

That same night at La Force, an escape had been concerted between Babet, Brujon, Gueulemer, and Thénardier, although Thénardier was in solitary. Montparnasse was to help them from without.

Brujon, having spent a month in a chamber of punishment, had had time, first, to twist a rope, secondly, to perfect a plan. Formerly these stern cells in which the discipline of the prison delivers the condemned to himself, were composed of four stone walls, a ceiling of stone, a pavement of tiles, a camp bed, a grated air-hole, a double iron door, and were called *dungeons;* but the dungeon has been thought too horrible; now it is composed of an iron door, a grated air-hole, a camp bed, a pavement of tiles, a ceiling of stone, four stone walls, and it is called *chamber of punishment*. There is a little light in them about noon.

Brujon had gone out of the chamber of punishment with a rope.

Brujon was a polished, gallant, intelligent robber, with an enticing look and an atrocious smile. His first studies in his art were directed towards roofs.

What rendered the moment peculiarly favourable for an attempt at escape, was that some workmen were taking off and relaying, at that very time, a part of the slating of the prison. There were scaffoldings and ladders up aloft; in other words, bridges and stairways leading towards deliverance.

Gueulemer and Brujon were in the same dormitory. It happened that the heads of their beds rested against the flue of the chimney.

Thénardier was exactly above them in a kind of large garret hall, closed with triple gratings and double sheet iron doors studded with monstrous nails. Entering at the north end, you had on your left four windows, and on your right, opposite the windows, four large square cages, with spaces between, separated by narrow passages, built breast-high of masonry with bars of iron to the roof.

Thénardier had been in solitary in one of these cages since the night of the 3rd of February. Nobody has ever discovered how, or by what contrivance, he had succeeded in procuring and hiding a bottle of that wine with which a narcotic is mixed. There are in many prisons treacherous employees, half jailers and half thieves, who aid in escapes, who sell a faithless service to the police, and who make much more than their salary.

On this same night, then, on which little Gavroche had picked up the two wandering children, Brujon and Gueulemer, knowing that Babet, who had escaped that very morning, was waiting for them in the street as well as Montparnasse, got up softly and began to pierce the flue of the chimney which touched their beds, with a nail which Brujon had found. The fragments fell upon Brujon's bed, so that nobody heard them. The hail storm and the thunder shook the doors upon their hinges, and made a frightful and convenient uproar in the prison. Those of the prisoners who awoke made a feint of going to sleep again, and let Gueulemer and Brujon alone. Brujon was adroit; Gueulemer was vigorous. Before any sound had reached the watchman who was lying in the grated cell with a window opening into the sleeping room, the wall was pierced, the chimney scaled, the iron trellis which closed the upper orifice of the flue forced, and the two formidable bandits were upon the roof. The rain and the wind redoubled, the roof was slippery.

"What a good *sorgue* for a *crampe*,"[1] said Brujon.

A gulf of six feet wide and eighty feet deep separated them from the encircling wall. At the bottom of this gulf they saw a sentinel's musket gleaming in the obscurity. They fastened one end of the rope which Brujon had woven in his cell, to the stumps of the bars of the chimney which they had just twisted off, threw the other end over the encircling wall, cleared the gulf at a bound, clung to the coping of the wall, bestrode it, let themselves glide one after the other down along the rope upon a little roof which adjoined the bath-house, pulled down their rope, leaped into the bath-house yard, crossed it, pushed open the porter's slide, near which hung the cord, pulled the cord, opened the porte-cochère, and were in the street.

It was not three-quarters of an hour since they had risen to their feet on their beds in the darkness, their nail in hand, their project in their heads.

[1] What a good night for an escape.

A few moments afterwards they had rejoined Babet and Montparnasse, who were prowling about the neighbourhood.

In drawing down their rope, they had broken it, and there was a piece remaining fastened to the chimney on the roof. They had received no other damage than having pretty thoroughly skinned their hands.

That night Thénardier had received a warning, it never could be ascertained in what manner, and did not go to sleep.

About one o'clock in the morning, the night being very dark, he saw two shadows passing on the roof, in the rain and in the raging wind, before the window opposite his cage. One stopped at the window long enough for a look. It was Brujon. Thénardier recognised him, and understood. That was enough for him. Thénardier, described as an assassin, and detained under the charge of lying in wait by night with force and arms, was kept constantly in sight. A sentinel, who was relieved every two hours, marched with loaded gun before his cage. The prisoner had irons on his feet weighing fifty pounds. Every day, at four o'clock in the afternoon, a warden, escorted by two dogs—this was customary at that period—entered his cage, laid down near his bed a two pound loaf of black bread, a jug of water, and a dish full of very thin soup in which a few beans were swimming, examined his irons, and struck upon the bars. This man, with his dogs, returned twice in the night.

Thénardier had obtained permission to keep a kind of an iron spike which he used to nail his bread into a crack in the wall, "in order," said he, "to preserve it from the rats." As Thénardier was constantly in sight, they imagined no danger from this spike. However, it was remembered afterwards that a warden had said: "It would be better to let him have nothing but a wooden pike."

At two o'clock in the morning, the sentinel, who was an old soldier, was relieved, and his place was taken by a conscript. A few moments afterwards, the man with the dogs made his visit, and went away without noticing anything, except the extreme youth and the "peasant air" of the "greenhorn." Two hours afterwards, at four o'clock, when they came to relieve the conscript, they found him asleep, and lying on the ground like a log near Thénardier's cage. As to Thénardier, he was not there. His broken irons were on the floor. There was a hole in the ceiling of his cage, and above, another hole in the roof. A board had been torn from his bed, and doubtless carried away, for it was not found again. There was also seized in the cell a half empty bottle, containing the rest of the drugged wine with which the soldier had been put to sleep. The soldier's bayonet had disappeared.

At the moment of his discovery, it was supposed that Thénardier was out of all reach. The reality is, that he was still in great danger.

Thénardier on reaching the roof found the remnant of Brujon's cord hanging to the bars of the upper trap of the chimney, but this broken end being much too short, he was unable to escape over the sentry's path as Brujon and Gueulemer had done.

On turning from the Rue des Ballets into the Rue du Roi de Sicile, on the right you meet almost immediately with a dirty recess. There was a house there in the last century, of which only the rear wall remains, a genuine ruin wall which rises to the height of the third story among the neighbouring buildings. This ruin can be recognised by two large square windows which may still be seen; the one in the middle, near the right gable, is crossed by a worm-eaten joist fitted like a cap-piece for a shore. Through these windows could formerly be discerned a high and dismal wall, which was a part of the encircling wall of La Force.

The void which the demolished house left upon the street is half filled by a palisade fence of rotten boards, supported by five stone posts. Hidden in this inclosure is a little shanty built against that part of the ruin which remains standing. The fence has a gate which a few years ago was fastened only by a latch.

Thénardier was upon the crest of this ruin a little after three o'clock in the morning.

How had he got there? That is what nobody has ever been able to explain or understand. The lightning must have both confused and helped him. Did he use the ladders and the scaffoldings of the slaters to get from roof to roof, from inclosure to inclosure? But there were gaps in this route which seemed to render it impossible. Did he lay down the plank from his bed as a bridge from the roof to the encircling wall, and did he crawl on his belly along the coping of the wall, all round the prison as far as the ruin? But the encircling wall of La Force followed an indented and uneven line, it rose and fell, it sank down to the barracks of the firemen, it rose up to the bathing-house, it was cut by buildings, it had slopes and right angles everywhere; and then the sentinels would have seen the dark outline of the fugitive; on this supposition again, the route taken by Thénardier is still almost inexplicable. Had Thénardier invented and extemporised a third method? It has never been known.

However this may be, dripping with sweat, soaked through by the rain, his clothes in strips, his hands skinned, his elbows bleeding, his knees torn, Thénardier had reached what children, in their figurative language, call the edge of the wall of the ruin, he had stretched himself on it at full length, and there his strength failed him. A steep escarpment, three stories high, separated him from the pavement of the street.

The rope was too short.

He was waiting there, pale, exhausted, having lost all the hope which he had had, still covered by night, but saying to himself that day was just about to dawn, dismayed at the idea of hearing in a few moments the neighbouring clock of Saint Paul's strike four, the hour when they would come to relieve the sentinel and would find him asleep under the broken roof, gazing with a kind of stupor through the fearful depth, by the glimmer of the lamps, upon the wet and black pavement, that longed for yet terrible pavement which was death yet which was liberty.

He asked himself if his three accomplices in escape had succeeded, if they had heard him, and if they would come to his aid. He listened. Except a patrolman, nobody had passed through the street since he had been there. Nearly all the travel of the gardeners of Montreuil, Charonne, Vincennes, and Bercy to the Market, is through the Rue Saint Antoine. The clock struck four. Thénardier shuddered. A few moments afterwards, that wild and confused noise which follows upon the discovery of an escape, broke out in the prison. The sounds of doors opening and shutting, the grinding of gratings upon their hinges, the tumult in the guard-house, the harsh calls of the gate-keepers, the sound of the butts of muskets upon the pavement of the yards reached him. Lights moved up and down in the grated windows of the dormitories, a torch ran along the attic, the firemen of the barracks alongside had been called. Their caps, which the torches lighted up in the rain, were going to and fro along the roofs. At the same time Thénardier saw in the direction of the Bastille a whitish cloud throwing a dismal pallor over the lower part of the sky.

He was on the top of a wall ten inches wide, stretched out beneath the storm, with two precipices, at the right and at the left, unable to stir, giddy at the prospect of falling, and horror-stricken at the certainty of arrest, and his thoughts, like the pendulum of a clock, went from one of these ideas to the other: "Dead if I fall, taken if I stay."

In this anguish, he suddenly saw, the street being still wrapped in obscurity, a man who was gliding along the walls, and who came from the direction of the Rue Pavée, stop in the recess above which Thénardier was as it were suspended. This man was joined by a second, who was walking with the same precaution, then by a third, then by a fourth. When these men were together, one of them lifted the latch of the gate in the fence, and they all four entered the inclosure of the shanty. They were exactly under Thénardier. These men had evidently selected this recess so as to be able to talk without being seen by the passers or by the sentinel who guards the gate of La Force a few steps off. It must also be stated that the rain kept this sentinel blockaded in his sentry-box. Thénardier, not being able to distinguish their faces, listened to their words with the desperate attention of a wretch who feels that he is lost.

Something which resembled hope passed before Thénardier's eyes; these men spoke argot.

The first said, in a low voice, but distinctly:

"*Décarrons*. What is it we *maquillons icigo?*"[1]

The second answered:

"*Il lansquine* enough to put out the *riffe* of the *rabouin*. And then the *coqueurs* are going by, there is a *grivier* there who carries a *gaffe*, shall we let them *emballer* us *icicaille?*"[2]

These two words, *icigo* and *icicaille*, which both mean *ici* [*here*], and which belong, the first to the argot of the Barrières, the second to the argot of the Temple, were revelations to Thénardier. By *icigo* he recognised

[1] Let us go, what are we doing here?

[2] It rains enough to put out the devil's fire. And then the police are going by. There is a soldier there who is standing sentinel. Shall we let them arrest us here?

Brujon, who was a prowler of the Barrières, and by *icicaille* Babet, who, among all his other trades, had been a second-hand dealer at the Temple.

The ancient argot of the age of Louis XIV., is now spoken only at the Temple, and Babet was the only one who spoke it quite purely. Without *icicaille*, Thénardier would not have recognised him, for he had entirely disguised his voice.

Meanwhile the third put in a word:

"Nothing is urgent yet, let us wait a little. How do we know that he doesn't need our help?"

By this, which was only French, Thénardier recognised Montparnasse, whose elegance consisted in understanding all argots and speaking none.

As to the fourth, he was silent, but his huge shoulders betrayed him. It was Gueulemer.

Montparnasse resisted but feebly; the truth is, that these four men, with that faithfulness which bandits exhibit in never abandoning each other, had been prowling all night about La Force at whatever risk, in hope of seeing Thénardier rise above some wall. But the night which was becoming really too fine, it was storming enough to keep all the streets empty, the cold which was growing upon them, their soaked clothing, their wet shoes, the alarming uproar which had just broken out in the prison, the passing hours, the patrolmen they had met, hope departing, fear returning, all this impelled them to retreat. Montparnasse himself, who was, perhaps, to some slight extent a son-in-law of Thénardier, yielded. A moment more, they were gone. Thénardier gasped upon his wall like the shipwrecked sailors of the *Méduse* on their raft when they saw the ship which had appeared, vanish in the horizon.

He dared not call them, a cry overheard might destroy all; he had an idea, a final one, a flash of light; he took from his pocket the end of Brujon's rope, which he had detached from the chimney, and threw it into the inclosure.

This rope fell at their feet.

"There is the innkeeper," said Montparnasse.

They raised their eyes. Thénardier advanced his head a little.

"Quick!" said Montparnasse, "have you the other end of the rope, Brujon?"

"Yes."

"Tie the two ends together, we will throw him the rope, he will fasten it to the wall, he will have enough to get down."

Thénardier ventured to speak:

"I am benumbed."

"We will warm you."

"I can't stir."

"Let yourself slip down, we will catch you."

"My hands are stiff."

"Only tie the rope to the wall."

"I can't."

"One of us must get up," said Montparnasse.

"Three stories!" said Brujon.

An old plaster flue, which had served for a stove which had formerly been in use in the shanty, crept along the wall, rising almost to the spot at which they saw Thénardier. This flue, then very much cracked and full of seams, has since fallen, but its traces can still be seen. It was very small.

"We could get up by that," said Montparnasse.

"By that flue!" exclaimed Babet, "an *orgue*,[1] never! it would take a *mion*."[2]

"It would take a *môme*,"[3] added Brujon.

"Where can we find a brat?" said Gueulemer.

"Wait," said Montparnasse, "I have the thing."

He opened the gate of the fence softly, made sure that nobody was passing in the street, went out carefully, shut the door after him, and started on a run in the direction of the Bastille.

Seven or eight minutes elapsed, eight thousand centuries to Thénardier; Babet, Brujon, and Gueulemer kept their teeth clenched; the door at last opened again, and Montparnasse appeared, out of breath, with Gavroche. The rain still kept the street entirely empty.

Little Gavroche entered the inclosure and looked upon these bandit forms with a quiet air. The water was dripping from his hair. Gueulemer addressed him:

"Brat, are you a man?"

Gavroche shrugged his shoulders.

"What is it you want?" said Gavroche.

Montparnasse answered:

"To climb up by this flue."

"And then?" said Gavroche.

"That's all!" said Gueulemer.

The *gamin* examined the rope, the flue, the wall, the windows, and made that inexpressible and disdainful sound with his lips which signifies:

"What's that?"

"There is a man up there whom you will save," replied Montparnasse.

"Will you?" added Brujon.

"Goosy!" answered the child, as if the question appeared to him absurd; and he took off his shoes.

Gueulemer caught up Gavroche with one hand, put him on the roof of the shanty, the worm-eaten boards of which bent beneath the child's weight, and handed him the rope which Brujon had tied together during the absence of Montparnasse. The *gamin* went towards the flue, which it was easy to enter, thanks to a large hole at the roof. Just as he was about to start, Thénardier, who saw safety and life approaching, bent over the edge of the wall; the first gleam of day lighted up his forehead reeking with sweat, his thin and savage nose, his grey bristly beard, and Gavroche recognised him:

[1] A man.

[2] A child (argot of the Temple).

[3] A child (argot of the Barrières).

"Hold on!" said he, "it is my father!—Well, that don't hinder!"

And taking the rope in his teeth, he resolutely commenced the ascent.

He reached the top of the ruin, bestrode the old wall like a horse, and tied the rope firmly to the upper cross-bar of the window.

A moment afterwards Thénardier was in the street.

As soon as he had touched the pavement, as soon as he felt himself out of danger, he was no longer either fatigued, benumbed, or trembling; the terrible things through which he had passed vanished like a whiff of smoke, all that strange and ferocious intellect awoke, and found itself erect and free, ready to march forward. The man's first words were these:

"Now, who are we going to eat?"

It is needless to explain the meaning of this frightfully transparent word, which signifies all at once to kill, to assassinate, and to plunder. *Eat*, real meaning: *devour*.

"Let us hide first," said Brujon, "finish in three words and we will separate immediately. There was an affair which had a good look in the Rue Plumet, a deserted street, an isolated house, an old rusty grating upon a garden, some lone women."

"Well, why not?" inquired Thénardier.

"Eponine has been to see the thing," answered Babet.

"And she brought a biscuit to Magnon," added Gueulemer, "nothing there."

"Still we must see," said Thénardier.

"Yes, yes," said Brujon, "we must see."

Meantime none of these men appeared longer to see Gavroche. He waited a few minutes, perhaps for his father to turn towards him, then he put on his shoes, and said:

"It is over? you have no more use for me? I am going."

And he went away.

XXIII.   M. GILLENORMAND

THE READER has understood that Eponine, having recognised through the grating the inhabitant of that Rue Plumet, to which Magnon had sent her, had begun by diverting the bandits from the Rue Plumet, had then conducted Marius thither, and that after several days of ecstasy before that grating, Marius, drawn by that force which pushes the iron towards the magnet and the lover towards the stones of which the house of her whom he loves is built, had finally entered Cosette's garden as Romeo did the garden of Juliet. It had even been easier for him than for Romeo; Romeo was obliged to scale a wall, Marius had only to push aside a little one of the bars of the decrepit grating, which was loosened in its rusty socket, like the teeth of old people. Marius was slender, and easily passed through.

As there was never anybody in the street, and as, moreover, Marius entered the garden only at night, he ran no risk of being seen.

From that blessed and holy hour when a kiss affianced these two souls, Marius came every evening. If, at this period of her life, Cosette had fallen into the love of a man who was unscrupulous and a libertine, she would have been ruined; for there are generous natures which give themselves, and Cosette was one. God willed that the love which Cosette met, should be one of those loves which save.

Through all the month of May of that year 1832, there were there, every night, in that poor, wild garden, under that shrubbery each day more odorous and more dense, two beings composed of every chastity and every innocence, overflowing with all the felicities of Heaven, pure, noble, intoxicated, radiant, resplendent to each other in the darkness. They touched each other, they beheld each other, they clasped each other's hands, they pressed closely to each other; but there was a distance which they did not pass. Not that they respected it; they were ignorant of it. Marius felt a barrier, the purity of Cosette, and Cosette felt a support, the loyalty of Marius. The first kiss was the last also. Marius, since, had not gone beyond touching Cosette's hand, or her neckerchief, or her ringlets, with his lips. She refused nothing and he asked nothing. Cosette was happy, and Marius was satisfied.

At that hour of love, an hour when passion is absolutely silent under the omnipotence of ecstasy, Marius, the pure and seraphic Marius, would have been capable rather of visiting a public woman than of lifting Cosette's dress to the height of her ankle. Once, on a moonlight night, Cosette stooped to pick up something from the ground, her dress loosened and displayed the rounding of her bosom. Marius turned away his eyes.

What passed between these two beings? Nothing. They were adoring each other.

Cosette said to Marius:

"Do you know my name is Euphrasie?"

"Euphrasie? Why no, your name is Cosette."

"Oh! Cosette is such an ugly name that they gave me somehow when I was little. But my real name is Euphrasie. Don't you like that name, Euphrasie?"

"Yes—but Cosette is not ugly."

"Do you like it better than Euphrasie?"

"Why—yes."

"Then I like it better, too. It is true it is pretty, Cosette. Call me Cosette."

Once Marius said to Cosette:

"Just think, I thought at one time that your name was Ursula."

This made them laugh the whole evening.

In the midst of another conversation, he happened to exclaim:

"Oh! one day at the Luxembourg I would have been glad to break the rest of the bones of an Invalide!"

But he stopped short and went no further. He would have been obliged to speak to Cosette of her garter, and that was impossible for him.

Marius imagined life with Cosette like this, without anything else: to come every evening to the Rue Plumet, to put aside the complaisant old bar of the president's grating, to sit side by side upon this seat, to behold through the trees the scintillation of the commencing night, to make the fold of the knee of his pantaloons intimate with the fulness of Cosette's dress, to caress her thumbnail, to say dearest to her, to inhale one after the other the odour of the same flower, for ever, indefinitely.

"Oh!" murmured Marius, "how beautiful you are! I dare not look at you. That is why I stare at you. I do not know what is the matter with me. The hem of your dress, when the tip of your shoe appears, completely overwhelms me. And then you reason astonishingly. O Cosette! how strange and charming it is! I am really mad. You are adorable, mademoiselle. I study your feet with the microscope and your soul with the telescope."

And Cosette answered:

"I have been loving you a little more every minute since this morning."

Cosette gave to him who saw her a sensation of April and of dawn. It was quite natural that Marius, adoring her, should admire her. But the truth is that this little schoolgirl, fresh from the convent mill, talked with an exquisite penetration and said at times all manner of true and delicate words. Her prattle was conversation. She made no mistakes, and saw clearly.

And, by the side of this—all these contradictions are the lightning play of love—they were fond of laughing, and laughed with a charming freedom, and so familiarly that they sometimes seemed almost like two boys.

Their existence was vague, bewildered with happiness. They did not perceive the cholera which decimated Paris that very month. They had been as confidential with each other as they could be, but this had not gone very far beyond their names. Marius had told Cosette that he was an orphan, that his name was Marius Pontmercy, that he was a lawyer, that he lived by writing things for publishers, that his father was a colonel, that he was a hero, and that he, Marius, had quarrelled with his grandfather who was rich. He had also said something about being a baron; but that had produced no effect upon Cosette. Marius a baron! She did not comprehend. She did not know what that word meant. Marius was Marius.

On her part she had confided that she had been brought up at the Convent of the Petit Picpus, that her mother was dead as well as his, that her father's name was M. Fauchelevent, that he was very kind, that he gave much to the poor, but that he was poor himself, and that he deprived himself of everything while he deprived her of nothing.

Strange to say, in the kind of symphony in which Marius had been living since he had seen Cosette, the past, even the most recent, had become so confused and distant to him that what Cosette told him satisfied him fully. He did not even think to speak to her of the night adventure at the Gorbeau tenement, the Thénardiers, the burning, and the strange attitude and the singular flight of her father. Marius had temporarily forgotten all that; he did not even know at night what he had done in the morning, nor where he had breakfasted, nor who had spoken to him; he had songs in his ear which rendered him deaf to every other thought; he existed only during the hours in which he saw Cosette. Then, as he was in Heaven, it was quite natural that he should forget the earth. They were both supporting with languor the undefinable burden of the immaterial pleasures. Thus live these somnambulists called lovers.

Jean Valjean suspected nothing.

Cosette, a little less dreamy than Marius, was cheerful, and that was enough to make Jean Valjean happy.

Old Toussaint who went to bed early, thought of nothing but going to sleep, once her work was done, and was ignorant of all, like Jean Valjean.

Never did Marius set foot into the house. When he was with Cosette they hid themselves in a recess near the steps, so that they could neither be seen nor heard from the street, and they sat there, contenting themselves often, by way of conversation, with pressing each other's hands twenty times a minute while looking into the branches of the trees. At such moments, a thunderbolt might have fallen within thirty paces of them, and they would not have suspected it, so deeply was the reverie of the one absorbed and buried in the reverie of the other.

Meanwhile various complications were approaching.

One evening Marius was making his way to the rendezvous by the Boulevard des Invalides; he usually walked with his head bent down; as he was just turning the corner of the Rue Plumet, he heard some one saying very near him:

"Good evening, Monsieur Marius."

He looked up, and recognised Eponine.

This produced a singular effect upon him. He had not thought even once of this girl since the day she brought him to the Rue Plumet, he had not seen her again, and she had completely gone out of his mind. He had motives of gratitude only towards her; he owed his present happiness to her, and still it was annoying to him to meet her.

He answered with some embarrassment:

"What! is it you, Eponine?"

"Why do you speak to me so sternly? Have I done anything to you?"

"No," answered he.

Certainly, he had nothing against her. Far from it. Only, he felt that he could not do otherwise, now that he had whispered to Cosette, than speak coldly to Eponine.

As he was silent, she exclaimed:

"Tell me now—"

Then she stopped. It seemed as if words failed this creature, once so reckless and so bold. She attempted to smile and could not. She resumed:

"Well?—"

Then she was silent again, and stood with her eyes cast down.

"Good evening, Monsieur Marius," said she all at once abruptly, and she went away.

The next day was the 3rd of June, the 3rd of June, 1832, a date which must be noted on account of the grave events which were at that time suspended over the horizon of Paris like thunder-clouds. Marius, at nightfall, was following the same path as the evening before, with the same rapturous thoughts in his heart, when he perceived, under the trees of the boulevard, Eponine approaching him. Two days in succession, this was too much. He turned hastily, left the boulevard, changed his route, and went to the Rue Plumet through the Rue Monsieur.

This caused Eponine to follow him to the Rue Plumet, a thing which she had not done before. She had been content until then to see him on his way through the boulevard without even seeking to meet him. The evening previous, only, had she tried to speak to him.

Eponine followed him then, without a suspicion on his part. She saw him push aside the bar of the grating, and glide into the garden.

"Why!" said she, "he is going into the house."

She approached the grating, felt of the bars one after another, and easily recognised the one which Marius had displaced.

She murmured in an undertone, with a mournful accent:

"I wouldn't be surprised if he came every evening!"

She sat down upon the surbase of the grating, close beside the bar, as if she were guarding it. It was just at the point at which the grating joined the neighbouring wall. There was an obscure corner there, in which Eponine was entirely hidden.

She remained thus for more than an hour.

About ten o'clock in the evening, six men, who were walking separately and at some distance from each other along the wall, entered the Rue Plumet.

The first to arrive at the grating of the garden stopped and waited for the others; in a second they were all six together.

These men began to talk in a low voice.

"It is *icicaille*," said one of them.

"Is there a *cab*[1] in the garden?" asked another.

"The grating is old," added one who had a voice like a ventriloquist.

The sixth man, who had not opened his mouth, began to examine the grating as Eponine had done an hour before, grasping each bar successively and shaking it carefully. In this way he came to the bar which Marius had loosened. Just as he was about to lay hold of this bar, a hand, starting abruptly from the shadow, fell upon his arm, he felt himself pushed sharply back by the middle of his breast, and a roughened voice said to him without crying out:

"There is a *cab*."

At the same time he saw a pale girl standing before him.

The man recoiled, and stammered:

"What is this creature?"

"Your daughter."

It was indeed Eponine who was speaking to Thénardier.

On the appearance of Eponine the five others, that is to say, Claquesous, Gueulemer, Babet, Montparnasse, and Brujon, approached without a sound,

[1]Dog.

without haste, without saying a word, with the ominous slowness peculiar to these men of the night.

In their hands might be distinguished some strangely hideous tools. Gueulemer had one of those crooked crowbars which the prowlers call *fanchons*.

"Ah, there, what are you doing here? what do you want of us? are you crazy?" exclaimed Thénardier, as much as one can exclaim in a whisper. "What do you come and hinder us in our work for?"

Eponine began to laugh.

"I am here, my darling father, because I am here. Is there any law against sitting upon the stones in these days? It is you who shouldn't be here. What are you coming here for, since it is a biscuit? There is nothing to do here. But embrace me now, my dear good father! What a long time since I have seen you! You are out then?"

Thénardier tried to free himself from Eponine's arms, and muttered:

"Very well. You have embraced me. Yes, I am out. I am not in. Now, be off."

But Eponine did not loose her hold and redoubled her caresses.

"My darling father, how did you do it? You must have a good deal of wit to get out of that! Tell me about it! And my mother? where is my mother? Give me some news of mamma."

Thénardier answered:

"She is well, I don't know, let me alone, I tell you to be off."

"I don't want to go away just now," said Eponine, with the pettishness of a spoiled child, "you send me away when here it is four months that I haven't seen you, and when I have hardly had time to embrace you."

And she caught her father again by the neck.

"Ah! come now, this is foolish," said Babet.

"Let us hurry!" said Gueulemer, "the *coqueurs* may come along."

Eponine turned towards the five bandits.

"Why, this is Monsieur Brujon. Good-day, Monsieur Babet. Good-day, Monsieur Claquesous. Don't you remember me, Monsieur Gueulemer? How goes it, Montparnasse?"

"Yes, they recognise you," said Thénardier. "But good-day, good-night, keep off! don't disturb us!"

"It is the hour for foxes, and not for pullets," said Montparnasse.

"My darling Montparnasse," answered Eponine very gently, "we must have confidence in people. I am my father's daughter, perhaps. Monsieur Babet, Monsieur Gueulemer, it is I who was charged with finding out about this affair."

She pressed in her little hand the great rough fingers of Gueulemer, and continued:

"You know very well that I am not a fool. Ordinarily you believe me. I have done you service on occasion. Well, I have learned all about this, you would expose yourself uselessly, do you see. I swear to you that there is nothing to be done in that house."

"There are lone women," said Gueulemer.

"No. The people have moved away."

"The candles have not, anyhow!" said Babet.

And he showed Eponine, through the top of the trees, a light which was moving about in the garret of the cottage. It was Toussaint, who had sat up to hang out her clothes to dry.

Eponine made a final effort.

"Well," said she, "they are very poor people, and it is a shanty where there isn't a sou."

"Go to the devil!" cried Thénardier. "When we have turned the house over, and when we have put the cellar at the top and the garret at the bottom, we will tell you what there is inside."

And he pushed her to pass by.

"My good friend Monsieur Montparnasse," said Eponine, "I beg you, you who are a good boy, don't go in!"

"Take care, you will cut yourself," replied Montparnasse.

Thénardier added, with his decisive tone:

"Clear out, and let men do their work!"

Eponine said:

"You will go into that house then?"

"Just a little!" said the ventriloquist, with a sneer.

Then she placed her back against the grating, faced the six bandits who were armed to the teeth, and to whom the night gave faces of demons, and said in a low and firm voice:

"Well, I, I won't have it."

They stopped astounded.

"Friends! listen to me. In the first place, if you touch this grating, I shall cry out, I shall rap on doors, I shall wake everybody up, I shall have all six of you arrested, I shall call the sergents de ville."

"She would do it," said Thénardier in a low tone to Brujon and the ventriloquist.

She shook her head, and added:

"Beginning with my father!"

Thénardier approached.

"Not so near, goodman!" said she.

He drew back, muttering between his teeth: "Why, what is the matter with her?" and he added:

"Slut!"

She began to laugh in a terrible way:

"As you will, you shall not go in, I am not the daughter of a dog, for I am the daughter of a wolf. There are six of you, what is that to me? You are men. Now, I am a woman. I am not afraid of you, not a bit. I tell you that you shall not go into this house, because it does not please me. If you approach, I shall bark. I told you so, I am the *cab*, I don't care for you. Go your ways, you annoy me. Go where you like, but don't come here, I forbid it! You have knives, I have feet and hands. That makes no difference, come on now!"

She took a step towards the bandits, she was terrible, she began to laugh.

"The devil! I am not afraid. This summer, I shall be hungry; this winter, I shall be cold. Are they fools, these geese of men, to think that they can make a girl afraid! Of what! afraid? Ah, pshaw, indeed! Because you have hussies of mistresses who hide under the bed when you raise your voice, it won't do here! I, I am not afraid of anything!"

She kept her eye fixed upon Thénardier, and said:

"Not even you, father!"

Then she went on, casting her ghastly bloodshot eyes over the bandits:

"What is it to me whether somebody picks me up to-morrow on the pavement of the Rue Plumet, beaten to death with a club by my father, or whether they find me in a year in the ditches of Saint Cloud, or at the Ile de Cygnes, among the old rotten rubbish and the dead dogs?"

She was obliged to stop; a dry cough seized her, her breath came like a rattle from her narrow and feeble chest.

She resumed:

"I have but to cry out, they come, bang! You are six; but I am everybody."

Thénardier made a movement towards her.

" 'Proach not!" cried she.

He stopped, and said to her mildly:

"Well, no; I will not approach, but don't speak so loud. Daughter, you want then to hinder us in our work? Still we must earn our living. Have you no love for your father now?"

"You bother me," said Eponine.

"Still we must live, we must eat—"

"Die."

Saying which, she sat down on the surbase of the grating, her elbow on her knee and her chin in her hand, and swinging her foot with an air of indifference. Her dress was full of holes, and showed her sharp shoulder-blades. The neighbouring lamp lit up her profile and her attitude. Nothing could be more resolute or more surprising.

The six assassins, sullen and abashed at being held in check by a girl, went under the protecting shade of the lantern and held counsel, with humiliated and furious shrugs of their shoulders.

She watched them the while with a quiet yet indomitable air.

"Something is the matter with her," said Babet. "Some reason. Is she in love with the *cab?* But it is a pity to lose it. Two women, an old fellow who lodges in a back-yard, there are pretty good curtains at the windows. I think it is a good thing."

"Well, go in, the rest of you," exclaimed Montparnasse. "Do the thing. I will stay here with the girl, and if she trips—"

He made the open knife which he had in his hand gleam in the light of the lantern.

Thénardier said not a word and seemed ready for anything.

Brujon, who was something of an oracle, and who had, as we know, "got up the thing," had not yet spoken. He appeared thoughtful. He had a reputation for recoiling from nothing, and they knew that he had plundered, from sheer bravado, a police station. Moreover he made verses and songs, which gave him a great authority.

Babet questioned him.

"You don't say anything, Brujon?"

Brujon remained silent a minute longer, then he shook his head in several different ways, and at last decided to speak.

"Here: I met two sparrows fighting this morning; to-night, I run against a woman quarrelling. All this is bad. Let us go away."

They went away.

As they went, Montparnasse murmured:

"No matter, if they had said so, I would have made her feel the weight of my hand."

Babet answered:

"Not I. I don't strike a lady."

At the corner of the street, they stopped and exchanged this enigmatic dialogue in a smothered voice:

"Where are we going to sleep to-night?"

"Under Paris."

"Have you the key of the grating with you, Thénardier?"

Eponine, who had not taken her eyes off from them, saw them turn back the way they had come. She began to creep along the walls and houses behind them. She followed them as far as the boulevard.

While the six bandits were slinking away before a girl, Marius was with Cosette.

Never had the sky been more studded with stars, the trees more tremulous, the odour of the shrubs more penetrating; never had Marius been more enamoured, more happy, more in ecstasy. But he had found Cosette sad. Cosette had been weeping. Her eyes were red.

It was the first cloud in this wonderful dream.

Marius' first word was:

"What is the matter?"

"See."

Then she sat down on the seat near the stairs, and as he took his place all trembling beside her, she continued:

"My father told me this morning to hold myself in readiness, that he had business, and that perhaps we should go away."

Marius shuddered from head to foot.

When we are at the end of life, to die means to go away; when we are at the beginning, to go away means to die.

For six weeks Marius, gradually, slowly, by degrees, had been each day taking possession of Cosette. A possession entirely ideal, but thorough. As we have entirely explained, in the first love, the soul is taken far before the body; afterwards the body is taken far before the soul; sometimes the soul is not taken at all. Marius then possessed Cosette, as minds possess; but he wrapped her in his whole soul, and clasped her jealously with an incredible conviction. Into the midst of this faith, of this intoxication, of this virginal possession, marvellous and absolute, of this sovereignty, these words: "We are going away," fell all at once, and the sharp voice of reality cried to him: "Cosette is not yours!"

Marius awoke. For six weeks Marius had lived, as we have said, outside of life; this word, going away, brought him roughly back to it.

He could not find a word. She said to him in her turn:

"What is the matter?"

She resumed:

"This morning my father told me to arrange all my little affairs and to be ready, that he would give me his clothes to pack, that he was obliged to take a journey, that we were going away, that we must have a large trunk for me and a small one for him, to get all that ready within a week from now, and that we should go perhaps to England."

"But it is monstrous!" exclaimed Marius.

It is certain that at that moment, in Marius' mind, no abuse of power, no violence, no abomination of the most cruel tyrants, no action of Tiberius, or Henry VIII., was equal in ferocity to this: M. Fauchelevent taking his daughter to England because he has business.

He asked in a feeble voice:

"And when would you start?"

"He didn't say when."

"And when should you return?"

"He didn't say when."

Marius arose, and said coldly:

"Cosette, shall you go?"

Cosette turned upon him her beautiful eyes full of anguish and answered with a sort of bewilderment:

"Where?"

"To England? shall you go?"

"Why do you speak so to me?"

"I ask you if you shall go?"

"What would you have me do?" said she, clasping her hands.

"So, you will go?"

"If my father goes."

"So, you will go?"

Cosette took Marius' hand and pressed it without answering.

"Very well," said Marius. "Then I shall go elsewhere."

Cosette felt the meaning of this word still more than she understood it. She turned so pale that her face became white in the darkness. She stammered:

"What do you mean?"

Marius looked at her, then slowly raised his eyes towards heaven and answered:

"Nothing."

When his eyes were lowered, he saw Cosette smiling upon him. The smile of the woman whom we love has a brilliancy which we can see by night.

"How stupid we are! Marius, I have an idea."

"What?"

"Go if we go! I will tell you where! Come and join me where I am!"

Marius was now a man entirely awakened. He had fallen back into reality. He cried to Cosette:

"Go with you? are you mad? But it takes money, and I have none! Go to England? Why I owe now, I don't know, more than ten louis to Courfeyrac, one of my friends whom you do not know! Why I have an old hat which is not worth three francs, I have a coat from which some of the buttons are gone in front, my shirt is all torn, my elbows are out, my boots let in the water; for six weeks I have not thought of it, and I have not told you about it. Cosette! I am a miserable wretch. You only see me at night, and you give me your love; if you should see me by day, you would give me a sou! Go to England? Ah! I have not the means to pay for a passport!"

He threw himself against a tree which was near by, standing with his arms above his head, his forehead against the bark, feeling neither the tree which was chafing his skin, nor the fever which was hammering his temples, motionless, and ready to fall, like 'a statue of Despair.

He was a long time thus. One might remain through eternity in such abysses. At last he turned. He heard behind him a little stifled sound, soft and sad.

It was Cosette sobbing.

He came to her, fell on his knees, and, prostrating himself slowly, he took the tip of her foot which peeped from under her dress and kissed it.

"Do not weep," said he.

She murmured:

"Because I am perhaps going away, and you cannot come!"

He continued:

"Do you love me?"

She answered him by sobbing out that word of Paradise which is never more enrapturing than when it comes through tears:

"I adore you."

He continued with a tone of voice which was an inexpressible caress:

"Do not weep. Tell me, will you do this for me, not to weep?"

"Do you love me, too?" said she.

He caught her hand.

"Cosette, I have never given my word of honour to anybody, because I stand in awe of my word of honour. I feel that my father is at my side. Now, I give you my most sacred word of honour that, if you go away, I shall die."

From the shock she ceased weeping.

"Now listen," said he, "do not expect me to-morrow."

"Why not?"

"Do not expect me till the day after to-morrow!"

"Oh! why not?"

"You will see."

"A day without seeing you! Why, that is impossible."

"Let us sacrifice one day to gain perhaps a whole life."

And Marius added in an undertone, and aside:

"He is a man who changes none of his habits, and he has never received anybody till evening."

"What man are you speaking of?" inquired Cosette.

"Me? I said nothing."

"What is it you hope for, then?"

"Wait till day after to-morrow."

"You wish it?"

"Yes, Cosette."

She took his head in both her hands, rising on tiptoe to reach his height, and striving to see his hope in his eyes.

Marius continued:

"It occurs to me, you must know my address, something may happen, we don't know; I live with that friend named Courfeyrac, Rue de la Verrerie, number 16."

He put his hand in his pocket, took out a penknife, and wrote with the blade upon the plastering of the wall:

16, *Rue de la Verrerie.*

Cosette, meanwhile, began to look into his eyes again.

"Tell me your idea. Marius, you have an idea. Tell me. Oh! tell me, so that I may pass a good night!"

"My idea is this: that it is impossible that God should wish to separate us. Expect me day after to-morrow."

"What shall I do till then?" said Cosette. "You, you are out doors, you go, you come! How happy men are. I have to stay alone. Oh! how sad I shall be! What is it you are going to do to-morrow evening, tell me?"

"I shall try a plan."

"Then I will pray God, and I will think of you from now till then, that you may succeed. I will not ask any more questions, since you wish me not to. But day after to-morrow you will come early; I shall expect you at night, at nine o'clock precisely. You understand;—when the clock strikes nine, I shall be in the garden."

"And I too."

When Marius went out, the street was empty. It was the moment when Eponine was following the bandits to the boulevard.

While Marius was thinking with his head against the tree, he had formed a desperate resolution.

Grandfather Gillenormand had, at this period, fully completed his ninety-first year. He still lived with Mademoiselle Gillenormand, Rue des Filles du Calvaire, No. 6, in that old house which belonged to him. He was one of those antique old men who await death still erect, whom age loads without making them stoop, and whom grief itself does not bend.

Still, for some time, his daughter had said: "My father is failing." He no longer beat the servants; he struck his cane with less animation on the landing of the stairs. The revolution of July had hardly exasperated him for six months. The fact is, that the old man was filled with dejection. He did not bend, he did not yield; but he felt himself failing. Four years he had been waiting for Marius, with his foot down, that is just the word, in the conviction that that naughty little scapegrace would ring at his door some day or other: now he had come, in certain gloomy hours, to say to himself that even if Marius should delay, but little longer— It was not death that was insupportable to him; it was the idea that perhaps he should never see Marius again.

He was beginning to lose his teeth, which added to his sadness.

M. Gillenormand, without however acknowledging it to himself, for he would have been furious and ashamed at it, had never loved a mistress as he loved Marius.

He had had hung in his room, at the foot of his bed, as the first thing which he wished to see on awaking, an old portrait of his other daughter, she who was dead, Madame Pontmercy, a portrait taken when she was eighteen years old. He looked at this portrait incessantly. He happened one day to say, while looking at it:

"I think it looks like the child."

"Like my sister?" replied Mademoiselle Gillenormand. "Why yes."

The old man added:

"And like him also."

Once, as he was sitting, his knees pressed together, and his eyes almost closed, in a posture of dejection, his daughter ventured to say to him:

"Father, are you still so angry with him?"

She stopped, not daring to go further.

"With whom?" asked he.

"With that poor Marius?"

He raised his old head, laid his thin and wrinkled fist upon the table, and cried in his most irritated and quivering tone:

"Poor Marius, you say? That gentleman is a rascal, a worthless knave, a little ungrateful vanity, with no heart, no soul, a proud, a wicked man!"

Three days later, after a silence which had lasted for four hours, he said to his daughter snappishly:

"I have had the honour to beg Mademoiselle Gillenormand never to speak to me of him."

Aunt Gillenormand gave up all attempts and came to this profound diagnosis: "My father never loved my sister very much after her folly. It is clear that he detests Marius."

"After her folly" meant: after she married the colonel.

Still, as may have been conjectured, Mademoiselle Gillenormand had failed in her attempt to substitute her favourite, the officer of lancers, for

Marius. The supplanter Théodule had not succeeded. Grandfather Gillenormand, at last, said to his daughter: "I have had enough of him, your Théodule. I have little taste for warriors in time of peace. Entertain him yourself, if you like."

It was of no use for his daughter to say: "Still he is your grand-nephew," it turned out that Monsieur Gillenormand, who was grandfather to the ends of his nails, was not grand-uncle at all.

One evening, it was the 4th of June, which did not prevent Monsieur Gillenormand from having a blazing fire in his fireplace, he had said good-night to his daughter who was sewing in the adjoining room. He was alone in his room with the rural scenery, his feet upon the andirons, half enveloped in his vast coromandel screen with nine folds, leaning upon his table on which two candles were burning under a green shade, buried in his tapestried armchair, a book in his hand, but not reading.

Monsieur Gillenormand thought of Marius lovingly and bitterly. He endeavoured to bring himself to the idea that it was over with, and that he would die without seeing "that gentleman" again.

In the deepest of this reverie, his old domestic, Basque, came in and asked: "Can monsieur receive Monsieur Marius?"

The old man straightened up.

"Monsieur Marius what?"

"I don't know," answered Basque, intimidated and thrown out of countenance by his master's appearance. "I have not seen him. Nicolette just told me: There is a young man here, say that it is Monsieur Marius."

M. Gillenormand stammered out in a whisper:

"Show him in."

Marius stopped at the door, as if waiting to be asked to come in.

His almost wretched dress was not perceived in the obscurity produced by the green shade. Only his face, calm and grave, but strangely sad, could be distinguished.

M. Gillenormand, as if congested with astonishment and joy, sat for some moments without seeing anything but a light, as when one is in presence of an apparition. At last! after four years! And through the contrast which was the groundwork of his nature, there came forth a harsh word. He said abruptly:

"What is it you come here for?"

Marius answered with embarrassment:

"Monsieur—"

M. Gillenormand would have had Marius throw himself into his arms. He was displeased with Marius and with himself. The old man continued, in a stern voice:

"Do you come to ask my pardon? have you seen your fault?"

Marius shuddered; it was the disavowal of his father which was asked of him; he cast down his eyes and answered:

"No, monsieur."

"And then," exclaimed the old man impetuously, with a grief which was bitter and full of anger, "what do you want with me?"

Marius clasped his hands, took a step, and said in a feeble and trembling voice:

"Monsieur, have pity on me."

This word moved M. Gillenormand; spoken sooner, it would have softened him, but it came too late. The grandfather arose; he supported himself upon his cane with both hands, his lips were white, his forehead quivered, but his tall stature commanded the stooping Marius.

"Pity on you, monsieur! The youth asks pity from the old man of ninety-one! You are entering life, I am leaving it; you go to the theatre, the ball, the café, the billiard-room; you have wit, you please the women, you are a handsome fellow, while I cannot leave my chimney corner in midsummer; you are rich, with the only riches there are, while I have all the poverties of old age; infirmity, isolation. You have your thirty-two teeth, a good stomach, a keen eye, strength, appetite, health, cheerfulness, a forest of black hair, while I have not even white hair left; I have lost my teeth, I am losing my legs, I am losing my memory, there are three names of streets which I am always confounding, the Rue Charlot, the Rue du Chaume, and the Rue Saint Claude, there is where I am; you have the whole future before you full of sunshine, while I am beginning not to see another drop of it, so deep am I getting into the night; you are in love, of course, I am not loved by anybody in the world; and you ask pity of me. Zounds, Molière forgot this. If that is the way you jest at the Palais, Messieurs Lawyers, I offer you my sincere compliments. You are funny fellows."

And the octogenarian resumed in an angry and stern voice:

"Come now, what do you want of me?"

"Monsieur," said Marius, "I know that my presence is displeasing to you, but I come only to ask one thing of you, and then I will go away immediately."

"You are a fool!" said the old man. "Who tells you to go away?"

This was the translation of those loving words which he had deep in his heart: *Come, ask my pardon now! Throw yourself on my neck!* M. Gillenormand continued:

"What! you have left my house to go nobody knows where; you have afflicted your aunt, you have been leading the life of a bachelor, playing the elegant, going home at all hours, amusing yourself; you have not given me a sign of life; and, at the end of four years, you come to my house, and have nothing to say but that!"

This violent method of pushing the grandson to tenderness produced only silence on the part of Marius. M. Gillenormand folded his arms, a posture which with him was particularly imperious, and apostrophised Marius bitterly.

"Let us make an end of it. You have come to ask something of me, say you? Well what? what is it? speak!"

"Monsieur," said Marius, with the look of a man who feels that he is about to fall into an abyss, "I come to ask your permission to marry."

M. Gillenormand rang. Basque half opened the door.

"Send my daughter in."

A second later—the door opened again. Mademoiselle Gillenormand did not come in, but showed herself. Marius was standing, mute, his arms hanging down, with the look of a criminal. M. Gillenormand was coming and going up and down the room. He turned towards his daughter and said to her:

"Nothing. It is Monsieur Marius. Bid him good evening. Monsieur wishes to marry. That is all. Go."

The crisp, harsh tones of the old man's voice announced a strange fulness of feeling. The aunt looked at Marius with a bewildered air, appeared hardly to recognise him, allowed neither a motion nor a syllable to escape her, and disappeared at a breath from her father, quicker than a dry leaf before a hurricane.

Meanwhile Grandfather Gillenormand had returned and stood with his back to the fireplace.

"You marry! at twenty-one! You have arranged that! You have nothing but a permission to ask! a formality. Sit down, monsieur. Well, you have had a revolution since I had the honour to see you. The Jacobins have had the upper hand. You ought to be satisfied. You are a republican, are you not, since you are a baron? You arrange that. The republic is sauce to the barony. Are you decorated by July?—did you take a bit of the Louvre, monsieur? There is close by here, in the Rue Saint Antoine, opposite the Rue des Nonaindières, a ball incrusted in the wall of the third story of a house with this inscription: July 28th, 1830. Go and see that. Pretty things those friends of yours do. By the way, are they not making a fountain in the square of the monument of M. the Duke de Berry? So you want to marry? Whom? can the question be asked without indiscretion?"

He stopped, and, before Marius had had time to answer, he added violently:

"Come now, you have a business? your fortune made? how much do you earn at your lawyer's trade?"

"Nothing," said Marius, with a firmness and resolution which were almost savage.

"Nothing? you have nothing to live on but the twelve hundred livres which I send you?"

Marius made no answer. M. Gillenormand continued:

"Then I understand the girl is rich?"

"As I am."

"What! no dowry?"

"No."

"Some expectations?"

"I believe not."

"With nothing to her back! and what is the father?"

"I do not know."

"What is her name?"

"Mademoiselle Fauchelevent."

"Fauchewhat?"

"Fauchelevent."

"Pttt!" said the old man.

"Monsieur!" exclaimed Marius.

M. Gillenormand interrupted him with the tone of a man who is talking to himself.

"That is it, twenty-one, no business, twelve hundred livres a year, Madame the Baroness Pontmercy will go to the market to buy two sous' worth of parsley."

"Monsieur," said Marius, in the desperation of the last vanishing hope, "I supplicate you! I conjure you, in the name of heaven, with clasped hands, monsieur, I throw myself at your feet, allow me to marry her!"

The old man burst into a shrill, dreary laugh, through which he coughed and spoke.

"Ha, ha, ha! you said to yourself, 'The devil! I will go and find that old wig, that silly dolt! What a pity that I am not twenty-five! how I would toss him a good respectful notice! how I would give him the go-by. Never mind, I will say to him: Old idiot, you are too happy to see me, I desire to marry, I desire to espouse mamselle no matter whom, daughter of monsieur no matter what, I have no shoes, she has no chemise, all right; I desire to throw to the dogs my career, my future, my youth, my life; I desire to make a plunge into misery with a wife at my neck, that is my idea, you must consent to it! and the old fossil will consent.' Go, my boy, as you like, tie your stone to yourself, espouse your Pousselevent, your Couplevent—Never, monsieur! never!"

"Father!"

"Never!"

At the tone in which this "never" was pronounced Marius lost all hope. He walked the room with slow steps, his head bowed down. M. Gillenormand followed him with his eyes, and, at the moment the door opened and Marius was going out, he took four steps with the senile vivacity of impetuous and self-willed old men, seized Marius by the collar, drew him back forcibly into the room, threw him into an armchair, and said to him:

"Tell me about it!"

It was that single word, *father*, dropped by Marius, which had caused this revolution.

Marius looked at him in bewilderment. The changing countenance of M. Gillenormand expressed nothing now but a rough and ineffable good-nature. The guardian had given place to the grandfather.

"Come, let us see, speak, tell me about your love scrapes, jabber, tell me all! Lord! how foolish these young folks are!"

"Father," resumed Marius—

He was sitting near the table, the light of the candle made the wretchedness of his dress apparent, and the grandfather gazed at it in astonishment.

"Well, father," said Marius—

"Come now," interrupted M. Gillenormand, "then you really haven't a sou? you are dressed like a robber."

He fumbled in a drawer and took out a purse, which he laid upon the table:

"Here, there is a hundred louis, buy yourself a hat."

"Father," pursued Marius, "if you knew. I love her. You don't realise it; the first time that I saw her was at the Luxembourg, she came there; in the beginning I did not pay much attention to her, and then I do not know how it came about, I fell in love with her. Oh! how wretched it has made me! Now at last I see her every day, at her own house, her father does not know it, only think that they are going away, we see each other in the garden in the evening, her father wants to take her to England, then I said to myself: I will go and see my grandfather and tell him about it. I should go crazy in the first place, I should die, I should make myself sick, I should throw myself into the river. I must marry her because I should go crazy. Now, that is the whole truth, I do not believe that I have forgotten anything. She lives in a garden where there is a railing, in the Rue Plumet. It is near the Invalides."

Grandfather Gillenormand, radiant with joy, had sat down by Marius' side. While listening to him and enjoying the sound of his voice, he enjoyed at the same time a long pinch of snuff. At that word, Rue Plumet, he checked his inspiration and let the rest of his snuff fall on his knees.

"Rue Plumet!—you say Rue Plumet?—Let us see now!—Are there not some barracks down there? Why yes, that is it. Your cousin Théodule has told me about her. The lancer, the officer.—A lassie, my good friend, a lassie!—Lord yes, Rue Plumet. That is what used to be called Rue Blomet. It comes back to me now. I have heard tell about this little girl of the grating in the Rue Plumet. In a garden, a Pamela. Your taste is not bad. They say she is nice. Between ourselves, I believe that ninny of a lancer has paid his court to her a little. I do not know how far it went. After all that does not amount to anything. And then, we must not believe him. He is a boaster. Marius! I think it is very well for a young man like you to be in love. It belongs to your age. I like you better in love than as a Jacobin. I like you better taken by a petticoat, Lord! by twenty petticoats, than by Monsieur de Robespierre. Pretty women are pretty women, the devil! there is no objection to that. As to the little girl, she receives you unknown to papa. That is all right. I have had adventures like that myself. More than one. Do you know how we do? we don't take the thing ferociously; we don't rush into the tragic; we don't conclude with marriage and with Monsieur the Mayor and his scarf. We are altogether a shrewd fellow. We have good sense. Slip over it, don't marry. We come and find grandfather who is a goodman at heart, and who almost always has a few rolls of louis in an old drawer; we say to him: 'Grandfather, that's how it is.' And grandfather says: 'That is all natural. Youth must fare and old age must wear. I have been young, you will be old. Go on, my boy, you will repay this to your grandson. There are two hundred pistoles. Amuse yourself, roundly! Nothing better! that is the way the thing should be done. We don't marry, but that doesn't hinder.' You understand me?"

Marius, petrified and unable to articulate a word, shook his head.

The goodman burst into a laugh, winked his old eye, gave him a tap on the knee, looked straight into his eyes with a significant and sparkling expression, and said to him with the most amorous shrug of the shoulders: "Stupid! make her your mistress."

Marius turned pale. He had understood nothing of all that his grandfather had been saying. This rigmarole of Rue Blomet, of Pamela, of barracks, of a lancer, had passed before Marius like a phantasmagoria. Nothing of all this could relate to Cosette, who was a lily. The goodman was wandering. But this wandering had terminated in a word which Marius did understand, and which was a deadly insult to Cosette. That phrase, *make her your mistress*, entered the heart of the chaste young man like a sword.

He rose, picked up his hat which was on the floor, and walked towards the door with a firm and assured step. There he turned, bowed profoundly before his grandfather, raised his head again, and said:

"Five years ago you outraged my father; to-day you have outraged my wife. I ask nothing more of you, monsieur. Adieu."

Grandfather Gillenormand, astounded, opened his mouth, stretched out his arms, attempted to rise, but before he could utter a word, the door closed and Marius had disappeared.

The old man was for a few moments motionless, unable to speak or breath, as if a hand were clutching his throat. At last he tore himself from his chair, ran to the door as fast as a man who is ninety-one can run, opened it and cried:

"Help! help!"

His daughter appeared, then the servants. He continued with a pitiful rattle in his voice:

"Run after him! catch him! what have I done to him! he is mad! he is going away! Oh! my God! oh! my God!—this time he will not come back!"

He went to the window which looked upon the street, opened it with his tremulous old hands, hung more than half his body outside, while Basque and Nicolette held him from behind, and cried:

"Marius! Marius! Marius! Marius!"

But Marius was already out of hearing, and was at that very moment turning the corner of the Rue Saint Louis.

XXIV.   JUNE 5, 1832

THAT very day, towards four o'clock in the afternoon, Jean Valjean was sitting alone upon the reverse of one of the most solitary embankments of

the Champ de Mars. Whether from prudence, or from a desire for meditation, or simply as a result of one of those insensible changes of habits
which creep little by little into all lives, he now rarely went out with
Cosette. He wore his working-man's waistcoat, brown linen trousers, and
his cap with the long visor hid his face. He was now calm and happy in
regard to Cosette; what had for some time alarmed and disturbed him was
dissipated; but within a week or two anxieties of a different nature had
come upon him. One day, when walking on the boulevard, he had seen
Thénardier; thanks to his disguise, Thénardier had not recognised him;
but since then Jean Valjean had seen him again several times, and he was
now certain that Thénardier was prowling about the quartier. This was
sufficient to make him take a serious step. Thénardier there! this was all
dangers at once.

Moreover, Paris was not quiet: the political troubles had this inconvenience for him who had anything in his life to conceal, that the police had
become very active, and very secret, and that in seeking to track out a
man like Pépin or Morey, they would be very likely to discover a man
like Jean Valjean. Jean Valjean had decided to leave Paris, and even
France, and to pass over to England. He had told Cosette. In less than a
week he wished to be gone. He was sitting on the embankment in the
Champ de Mars, revolving all manner of thoughts in his mind, Thénardier,
the police, the journey, and the difficulty of procuring a passport.

On all these points he was anxious.

Finally, an inexplicable circumstance which had just burst upon him,
and with which he was still warm, had added to his alarm. On the morning of that very day, being the only one up in the house, and walking in
the garden before Cosette's shutters were open, he had suddenly come
upon this line scratched upon the wall, probably with a nail: 16, *Rue de la
Verrerie.*

It was quite recent, the lines were white in the old black mortar, a tuft
of nettles at the foot of the wall was powdered with fresh fine plaster. It
had probably been written during the night. What was it? an address? a
signal for others? a warning for him? At all events, it was evident that
the garden had been violated, and that some persons unknown had penetrated into it. He recalled the strange incidents which had already alarmed
the house. He took good care not to speak to Cosette of the line written
on the wall, for fear of frightening her.

In the midst of these meditations, he perceived, by a shadow which the
sun had projected, that somebody had just stopped upon the crest of the
embankment immediately behind him. He was about to turn round, when
a folded paper fell upon his knees, as if a hand had dropped it from above
his head. He took the paper, unfolded it, and read on it this word, written
in large letters with a pencil:

REMOVE.

Jean Valjean rose hastily, there was no longer anybody on the embankment; he looked about him, and perceived a species of being larger than

a child, smaller than a man, dressed in a grey blouse, and trousers of dirt-coloured cotton velvet, which jumped over the parapet and let itself slide into the ditch of the Champ de Mars.

Jean Valjean returned home immediately, full of thought.

Marius had left M. Gillenormand's desolate. He had entered with a very small hope; he came out with an immense despair.

Still, and those who have observed the beginnings of the human heart will understand it, the lancer, the officer, the ninny, the cousin Théodule, had left no shadow in his mind. The dramatic poet might apparently hope for some complications from this revelation, made in the very teeth of the grandson by the grandfather. But what the drama would gain, the truth would lose. Marius was at that age when we believe no ill.

He began to walk the streets, the resource of those who suffer. At two o'clock in the morning he returned to Courfeyrac's, and threw himself, dressed as he was, upon his mattress. It was broad sunlight when he fell asleep, with that frightful, heavy slumber in which the ideas come and go in the brain. When he awoke, he saw standing in the room, their hats upon their heads, all ready to go out, and very busy, Courfeyrac, Enjolras, Feuilly, and Combeferre.

Courfeyrac said to him:

"Are you going to the funeral of General Lamarque?"

It seemed to him that Courfeyrac was speaking Chinese.

He went out some time after them. He put into his pocket the pistols which Javert had confided to him at the time of the adventure of the 3rd of February, and which had remained in his hands. These pistols were still loaded. It would be difficult to say what obscure thought he had in his mind in taking them with him.

He rambled about all day without knowing where; it rained at intervals, he did not perceive it; for his dinner he bought a penny roll at a baker's, put it in his pocket, and forgot it. It would appear that he took a bath in the Seine without being conscious of it. He waited for night with feverish impatience, he had but one clear idea; that was, that at nine o'clock he should see Cosette.

At intervals, while walking along the most deserted boulevards, he seemed to hear strange sounds in Paris. He roused himself from his reverie, and said: "Are they fighting?"

At nightfall, at precisely nine o'clock, as he had promised Cosette, he was in the Rue Plumet. When he approached the grating he forgot everything else. It was forty-eight hours since he had seen Cosette, he was going to see her again, every other thought faded away, and he felt now only a deep and wonderful joy.

Marius displaced the grating, and sprang into the garden. Cosette was not at the place where she usually waited for him. He crossed the thicket and went to the recess near the steps. "She is waiting for me there," said he. Cosette was not there. He raised his eyes, and saw the shutters of the house were closed. He took a turn around the garden, the garden was deserted. Then he returned to the house, and, mad with love, intoxicated, dismayed, exasperated with grief and anxiety, like a master who returns home in an untoward hour, he rapped on the shutters. He rapped, he rapped again, at the risk of seeing the window open and the forbidding face of the father appear and ask him: "What do you want?" This was nothing compared with what he now began to see. When he had rapped, he raised his voice and called Cosette. "Cosette!" cried he. "Cosette!" repeated he imperiously. There was no answer. It was settled. Nobody in the garden; nobody in the house.

Suddenly he heard a voice which appeared to come from the street, and which cried through the trees:

"Monsieur Marius!"

He arose.

"Hey?" said he.

"Monsieur Marius, is it you?"

"Yes."

"Monsieur Marius," added the voice, "your friends are expecting you at the barricade, in the Rue de la Chanvrerie."

This voice was not entirely unknown to him. It resembled the harsh and roughened voice of Eponine. Marius ran to the grating, pushed aside the movable bar, passed his head through, and saw somebody who appeared to him to be a young man rapidly disappearing in the twilight.

JEAN VALJEAN's purse was useless to M. Mabeuf. M. Mabeuf, in his venerable childlike austerity, had not accepted the gift of the stars; he did not admit that a star could coin itself into gold louis. He did not guess that what fell from the sky came from Gavroche. He carried the purse to the Commissary of Police of the quartier, as a lost article, placed by the finder at the disposition of claimants.

For the rest, M. Mabeuf had continued to descend.

The experiments upon indigo had succeeded no better at the Jardin des Plantes than in his garden at Austerlitz. The year before, he owed his housekeeper her wages; now, we have seen, he owed three quarters of his rent. The pawnbroker, at the expiration of thirteen months, had sold the plates of his *Flora*. Some coppersmith had made saucepans of them. His plates gone, being no longer able even to complete the broken sets of his *Flora* which he still possessed, he had given up engravings and text at a wretched price to a second-hand bookseller, as *odd copies*. He had now nothing left of the work of his whole life. He began to eat up the money from these copies. Before this, and for a long time before, he had given up the two eggs and the bit of beef which he used to eat from time to time. He dined on bread and potatoes. He had sold his last furniture, then all his spare bedding and clothing, then his collections of plants and his pictures; but he still had his most precious books, several of which were of great rarity. M. Mabeuf never made a fire in his room, and went to bed by daylight so as not to burn a candle. It seemed that he had now no neighbours, he was shunned when he went out; he was aware of it. The misery of a child is interesting to a mother, the misery of a young man is interesting to a young woman, the misery of an old man is interesting to nobody. This is of all miseries the coldest. Still Father Mabeuf had not entirely lost his childlike serenity. His eye regained some vivacity when it was fixed upon his books, and he smiled when he thought of the Diogenes Laertius, which was a unique copy. His glass bookcase was the only piece of furniture which he had preserved beyond what was indispensable.

One day Mother Plutarch said to him:

"I have nothing to buy the dinner with."

What she called the dinner was a loaf of bread and four or five potatoes.

"On credit?" said M. Mabeuf.

"You know well enough that they refuse me."

M. Mabeuf opened his library, looked long at all his books one after another, as a father, compelled to decimate his children, would look at them before choosing, then took one of them hastily, put it under his arm, and went out. He returned two hours afterwards with nothing under his arm, laid thirty sous on the table, and said:

"You will get some dinner."

From that moment, Mother Plutarch saw settling over the old man's white face a dark veil which was never lifted again.

The next day, the day after, every day, he had to begin again. M. Mabeuf went out with a book and came back with a piece of money. As the bookstall keepers saw that he was forced to sell, they bought from him for twenty sous what he had paid twenty francs for, sometimes to the same booksellers. Volume by volume, the whole library passed away. He said at times: "I am eighty years old however," as if he had some lingering hope of reaching the end of his days before reaching the end of his books. His sadness increased. Once, however, he had a pleasure. He went out with a Robert Estienne which he sold for thirty-five sous on the Quai Malaquais and returned with an Aldine which he had bought for forty sous in the Rue des Grès. "I owe five sous," said he to Mother Plutarch, glowing with joy.

That day he did not dine.

He belonged to the Society of Horticulture. His poverty was known there. The president of this society came to see him, promised to speak to the Minister of Agriculture and Commerce about him, and did so. "Why, how now!" exclaimed the minister. "I do believe! An old philosopher! a botanist! an inoffensive man! We must do something for him!" The next day M. Mabeuf received an invitation to dine at the minister's. Trembling with joy, he showed the letter to Mother Plutarch. "We are saved!" said he. On the appointed day, he went to the minister's. He perceived that his ragged cravat, his large, old, square coat, and his shoes polished with egg, astonished the ushers. Nobody spoke to him, not even the minister. About ten o'clock in the evening, as he was still expecting a word, he heard the minister's wife, a beautiful lady in a lownecked dress, whom he had not dared to approach, asking: "What can that old gentleman be?" He returned home on foot, at midnight, in a driving rain. He had sold an Elzevir to pay for a fiacre to go with.

Suddenly Mother Plutarch fell sick. There is one thing sadder than having nothing with which to buy bread from the baker; that is, having nothing with which to buy drugs from the apothecary. One night, the doctor had ordered a very dear potion. And then, the sickness was growing worse, a nurse was needed. M. Mabeuf opened his bookcase; the Diogenes Laertius alone remained.

He put the unique copy under his arm and went out; it was the 4th of June, 1832; he went to the Porte Saint Jacques, and returned with a hundred francs. He laid the pile of five-franc pieces on the old servant's bedroom table, and went back to his room without saying a word.

The next day, by dawn, he was seated on the stone post in the garden, and he might have been seen from over the hedge all the morning motionless, his head bowed down, his eye vaguely fixed upon the withered beds.

In the afternoon, extraordinary sounds broke out in Paris. They resembled musket shots, and the clamour of a multitude.

Father Mabeuf raised his head. He saw a gardener going by, and asked: "What is that?"

The gardener answered, his spade upon his shoulder, and in the most quiet tone:

"They are fighting."

"What are they fighting for?"

"Oh! Lordy!" said the gardener.

"Whereabouts?" continued M. Mabeuf.

"Near the Arsenal."

Father Mabeuf went into the house, took his hat, looked mechanically for a book to put under his arm, did not find any, said: "Ah! it is true!" and went away with a bewildered air.

In the spring of 1832, Paris had for a long time been ready for a commotion. As we have said, the great city resembles a piece of artillery; when it is loaded the falling of a spark is enough, the shot goes off. In June, 1832, the spark was the death of General Lamarque.

Lamarque was a man of renown and of action. He had had successively, under the Empire and under the Restoration, the bravery of the battlefield and the bravery of the rostrum. He sat between the left and the extreme left, loved by the people because he accepted the changes of the future, loved by the masses because he had served the emperor well. He hated Wellington with a direct hatred which pleased the multitude; and for seventeen years, hardly noticing intermediate events, he had majestically preserved the sadness of Waterloo.

His death was dreaded by the people as a loss, and by the government as an opportunity. This death was a mourning. Like everything which is bitter, mourning may turn into revolt. This is what happened.

The eve and the morning of the 5th of June, the day fixed for the funeral of Lamarque, the Faubourg Saint Antoine, through the edge of which the procession was to pass, assumed a formidable aspect. That tumultuous network of streets was full of rumour. Men armed themselves as they could. They were heard to say: *"Where is your pistol?" "Under my blouse." "And yours?" "Under my shirt."* Orders were passed about almost publicly.

On the 5th of June, then, a day of mingled rain and sunshine, the procession of General Lamarque passed through Paris with the official military pomp, somewhat increased by way of precaution. Two battalions, drums muffled, muskets reversed, ten thousand National Guards, their sabres at their sides, the batteries of artillery of the National Guard, escorted the coffin. The hearse was drawn by young men. The officers of the Invalides followed immediately bearing branches of laurel. Then came a countless multitude, strange and agitated, the sectionaries of the Friends of the People, the Law School, the Medical School, refugees from all nations, Spanish, Italian, German, Polish flags, horizontal tri-coloured flags, every possible banner, children waving green branches, stone-cutters and carpenters, who were on a strike at that very moment, printers recognisable by their paper caps, walking two by two, three by three, uttering cries, almost all brandishing clubs, a few swords. On the cross alleys of the boulevards, in the branches of the trees, on the balconies, at the windows, on the roofs, were swarms of heads, men, women, children; their eyes were full of anxiety. An armed multitude was passing by, a terrified multitude was looking on.

The government also was observing, with its hand upon the hilt of the sword. One might have seen, all ready to march, with full cartridge-boxes, guns and musquetoons loaded, in the Place Louis XV., four squadrons of carbineers, in the saddle, trumpets at their heads, in the Latin Quarter and at the Jardin des Plantes, the Municipal Guard, en échelon from street to street, at the Halle aux Vins a squadron of dragoons, at La Grève one half of the 12th Light, the other half at the Bastille, the 6th dragoons at the Célestins, the Court of the Louvre full of artillery. The rest of the troops were stationed in the barracks, without counting the regiments in the environs of Paris. Anxious authority held suspended over the threatening multitude twenty-four thousand soldiers in the city, and thirty thousand in the banlieue.

The hearse passed the Bastille, followed the canal, crossed the little bridge, and reached the esplanade of the Bridge of Austerlitz. There it stopped. A circle was formed about the hearse. Lafayette spoke and bade farewell to Lamarque. It was a touching and august moment, all heads were uncovered, all hearts throbbed. Suddenly a man on horseback, dressed in black, appeared in the midst of the throng with a red flag, others say with a pike surmounted by a red cap. Lafayette turned away his head.

This red flag raised a storm and disappeared in it. From the Boulevard Bourbon to the Bridge of Austerlitz one of those shouts which resemble billows moved the multitude. Two prodigious shouts arose: *Lamarque to the Pantheon! Lafayette to the Hôtel de Ville!* Some young men, amid the cheers of the throng, harnessed themselves, and began to draw Lamarque in the hearse over the Bridge of Austerlitz, and Lafayette in a fiacre along the Quai Morland.

In the crowd which surrounded and cheered Lafayette, was noticed and pointed out a German, named Ludwig Snyder, who afterwards died a centenarian, who had also been in the war of 1776, and who had fought at Trenton under Washington, and under Lafayette at Brandywine.

Meanwhile, on the left bank, the municipal cavalry was in motion, and had just barred the bridge, on the right bank the dragoons left the Célestins and deployed along the Quai Morland. The men who were drawing Lafayette suddenly perceived them at the corner of the Quai, and cried: "The dragoons!" The dragoons were advancing at a walk, in silence, their pistols in their holsters, their sabres in their sheaths, their musketoons in their rests, with an air of gloomy expectation.

At two hundred paces from the little bridge, they halted. The fiacre in which Lafayette was, made its way up to them, they opened their ranks, let it pass, and closed again behind it. At that moment the dragoons and the multitude came together. The women fled in terror.

What took place in that fatal moment? nobody could tell. Some say that a trumpet-flourish sounding the charge was heard from the direction of the Arsenal, others that a dagger-thrust was given by a child to a dragoon. The fact is that three shots were suddenly fired, the first killed the chief of the squadron, Cholet, the second killed an old deaf woman who was closing her window in the Rue Contrescarpe, the third singed the epaulet of an officer; a woman cried: "They are beginning too soon!" and all at once there was seen, from the side opposite the Quai Morland, a squadron of dragoons which had remained in barracks turning out on the gallop, with swords drawn, from the Rue Bassompierre and the Boulevard Bourdon, and sweeping all before them.

There are no more words, the tempest breaks loose, stones fall like hail, musketry bursts forth. They fire pistol-shots, a barricade is planned out, the young men pass the Bridge of Austerlitz with the hearse at a run, and charge on the Municipal Guard, the carbineers rush up, the dragoons ply the sabre, the mass scatters in every direction. A rumour of war flies to the four corners of Paris, men cry: "To arms!" Wrath sweeps along as the wind sweeps along a fire.

A quarter of an hour had not elapsed and here is what had taken place nearly at the same time at twenty different points in Paris.

In the Rue Sainte Croix de la Bretonnerie, some twenty young men, with beards and long hair, entered a smoking-room and came out again a moment afterwards, bearing a horizontal tri-colour flag covered with crape, and having at their head three men armed, one with a sword, another with a gun, the third with a pike.

In the Rue des Nonaindières, a well-dressed bourgeois, who was pursy, had a sonorous voice, a bald head, a high forehead, a black beard, and one of those rough moustaches which cannot be smoothed down, offered cartridges publicly to the passers-by.

In the Rue Saint Pierre Montmartre, some men with bare arms paraded a black flag on which these words could be read in white letters: *Republic or death.*

A manufactory of arms was rifled, on the Boulevard Saint Martin, and three armourer's shops, the first in the Rue Beaubourg, the second in the Rue Michel le Comte, the third in the Rue du Temple. In a few minutes the thousand hands of the multitude seized and carried off two hundred and thirty muskets nearly all double-barrelled, sixty-four swords, eighty-three pistols. To arm more people, one took the gun, another the bayonet.

The corpse of a mason killed by a musket shot was lying in the Rue de la Perle.

And then, right bank, left bank, on the quais, on the boulevards, in the Latin Quarter, in the region of the markets, breathless men, working-men, students, sectionaries, read proclamations, cried: "To arms!" broke the street lamps, unharnessed waggons, tore up the pavements, broke in the doors of the houses, uprooted the trees, ransacked the cellars, rolled hogsheads, heaped up paving stones, pebbles, pieces of furniture, boards, made barricades.

In the Quartier St. Jacques, the students came out of their hotels in swarms, and went up the Rue Saint Hyacinthe to the café Du Progrès or down to the café Des Sept Billards, on the Rue des Mathurins. There, before the doors, some young men standing upon the posts distributed arms. They pillaged the lumberyard on the Rue Transnonain to make barricades. At a single point, the inhabitants resisted, at the corner of the Rues Sainte Avoye and Simon le Franc where they destroyed the barricade themselves. At a single point, the insurgents gave way; they abandoned a barricade commenced in the Rue du Temple after having fired upon a detachment of the National Guard, and fled through the Rue de la Corderie. The detachment picked up in the barricade a red flag, a package of cartridges, and three hundred pistol balls. The National Guards tore up the flag and carried the shreds at the point of their bayonets.

Meanwhile the drums beat the long roll, the National Guards dressed and armed themselves in haste, the legions left the mairies, the regiments left their barracks.

In front of the Cour Batave, a detachment of National Guards found a red flag bearing this inscription: *Republican revolution, No. 127.* Was it a revolution, in fact?

The insurrection had made the centre of Paris a sort of inextricable, tortuous, colossal citadel.

In some regiments, the soldiers were doubtful, which added to the frightful obscurity of the crisis. They remembered the popular ovation which in July, 1830, had greeted the neutrality of the 53rd of the line. Enormous patrols, composed of battalions of the line surrounded by entire companies of the National Guard, and preceded by a commissary of police with his badge, went out reconnoitring the insurgent streets. On their side, the insurgents placed pickets at the corners of the streets and boldly sent patrols outside of the barricades. They kept watch on both sides. The government, with an army in its hand, hesitated; night was coming on, and the tocsin of Saint Merry began to be heard.

Solitude reigned at the Tuileries. Louis Philippe was full of serenity.

Evening came, the theatres did not open; the patrols made their round spitefully; passers were searched; the suspicious were arrested. At nine o'clock there were more than eight hundred persons under arrest; the prefecture of police was crowded, the Conciergerie was crowded, La Force was crowded. At the Conciergerie, in particular, the long vault which is called the Rue de Paris was strewn with bundles of straw, on which lay a throng of prisoners.

People barricaded themselves in their houses; wives and mothers were terrified; you heard only this: *Oh! my God! he has not come back!* People listened, on their door-sills, to the rumours, the cries, the tumults, the dull and indistinct sounds, things of which they said: *That is the cavalry*, or: *Those are the ammunition waggons galloping down*, the trumpets, the drums, the musketry, and above all, that mournful tocsin of Saint Merry. They expected the first cannon-shot. Men rose up at the corners of the streets and disappeared, crying: "Go home!" And they hastened to bolt their doors. They said: "How will it end?"

At the moment the insurrection, springing up at the shock of the people with the troops in front of the Arsenal, determined a backward movement in the multitude which was following the hearse, there was a frightful reflux. The mass wavered, the ranks broke, all ran, darted, slipped away, some with cries of attack, others with the pallor of flight. The great river which covered the boulevards divided in a twinkling, overflowed on the right and on the left, and poured in torrents into two hundred streets at once with the rushing of an opened mill-sluice.

At this moment a ragged child who was coming down the Rue Ménilmontant, holding in his hand a branch of laburnum in bloom, which he had just gathered on the heights of Belleville, caught sight, before a secondhand dealer's shop, of an old horse pistol. He threw his flowering branch upon the pavement, and cried:

"Mother What's-your-name, I'll borrow your machine."

And he ran off with the pistol.

It was little Gavroche going to war.

On the boulevard he perceived that the pistol had no hammer.

Whose was this refrain which served him to time his march, and all the other songs which, on occasion, he was fond of singing? we do not know. Who knows? his own perhaps. Gavroche besides kept up with all the popular airs in circulation, and mingled with them his own warbling. A sprite and a devil, he made a medley of the voices of nature and the voices of Paris. He combined the repertory of the birds with the repertory of the workshops. He knew some painter's boys, a tribe contiguous to his own. He had been, as it appears, three months a printer's apprentice. He had done an errand one day for Monsieur Baour-Lormian, one of the Forty. Gavroche was a *gamin* of letters.

On leaving the Rue des Ballets at early dawn, he had returned in haste to the elephant, artistically extracted the two *mômes*, shared with them such breakfast as he could invent, then went away, confiding them to that good mother, the street, who had almost brought him up himself. Gavroche had not seen them since.

Meanwhile he had reached, pistol in hand, the Rue du Pont aux Choux. He noticed that there was now, in that street, but one shop open, and, a matter worthy of reflection, a pastry-cook's shop. This was a providential opportunity to eat one more apple-puff before entering the unknown. Gavroche stopped, fumbled in his pockets, found nothing in them, not a sou. It is hard to lack the final cake.

Gavroche continued on his way.

Two minutes later, he was in the Rue Saint Louis. While passing through the Rue du Parc Royal he felt the need of some compensation for the impossible apple-puff, and he gave himself the immense pleasure of tearing down the theatre posters in broad day.

A little further along, seeing a group of well-to-do persons pass by, who appeared to him to be men of property, he shrugged his shoulders, and spit out at random this mouthful of philosophic bile:

"These rich men, how fat they are! they stuff themselves. They wallow in good dinners. Ask them what they do with their money. They don't know anything about it. They eat it, they do! How much of it the belly carries away."

The brandishing a pistol without a hammer, holding it in one's hand in the open street, is such a public function that Gavroche felt his spirits rise higher with every step. He cried, between the snatches of the Marseillaise which he was singing:

"It's all going well. I suffer a good deal in my left paw, I am broken with my rheumatism, but I am content, citizens. I come from the boulevard, my friends, it is getting hot, it is boiling over a little, it is simmering. It is time to skim the pot. Forward, men! let their impure blood water the furrows! I give my days for my country. I shall never see my concubine again, n-e-ver, over, yes. Never! but it's all the same, let us be joyful! let us fight, egad! I have had enough of despotism."

At that moment, the horse of a lancer of the National Guard, who was passing, having fallen down, Gavroche laid his pistol on the pavement, and raised up the man, then he helped to raise the horse. After which he picked up his pistol, and resumed his way.

The gossips of the Rue de Thorigny were busy only with their own affairs. They were three portresses and a rag-picker with her basket and hook.

Gavroche, who had stopped behind, was listening.

"Old women," said he, "what business have you now talking politics?"
A volley assailed him, composed of a quadruple hoot.

"There is another scoundrel!"

"What has he got in his stump? A pistol."

"I want to know, that beggar of a *môme!*"

"They are never quiet if they are not upsetting the government."

Gavroche, in disdain, made no other reply than merely to lift the end of his nose with his thumb while he opened his hand to its full extent.

The rag-picker cried:

"Spiteful go-bare-paws!"

She who answered to the name of Ma'am Patagon clapped her hands in horror.

"There is going to be troubles, that's sure. That rascal over there with a beard, I used to see him go by every morning with a young thing in a pink cap under his arm; to-day I see him go by, he was giving his arm to a musket. What would you have the government do with the scapegraces who do nothing but invent ways to disturb people, when we are beginning to be a little quiet, after all the troubles we have had, good Lord God, that poor queen that I see go by in the cart! And all this is going to make snuff dearer still. It is infamous! and surely I will go to see you guillotined, you scoundrel."

"You sniffle, my ancient," said Gavroche. "You do wrong to insult the Revolutionists, Mother Heap-in-the-corner. This pistol is in your interest. It is so that you may have more things good to eat in your basket."

The worthy barber, who drove away the two little boys to whom Gavroche opened the intestines of the elephant, was at this moment in his shop, busy shaving an old legionary soldier who had served under the empire. They were chatting. The barber had naturally spoken to the veteran of General Lamarque, and from Lamarque they had come to the emperor. Hence a conversation between a barber and a soldier, which Prudhomme, if he had been present, would have enriched with arabesques, and which he would have entitled: *Dialogue of the razor and the sabre.*

"Monsieur," said the wig-maker, "how did the emperor mount on horseback?"

"Badly. He didn't know how to fall. So he never fell."

"Did he have fine horses? he must have had fine horses!"

"The day he gave me the cross, I noticed his animal. She was a running mare, perfectly white. Her ears were very wide apart, saddle deep, head fine, marked with a black star, neck very long, knees strongly jointed, ribs protruding, shoulders sloping, hind quarters powerful. A little more than fifteen hands high."

"A pretty horse," said the barber.

"It was the animal of his majesty."

The barber felt that after this word a little silence was proper, he conformed to it, then resumed:

"The emperor was never wounded but once, was he, monsieur?"

The old soldier answered with the calm and sovereign tone of a man who was there:

"In the heel. At Ratisbon. I never saw him so well dressed as he was that day. He was as neat as a penny."

"And you, Monsieur Veteran, you must have been wounded often?"

"I?" said the soldier, "ah! no great thing. I got two sabre slashes in my neck at Marengo, a ball in my right arm at Austerlitz, another in my left hip at Jena, at Friedland a bayonet thrust—there,—at Moscow seven or eight lance thrusts, no matter where, at Lutzen a shell burst which crushed my finger—Ah! and then at Waterloo a bullet in my leg. That is all."

"How beautiful it is," exclaimed the barber, "to die on the field of battle! Upon my word, rather than die in my bed, of sickness, slowly, a little every day, with drugs, plasters, syringes, and medicine, I would prefer a cannon ball in my belly."

"You are not fastidious," said the soldier.

He had hardly finished when a frightful crash shook the shop. A pane of the window had been suddenly shattered.

The barber became pallid.

"O God!" cried he, "there is one!"

"What?"

"A cannon ball."

"Here it is," said the soldier.

And he picked up something which was rolling on the floor. It was a stone.

The barber ran to the broken window and saw Gavroche, who was running with all his might towards the Saint Jean market. On passing the barber's shop, Gavroche, who had the two *mômes* on his mind, could not resist the desire to bid him good day, and had sent a stone through his sash.

"See!" screamed the barber, who from white had become blue, "he makes mischief for the sake of mischief. What has anybody done to that *gamin?*"

Meanwhile Gavroche at the Saint Jean market had just effected his junction with a band led by Enjolras, Courfeyrac, Combeferre, and Feuilly. They were almost armed. Bahorel and Jean Prouvaire had joined them and enlarged the group. Enjolras had a double-barrelled fowling piece, Combeferre a National Guard's musket bearing the number of the legion, Jean Prouvaire an old cavalry musketoon, Bahorel a carbine; Courfeyrac was, brandishing an unsheathed sword-cane. Feuilly, a drawn sabre in his hand, marched in the van, crying: "Poland for ever!"

They came from the Quai Morland cravatless, hatless, breathless, soaked by the rain, lightning in their eyes. Gavroche approached them calmly:

"Where are we going?"

"Come on," said Courfeyrac.

Behind Feuilly marched, or rather bounded, Bahorel. His crimson waist-coat overcame a passer-by, who cried out in desperation:

"There are the reds!"

"The reds, the reds!" replied Bahorel. "A comical fear, bourgeois. As for

me, I don't tremble before a red poppy, the little red hood inspires me with
no dismay. Bourgeois, believe me, leave the fear of red to horned cattle."

A tumultuous cortège accompanied them, students, artists, workingmen,
rivermen, armed with clubs and bayonets; a few, like Combeferre, with pistols thrust into their waistbands. An old man, who appeared very old, was
marching with this band. He was not armed, and he was hurrying, that he
should not be left behind, although he had a thoughtful expression. Gavroche
perceived him:

"Whossat?" said he to Courfeyrac.

"That is an old man."

It was M. Mabeuf.

Enjolras and his friends were on the Boulevard Bourdon, near the ware-
houses, at the moment the dragoons charged. Enjolras, Courfeyrac, and
Combeferre were among those who took to the Rue Bassomipierre, crying:
"To the barricades!" In the Rue Lesdiguières they met an old man trudging
along. What attracted their attention was, that this goodman was walking
zigzag, as if he were drunk. Moreover, he had his hat in his hand, although
it had been raining all the morning, and was raining hard at that very
moment.

Courfeyrac recognised Father Mabeuf. He knew him from having seen
him many times accompanying Marius. Knowing the peaceful and more
than timid habits of the old church-warden-book-worm, and astounded at
seeing him in the midst of this tumult, within two steps of the cavalry
charges, almost in the midst of a fusillade, bareheaded in the rain, and walking among the bullets, he went up to him.

"Monsieur Mabeuf, go home."

"What for?"

"There is going to be a row."

"Very well."

"Sabre strokes, musket shots, Monsieur Mabeuf."

"Very well."

"Cannon shots."

"Very well. Where are you going, you boys?"

"We are going to pitch the government over."

"Very well."

And he followed them. From that moment he had not uttered a word.
His step had suddenly become firm; some workingmen had offered him an
arm, he refused with a shake of the head. He advanced almost to the front
rank of the column, having at once the motion of a man who is walking,
and the countenance of a man who is asleep.

"What a desperate goodman!" murmured the students. The rumour ran
through the assemblage that he was—an ancient Conventionist—an old regicide. The company had turned into the Rue de la Verrerie.

The band increased at every moment. Towards the Rue des Billettes a
man of tall stature, who was turning grey, whose rough and bold mien
Courfeyrac, Enjolras, and Combeferre noticed, but whom none of them

knew, joined them. Gavroche, busy singing, whistling, humming, going forward and rapping on the shutters of the shops with the butt of his hammerless pistol, paid no attention to this man.

It happened that, in the Rue de la Verrerie, they passed by Courfeyrac's door.

"That is lucky," said Courfeyrac, "I have forgotten my purse, and I have lost my hat." He left the company and went up to his room, four stairs at a time. He took an old hat and his purse. He took also a large square box, of the size of a big valise, which was hidden among his dirty clothes. As he was running down again, the portress hailed him:

"There is somebody who wishes to speak to you."

"Who is it?"

"I don't know."

"Where is he?"

"In my lodge."

"The devil!" said Courfeyrac.

"But he has been waiting more than an hour for you to come home!" replied the portress.

At the same time, a sort of young working-man, thin, pale, small, freckled, dressed in a torn blouse and patched pantaloons of ribbed velvet, and who had rather the appearance of a girl in boy's clothes than of a man, came out of the lodge and said to Courfeyrac in a voice which, to be sure, was not the least in the world like a woman's voice:

"Monsieur Marius, if you please?"

"He is not in."

"Will he be in this evening?"

"I don't know anything about it."

And Courfeyrac added: "As for myself, I shall not be in."

The young man looked fixedly at him, and asked him:

"Why so?"

"Because."

"Where are you going then?"

"What is that to you?"

"Do you want me to carry your box?"

"I am going to the barricades."

"Do you want me to go with you?"

"If you like," answered Courfeyrac. "The road is free; the streets belong to everybody."

And he ran off to rejoin his friends. When he had rejoined them, he gave the box to one of them to carry. It was not until a quarter of an hour afterwards that he perceived that the young man had in fact followed them.

A mob does not go precisely where it wishes. We have explained that a gust of wind carries it along. They went beyond Saint Merry and found themselves, without really knowing how, in the Rue Saint Denis.

XXV. THE BARRICADE

THE PARISIANS who, to-day, upon entering the Rue Rambuteau from the side of the markets, notice on their right, opposite the Rue Mondétour, a basket-maker's shop, with a basket for a sign, in the shape of the Emperor Napoleon the Great, do not suspect the terrible scenes which this very place saw thirty years ago.

Here were the Rue de la Chanvrerie, which the old signs spelled Chanverrerie, and the celebrated wine-shop called Corinth.

The room on the first floor, in which was "the restaurant," was a long and wide room, encumbered with stools, crickets, chairs, benches, and tables, and a rickety old billiard-table. It was reached by the spiral staircase which terminated at the corner of the room in a square hole like the hatchway of a ship.

Laigle de Meaux lived more with Joly than elsewhere. He had a lodging as the bird has a branch. The two friends lived together, ate together, slept together. Everything was in common with them, even Musichetta a little. On the morning of the 5th of June, they went to breakfast at Corinth. Joly, whose head was stopped up, had a bad cold, which Laigle was beginning to share. Laigle's coat was threadbare, but Joly was well dressed.

It was about nine o'clock in the morning when they opened the door of Corinth.

They went up to the first floor.

"Oysters, cheese, and ham," said Laigle.

And they sat down at a table.

The wine-shop was empty; they two only were there.

As they were at their first oysters, a head appeared at the hatchway of the stairs, and a voice said:

"I was passing. I smelt in the street a delicious odour of Brie cheese. I have come in."

Grantaire took a stool and sat down at the table.

The others had begun by eating. Grantaire began by drinking. A half bottle was quickly swallowed.

"Grantaire," asked Laigle, "do you come from the boulevard?"

"No."

"We just saw the head of the procession pass, Joly and I."

Grantaire was entering on his second bottle when a new actor emerged from the square hole of the stairway. It was a boy of less than ten years, ragged, very small, yellow, a mug of a face, a keen eye, monstrous long hair, wet to the skin, a complacent look.

The child, choosing without hesitation among the three, although he evidently knew none of them, addressed himself to Laigle de Meaux.

"Are you Monsieur Bossuet?" asked he.

"That is my nickname," answered Laigle. "What do you want of me?"

"This is it. A big light-complexioned fellow on the boulevard said to me: You will find Monsieur Bossuet, and you will tell him from me: A—B—C. It is a joke that somebody is playing on you, isn't it? He gave me ten sous."

"Joly, lend me ten sous," said Laigle, and turning towards Grantaire: "Grantaire, lend me ten sous."

This made twenty sous which Laigle gave the child.

"Thank you, monsieur," said the little fellow.

"What is your name?" asked Laigle.

"Navet, Gavroche's friend."

"Stop with us," said Laigle.

"Breakfast with us," said Grantaire.

The child answered:

"I can't, I am with the procession."

And giving his foot a long scrape behind him, which is the most respectful of all possible bows, he went away.

"A—B—C, that is to say: Lamarque's funeral."

"The big light-complexioned man," observed Grantaire, "is Enjolras, who sent to notify you."

"Shall we go?" said Bossuet.

"I stay here," said Grantaire. "I prefer a breakfast to a hearse."

This resolution taken, Bossuet, Joly, and Grantaire did not stir from the wine-shop. About two o'clock in the afternoon, the table on which they were leaning was covered with empty bottles. Two candles were burning, one in a perfectly green copper candlestick, the other in the neck of a cracked decanter. Grantaire had drawn Joly and Bossuet towards wine; Bossuet and Joly had led Grantaire towards joy.

Bossuet, very drunk, had preserved his calmness.

He sat in the open window, wetting his back with the falling rain, and gazed at his two friends.

Suddenly he heard a tumult behind him, hurried steps, cries *to arms!* He turned, and saw in the Rue Saint Denis, at the end of the Rue de la Chanvrerie, Enjolras passing, carbine in hand, and Gavroche with his pistol, Feuilly with his sabre, Courfeyrac with his sword, Jean Prouvaire with his musketoon, Combeferre with his musket, Bahorel with his musket, and all the armed and stormy gathering which followed them.

The Rue de la Chanvrerie was hardly as long as the range of a carbine. Bossuet improvised a speaking trumpet with his two hands, and shouted:

"Courfeyrac! Courfeyrac! ahoy!"

Courfeyrac heard the call, perceived Bossuet, and came a few steps into the Rue de la Chanvrerie, crying a "what do you want?" which was met on the way by a "where are you going?"

"To make a barricade," answered Courfeyrac.

"Well, here! this is a good place! make it here!"

"That is true, Eagle," said Courfeyrac.

And at a sign from Courfeyrac, the band rushed into the Rue de la Chanvrerie.

The place was indeed admirably chosen, the entrance of the street wide, the further end contracted and like a cul-de-sac, Corinth throttling it, Rue Mondétour easy to bar at the right and left, no attack possible except from the Rue Saint Denis, that is from the front, and without cover.

At the irruption of the mob, dismay seized the whole street, not a passer but had gone into eclipse. In a flash, at the end, on the right, on the left, shops, stalls, alley gates, windows, blinds, dormer-windows, shutters of every size, were closed from the ground to the roofs. One frightened old woman fixed a mattress before her window on two clothes poles, as a shield against the musketry.

Meanwhile, in a few minutes, twenty iron bars had been wrested from the grated front of the wine-shop, twenty yards of pavement had been torn up; Gavroche and Bahorel had seized on its passage and tipped over the dray of a lime merchant named Anceau; this dray contained three barrels full of lime, which they had placed under the piles of paving stones. Enjolras had opened the trapdoor of the cellar and all the widow Hucheloup's empty casks had gone to flank the lime barrels; Feuilly, with his fingers accustomed to colour the delicate folds of fans, had buttressed the barrels and the dray with two massive heaps of stones obtained nobody knows where. Some shoring-timbers had been pulled down from the front of a neighbouring house and laid upon the casks. When Bossuet and Courfeyrac turned round, half the street was already barred by a rampart higher than a man. There is nothing like the popular hand to build whatever can be built by demolishing.

An omnibus with two white horses passed at the end of the street. Bossuet sprang over the pavement, ran, stopped the driver, made the passengers get down, gave his hand "to the ladies," dismissed the conductor, and came back with the vehicle, leading the horses by the bridle. A moment later the horses were unhitched and going off at will through the Rue Mondétour, and the omnibus, lying on its side, completed the barring of the street.

Grantaire was attaining the highest regions of dithyramb. "Comrades, we will overturn the government. Messieurs, my father always detested me, because I could not understand mathematics. I only understand love and liberty. I am Grantaire, a good boy. Never having had any money, I have never got used to it, and by that means I have never felt the need of it; but if I had been rich, there would have been no more poor! you should have seen. Oh! if the good hearts had the fat purses, how much better everything would go! I imagine Jesus Christ with Rothschild's fortune! How much good he would have done!"

"Be still, wine-cask!" said Courfeyrac.

Grantaire answered:

"I am Capitoul and Master of Floral Games!"

Enjolras, who was standing on the crest of the barricade, musket in hand, raised his fine austere face. Enjolras, we know, had something of the Spartan and of the Puritan. He would have died at Thermopylæ with Leonidas, and would have burned Drogheda with Cromwell.

"Grantaire," cried he, "go sleep yourself sober away from here. This is the place for intoxication and not for drunkenness. Do not dishonour the barricade!"

This angry speech produced upon Grantaire a singular effect. One would have said that he had received a glass of cold water in his face. He appeared suddenly sobered. He sat down, leaned upon a table near the window, looked at Enjolras with an inexpressible gentleness, and said to him:

"Let me sleep here."

"Go sleep elsewhere," cried Enjolras.

But Grantaire, keeping his tender and troubled eyes fixed upon him, answered:

"Let me sleep here—until I die here."

Enjolras regarded him with a disdainful eye:

"Grantaire, you are incapable of belief, of thought, of will, of life, and of death."

He stammered out a few more unintelligible words, then his head fell heavily upon the table, and, a common effect of the second stage of inebriety into which Enjolras had rudely and suddenly pushed him, a moment later he was asleep.

Enjolras, Combeferre, and Courfeyrac directed everything. Two barricades were now building at the same time, both resting on the house of Corinth and making a right angle; the larger one closed the Rue de la Chanvrerie, the other closed the Rue Mondétour in the direction of the Rue du Cygne. This last barricade, very narrow, was constructed only of casks and paving stones. There were about fifty labourers there, some thirty armed with muskets.

Nothing could be more fantastic and more motley than this band. One had a short-jacket, a cavalry sabre, and two horse-pistols; another was in shirt sleeves, with a round hat, and a powder-horn hung at his side; a third had a breast-plate of nine sheets of brown paper, and was armed with a saddler's awl. There was one of them who cried: *Let us exterminate to the last man, and die on the point of our bayonets!* This man had no bayonet.

Another displayed over his coat a cross-belt and cartridge-box of the National Guard, with the box cover adorned with this inscription in red cloth: *Public Order.* Many muskets bearing the numbers of their legions, few hats, no cravats, many bare arms, some pikes; add to this all ages, all faces, small pale young men, bronzed wharfmen. All were hurrying, and, while helping each other, they talked about the possible chances—that they would have help by three o'clock in the morning—that they were sure of one regiment—that Paris would rise.

One would have said they were brothers; they did not know each other's names. Great perils have this beauty, that they bring to light the fraternity of strangers.

A fire had been kindled in the kitchen, and they were melting pitchers, dishes, forks, all the pewter ware of the wine-shop into bullets. They drank through it all. Percussion-caps and buck-shot rolled pell-mell upon the tables with glasses of wine.

The man of tall stature whom Courfeyrac, Combeferre, and Enjolras had noticed, at the moment he joined the company at the corner of the Rue des Billettes, was working on the little barricade, and making himself useful there. Gavroche worked on the large one. As for the young man who had waited for Courfeyrac at his house, and had asked him for Monsieur Marius, he had disappeared very nearly at the moment the omnibus was overturned.

Gavroche, completely carried away and radiant, had charged himself with making all ready. He went, came, mounted, descended, remounted, bustled, sparkled. He seemed to be there for the encouragement of all. Had he a spur? yes, certainly, his misery. They saw him incessantly, they heard him constantly. He filled the air, being everywhere at once. He vexed the loungers, he excited the idle, he reanimated the weary, he provoked the thoughtful, kept some in cheerfulness, others in breath, others in anger, all in motion, piqued a student, was biting to a working-man; took position, stopped, started on, flitted above the tumult and the effort, leaped from these to those, murmured, hummed, and stirred up the whole train; the fly on the revolutionary coach.

Perpetual motion was in his little arms, and perpetual clamour in his little lungs.

"More paving stones? more barrels? more machines? where are there any? A basket of plaster, to stop that hole. It is too small, your barricade. It must go higher. Pile on everything, brace it with everything. Break up the house. Hold on, there is a glass-door."

This made the labourers exclaim:

"A glass-door? what do you want us to do with a glass-door?"

"Then you have never hooked apples over a wall with broken bottles on it? A glass-door, it will cut the corns of the National Guards, when they try to climb over the barricade. Golly! glass is the devil. Ah, now, you haven't an unbridled imagination, my comrades."

Still, he was furious at his pistol without a hammer. He went from one to another, demanding: "A musket? I want a musket! Why don't you give me a musket?"

"A musket for you?" said Combeferre.

"Well?" replied Gavroche, "why not? I had one in 1830, in the dispute with Charles X."

Enjolras shrugged his shoulders.

"When there are enough for the men, we will give them to the children."

Gavroche turned fiercely, and answered him:

"If you are killed before me, I will take yours."

"*Gamin!*" said Enjolras.

"Smooth-face!" said Gavroche.

A stray dandy who was lounging at the end of the street made a diversion.

Gavroche cried to him:

"Come with us, young man? Well, this poor old country, you won't do anything for her then?"

The dandy fled.

The journals of the time which said that the barricade of the Rue de la Chanvrerie, that *almost inexpugnable construction,* as they call it, attained the level of a second story, were mistaken. The fact is, that it did not exceed an average height of six or seven feet. It was built in such a manner that the combatants could, at will, either disappear behind the wall, or look over it, and even scale the crest of it by means of a quadruple range of paving-stones superposed and arranged like steps on the inner side. The front of the barricade on the outside, composed of piles of paving-stones and of barrels bound together by timbers and boards which were interlocked in the wheels of the Anceau cart and the overturned omnibus, had a bristling and inextricable aspect.

An opening sufficient for a man to pass through had been left between the wall of the houses and the extremity of the barricade furthest from the wine-shop, so that a sortie was possible. The pole of the omnibus was turned directly up and held with ropes, and a red flag, fixed to this pole, floated over the barricade.

The two barricades finished, the flag run up, a table was dragged out of the wine-shop; and Courfeyrac mounted upon the table. Enjolras brought the square box and Courfeyrac opened it. This box was filled with cartridges.

Courfeyrac distributed them with a smile.

Each one received thirty cartridges. Many had powder and set about making others with the balls which they were moulding. As for the keg of powder, it was on a table by itself near the door.

The long roll which was running through all Paris was not discontinued, but it had got to be only a monotonous sound to which they paid no more attention, with melancholy undulations.

They loaded their muskets and their carbines all together, without precipitation, with a solemn gravity. Enjolras placed three sentinels outside the barricades.

Then, the barricades built, the posts assigned, the muskets loaded, the videttes placed, alone in these fearful streets in which there were now no passers, isolated, armed, determined, tranquil, they waited.

In these hours of waiting what did they do? This we must tell—for this is history.

While the men were making cartridges and the women lint, while a large frying-pan, full of melted pewter and lead, destined for the bullet-mould, was smoking over a burning furnace, while the videttes were watching the barricades with arms in their hands, while Enjolras, whom nothing could distract, was watching the videttes, Combeferre, Courfeyrac, Jean Prouvaire, Feuilly, Bossuet, Joly, Bahorel, a few others besides, sought each other as in the most peaceful student days, and in a corner of this wine-shop, their carbines primed and loaded resting on the backs of their chairs, these gallant young men, so near their last hour, began to sing love-rhymes.

Meanwhile they had lighted a lamp at the little barricade, and at the large one, one of those wax torches which are seen on Mardi Gras in front of the waggons loaded with masks, which are going to the Comtille. These torches, we have seen, came from the Faubourg Saint Antoine.

The torch had been placed in a kind of cage, closed in with paving-stones on three sides, to shelter it from the wind, and disposed in such a manner that all the light fell upon the flag. The street and the barricade remained plunged in obscurity, and nothing could be seen but the red flag, fearfully lighted up, as if by an enormous dark lantern.

It was now quite night. There were confused sounds, and at intervals volleys of musketry; but rare, ill-sustained, and distant. This respite, which was thus prolonged, was a sign that the government was taking its time, and massing its forces. These fifty men were awaiting sixty thousand.

Enjolras felt himself possessed by that impatience which seizes strong souls on the threshold of formidable events. He went to find Gavroche who had set himself to making cartridges in the basement room by the doubtful light of two candles placed upon the counter through precaution on account of the powder scattered over the tables. These two candles threw no rays outside. The insurgents moreover had taken care not to have any lights in the upper stories.

Gavroche at this moment was very much engaged, not exactly with his cartridges.

The man from the Rue des Billettes had just entered the basement room and had taken a seat at the table which was least lighted. An infantry musket of large model had fallen to his lot, and he held it between his knees. Gavroche hitherto, distracted by a hundred "amusing" things, had not even seen this man.

When he came in, Gavroche mechanically followed him with his eyes, admiring his musket, then, suddenly, when the man had sat down, the *gamin* arose. Had any one watched this man up to this time, he would have seen him observe everything in the barricade and in the band of insurgents with a singular attention; but since he had come into the room, he had fallen into a kind of meditation and appeared to see nothing more of what was going on. The *gamin* approached this thoughtful personage, and began to turn about him on the points of his toes as one walks when near somebody whom he fears to awake.

Enjolras accosted him.

"You are small," said Enjolras, "nobody will see you. Go out of the barricades, glide along by the houses, look about the streets a little, and come and tell me what is going on."

Gavroche straightened himself up.

"Little folks are good for something then! that is very lucky! I will go! meantime, trust the little folks, distrust the big—" And Gavroche, raising his head and lowering his voice, added, pointing to the man of the Rue des Billettes:

"You see that big fellow there?"

"Well?"

"He is a spy."

"You are sure?"

"It isn't a fortnight since he pulled me by the ear off the cornice of the Pont Royal where I was taking the air."

Enjolras hastily left the *gamin*, and murmured a few words very low to a working-man from the wine docks who was there. The working-man went out of the room and returned almost immediately, accompanied by three others. The four men, four broad-shouldered porters, placed themselves, without doing anything which could attract his attention, behind the table on which the man of the Rue des Billettes was leaning. They were evidently ready to throw themselves upon him.

Then Enjolras approached the man and asked him:

"Who are you?"

At this abrupt question, the man gave a start. He looked straight to the bottom of Enjolras' frank eye and appeared to catch his thought. He smiled with a smile which, of all things in the world, was the most disdainful, the most energetic, and the most resolute, and answered with a haughty gravity:

"I see how it is— Well, yes!"

"You are a spy?"

"I am an officer of the government."

"Your name is?"

"Javert."

Enjolras made a sign to the four men. In a twinkling, before Javert had time to turn around, he was collared, thrown down, bound, searched.

They found upon him a little round card framed between two glasses, and bearing on one side the arms of France, engraved with this legend: *Surveillance et vigilance,* and on the other side this endorsement: JAVERT, inspector of police, aged fifty-two, and the signature of the prefect of police of the time, M. Gisquet.

He had besides his watch and his purse, which contained a few gold pieces. They left him his purse and his watch. Under the watch, at the bottom of his fob, they felt and seized a paper in an envelope, which Enjolras opened, and on which he read these six lines, written by the prefect's own hand.

"As soon as his political mission is fulfilled, Inspector Javert will ascertain, by a special examination, whether it be true that malefactors have resorts on the slope of the right bank of the Seine, near the bridge of Jena."

The search finished, they raised Javert, tied his arms behind his back, fastened him in the middle of the basement-room to that celebrated post which had formerly given its name to the wine-shop.

Gavroche, who had witnessed the whole scene and approved the whole by silent nods of his head, approached Javert and said to him:

"The mouse has caught the cat."

All this was executed so rapidly that it was finished as soon as it was perceived about the wine-shop. Javert had not uttered a cry. Seeing Javert tied to the post, Courfeyrac, Bossuet, Joly, Combeferre, and the men scattered about the two barricades, ran in.

Javert, backed up against the post, and so surrounded with ropes that he could make no movement, held up his head with the intrepid serenity of the man who has never lied.

"It is a spy," said Enjolras.

And turning towards Javert:

"You will be shot ten minutes before the barricade is taken."

Javert replied in his most imperious tone:

"Why not immediately?"

"We are economising powder."

"Then do it with a knife."

"Spy," said the handsome Enjolras, "we are judges, not assassins."

Then he called Gavroche.

"You! go about your business! Do what I told you."

"I am going," cried Gavroche.

And stopping just as he was starting:

"By the way, you will give me his musket!"

Mobs are like snowballs, and gather a heap of tumultuous men as they roll. These men do not ask one another whence they come. Among the passers who had joined themselves to the company led by Enjolras, Combeferre, and Courfeyrac, there was a person wearing a porter's waistcoat worn out at the shoulders, who gesticulated and vociferated and had the appearance of a sort of savage drunkard. This man, who was named or nicknamed Le Cabuc, and who was moreover entirely unknown to those who attempted to recognise him, very drunk, or feigning to be, was seated with a few others at a table which they had brought outside of the wine-shop. This Cabuc, while inciting those to drink who were with him, seemed to gaze with an air of reflection upon the large house at the back of the barricade, the five stories of which overlooked the whole street and faced towards the Rue Saint Denis. Suddenly he exclaimed:

"Comrades, do you know? it is from that house that we must fire. If we are at the windows, devil a one can come into the street."

"Yes, but the house is shut up," said one of the drinkers.

"Knock!"

"They won't open."

"Stave the door in!"

Le Cabuc runs to the door, which had a very massive knocker, and raps. The door does not open. He raps a second time. Nobody answers. A third rap. The same silence.

"Is there anybody here?" cries Le Cabuc.

Nothing stirs.

Then he seizes a musket and begins to beat the door with the butt. It was an old alley door, arched, low, narrow, solid, entirely of oak, lined on the inside with sheet-iron and with iron braces, a genuine postern of a bastille. The blows made the house tremble, but did not shake the door.

Nevertheless it is probable that the inhabitants were alarmed, for they finally saw a little square window on the third story light up and open, and there appeared at this window a candle, and the pious and frightened face of a grey-haired goodman who was the porter.

The man who was knocking, stopped.

"Messieurs," asked the porter, "what do you wish?"

"Open!" said Le Cabuc.

"Messieurs, that cannot be."

"Open, I tell you!"

"Impossible, messieurs!"

Le Cabuc took his musket and aimed at the porter's head; but as he was below, and it was very dark, the porter did not see him.

"Yes, or no, will you open?"

"No, messieurs!"

"You say no?"

"I say no, my good—"

The porter did not finish. The musket went off; the ball entered under his chin and passed out at the back of the neck, passing through the jugular. The old man sank down without a sigh. The candle fell and was extinguished, and nothing could now be seen but an immovable head lying on the edge of the window, and a little whitish smoke floating towards the roof.

"That's it!" said Le Cabuc, letting the butt of his musket drop on the pavement.

Hardly had he uttered these words when he felt a hand pounce upon his shoulder with the weight of an eagle's talons, and heard a voice which said to him:

"On your knees."

The murderer turned and saw before him the white cold face of Enjolras. Enjolras had a pistol in his hand.

At the explosion, he had come up.

He had grasped with his left hand Le Cabuc's collar, blouse, shirt, and suspenders.

"On your knees," repeated he.

And with a majestic movement the slender young man of twenty bent the broad-shouldered and robust porter like a reed and made him kneel in the mud.

The whole barricade ran up, then all ranged in a circle at a distance, feeling that it was impossible to utter a word in presence of the act which they were about to witness.

Le Cabuc, vanquished, no longer attempted to defend himself. Enjolras let go of him and took out his watch.

"Collect your thoughts," said he. "Pray or think. You have one minute."

"Pardon!" murmured the murderer, then he bowed his head and mumbled some inarticulate oaths.

Enjolras did not take his eyes off his watch; he let the minute pass, then he put his watch back into his fob. This done, he took Le Cabuc, who was writhing against his knees and howling, by the hair, and placed the muzzle of his pistol at his ear. Many of those intrepid men, who had so tranquilly entered upon the most terrible of enterprises, turned away their heads.

They heard the explosion, the assassin fell face forward on the pavement, and Enjolras straightened up and cast about him his look determined and severe.

Then he pushed the body away with his foot, and said:

"Throw that outside."

Three men lifted the body and threw it over the small barricade into the little Rue Mondétour.

Enjolras raised his voice.

"Citizens," said Enjolras, "what that man did is horrible, and what I have done is terrible. He killed, that is why I killed him. I was forced to do it, for the insurrection must have its discipline. Assassination is a still greater crime here than elsewhere; we are under the eye of the revolution, we are the priests of the republic, we are the sacramental host of duty, and none must be able to calumniate our combat. I therefore judged and condemned that man to death. As for myself, compelled to do what I have done, but abhorring it, I have judged myself also, and you shall soon see to what I have sentenced myself."

"We will share your fate," cried Combeferre.

"So be it," added Enjolras. "A word more. In executing that man, I obeyed necessity; but necessity is a monster of the old world. Now the law of progress is, that monsters disappear before angels. Citizens, there shall be in the future neither darkness nor thunderbolts; neither ferocious ignorance nor blood for blood. In the future no man shall slay his fellow, the earth shall be radiant, the human race shall love. It will come, citizens, that day when all shall be concord, harmony, light, joy, and life; it will come, and it is that it may come that we are going to die."

Let us say that later, after the action, when the corpses were carried to the Morgue and searched, there was a police officer's card found on Le Cabuc. The author of this book had in his own hands, in 1848, the special report made on that subject to the prefect of police in 1832.

Let us add that, if we are to believe a police tradition, strange, but probably well founded, Le Cabuc was Claquesous. The fact is, that after the death of Le Cabuc, nothing more was heard of Claquesous. Claquesous left no trace on his disappearance, he would seem to have been amalgamated with the invisible. His life had been darkness, his end was night.

The whole insurgent group were still under the emotion of this tragic trial, so quickly instituted and so quickly terminated, when Courfeyrac again saw in the barricade the small young man who in the morning had called at his house for Marius.

This boy, who had a bold and reckless air, had come at night to rejoin the insurgents.

XXVI. GAVROCHE ATTACKS

THAT VOICE which through the twilight had called Marius to the barricade of the Rue de la Chanvrerie, sounded to him like the voice of destiny. Mad with grief, he had now but one desire: to make a quick end.

He began to walk rapidly. It happened that he was armed, having Javert's pistols with him.

The young man whom he thought he had seen was lost from his eyes in the streets.

Marius, who had left the Rue Plumet by the boulevard, crossed the Esplanade and the Bridge of the Invalides, the Champs Elysées, the Place Louis XV., and entered the Rue de Rivoli. The stores were open, the gas was burning under the arches, women were buying in the shops, people were taking ices at the Café Laiter, they were eating little cakes at the Pâtisserie Anglaise. However, a few post chaises were setting off at a gallop from the Hôtel des Princes and the Hôtel Meurice.

Marius entered through the Delorme arcade into the Rue Saint Honoré. The shops here were closed, the merchants were chatting before their half-open doors, people were moving about, the lamps were burning, above the first stories all the windows were lighted as usual. There was cavalry in the square of the Palais Royal.

Marius followed the Rue St. Honoré. As he receded from the Palais Royal, there were fewer lighted windows; the shops were entirely closed, nobody was chatting in the doors, the street grew gloomy, and at the same time the throng grew dense. For the passers now were a throng. Nobody was seen to speak in this throng, and still there came from it a deep and dull hum.

At the entrance of the Rue des Prouvaires, the throng no longer moved. It was a resisting, massive, solid, compact, almost impenetrable block of people, heaped together and talking in whispers. Black coats and round hats had almost disappeared. Frocks, blouses, caps, bristly and dirty faces. This multitude undulated confusedly in the misty night. Its whispering had the harsh sound of a roar. Although nobody was walking, a trampling was heard in the mud. The streets were not empty. Muskets could be distinguished in stacks, bayonets moving and troops bivouacking. The curious did not pass this bound. There circulation ceased. There the multitude ended and the army began.

Marius had been called, he must go. He found means to pass through the multitude, and to pass through the bivouac of the troops, he avoided the patrols, evaded the sentinels. He made a detour, reached the Rue de Béthisy, and made his way towards the markets.

By a circuitous route, he came to a little street which he judged to be the Rue de la Poterie; about the middle of this alley he ran against some obstacle.

He put out his hands. It was an overturned cart; his foot recognised puddles of water, mud-holes, paving-stones, scattered and heaped up. A barricade had been planned there and abandoned. He climbed over the stones and found himself on the other side of the obstruction. He walked very near the posts and guided himself by the walls of the houses. A little beyond the barricade, he seemed to catch a glimpse of something white in front of him. He approached, it took form. It was two white horses! the omnibus horses unharnessed by Bossuet in the morning, which had wandered at chance from street to street all day long, and had finally stopped there, with the exhausted patience of brutes, who no more comprehended the ways of man than man comprehends the ways of Providence.

Marius left the horses behind him. As he came to a street which struck him as being the Rue du Contrat Social, a shot from a musket coming nobody knows whence, passing at random through the obscurity, whistled close by him, and the ball pierced a copper shaving-dish suspended before a barber's shop. This shaving-dish with the bullet-hole could still be seen, in 1846, in the Rue du Contrat Social, at the corner of the pillars of the markets.

This musket-shot was life still. From that moment he met nothing more.

This whole route resembled a descent down dark stairs.

Marius none the less went forward.

At the markets, all was more calm, more obscure, and more motionless than in the neighbouring streets.

A red glare, however, cut out upon this dark background the high roofs of the houses which barred the Rue de la Chanvrerie on the side towards Saint Eustache. It was the reflection of the torch which was blazing in the barricade of Corinth. Marius directed his steps towards this glare. It led him to the Beet Market, and he dimly saw the dark mouth of the Rue des Prêcheurs. He entered it. The vidette of the insurgents who was on guard at the other end did not perceive him. He felt that he was very near what he had come to seek, and he walked upon tiptoe. He reached in this way the elbow of that short end of the Rue Mondétour, which was, as we remember, the only communication preserved by Enjolras with the outside.

A little beyond the black corner of the alley of the Rue de la Chanvrerie, which threw a broad shadow, in which he was himself buried, he perceived a light upon the pavement, a portion of the wine-shop, and behind, a lamp twinkling in a kind of shapeless wall, and men crouching down with muskets on their knees. All this was within twenty yards of him. It was the interior of the barricade.

The houses on the right of the alley hid from him the rest of the wine-shop, the great barricade, and the flag.

Marius had but one step more to take.

Then the unhappy young man sat down upon a stone, folded his arms, and thought of his father.

He thought of that heroic Colonel Pontmercy who had been so brave a soldier, who had defended the frontier of France under the republic, and reached the frontier of Asia under the emperor, who had seen Genoa,

Alessandria, Milan, Turin, Madrid, Vienna, Dresden, Berlin, Moscow, who had left upon every field of victory in Europe drops of that same blood which he, Marius, had in his veins, who had grown grey before his time in discipline and in command, who had lived with his sword-belt buckled in the barracks, in the camp, in the bivouac, in the ambulance, and who after twenty years had returned from the great wars with his cheek scarred, his face smiling, simple, tranquil, admirable, having done everything for France and nothing against her.

He said to himself that his day had come to him also, that his hour had at last struck, that after his father, he also was to be brave, intrepid, bold, to run amidst bullets, to bare his breast to the bayonets, to pour out his blood, to seek the enemy, to seek death, that he was to wage war in his turn and to enter upon the field of battle, and that that field of battle upon which he was about to enter, was the street, and that war which he was about to wage, was civil war!

He saw civil war yawning like an abyss before him, and that in it he was to fall.

He thought of that sword of his father which his grandfather had sold to a junk-shop, and which he himself had so painfully regretted. He said to himself that it was well that that chaste and valiant sword had escaped from him, and gone off in anger into the darkness; that if it had fled thus, it was because it was intelligent and because it foresaw the future; because it foreboded the war of the gutters, the war of the pavements, the firing from cellar windows, blows given and received from behind; because, coming from Marengo and Friedland, it would not go to the Rue de la Chanvrerie, because after what it had done with the father, it would not do this with the son!

But what could he do? Live without Cosette he could not. Since she had gone away, he must surely die. Had he not given her his word of honour that he should die? She had gone away knowing that; therefore it pleased her that Marius should die. And then it was clear that she no longer loved him, since she had gone away thus, without notifying him, without a word, without a letter, and she knew his address! What use in life and why live longer? And then, indeed! to have come so far, and to recoil! To abandon his friends who were expecting him! who perhaps had need of him! who were a handful against an army! To fail in all things at the same time, in his love, his friendship, his word! To give his poltroonery the pretext of patriotism! But this was impossible, and if his father's ghost were there in the shadow and saw him recoil, he would strike him with the flat of his sword and cry to him: "Advance, coward!"

A prey to the swaying of his thoughts, he bowed his head.

Suddenly he straightened up. A sort of splendid rectification was wrought in his spirit; to be near death makes us see the truth. The war of the street was suddenly transfigured before the eye of his mind.

Let us see, why should his father be indignant? are there not cases when insurrection rises to the dignity of duty? what would there be then belittling to the son of Colonel Pontmercy in the impending combat? It is no longer Montmirail or Champaubert; it is something else. It is no longer a question of a sacred territory, but of a holy idea. The country laments, so be it; but humanity applauds. Besides, is it true that the country mourns? France bleeds, but liberty smiles; and before the smile of liberty, France forgets her wound. And then, looking at the matter from a still higher stand, why do men talk of civil war?

Civil war? What does this mean? Is there any foreign war? Is not every war between men, war between brothers? War is modified only by its aim. There is neither foreign war, nor civil war; there is only unjust war and just war. Until the day when the great human concordat shall be concluded, war, that at least which is the struggle of the hurrying future against the lingering past, may be necessary.

War becomes shame, the sword becomes a dagger, only when it assassinates right, progress, reason, civilisation, truth. Then, civil war or foreign war, it is iniquitous; its name is crime. Outside of that holy thing, justice, by what right does one form of war despise another? by what right does the sword of Washington disown the pike of Camille Desmoulins? one is the defender, the other is the liberator. Despotism violates the moral frontier, as invasion violates the geographical frontier. To drive out the tyrant or to drive out the English is, in either case, to retake your territory. There comes an hour when protest no longer suffices; after philosophy there must be action; the strong hand finishes what the idea has planned. Down with the tyrant! But what? of whom do you speak? do you call Louis Philippe the tyrant? no; no more than Louis XVI. They are both what history is accustomed to call good kings; but principles cannot be parcelled out, and to wipe out the universal usurpation, it is necessary to fight; it is necessary, France always taking the initiative. When the master falls in France, he falls everywhere.

In short, to re-establish social truth, to give back to liberty her throne, to give back the people to the people, to give back sovereignty to man, to restore in their fulness reason and equity, to abolish the obstacle which royalty opposes to the immense universal concord, to replace the human race on a level with right, what cause more just, and, consequently, what war more grand? These wars construct peace. An enormous fortress of prejudices, of privileges, of superstitions, of lies, of exactions, of abuses, of violence, of iniquity, of darkness, is still standing upon the world with its towers of hatred. It must be thrown down. This monstrous pile must be made to fall. To conquer at Austerlitz is grand; to take the Bastille is immense.

This was Marius' state of mind.

Even while thinking thus, his gaze wandered into the interior of the barricade. The insurgents were chatting in undertone, without moving about; and that quasi-silence was felt which marks the last phase of delay. Above them, at a third story window, Marius distinguished a sort of spectator or witness who seemed to him singularly attentive. It was the porter killed by Le Cabuc. From below, by the reflection of the torch hidden among the paving-stones, this head was dimly perceptible. Nothing was more strange in that gloomy and uncertain light, than that livid, motionless, astonished face with its bristling hair, its staring eyes, and its gaping mouth, leaning over the street in an attitude of curiosity. One would have said that he who was dead was gazing at those who were about to die. A long trail of blood which had flowed from his head, descended in ruddy streaks from the window to the height of the first story, where it stopped.

Nothing came yet. The clock of Saint Merry had struck ten. Enjolras and Combeferre sat down, carbine in hand, near the opening of the great barricade. They were not talking, they were listening; seeking to catch even the faintest and most distant sound of a march.

Suddenly, in the midst of this dismal calm, a clear, young, cheerful voice, which seemed to come from the Rue Saint Denis, arose and began to sing distinctly to the old popular air, *Au clair de la lune,* these lines which ended in a sort of cry similar to the crow of a cock:

> *Mon nez est en larmes,*
> *Mon ami Bugeaud,*
> *Prêt-moi tes gendarmes*
> *Pour leur dire un mot.*
> *Encapote bleue,*
> *La poule au shako,*
> *Voici la banlieue!*
> *Co-cocorico!*[1]

They grasped each other by the hand:

"It is Gavroche," said Enjolras.

"He is warning us," said Combeferre.

A headlong run startled the empty street; they saw a creature nimbler than clown climb over the omnibus, and Gavroche bounded into the barricade all breathless, saying:

"My musket! Here they are."

An electric thrill ran through the whole barricade, and a moving of hands was heard, feeling for their muskets.

"Do you want my carbine?" said Enjolras to the *gamin.*

"I want the big musket," answered Gavroche.

And he took Javert's musket.

Two sentinels had been driven back, and had come in almost at the

[1] *My nose is in tears,*
My good friend Bugeaud,
Just lend me your spears
To tell them my woe.
In blue cassimere,
And feathered shako,
The banlieue is here!
Co-cocorico!

same time as Gavroche. They were the sentinel from the end of the street, and the vidette from la Petite Truanderie. The vidette in the little Rue des Prêcheurs remained at his post, which indicated that nothing was coming from the direction of the bridges and the markets.

The Rue de la Chanvrerie, in which a few paving-stones were dimly visible by the reflection of the light which was thrown upon the flag, offered to the insurgents the appearance of a great black porch opening into a cloud of smoke.

Every man had taken his post for the combat.

Forty-three insurgents, among them Enjolras, Combeferre, Courfeyrac, Bossuet, Joly, Bahorel, and Gavroche, were on their knees in the great barricade, their heads even with the crest of the wall, the barrels of their muskets and their carbines pointed over the paving-stones as through loopholes, watchful, silent, ready to fire. Six, commanded by Feuilly, were stationed with their muskets at their shoulders, in the windows of the two upper stories of Corinth.

A few moments more elapsed, then a sound of steps, measured, heavy, numerous, was distinctly heard. This sound, at first faint, then distinct, then heavy and sonorous, approached slowly, without halt, without interruption, with a tranquil and terrible continuity. They seemed to hear at the end of the street the breathing of many men. They saw nothing, however, only they discovered at the very end, in that dense obscurity, a multitude of metallic threads, as fine as needles and almost imperceptible, which moved about like those indescribable phosphoric networks which we perceive under our closed eyelids at the moment of going to sleep, in the first mists of slumber. They were bayonets and musket barrels dimly lighted up by the distant reflection of the torch.

There was still a pause, as if on both sides they were awaiting. Suddenly, from the depth of that shadow, a voice, so much the more ominous, because nobody could be seen, and because it seemed as if it were the obscurity itself which was speaking, cried:

"Who is there?"

At the same time they heard the click of the levelled muskets.

Enjolras answered in a lofty and ringing tone:

"French Revolution!"

"Fire!" said the voice.

A flash empurpled all the façades on the street, as if the door of a furnace were opened and suddenly closed.

A fearful explosion burst over the barricade. The red flag fell. The volley had been so heavy and so dense that it had cut the staff, that is to say, the very point of the pole of the omnibus. Some balls, which ricocheted from the cornices of the houses, entered the barricade and wounded several men.

The impression produced by this first charge was such as to make the boldest ponder. It was evident that they had to do with a whole regiment at least.

"Comrades," cried Courfeyrac, "don't waste the powder. Let us wait to reply till they come into the street."

"And first of all," said Enjolras, "let us hoist the flag again!"

He picked up the flag which had fallen just at his feet.

They heard from without the rattling of the ramrods in the muskets: the troops were reloading.

Enjolras continued:

"Who is there here who has courage? who replants the flag on the barricade?"

Nobody answered. To mount the barricade at the moment when without doubt it was aimed at anew, was simply death. The bravest hesitates to sentence himself, Enjolras himself felt a shudder. He repeated:

"Nobody volunteers!"

Since they had arrived at Corinth and had commenced building the barricade, hardly any attention had been paid to Father Mabeuf. M. Mabeuf, however, had not left the company. He had entered the ground floor of the wine-shop and sat down behind the counter. There he had been, so to speak, annihilated in himself. He no longer seemed to look or to think. Courfeyrac and others had accosted him two or three times, warning him of the danger, entreating him to withdraw, but he had not appeared to hear them. When nobody was speaking to him, his lips moved as if he were answering somebody; as soon as anybody addressed a word to him, his lips became still and his eyes lost all appearance of life.

When everybody had gone to take his place for the combat, there remained in the basement room only Javert tied to the post, an insurgent with drawn sabre watching Javert, and he, Mabeuf. At the moment of the attack, at the discharge, the physical shock reached him, and, as it were, awakened him; he rose suddenly, crossed the room, and at the instant when Enjolras repeated his appeal: "Nobody volunteers?" they saw the old man appear in the doorway of the wine-shop.

His presence produced some commotion in the group. A cry arose:

"It is the Voter! it is the Conventionist! it is the Representative of the people!"

It is probable that he did not hear.

He walked straight to Enjolras; the insurgents fell back before him with a religious awe. He snatched the flag from Enjolras, and then, nobody daring to stop him, or to aid him, this old man of eighty, with shaking head but firm foot, began to climb slowly up the stairway of paving-stones built into the barricade. It was so gloomy and so grand that all about him cried: "Hats off!" At each step it was frightful; his white hair, his decrepit face, his large forehead bald and wrinkled, his hollow eyes, his quivering and open mouth, his old arm raising the red banner, surged up out of the shadow and grew grand in the bloody light of the torch, and they seemed to see the ghost of '93 rising out of the earth, the flag of terror in its hand.

When he was on the top of the last step, standing in the face of death as if he were stronger, there was one of those silences which occur only in presence of prodigies. In the midst of this silence the old man waved the red flag and cried:

"*Vive la révolution! vive la république!* fraternity! equality! and death!"

They heard from the barricade a low and rapid muttering like the murmur of a hurried priest dispatching a prayer. It was probably the commissary of police making the legal summons at the other end of the street.

Then the same ringing voice which had cried: "Who is there?" cried: "Disperse!"

M. Mabeuf, pallid, haggard, his eyes illumined by the mournful fires of insanity, raised the flag above his head and repeated:

"*Vive la république!*"

"Fire!" said the voice.

A second discharge, like a shower of grape, beat against the barricade.

The old man fell upon his knees, then rose up, let the flag drop, and fell backwards upon the pavement within, like a log, at full length with his arms crossed.

Streams of blood ran from beneath him. His old face, pale and sad, seemed to behold the sky.

"What men these regicides are!" said Enjolras.

Then he raised his voice:

"Citizens! This is the example which the old give to the young. We hesitated, he came! we fell back, he advanced! Behold what those who tremble with old age teach those who tremble with fear!"

Enjolras stooped down, raised the old man's head, and timidly kissed him on the forehead; then handling the dead with a tender care, as if he feared to hurt him, he took off his coat, showed the bleeding holes to all, and said:

"There now is our flag."

They threw a long black shawl over Father Mabeuf. Six men made a barrow of their muskets, they laid the corpse upon it, and they bore it, bareheaded, with solemn slowness, to the large table in the basement room.

When the corpse passed near Javert, who was still impassible, Enjolras said to the spy:

"You! directly."

During this time little Gavroche, who alone had not left his post and had remained on the watch, thought he saw some men approaching the barricade with a stealthy step. Suddenly he cried:

"Take care!"

Courfeyrac, Enjolras, Jean Prouvaire, Combeferre, Joly, Bahorel, Bossuet, all sprang tumultuously from the wine-shop. There was hardly a moment to spare. They perceived a sparkling breadth of bayonets undulating above the barricade. Municipal Guards of tall stature were penetrating, some by climbing over the omnibus, others by the opening, pushing before them the *gamin*, who fell back, but did not fly.

The moment was critical. A second more, and the barricade had been taken.

Bahorel sprang upon the first Municipal Guard who entered, and killed him at the very muzzle of his carbine; the second killed Bahorel with his bayonet. Another had already prostrated Courfeyrac, who was crying "Help!" The largest of all, a kind of colossus, marched upon Gavroche with fixed bayonet. The *gamin* took Javert's enormous musket in his little arms, aimed it resolutely at the giant, and pulled the trigger. Nothing went off. Javert had not loaded his musket. The Municipal Guard burst into a laugh and raised his bayonet over the child.

Before the bayonet touched Gavroche the musket dropped from the soldier's hands, a ball had struck the Municipal Guard in the middle of the forehead, and he fell on his back. A second ball struck the other Guard, who had assailed Courfeyrac, full in the breast, and threw him upon the pavement.

It was Marius who had just entered the barricade.

Marius, still hidden in the corner of the Rue Mondétour, had watched the first phase of the combat, irresolute and shuddering. However, before the death of M. Mabeuf, that fatal enigma, before Bahorel slain, Courfeyrac crying "Help!" that child threatened, his friends to succour or to avenge, all hesitation had vanished, and he had rushed into the conflict, his two pistols in his hands. By the first shot he had saved Gavroche, and by the second delivered Courfeyrac.

At the shots, at the cries of the wounded Guards, the assailants had scaled the intrenchment, upon the summit of which could now be seen thronging Municipal Guards, soldiers of the Line, National Guards, musket in hand. They already covered more than two-thirds of the wall, but they did not leap into the inclosure; they seemed to hesitate, fearing some snare. They looked into the obscure barricade as one would look into a den of lions. The light of the torch only lighted up their bayonets, their bearskin caps, and the upper part of their anxious and angry faces.

Marius had now no arms, he had thrown away his discharged pistols, but he had noticed the keg of powder in the basement room near the door.

As he turned half round, looking in that direction, a soldier aimed at him. At the moment the soldier aimed at Marius, a hand was laid upon the muzzle of the musket, and stopped it. It was somebody who had sprung forward, the young working-man with velvet pantaloons. The shot went off, passed through the hand, and perhaps also through the working-man, for he fell. Marius, who was entering the basement room, hardly noticed it; he had caught a dim glimpse of that musket directed at him, and that hand which had stopped it, and he had heard the shot. But in moments like that the things which we see waver and rush headlong, and we stop for nothing.

The insurgents, surprised, but not dismayed, had rallied. Enjolras had cried: "Wait! don't fire at random!" In the first confusion, in fact, they might hit one another. Most of them had gone up to the window of the second story and to the dormer windows, whence they commanded the assailants. The most determined, with Enjolras, Courfeyrac, Jean Prouvaire, and Combeferre, had placed their backs to the houses in the rear, openly facing the ranks of soldiers and guards which crowded the barricade.

On both sides they were taking aim, the muzzles of the guns almost touching; they were so near that they could talk with each other in an ordinary tone. Just as the spark was about to fly, an officer in a gorget and with huge epaulets, extended his sword and said:

"Take aim!"

"Fire!" said Enjolras.

The two explosions were simultaneous, and everything disappeared in a stinging and stifling smoke amid which writhed the wounded and the dying.

When the smoke cleared away, on both sides the combatants were thinned out, but still in the same places, and reloading their pieces in silence.

Suddenly, a thundering voice was heard, crying:

"Begone, or I'll blow up the barricade!"

All turned in the direction whence the voice came.

Marius had entered the basement room, and had taken the keg of powder, then he had profited by the smoke and the kind of obscure fog which filled the intrenched inclosure, to glide along the barricade as far as that cage of paving-stones in which the torch was fixed. To pull out the torch, to put the keg of powder in its place, to push the pile of paving-stones upon the keg, which stove it in, with a sort of terrible self-control—all this had been for Marius the work of stooping down and rising up; and now all, National Guards, Municipal Guards, officers, soldiers, grouped at the other extremity of the barricade, beheld him with horror, his foot upon the stones, the torch in his hand, his stern face lighted by a deadly resolution, bending the flame of the torch towards that formidable pile in which they discerned the broken barrel of powder.

"Blow up the barricade!" said a sergeant, "and yourself also!"

Marius answered:

"And myself also."

And he approached the torch to the keg of powder.

But there was no longer anybody on the wall. The assailants, leaving their dead and wounded, fled pell-mell and in disorder towards the extremity of the street, and were again lost in the night. It was a rout.

The barricade was redeemed.

All flocked round Marius.

"You came in good time!" said Bossuet.

"Without you I should have been dead!" said Courfeyrac.

"Without you I'd been gobbled!" added Gavroche.

Marius inquired:

"Where is the chief?"

"You are the chief," said Enjolras.

Meanwhile the assailants made no movement, they were heard marching and swarming at the end of the street, but they did not venture forward, either that they were awaiting orders, or that before rushing anew upon that impregnable redoubt, they were awaiting reinforcements. The insurgents had posted sentinels, and some who were students in medicine had set about dressing the wounded.

They had thrown the tables out of the wine-shop, with the exception of two reserved for lint and cartridges, and that on which lay Father Mabeuf; they added them to the barricade, and had replaced them in the basement room by mattresses. Upon these mattresses they laid the wounded; as for the poor creatures who lived in Corinth, nobody knew what had become of them. They found them, at last, hidden in the cellar.

A bitter emotion came to darken their joy over the redeemed barricade. They called the roll. One of the insurgents was missing. And who? One of the dearest, one of the most valiant, Jean Prouvaire. They sought him among the wounded, he was not there. They sought him among the dead, he was not there. He was evidently a prisoner.

Combeferre said to Enjolras:

"They have our friend; we have their officer. Have you set your heart on the death of this spy?"

"Yes," said Enjolras; "but less than on the life of Jean Prouvaire."

This passed in the basement room near Javert's post. Javert had not moved his head during the attack upon the barricade, and beheld the revolt going on about him with the resignation of a martyr and the majesty of a judge.

"Well," replied Combeferre, "I am going to tie my handkerchief to my cane, and go with a flag of truce to offer to give them their man for ours."

"Listen," said Enjolras, laying his hand on Combeferre's arm.

There was a significant clicking of arms at the end of the street.

They heard a manly voice cry:

"*Vive la France! Vive l'avenir!*"

They recognized Prouvaire's voice.

There was a flash and an explosion.

Silence reigned again.

"They have killed him," exclaimed Combeferre.

Enjolras looked at Javert and said to him:

"Your friends have just shot you."

A peculiarity of this kind of war is that the attack on the barricades is almost always made in front, and that in general the assailants abstain from turning the positions, whether it be that they dread ambuscades, or that they fear to become entangled in the crooked streets. The whole attention of the insurgents therefore was directed to the great barricade, which was evidently the point still threatened, and where the struggle must infallibly recommence. Marius, however, thought of the little barricade and went to it. It was deserted, and the little Rue Mondétour, and the branch streets were perfectly quiet.

As Marius was retiring, he heard his name faintly pronounced in the obscurity:

"Monsieur Marius!"

He shuddered, for he recognised the voice which had called him two hours before, through the grating in the Rue Plumet.

Only this voice now seemed to be but a breath.

He looked about him and saw nobody.

Marius thought he was deceived, and that it was an illusion added by his mind to the extraordinary realities which were thronging about him. He started to leave the retired recess in which the barricade was situated.

"Monsieur Marius!" repeated the voice.

This time he could not doubt, he had heard distinctly; he looked, and saw nothing.

"At your feet," said the voice.

He stooped and saw a form in the shadow, which was dragging itself towards him. It was crawling along the pavement. It was this that had spoken to him.

The lamp enabled him to distinguish a blouse, a pair of torn pantaloons of coarse velvet, bare feet, and something which resembled a pool of blood. Marius caught a glimpse of a pale face which rose towards him and said to him:

"You do not know me?"

"No."

"Eponine."

Marius bent down quickly. It was indeed that unhappy child, dressed as a man.

"How came you here? what are you doing there?"

"I am dying," said she.

Marius exclaimed:

"You are wounded! Wait, I will carry you into the room! They will dress your wounds! Is it serious? how shall I take you up so as not to hurt you? Where are you hurt? my God! But what did you come here for?"

And he tried to pass his arm under her to lift her.

She uttered a feeble cry.

"Have I hurt you?" asked Marius.

"A little."

"But I have only touched your hand."

She raised her hand into Marius' sight, and Marius saw in the centre of that hand a black hole.

"What is the matter with your hand?" said he.

"It is pierced."

"Pierced?"

"Yes."

"By what?"

"By a ball."

"How?"

"Did you see a musket aimed at you?"

"Yes, and a hand which stopped it."

"That was mine."

Marius shuddered.

"What madness! Poor child! But that is not so bad, if that is all, it is nothing, let me carry you to a bed. They will care for you, people don't die from a shot in the hand."

She murmured:

"The ball passed through my hand, but it went out through my back. It is useless to take me from here. I will tell you how you can care for me, better than a surgeon. Sit down by me on that stone."

He obeyed; she laid her head on Marius' knees, and without looking at him, she said:

"Oh! how good it is! How kind he is! That is it! I don't suffer any more!"

She remained a moment in silence, then she turned her head with effort and looked at Marius.

"Do you know, Monsieur Marius? It worried me that you should go into that garden, it was silly, since it was I who had shown you the house, and then indeed I ought surely to have known that a young man like you—"

She stopped, and, leaping over the gloomy transitions which were doubtless in her mind, she added with a heartrending smile:

"You thought me ugly, didn't you?"

She continued:

"See, you are lost! Nobody will get out of the barricade, now. It was I who led you into this, it was! You are going to die, I am sure. And still when I saw him aiming at you, I put up my hand upon the muzzle of the musket. How droll it is! But it was because I wanted to die before you.

"When I got this ball, I dragged myself here, nobody saw me, nobody picked me up. I waited for you, I said: He will not come then? Oh! if you knew, I bit my blouse, I suffered so much! Now I am well. Do you remember the day when I came into your room, and when I looked at myself in your mirror, and the day when I met you on the boulevard near some work-women? How the birds sang! It was not very long ago. You gave me a hundred sous, and I said to you: I don't want your money. Did you pick up your piece? You are not rich. I didn't think to tell you to pick it up. The sun shone bright, I was not cold. Do you remember, Monsieur Marius? Oh! I am happy! We are all going to die."

She had a wandering, grave, and touching air. Her torn blouse showed her bare throat. While she was talking she rested her wounded hand upon her breast where there was another hole, from which there came with each pulsation a flow of blood like a jet of wine from an open bung.

"Oh!" she exclaimed suddenly, "it is coming back. I am stifling!"

She seized her blouse and bit it, and her legs writhed upon the pavement. At this moment the chicken voice of little Gavroche resounded through the barricade. The child had mounted upon a table to load his musket and was gaily singing the song then so popular:

En voyant Lafayette
Le gendarme répète
Sauvons-nous! sauvons-nous! sauvons-nous!

Eponine raised herself up, and listened, then she murmured:

"It is he."

And turning towards Marius:

"My brother is here. He must not see me. He would scold me."

"Your brother?" asked Marius, who thought in the bitterest and most sorrowful depths of his heart, of the duties which his father had bequeathed him towards the Thénardiers, "who is your brother?"

"That little boy."

"The one who is singing?"

"Yes."

Marius started.

"Oh! don't go away!" said she, "it will not be long now!"

She was sitting almost upright, but her voice was very low and broken by hiccoughs. She approached her face as near as she could to Marius' face. She added with a strange expression:

"Listen, I don't want to deceive you. I have a letter in my pocket for you. Since yesterday. I was told to put it in the post. I kept it. I didn't want it to reach you. But you would not like it of me perhaps when we meet again so soon. We do meet again, don't we? Take your letter."

She put Marius' hand into the pocket of her blouse. Marius felt a paper there.

"Take it," said she. "Now for my pains, promise me—"

And she hesitated.

"What?" asked Marius.

"Promise me!"

"I promise you."

"Promise to kiss me on the forehead when I am dead. I shall feel it."

She let her head fall back upon Marius' knees and her eyelids closed. He thought that poor soul had gone. Eponine lay motionless; but just when Marius supposed her for ever asleep, she slowly opened her eyes and said to him with an accent the sweetness of which already seemed to come from another world:

"And then, do you know, Monsieur Marius, I believe I was a little in love with you."

She essayed to smile again and expired.

Marius kept his promise. He kissed that forehead from which oozed an icy sweat. This was not infidelity to Cosette; it was a thoughtful and gentle farewell to an unhappy soul.

He had not taken the letter which Eponine had given him without a thrill. He was impatient to read it. The heart of man is thus made; the unfortunate child had hardly closed her eyes when Marius thought to unfold this paper. He laid her gently upon the ground, and went away.

He went to a candle in the basement-room. It was a little note, folded and sealed with the elegant care of woman. The address was in a woman's hand, and ran:

"To Monsieur, Monsieur Marius Pontmercy, at M. Courfeyrac's, Rue de la Verrerie, No. 16."

He broke the seal and read:

"My beloved, alas! my father wishes to start immediately. We shall be to-night in the Rue de l'Homme Armé, No. 7. In a week we shall be in London. COSETTE. June 4th."

Such was the innocence of this love that Marius did not even know Cosette's handwriting.

After the evening of the 3rd of June, Eponine had a double thought, to thwart the projects of her father and the bandits upon the house in the Rue Plumet, and to separate Marius from Cosette. She had changed rags with the first young rogue who thought it amusing to dress as a woman while Eponine disguised herself as a man. It was she who, in the Champ de Mars, had given Jean Valjean the expressive warning: *Remove.* Jean Valjean returned home, and said to Cosette: *we start to-night, and we are going to the Rue de l'Homme Armé with Toussaint. Next week we shall be in London.*

Cosette, prostrated by this unexpected blow, had hastily written two lines to Marius. But how should she get the letter to the post? She did not go out alone, and Toussaint, surprised at such an errand, would surely show the letter to M. Fauchelevent. In this anxiety, Cosette saw, through the grating, Eponine in men's clothes, who was now prowling continually about the garden. Cosette called "this young working-man" and handed him five francs and the letter, saying to him: "carry this letter to its address right away." Eponine put the letter in her pocket. The next day, June 5th, she went to Courfeyrac's to ask for Marius, not to give him the letter, but, a thing which every jealous and loving soul will understand, "to see." There she waited for Marius, or, at least, for Courfeyrac—still to see. When Courfeyrac said to her: we are going to the barricades, an idea flashed across her mind: to throw herself into that death as she would have thrown herself into any other, and to push Marius into it. She followed Courfeyrac, made sure of the post where they were building the barricade; and very sure, since Marius had received no notice, and she had intercepted the letter, that he would at nightfall be at his usual evening rendezvous, she went to the Rue Plumet, waited there for Marius, and sent him, in the name of his friends, that appeal which must, she thought, lead him to the barricade.

Marius covered Cosette's letter with kisses. She loved him then? He had for a moment the idea that now he need not die. Then he said to himself: "She is going away. Her father takes her to England, and my grandfather refuses to consent to the marriage. Nothing is changed in the fatality."

Then he thought that there were two duties remaining for him to fulfil: to inform Cosette of his death and to send her a last farewell, and to save from the imminent catastrophe which was approaching, this poor child, Eponine's brother and Thénardier's son.

He had a pocket-book with him; he tore out a leaf and wrote with a pencil:

"Our marriage was impossible. I have asked my grandfather, he has refused; I am without fortune, and you also. I ran to your house, I did not find you, you know the promise that I gave you? I keep it, I die, I love you. When you read this, my soul will be near you, and will smile upon you."

Having nothing to seal this letter with, he merely folded the paper, and wrote upon it this address:

"*To Mademoiselle Cosette Fauchelevent, at M. Fauchelevent's, Rue de l'Homme Armé, No. 7.*"

The letter folded, he remained a moment in thought, took his pocket-book again, opened it, and wrote these four lines on the first page with the same pencil:

"My name is Marius Pontmercy. Carry my corpse to my grandfather's, M. Gillenormand, Rue des Filles du Calvaire, No. 6, in the Marais."

Then he called Gavroche. The *gamin* ran up with his joyous and devoted face.

"Will you do something for me?"

"Anything," said Gavroche. "God of the good God! without you, I should have been cooked, sure."

"You see this letter?"

"Yes."

"Take it. Go out of the barricade immediately (Gavroche, disturbed, began to scratch his ear), and to-morrow morning you will carry it to its address, to Mademoiselle Cosette, at M. Fauchelevent's, Rue de l'Homme Armé, No. 7."

The heroic boy answered:

"Ah, well, but in that time they'll take the barricade, and I shan't be here."

"The barricade will not be attacked again before daybreak, according to all appearance, and will not be taken before to-morrow noon."

The new respite which the assailants allowed the barricade was, in fact, prolonged. It was one of those intermissions, frequent in night combats, which are always followed by a redoubled fury.

"Well," said Gavroche, "suppose I go and carry your letter in the morning?"

"It will be too late. The barricade will probably be blockaded; all the streets will be guarded, and you cannot get out. Go, right away!"

Gavroche had nothing more to say; he stood there, undecided, and sadly scratching his ear. Suddenly, with one of his birdlike motions, he took the letter:

"All right," said he.

And he started off on a run by the little Rue Mondétour.

Gavroche had an idea which decided him:

"It is hardly midnight, the Rue de l'Homme Armé is not far, I will carry the letter right away, and I shall get back in time."

On the eve of that same day, June 5th, Jean Valjean, accompanied by Cosette and Toussaint, had installed himself in the Rue de l'Homme Armé.

Cosette had not left the Rue Plumet without an attempt at resistance. For the first time since they had lived together, Cosette's will and Jean Valjean's will had shown themselves distinct, and had been, if not conflicting, at least contradictory. There was objection on one side and inflexibility on the other. The abrupt advice: *remove,* thrown to Jean Valjean by an unknown hand, had so far alarmed him as to render him absolute. He believed himself tracked out and pursued. Cosette had to yield.

They both arrived in the Rue de l'Homme Armé without opening their mouths or saying a word, absorbed in their personal meditations; Jean Valjean so anxious that he did not perceive Cosette's sadness, Cosette so sad that she did not perceive Jean Valjean's anxiety.

Jean Valjean had brought Toussaint, which he had never done in his preceding absences. He saw that possibly he should not return to the Rue Plumet, and he could neither leave Toussaint behind, nor tell her his secret. Besides he felt that she was devoted and safe.

In this departure from the Rue Plumet, which was almost a flight, Jean Valjean carried nothing but the little valise christened by Cosette the *inseparable.* Full trunks would have required porters, and porters are witnesses. It was with great difficulty that Toussaint obtained permission to pack up a little linen and clothing and a few toilet articles. Cosette herself carried only her writing-desk and her blotter. They arrived in the Rue de l'Homme Armé after nightfall; they went silently to bed.

Hardly was Jean Valjean in the Rue de l'Homme Armé, before his anxiety grew less, and by degrees was dissipated. Jean Valjean felt some strange contagion of tranquillity in that lane of the ancient Paris, so narrow that it was barred to carriages by a tranverse joist laid upon two posts, dumb and deaf in the midst of the noisy city, twilight in broad day, and so to speak, incapable of emotions between its two rows of lofty, century-old houses which are silent like the patriarchs that they are. There is stagnant oblivion in this street. Jean Valjean breathed there. By what means could anybody find him there?

As for Cosette, she shut herself in her bedroom upon pretext of a severe headache.

While Jean Valjean was making his frugal dinner, he became confusedly aware of the stammering of Toussaint, who said to him: "Monsieur, there is a row; they are fighting in Paris." But he paid no attention to it. To tell the truth, he had not heard.

He arose and began to walk from the window to the door, and from the door to the window. Not that he was troubled about this headache, a petty derangement of the nerves, a young girl's pouting, the cloud of a moment, in a day or two it would be gone; but he thought of the future. To have left the Rue Plumet without complication was already a piece of good fortune. Perhaps it would be prudent to leave the country, were it only for a few months, and go to London. Well, they would go. To be in France, to be in England, what did that matter, if he had Cosette with him? Cosette was his nation. Cosette sufficed for his happiness; the idea that perhaps he did not suffice for Cosette's happiness, this idea, once his fever and his bane, did not even present itself to his mind.

While yet walking up and down, with slow steps, his eye suddenly met something strange.

He perceived facing him, in the inclined mirror which hung above the sideboard, the lines which follow:

"My beloved, alas! my father wishes to start immediately. We shall be to-night in the Rue de l'Homme Armé, No. 7. In a week we shall be in London. COSETTE. June 4th."

Jean Valjean stood aghast.

Cosette, on arriving, had laid her blotter on the sideboard before the mirror, and, wholly absorbed in her sorrowful anguish, had forgotten it there, without even noticing that she left it wide open, and open exactly at the page upon which she had dried the five lines written by her, and which she had given in charge to the young workman passing through the Rue Plumet. The writing was imprinted upon the blotter.

The mirror reflected the writing.

There resulted what is called in geometry the symmetrical image; so that the writing reversed on the blotter was corrected by the mirror, and presented its original form; and Jean Valjean had beneath his eyes the letter written in the evening by Cosette to Marius.

Jean Valjean held the blotter in his hand and gazed at it. He understood, let the blotter fall, and sank down into the old armchair by the sideboard, his head drooping. He said to himself that it was clear, that the light of the world was for ever eclipsed. Cosette had written that to somebody.

Marius at that moment had not yet Cosette's letter; chance had brought it, like a traitor, to Jean Valjean before delivering it to Marius.

Jean Valjean till this day had never been vanquished when put to the proof. He had been subjected to fearful trials; no violence of ill fortune had been spared him; the ferocity of fate, armed with every vengeance and with every scorn of society, had taken him for a subject and had greedily pursued him. He had neither recoiled nor flinched before anything. He had given up his liberty, risked his head, lost all, suffered all, and he had remained so disinterested and stoical that at times one might have believed him translated, like a martyr.

Well, of all the tortures which he had undergone in that inquisition of destiny, this was the most fearful. Poor old Jean Valjean did not, certainly, love Cosette otherwise than as a father; but he loved Cosette as his daughter, and he loved her as his mother, and he loved her as his sister; and, as he had never had either sweetheart or wife, that sentiment, also, the most indestructible of all, was mingled with the others, vague, ignorant, pure with the purity of blindness.

His instinct did not hesitate. He put together certain circumstances, certain dates, certain blushes, and he said to himself: "It is he." With his first conjecture, he hit Marius. He did not know the name, but he found the man at once. He perceived distinctly the unknown prowler of the Luxembourg, that wretched seeker of amours, that romantic idler, that imbecile, that coward, for it is cowardice to come and make sweet eyes at girls who are beside their father who loves them.

After he had fully determined that that young man was at the bottom of this state of affairs, he, Jean Valjean, the regenerated man, the man who had laboured so much upon his soul, the man who had made so many efforts to resolve all life, all misery, and all misfortune into love, looked within himself, and there he saw hatred.

While he was thinking, Toussaint entered. Jean Valjean asked her: "In what direction is it? Do you know?"

Toussaint, astonished, could only answer:

"If you please?"

"Didn't you tell me just now that they were fighting?"

"Oh! yes, monsieur," answered Toussaint. "It is over by Saint Merry."

There are some mechanical impulses which come to us, without our knowledge even, from our deepest thoughts. It was doubtless under the influence of an impulse of this kind, and of which he was hardly conscious, that Jean Valjean five minutes afterwards found himself in the street.

He was bare-headed, seated upon the stone block by the door of his house. He seemed to be listening.

The street was empty. A few anxious bourgeois, who were rapidly returning home, hardly perceived him. The lamplighter came as usual to light the lamp which hung exactly opposite the door of No. 7, and went away. Jean Valjean, to one who had examined him in that shadow, would not have seemed a living man.

Suddenly he raised his eyes, somebody was walking in the street, he heard steps near him, he looked, and, by the light of the lamp, in the direction of the Archives, he perceived a young face.

Gavroche had just arrived in the Rue de l'Homme Armé.

Gavroche was looking in the air, and appeared to be searching for something. He saw Jean Valjean perfectly, but he took no notice of him.

Gavroche, after looking into the air, looked on the ground; he raised himself on tiptoe and felt of the doors and windows of the ground floors; they were all closed, bolted, and chained. After having found five or six houses barricaded in this way, the *gamin* shrugged his shoulders, and began to look into the air again.

Jean Valjean, who, the instant before, would not have spoken nor even replied to anybody, felt irresistibly impelled to address a word to this child.

"Small boy," said he, "what is the matter with you?"

"The matter is that I am hungry," answered Gavroche tartly. And he added: "Small yourself."

Jean Valjean felt in his pocket and took out a five-franc piece.

But Gavroche, who was of the wagtail species, and who passed quickly from one action to another, had picked up a stone. He had noticed a lamp.

"Hold on," said he, "you have your lamps here still. You are not regular, my friends. It is disorderly. Break me that."

And he threw the stone into the lamp, the glass from which fell with such a clatter that some bourgeois, hid behind their curtains in the opposite house, cried: "There is 'Ninety-three!'"

The lamp swung violently and went out. The street became suddenly dark.

"That's it, old street," said Gavroche, "put on your nightcap."

And turning towards Jean Valjean:

"What do you call that gigantic monument that you have got there at the end of the street? That's the Archives, isn't it? They ought to chip off these big fools of columns slightly, and make a genteel barricade of them."

Jean Valjean approached Gavroche.

"Poor creature," said he, in an undertone, and speaking to himself, "he is hungry."

And he put the hundred-sous piece into his hand.

Gavroche cocked up his nose, astonished at the size of this big sou; he looked at it in the dark, and the whiteness of the big sou dazzled him. He knew five-franc pieces by hearsay; their reputation was agreeable to him; he was delighted to see one so near.

He gazed at it for a few moments in ecstasy; then, turning towards Jean Valjean, he handed him the piece, and said majestically:

"Bourgeois, I prefer to break lamps. You don't corrupt me."

"Have you a mother?" inquired Jean Valjean.

Gavroche answered:

"Perhaps more than you have."

"Well," replied Jean Valjean, "keep this money for your mother."

Gavroche felt softened. Besides he had just noticed that the man who was talking to him, had no hat, and that inspired him with confidence.

"Really," said he, "it isn't to prevent my breaking the lamps?"

"Break all you like."

"You are a fine fellow," said Gavroche.

And he put the five-franc piece into one of his pockets.

His confidence increasing, he added:

"Do you belong in the street?"

"Yes; why?"

"Could you show me number seven?"

"What do you want with number seven?"

Here the boy stopped; he feared that he had said too much; he plunged his nails vigorously into his hair, and merely answered:

"Ah! that's it."

An idea flashed across Jean Valjean's mind. He said to the child:

"Have you brought the letter I am waiting for?"

"You?" said Gavroche. "You are not a woman."

"The letter is for Mademoiselle Cosette; isn't it?"

"Cosette?" muttered Gavroche, "yes, I believe it is that funny name."

"Well," resumed Jean Valjean, "I am to deliver the letter to her. Give it to me."

"In that case you must know that I am sent from the barricade?"

"Of course," said Jean Valjean.

Gavroche thrust his hand into another of his pockets, and drew out a folded paper.

Then he gave a military salute.

"Respect for the despatch," said he. "It comes from the provisional government."

"Give it to me," said Jean Valjean.

Gavroche held the paper raised above his head.

"Don't imagine that this is a love-letter. It is for a woman; but it is for the people. We men, we are fighting and we respect the sex. We don't do as they do in high life."

"Give it to me."

"The fact is," continued Gavroche, "you look to me like a fine fellow."

"Give it to me quick."

"Take it."

And he handed the paper to Jean Valjean.

"And hurry yourself, Monsieur What's-your-name, for Mamselle What's-her-name is waiting."

Jean Valjean asked:

"Is it to Saint Merry that the answer is to be sent?"

"That letter comes from the barricade in the Rue de la Chanvrerie, and I am going back there. Good night, citizen."

This said, Gavroche went away, or rather, plunged into the obscurity as if he made a hole in it, with the rapidity and precision of a projectile; the little Rue de l'Homme Armé again became silent and solitary. One might have thought him vanished, if, a few minutes after his disappearance, a loud crashing of glass and the splendid patatras of a lamp falling upon the pavement had not abruptly reawakened the indignant bourgeois. It was Gavroche passing along the Rue du Chaume.

Jean Valjean went in with Marius' letter.

He groped his way upstairs, opened and softly closed the door, listened to see if he heard any sound, decided that, according to all appearances, Cosette and Toussaint were asleep. His candle lighted, he leaned his elbows on the table, unfolded the paper, and read.

In Marius' note to Cosette, Jean Valjean saw only these words:
"——I die. When you read this, my soul will be near you."

Before these two lines, he was horribly dazzled; he looked at Marius' note with a sort of drunken astonishment; he had before his eyes that splendour, the death of the hated being.

So, it was finished. The end came sooner than he had dared to hope. The being who encumbered his destiny was going away of himself, freely, of his own accord. Without any intervention on his, Jean Valjean's part, without any fault of his, "that man" was about to die. Perhaps even he was already dead.—Here his fever began to calculate.—No. He is not dead yet. The letter was evidently written to be read by Cosette in the morning; since those two discharges which were heard between eleven o'clock and midnight, there had been nothing; the barricade will not be seriously attacked till daybreak; but it is all the same, for the moment "that man" meddled with this war, he was lost; he is caught in the net.

Jean Valjean felt that he was delivered. He would then find himself once more alone with Cosette. Rivalry ceased; the future recommenced. He had only to keep the note in his pocket. Cosette would never know what had become of "that man."

All this said within himself, he became gloomy.

Then he went down and waked the porter.

About an hour afterwards, Jean Valjean went out in the full dress of a National Guard, and armed. The porter had easily found in the neighbourhood what was necessary to complete his equipment. He had a loaded musket and a cartridge-box full of cartridges. He went in the direction of the markets.

In the recess of a porte-cochère was a hand-cart, an Auvergnat sleeping in it. The arms of the cart rested on the pavement and the Auvergnat's head rested on the tail-board of the cart. His body was curled up on the inclined plane and his feet touched the ground.

Gavroche, with his experience of the things of this world, recognised a drunken man. It was some corner-porter who had drunk too much.

"This," thought Gavroche, "is what summer nights are good for. The Auvergnat is asleep in his cart. We take the cart for the republic and we leave the Auvergnat to the monarchy."

Gavroche drew the cart softly by the back end and the Auvergnat by the forward end, that is to say, by the feet, and, in a minute, the Auvergnat, imperturbable, was lying flat on the pavement. The cart was delivered.

Gavroche, accustomed to face the unforeseen on all sides, always had everything about him. He felt in one of his pockets, and took out a scrap of paper and an end of a red pencil pilfered from some carpenter.

He wrote:

"French Republic

"Received your cart."
And he signed: "Gavroche."

This done, he put the paper into the pocket of the still snoring Auvergnat's velvet waistcoat, seized the cross-piece with both hands, and started off in the direction of the markets, pushing the cart before him at a full gallop with a glorious triumphal uproar.

This was perilous. There was a post at the Imprimerie Royale; Gavroche did not think of it. This post was occupied by the National Guards. A certain watchfulness began to excite the squad, and their heads were lifted from their camp-beds. Two lamps broken one after another, that song sung at the top of the voice, it was a good deal for streets so cowardly, which long to go to sleep at sunset, and put their extinguisher upon their candle so early. For an hour the *gamin* had been making, in this peaceful district, the uproar of a fly in a bottle. The sergeant of the banlieue listened. He waited. He was a prudent man.

"There is a whole band here," said he, "we must go softly."

And the sergeant ventured out of the post with stealthy tread.

All at once, Gavroche, pushing his cart, just as he was going to turn out of the Rue des Vieilles Haudriettes, found himself face to face with a uniform, a shako, a plume, and a musket.

For the second time, he stopped short.

"Hold on," said he, "that's him. Good morning, public order."

"Where are you going, vagabond?" cried the sergeant.

"Citizen," said Gavroche, "I haven't called you bourgeois yet. What do you insult me for?"

"Where are you going, rascal?"

"Monsieur," resumed Gavroche, "may have been a man of wit yesterday, but you were discharged this morning."

"I want to know where you are going, scoundrel?"

Gavroche answered.

"You talk genteelly. Really, nobody would guess your age. You ought to sell all your hairs at a hundred francs apiece. That would make you five hundred francs."

"Where are you going? where are you going? where are you going, bandit?"

Gavroche replied:

"Those are naughty words. They should wipe your mouth better."

The sergeant crossed his bayonet.

"Will you tell me where you are going, at last, wretch?"

"My general," said Gavroche, "I am going after the doctor for my wife, who is put to bed."

"To arms!" cried the sergeant.

To save yourself by means of that which has ruined you is the master-piece of great men; Gavroche measured the entire situation at a glance. It was the cart which had compromised him, it was for the cart to protect him.

At the moment the sergeant was about to rush upon Gavroche the cart became a projectile, and, hurled with all the *gamin's* might, ran against him furiously, and the sergeant, struck full in the stomach, fell backward into the gutter while his musket went off in the air.

At the sergeant's cry, the men of the post had rushed out pell-mell; the sound of the musket produced a general discharge at random, after which they reloaded and began again.

This musketry at blindman's buff lasted a full quarter of an hour, and killed several squares of glass.

Meanwhile Gavroche, who had run back desperately, stopped five or six streets off, and sat down breathless upon the block at the corner of the Enfants Rouges.

He listened attentively.

After breathing a few moments, he turned in the direction in which the firing was raging, raised his left hand to the level of his nose, and threw it forward three times, striking the back of his head with his right hand at the same time: a sovereign gestue into which the Parisian *gamin* has condensed French irony, and which is evidently effective, since it has lasted already for a half century.

This cheerfulness was marred by a bitter reflection:

"Yes," said he, "I grin, I twist myself, I run over with joy; but I am losing my way, I shall have to make a detour. If I only get to the barricade in time."

Thereupon, he resumed his course.

The taking up of arms at the post was not without result. The cart was conquered, the drunkard was taken prisoner. One was put on the wood-pile; the other afterwards tried before a court-martial, as an accomplice. The public ministry of the time availed itself of this circumstance to show its indefatigable zeal for the defence of society.

Gavroche's adventure, preserved among the traditions of the quartier of the Temple, is one of the most terrible reminiscences of the old bourgeois of the Marais, and is entitled in their memory: Nocturnal attack on the post of the Imprimerie Royale.

XXVII. THE PEOPLE

IT SOMETIMES HAPPENS that, even against principles, even against liberty, equality, and fraternity, even against universal suffrage, even against the government of all by all, from the depths of its anguish, of its discouragements, of its privations, of its fevers, of its distresses, of its miasmas, of its ignorance, of its darkness, that great madman, the rabble, protests, and the populace gives battle to the people.

Those are mournful days; for there is always a certain amount of right even in this madness, there is suicide in this duel, and these words, which are intended for insults, vagabonds, rabble, indicate, alas! rather the fault of those who reign than the fault of those who suffer; rather the fault of the privileged than the fault of the outcasts.

The insurgents, under the eye of Enjolras, for Marius no longer looked to anything, turned the night to advantage. The barricade was not only repaired, but made larger. They raised it two feet. Iron bars planted in the paving-stones resembled lances in rest. All sorts of rubbish added, and brought from all sides, increased the exterior intricacy. The redoubt was skilfully made over into a wall within and a thicket without.

They put the barricade in order, cleared up the basement room, took the kitchen for a hospital, completed the dressing of the wounds; gathered up the powder scattered over the floor and the tables, cast bullets, made cartridges, scraped lint, distributed the arms of the fallen, cleaned the interior of the redoubt, picked up the fragments, carried away the corpses.

They deposited the dead in a heap in the little Rue Mondétour, of which they were still masters. The pavement was red for a long time at that spot. Among the dead were four National Guards of the banlieue. Enjolras had their uniforms laid aside.

Enjolras advised two hours of sleep. Advice from Enjolras was an order. Still, three or four only profited by it. Feuilly employed these two hours in engraving this inscription on the wall which fronted the wine-shop:

"Vivent les Peuples!"

These three words, graven in the stone with a nail, were still legible on that wall in 1848.

Most of the wounded could and would still fight. There were, upon a straw mattress and some bunches of straw, in the kitchen now become a hospital, five men severely wounded, two of whom were Municipal Guards. The wounds of the Municipal Guards were dressed first.

Nothing now remained in the basement room but Mabeuf, under his black cloth, and Javert bound to the post. In the interior of this room, feebly lighted by a candle, a sort of large dim cross was produced by Javert standing, and Mabeuf lying.

The pole of the omnibus, although maimed by the musketry, was still high enough for them to hang a flag upon it.

Enjolras, who had this quality of a chief, always to do as he said, fastened the pierced and bloody coat of the slain old man to this pole.

No meals could now be had. There was neither bread nor meat. The fifty men of the barricade, in the sixteen hours that they had been there, had very soon exhausted the meagre provisions of the wine-shop. They must resign themselves to famine. They were in the early hours of that Spartan day of the 6th of June, when, in the barricade Saint Merry, Jeanne, surrounded by insurgents asking for bread, answered: "What for? it is three o'clock. At four o'clock we shall be dead."

As they could eat nothing, Enjolras prohibited wine.

They found in the cellar some fifteen bottles of brandy, full and hermetically sealed. Enjolras and Combeferre examined them.

"It ought to be genuine," observed Bossuet. "It is lucky that Grantaire is asleep. If he were on his feet, we should have hard work to save those bottles." Enjolras, in spite of the murmurs, put his veto upon the bottles, and in order that no one should touch them, he had them placed under the table on which Father Mabeuf lay.

About two o'clock in the morning, they took a count. There were left thirty-seven of them.

Day was beginning to dawn. They had just extinguished the torch which had been replaced in its socket of paving-stones. The interior of the barricade, that little court taken in on the street, was drowned in darkness, and seemed, through the dim twilight horror, the deck of a disabled ship. The combatants going back and forth, moved about in it like black forms. Above this frightful nest of shadow, the stories of the mute houses were lividly outlined; at the very top the wan chimneys appeared. The sky had that charming undecided hue, which is perhaps white, and perhaps blue. Some birds were flying with joyful notes. The tall house which formed the rear of the barricade, being towards the east, had a rosy reflection upon its roof. At the window on the third story, the morning breeze played with the grey hairs on the dead man's head.

"I am delighted that the torch is extinguished," said Courfeyrac to Feuilly. "That torch, startled in the wind, annoyed me. It appeared to be afraid. The light of a torch resembles the wisdom of a coward; it is not clear, because it trembles."

Enjolras had gone to make a reconnaissance. He went out by the little Rue Mondétour, creeping along by the houses.

The insurgents, we must say, were full of hope. The manner in which they had repelled the attack during the night, had led them almost to contempt in advance for the attack at daybreak. They had no more doubt of their success than of their cause. Moreover, help was evidently about to come. They counted on it. With that facility for triumphant prophecy which is a part of the strength of the fighting Frenchman, they divided into three distinct phases the day which was opening: at six o'clock in the morning a regiment, "which had been laboured with," would come over. At noon, insurrection of all Paris; at sundown, revolution.

They heard the tocsin of Saint Merry, a proof that the other barricade, the great one, that of Jeanne, still held out.

All these hopes were communicated from one to another in a sort of cheerful yet terrible whisper, which resembled the buzz of a hive of bees at war.

Enjolras reappeared. He returned from his gloomy eagle's walk in the obscurity without. He listened for a moment to all this joy with folded arms, one hand over his mouth. Then, fresh and rosy in the growing whiteness of the morning, he said:

"The whole army of Paris fights. A third of that army is pressing upon the barricade in which you are. Besides the National Guard, I distinguished the shakos of the Fifth of the Line and the colours of the Sixth Legion. You will be attacked in an hour. As for the people, they were boiling yesterday, but this morning they do not stir. Nothing to expect, nothing to hope. No more from a Faubourg than from a regiment. You are abandoned."

These words fell upon the buzzing of the groups, and wrought the effect which the first drops of the tempest produce upon the swarm. All were dumb.

This moment was short.

A voice, from the most obscure depths of the groups, cried to Enjolras: "So be it. Let us make the barricade twenty feet high, and let us all stand by it. Citizens, let us offer the protest of corpses. Let us show that, if the people abandon the republicans, the republicans do not abandon the people."

These words relieved the minds of all from the painful cloud of personal anxieties. They were greeted by an enthusiastic acclamation.

The name of the man who thus spoke was never known; it was some obscure blouse-wearer, an unknown, a forgotten man, a passing hero, that great anonymous always found in human crises and in social births, who, at the proper instant, speaks the decisive word supremely, and who vanishes into the darkness after having for a moment represented, in the light of a flash, the people and God.

This inexorable resolution so filled the air of June 6, 1832, that, almost at the same hour, in the barricade of Saint Merry, the insurgents raised this shout which was proved on the trial, and which has become historical: "Let them come to our aid or let them not come, what matter? Let us die here to the last man."

As we see, the two barricades, although essentially isolated, communicated.

Enjolras resumed:

"The position is good, the barricade is fine. Thirty men are enough. Why sacrifice forty?"

They replied:

"Because nobody wants to go away."

"Citizens," cried Enjolras, and there was in his voice almost an angry tremor, "the republic is not rich enough in men to incur useless expenditures. Vainglory is a squandering. If it is the duty of some to go away, that duty should be performed as well as any other."

Enjolras, the man of principle, had over his co-religionists that sort of omnipotence which emanates from the absolute. Still, notwithstanding this omnipotence, there was a murmur.

Chief to his finger-ends, Enjolras, seeing that they murmured, insisted. He resumed haughtily:

"Let those who fear to be one of but thirty, say so."

The murmurs redoubled.

"Besides," observed a voice from one of the groups, "to go away is easily said. The barricade is hemmed in."

"Not towards the markets," said Enjolras. "The Rue Mondétour is open, and by the Rue des Prêcheurs one can reach the Marché des Innocents."

"And there," put in another voice from the group, "he will be taken.

He will fall upon some grand guard of the line or the banlieue. They will see a man going by in cap and blouse. 'Where do you come from, fellow? you belong to the barricade, don't you?' And they look at your hands. You smell of powder. Shot."

Enjolras, without answering, touched Combeferre's shoulder, and they both went into the basement room.

They came back a moment afterwards. Enjolras held out in his hands the four uniforms which he had reserved. Combeferre followed him, bringing the cross belts and shakos.

"With this uniform," said Enjolras, "you can mingle with the ranks and escape. Here are enough for four."

And he threw the four uniforms upon the unpaved ground.

No wavering in the stoical auditory. Combeferre spoke:

"Come," said he, "we must have a little pity. Do you know what the question is now? It is a question of women. Let us see. Are there any wives, yes or no? are there any children, yes or no? Ah! you wish to die, I wish it also, I, who am speaking to you, but I do not wish to feel the ghosts of women wringing their hands about me. Die, so be it, but do not make others die. Suicides like those which will be accomplished here are sublime; but suicide is strict, and can have no extension; and as soon as it touches those next you, the name of suicide is murder. The mortality of abandoned children is fifty-five per cent. I repeat it, it is a question of wives, it is a question of mothers. Do I speak to you for yourselves? We know very well that you are all brave, good heavens! we know very well that your souls are filled with joy and glory at giving your life for the great cause; we know very well that you feel that you are elected to die usefully and magnificently, and that each of you clings to his share of the triumph. Well and good. But you are not alone in this world. We must not be selfish."

All bowed their heads with a gloomy air.

Strange contradictions of the human heart in its most sublime moments! Combeferre, who spoke thus, was not an orphan. He remembered the mothers of others, and he forgot his own. He was going to be killed. He was "selfish."

Marius, fasting, feverish, successively driven from every hope, saturated with violent emotions and feeling the end approach, was sinking deeper and deeper into that visionary stupor which always precedes the fatal hour. Still there was one point in this scene which woke him. He had now but one idea, to die, and he would not be diverted from it; but he thought, in his funereal somnambulism, that while destroying oneself it is not forbidden to save another.

He raised his voice:

"Enjolras and Combeferre are right," said he; "no useless sacrifice. I add my voice to theirs, and we must hasten. Combeferre has given the criteria. There are among you some who have families, mothers, sisters, wives, children. Let those leave the ranks."

Nobody stirred.

"Married men and supports of families, out of the ranks!" repeated Marius.

His authority was great. Enjolras was indeed the chief of the barricade, but Marius was its saviour.

"I order it," cried Enjolras.

"I beseech you," said Marius.

Then, roused by the words of Combeferre, shaken by the order of Enjolras, moved by the prayer of Marius, those heroic men began to inform against each other. "That is true," said a young man to a middle-aged man. "You are the father of a family. Go away." "It is you rather," answered the man, "you have two sisters whom you support."

"Make haste," said Courfeyrac, "in a quarter of an hour it will be too late."

"Citizens," continued Enjolras, "this is the republic, and universal suffrage reigns. Designate yourselves those who ought to go."

They obeyed. In a few minutes five were unanimously designated and left the ranks.

There were only four uniforms.

"Well," resumed the five, "one must stay."

And the generous quarrel recommenced.

"You, you have a wife who loves you." "As for you, you have your old mother." "You have neither father nor mother, what will become of your three little brothers?" "You are the father of five children." "You have a right to live, you are seventeen, it is too soon."

These grand revolutionary barricades were rendezvous of heroisms. The improbable there was natural. These men were not astonished at each other.

"Be quick," repeated Courfeyrac.

Somebody cried out from the group, to Marius:

"Designate yourself, which must stay."

"Yes," said the five, "choose. We will obey you."

Marius, in a stupor, counted them; there were still five! Then his eyes fell upon the four uniforms.

At this moment a fifth uniform dropped, as if from heaven, upon the four others.

Marius raised his eyes and saw M. Fauchelevent.

Jean Valjean had just entered the barricade.

Whether by information obtained, or by instinct, or by chance, he came by the little Rue Mondétour. Thanks to his National Guard dress, he had passed easily.

The sentry placed by the insurgents in the Rue Mondétour, had not given the signal of alarm for a single National Guard. He permitted him to get into the street, saying to himself: "he is a reinforcement, probably, and at the very worst a prisoner."

At the moment Jean Valjean entered the redoubt, nobody had noticed him, all eyes being fixed upon the five chosen ones and upon the four uniforms. Jean Valjean saw and understood, and, silently, he stripped off his coat, and threw it upon the pile with the others.

"Who is this man?" asked Bossuet.

"He is," answered Combeferre, "a man who saves others."

Marius added in a grave voice:

"I know him."

This assurance was enough for all.

Enjolras turned towards Jean Valjean:

"Citizen, you are welcome."

And he added:

"You know that we are going to die."

Jean Valjean, without answering, helped the insurgent whom he saved to put on his uniform.

The situation of all, in this hour of death, found its resultant and summit in Enjolras.

Enjolras had within himself the plenitude of revolution; he had come to accept, as its definitive and magnificent evolution, the transformation of the great French Republic into the immense human republic. As to the immediate means, in a condition of violence, he wished them to be violent; in that he had not varied; and he was still of that epic and formidable school, which is summed up in this word: 'Ninety-three.

Enjolras was standing on the paving-stone steps, his elbow upon the muzzle of his carbine. He was thinking. Suddenly he raised his head, his fair hair waved backwards, and Enjolras exclaimed:

"Citizens, do you picture to yourselves the future? The streets of the cities flooded with light, green branches upon the thresholds, the nations sisters, men just, the old men blessing the children, the past loving the present, thinkers in full liberty, believers in full equality, for religion the heavens; God priest direct, human conscience become the altar, no more hatred, the fraternity of the workshop and the school, for reward and for penalty notoriety, to all, labour, for all, law, over all, peace, no more bloodshed, no more war, mothers happy! To subdue matter is the first step; to realise the ideal is the second. Reflect upon what progress has already done. Once the early human races looked with terror upon the hydra which blew upon the waters, the dragon which vomited fire, the griffin, monster of the air, which flew with the wings of an eagle and the claws of a tiger; fearful animals which were above man. Man, however, has laid his snares, the sacred snares of intelligence, and has at last caught the monsters. We have tamed the hydra, and he is called the steamer; we have tamed the dragon, and he is called the locomotive; we are on the point of taming the griffin, we have him already, and he is called the balloon. The day when this promethean work shall be finished, and when man shall have definitely harnessed to his will the triple chimera of the ancients, the hydra, the dragon, and the griffin, he will be the master of the water, the fire, and the air, and he will be to the rest of the animated creation what the ancient gods were formerly to him. Courage, and forward!

"Citizens, whither are we tending? To science made government, to the force of things, recognised as the only public force, to the natural law having its sanction and its penalty in itself and promulgated by its self-evidence, to a dawn of truth, corresponding with the dawn of the day. We are tending towards the union of the peoples; we are tending towards the unity of man. No more fictions; no more parasites. The real governed by the true, such is the aim. Civilisation will hold its courts on the summit of Europe, and later at the centre of the continents, in a grand parliament of intelligence.

"Friends, the hour in which we live, and in which I speak to you, is a gloomy hour, but of such is the terrible price of the future. A revolution is a toll-gate. Oh! the human race shall be delivered, uplifted, and consoled! We affirm it on this barricade. Whence shall arise the shout of love, if it be not from the summit of sacrifice? O my brothers, here is the place of junction between those who think and those who suffer; this barricade is made neither of paving-stones, nor of timbers, nor of iron; it is made of two mounds, a mound of ideas and a mound of sorrows. Brothers, he who dies here dies in the radiance of the future, and we are entering a grave illuminated by the dawn."

Enjolras broke off rather than ceased, his lips moved noiselessly, as if he were continuing to speak to himself.

Marius no longer saw the faces of the living save with the eyes of one dead. How came M. Fauchelevent there? Why was he there? What did he come to do? Marius put none of these questions. Besides, our despair having this peculiarity that it enwraps others as well as ourselves, it seemed logical to him that everybody should come to die.

Only he thought of Cosette with an oppression of the heart.

The five men designated went out of the barricade by the little Rue Mondétour; they resembled National Guards perfectly; one of them went away weeping. Before starting, they embraced those who remained.

When the five men sent away into life had gone, Enjolras thought of the one condemned to death. He went into the basement room. Javert, tied to to the pillar, was thinking.

"Do you need anything?" Enjolras asked him.

Javert answered:

"When shall you kill me?"

"Wait. We need all our cartridges at present."

"Then, give me a drink," said Javert.

Enjolras presented him with a glass of water himself, and, as Javert was bound, he helped him to drink.

"Is that all?" resumed Enjolras.

"I am uncomfortable at this post," answered Javert. "It was not affectionate to leave me to pass the night here. Tie me as you please, but you can surely lay me on a table. Like the other."

And with a motion of his head he indicated M. Mabeuf's body.

There was, it will be remembered, at the back of the room, a long wide table, upon which they had cast balls and made cartridges. All the cartridges being made and all the powder used up, this table was free.

At Enjolras' order, four insurgents untied Javert from the post. While they were untying him, a fifth held a bayonet to his breast. They left his hands tied behind his back, they put a small yet strong whipcord about his feet, which permitted him to take fifteen-inch steps like those who are mounting the scaffold, and they made him walk to the table at the back of the room, on which they extended him, tightly bound by the middle of his body.

For greater security, by means of a rope fixed to his neck, they added to the system of bonds which rendered all escape impossible, that species of ligature, called in the prisons a martingale, which, starting from the back of the neck, divides over the stomach, and is fastened to the hands after passing between the legs.

While they were binding Javert, a man, on the threshold of the door, gazed at him with singular attention. The shade which this man produced made Javert turn his head. He raised his eyes and recognised Jean Valjean. He did not even start, he haughtily dropped his eyelids, and merely said: "It is very natural."

It was growing light rapidly. But not a window was opened, not a door stood ajar; it was the dawn, not the hour of awakening.

The barricade was stronger than at the time of the first attack. Since the departure of the five, it had been raised still higher.

On the report of the sentry who had been observing the region of the markets, Enjolras, for fear of a surprise from the rear, formed an important resolution. He had barricaded the little passage of the Rue Mondétour, which till then had been open. For this purpose they unpaved the length of a few more houses. In this way, the barricade, walled in upon three streets, in front upon the Rue de la Chanvrerie, at the left upon the Rue du Cygne and la Petite Truanderie, at the right upon the Rue Mondétour, was really almost impregnable; it is true that they were fatally shut in. It had three fronts, but no longer an outlet. "A fortress, but mousetrap," said Courfeyrac with a laugh.

Enjolras had piled up near the door of the wine-shop some thirty paving-stones, "torn up uselessly," said Bossuet.

The silence was now so profound on the side from which the attack must come, that Enjolras made each man resume his post for combat.

A ration of brandy was distributed to all.

Nothing is more singular than a barricade which is preparing for an assault. Each man chooses his place, as at a play. They lean on their sides, their elbows, their shoulders. There are some who make themselves stalls with paving-stones. There is a corner of a wall which is annoying, they move away from it; here is a redan which may be a protection, they take shelter in it. The left-handed are precious; they take places which are inconvenient for the rest. Many make arrangements to fight sitting down. They wish to be at their ease in killing, and comfortable in dying.

As soon as Enjolras had taken his double-barrelled carbine, and placed himself on a kind of battlement which he had reserved, all were silent.

A little dry snapping sound was heard confusedly along the wall of paving-stones. They were cocking their muskets.

They had not long to wait. A rattle of chains, the menacing jolt of a mass, a clicking of brass bounding over the pavement, a sort of solemn uproar, announced that an ominous body of iron was approaching. There was a shudder in the midst of those peaceful old streets, cut through and built up for the fruitful circulation of interests and ideas, and not made for the monstrous rumbling of the wheels of war.

A piece of artillery appeared.

The gunners pushed forward the piece; it was all ready to be loaded; the forewheels had been removed; two supported the carriage, four were at the wheels, others followed with the caisson. The smoke of the burning match was seen.

"Fire!" cried Enjolras.

The whole barricade flashed fire, the explosion was terrible; an avalanche of smoke covered and effaced the gun and the men; in a few seconds the cloud dissipated, and the cannon and the men reappeared; those in charge of the piece placed it in position in front of the barricade, slowly, correctly, and without haste. Not a man had been touched. Then the gunner, bearing his weight on the breech, to elevate the range, began to point the cannon with the gravity of an astronomer adjusting a telescope.

"Bravo for the gunners!" cried Bossuet.

And the whole barricade clapped hands.

A moment afterwards, placed squarely in the very middle of the street, astride of the gutter, the gun was in battery. A formidable mouth was opened upon the barricade.

"Come, be lively!" said Courfeyrac. "There is the brute. After the fillip, the knock-down. The army stretches out its big paw to us. The barricade is going to be seriously shaken. The musketry feels, the artillery takes."

"It is a bronze eight-pounder, new model," added Combeferre. "Those pieces, however little they exceed the proportion of ten parts of tin to a hundred of copper, are liable to burst. Upon the whole, artillery, that despot, cannot do all it would; strength is a great weakness. A cannon ball makes only two thousand miles an hour; light makes two hundred thousand miles a second. Such is the superiority of Jesus Christ over Napoleon."

"Reload arms," said Enjolras.

How was the facing of the barricade going to behave under fire? would the shot make a breach? That was the question. While the insurgents were reloading their muskets, the gunners loaded the cannon.

The gun went off; the detonation burst upon them.

"Present!" cried a cheerful voice.

And at the same time with the ball, Gavroche tumbled into the barricade.

He came by way of the Rue du Cygne, and he had nimbly clambered over the minor barricade, which fronted upon the labyrinth of the Petite Truanderie.

Gavroche produced more effect in the barricade than the ball.

The ball lost itself in the jumble of the rubbish. At the very utmost it broke a wheel of the omnibus, and finished the old Anceau cart. Seeing which, the barricade began to laugh.

"Proceed," cried Bossuet to the gunners.

They surrounded Gavroche, but he had no time to tell anything. Marius took him aside.

"What have you come here for?"

"Hold on!" said the boy. "What have you come for?"

And he looked straight at Marius with his epic effrontery. His eyes grew large with the proud light which was in them.

Marius continued, in a stern tone:

"Who told you to come back? At least you carried my letter to its address?"

Gavroche had some little remorse in relation to that letter. In his haste to return to the barricade, he had got rid of it rather than delivered it. He was compelled to acknowledge to himself that he had intrusted it rather rashly to that stranger, whose face even he could not distinguish. True, this man was bareheaded, but that was not enough. On the whole, he had some little interior remonstrances on this subject, and he feared Marius' reproaches. He took, to get out of the trouble, the simplest course; he lied abominably.

"Citizen, I carried the letter to the porter. The lady was asleep. She will get the letter when she wakes up."

Marius, in sending this letter, had two objects: to say farewell to Cosette, and to save Gavroche. He was obliged to be content with the half of what he intended.

The sending of his letter, and the presence of M. Fauchelevent in the barricade, this coincidence occurred to his mind. He pointed out M. Fauchelevent to Gavroche.

"Do you know that man?"

"No," said Gavroche.

Gavroche, in fact, had only seen Jean Valjean in the night.

The troubled conjectures which had arisen in Marius' mind were dissipated. Did he know M. Fauchelevent's opinions? M. Fauchelevent was a republican, perhaps. Hence his very natural presence in this conflict.

Meanwhile Gavroche was already at the other end of the barricade, crying: "My musket!"

Courfeyrac ordered it to be given to him.

Gavroche warned his "comrades" as he called them, that the barricade was surrounded. He had had great difficulty in getting through. A battalion of the line, whose muskets were stacked in la Petite Truanderie, were observing the side on the Rue du Cygne; on the opposite side the municipal guard occupied the Rue des Prêcheurs. In front, they had the bulk of the army.

This information given, Gavroche added:

"I authorise you to give them a dose of pills."

Meanwhile Enjolras, on his battlement, was watching, listening with intense attention.

The assailants, dissatisfied doubtless with the effect of their fire, had not repeated it. A company of infantry of the line had come in and occupied the extremity of the street, in the rear of the gun. The soldiers tore up the pavement, and with the stones constructed a little low wall, a sort of breastwork, hardly more than eighteen inches high, which fronted the barricade.

Enjolras, on the watch, thought he distinguished the peculiar sound which is made when canisters of grape are taken from the caisson, and he saw the gunner change the aim and incline the piece slightly to the left. Then the cannoneers began to load. The gunner seized the linstock himself and brought it near the touch-hole.

"Heads down, keep close to the wall!" cried Enjolras, "and all on your knees along the barricade!"

The insurgents, who were scattered in front of the wine-shop, and who had left their posts of combat on Gavroche's arrival, rushed pell-mell towards the barricade; but before Enjolras' order was executed, the discharge took place with the fearful rattle of grape-shot. The charge was directed at the opening of the redoubt, it ricocheted upon the wall, and this terrible ricochet killed two men and wounded three.

If that continued, the barricade was no longer tenable. It was not proof against grape.

"Let us prevent the second shot, at any rate," said Enjolras.

And, lowering his carbine, he aimed at the gunner, who, at that moment, bending over the breech of the gun, was correcting and finally adjusting the aim.

This gunner was a fine-looking sergeant of artillery, quite young, of fair complexion, with a very mild face, and the intelligent air peculiar to that predestined and formidable arm which, by perfecting itself in horror, must end in killing war.

Combeferre, standing near Enjolras, looked at this young man.

"What a pity!" said Combeferre. "What a hideous thing these butcheries are! Come, when there are no more kings, there will be no more war. Enjolras, you are aiming at that sergeant, you are not looking at him. Just think that he is a charming young man; he is intrepid; you see that he is a thinker; these young artillery-men are well educated; he has a father, a mother, a family; he is in love, probably; he is at most twenty-five years old; he might be your brother."

"He is," said Enjolras.

"Yes," said Combeferre, "and mine also. Well, don't let us kill him."

"Let me alone. We must do what we must."

And Enjolras pressed the trigger. The flash leaped forth. The artillery-man turned twice round, his arms stretched out before him, and his head raised as if to drink the air, then he fell over on his side upon the gun, and lay there motionless. His back could be seen, from the centre of which a stream of blood gushed upwards. The ball had entered his breast and passed through his body. He was dead.

It was necessary to carry him away and to replace him. It was indeed some minutes gained.

There was confusion in the counsel of the barricade. The gun was about to be fired again. They could not hold out a quarter of an hour in that storm of grape.

Enjolras threw out his command:

"We must put a mattress there."

"We have none," said Combeferre, "the wounded are on them."

Jean Valjean, seated apart at the corner of the wine-shop, his musket between his knees, had, up to this moment, taken no part in what was going on. He seemed not to hear the combatants about him say: "There is a musket which is doing nothing."

At the order given by Enjolras, he got up.

It will be remembered that on the arrival of the company in the Rue de la Chanvrerie, an old woman, foreseeing bullets, had put her mattress before her window. This window, a garret window, was on the roof of a house of six stories standing a little outside of the barricade. The mattress, placed crosswise, rested at the bottom upon two clothes-poles, and was sustained above by two ropes which, in the distance, seemed like threads, and which were fastened to nails driven into the window casing. These two ropes could be seen distinctly against the sky like hairs.

"Can somebody lend me a double-barrelled carbine?" said Jean Valjean.

Enjolras, who had just reloaded his, handed it to him.

Jean Valjean aimed at the window and fired.

One of the two ropes of the mattress was cut.

The mattress now hung only by one thread.

Jean Valjean fired the second barrel. The second rope struck the glass of the window. The mattress slid down between the two poles and fell into the street.

The barricade applauded.

All cried:

"There is a mattress."

"Yes," said Combeferre, "but who will go after it?"

The mattress had, in fact, fallen outside of the barricade, between the besieged and the besiegers. Now, the death of the gunner having exasperated the troops, the soldiers opened fire on the barricade. The insurgents made no response to this musketry, to spare their ammunition. The fusillade was broken against the barricade; but the street, which it filled with balls, was terrible.

Jean Valjean went out at the opening, entered the street, passed through the storm of balls, went to the mattress, picked it up, put it on his back, and returned to the barricade.

He put the mattress into the opening himself. He fixed it against the wall in such a way that the artillerymen did not see it.

This done, they awaited the charge of grape.

They had not long to wait.

The cannon vomited its package of shot with a roar. But there was no ricochet. The grape miscarried upon the mattress. The desired effect was obtained. The barricade was preserved.

"Citizen," said Enjolras to Jean Valjean, "the republic thanks you."

Bossuet admired and laughed. He exclaimed:

"It is immoral that a mattress should have so much power. Triumph of that which yields over that which thunders. But it is all the same; glory to the mattress which nullifies a cannon."

At that moment Cosette awoke.

Cosette had slept few hours, but well. Somebody who was Marius had appeared to her surrounded by a halo. She awoke with the sun in her eyes, which at first produced the effect of a continuation of her dream.

Her first emotion, on coming out of this dream, was joyous. Then came an oppression of the heart. Here were three days now that she had not seen Marius. But she said to herself that he must have received her letter, that he knew where she was, and that he had so much tact, that he would find means to reach her.

Cosette could not succeed in recalling what Marius had said to her on the subject of this absence which was to last but one day, or what explanation he had given her about it. She said to herself that it was very naughty of her and very wicked to have forgotten words uttered by Marius.

Cosette dressed herself very quickly, combed and arranged her hair, which was a very simple thing at that time, when women did not puff out their ringlets and plaits with cushions and rolls, and did not put crinoline in their hair. Then she opened the window and looked all about, hoping to discover something of the street, a corner of a house, a patch of pavement, and to be able to watch for Marius there. But she could see nothing. The backyard was surrounded with high walls, and a few gardens only were in view. Cosette pronounced these gardens hideous; for the first time in her life she found flowers ugly. The least bit of a street gutter would have been more to her mind. She finally began to look at the sky, as if she thought that Marius might come that way also.

Everybody was still in bed in the house. A rural silence reigned. No shutter had been opened. The porter's box was closed. Toussaint was not up, and Cosette very naturally thought that her father was asleep. She must have suffered indeed, and she must have been still suffering, for she said to herself that her father had been unkind; but she counted on Marius. At intervals she heard at some distance a kind of sullen jar, and she said: "It is singular that people are opening and shutting porte-cochères so early." It was the cannon battering the barricade.

THE fire of the assailants continued. The musketry and the grape alternated, without much damage indeed. The top of the façade of Corinth alone suffered; the window of the first story and the dormer windows on the roof, riddled with shot and ball, were slowly demolished. The combatants who were posted there, had to withdraw. Besides, this is the art of attacking barricades; to tease for a long time, in order to exhaust the ammunition of the insurgents, if they commit the blunder of replying. When it is perceived, from the slackening of their fire, that they have no longer either balls or powder, the assault is made. Enjolras did not fall into this snare; the barricade did not reply.

At each platoon fire, Gavroche thrust out his cheek with his tongue, a mark of lofty disdain:

"That's right," said he, "tear up the cloth. We want lint."

Courfeyrac jested with the grape about its lack of effect, and said to the cannon:

"You are getting diffuse, my goodman."

In a battle people force themselves upon acquaintance, as at a ball. It is probable that this silence of the redoubt began to perplex the besiegers, and make them fear some unlooked-for accident, and that they felt the need of seeing through that heap of paving-stones, and knowing what was going on behind that impassable wall, which was receiving their fire without answering it. The insurgents suddenly perceived a casque shining in the sun upon a neighbouring roof. A sapper was backed up against a tall chimney, and seemed to be there as a sentinel. He looked directly into the barricade.

"There is a troublesome overseer," said Enjolras.

Jean Valjean had returned his carbine to Enjolras, but he had his musket.

Without saying a word, he aimed at the sapper, and, a second afterwards, the casque, struck by a ball, fell noisily into the street. The startled soldier hastened to disappear.

A second observer took his place. This was an officer. Jean Valjean, who had reloaded his musket, aimed at the new comer, and sent the officer's casque to keep company with the soldier's. The officer was not obstinate, and withdrew very quickly. This time the warning was understood. Nobody appeared upon the roof again, and they gave up watching the barricade.

"Why didn't you kill the man?" asked Bossuet of Jean Valjean.

Jean Valjean did not answer.

Bossuet murmured in Combeferre's ear:

"He has not answered my question."

"He is a man who does kindness by musket shots," said Combeferre.

Those who retain some recollection of that now distant period, know that the National Guard was valiant against the insurrections. It was particularly eager and intrepid in the days of June, 1832. Many a good wineshopkeeper became leonine on seeing his dancing-hall deserted, and died to preserve order represented by the tavern. In those days, at once bourgeois and heroic, in presence of ideas which had their knights, interests had their paladins. The prosaic motive detracted nothing from the bravery of the action. The decrease of a pile of crowns made bankers sing the Marseillaise. They poured out their blood lyrically for the counter; and with enthusiasm they defended the shop, that immense diminutive of one's native land.

Civilisation, unfortunately represented at that epoch rather by an aggregation of interests than by a group of principles, was, or thought itself in peril; it raised the cry of alarm; every man making himself a centre, defended it, aided it, and protected it, in his own way; and anybody and everybody took it upon himself to save society.

Zeal sometimes goes to the extent of extermination. Such a platoon of National Guards constituted themselves, of their own private authority, a court-martial, and condemned and executed an insurgent prisoner in five minutes. Ferocious Lynch law, with which no party has the right to reproach others, for it is applied by the republic in America as well as by monarchy in Europe. This Lynch law is liable to mistakes.

The sun rose above the horizon.

An insurgent called to Enjolras:

"We are hungry here. Are we really going to die like this without eating?"

Enjolras, still leaning upon his battlement, without taking his eyes off the extremity of the street, nodded his head.

Courfeyrac, seated on a paving-stone beside Enjolras, continued his insults to the cannon, and every time that that gloomy cloud of projectiles which is known by the name of grape passed by, with its monstrous sound, he received it with an outburst of irony.

"You are tiring your lungs, my poor old brute, you trouble me, you are wasting your racket. That is not thunder; no, it is a cough."

And those about him laughed.

Bossuet was laughing still when Courfeyrac exclaimed:

"Something new!"

And, assuming the manner of an usher announcing an arrival, he added: "My name is Eight-Pounder."

In fact, a new personage had just entered upon the scene. It was a second piece of ordnance.

The artilleryman quickly executed the manœuvres, and placed this second piece in battery near the first.

A few moments afterwards, the two pieces, rapidly served, opened directly upon the redoubt; the platoon firing of the line supported the artillery.

Another cannonade was heard at some distance. At the same time that two cannon were raging against the redoubt in the Rue de la Chanvrerie, two other pieces of ordnance, pointed, one on the Rue Saint Denis, the other on the Rue Aubry le Boucher, were riddling the barricade St. Merry. The four cannon made dreary echo to one another.

Of the two pieces which were now battering the barricade in the Rue de la Chanvrerie, one fired grape, the other ball. The gun which threw balls was elevated a little, and the range was calculated so that the ball struck the extreme edge of the upper ridge of the barricade, dismantled it, and crumbled the paving-stones over the insurgents in showers. This peculiar aim announced the assault.

"We must at all events diminish the inconvenience of those pieces," said Enjolras, and he cried: "fire upon the cannoneers!"

The barricade, which had been silent for a long time, opened fire desperately; the street was filled with a blinding smoke, and after a few minutes, through this haze pierced by flame, they could confusedly make out two thirds of the cannoneers lying under the wheels of the guns. Those who remained standing continued to serve the pieces with rigid composure, but the fire was slackened.

"This goes well," said Bossuet to Enjolras. "Success."

Enjolras shook his head and answered:

"A quarter of an hour more of this success, and there will not be ten cartridges in the barricade."

It would seem that Gavroche heard this remark.

Courfeyrac suddenly perceived somebody at the foot of the barricade, outside in the street, under the balls.

Gavroche had taken a basket from the wine-shop, had gone out by the opening, and was quietly occupied in emptying into his basket the full cartridge-boxes of the National Guards who had been killed on the slope of the redoubt.

"What are you doing there?" said Courfeyrac.

Gavroche cocked up his nose.

"Citizen, I am filling my basket."

"Why, don't you see the grape?"

Gavroche answered:

"Well, it rains. What then?"

Courfeyrac cried:

"Come back!"

"Directly," said Gavroche.

And with a bound, he sprang into the street.

Some twenty dead lay scattered along the whole length of the street on the pavement. Twenty cartridge-boxes for Gavroche, a supply of cartridges for the barricade.

The smoke in the street was like a fog. Whoever has seen a cloud fall into a mountain gorge between two steep slopes can imagine this smoke crowded and thickened by two gloomy lines of tall houses. It rose slowly and was constantly renewed; hence the combatants could hardly perceive each other from end to end of the street, although it was very short.

This obscurity, calculated upon by the leaders who were to direct the assault upon the barricade, was of use to Gavroche. Under the folds of this veil of smoke, and thanks to his small size, he could advance far into the street without being seen. He emptied the first seven or eight cartridge-boxes without much danger.

He crawled on his belly, ran on his hands and feet, took his basket in his teeth, twisted, glided, writhed, wormed his way from one body to another, and emptied a cartridge-box as a monkey opens a nut.

From the barricade, of which he was still within hearing, they dared not call to him to return, for fear of attracting attention to him.

On one corpse, that of a corporal, he found a powder-flask.

"In case of thirst," said he as he put it into his pocket.

By successive advances, he reached a point where the fog from the firing became transparent. The sharp-shooters of the line drawn up and on the alert behind their wall of paving-stones, and the sharp-shooters of the banlieue massed at the corner of the street, suddenly discovered something moving in the smoke.

Just as Gavroche was relieving a sergeant who lay near a stone-block of his cartridges, a ball struck the body.

"The deuce!" said Gavroche. "So they are killing my dead for me."

A second ball splintered the pavement beside him. A third upset his basket.

Gavroche rose up straight, on his feet, his hair in the wind, his hands upon his hips, his eye fixed upon the National Guards who were firing, and he sang:

> *On est laid à Nanterre,*
> *C'est la faute à Voltaire,*
> *Et bête à Palaiseau,*
> *C'est la faute à Rousseau.*

Then he picked up his basket, put into it the cartridges which had fallen out, without losing a single one, and, advancing towards the fusillade, began to empty another cartridge-box. There a fourth ball just missed him again. Gavroche sang:

> *Je ne suis pas notaire,*
> *C'est la faute à Voltaire;*
> *Je suis petit oiseau,*
> *C'est la faute à Rousseau.*

A fifth ball succeeded only in drawing a third couplet from him.

> *Joie est mon caractère,*
> *C'est la faute à Voltaire;*
> *Misère est mon trousseau,*
> *C'est la faute à Rousseau.*

This continued thus for some time. Gavroche, fired at, mocked the firing. He appeared to be very much amused. It was the sparrow pecking at the hunters. He replied to each discharge by a couplet. They aimed at him incessantly, they always missed him. The National Guards and the soldiers laughed as they aimed at him. He lay down, then rose up, hid himself in a doorway, then sprang out, disappeared, reappeared, escaped, returned, retorted upon the volleys by wry faces, and meanwhile pillaged cartridges, emptied cartridge-boxes, and filled his basket. The insurgents, breathless with anxiety, followed him with their eyes. The barricade was trembling; he was singing. It was not a child; it was not a man; it was a strange fairy *gamin*. The bullets ran after him, he was more nimble than they. He was playing an indescribably terrible game of hide-and-seek with death; every time the flat-nosed face of the spectre approached, the *gamin* snapped his fingers.

One bullet, however, better aimed or more treacherous than the others, reached the Will-o'-the-wisp child. They saw Gavroche totter, then he fell. The whole barricade gave a cry; but for the *gamin* to touch the pavement is like the giant touching the earth; Gavroche had fallen only to rise again; he sat up, a long stream of blood rolled down his face, he raised both arms in air, looked in the direction whence the shot came, and began to sing:

> *Je suis tombé par terre,*
> *C'est la faute à Voltaire,*
> *La nez dans le ruisseau,*
> *C'est la faute à ——*

He did not finish. A second ball from the same marksman cut him short. This time he fell with his face upon the pavement, and did not stir again.

THERE were at that very moment in the garden of the Luxembourg—for the eye of the drama should be everywhere present—two children holding each other by the hand. One might have been seven years old, the other five. Having been soaked in the rain, they were walking in the paths on the sunny side; the elder was leading the little one; they were pale and in rags; they looked like wild birds. The smaller said: "I want something to eat."

The elder, already something of a protector, led his brother with his left hand and had a stick in his right hand.

They were alone in the garden. The garden was empty, the gates being closed by order of the police on account of the insurrection.

How came these children there? Had they escaped from some half-open guard-house; was there in the neighbourhood, at the Barrière d'Enfer, or on the esplanade of the Observatoire, some mountebank's tent from which they had fled; had they perchance, the evening before, evaded the eye of the garden-keepers at the hour of closing? The fact is, that they were wandering, and that they seemed free. To be wandering and to seem free is to be lost.

These two children were the same about whom Gavroche had been in trouble. These creatures belonged henceforth to the statistics of "abandoned children," whom the police report, collect, scatter, and find again on the streets of Paris.

If the officers had noticed them, they would have driven away these rags. Poor children cannot enter the public gardens; still one would think that, as children, they had a right in the flowers.

These were there, thanks to the closed gates. They were in violation of the rules. They had slipped into the garden, and they had stayed there. Closed gates do not dismiss the keepers, the oversight is supposed to continue, but it is relaxed and at its ease; and the keepers, also excited by the public anxiety and busier with matters without than within, no longer paid attention to the garden, and had not seen the two delinquents.

It had rained the night before, and even a little that morning. But in June showers are of no account. Nothing is so admirable as a verdure washed by the rain and wiped by the sunbeam; it is warm freshness. The gardens and the meadows, having water at their roots and sunshine in their flowers, become vases of incense, and exhale all their perfumes at once.

On the 6th June, 1832, towards eleven o'clock in the morning, the Luxembourg, solitary and unpeopled, was delightful. The parterres projected themselves into the light. The branches, wild with the noonday brilliance, seemed seeking to embrace each other. There was in the sycamores a chattering of linnets, the sparrows were jubilant, the woodpeckers climbed up the horse-chestnuts, tapping with their beaks the wrinkles in the bark. The flower beds accepted the legitimate royalty of the lilies; the most august of perfumes is that which comes from whiteness. You inhaled the spicy odour of the pinks. The old rooks of Marie de' Medici were amorous in the great trees. The sun gilded, empurpled, and kindled the tulips, which are nothing more nor less than all varieties of flame made flowers. All about the tulip beds whirled the bees, sparks from these flame-flowers. All was grace and gaiety, even the coming rain; that old offender, by whom the honeysuckles and the lilies of the valley would profit, produced no disquiet; the swallows flew low, charming menace. He who was there breathed happiness; life was sweet; all this nature exhaled candour, help, assistance, paternity, caress, dawn.

The statues under the trees, bare and white, had robes of shade torn by light; these goddesses were all tattered by the sunshine; it hung from them in shreds on all sides. Around the great basin, the earth was already so dry as to be almost baked.

The two little abandoned creatures were near the great basin, and, slightly disturbed by all this light, they endeavoured to hide, an instinct of the poor and feeble before magnificence, even impersonal, and they kept behind the shelter for the swans.

Here and there, at intervals, when the wind fell, they confusedly heard cries, a hum, a kind of tumultuous rattle, which was the musketry, and sullen jars, which were reports of cannon. There was smoke above the roofs in the direction of the markets. A bell, which appeared to be calling, sounded in the distance.

These children did not seem to notice these sounds. The smaller one repeated from time to time in an undertone: "I want something to eat."

Almost at the same time with the two children, another couple approached the great basin. This was a goodman of fifty, who was leading by the hand a goodman of six. Doubtless a father with his son. The goodman of six had a big bun in his hand.

At that period, certain adjoining houses, in the Rue Madame and the Rue d'Enfer, had keys to the Luxembourg which the occupants used when the gates were closed, a favour since suppressed. This father and this son probably came from one of those houses.

The two poor little fellows saw "this Monsieur" coming, and hid themselves a little more closely.

The father and son stopped near the basin in which the two swans were sporting. This bourgeois appeared to have a special admiration for the swans. He resembled them in this respect, that he walked like them.

For the moment, the swans were swimming, which is their principal talent, and they were superb.

If the two poor little fellows had listened, and had been of an age to understand, they might have gathered up the words of a grave man. The father said to the son:

"The sage lives content with little. Behold me, my son. I do not love pomp. Never am I seen with coats bedizened with gold and gems; I leave this false splendour to badly organised minds."

Here the deep sounds, which came from the direction of the markets, broke out with a redoubling of bell and of uproar.

"What is that?" inquired the child.

The father answered:

"There is the beginning."

Just then he noticed the two little ragged fellows standing motionless behind the green cottage of the swans.

And after a moment, he added:

"Anarchy is entering this garden."

Meanwhile the son bit the bun, spit it out, and suddenly began to cry.

"What are you crying for?" asked the father.

"I am not hungry any more," said the child.

The father's smile grew broad.

"You don't need to be hungry, to eat a cake."

"I am sick of my cake. It is stale."

"You don't want any more of it?"

"No."

"Throw it to those swans."

The child hesitated. Not to want any more of one's cake, is no reason for giving it away.

The father continued:

"Be humane. We must take pity on the animals."

And, taking the cake from his son, he threw it into the basin.

The cake fell near the edge.

The swans were at a distance, in the centre of the basin, and busy with some prey. They saw neither the bourgeois nor the bun.

The bourgeois, feeling that the cake was in danger of being lost, and aroused by this useless shipwreck, devoted himself to a telegraphic agitation which finally attracted the attention of the swans.

They perceived something floating, veered about like the ships they are, and directed themselves slowly towards the bun.

Just then the distant tumult in the city suddenly increased again. This time it was ominous. There are some gusts of wind that speak more distinctly than others. That which blew at that moment brought clearly the rolls of drums, shouts, platoon firing, and the dismal replies of the tocsin and the cannon. This was coincident with a black cloud which abruptly shut out the sun.

The swans had not yet reached the bun.

"Come home," said the father, "they are attacking the Tuileries."

He seized his son's hand again. Then he continued:

"From the Tuileries to the Luxembourg, there is only the distance which separates royalty from the peerage; it is not far. It is going to rain musket-balls."

He looked at the cloud.

"And perhaps also the rain itself is going to rain; the heavens are joining in. Come home, quick."

"I should like to see the swans eat the bun," said the child.

The father answered:

"That would be an imprudence."

And he led away his little bourgeois.

Meanwhile, at the same time with the swans, the two little wanderers had approached the bun. It was floating on the water. The smaller was looking at the cake, the larger was looking at the father and son. As soon as they were out of sight, the elder quickly lay down with his face over the rounded edge of the basin, and, holding by it with his left hand, hanging over the water, almost falling in, with his right hand reached his stick towards the cake. The swans, seeing the enemy, made haste, and in making haste produced an effect with their breasts which was useful to the little fisher; the water flowed back before the swans, and one of those smooth concentric waves pushed the bun gently towards the child's stick. As the swans came up, the stick touched the cake. The child made a quick movement, drew in the bun, frightened the swans, seized the cake, and got up. The cake was soaked; but they were hungry and thirsty. The eldest broke the bun into two pieces, one large and one small, took the small one for himself, gave the large one to his little brother, and said to him:

"*Stick that in your gun.*"

MARIUS had sprung out of the barricade. Combeferre had followed him. But it was too late. Gavroche was dead. Combeferre brought back the basket of cartridges; Marius brought back the child.

"Alas!" thought he. What the father had done for his father he was returning to the son; only Thénardier had brought back his father living, while he brought back the child dead.

When Marius re-entered the redoubt with Gavroche in his arms, his face, like the child's, was covered with blood.

Just as he had stooped down to pick up Gavroche, a ball grazed his skull; he did not perceive it.

Courfeyrac took off his cravat and bound up Marius' forehead.

They laid Gavroche on the same table with Mabeuf, and they stretched the black shawl over the two bodies. It was large enough for the old man and the child.

Combeferre distributed the cartridges from the basket which he had brought back. This gave each man fifteen shots.

Jean Valjean was still at the same place, motionless upon his block. When Combeferre presented him his fifteen cartridges, he shook his head.

"There is a rare eccentric," said Combeferre in a low tone to Enjolras. "He finds means not to fight in this barricade."

"Which does not prevent him from defending it," answered Enjolras.

A notable fact, the fire which was battering the barricade hardly disturbed the interior. Those who have never passed through the whirlwind of this kind of war can have no idea of the singular moments of tranquillity which are mingled with these convulsions. Men come and go, they chat, they joke, they lounge. Combeferre was dressing the wounded; Bossuet and Feuilly were making cartridges with the flask of powder taken by Gavroche from the dead corporal. Bossuet said to Feuilly: *We shall soon take the diligence for another planet.* Courfeyrac, upon the few paving-stones which he had reserved for himself near Enjolras, was disposing and arranging a whole arsenal, his sword-cane, his musket, two horse-pistols, and a pocket pistol.

Suddenly between two discharges they heard the distant sound of a clock striking.

"It is noon," said Combeferre.

The twelve strokes had not sounded when Enjolras sprang to his feet, and flung down from the top of the barricade this thundering shout:

"Carry some paving-stones into the house. Fortify the windows with them. Half the men to the muskets, the other half to the stones. Not a minute to lose."

A platoon of sappers, their axes on their shoulders, had just appeared in order of battle at the end of the street.

This could only be the head of a column of attack. The sappers, whose duty it is to demolish the barricade, must always precede the soldiers whose duty it is to scale it.

Enjolras' order was executed with the correct haste peculiar to ships and barricades, the only places of combat whence escape is impossible. In less than a minute, two-thirds of the paving-stones which Enjolras had had piled up at the door of Corinth were carried up to the first story and to the garret; and before a second minute had elapsed, these stones, artistically laid one upon another, walled up half the height of the window on the first story and the dormer windows of the attic. A few openings, carefully arranged by Feuilly, chief builder, allowed musket barrels to pass through. This armament of the windows could be performed the more easily since the grape had ceased. The two pieces were now firing balls upon the centre of the wall, in order to make a hole, and if it were possible, a breach for the assault.

When the paving-stones, destined for the last defence, were in position, Enjolras had them carry up to the first story the bottles which he had placed under the table where Mabeuf was.

"Who will drink that?" Bossuet asked him.

"They," answered Enjolras.

Then they barricaded the basement window, and they held in readiness the iron cross-pieces which served to bar the door of the wine-shop on the inside at night.

The fortress was complete. The barricade was the rampart, the wine-shop was the donjon.

With the paving-stones which remained, they closed up the opening beside the barricade.

As the defenders of a barricade are always obliged to husband their ammunition, and as the besiegers know it, the besiegers perfect their arrangements with a sort of provoking leisure, expose themselves to fire before the time, but in appearance more than in reality, and take their ease. The preparations for attack are always made with a certain methodical slowness, after which, the thunderbolt.

This slowness allowed Enjolras to look over the whole, and to perfect the whole. He felt that since such men were to die, their death should be a masterpiece.

He said to Marius: "We are the two chiefs; I will give the last orders within. You stay outside and watch."

Marius posted himself for observation upon the crest of the barricade.

Enjolras had the door of the kitchen, which, we remember, was the hospital, nailed up.

"No spattering on the wounded," said he.

He gave his last instructions in the basement-room in a quick, but deep and calm voice; Feuilly listened, and answered in the name of all.

"First story, hold your axes ready to cut the staircase. Have you them?"

"Yes," said Feuilly.

"How many?"

"Two axes and a pole-axe."

"Very well. There are twenty-six effective men left. How many muskets are there?"

"Thirty-four."

"Eight too many. Keep these eight muskets loaded like the rest, and at hand. Swords and pistols in your belts. Twenty men to the barricade. Six in ambush at the dormer windows and at the window on the first story to fire upon the assailants through the loopholes in the paving-stones. Let there be no useless labourer here. Immediately, when the drum beats the charge, let the twenty from below rush to the barricade. The first there will get the best places."

These dispositions made, he turned towards Javert, and said to him:
"I won't forget you."

And, laying a pistol on the table, he added:

"The last man to leave this room will blow out the spy's brains!"

"Here?" inquired a voice.

"No, do not leave this corpse with ours. You can climb over the little barricade on the Rue Mondétour. It is only four feet high. The man is well tied. You will take him there, and execute him there."

There was one man, at that moment, who was more impassible than Enjolras; it was Javert.

Here Jean Valjean appeared.

He was in the throng of insurgents. He stepped forward, and said to Enjolras:

"You are the commander?"

"Yes."

"You thanked me just now."

"In the name of the republic. The barricade has two saviours, Marius Pontmercy and you."

"Do you think that I deserve a reward?"

"Certainly."

"Well, I ask one."

"What?"

"To blow out that man's brains myself."

Javert raised his head, saw Jean Valjean, made an imperceptible movement, and said:

"That is appropriate."

As for Enjolras, he had begun to reload his carbine; he cast his eyes about him:

"No objection."

And turning towards Jean Valjean: "Take the spy."

Jean Valjean, in fact, took possession of Javert by sitting down on the end of the table. He caught up the pistol, and a slight click announced that he had cocked it.

Almost at the same moment, they heard a flourish of trumpets.

"Come on!" cried Marius, from the top of the barricade.

Javert began to laugh with that noiseless laugh which was peculiar to him, and, looking fixedly upon the insurgents, said to them:

"Your health is hardly better than mine."

"All outside?" cried Enjolras.

The insurgents sprang forward in a tumult, and, as they went out, they received this speech from Javert:

"Farewell till immediately!"

When Jean Valjean was alone with Javert, he untied the rope that held the prisoner by the middle of the body, the knot of which was under the table. Then he motioned to him to get up.

Javert obeyed, with that undefinable smile into which the supremacy of enchained authority is condensed.

Jean Valjean took Javert by the martingale as you would take a beast of burden by a strap, and, drawing him after him, went out of the wine-shop slowly, for Javert, with his legs fettered, could take only very short steps. Jean Valjean had the pistol in his hand.

They crossed thus the interior trapezium of the barricade. The insurgents, intent upon the imminent attack, were looking the other way. Marius, alone, placed towards the left extremity of the wall, saw them pass.

Jean Valjean, with some difficulty, bound as Javert was, but without letting go of him for a single instant, made him scale the little intrenchment on the Rue Mondétour.

When they had climbed over this wall, they found themselves alone in the little street. Nobody saw them now. The corner of the house hid them from insurgents. The corpses carried out from the barricades made a terrible mound a few steps off.

They distinguished in a heap of dead a face, a flowing head of hair, a wounded hand, and a woman's breast half naked. It was Éponine.

Javert looked aside at this dead body, and, perfectly calm, said in an undertone:

"It seems to me that I know that girl."

Then he turned towards Jean Valjean.

Jean Valjean put the pistol under his arm, and fixed upon Javert a look which had no need of words to say: "Javert, it is I."

Javert answered:

"Take your revenge."

Jean Valjean took a knife out of his pocket, and opened it.

"You are right. That suits you better," exclaimed Javert.

Jean Valjean cut the martingale which Javert had about his neck, then he cut the ropes which he had on his wrists, then, stooping down, he cut the cord which he had on his feet; and, rising, he said to him:

"You are free."

Javert was not easily astonished. Still, complete master as he was of himself, he could not escape an emotion. He stood aghast and motionless.

Jean Valjean continued:

"I don't expect to leave this place. Still, if by chance I should, I live, under the name of Fauchelevent, in the Rue de l'Homme Armé, Number Seven."

Javert had the scowl of a tiger half opening the corner of his mouth, and he muttered between his teeth:

"Take care."

"Go," said Jean Valjean.

Javert resumed:

"You said Fauchelevent, Rue de l'Homme Armé?"

"Number Seven."

Javert repeated in an undertone: "Number Seven." He buttoned his coat, restored the military stiffness between his shoulders, turned half round, folded his arms, supporting his chin with one hand, and walked off in the direction of the markets. Jean Valjean followed him with his eyes. After a few steps, Javert turned back, and cried to Jean Valjean:

"You annoy me. Kill me rather."

Javert did not notice that his tone was more respectful.

"Go away," said Jean Valjean.

Javert receded with slow steps. A moment afterwards, he turned the corner of the Rue des Prêcheurs.

When Javert was gone, Jean Valjean fired the pistol in the air.

Then he re-entered the barricade and said: "It is done."

Meanwhile Marius, busy rather with the street than the wine-shop, had not until then looked attentively at the spy who was bound in the dusky rear of the basement-room.

When he saw him in broad day clambering over the barricade on his way to die, he recognised him. A sudden reminiscence came into his mind. He remembered the inspector of the Rue de Pontoise, and the two pistols which he had handed him and which he had used, he, Marius, in this very barricade. Not only did he recollect the face, but he recalled the name.

This reminiscence, however, was a question: "Is not this that inspector of police who told me his name was Javert?"

Perhaps there was still time to interfere for this man? But he must first know if it were indeed that Javert.

Marius called to Enjolras, who had just taken his place at the other end of the barricade.

"Enjolras!"

"What?"

"What is that man's name?"

"Who?"

"The police officer. Do you know his name?"

"Of course. He told us."

"What is his name?"

"Javert."

Marius sprang up.

At that moment they heard the pistol-shot.

Jean Valjean reappeared and cried: "It is done."

A chill passed through the heart of Marius.

THE death-agony of the barricade was approaching.

For, since evening, the two rows of houses in the Rue de la Chanvrerie had become two walls; savage walls. Doors closed, windows closed, shutters closed.

A people cannot be surprised into a more rapid progress than it wills. Woe to him who attempts to force its hand! Then it abandons the insurrection to itself. The insurgents become pestiferous. A house is an escarpment, a door is a refusal, a façade is a wall. This wall sees, hears, and will not. It might open and save you. No. This wall is a judge. It looks upon you and condemns you. How gloomy are these closed houses! In the interior of this rock, people go and come, they lie down, they get up; they are at home there; they drink and eat; they are afraid there, a fearful thing! Fear excuses this terrible inhospitality.

Sometimes even, and this has been seen, fear becomes passion; fright may change into fury, as prudence into rage; hence this saying so profound: *The madmen of moderation.* There are flamings of supreme dismay from which rage springs like a dismal smoke. "What do these people want? They are never contented. They compromise peaceable men as if we had not had revolution enough like this! What do they come here for? Let them get out of it themselves. So much the worse for them. It is their own fault. They have only got what they deserve. It doesn't concern us. Here is our poor street riddled with balls. They are a parcel of scamps. Above all, don't open the door." And the house puts on the semblance of a tomb. The insurgent before that door is in his last agony; he sees the grape and the drawn sabres coming; if he calls, he knows that they hear him, but that they will not come.

Whom shall he accuse?

Nobody, and everybody. The imperfect age in which we live.

But is it ingratitude?

Yes, from the point of view of the race. No, from the point of view of the individual.

Progress is the mode of man. The general life of the human race is called Progress; the collective advance of the human race is called Progress. Progress marches; it makes the great human and terrestrial journey towards the celestial and the divine; it has its halts where it rallies the belated flock; it has its stations where it meditates, in sight of some splendid Canaan suddenly unveiling its horizon; it has its nights when it sleeps; and it is one of the bitter anxieties of the thinker to see the shadow upon the human soul, and to feel in the darkness progress asleep, without being able to waken it.

"*God is dead perhaps*," said one.

He who despairs is wrong. Progress infallibly awakens, and, in short, we might say that it advances even in sleep, for it has grown. When we see it standing again, we find it taller.

To be always peaceful belongs to progress no more than to the river; the obstacle makes water foam and humanity seethe. Hence troubles; but after these troubles, we recognise that there has been some ground gained. Until order, which is nothing more nor less than universal peace, be established, until harmony and unity reign, progress will have revolutions for stations.

Suddenly the drum beat the charge.

In the evening, in the obscurity, the barricade had been approached silently. Now, in broad day, in this open street, surprise was entirely impossible; the strong hand, moreover, was unmasked, the cannon had commenced the roar, the army rushed upon the barricade. Fury was now skill.

A powerful column of infantry of the line, intersected at equal intervals by National Guards and Municipal Guards on foot, and supported by deep masses heard but unseen, turned into the street at a quick step, drums beating, trumpets sounding, bayonets fixed, sappers at their head, and, unswerving under the projectiles, came straight upon the barricade with the weight of a bronze column upon a wall.

The wall held well.

The insurgents fired impetuously. The assault was so sudden that for a moment the barricade was overflowed by assailants; but it shook off the soldiers as the lion does the dogs, and it was covered with besiegers only as a cliff is with foam, to reappear, a moment afterwards, steep, black, and formidable.

The column, compelled to fall back, remained massed in the street, unsheltered, but terrible, and replied to the redoubt by a fearful fusillade. The street was covered with dead.

Enjolras was at one end of the barricade, and Marius at the other. Enjolras, who carried the whole barricade in his head, reserved and sheltered himself; three soldiers fell one after the other under his battlement, without even having perceived him; Marius fought without shelter. He took no aim. He stood with more than half his body above the summit of the redoubt. There is no man more fearful in action than a dreamer. Marius was in the battle as in a dream.

The cartridges of the besieged were becoming exhausted; not so their sarcasms.

"Does anybody understand these men," exclaimed Feuilly bitterly (and he cited the names, well-known names, famous even, some of the old army), "who promised to join us, and took an oath to help us, and who were bound to it in honour, and who are our generals, and who abandon us!"

And Combeferre simply answered with a grave smile:

"There are people who observe the rules of honour as we observe the stars, from afar off."

The interior of the barricade was so strewn with torn cartridges that one would have said it had been snowing.

The assailants had the numbers; the insurgents the position. There was assault after assault.

Then resounded over this pile of paving-stones, in this Rue de la Chanvrerie, a struggle worthy the walls of Troy. These men, wan, tattered, and exhausted, who had not eaten for twenty-four hours, who had not slept, who had but a few more shots to fire, who felt their pockets empty of cartridges, nearly all wounded, their heads or arms bound with a smutty and blackened cloth, with holes in their coats whence the blood was flowing, scarcely armed with worthless muskets and with old hacked swords, became Titans. The barricade was ten times approached, assaulted, scaled, and never taken.

Marius, still fighting, was so hacked with wounds, particularly about his head, that the countenance was lost in blood, and you would have said that he had his face covered with a red handkerchief.

Enjolras alone was untouched. When his weapon failed, he reached his hand to right or left, and an insurgent put whatever weapon he could in his grasp.

When there were none of the chiefs alive save Enjolras and Marius, who were at the extremities of the barricade, the centre, which Courfeyrac, Joly, Bossuet, Feuilly, and Combeferre had so long sustained, gave way. The artillery, without making a practicable breach, had deeply indented the centre of the redoubt; there, the summit of the wall had disappeared under the balls, and had tumbled down; and the rubbish which had fallen, sometimes on the interior, sometimes on the exterior, had finally made, as it was heaped up, on either side of the wall, a kind of talus, both on the inside, and on the outside. The exterior talus offered an inclined plane for attack.

A final assault was now attempted, and this assault succeeded. The mass bristling with bayonets and hurled at a double-quick step, came on irresistibly, and the dense battle-front of the attacking column appeared in the smoke at the top of the escarpment. This time, it was finished. The group of insurgents who defended the centre fell back pell-mell.

But Enjolras and Marius, with seven or eight who had been rallied about them, sprang forward and protected them. Enjolras cried to the soldiers: "Keep back!" and an officer not obeying, Enjolras killed the officer. He was now in the little interior court of the redoubt, with his back to the house of Corinth, his sword in one hand, his carbine in the other, keeping the door of the wine-shop open while he barred it against the assailants. He cried to the despairing: "There is but one door open. This one." And, covering them with his body, alone facing a battalion, he made them pass in behind him. All rushed in. Enjolras with his carbine, which he now used as a cane, beat down the bayonets about him and before him, entered last of all; and for an instant it was horrible, the soldiers struggling to get in, the insurgents to close the door. The door was closed with such violence that, in shutting into its frame, it exposed, cut off, and adhering to the casement, the thumb and fingers of a soldier who had caught hold of it.

Marius remained without. A ball had broken his shoulder-blade; he felt that he was falling. At that moment, his eyes already closed, he experienced the shock of a vigorous hand seizing him, and his fainting fit, in which he lost consciousness, left him hardly time for this thought, mingled with the last memory of Cosette: "I am taken prisoner. I shall be shot."

Enjolras, not seeing Marius among those who had taken refuge in the wine-shop, had the same idea. But they had reached that moment when each has only time to think of his own death. Enjolras fixed the bar of the door and bolted it, and fastened it with a double turn of lock and padlock, while they were beating furiously on the outside, the soldiers with the butts of their muskets, the sappers with their axes. The assailants were massed upon this door. The siege of the wine-shop was beginning.

The soldiers, we must say, were greatly irritated.

The death of the sergeant of artillery had angered them; and then, a more deadly thing, during the few hours which preceded the attack, it had been told among them that the insurgents mutilated prisoners, and that there was in the wine-shop the body of a soldier headless. This sort of unfortunate rumour is the ordinary accompaniment of civil wars.

When the door was barricaded, Enjolras said to the rest:

"Let us sell ourselves dearly."

Then he approached the table upon which Mabeuf and Gavroche were extended. Two straight and rigid forms could be seen under the black cloth, one large, the other small, and the two faces were vaguely outlined beneath the stiff folds of the shroud. A hand projected from below the pall, and hung towards the floor. It was the old man's.

Enjolras bent down and kissed that venerable hand, as in the evening he had kissed the forehead.

They were the only kisses which he had given in his life.

We must be brief. The barricade had struggled like a gate of Thebes; the wine-shop struggled like a house of Saragossa. Such resistances are dogged: no quarter, no parley possible. They are willing to die provided they kill.

At last, mounting on each other's shoulders, helping themselves by the skeleton of the staircase, cutting to pieces the last to resist, some twenty of the besiegers made an irruption into the first story. There was now but a single man there on his feet, Enjolras. Without cartridges, without a sword, he had in his hand only the barrel of his carbine, the stock of which he had broken over the heads of those who were entering. He had put the billiard table between the assailants and himself; he had retreated to the corner of the room, and there, with proud eye, haughty head, and that stump of a weapon in his grasp, he was still so formidable that a large space was left about him. A cry arose:

"This is the chief. It is he who killed the artilleryman. As he has put himself there, it is a good place. Let him stay. Let us shoot him on the spot."

"Shoot me," said Enjolras.

And, throwing away the stump of his carbine, and folding his arms, he presented his breast.

The boldness that dies well always moves men. As soon as Enjolras had folded his arms, accepting the end, the uproar of the conflict ceased. It seemed as if merely by the authority of his tranquil eye, this young man, who alone had no wound, superb, bloody, fascinating, indifferent as if he were invulnerable, compelled that sinister mob to kill him respectfully.

Twelve men formed in platoon in the corner opposite Enjolras and made their muskets ready in silence.

Then a sergeant cried: "Take aim!"

An officer intervened.

"Wait."

And addressing Enjolras:

"Do you wish your eyes bandaged?"

"No."

"Was it really you who killed the sergeant of artillery?"

"Yes."

Within a few seconds Grantaire had awakened.

Grantaire, it will be remembered, had been asleep since the day previous in the upper room of the wine-shop, sitting in a chair, leaning heavily forward on a table.

He realised, in all its energy, strength, the old metaphor: dead drunk. The hideous potion, absinthe-stout-alcohol, had thrown him into a lethargy. His table being small, and of no use in the barricade, they had left it to him. He had continued in the same posture, his breast doubled over the table, his head lying flat upon his arms, surrounded by glasses, jugs, and bottles. He slept with that crushing sleep of the torpid bear and the overfed leech. Nothing had affected him, neither the musketry, nor the balls, nor the grape which penetrated through the casement, nor the prodigious uproar of the assault. Only, he responded sometimes to the cannon with a snore. He seemed waiting there for a ball to come and save him the trouble of awaking. Several corpses lay about him; and, at the first glance, nothing distinguished him from those deep sleepers of death.

Noise does not waken a drunkard; silence wakens him. The halt in the tumult before Enjolras was a shock to his heavy sleep. Grantaire rose up with a start, stretched his arms, rubbed his eyes, looked, gaped, and understood.

Retired as he was in a corner and as it were sheltered behind the billiard-table, the soldiers, their eyes fixed upon Enjolras, had not even noticed Grantaire, and the sergeant was preparing to repeat the order: "Take aim!" when suddenly they heard a powerful voice cry out beside them:

"*Vive la République!* I belong to it."

Grantaire had arisen.

He repeated: "*Vive la République!*" crossed the room with a firm step, and took his place before the muskets beside Enjolras.

"Two at one shot," said he.

And, turning towards Enjolras gently, he said to him:

"Will you permit it?"

Enjolras grasped his hand with a smile.

The smile was not finished when the report was heard.

Enjolras, pierced by eight balls, remained backed against the wall as if the balls had nailed him there. Only he bowed his head.

Grantaire, stricken down, fell at his feet.

A few moments afterwards, the soldiers dislodged the last insurgents who had taken refuge in the top of the house. They fired through a wooden lattice into the garret. They fought in the attics. They threw the bodies out of the windows, some living. A soldier and an insurgent slipped together on the slope of the tiled roof, and would not let go of each other, and fell, clasped in a wild embrace. Similar struggle in the cellar, cries, shots, then silence; the barricade was taken.

The soldiers commenced the search of the houses round about and the pursuit of the fugitives.

XXVIII. UNDER PARIS

MARIUS was a prisoner of Jean Valjean.

The hand which had seized him at the moment he was falling, and the grasp of which he had felt in losing consciousness, was the hand of Jean Valjean.

Save for him, in that supreme phase of the death-struggle, nobody would have thought of the wounded. Thanks to him, those who fell were taken up, carried into the basement-room, and their wounds dressed. In the intervals, he repaired the barricade. But nothing which could resemble a blow, an attack, or even a personal defence came from his hands. He was silent, and gave aid. Moreover, he had only a few scratches. The balls refused him.

Jean Valjean, in the thick cloud of the combat, did not appear to see Marius; the fact is, that he did not take his eyes from him. When a shot struck down Marius, Jean Valjean bounded with the agility of a tiger, dropped upon him as upon a prey, and carried him away.

The whirlwind of the attack at that instant concentrated so fiercely upon Enjolras and the door of the wine-shop, that nobody saw Jean Valjean cross the unpaved field of the barricade, holding the senseless Marius in his arms, and disappear behind the corner of the house of Corinth.

It will be remembered that this corner was a sort of cape on the street; it sheltered from balls and grape, and from sight also, a few square feet of ground. Thus, there is sometimes in conflagrations a room which does not burn; and in the most furious seas, beyond a promontory or at the end of a cul-de-sac of shoals, a placid little haven. It was in this recess of the interior trapezium of the barricade that Eponine had died.

There Jean Valjean stopped; he let Marius slide to the ground, set his back to the wall, and cast his eyes about him.

For the moment, for two or three minutes, perhaps, this skirt of wall was a shelter; but how escape from this massacre? He remembered the anguish in which he was in the Rue Polonceau, eight years before, and how he had succeeded in escaping; difficult then, to-day it was impossible. Before him he had that deaf and implacable house of six stories, which seemed inhabited only by the dead man, leaning over his window; on his right he had the low barricade. To clamber over this obstacle appeared easy, but above the crest of the wall a range of bayonet-points could be seen. A company of the line was posted beyond this barricade, on the watch. At his left he had the field of combat. Death was behind the corner of the wall.

And he must decide upon the spot. They were fighting a few steps from him; by good luck all were fiercely intent upon a single point, the door of the wine-shop; but let one soldier conceive the idea of turning the house and all was over.

Jean Valjean looked at the house in front of him, he looked at the barricade by the side of him, then he looked upon the ground, in desperation, and as if he would have made a hole in it with his eyes.

Beneath his persistent look, something took form at his feet, as if there were a power in the eye to develop the thing desired. He perceived a few steps from him, at the foot of the little wall so pitilessly watched and guarded on the outside, under some fallen paving-stones which partly hid it, an iron grating laid flat and level with the ground. This grating, made of strong transverse bars, was about two feet square. The stone frame which held it had been torn up, and it was as it were unset. Through the bars a glimpse could be caught of an obscure opening, something like the flue of a chimney or the main of a cistern. Jean Valjean sprang forward. His old science of escape mounted to his brain like a flash. To remove the stones, to lift the grating, to load Marius, who was as inert as a dead body, upon his shoulders, to descend, with that burden upon his back, by the aid of his elbows and knees, into this kind of well, fortunately not very deep, to let fall over his head the heavy iron trapdoor upon which the stones were shaken back again, to find a foothold upon a flagged surface ten feet below the ground, required few moments.

Jean Valjean found himself, with Marius still senseless, in a sort of long underground passage.

He could now hardly hear above him, like a vague murmur, the fearful tumult of the wine-shop taken by assault.

It was in the sewer of Paris that Jean Valjean found himself. From the very centre of the city, Jean Valjean had gone out of the city, and, in the twinkling of an eye, the time of lifting a cover and closing it again, he had passed from broad day to complete obscurity, from noon to midnight, from uproar to silence, from the whirl of the thunder to the stagnation of the tomb, from the most extreme peril to the most absolute security.

Only, the wounded man did not stir, and Jean Valjean did not know whether what he was carrying away in this grave were alive or dead.

His first sensation was blindness. Suddenly he saw nothing more. It seemed to him also that in one minute he had become deaf. He heard nothing more. The frenzied storm of murder which was raging a few feet above him only reached him, as we have said, thanks to the thickness of the earth which separated him from it, stifled and indistinct, and like a rumbling at a great depth. He felt that it was solid under his feet; that was all; but that was enough. He reached out one hand, then the other, and touched the wall on both sides, and realised that the passage was narrow; he slipped, and realised that the pavement was wet. He advanced one foot with precaution, fearing a hole, a pit, some gulf; he made sure that the flagging continued. A whiff of fetidness informed him where he was.

After a few moments, he ceased to be blind. A little light fell from the air-hole through which he had slipped in, and his eye became accustomed to this cave. He began to distinguish something. The passage in which he was earthed, no other word better expresses the condition, was walled up behind him. It was one of those cul-de-sacs technically called branchments. Before him, there was another wall, a wall of night. The light from the air-hole died out ten or twelve paces from the point at which Jean Valjean stood. Beyond, the opaqueness was massive; to penetrate it appeared horrible, and to enter it seemed like being engulfed. He could, however, force his way into that wall of mist, and he must do it. He must even hasten. Jean Valjean thought that that grating, noticed by him under the paving-stones, might also be noticed by the soldiers, and that all depended upon that chance. They also could descend into the well and explore it. There was not a minute to be lost.

He had laid Marius upon the ground, he gathered him up, this is again the right word, replaced him upon his shoulders, and began his journey. He resolutely entered that obscurity.

The truth is, that they were not so safe as Jean Valjean supposed. Perils of another kind, and not less great, awaited them perhaps. After the flashing whirl of the combat, the cavern of miasmas and pitfalls; after chaos, the cloaca. Jean Valjean had fallen from one circle of Hell to another.

At the end of fifty paces he was obliged to stop. A question presented itself. The passage terminated in another which it met transversely. These two roads were offered. Which should he take? should he turn to the left or to the right? How guide himself in this black labyrinth? This labyrinth, as we have remarked, has a clue: its descent. To follow the descent is to go to the river.

Jean Valjean understood this at once.

He said to himself that he was probably in the sewer of the markets; that, if he should choose the left and follow the descent, he would come in less than a quarter of an hour to some mouth upon the Seine between the Pont au Change and the Pont Neuf, that is to say, he would reappear in broad day in the most populous portion of Paris. He might come out in some gathering of corner idlers. Amazement of the passers-by at seeing two bloody men come out of the ground under their feet. Arrival of sergent de ville, call to arms in the next guard-house. He would be seized before getting out. It was better to plunge into the labyrinth, to trust to this darkness, and to rely on Providence for the issue.

He chose the right, and went up the ascent.

When he had turned the corner of the gallery, the distant gleam of the air-hole disappeared, the curtain of obscurity fell back over him, and he again became blind. He went forward none the less, and as rapidly as he could. Marius' arms were passed about his neck, and his feet hung behind him. He held both arms with one hand, and groped for the wall with the other. Marius' cheek touched his and stuck to it, being bloody. He felt a warm stream flow over him and penetrate his clothing. Still, a moist warmth at his ear, which touched the wounded man's mouth, indicated respiration, and consequently life.

The passage through which Jean Valjean was now moving was not so small as the first. Jean Valjean walked in it with difficulty. The rains of the previous day had not yet run off, and made a little stream in the centre of the floor, and he was compelled to hug the wall, to keep his feet out of the water. Thus he went on in midnight.

However, little by little, whether that some distant air-holes sent a little floating light into this opaque mist, or that his eyes became accustomed to the obscurity, some dim vision came back to him.

To find his way was difficult.

The track of the sewers echoes, so to speak, the track of the streets which overlie them. There were in the Paris of that day two thousand two hundred streets. Picture to yourselves below then that forest of dark branches which is called the sewer. The sewers existing at that epoch, placed end to end, would have given a length of thirty miles.

Jean Valjean began with a mistake. He thought that he was under the Rue Saint Denis, and it was unfortunate that he was not there. There is beneath the Rue Saint Denis an old stone sewer, which dates from Louis XIII., and which goes straight to the collecting sewer, called the Grand Sewer. But the gallery of the Petite Truanderie, the entrance to which was near the wine-shop of Corinth, never communicated with the underground passage in the Rue Saint Denis; it runs into the Montmartre sewer, and it was in that that Jean Valjean was entangled. There, opportunities of losing one's self abound.

If Jean Valjean had had any notion of what we have here pointed out, he would have quickly perceived, merely from feeling the wall, that he was not in the underground gallery of the Rue Saint Denis. Instead of the old hewn stone, instead of the ancient architecture, haughty and royal even in the sewer, with floor and running courses of granite, and mortar of thick lime, which cost seventy-five dollars a yard, he would have felt beneath his hand the contemporary cheapness, the economical expedient, the millstone grit laid in hydraulic cement upon a bed of concrete, which cost thirty-five dollars a yard, the bourgeois masonry known as *small materials;* but he knew nothing of all this.

He went forward, with anxiety, but with calmness, seeing nothing, knowing nothing, plunged into chance, that is to say, swallowed up in Providence.

By degrees horror penetrated him. It is a dreary thing to be caught in this Paris of darkness. Jean Valjean was obliged to find and almost to invent his route without seeing it. In that unknown region, each step which he ventured might be the last. How should he get out? Should he find an outlet? Should he find it in time? Would this colossal subterranean sponge with cells of stone admit of being penetrated and pierced? Would he meet with some unlooked-for knot of obscurity? Would he encounter the inextricable and the insurmountable? Would Marius die of hæmorrhage, and he of hunger? Would they both perish there at last, and make two skeletons in some niche of that night? He did not know. He asked himself all this, and he could not answer. Like the prophet, he was in the belly of the monster.

Suddenly he was surprised. At the most unexpected moment, and without having diverged from a straight line, he discovered that he was no longer rising; the water of the brook struck coming against his heels instead of upon the top of his feet. The sewer now descended. What? would he then soon reach the Seine? This danger was great, but the peril of retreat was still greater. He continued to advance.

It was not towards the Seine that he was going. The saddleback which the topography of Paris forms upon the right bank, empties one of its slopes into the Seine and the other into the Grand Sewer. Jean Valjean was making his way towards the belt sewer; he was on the right road. But he knew nothing of it.

Whenever he came to a branch, he felt its angles, and if he found the opening not as wide as the corridor in which he was, he did not enter, and continued his route, deeming rightly that every narrower way must terminate in a cul-de-sac, and could only lead him away from his object, the outlet.

At a certain moment he felt that he was getting away from under the Paris in which the barricades had suppressed the circulation, and that he was coming beneath the Paris which was alive and normal. He heard suddenly above his head a sound like thunder, distant, but continuous. It was the rumbling of the vehicles.

He had been walking for about half an hour, at least by his own calculation, and had not yet thought of resting; only he had changed the hand which supported Marius. The darkness was deeper than ever, but this depth reassured him.

All at once he saw his shadow before him. It was marked out on a feeble ruddiness almost indistinct, which glided along the floor at his feet, and the arch over his head, and at his right and his left on the two slimy walls of the corridor. In amazement he turned round.

Behind him, flamed a sort of horrible star.

Behind this star were moving without order eight or ten black forms, straight, indistinct, terrible.

It was the gloomy star of the police which was rising in the sewer.

During the day of the 6th of June, a battue of the sewers had been ordered. It was feared that they would be taken as a refuge by the vanquished, and prefect Gisquet was to ransack the occult Paris, while General Bugeaud was sweeping the public Paris; a connected double operation which demanded a double strategy of the public power, represented above by the army and below by the police. Three platoons of officers and sewermen explored the subterranean streets of Paris. The officers were armed with carbines, clubs, swords, and daggers.

That which was at this moment directed upon Jean Valjean, was the lantern of the patrol of the right bank.

This patrol had just visited the crooked gallery and the three blind alleys which are beneath the Rue du Cadran. The policemen, on coming out from the gallery, had thought they heard the sound of steps in the direction of the belt sewer. The sergeant in command of the patrol lifted his lantern, and the squad began to look into the mist in the direction whence the sound came.

Luckily, if Jean Valjean saw the lantern well, the lantern saw him badly. It was light and he was shadow. He was far off, and merged in the blackness of the place. He drew close to the side of the wall, and stopped.

The men of the patrol listened and heard nothing, they looked and saw nothing. They consulted.

There was at that period a sort of square at this point of the Montmartre sewer, which has since been suppressed on account of the little interior lake which formed in it, by the damming up in heavy storms of the torrents of rain water. The patrol could gather in a group in this square. Jean Valjean saw these goblins form a kind of circle. These mastiffs' heads drew near each other and whispered.

The result of this council held by the watch-dogs was that they had been mistaken, that there had been no noise, that there was nobody there, that it was needless to trouble themselves with the belt sewer, but that they must hasten towards Saint Merry; if there were anything to do it was in that quarter.

The sergeant gave the order to file left towards the descent to the Seine. If they had conceived the idea of dividing into two squads and going in both directions, Jean Valjean would have been caught. It is probable that the instructions from the prefecture, foreseeing that the insurgents might be numerous, forbade the patrol to separate.

The patrol resumed its march, leaving Jean Valjean behind. Of all these movements, Jean Valjean perceived nothing except the eclipse of the lantern, which suddenly turned back.

Before going away, the sergeant, to ease the police conscience, discharged his carbine in the direction they were abandoning, towards Jean Valjean. The detonation rolled from echo to echo in the vault like the rumbling of this titanic bowel. Some plastering which fell into the stream and spattered the water a few steps from Jean Valjean made him aware that the ball had struck the arch above his head.

Slow and measured steps resounded upon the floor for some time; a glimmer oscillated and floated, making a ruddy circle in the vault, which decreased, then disappeared. The silence became deep again, the obscurity became again complete, blindness and deafness resumed possession of the darkness; and Jean Valjean, not yet daring to stir, stood for a long time with his back to the wall, his ear intent and eye dilated, watching the vanishing of that phantom patrol.

We must do the police of that period this justice that, even in the gravest public conjunctures, it imperturbably performed its duties watchful and sanitary.

In the midst of an incalculable political event, under the pressure of a possible revolution, without allowing himself to be diverted by the insurrection and the barricade, an officer would "spin" a thief.

Something precisely like this occurred in the afternoon of the 6th of June at the brink of the Seine, on the beach of the right bank, a little beyond the Pont des Invalides. On this beach, two men some distance apart seemed to be observing each other, one avoiding the other. The one who was going before was endeavouring to increase the distance, the one who came behind to lessen it.

If the other was allowing him to go on and did not yet seize him, it was, according to all appearance, in the hope of seeing him bring up at some significant rendezvous, some group of good prizes. This delicate operation is called "spinning."

What renders this conjecture the more probable is, that the closely buttoned man, perceiving from the shore a fiacre which was passing on the quai, beckoned to the driver; the driver understood, turned his horse, and began to follow the two men on the upper part of the quai at a walk.

One of the secret instructions of the police to officers contains this article: "Always have a vehicle within call, in case of need."

While manœuvring, each on his side, with an irreproachable strategy, these two men approached a slope of the quai descending to the beach, which, at that time, allowed the coach-drivers coming from Passy to go to the river to water their horses. It seemed probable that the man in the blouse would go up by this slope in order to attempt escape into the Champs Elysées, a place ornamented with trees, but on the other hand thickly dotted with officers, and where his pursuer would have easily seized him with a strong hand.

To the great surprise of his observer, the man pursued did not take the slope of the watering-place. He continued to advance on the beach along the quai.

If not to throw himself into the Seine, what was he going to do?

They were very near the spot, where the beach, narrowing more and more, is lost under the water. There he would inevitably find himself blockaded between the steep wall on his right, the river on the left and in front, and authority upon his heels.

It is true that this end of the beach was masked from sight by a mound of rubbish from six to seven feet high, the product of some demolition. But did this man hope to hide with any effect behind this heap of fragments? The innocence of robbers does not reach this extent.

The man pursued reached this little hill and doubled it, so that he ceased to be seen.

The other took advantage of this to abandon all dissimulation, and walk very rapidly. In a few seconds he came to the mound of rubbish, and turned it. There, he stopped in amazement. The man whom he was hunting was gone.

The beach beyond the mound of rubbish had scarcely a length of thirty yards, then it plunged beneath the water which beat against the wall of the quai. The fugitive could not have thrown himself into the Seine nor scaled the quai. What had become of him?

The man in the closely buttoned coat walked to the end of the beach, and stopped there a moment thoughtful, his eyes ferreting. Suddenly he slapped his forehead. He had noticed, at the point where the land and the water began, an iron grating, broad and low, arched, with a heavy lock and three massive hinges. This grating, a sort of door cut into the bottom of the quai, opened upon the river as much as upon the beach. A blackish stream flowed from beneath it. This stream emptied into the Seine.

Beyond its heavy rusty bars could be distinguished a sort of corridor arched and obscure.

The man looked at the grating reproachfully.

This look not sufficing, he tried to push it; he shook it, it resisted firmly. It was probable that it had just been opened, although no sound had been heard, a singular circumstance with a grating so rusty; but it was certain that it had been closed again. That indicated that he before whom this door had just turned, had not a hook but a key.

This evident fact burst immediately upon the mind of the man who was exerting himself to shake the grating.

"This is fine! a government key!"

This said, he posted himself on the watch behind the heap of rubbish, with the patient rage of a pointer.

For its part, the fiacre, which followed all his movements, had halted above him near the parapet. The driver, foreseeing a long stay, fitted the muzzles of his horses into the bag of wet oats.

Jean Valjean had resumed his advance, and had not stopped again.

This advance became more and more laborious. The level of these arches varies; the medium height is about five feet six inches, and was calculated for the stature of a man; Jean Valjean was compelled to bend so as not to hit Marius against the arch; he had to stoop every second, then rise up, to grope incessantly for the wall. The moisture of the stones and the sliminess of the floor made them bad points of support. He was wading in the hideous muck of the city. The occasional gleams from the air-holes appeared only at long intervals, and so ghastly were they that the noonday seemed but moonlight; all the rest was mist, miasma, opacity, blackness. Jean Valjean was hungry and thirsty, thirsty especially; and this place, like the sea, is one full of water where you cannot drink. His strength, which was prodigious, and very little diminished by age, thanks to his chaste and sober life, began to give way notwithstanding. Fatigue grew upon him, and as his strength diminished the weight of his load increased. Marius, dead perhaps, weighed heavily upon him as inert bodies do. Jean Valjean supported him in such a way that his breast was not compressed and his breathing could always be as free as possible. He felt the rapid gliding of the rats between his legs. One of them was so frightened as to bite him. There came to him from time to time through the aprons of the mouths of the sewer a breath of fresh air which revived him.

It might have been three o'clock in the afternoon when he arrived at the belt sewer.

He was first astonished at this sudden enlargement. He abruptly found himself in the gallery where his outstretched hands did not reach the two walls, and under an arch which his head did not touch. The Grand Sewer indeed is eight feet wide and seven high.

At the point where the Montmartre sewer joins the Grand Sewer, two other subterranean galleries, coming in, make a square. Between these four ways a less sagacious man would have been undecided. Jean Valjean took the widest, that is to say, the belt sewer. But there the question returned: to descend, or to ascend? He thought that the condition of affairs was urgent, and that he must, at whatever risk, now reach the Seine. In other words, descend. He turned to the left.

Well for him that he did so. Had Jean Valjean gone up the gallery, he would have come, after manifold efforts, exhausted by fatigue, expiring, in the darkness, to a wall. He would have been lost.

His instinct served him well. To descend was, in fact, possible safety.

A little beyond an affluent which was probably the branching of the Madeleine, he stopped. He was very tired. A large air-hole, probably the vista on the Rue d'Anjou, produced an almost vivid light. Jean Valjean, with the gentleness of movement of a brother for his wounded brother, laid Marius upon the side bank of the sewer. Marius' bloody face appeared, under the white gleam from the air-hole, as if at the bottom of a tomb. His eyes were closed, his hair adhered to his temples like brushes dried in red paint, his hands dropped down lifeless, his limbs were cold, there was coagulated blood at the corners of his mouth. A clot of blood had gathered in the tie of his cravat; his shirt was bedded in the wounds, the cloth of his coat chafed the gaping gashes in the living flesh. Jean Valjean, removing the garments with the ends of his fingers, laid his hand upon his breast; the heart still beat. Jean Valjean tore up his shirt, bandaged the wounds as well as he could, and staunched the flowing blood; then, bending in the twilight over Marius, who was still unconscious and almost lifeless, he looked at him with an inexpressible hatred.

In opening Marius' clothes, he had found two things in his pockets, the bread which had been forgotten there since the day previous, and Marius' pocket-book. He ate the bread and opened the pocket-book. On the first page he found the four lines written by Marius:

"My name is Marius Pontmercy. Carry my corpse to my grandfather's, M. Gillenormand, Rue des Filles du Calvaire, No. 6, in the Marais."

By the light of the air-hole, Jean Valjean read these four lines, and stopped a moment as if absorbed in himself, repeating in an undertone: "Rue des Filles du Calvaire, Number Six, Monsieur Gillenormand." He replaced the pocket-book in Marius' pocket. He had eaten, strength had returned to him: he took Marius on his back again, laid his head carefully upon his right shoulder, and began to descend the sewer.

The Grand Sewer, following the course of the valley of Ménilmontant, is almost two leagues in length. It is paved for a considerable part of its course.

Nothing told Jean Valjean what zone of the city he was passing through. Only the growing pallor of the gleams of light which he saw from time to time, indicated that the sun was withdrawing from the pavement, and that the day would soon be gone; and the rumblings of the waggons above his head having almost ceased, he concluded that he was under central Paris no longer, and that he was approaching some solitary region, in the vicinity of the outer boulevards or the furthest quais. Where there are fewer houses and fewer streets, the sewer has fewer air-holes. The darkness thickened about Jean Valjean. He none the less continued to advance, groping in the obscurity.

This obscurity suddenly became terrible. He felt that he was entering the water,.and that he had under his feet, pavement no longer, but mud.

It sometimes happens, on certain coasts of Brittany or Scotland, that a man, traveller or fisherman, walking on the beach at low tide far from the bank, suddenly notices that for several minutes he has been walking with some difficulty. The strand beneath his feet is like pitch; his soles stick to it; it is sand no longer, it is glue. All at once, he looks at his feet. His feet have disappeared. The sand covers them. He draws his feet out of the sand, he will retrace his steps, he turns back, he sinks in deeper. The sand comes up to his ankles, he pulls himself out and throws himself to the left, the sand is half-leg deep, he throws himself to the right, the sand comes up to his shins. Then he recognises with unspeakable terror that he is caught in the quicksand, and that he has beneath him the fearful medium in which man can no more walk than the fish can swim. He throws off his load if he has one, he lightens himself like a ship in distress; it is already too late, the sand is above his knees.

When, in 1836, they demolished the old stone sewer under the Faubourg Saint Honoré, in which we find Jean Valjean now entangled, the quicksand, which is the subsoil from the Champs Elysées to the Seine, was such an obstacle that the work lasted nearly six months, to the great outcry of the bordering proprietors of hotels and coaches. The work was more than difficult; it was dangerous. It is true that there were four months and a half of rain, and three risings of the Seine.

The fontis which Jean Valjean fell upon was caused by the showers of the previous day. A yielding of the pavement, imperfectly upheld by the underlying sand, had occasioned a damming of the rain-water. Infiltration having taken place, sinking had followed. The floor, broken up, had disappeared in the mire. For what distance? Impossible to say. It was a mudhole in the cavern of night.

Jean Valjean felt the pavement slipping away under him. This slime was water on the surface, mire at the bottom.

He must surely pass through. To retrace his steps was impossible. Marius was expiring, and Jean Valjean exhausted. Where else could he go? Jean Valjean advanced. Moreover, the quagmire appeared not very deep for a few steps. But in proportion as he advanced, his feet sank in. He very soon had the mire half-knee deep, and water above his knees. He walked on, holding Marius with both arms as high above the water as he could. The mud now came up to his knees, and the water to his waist. He could not longer turn back. He sank in deeper and deeper. This mire, dense enough for one man's weight, evidently could not bear two. Marius and Jean Valjean would have had a chance of escape separately. Jean Valjean continued to advance, supporting this dying man, who was perhaps a corpse.

The water came up to his armpits; he felt that he was foundering; it was with difficulty that he could move in the depth of mire in which he was. The density, which was the support, was also the obstacle. He still held Marius up, and, with an unparalleled outlay of strength, he advanced; but he sank deeper. He now had only his head out of the water, and his arms supporting Marius.

He sank still deeper, he threw his face back to escape the water, and to be able to breathe; he who should have seen him in this obscurity would have thought he saw a mask floating upon the darkness. He made a desperate effort, and thrust his foot forward; his foot struck something solid, a support. It was time.

He rose and writhed and rooted himself upon this support with a sort of fury. It produced the effect upon him of the first step of a staircase reascending towards life.

This support, discovered in the mire at the last moment, was the beginning of the other slope of the floor, which had bent without breaking, and had curved beneath the water like a board, and in a single piece. A well-constructed paving forms an arch. This fragment of the floor, partly submerged, but solid, was a real slope, and, once upon this slope, they were saved. Jean Valjean ascended this inclined plane, and reached the other side of the quagmire.

On coming out of the water, he struck against a stone, and fell upon his knees. This seemed to him fitting, and he remained thus for some time in unspoken prayer to God.

He resumed his route once more.

However, if he had not left his life in the fontis, he seemed to have left his strength. This supreme effort had exhausted him. His exhaustion was so great, that every three or four steps he was obliged to take breath, and leaned against the wall. Once he had to sit down upon the curb to change Marius' position and he thought he should stay there. But if his vigour were dead his energy was not. He rose again. He walked with desperation, almost with rapidity, for a hundred paces, without raising his head, almost without breathing, and suddenly struck against the wall. He had reached an angle of the sewer. At the extremity of the passage, very far away, he perceived a light. This time, it was not the terrible light; it was the good and white light of day.

Jean Valjean felt exhaustion no more, he felt Marius' weight no longer, he found again his knees of steel, he ran rather than walked. As he approached, the outlet assumed more and more distinct outline. It was a circular arch, not so high as the vault which sank down by degrees, and not so wide as the gallery which narrowed as the top grew lower. The tunnel ended on the inside in the form of a funnel; a vicious contraction, copied from the wickets of houses of detention, logical in a prison, illogical in a sewer, and which has since been corrected.

Jean Valjean reached the outlet.

There he stopped.

It was indeed the outlet, but it did not let him out.

The arch was closed by a strong grating, and the grating which, according to all appearance, rarely turned upon its rusty hinges, was held in its stone frame by a stout lock which, red with rust, seemed an enormous brick. He could see the keyhole, and the strong bolt deeply plunged into the iron staple. The lock was plainly a double-lock. It was one of those Bastille locks of which the old Paris was so lavish.

Beyond the grating, the open air, the river, the daylight, the beach, very narrow, but sufficient to get away; the distant quais, Paris, that gulf in which one is so easily lost, the wide horizon, liberty. He distinguished at his right, below him, the Pont d'Iéna, and at his left, above, the Pont des Invalides; the spot would have been propitious for awaiting night and escaping. It was one of the most solitary points in Paris. The flies came in and went out through the bars of the grating.

It might have been half-past eight o'clock in the evening. The day was declining.

Jean Valjean laid Marius along the wall on the dry part of the floor, then walked to the grating and clenched the bars with both hands; the shaking was frenzied, the shock nothing. The grating did not stir. Jean Valjean seized the bars one after another, hoping to be able to tear out the least solid one, and to make a lever of it to lift the door or break the lock. Not a bar yielded. No lever; no possible purchase. The obstacle was invincible. No means of opening the door.

Must he then perish there? What should he do? what would become of them? go back; recommence the terrible road which he had already traversed; he had not the strength. Besides, how cross that quagmire again, from which he had escaped only by a miracle? And after the quagmire, was there not that police patrol from which, certainly, one would not escape twice? And then where should he go? what direction take? to follow the descent was not to reach the goal. Should he come to another outlet, he would find it obstructed by a door or a grating. All the outlets were undoubtedly closed in this way. Chance had unsealed the grating by which they had entered, but evidently all the other mouths of the sewer were fastened. He had succeeded in escaping into a prison.

It was over. All that Jean Valjean had done was useless.

He turned his back to the grating, and dropped upon the pavement, rather prostrate than sitting, beside the yet motionless Marius and his head sank between his knees.

Of whom did he think in this overwhelming dejection? Neither of himself nor of Marius. He thought of Cosette.

In the midst of this annihilation, a hand was laid upon his shoulder, and a voice which spoke low, said to him:

"Go halves."

Somebody in that darkness? Nothing is so like a dream as despair; Jean Valjean thought he was dreaming. He had heard no steps. Was it possible? he raised his eyes.

A man was before him.

This man was dressed in a blouse; he was barefooted; he held his shoes in his left hand; he had evidently taken them off to be able to reach Jean Valjean without being heard.

Unforeseen as was the encounter, this man was known. This man was Thénardier.

Although wakened, so to speak, with a start, Jean Valjean, accustomed to be on the alert and on the watch for unexpected blows which he must quickly parry, instantly regained possession of all his presence of mind. Besides, the condition of affairs could not be worse, a certain degree of distress is no longer capable of crescendo, and Thénardier himself could not add to the blackness of this night.

There was a moment of delay.

Thénardier, lifting his right hand to the height of his forehead, shaded his eyes with it, then brought his brows together while he winked his eyes, which, with a slight pursing of the mouth, characterises the sagacious attention of a man who is seeking to recognise another. He did not succeed. Jean Valjean, we have just said, turned his back to the light, and was moreover so disfigured, so muddy and so blood-stained, that in full noon he would have been unrecognisable. On the other hand, the light from the grating shining in his face struck Thénardier. This inequality of conditions was enough to insure Jean Valjean some advantage; the encounter took place between Jean Valjean veiled and Thénardier unmasked.

Jean Valjean perceived immediately that Thénardier did not recognise him.

They gazed at each other for a moment as if they were taking each other's measure. Thénardier was first to break the silence.

"How are you going to manage to get out?"

Jean Valjean did not answer.

Thénardier continued:

"Impossible to pick the lock. Still you must get away from here."

"That is true," said Jean Valjean.

"Well, go halves."

"What do you mean?"

"You have killed the man; very well. For my part, I have the key."

Thénardier pointed to Marius. He went on:

"I don't know you, but I would like to help you. You must be a friend."

Jean Valjean began to understand. Thénardier took him for an assassin. Thénardier resumed:

"Listen, comrade. You haven't killed that man without looking to what he had in his pockets. Give me my half. I will open the door for you."

And, drawing a big key half out from under his blouse, which was full of holes, he added:

"Would you like to see how the key of the fields is made? There it is."

Thénardier plunged his fist into a huge pocket hidden under his blouse, pulled out a rope, and handed it to Jean Valjean.

"Here," said he, "I'll give you the rope to boot."

"A rope, what for?"

"You want a stone too, but you'll find one outside. There is a heap of rubbish there."

"A stone, what for?"

"Fool, as you are going to throw the *pantre*[1] into the river, you want a stone and a rope; without them it would float on the water."

Jean Valjean took the rope. Everybody has accepted things thus mechanically.

Thénardier snapped his fingers as over the arrival of a sudden idea:

"Ah, now, comrade, how did you manage to get out of the quagmire yonder? I haven't dared to risk myself there. Pugh! you don't smell good."

After a pause, he added:

"I ask you questions, but you are right in not answering them. That is an apprenticeship for the examining judge's cursed quarter of an hour. And then by not speaking at all, you run no risk of speaking too loud. It is all the same, because I don't see your face, and because I don't know your name, you would do wrong to suppose that I don't know who you are and what you want. Understood. You have smashed this gentleman a little; now you want to squeeze him somewhere. You need the river, the great hide-folly. I am going to get you out of the scrape. To help a good fellow in trouble that puts my boots on."

While approving Jean Valjean for keeping silence, he was evidently seeking to make him speak. He pushed his shoulders, so as to endeavour to see his side-face, and exclaimed, without however rising above the moderate tone in which he kept his voice:

"Speaking of the quagmire, you are a proud animal. Why didn't you throw the man in there?"

Jean Valjean preserved silence.

Thénardier resumed, raising the rag which served him as a cravat up to his Adam's apple, a gesture which completes the air of sagacity of a serious man:

"Indeed, perhaps you have acted prudently. The workmen when they
[1]Corpse.

come to-morrow to stop the hole, would certainly have found the *pantinois* forgotten there, and they would have been able, thread by thread, straw by straw, to *pincer* the trace, and to reach you. Something has passed through the sewer? Who? Where did he come out? Did anybody see him come out? The police has plenty of brains. The sewer is treacherous and informs against you. Such a discovery is a rarity, it attracts attention, few people use the sewer in their business while the river is at everybody's service. The river is the true grave. At the month's end, they fish you up the man at the nets of Saint Cloud. Who killed this man? Paris. And justice don't even inquire into it. You have done right."

The more loquacious Thénardier was, the more dumb was Jean Valjean. Thénardier pushed his shoulder anew.

"Now, let us finish the business. Let us divide. You have seen my key, show me your money."

Thénardier was haggard, tawny, equivocal, a little threatening, nevertheless friendly.

There was one strange circumstance; Thénardier's manner was not natural; he did not appear entirely at his ease; while he did not affect an air of mystery, he talked low; from time to time he laid his finger on his mouth, and muttered: "Hush!" It was difficult to guess why. There was nobody there but them. Jean Valjean thought that perhaps some other bandits were hidden in some recess not far off, and that Thénardier did not care to share with them.

Thénardier resumed:

"Let us finish. How much did the *pantre* have in his deeps?"

Jean Valjean felt in his pockets.

It was, as will be remembered, his custom always to have money about him. The gloomy life of expedients to which he was condemned, made this a law to him. This time, however, he was caught unprovided. On putting on his National Guard's uniform, the evening before, he had forgotten, gloomily absorbed as he was, to take his pocket-book with him. He had only some coins in his waistcoat pocket. He turned out his pocket, all soaked with filth, and displayed upon the curb of the sewer a louis d'or, two five-franc pieces, and five or six big sous.

Thénardier thrust out his under lip with a significant twist of the neck.

"You didn't kill him very dear," said he.

He began to handle the pockets of Jean Valjean and Marius. Jean Valjean, concerned in keeping his back to the light, did not interfere. While he was feeling of Marius' coat, Thénardier, with the dexterity of a juggler, found means, without attracting Jean Valjean's attention, to tear off a strip, which he hid under his blouse, probably thinking that this scrap of cloth might assist him afterwards to identify the assassinated man and the assassin. He found, however, nothing more than the thirty francs.

"It is true," said he, "both together, you have no more than that."

And, forgetting his words, *go halves*, he took the whole.

He hesitated a little before the big sous. Upon reflection, he took them also, mumbling:

"No matter! this is to *suriner* people too cheap."

This said, he took the key from under his blouse anew.

"Now, friend, you must go out."

And he began to laugh.

Thénardier helped Jean Valjean to replace Marius upon his shoulders; then he went towards the grating upon his bare feet, beckoning to Jean Valjean to follow him, he looked outside, laid his finger on his mouth, and stood a few seconds as if in suspense; the inspection over, he put the key into the lock. The bolt slid and the door turned. There was neither snapping nor grinding. It was done very quietly. It was plain that this grating and its hinges, oiled with care, were opened oftener than would have been guessed. This quiet was ominous; you felt in it the furtive goings and comings, the silent entrances and exits of the men of the night. The sewer was evidently in complicity with some mysterious band. This taciturn grating was a receiver.

Thénardier half opened the door, left just a passage for Jean Valjean, closed the grating again, turned the key twice in the lock, and plunged back into the obscurity, without making more noise than a breath. He seemed to walk with the velvet paws of a tiger. A moment afterwards, this hideous providence had entered again into the invisible.

Jean Valjean found himself outside.

He let Marius slide down upon the beach.

The miasmas, the obscurity, the horror, were behind him. The balmy air, pure, living, joyful, flowed around him. Everywhere about him silence, but the charming silence of a sunset in a clear sky. Twilight had fallen; night was coming. There was already night enough for one to be lost in it at a little distance, and still day enough for one to be recognised near at hand.

Jean Valjean was for a few seconds overcome by all this august and caressing serenity. Then, hastily, as if a feeling of duty came back to him, he bent over Marius, and, dipping up some water in the hollow of his hand, he threw a few drops gently into his face. Marius' eyelids did not part; but his half-open mouth breathed.

Jean Valjean was plunging his hand into the river again, when suddenly he felt an indescribable uneasiness, such as we feel when we have somebody behind us, without seeing him.

He turned round. Somebody was indeed behind him.

A man of tall stature, wrapped in a long overcoat, with folded arms, and holding in his right hand a club, the leaden knob of which could be seen, stood erect a few steps in the rear of Jean Valjean, who was stooping over Marius.

Jean Valjean recognised Javert.

The reader has doubtless guessed that Thénardier's pursuer was none other than Javert. Javert, after his unhoped-for departure from the barricade, had gone to the prefecture of police, had given an account verbally to the prefect in person in short audience, had then immediately returned to his duty, which implied—the note found upon him will be remembered—a certain surveillance of the shore on the right bank of the Champs Elysées, which for some time had excited the attention of the police. There he had seen Thénardier, and had followed him. The rest is known.

It is understood also that the opening of that grating so obligingly before Jean Valjean was a piece of shrewdness on the part of Thénardier. Thénardier felt that Javert was still there; a bone must be thrown to this hound. An assassin, what a godsend! It was the scapegoat, which must never be refused. Thénardier, by putting Jean Valjean out in his place, gave a victim to the police, threw them off his own track, caused himself to be forgotten in a larger matter, rewarded Javert for his delay, gained thirty francs, and counted surely upon escaping by the aid of this diversion.

Javert did not recognise Jean Valjean, who, as we have said, no longer resembled himself. He did not unfold his arms, he secured his club in his grasp by an imperceptible movement, and said in a quick and calm voice:

"Who are you?"

"I."

"What you?"

"Jean Valjean."

Javert put the club between his teeth, bent his knees, inclined his body, laid his two powerful hands upon Jean Valjean's shoulders.

Jean Valjean stood inert under the grasp of Javert like a lion who should submit to the claw of a lynx.

"Inspector Javert," said he, "you have got me. Besides, since this morning, I have considered myself your prisoner. I did not give you my address to try to escape you. Take me. Only grant me one thing."

Javert seemed not to hear. He rested his fixed eye upon Jean Valjean. His rising chin pushed his lips towards his nose. At last, he let go, rose up as straight as a stick, took his club firmly in his grasp, and murmured:

"What are you doing here? and who is this man?"

Jean Valjean answered:

"It is precisely of him that I wish to speak. Dispose of me as you please; but help me first to carry him home. I only ask that of you."

Javert's face contracted, as it happened to him whenever anybody seemed to consider him capable of a concession. Still he did not say no.

He stooped down again, took a handkerchief from his pocket, which he dipped in the water, and wiped Marius' bloodstained forehead.

"This man was in the barricade," said he in an undertone, and as if speaking to himself. "This is he whom they called Marius."

A spy of the first quality, who had observed everything, listened to everything, heard everything, and recollected everything, believing he was about to die; who spied even in his death-agony, and who, leaning upon the first step of the grave, had taken notes.

He seized Marius' hand, seeking for his pulse.

"He is wounded," said Jean Valjean.

"He is dead," said Javert.

Jean Valjean answered:

"No. Not yet."

"You have brought him, then, from the barricade here?" observed Javert.

His preoccupation must have been deep, as he did not dwell longer upon this perplexing escape through the sewer, and did not even notice Jean Valjean's silence after his question.

Jean Valjean, for his part, seemed to have but one idea. He resumed:

"He lives in the Marais, Rue des Filles du Calvaire, at his grandfather's— I forget the name."

Jean Valjean felt in Marius' coat, took out the pocket-book, opened it at the page pencilled by Marius, and handed it to Javert.

There was still enough light to enable one to read. Javert deciphered the few lines written by Marius, and muttered: "Gillenormand, Rue des Filles du Calvaire, No. 6."

Then he cried: "Driver?"

The reader will remember the fiacre which was waiting, in case of need. Javert kept Marius' pocket-book.

A moment later, the carriage, descending by the slope of the watering-place, was on the beach. Marius was laid upon the back seat, and Javert sat down by the side of Jean Valjean on the front seat.

When the door was shut, the fiacre moved rapidly off, going up the quais in the direction of the Bastille. The driver, a black silhouette upon his box, whipped up his bony horses. Icy silence in the coach. Marius, motionless, his body braced in the corner of the carriage, his head dropping down upon his breast, his arms hanging, his legs rigid, appeared to await nothing now but a coffin; Jean Valjean seemed made of shadow, and Javert of stone.

XXIX. THE RIVER

AT EVERY JOLT over the pavement, a drop of blood fell from Marius' hair.

It was after nightfall when the fiacre arrived at No. 6, in the Rue des Filles du Calvaire.

Javert first set foot on the ground, verified by a glance the number above the porte-cochère, and, lifting the heavy wrought-iron knocker, embellished in the old fashion, with a goat and a satyr defying each other, struck a violent blow. The fold of the door partly opened, and Javert pushed it. The porter showed himself, gaping and half-awake, a candle in his hand.

Everybody in the house was asleep. People go to bed early in the Marais.

Meanwhile Jean Valjean and the driver lifted Marius out of the coach, Jean Valjean supporting him by the armpits, and the coachman by the knees. While he was carrying Marius in this way, Jean Valjean slipped his hand under his clothes, which were much torn, felt his breast, and assured himself that the heart still beat. It beat even a little less feebly, as if the motion of the carriage had determined a certain renewal of life.

Javert called out to the porter in the tone which befits the government, "Somebody whose name is Gillenormand?"

"It is here. What do you want with him?"

"His son is brought home."

"His son?" said the porter with amazement.

"He is dead."

Jean Valjean, who came ragged and dirty, behind Javert, and whom the porter beheld with some horror, motioned to him with his head that he was not.

The porter did not appear to understand either Javert's words, or Jean Valjean's signs.

Javert continued:

"He has been to the barricade, and here he is."

"To the barricade!" exclaimed the porter.

"He has got himself killed. Go and wake his father."

The porter did not stir.

"Why don't you go?" resumed Javert.

And he added:

"There will be a funeral here to-morrow."

The porter merely woke Basque. Basque woke Nicolette; Nicolette woke Aunt Gillenormand. As to the grandfather, they let him sleep, thinking that he would know it soon enough at all events.

They carried Marius up to the first story, without anybody perceiving it in the other portions of the house, and they laid him on an old couch in M. Gillenormand's ante-chamber; and, while Basque went for a doctor and Nicolette was opening the linen closets, Jean Valjean felt Javert touch him on the shoulder. He understood, and went down stairs, having behind him Javert's following steps.

The porter saw them depart as he had seen them arrive, with drowsy dismay.

They got into the fiacre again, and the driver mounted upon his box.

"Inspector Javert," said Jean Valjean, "grant me one thing more."

"What?" asked Javert roughly.

"Let me go home a moment. Then you shall do with me what you will."

Javert remained silent for a few seconds, his chin drawn back into the collar of his overcoat, then he let down the window in front.

"Driver," said he, "Rue de l'Homme Armé, No. 7."

They did not open their mouths again for the whole distance.

What did Jean Valjean desire? To finish what he had begun; to inform Cosette, to tell her where Marius was, to give her perhaps some other useful information, to make, if he could, certain final dispositions. As to himself, as to what concerned him personally, it was all over; he had been seized by Javert and did not resist.

At the entrance of the Rue de l'Homme Armé, the fiacre stopped, this street being too narrow for carriages to enter. Javert and Jean Valjean got out.

The driver humbly represented to monsieur the inspector that the Utrecht velvet of his carriage was all stained with the blood of the assassinated man and with the mud of the assassin. That was what he had understood. He added that an indemnity was due him. At the same time, taking his little book from his pocket, he begged monsieur the inspector to have the goodness to write him "a little scrap of certificate as to what."

Javert pushed back the little book which the driver handed him, and said: "How much must you have, including your stop and your trip?"

"It is seven hours and a quarter," answered the driver, "and my velvet was brand new. Eighty francs, monsieur the inspector."

Javert took four napoleons from his pocket and dismissed the fiacre.

Jean Valjean thought that Javert's intention was to take him on foot to the post of the Blancs-Manteaux or to the post of the Archives which are quite near by.

They entered the street. It was, as usual, empty. Javert followed Jean Valjean. They reached No. 7. Jean Valjean rapped. The door opened.

"Very well," said Javert. "Go up."

He added with a strange expression and as if he were making an effort in speaking in such a way:

"I will wait here for you."

Jean Valjean looked at Javert. This manner of proceeding was little in accordance with Javert's habits. Still, that Javert should now have a sort of haughty confidence in him, the confidence of the cat which grants the mouse the liberty of the length of her claw, resolved as Jean Valjean was to deliver himself up and make an end of it, could not surprise him very much. He opened the door, went into the house, cried to the porter who was in bed and who had drawn the cord without getting up: "It is I!" and mounted the stairs.

On reaching the first story, he paused. All painful paths have their halting-places. The window on the landing, which was a sliding window, was open. As in many old houses, the stairway admitted the light, and had a view upon the street. The street lamp, which stood exactly opposite, threw some rays upon the stairs, which produced an economy in light.

Jean Valjean, either to take breath or mechanically, looked out of this window. He leaned over the street. It is short, and the lamp lighted it from one end to the other. Jean Valjean was bewildered with amazement; there was nobody there.

Javert was gone.

BASQUE and the porter had carried Marius into the parlour, still stretched motionless upon the couch on which he had been first laid. The doctor, who had been sent for, had arrived. Aunt Gillenormand had got up.

Aunt Gillenormand went to and fro, in terror, clasping her hands, and incapable of doing anything but to say: "My God, is it possible?" She added at intervals: "Everything will be covered with blood!" When the first horror was over, a certain philosophy of the situation dawned upon her mind; "it must have turned out this way!" She did not attain to: "*I always said so!*" which is customary on occasions of this kind.

On the doctor's order, a cot-bed had been set up near the couch. The doctor examined Marius, and, after having determined that the pulse still beat, that the sufferer had no wound penetrating his breast, and that the blood at the corners of his mouth came from the nasal cavities, he had him laid flat upon the bed, without a pillow, his head on a level with his body, and even a little lower, with his chest bare, in order to facilitate respiration. Mademoiselle Gillenormand, seeing that they were taking off Marius' clothes, withdrew. She began to tell her beads in her room.

The body had not received any interior lesion; a ball, deadened by the pocket-book, had turned aside, and made the tour of the ribs with a hideous gash, but not deep, and consequently not dangerous. The long walk underground had completed the dislocation of the broken shoulder-blade, and there were serious difficulties there. There were sword cuts on the arms. No scar disfigured his face; the head, however, was as it were covered with hacks; what would be the result of these wounds on the head? did they stop at the scalp? did they affect the skull? That could not yet be told.

Basque and Nicolette tore up linen and made bandages; Nicolette sewed them, Basque folded them. There being no lint, the doctor stopped the flow of blood from the wounds temporarily with rolls of wadding. By the side of the bed, three candles were burning on a table upon which the surgical instruments were spread out. The doctor washed Marius' face and hair with cold water. A bucketful was red in a moment. The porter, candle in hand, stood by.

The physician seemed reflecting sadly. From time to time he shook his head, as if he were answering some question which he had put to himself internally. A bad sign for the patient, these mysterious dialogues of the physician with himself.

At the moment the doctor was wiping the face and touching the still closed eyelids lightly with his finger, a door opened at the rear end of the parlour, and a long, pale figure approached.

The slumbers of old men are easily broken; M. Gillenormand's room was next the parlour, and, in spite of the precautions they had taken, the noise had awakened him. Surprised by the light which he saw at the crack of his door, he had got out of bed, and groped his way along.

He was on the threshold, one hand on the knob of the half-opened door, his head bent a little forward and shaking, his body wrapped in a white nightgown, straight and without folds like a shroud; he was astounded; and he had the appearance of a phantom who is looking into a tomb.

He perceived the bed, and on the mattress that bleeding young man, white with a waxy whiteness, his eyes closed, his mouth open, his lips pallid, naked to the waist, gashed everywhere with red wounds, motionless.

The grandfather had, from head to foot, as much of a shiver as ossified limbs can have; his knees bent forward, showing through the opening of his nightgown his poor naked legs bristling with white hairs, and he murmured:

"Marius!"

"Monsieur," said Basque, "monsieur has just been brought home. He has been to the barricade, and—"

"He is dead!" cried the old man in a terrible voice. "Oh! the brigand."

Then a sort of sepulchral transfiguration made this octogenarian as straight as a young man.

"Monsieur," said he, "you are the doctor. Come, tell me one thing. He is dead, isn't he?"

The physician, in the height of anxiety, kept silence.

M. Gillenormand wrung his hands with a terrific burst of laughter.

"He is dead! he is dead! He has got killed at the barricade! in hatred of me! It is against me that he did this! Ah, the blood-drinker! This is the way he comes back to me! Misery of my life, he is dead!"

He went to a window, opened it wide as if he were stifling, and, standing before the shadow, he began to talk into the street to the night:

"Pierced, sabred, slaughtered, exterminated, slashed, cut in pieces! do you see that, the vagabond! He knew very well that I was waiting for him, and that I had had his room arranged for him, and that I had had his portrait of the time when he was a little boy hung at the head of my bed! He knew very well that he had only to come back, and that for years I had been calling him, and that I sat at night in my chimney corner, with my hands on my knees, not knowing what to do, and that I was a fool for his sake! You knew it very well, that you had only to come in and say: 'It is I,' and that you would be the master of the house, and that I would obey you, and that you would do whatever you liked with your old booby of a grandfather. You knew it very well, and you said: 'No, he is a royalist; I won't go!' And you went to the barricades, and you got yourself killed, out of spite! to revenge yourself for what I said to you about Monsieur the Duke de Berry! That is infamous! Go to bed, then, and sleep quietly! He is dead! That is my waking."

The physician, who began to be anxious on two accounts, left Marius a moment, and went to M. Gillenormand and took his arm. The grandfather turned round, looked at him with eyes which seemed swollen and bloody, and said quietly:

"Monsieur, I thank you. I am calm, I am a man, I saw the death of Louis XVI., I know how to bear up under events. There is one thing which is terrible, to think that it is your newspapers that do all the harm. You will have scribblers, talkers, lawyers, orators, tribunes, discussions, progress, lights, rights of man, freedom of the press, and this is the way they bring home your children for you. Oh! Marius! it is abominable! Killed! dead before me! A barricade! Oh! the bandit! Doctor, you live in the quartier, I believe? Oh! I know you well. I see your carriage pass from my window.

I am going to tell you. You would be wrong to think I am angry. We don't get angry with a dead man; that would be stupid. That is a child I brought up. I was an old man when he was yet quite small. He played at the Tuileries with his little spade and his little chair, and, so that the keeper should not scold, with my cane I filled up the holes in the ground that he made with his spade. One day he cried: 'Down with Louis XVIII!' and went away. It is not my fault."

Little by little, as internal eruptions must always make their way out, the connection of his words returned, but the grandfather appeared to have lost the strength to utter them, his voice was so dull and faint that it seemed to come from the other side of an abyss:

"It is all the same to me, I am going to die too, myself. And to say that there is no little creature in Paris who would have been glad to make the wretch happy! A rascal who, instead of amusing himself and enjoying life, went to fight and got himself riddled like a brute! And for whom? for what? For the republic! Instead of going to dance at the Chaumière, as young people should! He hasn't done the thing halfway. Yes, these times are infamous, infamous, infamous, and that is what I think of you, of your ideas, of your systems, of your masters, of your oracles, of your doctors, of your scamps of writers, of your beggars of philosophers, and of all the revolutions which for sixty years have frightened the flocks of crows in the Tuileries! And as you had no pity in getting yourself killed like that, I shall not have even any grief for your death, do you understand, assassin?"

At this moment, Marius slowly raised his lids, and his gaze, still veiled in the astonishment of lethargy, rested upon M. Gillenormand.

"Marius!" cried the old man. "Marius! my darling Marius! my child! my dear son! You are opening your eyes, you are looking at me, you are alive!"

JAVERT made his way with slow steps from the Rue de l'Homme Armé.

He walked with his head down, for the first time in his life, and, for the first time in his life as well, with his hands behind his back.

Until that day, Javert had taken, of the two attitudes of Napoleon, only that which expresses resolution, the arms folded upon the breast; that which expresses uncertainty, the hands behind the back, was unknown to him. Now, a change had taken place; his whole person, slow and gloomy, bore the impress of anxiety.

He plunged into the silent streets.

He took the shortest route towards the Seine, reached the Quai des Ormes, went along the quai, and stopped, at the corner of the Point Notre Dame. The Seine there forms between the Pont Notre Dame and the Pont au Change in one direction, and in the other between the Quai de la Mégisserie and the Quai aux Fleurs, a sort of square lake crossed by a rapid.

This point of the Seine is dreaded by mariners. Nothing is more dangerous than this rapid, narrowed at that period and vexed by the piles of the mill of the bridge, since removed. The two bridges, so near each other, increase the danger, the water hurrying fearfully under the arches. It rolls on with broad, terrible folds; it gathers and heaps up; the flood strains at the piles of the bridge as if to tear them out with huge liquid ropes. Men who fall in there, one never sees again; the best swimmers are drowned.

Javert leaned both elbows on the parapet, with his chin in his hands, and while his fingers were clenched mechanically in the thickest of his whiskers, he reflected.

There had been a new thing, a revolution, a catastrophe in the depths of his being; and Javert was suffering frightfully.

Javert felt that duty was growing weaker in his conscience, and he could not hide it from himself. He saw before him two roads, both equally straight; but he saw two; and that terrified him—him, who had never in his life known but one straight line. And, bitter anguish, these two roads were contradictory. One of these two straight lines excluded the other. Which of the two was the true one?

To owe life to a malefactor, to accept that debt and to pay it, to be on a level with a fugitive from justice, and pay him for one service with another service; to allow him to say: "Go away," and to say to him in turn: "Be free;" to sacrifice duty to personal motives, and to feel in these personal motives something general also, and perhaps superior; to betray society in order to be true to his own conscience; that all these absurdities should be realised and that they should be accumulated upon himself, this it was by which he was prostrated.

One thing had astonished him, that Jean Valjean had spared him, and one thing had petrified him, that he, Javert, had spared Jean Valjean.

Where was he? He sought himself and found himself no longer.

What should he do now? Give up Jean Valjean, that was wrong; leave Jean Valjean free, that was wrong. In the first case, the man of authority would fall lower than the man of the galley; in the second, a convict rose higher than the law and set his foot upon it. In both cases, dishonour to him, Javert. In every course which was open to him, there was a fall.

One of his causes of anxiety was, that he was compelled to think. The very violence of all these contradictory emotions forced him to it. Thought, an unaccustomed thing to him, and singularly painful.

What he had just done made him shudder. He, Javert, had thought good to decide, against all the regulations of the police, against the entire code, in favour of a release. He had substituted his own affairs for the public affairs. Every time that he set himself face to face with this nameless act which he had committed, he trembled from head to foot. Upon what should he resolve? A single resource remained: to return immediately to the Rue de l'Homme Armé, and have Jean Valjean arrested. It was clear that that was what he must do. He could not.

Something barred the way to him on that side.

Something? What? Is there anything else in the world besides tribunals, sentences, police, and authority? Javert's ideas were overturned.

A galley-slave sacred! a convict not to be taken by justice! and that by the act of Javert!

That Javert and Jean Valjean, the man made to be severe, the man made to be submissive, that these two men, who were each the thing of the law, should have come to this point of setting themselves both above the law, was not this terrible?

What then! such enormities should happen and nobody should be punished? Jean Valjean, stronger than the entire social order, should be free and he, Javert, continue to eat the bread of the government!

This could not last.

His supreme anguish was the loss of all certainty. He felt that he was uprooted. The code was now but a stump in his hand. He had to do with scruples of an unknown species. There was in him a revelation of feeling entirely distinct from the declarations of the law, his only standard hitherto. To retain his old virtue, that no longer sufficed. An entire order of unexpected facts arose and subjugated him. An entire new world appeared to his soul; favour accepted and returned, devotion, compassion, indulgence, acts of violence committed by pity upon austerity, respect of persons, no more final condemnation, no more damnation, the possibility of a tear in the eye of the law, a mysterious justice according to God going counter to justice according to men. He perceived in the darkness the fearful rising of an unknown moral sun; he was horrified and blinded by it.

Javert's ideal was not to be humane, not to be great, not to be sublime; it was to be irreproachable. Now he had just failed.

He had lost his bearings in this unexpected presence; he did not know what to do with this superior; he who was not ignorant that the subordinate is bound always to yield, that he ought neither to disobey, nor to blame, nor to discuss, and that, in presence of a superior who astonishes him too much, the inferior has no resource but resignation.

But how manage to send in his resignation to God?

However this might be, and it was always to this that he returned, one thing overruled all else for him, that was, that he had just committed an appalling infraction. He had closed his eyes upon a convicted second offender in breach of his ban. He had set a galley-slave at large. He had robbed the laws of a man who belonged to them. He had done that. He could not understand himself. He was not sure of being himself. The very reasons of his action escaped him; he caught only the whirl of them. He had lived up to this moment by that blind faith which a dark probity engenders. This faith was leaving him, this probity was failing him. All that he had believed was dissipated. Truths which he had no wish for inexorably besieged him. He must henceforth be another man. He suffered the strange pangs of a conscience suddenly operated upon for the cataract. He saw what he revolted at seeing. He felt that he was emptied, useless, broken off from his past life, destitute, dissolved. Authority was dead in him. He had no further reason for existence.

Terrible situation! to be moved.

Unnatural state, if ever there was one. There were only two ways to get out of it. One, to go resolutely to Jean Valjean, and to return the man of the galleys to the dungeon. The other—

The darkness was complete. It was the sepulchral moment which follows midnight. A ceiling of clouds concealed the stars. The sky was only an ominous depth. The houses in the city no longer showed a single light; nobody was passing; all that he could see of the streets and the quais was deserted; Notre Dame and the towers of the Palais de Justice seemed like features of the night. A lamp reddened the curb of the quai. The silhouettes of the bridges were distorted in the mist, one behind the other. The rains had swelled the river.

The place where Javert was leaning was, it will be remembered, situated exactly over the rapids of the Seine, perpendicularly over that formidable whirlpool which knots and unknots itself like an endless screw.

Javert bent his head and looked. All was black. He could distinguish nothing. He heard a frothing sound; but he did not see the river. At intervals, in that giddy depth, a gleam appeared in dim serpentine contortions, the water having this power, in the most complete night, of taking light, nobody knows whence, and changing it into an adder. The gleam vanished, and all became again indistinct. Immensity seemed open there. What was beneath was not water, it was chasm. The wall of the quai, abrupt, confused, mingled with vapour, suddenly lost to sight, seemed like an escarpment of the infinite.

He saw nothing, but he perceived the hostile chill of the water, and the insipid odour of the moist stones. A fierce breath rose from that abyss. The swollen river guessed at rather than perceived, the tragical whispering of the flood, the dismal vastness of the arches of the bridge, the imaginable fall into that gloomy void, all that shadow was full of horror.

Javert remained for some minutes motionless, gazing into that opening of darkness; he contemplated the invisible with a fixedness which resembled attention. The water gurgled. Suddenly he took off his hat and laid it on the edge of the quai. A moment afterwards, a tall and black form, which from a distance some belated passer might have taken for a phantom, appeared standing on the parapet, bent towards the Seine, then sprang up, and fell straight into the darkness; there was a dull splash; and the shadow alone was in the secret of the convulsions of that obscure form which had disappeared under the water.

XXX. THE WEDDING

SOME TIME after the events which we have just related, the Sieur Boulatruelle had a vivid emotion.

Boulatruelle, it will perhaps be remembered, was a man occupied with troublous and various things. He broke stones and damaged travellers on the highway. Digger and robber, he had a dream; he believed in treasures buried in the forest of Montfermeil. He hoped one day to find money in the ground at the foot of a tree; in the meantime, he was willing to search for it in the pockets of the passers-by.

Nevertheless, for the moment, he was prudent. He had just had a narrow escape. He had been picked up in the Jondrette garret with the other bandits; his drunkenness had saved him. It could never be clearly made out whether he was there as a robber or as robbed. An order of *nol. pros.*, founded upon his clearly proved state of drunkenness on the evening of the ambuscade, had set him at liberty. He regained the freedom of the woods. He returned to his road from Gagny to Lagny to break stones for the use of the state, under administrative surveillance, a little cooled towards robbery, which had nearly ruined him, but turning with the more affection towards wine, which had just saved him.

As to the vivid emotion which he had a little while after his return beneath the thatched roof of his road-labourer's hut, it was this:

One morning a little before the break of day, Boulatruelle, while on the way to his work according to his habit, and upon the watch, perhaps, perceived a man among the branches, whose back only he could see, but whose form, as it seemed to him, through the distance and the twilight, was not altogether unknown to him. Boulatruelle, although a drunkard, had a correct and lucid memory, an indispensable defensive arm to him who is slightly in conflict with legal order.

"Where the devil have I seen something like that man?" inquired he of himself.

Boulatruelle thought of the treasure. By dint of digging into his memory he dimly recollected having already had, several years before, a similar surprise.

While he was meditating, he had bowed his head, which was natural, but not very cunning. When he raised it again there was no longer anything there. The man had vanished in the forest and the twilight.

"The deuce," said Boulatruelle, "I will find him again. I will discover the parish of that parishioner. This Patron-Minette prowler has a why, I will find it out. Nobody has a secret in my woods without I have a finger in it."

He took his pickaxe, which was very sharp.

"Here is something," he muttered, "to pry into the ground or a man with."

And, limping along at his best in the path which the man must have followed, he took his way through the thicket.

When he had gone a hundred yards, daylight, which began to break, aided him. Footsteps printed on the sand here and there, grass matted down, heath broken off, young branches bent into the bushes and rising again with a graceful slowness, like the arms of a pretty woman who stretches herself on awaking, indicated to him a sort of track. He followed it, then he lost it.

Time was passing. He pushed further forward into the wood and reached a kind of eminence. A morning hunter who passed along a path in the distance, whistling, inspired him with the idea of climbing a tree. Although old, he was agile. There was near by a beech tree of great height; Boulatruelle climbed the beech as high as he could.

The idea was good. In exploring the solitude on the side where the wood was entirely wild and tangled, Boulatruelle suddenly perceived the man.

Hardly had he perceived him when he lost sight of him.

The man entered, or rather glided, into a distant glade, masked by tall trees, but which Boulatruelle knew very well from having noticed there, near a great heap of burrstone, a wounded chestnut tree bandaged with a plate of zinc nailed upon the bark. The heap of stones, intended for nobody knows what use, which could be seen there thirty years ago, is doubtless there still.

Boulatruelle, with the rapidity of joy, let himself fall from the tree rather than descended. The lair was found, the problem was to catch that famous treasure of his dreams.

It was no easy matter to reach that glade. By the beaten paths, it required a good quarter of an hour. In a straight line, through the underbrush, which is there singularly thick, very thorny, and very aggressive, it required a long half-hour. There was Boulatruelle's mistake. Accustomed to going astray, this time he made the blunder of going straight.

He threw himself resolutely into the thickest of the bushes. He had to deal with hollies, with nettles, with hawthorns, with sweetbriers, with thistles, with exceedingly irascible brambles. He was very much scratched. At the bottom of a ravine he found a stream which must be crossed.

He finally reached the glade, at the end of forty minutes, sweating, soaked, breathless, torn, ferocious.

Nobody in the glade.

Boulatruelle ran to the heap of stones. It was in its place. Nobody had carried it away.

As for the man, he had vanished into the forest. He had escaped. Where? on which side? in what thicket? Impossible to guess.

And, a bitter thing, there was behind the heap of stones, before the tree with the plate of zinc, some fresh earth, a pick, forgotten or abandoned, and a hole.

This hole was empty.

"Robber!" cried Boulatruelle, showing both fists to the horizon.

MARIUS was for a long time neither dead nor alive. He had for several weeks a fever accompanied with delirium, and serious cerebral symptoms resulting rather from the concussion produced by the wounds in the head than from the wounds themselves.

He repeated the name of Cosette during entire nights in the dismal loquacity of fever and with the gloomy obstinacy of agony. The physician was anxious. "Above all, let the wounded man have no excitement," he repeated. As long as there was danger, M. Gillenormand, in despair at the bedside of his grandson, was, like Marius, neither dead nor alive.

Every day, and sometimes twice a day, a very well-dressed gentleman with white hair came to inquire after the wounded man, and left a large package of lint for the dressings.

At last, on the 7th of September, four months, to a day, after the sorrowful night when they had brought him home dying to his grandfather, the physician declared him out of danger.

This long sickness and long convalescence saved him from pursuit. In France, there is no anger, even governmental, which six months does not extinguish.

At each new phase of improvement, which continued to grow more and more visible, the grandfather raved. He did a thousand mirthful things mechanically; he ran up and down stairs without knowing why. A neighbour, a pretty woman withal, was amazed at receiving a large bouquet one morning; it was M. Gillenormand who sent it to her. The husband made a scene. M. Gillenormand attempted to take Nicolette upon his knees. He called Marius Monsieur the Baron.

He cried, *"Vive la République!"*

In this lightness of heart which possessed him, he was the most venerable of children. For fear of fatiguing or of annoying the convalescent, he got behind him to smile upon him. He was contented, joyous, enraptured, delightful, young. His white hairs added a sweet majesty to the cheerful light upon his face. When grace is joined with wrinkles, it is adorable. There is an unspeakable dawn in happy old age.

As for Marius, while he let them dress his wounds and care for him, he had one fixed idea: Cosette.

He did not know what had become of Cosette; the whole affair of the Rue de la Chanvrerie was like a cloud in his memory. Eponine, Gavroche, Mabeuf, the Thénardiers, all his friends mingled drearily with the smoke of the barricade; the strange passage of M. Fauchelevent in that bloody drama produced upon him the effect of an enigma in a tempest; he understood nothing in regard to his own life; he neither knew how, nor by whom, he had been saved, and nobody about him knew; all that they could tell him was that he had been brought to the Rue des Filles du Calvaire in a fiacre by night. Past, present, future, all was now to him but the mist of a vague idea; but there was within this mist an immovable point, one clear and precise feature, something which was granite, a resolution, a will: to find Cosette again.

He was not won over, and was little softened by all the solicitude and all the tenderness of his grandfather. In the first place, he was not in the secret at all; then, in his sick man's reveries, still feverish perhaps, he distrusted this gentleness as a new and strange thing, the object of which was to subdue him. He remained cold. The grandfather expended his poor old smile for nothing. Marius said to himself it was well so long as he, Marius, did not speak and offered no resistance; but that, when the question of

Cosette was raised, he would find another face, and his grandfather's real attitude would be unmasked. Then it would be harsh recrudescence of family questions, every sarcasm and every objection at once: Fauchelevent, Coupelevent, fortune, poverty, misery, the stone at the neck, the future. Violent opposition; conclusion, refusal. Marius was bracing himself in advance.

As it almost always happens in similar cases, Marius, in order to try himself, skirmished before offering battle. This is called feeling the ground. One morning it happened that M. Gillenormand, over a newspaper which had fallen into his hands, spoke lightly of the Convention and discharged a royalist epiphonema upon Danton, Saint Just, and Robespierre. "The men of '93 were giants," said Marius, sternly. The old man was silent, and did not whisper for the rest of the day.

He determined that in case of refusal he would tear off his bandages, dislocate his shoulder, lay bare and open his remaining wounds, and refuse all nourishment. His wounds were his ammunition. To have Cosette or to die.

He waited for the favourable moment with the crafty patience of the sick.

One day M. Gillenormand, while his daughter was putting in order the vials and the cups upon the marble top of the bureau, bent over Marius and said to him in his most tender tone:

"Do you see, my darling Marius, in your place I would eat meat now rather than fish. A fried sole is excellent to begin a convalescence, but, to put the sick man on his legs, it takes a good cutlet."

Marius, nearly all whose strength had returned, gathered it together, sat up in bed, rested his clenched hands on the sheets, looked his grandfather in the face, assumed a terrible air, and said:

"This leads me to say something to you."

"What is it?"

"It is that I wish to marry."

"Foreseen," said the grandfather. And he burst out laughing.

"How foreseen?"

"Yes, foreseen. You shall have her, your lassie."

Marius, astounded, and overwhelmed by the dazzling burst of happiness, trembled in every limb.

M. Gillenormand continued:

"Yes, you shall have her, your handsome, pretty little girl. She comes every day in the shape of an old gentleman to inquire after you. Since you were wounded, she has passed her time in weeping and making lint. I have made inquiry. She lives in the Rue de l'Homme Armé, Number Seven. Ah, we are ready! Ah! you want her! Well, you shall have her. That catches you. You had arranged your little plot; you said to yourself: I am going to make it known bluntly to that grandfather, to that mummy of the Regency and of the Directory, to that old beau. We shall see. Battle. Ah! that is good. I propose a cutlet, and you answer: 'A propos, I wish to marry.' That is what I call a transition. Ah! you had reckoned upon some bickering. You didn't know that I was an old coward. What do you say to that? You are spited. To find your grandfather still more stupid than yourself, you didn't expect that, you lose the argument which you were to have made to me, monsieur advocate; it is provoking. Well, it is all the same, rage. I do what you wish, that cuts you out of it, idiot. Listen. I have made inquiries, I am sly too; she is charming, she is modest, the lancer is not true, she has made heaps of lint, she is a jewel, she worships you. Cosette, so be it; love, so be it; I ask nothing better. Monsieur, take the trouble to marry. Be happy, my dear child."

This said, the old man burst into sobs.

And he took Marius' head, and he hugged it in both arms against his old breast, and they both began to weep. That is one of the forms of supreme happiness.

"Father!" exclaimed Marius.

"Ah! you love me then!" said the old man.

They choked and could not speak.

Marius released his head from his grandfather's arms, and said softly:

"But, father, now that I am well, it seems to me that I could see her."

"Foreseen again, you shall see her to-morrow."

"Father!"

"What?"

"Why not to-day?"

"Well, to-day. Here goes for to-day. You have called me 'Father,' three times, it is well worth that. I will see to it. She shall be brought to you. Foreseen, I tell you. This has already been put into verse. It is the conclusion of André Chénier's elegy of the *Jeune malade*, André Chénier who was murdered by the scound—, by the giants of '93."

M. Gillenormand thought he perceived a slight frown on Marius' brow, although, in truth, he was no longer listening. The grandfather, trembling at having introduced André Chénier so inopportunely, resumed precipitately:

"Murdered is not the word. The fact is that the great revolutionary geniuses, who were not evilly disposed, that is incontestable, who were heroes, egad! found that André Chénier embarrassed them a little, and they had him gillout— That is to say that those great men, on the seventh of Thermidor, in the interest of the public safety, begged André Chénier to have the kindness to go—"

M. Gillenormand, choked by his own sentence, could not continue; the old man, overwhelmed by so many emotions, threw himself, as quickly as his age permitted, out of the bedroom, pushed the door to behind him, and, purple, strangling, foaming, his eyes starting from his head, found himself face to face with honest Basque who was polishing boots in the antechamber. He seized Basque by the collar and cried full in his face with fury: "By the hundred thousand Javottes of the devil, those brigands assassinated him!"

"Who, monsieur?"

"André Chénier!"

"Yes, monsieur," said Basque in dismay.

THE whole family, including Basque and Nicolette, were assembled in Marius' room when Cosette entered.

Just at that instant the grandfather was about to blow his nose; he stopped short, holding his nose in his handkerchief, and looking at Cosette above it:

"Adorable!" he exclaimed.

Then he blew his nose with a loud noise.

Cosette was intoxicated, enraptured, startled, in Heaven. She was as frightened as one can be by happiness. She stammered, quite pale, quite red, wishing to throw herself into Marius' arms, and ashamed to show her love before all those people.

With Cosette and behind her had entered a man with white hair, grave, smiling nevertheless, but with a vague and poignant smile. This was "Monsieur Fauchelevent;" this was Jean Valjean.

He was *very well dressed*, as the porter had said, in a new black suit, with a white cravat.

The porter was a thousand miles from recognising in this correct bourgeois, in this probable notary, the frightful corpse-bearer who had landed at his door on the night of the 7th of June, ragged, muddy, hideous, haggard, his face masked by blood and dirt, supporting the fainting Marius in his arms; still his porter's scent was awakened. When M. Fauchelevent had arrived with Cosette, the porter could not help confiding this remark to his wife: "I don't know why I always imagine that I have seen that face somewhere."

Monsieur Fauchelevent, in Marius' room, stayed near the door, as if apart. He had under his arm a package similar in appearance to an octavo volume, wrapped in paper. The paper of the envelope was greenish, and seemed mouldy.

"Does this gentleman always have books under his arm like that?" asked Mademoiselle Gillenormand, who did not like books, in a low voice of Nicolette.

"Well," answered M. Gillenormand, who had heard her, in the same tone, "he is a scholar. What then? is it his fault?"

And bowing, he said, in a low voice:

"Monsieur Tranchelevent—"

Father Gillenormand did not do this on purpose, but inattention to proper names was an aristocratic way he had.

"Monsieur Tranchelevent, I have the honour of asking of you for my grandson, Monsieur the Baron Marius Pontmercy, the hand of mademoiselle."

Monsieur Tranchelevent bowed.

"It is done," said the grandfather.

And, turning towards Marius and Cosette, with arms extended and blessing, he cried:

"Permission to adore each other."

They did not make him say it twice. It was all the same! The cooing began. They talked low, Marius leaning on his long chair, Cosette standing near him. "Oh, my God!" murmured Cosette, "I see you again! It is you! it is you! To have gone to fight like that! But why? It is horrible. For four months I have been dead. Oh, how naughty it is to have been in that battle! What had I done to you? I pardon you, but you won't do it again. I have been making lint all the time. Here, monsieur, look, it is your fault, my fingers are callous." "Angel!" said Marius.

Then, as there were spectators, they stopped, and did not say another word, contenting themselves with touching each other's hands very gently.

M. Gillenormand turned towards all those who were in the room, and cried:

"Why don't you talk loud, the rest of you? Make a noise, behind the scenes. Come, a little uproar, the devil! so that these children can chatter at their ease."

And, approaching Marius and Cosette, he said to them very low:

"Make love. Adore each other. Only," added he, suddenly darkening, "what a misfortune! This is what I am thinking of! More than half of what I have is in annuity; as long as I live, it's all well enough, but after my death, twenty years from now, ah! my poor children, you will not have a sou."

"Mademoiselle Euphrasie Fauchelevent has six hundred thousand francs."

It was Jean Valjean's voice.

He had not yet uttered a word, nobody seemed even to remember that he was there, and he stood erect and motionless behind all these happy people.

"How is Mademoiselle Euphrasie in question?" asked the grandfather, startled.

"That is me," answered Cosette.

"Six hundred thousand francs!" resumed M. Gillenormand.

"Less fourteen or fifteen thousand francs, perhaps," said Jean Valjean.

And he laid on the table the package which Aunt Gillenormand had taken for a book.

Jean Valjean opened the package himself; it was a bundle of banknotes. They ran through them, and they counted them. There were five hundred bills of a thousand francs, and a hundred and sixty-eight of five hundred. In all, five hundred and eighty-four thousand francs.

"That is a good book," said M. Gillenormand.

"Five hundred and eighty-four thousand francs!" murmured the aunt. "Five hundred and eighty-four! you might call it six hundred thousand, indeed!"

As for Marius and Cosette, they were looking at each other during this time; they paid little attention to this incident.

The reader has doubtless understood that Jean Valjean had been able, thanks to his first escape after the Champmathieu affair, to withdraw the sum made by him, under the name of Monsieur Madeleine, from Laffitte's; and that, in the fear of being retaken, he had concealed and buried that sum in the forest of Montfermeil. The sum, six hundred and thirty thousand francs, all in bank-notes, was of small bulk, and was contained in a box; but to preserve the box from moisture he had placed it in an oaken chest, full of chestnut shavings. In the same chest, he had put his other treasure, the bishop's candlesticks. It will be remembered that he carried away these candlesticks when he escaped from M— sur M—. The man perceived one evening, for the first time, by Boulatruelle, was Jean Valjean. Afterwards, whenever Jean Valjean was in need of money, he went to the glade for it. Hence the absences of which we have spoken. He had a pickaxe somewhere in the bushes, in a hiding-place known only to himself. When he saw Marius convalescent, feeling that the hour was approaching when this money might be useful, he had gone after it; and it was he again whom Boulatruelle saw in the wood, but this time in the morning, and not at night. Boulatruelle inherited the pickaxe.

The real sum was five hundred and eighty-four thousand five hundred francs. Jean Valjean took out five hundred francs for himself. "We will see afterwards," thought he.

The difference between this sum and the six hundred and thirty thousand francs withdrawn from Laffitte's represented the expenses of ten years, from 1823 to 1833. The five years spent in the convent had cost only five thousand francs.

Jean Valjean put the two silver candlesticks upon the mantel, where they shone, to Toussaint's great admiration.

Moreover, Jean Valjean knew that he was delivered from Javert. It had been mentioned in his presence, and he had verified the fact in the *Moniteur*, that an inspector of police, named Javert, had been found drowned under a washerwoman's boat between the Pont au Change and Pont Neuf.

All the preparations were made for the marriage. The physician said that it might take place in February. This was in December. Some ravishing weeks of perfect happiness rolled away.

Jean Valjean did all, smoothed all, conciliated all, made all easy. He hastened towards Cosette's happiness with as much eagerness, and apparently as much joy, as Cosette herself.

As he had been a mayor, he knew how to solve a delicate problem, Cosette's civil state. To bluntly give her origin, who knows? that might prevent the marriage. He arranged a family of dead people for her, a sure means of incurring no objection. Cosette was what remained of an extinct family; Cosette was not his daughter, but the daughter of another Fauchelevent. Two brothers Fauchelevent had been gardeners at the convent of the Petit Picpus. They went to this convent, the best recommendations and the most respectable testimonials abounded; the good nuns, little apt and little inclined to fathom questions of paternity, and understanding no malice, had never known very exactly of which of the two Fauchelevents little Cosette was the daughter. They said what was wanted of them, and said it with zeal. A notary's act was drawn up. Cosette became before the law Mademoiselle Euphrasie Fauchelevent. She was declared an orphan. Jean

Valjean arranged matters in such a way as to be designated, under the name of Fauchelevent, as Cosette's guardian, with M. Gillenormand as overseeing guardian.

As for the five hundred and eighty-four thousand francs, that was a legacy left to Cosette by a dead person who desired to remain unknown.

Cosette learned that she was not the daughter of that old man whom she had so long called father. He was only a relative; another Fauchelevent was her real father. At any other time, this would have broken her heart. But at this ineffable hour, it was only a little shadow, a darkening, and she had so much joy that this cloud was of short duration. She had Marius.

She continued, however, to say "Father" to Jean Valjean.

Cosette, in raptures, was enthusiastic about Grandfather Gillenormand. It is true that he loaded her with presents. Nothing amused him so much as being magnificent. He had given Cosette a dress of Binche guipure which descended to him from his own grandmother. "These fashions have come round again," said he, "old things are the rage, and the young women of my age dress like the old women of my childhood."

He rifled his respectable round-bellied bureaus of Coromandel lac which had not been opened for years. "Let us put these dowagers to the confession," said he; "let us see what they have in them." He noisily stripped the deep drawers full of toilets of all his wives, of all his mistresses, and of all his ancestresses. Pekins, damasks, lampas, painted moires, dresses of gros de Tours, Indian handkerchiefs embroidered with a gold which could be washed, dauphines in the piece finished on both sides, Genoa and Alençon point, antique jewellery, comfit-boxes of ivory ornamented with microscopic battles, clothes, ribbons, he lavished all upon Cosette. Cosette, astonished, desperately in love with Marius and wild with gratitude towards M. Gillenormand, dreamed of a boundless happiness clad in satin and velvet. Her soul soared into the azure on wings of Mechlin lace.

Aunt Gillenormand beheld it all with her imperturbable placidity. She had had within five or six months a certain number of emotions; Marius returned, Marius brought back bleeding, Marius brought back from a barricade, Marius dead, then alive, Marius reconciled, Marius betrothed, Marius marrying a pauper, Marius marrying a millionaire. The six hundred thousand francs had been her last surprise.

It is probable that, if the marriage had been poor, she would have left it poor. So much the worse for monsieur, my nephew! He marries a beggar, let him be a beggar. But Cosette's half-million pleased the aunt, and changed her feelings in regard to this pair of lovers. Some consideration is due to six hundred thousand francs, and it was clear that she could not do otherwise than leave her fortune to these young people, since they no longer needed it.

It was arranged that the couple should live with the grandfather. M. Gillenormand absolutely insisted upon giving them his room, the finest in the house. "It will rejuvenate me," he declared. "It is an old project. I always had the idea of making a wedding in my room." He filled this room with a profusion of gay old furniture. He hung the walls and the ceiling with an extraordinary stuff which he had in the piece, and which he believed to be from Utrecht, a satin background with golden immortelles, and velvet auriculas. "With this stuff," said he, "the Duchess d'Anville's bed was draped at La Roche Guyon." He put a little Saxony figure on the mantel, holding a muff over her naked belly.

M. Gillenormand's library became the attorney's office which Marius required; an office, it will be remembered, being rendered necessary by the rules of the order.

The lovers saw each other every day. Cosette came with M. Fauchelevent. "It is reversing the order of things," said Mademoiselle Gillenormand, "that the intended should come to the house to be courted like this." But Marius' convalescence had led to the habit: and the armchairs in the Rue des Filles du Calvaire, better for long talks than the straw chairs of the Rue de l'Homme Armé, had rooted it. Marius and M. Fauchelevent saw one another, but did not speak to each other. That seemed to be understood. Every girl needs a chaperon. Cosette could not have come without M. Fauchelevent. To Marius, M. Fauchelevent was the condition of Cosette. He accepted it. Once, on the subject of education, which Marius wished gratuitous and obligatory, multiplied under all forms, lavished upon all like the air and the sunshine, in one word, respirable by the entire people, they fell into unison and almost into a conversation. Marius remarked on this occasion that M. Fauchelevent talked well, and even with a certain elevation of language. There was, however, something wanting. M. Fauchelevent had something less than a man of the world, and something more.

Marius, inwardly and in the depth of his thought, surrounded this M. Fauchelevent, who was to him simply benevolent and cold, with all sorts of silent questions. There came to him at intervals doubts about his own recollections. In his memory there was a hole, a black place, an abyss scooped out by four months of agony. Many things were lost in it. At moments, Marius covered his face with his hands, and saw Mabeuf fall again, he heard Gavroche singing beneath the grape, he felt upon his lip the chill of Eponine's forehead; Enjolras, Courfeyrac, Jean Prouvaire, Combeferre, Bossuet, Grantaire, all his friends, rose up before him, then dissipated. All these beings, dear, sorrowful, valiant, charming or tragical, were they dreams? had they really existed?

Once only, Marius brought the Rue de la Chanvrerie into the conversation, and, turning towards M. Fauchelevent, he said to him:

"You are well acquainted with that street?"

"What street?"

"The Rue de la Chanvrerie."

"I have no idea of the name of that street," answered M. Fauchelevent in the most natural tone in the world.

The answer, which bore upon the name of the street, and not upon the street itself, appeared to Marius more conclusive than it was.

"Decidedly," thought he, "I have been dreaming. I have had a hallucination. It was somebody who resembled him. M. Fauchelevent was not there."

The enchantment, great as it was, did not efface other preoccupations from Marius' mind.

There was Thénardier; there was the unknown man who had brought him, Marius, to M. Gillenormand's.

Marius persisted in trying to find these two men, not intending to be happy and forget them, and fearing lest these debts of duty unpaid might cast a shadow over his life, so luminous henceforth.

That Thénardier was a scoundrel, took away nothing from this fact that he had saved Colonel Pontmercy. Thénardier was a bandit to everybody except Marius.

And Marius, ignorant of the real scene of the battle-field of Waterloo, did not know that his father owed his life to Thénardier without owing him any thanks.

None of the various agents whom Marius employed, succeeded in finding Thénardier's track. The Thénardiess had died in prison pending the examination on the charge. Thénardier and his daughter Azelma, the two who alone remained of that woeful group, had plunged back into the shadow.

As for the unknown man who had saved Marius, the researches at first had some result, then stopped short. They succeeded in finding the fiacre which had brought Marius to the Rue des Filles du Calvaire on the evening of the 6th of June. The driver declared that on the 6th of June, by order of a police officer, he had been "stationed," from three o'clock in the afternoon until night, on the quai of the Champs Elysées, above the outlet of the Grand Sewer; that, about nine o'clock in the evening, the grating of the sewer, which overlooks the river beach, was opened; that a man came out, carrying another man on his shoulders, who seemed to be dead; that the officer watching at that point arrested the living man, and seized the dead man; that, on the order of the officer, he, the driver, received "all those people" into the fiacre; that they went first to the Rue des Filles du Calvaire; that they left the dead man there; that the dead man was Monsieur Marius, and that he, the driver, recognised him plainly, although he was alive "this time;" that they then got into his carriage again; that he whipped up his horses; that, within a few steps of the door of the Archives, he had been called to stop; that there, in the street, he had been paid and left, and that the officer took away the other man; that he knew nothing more, that the night was very dark.

Marius, we have said, recollected nothing. He merely remembered having been seized from behind by a vigorous hand at the moment he fell backwards into the barricades, then all became a blank to him. He had recovered consciousness only at M. Gillenormand's.

He could not doubt his own identity. How did it come about, however, that, falling in the Rue de la Chanvrerie, he had been picked up by the police officer on the banks of the Seine, near the Pont des Invalides? Somebody had carried him from the quartier of the markets to the Champs Elysées. And how? By the sewer. Unparalleled devotion!

Somebody? who?

It was this man whom Marius sought.

Marius pushed his researches as far as the prefecture of police. The prefecture knew less than the driver of the fiacre. They had no knowledge of any arrest made on the 6th of June at the grating of the Grand Sewer; they had received no officer's report upon that fact, which, at the prefecture, was regarded as a fable. They attributed the invention of this fable to the driver.

In the hope of aid in his researches, Marius had had preserved the bloody clothes which he wore when he was brought back to his grandfather's. On examining the coat, it was noticed that one skirt was oddly torn. A piece was missing.

One evening, Marius spoke, before Cosette and Jean Valjean, of all this singular adventure, of the numberless inquiries which he had made, and of the uselessness of his efforts. The cold countenance of "Monsieur Fauchelevent" made him impatient. He exclaimed with a vivacity which had almost the vibration of anger:

"Yes, that man, whoever he may be, was sublime. Do you know what he did, monsieur? He intervened like the archangel. He must have thrown himself into the midst of the combat, have snatched me out of it, have opened the sewer, have drawn me into it, have borne me through it! He must have made his way for more than four miles through hideous subterranean galleries, bent, stooping, in the darkness, in the cloaca, more than four miles, monsieur, with a corpse upon his back! And with what object? With the single object of saving that corpse. And that corpse was I. He said to himself: 'There is perhaps a glimmer of life still there; I will risk my own life for that miserable spark!' And his life, he did not risk it once, but twenty times! And each step was a danger. The proof is, that on coming out of the sewer he was arrested. Do you know, monsieur, that that man did all that? And he could expect no recompense. What was I? An insurgent. What was I? A vanquished man. Oh! if Cosette's six hundred thousand francs were mine—"

"They are yours," interrupted Jean Valjean.

"Well," resumed Marius, "I would give them to find that man!"

Jean Valjean kept silence.

THE NIGHT of the 16th of February, 1833, was a blessed night. Above its shade the heavens were opened. It was the wedding night of Marius and Cosette.

The day had been adorable. It rained that day, but there is always a little patch of blue in the sky which lovers see, even though the rest of creation be under an umbrella.

A few days before the day fixed for the marriage, an accident happened to Jean Valjean; he slightly bruised the thumb of his right hand. It was not serious; and he had allowed nobody to take any trouble about it, nor to dress it, nor even to see his hurt, not even Cosette. It compelled him, however, to muffle his hand in a bandage, and to carry his arm in a sling, and prevented his signing anything. M. Gillenormand, as Cosette's overseeing guardian, took his place.

We shall take the reader neither to the mairie nor to the church. We generally turn our backs upon the drama as soon as it puts its bridegroom's bouquet into his buttonhole. We shall merely mention an incident which, although unnoticed by the wedding party, marked its progress from the Rue des Filles du Calvaire to Saint Paul's.

They were repaving, at that time, the northern extremity of the Rue Saint Louis. It was impossible for the wedding carriages to go directly to Saint Paul's. It was necessary to change the route, and the shortest way was to turn off by the boulevard. One of the guests observed that it was Mardi Gras, and that the boulevard would be encumbered with carriages. "Why?" asked M. Gillenormand. "On account of the masks." "Capital!" said the grandfather; "let us go that way. These young folks are marrying; they are going to enter upon the serious things of life. It will prepare them for it to see a bit of masquerade."

Masks abounded on the boulevard. It was of no avail that it rained at intervals; Pantaloon and Harlequin were obstinate. In the good-humour of that winter of 1833, Paris had disguised herself as Venice. We see no such Mardi Gras nowadays. Everything being an expanded carnival, there is no longer any carnival.

From time to time, there was a block somewhere in the procession of vehicles; one or the other of the two lateral files stopped until the knot was disentangled; one carriage obstructed was enough to paralyse the whole line. Then they resumed their course.

Chance determined that one of these shapeless bunches of masked women and men, drawn along in a huge calash, stopped on the left of the boulevard while the wedding cortège was stopping on the right. From one side of the boulevard to the other, the carriage in which the masks were, looked into the carriage opposite, in which was the bride.

"Hullo!" said a mask, " a wedding."

"A sham wedding," replied another. "We are the genuine."

Meanwhile, two other masks in the same carriage, a huge-nosed Spaniard with an oldish air and enormous black moustaches, and a puny jade, a very young girl, with a black velvet mask, had also noticed the wedding party, and, while their companions and the passers-by were lampooning one another, carried on a dialogue in a low tone.

Their aside was covered by the tumult and lost in it. The gusts of rain had soaked the carriage, which was thrown wide open; the February wind is not warm; even while answering the Spaniard, the girl, with her low-necked dress, shivered, laughed, and coughed.

This was the dialogue:

"Say, now. Do you see that old fellow?"

"Well?"

"I am sure I know him."

"Ah!"

"Bend forward well and try to see the bride."

"I can't."

"It's all the same, that old fellow who has something the matter with his paw, I am sure I know him."

"And what good does it do you to know him?"

"Listen."

"What?"

"For my part, I can hardly go out unless I am masked. I must get back to my hole. You are free."

"Not too much so."

"More than I, still."

"Well, what then?"

"You must try to find out where this wedding party have gone."

"Where it is going?"

"Yes."

"I know that."

"That isn't all. I tell you that you must try to let me know what that wedding party is, that this old fellow belongs to, and where that wedding party lives."

"Not often! that will be funny. It is convenient to find, a week afterwards, a wedding party which passed by in Paris on Mardi Gras. Is it possible!"

"No matter, you must try. Do you understand, Azelma?"

The two files resumed their movement in opposite directions on the two sides of the boulevard, and the carriage of the masks lost sight of the bride's.

Cosette wore her dress of Binche guipure over a skirt of white taffeta, a veil of English point, a necklace of fine pearls, a crown of orange flowers; all this was white, and, in this whiteness, she was radiant.

Jean Valjean, in black, followed and smiled.

"Monsieur Fauchelevent," said the grandfather to him, "this is a happy day. I vote for the end of afflictions and sorrows. There must no longer be any sadness anywhere henceforth. By Jove! I decree joy! Evil has no right to be. That there should be unfortunate men—in truth, it is a shame to the blue sky. Evil does not come from man, who, in reality, is good. All human miseries have for their chief seat and central government Hell, otherwise called the Tuileries of the devil. Good, here am I saying demagogical words now! As for me, I no longer have any political opinions; that all men may be rich, that is to say, happy, that is all I ask for."

When, at the completion of all the ceremonies, after having pronounced before the mayor and the priest every possible yes, after having signed the registers at the municipality and at the sacristy, after having exchanged their rings, after having been on their knees elbow to elbow under the canopy of white moire in the smoke of the censer, hand in hand, admired and envied by all, Marius in black, she in white, preceded by the usher in colonel's epaulets, striking the pavement with his halberd, between two hedges of marvelling spectators, they arrived under the portal of the church where the folding-doors were both open, ready to get into the carriage again, and all was over, Cosette could not yet believe it. She looked at Marius, she looked at the throng, she looked at the sky; it seemed as if she were afraid of awaking.

Then they returned to the Rue des Filles du Calvaire, to their home.

The officer Théodule Gillenormand, now a captain, had come from Chartres, where he was now in garrison, to attend the wedding of his cousin Pontmercy. Cosette did not recognise him.

He, for his part, accustomed to being thought handsome by the women, remembered Cosette no more than any other.

"I was right in not believing that lancer's story!" said Grandfather Gillenormand to himself.

Cosette had never been more tender towards Jean Valjean. She was in unison with Grandfather Gillenormand; while he embodied joy in aphorisms and in maxims, she exhaled love and kindness like a perfume. Happiness wishes everybody happy.

She went back, in speaking to Jean Valjean, to the tones of voice of the time when she was a little girl. She caressed him with smiles.

The dining-room was a furnace of cheerful things. In the centre above the white and glittering table, a Venetian lustre with flat drops, with all sorts of coloured birds, blue, violet, red, green, perched in the midst of the candles; about the lustre girandoles, upon the wall reflectors with triple and quintuple branches; glasses, crystals, glassware, vessels, porcelains, Faënza-ware, pottery, gold and silver ware, all sparkled and rejoiced. The spaces between the candelabra were filled with bouquets, so that, wherever there was not a light, there was a flower.

Jean Valjean sat in a chair in the parlour, behind the door, which shut back upon him in such a way as almost to hide him. A few moments before they took their seats at the table, Cosette came, as if from a sudden impulse, and made him a low curtsy, spreading out her bridal dress with both hands, and, with a tenderly frolicsome look, she asked him:

"Father, are you pleased?"

"Yes," said Jean Valjean, "I am pleased."

"Well, then, laugh."

Jean Valjean began to laugh.

A few moments afterward, Basque announced dinner.

Two large arm-chairs were placed, on the right and on the left of the bride, the first for M. Gillenormand, the second for Jean Valjean. M. Gillenormand took his seat. The other arm-chair remained empty.

All eyes sought "Monsieur Fauchelevent."

He was not there.

M. Gillenormand called Basque.

"Do you know where Monsieur Fauchelevent is?"

"Monsieur," answered Basque. "Exactly. Monsieur Fauchelevent told me to say to monsieur that he was suffering a little from his sore hand, and could not dine with Monsieur the Baron and Madame the Baroness. That he begged they would excuse him, that he would come to-morrow morning. He has just gone away."

This empty arm-chair chilled for a moment the effusion of the nuptial repast. But, M. Fauchelevent absent, M. Gillenormand was there, and the grandfather was brilliant enough for two. He declared that M. Fauchelevent did well to go to bed early, if he was suffering, but that it was only a "scratch." This declaration was enough. Besides, what is one dark corner in such a deluge of joy? Cosette and Marius were in one of those selfish and blessed moments when we have no faculty save for the perception of happiness. And then, M. Gillenormand had an idea. "By Jove, this armchair is empty. Come here, Marius. Your aunt, although she has a right to you, will allow it. This arm-chair is for you. It is legal, and it is proper." Applause from the whole table. Marius took Jean Valjean's place at Cosette's side; and things arranged themselves in such a way that Cosette, at first saddened by Jean Valjean's absence, was finally satisfied with it. From the moment that Marius was the substitute, Cosette would not have regretted God. She put her soft little foot encased in white satin upon Marius' foot.

The arm-chair occupied, M. Fauchelevent was effaced; and nothing was missed. And, five minutes later, the whole table was laughing from one end to the other with all the spirit of forgetfulness.

At the dessert, M. Gillenormand standing, a glass of champagne in his hand, filled half full so that the trembling of his ninety-two years should not spill it, gave the health of the married pair.

"You shall not escape two sermons," exclaimed he. "This morning you had the curé's, to-night you shall have the grandfather's. Listen to me; I am going to give you a piece of advice: Adore one another. I don't make a heap of flourishes. I go to the end, be happy. The only sages in creation are the turtle-doves."

The evening was lively, gay, delightful. The sovereign good-humour of the grandfather gave the key-note to the whole festival, and everybody regulated himself by this almost centenarian cordiality. They danced a little, they laughed much; it was a good childlike wedding.

What had become of Jean Valjean?

Immediately after having laughed, upon Cosette's playful injunction, nobody observing him, Jean Valjean had left his seat, got up, and, un-perceived, had reached the antechamber. It was that same room which eight months before he had entered, black with mire, blood, and powder, bringing the grandson home to the grandfather. The old woodwork was garlanded with leaves and flowers; the musicians were seated on the couch upon which they had placed Marius. Basque, in a black coat, short breeches, white stockings, and white gloves, was arranging crowns of roses about each of the dishes which was to be served up. Jean Valjean had shown him his arm in a sling, charged him to explain his absence, and gone away.

The windows of the dining-room looked upon the street. Jean Valjean stood for some minutes motionless in the obscurity under those radiant windows. He listened. The confused sounds of the banquet reached him. He heard the loud and authoritative words of the grandfather, the violins, the clatter of the plates and glasses, the bursts of laughter, and through all that gay uproar he distinguished Cosette's sweet joyous voice.

He left the Rue des Filles du Calvaire and returned to the Rue de l'Homme Armé.

He lighted his candle and went upstairs. The apartment was empty. Toussaint herself was no longer there. Jean Valjean's step made more noise than usual in the rooms. All the closets were open. He went into Cosette's room. There were no sheets on the bed. The pillow, without a pillow-case and without laces, was laid upon the coverlets folded at the foot of the mattress of which the ticking was to be seen and on which nobody should sleep henceforth. All the little feminine objects to which Cosette clung had been carried away; there remained only the heavy furniture and the four walls. Toussaint's bed was also stripped. A single bed was made and seemed waiting for somebody, that was Jean Valjean's.

Jean Valjean looked at the walls, shut some closet doors, went and came from one room to the other.

Then he found himself again in his own room, and he put his candle on the table.

He had released his arm from the sling, and he helped himself with his right hand as if he did not suffer from it.

He approached his bed, and his eye fell, was it by chance? was it with intention? upon the *inseparable*, of which Cosette had been jealous, upon the little trunk which never left him. On the 4th of June, on arriving in the Rue de l'Homme Armé, he had placed it upon a candle-stand at the head of his bed. He went to this stand with a sort of vivacity, took a key from his pocket, and opened the valise.

He took out slowly the garments in which, ten years before, Cosette had left Montfermeil; first the little dress, then the black scarf, then the great heavy child's shoes which Cosette could have almost put on still, so small a foot she had, then the bodice of very thick fustian, then the knit-skirt, then the apron with pockets, then the woollen stockings. Those stockings, on which the shape of a little leg was still gracefully marked, were hardly longer than Jean Valjean's hand. These were all black. He had carried these garments for her to Montfermeil. As he took them out of the valise, he laid them on the bed. He was thinking. He remembered. It was in winter, a very cold December, she shivered half-naked in rags, her poor little feet all red in her wooden shoes. He, Jean Valjean, he had taken her away from those rags to clothe her in this mourning garb. The mother must have been pleased in her tomb to see her daughter wear mourning for her, and especially to see that she was clad, and that she was warm. He thought of that forest of Montfermeil; they had crossed it together, Cosette and he; he thought of the weather, of the trees without leaves, of the forest without birds, of the sky without sun; it is all the same, it was charming. He arranged the little things upon the bed, the scarf next the skirt, the stockings beside the shoes, the bodice beside the dress, and he looked at them one after another. She was no higher than that, she had her great doll in her arms, she had put her louis d'or in the pocket of this apron, she laughed, they walked holding each other by the hand, she had nobody but him in the world.

Then his venerable white head fell upon the bed, this old stoical heart broke, his face was swallowed up, so to speak, in Cosette's garments, and anybody who had passed along the staircase at that moment, would have heard fearful sobs.

XXXI. MONSIEUR JEAN

JACOB wrestled with the angel but one night. Alas! how many times have we seen Jean Valjean clenched, body to body, in the darkness with his conscience, and wrestling desperately against it.

In what manner should Jean Valjean comport himself in regard to the happiness of Cosette and Marius? This happiness, it was he who had willed it, it was he who had made it; he had thrust it into his own heart, and at this hour, looking upon it, he might have the same satisfaction that an armourer would have, who should recognise his own mark upon a blade, on withdrawing it all reeking from his breast.

Cosette had Marius, Marius possessed Cosette. They had everything, even riches. And it was his work.

But this happiness, now that it existed, now that it was here, what was he to do with it, he, Jean Valjean? Should he impose himself upon this happiness? Should he treat it as belonging to him? Unquestionably, Cosette was another's; but should he, Jean Valjean, retain all of Cosette that he could retain?

Thus bitterly he held counsel with his thoughts, or, to speak more truthfully, he struggled; he rushed, furious, within himself, sometimes against his will, sometimes against his conviction.

We are never done with conscience. It is bottomless, being God. We cast into this pit the labour of our whole life, we cast in our fortune, we cast in our riches, we cast in our success, we cast in our liberty or our country, we cast in our well-being, we cast in our repose, we cast in our happiness. More! more! more! We must at last cast in our heart.

The first step is nothing; it is the last which is difficult. What was the Champmathieu affair compared with Cosette's marriage and all that it involved? What is this: to return to the galleys, compared with this: to enter into nothingness?

Jean Valjean weighed, he thought, he considered the alternatives. His reverie lasted all night.

The day after a wedding is solitary. The privacy of the happy is respected. And thus their slumber is a little belated. The tumult of visits and felicitations does not commence until later. On the morning of the 17th of February, it was a little after noon, when Basque, his napkin and duster under his arm, busy "doing his antechamber," heard a light rap at the door. There was no ring, which is considerate on such a day. Basque opened and saw M. Fauchelevent. He introduced him into the parlour, still cumbered and topsy-turvy, and which had the appearance of the battle-field of the evening's festivities.

"Faith, monsieur," observed Basque, "we are waking up late."

"Has your master risen?" inquired Jean Valjean.

"How is monsieur's arm?" answered Basque.

"Better. Has your master risen?"

"Which? the old or the new one?"

"Monsieur Pontmercy."

"Monsieur the Baron?" said Basque, drawing himself up.

One is baron to his domestics above all. Something of it is reflected upon them; they have what a philosopher would call the spattering of the title, and it flatters them. Marius, to speak of it in passing, a republican militant, and he had proved it, was now a baron in spite of himself. A slight revolution had taken place in the family in regard to this title. At present it was M. Gillenormand who clung to it and Marius who made light of it. But Colonel Pontmercy had written: *My son will bear my title.* Marius obeyed. And then Cosette, in whom the woman was beginning to dawn, was in raptures at being a baroness.

"Monsieur the Baron?" repeated Basque. "I will go and see. I will tell him that Monsieur Fauchelevent is here."

"No. Do not tell him that it is I. Tell him that somebody asks to speak with him in private, and do not give him any name."

"Ah!" said Basque.

"I wish to give him a surprise."

"Ah!" resumed Basque, giving himself his second ah! as an explanation of the first.

And he went out.

Jean Valjean remained alone.

The parlour, as we have just said, was all in disorder. It seemed that by lending the ear the vague rumour of the wedding might still have been heard. There were all sorts of flowers, which had fallen from garlands and head-dresses, upon the floor. The candles, burned to the socket, added stalactites of wax to the pendents of the lustres. Not a piece of furniture was in its place. In the corners, three or four arm-chairs drawn up had the ap-pearance of continuing a conversation. Altogether it was joyous. There is still a certain grace in a dead festival. It has been happy. Upon those chairs in disarray, among those flowers which are withering, under those extinguished lights, there have been thoughts of joy. The sun succeeded to the chandelier, and entered cheerfully into the parlour.

A few minutes elapsed. Jean Valjean was motionless in the spot where Basque had left him. He was very pale. His eyes were hollow, and sunken in their sockets from want of sleep. His black coat had the weary folds of a garment which has passed the night. The elbows were whitened with that down which is left upon cloth by the chafing of linen. Jean Valjean was looking at the window marked out by the sun upon the floor at his feet.

There was a noise at the door, he raised his eyes.

Marius entered, his head erect, his mouth smiling, an indescribable light upon his face, his forehead radiant, his eye triumphant. He also had not slept.

"It is you, father!" exclaimed he on perceiving Jean Valjean; "that idiot of a Basque with his mysterious air! But you come too early. It is only half an hour after noon yet. Cosette is asleep."

That word: Father, said to M. Fauchelevent by Marius, signified: Supreme felicity. There had always been, as we know, barrier, coldness, and constraint between them; ice to break or to melt. Marius had reached that degree of intoxication where the barrier was falling, the ice was dissolving, and M. Fauchelevent was to him, as to Cosette, a father.

He continued; words overflowed from him, which is characteristic of these divine paroxysms of joy:

"How glad I am to see you! If you knew how we missed you yesterday! Good morning, father. How is your hand? Better, is it not?"

And, satisfied with the good answer which he made to himself, he went on:

"We have both of us talked much about you. Cosette loves you so much! You will not forget that your room is here. We will have no more of the Rue de l'Homme Armé. We will have no more of it at all. You have conquered my grandfather, you suit him. We will live together. Do you know whist? you will overjoy my grandfather, if you know whist. You will take Cosette to walk on my court-days, you will give her your arm, you know, as at the Luxembourg, formerly. We have absolutely decided to be very happy. And you are part of our happiness, do you understand, father? Come now, you breakfast with us to-day?"

"Monsieur," said Jean Valjean, "I have one thing to tell you. I am an old convict."

The limit of perceptible acute sounds may be passed quite as easily for the mind as for the ear. Those words: *I am an old convict*, coming from M. Fauchelevent's mouth and entering Marius' ear, went beyond the possible. Marius did not hear. It seemed to him that something had just been said to him; but he knew not what. He stood aghast.

Jean Valjean untied the black cravat which sustained his right arm, took off the cloth wound about his head, laid his thumb bare, and showed it to Marius.

"There is nothing the matter with my hand," said he.

Marius looked at the thumb.

"There has never been anything the matter with it," continued Jean Valjean.

Jean Valjean pursued:

"It was best that I should be absent from your marriage. I absented myself as much as I could. I feigned this wound so as not to commit a forgery, not to introduce a nullity into the marriage acts, to be excused from signing."

Marius stammered out:

"What does this mean?"

"It means," answered Jean Valjean, "that I have been in the galleys."

"You drive me mad!" exclaimed Marius in dismay.

"Monsieur Pontmercy," said Jean Valjean, "I was nineteen years in the galleys. For robbery. Then I was sentenced for life. For robbery. For a second offence. At this hour I am in breach of ban."

It was useless for Marius to recoil before the reality, to refuse the fact, to resist the evidence; he was compelled to yield. He began to comprehend, and as always happens in such a case, he comprehended beyond the truth. He felt the shiver of a horrible interior flash; an idea which made him shudder, crossed his mind. He caught a glimpse in the future of a hideous destiny for himself.

"Tell all, tell all!" cried he. "You are Cosette's father!"

And he took two steps backward with an expression of unspeakable horror.

Jean Valjean raised his head with such a majesty of attitude that he seemed to rise to the ceiling.

"It is necessary that you believe me in this, monsieur; although the oath of such as I be not received."

Here he made a pause; then, with a sort of sovereign and sepulchral authority, he added, articulating slowly and emphasising his syllables:

"—You will believe me. I, the father of Cosette! before God, no. Monsieur Baron Pontmercy, I am a peasant of Faverolles. I earned my living by pruning trees. My name is not Fauchelevent, my name is Jean Valjean. I am nothing to Cosette. Compose yourself."

Marius faltered:

"Who proves it to me—"

"I. Since I say so."

Marius looked at this man. He was mournful, yet self-possessed. No lie could come out of such a calmness. That which is frozen is sincere. We feel the truth in that sepulchral coldness.

"I believe you," said Marius.

Jean Valjean inclined his head as if making oath, and continued:

"What am I to Cosette? a passer-by. Ten years ago, I did not know that she existed. I love her, it is true. A child whom one has seen when little, being himself already old, he loves. When a man is old, he feels like a grandfather towards all little children. You can, it seems to me, suppose that I have something which resembles a heart. She was an orphan. Without father or mother. She had need of me. That is why I began to love her. Children are so weak, that anybody, even a man like me, may be their protector. I performed that duty with regard to Cosette. I do not think that one could truly call so little a thing a good deed; but if it is a good deed, well, set it down that I have done it. Record that mitigating circumstance. Today Cosette leaves my life; our two roads separate. Henceforth I can do nothing more for her. She is Madame Pontmercy. Her protector is changed. And Cosette gains by the change. All is well. As for the six hundred thousand francs, you have not spoken of them to me, but I anticipate your thought; that is a trust. How did this trust come into my hands? What matters it? I make over the trust. Nothing more can be asked of me. I complete the restitution by telling my real name. This again concerns me. I desire, myself, that you should know who I am."

And Jean Valjean looked Marius in the face.

All that Marius felt was tumultuous and incoherent.

We have all had such moments of trouble, in which everything within us is dispersed; we say the first things that come to mind, which are not always precisely those that we should say. There are sudden revelations which we cannot bear, and which intoxicate like a noxious wine. Marius was so stupefied at the new condition of affairs which opened before him that he spoke to this man almost as though he were angry with him for his avowal.

"But after all," exclaimed he, "why do you tell me all this? What compels you to do so? You could have kept the secret to yourself. You are neither denounced, nor pursued, nor hunted. You have some reason for making, from mere wantonness, such a revelation. Finish it. There is something else. In connection with what do you make this avowal? From what motive?"

"From what motive?" answered Jean Valjean, in a voice so low and so hollow that one would have said it was to himself he was speaking rather than to Marius. "From what motive, indeed, does this convict come and say: I am a convict? Well, yes! the motive is strange. It is from honour. As long as it was for her, I could lie; but now it would be for myself, I must not do it. I should have been a detestable imposter! What for? to be happy. To be happy, I! Have I the right to be happy? I am outside of life, monsieur."

Jean Valjean stopped. Marius listened. Jean Valjean lowered his voice anew, but it was no longer a hollow voice, it was an ominous voice.

"To live, once I stole a loaf of bread; to-day, to live, I will not steal a name."

"To live!" interrupted Marius. "You have no need of that name to live!"

"Ah! I understand," answered Jean Valjean, raising and lowering his head several times in succession.

There was a pause. Both were silent, each sunk in an abyss of thought. Marius had seated himself beside a table, and was resting the corner of his mouth on one of his bent fingers. Jean Valjean was walking back and forth. Just as he began to turn, he perceived that Marius was noticing his walk. He said to him:

"I drag one leg a little. You understand why now."

Then he turned quite round towards Marius:

"And now, monsieur, picture this to yourself: I have said nothing, I have remained Monsieur Fauchelevent, I have taken my place in your house, I am one of you, I am in my room, I come to breakfast in the morning in slippers, at night we all three go to the theatre, I accompany Madame Pontmercy to the Tuileries and to the Place Royale, we are together, you suppose me your equal; some fine day I am there, you are there, we are chatting, we are laughing, suddenly you hear a voice shout this name: Jean Valjean! and you see that appalling hand, the police, spring out of the shadow and abruptly tear off my mask!"

He ceased again; Marius had risen with a shudder. Jean Valjean resumed: "What say you?"

Marius crossed the parlour slowly, and, when he was near Jean Valjean, extended him his hand.

But Marius had to take that hand which did not offer itself, Jean Valjean was passive, and it seemed to Marius that he was grasping a hand of marble.

"My grandfather has friends," said Marius. "I will procure your pardon."

"It is useless," answered Jean Valjean. "They think me dead, that is enough. The dead are not subjected to surveillance. They are supposed to moulder tranquilly. Death is the same thing as pardon."

And, disengaging his hand, which Marius held, he added with a sort of inexorable dignity:

"Besides, to do my duty, that is the friend to which I have recourse; and I need pardon of but one, that is my conscience."

Just then, at the other end of the parlour, the door was softly opened a little way, and Cosette's head made its appearance. They saw only her sweet face, her hair was in charming disorder, her eyelids were still swollen with sleep. She made the movement of a bird passing its head out of its nest, looked first at her husband, then at Jean Valjean, and called to them:

"I'll wager that you're talking politics. How stupid that is, instead of being with me!"

"Cosette," faltered Marius—and he stopped. One would have said that they were two culprits.

"I catch you in the very act," said Cosette. "I just heard my father Fauchelevent say, through the door: 'Conscience—Do his duty.'—It is politics, that is. I will not have it. You ought not to talk politics the very next day. It is not right."

And, passing resolutely through the door, she came into the parlour. She was dressed in a full white morning gown, with a thousand folds and with wide sleeves which, starting from the neck, fell to her feet. There are in the golden skies of old Gothic pictures such charming robes for angels to wear.

She viewed herself from head to foot in a large glass, then exclaimed with an explosion of ineffable ecstasy:

"Once there was a king and a queen. Oh! how happy I am!"

So saying, she made a reverence to Marius and to Jean Valjean. "There," said she, "I am going to install myself by you in an arm-chair; we breakfast in half an hour, you shall say all you wish to; I know very well that men must talk, I shall be very good."

Marius took her arm, and said to her lovingly:

"We are talking figures. It will tire you."

"You have put on a charming cravat this morning, Marius. You are very coquettish, monseigneur. It will not tire me."

"I swear to you that we must be alone."

"Well, am I anybody?"

Jean Valjean did not utter a word. Cosette turned towards him.

"In the first place, father, I want you to come and kiss me. What are you doing there, saying nothing, instead of taking my part? who gave me such a father as that? You see plainly that I am very unfortunate in my domestic affairs. My husband beats me. Come, kiss me this instant."

Jean Valjean approached.

"Father, you are pale. Does your arm hurt you?"

"It is well," said Jean Valjean.

"Have you slept badly?"

"No."

"Are you sad?"

"No."

"Smile."

Jean Valjean obeyed. It was the smile of a spectre.

"Now defend me against my husband."

"Cosette!—" said Marius.

"Get angry, father. Tell him that I must stay. You can surely talk before me. So you think me very silly. It is very astonishing then what you are saying! business, putting money in a bank, that is a great affair. Men play the mysterious for nothing. I want to stay. I am very pretty this morning. Look at me, Marius."

And with an adorable shrug of the shoulders and an inexpressibly exquisite pout, she looked at Marius. That somebody was there mattered little.

"I love you!" said Marius.

"I adore you!" said Cosette.

And they fell irresistibly into each other's arms.

"Now," resumed Cosette, readjusting a fold of her gown with a little triumphant pout, "I shall stay."

"What, no," answered Marius, in a tone of entreaty, "we have something to finish."

"No, still?"

Marius assumed a grave tone of voice:

"I assure you, Cosette, that it is impossible."

"Ah! you put on your man's voice, monsieur. Very well, I'll go. You, father, you have not sustained me. Monsieur my husband, monsieur my papa, you are tyrants. I am going to tell grandfather of you. If you think that I shall come back and talk nonsense to you, you are mistaken. I am proud. I wait for you now, you will see that it is you who will get tired without me. I am going away, very well."

And she went out.

Two seconds later, the door opened again, her fresh rosy face passed once more between the two folding doors, and she cried to them:

"I am very angry."

The door closed again and the darkness returned.

Marius made sure that the door was well closed.

"Poor Cosette!" murmured he, "when she knows—"

At these words, Jean Valjean fixed upon Marius a bewildered eye.

"Cosette! Oh, yes, it is true, you will tell this to Cosette. That is right. Stop, I had not thought of that. People have the strength for some things, but not for others. Monsieur, I beseech you, I entreat you, Monsieur, give me your most sacred word, do not tell her. Is it not enough that you know it yourself? I could have told it of myself without being forced to it, I would have told it to the universe, to all the world, that would be nothing to me. But she, she doesn't know what it is, it would appal her. A convict, why! you would have to explain it to her, to tell her: It is a man who has been in the galleys. She saw the Chain pass by one day. Oh, my God!"

He sank into an arm-chair and hid his face in both hands.

"Be calm," said Marius, "I will keep your secret for myself alone."

And, less softened perhaps than he should have been, but obliged for an hour past to familiarise himself with a fearful surprise, seeing by degrees a convict superimposed before his eyes upon M. Fauchelevent, and led by the natural tendency of the position to determine the distance which had just been put between this man and himself, Marius added:

"It is impossible that I should not say a word to you of the trust which you have so faithfully and so honestly restored. That is an act of probity. It is just that a recompense should be given you. Fix the sum yourself, it shall be counted out to you. Do not be afraid to fix it very high."

"I thank you, monsieur," answered Jean Valjean gently.

He remained thoughtful a moment, passing the end of his forefinger over his thumb-nail mechanically, then he raised his voice:

"It is all nearly finished. There is one thing left—"

"What?"

Jean Valjean had as it were a supreme hesitation, and, voiceless, almost breathless, he faltered out rather than said:

"Now that you know, do you think, monsieur, you who are the master, that I ought not to see Cosette again?"

"I think that would be best," answered Marius coldly.

"I shall not see her again," murmured Jean Valjean.

And he walked towards the door.

He placed his hand upon the knob, the door started, Jean Valjean opened it wide enough to enable him to pass out; then shut the door, and turned towards Marius.

There were no longer tears in his eyes, but a sort of tragical flame. His voice had again become strangely calm.

"But, monsieur," said he, "if you are willing, I will come and see her. I assure you that I desire it very much. If I had not clung to seeing Cosette, I should not have made the avowal which I have made, I should have gone away; but wishing to stay in the place where Cosette is and to continue to see her, I was compelled in honour to tell you all. You follow my reasoning, do you not? that is a thing which explains itself. You see, for nine years past, I have had her near me. We lived first in that ruin on the boulevard, then in the convent, then near the Luxembourg. It was there that you saw her for the first time. You remember her blue plush hat. We were afterwards in the quartier of the Invalides where there was a grating and a garden. Rue Plumet. I lived in a little back-yard where I heard her piano. That was my life. We never left each other. That lasted nine years and some months. I was like her father, and she was my child. I don't know whether you understand me, Monsieur Pontmercy, but from the present time, to see her no more, to speak to her no more, to have nothing more, that would be hard. If you do not think it wrong, I will come from time to time to see Cosette. I should not come often. I would not stay long. You might say I should be received in the little low room. On the ground floor. I would willingly come in by the back-door, which is for the servants, but that would excite wonder, perhaps. It is better, I suppose, that I should enter by the usual door. Monsieur, indeed, I would really like to see Cosette a little still. As rarely as you please. Put yourself in my place, it is all that I have. And then, we must take care. If I should not come at all, it would have a bad effect, it would be thought singular. For instance, what I can do, is to come in the evening, at nightfall."

"You will come every evening," said Marius, "and Cosette will expect you."

"You are kind, monsieur," said Jean Valjean.

Marius bowed to Jean Valjean, happiness conducted despair to the door, and these two men separated.

Marius was completely unnerved.

The kind of repulsion which he had always felt for the man with whom he saw Cosette was now explained. There was something strangely enigmatic in this person, of which his instinct had warned him. This enigma was the most hideous of disgraces, the galleys.

Confused as Marius' recollections were, some shadow of them returned to him. What was the exact nature of that affair in the Jondrette garret? Why, on the arrival of the police, did this man, instead of making his complaint, make his escape? Here Marius found the answer. Because this man was a fugitive from justice in breach of ban.

Another question: Why had this man come into the barricade? For now Marius saw that reminiscence again distinctly, reappearing in these emotions like sympathetic ink before the fire. This man was in the barricade. He did not fight there. What did he come there for? Before this question a spectre arose, and made response. Javert. Marius recalled perfectly to mind at this hour the fatal sight of Jean Valjean dragging Javert bound outside the barricade, and he again heard the frightful pistol-shot behind the corner of the little Rue Mondétour. There was, probably, hatred between the spy and this galley-slave. Jean Valjean had gone to the barricade to avenge himself. He had arrived late. He knew probably that Javert was a prisoner there. The Corsican vendetta has penetrated into certain lower depths and is their law; it is so natural that it does not astonish souls half turned back towards the good; and these hearts are so constituted that a criminal, in the path of repentance, may be scrupulous in regard to robbery and not be so in regard to vengeance. Jean Valjean had killed Javert. At least, that seemed evident.

In this frame of mind it was a bitter perplexity to Marius to think that this man should have henceforth any contact whatever with Cosette. These fearful questions, before which he had shrunk, and from which an implacable and definitive decision might have sprung, he now reproached himself almost, for not having put. He thought himself too good, too mild, let us say the word, too weak. This weakness had led him to an imprudent concession. He had allowed himself to be moved. He had done wrong. He should have merely and simply cast off Jean Valjean. Jean Valjean was the Jonah, he should have done it, and relieved his house of this man.

The next day, at nightfall, Jean Valjean knocked at the M. Gillenormand porte-cochère. Basque received him. Basque happened to be in the court-yard very conveniently, and as if he had had orders. It sometimes happens that one says to a servant: "You will be on the watch for Monsieur So-and-so, when he comes."

Basque, without waiting for Jean Valjean to come up to him, addressed him as follows:

"Monsieur the Baron told me to ask monsieur whether he desires to go upstairs or to remain below?"

"To remain below," answered Jean Valjean.

Basque, who was moreover absolutely respectful, opened the door of the basement room and said: "I will inform madame."

The room which Jean Valjean entered was an arched and damp basement, used as a cellar when necessary, looking upon the street, paved with red tiles, and dimly lighted by a window with an iron grating.

The room was not of those which are harassed by the brush, the duster, and the broom. In it the dust was tranquil. There the persecution of the spiders had not been organised. A fine web, broadly spread out, very black, adorned with dead flies, ornamented one of the window-panes. The room, small and low, was furnished with a pile of empty bottles heaped up in one corner. The wall had been washed with a wash of yellow ochre, which was scaling off in large flakes. At the end was a wooden mantel, painted black, with a narrow shelf. A fire was kindled, which indicated that somebody had anticipated Jean Valjean's answer: *To remain below.*

Two arm-chairs were placed at the corners of the fireplace. Between the chairs was spread, in guise of a carpet, an old bed-side rug, showing more warp than wool.

The room was lighted by the fire in the fireplace and the twilight from the window.

Jean Valjean was fatigued. For some days he had neither eaten nor slept. He let himself fall into one of the arm-chairs.

Basque returned, set a lighted candle upon the mantel, and retired. Jean Valjean, his head bent down and his chin upon his breast, noticed neither Basque nor the candle.

Suddenly he started up. Cosette was behind him.

He had not seen her come in, but he had felt that she was coming.

He turned. He gazed at her. She was adorably beautiful.

"Ah, well!" exclaimed Cosette, "father, I knew that you were singular, but I should never have thought this. What an idea! Marius tells me that it is you who wish me to receive you here."

"Yes, it is I."

"I expected the answer. Well, I warn you that I am going to make a scene. Let us begin at the beginning. Father, kiss me."

And she offered her cheek.

Jean Valjean remained motionless.

"You do not stir. I see it. You act guilty. But it is all the same, I forgive you. Jesus Christ said: 'Offer the other cheek.' Here it is."

And she offered the other cheek.

Jean Valjean did not move. It seemed as if his feet were nailed to the floor.

"This is getting serious," said Cosette. "What have I done to you? I declare I am confounded. You owe me amends. You will dine with us."

"I have dined."

"That is not true. I will have Monsieur Gillenormand scold you. Grand-fathers are made to scold fathers. Come. Go up to the parlour with me. Immediately."

"Impossible."

Cosette here lost ground a little. She ceased to order and passed to questions.

"But why not? and you choose the ugliest room in the house to see me in. It is horrible here."

"You know, madame, I am peculiar, I have my whims."

Cosette clapped her little hands together.

"Madame! Still again! What does this mean?"

Jean Valjean fixed upon her that distressing smile to which he some-times had recourse:

"You have wished to be madame. You are so."

"Not to you, father."

"Don't call me father any more."

"What?"

"Call me Monsieur Jean. Jean, if you will."

"You are no longer father? I am no longer Cosette? Monsieur Jean? What does this mean? but these are revolutions, these are! what then has happened? look me in the face now. And you will not live with us! And you will not have my room! What have I done to you? what have I done to you? Is there anything the matter?"

"Nothing."

"Well then?"

"All is as usual."

"Why do you change your name?"

"You have certainly changed yours."

He smiled again with that same smile and added:

"Since you are Madame Pontmercy I can surely be Monsieur Jean."

"I don't understand anything about it. It is all nonsense; I shall ask my husband's permission for you to be Monsieur Jean. I hope that he will not consent to it. You make me a great deal of trouble. You may have whims, but you must not grieve your darling Cosette. It is wrong. You have no right to be naughty, you are too good."

He made no answer.

She seized both his hands hastily and, with an irresistible impulse, raising them towards her face, she pressed them against her neck under her chin, which is a deep token of affection.

"Oh!" said she to him, "be good!"

And she continued:

"This is what I call being good: being nice, coming to stay here, there are birds here as well as in the Rue Plumet, living with us, leaving that hole in the Rue de l'Homme Armé, not giving us riddles to guess, being like other people, dining with us, breakfasting with us, being my father."

He disengaged his hands.

"You have no more need of a father, you have a husband."

Cosette could not contain herself.

"I no more need of a father! To things like that which have no common sense, one really doesn't know what to say!"

"If Toussaint was here," replied Jean Valjean, like one who is in search of authorities and who catches at every straw, "she would be the first to acknowledge that it is true that I always had my peculiar ways. There is nothing new in this. I have always liked my dark corner."

"But it is cold here. We can't see clearly. It is horrid, too, to want to be Monsieur Jean. I don't want you to talk so to me."

"Just now, on my way here," answered Jean Valjean, "I saw a piece of furniture in the Rue Saint Louis. At a cabinet maker's. If I were a pretty woman, I should make myself a present of that piece of furniture. A very fine toilet table; in the present style. What you call rosewood, I think. It is inlaid. A pretty large glass. There are drawers in it. It is handsome."

"Oh! the ugly bear!" replied Cosette. "Since yesterday, you all make me rage. Everybody spites me. I don't understand. You don't defend me against Marius. Marius doesn't uphold me against you, I am all alone. I arrange a room handsomely. If I could have put the good God into it, I would have done it. You leave me my room upon my hands. My tenant bankrupts me. I order Nicolette to have a nice little dinner. Nobody wants your dinner, madame. And my father Fauchelevent wishes me to call him Monsieur Jean, and to receive him in a hideous, old, ugly, mouldy cellar, where there are empty bottles for vases, and spiders' webs for curtains. You are singular, I admit, that is your way, but a truce is granted to people who get married. You should not have gone back to being singular immediately. So you are going to be well satisfied with your horrid Rue de l'Homme Armé. I was very forlorn there, myself! What have you against me? You give me a great deal of trouble. Fie!"

And, growing suddenly serious, she looked fixedly at Jean Valjean, and added:

"So you don't like it that I am happy?"

Artlessness, unconsciously, sometimes penetrates very deep. This question, simple to Cosette, was severe to Jean Valjean. Cosette wished to scratch; she tore.

For a moment Jean Valjean did not answer, then, talking to himself, he murmured:

"Her happiness was the aim of my life. Now, God may beckon me away. Cosette, you are happy; my time is full."

"Ah, you have called me Cosette!" exclaimed she.

And she sprang upon his neck.

Jean Valjean, in desperation, clasped her to his breast wildly. It seemed to him almost as if he were taking her back.

"Thank you, father!" said Cosette to him.

The transport was becoming poignant to Jean Valjean. He gently put away Cosette's arms, and took his hat.

"Well?" said Cosette.

Jean Valjean answered:

"I will leave you madame; they are waiting for you."

And, from the door, he added:

"I called you Cosette. Tell your husband that that shall not happen again. Pardon me."

Jean Valjean went out, leaving Cosette astounded at that enigmatic farewell.

The following day, at the same hour, Jean Valjean came.

Cosette put no questions to him, was no longer astonished, no longer exclaimed that she was cold, no longer talked of the parlour; she avoided saying either father or Monsieur Jean. She let him speak as he would. She allowed herself to be called madame. Only she betrayed a certain diminution of joy. She would have been sad, if sadness had been possible for her.

It is probable that she had had one of those conversations with Marius, in which the beloved man says what he pleases, explains nothing, and satisfies the beloved woman. The curiosity of lovers does not go very far beyond their love.

The basement room had made its toilet a little. Basque had suppressed the bottles, and Nicolette the spiders.

Every succeeding morrow brought Jean Valjean at the same hour. He came every day, not having the strength to take Marius' words otherwise than to the letter. Marius made his arrangements, so as to be absent at the hours when Jean Valjean came. The house became accustomed to M. Fauchelevent's new mode of life. Toussaint aided: *"Monsieur always was just so,"* she repeated. The grandfather issued this decree: "He is an original!" and all was said. Besides, at ninety, no further tie is possible; all is juxtaposition; a new-comer is an annoyance. There is no more room; all the habits are formed. M. Fauchelevent, M. Tranchelevent, Grandfather Gillenormand asked nothing better than to be relieved of "that gentleman." He added: "Nothing is more common than these originals. They do all sorts of odd things. No motive. The Marquis de Canaples was worse. He bought a palace to live in the barn."

Several weeks passed thus. A new life gradually took possession of Cosette; the relations which marriage creates, the visits, the care of the house, the pleasures, those grand affairs. Cosette's pleasures were not costly; they consisted in a single one: being with Marius. Going out with him, staying at home with him, this was the great occupation of her life. It was a joy to them for ever new, to go out arm in arm, in the face of the sun, in the open street, without hiding, in sight of everybody, all alone with each other. Cosette had one vexation. Toussaint could not agree with Nicolette, the wedding of two old maids being impossible, and went away. The grandfather was in good health; Marius argued a few cases now and then; Aunt Gillenormand peacefully led by the side of the new household, that lateral life which was enough for her. Jean Valjean came every day.

The disappearance of familiarity, the madame, the Monsieur Jean, all this made him different to Cosette. The care which he had taken to detach her from him, succeeded with her. She became more and more cheerful, and less and less affectionate. However, she still loved him very much, and he felt it. One day she suddenly said to him, "You were my father, you are no longer my father, you were my uncle, you are no longer my uncle, you were Monsieur Fauchelevent, you are Jean. Who are you then? I don't like all that. If I did not know you were so good, I should be afraid of you."

He still lived in the Rue de l'Homme Armé, unable to resolve to move further from the quartier in which Cosette dwelt.

At first he stayed with Cosette only a few minutes, then went away.

Little by little he got into the habit of making his visits longer. One would have said that he took advantage of the example of the days which were growing longer: he came earlier and went away later.

One day Cosette inadvertently said to him: "Father." A flash of joy illuminated Jean Valjean's gloomy old face.

That was the last time. From that last gleam onward, there was complete extinction. No more familiarity, no more good-day with a kiss, never again that word so intensely sweet: Father! he was, upon his own demand, driven in succession from every happiness.

The eye at last becomes accustomed to the light of a cellar; to have a vision of Cosette every day sufficed him. His whole life was concentrated in that hour. He sat by her side, he looked at her in silence, or rather he talked to her of the years long gone, of her childhood, of the convent, of her friends of those days.

One afternoon—it was one of the early days of April, the hawthorn was beginning to peep, a jewelled array of gilliflowers displayed themselves upon the old walls, there was a charming beginning of daisies and butter-cups in the grass, the white butterflies of the year made their first appear-ance—Marius said to Cosette: "We have said that we would go to see our garden in the Rue Plumet again. Let us go. We must not be ungrateful." And they flew away like two swallows towards the spring. This garden in the Rue Plumet had the effect of the dawn upon them. In it they found themselves again; they forgot themselves. At night, at the usual hour, Jean Valjean came to the Rue des Filles du Calvaire. "Madame has gone out with monsieur, and has not returned yet," said Basque to him. He sat down in silence, and waited an hour. Cosette did not return. He bowed his head and went away.

Cosette was so intoxicated with her walk to "the garden," and so happy over having "lived a whole day in her past," that she did not speak of any-thing else the next day. It did not occur to her that she had not seen Jean Valjean.

"How did you go there?" Jean Valjean asked her.

"We walked."

"And how did you return?"

"In a fiacre."

For some time Jean Valjean had noticed the frugal life which the young couple led. He was annoyed at it. Marius' economy was severe, and the word to Jean Valjean had its absolute sense. He ventured a question:

"Why have you no carriage of your own? A pretty brougham would cost you only five hundred francs a month. You are rich."

"I don't know," answered Cosette.

"So with Toussaint," continued Jean Valjean. "She has gone away. You have not replaced her. Why not?"

"Nicolette is enough."

"But you must have a waiting maid."

"Have not I Marius?"

"You ought to have a house of your own, servants of your own, a car-riage, a box at the theatre. There is nothing too good for you. Why not have the advantages of being rich? Riches add to happiness."

Cosette made no answer.

Jean Valjean's visits did not grow shorter. When Jean Valjean desired to prolong his visit, and to make the hours pass unnoticed, he eulogised Marius; he thought him beautiful, noble, courageous, intellectual, eloquent, good. Cosette surpassed him. Jean Valjean began again. They were never silent. Marius, this word was inexhaustible; there were volumes in these six letters. In this way Jean Valjean succeeded in staying a long time. It happened several times that Basque came down twice to say: "Monsieur Gillenormand sends me to remind Madame the Baroness that dinner is served."

On those days, Jean Valjean returned home very thoughtful.

One day he stayed longer than usual. The next day, he noticed that there was no fire in the fireplace. "What!" thought he. "No fire." And he made the explanation to himself: "It is a matter of course. We are in April. The cold weather is over."

"Goodness! how cold it is here!" exclaimed Cosette as she came in.

"Why no," said Jean Valjean.

"So it is you who told Basque not to make a fire?"

"Yes. We are close upon May."

"But we have fire until the month of June. In this cellar, it is needed the year round."

"I thought that the fire was unnecessary."

"That is just one of your ideas!" replied Cosette.

The next day there was a fire. But the two arm-chairs were placed at the other end of the room, near the door. "What does that mean?" thought Jean Valjean.

He went for the arm-chairs, and put them back in their usual place near the chimney.

This fire being kindled again encouraged him, however. He continued the conversation still longer than usual. As he was getting up to go away, Cosette said to him:

"My husband said a funny thing to me yesterday."

"What was it?"

"He said: 'Cosette, we have an income of thirty thousand francs. Twenty-seven that you have, three that my grandfather allows me.' I answered: 'That makes thirty.' 'Would you have the courage to live on three thousand?' I answered: 'Yes, on nothing. Provided it be with you.' And then I asked: 'Why do you say this?' He answered: 'To know.' "

Jean Valjean did not say a word. Cosette probably expected some explanation from him; he listened to her in a mournful silence. He went back to the Rue de l'Homme Armé; he was so deeply absorbed that he mistook the door, and instead of entering his own house, he entered the next one. Not until he had gone up almost to the second story did he perceive his mistake, and go down again.

It was evident that Marius had doubts in regard to the origin of these six hundred thousand francs, that he feared some impure source, who knows? that he had perhaps discovered that this money came from him, Jean Valjean, that he hesitated before this suspicious fortune, and disliked to take it as his own, preferring to remain poor, himself and Cosette, than to be rich with a doubtful wealth.

Besides, Jean Valjean began to feel that the door was shown him. The next day, he received, on entering the basement room, something like a shock. The arm-chairs had disappeared. There was not even a chair of any kind.

"Ah now," exclaimed Cosette as she came in, "no chairs! Where are the arm-chairs, then?"

"They are gone," answered Jean Valjean.

"That is a pretty business!"

Jean Valjean stammered:

"I told Basque to take them away."

"And what for?"

"I shall stay only a few minutes to-day."

"Staying a little while is no reason for standing while you do stay."

"I believe that Basque needed some arm-chairs for the parlour."

"What for?"

"You doubtless have company this evening."

"We have nobody."

Jean Valjean could not say a word more.

Cosette shrugged her shoulders.

"To have the chairs carried away! The other day you had the fire put out. How singular you are!"

"Good-bye," murmured Jean Valjean.

He did not say: "Good-bye, Cosette." But he had not the strength to say: "Good-bye, madame."

He went away overwhelmed. This time he had understood.

The next day he did not come. Cosette did not notice it until night.

"Why," said she, "Monsieur Jean has not come to-day."

She felt something like a slight oppression of the heart, but she hardly perceived it, being immediately diverted by a kiss from Marius.

The next day he did not come.

Cosette paid no attention to it, passed the evening and slept as usual, and thought of it only on awaking. She was so happy! She sent Nicolette very quickly to Monsieur Jean's to know if he were sick, and why he had not come the day before. Nicolette brought back Monsieur Jean's answer. He was not sick. He was busy. He would come very soon. As soon as he could. However, he was going to make a little journey. Madame must remember that he was in the habit of making journeys from time to time. Let there be no anxiety. Let them not be troubled about him.

Nicolette, on entering Monsieur Jean's house, had repeated to him the very words of her mistress. That madame sent to know "why Monsieur Jean had not come the day before." "It is two days that I have not been there," said Jean Valjean mildly.

But the remark escaped the notice of Nicolette, who reported nothing of it to Cosette.

During the last months of the spring and the first months of the summer of 1833, the scattered wayfarers in the Marais, the storekeepers, the idlers upon the doorsteps, noticed an old man neatly dressed in black, every day, about the same hour, at night-fall, come out of the Rue de l'Homme Armé, pass by to the Rue Culture Sainte Catherine, turn to the left, and enter the Rue Saint Louis.

There he walked with slow steps, his head bent forward, seeing nothing, hearing nothing, his eye immovably fixed upon one point, which was the corner of the Rue des Filles du Calvaire. As he approached the corner of that street, his face lighted up; he had a fascinated and softened expression, his lips moved vaguely, as if he were speaking to some one whom he did not see, he smiled faintly, and he advanced as slowly as he could. You would have said that even while wishing to reach some destination, he dreaded the moment when he should be near it. When there were but a few houses left between him and that street which appeared to attract him, his pace became so slow, that at times you might have supposed he had ceased to move. However long he succeeded in deferring it, he must arrive at last; he reached the Rue des Filles du Calvaire; then he stopped, he put his head with a kind of gloomy timidity beyond the corner of the last house, and he looked into that street. He remained thus a few minutes, as if he had been stone; then he returned by the same route and at the same pace.

Little by little, this old man ceased to go as far as the corner of the Rue des Filles du Calvaire; he stopped half way down the Rue Saint Louis; sometimes a little further, sometimes a little nearer. One day, he stopped at the corner of the Rue Culture Sainte Catherine, and looked at the Rue des Filles du Calvaire from the distance. Then he silently moved his head from right to left as if he were refusing himself something, and retraced his steps.

Very soon he no longer came even as far as the Rue Saint Louis. You would have said a pendulum which has not been wound up, and the oscillations of which are growing shorter ere they stop.

Every day, he came out of his house at the same hour, he commenced the same walk, but he did not finish it, and, perhaps unconsciously, he continually shortened it. His whole countenance expressed this single idea: What is the use? The old man's head was still bent forward; his chin quivered at times; the wrinkles of his thin neck were painful to behold. Sometimes, when the weather was bad, he carried an umbrella under his arm, which he never opened. The good women of the quartier said: "He is a natural." The children followed him laughing.

XXXII. WHAT JEAN VALJEAN WANTED

IT IS A TERRIBLE THING to be happy! How pleased we are with it! How all-sufficient we think it! How, being in possession of the false aim of life, happiness, we forget the true aim, duty!

We must say, however, that it would be unjust to blame Marius.

Marius as we have explained, before his marriage, had put no questions to M. Fauchelevent, and, since, he had feared to put any to Jean Valjean. He had regretted the promise into which he had allowed himself to be led. He had reiterated to himself many times that he had done wrong in making that concession to despair. He did nothing more than gradually to banish Jean Valjean from his house, and to obliterate him as much as possible from Cosette's mind. He had in some sort constantly placed himself between Cosette and Jean Valjean, sure that in that way she would not notice him, and would never think of him. It was more than obliteration, it was eclipse.

Marius did what he deemed necessary and just. He supposed he had serious reasons. Having chanced to meet, in a cause in which he was engaged, an old clerk of the house of Laffitte, he had obtained, without seeking it, some mysterious information which he could not, in truth, probe to the bottom, from respect for the secret which he had promised to keep, and from care for Jean Valjean's perilous situation. He believed, at that very time, that he had a solemn duty to perform, the restitution of the six hundred thousand francs to somebody whom he was seeking as cautiously as possible. In the meantime, he abstained from using that money.

As for Cosette, she was in none of these secrets; but it would be hard to condemn her also.

There was an all-powerful magnetism flowing from Marius to her, which compelled her to do, instinctively and almost mechanically, what Marius wished. She felt, in regard to "Monsieur Jean," a will from Marius; she conformed to it. Her husband had had nothing to say to her; she experienced the vague, but clear pressure of his unspoken wishes, and obeyed blindly. Her obedience in this consisted in not remembering what Marius forgot. She had to make no effort for that. Without knowing why herself, and without affording any grounds for censure, her soul had so thoroughly become her husband's soul, that whatever was covered with shadow in Marius' thought, was obscured in hers. She was rather thoughtless than forgetful. At heart, she really loved him whom she had so long called father. But she loved her husband still more.

It sometimes happened that Cosette spoke of Jean Valjean, and wondered. Then Marius calmed her: "He is absent, I think. Didn't he say that he was going away on a journey?" "That is true," thought Cosette. "He was in the habit of disappearing in this way. But not for so long." Two or three times she sent Nicolette to inquire in the Rue de l'Homme Armé if Monsieur Jean had returned from his journey. Jean Valjean had the answer returned that he had not.

One day Jean Valjean went down stairs, took three steps into the street, sat down upon a stone block, upon that same block where Gavroche, on the night of the 5th of June, had found him musing; he remained there a few minutes, then went upstairs again. This was the last oscillation of the pendulum. The next day, he did not leave his room. The day after he did not leave his bed.

His portress, who prepared his frugal meal, some cabbage, a few potatoes with a little pork, looked into the brown earthen plate, and exclaimed:

"Why, you didn't eat anything yesterday, poor dear man!"

"Yes, I did," answered Jean Valjean.

"The plate is all full."

"Look at the water-pitcher. That is empty."

"That shows that you have drunk; it don't show that you have eaten."

"Well," said Jean Valjean, "suppose I have only been hungry for water?"

"That is called thirst, and, when people don't eat at the same time, it is called fever."

"I will eat to-morrow."

"Or at Christmas. Why not eat to-day? Do people say: I will eat to-morrow! To leave me my whole plateful without touching it! My cole slaugh, which was so good!"

Jean Valjean took the old woman's hand:

"I promise to eat it," said he to her in his benevolent voice.

"I am not satisfied with you," answered the portress.

Jean Valjean scarcely ever saw any other human being than this good woman. There are streets in Paris in which nobody walks, and houses into which nobody comes. He was in one of those streets, and in one of those houses.

While he still went out, he had bought for a few sous a little copper crucifix, which he had hung upon a nail before his bed. The cross is always good to look upon.

A week elapsed, and Jean Valjean had not taken a step in his room. He was still in bed. The portress said to her husband: "The goodman upstairs does not get up any more, he does not eat any more, he won't last long. He has trouble, he has. Nobody can get it out of my head that his daughter has made a bad match."

The porter replied, with the accent of the marital sovereignty:

"If he is rich, let him have a doctor. If he is not rich, let him not have any. If he doesn't have a doctor, he will die."

"And if he does have one?"

"He will die," said the porter.

The portress began to dig up with an old knife some grass which was sprouting in what she called her pavement, and, while she was pulling up the grass, she muttered:

"It is a pity. An old man who is so nice! He is white as a chicken."

She saw a physician of the quartier passing at the end of the street; she took it upon herself to beg him to go up.

"It is on the second floor," said she to him. "You will have nothing to do but go in. As the goodman does not stir from his bed now, the key is in the door all the time."

The physician saw Jean Valjean, and spoke with him.

When he came down, the portress questioned him:

"Well, doctor?"

"Your sick man is very sick."

"What is the matter with him?"

"Everything and nothing. He is a man who, to all appearance has lost some dear friend. People die of that."

"What did he tell you?"

"He told me that he was well."

"Will you come again, doctor?"

"Yes," answered the physician. "But another than I must come again."

One evening Jean Valjean had difficulty in raising himself upon his elbow; he felt his wrist and found no pulse; his breathing was short, and stopped at intervals; he realised that he was weaker than he had been before. Then he made an effort, sat up in bed, and dressed himself. He put on his old working-man's garb. He was obliged to stop several times while dressing; the mere effort of putting on his waistcoat made the sweat roll down his forehead.

He opened the valise and took out Cosette's suit.

He spread it out upon his bed.

The bishop's candlesticks were in their place, on the mantel. He took two wax tapers from a drawer, and put them into the candlesticks. Then, although it was still broad daylight, it was in summer, he lighted them. We sometimes see torches lighted thus in broad day, in rooms where the dead lie.

Each step that he took in going from one piece of furniture to another, exhausted him, and he was obliged to sit down. It was not ordinary fatigue which spends the strength that it may be renewed; it was the remnant of possible motion; it was exhausted life pressed out drop by drop in overwhelming efforts, never to be made again.

One of the chairs upon which he sank, was standing before that mirror, so providential for Marius, in which he had read Cosette's note reversed on the blotter. He saw himself in this mirror, and did not recognise himself. He was eighty years old; before Marius' marriage, one would hardly have thought him fifty; this year had counted thirty. What was now upon his forehead was not the wrinkle of age, it was the mysterious mark of death.

Night had come. With much labour he drew a table and an old arm-chair near the fireplace, and put upon the table pen, ink, and paper.

Then he fainted. When he regained consciousness he was thirsty. Being unable to lift the water-pitcher, with great effort he tipped it towards his mouth, and drank a swallow.

Then he turned to the bed, and, still sitting, for he could stand but a moment, he looked at the little black dress, and all those dear objects.

Suddenly he shivered, he felt that the chill was coming; he leaned upon the table which was lighted by the bishop's candlesticks, and took the pen.

As neither the pen nor the ink had been used for a long time, the tip of the pen was bent back, the ink was dried, he was obliged to get up and put a few drops of water into the ink, which he could not do without stopping and sitting down two or three times, and he was compelled to write with the back of the pen. He wiped his forehead from time to time. His hand trembled. He slowly wrote:

"Cosette, I bless you. I am going to make an explanation to you. Your husband was quite right in giving me to understand that I ought to leave; still there is some mistake in what he believed, but he was right. He is very good. Always love him well when I am dead. Monsieur Pontmercy, always love my darling child. Cosette, this paper will be found, this is what I want to tell you, you shall see the figures, if I have the strength to recall them, listen well, this money is really your own. This is the whole story: The white jet comes from Norway, the black jet comes from England, the black-glass imitation comes from Germany. The jet is lighter, more precious, more costly. We can make imitations in France as well as in Germany. It requires a little anvil two inches square, and a spirit-lamp to soften the wax. The wax was formerly made with resin and lamp-black, and cost four francs a pound. I hit upon making it with gum lac and turpentine. This costs only thirty sous, and it is much better. The buckles are made of violet glass, which is fastened by means of this wax to a narrow rim of black iron. The glass should be violet for iron trinkets, and black for gold trinkets. Spain purchases many of them. That is the country of jet—"

Here he stopped, the pen fell from his fingers, he gave way to one of those despairing sobs which rose at times from the depths of his being, the poor man clasped his head with both hands, and reflected.

"Oh!" exclaimed he within himself (pitiful cries, heard by God alone), "it is all over. I shall never see her more. I am going to enter into the night without even seeing her again. Oh! a minute, an instant, to hear her voice, to touch her dress, to look at her, the angel! and then to die! It is nothing to die, but it is dreadful to die without seeing her. She would smile upon me, she would say a word to me. Would that harm anybody? No, it is over, forever. Here I am, all alone. My God! my God! I shall never see her again."

At this moment there was a rap at his door.

THAT very day, or rather that very evening, just as Marius had left the table and retired into his office, having a bundle of papers to study over, Basque had handed him a letter, saying: "the person who wrote the letter is in the antechamber."

Cosette had taken grandfather's arm, and was walking in the garden.

A letter, as well as a man, may have a forbidding appearance. Coarse paper, clumsy fold, the mere sight of certain missives displeases. The letter which Basque brought was of this kind.

Marius took it. It smelt of tobacco. Nothing awakens a reminiscence like an odour. Marius recognised this tobacco. He looked at the address: *To Monsieur, Monsieur the Baron Pommerci. In his hôtel.* The tobacco made him recognise the handwriting. Here was the very paper, the manner of folding, the paleness of the ink; here was, indeed, the well-known handwriting; above all, here was the tobacco. The Jondrette garret appeared before him.

He broke the seal eagerly, and read:—

"Monsieur Baron,—If the Supreme Being had given me the talents for it, I could have been Baron Thénard, member of the Institute (Academy of Ciences), but I am not so. I merely bear the same name that he does, happy if this remembrance commends me to the excellence of your bounties. The benefit with which you honour me will be reciprocal. I am in possession of a secret conserning an individual. This individual conserns you. I hold the secret at your disposition, desiring to have the honour of being yuseful to you. I will give you the simple means of drivving from your honourable family this individual who has no right in it, Madame the Baroness being of high birth. The sanctuary of virtue could not coabit longer with crime without abdicating.

"I atend in the entichamber the orders of Monsieur the Baron.—With respect."

The letter was signed "THÉNARD."

Besides the rigmarole and the orthography completed the revelation. The certificate of origin was perfect. There was no doubt possible.

After the feeling of surprise, Marius had a feeling of happiness. Let him now find the other man whom he sought, the man who had saved him, and he would have nothing more to wish.

He opened one of his secretary drawers, took out some banknotes, put them in his pockets, closed the secretary, and rang. Basque appeared.

"Show him in," said Marius.

Basque announced:

"Monsieur Thénard."

A man entered, a new surprise for Marius. The man who came in was perfectly unknown to him.

This man had a large nose, his chin in his cravat, green spectacles, with double shade of green silk over his eyes, his hair polished and smoothed down, his forehead close to the eyebrows, like the wigs of English coachmen in high life. His hair was grey. He was dressed in black from head to foot, in a well worn but tidy black; a bunch of trinkets, hanging from his fob, suggested a watch. He held an old hat in his hand. He walked with a stoop, and the crook of his back increased the lowliness of his bow.

What was striking at first sight was, that this person's coat, too full, although carefully buttoned, did not seem to have been made for him. Here a short digression is necessary.

There was in Paris, at that period, in an old shanty, in the Rue Beautreillis, near the Arsenal, an ingenious renter of costumes called *the Changer;* the Parisian thieves had given him this name, and knew him by no other. He had a tolerably complete wardrobe. The rags with which he tricked out his people were almost respectable. He had specialties and categories; upon each nail in his shop, hung, worn and rumpled, a social condition; here the magistrate's dress, there the curé's dress, there the banker's dress, in one corner the retired soldier's dress, in another the literary man's dress, further on the statesman's dress. This man was the costumer of the immense drama which knavery plays in Paris. His hut was the green-room whence robbery came forth, and whither swindling returned. A ragged rogue came to this wardrobe, laid down thirty sous, and chose, according to the part which he wished to play that day, the dress which suited him, and, when he returned to the street, the rogue was somebody. The next day the clothes were faithfully brought back, and the Changer, who trusted everything to the robbers, was never robbed.

These garments had one inconvenience, they were not a fit; not having been made for those who wore them, they were tight for this man, baggy for that, and fitted nobody.

Marius' disappointment, on seeing another man enter than the one he was expecting, turned into dislike towards the new comer. He examined him from head to foot, while the personage bowed without measure, and asked him in a sharp tone:

"What do you want?"

The man answered with an amiable grin of which the caressing smile of a crocodile would give some idea:

"It seems to me impossible that I have not already had the honour of seeing Monsieur the Baron in society. I really think that I met him privately some years ago, at Madame the Princess Bagration's and in the salons of his lordship the Viscount Dambray, peer of France."

Marius listened attentively to the voice of this man. He watched for the tone and gesture eagerly, but his disappointment increased; it was a whining pronunciation, entirely different from the sharp and dry sound of voice which he expected. He was completely bewildered.

"I don't know," said he, "either Madame Bagration or M. Dambray. I have never in my life set foot in the house of either the one or the other."

The answer was testy. The person, gracious notwithstanding, persisted:

"Then it must be at Chateaubriand's that I have seen monsieur? I know Chateaubriand well. He is very affable. He says to me sometimes: 'Thénard, my friend, won't you drink a glass of wine with me?'"

Marius' brow grew more and more severe:

"I have never had the honour of being received at Monsieur de Chateaubriand's. Come to the point. What is it you wish?"

"Certainly, Monsieur the Baron. I will explain. I have a secret to sell you."

"Which concerns me?"

"Somewhat."

"What is this secret?"

"Monsieur Baron, you have in your house a robber and an assassin."

Marius shuddered.

"In my house? no," said he.

The stranger, imperturbable, brushed his hat with his sleeve, and continued:

"Assassin and robber. Observe, Monsieur Baron, that I do not speak here of acts, old, by-gone, and withered, which may be cancelled by prescription in the eye of the law, and by repentance in the eye of God. I speak of recent acts, present acts, acts yet unknown to justice at this hour. I will proceed. This man has glided into your confidence, and almost into your family, under a false name. I am going to tell you his true name. And to tell it to you for nothing."

"I am listening."

"His name is Jean Valjean."

"I know it."

"I am going to tell you, also for nothing, who he is."

"Say on."

"He is an old convict."

"I know it."

"You know it since I have had the honour of telling you."

"No. I knew it before."

Marius' cool tone, that double reply, *I know it*, his laconic method of speech, embarrassing to conversation, excited some suppressed anger in the stranger. He shot furtively at Marius a furious look, which was immediately extinguished.

"I do not permit myself to contradict Monsieur the Baron. At all events, you must see that I am informed. Now, what I have to acquaint you with, is known to myself alone. It concerns the fortune of Madame the Baroness. It is an extraordinary secret. It is for sale. I offer it to you first. Cheap. Twenty thousand francs."

"I know that secret as well as the others," said Marius.

The person felt the necessity of lowering his price a little.

"Monsieur Baron, say ten thousand francs, and I will go on."

"I repeat, that you have nothing to acquaint me with. I know what you wish to tell me."

There was a new flash in the man's eye. He exclaimed:

"Still I must dine to-day. It is an extraordinary secret, I tell you. Monsieur the Baron, I am going to speak. I will speak. Give me twenty francs."

Marius looked at him steadily:

"I know your extraordinary secret; just as I knew Jean Valjean's name: just as I know your name."

"My name?"

"Yes."

"That is not difficult, Monsieur Baron. I have had the honour of writing it to you and telling it to you. Thénard."

"Dier."

"Eh?"

"Thénardier."

"Who is that?"

In danger the porcupine bristles, the beetle feigns death, the Old Guard forms a square; this man began to laugh.

Then, with a fillip, he brushed a speck of dust from his coat-sleeve. Marius continued:

"You are also the working-man Jondrette, the comedian Fabantou, the poet Genflot, the Spaniard Don Alvarès, and the woman Balizard."

"The woman what?"

"And you have kept a chop-house at Montfermeil."

"A chop-house! never."

"And I tell you that you are Thénardier."

"I deny it."

"And that you are a scoundrel. Here."

And Marius, taking a bank-note from his pocket, threw it in his face.

"Thanks! pardon! five hundred francs! Monsieur Baron!"

And the man, bewildered, bowing, catching the note, examined it.

"Five hundred francs!" he repeated in astonishment.

Then bluntly:

"Well, so be it," exclaimed he. "Let us make ourselves comfortable."

And, with the agility of a monkey, throwing his hair off backwards, pulling off his spectacles, taking out of his nose and pocketing two quill tubes, he took off his countenance as one takes off his hat.

His eye kindled; his forehead, uneven, ravined, humped in spots, hideously wrinkled at the top, emerged; his nose became as sharp as a beak; the fierce and cunning profile of the man of prey appeared again.

"Monsieur the Baron is infallible," said he in a clear voice from which all nasality had disappeared, "I am Thénardier."

And he straightened his bent back.

Thénardier was strangely surprised. He saw this Baron Pontmercy for the first time, and, in spite of his disguise, this Baron Pontmercy recognised him. And not only was this baron fully informed, in regard to Thénardier, but he seemed fully informed in regard to Jean Valjean. Who was this almost beardless young man, so icy and so generous, who knew people's names, who knew all their names, who abused rogues like a judge and who paid them like a dupe?

Thénardier, it will be remembered, although he had been a neighbour of Marius, had never seen him, which is frequent in Paris; he had once heard some talk of his daughters about a very poor young man named Marius who lived in the house. He had written to him, without knowing him, the letter which we have seen. No connection was possible in his mind between that Marius and M. the Baron Pontmercy.

Through his daughter Azelma, however, whom he had put upon the track of the couple married on the 16th of February, and through his own researches, he had succeeded in finding out many things, and, from the depth of his darkness, he had been able to seize more than one mysterious clue. He had, by dint of industry, discovered, or at least guessed who the man was whom he had met on a certain day in the Grand Sewer. From the man, he had easily arrived at the name. He knew that Madame the Baroness Pontmercy was Cosette. But, in that respect, he intended to be prudent. Who was Cosette? He did not know exactly himself. He suspected indeed some illegitimacy. Fantine's story had always seemed to him ambiguous; but why speak of it? to get paid for his silence? He had, or thought he had, something better to sell than that.

In Thénardier's opinion, the conversation with Marius had not yet commenced. He had been obliged to retreat, to modify his strategy, to abandon a position, to change his base; but nothing essential was yet lost, and he had five hundred francs in his pocket.

Thénardier was looking at Marius with an almost affectionate humility. Marius interrupted the silence.

"Thénardier, I have told you your name. Now your secret, what you came to make known to me, do you want me to tell you that? I too have my means of information. You shall see that I know more about it than you do. Jean Valjean, as you have said, is an assassin and a robber. A robber, because he robbed a rich manufacturer, M. Madeleine, whose ruin he caused. An assassin, because he assassinated the police-officer, Javert."

"I don't understand, Monsieur Baron," said Thénardier.

"I will make myself understood. Listen. There was, in an arrondissement of the Pas-de-Calais, about 1822, a man who had had some old difficulty with justice, and who, under the name of M. Madeleine, had reformed and re-established himself. He had become in the full force of the term an upright man. By means of a manufacture, that of black glass trinkets, he had made the fortune of an entire city. As for his own personal fortune, he had made it also. He was the foster-father of the poor. He founded hospitals, opened schools, visited the sick, endowed daughters, supported widows, adopted orphans; he was, as it were, the guardian of the country. He had refused the Cross, he had been appointed mayor. A liberated convict knew the secret of a penalty once incurred by this man; he informed against him and had him arrested, and took advantage of the arrest to come to Paris and draw from the banker, Laffitte—I have the fact from the cashier himself—by means of a false signature, a sum of more than half a million which belonged to M. Madeleine. This convict who robbed M. Madeleine is Jean Valjean. As to the other act, you have just as little to tell me. Jean Valjean killed the officer Javert; he killed him with a pistol. I, who am now speaking to you, I was present."

Thénardier cast upon Marius the sovereign glance of a beaten man who lays hold on victory again, and who has just recovered in one minute all the ground which he had lost. But Thénardier merely said to Marius:

"Monsieur Baron, we are on the wrong track."

And he emphasised this phrase by giving his bunch of trinkets an expressive twirl.

"What!" replied Marius, "do you deny that? These are facts."

"They are chimeras. The confidence with which Monsieur the Baron honours me makes it my duty to tell him so. Before all things, truth and justice. I do not like to see people accused unjustly. Monsieur Baron, Jean

Valjean never robbed Monsieur Madeleine, and Jean Valjean never killed Javert."

"You speak strongly! how is that?"

"For two reasons."

"What are they? tell me."

"The first is this: he did not rob Monsieur Madeleine, since it is Jean Valjean himself who was Monsieur Madeleine."

"What is that you are telling me?"

"And the second is this: he did not assassinate Javert, since Javert himself killed Javert."

"What do you mean?"

"That Javert committed suicide."

"Prove it! prove it!" cried Marius, beside himself.

"The—police—of—ficer—Ja—vert—was—found—drowned—under—a—boat—by—the—Pont—au—Change."

"But prove it now!"

Thénardier took from his pocket a large envelope of grey paper, which seemed to contain folded sheets of different sizes.

"I have my documents," said he, with calmness.

And he added:

"Monsieur Baron, in your interest, I wished to find out Jean Valjean to the bottom. I say that Jean Valjean and Madeleine are the same man; and I say that Javert had no other assassin than Javert; and when I speak I have the proofs. Not manuscript proofs; writing is suspicious; proofs in print."

While speaking, Thénardier took out of the envelope two newspapers, yellow, faded, and strongly saturated with tobacco. One of these two newspapers, broken at all the folds, and falling in square pieces, seemed much older than the other.

"Two facts, two proofs," said Thénardier. And unfolding the two papers, he handed them to Marius.

With these two newspapers the reader is acquainted. One, the oldest, a copy of the *Drapeau Blanc*, of the 25th of July, 1823, established the identity of M. Madeleine and Jean Valjean. The other, a *Moniteur* of the 15th of June, 1832, verified the suicide of Javert, adding that it appeared from a verbal report made by Javert to the prefect that, taken prisoner in the barricade of the Rue de la Chanvrerie, he had owed his life to the magnanimity of an insurgent who, though he had him at the muzzle of his pistol, had fired into the air.

Marius read. There was evidence, certain date, unquestionable proof; these two newspapers had not been printed expressly to support Thénardier's words. The note published in the *Moniteur* was an official communication from the prefecture of police. Marius could not doubt. The information derived from the cashier was false, and he himself was mistaken. Marius could not restrain a cry of joy:

"Well, then, this unhappy man is a wonderful man! all that fortune was really his own! he is Madeleine, the providence of a whole region! he is Jean Valjean, the saviour of Javert! he is a hero! he is a saint!"

"He is not a saint, and he is not a hero," said Thénardier. "He is an assassin and a robber."

And he added with the tone of a man who begins to feel some authority in himself: "Let us be calm."

Robber, assassin; these words, which Marius supposed were gone, yet which came back, fell upon him like a shower of ice.

"Again," said he.

"Still," said Thénardier. "Jean Valjean did not rob Madeleine, but he is a robber. He did not kill Javert, but he is a murderer."

"Will you speak," resumed Marius, "of that petty theft of forty years ago, expiated, as appears from your newspapers themselves, by a whole life of repentance, abnegation, and virtue?"

"I said assassination and robbery, Monsieur Baron. And I repeat that I speak of recent facts. What I have to reveal to you is absolutely unknown. It belongs to the unpublished. And perhaps you will find in it the source of the fortune adroitly presented by Jean Valjean to Madame the Baroness. I say adroitly, for, by a donation of this kind, to glide into an honourable house, the comforts of which he will share, and, by the same stroke, to conceal his crime, to enjoy his robbery, to bury his name, and to create himself a family, that would not be very unskilful."

"I might interrupt you here," observed Marius; "but continue."

"Monsieur Baron, I will tell you all, leaving the recompense to your generosity. This secret is worth a pile of gold. You will say to me: why have you not gone to Jean Valjean? For a very simple reason: I know that he has dispossessed himself, and dispossessed in your favour, and I think the contrivance ingenious; but he has not a sou left, he would show me his empty hands, and, since I need some money, I prefer you, who have all, to him who has nothing. I am somewhat fatigued; allow me to take a chair."

Marius sat down, and made a sign to him to sit down.

Thénardier installed himself in a chair, took up the two newspapers, thrust them back into the envelope, and muttered, striking the *Drapeau Blanc* with his nail: "It cost me some hard work to get this one." This done, he crossed his legs and lay back in his chair, an attitude characteristic of people who are sure of what they are saying, then entered into the subject seriously, and emphasising his words:

"Monsieur Baron, on the 6th of June, 1832, about a year ago, a man was in the Grand Sewer of Paris, near where the sewer empties into the Seine, between the Pont des Invalides and the Pont d'Iéna."

Marius suddenly drew his chair near Thénardier's. Thénardier noticed this movement, and continued with the deliberation of a speaker who feels the palpitation of his adversary beneath his words:

"This man, compelled to conceal himself, for reasons foreign to politics, however, had taken the sewer for his dwelling, and had a key to it. It was,

I repeat it, the 6th of June; it might have been eight o'clock in the evening. The man heard a noise in the sewer. Very much surprised, he hid himself, and watched. It was a sound of steps, somebody was walking in the darkness; somebody was coming in his direction. Strange to say, there was another man in the sewer beside him. The grating of the outlet of the sewer was not far off. A little light which came from it enabled him to recognise the newcomer, and to see that this man was carrying something on his back. He walked bent over. The man who was walking bent over was an old convict, and what he was carrying upon his shoulders was a corpse. Assassination *in flagrante delicto,* if ever there was such a thing. As for the robbery, it follows of course; nobody kills a man for nothing. This convict was going to throw his corpse into the river. It is a noteworthy fact, that before reaching the grating of the outlet, this convict, who came from a distance in the sewer, had been compelled to pass through a horrible quagmire in which it would seem that he might have left the corpse; but, the sewer-men working upon the quagmire might, the very next day, have found the assassinated man, and that was not the assassin's game. He preferred to go through the quagmire with his load, and his efforts must have been terrible; it is impossible to put one's life in greater peril; I do not understand how he came out of it alive."

Marius' chair drew still nearer. Thénardier took advantage of it to draw a long breath. He continued:

"Monsieur Baron, a sewer is not the Champ de Mars. One lacks everything there, even room. When two men are in a sewer, they must meet each other. That is what happened. The resident and the traveller were compelled to say good-day to each other, to their mutual regret. The traveller said to the resident: *"You see what I have on my back, I must get out, you have the key, give it to me."* This convict was a man of terrible strength. There was no refusing him. Still he who had the key parleyed, merely to gain time. He examined the dead man, but he could see nothing, except that he was young, well dressed, apparently a rich man, and all disfigured with blood. While he was talking, he found means to cut and tear off from behind, without the assassin perceiving it, a piece of the assassinated man's coat. A piece of evidence, you understand; means of getting trace of the affair, and proving the crime upon the criminal. He put this piece of evidence in his pocket. After which he opened the grating, let the man out with his incumbrance on his back, shut the grating again and escaped, little caring to be mixed up with the remainder of the adventure, and especially desiring not to be present when the assassin should throw the assassinated man into the river. You understand now. He who was carrying the corpse was Jean Valjean; he who had the key is now speaking to you, and the piece of the coat—"

Thénardier finished the phrase by drawing from his pocket and holding up, on a level with his eyes, between his thumbs and his forefingers, a strip of ragged black cloth, covered with dark stains.

Marius had risen, hardly breathing, his eye fixed upon the scrap of black cloth. Without uttering a word, without losing sight of this rag, he retreated to the wall, and, with his right hand stretched behind him, groped about for a key which was in the lock of a closet near the chimney. He found this key, opened the closet, and thrust his arm into it without looking, and without removing his startled eyes from the fragment that Thénardier held up.

Meanwhile Thénardier continued:

"Monsieur Baron, I have the strongest reasons to believe that the assassinated young man was an opulent stranger drawn into a snare by Jean Valjean, and the bearer of an enormous sum."

"The young man was myself, and there is the coat!" cried Marius, and he threw an old black coat covered with blood upon the carpet.

Then, snatching the fragment from Thénardier's hands, he bent down over the coat, and applied the piece to the cut skirt. The edges fitted exactly, and the strip completed the coat.

Marius rose up, quivering, desperate, flashing.

He felt in his pocket, and walked, furious, towards Thénardier, offering him and almost pushing into his face his fist full of five hundred and thousand franc notes.

"You are a wretch! you are a liar, a slanderer, a scoundrel. You came to accuse this man, you have justified him; you wanted to destroy him, you have succeeded only in glorifying him. And it is you who are a robber! and it is you who are an assassin. I saw you, Thénardier, Jondrette, in that den on the Boulevard de l'Hôpital. I know enough about you to send you to the galleys, and further even, if I wished. Here, there are a thousand francs, braggart that you are!"

And he threw a bill for a thousand francs to Thénardier.

"Ah! Jondrette Thénardier, vile knave! let this be a lesson to you, pedlar of secrets, trader in mysteries, fumbler in the dark, wretch! Take these five hundred francs, and leave this place! Waterloo protects you."

"Waterloo!" muttered Thénardier, pocketing the five hundred francs with the thousand francs.

"Yes, assassin! you saved the life of a colonel there—"

"Of a general," said Thénardier, raising his head.

"Of a colonel!" replied Marius with a burst of passion. "I would not give a farthing for a general. And you came here to act out your infamy! I tell you that you have committed every crime. Go! out of my sight! Be happy only, that is all that I desire. Ah! monster! there are three thousand francs more. Take them. You will start to-morrow for America. I will see to your departure, bandit, and I will count out to you then twenty thousand francs. Go and get hung elsewhere!"

"Monsieur Baron," answered Thénardier, bowing to the ground, "eternal gratitude."

And Thénardier went out, comprehending nothing, astounded and transported with this sweet crushing under sacks of gold and with this thunderbolt bursting upon his head in bank-notes.

Let us finish with this man at once. Two days after the events which we are now relating, he left, through Marius' care, for America, under a false name, with his daughter Azelma, provided with a draft upon New York for twenty thousand francs. Thénardier, the moral misery of Thénardier, the brokendown bourgeois, was irremediable; he was in America what he had been in Europe. The touch of a wicked man is often enough to corrupt a good deed and to make an evil result spring from it. With Marius' money, Thénardier became a slaver.

As soon as Thénardier was out of doors, Marius ran to the garden where Cosette was still walking:

"Cosette! Cosette!" cried he. "Come! come quick! Let us go. Basque, a fiacre! Cosette, come. Oh! my God! It was he who saved my life! Let us not lose a minute! Put on your shawl."

Cosette thought him mad, and obeyed.

Marius began to see in this Jean Valjean a strangely lofty and saddened form. An unparalleled virtue appeared before him, supreme and mild, humble in its immensity. The convict was transfigured into Christ. Marius was bewildered by this marvel. He did not know exactly what he saw, but it was grand.

In a moment, a fiacre was at the door.

Marius helped Cosette in and sprang in himself.

"Driver," said he, "Rue de l'Homme Armé, Number 7."

The fiacre started.

"Oh! what happiness!" said Cosette. "Rue de l'Homme Armé! I dared not speak to you of it again. We are going to see Monsieur Jean."

"Your father! Cosette, your father more than ever. Cosette, I see it. You told me that you never received the letter which I sent you by Gavroche. It must have fallen into his hands. Cosette, he went to the barricade to save me. As it is a necessity for him to be an angel, on the way, he saved others; he saved Javert. He snatched me out of that gulf to give me to you. He carried me on his back in that frightful sewer. Oh! I am an unnatural ingrate. Cosette, after having been your providence, he was mine. Only think that there was a horrible quagmire, enough to drown him a hundred times, to drown him in the mire, Cosette! he carried me through that. I had fainted; I saw nothing, I heard nothing, I could know nothing of my own fate. We are going to bring him back, take him with us, whether he will or no, he shall never leave us again. If he is only at home! If we only find him! I will pass the rest of my life in venerating him. Yes, that must be it, do you see, Cosette? Gavroche must have handed my letter to him. It is all explained. You understand."

Cosette did not understand a word.

"You are right," said she to him.

Meanwhile the fiacre rolled on.

At the knock which he heard at his door, Jean Valjean turned his head.

"Come in," said he feebly.

The door opened. Cosette and Marius appeared.

Cosette rushed into the room.

Marius remained upon the threshold, leaning against the casing of the door.

"Cosette!" said Jean Valjean, and he rose in his chair, his arms stretched out and trembling.

Cosette, stifled with emotion, fell upon Jean Valjean's breast.

"Father!" said she.

Jean Valjean, beside himself, stammered:

"Cosette! she? you, madame? it is you, Cosette? Oh, my God!"

And, clasped in Cosette's arms, he exclaimed:

"It is you, Cosette? you are here? You forgive me then!"

Marius stepped forward and murmured:

"Father!"

"And you too, you forgive me!" said Jean Valjean.

Marius could not utter a word.

Cosette took off her shawl and threw her hat upon the bed. And, seating herself upon the old man's knees, she stroked away his white hair with an adorable grace, and kissed his forehead.

Jean Valjean, bewildered, faltered:

"How foolish we are! I thought I should never see her again. Only think, Monsieur Pontmercy, that at the moment you came in, I was saying to myself: It is over. There is her little dress, I am a miserable man, I shall never see Cosette again, I was saying that at the very moment you were coming up the stairs. Was I not silly? I was as silly as that! But we reckon without God. God said: You think that you are going to be abandoned, dolt? No. No, it shall not come to pass like that. Come, here is a poor goodman who has need of an angel. And the angel comes; and I see my Cosette again! and I see my darling Cosette again! Oh! I was very miserable!"

For a moment he could not speak, then he continued:

"I really needed to see Cosette a little while from time to time. A heart does want a bone to gnaw. Still I felt plainly that I was in the way. I gave myself reasons: they have no need of you, stay in your corner, you have no right to continue for ever. Oh! bless God, I see her again! Do you know, Cosette, that your husband is very handsome? Ah, you have a pretty embroidered collar, yes, yes. I like that pattern. Your husband chose it, did not he? And then, Cosette, you must have cashmeres. Monsieur Pontmercy, let me call her Cosette. It will not be very long."

And Cosette continued again:

"How naughty to have left us in this way! Where have you been? why were you away so long? Your journeys did not use to last more than three or four days. I sent Nicolette, the answer always was: He is absent. How long since you returned? Why did not you let us know? Do you know that you are very much changed? Oh! the naughty father! he has been sick, and we did not know it! Here, Marius, feel his hand, how cold it is!"

"So you are here, Monsieur Pontmercy, you forgive me!" repeated Jean Valjean.

At these words, which Jean Valjean now said for the second time, all that was swelling in Marius' heart found an outlet, he broke forth:

"Cosette, do you hear? that is the way with him! he begs my pardon, and do you know what he has done for me, Cosette? he has saved my life. He has done more. He has given you to me. And, after having saved me, and after having given you to me, Cosette, what did he do with himself? he sacrificed himself. There is the man. And, to me the ungrateful, to me the forgetful, to me the pitiless, to me the guilty, he says: Thanks! Cosette, my whole life passed at the feet of this man would be too little. That barricade, that sewer, that furnace, that cloaca, he went through everything for me, for you, Cosette! He bore me through death in every form which he put aside from me, and which he accepted for himself. All courage, all virtue, all heroism, all sanctity, he has it all, Cosette, that man is an angel!"

"Hush! hush!" said Jean Valjean in a whisper. "Why tell all that?"

"But you!" exclaimed Marius, with a passion in which veneration was mingled, "why have not you told it? It is your fault, too. You save people's lives, and you hide it from them! You do more, under pretence of unmasking yourself, you calumniate yourself. It is frightful."

"I told the truth," answered Jean Valjean.

"No," replied Marius, "the truth is the whole truth; and you did not tell it. You were Monsieur Madeleine, why not have said so? You had saved Javert, why not have said so? I owe my life to you, why not have said so?"

"Because I thought as you did. I felt that you were right. It was necessary that I should go away. If you had known that affair of the sewer you would have made me stay with you. I should then have had to keep silent. If I had spoken, it would have embarrassed all."

"Embarrassed what? embarrassed whom?" replied Marius. "Do you suppose you are going to stay here? We are going to carry you back. Oh! my God! when I think it was by accident that I learned it all! We are going to carry you back. You are a part of us. You are her father and mine. You shall not spend another day in this horrid house. Do not imagine that you will be here to-morrow."

"To-morrow," said Jean Valjean, "I shall not be here, but I shall not be at your house."

"What do you mean?" replied Marius. "Ah now, we shall allow no more journeys. You shall never leave us again. You belong to us. We will not let you go."

"This time, it is for good," added Cosette. "We have a carriage below. I am going to carry you off. If necessary, I shall use force."

And laughing, she made as if she would lift the old man in her arms.

"Your room is still in our house," she continued. "If you knew how pretty the garden is now. The azalias are growing finely. The paths are sanded with river sand: there are some little violet shells. You shall eat some of my strawberries. I water them myself. And no more madame, and no more Monsieur Jean, we are a republic, are we not, Marius? The programme is changed. If you knew, father, I have had some trouble, there was a red-breast which had made her nest in a hole in the wall a horrid cat ate her up for me. My poor pretty little red-breast who put her head out at her window and looked at me! I cried over it. I would have killed the cat! But now, nobody cries any more. Everybody laughs, everybody is happy. You are coming with us. How glad grandfather will be. You shall have your bed in the garden, you shall tend it, and we will see if your strawberries are as fine as mine. And then, I will do what ever you wish, and then, you will obey me."

Jean Valjean listened to her without hearing her. He heard the music of her voice rather than the meaning of her words. He murmured:

"The proof that God is good is that she is here."

Jean Valjean continued:

"It is very true that it would be charming to live together. They have their trees full of birds. I would walk with Cosette. To be with people who live, who bid each other good morning, who call each other into the garden, would be sweet. We would see each other as soon as it was morning. We would each cultivate our little corner. She would have me eat her strawberries. I would have her pick my roses. It would be charming. Only—"

He paused and said mildly:

"It is a pity."

Cosette took both the old man's hands in her own.

"My God!" said she, "your hands are colder yet. Are you sick? Are you suffering?"

"No," answered Jean Valjean. "I am very well. Only—"

He stopped.

"Only what?"

"I shall die in a few minutes."

Cosette and Marius shuddered.

"Die!" exclaimed Marius.

"Yes, but that is nothing," said Jean Valjean.

He breathed, smiled, and continued:

"Cosette, you are speaking to me, go on, speak again, your little red-breast is dead then, speak, let me hear your voice!"

Marius, petrified, gazed upon the old man.

Cosette uttered a piercing cry:

"Father! my father! you shall live. You are going to live. I will have you live, do you hear!"

Jean Valjean raised his head towards her with adoration.

"Oh yes, forbid me to die. Who knows? I shall obey perhaps. I was just dying when you came. That stopped me, it seemed to me that I was born again."

"You are full of strength and life," exclaimed Marius. "Do you think people die like that? You have had trouble, you shall have no more. I ask your pardon now, and that on my knees! You shall live, and live with us and live long. We will take you back. Both of us here will have but one thought henceforth, your happiness!"

"You see," added Cosette in tears, "that Marius says you will not die."

There was a noise at the door. It was the physician coming in.

"Good day and good-bye, doctor," said Jean Valjean. "Here are my poor children."

Marius approached the physician. He addressed this single word to him: "Monsieur?"

The physician answered the question by an expressive glance.

Because things are unpleasant," said Jean Valjean, "that is no reason for being unjust towards God."

There was a silence. All hearts were oppressed.

Jean Valjean turned towards Cosette. He began to gaze at her as if he would take a look which should endure through eternity. At the depth of shadow to which he had already descended, ecstasy was still possible to him while beholding Cosette.

The physician felt his pulse.

"Ah! it was you he needed!" murmured he, looking at Cosette and Marius.

And, bending towards Marius' ear he added very low:

"Too late."

Jean Valjean, almost without ceasing to gaze upon Cosette, turned upon Marius and the physician a look of serenity. They heard these almost inarticulate words come from his lips:

"It is nothing to die; it is frightful not to live."

Cosette supported his shoulders, and sobbed, and attempted to speak to him, but could not.

"He is reviving! doctor, he is reviving!" cried Marius.

"You are both kind," said Jean Valjean. "I will tell you what has given me pain. What has given me pain, Monsieur Pontmercy, was that you have been unwilling to touch that money. That money really belongs to your wife. I will explain it to you, my children, on that account I am glad to see you. The black jet comes from England, the white jet comes from Norway. All this is in the paper you see there, which you will read. For bracelets, I invented the substitution of clasps made by bending the metal, for clasps made by soldering the metal. They are handsomer, better, and cheaper. You understand how much money can be made. So Cosette's fortune is really her own. I give you these particulars so that your minds may be at rest."

The portress had come up, and was looking through the half-open door. The physician motioned her away, but could not prevent that good, zealous woman from crying to the dying man before she went:

"Do you want a priest?"

"I have one," answered Jean Valjean.

And, with his finger, he seemed to designate a point above his head, where, you would have said, he saw some one.

It is probable that the Bishop was indeed a witness of this death-agony.

From moment to moment, Jean Valjean grew weaker.

He motioned to Cosette to approach, then to Marius; it was evidently the last minute of the last hour, and he began to speak to them in a voice so faint it seemed to come from afar, and you would have said that there was already a wall between them and him.

"Come closer, come closer, both of you. I love you dearly. You too, you love me, my Cosette. I knew very well that you still had some affection for your old goodman. How kind you are to put this cushion under my back! You will weep for me a little, will you not? Not too much. I do not wish you to have any deep grief. You must amuse yourselves a great deal, my children. I forgot to tell you that on buckles without tongues still more is made than on anything else. A gross, twelve dozen, costs ten francs, and sells for sixty. That is really a good business. Cosette, do you see your little dress, there on the bed? do you recognise it? How time passes! We have been very happy. It is over. My children, do not weep, I am not going very far, I shall see you from there.

"Cosette, do you remember Montfermeil? You were in the wood, you were very much frightened; do you remember when I took the handle of the water-bucket? That was the first time I touched your poor little hand. It was so cold! Ah! you had red hands in those days, mademoiselle, your hands are very white now. And the great doll! do you remember? you called her Catharine. You regretted that you did not carry her to the convent. How you made me laugh sometimes, my sweet angel! When it had rained you launched spears of straw in the gutters, and you watched them. One day, I gave you a willow battledore, and a shuttlecock with yellow, blue, and green feathers. You have forgotten it. You were so cunning when you were little! You played. You put cherries in your ears.

"So I am going away, my children. Love each other dearly always. There is scarcely anything else in the world but that: to love one another. You will think sometimes of the poor old man who died here. O my Cosette! it is not my fault, indeed, if I have not seen you all this time, it broke my heart; I went as far as the corner of the street, I must have seemed strange to the people who saw me pass, I looked like a crazy man, once I went out with no hat. My children, I do not see very clearly now, I had some more things to say, but it makes no difference. Think of me a little. You are blessed creatures. I do not know what is the matter with me, I see a light. Come nearer. I die happy. Let me put my hands upon your dear beloved heads."

Cosette and Marius fell on their knees, choked with tears, each grasping one of Jean Valjean's hands. Those hands moved no more.

The night was starless and very dark. Without doubt, in the gloom some mighty angel was standing, with outstretched wings, awaiting the soul.